DARK RIVERS OF THE HEART

▼

INTENSITY

▼

SOLE SURVIVOR

▼

THREE COMPLETE NOVELS BY

Dean Koontz

▲

bright sky press

A bright sky press book
Published by arrangement with Alfred A. Knopf,
a division of Random House, Inc.

Library of Congress Catalog Card Number   2001   132544
ISBN 0-9709987-1-6

Cover design by Jeffrey Faust

Distributed by: Sterling Publishing Co., Inc.

10 9 8 7 6 5 4 3 2 1

Printed in China

DARK RIVERS
OF THE HEART

▼

To Gary and Zov Karamardian
for their valued friendship,
for being the kind of people who
make life a joy for others,
and for giving us a home
away from home.
We've decided to move in permanently
next week!

PART ONE

ON A STRANGE SEA

▼

All of us are travelers lost,
our tickets arranged at a cost
unknown but beyond our means.
This odd itinerary of scenes
—enigmatic, strange, unreal—
leaves us unsure how to feel.
No postmortem journey is rife
with more mystery than life.
        —*The Book of Counted Sorrows*

Tremulous skeins of destiny
flutter so ethereally
around me—but then I feel
its embrace is that of steel.
        —*The Book of Counted Sorrows*

ONE

With the woman on his mind and a deep uneasiness in his heart, Spencer Grant drove through the glistening night, searching for the red door. The vigilant dog sat silently beside him. Rain ticked on the roof of the truck.

Without thunder or lightning, without wind, the storm had come in from the Pacific at the end of a somber February twilight. More than a drizzle but less than a downpour, it sluiced all the energy out of the city. Los Angeles and environs became a metropolis without sharp edges, urgency, or spirit. Buildings blurred into one another, traffic flowed sluggishly, and streets deliquesced into gray mists.

In Santa Monica, with the beaches and the black ocean to his right, Spencer stopped at a traffic light.

Rocky, a mixed breed not quite as large as a Labrador, studied the road ahead with interest. When they were in the truck—a Ford Explorer—Rocky sometimes peered out the side windows at the passing scene, though he was more interested in what lay before them.

Even when he was riding in the cargo area behind the front seats, the mutt rarely glanced out the rear window. He was skittish about watching the scenery recede. Maybe the motion made him dizzy in a way that oncoming scenery did not.

Or perhaps Rocky associated the dwindling highway behind them with the past. He had good reason not to dwell on the past.

So did Spencer.

Waiting for the traffic signal, he raised one hand to his face. He had a habit of meditatively stroking his scar when troubled, as another man might finger a strand of worry beads. The feel of it soothed him, perhaps because it was a reminder that he'd survived the worst terror he would ever know, that life could have no more surprises dark enough to destroy him.

The scar defined Spencer. He was a damaged man.

Pale, slightly glossy, extending from his right ear to his chin, the mark varied between one quarter and one half an inch in width. Extremes of cold and heat bleached it whiter than usual. In wintry air, though the thin ribbon of connective tissue contained no nerve endings, it felt like a hot wire laid on his face. In summer sun, the scar was cold.

The traffic signal changed from red to green.

The dog stretched his furry head forward in anticipation.

Spencer drove slowly southward along the dark coast, both hands on the wheel again. He nervously searched for the red door on the eastern side of the street, among the many shops and restaurants.

Though no longer touching the fault line in his face, he remained conscious of it. He was never unaware that he was branded. If he smiled or frowned, he would feel the scar cinching one half of his countenance. If he laughed, his amusement would be tempered by the tension in that inelastic tissue.

The metronomic windshield wipers timed the rhythm of the rain.

Spencer's mouth was dry, but the palms of his hands were damp. The tightness in his chest arose as much from anxiety as from the pleasant anticipation of seeing Valerie again.

He was of half a mind to go home. The new hope he harbored was surely the emotional equivalent of fool's gold. He was alone, and he was always going to be alone, except for Rocky. He was ashamed of this fresh glimmer of optimism, of the naivete it revealed, the secret need, the quiet desperation. But he kept driving.

Rocky couldn't know what they were searching for, but he chuffed softly when the red landmark appeared. No doubt he was responding to a subtle change in Spencer's mood at the sight of the door.

The cocktail lounge was between a Thai restaurant with steam-streaked windows and an empty storefront that had once been an art gallery. The windows of the gallery were boarded over, and squares of travertine were missing from the once elegant facade, as if the enterprise had not merely failed but been bombed out of business. Through the silver rain, a downfall of light at the lounge entrance revealed the red door that he remembered from the previous night.

Spencer hadn't been able to recall the name of the place. That lapse of memory now seemed willful, considering the scarlet neon above the entrance: THE RED DOOR. A humorless laugh escaped him.

After haunting so many barrooms over the years, he had ceased to notice enough differences, one from another, to be able to attach names to them. In scores of towns, those countless taverns were, in their essence, the same church confessional; sitting on a barstool instead of kneeling on a prie-dieu, he murmured the same admissions to strangers who were not priests and could not give him absolution.

His confessors were drunkards, spiritual guides as lost as he was. They could never tell him the appropriate penance he must do to find peace. Discussing the meaning of life, they were incoherent.

Unlike those strangers to whom he often quietly revealed his soul, Spencer had never been drunk. Inebriation was as dreadful for him to contemplate as was suicide. To be drunk was to relinquish control. Intolerable. Control was the only thing he had.

At the end of the block, Spencer turned left and parked on the secondary street.

He went to bars not to drink but to avoid being alone—and to tell his story to someone who would not remember it in the morning. He often nursed a beer or two through a long evening. Later, in his bedroom, after staring toward the hidden heavens, he would finally close his eyes only when the patterns of shadows on the ceiling inevitably reminded him of things he preferred to forget.

When he switched off the engine, the rain drummed louder than before—a cold sound, as chilling as the voices of dead children that sometimes called to him with wordless urgency in his worst dreams.

The yellowish glow of a nearby streetlamp bathed the interior of the truck, so Rocky was clearly visible. His large and expressive eyes solemnly regarded Spencer.

"Maybe this is a bad idea," Spencer said.

The dog craned his head forward to lick his master's right hand, which was still clenched around the wheel. He seemed to be saying that Spencer should relax and just do what he had come there to do.

As Spencer moved his hand to pet the mutt, Rocky bowed his head, not to make the backs of his ears or his neck more accessible to stroking fingers, but to indicate that he was subservient and harmless.

"How long have we been together?" Spencer asked the dog.

Rocky kept his head down, huddling warily but not actually trembling under his master's gentle hand.

"Almost two years," Spencer said, answering his own question. "Two years of kindness, long walks, chasing Frisbees on the beach, regular meals . . . and still sometimes you think I'm going to hit you."

Rocky remained in a humble posture on the passenger seat.

Spencer slipped one hand under the dog's chin, forced his head up. After briefly trying to pull away, Rocky ceased all resistance.

When they were eye-to-eye, Spencer said, "Do you trust me?"

The dog self-consciously looked away, down and to the left.

Spencer shook the mutt gently by the muzzle, commanding his attention again. "We keep our heads up, okay? Always proud, okay? Confident. Keep our heads up, look people in the eye. You got that?"

Rocky slipped his tongue between his half-clenched teeth and licked the fingers with which Spencer was gripping his muzzle.

"I'll interpret that as 'yes.' " He let go of the dog. "This cocktail lounge isn't a place I can take you. No offense."

In certain taverns, though Rocky was not a guide dog, he could lie at Spencer's feet, even sit on a stool, and no one would object to the violation of health laws. Usually a dog was the least of the infractions for which the joint would be cited if a city inspector happened to visit. The Red Door, however, still had pretensions to class, and Rocky wouldn't be welcome.

Spencer got out of the truck, slammed the door. He engaged the locks and security system with the remote control on his key chain.

He could not count on Rocky to protect the Explorer. This was one dog who would never scare off a determined car thief—unless the would-be thief suffered an extreme phobic aversion to having his hand licked.

After sprinting through the cold rain to the shelter of an awning that skirted the corner building, Spencer paused to look back.

Having moved onto the driver's seat, the dog stared out, nose pressed to the side window, one ear pricked, one ear drooping. His breath was fogging the glass, but he wasn't barking. Rocky never barked. He just stared, waited. He was seventy pounds of pure love and patience.

Spencer turned away from the truck and the side street, rounded the corner, and hunched his shoulders against the chilly air.

Judging by the liquid sounds of the night, the coast and all the works of civilization that stood upon it might have been merely ramparts of ice melting into the black Pacific maw. Rain drizzled off the awning, gurgled in gutters, and splashed beneath the tires of passing cars. At the threshold of audibility, more sensed than heard, the ceaseless rumble of surf announced the steady erosion of beaches and bluffs.

As Spencer was passing the boarded-up art gallery, someone spoke from the shadows in the deeply recessed entrance. The voice was as dry as the night was damp, hoarse and grating: "I know what you are."

Halting, Spencer squinted into the gloom. A man sat in the entryway, legs splayed, back against the gallery door. Unwashed and unbarbered, he seemed less a man than a heap of black rags saturated with so much organic filth that malignant life had arisen in it by spontaneous generation.

"I know what you are," the vagrant repeated softly but clearly.

A miasma of body odor and urine and the fumes of cheap wine rose out of the doorway.

The number of shambling, drug-addicted, psychotic denizens of the streets had increased steadily since the late seventies, when most of the mentally ill had been freed from sanitariums in the name of civil liberties and compassion. They roamed America's cities, championed by politicians but untended, an army of the living dead.

The penetrating whisper was as desiccated and eerie as the voice of a reanimated mummy. "*I know what you are.*"

The prudent response was to keep moving.

The paleness of the vagrant's face, above the beard and below the tangled hair, became dimly visible in the gloom. His sunken eyes were as bottomless as abandoned wells. "*I know what you are.*"

"Nobody knows," Spencer said.

Sliding the fingertips of his right hand along his scar, he walked past the shuttered gallery and the ruined man.

"Nobody knows," whispered the vagrant. Perhaps his commentary on passersby, which at first had seemed eerily perceptive, even portentous, was nothing more than mindless repetition of the last thing he had heard from the most recent scornful citizen to reply to him. *"Nobody knows."*

Spencer stopped in front of the cocktail lounge. Was he making a dreadful mistake? He hesitated with his hand on the red door.

Once more the hobo spoke from the shadows. Through the sizzle of the rain, his admonition now had the haunting quality of a static-shredded voice on the radio, speaking from a distant station in some far corner of the world. *"Nobody knows. . . ."*

Spencer opened the red door and went inside.

On a Wednesday night, no host was at the reservations podium in the vestibule. Maybe there wasn't a front man on Fridays and Saturdays, either. The joint wasn't exactly jumping.

The warm air was stale and filigreed with blue cigarette smoke. In the far left corner of the rectangular main room, a piano player under a spotlight worked through a spiritless rendition of "Tangerine."

Decorated in black and gray and polished steel, with mirrored walls, with Art Deco fixtures that cast overlapping rings of moody sapphire-blue light on the ceiling, the lounge once had recaptured a lost age with style. Now the upholstery was scuffed, the mirrors streaked. The steel was dull under a residue of old smoke.

Most tables were empty. A few older couples sat near the piano.

Spencer went to the bar, which was to the right, and settled on the stool at the end, as far from the musician as he could get.

The bartender had thinning hair, a sallow complexion, and watery gray eyes. His practiced politeness and pale smile couldn't conceal his boredom. He functioned with robotic efficiency and detachment, discouraging conversation by never making eye contact.

Two fiftyish men in suits sat farther along the bar, each alone, each frowning at his drink. Their shirt collars were unbuttoned, ties askew. They looked dazed, glum, as if they were advertising-agency executives who had been pink-slipped ten years ago but still got up every morning and dressed for success because they didn't know what else to do; maybe they came to The Red Door because it had been where they'd unwound after work, in the days when they'd still had hope.

The only waitress serving the tables was strikingly beautiful, half Vietnamese and half black. She wore the costume that she—and Valerie—had worn the previous evening: black heels, short black skirt, short-sleeved black sweater. Valerie had called her Rosie.

After fifteen minutes, Spencer stopped Rosie when she passed nearby with a tray of drinks. "Is Valerie working tonight?"

"Supposed to be," she said.

He was relieved. Valerie hadn't lied. He had thought perhaps she'd misled him, as a gentle way of brushing him off.

"I'm kinda worried about her," Rosie said.

"Why's that?"

"Well, the shift started an hour ago." Her gaze kept straying to his scar. "She hasn't called in."

"She's not often late?"

"Val? Not her. She's *organized*."

"How long has she worked here?"

"About two months. She . . ." The woman shifted her gaze from the scar to his eyes. "Are you a friend of hers or something?"

"I was here last night. This same stool. Things were slow, so Valerie and I talked awhile."

"Yeah, I remember you," Rosie said, and it was obvious that she couldn't understand why Valerie had spent time with him.

He didn't look like any woman's dream man. He wore running shoes, jeans, a work shirt, and a denim jacket purchased at Kmart—essentially the same outfit that he'd worn on his first visit. No jewelry. His watch was a Timex. And the scar, of course. Always the scar.

"Called her place," Rosie said. "No answer. I'm worried."

"An hour late, that's not so much. Could've had a flat tire."

"In this city," Rosie said, her face hardening with anger that aged her ten years in an instant, "she could've been gang-raped, stabbed by some twelve-year-old punk wrecked on crack, maybe even shot dead by a carjacker in her own driveway."

"You're a real optimist, huh?"

"I watch the news."

She carried the drinks to a table at which sat two older couples whose expressions were more sour than celebratory. Having missed the new Puritanism that had captured many Californians, they were puffing furiously on cigarettes. They appeared to be afraid that the recent total ban on smoking in restaurants might be extended tonight to barrooms and homes, and that each cigarette might be their last.

While the piano player clinked through "The Last Time I Saw Paris," Spencer took two small sips of beer.

Judging by the palpable melancholy of the patrons in the bar, it might actually have been June 1940, with German tanks rolling down the Champs-Élysées, and with omens of doom blazing in the night sky.

A few minutes later, the waitress approached Spencer again. "I guess I sounded a little paranoid," she said.

"Not at all. I watch the news too."

"It's just that Valerie is so . . ."

"Special," Spencer said, finishing her thought so accurately that she stared at him with a mixture of surprise and vague alarm, as if she suspected that he had actually read her mind.

"Yeah. Special. You can know her only a week, and . . . well, you want her to be happy. You want good things to happen to her."

It doesn't take a week, Spencer thought. One evening.

Rosie said, "Maybe because there's this hurt in her. She's been hurt a lot."

"How?" he asked. "Who?"

She shrugged. "It's nothing I know, nothing she ever said. You just feel it about her."

He also had sensed a vulnerability in Valerie.

"But she's tough too," Rosie said. "Gee, I don't know why I'm so jumpy about this. It's not like I'm her big sister. Anyway, everyone's got a right to be late now and then."

The waitress turned away, and Spencer sipped his warm beer.

The piano player launched into "It Was a Very Good Year," which Spencer disliked even when Sinatra sang it, though he was a Sinatra fan. He knew the song was intended to be reflective in tone, even mildly pensive; however, it seemed terribly sad to him, not the sweet wistfulness of an older man reminiscing about the women he had loved, but the grim ballad of someone at the bitter end of his days, looking back on a barren life devoid of deep relationships.

He supposed that his interpretation of the lyrics was an expression of his fear that decades hence, when his own life burned out, he would fade away in loneliness and remorse.

He checked his watch. Valerie was now an hour and a half late.

The waitress's uneasiness had infected him. An insistent image rose in his mind's eye: Valerie's face, half concealed by a spill of dark hair and a delicate scrollwork of blood, one cheek pressed against the floor, eyes wide and unblinking. He knew his concern was irrational. She was merely late for work. There was nothing ominous about that. Yet, minute by minute, his apprehension deepened.

He put his unfinished beer on the bar, got off the stool, and walked through the blue light to the red door and into the chilly night, where the sound of marching armies was only the rain beating on the canvas awnings.

As he passed the art gallery doorway, he heard the shadow-wrapped vagrant weeping softly. He paused, affected.

Between strangled sounds of grief, the half-seen stranger whispered the last thing Spencer had said to him earlier: "*Nobody knows . . . nobody knows. . . .*" That short declaration evidently had acquired a personal and profound meaning for him, because he spoke the two words not in the tone in which Spencer had spoken but with quiet, intense anguish. "*Nobody knows.*"

Though Spencer knew that he was a fool for funding the wretch's further self-destruction, he fished a crisp ten-dollar bill from his wallet. He leaned into the gloomy entryway, into the fetid stink that the hobo exuded, and held out the money. "Here, take this."

The hand that rose to the offering was either clad in a dark glove or exceedingly filthy; it was barely discernible in the shadows. As the bill was plucked out of Spencer's fingers, the vagrant keened thinly: "*Nobody . . . nobody. . . .*"

"You'll be all right," Spencer said sympathetically. "It's only life. We all get through it."

"*It's only life, we all get through it,*" the vagrant whispered.

Plagued once more by the mental image of Valerie's dead face, Spencer hurried to the corner, into the rain, to the Explorer.

Through the side window, Rocky watched him approaching. As Spencer opened the door, the dog retreated to the passenger seat.

Spencer got in the truck and pulled the door shut, bringing with him the smell of damp denim and the ozone odor of the storm. "You miss me, killer?"

Rocky shifted his weight from side to side a couple of times, and he tried to wag his tail even while sitting on it.

As he started the engine, Spencer said, "You'll be pleased to hear that I didn't make an ass of myself in there."

The dog sneezed.

"But only because she didn't show up."

The dog cocked his head curiously.

Putting the car in gear, popping the hand brake, Spencer said, "So instead of quitting and going home while I'm ahead of the game, what do you think I'm going to do now? Hmmm?"

Apparently the dog didn't have a clue.

"I'm going to poke in where it's none of my business, give myself a second chance to screw up. Tell me straight, pal, do you think I've lost my mind?"

Rocky merely panted.

Pulling the truck away from the curb, Spencer said, "Yeah, you're right. I'm a basket case."

He headed directly for Valerie's house. She lived ten minutes from the bar.

The previous night, he had waited with Rocky in the Explorer, outside The Red Door, until two o'clock in the morning, and had followed Valerie when she drove home shortly after closing time. Because of his surveillance training, he knew how to tail a subject discreetly. He was confident that she hadn't spotted him.

He was not equally confident, however, about his ability to explain to her—or to himself—*why* he had followed her. After one evening of conversation with her, periodically interrupted by her attention to the few customers in the nearly deserted lounge, Spencer was overcome by the desire to know everything about her. Everything.

In fact, it was more than a desire. It was a need, and he was compelled to satisfy it.

Although his intentions were innocent, he was mildly ashamed of his budding obsession. The night before, he had sat in the Explorer, across the street from her house, staring at her lighted windows; all were covered with translucent drapes, and on one occasion her shadow played briefly across the folds of cloth, like a spirit glimpsed in candlelight at a séance. Shortly before three-thirty in the morning, the last light went out. While Rocky lay curled in sleep on the backseat, Spencer had remained on watch another hour, gazing at the dark house, wondering what books Valerie read, what she enjoyed doing on her days off, what her parents were like, where she had lived as a child, what she dreamed about when she was contented, and what shape her nightmares took when she was disturbed.

Now, less than twenty-four hours later, he headed to her place again, with a fine-grain anxiety abrading his nerves. She was late for work. Just late. His excessive concern told him more than he cared to know about the inappropriate intensity of his interest in this woman.

Traffic thinned as he drove farther from Ocean Avenue into residential neighborhoods. The languorous, liquid glimmer of wet blacktop fostered a false impression of movement, as if every street might be a lazy river easing toward its own far delta.

Valerie Keene lived in a quiet neighborhood of stucco and clapboard bungalows built in the late forties. Those two- and three-bedroom homes offered more charm than space: trellised front porches, from which hung great capes of bougainvillea; decorative shutters flanking windows; interestingly scalloped or molded or carved fascia boards under the eaves; fanciful rooflines; deeply recessed dormers.

Because Spencer didn't want to draw attention to himself, he drove past the woman's place without slowing. He glanced casually to the right, toward her dark bungalow on the south side of the block. Rocky mimicked him, but the dog seemed to find nothing more alarming about the house than did his master.

At the end of the block, Spencer turned right and drove south. The next few streets to the right were cul-de-sacs. He passed them by. He didn't want to park on a dead-end street. That was a trap. At the next main avenue, he hung a right again and parked at the curb in a neighborhood similar to the one in which Valerie lived. He turned off the thumping windshield wipers but not the engine.

He still hoped that he might regain his senses, put the truck in gear, and go home.

Rocky looked at him expectantly. One ear up. One ear down.

"I'm not in control," Spencer said, as much to himself as to the curious dog. "And I don't know why."

Rain sluiced down the windshield. Through the film of rippling water, the streetlights shimmered.

He sighed and switched off the engine.

When he'd left home, he'd forgotten an umbrella. The short dash to and from The Red Door had left him slightly damp, but the longer walk back to Valerie's house would leave him soaked.

He was not sure why he hadn't parked in front of her place. Training, perhaps. Instinct. Paranoia. Maybe all three.

Leaning past Rocky and enduring a warm, affectionate tongue in his ear, Spencer retrieved a flashlight from the glove compartment and tucked it in a pocket of his jacket.

"Anybody messes with the truck," he said to the dog, "you rip the bastard's guts out."

As Rocky yawned, Spencer got out of the Explorer. He locked it with the remote control as he walked away and turned north at the corner. He didn't bother running. Regardless of his pace, he would be soaked before he reached the bungalow.

The north-south street was lined with jacarandas. They would have provided little cover even when fully dressed with leaves and cascades of purple blossoms. Now, in winter, the branches were bare.

Spencer was sodden by the time he reached Valerie's street, where the jacarandas gave way to huge Indian laurels. The aggressive roots of the trees had cracked and canted the sidewalk; however, the canopy of branches and generous foliage held back the cold rain.

The big trees also prevented most of the yellowish light of the sodium-vapor streetlamps from reaching even the front lawns of the properties along that cloistered avenue. The trees and shrubs around the houses also were mature; some were overgrown. If any residents were looking out windows, they would most likely be unable to see him through the screen of greenery, on the deeply shadowed sidewalk.

As he walked, he scanned the vehicles parked along the street. As far as he could tell, no one was sitting in any of them.

A Mayflower moving van was parked across the street from Valerie's bungalow. That was convenient for Spencer, because the large truck blocked those neighbors' view. No men were working at the van; the move-in or move-out must be scheduled for the morning.

Spencer followed the front walkway and climbed three steps to the porch. The trellises at both ends supported not bougainvillea but night-blooming jasmine. Though it wasn't at its seasonal peak, the jasmine sweetened the air with its singular fragrance.

The shadows on the porch were deep. He doubted that he could even be seen from the street.

In the gloom, he had to feel along the door frame to find the button. He could hear the doorbell ringing softly inside the house.

He waited. No lights came on.

The flesh creped on the back of his neck, and he sensed that he was being watched.

Two windows flanked the front door and looked onto the porch. As far as he could discern, the dimly visible folds of the draperies on the other side of the glass were without any gaps through which an observer could have been studying him.

He looked back at the street. Sodium-yellow light transformed the downpour into glittering skeins of molten gold. At the far curb, the moving van stood half in shadows, half in the glow of the streetlamps. A late-model Honda and an older Pontiac were parked at the nearer curb. No pedestrians. No passing traffic. The night was silent except for the incessant rataplan of the rain.

He rang the bell once more.

The crawling feeling on the nape of his neck didn't subside. He put a hand back there, half convinced that he would find a spider negotiating his rain-slick skin. No spider.

As he turned to the street again, he thought that he saw furtive movement from the corner of his eye, near the back of the Mayflower van. He stared for half a minute, but nothing moved in the windless night except torrents of golden rain falling to the pavement as straight as if they were, in fact, heavy droplets of precious metal.

He knew why he was jumpy. He didn't belong here. Guilt was twisting his nerves.

Facing the door again, he slipped his wallet out of his right hip pocket and removed his MasterCard.

Though he could not have admitted it to himself until now, he would have been disappointed if he had found lights on and Valerie at home. He *was* concerned about her, but he doubted that she was lying, either injured or dead, in her darkened house. He was not psychic: The image of her bloodstained face, which he'd conjured in his mind's eye, was only an excuse to make the trip here from The Red Door.

His need to know everything about Valerie was perilously close to an adolescent longing. At the moment, his judgment was not sound.

He frightened himself. But he couldn't turn back.

By inserting the MasterCard between the door and jamb, he could pop the spring latch. He assumed there would be a deadbolt as well, because Santa Monica was as crime-ridden as any town in or around Los Angeles, but maybe he would get lucky.

He was luckier than he hoped: The front door was unlocked. Even the spring latch wasn't fully engaged. When he twisted the knob, the door clicked open.

Surprised, stricken by another tremor of guilt, he glanced back at the street again. The Indian laurels. The moving van. The cars. The rain, rain, rain.

He went inside. He closed the door and stood with his back against it, dripping on the carpet, shivering.

At first the room in front of him was unrelievedly black. After a while, his vision adjusted enough for him to make out a drapery-covered window—and then a second and a third—illuminated only by the faint gray ambient light of the night beyond.

For all that he could see, the blackness before him might have harbored a crowd, but he knew that he was alone. The house felt not merely unoccupied but deserted, abandoned.

Spencer took the flashlight from his jacket pocket. He hooded the beam with his left hand to ensure, as much as possible, that it would not be noticed by anyone outside.

The beam revealed an unfurnished living room, barren from wall to wall. The carpet was milk-chocolate brown. The unlined draperies were beige. The two-bulb light fixture in the ceiling could probably be operated by one of the three switches beside the front door, but he didn't try them.

His soaked athletic shoes and socks squished as he crossed the living room. He stepped through an archway into a small and equally empty dining room.

Spencer thought of the Mayflower van across the street, but he didn't believe that Valerie's belongings were in it or that she had moved out of the bungalow since four-thirty the previous morning, when he'd left his watch post in front of her house and returned to his own bed. Instead, he suspected that she had never actually moved *in*. The carpet was not marked by the pressure lines and foot indentations of furniture; no tables, chairs, cabinets, credenzas, or floor lamps had stood on it recently. If Valerie had lived in the bungalow during the two months that she had worked at The Red Door, she evidently hadn't furnished it and hadn't intended to call it home for any great length of time.

To the left of the dining room, through an archway half the size of the first, he found a small kitchen with knotty pine cabinets and red Formica countertops. Unavoidably, he left wet shoe prints on the gray tile floor.

Stacked beside the two-basin sink were a single dinner plate, a bread plate, a soup bowl, a saucer, and a cup—all clean and ready for use. One drinking glass stood with the dinnerware. Next to the glass lay a dinner fork, a knife, and a spoon, which were also clean.

He shifted the flashlight in his right hand, splaying a couple of fingers across the lens to partly suppress the beam, thus freeing his left hand to touch the drinking glass. He traced the rim with his fingertips. Even if the glass had been washed since Valerie had taken a drink from it, her lips had once touched the rim.

He had never kissed her. Perhaps he never would.

That thought embarrassed him, made him feel foolish, and forced him to consider, yet again, the impropriety of his obsession with this woman. He didn't belong here. He was trespassing not merely in her home but in her life. Until now, he had lived an honest life, if not always with undeviating respect for the law. Upon entering her house, however, he had crossed a sharp line that had scaled away his innocence, and what he had lost couldn't be regained.

Nevertheless, he did not leave the bungalow.

When he opened kitchen drawers and cabinets, he found them empty except for a combination bottle-and-can opener. The woman owned no plates or utensils other than those stacked beside the sink.

Most of the shelves in the narrow pantry were bare. Her stock of food was limited to three cans of peaches, two cans of pears, two cans of pineapple rings, one box of a sugar substitute in small blue packets, two boxes of cereal, and a jar of instant coffee.

The refrigerator was nearly empty, but the freezer compartment was well stocked with gourmet microwave dinners.

By the refrigerator was a door with a mullioned window. The four panes were covered by a yellow curtain, which he pushed aside far enough to see a side porch and a dark yard hammered by rain.

He allowed the curtain to fall back into place. He wasn't interested in the outside world, only in the interior spaces where Valerie had breathed the air, taken her meals, and slept.

As Spencer left the kitchen, the rubber soles of his shoes squeaked on the wet tiles. Shadows retreated before him and huddled in the corners while darkness crowded his back again.

He could not stop shivering. The damp chill in the house was as penetrating as that of the February air outside. The heat must have been off all day, which meant that Valerie had left early.

On his cold face, the scar burned.

A closed door was centered in the back wall of the dining room. He opened it and discovered a narrow hallway that led about fifteen feet to the left and fifteen to the right. Directly across the hall, another door stood half open; beyond, he glimpsed a white tile floor and a bathroom sink.

As he was about to enter the hall, he heard sounds other than the monotonous and hollow drumming of the rain on the roof. A thump and a soft scrape.

He immediately switched off the flashlight. The darkness was as perfect as that in any carnival fun house just before flickering strobe lights revealed a leering, mechanical corpse.

At first the sounds had seemed stealthy, as if a prowler outside had slipped on the wet grass and bumped against the house. However, the longer Spencer listened, the more he became convinced that the source of noise might have been distant rather than nearby, and that he might have heard nothing more than a car door slamming shut, out on the street or in a neighbor's driveway.

He switched on the flashlight and continued his search in the bathroom. A bath towel, a hand towel, and a washcloth hung on the rack. A half-used bar of Ivory lay in the plastic soap dish, but the medicine cabinet was empty.

To the right of the bathroom was a small bedroom, as unfurnished as the rest of the house. The closet was empty.

The second bedroom, to the left of the bath, was larger than the first, and it was obviously where she had slept. An inflated air mattress lay on the floor. Atop the mattress were a tangle of sheets, a single wool blanket, and a pillow. The bifold closet doors stood open, revealing wire hangers dangling from an unpainted wooden pole.

Although the rest of the bungalow was unadorned by artwork or decoration, something was fixed to the center of the longest wall in that bedroom. Spencer approached it, directed the light at it, and saw a full-color, closeup photograph of a cockroach. It seemed to be a page from a book, perhaps an entomology text, because the caption under the photograph was in dry academic English. In closeup, the roach was about six inches long. It had been fixed to the wall with a single large nail that had been driven through the center of the beetle's carapace. On the floor, directly below the photograph, lay the hammer with which the spike had been pounded into the plaster.

The photograph had not been decoration. Surely, no one would hang a picture of a cockroach with the intention of beautifying a bedroom. Furthermore, the use of a nail—rather than pushpins or staples or Scotch tape—implied that the person wielding the hammer had done so in considerable anger.

Clearly, the roach was meant to be a symbol for something else.

Spencer wondered uneasily if Valerie had nailed it there. That seemed unlikely. The woman with whom he'd talked the previous evening at The Red Door had seemed uncommonly gentle, kind, and all but incapable of serious anger.

If not Valerie—who?

As Spencer moved the flashlight beam across the glossy paper, the roach's carapace glistened as if wet. The shadows of his fingers, which half blocked the lens, created the illusion that the beetle's spindly legs and antennae jittered briefly.

Sometimes, serial killers left behind signatures at the scenes of their crimes to identify their work. In Spencer's experience, that could be anything from a specific playing card, to a Satanic symbol carved in some part of the victim's anatomy, to a single word or a line of poetry scrawled in blood upon a wall. The nailed photo had the feeling of such a signature, although it was stranger than anything he had seen or about which he had read in the hundreds of case studies with which he was familiar.

A faint nausea rippled through him. He had encountered no signs of violence in the house, but he had not yet looked in the attached single-car garage. Perhaps he would find Valerie on that cold slab of concrete, as he had seen her earlier in his mind's eye: lying with one side of her face pressed to the floor, unblinking eyes open wide, a scrollwork of blood obscuring some of her features.

He knew that he was jumping to conclusions. These days, the average American routinely lived in anticipation of sudden, mindless violence, but Spencer was more sensitized to the dark possibilities of modern life than were most people. He had endured pain and terror that had marked him in many ways, and his tendency now was to expect savagery as surely as sunrises and sunsets.

As he turned away from the photograph of the roach, wondering if he dared to investigate the garage, the bedroom window shattered inward, and a small black object hurtled through the draperies. At a glimpse, tumbling and airborne, it resembled a grenade.

Reflexively, he switched off the flashlight even as broken glass was still falling. In the gloom, the grenade thumped softly against the carpet.

Before Spencer could turn away, he was hit by the explosion. No flash of light accompanied it, only ear-shattering sound—and hard shrapnel snapping into him from his shins to his forehead. He cried out. Fell. Twisted. Writhed. Pain in his legs, hands, face. His torso was protected by his denim jacket. But his hands, God, his hands. He wrung his burning hands. Hot pain. Pure torment. How many fingers lost, bones shattered? Jesus, Jesus, his hands were spastic with pain yet half numb, so he couldn't assess the damage.

The worst of it was the fiery agony in his forehead, cheeks, the left corner of his mouth. Excruciating. Desperate to quell the pain, he pressed his hands to his face. He was afraid of what he would find, of the damage he would feel, but his hands throbbed so fiercely that his sense of touch wasn't trustworthy.

How many new scars if he survived—how many pale and puckered cicatricial welts or red keloid monstrosities from hairline to chin?

Get out, get away, find help.

He kicked-crawled-clawed-twitched like a wounded crab through the darkness. Disoriented and terrified, he nevertheless scrambled in the right direction, across a floor now littered with what seemed to be small marbles, into the bedroom doorway. He clambered to his feet.

He figured he was caught in a gang war over disputed turf. Los Angeles in the nineties was more violent than Chicago during Prohibition. Modern youth gangs were more savage and better armed than the Mafia, pumped up with drugs and their own brand of racism, as cold-blooded and merciless as snakes.

Gasping for breath, feeling blindly with aching hands, he stumbled into the hall. Pain coruscated through his legs, weakening him and testing his balance. Staying on his feet was as difficult as it would have been in a revolving fun-house barrel.

Windows shattered in other rooms, followed by a few muffled explosions. The hallway was windowless, so he wasn't hit again.

In spite of his confusion and fear, Spencer realized he didn't smell blood. Didn't taste it. In fact, he wasn't bleeding.

Suddenly he understood what was happening. Not a gang war. The shrapnel hadn't cut him, so it wasn't actually shrapnel. Not marbles, either, littering the floor. Hard rubber pellets. From a sting grenade. Only law-enforcement agencies had sting grenades. He had used them himself. Seconds ago a SWAT team of some kind must have initiated an assault on the bungalow, launching the grenades to disable any occupants.

The moving van had no doubt been covert transport for the assault force. The movement he had seen at the back of it, out of the corner of his eye, hadn't been imaginary after all.

He should have been relieved. The assault was an action of the local police, the Drug Enforcement Administration, the FBI, or another law-enforcement organization. Apparently he had stumbled into one of their operations. He knew the drill. If he dropped to the floor, facedown, arms extended over his head, hands spread to prove they were empty, he would be fine; he wouldn't be shot; they would handcuff him, question him, but they wouldn't harm him further.

Except that he had a big problem: He didn't belong in that bungalow. He was a trespasser. From their point of view, he might even be a burglar. To them, his explanation for being there would seem lame at best. Hell, they would think it was crazy. He didn't really understand it himself—why he was so stricken with Valerie, why he had needed to know about her, why he had been bold enough and stupid enough to enter her house.

He didn't drop to the floor. On wobbly legs, he staggered through the tunnel-black hall, sliding one hand along the wall.

The woman was mixed up in something illegal, and at first the authorities would think that he was involved as well. He would be taken into custody, detained for questioning, maybe even booked on suspicion of aiding and abetting Valerie in whatever she had done.

They would find out who he was.

The news media would dredge up his past. His face would be on television, in newspapers and magazines. He had lived many years in blessed anonymity, his new name unknown, his appearance altered by time, no longer recognizable. But his privacy was about to be stolen. He would be center ring at the circus again, harassed by reporters, whispered about every time he went out in public.

No. Intolerable. He couldn't go through that again. He would rather die.

They were cops of some kind, and he was innocent of any serious offense; but they were not on his side right now. Without meaning to destroy him, they would do so simply by exposing him to the press.

More shattering glass. Two explosions.

The officers on the SWAT team were taking no chances, as if they thought they were up against people crazed on PCP or something worse.

Spencer had reached the midpoint of the hall, where he stood between two doorways. A dim grayness beyond the right-hand door: the dining room. On his left: the bathroom.

He stepped into the bathroom, closed the door, hoping to buy time to think.

The stinging in his face, hands, and legs was slowly subsiding. Rapidly, repeatedly, he clenched his hands, then relaxed them, trying to improve the circulation and work off the numbness.

From the far end of the house came a wood-splintering crash, hard enough to make the walls shudder. It was probably the front door slamming open or going down.

Another crash. The kitchen door.

They were in the house.

They were coming.

No time to think. He had to move, relying on instinct and on military training that was, he hoped, at least as extensive as that of the men who were hunting him.

In the back wall of the cramped room, above the bathtub, the blackness was broken by a rectangle of faint gray light. He stepped into the tub and, with both hands, quickly explored the frame of that small window. He wasn't convinced that it was big enough to provide a way out, but it was the only possible route of escape.

If it had been fixed or jalousied, he would have been trapped. Fortunately, it was a single pane that opened inward from the top on a heavy-duty piano hinge. Collapsible elbow braces on both sides clicked softly when fully extended, locking the window open.

He expected the faint squeak of the hinge and the click of the braces to elicit a shout from someone outside. But the unrelenting drone of the rain screened what sounds he made. No alarm was raised.

Spencer gripped the window ledge and levered himself into the opening. Cold rain spattered his face. The humid air was heavy with the fecund smells of saturated earth, jasmine, and grass.

The backyard was a tapestry of gloom, woven exclusively from shades of black and graveyard grays, washed by rain that blurred its details. At least one man—more likely two—from the SWAT team had to be covering the rear of the house. However, though Spencer's vision was keen, he could not force any of the interwoven shadows to resolve into a human form.

For a moment his upper body seemed wider than the frame, but he hunched his shoulders, twisted, wriggled, and scraped through the opening. The ground was a short drop from the window. He rolled once on the wet grass and then lay flat on his stomach, head raised, surveying the night, still unable to spot any adversaries.

In the planting beds and along the property line, the shrubbery was overgrown. Several old fig trees, long untrimmed, were mighty towers of foliage.

Glimpsed between the branches of those mammoth ficuses, the heavens were not black. The lights of the sprawling metropolis reflected off the bellies of the eastbound storm clouds, painting the vault of the night with deep and sour yellows that, toward the oceanic west, faded into charcoal gray.

Though familiar to Spencer, the unnatural color of the city sky filled him with a surprising and superstitious dread, for it seemed to be a malevolent firmament under which men were meant to die—and to the sight of which they might wake in Hell. It was a mystery how the yard could remain unlit under that sulfurous glow, yet he could have sworn that it grew blacker the longer he squinted at it.

The stinging in his legs subsided. His hands still ached but not disablingly, and the burning in his face was less intense than it had been.

Inside the dark house, an automatic weapon stuttered briefly, spitting out several rounds. One of the cops must be trigger-happy, shooting at shadows or ghosts. Curious. Hair-trigger nerves were uncommon among special-forces officers.

Spencer scuttled across the sodden grass to the shelter of a nearby triple-trunk ficus. Rising to his feet, with his back against the bark, he surveyed the lawn, the shrubs, and the line of trees along the rear property wall, half convinced he should make a break for it, but also half convinced that he would be spotted and brought down if he stepped into the open.

Flexing his hands to work off the pain, he considered climbing into the web of wood above him and hiding in the higher bowers. Useless, of course. They would find him in the tree, because they would not admit to his escape until they had searched every shadow and cloak of greenery, both high and low.

In the bungalow: voices, a door slamming, not even a pretense of stealth and caution any longer, not after the precipitous gunfire. Still no lights.

Time was running out.

Arrest, revelation, the glare of videocam lights, reporters shouting questions. Intolerable.

He silently cursed himself for being so indecisive.

Rain rattled the leaves above.

Newspaper stories, magazine spreads, the hateful past alive again, the gaping stares of thoughtless strangers to whom he would be the walking, breathing equivalent of a spectacular train wreck.

His booming heart counted cadence for the ever quickening march of his fear.

He could not move. Paralyzed.

Paralysis served him well, however, when a man dressed in black crept past the tree, holding a weapon that resembled an Uzi. Though he was no more than two strides from Spencer, the guy was focused on the house, ready if his quarry crashed through a window into the night, unaware that the very fugitive he sought was within reach. Then the man saw the open window at the bathroom, and he froze.

Spencer was moving before his target began to turn. Anyone with SWAT-team training—

whether local cop or federal agent—would not go down easily. The only chance of taking the guy quickly and quietly was to hit him hard while he was in the grip of surprise.

Spencer rammed his right knee into the cop's crotch, putting everything he had behind it, trying to lift the guy off the ground.

Some special-forces officers wore jockstraps with aluminum cups on every enter-and-subdue operation, as surely as they wore bullet-resistant Kevlar body jackets or vests. This one was unprotected. He exhaled explosively, a sound that wouldn't have carried ten feet in the rainy night.

Even as Spencer was driving his knee upward, he seized the automatic weapon with both hands, wrenching it violently clockwise. It twisted out of the other man's grasp before he could convulsively squeeze off a burst of warning fire.

The gunman fell backward on the wet grass. Spencer dropped atop him, carried forward by momentum.

Though the cop tried to cry out, the agony of that intimate blow had robbed him of his voice. He couldn't even inhale.

Spencer could have slammed the weapon—a compact submachine gun, judging by the feel of it—into his adversary's throat, crushing his windpipe, asphyxiating him on his own blood. A blow to the face would have shattered the nose and driven splinters of bone into the brain.

But he didn't want to kill or seriously injure anyone. He just needed time to get the hell out of there. He hammered the gun against the cop's temple, half checking the blow but knocking the poor bastard unconscious.

The guy was wearing night-vision goggles. The SWAT team was conducting a night stalk with full technological assistance, which was why no lights had come on in the house. They had the vision of cats, and Spencer was the mouse.

He rolled onto the grass, rose into a crouch, clutching the submachine gun in both hands. It was an Uzi: He recognized the shape and heft of it. He swept the muzzle left and right, anticipating the charge of another adversary. No one came at him.

Perhaps five seconds had passed since the man in black had crept past the ficus tree.

Spencer sprinted across the lawn, away from the bungalow, into flowers and shrubs. Greenery lashed his legs. Woody azaleas poked his calves, snagged his jeans.

He dropped the Uzi. He wasn't going to shoot at anyone. Even if it meant being taken into custody and exposed to the news media, he would surrender rather than use the gun.

He waded through the shrubs, between two trees, past a eugenia with phosphorescent white blossoms, and reached the property wall.

He was as good as gone. If they spotted him now, they wouldn't shoot him in the back. They'd shout a warning, identify themselves, order him to freeze, and come after him, but they wouldn't shoot.

The stucco-sheathed, concrete-block wall was six feet high, capped with bull-nose bricks that were slippery with rain. He got a grip, pulled himself up, scrabbling at the stucco with the toes of his athletic shoes.

As he slid onto the top of the wall, belly against the cold bricks, and drew up his legs, gunfire erupted behind him. Bullets smacked into the concrete blocks, so close that chips of stucco sprayed his face.

Nobody shouted a goddamned warning.

He rolled off the wall into the neighboring property, and automatic weapons chattered again—a longer burst than before.

Submachine guns in a residential neighborhood. Craziness. What the hell kind of cops were these?

He fell into a tangle of rosebushes. It was winter; the roses had been pruned; even in the colder months, however, the California climate was sufficiently mild to encourage some growth, and thorny trailers snared his clothes, pricked his skin.

Voices, flat and strange, muffled by the static of the rain, came from beyond the wall: "This way, back here, come on!"

Spencer sprang to his feet and flailed through the rose brambles. A spiny trailer scraped the unscarred side of his face and curled around his head as if intent on fitting him with a crown, and he broke free only at the cost of punctured hands.

He was in the backyard of another house. Lights in some of the ground-floor rooms. A face at a rain-jeweled window. A young girl. Spencer had the terrible feeling that he'd be putting her in mortal jeopardy if he didn't get out of there before his pursuers arrived.

After negotiating a maze of yards, block walls, wrought iron fences, cul-de-sacs, and service alleys, never sure if he had lost his pursuers or if they were, in fact, at his heels, Spencer found the street on which he had parked the Explorer. He ran to it and jerked on the door.

Locked, of course.

He fumbled in his pockets for the keys. Couldn't find them. He hoped to God he hadn't lost them along the way.

Rocky was watching him through the driver's window. Apparently he found Spencer's frantic search amusing. He was grinning.

Spencer glanced back along the rain-swept street. Deserted.

One more pocket. Yes. He pressed the deactivating button on the key chain. The security system issued an electronic bleat, the locks popped open, and he clambered into the truck.

As he tried to start the engine, the keys slipped through his wet fingers and fell to the floor.

"Damn!"

Reacting to his master's fear, no longer amused, Rocky huddled timidly in the corner formed by the passenger seat and the door. He made a thin, interrogatory sound of concern.

Though Spencer's hands tingled from the rubber pellets that had stung them, they were no longer numb. Yet he fumbled after the keys for what seemed an age.

Maybe it was best to lie on the seats, out of sight, and keep Rocky below window level. Wait for the cops to come . . . and go. If they arrived just as he was pulling away from the curb, they would suspect he was the one who had been in Valerie's house, and they would stop him one way or another.

On the other hand, he had stumbled into a major operation with a lot of manpower. They weren't going to give up easily. While he was hiding in the truck, they might cordon off the area and initiate a house-to-house search. They would also inspect parked cars as best they could, peering in windows; he would be pinned by a flashlight beam, trapped in his own vehicle.

The engine started with a roar.

He popped the hand brake, shifted gears, and pulled away from the curb, switching on windshield wipers and headlights as he went. He had parked near the corner, so he hung a U-turn.

He glanced at the rearview mirror, the side mirror. No armed men in black uniforms.

A couple of cars sped through the intersection, heading south on the other avenue. Plumes of spray fanned behind them.

Without even pausing at the stop sign, Spencer turned right and entered the southbound flow of traffic, away from Valerie's neighborhood. He resisted the urge to tramp the accelerator into the floorboards. He couldn't risk being stopped for speeding.

"What the hell?" he asked shakily.

The dog replied with a soft whine.

"What's she done, why're they after her?"

Water trickled down his brow into his eyes. He was soaked. He shook his head, and a spray of cold water flew from his hair, spattering the dashboard, the upholstery, and the dog. Rocky flinched.

Spencer turned up the heater.

He drove five blocks and made two changes of direction before he began to feel safe. "Who is she? What the *hell* has she done?"

Rocky had adopted his master's change of mood. He no longer huddled in the corner. Having resumed his vigilant posture in the center of his seat, he was wary but not fearful. He divided his attention between the storm-drenched city ahead and Spencer, favoring the former with guarded anticipation and the latter with a cocked-head expression of puzzlement.

"Jesus, what was I doing there anyway?" Spencer wondered aloud.

Though bathed in hot air from the dashboard vents, he continued to shiver. Part of his chill had nothing to do with being rain-soaked, and no quantity of heat could dispel it.

"Didn't belong there, shouldn't have gone. Do *you* have a clue what I was doing in that place, pal? Hmmmm? Because I sure as hell don't. That was *stupid*."

He reduced speed to negotiate a flooded intersection, where an armada of trash was adrift on the dirty water.

His face felt hot. He glanced at Rocky.

He had just lied to the dog.

Long ago he had sworn never to lie to himself. He kept that oath only somewhat more faithfully than the average drunkard kept his New Year's Eve resolution never to allow demon rum to touch his lips again. In fact, he probably indulged in less self-delusion and self-deception than most people did, but he could not claim, with a straight face, that he invariably told himself the truth. Or even that he invariably wanted to hear it. What it came down to was that he *tried* always to be truthful with himself, but he often accepted a half-truth and a wink instead of the real thing—and he could live comfortably with whatever omission the wink implied.

But he never lied to the dog.

Never.

Theirs was the only entirely honest relationship that Spencer had ever known; therefore, it was special to him. No. More than merely special. Sacred.

Rocky, with his hugely expressive eyes and guileless heart, with his body language and his soul-revealing tail, was incapable of deceit. If he'd been able to talk, he would have been perfectly ingenuous because he was a perfect innocent. Lying to the dog was worse than lying to a small child. Hell, he wouldn't have felt as bad if he had lied to God, because God unquestionably expected less of him than did poor Rocky.

Never lie to the dog.

"Okay," he said, braking for a red traffic light, "so I know why I went to her house. I know what I was looking for."

Rocky regarded him with interest.

"You want me to say it, huh?"

The dog waited.

"That's important to you, is it—for me to say it?"

The dog chuffed, licked his chops, cocked his head.

"All right. I went to her house because—"

The dog stared.

"—because she's a very nice-looking woman."

The rain drummed. The windshield wipers thumped.

"Okay, she's pretty but she's not gorgeous. It isn't her looks. There's just . . . something about her. She's special."

The idling engine rumbled.

Spencer sighed and said, "Okay, I'll be straight this time. Right to the heart of it, huh? No more dancing around the edges. I went to her house because—"

Rocky stared.

"—because I wanted to find a life."

The dog looked away from him, toward the street ahead, evidently satisfied with that final explanation.

Spencer thought about what he had revealed to himself by being honest with Rocky. *I wanted to find a life.*

He didn't know whether to laugh at himself or weep. In the end, he did neither. He just moved on, which was what he'd been doing for at least the past sixteen years.

The traffic light turned green.

With Rocky looking ahead, only ahead, Spencer drove home through the streaming night, through the loneliness of the vast city, under a strangely mottled sky that was as yellow as a rancid egg yolk, as gray as crematorium ashes, and fearfully black along one far horizon.

TWO

At nine o'clock, after the fiasco in Santa Monica, eastbound on the freeway, returning to his hotel in Westwood, Roy Miro noticed a Cadillac stopped on the shoulder of the highway. Serpents of red light from its emergency flashers wriggled across his rain-streaked windshield. The rear tire on the driver's side was flat.

A woman sat behind the steering wheel, evidently waiting for help. She appeared to be the only person in the car.

The thought of a woman alone in such circumstances, in *any* part of greater Los Angeles, worried Roy. These days, the City of Angels wasn't the easygoing place it had once been— and the hope of actually finding anyone living even an approximation of an angelic existence was slim indeed. Devils, yes: Those were relatively easy to locate.

He stopped on the shoulder ahead of the Cadillac.

The downpour was heavier than it had been earlier. A wind had sailed in from the ocean. Silvery sheets of rain, billowing like the transparent canvases of a ghost ship, flapped through the darkness.

He plucked his floppy-brimmed vinyl hat off the passenger seat and squashed it down on his head. As always in bad weather, he was wearing a raincoat and galoshes. In spite of his precautionary dress, he was going to get soaked, but he couldn't in good conscience drive on as if he'd never seen the stranded motorist.

As Roy walked back to the Cadillac, the passing traffic cast an all but continuous spray of filthy water across his legs, pasting his pants to his skin. Well, the suit needed to be dry-cleaned anyway.

When he reached the car, the woman did not put down her window. Staring warily at him through the glass, she reflexively checked the door locks to be sure they were engaged.

He wasn't offended by her suspicion. She was merely wise to the ways of the city and understandably skeptical of his intentions.

He raised his voice to be heard through the closed window: "You need some help?"

She held up a cellular phone. "Called a service station. They said they'll send somebody."

Roy glanced toward the oncoming traffic in the eastbound lanes. "How long have they kept you waiting?"

After a hesitation, she said exasperatedly, "Forever."

"I'll change the tire. You don't have to get out or give me your keys. This car—I've driven one like it. There's a trunk-release knob. Just pop it, so I can get the jack and the spare."

"You could get hurt," she said.

The narrow shoulder offered little safety margin, and the fast-moving traffic *was* unnervingly close. "I've got flares," he said.

Turning away before she could object, Roy hurried to his own car and retrieved all six flares from the roadside-emergency kit in the trunk. He strung them out along the freeway for fifty yards behind the Cadillac, closing off most of the nearest traffic lane.

If a drunk driver barreled out of the night, of course, no precautions would be sufficient. And these days it seemed that sober motorists were outnumbered by those who were high on booze or drugs.

It was an age plagued by social irresponsibility—which was why Roy tried to be a good Samaritan whenever an opportunity arose. If everyone lit just one little candle, what a bright world it would be: He really believed in that.

The woman had released the trunk lock. The lid was ajar.

Roy Miro was happier than he had been all day. Battered by wind and rain, splashed by the passing traffic, he labored with a smile. The more hardship involved, the more rewarding the good deed. As he struggled with a tight lug nut, the wrench slipped and he skinned one knuckle; instead of cursing, he began to whistle while he worked.

When the job was done, the woman lowered the window two inches, so he didn't have to shout. "You're all set," he said.

Sheepishly, she began to apologize for having been so wary of him, but he interrupted to assure her that he understood.

She reminded Roy of his mother, which made him feel even better about helping her. She was attractive, in her early fifties, perhaps twenty years older than Roy, with auburn hair and blue eyes. His mother had been a brunette with hazel eyes, but this woman and his mother had in common an aura of gentleness and refinement.

"This is my husband's business card," she said, passing it through the gap in the window. "He's an accountant. If you need any advice along those lines, no charge."

"I haven't done all that much," Roy said, accepting the card.

"These days, running into someone like you, it's a miracle. I'd have called Sam instead of that damn service station, but he's working late at a client's. Seems we work around the clock these days."

"This recession," Roy sympathized.

"Isn't it ever going to end?" she wondered, rummaging in her purse for something more.

He cupped the business card in his hand to protect it from the rain, turning it so the red glow of the nearest flare illuminated the print. The husband had an office in Century City, where rents were high; no wonder the poor guy was working late to remain afloat.

"And here's my card," the woman said, extracting it from her purse and passing it to him.

Penelope Bettonfield. Interior Designer. 213–555–6868.

She said, "I work out of my home. Used to have an office, but this dreadful recession . . ." She sighed and smiled up at him through the partly open window. "Anyway, if I can ever be of help . . ."

He fished one of his own cards from his wallet and passed it in to her. She thanked him again, closed her window, and drove away.

Roy walked back along the highway, clearing the flares off the pavement so they would not continue to obstruct traffic.

In his car once more, heading for his hotel in Westwood, he was exhilarated to have lit his one little candle for the day. Sometimes he wondered if there was any hope for modern society, if it was going to spiral down into a hell of hatred and crime and greed—but then he encountered someone like Penelope Bettonfield, with her sweet smile and her aura of gentleness and refinement, and he found it possible to be hopeful again. She was a caring person who would repay his kindness to her by being kind to someone else.

In spite of Mrs. Bettonfield, Roy's fine mood didn't last. By the time he left the freeway for Wilshire Boulevard and drove into Westwood, a sadness had crept over him.

He saw signs of social devolution everywhere. Spray-painted graffiti defaced the retaining walls of the freeway exit ramp and obscured the directions on a couple of traffic signs, in an area of the city previously spared such dreary vandalism. A homeless man, pushing a shopping cart full of pathetic possessions, trudged through the rain, his face expressionless, as if he were a zombie shuffling along the aisles of a Kmart in Hell.

At a stoplight, in the lane beside Roy, a car full of fierce-looking young men—skinheads, each with one glittering earring—glared at him malevolently, perhaps trying to decide if he looked like a Jew. They mouthed obscenities with care, to be sure he could read their lips.

He passed a movie theater where the films were all swill of one kind or another. Extravaganzas of violence. Seamy tales of raw sex. Films from big studios, with famous stars, but swill nonetheless.

Gradually, his impression of his encounter with Mrs. Bettonfield changed. He remembered what she'd said about the recession, about the long hours that she and her husband were working, about the poor economy that had forced her to close her design office and run her faltering business from her home. She was such a nice lady. He was saddened to think that she had financial worries. Like all of them, she was a victim of the system, trapped in a society that was awash in drugs and guns but that was bereft of compassion and commitment to high ideals. She deserved better.

By the time he reached his hotel, the Westwood Marquis, Roy was in no mood to go to his room, order a late dinner from room service, and turn in for the night—which was what he'd been planning to do. He drove past the place, kept going to Sunset Boulevard, turned left, and just cruised in circles for a while.

Eventually he parked at the curb two blocks from UCLA, but he didn't switch off the engine. He clambered across the gearshift into the passenger seat, where the steering wheel would not interfere with his work.

His cellular phone was fully charged. He unplugged it from the cigarette lighter.

From the backseat, he retrieved an attaché case. He opened it on his lap, revealing a compact computer with a built-in modem. He plugged it into the cigarette lighter and switched it on. The display screen lit. The basic menu appeared, from which he made a selection.

He married the cellular phone to the modem, and then called the direct-access number that would link his terminal with the dual Cray supercomputers in the home office. In seconds, the connection was made, and the familiar security litany began with three words that appeared on his screen: WHO GOES THERE?

He typed his name: ROY MIRO.

YOUR IDENTIFICATION NUMBER?

Roy provided it.

YOUR PERSONAL CODE PHRASE?

POOH, he typed, which he had chosen as his code because it was the name of his favorite fictional character of all time, the honey-seeking and unfailingly good-natured bear.

RIGHT THUMBPRINT PLEASE.

A two-inch-square white box appeared in the upper-right quadrant of the blue screen. He pressed his thumb in the indicated space and waited while sensors in the monitor modeled the whorls in his skin by directing microbursts of intense light at them and then contrasting the comparative shadowiness of the troughs to the marginally more reflective ridges. After a minute, a soft beep indicated that the scanning was completed. When he lifted his thumb, a detailed black-line image of his print filled the center of the white box. After an additional thirty seconds, the print vanished from the screen; it had been digitized, transmitted by phone to the home-office computer, electronically compared to his print on file, and approved.

Roy had access to considerably more sophisticated technology than the average hacker with a few thousand dollars and the address of the nearest Computer City store. Neither the electronics in his attaché case nor the software that had been installed in the machine could be purchased by the general public.

A message appeared on the display: ACCESS TO MAMA IS GRANTED.

Mama was the name of the home-office computer. Three thousand miles away on the East Coast, all her programs were now available for Roy's use, through his cellular phone. A long menu appeared on the screen before him. He scrolled through, found a program titled LOCATE, and selected it.

He typed in a telephone number and requested the street address at which it was located.

While he waited for Mama to access phone company records and trace the listing, Roy studied the storm-lashed street. At that moment, no pedestrians or moving cars were in sight. Some houses were dark, and the lights of the others were dimmed by the seemingly eternal torrents of rain. He could almost believe that a strange, silent apocalypse had transpired, eliminating all human life on earth while leaving the works of civilization untouched.

A real apocalypse *was* coming, he supposed. Sooner than later, a great war: nation against nation or race against race, religions clashing violently or ideology battling ideology. Humanity was drawn to turmoil and self-destruction as inevitably as the earth was drawn to complete its annual revolution of the sun.

His sadness deepened.

Under the telephone number on the video display, the correct name appeared. The address, however, was listed as unpublished by request of the customer.

Roy instructed the home-office computer to access and search the phone company's electronically stored installation and billing records to find the address. Such an invasion of private-sector data was illegal, of course, without a court order, but Mama was exceedingly discreet. Because all the computer systems in the national telephone network were already in Mama's directory of previously violated entities, she was able to enter any of them virtually instantaneously, explore at will, retrieve whatever was requested, and disengage without leaving the slightest trace that she had been there; Mama was a ghost in their machines.

In seconds, a Beverly Hills address appeared on the screen.

He cleared the screen and then asked Mama for a street map of Beverly Hills. She supplied it after a brief hesitation. Seen in its entirety, it was too compressed to be read.

Roy typed in the address that he'd been given. The computer filled the screen with the quadrant that was of interest to him, and then with a quarter of that quadrant. The house was only a couple of blocks south of Wilshire Boulevard, in the less prestigious "flats" of Beverly Hills, and easy to find.

He typed POOH OUT, which disengaged his portable terminal from Mama in her cool, dry bunker in Virginia.

The large brick house—which was painted white, with hunter-green shutters—stood behind a white picket fence. The front lawn featured two enormous bare-limbed sycamores.

Lights were on inside, but only at the back of the house and only on the first floor.

Standing at the front door, sheltered from the rain by a deep portico supported on tall white columns, Roy could hear music inside: a Beatles number, "When I'm Sixty-four." He was thirty-three; the Beatles were before his time, but he liked their music because much of it embodied an endearing compassion.

Softly humming along with the lads from Liverpool, Roy slipped a credit card between the door and the jamb. He worked it upward until it forced open the first—and least formidable—of the two locks. He wedged the card in place to hold the simple spring latch out of the niche in the striker plate.

To open the heavy-duty deadbolt, he needed a more sophisticated tool than a credit card: a Lockaid lock-release gun, sold only to law-enforcement agencies. He slipped the thin pick of the gun into the key channel, under the pin tumblers, and pulled the trigger. The flat steel spring in the Lockaid caused the pick to jump upward and to lodge some of the pins at the shear line. He had to pull the trigger half a dozen times to fully disengage the lock.

The snapping of hammer against spring and the clicking of pick against pin tumblers were not thunderous sounds, by any measure, but he was grateful for the cover provided by the music. "When I'm Sixty-four" ended as he opened the door. Before his credit card could fall, he caught it, froze, and waited for the next song. To the opening bars of "Lovely Rita," he stepped across the threshold.

He put the lock-release gun on the floor, to the right of the entrance. Quietly, he closed the door behind him.

The foyer welcomed him with gloom. He stood with his back against the door, letting his eyes adjust to the shadows.

When he was confident that he would not blindly knock over any furniture, he proceeded from room to room, toward the light at the back of the house.

He regretted that his clothes were so saturated and his galoshes so dirty. He was probably making a mess of the carpet.

She was in the kitchen, at the sink, washing a head of lettuce, her back to the swinging door through which he entered. Judging by the vegetables on the cutting board, she was preparing a salad.

Easing the door shut behind him, hoping to avoid startling her, he debated whether or not to announce himself. He wanted her to know that it was a concerned friend who had come to comfort her, not a stranger with sick motives.

She turned off the running water and placed the lettuce in a plastic colander to drain. Wiping her hands on a dish towel, turning away from the sink, she finally discovered him as "Lovely Rita" drew to an end.

Mrs. Bettonfield looked surprised but not, in the first instant, afraid—which was, he knew, a tribute to his appealing, soft-featured face. He was slightly pudgy, with dimples, and had skin so beardless that it was almost as smooth as a boy's. With his twinkling blue eyes and warm smile, he would make a convincing Santa Claus in another thirty years. He believed that his kindheartedness and his genuine love of people were also apparent, because strangers usually warmed to him more quickly than a merry face alone could explain.

While Roy still was able to believe that her wide-eyed surprise would fade into a smile of welcome rather than a grimace of fear, he raised the Beretta 93-R and shot her twice in the chest. A silencer was screwed to the barrel; both rounds made only soft popping sounds.

Penelope Bettonfield dropped to the floor and lay motionless on her side, with her hands still entangled in the dish towel. Her eyes were open, staring across the floor at his wet, dirty galoshes.

The Beatles began "Good Morning, Good Morning." It must be the *Sgt. Pepper* album.

He crossed the kitchen, put the pistol on the counter, and crouched beside Mrs. Bettonfield. He pulled off one of his supple leather gloves and placed his fingertips to her throat, searching for a pulse in her carotid artery. She was dead.

One of the two rounds was so perfectly placed that it must have pierced her heart. Consequently, with circulation halted in an instant, she had not bled much.

Her death had been a graceful escape: quick and clean, painless and without fear.

He pulled on his right glove again, then rubbed gently at her neck where he had touched it. Gloved, he had no concern that his fingerprints might be lifted off the body by laser technology.

Precautions must be taken. Not every judge and juror would be able to grasp the purity of his motives.

He closed the lid over her left eye and held it in place for a minute or so, to be sure that it would stay shut.

"Sleep, dear lady," he said with a mixture of affection and regret, as he also closed the lid over her right eye. "No more worrying about finances, no more working late, no more stress and strife. You were too good for this world."

It was both a sad and a joyous moment. Sad, because her beauty and elegance no longer brightened the world; nevermore would her smile lift anyone's spirits; her courtesy and consideration would no longer counter the tides of barbarity washing over this troubled society. Joyous, because she would never again be afraid, spill tears, know grief, feel pain.

"Good Morning, Good Morning" gave way to the marvelously bouncy, syncopated reprise of "Sgt. Pepper's Lonely Hearts Club Band," which was better than the first rendition of the song at the start of the album and which seemed a suitably upbeat celebration of Mrs. Bettonfield's passage to a better world.

Roy pulled out one of the chairs from the kitchen table, sat, and removed his galoshes. He rolled up the damp and muddy legs of his trousers as well, determined to cause no more mess.

The reprise of the album theme song was short, and by the time he got to his feet again, "A Day in the Life" had begun. That was a singularly melancholy piece, too somber to be in sync with the moment. He had to shut it off before it depressed him. He was a sensitive man, more vulnerable than most to the emotional effects of music, poetry, fine paintings, fiction, and the other arts.

He found the central music system in a long wall of beautifully crafted mahogany cabinets in the study. He stopped the music and searched two drawers that were filled with compact discs. Still in the mood for the Beatles, he selected *A Hard Day's Night* because none of the songs on that album were downbeat.

Singing along to the title track, Roy returned to the kitchen, where he lifted Mrs. Bettonfield off the floor. She was more petite than she had seemed when he'd been talking with her through the car window. She weighed no more than a hundred and five pounds, with slender wrists, a swan neck, and delicate features. Roy was deeply touched by the woman's fragility, and he bore her in his arms with more than mere care and respect, almost with reverence.

Nudging light switches with his shoulder, he carried Penelope Bettonfield to the front of the house, upstairs, along the hallway, checking door by door until he found the master bedroom. There, he placed her gently on a chaise lounge.

He folded back the quilted bedspread and then the bedclothes, revealing the bottom sheet. He plumped the pillows, which were in Egyptian-cotton shams trimmed with cutwork lace as lovely as any he had ever seen.

He took off Mrs. Bettonfield's shoes and put them in her closet. Her feet were as small as those of a girl.

Leaving her fully dressed, he carried Penelope to the bed and put her down on her back, with her head elevated on two pillows. He left the spread folded at the bottom of the bed, but he drew the blanket cover, blanket, and top sheet over her breasts. Her arms remained free.

With a brush that he found in the master bathroom, he smoothed her hair. The Beatles were singing "If I Fell" when he began to groom her, but they were well into "I'm Happy Just to Dance with You" by the time her lustrous auburn locks were perfectly arranged around her lovely face.

After switching on the bronze floor lamp that stood beside the chaise lounge, he turned off the harsher ceiling light. Soft shadows fell across the recumbent woman, like the enfolding wings of angels who had come to carry her away from this vale of tears and into a higher land of eternal peace.

He went to the Louis XVI vanity, removed its matching chair, and put it beside the bed. He sat next to Mrs. Bettonfield, stripped off his gloves, and took one of her hands in both of his. Her flesh was cooling but still somewhat warm.

He couldn't linger for long. There was much yet to do and not a lot of time in which to do it. Nevertheless, he wanted to spend a few minutes of quality time with Mrs. Bettonfield.

While the Beatles sang "And I Love Her" and "Tell Me Why," Roy Miro tenderly held his late friend's hand and took a moment to appreciate the exquisite furniture, the paintings, the art objects, the warm color scheme, and the array of fabrics in different but wonderfully complementary patterns and textures.

"It's so very unfair that you had to close your shop," he told Penelope. "You were a fine interior designer. You really were, dear lady. You really were."

The Beatles sang.

Rain beat upon the windows.

Roy's heart swelled with emotion.

THREE

Rocky recognized the route home. Periodically, as they passed one landmark or another, he chuffed softly with pleasure.

Spencer lived in a part of Malibu that was without glamour but that had its own wild beauty.

All the forty-room Mediterranean and French mansions, the ultra modern cliff side dwellings of tinted glass and redwood and steel, the Cape Cod cottages as large as ocean liners, the twenty-thousand-square-foot Southwest adobes with authentic lodgepole ceilings and authentic twenty-seat personal screening rooms with THX sound, were on the beaches, on the bluffs above the beaches—and inland of the Pacific Coast Highway, on hills with a view of the sea.

Spencer's place was east of any home that *Architectural Digest* would choose to photograph, halfway up an unfashionable and sparsely populated canyon. The two-lane blacktop was textured by patches atop patches and by numerous cracks courtesy of the earthquakes that regularly quivered through the entire coast. A pipe-and-chain-link gate, between a pair of mammoth eucalyptuses, marked the entrance to his two-hundred-yard-long gravel driveway.

Wired to the gate was a rusted sign with fading red letters: DANGER / ATTACK DOG. He had fixed it there when he first purchased the place, long before Rocky had come to live with him. There had been no dog then, let alone one trained to kill. The sign was an empty threat, but effective. No one ever bothered him in his retreat.

The gate was not electrically operated. He had to get out in the rain to unlock it and to relock it after he'd driven through.

With only one bedroom, a living room, and a large kitchen, the structure at the end of the driveway was not a house, really, but a cabin. The cedar-clad exterior, perched on a stone foundation to foil termites, weathered to a lustrous silver gray, might have appeared shabby to an unappreciative eye; to Spencer it was beautiful and full of character in the wash of the Explorer's headlights.

The cabin was sheltered—surrounded, shrouded, *encased*—by a eucalyptus grove. The trees were red gums, safe from the Australian beetles that had been devouring California blue gums for more than a decade. They had not been topped since Spencer had bought the place.

Beyond the grove, brush and scrub oak covered the canyon floor and the steep slopes to the ridges. Summer through autumn, leached of moisture by dry Santa Ana winds, the hills and the ravines became tinder. Twice in eight years, firefighters had ordered Spencer to evacuate, when blazes in neighboring canyons might have swept down on him as mercilessly as judgment day. Wind-driven flames could move at express-train speeds. One night they might overwhelm him in his sleep. But the beauty and privacy of the canyon justified the risk.

At various times in his life, he had fought hard to stay alive, but he was not afraid to die. Sometimes he even embraced the thought of going to sleep and never waking. When fears of fire troubled him, he worried not about himself but about Rocky.

That Wednesday night in February, the burning season was months away. Every tree and bush and blade of wild grass dripped rain and seemed as if it would be forever impervious to fire.

The house was cold. It could be heated by a big river-rock fireplace in the living room, but each room also had its own in-wall electric heater. Spencer preferred the dancing light, the crackle, and the smell of a log fire, but he switched on the heaters because he was in a hurry.

After changing from his damp clothes into a comfortable gray jogging suit and athletic socks, he brewed a pot of coffee. For Rocky, he set out a bowl of orange juice.

The mutt had many peculiarities besides a taste for orange juice. For one thing, though he enjoyed going for walks during the day, he had none of a dog's usual frisky interest in the nocturnal world, preferring to keep at least a window between himself and the night; if he *had* to go outside after sunset, he stayed close to Spencer and regarded the darkness with suspicion. Then there was Paul Simon. Rocky was indifferent to most music, but Simon's voice enchanted him; if Spencer put on a Simon album, especially *Graceland*, Rocky would sit in front of the speakers, staring intently, or pace the floor in lazy, looping patterns—off the beat, lost in reverie—to "Diamonds on the Soles of Her Shoes" or "You Can Call Me Al." Not a doggy thing to do. Less doggy still was his bashfulness about bodily functions, for he wouldn't make his toilet if watched; Spencer had to turn his back before Rocky would get down to business.

Sometimes Spencer thought that the dog, having suffered a hard life until two years ago and having had little reason to find joy in a canine's place in the world, wanted to be a human being.

That was a big mistake. People were more likely to live a dog's life, in the negative sense of the phrase, than were most dogs.

"Greater self-awareness," he'd told Rocky on a night when sleep wouldn't come, "doesn't make a species any happier, pal. If it did, we'd have fewer psychiatrists and barrooms than you dogs have—and it's not that way, is it?"

Now, as Rocky lapped at the juice in the bowl on the kitchen floor, Spencer carried a mug of coffee to the expansive L-shaped desk in one corner of the living room. Two computers with large hard-disk capacities, a full-color laser printer, and other pieces of equipment were arrayed from one end of the work surface to the other.

That corner of the living room was his office, though he had not held a real job in ten months. Since leaving the Los Angeles Police Department—where, during his last two years, he'd been on assignment to the California Multi-Agency Task Force on Computer Crime—he had spent several hours a day on-line with his own computers.

Sometimes he researched subjects of interest to him, through Prodigy and GEnie. More often, however, he explored ways to gain unapproved access to private and government computers that were protected by sophisticated security programs.

Once entry was achieved, he was engaged in illegal activity. He never destroyed any company's or agency's files, never inserted false data. Still, he was guilty of trespassing in private domains.

He could live with that.

He was not seeking material rewards. His compensation was knowledge—and the occasional satisfaction of righting a wrong.

Like the Beckwatt case.

The previous December, when a serial child molester—Henry Beckwatt—was to be released from prison after serving less than five years, the California State Parole Board had refused, in the interest of prisoners' rights, to divulge the name of the community in which he would be residing during the term of his parole. Because Beckwatt had beaten some of his victims and expressed no remorse, his pending release raised anxiety levels in parents statewide.

Taking great pains to cover his tracks, Spencer had first gained entry to the Los Angeles Police Department's computers, stepped from there to the state attorney general's system in Sacramento, and from there into the parole board's computer, where he finessed the address to which Beckwatt would be paroled. Anonymous tips to a few reporters forced the parole board to delay action until a secret new placement could be worked out. During the following five weeks, Spencer exposed three more addresses for Beckwatt, shortly after each was arranged.

Although officials had been in a frenzy to uncover an imagined snitch within the parole system, no one had wondered, at least not publicly, if the leak had been from their electronic-data files, sprung by a clever hacker. Finally admitting defeat, they paroled Beckwatt to an empty caretaker's house on the grounds of San Quentin.

In a couple of years, when his period of post-prison supervision ended, Beckwatt would be free to prowl again, and he would surely destroy more children psychologically if not physically. For the time being, however, he was unable to settle into a lair in the middle of a neighborhood of unsuspecting innocents.

If Spencer could have discovered a way to access God's computer, he would have tampered with Henry Beckwatt's destiny by giving him an immediate and mortal stroke or by walking him into the path of a runaway truck. He wouldn't have hesitated to ensure the justice that modern society, in its Freudian confusion and moral paralysis, found difficult to impose.

He was not a hero, not a scarred and computer-wielding cousin of Batman, not out to save the world. Mostly, he sailed cyberspace—that eerie dimension of energy and information within computers and computer networks—simply because it fascinated him as much as Tahiti and far Tortuga fascinated some people, enticed him in the way that the moon and Mars enticed the men and women who became astronauts.

Perhaps the most appealing aspect of that other dimension was the potential for exploration and discovery that it offered—*without direct human interaction.* When Spencer avoided computer bulletin boards and other user-to-user conversations, cyberspace was an uninhabited universe, created by human beings yet strangely devoid of them. He wandered through vast structures of data, which were infinitely more grand than the pyramids of Egypt, the ruins of ancient Rome, or the rococo hives of the world's great cities—yet saw no human face, heard no human voice. He was Columbus without shipmates, Magellan walking alone across electronic highways and through metropolises of data as unpopulated as ghost towns in the Nevada wastelands.

Now, he sat before one of his computers, switched it on, and sipped coffee while it went through its start-up procedures. These included the Norton AntiVirus program, to be sure that none of his files had been contaminated by a destructive bug during his previous venture into the national data webs. The machine was uninfected.

The first telephone number that he entered was for a service offering twenty-four-hour-a-day stock market quotations. In seconds, the connection was made, and a greeting appeared on his computer screen: WELCOME TO WORLDWIDE STOCK MARKET INFORMATION, INC.

Using his subscriber ID, Spencer requested information about Japanese stocks. Simultaneously he activated a parallel program that he had designed himself and that searched the open phone line for the subtle electronic signature of a listening device. Worldwide Stock Market Information was a legitimate data service, and no police agency had reason to eavesdrop on its lines; therefore, evidence of a tap would indicate that his own telephone was being monitored.

Rocky padded in from the kitchen and rubbed his head against Spencer's leg. The mutt couldn't have finished his orange juice so quickly. He was evidently more lonely than thirsty.

Keeping his attention on the video display, waiting for an alarm or an all-clear, Spencer reached down with one hand and gently scratched behind the dog's ears.

Nothing he had done as a hacker could have drawn the attention of the authorities, but caution was advisable. In recent years, the National Security Agency, the Federal Bureau of Investigation, and other organizations had established computer-crime divisions, all of which zealously prosecuted offenders.

Sometimes they were almost criminally zealous. Like every overstaffed government agency, each computer-crime project was eager to justify its ever increasing budget. Every year a greater number of arrests and convictions was required to support the contention that electronic theft and vandalism were escalating at a frightening rate. Consequently, from time to time, hackers who had stolen nothing and who had wrought no destruction were brought to trial on flimsy charges. They weren't prosecuted with any intention that, by their example, they would deter crime; their convictions were sought merely to create the statistics that ensured higher funding for the project.

Some of them were sent to prison.

Sacrifices on the altars of bureaucracy.

Martyrs to the cyberspace underground.

Spencer was determined never to become one of them.

As the rain rattled against the cabin roof and the wind stirred a whispery chorus of lamenting ghosts from the eucalyptus grove, he waited, with his gaze fixed on the upper-right corner of the video screen. In red letters, a single word appeared: CLEAR.

No taps were in operation.

After logging off Worldwide Stock Market, he dialed the main computer of the California Multi-Agency Task Force on Computer Crime. He entered that system by a deeply concealed back door that he had inserted prior to resigning as second in command of the unit.

Because he was accepted at the system-manager level (the highest security clearance), all functions were available to him. He could use the task force's computer as long as he wanted, for whatever purpose he wished, and his presence wouldn't be observed or recorded.

He had no interest in their files. He used their computer only as a jumping-off point into the Los Angeles Police Department system, to which they had direct access. The irony of employing a computer-crime unit's hardware and software to commit even a minor computer crime was appealing.

It was also dangerous.

Nearly everything that was fun, of course, was also a little dangerous: riding roller coasters, skydiving, gambling, sex.

From the LAPD system, he entered the California Department of Motor Vehicles computer in Sacramento. He got such a kick from making those leaps that he felt almost as though he had traveled physically, teleporting from his canyon in Malibu to Los Angeles to Sacramento, in the manner of a character in a science fiction novel.

Rocky jumped onto his hind legs, planted his forepaws on the edge of the desk, and peered at the computer screen.

"You wouldn't enjoy this," Spencer said.

Rocky looked at him and issued a short, soft whine.

"I'm sure you'd get a lot more pleasure from chewing on that new rawhide bone I got you."

Peering at the screen again, Rocky inquisitively cocked his furry head.

"Or I could put on some Paul Simon for you."

Another whine. Longer and louder than before.

Sighing, Spencer pulled another chair next to his own. "All right. When a fella has a bad case of the lonelies, I guess chewing on a rawhide bone just isn't as good as having a little company. Never works for me, anyway."

Rocky hopped into the chair, panting and grinning.

Together, they went voyaging in cyberspace, plunging illegally into the galaxy of DMV records, searching for Valerie Keene.

They found her in seconds. Spencer had hoped for an address different from the one he already knew, but he was disappointed. She was listed at the bungalow in Santa Monica, where he had discovered unfurnished rooms and the photo of a cockroach nailed to one wall.

According to the data that scrolled up the screen, she had a Class C license, without restrictions. It would expire in a little less than four years. She had applied for the license and taken a written test in early December, two months ago.

Her middle name was Ann.

She was twenty-nine. Spencer had guessed twenty-five.

Her driving record was free of violations.

In the event that she was gravely injured and her own life could not be saved, she had authorized the donation of her vital organs.

Otherwise, the DMV offered little information about her:

SEX:	F	HAIR:	BRN	EYES:	BRN
HT:	5–4	WT:	115		

That bureaucratic thumbnail description wouldn't be of much help when Spencer needed to describe her to someone. It was insufficient to conjure an image that included the things that truly distinguished her: the direct and clear-eyed stare, the slightly lopsided smile, the dimple in her right cheek, the delicate line of her jaw.

Since last year, with federal funding from the National Crime and Terrorism Prevention Act, the California DMV had been digitizing and electronically storing photographs and thumbprints of new and renewing drivers. Eventually, there would be mug shots and prints on file for every resident with a driver's license, though the vast majority had never been accused of a crime, let alone convicted.

Spencer considered this the first step toward a national ID card, an internal passport of the type that had been required in the communist states before they had collapsed, and he was opposed to it on principle. In this instance, however, his principles didn't prevent him from calling up the photo from Valerie's license.

The screen flickered, and she appeared. Smiling.

The banshee eucalyptuses whisper-wailed complaints of eternity's indifference, and the rain drummed, drummed.

Spencer realized that he was holding his breath. He exhaled.

Peripherally, he was aware of Rocky staring at him curiously, then at the screen, then at him again.

He picked up the mug and sipped some black coffee. His hand was shaking.

Valerie had known that authorities of one kind or another were hunting her, and she had known that they were getting close—because she had vacated her bungalow only hours before they'd come for her. If she was innocent, why would she settle for the unstable and fear-filled life of a fugitive?

Putting the mug aside and his fingers to the keyboard, he asked for a hard copy of the photo on the screen.

The laser printer hummed. A single sheet of white paper slid out of the machine.

Valerie. Smiling.

In Santa Monica, no one had called for surrender before the assault on the bungalow had begun. When the attackers burst inside, there had been no warning shouts of *Police*!

Yet Spencer was certain that those men had been officers of one law-enforcement agency or another because of their uniformlike dress, night-vision goggles, weaponry, and military methodology.

Valerie. Smiling.

That soft-voiced woman with whom Spencer had talked last night at The Red Door had seemed gentle and honest, less capable of deceit than were most people. First thing, she had looked boldly at his scar and had asked about it, not with pity welling in her eyes, not with an edge of morbid curiosity in her voice, but in the same way that she might have asked where he'd bought the shirt he'd been wearing. Most people studied the scar surreptitiously and managed to speak of it, if at all, only when they realized that he was aware of their intense curiosity. Valerie's frankness had been refreshing. When he'd told her only that he'd been in an accident when he was a child, Valerie had sensed that he either didn't want or wasn't able to talk about it, and she had dropped the subject as if it mattered no more than his hairstyle. Thereafter, he never caught her gaze straying to the pallid brand on his face; more important, he never had the feeling that she was struggling *not* to look. She found other things about him more interesting than that pale welt from ear to chin.

Valerie. In black and white.

He could not believe that this woman was capable of committing a major crime, and certainly not one so heinous that a SWAT team would come after her in utmost silence, with submachine guns and every high-tech advantage.

She might be traveling with someone dangerous.

Spencer doubted that. He reviewed the few clues: one set of dinnerware, one drinking glass, one set of stainless steel flatware, an air mattress adequate for one but too small for two.

Yet the possibility remained: She might not be alone, and the person with her might rate the extreme caution of the SWAT team.

The photo, printed from the computer screen, was too dark to do her justice. Spencer directed the laser printer to produce another, just a shade lighter than the first.

That printout was better, and he asked for five more copies.

Until he held her likeness in his hands, Spencer had not been consciously aware that he was going to follow Valerie Keene wherever she had gone, find her, and help her. Regardless of what she might have done, even if she was guilty of a crime, regardless of the cost to himself, whether or not she could ever care for him, Spencer was going to stand with this woman against whatever darkness she faced.

As he realized the deeper implications of the commitment that he was making, a chill of wonder shivered him, for until that moment he had thought of himself as a thoroughly modern man who believed in no one and nothing, neither in God Almighty nor in himself.

Softly, touched by awe and unable fully to understand his own motivations, he said, "I'll be damned."

The dog sneezed.

FOUR

By the time the Beatles were singing "I'll Cry Instead," Roy Miro detected a cooling in the dead woman's hand that began to seep into his own flesh.

He let go of her and put on his gloves. He wiped her hands with one corner of the top sheet to smear any oils from his own skin that might have left the patterns of his fingertips.

Filled with conflicting emotions—grief at the death of a good woman, joy at her release from a world of pain and disappointment—he went downstairs to the kitchen. He wanted to be in a position to hear the automatic garage door when Penelope's husband came home.

A few spots of blood had congealed on the tile floor. Roy used paper towels and a spray bottle of Fantastik, which he found in the cabinet under the kitchen sink, to clean away the mess.

After he wiped up the dirty prints of his galoshes as well, he noticed that the stainless steel sink wasn't as well kept as it could have been, and he scrubbed until it was spotless.

The window in the microwave was smeared. It sparkled when he was done with it.

By the time the Beatles were halfway through "I'll Be Back" and Roy had wiped down the front of the Sub-Zero refrigerator, the garage door rumbled upward. He threw the used paper towels into the trash compactor, put away the Fantastik, and retrieved the Beretta that he had left on the counter after delivering Penelope from her suffering.

The kitchen and garage were separated only by a small laundry room. He turned to that closed door.

The rumble of the car engine echoed off the garage walls as Sam Bettonfield drove inside. The engine cut off. The big door clattered and creaked as it rolled down behind the car.

Home from the accountant wars at last. Weary of working late, crunching numbers. Weary of paying high office rents in Century City, trying to stay afloat in a system that valued money more than people.

In the garage, a car door slammed.

Burned out from the stress of life in a city that was riddled with injustice and at war with itself, Sam would be looking forward to a drink, a kiss from Penelope, a late dinner, perhaps an hour of television. Those simple pleasures and eight hours of restful sleep constituted the poor man's only respite from his greedy and demanding clients—and his sleep was likely to be tormented by bad dreams.

Roy had something better to offer. Blessed escape.

The sound of a key in the lock between the garage and the house, the *clack* of the dead bolt, a door opening: Sam entered the laundry.

Roy raised the Beretta as the inner door opened.

Wearing a raincoat, carrying a briefcase, Sam stepped into the kitchen. He was a balding man with quick dark eyes. He looked startled but sounded at ease. "You must have the wrong house."

Eyes misting with tears, Roy said, "I know what you're going through," and he squeezed off three quick shots.

Sam was not a large man, perhaps fifty pounds heavier than his wife. Nevertheless, getting him upstairs to the bedroom, wrestling him out of his raincoat, pulling off his shoes, and hoisting him into bed was not easy. When the task had been accomplished, Roy felt good about himself because he knew that he had done the right thing by placing Sam and Penelope together and in dignified circumstances.

He pulled the bedclothes over Sam's chest. The top sheet was trimmed with cut-work lace to match the pillow shams, so the dead couple appeared to be dressed in fancy surplices of the sort that angels might wear.

The Beatles had stopped singing a while ago. Outside, the soft and somber sound of the rain was as cold as the city that received it—as relentless as the passage of time and the fading of all light.

Though he had done a caring thing, and though there was joy in the end of these people's suffering, Roy was sad. It was a strangely sweet sadness, and the tears that it wrung from him were cleansing.

Eventually he went downstairs to clean up the few drops of Sam's blood that spotted the kitchen floor. He found the vacuum cleaner in the big closet under the stairs, and he swept away the dirt that he had tracked on the carpet when he'd first come into the house.

In Penelope's purse, he searched for the business card that he had given her. The name on it was phony, but he retrieved it anyway.

Finally, using the telephone in the study, he dialed 911.

When a policewoman answered, Roy said, "It's very sad here. It's very sad. Someone should come right away."

He did not return the handset to the cradle, but put it down on the desk, leaving the line open. The Bettonfields' address should have appeared on a computer screen in front of the policewoman who had answered the call, but Roy didn't want to take a chance that Sam and Penelope might be there for hours or even days before they were found. They were good people and did not deserve the indignity of being discovered stiff, gray, and reeking of decomposition.

He carried his galoshes and shoes to the front door, where he quickly put them on again. He remembered to pick up the lock-release gun from the foyer floor.

He walked through the rain to his car and drove away from there.

According to his watch, the time was twenty minutes past ten. Although it was three hours later on the East Coast, Roy was sure that his contact in Virginia would be waiting.

At the first red traffic light, he popped open the attaché case on the passenger seat. He plugged in the computer, which was still married to the cellular phone; he didn't separate the devices because he needed both. With a few quick keystrokes, he set up the cellular unit to respond to preprogrammed vocal instructions and to function as a speakerphone, which freed both his hands for driving.

As the traffic light turned green, he crossed the intersection and made the long-distance call by saying, "Please connect," and then reciting the number in Virginia.

After the second ring, the familiar voice of Thomas Summerton came down the line, recognizable by a single word, as smooth and as southern as pecan butter. "Hello?"

Roy said, "May I speak to Jerry, please?"

"Sorry, wrong number." Summerton hung up.

Roy terminated the resultant dial tone by saying: "Please disconnect now."

In ten minutes, Summerton would call back from a secure phone, and they could speak freely without fear of being recorded.

Roy drove past the glitzy shops on Rodeo Drive to Santa Monica Boulevard, and then west into residential streets. Large, expensive houses stood among huge trees, palaces of privilege that he found offensive.

When the phone rang, he didn't reach for the keypad but said, "Please accept call."

The connection was made with an audible click.

"Please scramble now," Roy said.

The computer beeped to indicate that everything he said would be rendered unintelligible to anyone between him and Summerton. As it was transmitted, their speech would be broken into small pieces of sound and rearranged by a randomlike control factor. Both phones were synchronized with the *same* control factor, so the meaningless streams of transmitted sound would be reassembled into intelligible speech when received.

"I've seen the early report on Santa Monica," Summerton said.

"According to neighbors, she was there this morning. But she must've skipped by the time we set up surveillance this afternoon."

"What tipped her off?"

"I swear she has a sixth sense about us." Roy turned west on Sunset Boulevard, joining the heavy flow of traffic that gilded the wet pavement with headlight beams. "You heard about the man who showed up?"

"And got away."

"We weren't sloppy."

"So he was just lucky?"

"No. Worse than that. He knew what he was doing."

"You saying he's somebody with a history?"

"Yeah."

"Local, state, or federal history?"

"He took out a team member, neat as you please."

"So he's had a few lessons beyond the local level."

Roy turned right off Sunset Boulevard onto a less traveled street, where mansions were hidden behind walls, high hedges, and wind-tossed trees. "If we're able to chase him down, what's our priority with him?"

Summerton considered for a moment before he spoke. "Find out who he is, who he's working for."

"Then detain him?"

"No. Too much is at stake. Make him disappear."

The serpentine streets wound through the wooded hills, among secluded estates, overhung by dripping branches, through blind turn after blind turn.

Roy said, "Does this change our priority with the woman?"

"No. Whack her on sight. Anything else happening at your end?"

Roy thought of Mr. and Mrs. Bettonfield, but he didn't mention them. The extreme kindness he had extended to them had nothing to do with his job, and Summerton would not understand.

Instead, Roy said, "She left something for us."

Summerton said nothing, perhaps because he intuited what the woman had left.

Roy said, "A photo of a cockroach, nailed to the wall."

"Whack her hard," Summerton said, and he hung up.

As Roy followed a long curve under drooping magnolia boughs, past a wrought-iron fence beyond which a replica of Tara stood spotlighted in the rain-swept darkness, he said, "Cease scrambling."

The computer beeped to indicate compliance.

"Please connect," he said, and recited the telephone number that would bring him into Mama's arms.

The video display flickered. When Roy glanced at the screen, he saw the opening question: WHO GOES THERE?

Though the phone would react to vocal commands, Mama would not; therefore, Roy pulled off the narrow road and stopped in a driveway, before a pair of nine-foot-high wrought-iron gates, to type in his responses to the security interrogation. After the transmission of his thumbprint, he was granted access to Mama in Virginia.

From her basic menu, he chose FIELD OFFICES. From that submenu, he chose LOS ANGELES, and he was thereby connected to the largest of Mama's babies on the West Coast.

He went through a few menus in the Los Angeles computer until he arrived at the files of the photo-analysis department. The file that interested him was currently in play, as he knew it would be, and he tapped in to observe.

The screen of his portable computer went to black and white, and then it filled with a photograph of a man's head from the neck up. His face was half turned away from the camera, dappled with shadows, blurred by a curtain of rain.

Roy was disappointed. He had hoped for a clearer picture.

This was dismayingly like an impressionist painting: in general, recognizable; in specific, mysterious.

Earlier in the evening, in Santa Monica, the surveillance team had taken photographs of the stranger who had gone into the bungalow minutes prior to the SWAT team assault. The night, the heavy rain, and the overgrown trees that prevented the streetlamps from casting much light on the sidewalk—all conspired to make it difficult to get a clear look at the man. Furthermore, they had not been expecting him, had thought that he was only an ordinary pedestrian who would pass by, and had been unpleasantly surprised when he'd turned in at the woman's house. Consequently, they had gotten precious few shots, none of quality, and none that revealed the full face of the mystery man, though the camera had been equipped with a telephoto lens.

The best of the photographs already had been scanned into the local-office computer, where it was being processed by an enhancement program. The computer would attempt to identify rain distortion and eliminate it. Then it would gradually lighten all areas of the shot uniformly, until it was able to identify biological structures in the deepest shadows that fell across the face; employing its extensive knowledge of human skull formation—with an enormous catalogue of the variations that occurred between the sexes, among the races, and among age groups—the computer would interpret the structures it glimpsed and develop them on a best-guess basis.

The process was laborious even at the lightning speed with which the program operated. Any photograph could ultimately be broken down into tiny dots of light and shadow called pixels: puzzle pieces that were identically shaped but varied subtly in texture and shading. Every one of the hundreds of thousands of pixels in this photograph had to be analyzed, to decipher not merely what it represented but what its undistorted relationship was to each of the many pixels surrounding it, which meant that the computer had to make hundreds of millions of comparisons and decisions in order to clarify the image.

Even then, there was no guarantee that the face finally rising from the murk would be an entirely accurate depiction of the man who had been photographed. Any analysis of this kind was as much an art—or guesswork—as it was a reliable technological process. Roy had seen instances in which a computer-enhanced portrait was as off the mark as any amateur artist's paint-by-the-numbers canvas of the Arc de Triomphe or of Manhattan at twilight. However, the face that they eventually got from the computer most likely would be so close to the man's true appearance as to be an exact likeness.

Now, as the computer made decisions and adjusted thousands of pixels, the image on the video display rippled from left to right. Still disappointing. Although changes had occurred, their effect was imperceptible. Roy was unable to see how the man's face was any different from what it had been before the adjustment.

For the next several hours, the image on the screen would ripple every six to ten seconds. The cumulative effect could be appreciated only by checking it at widely spaced intervals.

Roy backed out of the driveway, leaving the computer plugged in and the VDT angled toward him.

For a while he chased his headlights up and down hills, around blind turns, searching for a way out of the folded darkness, where the tree-filtered lights of cloistered mansions hinted at mysterious lives of wealth and power beyond his understanding.

From time to time, he glanced at the computer screen. The rippling face. Half averted. Shadowy and strange.

When at last he found Sunset Boulevard again and then the lower streets of Westwood, not far from his hotel, he was relieved to be back among people who were more like himself than those who lived in the monied hills. In the lower lands, the citizens knew suffering and uncertainty; they were people whose lives he could affect for the better, people to whom he could bring a measure of justice and mercy—one way or another.

The face on the computer screen was still that of a phantom, amorphous and possibly malignant. The face of chaos.

The stranger was a man who, like the fugitive woman, stood in the way of order, stability, and justice. He might be evil or merely troubled and confused. In the end, it didn't matter which.

"I'll give you peace," Roy Miro promised, glancing at the slowly mutating face on the video display terminal. "I'll find you and give you peace."

FIVE

While hooves of rain beat across the roof, while the troll-deep voice of the wind grumbled at the windows, and while the dog lay curled and dozing on the adjacent chair, Spencer used his computer expertise to try to build a file on Valerie Keene.

According to the records of the Department of Motor Vehicles, the driver's license for which she'd applied had been her first, not a renewal, and to get it, she had supplied a Social Security card as proof of identity. The DMV had verified that her name and number were indeed paired in the Social Security Administration's files.

That gave Spencer four indices with which to locate her in other databases where she was likely to appear: name, date of birth, driver's license number, and Social Security number. Learning more about her should be a snap.

Last year, with much patience and cunning, he'd made a game of getting into all the major nationwide credit-reporting agencies—like TRW—which were among the most secure of all systems. Now, he wormed into the largest of those apples again, seeking Valerie Ann Keene.

Their files included forty-two women by that name, fifty-nine when the surname was spelled either "Keene" or "Keane," and sixty-four when a third spelling—"Keen"—was added. Spencer entered her Social Security number, expecting to winnow away sixty-three of the sixty-four, but *none* had the same number as that in the DMV records.

Frowning at the screen, he entered Valerie's birthday and asked the system to locate her with that. One of the sixty-four Valeries was born on the same day of the same month as the woman whom he was hunting—but twenty years earlier.

With the dog snoring beside him, he entered the driver's license number and waited while the system cross-checked the Valeries. Of those who were licensed drivers, five were in California, but none had a number that matched hers. Another dead end.

Convinced that mistakes must have been made in the data entries, Spencer examined the file for each of the five California Valeries, looking for a driver's license or date of birth that was one number different from the information he had gotten out of the DMV. He was sure he would discover that a data-entry clerk had typed a six when a nine was required or had transposed two numbers.

Nothing. No mistakes. And judging by the information in each file, none of those women could possibly be the right Valerie.

Incredibly, the Valerie Ann Keene who had recently worked at The Red Door was absent from credit-agency files, utterly without a credit history. That was possible only if she had never purchased anything on time payments, had never possessed a credit card of any kind, had never opened a checking or savings account, and had never been the subject of a background check by an employer or landlord.

To be twenty-nine years old without acquiring a credit history in modern America, she would have to have been a Gypsy or a jobless vagrant most of her life, at least since she'd been a teenager. Manifestly she had not been any such thing.

Okay. Think. The raid on her bungalow meant one kind of police agency or another was after her. So she must be a wanted felon with a criminal record.

Spencer returned along electronic freeways to the Los Angeles Police Department computer, through which he searched city, county, and state court records to see if anyone by the name of Valerie Ann Keene had ever been convicted of a crime or had an outstanding arrest warrant in those jurisdictions.

The city system flashed NEGATIVE on the video screen.

NO FILE, reported the county.

NOT FOUND, said the state.

Nothing, nada, zero, zip.

Using the LAPD's electronic information-sharing arrangement with the FBI, he accessed the Washington-based Justice Department files of people convicted of federal offenses. She wasn't included in those, either.

In addition to its famous ten-most-wanted list, the FBI was, at any given time, seeking hundreds of other people related to criminal investigations—either suspects or potential witnesses. Spencer inquired if her name appeared on any of those lists, but it did not.

She was a woman without a past.

Yet something that she'd done had made her a wanted woman. Desperately wanted.

Spencer did not get to bed until ten minutes past one o'clock in the morning.

Although he was exhausted, and although the rhythm of the rain should have served as a sedative, he couldn't sleep. He lay on his back, staring alternately at the shadowy ceiling and at the thrashing foliage of the trees beyond the window, listening to the meaningless monologue of the blustery wind.

At first he could think of nothing but the woman. The look of her. Those eyes. That voice. That smile. The mystery.

In time, however, his thoughts drifted to the past, as they did too often, too easily. For him, reminiscence was a highway with one destination: that certain summer night when he was fourteen, when a dark world became darker, when everything he knew was proved false, when hope died and a dread of destiny became his constant companion, when he awakened to the cry of a persistent owl whose single inquiry thereafter became the central question of his own life.

Rocky, who was usually so well attuned to his master's moods, was still restlessly pacing; he seemed to be unaware that Spencer was sinking into the quiet anguish of stubborn memory and that he needed company. The dog didn't respond to his name when called.

In the gloom, Rocky padded restlessly back and forth between the open bedroom door (where he stood on the threshold and listened to the storm that huffed in the fireplace chimney) and the bedroom window (where he put his forepaws upon the sill and stared out at the rampage of the wind through the eucalyptus grove). Although he neither whined nor grumbled, he had about him an air of anxiety, as if the bad weather had blown an unwanted memory out of his own past, leaving him bedeviled and unable to regain the peace he had known while dozing on the chair in the living room.

"Here, boy," Spencer said softly. "Come here."

Unheeding, the dog padded to the door, a shadow among shadows.

Tuesday evening, Spencer had gone to The Red Door to talk about a night in July, sixteen years past. Instead, he met Valerie Keene and, to his surprise, talked of other things. That distant July, however, still haunted him.

"Rocky, come here." Spencer patted the mattress.

A minute or so of further encouragement finally brought the dog onto the bed. Rocky lay with his head on Spencer's chest, shivering at first but quickly soothed by his master's hand. One ear up, one ear down, he was attentive to the story that he'd heard on countless nights like this, when he was the entire audience, and on nights when he accompanied Spencer into barrooms, where drinks were bought for strangers who would listen in an alcoholic haze.

"I was fourteen," Spencer began. "It was the middle of July, and the night was warm, humid. I was asleep under just one sheet, with my bedroom window open so the air could circulate. I remember . . . I was dreaming about my mother, who'd been dead more than six years by then, but I can't remember anything that happened in the dream, only the warmth of it, the contentment, the comfort of being with her . . . and maybe the music of her laughter. She had a wonderful laugh. But it was another sound that woke me, not because it was loud but because it was recurring—so hollow and strange. I sat up in bed, confused, half drugged with sleep, but not frightened at all. I heard someone asking 'Who?' again and again. There would be a pause, silence, but then it would repeat as before: 'Who, who, who?' Of course, as I came all the way awake, I realized it was an owl perched on the roof, just above my open window."

Spencer was again drawn to that distant July night, like an asteroid captured by the greater gravity of the earth and doomed to a declining orbit that would end in impact.

. . . *it's an owl perched on the roof, just above my open window, calling out in the night for whatever reason owls call out.*

In the humid dark, I get up from my bed and go to the bathroom, expecting the hooting to stop when the hungry owl takes wing and goes hunting for mice again. But even after I return to bed, he seems to be content on the roof and pleased by his one-word, one-note song.

Finally, I go to the open window and quietly slide up the double-hung screen, trying not to startle him into flight. But when I lean outside, turning my head to look up, half expecting to see his talons hooked over the shingles and curled in toward the eaves, another and far different cry arises before I can say "Shoo" or the owl can ask "Who." This new sound is thin and bleak, a fragile wail of terror from a far place in the summer night. I look out toward the barn, which stands two hundred yards behind the house, toward the moonlit fields beyond the barn, toward the wooded hills beyond the fields. The cry comes again, shorter this time, but even more pathetic and therefore more piercing.

Having lived in the country since the day I was born, I know that nature is one great killing ground, governed by the cruelest of all laws—the law of natural selection—and ruled by the ruthless. Many nights, I've heard the eerie, quavery yowling of coyote packs chasing prey and celebrating slaughter. The triumphant shriek of a mountain lion after it has torn the life out of a rabbit sometimes echoes out of the highlands, a sound which makes it easy to believe that Hell is real and that the damned have flung open the gates.

This cry that catches my attention as I lean out the window—and that silences the owl on the roof—comes not from a predator but from prey. It's the voice of something weak, vulnerable. The forests and fields are filled with timid and meek creatures, which live only to perish violently, which do so every hour of every day without surcease, whose terror may actually be noticed by a god who knows of every sparrow's fall but seems unmoved.

Suddenly the night is profoundly quiet, uncannily still, as if the distant bleat of fear was, in fact, the sound of creation's engines grinding to a halt. The stars are hard points of light that have stopped twinkling, and the moon might well be painted on canvas. The landscape—trees, shrubs, summer flowers, fields, hills, and far mountains—appears to be nothing but crystalized shadows in various dark hues, as brittle as ice. The air must still be warm, but I am nonetheless frigid.

I quietly close the window, turn away from it, and move toward the bed again. I feel heavy-eyed, wearier than I've ever been.

But then I realize that I'm in a strange state of denial, that my weariness is less physical than psychological, that I desire sleep more than I really need it. Sleep is an escape. From fear. I'm shaking but not because I'm cold. The air is as warm as it was earlier. I'm shaking with fear.

Fear of what? I can't quite identify the source of my anxiety.

I know that the thing I heard was no ordinary wild cry. It reverberates in my mind, an icy sound that recalls something I've heard once before, although I can't remember what, when, where. The longer the forlorn wail echoes in my memory, the faster my heart beats.

I desperately want to lie down, forget the cry, the night, the owl and his question, but I know I can't sleep.

I'm wearing only briefs, so I quickly pull on a pair of jeans. Now that I'm committed to act, denial and sleep have no attraction for me. In fact, I'm in the grip of an urgency at least as strange as the previous denial. Bare-chested and barefoot, I'm drawn out of my bedroom by intense curiosity, by the sense of post-midnight adventure that all boys share—and by a terrible truth, which I don't yet know that I know.

Beyond my door, the house is cool, because my room is the only one not air-conditioned. For several summers, I've closed the vents against that chill flow because I prefer the benefits of fresh air even on a humid July night . . . and because, for some years, I've been unable to sleep with the hiss and hum that the icy air makes as it rushes through the ductwork and seethes through the vanes in the vent grille. I've long been afraid that this incessant if subtle noise will mask some other sound in the night that I must hear in order to survive. I have no idea what that other sound would be. It's a groundless and childish fear, and I'm embarrassed by it. Yet it dictates my sleeping habits.

The upstairs hallway is silvered with moonlight, which streams through a pair of sky-lights. Here and there along both walls, the polished-pine floor glimmers softly. Down the middle of the hall is an intricately patterned Persian runner, in which the curved and curled and undulant shapes absorb the radiance of the full moon and glow dimly with it: Hundreds of pale, luminous coelenterate forms seem to be not immediately under my feet but well below me, as if I am not on a carpet but am walking Christlike on the surface of a tidepool while gazing down at the mysterious denizens at the bottom.

I pass my father's room. The door is closed.

I reach the head of the stairs, where I hesitate.

The house is silent.

I descend the stairs, quaking, rubbing my bare arms with my hands, wondering at my inexplicable fear. Perhaps even at that moment, I dimly realize that I am going down to a place from which I'll never again quite be able to ascend. . . .

With the dog as his confessor, Spencer spun his story all the way through that long-ago night, to the hidden door, to the secret place, to the beating heart of the nightmare. As he recounted the experience, step by barefoot step, his voice faded to a whisper.

When he finished, he was in a temporary state of grace that would burn away with the coming of the dawn, but it was even sweeter for being so tenuous and brief. Purged, he was at last able to close his eyes and know that dreamless sleep would come to him.

In the morning he would begin to search for the woman.

He had the uneasy feeling that he was walking into a living hell to rival the one that he had so often described to the patient dog. He could do nothing else. Only one acceptable road lay ahead of him, and he was compelled to follow it.

Now sleep.

Rain washed the world, and its susurration was the sound of absolution—though some stains could never be permanently removed.

SIX

In the morning, Spencer had a few tiny bruises and red marks on his face and hands, from the sting-grenade pellets. Compared with his scar, they would draw no comments.

For breakfast, he had English muffins and coffee at his desk in the living room while he hacked into the county tax collector's computer. He discovered that the bungalow in Santa Monica, where Valerie had been living until the previous day, was owned by the Louis and Mae Lee Family Trust. Property tax bills were mailed in care of something called China Dream, in West Hollywood.

Out of curiosity, he requested a list of other properties—if any—owned by that trust. There were fourteen: five more homes in Santa Monica; a pair of eight-unit apartment buildings in Westwood; three single-family homes in Bel Air; and four adjacent commercial buildings in West Hollywood, including the address for China Dream.

Louis and Mae Lee had done all right for themselves.

After switching off the computer, Spencer stared at the blank screen and finished his coffee. It was bitter. He drank it anyway.

By ten o'clock, he and Rocky were heading south on the Pacific Coast Highway. Traffic passed him at every opportunity, because he obeyed the speed limit.

The storm had moved east during the night, taking every cloud with it. The morning sun was white, and in its hard light, the westward-tilting shadows had edges as sharp as steel blades. The Pacific was bottle green and slate gray.

Spencer tuned the radio to an all-news station. He hoped to hear a story about the SWAT-team raid the night before and to learn who had been in charge of it and why Valerie was wanted.

The news reader informed him that taxes were going up again. The economy was slipping deeper into recession. The government was further restricting gun ownership and television violence. Robbery, rape, and homicide rates were at all-time highs. The Chinese were accusing us of possessing "orbiting laser death rays," and we were accusing them of the same. Some people believed that the world would end in fire; others said ice; both were testifying before Congress on behalf of competing legislative agendas designed to save the world.

When he found himself listening to a story about a dog show that was being picketed by protesters who were demanding an end to selective breeding and to the "exploitation of animal beauty in an exhibitionistic performance no less repugnant than the degrading of young women in topless bars," Spencer knew that there would be no report of the incident at the bungalow in Santa Monica. Surely a SWAT-team operation would rate higher on any reporter's agenda than unseemly displays of canine comeliness.

Either the media had found nothing newsworthy in an assault on a private home by cops with machine guns—or the agency conducting the operation had done a first-rate job of misdirecting the press. They had turned what should have been a public spectacle into what amounted to a covert action.

He switched off the radio and entered the Santa Monica Freeway. East by northeast, in the lower hills, the China Dream awaited them.

To Rocky, he said, "What's your opinion of this dog-show thing?"

Rocky looked at him curiously.

"You're a dog, after all. You must have an opinion. These are your people being exploited."

Either he was a dog of extreme circumspection when it came to discussing current affairs or he was just a carefree, culturally disengaged mutt with no positions on the weightiest social issues of his time and species.

"I would hate to think," Spencer said, "that you are a dropout, resigned to the status of a lumpen mammal, unconcerned about being exploited, all fur and no fury."

Rocky peered forward at the highway again.

"Aren't you outraged that purebred females are forbidden to have sex with mongrels like you, forced to submit only to purebred males? Just to make puppies destined for the degradation of showrings?"

The mutt's tail thumped against the passenger door.

"Good dog." Spencer held the steering wheel with his left hand and petted Rocky with his right. The dog submitted with pleasure. Thump-thump went the tail. "A good, accepting dog. You don't even think it's strange that your master talks to himself."

They exited the freeway at Robertson Boulevard and drove toward the fabled hills.

After the night of rain and wind, the sprawling metropolis was as free of smog as the seacoast from which they had traveled. The palms, ficuses, magnolias, and early-blooming bottlebrush trees with red flowers were so green and gleaming that they appeared to have been hand-polished, leaf by leaf, frond by frond. The streets were washed clean, the glass walls of the tall buildings sparkled in the sunshine, birds wheeled across the piercingly blue sky, and it was easy to be deceived into believing that all was right with the world.

Thursday morning, while other agents used the assets of several law-enforcement organizations to search for the nine-year-old Pontiac that was registered to Valerie Keene, Roy Miro personally took charge of the effort to identify the man who had nearly been captured in the previous night's operation. From his Westwood hotel, he drove into the heart of Los Angeles, to the agency's California headquarters.

Downtown, the volume of office space occupied by city, county, state, and federal governments was rivaled only by the space occupied by banks. At lunchtime the conversation in the restaurants was more often than not about money—massive, raw slabs of money— whether the diners were from the political or the financial community.

In this opulent wallow, the agency owned a handsome ten-story building on a desirable street near city hall. Bankers, politicians, bureaucrats, and wine-swilling derelicts shared the sidewalks with mutual respect—except for those regrettable occasions when one of them suddenly snapped, screamed incoherent deprecations, and savagely stabbed one of his fellow Angelenos. The wielder of the knife (or gun or blunt instrument) frequently suffered delusions of persecution by extraterrestrials or the CIA and was more likely to be a derelict than a banker, or a politician, or a bureaucrat.

Just six months ago, however, a middle-aged banker had gone on a killing spree with two 9mm pistols. The incident had traumatized the entire society of downtown vagrants and had made them more wary of the unpredictable "suits" who shared the streets with them.

The agency's building—clad in limestone, with acres of bronze windows as dark as any movie star's sunglasses—did not bear the agency's name. The people with whom Roy worked weren't glory seekers; they preferred to function in obscurity. Besides, the agency that employed them did not officially exist, was funded by the clandestine redirection of money from other bureaus that were under the control of the Justice Department, and actually had no name itself.

Over the main entrance, the street address gleamed in polished copper numbers. Under the numbers were four names and one ampersand, also in copper: CARVER, GUNMANN, GARROTE & HEMLOCK.

A passerby, if he wondered about the building's occupant, might think it was a partnership of attorneys or accountants. If he made inquiries of the uniformed guard in the lobby, he would be told that the firm was an "international property-management company."

Roy drove down a ramp to the underground parking facility. At the bottom of the ramp, the way was barred by a sturdy steel gate.

He gained admittance neither by plucking a time-stamped ticket from an automatic dispenser nor by identifying himself to a guard in a booth. Instead, he stared directly into the lens of a high-definition video camera that was mounted on a post two feet from the side window of his car and waited to be recognized.

The image of his face was transmitted to a windowless room in the basement. There, Roy knew, a guard at a display terminal watched as the computer dropped everything out of the image except the eyes, enlarged them without compromising the high resolution, scanned the striation and vessel patterns of the retinas, compared them with on-file retinal patterns, and acknowledged Roy as one of the select.

The guard then pushed a button to raise the gate.

The entire procedure could have been accomplished without the guard—if not for one contingency against which precautions had to be taken. An operative bent on penetrating the agency might have killed Roy, cut out his eyes, and held them up to the camera to be scanned. While the computer conceivably could have been deceived, a guard surely would have noticed this messy ruse.

It was unlikely that anyone would go to such extremes to breach the agency's security. But not impossible. These days, sociopaths of singular viciousness were loose in the land.

Roy drove into the subterranean garage. By the time he parked and got out of the car, the steel gate had clattered shut again. The dangers of Los Angeles, of democracy run amok, were locked out.

His footsteps echoed off the concrete walls and the low ceiling, and he knew that the guard in the basement room could hear them too. The garage was under audio as well as video surveillance.

Access to the high-security elevator was achieved by pressing his right thumb to the glass face of a print scanner. A camera above the lift doors gazed down at him, so the distant guard could prevent anyone from entering merely by placing a severed thumb to the glass.

No matter how smart machines eventually became, human beings would always be needed. Sometimes that thought encouraged Roy. Sometimes it depressed him, though he wasn't sure why.

He rode the elevator to the fourth floor, which was shared by Document Analysis, Substance Analysis, and Photo Analysis.

In the Photo Analysis computer lab, two young men and a middle-aged woman were working at arcane tasks. They all smiled and said good morning, because Roy had one of those faces that encouraged smiles and familiarity.

Melissa Wicklun, their chief photo analyst in Los Angeles, was sitting at the desk in her office, which was in a corner of the lab. The office had no windows to the outside but featured two glass walls through which she could watch her subordinates in the larger room.

When Roy knocked on the glass door, she looked up from a file that she was reading. "Come in."

Melissa, a blonde in her early thirties, was at the same time an elf and a succubus. Her green eyes were large and guileless—yet simultaneously smoky, mysterious. Her nose was pert—but her mouth was sensuous, the essence of allerotic orifices. She had large breasts, a slim waist, and long legs—but she chose to conceal those attributes in loose white blouses, white lab coats, and baggy chinos. In her scuffed Nikes, her feet were no doubt so feminine and delicate that Roy would have been delighted to spend hours kissing them.

He had never made a pass at her, because she was reserved and businesslike—and because he suspected that she was a lesbian. He had nothing against lesbians. Live and let live. At the same time, however, he was loath to reveal his interest only to be rejected.

Melissa said crisply, "Good morning, Roy."

"How have you been? Good heavens, you know that I haven't been in L.A., haven't seen you since—"

"I was just examining the file." Straight to business. She was never interested in small talk. "We have a finished enhancement."

When Melissa was talking, Roy was never able to decide whether to look at her eyes or her mouth. Her gaze was direct, with a challenge that he found appealing. But her lips were so deliciously ripe.

She pushed a photograph across the desk.

Roy looked away from her lips.

The picture was a drastically improved, full-color version of the shot that he had seen on his attaché case computer terminal the night before: a man's head from the neck up, in profile. Shadows still dappled the face, but they were lighter and less obscuring than they had been. The blurring screen of rain had been removed entirely.

"It's a fine piece of work," Roy said. "But it still doesn't give us a good enough look at him to make an identification."

"On the contrary, it tells us a lot about him," Melissa said. "He's between twenty-eight and thirty-two."

"How do you figure?"

"Computer projection based on an analysis of lines radiating from the corner of his eye, percentage of gray in his hair, and the apparent degree of firmness of facial muscles and throat skin."

"That's projecting quite a lot from such few—"

"Not at all," she interrupted. "The system makes analytic projections operating from a ten-megabyte database of biological information, and I'd pretty much bet the house on what it says."

He was thrilled by the way her supple lips formed the words "ten-megabyte database of biological information." Her mouth was better than her eyes. Perfect. He cleared his throat. "Well—"

"Brown hair, brown eyes."

Roy frowned. "The hair, okay. But you can't see his eyes here."

Rising from her chair, Melissa took the photograph out of his hand and put it on the desk. With a pencil, she pointed to the beginning curve of the man's eyeball as viewed from the side. "He's not looking at the camera, so if you or I examined the photo under a microscope, we still wouldn't be able to see enough of the iris to determine color. But even from an oblique perspective like this, the computer can detect a few pixels of color."

"So he has brown eyes."

"Dark brown." She put down the pencil and stood with her left hand fisted on her hip, as delicate as a flower and as resolute as an army general. "Absolutely dark brown."

Roy liked her unshakable self-confidence, the brisk certitude with which she spoke. And that *mouth*.

"Based on the computer's analysis of his physical relationship to measurable objects in the photograph, he's five feet eleven inches tall." She clipped her words, so the facts came out of her with the staccato energy of bullets from a submachine gun. "He weighs one hundred and sixty-five, give or take five pounds. He's Caucasian, clean-shaven, in good physical shape, recently had a haircut."

"Anything else?"

From the file folder, Melissa removed another photograph. "This is him. From the front, straight on. His full face."

Roy looked up from the new photo, surprised. "I didn't know we got a shot like this."

"We didn't," she said, studying the portrait with evident pride. "This isn't an actual photograph. It's a projection of what the guy ought to look like, based on what the computer can determine of his bone structure and fat-deposit patterns from the partial profile."

"It can do that?"

"It's a recent innovation in the program."

"Reliable?"

"Considering the view the computer had to work with in this case," she assured Roy, "there's a ninety-four-percent probability that this face will precisely match the real face in any ninety of one hundred reference details."

"I guess that's better than a police artist's sketch," he said.

"Much better." After a beat, she said, "Is something wrong?"

Roy realized that she had shifted her gaze from the computer portrait to him—and that he was staring at her mouth.

"Uh," he said, looking down at the full portrait of the mystery man, "I was wondering . . . what's this line across his right cheek?"

"A scar."

"Really? You're sure? From the ear to the point of the chin?"

"A major scar," she said, opening a desk drawer. "Cicatricial welt—mostly smooth tissue, crimped here and there along the edges."

Roy referred to the original profile shot and saw that a portion of the scar was there, although he had not correctly identified it. "I thought it was just a line of light between shadows, light from the streetlamp, falling across his cheek."

"No."

"It couldn't be that?"

"No. A scar," Melissa said firmly, and she took a Kleenex from a box in the open drawer.

"This is great. Makes for an easier ID. This guy seems to've had special-forces training, either military or paramilitary, and with a scar like this—it's a good bet he was wounded while on duty. Badly wounded. Maybe badly enough that he was discharged or retired on psychological if not physical disability."

"Police and military organizations keep records forever."

"Exactly. We'll have him in seventy-two hours. Hell, forty-eight." Roy looked up from the portrait. "Thanks, Melissa."

She was wiping her mouth with the Kleenex. She didn't have to be concerned about smearing her lipstick, because she wasn't wearing any. She didn't need lipstick. It couldn't improve her.

Roy was fascinated by the way in which her full and pliant lips compressed so tenderly under the soft Kleenex.

He realized that he was staring and that again she was aware of it. His gaze drifted up to her eyes.

Melissa blushed faintly, looked away from him, and threw the crumpled Kleenex in the waste can.

"May I keep this copy?" he asked, indicating the full-face computer-generated portrait.

Withdrawing a manila envelope from beneath the file folder on the desk, handing it to him, she said, "I've put five prints in here, plus two diskettes that contain the portrait."

"Thanks, Melissa."

"Sure."

The warm pink blush was still on her cheeks.

Roy felt that he had penetrated her cool, businesslike veneer for the first time since he'd known her, and that he was in touch, however tenuously, with the inner Melissa, with the exquisitely sensuous self that she usually strove to conceal. He wondered if he should ask her for a date.

Turning his head, he looked through the glass walls at the workers in the computer lab, certain that they must be aware of the erotic tension in their boss's office. All three seemed to be absorbed in their work.

When Roy turned to Melissa Wicklun again, prepared to ask her to dinner, she was surreptitiously wiping at one corner of her mouth with a fingertip. She tried to cover by spreading her hand across her mouth and faking a cough.

With dismay, Roy realized that the woman had misinterpreted his salacious stare. Apparently she thought that his attention had been drawn to her mouth by a smear or crumb of food left over, perhaps, from a mid-morning doughnut.

She had been oblivious of his lust. If she *was* a lesbian, she must have assumed that Roy knew as much and would have no interest in her. If she wasn't a lesbian, perhaps she simply couldn't imagine being attracted—or being an object of desire—to a man with round cheeks, a soft chin, and ten extra pounds on his waist. He had met with that prejudice before: looksism. Many women, brainwashed by a consumer culture that sold the wrong values, were interested only in men like those who appeared in advertisements for Marlboro or Calvin Klein. They could not understand that a man with the merry face of a favorite uncle might be kinder, wiser, more compassionate, and a better lover than a hunk who spent too much time at the gym. How sad to think that Melissa might be that shallow. How very sad.

"Can I help you with anything else?" she asked.

"No, this is fine. This is a lot. We'll nail him with this."

She nodded.

"I have to get down to the print lab, see if they got anything off that flashlight or bathroom window."

"Yes, of course," she said awkwardly.

He indulged in one last look at her *perfect* mouth, sighed, and said, "See you later."

After he had stepped out of her office, closed the door behind him, and crossed two-thirds of the long computer lab, he looked back, half hoping that she would be staring wistfully after him. Instead, she was sitting at her desk again, holding a compact in one hand, examining her mouth in that small mirror.

China Dream was a West Hollywood restaurant in a quaint three-story brick building, in an area of trendy shops. Spencer parked a block away, left Rocky in the truck again, and walked back.

The air was pleasantly warm. The breeze was refreshing. It was one of those days when the struggles of life seemed worth waging.

The restaurant was not yet open for lunch. Nevertheless, the door was unlocked, and he went inside.

The China Dream indulged in none of the decor common to many Chinese restaurants: no dragons or foo dogs, no brass ideograms on the walls. It was starkly modern, pearl gray and black, with white linen on the thirty to forty tables. The only Chinese art object was a life-size, carved-wood statue of a gentle-faced, robed woman holding what appeared to be an inverted bottle or a gourd; it was standing just inside the door.

Two Asian men in their twenties were arranging flatware and wineglasses. A third man, Asian but a decade older than his coworkers, was rapidly folding white cloth napkins into fanciful, peaked shapes. His hands were as dexterous as those of a magician. All three men wore black shoes, black slacks, white shirts, and black ties.

Smiling, the oldest approached Spencer. "Sorry, sir. We don't open for lunch until eleven-thirty."

He had a mellow voice and only a faint accent.

"I'm here to see Louis Lee, if I may," Spencer said.

"Do you have an appointment, sir?"

"No, I'm afraid not."

"Can you please tell me what you wish to discuss with him?"

"A tenant who lives in one of his rental properties."

The man nodded. "May I assume this would be Ms. Valerie Keene?"

The soft voice, smile, and unfailing politeness combined to project an image of humility, which was like a veil that made it more difficult to see, until now, that the napkin folder was also quite intelligent and observant.

"Yes," Spencer said. "My name's Spencer Grant. I'm a . . . I'm a friend of Valerie's. I'm worried about her."

From a pocket of his trousers, the man withdrew an object about the size—but less than the thickness—of a deck of cards. It was hinged at one end; unfolded, it proved to be the smallest cellular telephone that Spencer had ever seen.

Aware of Spencer's interest, the man said, "Made in Korea."

"Very James Bond."

"Mr. Lee has just begun to import them."

"I thought he was a restaurateur."

"Yes, sir. But he is many things." The napkin folder pushed a single button, waited while the seven-digit programmed number was transmitted, and then surprised Spencer again by speaking in neither English nor Chinese, but in French, to the person on the other end.

Collapsing the phone and tucking it into his pocket, the napkin folder said, "Mr. Lee will see you, sir. This way, please."

Spencer followed him among the tables, to the right rear corner of the front room, through a swinging door with a round window in the center, into clouds of appetizing aromas: garlic, onions, ginger, hot peanut oil, mushroom soup, roasting duck, almond essence.

The immense and spotlessly clean kitchen was filled with ovens, cooktops, griddles, huge woks, deep fryers, warming tables, sinks, chopping blocks. Sparkling white ceramic tile and stainless steel dominated. At least a dozen chefs and cooks and assistants, dressed in white from head to foot, were busy at a variety of culinary tasks.

The operation was as organized and precise as the mechanism in an elaborate Swiss clock with twirling ballerina dolls, marching toy soldiers, prancing wooden horses. Reliably tick-tick-ticking along.

Spencer trailed his escort through another swinging door, into a corridor, past storage rooms and staff rest rooms, to an elevator. He expected to go up. In silence, they went down one floor. When the doors opened, the escort motioned for Spencer to exit first.

The basement was not dank and dreary. They were in a mahogany-paneled lounge with handsome teak chairs upholstered in teal fabric.

The receptionist at the teak and polished-steel desk was a man: Asian, totally bald, six feet tall, with broad shoulders and a thick neck. He was typing furiously at a computer keyboard. When he turned from the keyboard and smiled, his gray suit jacket stretched tautly across a concealed handgun in a shoulder holster.

He said, "Good morning," and Spencer replied in kind.

"Can we go in?" asked the napkin folder.

The bald man nodded. "Everything's fine."

As the escort led Spencer to an inner door, an electrically operated deadbolt clacked open, triggered by the receptionist.

Behind them, the bald man began to type again. His fingers raced across the keys. If he could use a gun as well as he could type, he would be a deadly adversary.

Beyond the lounge, they followed a white corridor with a gray vinyl-tile floor. It served windowless offices on both sides. Most of the doors were open, and Spencer saw men and women—many but not all of them Asian—working at desks, filing cabinets, and computers just like office workers in the real world.

The door at the end of the hall led into Louis Lee's office, which was another surprise. Travertine floor. A beautiful Persian carpet: mostly grays, lavender, and greens. Tapestry-covered walls. Early-nineteenth-century French furniture, with elaborate marquetry and ormolu. Leather-bound books in cases with glass doors. The large room was warmly but not brightly lighted by Tiffany floor and table lamps, some with stained-glass and some with blown-glass shades, and Spencer was sure that none was a reproduction.

"Mr. Lee, this is Mr. Grant," said the escort.

The man who came out from behind the ornate desk was five feet seven, slender, in his fifties. His thick jet-black hair had begun to turn gray at the temples. He wore black wingtips, dark blue trousers with suspenders, a white shirt, a bow tie with small red polka dots against a blue background, and horn-rimmed glasses.

"Welcome, Mr. Grant." He had a musical accent as European as it was Chinese. His hand was small, but his grip was firm.

"Thank you for seeing me," Spencer said, feeling as disoriented as he might have felt if he had followed Alice's white rabbit into this windowless, Tiffany-illumined hole.

Lee's eyes were anthracite black. They fixed Spencer with a stare that penetrated him almost as effectively as a scalpel.

The escort and erstwhile napkin folder stood to one side of the door, his hands clasped behind him. He had not grown, but he now seemed as much of a bodyguard as the huge, bald receptionist.

Louis Lee invited Spencer to one of a pair of armchairs that faced each other across a low table. A nearby Tiffany floor lamp cast blue, green, and scarlet light.

Lee took the chair opposite Spencer and sat very erect. With his spectacles, bow tie, and suspenders, and with the backdrop of books, he might have been a professor of literature in the study of his home, near the campus of Yale or another Ivy League university.

His manner was reserved but friendly. "So you are a friend of Ms. Keene's? Perhaps you went to high school together? College?"

"No, sir. I haven't known her that long. I met her where she works. I'm a recent . . . friend. But I do care about her and . . . well, I'm concerned that something's happened to her."

"What do you think might have happened to her?"

"I don't know. But I'm sure you're aware of the SWAT-team raid on your house last night, the bungalow she was renting from you."

Lee was silent for a moment. Then: "Yes, the authorities came to my own home last evening, after the raid, to ask about her."

"Mr. Lee, these authorities . . . who were they?"

"Three men. They claimed to be with the FBI."

"Claimed?"

"They showed me credentials, but they were lying."

Frowning, Spencer said, "How can you be sure of that?"

"In my life, I've had considerable experience of deceit and treachery," Lee said. He didn't seem either angry or bitter. "I've developed a good nose for it."

Spencer wondered if that was as much a warning as it was an explanation. Whichever the case, he knew that he was not in the presence of an ordinary businessman. "If they weren't actually government agents—"

"Oh, I'm sure they were government agents. However, I believe the FBI credentials were simply a convenience."

"Yes, but if they were with another bureau, why not flash their real ID?"

Lee shrugged. "Rogue agents, operating without the authority of their bureau, hoping to confiscate a cache of drug profits for their own benefit, would have reason to mislead with false ID."

Spencer knew that such things had happened. "But I don't . . . I *can't* believe that Valerie is involved with drug peddling."

"I'm sure she isn't. If I'd thought so, I wouldn't have rented to her. Those people are scum—corrupting children, ruining lives. Besides, although Ms. Keene paid her rent in cash, she wasn't rolling in money. And she worked at a full-time job."

"So if these weren't, let's say, rogue Drug Enforcement Administration operatives looking to line their own pockets with cocaine profits, and if they weren't actually with the FBI—who were they?"

Louis Lee shifted slightly in his chair, still sitting erect but tilting his head in such a way that reflections of the stained glass Tiffany lamp painted both lenses of his spectacles and obscured his eyes. "Sometimes a government—or a bureau within a government—becomes frustrated when it has to play by the rules. With oceans of tax money washing around, with bookkeeping systems that would be laughable in any private enterprise, it's easy for some government officials to fund covert organizations to achieve results that can't be achieved through legal means."

"Mr. Lee, do you read a lot of espionage novels?"

Louis Lee smiled thinly. "They're not of interest to me."

"Excuse me, sir, but this sounds a little paranoid."

"It's only experience speaking."

"Then your life's been even more interesting than I'd guess from appearances."

"Yes," Lee said, but didn't elaborate. After a pause, with his eyes still hidden by the patterns of reflected color that glimmered in his eyeglasses, he continued: "The larger a government, the more likely it is to be riddled with such covert organizations—some small but some not. We have a very big government, Mr. Grant."

"Yes, but—"

"Direct and indirect taxes require the average citizen to work from January until the middle of July to pay for that government. *Then* working men and women begin to labor for themselves."

"I've heard that figure too."

"When government grows so large, it also grows arrogant."

Louis Lee did not seem to be a fanatic. No anger or bitterness strained his voice. In fact, although he chose to surround himself with highly ornamented French furniture, he had a calm air of Zen simplicity and a distinctly Asian resignation to the ways of the world. He seemed more of a pragmatist than a crusader.

"Ms. Keene's enemies, Mr. Grant, are my enemies too."

"And mine."

"However, I don't intend to make a target of myself—as you are doing. Last night, I didn't express my doubt about their credentials when they presented themselves as FBI agents. That would not have been prudent. I was unhelpful, yes, but *cooperatively* unhelpful—if you know what I mean."

Spencer sighed and slumped in his chair.

Leaning forward with his hands on his knees, his intense black eyes becoming visible again as the reflections of the lamp moved off his glasses, Lee said, "You were the man in her house last night."

Spencer was surprised again. "How do you know anyone was there?"

"They were asking about a man she might have been living with. Your height, weight. What were you doing there, if I may ask?"

"She was late for work. I was worried about her. I went to her place to see if anything was wrong."

"You work at The Red Door too?"

"No. I was waiting there for her." That was all he chose to say. The rest was too complicated—and embarrassing. "What can you tell me about Valerie that might help me locate her?"

"Nothing, really."

"I only want to help her, Mr. Lee."

"I believe you."

"Well, sir, then why not cooperate with me? What was on her renter's application? Previous residence, previous jobs, credit references—anything like that would be helpful."

The businessman leaned back, moving his small hands from his knees to the arms of his chair. "There was no renter's application."

"With as many properties as you have, sir, I'm sure whoever manages them must use applications."

Louis Lee raised his eyebrows, which was a theatrical expression for such a placid man. "You've done some research on me. Very good. Well, in Ms. Keene's case, there was no application, because she was recommended by someone at The Red Door who's also a tenant of mine."

Spencer thought of the beautiful waitress who appeared to be half Vietnamese and half black. "Would that be Rosie?"

"It would."

"She was friends with Valerie?"

"She is. I met Ms. Keene and approved of her. She impressed me as a reliable person. That's all I needed to know about her."

Spencer said, "I've got to speak to Rosie."

"No doubt she'll be working again this evening."

"I need to talk to her before this evening. Partly because of this conversation with you, Mr. Lee, I have the distinct feeling that I'm being hunted and that time may be running out."

"I think that's an accurate assessment."

"Then I'll need her last name, sir, and her address."

Louis Lee was silent for so long that Spencer grew nervous. Finally: "Mr. Grant, I was born in China. When I was a child, we fled the Communists and emigrated to Hanoi, Vietnam, which was then controlled by the French. We lost everything—but that was better than being among the tens of millions liquidated by Chairman Mao."

Although Spencer was unsure what the businessman's personal history might have to do with his own problems, he knew there would be a connection and that it would soon become apparent. Louis Lee was Chinese but not inscrutable. Indeed, he was as direct, in his way, as was any rural New Englander.

"Chinese in Vietnam were oppressed. Life was hard. But the French promised to protect us from the Communists. They failed. When Vietnam was partitioned in nineteen fifty-four, I was still a young boy. Again we fled, to South Vietnam—and lost everything."

"I see."

"No. You begin to perceive. But you don't yet see. Within a year, civil war began. In nineteen fifty-nine, my younger sister was killed in the street by sniper fire. Three years later, one week after John Kennedy promised that the United States would ensure our freedom, my father was killed by a terrorist bomb on a Saigon bus."

Lee closed his eyes and folded his hands in his lap. He almost seemed to be meditating rather than remembering.

Spencer waited.

"By late April, nineteen seventy-five, when Saigon fell, I was thirty, with four children, my wife Mae. My mother was still alive, and one of my three brothers, two of his children. Ten of us. After six months of terror, my mother, brother, one of my nieces, and one of my sons were dead. I failed to save them. The remaining six of us . . . we joined thirty-two others in an attempt to escape by sea."

"Boat people," Spencer said respectfully, for in his own way he knew what it meant to be cut off from one's past, adrift and afraid, struggling daily to survive.

Eyes still closed, speaking as serenely as if recounting the details of a walk in the country, Lee said: "In bad weather, pirates tried to board our vessel. Vietcong gunboat. Same as pirates. They would have killed the men, raped and killed the women, stolen our meager possessions. Eighteen of our thirty-eight perished attempting to repel them. One was my son. Ten years old. Shot. I could do nothing. The rest of us were saved because the weather grew so bad, so quickly—the gunboat withdrew to save itself. The storm separated us from the pirates. Two people were washed overboard in high waves. Leaving eighteen. When good weather returned, our boat was damaged, no engine or sails, no radio, far out on the South China Sea."

Spencer could no longer bear to look at the placid man. But he was incapable of looking away.

"We were adrift six days in fierce heat. No fresh water. Little food. One woman and four children died before we crossed a sea-lane and were rescued by a U.S. Navy ship. One of the children who died of thirst was my daughter. I couldn't save her. I wasn't able to save anyone. Of the ten in my family who survived the fall of Saigon, four remained to be pulled from that boat. My wife, my remaining daughter—who was then my only child—one of my nieces. And me."

"I'm sorry," Spencer said, and those words were so inadequate that he wished he hadn't spoken them.

Louis Lee opened his eyes. "Nine other people were rescued from that disintegrating boat, more than twenty years ago. As I did, they took American first names, and today all nine are partners with me in the restaurant, other businesses. I consider them my family also. We're a nation unto ourselves, Mr. Grant. I am an American because I believe in America's ideals. I love this country, its people. I do not love its government. I can't love what I can't trust, and I will never trust a government again, anywhere. That disturbs you?"

"Yes. It's understandable. But depressing."

"As individuals, as families, as neighbors, as members of one community," Lee said, "people of all races and political views are usually decent, kind, compassionate. But in large corporations or governments, when great power accumulates in their hands, some become monsters even with good intentions. I can't be loyal to monsters. But I will be loyal to my family, my neighbors, my community."

"Fair enough, I guess."

"Rosie, the waitress at The Red Door, was not one of the people on that boat with us. Her mother was Vietnamese, however, and her father was an American who died over there, so she is a member of my community."

Spencer had been so mesmerized by Louis Lee's story that he had forgotten the request that had triggered those grisly recollections. He wanted to talk to Rosie as soon as possible. He needed her last name and address.

"Rosie must not be any more involved in this than she is now," Lee said. "She's told these phony FBI men that she knows little about Ms. Keene, and I don't want you to drag her deeper into this."

"I only want to ask her a few questions."

"If the wrong people saw you with her and identified you as the man at the house last night, they'd think Rosie was more than just a friend at work to Ms. Keene—though that is, in fact, all she was."

"I'll be discreet, Mr. Lee."

"Yes. That is the only choice I'm giving you."

A door opened softly, and Spencer turned in his armchair to see the napkin folder, his polite escort from the front door of the restaurant, returning to the room. He hadn't heard the man leave.

"She remembers him. It's arranged," the escort told Louis Lee, as he approached Spencer and handed him a piece of notepaper.

"At one o'clock," Louis Lee said, "Rosie will meet you at that address. It's not her apartment—in case her place is being watched."

The swiftness with which a meeting had been arranged, without a word between Lee and the other man, seemed magical to Spencer.

"She will not be followed," Lee said, getting up from his chair. "Make sure that you are not followed, either."

Also rising, Spencer said, "Mr. Lee, you and your family . . ."

"Yes?"

"Impressive."

Louis Lee bowed slightly from the waist. Then, turning away and walking to his desk, he said, "One more thing, Mr. Grant."

When Lee opened a desk drawer, Spencer had the crazy feeling that this soft-spoken, mild-looking, professorial gentleman was going to withdraw a silencer-equipped gun and shoot him dead. Paranoia was like an injection of amphetamines administered directly to his heart.

Lee came up with what appeared to be a jade medallion on a gold chain. "I sometimes give one of these to people who seem to need it."

Half afraid that the two men would hear his heart thundering, Spencer joined Lee at the desk and accepted the gift.

It was two inches in diameter. Carved on one side was the head of a dragon. On the other side was an equally stylized pheasant.

"This looks too expensive to—"

"It's only soapstone. Pheasants and dragons, Mr. Grant. You need their power. Pheasants and dragons. Prosperity and long life."

Dangling the medallion from its chain, Spencer said, "A charm?"

"Effective," Lee said. "Did you see the Quan Yin when you came in the restaurant?"

"Excuse me?"

"The wooden statue, by the front door?"

"Yes, I did. The woman with the gentle face."

"A spirit resides in her and prevents enemies from crossing my threshold." Lee was as solemn as when he'd recounted his escape from Vietnam. "She is especially good at barring envious people, and envy is second only to self-pity as the most dangerous of all emotions."

"After a life like yours, you can believe in this?"

"We must believe in something, Mr. Grant."

They shook hands.

Carrying the notepaper and the medallion, Spencer followed the escort out of the room.

In the elevator, recalling the brief exchange between the escort and the bald man when they had first entered the reception lounge, Spencer said, "I was scanned for weapons on the way down, wasn't I?"

The escort seemed amused by the question but didn't answer.

A minute later, at the front door, Spencer paused to study the Quan Yin. "He really thinks she works, keeps out his enemies?"

"If he thinks so, then she must," said the escort. "Mr. Lee is a great man."

Spencer looked at him. "You were in the boat?"

"I was only eight. My mother was the woman who died of thirst the day before we were rescued."

"He says he saved no one."

"He saved us all," the escort said, and he opened the door.

On the sidewalk in front of the restaurant, half blinded by the harsh sunlight, jarred by the noise of the passing traffic and a jet overhead, Spencer felt as if he had awakened suddenly from a dream. Or had just plunged into one.

During the entire time he'd been in the restaurant and the rooms beneath it, no one had looked at his scar.

He turned and gazed through the glass door of the restaurant.

The man whose mother had died of thirst on the South China Sea now stood among the tables again, folding white cloth napkins into fanciful, peaked shapes.

The print lab, where David Davis and a young male assistant were waiting for Roy Miro, was one of four rooms occupied by Fingerprint Analysis. Image-processing computers, high-definition monitors, and more exotic pieces of equipment were provided in generous quantity.

Davis was preparing to develop latent fingerprints on the bathroom window that had been carefully removed from the Santa Monica bungalow. It lay on the marble top of a lab bench—the entire frame, with the glass intact and the corroded brass piano hinge attached.

"This one's important," Roy warned as he approached them.

"Of course, yes, every case is important," Davis said.

"This one's more important. And urgent."

Roy disliked Davis, not merely because the man had an annoying name, but because he was exhaustingly enthusiastic. Tall, thin, storklike, with wiry blond hair, David Davis never merely walked anywhere but bustled, scurried, sprinted. Instead of just turning, he always seemed to *spin*. He never pointed at anything but *thrust* a finger at it. To Roy Miro, who avoided extremes of appearance and of public behavior, Davis was embarrassingly theatrical.

The assistant—known to Roy only as Wertz—was a pale creature who wore his lab coat as if it were the cassock of a humble novice in a seminary. When he wasn't rushing off to fetch something for Davis, he orbited his boss with fidgety reverence. He made Roy sick.

"The flashlight gave us nothing," David Davis said, flamboyantly whirling one hand to indicate a big zero. "Zero! Not even a partial. Crap. A piece of *crap*—that flashlight! No smooth surface on it. Brushed steel, ribbed steel, checked steel, but no *smooth* steel."

"Too bad," Roy said.

"Too bad?" Davis said, eyes widening as if Roy had responded to news of the Pope's assassination with a shrug and a chuckle. "It's as if the damned thing was *designed* for burglars and thugs—the official Mafia flashlight, for God's sake."

Wertz mumbled an affirmative, "For God's sake."

"So let's do the window," Roy said impatiently.

"Yes, we have big hopes for the window," Davis said, his head bobbing up and down like that of a parrot listening to reggae music. "Lacquer. Painted with multiple coats of mustard-yellow lacquer to resist the steam from the shower, you see. Smooth." Davis beamed at the small window that lay on the marble lab bench. "If there's anything on it, we'll fume it up."

"The quicker the better," Roy stressed.

In one corner of the room, under a ventilation hood, stood an empty ten-gallon fish tank. Wearing surgical gloves, handling the window by the edges, Wertz conveyed it to the tank. A smaller object would have been suspended on wires, with spring-loaded clips. The window was too heavy and cumbersome for that, so Wertz stood it in the tank, at an angle, against one of the glass walls. It just fit.

Davis put three cotton balls in a petri dish and placed the dish in the bottom of the tank. He used a pipette to transfer a few drops of liquid cyanoacrylate methyl ester to the cotton. With a second pipette, he applied a similar quantity of sodium hydroxide solution.

Immediately, a cloud of cyanoacrylate fumes billowed through the fish tank, up toward the ventilation hood.

Latent prints, left by small amounts of skin oils and sweat and dirt, were generally invisible to the naked eye until developed with one of several substances: powders, iodine, silver nitrate solution, ninhydrin solution—or cyanoacrylate fumes, which often achieved the best results on nonporous materials like glass, metal, plastic, and hard lacquers. The fumes readily condensed into resin on any surface but more heavily on the oils of which latent prints were formed.

The process could take as little as thirty minutes. If they left the window in the tank more than sixty minutes, so much resin might be deposited that print details would be lost. Davis settled on forty minutes and left Wertz to watch over the fuming.

Those were forty cruel minutes for Roy, because David Davis, a techno geek without equal, insisted on demonstrating some new, state-of-the-art lab equipment. With much gesticulating and exclaiming, his eyes as beady and bright as those of a bird, the technician dwelt on every mechanical detail at excruciating length.

By the time Wertz announced that the window was out of the fish tank, Roy was exhausted from being attentive to Davis. Wistfully, he recalled the Bettonfields' bedroom the night before: holding lovely Penelope's hand, listening to the Beatles. He'd been so relaxed.

The dead were often better company than the living.

Wertz led them to the photography table, on which lay the bathroom window. A Polaroid CU-5 was fixed to a rack over the table, lens downward, to take closeups of any prints that might be found.

The side of the window that was facing up had been on the inside of the bungalow, and the mystery man must have touched it when he escaped. The outside, of course, had been washed with rain.

Although a black background would have been ideal, the mustard-yellow lacquer should have been sufficiently dark to contrast with a friction-ridge pattern of white cyano-acrylate deposits. A close examination revealed nothing on either the frame or the glass itself.

Wertz switched off the overhead fluorescent panels, leaving the lab dark except for what little daylight leaked around the closed Levolor blinds. His pale face seemed vaguely phosphorescent in the murk, like the flesh of a creature that lived in a deep-sea trench.

"A little oblique light will make something pop up," Davis said.

A halogen lamp, with a cone-shaped shade and a flexible metal cable for a neck, hung on a wall bracket nearby. Davis unhooked it, switched it on, and slowly moved it around the bathroom window, aiming the focused light at severe angles across the frame.

"Nothing," Roy said impatiently.

"Let's try the glass," Davis said, angling light from first one direction then another, studying the pane as he'd studied the frame.

Nothing.

"Magnetic powder," Davis said. "That's the ticket."

Wertz flicked on the fluorescent lights. He went to a supply cabinet and returned with a jar of magnetic powder and a magnetic applicator called a Magna-Brush, which Roy had seen used before.

Streamers of black powder flowed in rays from the applicator and stuck where there were traces of grease or oil, but loose grains were drawn back by the magnetized brush. The advantage of the magnetized over other fingerprint powders was that it did not leave the suspect surface coated with excess material.

Wertz covered every inch of the frame and pane. No prints.

"Okay, all right, fine, so be it!" Davis exclaimed, rubbing his long-fingered hands together, bobbing his head, happily rising to the challenge. "Shoot, we're not stumped yet. Damned if we are! This is what makes the job fun."

"If it's easy, it's for assholes," Wertz said with a grin, obviously repeating one of their favorite aphorisms.

"Exactly!" Davis said. "Right you are, young master Wertz. And we are not just *any* assholes."

The challenge seemed to have made them dangerously giddy.

Roy looked pointedly at his wristwatch.

While Wertz put away the Magna-Brush and jar of powder, David Davis pulled on a pair of latex gloves and carefully transferred the window to an adjoining room that was smaller than the main lab. He stood it in a metal sink and snatched one of two plastic laboratory wash bottles that stood on the counter, with which he washed down the lacquered frame and glass. "Methanol solution of rhodamine 6G," Davis explained, as though Roy would know what that was or as if he might even keep it in his refrigerator at home.

Wertz came in just then and said, "I used to know a Rhodamine, lived in apartment 6G, just across the hall."

"This smell like her?" Davis asked.

"She was more pungent," Wertz said, and he laughed with Davis.

Nerd humor. Roy found it tedious, not funny. He supposed he should be relieved about that.

Trading the first wash bottle for the second, David Davis said, "Straight methanol. Washes away excess rhodamine."

"Rhodamine always went to excess, and you couldn't wash her away for weeks," said Wertz, and they laughed again.

Sometimes Roy hated his job.

Wertz powered up a water-cooled argon ion laser generator that stood along one wall. He fiddled with the controls.

Davis carried the window to the laser-examination table.

Satisfied that the machine was ready, Wertz distributed laser goggles. Davis switched off the fluorescents. The only light was the pale wedge that came through the door from the adjoining lab.

Putting on his goggles, Roy crowded close to the table with the two technicians.

Davis switched on the laser. As the eerie beam of light played across the bottom of the window frame, a print appeared almost at once, limed in rhodamine: strange, luminescent whorls.

"There's the sonofabitch!" Davis said.

"Could be anybody's print," Roy said. "We'll see."

Wertz said, "That one looks like a thumb."

The light moved on. More prints magically glowed around the handle and the latch hasp in the center of the bottom member of the frame. A cluster: some partial, some smeared, some whole and clear.

"If I was a betting man," Davis said, "I'd wager a bundle that the window had been cleaned recently, wiped with a cloth, which gives us a pristine field. I'd bet all these prints belong to the same person, were laid down at the same time, by your man last night. They were harder to detect than usual because there wasn't much oil on his fingertips."

"Yeah, that's right, he'd just been walking in the rain," Wertz said excitedly.

Davis said, "And maybe he dried his hands on something when he entered the house."

"There aren't any oil glands in the underside of the hand," Wertz felt obliged to tell Roy. "Fingertips get oily from touching the face, the hair, other parts of the body. Human beings seem to be incessantly touching themselves."

"Hey, now," Davis said in a mock-stern voice, "none of that here, young master Wertz."

They both laughed.

The goggles pinched the bridge of Roy's nose. They were giving him a headache.

Under the lambent light of the laser, another print appeared.

Even Mother Teresa on powerful methamphetamines would have been stricken by depression in the company of David Davis and the Wertz thing. Nevertheless, Roy felt his spirits rise with the appearance of each new luminous print.

The mystery man would not be a mystery much longer.

SEVEN

The day was mild, though not warm enough for sunbathing. At Venice Beach, however, Spencer saw six well-tanned young women in bikinis and two guys in flowered Hawaiian swim trunks, all lying on big towels and soaking up the rays, goose-pimpled but game.

Two muscular, barefoot men in shorts had set up a volleyball net in the sand. They were playing an energetic game, with much leaping, whooping, and grunting. On the paved promenade, a few people glided along on roller skates and Rollerblades, some in swimwear and some not. A bearded man, wearing jeans and a black T-shirt, was flying a red kite with a long tail of red ribbons.

Everyone was too old for high school, old enough so they should have been at work on a Thursday afternoon. Spencer wondered how many were victims of the latest recession and how many were just perpetual adolescents who scammed a living from parents or society. California had long been home to a sizable community of the latter and, with its economic policies, had recently created the former in hordes to rival the affluent legions that it had spawned in previous decades.

On a grassy area adjacent to the sand, Rosie was sitting on a concrete-and-redwood bench, with her back to the matching picnic table. The feathery shadows of an enormous palm tree caressed her.

In white sandals, white slacks, and a purple blouse, she was even more exotic and strikingly beautiful than she had been in the moody Deco lighting at The Red Door. The blood of her Vietnamese mother and that of her African-American father were both visible in her features, yet she didn't call to mind either of the ethnic heritages that she embodied. Instead, she seemed to be the exquisite Eve of a new race: a perfect, innocent woman made for a new Eden.

The peace of the innocent didn't fill her, however. She looked tense and hostile as she stared out to sea, no less so when she turned and saw Spencer approaching. But then she smiled broadly when she saw Rocky. "What a cutie!" She leaned forward on the bench and made come-to-me motions with her hands. "Here, baby. Here, cutie."

Rocky had been happily padding along, tail wagging, taking in the beach scene—but he froze when confronted by the reaching, cooing beauty on the bench. His tail slipped between his legs, fell still. He tensed and prepared to spring away if she moved toward him.

"What's his name?" Rosie asked.

"Rocky. He's shy." Spencer sat on the other end of the bench.

"Come here, Rocky," she coaxed. "Come here, you sweet thing."

Rocky cocked his head and studied her warily.

"What's wrong, cutie? Don't you want to be cuddled and petted?"

Rocky whined. He dropped low on his front paws and wiggled his rear end, though he couldn't bring himself to wag his tail. Indeed, he wanted to be cuddled. He just didn't quite trust her.

"The more you come on to him," Spencer advised, "the more he'll withdraw. Ignore him, and there's a chance he'll decide you're okay."

When Rosie stopped coaxing and sat up straight again, Rocky was frightened by the sudden movement. He scrambled backward a few feet and studied her more warily than before.

"Has he always been this shy?" Rosie asked.

"Since I've known him. He's four or five years old, but I've only had him for two. Saw one of those little spots the newspaper runs every Friday for the animal shelter. Nobody would adopt him, so they were going to have to put him to sleep."

"He's so cute. Anyone would adopt him."

"He was a lot worse then."

"You can't mean he'd bite anyone. Not this sweetie."

"No. Never tried to bite. He was too beaten down for that. He whined and trembled anytime you tried to approach him. When you touched him, he just sort of curled into a ball, closed his eyes, and whimpered, shivering like crazy, as if it hurt to be touched."

"Abused?" she said grimly.

"Yeah. Normally, the people at the pound wouldn't have featured him in the paper. He wasn't a good prospect for adoption. They told me—when a dog's as emotionally crippled as he was, it's usually best not even to try to place him, just put him to sleep."

Still watching the dog as he watched her, Rosie asked, "What happened to him?"

"I didn't ask. Didn't want to know. There are too many things in life I wish I'd never learned . . . 'cause now I can't forget."

The woman looked away from the dog and met Spencer's eyes.

He said, "Ignorance isn't bliss, but sometimes . . ."

". . . ignorance makes it possible for us to sleep at night," she finished.

She was in her late twenties, perhaps thirty. She had been well out of infancy when bombs and gunfire shattered the Asian days, when Saigon fell, when conquering soldiers seized the spoils of war in drunken celebration, when the reeducation camps opened. Maybe as old as eight or nine. Pretty even then: silky black hair, enormous eyes. And far too old for the memories of those terrors ever to fade, as did the forgotten pain of birth and the night fears of the crib.

Last evening at The Red Door, when Rosie had said that Valerie Keene's past was full of suffering, she hadn't merely been guessing or expressing an intuition. She had meant that she'd seen a torment in Valerie that was akin to her own pain.

Spencer looked away from her and stared at the combers that broke gently on the shore. They cast an ever changing lacework of foam across the sand.

"Anyway," he said, "if you ignore Rocky, he might come around. Probably not. But he might."

He shifted his gaze to the red kite. It bobbed and darted on rising thermals, high in the blue sky.

"Why do you want to help Val?" she asked finally.

"Because she's in trouble. And like you said yourself last night, she's special."

"You like her."

"Yes. No. Well, not in the way you mean."

"In what way, then?" Rosie asked.

Spencer couldn't explain what he couldn't understand.

He looked down from the red kite but not at the woman. Rocky was creeping past the far end of the bench, watching Rosie intently as she studiously ignored him. The dog was keeping well out of her reach in case she suddenly turned and snatched at him.

"Why do you want to help her?" Rosie pressed.

The dog was close enough to hear him.

Never lie to the dog.

As he had admitted in the truck last night, Spencer said, "Because I want to find a life."

"And you think you can find it by helping her?"

"Yes."

"How?"

"I don't know."

The dog crept out of sight, circling the bench behind them.

Rosie said, "You think she's part of this life you're looking for. But what if she isn't?"

He stared at the roller skaters on the promenade. They were gliding away from him, as if they were gossamer people blown by the wind, gliding, gliding away.

At last he said, "Then I'll be no worse off than I am now."

"And her?"

"I don't want anything from her that she doesn't want to give."

After a silence, she said, "You're a strange one, Spencer."

"I know."

"Very strange. Are you also special?"

"Me? No."

"Special like Valerie?"

"No."

"She deserves special."

"I'm not."

He heard stealthy sounds behind them, and he knew the dog was squirming on its belly, under the bench on the other side of the picnic table, under the table itself, trying to get closer to the woman, the better to detect and ponder her scent.

"She *did* talk to you quite a while Tuesday night," Rosie said.

He said nothing, letting her make up her mind about him.

"And I saw . . . a couple of times . . . you made her laugh."

He waited.

"Okay," Rosie said, "since Mr. Lee called, I've been trying to remember anything Val said that might help you find her. But there's not much. We liked each other right off, we got close pretty quickly. But mostly we just talked about work, about movies and books, about stuff in the news and things *now*, not about things in the past."

"Where'd she live before she moved to Santa Monica?"

"She never said."

"You didn't ask? You think it might've been somewhere around Los Angeles?"

"No. She wasn't familiar with the city."

"She ever mention where she was born, where she grew up?"

"I don't know why, but I think it was back east somewhere."

"She ever tell you anything about her mom and dad, about having any brothers or sisters?"

"No. But when anyone was talking about family, she'd get this sadness in her eyes. I think maybe . . . her folks are all dead."

He looked at Rosie. "You didn't ask her about them?"

"No. It's just a feeling."

"Was she ever married?"

"Maybe. I didn't ask."

"For a friend, there's a lot you didn't ask."

Rosie nodded. "Because I knew she couldn't tell me the truth. I don't have that many close friends, Mr. Grant, so I didn't want to spoil our relationship by putting her in a position where she'd have to lie to me."

Spencer put his right hand to his face. In the warm air, the scar felt icy under his fingertips.

The bearded man slowly reeled in the kite. That big red diamond blazed against the sky. Its tail of ribbons fluttered like flames.

"So," Spencer said, "you sensed she was running from something?"

"I figured it might be a bad husband, you know, who beat her."

"Do wives regularly run away, start their lives over from scratch, because of a bad husband, instead of just divorcing him?"

"They do in the movies," she said. "If he's violent enough."

Rocky had slipped out from under the table. He appeared at Spencer's side, having fully circled them. His tail was no longer between his legs, but he wasn't wagging it, either. He watched Rosie intently as he continued to slink around to the front of the table.

Pretending to be unaware of the dog, Rosie said, "I don't know if it helps . . . but from little things she said, I think she knows Las Vegas. She's been there more than once, maybe a lot of times."

"Could she have lived there?"

Rosie shrugged. "She liked games. She's good at games. Scrabble, checkers, Monopoly . . . And sometimes we played cards—five-hundred rummy or two-hand pinochle. You should see her shuffle and deal out cards. She can really make them fly through her hands."

"You think she picked that up in Vegas?"

She shrugged again.

Rocky sat on the grass in front of Rosie and stared at her with obvious yearning, but he remained ten feet away, safely out of reach.

"He's decided he can't trust me," she said.

"Nothing personal," Spencer assured her, getting to his feet.

"Maybe he knows."

"Knows what?"

"Animals know things," she said solemnly. "They can see into a person. They see the stains."

"All Rocky sees is a beautiful lady who wants to cuddle him, and he's going crazy because there's nothing to fear but fear itself."

As if he understood his master, Rocky whined pathetically.

"He sees the stains," she said softly. "He knows."

"All I see," Spencer said, "is a lovely woman on a sunny day."

"A person does terrible things to survive."

"That's true of everyone," he said, though he sensed that she was talking to herself more than to him. "Old stains, long faded."

"Never entirely." She seemed no longer to be staring at the dog but at something on the far side of an invisible bridge of time.

Though he was reluctant to leave her in that suddenly strange mood, Spencer could think of nothing more to say.

Where the white sand met the grass, the bearded man cranked the reel in his hands and appeared to be fishing the heavens. The blood-red kite gradually descended, its tail snapping like a whip of fire.

Finally Spencer thanked Rosie for talking with him. She wished him luck, and he walked away with Rocky.

The dog repeatedly stopped to glance back at the woman on the bench, then scurried to catch up with Spencer. When they had covered fifty yards and were halfway to the parking lot, Rocky issued a short yelp of decision and bolted back to the picnic table.

Spencer turned to watch.

In the last few feet, the mutt lost courage. He skidded nearly to a halt and approached her with his head lowered timidly, with much shivering and tail wagging.

Rosie slipped off the bench onto the grass, and pulled Rocky into her arms. Her sweet, clean laughter trilled across the park.

"Good dog," Spencer said quietly.

The muscular volleyball players took a break from their game to get a couple of cans of Pepsi out of a Styrofoam cooler.

Having reeled his kite all the way to the earth, the bearded man headed for the parking lot by a route that brought him past Spencer. He looked like a mad prophet: untrimmed; unwashed; with deeply set, wild blue eyes; a beaky nose; pale lips; broken, yellow teeth. On his black T-shirt, in red letters, were five words: ANOTHER BEAUTIFUL DAY IN HELL. He cast a fierce glance at Spencer, clutched his kite as if he thought every blackguard in creation wanted nothing more than to steal it, and stalked out of the park.

Spencer realized he had put a hand over his scar when the man had glanced at him. He lowered it.

Rosie was standing a few steps in front of the picnic table now, shooing Rocky away, apparently admonishing him not to keep his master waiting. She was beyond the reach of the palm shadows, in sunlight.

As the dog reluctantly left his new friend and trotted toward his master, Spencer was once again aware of the woman's exceptional beauty, which was far greater than Valerie's. And if it was the role of savior and healer that he yearned to fill, this woman most likely needed him more than the one he sought. Yet he was drawn to Valerie, not to Rosie, for reasons he could not explain—except to accuse himself of obsession, of being swept away by the fathomless currents of his subconscious, regardless of where they might take him.

The dog reached him, panting and grinning.

Rosie raised one hand over her head and waved good-bye.

Spencer waved too.

Maybe his search for Valerie Keene wasn't merely an obsession. He had the uncanny feeling that he was the kite and that she was the reel. Some strange power—call it destiny—turned the crank, wound the line around the spool, drawing him inexorably toward her, and he had no choice in the matter whatsoever.

While the sea rolled in from faraway China and lapped at the beach, while the sunshine traveled ninety-three million miles through airless space to caress the golden bodies of the young women in their bikinis, Spencer and Rocky walked back to the truck.

With Roy Miro trailing after him at a more sedate pace, David Davis rushed into the main data processing room with the photographs of the two best prints on the bathroom window. He took them to Nella Shire, at one of the workstations. "One is clearly a thumb, clearly, no question," Davis told her. "The other might be an index finger."

Shire was about forty-five, with a face as sharp as that of a fox, frizzy orange hair, and green fingernail polish. Her half-walled cubicle was decorated with three photographs clipped from bodybuilding magazines: hugely pumped-up men in bikini briefs.

Noticing the musclemen, Davis frowned and said, "Ms. Shire, I've told you this is unacceptable. You must remove these pinups."

"The human body is art."

Davis was red-faced. "You *know* this can be construed as sexual harassment in the workplace."

"Yeah?" She took the fingerprint photos from him. "By who?"

"By any male worker in this room, that's by *whom*."

"None of the men working here looks like these hunks. Until one of them does, nobody has anything to worry about from me."

Davis tore one of the clippings from the cubicle wall, then another. "The last thing I need is a notation on my management record, saying I allowed harassment in my division."

Although Roy believed in the law of which Nella Shire was in violation, he was aware of the irony of Davis worrying about his management record being soiled by a tolerance-of-harassment entry. After all, the nameless agency for which they worked was an illegal organization, answering to no elected official; therefore, every act of Davis's working day was in violation of one law or another.

Of course, like nearly all of the agency's personnel, Davis didn't know that he was an instrument of a conspiracy. He received his paycheck from the Department of Justice and thought he was on their records as an employee. He had signed a secrecy oath, but he believed that he was part of a legal—if potentially controversial—offensive against organized crime and international terrorism.

As Davis tore the third pinup off the cubicle walls and wadded it in his fist, Nella Shire said, "Maybe you hate those pictures so much because they turn *you* on, which is something you can't accept about yourself. Did you ever think of that?" She glanced at the fingerprint photos. "So what do you want me to do with these?"

Roy saw that David Davis had to struggle not to answer with the first thing that came to his mind.

Instead, Davis said, "We need to know whose prints these are. Go through Mama, get on-line with the FBI's Automated Identification Division. Start with the Latent Descriptor Index."

The Federal Bureau of Investigation had one hundred ninety million fingerprints on file. Though its newest computer could make thousands of comparisons a minute, a lot of time could be expended if it had to shuffle through its entire vast storehouse of prints.

With the help of clever software called the Latent Descriptor Index, the field of search could be drastically reduced and results achieved quickly. If they had been seeking suspects in a series of killings, they would have listed the prime characteristics of the crimes—the sex and age of each victim, the methods of murder, any similarities in the conditions of the corpses, the locations at which the bodies had been found—and the index would have compared those facts to the modus operandi of known offenders, eventually producing a list of suspects and their fingerprints. Then a few hundred—or even just a few—comparisons might be necessary instead of millions.

Nella Shire turned to her computer and said, "So give me the telltales, and I'll create a three-oh-two."

"We aren't seeking a known criminal," Davis said.

Roy said, "We think our man was in special forces, or maybe he had special-weapons-and-tactics training."

"Those guys are all hardbodies, for sure," Shire said, eliciting a scowl from David Davis. "Army, navy, marines, or air force?"

"We don't know," Roy said. "Maybe he was never in the service. Could have been with a state or local police department. Could have been a Bureau agent, as far as we know, or DEA or ATF."

"The way this works," Shire said impatiently, "is, I need to put in telltales that limit the field."

A hundred million of the prints in the Bureau's system were in criminal-history files, which left ninety million that covered federal employees, military personnel, intelligence services, state and local law-enforcement officers, and registered aliens. If they knew that their mystery man was, say, an ex-marine, they wouldn't have to search most of those ninety million files.

Roy opened the envelope that Melissa Wicklun had given him a short while ago, in Photo Analysis. He took out one of the computer-projected portraits of the man they were hunting. On the back of it was the data that the photo-analysis software had deduced from the rain-veiled profile of the man at the bungalow the previous night.

"Male, Caucasian, twenty-eight to thirty-two," Roy said.

Nella Shire typed swiftly. A list appeared on the screen.

"Five feet eleven inches tall," Roy continued. "One hundred and sixty-five pounds, give or take five. Brown hair, brown eyes."

He turned the photo over to stare at the full-face portrait, and David Davis bent down to look as well. "Severe facial scarring," Roy said. "Right side. Beginning at the ear, terminating near the chin."

"Was that sustained on duty?" David wondered.

"Probably. So a conditional telltale might be an honorable early discharge or even a service disability."

"Whether he was discharged or disabled," Davis said excitedly, "you can bet he was required to undergo psychological counseling. A scar like this—it's a terrible blow to self-esteem. Terrible."

Nella Shire swiveled in her chair, snatched the portrait out of Roy's hand, and looked at it. "I don't know . . . I think it makes him look sexy. Dangerous and sexy."

Ignoring her, Davis said, "The government's very concerned about self-esteem these days. A lack of self-esteem is the root of crime and social unrest. You can't hold up a bank or mug an old lady unless you first think you're nothing but a lowlife thief."

"Yeah?" Nella Shire said, returning the portrait to Roy. "Well, I've known a thousand jerks who thought they were God's best work."

Davis said firmly, "Make psychological counseling a telltale."

She added that item to her list. "Anything else?"

"That's all," Roy said. "How long is this going to take?"

Shire read through the list on the screen. "Hard to say. No more than eight or ten hours. Maybe less. Maybe a lot less. Could be, in an hour or two, I'll have his name, address, phone number, and be able to tell you which side of his pants he hangs on."

David Davis, still clutching a fistful of crumpled musclemen and worried about his management record, appeared offended by her remark.

Roy was merely intrigued. "Really? Maybe only an hour or two?"

"Why would I be jerking your chain?" she asked impatiently.

"Then I'll hang around. We need this guy real bad."

"He's almost yours," Nella Shire promised as she set to work.

At three o'clock they had a late lunch on the back porch while the long shadows of euca-lyptuses crept up the canyon in the yellowing light of the westering sun. Sitting in a rock-ing chair, Spencer ate a ham-and-cheese sandwich and drank a bottle of beer. After polishing off a bowl of Purina, Rocky used his grin, his best sad-eyed look, his most pa-thetic whine, his wagging tail, and a master thespian's store of tricks to cadge bits of the sandwich.

"Laurence Olivier had nothing on you," Spencer told him.

When the sandwich was gone, Rocky padded down the porch steps and started across the backyard toward the nearest cluster of wild brush, characteristically seeking privacy for his toilet.

"Wait, wait, wait," Spencer said, and the dog stopped to look at him. "You'll come back with your coat full of burrs, and it'll take me an hour to comb them all out. I don't have time for that."

He got up from the rocking chair, turned his back to the dog, and stared at the cabin wall while he finished the last of the beer.

When Rocky returned, they went inside, leaving the tree shadows to grow unwatched.

While the dog napped on the sofa, Spencer sat at the computer and began his search for Valerie Keene. From that bungalow in Santa Monica, she could have gone anywhere in the world, and he would have been as well advised to start looking in far Borneo as in nearby Ventura. Therefore, he could only go backward, into the past.

He had a single clue: Vegas. *Cards. She can really make them fly through her hands.*

Her familiarity with Vegas and her facility with cards might mean that she had lived there and earned her living as a dealer.

By his usual route, Spencer hacked into the main LAPD computer. From there he springboarded into an interstate police data-sharing network, which he had often used be-fore, and bounced across borders into the computer of the Clark County Sheriff's Depart-ment in Nevada, which had jurisdiction over the city of Las Vegas.

On the sofa, the snoring dog pumped his legs, chasing rabbits in his sleep. In Rocky's case, the rabbits were probably chasing him.

After exploring the sheriff's computer for a while and finding his way into—among other things—the department's personnel records, Spencer finally discovered a file labeled NEV CODES. He was pretty sure he knew what it was, and he wanted in.

NEV CODES was specially protected. To use it, he required an access number. Incredibly, in many police agencies, that would be either an officer's badge number or, in the case of office workers, an employee ID number—all obtainable from personnel records, which were not well guarded. He had already collected a few badge numbers in case he needed them. Now he used one, and NEV CODES opened to him.

It was a list of numerical codes with which he could access the computer-stored data of any government agency in the state of Nevada. In a wink he followed the cyberspace high-way from Las Vegas to the Nevada Gaming Commission in Carson City, the capital.

The commission licensed all casinos in the state and enforced the laws and regulations that governed them. Anyone who wished to invest—or serve as an executive—in the gam-ing industry was required to submit to a background investigation and to be proved free of ties to known criminals. In the 1970s, a strengthened commission squeezed out most of the mobsters and Mafia front men who had founded Nevada's biggest industry, in favor of companies like Metro-Goldwyn-Mayer and Hilton Hotels.

It was logical to suppose that other casino employees below management level—from pit bosses to cocktail waitresses—underwent similar although less exhaustive background checks and were issued ID cards. Spencer explored menus and directories, and in another twenty minutes, he found the records that he needed.

The data related to casino-employee work permits was divided into three primary files: Expired, Current, Pending. Because Valerie had been working at The Red Door in Santa Monica for two months, Spencer accessed the Expired list first.

In his rambles through cyberspace, he had seen few files so extensively cross-referenced as this one—and those others had been related to grave national defense matters. The system allowed him to search for a subject in the Expired category by means of twenty-two indices ranging from eye color to most recent place of employment.

He typed VALERIE ANN KEENE.

In a few seconds the system replied: UNKNOWN.

He shifted to the file labeled Current and typed in her name.

UNKNOWN.

Spencer tried the Pending file with the same result. Valerie Ann Keene was unknown to the Nevada gaming authorities.

For a moment he stared at the screen, despondent because his only clue had proved to be a dead end. Then he realized that a woman on the run was unlikely to use the same name everywhere she went and thereby make herself easy to track. If Valerie had lived and worked in Vegas, her name almost surely had been different then.

To find her in the file, Spencer would have to be clever.

While waiting for Nella Shire to find the scarred man, Roy Miro was in terrible danger of being dragooned into hours of sociable conversation with David Davis. He would almost rather have eaten a cyanide-laced muffin and washed it down with a big, frosty beaker of carbolic acid than spend any more time with the fingerprint maven.

Claiming not to have slept the night before, when in fact he had slept the innocent sleep of a saint after the priceless gift he had given to Penelope Bettonfield and her husband, Roy charmed Davis into offering the use of his office. "I insist, I really do, I will listen to no argument, none!" Davis said with considerable gesturing and bobbing of his head. "I've got a couch in there. You can stretch out on it, you won't be inconveniencing me. I've got plenty of lab work to do. I don't need to be at my desk today."

Roy didn't expect to sleep. In the cool dimness of the office, with the California sun banished by the tightly closed Levolors, he thought he would lie on his back, stare at the ceiling, visualize the nexus of his spiritual being—where his soul connected with the mysterious power that ruled the cosmos—and meditate on the meaning of existence. He pursued deeper self-awareness every day. He was a seeker, and the search for enlightenment was endlessly exciting to him. Strangely, however, he fell asleep.

He dreamed of a perfect world. There was no greed or envy or despair, because everyone was identical to everyone else. There was a single sex, and human beings reproduced by discreet parthenogenesis in the privacy of their bathrooms—though not often. The only skin color was a pale and slightly radiant blue. Everyone was beautiful in an androgynous way. No one was dumb, but no one was too smart, either. Everyone wore the same clothes and lived in houses that all looked alike. Every Friday evening, there was a planetwide bingo game, which everyone won, and on Saturdays—

Wertz woke him, and Roy was paralyzed by terror because he confused the dream and reality. Gazing up into the slug-pale, moon-round face of Davis's assistant, which was revealed by a desk lamp, Roy thought that he himself, along with everyone else in the world, looked exactly like Wertz. He tried to scream but couldn't find his voice.

Then Wertz spoke, bringing Roy fully awake: "Mrs. Shire's found him. The scarred man. She's found him."

Alternately yawning and grimacing at the sour taste in his mouth, Roy followed Wertz to the data processing room. David Davis and Nella Shire were standing at her workstation, each with a sheaf of papers. In the fluorescent glare, Roy squinted with dis-comfort, then with interest, as Davis passed to him, page by page, computer printouts on which both he and Nella Shire commented excitedly.

"His name's Spencer Grant," Davis said. "No middle name. At eighteen, out of high school, he joined the army."

"High IQ, equally high motivation," Mrs. Shire said. "He applied for special-forces training. Army Rangers."

"He left the army after six years," Davis said, passing another printout to Roy, "used his service benefits to go to UCLA."

Scanning the latest page, Roy said, "Majored in criminology."

"Minored in criminal psychology," said Davis. "Went to school year-round, kept a heavy class load, got a degree in three years."

"Young man in a hurry," Wertz said, apparently so they would remember that he was part of the team and would not, accidentally, step on him and crush him like a bug.

As Davis handed Roy another page, Nella Shire said, "Then he applied to the L.A. Po-lice Academy. Graduated at the top of his class."

"One day, after less than a year on the street," Davis said, "he walked into the middle of a carjacking in progress. Two armed men. They saw him coming, tried to take the woman motorist hostage."

"He killed them both," Shire said. "The woman wasn't scratched."

"Grant get crucified?"

"No. Everyone felt these were righteous shootings."

Glancing at another page that Davis handed to him, Roy said, "According to this, he was transferred off the street."

"Grant has computer skills and high aptitude," Davis said, "so they put him on a computer-crime task force. Strictly desk work."

Roy frowned. "Why? Was he traumatized by the shootings?"

"Some of them can't handle it," Wertz said knowingly. "They don't have the right stuff, don't have the stomach for it, they just come apart."

"According to the records from his mandatory therapy sessions," Nella Shire said, "he wasn't traumatized. He handled it well. He asked for the transfer, but not because he was traumatized."

"Probably in denial," Wertz said, "being macho, too ashamed of his weakness to ad-mit to it."

"Whatever the reason," Davis said, "he asked for the transfer. Then, ten months ago, after putting in twenty-one months with the task force, he just up and resigned from the LAPD altogether."

"Where's he working now?" Roy asked.

"We don't know that, but we *do* know where he lives," David Davis said, producing another printout with a dramatic flourish.

Staring at the address, Roy said, "You're sure this is our man?"

Shire shuffled her own sheaf of papers. She produced a high-resolution printout of a Los Angeles Police Department personnel fingerprint ID sheet while Davis provided the photos of the prints they had lifted from the frame of the bathroom window.

Davis said, "If you know how to make comparisons, you'll see the computer's right when it says they're a perfect match. Perfect. This is our guy. No doubt about it, none."

Handing another printout to Roy, Nella Shire said, "This is his most recent photo ID from the police records."

Full-face and in profile, Grant bore an uncanny resemblance to the computer-projected portrait that had been given to Roy by Melissa Wicklun in Photo Analysis.

"Is this a recent photo?" Roy asked.

"The most recent the LAPD has on file," Shire said.

"Taken a long time after the carjacking incident?"

"That would have been two and a half years ago. Yeah, I'm sure this picture is a lot more recent than that. Why?"

"The scar looks fully healed," Roy noted.

"Oh," Davis said, "he didn't get the scar in that shootout, no, not then. He's had it a long time, a very long time, had it when he entered the army. It's from a childhood injury."

Roy looked up from the picture. "What injury?"

Davis shrugged his angular shoulders, and his long arms flapped against his white lab coat. "We don't know. None of the records tell us about it. They just list it as his most prominent identifying feature. 'Cicatricial scar from right ear to point of chin, result of childhood injury.' That's all."

"He looks like Igor," Wertz said with a snicker.

"I think he's sexy," Nella Shire disagreed.

"Igor," Wertz insisted.

Roy turned to him. "Igor who?"

"Igor. You remember—from those old Frankenstein movies, Dr. Frankenstein's sidekick. Igor. The grisly old hunchback with the twisted neck."

"I don't care for that kind of entertainment," Roy said. "It glorifies violence and deformity. It's sick." Studying the photo, Roy wondered how young Spencer Grant had been when he'd suffered such a grievous wound. Just a boy, apparently. "The poor kid," he said. "The poor, poor kid. What quality of life could he have had with a face as damaged as that? What psychological burdens does he carry?"

Frowning, Wertz said, "I thought this was a bad guy, mixed up in terrorism somehow?"

"Even bad guys," Roy said patiently, "deserve compassion. This man has suffered. You can see that. I need to get my hands on him, yes, and be sure that society's safe from him— but he still deserves to be treated with compassion, with as much mercy as possible."

Davis and Wertz stared uncomprehendingly.

But Nella Shire said, "You're a nice man, Roy."

Roy shrugged.

"No," she said, "you really are. It makes me feel good to know there are men like you in law enforcement."

The heat of a blush rose in Roy's face. "Well, thank you, that's very kind, but there's nothing special about me."

Because Nella was clearly not a lesbian, even though she was as much as fifteen years older than he, Roy wished that at least one feature about her was as attractive as Melissa Wicklun's exquisite mouth. But her hair was too frizzy and too orange. Her eyes were too cold a blue, her nose and chin too pointed, her lips too severe. Her body was reasonably well proportioned but not exceptional in any regard.

"Well," Roy said with a sigh, "I'd better pay a visit to this Mr. Grant, ask him what he was doing in Santa Monica last night."

Sitting at the computer in his Malibu cabin but prowling deep into the Nevada Gaming Commission in Carson City, Spencer searched the file of current casino-worker permits by asking to be given the names of all card dealers who were female, between the ages of twenty-eight and thirty, five feet four inches tall, one hundred ten to one hundred twenty pounds, with brown hair and brown eyes. Those were sufficient parameters to result in a comparatively small number of candidates—just fourteen. He directed the computer to print the list of names in alphabetical order.

He started at the top of the printout and summoned the file on Janet Francine Arbonhall. The first page of the electronic dossier that appeared on the screen featured her basic physical description, the date on which her work permit had been approved, and a full-face photograph. She looked nothing like Valerie, so Spencer exited her file without reading it.

He called up another file: Theresa Elisabeth Dunbury. Not her.

Bianca Marie Haguerro. Not her, either.

Corrine Serise Huddleston. No.

Laura Linsey Langston. No.

Rachael Sarah Marks. Nothing like Valerie.

Jacqueline Ethel Mung. Seven down and seven to go.

Hannah May Rainey.

On the screen, Valerie Ann Keene appeared, her hair different from the way she had worn it at The Red Door, lovely but unsmiling.

Spencer ordered a complete printout of Hannah May Rainey's file, which was only three pages long. He read it end to end while the woman continued to stare at him from the computer.

Under the Rainey name, she had worked for over four months of the previous year as a blackjack dealer in the casino of the Mirage Hotel in Las Vegas. Her last day on the job had been November 26, not quite two and a half months ago, and according to the casino manager's report to the commission, she had quit without notice.

They—whoever "they" might be—must have tracked her down on the twenty-sixth of November, and she must have eluded them as they were reaching out for her, just as she eluded them in Santa Monica.

In a corner of the parking garage beneath the agency's building in downtown Los Angeles, Roy Miro had a final word with the three agents who would accompany him to Spencer Grant's house and take the man into custody. Because their agency did not officially exist, the word "custody" was being stretched beyond its usual definition; "kidnapping" was a more accurate description of their intentions.

Roy had no problem with either term. Morality was relative, and nothing done in the service of correct ideals could be a crime.

They were all carrying Drug Enforcement Administration credentials, so Grant would believe that he was being taken to a federal facility to be questioned—and that upon arrival there, he would be permitted to call an attorney. Actually, he was more likely to see the Lord God Almighty on a golden airborne throne than anyone with a law degree.

Using whatever methods might be necessary to obtain truthful answers, they would question him about his relationship with the woman and her current whereabouts. When they had what they needed—or were convinced that they had squeezed out of him all that he knew—they would dispose of him.

Roy would conduct the disposal himself, releasing the poor scarred devil from the misery of this troubled world.

The first of the other three agents, Cal Dormon, wore white slacks and a white shirt with the logo of a pizza parlor stitched on the breast. He would be driving a small white van with a matching logo, which was one of many magnetic-mat signs that could be attached to the vehicle to change its character, depending on what was needed for any particular operation.

Alfonse Johnson was dressed in work shoes, khaki slacks, and a denim jacket. Mike Vecchio wore sweats and a pair of Nikes.

Roy was the only one of them in a suit. Because he had napped fully clothed on Davis's couch, however, he didn't fit the stereotype of a neat and well-pressed federal agent.

"All right, this isn't like last night," Roy said. They had all been part of the SWAT team in Santa Monica. "We need to *talk* to this guy."

The previous night, if any of them had seen the woman, he would have cut her down instantly. For the benefit of any local police who might have shown up, a weapon would have been planted in her hand: a Desert Eagle .50 Magnum, such a powerful handgun that a shot from it would leave an exit wound as large as a man's fist, a piece obviously meant solely for killing people. The story would have been that the agent had gunned her down in self-defense.

"But we can't let him slip away," Roy continued. "And he's a boy with schooling, as well trained as any of you, so he might not just hold out his hands for the bracelets. If you can't make him behave and he looks to be gone, then shoot his legs out from under him. Chop him up good if you have to. He isn't going to need to walk again anyway. Just don't get carried away—okay? Remember, we absolutely *must* talk to him."

Spencer had obtained all the information of interest to him that was contained in the files of the Nevada Gaming Commission. He retreated along the cyberspace highways as far as the Los Angeles Police Department computer.

From there he linked with the Santa Monica Police Department and examined its file of cases initiated within the past twenty-four hours. No case could be referenced either by the name Valerie Ann Keene or by the street address of the bungalow that she had been renting.

He exited the case files and checked call reports for Wednesday night, because it was possible that SMPD officers had answered a call related to the fracas at the bungalow but had not given the incident a case number. This time, he found the address.

The last of the officer's notations indicated why no case number had been assigned: ATF OP IN PROG. FED ASSERTED. Which meant: Bureau of Alcohol, Tobacco and Firearms operation in progress; federal jurisdiction asserted.

The local cops had been frozen out.

On the nearby couch, Rocky exploded from sleep with a shrill yelp, fell to the floor, scrambled to his feet, started to chase his tail, then whipped his head left and right in confusion, searching for whatever threat had pursued him out of his dream.

"Just a nightmare," Spencer assured the dog.

Rocky looked at him doubtfully and whined.

"What was it this time— a giant prehistoric cat?"

The mutt padded quickly across the room and jumped up to plant his forepaws on a windowsill. He stared out at the driveway and the surrounding woods.

The short February day was drawing toward a colorful twilight. The undersides of the eucalyptuses' oval leaves, which were usually silver, now reflected the golden light that poured through gaps in the foliage; they glimmered in a faint breeze, so it appeared as if the trees had been hung with ornaments for the Christmas season that was now more than a month past.

Rocky whined worriedly again.

"A pterodactyl cat?" Spencer suggested. "Huge wings and giant fangs and a purr loud enough to crack stone?"

Not amused, the dog dropped from the window and hurried into the kitchen. He was always like this when he woke abruptly from a bad dream. He would circle the house, from window to window, convinced that the enemy in the land of dreams was every bit as dangerous to him in the real world.

Spencer looked at the computer screen again.

ATF OP IN PROG. FED ASSERTED.

Something was wrong.

If the SWAT team that hit the bungalow the previous night had been composed of agents of the Bureau of Alcohol, Tobacco and Firearms, why had the men who showed up at Louis Lee's home in Bel Air been carrying FBI credentials? The former bureau was under the control of the United States Secretary of the Treasury, while the latter was ultimately answerable to the Attorney General—though changes in that structure were being contemplated. The different organizations sometimes cooperated in operations of mutual interest; however, considering the usual intensity of interagency rivalry and suspicion, *both* would have had representatives present at the questioning of Louis Lee or of anyone else from whom a lead might have been developed.

Grumbling to himself as if he were the White Rabbit running late for tea with the Mad Hatter, Rocky scampered out of the kitchen and hurried through the open door to the bedroom.

ATF OP IN PROG.

Something wrong . . .

The FBI was by far the more powerful of the two bureaus, and if it was interested enough to be on the scene, it would never agree to surrender all jurisdiction entirely to the ATF. In fact, there was legislation being written in Congress, at the request of the White House, to fold the ATF into the FBI. The cop's note in the SMPD call report should have read: FBI/ATF OP IN PROG.

Brooding about all that, Spencer retreated from Santa Monica to the LAPD, floated there a moment as he tried to decide if he was finished, then backed into the task-force computer, closing doors as he went, neatly cleaning up any traces of his invasion.

Rocky bolted out of the bedroom, past Spencer, to the living room window once more.

Home again, Spencer shut down his computer. He got up from the desk and went to the window to stand beside Rocky.

The tip of the dog's black nose was against the glass. One ear up, one down.

"What do you dream about?" Spencer wondered.

Rocky whimpered softly, his attention fixed on the deep purple shadows and the golden glimmerings of the twilit eucalyptus grove.

"Fanciful monsters, things that could never be?" Spencer asked. "Or just . . . the past?"

The dog was shivering.

Spencer put one hand on the nape of Rocky's neck and stroked him gently.

The dog glanced up, then immediately returned his attention to the eucalyptuses, perhaps because a great darkness was descending slowly over the shrinking twilight. Rocky had always been afraid of the night.

EIGHT

The fading light congealed into a luminous red scum across the western sky. The crimson sun was reflected by every microscopic particle of pollution and water vapor in the air, so it seemed as though the city lay under a thin mist of blood.

Cal Dormon retrieved a large pizza box from the back of the white van and walked toward the house.

Roy Miro was on the other side of the street from the van, having entered the block from the opposite direction. He got out of his car and quietly closed the door.

By now, Johnson and Vecchio would have made their way to the back of the house by neighboring properties.

Roy started across the street.

Dormon was halfway along the front walk. He didn't have a pizza in the box, but a Desert Eagle .44 Magnum pistol equipped with a heavy-duty sound suppressor. The uniform and the prop were solely to allay suspicion if Spencer Grant happened to glance out a window just as Dormon was approaching the house.

Roy reached the back of the white van.

Dormon was at the front stoop.

Putting one hand across his mouth as if to muffle a cough, Roy spoke into the transmitter microphone that was clipped to his shirt cuff. "Count five and go," he whispered to the men at the back of the house.

At the front door, Cal Dormon didn't bother to ring the bell or knock. He tried the knob. The lock must have been engaged, because he opened the pizza box, let it fall to the ground, and brought up the powerful Israeli pistol.

Roy picked up his pace, no longer casual.

In spite of its high-quality silencer, the .44 emitted a hard thud each time it was fired. The sound wasn't like gunfire, but it was loud enough to draw the attention of passersby if there had been any. The gun was, after all, a door-buster: Three quick rounds tore the hell out of the jamb and striker plate. Even if the deadbolt remained intact, the notch in which it had been seated was not a notch anymore; it was just a bristle of splinters.

Dormon went inside, with Roy behind him, and a guy in stocking feet was coming up from a blue vinyl Barcalounger, a can of beer in one hand, wearing faded jeans and a T-shirt, saying "Jesus Christ," looking terrified and bewildered because the last bits of wood and brass from the door had just hit the living room carpet around him. Dormon drove him backward into the chair again, hard enough to knock the breath out of him, and the can of beer tumbled to the floor, rolled across the carpet, spewing gouts of foam.

The guy wasn't Spencer Grant.

Holding his silencer-fitted Beretta in both hands, Roy quickly crossed the living room, went through an archway into a dining room, and then through an open door into a kitchen.

A blonde of about thirty was facedown on the kitchen floor, her head turned toward Roy, her left arm extended as she tried to recover a butcher knife that had been knocked out of her hand and that was an inch or two beyond her reach. She couldn't move toward it, because Vecchio had a knee in the small of her back and the muzzle of his pistol against her neck, just behind her left ear.

"You bastard, you bastard, you *bastard*," the woman squealed. Her shrill words were neither loud nor clear, because her face was jammed against the linoleum. And she couldn't draw much breath with Vecchio's knee in her back.

"Easy, lady, easy," Vecchio said. "Be still, damn it!"

Alfonse Johnson was one step inside the back door, which must have been unlocked because they hadn't needed to break it down. Johnson was covering the only other person in the room: a little girl, perhaps five, who stood with her back pressed into a corner, wide-eyed and pale, too frightened yet to cry.

The air smelled of hot tomato sauce and onions. On the cutting board were sliced green peppers. The woman had been making dinner.

"Come on," Roy said to Johnson.

Together, they searched the rest of the house, moving fast. The element of surprise was gone, but momentum was still on their side. Hall closet. Bathroom. Girl's bedroom: teddy bears and dolls, the closet door standing open, nobody there. Another small room: a sewing machine, a half-finished green dress on a dressmaker's dummy, closet packed full, no place for anyone to hide. Then the master bedroom, closet, closet, bathroom: nobody.

Johnson said, "Unless that's him in a blond wig on the kitchen floor . . ."

Roy returned to the living room, where the guy in the lounge chair was tilted as far back as he could go, staring into the bore of the .44 while Cal Dormon screamed in his face, spraying him with spittle: "One more time. You hear me, asshole? I'm asking just one more time—where is he?"

"I told you," the guy said, "Jesus, nobody's here but us."

"Where's Grant?" Dormon insisted.

The man was shaking as if the Barcalounger was equipped with a vibrating massage unit. "I don't know him, I swear, never heard of him. So will you just, will you just please, will you point that cannon somewhere else?"

Roy was saddened that it was so often necessary to deny people their dignity in order to get them to cooperate. He left Johnson in the living room with Dormon and returned to the kitchen.

The woman was still flat on the floor, with Vecchio's knee in her back, but she was no longer trying to reach the butcher knife. She wasn't calling him a bastard anymore, either. Fury having given way to fear, she was begging him not to hurt her little girl.

The child was in the corner, sucking on her thumb. Tears tracked down her cheeks, but she made no sound.

Roy picked up the butcher knife and put it on the counter, out of the woman's reach.

She rolled one eye to look up at him. "Don't hurt my baby."

"We aren't going to hurt anyone," Roy said.

He went to the little girl, crouched beside her, and said in his softest voice, "Are you scared, honey?"

She turned her eyes from her mother to Roy.

"Of course, you're scared, aren't you?" he said.

With her thumb stuck in her mouth, sucking fiercely, she nodded.

"Well, there's no reason to be scared of me. I'd never hurt a fly. Not even if it buzzed and buzzed around my face and danced in my ears and went skiing down my nose."

The child stared solemnly at him through tears.

Roy said, "When a mosquito lands on me and tries to take a bite, do I swat him? Noooooo. I lay out a tiny napkin for him, a teeny tiny little knife and fork, and I say, 'No one in this world should go hungry. Dinner's on me, Mr. Mosquito.' "

The tears seemed to be clearing from her eyes.

"I remember one time," Roy told her, "when this elephant was on his way to a super-market to buy peanuts. He was in ever so great a hurry, and he just ran my car off the road. Most people, they would have followed that elephant to the market and punched him right on the tender tip of his trunk. But did I do that? Noooooo. 'When an elephant is out of peanuts,' I told myself, 'he just can't be held responsible for his actions.' However, I must admit I drove to that market after him and let the air out of the tires on his bicycle, but that was not done in anger. I only wanted to keep him off the road until he'd had time to eat some peanuts and calm down."

She was an adorable child. He wished he could see her smile.

"Now," he said, "do you really think I'd hurt anyone?"

The girl shook her head: no.

"Then give me your hand, honey," Roy said.

She let him take her left hand, the one without a wet thumb, and he led her across the kitchen.

Vecchio released the mother. The woman scrambled to her knees and, weeping, em-braced the child.

Letting go of the girl's hand and crouching again, touched by the mother's tears, Roy said, "I'm sorry. I abhor violence, I really do. But we thought a dangerous man was here, and we couldn't very well just knock and ask him to come out and play. You understand?"

The woman's lower lip quivered. "I . . . I don't know. Who are you, what do you want?"

"What's your name?"

"Mary. Mary Z-Zelinsky."

"Your husband's name?"

"Peter."

Mary Zelinsky had a lovely nose. The bridge was a perfect wedge, all the lines straight and true. Such delicate nostrils. A septum that seemed crafted of finest porcelain. He didn't think he had ever seen a nose quite as wonderful before.

Smiling, he said, "Well, Mary, we need to know where he is."

"Who?" the woman asked.

"I'm sure you know who. Spencer Grant, of course."

"I don't know him."

Just as she answered him, he looked up from her nose into her eyes, and he saw no deception there.

"I've never heard of him," she said.

To Vecchio, Roy said, "Turn the gas off under that tomato sauce. I'm afraid it's going to burn."

"I swear I've never heard of him," the woman insisted.

Roy was inclined to believe her. Helen of Troy could not have had a nose any finer than Mary Zelinsky's. Of course, indirectly, Helen of Troy had been responsible for the deaths of thousands, and many others had suffered because of her, so beauty was no guarantee of innocence. And in the tens of centuries since the time of Helen, human beings had become masters at the concealment of evil, so even the most guileless-looking creatures sometimes proved to be depraved.

Roy had to be sure, so he said, "If I feel you're lying to me—"

"I'm not lying," Mary said tremulously.

He held up one hand to silence her, and he continued where he had been interrupted:

"—I might take this precious girl to her room, undress her—"

The woman closed her eyes tightly, in horror, as if she could block out the scene that he was so delicately describing for her.

"—and there, among the teddy bears and dolls, I could teach her some grown-up games."

The woman's nostrils flared with terror. Hers really was an exquisite nose.

"Now, Mary, look me in the eyes," he said, "and tell me again if you know a man named Spencer Grant."

She opened her eyes and met his gaze.

They were face-to-face.

He put one hand on the child's head, stroked her hair, smiled

Mary Zelinsky clutched her daughter with pitiful desperation. "I swear to God I never heard of him. I don't know him. I don't understand what's happening here."

"I believe you," he said. "Rest easy, Mary. I believe you, dear lady. I'm sorry it was necessary to resort to such crudity."

Though the tone of his voice was tender and apologetic, a tide of rage washed through Roy. His fury was directed at Grant, who had somehow hoodwinked them, not at this woman or her daughter or her hapless husband in the Barcalounger.

Although Roy strove to repress his anger, the woman must have glimpsed it in his eyes, which were ordinarily of such a kindly aspect, for she flinched from him.

At the stove, where he had turned off the gas under the sauce and under a pot of boiling water as well, Vecchio said, "He doesn't live here anymore."

"I don't think he ever did," Roy said tightly.

Spencer took two suitcases from the closet, considered them, put the smaller of the two aside, and opened the larger bag on his bed. He selected enough clothes for a week. He didn't own a suit, a white shirt, or even one necktie. In his closet hung half a dozen pairs of blue jeans, half a dozen pairs of tan chinos, khaki shirts, and denim shirts. In the top drawer of the highboy, he kept four warm sweaters—two blue, two green—and he packed one of each.

While Spencer filled the suitcase, Rocky paced from room to room, standing worried sentry duty at every window he could reach. The poor mutt was having a hard time shaking off the nightmare.

Leaving his men to watch over the Zelinsky family, Roy stepped out of the house and crossed the street toward his car.

The twilight had darkened from red to deep purple. The streetlamps had come on. The air was still, and for a moment the silence was almost as deep as if he had been in a country field.

They were lucky that the Zelinskys' neighbors had not heard anything to arouse suspicion.

On the other hand, no lights showed in the houses flanking the Zelinsky place. Many families in that pleasant middle-class neighborhood were probably able to maintain their standard of living only if both husband and wife held full-time jobs. In fact, in this precarious economy, with take-home pay declining, many were holding on by their fingernails even with two breadwinners. Now, at the height of the rush hour, two-thirds of the homes on both sides of the street were dark, untenanted; their owners were battling freeway traffic, picking up their kids at sitters and day schools that they could not easily afford, and struggling to get home to enjoy a few hours of peace before climbing back on the treadmill in the morning.

Sometimes Roy was so sensitive to the plight of the average person that he was brought to tears.

Right now, however, he could not allow himself to surrender to the empathy that came so easily to him. He had to find Spencer Grant.

In the car, after starting the engine and slipping into the passenger seat, he plugged in the attaché case computer. He married the cellular telephone to it.

He called Mama and asked her to find a phone number for Spencer Grant, in the greater L.A. area, and from the center of her web in Virginia, she began the search. He hoped to get an address for Grant from the phone company, as he had gotten one for the Bettonfields.

David Davis and Nella Shire would have left the downtown office for the day, so he couldn't call there to rail at them. In any case, the problem wasn't their fault, though he would have liked to place the blame on Davis—and on Wertz, whose first name was probably Igor.

In a few minutes, Mama reported that no one named Spencer Grant possessed a telephone, listed or unlisted, in the Los Angeles area.

Roy didn't believe it. He fully trusted Mama. The problem wasn't with her. She was as faultless as his own dear, departed mother had been. But Grant was clever. Too damned clever.

Roy asked Mama to search telephone-company *billing* records for the same name. Grant might have been listed under a pseudonym, but before providing service, the phone company had surely required the signature of a real person with a good credit history.

As Mama worked, Roy watched a car cruise past and pull into a driveway a few houses farther along the street.

Night ruled the city. To the far edge of the western horizon, twilight had abdicated; no trace of its royal-purple light remained.

The display screen flashed dimly, and Roy looked down at the computer on his lap. According to Mama, Spencer Grant's name did not appear in telephone billing records, either.

First, the guy had gone back into his employment files in the LAPD computer and inserted the Zelinsky address, evidently chosen at random, in place of his own. And now, although he still lived in the L.A. area and almost certainly had a telephone, he had expunged his name from the records of whichever company—Pacific Bell or GTE—provided his local service.

Grant seemed to be trying to make himself invisible.

"Who the hell is this guy?" Roy wondered aloud.

Because of what Nella Shire had found, Roy had been convinced that he knew the man he was seeking. Now he suddenly felt that he didn't know Spencer Grant at all, not in any fundamental sense. He knew only generalities, superficialities—but it was in the details where his damnation might lie.

What had Grant been doing at the bungalow in Santa Monica? How was he involved with the woman? What did he know?

Getting answers to those questions was of increasing urgency.

Two more cars disappeared into garages at different houses.

Roy sensed that his chances of finding Grant were diminishing with the passage of time.

Feverishly, he considered his options, and then went through Mama to penetrate the computer at the California Department of Motor Vehicles in Sacramento. In moments, a picture of Grant was on his display screen, one taken by the DMV specifically for a new driver's license. All vital statistics were provided. And a street address.

"All right," Roy said softly, as if to speak loudly would be to undo this bit of good luck.

He ordered and received three printouts of the data on the screen, exited the DMV, said good-bye to Mama, switched off the computer, and went back across the street to the Zelinsky house.

Mary, Peter, and the daughter sat on the living room sofa. They were pale, silent, holding hands. They looked like three ghosts in a celestial waiting room, anticipating the imminent arrival of their judgment documents, more than half expecting to be served with one-way tickets to Hell.

Dormon, Johnson, and Vecchio stood guard, heavily armed and expressionless. Without comment, Roy gave them printouts of the new address for Grant that he had gotten from the DMV.

With a few questions, he established that both Mary and Peter Zelinsky were out of work and on unemployment compensation. That was why they were at home, about to have dinner, when most neighbors were still in schools of steel fish on the concrete seas of the freeway system. They had been searching the want ads in the Los Angeles Times every day, applying for new jobs at numerous companies, and worrying so unrelentingly about the future that the explosive arrival of Dormon, Johnson, Vecchio, and Roy had seemed, on some level, not surprising but a natural progression of their ongoing catastrophe.

Roy was prepared to flash his Drug Enforcement Administration ID and to use every technique of intimidation in his repertoire to reduce the Zelinsky family to total submission and to ensure that they never filed a complaint, either with the local police or with the federal government. However, they were obviously already so cowed by the economic turmoil that had taken their jobs—and by city life in general—that Roy did not need to provide even phony identification.

They would be grateful to escape from this encounter with their lives. They would meekly repair their front door, clean up the mess, and probably conclude that they had been terrorized by drug dealers who had burst into the wrong house in search of a hated competitor.

No one filed complaints against drug dealers. Drug dealers in modern America were akin to a force of nature. It made as much sense—and was far safer—to file an angry complaint about a hurricane, a tornado, a lightning storm.

Adopting the imperious manner of a cocaine king, Roy warned them: "Unless you want to see what it's like having your brains blown out, better sit still for ten minutes after we leave. Zelinsky, you have a watch. You think you can count off ten minutes?"

"Yes, sir," Peter Zelinsky said.

Mary would not look at Roy. She kept her head down. He could not see much of her splendid nose.

"You know I'm serious?" Roy asked the husband, and was answered with a nod. "Are you going to be a good boy?"

"We don't want any trouble."

"I'm glad to hear that."

The reflexive meekness of these people was a sorry comment on the brutalization of American society. It depressed Roy.

On the other hand, their pliability made his job a hell of a lot easier than it otherwise might have been.

He followed Dormon, Johnson, and Vecchio outside, and he was the last to drive away. He glanced repeatedly at the house, but no faces appeared at the door or at any of the windows.

A disaster had been narrowly averted.

Roy, who prided himself on his generally even temper, could not remember being as angry with anyone in a long time as he was with Spencer Grant. He couldn't wait to get his hands on the guy.

Spencer packed a canvas satchel with several cans of dog food, a box of biscuit treats, a new rawhide bone, Rocky's water and food bowls, and a rubber toy that looked convincingly like a cheeseburger in a sesame-seed bun. He stood the satchel beside his own suitcase, near the front door.

The dog was still checking the windows from time to time, but not as obsessively as before. For the most part, he had overcome the nameless terror that propelled him out of his dream. Now his fear was of a more mundane and quieter variety: the anxiety that always possessed him when he sensed that they were about to do something out of their daily routine, a wariness of change. He padded after Spencer to see if any alarming actions were being taken, returned repeatedly to the suitcase to sniff it, and visited his favorite corners of the house to sigh over them as though he suspected that he might never have the chance to enjoy their comforts again.

Spencer removed a laptop computer from a storage shelf above his desk and put it beside the satchel and suitcase. He'd purchased it in September, so he could develop his own programs while sitting on the porch, enjoying the fresh air and the soothing susurration of autumn breezes stirring the eucalyptus grove. Now it would keep him wired into the great American info network during his travels.

He returned to his desk and switched on the larger computer. He made floppy-disk copies of some of the programs he had designed, including the one that could detect the faint electronic signature of an eavesdropper on a phone line being used for a computer-to-computer dialogue. Another would warn him if, while he was hacking, someone began hunting him down with sophisticated trace-back technology.

Rocky was at a window again, alternately grumbling and whining softly at the night.

At the west end of the San Fernando Valley, Roy drove into hills and across canyons. He was not yet beyond the web of interlocking cities, but there were pockets of primordial blackness between the clustered lights of the suburban blaze.

This time, he would proceed with more caution than he had shown previously. If the address from the DMV proved to be the home of another family who, like the Zelinskys, had never heard of Spencer Grant, Roy preferred to find that out *before* he smashed down their door, terrorized them with guns, ruined the spaghetti sauce that was on the stove, and risked being shot by an irate homeowner who perhaps also happened to be a heavily armed fanatic of one kind or another.

In this age of impending social chaos, breaking into a private home—whether behind the authority of a genuine badge or not—was a riskier business than it had once been. The residents might be anything from child-molesting worshipers of Satan to cohabiting serial killers with cannibalistic tendencies, refrigerators full of body parts, and eating utensils prettily hand-carved out of human bones. On the cusp of the millennium, some damned strange people were loose out there in fun-house America.

Following a two-lane road into a dark hollow that was threaded with gossamer fog, Roy began to suspect he wouldn't be confronted with an ordinary suburban house or with the simple question of whether or not it was occupied by Spencer Grant. Something else awaited him.

The blacktop became one lane of loose gravel, flanked by sickly palms that had not been trimmed in years and that sported long ruffs of dead fronds. At last it came to a gate in a chain-link fence.

The phony pizza-shop truck was already there; its red taillights were refracted by the thin mist. Roy checked his rearview mirror and saw headlights a hundred yards behind him: Johnson and Vecchio.

He walked to the gate. Cal Dormon was waiting for him.

Beyond the chain-link, in the headlight-silvered fog, strange machines moved rhythmically, in counterpoint to one another, like giant prehistoric birds bobbing for worms in the soil. Wellhead pumps. It was a producing oil field, of which many were scattered throughout southern California.

Johnson and Vecchio joined Roy and Dormon at the gate.

"Oil wells," Vecchio said.

"Goddamned oil wells," Johnson said.

"Just a bunch of goddamned oil wells," Vecchio said.

At Roy's direction, Dormon went to the van to get flashlights and a bolt cutter. It was not just a fake pizza-delivery truck, but a well-equipped support unit with all the tools and electronic gear that might be needed in a field operation.

"We going in there?" Vecchio asked. "Why?"

"There might be a caretaker's cottage," Roy said. "Grant might be an on-site caretaker, living here."

Roy sensed that they were as anxious as he to avoid being made fools of twice in one evening. Nevertheless, they knew, as he did, that Grant had likely inserted a phony address in his DMV records and that the chance of finding him in the oil field was between slim and nil.

After Dormon snapped the gate chain, they followed the gravel lane, using their flashlights to probe between the seesawing pumps. In places, the previous night's torrential rain had washed away the gravel, leaving mud. By the time they looped through the creaking-squeaking-clicking machinery and returned to the gate, without finding a caretaker, Roy had ruined his new shoes.

In silence, they cleaned off their shoes as best they could by shuffling their feet in the wild grass beside the lane.

While the others waited to be told what to do next, Roy returned to his car. He intended to link with Mama and find another address for Spencer snake-humping-crap-eating-piece-of-human-garbage Grant.

He was angry, which wasn't good. Anger inhibited clear thinking. No problem had ever been solved in a rage.

He breathed deeply, inhaling both air and tranquility. With each exhalation, he expelled his tension. He visualized tranquility as a pale-peach vapor; he saw tension, however, as a bile-green mist that seethed from his nostrils in twin plumes.

From a book of Tibetan wisdom, he had learned this meditative technique of managing his emotions. Maybe it was a Chinese book. Or Indian. He wasn't sure. He had explored many Eastern philosophies in his endless search for deeper self-awareness and transcendence.

When he got in the car, his pager was beeping. He unclipped it from the sun visor. In the message window he saw the name Kleck and a telephone number in the 714 area code.

John Kleck was leading the search for the nine-year-old Pontiac registered to "Valerie Keene." If she'd followed her usual pattern, the car had been abandoned in a parking lot or along a city street.

When Roy called the number on the pager, the answering voice was unmistakably Kleck's. He was in his twenties, thin and gangly, with a huge Adam's apple and a face resembling that of a trout, but his voice was deep, mellifluous, and impressive.

"It's me," Roy said. "Where are you?"

The words rolled off Kleck's tongue with sonorous splendor: "John Wayne Airport, down in Orange County." The search had begun in L.A. but had been widening all day. "The Pontiac's here, in one of the long-term parking garages. We're collecting the names of the airline ticket agents working yesterday afternoon and evening. We've got photographs of her. Someone may remember selling her a ticket."

"Follow through, but it's a dead end. She's too smart to dump the car where she made her next connection. It's misdirection. She knows we can't be sure, so we'll have to waste time checking it out."

"We're also trying to talk to all the cab drivers who worked the airport during that time. Maybe she didn't fly out but took a taxi."

"Better carry it one step further. She might have walked from the airport to one of the hotels around there. See if any doormen, parking valets, or bellmen remember her asking for a cab."

"Will do," Kleck said. "She's not going to get far this time, Roy. We're going to stay right on her ass."

Roy might have been reassured by Kleck's confidence and by the rich timbre of his voice—if he hadn't known that Kleck looked like a fish trying to swallow a cantaloupe. "Later." He hung up.

He married the phone to the attaché case computer, started the car, and linked with Mama in Virginia. He gave her a daunting task, even considering her considerable talents and connections: Search for Spencer Grant in the computerized records of water and power companies, gas companies, tax collectors' offices; in fact, search the electronic files of every state, county, regional, and city agency, as well as those of any company regulated by any public agency in Ventura, Kern, Los Angeles, Orange, San Diego, Riverside, and San Bernardino Counties; furthermore, access customer records of every banking institution in California—their checking, savings, loan, and credit-card accounts; on a national level, search Social Security Administration and Internal Revenue Service files beginning with California and working eastward state by state.

Finally, after indicating that he would call in the morning for the results of Mama's investigation, he closed the electronic door in Virginia. He switched off his computer.

The fog was growing thicker and the air chillier by the minute. The three men were still waiting for him by the gate, shivering.

"We might as well wrap it up for tonight," Roy told them. "Get a fresh start in the morning."

They looked relieved. Who knew where Grant might send them next?

Roy slapped their backs and gave them cheerful encouragement as they returned to their vehicles. He wanted them to feel good about themselves. Everyone had a right to feel good about himself.

In his car, reversing along the gravel to the two-lane blacktop, Roy breathed deeply, slowly. In with the pale-peach vapor of blessed tranquility. Out with the bile-green mist of anger, tension, stress. Peach in. Green out. Peach in.

He was still furious.

• • •

Because they had eaten a late lunch, Spencer drove across a long stretch of barren Mojave, all the way to Barstow, before pulling off Interstate 15 and stopping for dinner. At the drive-through window of a McDonald's, he ordered a Big Mac, fries, and a small vanilla milkshake for himself. Rather than fuss with the cans of dog food in the canvas satchel, he also ordered two hamburgers and a large water for Rocky—then relented and ordered a second vanilla shake.

He parked at the rear of the well-lighted restaurant lot, left the engine running to keep the Explorer warm, and sat in the cargo area to eat, with his back against the front seat and legs stretched out in front of him. Rocky licked his chops in anticipation as the paper bags were opened and the truck filled with wonderful aromas. Spencer had folded down the rear seats before leaving Malibu, so even with the suitcase and other gear, he and the dog had plenty of room.

He opened Rocky's burgers and put them on their wrappers. By the time Spencer had extracted his own Big Mac from its container and had taken a single bite, Rocky had wolfed down the meat patties that he'd been given and most of one bun, which was all the bread he wanted. He gazed yearningly at Spencer's sandwich, and he whined.

"Mine," Spencer said.

Rocky whined again. Not a frightened whine. Not a whine of pain. It was a whine that said oh-look-at-poor-cute-me-and-realize-how-much-I'd-like-that-hamburger-and-cheese-and-special-sauce-and-maybe-even-the-pickles.

"Do you understand the meaning of *mine*?"

Rocky looked at the bag of french fries in Spencer's lap.

"Mine."

The dog looked dubious.

"Yours," Spencer said, pointing to the uneaten hamburger bun.

Rocky sorrowfully regarded the dry bun—then the juicy Big Mac.

After taking another bite and washing it down with some vanilla milkshake, Spencer checked his watch. "We'll gas up and be back on the interstate by nine o'clock. It's about a hundred and sixty miles to Las Vegas. Even without pushing hard, we can make it by midnight."

Rocky was fixated on the french fries again.

Spencer relented and dropped four of them onto one of the burger wrappers. "You ever been to Vegas?" he asked.

The four fries had vanished. Rocky stared longingly at the others that bristled from the bag in his master's lap.

"It's a tough town. And I've got a bad feeling that things are going to get nasty for us real fast once we get there."

Spencer finished his sandwich, fries, and milkshake, sharing no more of anything in spite of the mutt's reproachful expression. He gathered up the paper debris and put it in one of the bags.

"I want to make this clear to you, pal. Whoever's after her—they're damned powerful. Dangerous. Trigger-happy, on edge—the way they shot at shadows last night. Must be a lot at stake for them."

Spencer took the lid off the second vanilla milkshake, and the dog cocked his head with interest.

"See what I saved for you? Now, aren't you ashamed for thinking bad thoughts about me when I wouldn't give you more fries?"

Spencer held the container so Rocky wouldn't tip it over.

The dog attacked the milkshake with the fastest tongue west of Kansas City, consuming it in a frenzy of lapping, and in seconds his snout went deep into the cup in quest of the swiftly vanishing treat.

"If they had that house under observation last night, maybe they have a photograph of me."

Withdrawing from the cup, Rocky stared curiously at Spencer. The mutt's snout was smeared with milkshake.

"You have disgusting table manners."

Rocky stuck his snout back in the cup, and the Explorer was filled with the slurping noises of canine gluttony.

"If they have a photo, they'll find me eventually. And trying to get a lead on Valerie by going back into her past, I'm liable to blunder across a tripwire and call attention to myself."

The cup was empty, and Rocky was no longer interested in it. With an amazing extended rotation of his tongue, he licked most of the mess off his snout.

"Whoever she's up against, I'm the world's biggest fool to think I can handle them. I know that. I'm *acutely* aware of that. But here I am, on my way to Vegas, just the same."

Rocky hacked. Milkshake residue was cloying in his throat.

Spencer opened the cup of water and held it while the dog drank.

"What I'm doing, getting involved like this . . . it's not really fair to you. I'm aware of that too."

Rocky wanted no more water. His entire muzzle was dripping.

After capping the cup again, Spencer put it in the bag of trash. He picked up a handful of paper napkins and took Rocky by the collar.

"Come here, slob."

Rocky patiently allowed his snout and chin to be blotted dry.

Eye-to-eye with the dog, Spencer said, "You're the best friend I have. Do you know that? Of course, you know. I'm the best friend you have too. And if I get myself killed—who'll take care of you?"

The dog solemnly met Spencer's gaze, as if aware that the issue at hand was important.

"Don't tell me you can take care of yourself. You're better than when I took you in—but you're not self-sufficient yet. You probably never will be."

The dog chuffed as if to disagree, but they both knew the truth.

"If anything happens to me, I think you'll come apart. Revert. Be like you were in the pound. And who else will ever give you the time and attention you'll need to come back again? Hmmm? Nobody."

He let go of the collar.

"So I want you to know I'm not as good a friend to you as I ought to be. I want to have a chance with this woman. I want to find out if she's special enough to care about . . . about someone like me. I'm willing to risk my life to find that out . . . but I shouldn't be willing to risk yours too."

Never lie to the dog.

"I don't have it in me to be as faithful a friend as you can be. I'm just a human being, after all. Look deep enough inside any of us, you'll find a selfish bastard."

Rocky wagged his tail.

"Stop that. Are you trying to make me feel even worse?"

With his tail swishing furiously back and forth, Rocky clambered into Spencer's lap to be petted.

Spencer sighed. "Well, I'll just have to avoid getting killed."

Never lie to the dog.

"Though I think the odds are against me," he added.

In the suburban maze of the valley once more, Roy Miro cruised through a series of commercial districts, unsure where one community ended and the next began. He was still angry but also on the edge of a depression. With increasing desperation, he sought a convenience store, where he could expect to find a full array of newspaper-vending machines. He needed a *special* newspaper.

Interestingly, in two widely separated neighborhoods, he passed what he was certain were two sophisticated surveillance operations.

The first was being conducted out of a tricked-up van with an extended wheelbase and chrome-plated wire wheels. The side of the vehicle had been decorated with an airbrush mural of palm trees, waves breaking on a beach, and a red sunset. Two surfboards were strapped to the luggage rack on the roof. To the uninitiated, it might appear to belong to a surf Gypsy who'd won the lottery.

The clues to the van's real purpose were apparent to Roy. All glass on the vehicle, including the windshield, was heavily tinted, but two large windows on the side, around which the mural wrapped, were so black that they had to be two-way mirrors disguised with a layer of tinted film on the exterior, making it impossible to see inside, but providing agents in the van—and their video cameras—a clear view of the world beyond. Four spotlights were side by side on the roof, above the windshield; none was lit, but each bulb was seated in a cone-shaped fixture, like a small megaphone, which might have been a reflector that focused the beam forward—although, in fact, it was no such thing. One cone would be the antenna for a microwave transceiver linked to computers inside the van, allowing high volumes of encoded data to be received and sent from—or to—more than one communicant at a time. The remaining three cones were collection dishes for directional microphones.

One unlit spotlight was turned not toward the front of the van, as it should have been and as the other three were, but toward a busy sandwich shop—Submarine Dive—across the street. The agents were recording the jumble of conversations among the eight or ten people socializing on the sidewalk in front of the place. Later, a computer would analyze the host of voices: It would isolate each speaker, identify him with a number, associate one number to another based on word flow and inflection, delete most background noise such as traffic and wind, and record each conversation as a separate track.

The second surveillance operation was a mile from the first, on a cross street. It was being run out of a van disguised as a commercial vehicle that supposedly belonged to a glass-and-mirror company called Jerry's Glass Magic. Two-way mirrors were featured boldly on the side, incorporated into the fictitious company's logo.

Roy was always gladdened to see surveillance teams, especially super-high-tech units, because they were likely to be federal rather than local. Their discreet presence indicated that *somebody* cared about social stability and peace in the streets.

When he saw them, he usually felt safer—and less alone.

Tonight, however, his spirits were not lifted. Tonight, he was caught in a whirlpool of negative emotions. Tonight, he could not find solace in the surveillance teams, in the good work he was doing for Thomas Summerton, or in anything else that this world had to offer.

He needed to locate his center, open the door in his soul, and stand face-to-face with the cosmic.

Before he spotted a 7-Eleven or any other convenience store, Roy saw a post office, which had what he needed. In front of it were ten or twelve battered newspaper-vending machines.

He parked at a red curb, left the car, and checked the machines. He wasn't interested in the *Times* or the *Daily News*. What he required could be found only in the alternative press. Most such publications sold sex: focusing on swinging singles, mate-swapping couples, gays—or on adult entertainment and services. He ignored the salacious tabloids. Sex would never suffice when the soul sought transcendence.

Many large cities supported a weekly New Age newspaper that reported on natural foods, holistic healing, and spiritual matters ranging from reincarnation therapy to spirit channeling.

Los Angeles had three.

Roy bought them all and returned to the car.

By the dim glow of the ceiling light, he flipped through each publication, scanning only the space ads and classifieds. Gurus, swamis, psychics, Tarot-card readers, acupuncturists, herbalists to movie stars, channelers, aura interpreters, palm readers, chaos-theory dice counselors, past-life guides, high-colonic therapists, and other specialists offered their services in heartening numbers.

Roy lived in Washington, D.C., but his work took him all over the country. He had visited all the sacred places where the land, like a giant battery, accumulated vast stores of spiritual energy: Santa Fe, Taos, Woodstock, Key West, Spirit Lake, Meteor Crater, and others. He'd had moving experiences in those hallowed confluences of cosmic energy— yet he had long suspected that Los Angeles was an undiscovered nexus as powerful as any. Now, the sheer plenitude of consciousness-raising guides in the ads strengthened his suspicion.

From the myriad choices, Roy selected The Place Of The Way in Burbank. He was intrigued that they had capitalized every word in the name of their establishment, instead of using lowercase for the preposition and second article. They offered numerous methods for "seeking the self and finding the eye of the universal storm," not from a shabby storefront but "from the peaceful sphere of our home." He also liked the proprietors' names— and that they were thoughtful enough to identify themselves in their ad: Guinevere and Chester.

He checked his watch. Past nine o'clock.

Still parked illegally in front of the post office, he called the number in the ad. A man answered: "This is Chester at The Place Of The Way. How may I assist you?"

Roy apologized for calling at that hour, since The Place Of The Way was located in their home, but he explained that he was slipping into a spiritual void and needed to find firm ground as quickly as possible. He was grateful to be assured that Chester and Guinevere fulfilled their mission at all hours. After he received directions, he estimated that he could be at their door by ten o'clock.

He arrived at nine-fifty.

The attractive two-story Spanish house had a tile roof and deep-set leaded windows. In the artful landscape lighting, lush palms and Australian tree ferns threw mysterious shadows against pale-yellow stucco walls.

When Roy rang the bell, he noticed an alarm-company sticker on the window next to the door. A moment later, Chester spoke to him from an intercom box. "Who's there, please?"

Roy was only mildly surprised that an enlightened couple like this, in touch with their psychic talents, found it necessary to take security precautions. Such was the sorry state of the world in which they lived. Even mystics were marked for mayhem.

Smiling and friendly, Chester welcomed Roy into The Place Of The Way. He was pot-bellied, about fifty, mostly bald but with a Friar Tuck fringe of hair, deeply tanned in midwinter, bearish and strong looking in spite of his gut. He wore Rockports, khaki slacks, and a khaki shirt with the sleeves rolled to expose thick, hairy forearms.

Chester led Roy through rooms with yellow pine floors buffed to a high polish, Navajo rugs, and rough-hewn furniture that looked more suitable to a lodge in the Sangre de Cristo Mountains than to a home in Burbank. Beyond the family room, which boasted a giant-screen TV, they entered a vestibule and then a round room that was about twelve feet in diameter, with white walls and no windows other than the round skylight in the domed ceiling.

A round pine table stood in the center of the round room. Chester indicated a chair at the table. Roy sat. Chester offered a beverage—"anything from diet Coke to herbal tea"— but Roy declined because his only thirst was of the soul.

In the center of the table was a basket of plaited palm leaves, which Chester indicated. "I'm only an assistant in these matters. Guinevere is the spiritual adept. Her hands must never touch money. Though she's transcended earthly concerns, she must eat, of course."

"Of course," Roy said.

From his wallet, Roy extracted three hundred dollars and put the cash in the basket. Chester seemed to be pleasantly surprised by the offering, but Roy had always believed that a person could expect only the quality of enlightenment for which he was willing to pay.

Chester left the room with the basket.

From the ceiling, pin spots had washed the walls with arcs of white light. Now they dimmed until the chamber filled with shadows and a moody amber radiance that approximated candlelight.

"Hi, I'm Guinevere! No, please, don't get up."

Breezing into the room with girlish insouciance, head held high, shoulders back, she went around the table to a chair opposite the one in which Roy sat.

Guinevere, about forty, was exceedingly beautiful, in spite of wearing her long blond hair in medusan cascades of cornrows, which Roy disliked. Her jade-green eyes flared with inner light, and every angle of her face was reminiscent of every mythological goddess Roy had seen portrayed in classical art. In tight blue jeans and a snug white T-shirt, her lean and supple body moved with fluid grace, and her large breasts swayed alluringly. He could see the points of her nipples straining against her cotton shirt.

"How ya doin'?" she asked perkily.

"Not so good."

"We'll fix that. What's your name?"

"Roy."

"What are you seeking, Roy?"

"I want a world with justice and peace, a world that's perfect in every way. But people are flawed. There's so little perfection anywhere. Yet I want it so badly. Sometimes I get depressed."

"You need to understand the meaning of the world's imperfection and your own obsession with it. What road of enlightenment do you prefer to take?"

"Any road, all roads."

"Excellent!" said the beautiful Nordic Rastafarian, with such enthusiasm that her cornrows bounced and swayed, and the clusters of red beads dangling from the ends clicked together. "Maybe we'll start with crystals."

Chester returned, pushing a large wheeled box around the table to Guinevere's right side.

Roy saw that it was a gray-and-black metal tool cabinet: four feet high, three feet wide, two feet deep, with doors on the bottom third and drawers of various widths and depths above the doors. The Sears Craftsman logo gleamed dully in the amber light.

While Chester sat in the third and last chair, which was two feet to the left and a foot behind the woman, Guinevere opened one of the drawers in the cabinet and removed a crystal sphere slightly larger than a billiard ball. Cupping it in both hands, she held it out to Roy, and he accepted it.

"Your aura's dark, disturbed. Let's clean that up first. Hold this crystal in both hands, close your eyes, seek a meditative calm. Think about only one thing, only this clean image: hills covered with snow. Gently rolling hills with fresh snow, whiter than sugar, softer than flour. Gentle hills to all horizons, hills upon hills, mantled with new snow, white on white, under a white sky, snowflakes drifting down, whiteness through whiteness over whiteness on whiteness . . ."

Guinevere went on like that for a while, but Roy couldn't see the snow-mantled hills or the falling snow regardless of how hard he tried. Instead, in his mind's eye, he could see only one thing: her hands. Her lovely hands. Her incredible *hands*.

She was altogether so spectacular looking that he hadn't noticed her hands until she was passing the crystal ball to him. He had never seen hands like hers. Exceptional hands. His mouth went dry at the mere thought of kissing her palms, and his heart pounded fiercely at the memory of her slender fingers. They had seemed *perfect*.

"Okay, that's better," Guinevere said cheerily, after a time. "Your aura's much lighter. You can open your eyes now."

He was afraid that he had imagined the perfection of her hands and that when he saw them again he would discover that they were no different from the hands of other women—not the hands of an angel after all. Oh, but they *were*. Delicate, graceful, ethereal. They took the crystal ball from him, returned it to the open drawer of the tool cabinet, and then gestured—like the spreading wings of doves—to seven new crystals that she had placed on a square of black velvet in the center of the table while his eyes had been closed.

"Arrange these in any pattern that seems appropriate to you," she said, "and then I'll read them."

The objects appeared to be half-inch-thick crystal snow flakes that had been sold as Christmas ornaments. None was like another.

As Roy tried to focus on the task before him, his gaze kept sliding surreptitiously to Guinevere's hands. Each time he glimpsed them, his breath caught in his throat. His own hands were trembling, and he wondered if she noticed.

Guinevere progressed from crystals to the reading of his aura through prismatic lenses, to Tarot cards, to rune stones, and her fabulous hands became ever more beautiful. Somehow he answered her questions, followed instructions, and appeared to be listening to the wisdom that she imparted. She must have thought him dim-witted or drunk, because his speech was thick and his eyelids drooped as he became increasingly intoxicated by the sight of her hands.

Roy glanced guiltily at Chester, suddenly certain that the man—perhaps Guinevere's husband—was angrily aware of the lascivious desire that her hands engendered. But Chester wasn't paying attention to either of them. His bald head was bowed, and he was cleaning the fingernails of his left hand with the fingernails of his right.

Roy was convinced that the Mother of God could not have had hands more gentle than Guinevere's, nor could the greatest succubus in Hell have had hands more erotic. Guinevere's hands were, to her, what Melissa Wicklun's sensuous lips were to *her*, oh, but a thousand times more so, *ten* thousand times more so. Perfect, perfect, perfect.

She shook the bag of runes and cast them again.

Roy wondered if he dared ask for a palm reading. She would have to hold his hands in hers.

He shivered at that delicious thought, and a spiral of dizziness spun through him. He could not walk out of that room and leave her to touch other men with those exquisite, unearthly hands.

He reached under his suit jacket, drew the Beretta from his shoulder holster, and said, "Chester."

The bald man looked up, and Roy shot him in the face. Chester tipped backward in his chair, out of sight, and thudded to the floor.

The silencer needed to be replaced soon. The baffles were worn from use. The muffled shot had been loud enough to carry out of the room, though fortunately not beyond the walls of the house.

Guinevere was gazing at the rune stones on the table when Roy shot Chester. She must have been deeply immersed in her reading, for she seemed confused when she looked up and saw the gun.

Before she could raise her hands in defense and force Roy to damage them, which was unthinkable, he shot her in the forehead. She crashed backward in her chair, joining Chester on the floor.

Roy put the gun away, got up, went around the table. Chester and Guinevere stared, unblinking, at the skylight and the infinite night beyond. They had died instantly, so the scene was almost bloodless. Their deaths had been quick and painless.

The moment, as always, was sad and joyous. Sad, because the world had lost two enlightened people who were kind of heart and deep-seeing. Joyous, because Guinevere and Chester no longer had to live in a society of the unenlightened and uncaring.

Roy envied them.

He withdrew his gloves from an inside coat pocket and dressed his hands for the tender ceremony ahead.

He tipped Guinevere's chair back onto its feet. Holding her in it, he pushed the chair to the table, wedging the dead woman in a seated position. Her head flopped forward, chin on her breast, and her cornrows rattled softly, falling like a beaded curtain to conceal her face. He lifted her right arm, which hung at her side, and put it on the table, then her left.

Her hands. For a while he stared at her hands, which were as appealing in death as in life. Graceful. Elegant. Radiant.

They gave him hope. If perfection could exist anywhere, in any form, no matter how small, even in a pair of hands, then his dream of an *entirely* perfect world might one day be realized.

He put his own hands atop hers. Even through his gloves, the contact was electrifying. He shuddered with pleasure.

Dealing with Chester was more difficult because of his greater weight. Nevertheless, Roy managed to move him around the table until he was opposite Guinevere, but slumped in his own chair rather than in the one Roy had been using.

In the kitchen, Roy explored the cabinets and pantry, collecting what he needed to finish the ceremony. He looked in the garage as well, for the final implement he required. Then he carried those items to the round room and placed them atop the wheeled chest in which Guinevere stored her divining aids.

He used a dish towel to wipe off the chair in which he had been sitting, for at the time he had not been wearing gloves and might have left fingerprints. He also buffed that side of the table, the crystal ball, and the snowflake crystals that he had arranged earlier for the psychic reading. He had touched nothing else in the room.

For a few minutes he pulled open drawers and doors in the tool chest, examining the magical contents, until he found an item that seemed appropriate to the circumstances. It was a pentalpha, also called a pentagram, in green on a field of black felt, used in more serious matters—such as attempted communication with the spirits of the dead—than the mere reading of runes, crystals, and Tarot cards.

Unfolded, it was an eighteen-inch square. He placed it in the center of the table, as a symbol of the life beyond this one.

He plugged in the small electric reciprocating saw that he had found among the tools in the garage, and he relieved Guinevere of her right hand. Gently, he placed the hand in a rectangular Tupperware container on another soft dish towel that he had arranged as a bed for it. He snapped the lid on the container.

Although he wanted to take her left hand, too, he felt that it would be selfish to insist on possessing both. The right thing was to leave one with the body, so the police and coroner and mortician and everyone else who dealt with Guinevere's remains would know that she'd possessed the most beautiful hands in the world.

He lifted Chester's arms onto the table. He placed the dead man's right hand over Guinevere's left, on top of the pentalpha, to express his conviction that they were together in the next world.

Roy wished he had the psychic power or purity or whatever was required to be able to channel the spirits of the dead. He would have channeled Guinevere there and then, to ask if she would really mind if he acquired her left hand as well.

He sighed, picked up the Tupperware container, and reluctantly left the round room. In the kitchen, he phoned 911 and spoke to the police operator: "The Place Of The Way is just a place now. It's very sad. Please come."

Leaving the telephone off the hook, he snatched another dish towel from a drawer and hurried to the front door. As far as he could recall, when he had first entered the house and followed Chester to the round room, he had touched nothing. Now, he needed only to wipe the doorbell-push and drop the dish towel on the way to his car.

He drove out of Burbank, over the hills, into the Los Angeles basin, through a seedy section of Hollywood. The bright splashes of graffiti on walls and highway structures, the cars full of young thugs cruising in search of trouble, the pornographic bookstores and movie theaters, the empty shops and the littered gutters and the other evidence of economic and moral collapse, the hatred and envy and greed and lust that thickened the air more effectively than the smog—none of that dismayed him for the time being, because he carried with him an object of such perfect beauty that it proved there was a powerful and wise creative force at work in the universe. He had evidence of God's existence secured in a Tupperware container.

Out on the vast Mojave, where the night ruled, where the works of humankind were limited to the dark highway and the vehicles upon it, where the radio reception of distant stations was poor, Spencer found his thoughts drawn, against his will, to the deeper darkness and even stranger silence of that night sixteen years in the past. Once captured in that loop of memory, he could not escape until he had purged himself by talking about what he had seen and endured.

The barren plains and hills provided no convenient taverns to serve as confessionals. The only sympathetic ears were those of the dog.

. . . bare-chested and barefoot, I descend the stairs, shivering, rubbing my arms, wondering why I'm so afraid. Perhaps even at that moment, I dimly realize that I'm going down to a place from which I'll never be able to ascend.

I'm drawn forward by the cry that I heard while leaning out the window to find the owl. Although it was brief and came just twice, and then only faintly, it was so piercing and pathetic that the memory of it bewitches me, the way a fourteen-year-old boy can sometimes be seduced as easily by the prospect of strangeness and terror as by the mysteries of sex.

Off the stairs. Through rooms where the moonlit windows glow softly, like video screens, and where the museum-quality Stickley furniture is visible only as angular black shadows within the blue-black gloom. Past artworks by Edward Hopper and Thomas Hart Benton and Steven Ackblom, from the latter of which peer vaguely luminous faces with eerie expressions as inscrutable as the ideograms of an alien language evolved on a world millions of light-years from Earth.

In the kitchen, the honed-limestone floor is cold beneath my feet. During the long day and all night it has absorbed the chill from the Freon-cooled air, and now it steals the heat from my soles.

Beside the back door, a small red light burns on the security-system keypad. In the readout window are three words in radiant green letters: ARMED AND SECURE. I key in the code to disarm the system. The red light turns green. The words change: READY TO ARM.

This is no ordinary farmhouse. It isn't the home of folks who earn their living from the bounty of the land and who have simple tastes. There are treasures within—fine furnishings and art—and even in rural Colorado, precautions must be taken.

I disengage both deadbolts, open the door, and step onto the back porch, out of the frigid house, into the sultry July night. I walk barefoot across the boards to the steps, down to the flagstone patio that surrounds the swimming pool, past the darkly glimmering water in the pool, into the yard, almost like a boy sleepwalking while in a dream, drawn through the silence by the remembered cry.

The ghostly silver face of the full moon behind me casts its reflection on every blade of grass, so the lawn appears to be filmed by a frost far out of season. Strangely, I am suddenly afraid not merely for myself but for my mother, although she has been dead for *more than six years and is far beyond the reach of any danger. My fear becomes so intense that I am halted by it. Halfway across the backyard, I stand alert and still in the uncertain silence. My moonshadow is a blot on the faux frost before me.*

Ahead of me looms the barn, where no animals or hay or tractors have been kept for at least fifteen years, since before I was born. To anyone driving past on the county road, the property looks like a farm, but it isn't what it appears to be. Nothing is what it appears to be.

The night is hot, and sweat beads on my face and bare chest. Nevertheless, the stubborn chill is beneath my skin and in my blood and in the deepest hollows of my boyish bones, and the July heat can't dispel it.

It occurs to me that I'm chilled because, for some reason, I'm remembering too clearly the late-winter coldness of the bleak day in March, six years ago, when they found my mother after she had been missing for three days. Rather, they had found her brutalized body, crumpled in a ditch along a back road, eighty miles from home, where she had been dumped by the sonofabitch who kidnapped and killed her. Only eight years old, I'd been too young to understand the full meaning of death. And no one dared tell me, that day, how savagely she'd been treated, how terribly she had suffered; those were horrors still to be revealed to me by a few of my schoolmates—who had the capacity for cruelty that is possessed only by certain children and by those adults who, on some primitive level, have never matured. Yet, even in my youth and innocence, I had understood enough of death to realize at once that I would never see my mother again, and the chill of that March day had been the most penetrating cold that I'd ever known.

Now I stand on the moonlit lawn, wondering why my thoughts leap repeatedly to my lost mother, why the eerie cry that I heard when I leaned out my bedroom window strikes me as both infinitely strange and familiar, why I fear for my mother even though she's dead, and why I fear so intensely for my own life when the summer night holds no immediate threat that I can see.

I begin to move again, toward the barn, which has become the focus of my attention, though initially I had thought that the cry had come from some animal out in the fields or in the lower hills. My shadow floats ahead of me, so that no step I take is on the carpet of moonlight but, instead, into a darkness of my own making.

Instead of going directly to the huge main doors in the south wall of the barn, in which a smaller, man-size door is inset, I obey instinct and head toward the southeast corner, crossing the macadam driveway that leads past the house and garage. In grass again, I round the corner of the barn and follow the east wall, stealthy in my bare feet, treading on the cushion of my moonshadow all the way to the northeast corner.

There I halt, because a vehicle I've never seen before is parked behind the barn: a customized Chevy van that no doubt isn't charcoal, as it appears to be, for the moonlight alchemizes every color into silver or gray. Painted on the side is a rainbow, which also seems to be in shades of gray. The rear door stands open.

The silence is deep.

No one is in sight.

Even at the impressionable age of fourteen, with a childhood of Halloweens and nightmares behind me, I've never known strangeness and terror to be more seductive, and I can't resist their perverse allure. I take one step toward the van, and—

—something slices the air close overhead with a whoosh and a flutter, startling me. I stumble, fall, roll, and look up in time to see enormous white wings spread above me. A shadow sweeps over the moonlit grass, and I have the crazy notion that my mother, in some angelic form, has swooped down from Heaven to warn me away from the van. Then the celestial presence arcs higher into the darkness, and I see that it's only a great white owl, with a wingspan of five feet, sailing the summer night in search of field mice or other prey.

The owl vanishes.

The night remains.

I rise to my feet.

I creep toward the van, powerfully drawn by the mystery of it, by the promise of adventure. And by a terrible truth, which I don't yet know that I know.

The sound of the owl's wings, though so recent and frightening, doesn't remain with me. But that pitiful cry, heard at the open window, echoes unrelentingly in my memory. Perhaps I'm beginning to acknowledge that it wasn't the plaint of any wild animal meeting its end in the fields and forests, but the wretched and desperate plea of a human being in the grip of extreme terror. . . .

In the Explorer, speeding across the moonlit Mojave, wingless but now as wise as any owl, Spencer followed insistent memory all the way into the heart of darkness, to the flash of steel from out of shadows, to the sudden pain and the scent of hot blood, to the wound that would become his scar, forcing himself toward the ultimate revelation that always eluded him.

It eluded him again.

He could recall nothing of what happened in the final moments of that hellish, long-ago encounter, after he pulled the trigger of the revolver and returned to the slaughter-house. The police had told him how it must have ended. He had read accounts of what he'd done, by writers who based their articles and books upon the evidence. But none of them had been there. They couldn't know the truth beyond a doubt. Only he had been there. Up to a point, his memories were so vivid as to be profoundly tormenting, but memory ended at a black hole of amnesia; after sixteen years, he'd still not been able to focus even one beam of light into that darkness.

If he ever recalled the rest, he might earn lasting peace. Or remembrance might destroy him. In that black tunnel of amnesia, he might find a shame with which he could not live, and the memory might be less desirable than a self-administered bullet to the brain.

Nevertheless, by periodically unburdening himself of everything that he *did* remember, he always found temporary relief from anguish. He found it again in the Mojave Desert, at fifty-five miles an hour.

When Spencer glanced at Rocky, he saw that the dog was curled on the other seat, dozing. The mutt's position seemed awkward, if not precarious, with his tail dangling down into the leg space under the dashboard, but he was evidently comfortable.

Spencer supposed that the rhythms of his speech and the tone of his voice, after countless repetitions of his story over the years, had become soporific whenever he turned to that subject. The poor dog couldn't have stayed awake even if they'd been in a thunderstorm.

Or perhaps, for some time, he had not actually been talking aloud. Perhaps his soliloquy had early faded to a whisper and then into silence while he continued to speak only with an inner voice. The identity of his confessor didn't matter—a dog was as acceptable as a stranger in a barroom—so it followed that it was not important to him if his confessor listened. Having a willing listener was merely an excuse to talk *himself* through it once more, in search of temporary absolution or—if he could shine a light into that final darkness—a permanent peace of one kind or another.

He was fifty miles from Vegas.

Windblown tumbleweeds as big as wheelbarrows rolled across the highway, through his headlight beams, from nowhere to nowhere.

The clear, dry desert air did little to inhibit his view of the universe. Millions of stars blazed from horizon to horizon, beautiful but cold, alluring but unreachable, shedding surprisingly little light on the alkaline plains that flanked the highway—and, for all their grandeur, revealing nothing.

When Roy Miro woke in his Westwood hotel room, the digital clock on the nightstand read 4:19. He had slept less than five hours, but he felt rested, so he switched on the lamp.

He threw back the covers, sat on the edge of the bed in his pajamas, squinted as his eyes adjusted to the brightness—then smiled at the Tupperware container that stood beside the clock. The plastic was translucent, so he could see only a vague shape within.

He put the container on his lap and removed the lid. Guinevere's hand. He felt blessed to possess an object of such great beauty.

How sad, however, that its ravishing splendor wouldn't last much longer. In twenty-four hours, if not sooner, the hand would have deteriorated visibly. Its comeliness would be but a memory.

Already it had undergone a color change. Fortunately, a certain chalkiness only emphasized the exquisite bone structure in the long, elegantly tapered fingers.

Reluctantly, Roy replaced the lid, made sure the seal was tight, and put the container aside.

He went into the living room of the two-room suite. His attaché case computer and cellular phone were already connected, plugged in, and arranged on a luncheon table by a large window.

Soon he was in touch with Mama. He requested the results of the investigation that he'd asked her to undertake the previous evening, when he and his men had discovered that the DMV address for Spencer Grant was an uninhabited oil field.

He had been so furious then.

He was calm now. Cool. In control.

Reading Mama's report from the screen, tapping the PAGE DOWN key each time he wanted to continue, Roy quickly saw that the search for Spencer Grant's true address hadn't been easy.

During Grant's months with the California Multi-Agency Task Force on Computer Crime, he'd learned a lot about the nationwide Infonet and the vulnerabilities of the thousands of computer systems it comprised. Evidently, he had acquired codes-and-procedures books and master programming atlases for the computer systems of various telephone companies, credit agencies, and government offices. Then he must have managed to carry or electronically transmit them from the task-force offices to his own computer.

After quitting his job, he had erased every reference to his whereabouts from public and private records. His name appeared only in his military, DMV, Social Security, and police department files, and in every case the given address was one of the two that had already proved to be false. The national file of the Internal Revenue Service contained other men with his name; however, none was his age, had his Social Security number, lived in California, or had paid withholding taxes as an employee of the LAPD. Grant was missing, as well, from the records of the State of California tax authorities.

If nothing else, he was apparently a tax evader. Roy hated tax evaders. They were the epitome of social irresponsibility.

According to Mama, no utility company currently billed Spencer Grant—yet no matter where he lived, he needed electricity, water, telephone, garbage pickup, and probably natural gas. Even if he had erased his name from billing lists to avoid paying for utilities, he couldn't exit their *service* records without triggering disconnection of essential services. Yet he could not be found.

Mama assumed two possibilities. First: Grant was honest enough to pay for utilities; however, he altered the companies' billing and service records to transfer his accounts to a false name that he had created for himself. The sole purpose of those actions would be to further his apparent goal of disappearing from public record, making himself hard to find if any police agency or governmental body wanted to talk to him. Like now. Or, second: He was dishonest, eliminating himself from billing records, paying for nothing—while maintaining service under a false name. In either case, he and his address were *somewhere* in those companies' files, under the name that was his secret identity; he could be located if his alias could be uncovered.

Roy froze Mama's report and returned to the bedroom to get the envelope that contained the computer-projected portrait of Spencer Grant. This man was an unusually crafty adversary. Roy wanted to have the clever bastard's face for reference while reading about him.

At the computer again, he paged forward in the report.

Mama had been unable to find an account for Spencer Grant at any bank or savings and loan association. Either he paid for everything with cash, or he maintained accounts under an alias. Probably the former. There was unmistakable paranoia in this man's actions, so he wouldn't trust his funds in a bank under any circumstances.

Roy glanced at the portrait beside the computer. Grant's eyes *did* look strange. Feverish. No doubt about it. A trace of madness in his eyes. Maybe even more than a trace.

Because Grant might have formed an S-chapter corporation through which he did his banking and bill paying, Mama had searched the files of the California Secretary of the Treasury and various regulatory bodies, seeking his name as a registered corporate officer. Nothing.

Every bank account had to be tied to a Social Security number, so Mama looked for a savings or checking account with Grant's number, regardless of the name under which the money was deposited. Nothing.

He might own the home in which he lived, so Mama had checked property tax records in the counties that Roy targeted. Nothing. If he *did* own a home, he held title under a false name.

Another hope: If Grant had ever taken a university class or been a hospital patient, he might not have remembered that he'd supplied his home address on applications and admissions forms, and he might not have deleted them. Most educational and medical institutions were regulated by federal laws; therefore, their records were accessible to numerous government agencies. Considering the number of such institutions even in a limited geographical area, Mama needed the patience of a saint or a machine, the latter of which she possessed. And for all her efforts, she found nothing.

Roy glanced at the portrait of Spencer Grant. He was beginning to think that this man was not merely mentally disturbed, but something far darker than that. An actively *evil* person. Anyone this obsessed with his privacy was surely an enemy of the people.

Chilled, Roy returned his attention to the computer.

When Mama undertook a search as extensive as the one that Roy had requested of her and when that search was fruitless, she didn't give up. She was programmed to apply her spare logic circuits—during periods of lighter work and between assignments—to riffle through a large store of mailing lists that the agency had accumulated, looking for the name that couldn't be found elsewhere. Name soup. That was what the lists were called. They were lifted from book and record clubs, national magazines, Publishers Clearing House, major political parties, catalogue-sales companies peddling everything from sexy lingerie to electronic gadgetry to meat by mail, interest groups like antique-car enthusiasts and stamp collectors, as well as from numerous other sources.

In the name soup, Mama had found a Spencer Grant different from the others in the Internal Revenue Service records.

Intrigued, Roy sat up straighter in his chair.

Almost two years ago, *this* Spencer Grant had ordered a dog toy from a mail-order catalogue aimed at pet owners: a hard-rubber, musical bone. The address on that list was in California. Malibu.

Mama had returned to the utility companies' files, to see whether services were maintained at that address. They were.

The electrical connection was in the name of Stewart Peck.

The water service and trash collection account was in the name of Mr. Henry Holden.

Natural gas was billed to James Gable.

The telephone company provided service to one John Humphrey. They also billed a cellular phone to William Clark at that address.

AT&T provided long-distance service for Wayne Gregory.

Property tax records listed the owner as Robert Tracy.

Mama had found the scarred man.

In spite of his efforts to vanish behind an elaborate screen of multifarious identities, though he had diligently attempted to erase his past and to make his current existence as difficult to prove as that of the Loch Ness monster, and though he had nearly succeeded in being as elusive as a ghost, he had been tripped up by a musical rubber bone. A dog toy. Grant had seemed inhumanly clever, but the simple human desire to please a beloved pet had brought him down.

NINE

Roy Miro watched from the blue shadows of the eucalyptus grove, enjoying the medicinal but pleasant odor of the oil-rich leaves.

The rapidly assembled SWAT team hit the cabin an hour after dawn, when the canyon was quiet except for the faintest rustle of the trees in an offshore breeze. The stillness was broken by shattering glass, the *whomp* of stun grenades, and the crash of the front and back doors going down simultaneously.

The place was small, and the initial search required little more than a minute. Toting a Micro Uzi, wearing a Kevlar jacket so heavy that it appeared to be capable of stopping even Teflon-coated slugs, Alfonse Johnson stepped out onto the back porch to signal that the cabin was deserted.

Dismayed, Roy came out of the grove and followed Johnson through the rear entrance into the kitchen, where shards of glass crunched under his shoes.

"He's taken a trip somewhere," Johnson said.

"How do you figure?"

"In here."

Roy followed Johnson into the only bedroom. It was almost as sparsely furnished as a monk's cell. No art brightened the roughly plastered walls. Instead of drapes or curtains, white vinyl blinds hung at the windows.

A suitcase stood near the bed, in front of the only nightstand.

"Must have decided he didn't need that one," said Johnson.

The simple cotton bedspread was slightly mussed—as if Grant had put another suitcase there to pack for his trip.

The closet door stood open. A few shirts, jeans, and chinos hung from the wooden rod, but half the hangers were empty.

One by one, Roy pulled out the drawers on a highboy. They contained a few items of clothing—mostly socks and underwear. A belt. One green sweater, one blue.

Even the contents of a large suitcase, if returned to the drawers, would not have filled them. Therefore, Grant had either packed two or more suitcases—or his clothing and home-decorating budgets were equally frugal.

"Any signs of a dog?" Roy asked.

Johnson shook his head. "Not that I noticed."

"Look around, inside and out," Roy ordered, leaving the bedroom.

Three members of the SWAT team, men with whom Roy had not worked before, were standing in the living room. They were tall, beefy guys. In that confined space, their protective gear, combat boots, and bristling weapons made them appear to be even larger than they were. With no one to shoot or subdue, they were as awkward and uncertain as professional wrestlers invited to tea with the octogenarian members of a ladies' knitting club.

Roy was about to send them outside when he saw that the screen was lit on one of the computers in the array of electronic equipment that covered the surface of an L-shaped corner desk. White letters glowed on a blue background.

"Who turned that on?" he asked the three men.

They gazed at the computer, baffled.

"Must've been on when we came in," one of them said.

"Wouldn't you have noticed?"

"Maybe not."

"Grant must've left in a hurry," said another.

Alfonse Johnson, just entering the room, disagreed: "It wasn't on when I came through the front door. I'd bet anything."

Roy went to the desk. On the computer screen was the same number repeated three times down the center:

$$31$$
$$31$$
$$31$$

Suddenly the numbers changed, beginning at the top, continuing slowly down the column, until all were the same:

$$32$$
$$32$$
$$32$$

Simultaneously with the appearance of the third thirty-two, a soft *whirrrrr* arose from one of the electronic devices on the large desk. It lasted only a couple of seconds, and Roy couldn't identify the unit in which it originated.

The numbers changed from top to bottom, as before: 33, 33, 33. Again: that whispery two-second *whirrrrr*.

Although Roy was far better acquainted with the capabilities and operation of sophisticated computers than was the average citizen, he had never seen most of the gadgetry on the desk. Some items appeared to be homemade. Small red and green bulbs shone on several peculiar devices, indicating that they were powered up. Tangles of cables, in various diameters, linked much of the familiar equipment with the units that were mysterious to him.

$$34$$
$$34$$
$$34$$

Whirrrrr.

Something important was happening. Intuition told Roy that much. But *what*? He couldn't understand, and with growing urgency he studied the equipment.

On the screen, the numbers advanced, from top to bottom, until all of them were thirty-five. *Whirrrrr.*

If the numbers had been descending, Roy might have thought that he was watching a countdown toward a detonation. A bomb. Of course, no cosmic law required that a time bomb had to be triggered at the end of a count*down*. Why not a count*up*? Start at zero, detonate at one hundred. Or at fifty. Or forty.

36
36
36

Whirrrrr.

No, not a bomb. That didn't make sense. Why would Grant want to blow up his own home?

Easy question. Because he was crazy. Paranoid. Remember the eyes in the computer-generated portrait: feverish, touched with madness.

Thirty-seven, top to bottom. *Whirrrrr.*

Roy started exploring the tangle of cables, hoping to learn something from the way in which the devices were linked.

A fly crept along his left temple. He brushed impatiently at it. Not a fly. A bead of sweat.

"What's wrong?" Alfonse Johnson asked. He loomed at Roy's side—abnormally tall, armored, and armed, as if he were a basketball player from some future society in which the game had evolved into a form of mortal combat.

On the screen, the count had reached forty. Roy paused with his hands full of cables, listened to the *whirrrrr*, and was relieved when the cabin didn't blow up.

If it wasn't a bomb, what was it?

To grasp what was happening, he needed to think like Grant. Try to imagine how a paranoid sociopath might view the world. Look out through the eyes of madness. Not easy.

Well, all right, even if Grant was psychotic, he was also cunning, so after nearly being apprehended in the assault on the bungalow Wednesday night in Santa Monica, he had figured that a surveillance unit had photographed him and that he had become the subject of an intense search. He was an ex-cop, after all. He knew the routine. Although he'd spent the past year performing a gradual disappearing act from every public record, he hadn't yet taken the final step into invisibility, and he'd been acutely aware that they would find his cabin sooner or later.

"What's wrong?" Johnson repeated.

Grant would have expected them to break into his home in the same manner as they had broken into the bungalow. An entire SWAT team. Searching the place. Milling around.

Roy's mouth was dry. His heart was racing. "Check the door frame. We must've set off an alarm."

"Alarm? In this old shack?" Johnson said doubtfully.

"Do it," Roy ordered.

Johnson hurried away.

Roy frantically sorted through the loops and knots of cables. The computer in action was the one with the most powerful logic unit among Grant's collection. It was connected to a lot of things, including an unmarked green box that was, in turn, linked to a modem that was itself linked to a six-line telephone.

For the first time he realized that one of the red power-on lights gleaming in the equipment was actually the in-use indicator on line one of the telephone. An outgoing call was in progress.

He picked up the handset and listened. Data transmission was under way in the form of a cascade of electronic tones, a high-speed language of weird music without melody or rhythm.

"Magnetic contact here on the doorsill!" Johnson called from the front entrance.

"Visible wires?" Roy asked, dropping the telephone handset into the cradle.

"Yeah. And this was just hooked up. Bright, new copper at the contact point."

"Follow the wires," Roy said.

He glanced at the computer again.

On the screen, the count was up to forty-five.

Roy returned to the green box that linked computer and modem, and he grabbed another gray cable that led from it to something that he had not yet found. He traced it across the desk, through snarled cords, behind equipment, to the edge of the desk, and then to the floor.

On the other side of the room, Johnson was ripping up the alarm wire from the baseboard to which it was stapled, and winding it around one gloved fist. The other three men were watching him and edging backward, out of the way.

Roy followed the gray cable along the floor. It disappeared behind a tall bookcase.

Following the alarm wire, Johnson reached the other side of the same bookcase.

Roy jerked on the gray cable, and Johnson jerked on the alarm wire. Books wobbled noisily on the next to the highest shelf.

Roy looked up from the cable on which his attention had been fixed. Almost directly in front of him, slightly higher than eye level, a one-inch lens peered darkly at him from between the spines of thick volumes of history. He pulled books off the shelf, revealing a compact videocamera.

"What the hell's this?" Johnson asked.

On the display screen, the count had just reached forty-eight at the top of the column.

"When you broke the magnetic contact at the door, you started the videocamera," Roy explained.

He dropped the cable and snatched another book from the shelf.

Johnson said, "So we just destroy the videotape, and no one knows we were here."

Opening the book and tearing off one corner of a page, Roy said, "It's not so easy as that. When you turned on the camera, you also activated the computer, the whole system, and it placed an outgoing phone call."

"What system?"

"The videocamera feeds to that oblong green box on the desk."

"Yeah? What's it do?"

After working up a thick gob of saliva, Roy spat on the page fragment that he had torn from the book, and he pasted the paper to the lens. "I'm not sure exactly what it does, but somehow the box processes the video image, translates it from visuals to another form of information, and feeds it to the computer."

He stepped to the display screen. He was less tense than he had been before finding the camera, for now he knew what was happening. He wasn't happy about it—but at least he understood.

51

50

50

The second number changed to fifty-one. Then the third.

Whirrrr.

"Every four or five seconds, the computer freezes a frame's worth of data from the videotape and sends it back to the green box. That's when the first number changes."

They waited. Not long.

52

51

51

"The green box," Roy continued, "passes that frame of data to the modem, and that's when the second number changes."

52
52
51

"The modem translates the data into tonal code, sends it to the telephone, then the third number changes and—"

52
52
52

"—at the far end of the phone line, the process is reversed, translating the encoded data back into a picture again."

"Picture?" Johnson said. "Pictures of us?"

"He's just received his fifty-second picture since you entered the cabin."

"Damn."

"Fifty of them were nice and clear—before I blocked the camera lens."

"Where? Where's he receiving them?"

"We'll have to trace the phone call the computer made when you broke down the door," Roy said, pointing to the red indicator light on line one of the six-line phone. "Grant didn't want to meet us face-to-face, but he wanted to know what we look like."

"So he's looking at printouts of us right now?"

"Probably not. The other end could be just as automated as this. But he'll stop by there eventually to see if anything's been transmitted. By then, with a little luck, we'll find the phone to which the call was placed, and we'll be waiting there for him."

The three other men had backed farther away from the computers. They regarded the equipment with superstition.

One of them said, "Who *is* this guy?"

Roy said, "He's nothing special. Just a sick and hateful man."

"Why didn't you pull the plug the minute you realized he was filming us?" Johnson demanded.

"He already had us by then, so it didn't matter. And maybe he set up the system so the hard disk will erase if the plug is pulled. Then we wouldn't know what programs and information had been in the machine. As long as the system's intact, we might get a pretty good idea of what this guy's been up to here. Maybe we can reconstruct his activities for the past few days, weeks, even months. We should be able to turn up a few clues about where he's gone—and maybe even find the woman through him."

55
55
55

Whirrrr.

The screen flashed, and Roy flinched. The column of numbers was replaced by three words: THE MAGIC NUMBER.

The phone disconnected. The red indicator light on line one blinked off.

"That's all right," Roy said. "We can still trace it through the phone company's automated records."

The display screen went blank again.

"What's happening?" Johnson asked.

Two new words appeared: BRAIN DEAD.

Roy said, "You sonofabitch, bastard, scar-faced geek!"

Alfonse Johnson backed off a step, obviously surprised by such fury in a man who had always been good-natured and even-tempered.

Roy pulled the chair out from the desk and sat down. As he put his hands to the keyboard, BRAIN DEAD blinked off the screen.

A field of soft blue confronted him.

Cursing, Roy tried to call up a basic menu.

Blue. Serene blue.

His fingers flew over the keys.

Serene. Unchanging. Blue.

The hard disk was blank. Even the operating system, which was surely still intact, was frozen and dysfunctional.

Grant had cleaned up after himself, and then he had mocked them with the BRAIN DEAD announcement.

Breathe deeply. Slowly and deeply. Inhale the pale-peach vapor of tranquility. Exhale the bile-green mist of anger and tension. In with the good, out with the bad.

When Spencer and Rocky had arrived in Vegas near midnight, the towering ramparts of blinking-rippling-swirling-pulsing neon along the famous Strip had made the night nearly as bright as a sunny day. Even at that hour, traffic clogged Las Vegas Boulevard South. Swarms of people had filled the sidewalks, their faces strange and sometimes demonic in the reflected phantasmagoria of neon; they churned from casino to casino and then back again, like insects seeking something that only insects could want or understand.

The frenetic energy of the scene had disturbed Rocky. Even viewing it from the safety of the Explorer, with the windows tightly closed, the dog had begun to shiver before they had gone far. Then he'd whimpered and turned his head anxiously left and right, as if certain that a vicious attack was imminent, but unable to discern from which direction to expect danger. Perhaps, with a sixth sense, the mutt had perceived the fevered need of the most compulsive gamblers, the predatory greed of con men and prostitutes, and the desperation of the big losers in the crowd.

They had driven out of the turmoil and had stayed overnight in a motel on Maryland Parkway, two long blocks from the Strip. Without a casino or cocktail lounge, the place was quiet.

Exhausted, Spencer had found that sleep came easily even on the too-soft bed. He dreamed of a red door, which he opened repeatedly, ten times, twenty, a hundred. Sometimes he found only darkness on the other side, a blackness that smelled of blood and that wrenched a sudden thunder from his heart. Sometimes Valerie Keene was there, but when he reached for her, she receded, and the door slammed shut.

Friday morning, after shaving and showering, Spencer filled one bowl with dog food, another with water, put them on the floor by the bed, and went to the door. "They have a coffee shop. I'll have breakfast, and we'll check out when I get back."

The dog didn't want to be left alone. He whined pleadingly.

"You're safe here," Spencer said.

Guardedly, he opened the door, expecting Rocky to rush outside.

Instead of making a break for freedom, the dog sat on his butt, huddled pathetically, and hung his head.

Spencer stepped outside onto the covered promenade. He looked back into the room.

Rocky hadn't moved. His head hung low. He was shivering.

Sighing, Spencer reentered the room and closed the door. "Okay, have your breakfast, then come with me while I have mine."

Rocky rolled his eyes to watch from under his furry brows as his master settled in the armchair. He went to his food bowl, glanced at Spencer, then looked back uneasily at the door.

"I'm not going anywhere," Spencer assured him.

Instead of wolfing down his food as usual, Rocky ate with a delicacy and at a pace not characteristically canine. As if he believed that this would be his last meal, he savored it.

When the mutt was finally finished, Spencer rinsed the bowls, dried them, and loaded all the luggage into the Explorer.

In February, Vegas could be as warm as a late-spring day, but the high desert was also subject to an inconstant winter that had sharp teeth when it chose to bite. That Friday morning, the sky was gray, and the temperature was in the low forties. From the western mountains came a wind as cold as a pit boss's heart.

After the luggage was loaded, they visited a suitably private corner of a brushy vacant lot behind the motel. Spencer stood guard, with his back turned and his shoulders hunched and his hands jammed in his jeans pockets, while Rocky attended to the call of nature.

With that moment successfully negotiated, they returned to the Explorer, and Spencer drove from the south wing of the motel to the north wing, where the coffee shop was located. He parked at the curb, facing the big plate-glass windows.

Inside the restaurant, he selected a booth by the windows, in a direct line with the Explorer, which was less than twenty feet away. Rocky sat as tall as he could in the passenger seat of the truck, watching his master through the windshield.

Spencer ordered eggs, home fries, toast, coffee. While he ate, he glanced frequently at the Explorer, and Rocky was always watching.

A few times, Spencer waved.

The dog liked that. He wagged his tail every time that Spencer acknowledged him. Once, he put his paws on the dashboard and pressed his nose to the windshield, grinning.

"What did they do to you, pal? What did they do to make you like this?" Spencer wondered aloud, over his coffee, as he watched the adoring dog.

Roy Miro left Alfonse Johnson and the other men to search every inch of the cabin in Malibu while he returned to Los Angeles. With luck, they would find something in Grant's belongings that would shed light upon his psychology, reveal an unknown aspect of his past, or give them a lead on his whereabouts.

Agents in the downtown office were already penetrating the phone company system to trace the call placed earlier by Grant's computer. Grant had probably covered his trail. They would be lucky if they discovered, even by this time tomorrow, at what number and location he had received those fifty images from the videocamera.

Driving south on the Coast Highway, toward L.A., Roy put his cellular unit on speakerphone mode and called Kleck in Orange County.

Although he sounded weary, John Kleck was in fine, deep voice. "I'm getting to hate this tricky bitch," he said, referring to the woman who had been Valerie Keene until she abandoned her car at John Wayne Airport on Wednesday and became, yet again, someone new.

As he listened, Roy had difficulty picturing the thin, gangly young agent with the startled-trout face. Because of the reverberant bass voice, it was easier to believe that Kleck was a tall, broad-chested, black rock singer from the doo-wop era.

Every report that Kleck delivered sounded vitally important—even when he had nothing to report. Like now. Kleck and his team still had no idea where the woman had gone.

"We're widening the search to rental-car agencies countywide," Kleck intoned. "Also checking stolen-car reports. Any set of wheels heisted anytime Wednesday—we're putting it on our must-find sheet."

"She never stole a car before," Roy noted.

"Which is why she might this time—to keep us off balance. I'm just worried she hitchhiked. Can't track her on the thumb express."

"If she hitchhiked, with all the crazies out there these days," Roy said, "then we don't have to worry about her anymore. She's already been raped, murdered, beheaded, gutted, and dismembered."

"That's all right with me," Kleck said. "Just so I can get a piece of the body for a positive ID."

After talking to Kleck, though the morning was still fresh, Roy was convinced that the day would feature nothing but bad news.

Negative thinking usually wasn't his style. He loathed negative thinkers. If too many of them radiated pessimism at the same time, they could distort the fabric of reality, resulting in earthquakes, tornadoes, train wrecks, plane crashes, acid rain, cancer clusters, disruptions in microwave communications, and a dangerous surliness in the general population. Yet he couldn't shake his bad mood.

Seeking to lift his spirits, he drove with only his left hand until he'd gently extracted Guinevere's treasure from the Tupperware container and put it on the seat beside him.

Five exquisite digits. Perfect, natural, unpainted fingernails, each with its precisely symmetrical, crescent-shaped lunula. And the fourteen finest phalanges that he'd ever seen: None was a millimeter more or less than ideal length. Across the gracefully arched back of the hand, pulling the skin taut: the five most flawlessly formed metacarpals he ever hoped to see. The skin was pale but unblemished, as smooth as melted wax from the candles on God's own high table.

Driving east, heading downtown, Roy let his gaze drift now and then to Guinevere's treasure, and with each stolen glimpse, his mood improved. By the time he was near Parker Center, the administrative headquarters of the Los Angeles Police Department, he was buoyant.

Reluctantly, while stopped at a traffic light, he returned the hand to the container. He put that reliquary and its precious contents under the driver's seat.

At Parker Center, after leaving his car in a visitor's stall, he took an elevator from the garage and, using his FBI credentials, went up to the fifth floor. The appointment was with Captain Harris Descoteaux, who was in his office and waiting.

Roy had spoken briefly to Descoteaux from Malibu, so it was no surprise that the captain was black. He had that almost glossy, midnight-dark, beautiful skin sometimes enjoyed by those of Caribbean extraction, and although he evidently had been an Angeleno for years, a faint island lilt still lent a musical quality to his speech.

In navy-blue slacks, striped suspenders, white shirt, and blue tie with diagonal red stripes, Descoteaux had the poise, dignity, and gravitas of a Supreme Court justice, even though his sleeves were rolled up and his jacket was hanging on the back of his chair.

After shaking Roy's hand, Harris Descoteaux indicated the only visitor's chair and said, "Please sit down."

The small office was not equal to the man who occupied it. Poorly ventilated. Poorly lighted. Shabbily furnished.

Roy felt sorry for Descoteaux. No government employee at the executive level, whether in a law-enforcement organization or not, should have to work in such a cramped office. Public service was a noble calling, and Roy was of the opinion that those who were willing to serve should be treated with respect, gratitude, and generosity.

Settling into the chair behind the desk, Descoteaux said, "The Bureau verifies your ID, but they won't say what case you're on."

"National security matter," Roy assured him.

Any query about Roy that was placed with the FBI would have been routed to Cassandra Solinko, a valued administrative assistant to the director. She would support the lie (though not in writing) that Roy was a Bureau agent; however, she could not discuss the nature of his investigation, because she didn't know what the hell he was doing.

Descoteaux frowned. "Security matter—that's pretty vague."

If Roy got into deep trouble—the kind to inspire congressional investigations and newspaper headlines—Cassandra Solinko would deny that she'd ever verified his claim to be with the FBI. If she was disbelieved and subpoenaed to testify about what little she knew of Roy and his nameless agency, there was a stunningly high statistical probability that she would suffer a deadly cerebral embolism, or a massive cardiac infarction, or a high-speed, head-on collision with a bridge abutment. She was aware of the consequences of cooperation.

"Sorry, Captain Descoteaux, but I can't be more specific."

Roy would experience consequences similar to Ms. Solinko's if he himself screwed up. Public service could sometimes be a brutally stressful career—which was one reason why comfortable offices, a generous package of fringe benefits, and virtually unlimited perks were, in Roy's estimation, entirely justified.

Descoteaux didn't like being frozen out. Trading his frown for a smile, speaking with soft island ease, he said, "It's difficult to lend assistance without knowing the whole picture."

It would be easy to succumb to Descoteaux's charm, to mistake his deliberate yet fluid movements for the sloth of a tropical soul, and to be deceived by his musical voice into believing that he was a frivolous man.

Roy saw the truth, however, in the captain's eyes, which were huge, as black and liquid as ink, as direct and penetrating as those in a Rembrandt portrait. His eyes revealed an intelligence, patience, and relentless curiosity that defined the kind of man who posed the greatest threat to someone in Roy's line of work.

Returning Descoteaux's smile with an even sweeter smile of his own, convinced that his younger-slimmer-Santa-Claus look was a match for Caribbean charm, Roy said, "Actually, I don't need help, not in the sense of services and support. Just a little information."

"Be pleased to provide it, if I can," said the captain.

The wattage of their two smiles had temporarily rectified the problem of inadequate lighting in the small office.

"Before you were promoted to central administration," Roy said, "I believe you were a division captain."

"Yes. I commanded the West Los Angeles Division."

"Do you remember a young officer who served under you for a little more than a year—Spencer Grant?"

Descoteaux's eyes widened slightly. "Yes, of course, I remember Spence. I remember him well."

"Was he a good cop?"

"The best," Descoteaux said without hesitation. "Police academy, criminology degree, army special services—he had *substance*."

"A very competent man, then?"

" 'Competence' is hardly an adequate word in Spence's case."

"And intelligent?"

"Extremely so."

"The two carjackers he killed—was that a righteous shooting?"

"Hell, yes, as righteous as they get. One perp was wanted for murder, and there were three felony warrants out on the second loser. Both were carrying, shot at him. Spence had no choice. The review board cleared him as quick as God let Saint Peter into Heaven."

Roy said, "Yet he didn't go back out on the street."

"He didn't want to carry a gun anymore."

"He'd been a U.S. Army Ranger."

Descoteaux nodded. "He was in action a few times—in Central America and the Middle East. He'd had to kill before, and finally he was forced to admit to himself he couldn't make a career of the service."

"Because of how killing made him feel."

"No. More because . . . I think because he wasn't always convinced that the killing was justified, no matter what the politicians said. But I'm guessing. I don't know for sure what his thinking was."

"A man has trouble using a gun against another human being—that's understandable," Roy said. "But the same man trading the army for the police department—that baffles me."

"As a cop, he thought he'd have more control over when to use deadly force. Anyway, it was his dream. Dreams die hard."

"Being a cop was his dream?"

"Not necessarily a cop. Just being the good guy in a uniform, risking his life to help people, saving lives, upholding the law."

"Altruistic young man," Roy said with an edge of sarcasm.

"We get some. Fact is, a lot are like that—in the beginning, at least." He stared at his coal-black hands, which were folded on the green blotter on his desk. "In Spence's case, high ideals led him to the army, then the force . . . but there was something more than that. Somehow . . . by helping people in all the ways a cop can help, Spence was trying to understand himself, come to terms with himself."

Roy said, "So he's psychologically troubled?"

"Not in any way that would prevent him from being a good cop."

"Oh? Then what is it he's trying to understand about himself?"

"I don't know. It goes back, I think."

"Back?"

"The past. He carries it like a ton of stone on his shoulders."

"Something to do with the scar?" Roy asked.

"Everything to do with it, I suspect."

Descoteaux looked up from his hands. His huge, dark eyes were full of compassion. They were exceptional, expressive eyes. Roy might have wanted to possess them if they had belonged to a woman.

"How was he scarred, how did it happen?" Roy asked.

"All he ever said was he'd been in an accident when he was a boy. A car accident, I guess. He didn't really want to talk about it."

"He have any close friends on the force?"

"Not close, no. He was a likable guy. But self-contained."

"A loner," Roy said, nodding with understanding.

"No. Not the way you mean it. He'll never wind up in a tower with a rifle, shooting everyone in sight. People liked him, and he liked people. He just had this . . . reserve."

"After the shooting, he wanted a desk job. Specifically, he applied for a transfer to the Task Force on Computer Crime."

"No, *they* came to *him*. Most people would be surprised—but I'm sure you're aware—we have officers with degrees in law, psychology, and criminology like Spence. Many get the education not because they want to change careers or move up to administration. They want to stay on the street. They love their work, and they think a little advanced education will help them do a better job. They're committed, dedicated. They only want to be *cops*, and they—"

"Admirable, I'm sure. Though some might see them as hard-core reactionaries, unable to give up the *power* of being a cop."

Descoteaux blinked. "Well, anyway, if one of them wants off the street, he doesn't wind up processing paperwork. The department uses his knowledge. The Administrative Office, Internal Affairs, Organized Crime Intelligence Division, most divisions of the Detective Services Group—they all wanted Spence. He chose the task force."

"He didn't perhaps *solicit* the interest of the task force?"

"He didn't need to solicit. Like I said, they came to him."

"Before he went to the task force, had he been a computer nut?"

"Nut?" Descoteaux was no longer able to repress his impatience. "He knew how to use computers on the job, but he wasn't obsessed with them. Spence wasn't a nut about anything. He's a very solid man, dependable, together."

"Except that—and these are your words—he's still trying to understand himself, come to terms with himself."

"Aren't we all?" the captain said crisply. He rose and turned from Roy to the small window beside his desk. The angled slats of the blind were dusty. He stared between them at the smog-cloaked city.

Roy waited. It was best to let Descoteaux have his tantrum. The poor man had earned it. His office was dreadfully small. He didn't even have a private bathroom with it.

Turning to face Roy again, the captain said, "I don't know what you think Spence has done. And there's no point in my asking—"

"National security," Roy confirmed smugly.

"—but you're wrong about him. He's not a man who's ever going to turn bad."

Roy raised his eyebrows. "What makes you so sure of that?"

"Because he agonizes."

"Does he? About what?"

"About what's right, what's wrong. About what he does, the decisions he makes. Quietly, privately—but he agonizes."

"Don't we all?" Roy said, getting to his feet.

"No," Descoteaux said. "Not these days. Most people believe everything's relative, including morality."

Roy didn't think Descoteaux was in a hand-shaking mood, so he just said, "Well, thank you for your time, Captain."

"Whatever the crime, Mr. Miro, the kind of man you want to be looking for is one who's absolutely certain of his righteousness."

"I'll keep that in mind."

"No one's more dangerous than a man who's convinced of his own moral superiority," Descoteaux said pointedly.

"How true," Roy replied, opening the door.

"Someone like Spence—he's not the enemy. In fact, people like that are the only reason the whole damn civilization hasn't fallen down around our ears already."

Stepping into the hall, Roy said, "Have a nice day."

"Whatever side Spence settles on," said Descoteaux with quiet but unmistakable belligerence, "I'd bet my ass it's the right side."

Roy closed the office door behind him. By the time he reached the elevators, he'd decided to have Harris Descoteaux killed. Maybe he would do it himself, as soon as he had dealt with Spencer Grant.

On the way to his car, he cooled down. On the street once more, with Guinevere's treasure on the car seat beside him exerting its calming influence, Roy was sufficiently in control again to realize that summary execution wasn't an appropriate response to Descoteaux's insulting insinuations. Greater punishments than death were within his power to bestow.

The three wings of the two-story apartment complex embraced a modest swimming pool. Cold wind chopped the water into wavelets that slapped at the blue tile under the coping, and Spencer detected the scent of chlorine as he crossed the courtyard.

The burned-out sky was lower than it had been before breakfast, as if it were a pall of gray ashes settling toward the earth. The lush fronds of the wind-tossed palm trees rustled and clicked and clattered with what might have been a storm warning.

Padding along at Spencer's side, Rocky sneezed a couple of times at the chlorine smell, but he was unfazed by the thrashing palms. He had never met a tree that scared him. Which was not to say that such a devil tree didn't exist. When he was in one of his stranger moods, when he had the heebie-jeebies and sensed evil mojo at work in every shadow, when the circumstances were *just right*, he probably could be terrorized by a wilted sapling in a five-inch pot.

According to the information that Valerie—then calling herself Hannah May Rainey—had supplied to obtain a work card for a job as a dealer in a casino, she'd lived at this apartment complex. Unit 2-D.

The apartments on the second floor opened onto a roofed balcony that overlooked the courtyard and that sheltered the walkway in front of the ground-floor units. As Spencer and Rocky climbed concrete stairs, wind rattled a loose picket in the rust-spotted iron railing.

He'd brought Rocky because a cute dog was a great icebreaker. People tended to trust a man who was trusted by a dog, and they were more likely to open up and talk to a stranger who had an appealing mutt at his side—even if that stranger had a dark intensity about him and a scar from ear to chin. Such was the power of canine charm.

Hannah-Valerie's former apartment was in the center wing of the U-shaped structure, at the rear of the courtyard. A large window to the right of the door was covered by draperies. To the left, a small window revealed a kitchen. The name above the doorbell was Traven.

Spencer rang the bell and waited.

His highest hope was that Valerie had shared the apartment and that the other tenant remained in residence. She had lived there at least four months, the duration of her employment at the Mirage. In that much time, though Valerie would have been living as much of a lie as in California, her roommate might have made an observation that would enable Spencer to track her backward from Nevada, the same way that Rosie had pointed him from Santa Monica to Vegas.

He rang the bell again.

Odd as it was to try to find her by seeking to learn where she'd come from instead of where she'd gone, Spencer had no better choice. He didn't have the resources to track her forward from Santa Monica. Besides, by going backward, he was less likely to collide with the federal agents—or whatever they were—following her.

He had heard the doorbell ringing inside. Nevertheless, he tried knocking.

The knock was answered—though not by anyone in Valerie's former apartment. Farther to the right along the balcony, the door to 2-E opened, and a gray-haired woman in her seventies leaned her head out to peek at him. "Can I help you?"

"I'm looking for Miss Traven."

"Oh, she works the early shift at Caesars Palace. Won't be home for hours yet."

She moved into the doorway: a short, plump, sweet-faced woman in clunky orthopedic shoes, support stockings as thick as dinosaur hide, a yellow-and-gray housedress, and a forest-green cardigan.

Spencer said, "Well, who I'm really looking for is—"

Rocky, hiding behind Spencer, risked poking his head around his master's legs to get a look at the grandmotherly soul from 2-E, and the old woman squealed with delight when she spotted him. Although she toddled more than walked, she launched herself off the threshold with the exuberance of a child who didn't know the meaning of the word "arthritis." Burbling baby talk, she approached at a velocity that startled Spencer and alarmed the hell out of Rocky. The dog yelped, the woman bore down on them with exclamations of adoration, the dog tried to climb Spencer's right leg as if to hide under his jacket, the woman said "Sweetums, sweetums, sweetums," and Rocky dropped to the balcony floor in a swoon of terror and curled into a ball and crossed his forepaws over his eyes and prepared himself for the inevitability of violent death.

Bosley Donner's left leg slipped off the foot brace on his electric wheelchair and scraped along the walkway. Laughing, letting his chair coast to a halt, Donner lifted his unfeeling leg with both hands and slammed it back where it belonged.

Equipped with a high-capacity battery and a golf-cart propulsion system, Donner's transportation was capable of considerably greater speeds than any ordinary electric wheelchair. Roy Miro caught up with him, breathing heavily.

"I told you this baby can *move*," Donner said.

"Yes. I see. Impressive," Roy puffed.

They were in the backyard of Donner's four-acre estate in Bel Air, where a wide ribbon of brick-colored concrete had been installed to allow the disabled owner to access every corner of his elaborately landscaped property. The walkway rose and fell repeatedly, passed through a tunnel under one end of the pool patio, and serpentined among phoenix palms, queen palms, king palms, huge Indian laurels, and melaleucas in their jackets of shaggy bark. Evidently, Donner had designed the walkway to serve as his private roller coaster.

"It's illegal, you know," Donner said.

"Illegal?"

"It's against the law to modify a wheelchair the way I've done."

"Well, yes, I can see why it would be."

"You can?" Donner was amazed. "I can't. It's *my* chair."

"Whipping around this track the way you do, you could wind up not just a paraplegic but a quadriplegic."

Donner grinned and shrugged. "Then I'd computerize the chair so I could operate it with vocal commands."

At thirty-two, Bosley Donner had been without the use of his legs for eight years, after taking a chunk of shrapnel in the spine during a Middle East police action that had involved the unit of U.S. Army Rangers in which he had served. He was stocky, deeply tanned, with brush-cut blond hair and blue-gray eyes that were even merrier than Roy's. If he'd ever been depressed about his disability, he had gotten over it long ago—or maybe he'd learned to hide it well.

Roy disliked the man because of his extravagant lifestyle, his annoyingly high spirits, his unspeakably garish Hawaiian shirt—and for other reasons not quite definable. "But is this recklessness socially responsible?"

Donner frowned with confusion, but then his face brightened. "Oh, you mean I might be a burden to society. Hell, I'd never use government health care anyway. They'd triage me into the grave in six seconds flat. Look around, Mr. Miro. I can pay what's necessary. Come on, I want to show you the temple. It's really something."

Rapidly gaining speed, Donner streaked away from Roy, downhill through feathery palm shadows and spangles of red-gold sunshine.

Straining to repress his annoyance, Roy followed.

After being discharged from the army, Donner had fallen back on a lifelong talent for drawing inventive cartoon characters. His portfolio had won him a job with a greeting card company. In his spare time, he developed a comic strip and was offered a contract by the first newspaper syndicate to see it. Within two years, he was the hottest cartoonist in the country. Now, through those widely loved cartoon characters—which Roy found idiotic—Bosley Donner was an industry: best-selling books, TV shows, toys, T-shirts, his own line of greeting cards, product endorsements, records, and much more.

At the bottom of a long slope, the walkway led to a balustraded garden temple in the classical style. Five columns stood on a limestone floor, supporting a heavy cornice and a dome with a ball finial. The structure was surrounded by English primrose laden with blossoms in intense shades of yellow, red, pink, and purple.

Donner sat in his chair, in the center of the open-air temple, swathed in shadows, waiting for Roy. In that setting, he should have been a mysterious figure; however, his stockiness and broad face and brush-cut hair and loud Hawaiian shirt all combined to make him seem like one of his own cartoon characters.

Stepping into the temple, Roy said, "You were telling me about Spencer Grant."

"Was I?" Donner said with a note of irony.

In fact, for the past twenty minutes, while leading Roy on a chase around the estate, Donner had said quite a lot about Grant—with whom he had served in the Army Rangers—and yet had said nothing that revealed either the inner man or any important details of his life prior to joining the army.

"I liked Hollywood," Donner said. "He was the quietest man I've ever known, one of the most polite, one of the smartest—and sure as hell the most self-effacing. Last guy in the world to brag. And he could be a lot of fun when he was in the right mood. But he was very self-contained. No one ever really got to know him."

"Hollywood?" Roy asked.

"That's just a name we had for him, when we wanted to kid him. He loved old movies. I mean, he was almost obsessed with them."

"Any particular kind of movies?"

"Suspense flicks and dramas with old-fashioned heroes. These days, he said, movies have forgotten what heroes are all about."

"How so?"

"He said heroes used to have a better sense of right and wrong than they do now. He loved *North by Northwest, Notorious, To Kill a Mockingbird,* because the heroes had strong principles, morals. They used their wits more than guns."

"Now," Roy said, "you have movies where a couple of buddy cops smash and shoot up half a city to get one bad guy—"

"—use four-letter words, all kinds of trash talk—"

"—jump into bed with women they met only two hours ago—"

"—and strut around with half their clothes off to show their muscles, totally *full* of themselves."

Roy nodded. "He had a point."

"Hollywood's favorite old movie stars were Cary Grant and Spencer Tracy, so of course he took a lot of ribbing about that."

Roy was surprised that his and the scarred man's opinions of current movies were in harmony. He was disturbed to find himself in agreement on *any* issue with a dangerous sociopath like Grant.

Thus preoccupied, he'd only half heard what Donner had told him. "I'm sorry—took a lot of ribbing about what?"

"Well, it wasn't particularly funny that Spencer Tracy and Cary Grant must've been his mom's favorite stars too, or that she named him after them. But a guy like Hollywood, as modest and quiet as he was, shy around girls, a guy who didn't hardly seem to *have* an ego—well, it just struck us funny that he identified so strongly with a couple of movie stars, the heroes they played. He was still nineteen when he went into Ranger training, but in most ways he seemed twenty years older than the rest of us. You could see the kid in him only when he was talking about old movies or watching them."

Roy sensed that what he had just learned was of great importance—but he didn't understand why. He stood on the brink of a revelation yet could not quite see the shape of it.

He held his breath, afraid that even exhaling would blow him away from the understanding that seemed within reach.

A warm breeze soughed through the temple.

On the limestone floor near Roy's left foot, a slow black beetle crawled laboriously toward its own strange destiny.

Then, almost eerily, Roy heard himself asking a question that he had not first consciously considered. "You're sure his mother named him after Spencer Tracy and Cary Grant?"

"Isn't it obvious?" Donner replied.

"Is it?"

"It is to me."

"He actually told you that's why she named him what she did?"

"I guess so. I don't remember. But he must have."

The soft breeze soughed, the beetle crawled, and a chill of enlightenment shivered through Roy.

Bosley Donner said, "You haven't seen the waterfall yet. It's terrific. It's really, really neat. Come on, you've got to see it."

The wheelchair purred out of the temple.

Roy turned to watch between the limestone columns as Donner sped recklessly along another down-sloping pathway into the cool shadows of a green glen. His brightly patterned Hawaiian shirt seemed to flare with fire when he flashed through shafts of red-gold sunshine, and then he vanished past a stand of Australian tree ferns.

By now Roy understood the primary thing about Bosley Donner that so annoyed him: The cartoonist was just too damned self-confident and independent. Even disabled, he was utterly self-possessed and self-sufficient.

Such people were a grave danger to the system. Civil order was not sustainable in a society populated by rugged individualists. The dependency of the people was the source of the state's power, and if the state didn't have enormous power, progress could not be achieved or peace sustained in the streets.

He might have followed Donner and terminated him in the name of social stability, lest others be inspired by the cartoonist's example, but the risk of being observed by witnesses was too great. A couple of gardeners were at work on the grounds, and Mrs. Donner or a member of the household staff might be looking out a window at the most inconvenient of all moments.

Besides, chilled and excited by what he believed he'd discovered about Spencer Grant, Roy was eager to confirm his suspicion.

He left the temple, being careful not to crush the slow black beetle, and turned in the opposite direction from that in which Donner had vanished. He swiftly ascended to higher levels of the backyard, hurried past the side of the enormous house, and got in his car, which was parked in the circular driveway.

From the manila envelope that Melissa Wicklun had given him, he withdrew one of the pictures of Grant and put it on the seat. But for the terrible scar, that face initially had seemed quite ordinary. Now he knew that it was the face of a monster.

From the same envelope, he took a printout of the report that he'd requested from Mama the previous night and that he'd read off the computer screen in his hotel a few hours ago. He paged to the false names under which Grant had acquired and paid for utilities.

Stewart Peck
Henry Holden
James Gable
John Humphrey
William Clark
Wayne Gregory
Robert Tracy

Roy withdrew a pen from his inside jacket pocket and rearranged first and last names into a new list of his own:

Gregory Peck
William Holden
Clark Gable
James Stewart
John Wayne

That left Roy with four names from the original list: Henry, Humphrey, Robert, and Tracy.

Tracy, of course, matched the bastard's first name—Spencer. And for a purpose that neither Mama nor Roy had yet discovered, the tricky, scarfaced son of a bitch was probably using another false identity that incorporated the name Cary, which was missing from the first list but was the logical match for his last name—Grant.

That left Henry, Humphrey, and Robert.

Henry. No doubt Grant sometimes operated under the name Fonda, perhaps with a first name lifted from Burt Lancaster or Gary Cooper.

Humphrey. In some circle, somewhere, Grant was known as Mr. Bogart—first name courtesy of yet another movie star of yesteryear.

Robert. Eventually they were certain to find that Grant also employed the surname Mitchum or Montgomery.

As casually as other men changed shirts, Spencer Grant changed identities.

They were searching for a phantom.

Although he couldn't yet prove it, Roy was now convinced that the name Spencer Grant was as phony as all the others. Grant was not the surname that this man had inherited from his father, nor was Spencer the Christian name that his mother had given him. He had named himself after favorite actors who had played old-fashioned heroes.

His real name was cipher. His real name was mystery, shadow, ghost, smoke.

Roy picked up the computer-enhanced portrait and studied the scarred face.

This dark-eyed cipher had joined the army under the name Spencer Grant, when he was just eighteen. What teenager knew how to establish a false identity, with convincing credentials, and get away with it? What had this enigmatic man been running from at even that young age?

How in the *hell* was he involved with the woman?

On the sofa, Rocky lay on his back, all four legs in the air, paws limp, his head in Theda Davidowitz's ample lap, gazing up in rapture at the plump, gray-haired woman. Theda stroked his tummy, scratched under his chin, and called him "sweetums" and "cutie" and "pretty eyes" and "snookums." She told him that he was God's own little furry angel, the handsomest canine in all creation, wonderful, marvelous, cuddly, adorable, perfect. She fed him thin little slices of ham, and he took each morsel from her fingertips with a delicacy more characteristic of a duchess than of a dog.

Ensconced in an overstuffed armchair with antimacassars on the back and arms, Spencer sipped from a cup of rich coffee that Theda had improved with a pinch of cinnamon. On the table beside his chair, a china pot held additional coffee. A plate was heaped with homemade chocolate-chip cookies. He had politely declined imported English tea biscuits, Italian anisette biscotti, a slice of lemon-coconut cake, a blueberry muffin, gingersnaps, shortbread, and a raisin scone; exhausted by Theda's hospitable perseverance, he had at last agreed to a cookie, only to be presented with twelve of them, each the size of a saucer.

Between cooing at the dog and urging Spencer to eat another cookie, Theda revealed that she was seventy-six and that her husband—Bernie—had died eleven years ago. She and Bernie had brought two children into the world: Rachel and Robert. Robert—the finest boy who ever lived, thoughtful and kind—served in Vietnam, was a *hero*, won more medals than you would believe . . . and died there. Rachel—oh, you should have seen her, so beautiful, her picture was there on the mantel, but it didn't do her justice, no photo could do her justice—had been killed in a traffic accident fourteen years ago. It was a terrible thing to outlive your children; it made you wonder if God was paying attention. Theda and Bernie had lived most of their married life in California, where Bernie had been an accountant and she'd been a third-grade teacher. On retirement, they sold their home, reaped a big capital gain, and moved to Vegas not because they were gamblers—well, twenty dollars, wasted on slot machines, once a month—but because real estate was cheap compared with California. Retirees had moved there by the thousands for that very reason. She and Bernie bought a small house for cash and were still able to bank sixty percent of what they'd gotten from the sale of their home in California. Bernie died three years later. He was the sweetest man, gentle and considerate, the greatest good fortune in her life had been to marry him—and after his death, the house was too large for a widow, so Theda sold it and moved to the apartment. For ten years, she'd had a dog—his name was Sparkle and it suited him, he was an adorable cocker spaniel—but, two months ago, Sparkle had gone the way of all things. God, how she'd cried, a foolish old woman, cried rivers, but she'd loved him. Since then she'd occupied herself with cleaning, baking, watching TV, and playing cards with friends twice a week. She hadn't considered getting another dog after Sparkle, because she wouldn't outlive another pet, and she didn't want to die and leave a sad little dog to fend for itself. Then she saw Rocky, and her heart melted, and now she knew she would have to get another dog. If she got one from the pound, a cute pooch destined to be put to sleep anyway, then every good day she could give him was more than he would have had without her. And who knew? Maybe she *would* outlive another pet and make a home for him until *his* time came, because two of her friends were in their mid-eighties and still going strong.

To please her, Spencer had a third cup of coffee and a second of the immense chocolate-chip cookies.

Rocky was gracious enough to accept more paper-thin slices of ham and submit to more belly stroking and chin scratching. From time to time he rolled his eyes toward Spencer, as if to say, *Why didn't you tell me about this lady a long time ago?*

Spencer had never seen the dog so completely, quickly charmed as he'd been by Theda. When his tail periodically swished back and forth, the motion was so vigorous that the upholstery was in danger of being worn to tatters.

"What I wanted to ask you," Spencer said when Theda paused for breath, "is if you knew a young woman who lived in the next apartment until late last November. Her name was Hannah Rainey and she—"

At the mention of Hannah—whom Spencer knew as Valerie—Theda launched into an enthusiastic monologue seasoned with superlatives. This girl, this special girl, oh, she'd been the best neighbor, so considerate, such a good heart in that dear girl. Hannah worked at the Mirage, a blackjack dealer on the graveyard shift, and she slept mornings through early afternoons. More often than not, Hannah and Theda had eaten dinner together, sometimes in Theda's apartment, sometimes in Hannah's. Last October Theda had been desperately ill with the flu and Hannah had looked after her, nursed her, been like a *daughter* to her. No, Hannah never talked about her past, never said where she was from, never talked about family, because she was trying to put something terrible behind her—that much was obvious—and she was looking only to the future, always forward, never back. For a while Theda had figured maybe it was an abusive husband, still out there somewhere, stalking her, and she'd had to leave her old life to avoid being killed. These days, you heard so much about such things, the world was a mess, everything turned upside down, getting worse all the time. Then the Drug Enforcement Administration had raided Hannah's apartment last November, at eleven in the morning, when she should have been sound asleep, but the girl was gone, packed up and moved overnight, without a word to her friend Theda, as if she'd known that she was about to be found. The federal agents were furious, and they questioned Theda at length, as if she might be a criminal mastermind herself, for God's sake. They said Hannah Rainey was a fugitive from justice, a partner in one of the most successful cocaine-importing rings in the country, and that she had shot and killed two undercover police officers in a sting operation that had gone sour.

"So she's wanted for murder?" Spencer asked.

Making a fist of one liver-spotted hand, stamping one foot so hard that her orthopedic shoe hammered the floor with a resounding *thud* in spite of the carpet, Theda Davidowitz said, "Bullshit!"

Eve Marie Jammer worked in a windowless chamber at the bottom of an office tower, four stories below downtown Las Vegas. Sometimes she thought of herself as being like the hunchback of Notre Dame in his bell tower, or like the phantom in his lonely realm beneath the Paris Opera House, or like Dracula in the solitude of his crypt: a figure of mystery, in possession of terrible secrets. One day, she hoped to be feared more intensely, by more people, than all those who had feared the hunchback, the phantom, and the count combined.

Unlike the monsters in movies, Eve Jammer was not physically disfigured. She was thirty-three, an ex-showgirl, blond, green-eyed, breathtaking. Her face caused men to turn their heads and walk into lampposts. Her perfectly proportioned body existed nowhere else but in the moist, erotic dreams of pubescent boys.

She was aware of her exceptional beauty. She reveled in it, for it was a source of power, and Eve loved nothing as much as power.

In her deep domain, the walls and the concrete floor were gray, and the banks of fluorescent bulbs shed a cold, unflattering light in which she was nonetheless gorgeous. Though the space was heated, and though she occasionally turned the thermostat to ninety degrees, the concrete vault resisted every effort to warm it, and Eve often wore a sweater to ward off the chill. As the sole worker in her office, she shared the room only with a few varieties of spiders, all unwelcome, which no quantity of insecticide could eradicate entirely.

That Friday morning in February, Eve was diligently tending the banks of recording machines on the metal shelves that nearly covered one wall. One hundred twenty-eight private telephone lines served her bunker, and all but two were connected to recorders, although not all the recorders were on active status. Currently, the agency had eighty taps operating in Las Vegas.

The sophisticated recording devices employed laser discs rather than tape, and all the phone taps were voice activated, so the discs would not become filled with long stretches of silence. Because of the enormous capacity for data storage allowed by the laser format, the discs seldom had to be replaced.

Nevertheless, Eve checked the digital readout on each machine, which indicated available recording capacity. And although an alarm would draw attention to any malfunctioning recorder, she tested each unit to be certain that it was working. If even one disc or machine failed, the agency might lose information of incalculable value: Las Vegas was the heart of the country's underground economy, which meant that it was a nexus of criminal activity and political conspiracy.

Casino gambling was primarily a cash business, and Las Vegas was like a huge, brightly lighted pleasure ship afloat on a sea of coins and paper currency. Even the casinos that were owned by respectable conglomerates were believed to be skimming fifteen to thirty percent of receipts, which never appeared on their books or tax returns. A portion of that secret treasure circulated through the local economy.

Then there were tips. Tens of millions in gratuities were given by winning gamblers to card dealers and roulette croupiers and craps-table crews, and most of that vanished into the deep pockets of the city. To obtain a three- or five-year contract as the maître d' at main showrooms in most major hotels, a winning applicant had to pay a quarter million in cash—or more—as "key money" to those who were in a position to grant the job; tips reaped from tourists seeking good seats for the shows quickly made the investment pay off.

The most beautiful call girls, referred by casino management to high rollers, could make half a million a year—tax free.

Houses frequently were bought with hundred-dollar bills packed in grocery bags or Styrofoam coolers. Each such sale was by private contract, with no escrow company involved and no official recording of a new deed, which prevented any taxing authority from discovering either that a seller had made a capital gain or that a buyer had made the purchase with undeclared income. Some of the finest mansions in the city had changed hands three or four times over two decades, but the name on the deed of record remained that of the original owner, to whom all official notices were mailed even after his death.

The IRS and numerous other federal agencies maintained large offices in Vegas. Nothing interested the government more than money—especially money from which it had never taken its bite.

The high-rise above Eve's windowless realm was occupied by an agency that maintained as formidable a presence in Las Vegas as any arm of government. She was supposed to believe that she worked for a secret though legitimate operation of the National Security Agency, but she knew that was not the truth. This was a nameless outfit, engaged in wide-ranging and mysterious tasks, intricately structured, operating outside the law, manipulating legislative and judicial branches of government (perhaps the executive branch as well), acting as judge and jury and executioner when it wished—a discreet gestapo.

They had put her in one of the most sensitive positions in the Vegas office partly because of her father's influence. However, they also trusted her in that subterranean recording studio because they thought that she was too dumb to realize the personal advantage to be made of the information therein. Her face was the purest distillation of male sex fantasies, and her legs were the most lithe and erotic ever to grace a Vegas stage, and her breasts were enormous, defiantly upswept—so they assumed that she was barely bright enough to change the laser discs from time to time and, when necessary, to call an in-house technician to repair malfunctioning machines.

Although Eve had developed a convincing dumb-blonde act, she was smarter than any of the Machiavellian crowd in the offices above her. During two years with the agency, she had secretly listened to the wiretaps on the most important of the casino owners, Mafia bosses, businessmen, and politicians being monitored.

She had profited by obtaining the details of secret corporate-stock manipulations, which allowed her to buy and sell for her own portfolio without risk. She was well informed about the guaranteed point spreads on national sporting events on those occasions when they were rigged to ensure gigantic profits for certain casino sports books. Usually, when a boxer had been paid to take a dive, Eve had placed a wager on his opponent—through a sports book in Reno, where her amazing luck was less likely to be noticed by anyone she knew.

Most of the people under agency surveillance were sufficiently experienced—and larcenous—to know the danger of conducting illegal activities over the phone, so they monitored their own lines twenty-four hours a day for evidence of electronic eavesdropping. Some of them also used scrambling devices. They were, therefore, arrogantly convinced that their communications couldn't be intercepted.

However, the agency employed technology available nowhere else outside the inner sanctums of the Pentagon. No detection equipment in existence could sniff out the electronic spoor of their devices. To Eve's certain knowledge, they operated an undiscovered tap on the "secure" phone of the special agent in charge of the Las Vegas office of the FBI; she wouldn't have been surprised to learn that the agency enjoyed equal coverage of the director of the Bureau in Washington.

In two years, making a long series of small profits that no one noticed, she had amassed more than five million dollars. Her only large score had been a million in cash, which had been intended as a payoff from the Chicago mob to a United States Senator on a fact-finding junket to Vegas. After covering her tracks by destroying the laser disc on which a conversation about the bribe had been recorded, Eve intercepted the two couriers in a hotel elevator on their way from a penthouse suite to the lobby. They were carrying the money in a canvas book bag that was decorated with the face of Mickey Mouse. Big guys. Hard faces. Cold eyes. Brightly patterned Italian silk shirts under black linen sport coats. Eve was rummaging in her big straw purse even as she entered the elevator, but the two thugs could see only her boobs stretching the low neckline of her sweater. Because they might have been quicker than they looked, she didn't risk taking the Korth .38 out of the handbag, just shot them through the straw, two rounds each. They hit the floor so hard that the elevator shook, and then the money was hers.

The only thing she regretted about the operation was the third man. He was a little guy with thinning hair and bags under his eyes, squeezing into the corner of the cab as if trying to make himself too small to be noticed. According to the tag pinned to his shirt, he was with a convention of dentists and his name was Thurmon Stookey. The poor bastard was a witness. After stopping the elevator between the twelfth and eleventh floors, Eve shot him in the head, but she didn't like doing it.

After she reloaded the Korth and stuffed the ruined straw purse into the canvas book bag with the money, she descended to the ninth floor. She was prepared to kill anyone who might be waiting in the elevator alcove—but, thank God, no one was there. Minutes later she was out of the hotel, heading home, with one million bucks and a handy Mickey Mouse tote bag.

She felt terrible about Thurmon Stookey. He shouldn't have been in that elevator. The wrong place, the wrong time. Blind fate. Life sure was full of surprises. In her entire thirty-three years, Eve Jammer had killed only five people, and Thurmon Stookey had been the sole innocent bystander among them. Nevertheless, for a while, she kept seeing the little guy's face in her mind's eye, as he had looked before she'd wasted him, and it had taken her the better part of a day to stop feeling bad about what had happened to him.

Within a year, she would not need to kill anyone again. She would be able to order people to carry out executions for her.

Soon, though unknown to the general populace, Eve Jammer would be the most feared person in the country, and safely beyond the reach of all enemies. The money she socked away was growing geometrically, but it was not money that would make her untouchable. Her *real* power would come from the trove of incriminating evidence on politicians, businessmen, and celebrities that she had transmitted at high speed, in the form of supercompressed digitized data, from the discs in her bunker to an automated recording device of her own, on a dedicated telephone line, in a bungalow in Boulder City that she had leased through an elaborate series of corporate blinds and false identities.

This was, after all, the Information Age, which had followed the Service Age, which itself had replaced the Industrial Age. She'd read all about it in *Fortune* and *Forbes* and *Business Week*. The future was now, and information was wealth.

Information was power.

Eve had finished examining the eighty active recorders and had begun to select new material for transmission to Boulder City when an electronic tone alerted her to a significant development on one of the taps.

If she had been out of the office, at home or elsewhere, the computer would have alerted her by beeper, whereupon she would have returned to the office immediately. She didn't mind being on call twenty-four hours a day. That was preferable to having assistants manning the room on two other shifts, because she simply didn't *trust* anyone else with the sensitive information on the discs.

A blinking red light drew her to the correct machine. She pushed a button to turn off the alarm.

On the front of the recorder, a label provided information about the wiretap. The first line was a case-file number. The next two lines were the address at which the tap was located. On the fourth line was the name of the subject being monitored: THEDA DAVIDOWITZ.

The surveillance of Mrs. Davidowitz was not the standard fishing expedition in which every word of every conversation was preserved on disc. After all, she was only an elderly widow, an ordinary prole whose general activities were no threat to the system—and therefore were of no interest to the agency. By merest chance, Davidowitz had established a short-lived friendship with the woman who was, at the moment, the most urgently sought fugitive in the nation, and the agency was interested in the widow only in the unlikely event that she received a telephone call or was paid a visit by her special friend. Monitoring the old woman's dreary chats with other friends and neighbors would have been a waste of time.

Instead, the bunker's autonomous computer, which controlled all the recording machines, was programmed to monitor the Davidowitz wiretap continuously and to activate the laser disc only upon the recognition of a key word that was related to the fugitive. That recognition had occurred moments ago. Now the key word appeared on a small display screen on the recorder: HANNAH.

Eve pressed a button marked MONITOR and heard Theda Davidowitz talking to someone in her living room on the other side of the city.

In the handset of each telephone in the widow's apartment, the standard microphone had been replaced with one that could pick up not only what was said in a phone conversation but what was said in any of her rooms, even when none of the phones were in use, and pass it down the line to a monitoring station on a continuous basis. This was a variation on a device known in the intelligence trade as an infinity transmitter.

The agency used infinity transmitters that were considerably improved over the models available on the open market. This one could operate twenty-four hours a day without compromising the function of the telephone in which it was concealed; therefore, Mrs. Davidowitz always heard a dial tone when she picked up a receiver, and callers trying to reach her were never frustrated by a busy signal related to the infinity transmitter's operation.

Eve Jammer listened patiently as the old woman rambled on about Hannah Rainey. Davidowitz was obviously talking *about* rather than *to* her friend the fugitive.

When the widow paused, a young-sounding man in the room with her asked a question about Hannah. Before Davidowitz answered, she called her visitor "my pretty-eyed snookie-wookums" and asked him to "give me a kissie, come on, give me a little lick, show Theda you love her, you little sweetums, sweet little sweetums, yeah, that's right, shake that tail and give Theda a little lick, a little kissie."

"Good God," Eve said, grimacing with disgust. Davidowitz was going on eighty. From the sound of him, the man with her was forty or fifty years her junior. Sick. Sick and perverted. What was the world coming to?

"A cockroach," Theda said as she gently rubbed Rocky's tummy. "Big. About four or five feet long, not counting the antennae."

After the Drug Enforcement Administration raided Hannah Rainey's place with a force of eight agents and discovered that she'd already fled, they grilled Theda and other neighbors for hours, asking the dumbest questions, all those grown men insisting Hannah was a dangerous criminal, when anyone who had ever met the precious girl for five minutes knew she was *incapable* of dealing drugs and murdering police officers. What absolute, total, stupid, silly nonsense. Then, unable to learn anything from neighbors, the agents had spent still more hours in Hannah's apartment, searching for God-knew-what.

Later that same evening, long after the Keystone Kops had departed—such a loud, rude group of nitwits—Theda went to 2-D with the spare key that Hannah had given her. Instead of breaking down the door to get into the apartment, the DEA had smashed the big window in the dining area that overlooked the balcony and courtyard. The landlord already had boarded over the window with sheets of plywood, until the glazier could fix it. But the front door was intact, and the lock hadn't been changed, so Theda let herself in. The apartment—unlike Theda's own—was rented furnished. Hannah had always kept it spotless, treated the furniture as though it were her own, a fastidious and *thoughtful* girl, so Theda wanted to see what damage the nitwits had done and be sure that the landlord didn't try to blame it on Hannah. In case Hannah turned up, Theda would testify about her immaculate housekeeping and her respect for the landlord's property. By God, she wouldn't let them make the dear girl pay for the damage *plus* stand trial for murdering police officers whom she obviously never murdered. And, of course, the apartment was a mess, the agents were pigs: They had ground out cigarettes on the kitchen floor, spilled cups of take-out coffee from the diner down the block, and even left the toilet unflushed, if you could believe such a thing, since they were grown men and must have had mothers who taught them *something*. But the strangest thing was the cockroach, which they'd drawn on a bedroom wall, with one of those wide-point felt-tip markers.

"Not well drawn, you understand, more or less just the outline of a cockroach, but you could see what it was meant to be," Theda said. "Just a sort of line drawing but ugly all the same. What on earth were those nitwits trying to prove, scrawling on the walls?"

Spencer was pretty sure that Hannah-Valerie herself had drawn the cockroach—just as she had nailed the textbook photograph of a roach to the wall of the bungalow in Santa Monica. He sensed it was meant to taunt and aggravate the men who had come looking for her, though he had no idea what it signified or why she knew that it would anger her pursuers.

Sitting at her desk in her windowless jurisdiction, Eve Jammer telephoned the operations office, upstairs, on the ground floor of the Las Vegas quarters of Carver, Gunmann, Garrote & Hemlock. The morning duty officer was John Cottcole, and Eve alerted him to the situation at Theda Davidowitz's apartment.

Cottcole was electrified by the news and unable to conceal his excitement. He was shouting orders to people in his office even while he was still on the line with Eve.

"Ms. Jammer," Cottcole said, "I'll want a copy of that disc, every word on that disc, you understand?"

"Sure," she said, but he hung up even as she was replying.

They thought that Eve didn't know who Hannah Rainey had been before becoming Hannah Rainey, but she knew the whole story. She also knew that there was an enormous opportunity for her in that case, a chance to hasten the growth of her fortune and power, but she hadn't quite yet decided how to exploit it.

A fat spider scurried across her desk.

She slammed one hand down, crushing the bug against her palm.

Driving back to Spencer Grant's cabin in Malibu, Roy Miro opened the Tupperware container. He needed the mood boost that the sight of Guinevere's treasure was sure to give him.

He was shocked and dismayed to see a bluish-greenish-brownish spot of discoloration spreading from the web between the first and second fingers. He hadn't expected anything like that for *hours* yet. He was irrationally upset with the dead woman for being so fragile.

Although he told himself that the spot of corruption was small, that the rest of the hand was still exquisite, that he should focus more on the unchanged and perfect form of it than on the coloration, Roy could not rekindle his previous passion for Guinevere's treasure. In fact, though it didn't yet emit a foul odor, it wasn't a treasure any longer: It was just garbage.

Deeply saddened, he put the lid on the plastic box.

He drove another couple of miles before pulling off Pacific Coast Highway and parking in the lot at the foot of a public pier. But for his sedan, the lot was empty.

Taking the Tupperware container with him, he got out of the car, climbed the steps to the pier, and walked toward the end.

His footsteps echoed hollowly off the boardwalk. Under those tightly set beams, breakers rolled between the pilings, rumbling and sloshing.

The pier was deserted. No fishermen. No young lovers leaning against the railing. No tourists. Roy was alone with his corrupted treasure and with his thoughts.

At the end of the pier he stood for a moment, gazing at the vast expanse of glimmering water and at the azure heavens that curved down to meet it at the far horizon. The sky would be there tomorrow and a thousand years from tomorrow, and the sea would roll eternally, but all else passed away.

He strove to avoid negative thoughts. It wasn't easy.

He opened the Tupperware container and threw the five-fingered garbage into the Pacific. It disappeared into the golden spangles of sunlight that gilded the backs of the low waves.

He wasn't concerned that his fingerprints might be lifted by laser from the pallid skin of the severed hand. If the fish didn't eat that last bit of Guinevere, the salt water would scrub away evidence of his touch.

He tossed the Tupperware container and its lid into the sea as well, although he was stricken with a pang of guilt even as the two objects arced toward the waves. He was usually sensitive to the environment, and he never littered.

He was not concerned about the hand, because it was organic. It would become a part of the ocean, and the ocean would not be changed.

Plastic, however, would take more than three hundred years to completely disintegrate. And throughout that period, toxic chemicals would leach from it into the suffering sea.

He should have dumped the Tupperware in one of the trash cans that stood at intervals along the pier railing.

Well. Too late. He was human. That was always the problem.

For a while Roy leaned against the railing. He stared into an infinity of sky and water, brooding about the human condition.

As far as Roy was concerned, the saddest thing in the world was that human beings, for all their ardent striving and desire, could never achieve physical, emotional, or intellectual perfection. The species was doomed to imperfection; it thrashed forever in despair or denial of that fact.

Though she had been undeniably attractive, Guinevere had been perfect in only one regard. Her hands.

Now those were gone too.

Even so, she had been one of the fortunate, because the vast majority of people were imperfect in *every* detail. They would never know the singular confidence and pleasure that must surely arise from the possession of even one flawless feature.

Roy was blessed with a repetitive dream, which came to him two or three nights every month, and from which he always woke in a state of rapture. In the dream, he searched the world over for women like Guinevere, and from each he harvested her perfect feature: from this one, a pair of ears so beautiful that they made his foolish heart pound almost painfully; from that one, the most exquisite ankles that it was within the mind of man to contemplate; from yet another, the snow-white, sculptured teeth of a goddess. He kept these treasures in magic jars, where they did not in the least deteriorate, and when he had collected all the parts of an ideal woman, he assembled them into the lover for whom he had always longed. She was so radiant in her unearthly perfection that he was half blinded when he looked upon her, and her slightest touch was purest ecstasy.

Unfortunately, he always woke from the paradise of her arms.

In life he would never know such beauty. Dreams were the only refuge for a man who would settle for nothing less than perfection.

Gazing into the sea and sky. A solitary man at the end of a deserted pier. Imperfect in every aspect of his own face and form. Aching for the unattainable.

He knew that he was both a romantic and a tragic figure. There were those who would even call him a fool. But at least he dared to dream and to dream big.

Sighing, he turned away from the uncaring sea and walked back to his car in the parking lot.

Behind the steering wheel, after he switched on the engine but before he put the car in gear, Roy allowed himself to withdraw the color snapshot from his wallet. He had carried it with him for more than a year, and he had studied it often. Indeed, it had such power to mesmerize him that he could have spent half the day staring at it in dreamy contemplation.

The photo was of the woman who had most recently called herself Valerie Ann Keene. She was attractive by anyone's standards, perhaps even as attractive as Guinevere.

What made her special, however, what filled Roy with reverence for the divine power that had created humankind, was her perfect eyes. They were more arresting and compelling than even the eyes of Captain Harris Descoteaux of the Los Angeles Police Department.

Dark yet limpid, enormous yet perfectly proportioned to her face, direct yet enigmatic, they were eyes that had seen what lay at the heart of all meaningful mysteries. They were the eyes of a sinless soul yet somehow also the eyes of a shameless voluptuary, simultaneously coy and direct, eyes to which every deceit was as transparent as glass, filled with spirituality and sexuality and a complete understanding of destiny.

He was confident that in reality her eyes would be more, not less, powerful than they were in the snapshot. He had seen other photographs of her, as well as numerous videotapes, and each image had battered his heart more punishingly than the one before it.

When he found her, he would kill her for the agency and for Thomas Summerton and for all those well-meaning others who labored to make this a better country and a better world. She had earned no mercy. Except for her single perfect feature, she was an evil woman.

But after Roy had fulfilled his duty, he would take her eyes. He deserved them. For too brief a time, those enchanting eyes would bring him desperately needed solace in a world that was sometimes too cruel and cold to bear, even for someone with an attitude as positive as that which he cultivated.

By the time Spencer was able to make it to the front door of the apartment with Rocky in his arms (the dog might not have left under his own power), Theda filled a plastic bag with the remaining ten chocolate-chip cookies from the plate beside the armchair, and she insisted that he take them. She also toddled into the kitchen and returned with a homemade blueberry muffin in a small brown paper bag—and then made another trip to bring him two slices of lemon-coconut cake in a Tupperware container.

Spencer protested only the cake, because he wouldn't be able to return the container to her.

"Nonsense," she said. "You don't need to return it. I've got enough Tupperware to last two lifetimes. For years I collected and collected it, because you can keep just anything in Tupperware, it has so many uses, but enough is enough, and I have more than enough, so just enjoy the cake and throw the container away. Enjoy!"

In addition to all the edible treats, Spencer had acquired two pieces of information about Hannah-Valerie. The first was Theda's story about the portrait of the cockroach on the wall of Hannah's bedroom, but he still didn't know what to make of that. The second concerned something that Theda remembered Hannah saying during idle dinner conversation one evening shortly before packing up her things and dusting Vegas off her heels.

They had been discussing places in which they had always dreamed of living, and although Theda couldn't make up her mind between Hawaii and England, Hannah had been adamant that only the small coastal town of Carmel, California, had all the peace and beauty that anyone could ever desire.

Spencer supposed that Carmel was a long shot, but at the moment it was the best lead he had. On one hand, she hadn't gone straight there from Las Vegas; she had stopped in the Los Angeles metropolitan area and tried to make a life as Valerie Keene. On the other hand, perhaps now, after her mysterious enemies had found her twice in large cities, she would decide to see if they could locate her as easily in a far smaller community.

Theda had not informed the band of loud, rude, window-shattering nitwits about Hannah's mention of Carmel. Maybe that gave Spencer an advantage.

He was loath to leave her alone with the memories of her beloved husband, long-mourned children, and vanished friend. Nevertheless, thanking her effusively, he stepped across the threshold onto the balcony and walked to the stairs that led down into the courtyard.

The mottled gray-black sky and the blustery wind surprised him, for when he had been in Thedaworld, he had all but forgotten that anything else existed beyond its walls. The crowns of the palms still thrashed, and the air was chillier than before.

Carrying a seventy-pound dog, a plastic bag full of cookies, a blueberry muffin in a paper sack, and a Tupperware container heavy with cake, he found the stairs precarious. He lugged Rocky all the way to the bottom, however, because he was certain that the dog would race straight back to Thedaworld if put down on the balcony.

When Spencer finally released the mutt, Rocky turned and gazed longingly up the stairs toward that little piece of canine heaven.

"Time to plunge back into reality," Spencer said.

The dog whined.

Spencer walked toward the front of the complex, under the windwhipped trees. Halfway past the swimming pool he looked back.

Rocky was still at the stairs.

"Hey, pal."

Rocky looked at him.

"Whose hound are you anyway?"

An expression of doggy guilt overcame the mutt, and at last he padded toward Spencer.

"Lassie would never leave Timmy, even for God's *own* grandmother."

Rocky sneezed, sneezed, and sneezed again at the pungent scent of chlorine.

"What if," Spencer said as the dog caught up to him, "I'd been trapped here, under an overturned tractor, unable to save myself, or maybe cornered by an angry bear?"

Rocky whined as if in apology.

"Accepted," Spencer said.

On the street, in the Explorer again, Spencer said, "Actually, I'm proud of you, pal."

Rocky cocked his head.

Starting the engine, Spencer said, "You're getting more sociable every day. If I didn't know better, I'd think you've been raiding my cash supply to pay for some high-priced Beverly Hills therapist."

Half a block ahead, a mold-green Chevy rounded the corner in a high-speed slide, tires screaming and smoking, and almost rolled like a stock car in a demolition derby. Somehow it stayed on two wheels, accelerated toward them, and shrieked to a stop at the curb on the other side of the street.

Spencer assumed the car was driven by a drunk or by a kid hopped up on something stronger than Pepsi—until the doors flew open and four men, of a type he recognized too well, exploded out of it. They hurried toward the entrance to the apartment-house courtyard.

Spencer popped the hand brake and shifted into drive.

One of the running men spotted him, pointed, shouted. All four of them turned toward the Explorer.

"Better hold tight, pal."

Spencer tramped on the accelerator, and the Explorer shot into the street, away from the men, toward the corner.

He heard gunfire.

TEN

A bullet smacked into the tailgate of the Explorer. Another ricocheted off metal with a piercing whine. The fuel tank didn't explode. No glass shattered. No tires blew out. Spencer hung a hard right turn past the coffee shop on the corner, felt the truck lifting, trying to tip over, so he pushed it into a slide instead. Rubber barked against blacktop as the rear tires stuttered sideways across the pavement. Then they were into the side street, out of sight of the gunmen, and Spencer accelerated.

Rocky, who was afraid of darkness and wind and lightning and cats and being seen at his toilet, among a dauntingly long list of other things, was not in the least frightened by the gunfire or by Spencer's stunt driving. He sat up straight, his claws sunk into the upholstery, swaying with the movement of the truck, panting and grinning.

Glancing at the speedometer, Spencer saw that they were doing sixty-five in a thirty-mile-per-hour zone. He accelerated.

In the passenger seat, Rocky did something that he had never done before: He began to bob his head up and down, as if encouraging Spencer to greater speed, *yesyesyesyes.*

"This is serious stuff," Spencer reminded him.

Rocky chuffed, as though scoffing at the danger.

"They must have been running audio surveillance on Theda's apartment."

Yesyesyesyesyes.

"Wasting precious resources monitoring *Theda*—and ever since last November? What the *hell* do they want with Valerie, what's so damned important that it's worth all this?"

Spencer looked at the rearview mirror. One and a half blocks behind them, the Chevy rounded the corner at the coffee shop.

He had wanted to get two blocks away before swinging left, out of sight, hoping that the trigger-happy torpedoes in the mold-green sedan would be deceived into thinking that he had turned at the first cross street rather than the second. Now they were on to him again. The Chevy was closing the distance between them, and it was a hell of a lot faster than it looked, a souped-up street rod disguised as one of the stripped-down wheezemobiles that the government assigned to Agriculture Department inspectors and agents of the Bureau of Dental Floss Management.

Though in their sights, Spencer hung a left at the end of the second block, as planned. This time he entered the new street in a wide turn to avoid another time-wasting, tire-stressing slide.

Nevertheless, he was going so fast that he spooked the driver of an approaching Honda. The guy wheeled hard right, bounced up onto the sidewalk, grazed a fire hydrant, and rammed a sagging chain-link fence that surrounded an abandoned service station.

From the corner of his eye, Spencer saw Rocky leaning against the passenger door, pushed there by centrifugal force, yet bobbing his head enthusiastically: *Yesyesyesyesyes.*

Pillowy hammers of cold wind buffeted the Explorer. From out of several empty acres on the right, dense clouds of sand churned into the street.

Vegas had grown haphazardly across the floor of a vast desert valley, and even most of the developed sectors of the city embraced big expanses of barren land. At a glance they seemed to be only enormous vacant lots—but, in fact, they were manifestations of the brooding desert, which was just biding its time. When the wind blew hard enough, the encircled desert angrily flung off its thin disguise, storming into the surrounding neighborhoods.

Half blinded by the seething tempest of sand, with shatters of dust hissing across the windshield, Spencer prayed for more: more wind, more clouds of grit. He wanted to vanish like a ghost ship disappearing into a fog.

He glanced at the rearview mirror. Behind him, visibility was limited to ten or fifteen feet.

He started to accelerate but reconsidered. Already he was plunging into the dry blizzard at suicidal speed. The street was no more visible ahead than it was behind. If he encountered a stopped or slow-moving vehicle, or if he suddenly crossed an intersection against the flow of traffic, the least of his worries would be the four homicidal men in the supercharged fedwagon.

One day, when the axis of the earth shifted just the tiniest fraction of a degree or when the jet streams of the upper troposphere suddenly deepened and accelerated for reasons mysterious, the wind and desert would no doubt conspire to tumble Vegas into ruin and bury the remains beneath billions of cubic yards of dry, white, triumphant sand. Maybe that moment had arrived.

Something thumped into the back end of the Explorer, jolting Spencer. The rearview mirror. The Chevy. On his ass. The fedwagon receded a few feet into the swirling sand, then leaped forward again, tapping the truck, maybe trying to make him spin out, maybe just letting him know they were there.

He was aware of Rocky looking at him, so he looked at Rocky.

The dog seemed to be saying, *Okay, now what?*

They passed the last of the undeveloped land and exploded into a silent clarity of sandless air. In the cold steely light of the pending storm, they had to abandon all hope of slipping away like Lawrence of Arabia into the swirling silicate cloaks of the desert.

An intersection lay half a block ahead. The signal light was red. The flow of traffic was against him.

He kept his foot on the accelerator, praying for a gap in the passing traffic, but at the last moment he rammed the brake pedal to the floor, to avoid colliding with a bus. The Explorer seemed to lift onto its front wheels, then rocked to a halt in a shallow drainage swale that marked the brink of the intersection.

Rocky yelped, lost his grip on the upholstery, and slid into the leg space in front of his seat, under the dashboard.

Belching pale-blue fumes, the bus trundled past in the nearest of the four traffic lanes.

Rocky eeled around in the cramped leg space and grinned up at Spencer.

"Stay there, pal. It's safer."

Ignoring the advice, the dog scrambled onto the seat again as Spencer accelerated into traffic in the reeking wake of the bus.

As Spencer turned right and swung around the bus, the rearview mirror captured the mold-green sedan bouncing across the same shallow swale in the pavement and arcing right into the street, as smoothly as if it were airborne.

"That sonofabitch knows how to drive."

Behind him, the Chevy appeared around the side of the city bus. It was coming fast.

Spencer was less concerned about losing them than about being shot at again before he could get away.

They would have to be crazy to open fire from a moving car, in traffic, where stray bullets could kill uninvolved motorists or pedestrians. This wasn't Chicago in the Roaring Twenties, wasn't Beirut or Belfast, wasn't even Los Angeles, for God's sake.

On the other hand, they hadn't hesitated to blast away at him on the street in front of Theda Davidowitz's apartment building. *Shot* at him. No questions first. No polite reading of his constitutional rights. Hell, they hadn't even made a serious effort to confirm that he was, in fact, the person they believed him to be. They wanted him badly enough to risk killing the wrong man.

They seemed convinced that he'd learned something of staggering importance about Valerie and that he must be terminated. In truth, he knew less about the woman's past than he knew about Rocky's.

If they ran him down in traffic and shot him, they would flash real or fake ID from one federal agency or another, and no one would hold them responsible for murder. They would claim that Spencer had been a fugitive, armed and dangerous, a cop killer. No doubt they'd be able to produce a warrant for his arrest, issued after the fact and post-dated, and they would clamp his dead hand around a drop gun that could be linked to a series of unsolved homicides.

He accelerated through a yellow traffic light as it turned red. The Chevy stayed close behind him.

If they didn't kill him on the spot, but wounded him and took him alive, they would probably haul him away to a soundproofed room and use creative methods of interrogation. His protestations of ignorance would not be believed, and they would kill him slowly, by degrees, in a vain attempt to extract secrets that he didn't possess.

He had no gun of his own. He had only his hands. His training. And a dog. "We're in big trouble," he told Rocky.

In the cozy kitchen of the cabin in the Malibu canyon, Roy Miro sat alone at the dining table, sorting through forty photographs. His men had found them in a shoe box on the top shelf in the bedroom closet. Thirty-nine of the pictures were loose, and the fortieth was in an envelope.

Six of the loose snapshots were of a dog—mixed breed, tan and black, with one floppy ear. It was most likely the pet for which Grant had bought the musical rubber bone from the mail-order firm that still kept his name and address on file two years later.

Thirty-three of the remaining photographs were of the same woman. In some she appeared to be as young as twenty, in others as old as her early thirties. Here: wearing blue jeans and a reindeer sweater, decorating a Christmas tree. And here: in a simple summer dress and white shoes, holding a white purse, smiling at the camera, dappled in sun and shadow, standing by a tree that was dripping clusters of white flowers. In more than a few, she was grooming horses, riding horses, or feeding apples to them.

Something about her haunted Roy, but he couldn't understand why she so affected him.

She was an undeniably attractive woman, but she was far from drop-dead gorgeous. Though shapely, blond, blue-eyed, she nonetheless lacked any single transcendent feature that would have put her in the pantheon of true beauty.

Her smile was the only truly striking thing about her. It was the most consistent element of her appearance from one snapshot to the next: warm, open, easy, a charming smile that never seemed to be false, that revealed a gentle heart.

A smile, however, was not a *feature*. That was especially true in this woman's case, for her lips weren't particularly luscious, as were Melissa Wicklun's lips. Nothing about the set or width of her mouth, the contours of her philtrum, or the shape of her teeth was even intriguing, let alone electrifying. Her smile was greater than the sum of its parts, like the dazzling reflection of sunlight on the otherwise unremarkable surface of a pond.

He could find nothing about her that he yearned to possess.

Yet she haunted him. Though he doubted that he had ever met her, he felt that he ought to know who she was. Somewhere, he had seen her before.

Staring at her face, at her radiant smile, he sensed a terrible presence hovering over her, just beyond the frame of the photograph. A cold darkness was descending, of which she was unaware.

The newest of the photographs were at least twenty years old, and many were surely three decades out of the darkroom tray. The colors of even the more recent shots were faded. The older ones held only the faintest suggestions of color, were mostly gray and white, and were slightly yellowed in places.

Roy turned each photo over, hoping to find a few identifying words on the reverse, but the backs were all blank. Not even a single name or date.

Two of the pictures showed her with a young boy. Roy was so mystified by his strong response to the woman's face and so fixated on figuring out why she seemed familiar that he did not at first realize that the boy was Spencer Grant. When he made the connection, he put the two snapshots side by side on the table.

It was Grant in the days before he had sustained his scar.

In his case, more than with most people, the face of the man reflected the child he had been.

He was about six or seven years old in the first photo, a skinny kid in swimming trunks, dripping wet, standing by the edge of a pool. The woman was in a one-piece bathing suit beside him, playing a silly practical joke for the camera: one hand behind Grant's head, two of her fingers secretly raised and spread to make it appear as though he had a small pair of horns or antennae.

In the second photograph, the woman and the boy were sitting at a picnic table. The kid was a year or two older than in the first picture, wearing jeans, a T-shirt, and a baseball cap. She had one arm around him, pulling him against her side, knocking his cap askew.

In both snapshots, the woman's smile was as radiant as in all those without the boy, but her face was also brightened by affection and love. Roy felt confident that he'd found Spencer Grant's mother.

He remained baffled, however, as to why the woman was familiar to him. Eerily familiar. The longer he stared at the pictures of her, with or without the boy at her side, the more certain he became that he knew her—and that the context in which he had previously seen her was deeply disturbing, dark, and strange.

He turned his attention again to the snapshot in which mother and son stood beside the swimming pool. In the background, at some distance, was a large barn; even in the faded photograph, traces of red paint were visible on its high, blank walls.

The woman, the boy, the barn.

On a deep subconscious level, a memory must have stirred, for suddenly the skin prickled across Roy's scalp.

The woman. The boy. The barn.

A chill quivered through him.

He looked up from the photographs on the kitchen table, at the window above the sink, at the crowded grove of trees beyond the window, at the meager coins of noontime sunlight tumbling through the wealth of shadows, and he willed memory to glimmer forth, as well, from the eucalyptic dark.

The woman. The boy. The barn.

For all his straining, enlightenment eluded him, although another chill walked through his bones.

The barn.

Through residential streets of stucco homes, where cacti and yucca plants and hardy olive trees were featured in low-maintenance desert landscaping, through a shopping center parking lot, through an industrial area, through the maze of a self-storage yard filled with corrugated-steel sheds, off the pavement and through a sprawling park, where the fronds of the palms tossed and lashed in a frenzied welcome to the oncoming storm, Spencer sought without success to shake off the pursuing Chevrolet.

Sooner or later, they were going to cross the path of a police patrol. As soon as one unit of local cops became involved, Spencer would find it even more difficult to get away.

Disoriented by the twisting route taken to elude his pursuers, Spencer was surprised to be flashing past one of the newest resort hotels, on the right. Las Vegas Boulevard South was only a few hundred yards ahead. The traffic light was red, but he decided to bet everything that it would change by the time he got there.

The Chevy remained close behind him. If he stopped, the bastards would be out of their car and all over the Explorer, bristling with more guns than a porcupine had quills.

Three hundred yards to the intersection. Two hundred fifty.

The signal was still red. Cross traffic wasn't as heavy as it could get farther north along the Strip, but it was not light, either.

Running out of time, Spencer slowed slightly, enough to allow himself more maneuverability at the moment of decision but not enough to encourage the driver of the Chevy to try to pull alongside him.

A hundred yards. Seventy-five. Fifty.

Lady Luck wasn't with him. He was still playing the green, but the red kept turning up.

A gasoline tanker truck was approaching the intersection from the left, taking advantage of the rare chance to make a little speed on the Strip, going faster than the legal limit.

Rocky began bobbing his head up and down again.

Finally the driver of the tanker saw the Explorer coming and tried to brake quickly without jackknifing.

"All right, okay, okay, gonna make it," Spencer heard himself saying, almost chanting, as if he were crazily determined to shape reality with positive thought.

Never lie to the dog.

"We're in deep shit, pal," he amended as he curved into the intersection in a wide arc, around the front of the oncoming truck.

As panic shifted his perceptions into slo-mo, Spencer saw the tanker sweep toward them, the giant tires rolling and bouncing and rolling and bouncing while the terrified driver adroitly pumped the brakes as much as he dared. And now it was not merely approaching but looming over them, huge, an inexorable and inescapable behemoth, far bigger than it had seemed only a split second ago, and now bigger still, towering, immense. Good God, it seemed bigger than a jumbo jet, and he was nothing but a bug on the runway. The Explorer began to cant to starboard, as if it would tip over, and Spencer corrected with a slight pull to the right and a tap of the brakes. The energy of the aborted rollover was channeled into a slide, however, and the back end traveled sideways with a shriek of tormented tires. The steering wheel spun back and forth through his sweat-dampened hands. The Explorer was out of control, and the gasoline tanker was on top of them, as large as God, but at least they were sliding in the right direction, away from the big rig, although probably not fast enough to escape it. Then the sixteen-wheel monster shrieked by with only inches to spare, a curved wall of polished steel passing in a mirrored blur, in a gale of wind that Spencer was certain he could feel even through the tightly closed windows.

The Explorer spun three hundred sixty degrees, then kept going for another ninety. It shuddered to a halt, facing the opposite direction—and on the far side of the divided boulevard—from the gasoline tanker, even as that behemoth was still passing it.

The southbound traffic, into the lanes of which Spencer had careened, stopped before running him down, although not without a chorus of screaming brakes and blaring horns.

Rocky was on the floor again.

Spencer didn't know if the dog had been thrown off the seat again or, in a sudden attack of prudence, had scrambled down there.

He said, "Stay!" even as Rocky clambered up onto the seat.

The roar of an engine. From the left. Coming across the broad intersection. The Chevy. Hurtling past the back of the halted tanker, toward the side of the Explorer.

He jammed his foot down hard on the accelerator. The tires spun, then rubber got a bite of pavement. The Explorer bulleted south on the boulevard—just as the Chevy shot past the rear bumper. With a cold squeal, metal kissed metal.

Gunshots erupted. Three or four rounds. None seemed to strike the Explorer.

Rocky remained on the seat, panting, claws dug in, determined to hold fast this time.

Spencer was headed out of Vegas, which was both good and bad. It was good because as he proceeded farther south, toward the open desert and the last entrance to Interstate 15, the risk of being brought to a stop by a traffic jam would quickly diminish. It was bad, however, because beyond the forest of hotels, the barren land would provide few easy routes of escape and even fewer places to hide. Out on the vast panoramas of the Mojave, the thugs in the Chevy could slip a mile or two behind and still keep a watch on him.

Nevertheless, leaving town was the only sane choice. The turmoil at the intersection behind him was sure to bring the cops.

As he was speeding past the newest hotel-casino in town—which included a two-hundred-acre amusement park, Spaceport Vegas—his only sane choice became no real choice at all. From across the boulevard, a hundred yards ahead, a northbound car swung out of the oncoming traffic, jumped the far side of the low median strip, smashed through a row of shrubs, and bounced into the southbound lanes. It slid to a stop at an angle, blocking the way, ready to ram Spencer if he tried to squeeze around either end of it.

He stopped thirty yards from the blockade.

The new car was a Chrysler but, otherwise, so like the Chevy that the two might have been born of the same factory.

The driver stayed behind the wheel of the Chrysler, but the other doors opened. Big, troublesome-looking men got out.

The rearview mirror revealed what he'd expected: The Chevy also had halted at an angle across the boulevard, fifteen yards behind him. Men were getting out of that vehicle too—and they had guns.

In front of him, the men at the Chrysler had guns too. Somehow that didn't come as a surprise.

The final picture had been kept in a white envelope, which had been fastened shut with a length of Scotch tape.

Because of the shape and thinness of the object, Roy knew that it was another photograph before he opened the envelope, though it was larger than a snapshot. As he peeled off the tape, he expected to find a five-by-seven studio portrait of the mother, a memento of special importance to Grant.

It was a black-and-white studio photograph, sure enough, but it was of a man in his middle thirties.

For a strange moment, for Roy, there was neither a eucalyptus grove beyond the windows nor a window through which to see it. The kitchen itself faded from his awareness, until nothing existed except him and that single picture, to which he related even more powerfully than to the photos of the woman.

He could breathe but shallowly.

If anyone had entered the room to ask a question, he could not have spoken.

He felt detached from reality, as if in a fever, but he was not feverish. Indeed, he was cold, though not uncomfortably so: It was the cold of a watchful chameleon, pretending to be stone on a stone, on an autumn morning; it was a cold that invigorated, that focused his entire consciousness, that contracted the gears of his mind and allowed his thoughts to spin without friction. His heart didn't race, as it would have in a fever. Indeed, his pulse rate declined, until it was as ponderously slow as that of a sleeper, and throughout his body, each beat reverberated like a recording of a cathedral bell played at quarter speed: protracted, solemn, heavy tolling.

Obviously, the shot had been taken by a talented professional, under studio conditions, with much attention to the lighting and to the selection of the ideal lens. The subject, wearing a white shirt open at the throat and a leather jacket, was presented from the waist up, posed against a whitewall, arms folded across his chest. He was strikingly handsome, with thick dark hair combed straight back from his forehead. The publicity photograph, of a type usually associated with young actors, was a blatant glamour shot but a good one, because the subject possessed natural glamour, an aura of mystery and drama that the photographer didn't have to create with bravura technique.

The portrait was a study in light and shadow, with more of the latter than the former. Peculiar shadows, cast by objects beyond the frame, appeared to swarm across the wall, drawn to the man as night itself was drawn across the evening sky by the terrible weight of the sinking sun.

His direct and piercing stare, the firm set of his mouth, his aristocratic features, and even his deceptively casual posture seemed to reveal a man who had never known self-doubt, depression, or fear. He was more than merely confident and self-possessed. In the photo, he projected a subtle but unmistakable arrogance. His expression seemed to say that, without exception, he regarded all other members of the human race with amusement and contempt.

Yet he remained enormously appealing, as though his intelligence and experience had earned him the right to feel superior. Studying the photograph, Roy sensed that here was a man who would make an interesting, unpredictable, entertaining friend. Peering out from his shadows, this singular individual had an animal magnetism that made his expression of contempt seem inoffensive. Indeed, an air of arrogance seemed *right* for him—just as any lion must walk with feline arrogance if it was to seem at all like a lion.

Gradually, the spell cast by the photograph diminished in power but didn't altogether fade. The kitchen reestablished itself from the mists of Roy's fixation, as did the window and the eucalyptuses.

He knew this man. He had seen him before.

A long time ago . . .

Familiarity was part of the reason that the picture affected him so strongly. As with the woman, however, Roy was unable to put a name to the face or to recall the circumstances under which he had seen this person previously.

He wished the photographer had allowed more light to reach his subject's face. But the shadows seemed to love the dark-eyed man.

Roy placed that photo on the kitchen table, beside the snapshot of the mother and her son at poolside.

The woman. The boy. The barn in the background. The man in the shadows.

At a full stop on Las Vegas Boulevard South, confronted by armed men in front of and behind him, Spencer pounded the horn, pulled the wheel hard to the right, and tramped on the accelerator. The Explorer rocketed toward the amusement park, Spaceport Vegas, pressing him and Rocky against their seats as if they were astronauts moonward bound.

The cocksure boldness of the gunmen proved that they *were* feds of some kind, even if they used fake credentials to conceal their true identity. They would never ambush him on a major street, before witnesses, unless they were confident of pulling rank on local cops.

On the sidewalk in front of Spaceport Vegas, on their way from casino to casino, pedestrians scattered, and the Explorer shot into a driveway posted for buses only, though no buses were in sight.

Perhaps because of the February cold snap and the pending storm, or maybe because it was only noon, Spaceport Vegas wasn't open. The ticket booths were shuttered, and the thrill rides that were high enough to be seen behind the park walls were in suspended animation.

Nevertheless, neon and futuristic applications of fiber optics throbbed and flashed along the perimeter wall, which was nine feet high and painted like the armored hull of a starfighter. A photosensitive cell must have switched on the lights, mistaking the midday gloom of the advancing storm for the onset of evening.

Spencer drove between two rocket-shaped ticket booths, toward a twelve-foot-diameter tunnel of polished steel that penetrated the park walls. In blue neon, the words TIME TUNNEL TO SPACEPORT VEGAS promised more escape than he needed.

He flew up the gentle ramp, never tapping the brakes, and raced unheeding through time.

The massive pipe was two hundred feet long. Tubes of brilliant blue neon curved up the walls, across the ceiling. They blinked in rapid sequence from the entrance to the exit, creating an illusion of a funnel of lightning.

Under ordinary circumstances, patrons were conveyed into the park on lumbering trams, but the half-blinding surges of light were more effective at greater speed. Spencer's eyes throbbed, and he could almost believe that he *had* been catapulted into a distant era.

Rocky was doing the head-bobbing bit again.

"Never knew I had a dog," Spencer said, "with a need for speed."

He fled into the far reaches of the park, where the lights had not been activated like those on the wall and in the tunnel. The deserted and seemingly endless midway rose and fell, narrowed and widened and narrowed again, and repeatedly looped back on itself.

Spaceport Vegas featured corkscrew roller coasters, dive-bombers, scramblers, whips, and the other usual gut churners, all tricked up with lavish science fiction facades, gimmicks, and names. Lightsled to Ganymede. Hyperspace Hammer. Solar Radiation Hell. Asteroid Collision. Devolution Drop. The park also offered elaborate flight-simulator adventures and virtual-reality experiences in buildings of futuristic or bizarrely alien architecture: Planet of the Snakemen, Blood Moon, Vortex Blaster, Deathworld. At Robot Wars, homicidal machines with red eyes guarded the entrance, and the portal to Star Monster looked like a glistening orifice at one end or the other of an extraterrestrial leviathan's digestive tract.

Under the bleak sky, swept by cold wind, with the gray prestorm light sucking the color out of everything, the future as imagined by the creators of Spaceport Vegas was unremittingly hostile.

Curiously, that made it appear more realistic to Spencer, more like a true vision and less like an amusement park than its designers ever intended. Alien, machine, and human predators were everywhere on the prowl. Cosmic disasters loomed at every turn: The Exploding Sun, Comet Strike, Time Snap, The Big Bang, Wasteland. The End of Time was on the same avenue of the midway that offered an adventure called Extinction. It was possible to look at the ominous attractions and believe that this grim future—in its mood if not its specifics—was sufficiently terrifying to be one that contemporary society might make for itself.

In search of a service exit, Spencer drove recklessly along the winding promenades, weaving among the attractions. He repeatedly glimpsed the Chevy and the Chrysler between the rides and the exotic structures, though never dangerously close. They were like sharks cruising in the distance. Each time he spotted them, he whipped out of sight into another branch of the midway maze.

Around the corner from the Galactic Prison, past the Palace of the Parasites, beyond a screen of ficus trees and a red-flowering oleander hedge that were surely drab compared with the shrubs that grew on the planets of the Crab Nebula, he found a two-lane service road that marked the back of the park. He followed it.

To his left were the trees, aligned twenty feet on center, with the six-foot-high hedge between the trunks. On his right, instead of the neon-lit wall that was featured in the public portions of the perimeter, a chain-link fence rose ten feet high, topped with coils of barbed wire, and beyond it lay a sward of desert scrub.

He rounded a corner, and a hundred yards ahead was a pipe-and-chain-link gate, on wheels, controlled by overhead hydraulic arms. It would roll out of the way at the touch of the right remote-control device—which Spencer didn't possess.

He increased speed. He'd have to ram the gate.

Reverting to his customary prudence, the dog scrambled off the passenger seat and curled in the leg space before he could be thrown there by the upcoming impact.

"Neurotic but not stupid," Spencer said approvingly.

He was more than halfway to the gate when he caught a flicker of motion out of the corner of his left eye. The Chrysler erupted from between two ficus trees, tearing the hell out of the oleander hedge, and crashed into the service way in showers of green leaves and red flowers. It crossed Spencer's wake and rammed the fence so hard that the chain-link billowed, as if made of cloth, to the end of the lane.

The Explorer trailed that billow by a split second and hit the gate with enough force to crumple the hood without popping it open, to make Spencer's restraining harness tighten painfully across his chest, to knock the breath out of him, to clack his teeth together, to make his luggage rattle under the restraining net in the cargo area—but not hard enough to take out the gate. That barrier was torqued, sagging, half collapsed, trailing tangles of barbed wire like dreadlocks—but still intact.

He shifted gears and shot backward as if he were a cannonball returning to the barrel in a counterclockwise world.

The hitmen in the Chrysler were opening the doors, getting out, drawing their guns—until they saw the truck reversing toward them. They reversed too, scrambling inside the car, pulling the doors shut.

He rammed backward into the sedan, and the collision was loud enough to convince him that he'd overdone it, disabled the Explorer.

When he shifted into drive, however, the truck sprang forward. No tires were flat or obstructed by crumpled fenders. No windows had shattered. No smell of gasoline, so the tank wasn't ruptured. The battered Explorer rattled, clinked, ticked, and creaked—but it *moved*, with power and grace.

The second impact took down the gate. The truck clambered over the fallen chain-link, away from Spaceport Vegas, into an enormous plot of desert scrub on which no one had yet built a theme park, a hotel, a casino, or a parking lot.

Engaging the four-wheel drive, Spencer angled west, away from the Strip, toward Interstate 15.

He remembered Rocky and glanced down at the leg space in front of the passenger seat. The dog was curled up, with his eyes squeezed shut, as if anticipating another collision.

"It's okay, pal."

Rocky continued to grimace in anticipation of disaster.

"Trust me."

Rocky opened his eyes and returned to his seat, where the vinyl upholstery had been well scratched and punctured by his claws.

They rocked and rolled across the eroded and barren land, to the base of the superhighway.

A steep slope of gravel and shale rose thirty or forty feet to the east-west lanes. Even if he could find a break in the guardrail above him, no escape could be found—and certainly no salvation—on that highway. The people who were seeking him would establish checkpoints in both directions.

After a brief hesitation, he turned south, following the base of the elevated interstate.

From the east, across the white sand and the pink-gray slate, came the mold-green Chevrolet. It was like a heat mirage, although the day was cool. The low dunes and shallow washes would defeat it. The Explorer was made for overland travel; the Chevrolet was not.

Spencer came to a waterless riverbed, which the interstate crossed on a low concrete bridge. He drove into that declivity, onto a soft bed of silt, where driftwood slept and where dead tumbleweeds moved as ceaselessly as strange shadows in a bad dream.

He followed the dry wash under the interstate, west into the inhospitable Mojave.

The forbidding sky, as hard and dark as sarcophagus granite, hung within inches of the iron mountains. Desolate plains rose gradually toward those more sterile elevations, with a steadily decreasing burden of withered mesquite, dry bunchgrass, and cactus.

He drove out of the arroyo but continued to follow it upslope, toward distant peaks as bare as ancient bones.

The Chevrolet was no longer in sight.

Finally, when he was sure that he was far beyond the casual notice of any surveillance teams posted to watch the traffic on the interstate, he turned south and paralleled that highway. Without it as a reference, he would be lost. Whirling dust devils spun across the desert, masking the telltale plumes cast up behind the Explorer.

Although no rain yet fell, lightning scored the sky. The shadows of low stone formations leaped, fell back, and leaped again across the alabaster land.

Rocky's cloaks of courage had been cast off as the Explorer's speed had fallen. He was huddled once more in folds of cold timidity. He whined periodically and looked at his master for reassurance.

The sky cracked with fissures of fire.

Roy Miro pushed the troubling photographs aside and set up his attaché case computer on the kitchen table in the Malibu cabin. He plugged it into a wall outlet and connected with Mama in Virginia.

When Spencer Grant had joined the United States Army, as a boy of eighteen, more than twelve years ago, he must have completed the standard enlistment forms. Among other things, he'd been required to provide information about his schooling, his place of birth, his father's name, his mother's maiden name, and his next of kin.

The recruiting officer through whom he had enlisted would have verified that basic information. It would have been verified again, at a higher level, prior to Grant's induction into the service.

If "Spencer Grant" was a phony identity, the boy would have had considerable difficulty getting into the army with it. Nevertheless, Roy remained convinced that it was not the name on Grant's original birth certificate, and he was determined to discover what that birth name had been.

At Roy's request, Mama accessed the Department of Defense dead files on former army personnel. She brought Spencer Grant's basic information sheet onto the display screen.

According to the data on the VDT, Grant's mother's name, which he had given to the army, was Jennifer Corrine Porth.

The young recruit had listed her as "deceased."

The father was said to be "unknown."

Roy blinked in surprise at the screen. UNKNOWN.

That was extraordinary. Grant had not simply claimed to be a bastard child, but had implied that his mother's promiscuity had made it impossible to pinpoint the man who fathered him. Anyone else might have cited a false name, a convenient fictional father, to spare himself and his late mother some embarrassment.

Logically, if the father was genuinely unknown, Spencer's last name should have been Porth. Therefore, either his mother borrowed the "Grant" from a favorite movie star, as Bosley Donner believed she'd done, or she named her son after one of the men in her life even without being certain that he had fathered the boy.

Or the "unknown" was a lie, and the name "Spencer Grant" was just another false identity, perhaps the first of many, that this phantom had manufactured for himself.

At the time of Grant's enlistment, with his mother already dead and his father unknown, he had given his next of kin as "Ethel Marie and George Daniel Porth, grandparents." They had to be his mother's parents, since Porth was also her maiden name.

Roy noticed that the address for Ethel and George Porth—in San Francisco—had been the same as Grant's current address at the time that he'd enlisted. Apparently the grandparents had taken him in, subsequent to the death of his mother, whenever that had been.

If anyone knew the true story of Grant's provenance and the source of his scar, it would be Ethel and George Porth. Assuming that they actually existed and were not just names on a form that a recruitment officer had failed to verify twelve years ago.

Roy asked for a printout of the pertinent portion of Grant's service file. Even with what seemed to be a good lead in the Porths, Roy wasn't confident of learning anything in San Francisco that would give more substance to this elusive phantom whom he'd first glimpsed less than forty-eight hours ago in the rainy night in Santa Monica.

Having erased himself entirely from all utility-company records, from property tax rolls, and even from the Internal Revenue Service files—why had Grant allowed his name to remain in the DMV, Social Security Administration, LAPD, and military files? He had tampered with those records to the extent of replacing his true address with a series of phony addresses, but he could have entirely eliminated them. He had the knowledge and the skill to do so. Therefore, he must have maintained a presence in some data banks for a purpose.

Roy felt that somehow he was playing into Grant's hands even by trying to track him down.

Frustrated, he turned his attention once more to the two most affecting of the forty photographs. The woman, the boy, and the barn in the background. The man in the shadows.

On all sides of the Explorer lay sand as white as powdered bones, ash-gray volcanic rock, and slopes of shale shattered by millions of years of heat, cold, and quaking earth. The few plants were crisp and bristly. Except for the dust and vegetation stirred by the wind, the only movement was the creeping and slithering of scorpions, spiders, scarabs, poisonous snakes, and the other cold-blooded or bloodless creatures that thrived in that arid wasteland.

Silvery quills and nibs of lightning flashed continually, and fast-moving thunderheads as black as ink wrote a promise of rain across the sky. The bellies of the clouds hung heavy. With great crashes of thunder, the storm struggled to create itself.

Captured between the dead earth and tumultuous heavens, Spencer paralleled the distant interstate highway as much as possible. He detoured only when the contours of the land required compromise.

Rocky sat with head bowed, gazing at his paws rather than at the stormy day. His flanks quivered as currents of fear flowed through him like electricity through a closed circuit.

On another day, in a different place and in a different storm, Spencer would have kept up a steady line of patter to soothe the dog. Now, however, he was in a mood that darkened with the sky, and he was able to focus only on his own turmoil.

For the woman, he had walked away from his life, such as it was. He had left behind the quiet comfort of the cabin, the beauty of the eucalyptus grove, the peace of the canyon—and most likely he would never be able to return to that. He had made a target of himself and had put his precious anonymity in jeopardy.

He regretted none of that—because he still had the hope of gaining a real life with some kind of meaning and purpose. Although he had wanted to help the woman, he had also wanted to help himself.

But the stakes suddenly had been raised. Death and disclosure were not the only risks he was going to have to take if he continued to involve himself in Valerie Keene's problems. Sooner or later, he was going to have to kill someone. They would give him no choice.

After escaping the assault on the bungalow in Santa Monica on Wednesday night, he had avoided thinking about the most disturbing implications of the SWAT team's extreme violence. Now he recalled the gunfire directed at imagined targets inside the dark house and the rounds fired at him as he had scaled the property wall.

That was not merely the response of a few edgy law-enforcement officers intimidated by their quarry. It was a criminally excessive use of force, evidence of an agency out of control and arrogantly confident that it wasn't accountable for any atrocities it committed.

A short while ago, he had encountered equivalent arrogance in the reckless behavior of the men who harried him out of Las Vegas.

He thought about Louis Lee in that elegant office under China Dream. The restaurateur had said that governments, when big enough, often ceased to play by the codes of justice under which they were established.

All governments, even democracies, maintained control by the threat of violence and imprisonment. When that threat was divorced from the rule of law, however, even if with the best of intentions, there was a fearfully thin line between a federal agent and a thug.

If Spencer located Valerie and learned why she was on the run, helping her would not be simply a matter of dipping into his cash reserves and finding the best attorney to represent her. Naively, that had been his nebulous plan, on those few occasions when he had bothered to think about what he might do if he tracked her down.

But the ruthlessness of these enemies ruled out a solution in any court of law.

Faced with the choice of violence or flight, he would always choose to flee and risk a bullet in the back—at least when no life but his own was at stake. When he eventually took responsibility for this woman's life, however, he could not expect her to turn her own back on a gun; sooner or later he would have to meet the violence of those men with violence of his own.

Brooding about that, Spencer drove south between the too-solid desert and the amorphous sky. The distant highway was only barely visible to the east, and no clear path lay before him.

Out of the west came rain in blinding cataracts of rare ferocity for the Mojave, a towering gray tide behind which the desert began to disappear.

Spencer could smell the rain even though it hadn't reached them yet. It was a cold, wet, ozone-tainted scent, refreshing at first but then strange and profoundly chilling.

"It's not that I'm worried about being able to kill someone if it comes to that," he told the huddled dog.

The gray wall rushed toward them, faster by the second, and it seemed to be more than mere rain that loomed. It was the future too, and it was all that he feared knowing about the past.

"I've done it before. I can do it again if I have to."

Over the rumble of the Explorer's engine, he could hear the rain now, like a million pounding hearts.

"And if some sonofabitch deserves killing, I can do him and feel no guilt, no remorse. Sometimes it's right. It's justice. I don't have a problem with that."

The rain swept over them, billowing like a magician's scarves, bringing sorcerous change. The pale land darkened dramatically with the first splash. In the peculiar storm light, the desiccated vegetation, more brown than green, suddenly became glossy, verdant; in seconds, withered leaves and grass appeared to swell into plump tropical forms, though it was all illusion.

Switching on the windshield wipers, shifting the Explorer into four-wheel drive, Spencer said, "What worries me . . . what scares me is . . . maybe I waste some sonofabitch who deserves it . . . some piece of walking garbage . . . and *this* time I like it."

The downpour could have been no less cataclysmic than that which had launched Noah upon the Flood, and the fierce drumming of rain on the truck was deafening. The storm-cowed dog probably could not hear his master above the roar, yet Spencer used Rocky's presence as an excuse to acknowledge a truth that he preferred not to hear, speaking aloud because he might lie if he spoke only to himself.

"I never liked it before. Never felt like a hero for doing it. But it didn't sicken me, either. I didn't puke or lose any sleep over it. So . . . what if the next time . . . or the time after that . . . ?"

Beneath the glowering thunderheads, in the velvet-heavy shrouds of rain, the early afternoon had grown as dark as twilight. Driving out of murk into mystery, he switched on the headlights, surprised to find that both had survived the impact with the amusement-park gate.

Rain fell straight to the earth in such tremendous tonnage that it dissolved and washed away the wind that had previously stirred the desert into sand spouts.

They came to a ten-foot-deep wash with gently sloping walls. In the headlight beams, a stream of silvery water, a foot wide and a few inches deep, glimmered along the center of that depression. Spencer crossed the twenty-foot-wide arroyo to higher ground on the far side.

As the Explorer crested the second bank, a series of massive lightning bolts blazed across the desert, accompanied by crashes of thunder that vibrated through the truck. The rain came down even harder than before, harder than he had ever seen it fall.

Driving with one hand, Spencer stroked Rocky's head. The dog was too frightened to look up or to lean into the consoling hand.

They went no more than fifty yards from the first arroyo when Spencer saw the earth moving ahead of them. It rolled sinuously, as though swarms of giant serpents were traveling just below the surface of the desert. By the time he braked to a full stop, the headlights revealed a less fanciful but no less frightening explanation: The earth wasn't moving, but a swift muddy river was churning from west to east along the gently sloping plain, blocking travel to the south.

The depths of this new arroyo were mostly hidden. The racing water was already within a few inches of its banks.

Such torrents couldn't have risen just since the storm had swept across the plains minutes ago. The runoff was from the mountains, where rain had been falling for a while and where the stony, treeless slopes absorbed little of it. The desert seldom received downpours of that magnitude; but on rare occasions, with breathtaking suddenness, flash floods could inundate even portions of the elevated interstate highway or pour into low-lying areas of the now distant Las Vegas Strip and sweep cars out of casino parking lots.

Spencer couldn't judge the depth of the water. It might have been two feet or twenty.

Even if only two feet deep, the water was moving so fast, with such power, that he didn't dare attempt to ford it. The second wash was wider than the first, forty feet across. Before he'd traveled half that distance, the truck would be lifted and carried downriver, rolling and bobbing, as if it were driftwood.

He backed the Explorer away from the churning flow, turned, and retraced his route, arriving at the first arroyo, to the south, more quickly than he expected. In the brief time since he had crossed it, the silvery freshet had become a turbulent river that nearly filled the wash.

Bracketed by impassable cataracts, Spencer was no longer able to parallel the distant north-south interstate.

He considered parking right there, to wait for the storm to pass. When the rain ended, the arroyos would empty as swiftly as they had filled. But he sensed that the situation was more dangerous than it appeared.

He opened the door, stepped into the downpour, and was soaked by the time he walked to the front of the Explorer. The pummeling rain hammered a chill deep into his flesh.

The cold and the wet contributed to his misery less than did the incredible *noise*. The oppressive roar of the storm blocked all other sounds. The rattle of the rain against the desert, the swash and rumble of the river, and the booming thunder combined to make the vast Mojave as confining and claustrophobia-inducing as the interior of a stuntman's barrel on the brink of Niagara.

He wanted a better view of the surging flux than he'd gotten from inside the truck, but a closer look alarmed him. Moment by moment, water lapped higher on the banks of the wash; soon it would flood across the plain. Sections of the soft arroyo walls collapsed, dissolved into the muddy currents, and were carried away. Even as the violent gush eroded a wider channel, it swelled tremendously in volume, simultaneously rising and growing broader. Spencer turned from the first arroyo and hurried toward the second, to the south of the truck. He reached that other impromptu river sooner than he expected. It was brimming and widening like the first channel. Fifty yards had separated the two arroyos when he'd first driven between them, but that gap had shrunk to thirty.

Thirty yards was still a considerable distance. He found it difficult to believe that those two spates were powerful enough to eat through so much remaining land and ultimately converge.

Then, immediately in front of his shoes, a crack opened in the ground. A long, jagged leer. The earth grinned, and a six-foot-wide slab of riverbank collapsed into the onrushing water.

Spencer stumbled backward, out of immediate danger. The sodden land around him was turning mushy underfoot.

The unthinkable suddenly seemed inevitable. Large portions of the desert were all shale and volcanic rock and quartzite, but he had the misfortune to be caught in a cloudburst while traveling over a fathomless sea of sand. Unless a hidden spine of rock was buried between the two arroyos, the intervening land might indeed be washed away and the entire plain recontoured, depending on how long the storm raged at its current intensity.

The impossibly heavy downfall abruptly grew heavier still.

He sprinted for the Explorer, clambered inside, and pulled his door shut. Shivering, streaming water, he backed the truck farther from the northern arroyo, afraid that the wheels would be undermined.

With head still downcast, from under his lowered brow, Rocky looked up worriedly at his master.

"Have to drive between arroyos, east or west," Spencer thought aloud, "while there's still something to drive *on*."

The windshield wipers weren't coping well with the cascades that poured across the glass, and the rain-blurred landscape settled into deeper degrees of false twilight. He tried turning the wiper control to a higher setting. It was already as high as it would go.

"Shouldn't head toward lower land. Water's gaining velocity as it goes. More likely to wash out down there."

He switched the headlamps to high beams. The extra light didn't clarify anything: It bounced off the skeins of rain, so the way ahead seemed to be obscured by curtain after curtain of mirrored beads. He selected the low beams again.

"Safer ground uphill. Ought to be more rock."

The dog only trembled.

"The space between arroyos will probably widen out."

Spencer shifted gears again. The plain sloped gradually up to the west, into obscure terrain.

As giant needles of lightning stitched the heavens to the earth, he drove into the resultant narrow pocket of gloom.

At Roy Miro's direction, agents in San Francisco were seeking Ethel and George Porth, the maternal grandparents who had raised Spencer Grant following the death of his mother. Meanwhile, Roy drove to the offices of Dr. Nero Mondello in Beverly Hills.

Mondello was the most prominent plastic surgeon in a community where God's work was revised more frequently than anywhere except Palm Springs and Palm Beach. On a misshapen nose, he could perform miracles equivalent to those that Michelangelo had performed on giant cubes of Carrara marble—though Mondello's fees were substantially higher than those of the Italian master.

He had agreed to make changes in a busy schedule to meet with Roy, because he believed that he was assisting the FBI in a desperate search for a particularly savage serial killer.

They met in the doctor's spacious inner office: white marble floor, white walls and ceiling, white shell sconces. Two abstract paintings hung in white frames: The only color was white, and the artist achieved his effects solely with the textures of the heavily layered pigment. Two white-washed lacewood chairs with white leather cushions flanked a glass-and-steel table and stood before a whitewashed burled-wood desk, against a backdrop of white silk draperies.

Roy sat in one of the lacewood chairs, like a blot of soil in all that whiteness, and wondered what view would be revealed if the draperies were opened. He had the crazy notion that beyond the window, in downtown Beverly Hills, lay a landscape swaddled in snow.

Other than the photographs of Spencer Grant that Roy had brought with him, the only object on the polished surface of the desk was a single blood-red rose in a Waterford cut-crystal vase. The flower was a testament to the possibility of perfection—and drew the visitor's attention to the man who sat beyond it, behind the desk.

Tall, slender, handsome, fortyish, Dr. Nero Mondello was the focal point of his bleached domain. With his thick jet-black hair combed back from his forehead, warm-toned olive complexion, and eyes the precise purple-black of ripe plums, the surgeon had an impact almost as powerful as that of a spirit manifestation. He wore a white lab coat over a white shirt and red silk necktie. Around the face of his gold Rolex, matched diamonds sparkled as though charged with supernatural energy.

The room and the man were no less impressive for being blatantly theatrical. Mondello was in the business of replacing nature's truth with convincing illusions, and all good magicians were theatrical.

Studying the DMV photograph of Grant and the computer-generated portrait, Mondello said, "Yes, this would have been a dreadful wound, quite terrible."

"What might've caused it?" Roy asked.

Mondello opened a desk drawer and removed a magnifying glass with a silver handle. He studied the photographs more closely.

At last he said, "It was more a cut than a tear, so it must have been a relatively sharp instrument."

"A knife?"

"Or glass. But it wasn't an entirely even cutting edge. Very sharp but slightly irregular like glass—or a serrated blade. An even blade would produce a cleaner wound and a narrower scar."

Watching Mondello pore over the photographs, Roy realized that the surgeon's facial features were so refined and so uncannily well proportioned that a talented colleague had been at work on them.

"It's a cicatricial scar."

"Excuse me?" Roy said.

"Connective tissue that's contracted—pinched or wrinkled," Mondello said, without looking up from the photographs. "Though this one is relatively smooth, considering its width." He returned the magnifying glass to the drawer. "I can't tell you much more—except that it's not a recent scar."

"Could surgery eliminate it, skin grafts?"

"Not entirely, but it could be made far less visible, just a thin line, a thread of discoloration."

"Painful?" Roy asked.

"Yes, but this"—he tapped the photo—"wouldn't require a long series of surgeries over a number of years, as burns might."

Mondello's face was exceptional because the proportions were so studied, as though the guiding aesthetic behind his surgery had been not merely the intuition of an artist but the logical rigor of a mathematician. The doctor had remade himself with the same iron control that great politicians applied to society to transform its imperfect citizens into better people. Roy had long understood that human beings were so deeply flawed that no society could have perfect justice without imposing mathematically rigorous planning and stern guidance from the top. Yet he'd never perceived, until now, that his passion for ideal beauty and his desire for justice were both aspects of the same longing for Utopia.

Sometimes Roy was amazed by his intellectual complexity.

"Why," he asked Mondello, "would a man live with that scar if it could be made all but invisible? Aside, that is, from being unable to pay for the surgery."

"Oh, cost wouldn't be a deterrent. If the patient had no money and the government wouldn't pay, he'd still receive treatment. Most surgeons have always dedicated a portion of their professional time to charity work like this."

"Then why?"

Mondello shrugged and pushed the photographs across the desk. "Perhaps he's afraid of pain."

"I don't think so. Not this man."

"Or afraid of doctors, hospitals, sharp instruments, anesthesia. There are countless phobias that prevent people from having surgery."

"This man's not a phobic personality," Roy said, returning the photos to the manila envelope.

"Could be guilt. If he lived through an accident in which others were killed, he could have survivor's guilt. Especially if loved ones died. He feels he's no better than they were, and he wonders why he was spared when they were taken. He feels guilty just for living. Suffering with the scar is a way of atoning."

Frowning, Roy got to his feet. "Maybe."

"I've had patients with that problem. They didn't want surgery because survivor's guilt led them to feel they deserved their scars."

"That doesn't sound right, either. Not for this guy."

"If he's not either phobic or suffering from survivor's guilt," said Mondello, coming around the desk and walking Roy to the door, "then you can bet it's guilt over *something*. He's punishing himself with the scar. Reminding himself of something he would like to forget but feels obligated to remember. I've seen that before as well."

As the surgeon talked, Roy studied his face, fascinated by the finely honed bone structure. He wondered how much of the effect had been achieved with real bone and how much with plastic implants, but he knew that it would be gauche to ask.

At the door, he said, "Doctor, do you believe in perfection?"

Pausing with his hand on the doorknob, Mondello appeared mildly puzzled. "Perfection?"

"Personal and societal perfection. A better world."

"Well . . . I believe in always striving for it."

"Good." Roy smiled. "I knew you did."

"But I don't believe it can be achieved."

Roy's smile froze. "Oh, but I've seen perfection now and then. Not perfection in the whole of anything, perhaps, but in part."

Mondello smiled indulgently and shook his head. "One man's idea of perfect order is another man's chaos. One man's vision of perfect beauty is another man's notion of deformity."

Roy did not appreciate such talk. The implication was that any Utopia was also Hell. Eager to convince Mondello of an alternate view, he said, "Perfect beauty exists in nature."

"There's always a flaw. Nature abhors symmetry, smoothness, straight lines, order—all the things we associate with beauty."

"I recently saw a woman with perfect hands. Flawless hands, without a blemish, exquisitely shaped."

"A cosmetic surgeon looks at the human form with a more critical eye than other people do. I'd have seen a lot of flaws, I'm sure."

The doctor's smugness irritated Roy, and he said, "I wish I'd brought those hands to you—the one, anyway. If I'd brought it, if you'd seen it, you would have agreed."

Suddenly Roy realized that he had come close to revealing things that would have necessitated the surgeon's immediate execution.

Concerned that his agitated state of mind would lead him to make another and more egregious error, Roy dawdled no longer. He thanked Mondello for his cooperation, and he got out of the white room.

In the medical building parking lot, the February sunshine was more white than golden, with a harsh edge, and a border of palm trees cast eastward-leaning shadows. The afternoon was turning cool.

As he twisted the key in the ignition and started the car, his pager beeped. He checked the small display window, saw a number with the prefix of the regional offices in downtown Los Angeles, and made the call on his cellular phone.

They had big news for him. Spencer Grant had almost been chased down in Las Vegas; he was now on the run, overland, across the Mojave Desert. A Learjet was standing by at LAX to take Roy to Nevada.

Driving up the barely perceptible slope between two rushing rivers, on a steadily narrowing peninsula of sodden sand, searching for an intruding formation of rock on which to batten down and wait out the storm, Spencer was hampered by decreasing visibility. The clouds were so thick, so black, that daylight on the desert was as murky as that a few fathoms under any sea. Rain fell in Biblical quantities, overwhelming the windshield wipers, and although the headlights were on, clear glimpses of the ground ahead were brief.

Great fiery lashes tortured the sky. The blinding pyrotechnics escalated into nearly continuous chain lightning, and brilliant links rattled down the heavens as though an evil angel, imprisoned in the storm, were angrily testing his bonds. Even then, the inconstant light illuminated nothing while swarms of stroboscopic shadows flickered across the landscape, adding to the gloom and confusion.

Suddenly, ahead and a quarter mile to the west, at ground level, a blue light appeared as if from out of another dimension. At once, it moved off to the south at high speed.

Spencer squinted through rain and shadow, trying to discern the nature and size of the light source. The details remained obscure.

The blue traveler turned east, proceeded a few hundred yards, then swung north toward the Explorer. Spherical. Incandescent.

"What the hell?" Spencer slowed the Explorer to a crawl to watch the eerie luminosity.

When it was still a hundred yards from him, the thing swerved west, toward the place where it had first appeared, then dwindled past that point, rose, flared, and vanished.

Even before the first light winked out, Spencer saw a second from the corner of his eye. He stopped and looked west-northwest.

The new object—blue, throbbing—moved incredibly fast, on an erratic serpentine course that brought it closer before it angled east. Abruptly it spun like pinwheel fireworks and disappeared.

Both objects had been silent, gliding like apparitions across the storm-washed desert.

The skin prickled on his arms and along the nape of his neck.

For the past few days, although he was usually skeptical of all things mystical, he had felt that he was venturing into the unknown, the uncanny. In his country, in his time, real life had become a dark fantasy, as full of sorcery as any novel about lands where wizards ruled, dragons roamed, and trolls ate children. Wednesday night, he had stepped through an invisible doorway that separated his lifelong reality from another place. In this new reality, Valerie was his destiny. Once found, she would be a magic lens that would forever alter his vision. All that was mysterious would become clear, but things long known and understood would become mysterious once more.

He felt all that in his bones, as an arthritic man might feel the approach of a storm before the first cloud crossed the horizon. He felt more than understood it, and the visitations of the two blue spheres seemed to confirm that he was on the right trail to find Valerie, traveling to a strange place that would transform him.

He glanced at his four-legged companion, hoping that Rocky was staring toward where the second light had vanished. He needed confirmation that he had not imagined the thing, even if his only reassurance came from a dog. But Rocky was huddled and shivering in terror. His head remained bowed, and his eyes were downcast.

To the right of the Explorer, lightning was reflected in raging water. The river was much closer than he expected. The right-hand arroyo had widened dramatically in the past minute.

Hunched over the wheel, he angled to the new midpoint of the ever narrower strip of high ground and drove forward, seeking stable rock, wondering if the mysterious Mojave had more surprises for him.

The third blue enigma plunged out of the sky, as fast and plumb as an express elevator, two hundred yards ahead and to the left. It halted smoothly and hovered just above the ground, revolving rapidly.

Spencer's heart thudded painfully against his ribs. He eased off the accelerator. He was balanced between wonder and dread.

The glowing object shot straight at him: as large as the truck, still without detail, silent, otherworldly, on a collision course. He tramped the accelerator. The light swerved to counter his move, swelled brighter, filled the Explorer with blue-blue light. To make a smaller target of himself, he turned right, braked hard, putting the back end of the truck to the oncoming object. It struck without force but with sprays of sapphire sparks, and scores of electrical arcs blazed from one prominent point of the truck to another.

Spencer was encapsulated in a dazzling blue sphere of hissing, crackling light. And knew what it was. One of the rarest of all weather phenomena. Ball lightning. It wasn't a conscious entity, not the extraterrestrial force he had half imagined, neither stalking nor seducing him. It was simply one more element of the storm, as impersonal as ordinary lightning, thunder, rain.

Perched on four tires, the Explorer was safe. As soon as the ball burst upon them, its energy began to dissipate. Sizzling and snapping, it swiftly faded to a fainter blue: dimmer, dimmer.

His heart had been pounding with a strange jubilation, as though he desperately wanted to encounter something paranormal, even if it proved hostile, rather than return to a life without wonder. Though rare, ball lightning was too mundane to satisfy his expectations, and disappointment brought his heart rate almost back to normal.

With a jolt, the front of the truck dropped precipitously, and the cab tipped forward. As a final arc of electricity crackled from the left headlight rim to the top right corner of the windshield frame, dirty water sloshed over the hood.

In his panic, as he had tried to avoid the blue light, Spencer had swung too far to the right, braking at the brink of the arroyo. The soft wall of sand was eroding beneath him.

His heart raced again, his disappointment forgotten.

He shifted into reverse and *eased* down on the accelerator. The truck moved backward, up the disintegrating slope.

Another slab of the bank gave way. The Explorer tipped farther forward. Water surged across the hood, almost to the windshield.

Spencer abandoned caution, accelerated hard. The truck *jumped* backward. Out of the water. Tires eating through the soft, wet ground. Tipping back, back, almost horizontal again.

The arroyo wall was too unstable to endure. The churning wheels destabilized the gélatinous ground. Engine shrieking, tires spinning in the treacherous muck, the Explorer slid into the flood, protesting as noisily as a mastodon being sucked into a tar pit.

"Sonofabitch." Spencer inhaled deeply and held his breath as though he were a schoolboy leaping into a pond.

The truck splashed beneath the surface, fully submerged.

Unnerved by the calamitous sound and motion, Rocky wailed in misery, as though responding not only to current events but to the cumulative terrors of his entire troubled life.

The Explorer broke the surface, wallowing like a boat in rough seas. The windows were closed, preventing an inrush of cold water, but the engine had gone dead.

The truck was swept downstream, pitching and yawing, riding higher in the flood than Spencer had expected. The choppy surface lapped four to six inches below the sill of his side window.

He was assaulted by liquid noises, a symphonic Chinese water torture: the hollow paradiddle of rain on the roof, the whoosh and swish and plash and gurgle of the churning flow against the Explorer.

Above all the competing sounds, a drizzling noise drew Spencer's attention, because it was intimate, not muffled by sheet metal or glass. The maracas of a rattlesnake wouldn't have been more alarming. Somewhere, water was getting into the truck.

The breach wasn't catastrophic—a drizzle, not a gush. With every pound of water taken aboard, however, the truck would ride lower, until it sank. Then it would tumble along the river bottom, pushed rather than buoyed, body crumpling, windows shattering.

Both front doors were secure. No leaks.

As the truck heaved and plunged downstream, Spencer turned in his seat, snared by his safety harness, and examined the cargo hold. All windows were intact. The tailgate wasn't leaking. The backseat was folded down, so he couldn't see the floor concealed under it, but he doubted that the river was getting through the rear doors, either.

When he faced front again, his feet sloshed in an inch of water.

Rocky whined, and Spencer said, "It's okay."

Don't alarm the dog. Don't lie, but don't alarm.

Heater. The engine was dead, but the heater still functioned. The river was invading through the lower vents. Spencer switched off the system, closed the air intakes. The drizzle was silenced.

As the truck pitched, the headlights slashed the bruised sky and glistered in the mortal torrents of rain. Then the truck yawed, and the beams cut wildly left and right, seeming to carve the arroyo walls; slabs of earth crashed into the dirty tide, spewing gouts of pearlescent foam. He killed the lights, and the resultant gray-on-gray world was less chaotic.

The windshield wipers were running on battery power. He didn't switch them off. He needed to see what was coming, as best he could.

He would be less stressed—and no worse off—if he lowered his head and closed his eyes, like Rocky, and waited for fate to deal with him as it wished. A week ago, he might have done that. Now he peered forward anxiously, hands locked to the useless steering wheel.

He was surprised by the fierceness of his desire to survive. Until he had walked into The Red Door, he had expected nothing from life: only to keep a degree of dignity and to die without shame.

Blackened tumbleweed, thorny limbs of uprooted cacti, masses of desert bunchgrass that might have been the blond hair of drowned women, and pale driftwood rode the rolling river with the Explorer, scraping and thumping against it. In emotional turmoil equal to the tumult of the natural world, Spencer knew that he had been traveling the years as if he himself were driftwood, but at last he was *alive*.

The watercourse abruptly dropped ten or twelve feet, and the truck sailed over a roaring cataract, airborne, tipping forward. It dove into the rampaging water, into a diluvial darkness. Spencer was first jerked forward in his harness, then slammed backward. His head bounced off the headrest. The Explorer failed to hit bottom, exploded through the surface, and rollicked on downriver.

Rocky was still on the passenger seat, huddled and miserable, claws hooked in the upholstery.

Spencer gently stroked and squeezed the back of the mutt's neck.

Rocky didn't raise his bowed head but turned toward his master and rolled his eyes to look up from under his brow.

Interstate 15 was a quarter mile ahead. Spencer was stunned that the truck had been carried so far in so little time. The currents were even faster than they seemed.

The highway spanned the arroyo—usually a dry wash—on massive concrete columns. Through the smeary windshield and heavy rain, the bridge supports appeared to be absurdly numerous, as if government engineers had designed the structure primarily to funnel millions of dollars to a senator's nephew in the concrete business.

The central passage between the bridge supports was broad enough to let five trucks pass abreast. But half the flood churned through the narrower races between the closely ranked columns on each side of the main channel. Impact with the bridge supports would be deadly.

Swooping, plunging, they rode a series of rapids. Water splashed against the windows. The river picked up speed. A lot of speed.

Rocky was shaking more violently than ever and panting raggedly.

"Easy, pal, easy. You better not pee on the seat. You hear?"

On I-15, the headlights of big rigs and cars moved through the storm-darkened day. Emergency flashers threw red light into the rain where motorists had stopped on the shoulder to wait out the downpour.

The bridge loomed. Exploding ceaselessly against the concrete columns, the river threw sheets of spray into the rain-choked air.

The truck had attained a fearful velocity, *shooting* downstream. It rolled violently, and waves of nausea swelled through Spencer.

"Better not pee on the seat," he repeated, no longer speaking only to the dog.

He reached under his fleece-lined denim jacket, under his soaked shirt, and withdrew the jade-green soapstone medallion that hung on a gold chain around his neck. On one side was the carved head of a dragon. On the other side was an equally stylized pheasant.

Spencer vividly recalled the elegant, windowless office beneath China Dream. Louis

Lee's smile. The bow tie, suspenders. The gentle voice: *I sometimes give one of these to people who seem to need it.*

Without slipping the chain over his head, he held the medallion in one hand. He felt childish, but he held it tightly nonetheless.

The bridge was fifty yards ahead. The Explorer was going to pass dangerously close to the forest of columns on the right.

Pheasants and dragons. Prosperity and long life.

He remembered the statue of Quan Yin by the front door of the restaurant. Serene but vigilant. Guarding against envious people.

After a life like yours, you can believe in this?

We must believe in something, Mr. Grant.

Ten yards from the bridge, ferocious currents caught the truck, lifted it, dropped it, tipped it half onto its right side, rolled it back to the left, and slapped loudly against the doors.

Sailing out of the storm into the eclipsing shadow of the highway above, they passed the first of the bridge columns in the row immediately to the right. Passed the second. At horrendous speed. The river was so high that the solid underside of the bridge was only a foot above the truck. They surged nearer to the columns, bulleting past the third, the fourth, nearer still.

Pheasants and dragons. Pheasants and dragons.

The currents pulled the truck away from the concrete supports and dropped it into a sudden swale in the turbulent surface, where it wallowed with filthy water to its windowsills. The river teased Spencer with the possibility of safe passage in that trough, pushing them along as if they were on a bobsled in a luge chute—but then it mocked his brief flicker of hope by lifting the truck again and tossing it passenger-side-first into the next column. The crash was as loud as a bomb blast, metal shrieked, and Rocky howled.

The impact pitched Spencer to his left, a move that the safety harness couldn't check. The side of his head slammed into the window. In spite of all the other clamor, he heard the tempered glass webbing with a million hairline cracks, a sound like a crisp slice of toast being crushed with a sudden clench of a fist.

Cursing, he put his left hand to the side of his head. No blood. Only a rapid throbbing that was in time with his heartbeat.

The window was a mosaic of thousands of tiny chips of glass, held together by the gummy film in the center of the sandwiched pane.

Miraculously, the windows on Rocky's side were undamaged. But the front door bulged inward. Water dribbled around the frame.

Rocky lifted his head, suddenly afraid *not* to look. He whimpered as he peered at the wild river, at the low concrete ceiling, and at the rectangle of cheerless gray storm light beyond the bridge.

"Hell," Spencer said, "pee on the seat if you want to."

The truck sank into another swale.

They were two-thirds of the way through the tunnel.

A hissing, needle-thin stream of water *squirted* through a tiny breach in the twisted door frame. Rocky yelped as it spattered him.

When the truck soared out of the trough, it wasn't thrown into the columns after all. Worse, the river heaved as if passing over an enormous obstruction on the floor of the wash, and it slammed the Explorer straight up into the low concrete underside of the bridge.

Braced with both hands on the steering wheel, determined not to be thrown into the side window, Spencer was unprepared for the upward rush. He dropped in his seat as the roof crumpled inward, but he was not quick enough. The ceiling cracked against the top of his skull.

Bright bolts of pain flashed behind his eyes, along his spine. Blood streamed down his face. Scalding tears. His vision blurred.

The river carried the truck down from the underside of the bridge, and Spencer tried to push up in his seat. The effort made him dizzy, so he slumped again, breathing hard.

His tears swiftly darkened, as if polluted. His blurred vision faded. Soon the tears were as black as ink, and he was blind.

The prospect of blindness panicked him, and panic opened a door to understanding: He wasn't blind, thank God, but he *was* passing out.

He held desperately to consciousness. If he fainted, he might never wake. He balanced on the edge of a swoon. Then hundreds of gray dots appeared in the blackness, expanded into elaborate matrices of light and shadow, until he could see the interior of the truck.

Pulling himself up in the seat as far as the crumpled roof would allow, he again almost passed out. Gingerly, he touched his bleeding scalp. The wound seeped rather than gushed, not a mortal laceration.

They were in the open once more. Rain hammered on the truck.

The battery wasn't dead yet. Wipers still swept the windshield.

The Explorer gamely wallowed down the center of the river, which was broader than ever. Perhaps a hundred twenty feet wide. Brimming against its banks, within inches of spilling over. God knew how deep it might be. The water was calmer than it had been but moving fast.

Gazing worriedly at the liquid road ahead, Rocky made pitiful sounds of distress. He wasn't bobbing his head, wasn't delighted by their speed, as on the streets of Vegas. He didn't seem to trust nature as much as he had trusted his master.

"Good old Mr. Rocky Dog," Spencer said affectionately, and was unnerved to hear that his speech was slurred.

In spite of Rocky's concern, Spencer couldn't see any unusual dangers immediately ahead, nothing like the bridge. For a couple of miles the flow appeared to proceed unimpeded, until it vanished into rain, mist, and the iron-colored light of thunderhead-filtered sun.

Desert plains lay on both sides, bleak but not entirely barren. Mesquite bristled. Clumps of wiry grass. Outcroppings of gnarled rock also grew out of the plains. They were natural formations but achieved the strange geometry of ancient Druid structures.

A new pain blossomed in Spencer's skull. Irresistible darkness flowered behind his eyes. He might have been out for a minute or an hour. He didn't dream. He just went away into a timeless dark.

When he revived, cool air fluttered feebly across his brow, and cold rain spattered his face. The many liquid voices of the river grumbled, hissed, and chuckled louder than before.

He sat for a while, wondering why the sound was so much louder. His thoughts were muddled. Eventually, he realized that the side window had collapsed while he'd been unconscious. Gummy laces of highly fragmented tempered glass lay in his lap.

Water was ankle-deep on the floor. His feet were half numb with cold. He propped them on the brake pedal and flexed his toes in his saturated shoes. The Explorer was riding lower than when last he'd noticed. The water was only an inch below the bottom of the window. Though moving fast, the river was less turbulent, perhaps because it had broadened. If the arroyo narrowed or the terrain changed, the flow might become tempestuous again, lap inside, and sink them.

Spencer was barely clearheaded enough to know that he should be alarmed. Nevertheless, he could muster only a mild concern.

He should find a way to seal the dangerous gap where the window had been. But the problem seemed insurmountable. For one thing, he would have to move to accomplish it, and he didn't want to move.

All he wanted to do was sleep. He was so tired. Exhausted.

His head lolled to the right against the headrest, and he saw the dog sitting on the passenger seat. "How you doin', fur butt?" he asked thickly, as if he had been pouring down beer after beer.

Rocky glanced at him, then looked again at the river ahead.

"Don't be afraid, pal. He wins if you're afraid. Don't let the bastard win. Can't let him win. Got to find Valerie. Before he does. He's out there. He's forever . . . on the prowl. . . ."

With the woman on his mind and a deep uneasiness in his heart, Spencer Grant rode through the glistening day, muttering feverishly, searching for something unknown, unknowable. The vigilant dog sat silently beside him. Rain ticked on the crumpled roof of the truck.

Maybe he passed out again, maybe he only closed his eyes, but when his feet slipped off the brake pedal and splashed into water that was now halfway up his calves, Spencer lifted his throbbing head and saw that the windshield wipers had stopped. Dead battery.

The river was as fast as an express train. Some turbulence had returned. Muddy water licked at the sill of the broken window.

Inches beyond that gap, a dead rat floated on the surface of the flow, pacing the truck. Long and sleek. One unblinking, glassy eye fixed on Spencer. Lips skinned back from sharp teeth. The long, disgusting tail was as stiff as wire, strangely curled and kinked.

The sight of the rat alarmed Spencer as he had not been alarmed by the flood lapping at the windowsill. With the breathless, heart-pounding fear familiar from nightmares, he knew he would die if the rat washed into the truck, because it was not merely a rat. It was Death. It was a cry in the night and the hoot of an owl, a flashing blade and the smell of hot blood, it was the catacombs, it was the smell of lime and worse, it was the door out of boyhood innocence, the passageway to Hell, the room at the end of nowhere: It was all that in the cold flesh of one dead rodent. If it touched him, he'd scream until his lungs burst, and his last breath would be darkness.

If only he could find an object with which to reach through the window and shove the thing away without having to touch it directly. But he was too weak to search for anything that could serve as a prod. His hands lay in his lap, palms up, and even contracting his fingers into fists required more strength than he possessed.

Maybe more damage had been done than he had first realized, when the top of his head had hit the ceiling. He wondered if paralysis had begun to creep through him. If so, he wondered if it mattered.

Lightning scarred the sky. A bright reflection transformed the rat's tenebrous eye into a flaring white orb that seemed to swivel in the socket to glare even more directly at Spencer.

He sensed that his fixation on the rat would draw it toward him, that his horrified gaze was a magnet to its iron-black eye. He looked away from it. Ahead. At the river.

Though he was sweating profusely, he was colder than ever. Even his scar was cold, not ablaze any longer. The coldest part of him. His skin was ice, but his scar was frozen steel.

Blinking away the rain as it slanted through the window, Spencer watched the river gain speed, racing toward the only interesting feature in an otherwise tedious landscape of gently declining plains.

North to south across the Mojave, vanishing in mist, a spine of rock jutted as high as twenty or thirty feet in some places, as low as three feet in others. Though it was a natural geological feature, the formation was weathered curiously, with wind-carved windows, and appeared to be the ruined ramparts of an immense fortification erected and destroyed in a warring age a thousand years prior to recorded history. Along some of the highest portions of the expanse were suggestions of crumbling and unevenly crenelated parapets. In places the wall was breached from top to bottom, as though an enemy army had battered into the fortress at those points.

Spencer concentrated on the fantasy of the ancient castle, superimposing it upon the escarpment of stone, to distract himself from the dead rat floating just beyond the broken window at his side.

In his mental confusion, he was not initially concerned that the river was carrying him toward those battlements. Gradually, however, he realized that the approaching encounter might be as devastating to the truck as had been the brutal game of pinball with the bridge. If the currents conveyed the Explorer through one of the sluiceways and along the river, the queer rock formations would be just interesting scenery. But if the truck clipped one of those natural gateposts . . .

The spine of rock traversed the arroyo but was breached in three places by the flow. The widest gap was fifty feet across and lay to the right, framed by the south shore and by a six-foot-wide, twenty-foot-high tower of dark stone that rose from the water. The narrowest passage, not even eight feet wide, lay in the center, between that first tower and another pile of rocks ten feet wide and twelve high. Between *that* pile and the left-hand shore, where the battlements soared again and ran uninterrupted far to the north, lay the third passage, which must have been twenty to thirty feet across.

"Gonna make it." He tried to reach out to the dog. Couldn't.

With a hundred yards to go, the Explorer seemed to be drifting swiftly toward the southernmost and widest gateway.

Spencer wasn't able to stop himself from glancing to the left. Through the missing window. At the rat. Floating. Closer than before. The stiff tail was mottled pink and black.

A memory scuttled through his mind: *rats in a cramped place, hateful red eyes in the shadows, rats in the catacombs, down in the catacombs, and ahead lies the room at the end of nowhere.*

With a quiver of revulsion, he looked forward. The windshield was blurred by rain. Nevertheless, he could see too much. Having closed within fifty yards of the point at which the river divided, the truck no longer sailed toward the widest passage. It angled left, toward the center gate, the most dangerous of the three.

The channel narrowed. The water accelerated.

"Hold on, pal. Hold on."

Spencer hoped to be carried sharply to the left, past the center gate, into the north passage. Twenty yards from the sluiceways, the lateral drift of the truck slowed. It would never reach the north gate. It was going to race through the center.

Fifteen yards. Ten.

Even to transit the center passage, they would need some luck. At the moment, they were rocketing toward the twenty-foot-high gatepost of solid rock on the right of that opening.

Maybe they would just graze the pillar or even slide by with a finger's width to spare.

They were so close that Spencer could no longer see the base of the stone tower past the front of the Explorer. "Please, God."

The bumper rammed the rock as though to cleave it. The impact was so great that Rocky slid onto the floor again. The right front fender tore loose, flew away. The hood buckled as if made of tinfoil. The windshield imploded, but instead of spraying Spencer, tempered glass cascaded over the dashboard in glutinous, prickly wads.

For an instant after the collision, the Explorer was at a dead stop in the water and at an angle to the direction of the flow. Then the raging current caught the side of the truck and began to push the back end around to the left.

Spencer opened his eyes and watched in disbelief as the Explorer turned crosswise to the flow. It could never pass sideways between the two masses of rock and through the center sluiceway. The gap was too narrow; the truck would wedge tight. Then the rampaging river would hammer the passenger side until it flooded the interior or maybe hurled a driftwood log through the open window at his head.

Shuddering, grinding, the front of the Explorer worked along the rock, deeper into the passage, and the back end continued to arc to the left. The river pushed hard on the passenger side, surging halfway up the windows. In turn, as the driver's side of the truck was shoved fully around toward the narrow sluiceway, it created a small swell that rose over the windowsill. The back end slammed into the second gatepost, and water poured inside, onto Spencer, carrying the dead rodent, which had remained in the orbit of the truck.

The rat slipped greasily through his upturned palms and onto the seat between his legs. Its stiff tail trailed across his right hand.

The catacombs. The fiery eyes watching from the shadows. The room, the room, the room at the end of nowhere.

He tried to scream, but what he heard was a choked and broken sobbing, like that of a child terrified beyond endurance.

Possibly half paralyzed from the blow to his head, without a doubt paralyzed by fear, he still managed a spasmodic twitch of both hands, casting the rat off the seat. It splashed into a calf-deep pool of muddy water on the floor. Now it was out of sight. But not gone. Down there. Floating between his legs.

Don't think about that.

He was as dizzy as if he had spent hours on a carousel, and a fun-house darkness was bleeding in at the edges of his vision.

He wasn't sobbing anymore. He repeated the same two words, in a hoarse, agonized voice: "I'm sorry, I'm sorry, I'm sorry. . . ."

In his deepening delirium, he knew that he was not apologizing to the dog or to Valerie Keene, whom he would now never save, but to his mother for not having saved her, either. She had been dead for more than twenty-two years. He had been only eight years old when she'd died, too small to have saved her, too small then to feel such enormous guilt now, yet "I'm sorry" spilled from his lips.

The river industriously shoved the Explorer deeper into the sluiceway, although the truck was now entirely crosswise to the flow. Both front and rear bumpers scraped and rattled along the rock walls. The tortured Ford squealed, groaned, creaked: It was at most one inch shorter from back to front than the width of the water-smoothed gap through which it was struggling to be borne. The river wiggled it, wrenched it, alternately jammed and finessed it, crumpled it at each end to force it forward a foot, an inch, grudgingly forward.

Simultaneously, gradually, the tremendous power of the thwarted currents actually lifted the truck a foot. The dark water surged against the passenger side, no longer halfway up the windows on that flank but swirling at the base of them.

Rocky remained down in the half-flooded leg space, enduring.

When Spencer had quelled his dizziness with sheer willpower, he saw that the spine of rock bisecting the arroyo was not as thick as he had thought. From the entrance to the exit of the sluiceway, that corridor of stone would measure no more than twelve feet.

The jackhammering river pushed the Explorer nine feet into the passage, and then with a *skreek* of tearing metal and an ugly binding sound, the truck wedged tight. If it had made only three more feet, the Explorer would have flowed with the river once more, clear and free. So close.

Now that the truck was held fast, no longer protesting the grip of the rock, the rain was again the loudest sound in the day. It was more thunderous than before, although falling no harder. Maybe it only *seemed* louder because he was sick to death of it.

Rocky had scrambled onto the seat again, out of the water on the floor, dripping and miserable.

"I'm so sorry," Spencer said.

Fending off despair and the insistent darkness that constricted his vision, incapable of meeting the dog's trusting eyes, Spencer turned to the side window, to the river, which so recently he had feared and hated but which he now longed to embrace.

The river wasn't there.

He thought he was hallucinating.

Far away, veiled by furies of rain, a range of desert mountains defined the horizon, and the highest elevations were lost in clouds. No river dwindled from him toward those distant peaks. In fact, nothing whatsoever seemed to lie between the truck and the mountains. The vista was like a painting in which the artist had left the foreground of the canvas entirely blank.

Then, almost dreamily, Spencer realized that he had not seen what was there to see. His perception had been hampered as much by his expectations as by his befuddled senses. The canvas wasn't blank after all. Spencer needed only to alter his point of view, lower his gaze from his own plane, to see the thousand-foot chasm into which the river plunged.

The miles-long spine of weathered rock that he had thought marched across otherwise flat desert terrain was actually the irregular parapet of a perilous cliff. On his side, the sandy plain had eroded, over eons, to a somewhat lower level than the rock. On the other side was not another plain but a sheer face of stone, down which the river fell with a cataclysmic roar.

He had also wrongly assumed that the increased rumble of rain was imaginary. In fact, the greater roar was a trio of waterfalls, altogether more than one hundred feet across, crashing a hundred stories to the valley floor below.

Spencer couldn't see the foaming cataracts, because the Explorer was suspended directly over them. He lacked the strength to pull himself against the door and lean out the window to look. With the flood pushing hard against the passenger side, as well as slipping under it and away, the truck actually hung half *in* the narrowest of the three falls, prevented from being carried over the brink only by the jaws of the rock vise.

He wondered how in God's name he was going to get out of the truck and out of the river alive. Then he rejected all consideration of the challenge. The fearfulness of it sapped what meager energy he still had. He must rest first, think later.

From where Spencer slumped in the driver's seat, though he had no view of the river gone vertical, he could see the broad valley beneath him and the serpentine course of the water as it flowed horizontally again across the lower land. That long drop and the tilted panorama at the bottom caused a new attack of vertigo, and he turned away to avoid passing out.

Too late. The motion of a phantom carousel afflicted him, and the spinning view of rock and rain became a tight spiral of darkness into which he tumbled, around and around and down and away.

. . . and there in the night behind the barn, I'm still spooked by the swooping angel that was only an owl. Inexplicably, when the vision of my mother in celestial robes and wings proves to be a fantasy, I am overcome by another image of her: bloody, crumpled, naked, dead in a ditch, eighty miles from home, as she had been found six years before. I never actually saw her that way, not even in a newspaper photograph, only heard the scene described by a few kids in school, vicious little bastards. Yet, after the owl has vanished into the moonlight, I can't retain the vision of an angel, though I try, and I can't shed the gruesome mental picture of the battered corpse, although both images are products of my imagination and should be subject to my control.

Bare-chested and barefoot, I move farther behind the barn, which hasn't been a real working barn for more than fifteen years. It's a well-known place to me, part of my life since I can remember—yet tonight it seems different from the barn I've always known, changed in some way that I can't define but that makes me uneasy.

It's a strange night, stranger than I yet realize. And I'm a strange boy, full of questions I've never dared to ask myself, seeking answers in that July darkness when the answers are within me, if I would only look for them there. I am a strange boy who feels the warp in the wood of a life gone wrong, but who convinces himself that the warped line is really true and straight. I am a strange boy who keeps secrets from himself—and keeps them as well as the world keeps the secret of its meaning.

In the eerily quiet night, behind the barn, I creep cautiously toward the Chevy van, which I've never seen before. No one is behind the wheel or in the other front seat. When I place my hand on the hood, it's warm with engine heat. The metal is still cooling with faint ticks and pings. I slip past the rainbow mural on the side of the van to the open rear door.

Although the interior of the cargo section is dark, enough pale moonlight filters back from the windshield to reveal that no one is in there, either. I'm also able to see this is only a two-seater, with no apparent amenities, though the customized exterior led me to expect a plush recreational vehicle.

I still sense there's something ominous about the van—other than the simple fact that it doesn't belong here. Seeking a reason for that ominousness, leaning through the open door, squinting, wishing I'd brought a flashlight, I'm hit by the stink of urine. Someone has pissed in the back of the van. Weird. Jesus. Of course, maybe it's only a dog that made the mess, which isn't so weird after all, but it's still disgusting.

Holding my breath, wrinkling my nose, I step back from the door and hunker down to get a closer look at the license plate. It's from Colorado, not out of state.

I stand.

I listen. Silence.

The barn waits.

Like many barns built in snow country, it had been essentially windowless when constructed. Even after the radical conversion of the interior, the only windows are two on the first floor, the south side, and four second-floor panes in this face. Those four above me are tall and wide to capture the north light from dawn to dusk.

The windows are dark. The barn is silent.

The north wall features a single entrance. One man-size door.

After moving around to the far side of the van, finding no one there, either, I'm indecisive for precious seconds.

From a distance of twenty feet, under a moon that seems to conceal as much with its shadows as it reveals with its milky light, I nevertheless can see that the north door is ajar.

On some deep level, perhaps I know what I should do, what I must do. But the part of me that keeps secrets so well is insistent that I return to my bed, forget the cry that woke me from a dream of my mother, and sleep the last of the night away. In the morning, of course, I'll have to continue living in the dream that I've made for myself, a prisoner of this life of self-deception, with truth and reality tucked into a forgotten pocket at the back of my mind. Maybe the burden of that pocket has become too heavy for the fabric to contain it, and maybe the threads of the seams have begun to break. On some deep level, maybe I have decided to end my waking dream.

Or maybe the choice I make is preordained, having less to do with either my subconscious agonies or my conscience than with the track of destiny on which I've traveled since the day I was born. Maybe choice is an illusion, and maybe the only routes we can take in life are those marked on a map at the moment of our conception. I pray to God that destiny isn't a thing of iron, that it can be flexed and reshaped, that it bends to the power of mercy, honesty, kindness, and virtue—because otherwise, I can't tolerate the person I will become, the things I will do, or the end that will be mine.

That hot July night, beaded with sweat but chilled, fourteen in moonlight, I am thinking about none of that: no brooding about hidden secrets or destiny. That night, I'm driven by emotion rather than intellect, by sheer intuition rather than reason, by need rather than curiosity. I'm only fourteen years old, after all. Only fourteen.

The barn waits.

I go to the door, which is ajar.

I listen at the gap between the door and the jamb.

Silence within.

I push the door inward. The hinges are well oiled, my feet are bare, and I enter with a silence as perfect as that of the darkness that welcomes me. . . .

Spencer opened his eyes from the dark interior of the barn in the dream to the dark interior of the rock-pinned Explorer, and he realized that night had come to the desert. He had been unconscious for at least five or six hours.

His head was tipped forward, his chin on his chest. He gazed down into his own up-turned palms, chalk white and supplicant.

The rat was on the floor. Couldn't see it. But it was there. In the darkness. Floating. *Don't think about that.*

The rain had stopped. No drumming on the roof.

He was thirsty. Parched. Raspy tongue. Chapped lips.

The truck rocked slightly. The river was trying to push it over the cliff. The tireless damned river.

No. That couldn't be the explanation. The roar of the waterfall was gone. The night was silent. No thunder. No lightning. No water sounds out there anymore.

He ached all over. His head and neck were the worst.

He could barely find the strength to look up from his hands.

Rocky was gone.

The passenger door hung open.

The truck rocked again. Rattled and creaked.

The woman appeared at the bottom of the open door. First her head, then her shoulders, as if she were levitating up out of the flood. Except, judging by the comparative quiet, the flood was gone.

Because his eyes were adapted to darkness and cool moonlight shone between ragged clouds, Spencer was able to recognize her.

In a voice as dry as cinders, but without a slur, he said, "Hi."

"Hi, yourself," she said.

"Come in."

"Thank you, I think I will."

"This is nice," he said.

"You like it here?"

"Better than the other dream."

She levered herself into the truck, and it wobbled more than before, grinding against rock at both ends.

The motion disturbed him—not because he was concerned that the truck would shift and break loose and fall, but because it stirred up his vertigo again. He was afraid of spiraling out of this dream, back into the nightmare of July and Colorado.

Sitting where Rocky had once sat, she remained still for a moment, waiting for the truck to stop moving. "This is one tricky damned situation you've gotten into."

"Ball lightning," he said.

"Excuse me?"

"Ball lightning."

"Of course."

"Knocked the truck into the arroyo."

"Why not," she said.

It was so hard to think, to express himself clearly. Thinking hurt. Thinking made him dizzy.

"Thought it was aliens," he explained.

"Aliens?"

"Little guys. Big eyes. Spielberg."

"Why would you think it was aliens?"

"Because you're wonderful," he said, though the words didn't convey what he meant. In spite of the poor light, he could see that the look she gave him was peculiar. Straining to find better words, made dizzier by the effort, he said, "Wonderful things must happen around you . . . happen around you all the time."

"Oh, yeah, I'm the center of a regular *festival*."

"You must know some wonderful thing. That's why they're after you. Because you know some wonderful thing."

"You been taking drugs?"

"I could use a couple aspirin. Anyway . . . they're not after you because you're a bad person."

"Aren't they?"

"No. Because you're not. A bad person, I mean."

She leaned toward him and put a hand against his forehead. Even her light touch made him wince with pain.

"How do you know I'm not a bad person?" she asked.

"You were nice to me."

"Maybe it was an act."

She produced a penlight from her jacket, peeled back his left eyelid, directed the beam at his eye. The light hurt. Everything hurt. The cool air hurt his face. Pain accelerated his vertigo.

"You were nice to Theda."

"Maybe that was an act too," she said, now examining his right eye with the penlight.

"Can't fool Theda."

"Why not?"

"She's wise."

"Well, that's true."

"And she makes *huge* cookies."

Finished examining his eyes, she tipped his head forward to have a look at the gash in the top of his skull. "Nasty. Coagulated now, but it needs cleaned and stitched."

"Ouch!"

"How long were you bleeding?"

"Dreams don't hurt."

"Do you think you lost a lot of blood?"

"This hurts."

" 'Cause you're not dreaming."

He licked his chapped lips. His tongue was dry. "Thirsty."

"I'll get you a drink in just a minute," she said, putting two fingers under his chin and tipping his head up again.

All this head tipping was making him dangerously dizzy, but he managed to say, "Not dreaming? You're sure?"

"Positive." She touched his upturned right palm. "Can you squeeze my hand?"

"Yes."

"Go ahead."

"All right."

"I mean now."

"Oh." He closed his hand around hers.

"That's not bad," she said.

"It's nice."

"A good grip. Probably no spinal damage. I expected the worst."

She had a warm, strong hand. He said, "Nice."

He closed his eyes. An inner darkness leaped at him.He opened his eyes at once, before he could fall back into the dream.

"You can let go of my hand now," she said.

"Not a dream, huh?"

"No dream."

She clicked on the penlight again and directed it down between his seat and the center console.

"This is really strange," he said.

She was peering along the narrow shaft of light.

"Not dreaming," he said, "must be hallucinating."

She popped the release button that disengaged the buckle on his safety harness from the latch between his seat and the console.

"It's okay," he said.

"What's okay?" she asked, switching off the light and returning it to her jacket pocket.

"That you peed on the seat."

She laughed.

"I like to hear you laugh."

She was still laughing as she carefully extricated him from the harness.

"You've never laughed before," he said.

"Well," she said, "not much recently."

"Not ever before. You've never barked either."

She laughed again.

"I'm going to get you a new rawhide bone."

"You're very kind."

He said, "This is damned interesting."

"That's for sure."

"It's so real."

"Seems *un*real to me."

Even though Spencer remained mostly passive through the process, getting out of the harness left him so dizzy that he saw three of the woman and three of every shadow in the car, like superimposed images on a photograph.

Afraid that he would pass out before he had a chance to express himself, he spoke in a raspy rush of words: "You're a real friend, pal, you really are, you're a perfect friend."

"We'll see if that's how it turns out."

"You're the only friend I have."

"Okay, my friend, now we've come to the hard part. How the hell am I going to get you out of this junker when you can't help yourself at all?"

"I can help myself."

"You think you can?"

"I was an Army Ranger once. And a cop."

"Yes, I know."

"I've been trained in tae kwon do."

"That would really be handy if we were under assault by a bunch of ninja assassins. But can you help me get you out of here?"

"A little."

"I guess we've got to give it a try."

"Okay."

"Can you lift your legs out of there, swing them to me?"

"Don't want to disturb the rat."

"There's a rat?"

"He's dead already but . . . you know."

"Of course."

"I'm very dizzy."

"Then let's wait a minute, rest a minute."

"Very, very dizzy."

"Just take it easy."

"Goodbye," he said, and surrendered to a black vortex that spun him around and away. For some reason, as he went, he thought of Dorothy and Toto and Oz.

The back door of the barn opens into a short hallway. I step inside. No lights. No windows. The green glow from the security-system readout—NOT READY TO ARM—in the right-hand wall provides just enough light for me to see that I am alone in the corridor. I don't ease the door all the way shut behind me but leave it ajar, as I found it.

The floor appears to be black beneath me, but I'm on polished pine. To the left are a bathroom and a room where art supplies are stored. Those doorways are barely discernible in the faint green wash, which is like the unearthly illumination in a dream, less like real light than like a lingering memory of neon. To the right is a file room. Ahead, at the end of the hallway, is the door to the large first-floor gallery, where a switchback staircase leads to my father's studio. That upper chamber occupies the entire second floor and features the big north-facing windows under which the van is parked outside.

I listen to the hallway darkness.

It doesn't speak or breathe.

The light switch is to the right, but I leave it untouched.

In the green-black gloom, I ease the bathroom door all the way open. Step inside. Wait for a sound, a sense of movement, a blow. Nothing.

The supply room is also deserted.

I move to the right side of the hall and quietly open the door to the file room. I step across the threshold.

The overhead fluorescent tubes are dark, but there is other light where no light should be. Yellow and sour. Dim and strange. From a mysterious source at the far end of the room.

A long worktable occupies the center of that rectangular space. Two chairs. File cabinets stand against one of the long walls.

My heart is knocking so hard it shakes my arms. I make fists of my hands and hold them at my sides, struggling to control myself.

I decide to return to the house, to bed, to sleep.

Then I'm at the far end of the file room, though I don't recall having taken a single step in that direction. I seem to have walked those twenty feet in a sudden spell of sleep. Called forward by something, someone. As if responding to a powerful hypnotic command. To a wordless, silent summons.

I am standing in front of a knotty-pine cabinet that extends from floor to ceiling and from corner to corner of the thirteen-foot-wide room. The cabinet features three pairs of tall, narrow doors.

The center pair stand open.

Behind those doors, there should be nothing but shelves. On the shelves should be boxes of old tax records, correspondence, and dead files no longer kept in the metal cabinets along the other wall.

This night, the shelves and their contents, along with the back wall of the pine cabinet, have been pushed backward four or five feet into a secret space behind the file room, into a hidden chamber I've never seen before. The sour yellow light comes from a place beyond the closet.

Before me is the essence of all boyish fantasies: the secret passage to a world of danger and adventure, to far stars, to stars farther still, to the very center of the earth, to lands of trolls or pirates or intelligent apes or robots, to the distant future or to the age of dinosaurs. Here is a stairway to mystery, a tunnel through which I might set out upon heroic quests, or a way station on a strange highway to dimensions unknown.

Briefly, I thrill to the thought of what exotic travels and magical discoveries might lay ahead. But instinct quickly tells me that on the far side of this secret passage, there is something stranger and deadlier than an alien world or a Morlock dungeon. I want to return to the house, to my bedroom, to the protection of my sheets, immediately, as fast as I can run. The perverse allure of terror and the unknown deserts me, and I'm suddenly eager to leave this waking dream for the less threatening lands to be found on the dark side of sleep.

Although I can't recall crossing the threshold, I find myself inside the tall cabinet instead of hurrying to the house, through the night, the moonlight, and the owl shadows. I blink, and then I find that I've gone farther still, not back one step but forward into the secret space beyond.

It's a vestibule of sorts, six feet by six feet. Concrete floor. Concrete-block walls. Bare yellow bulb in a ceiling socket.

A cursory investigation reveals that the back wall of the pine cabinet, complete with the attached and laden shelves, is fitted with small concealed wheels. It's been shoved inward on a pair of sliding-door tracks.

To the right is a door out of the vestibule. An ordinary door in many ways. Heavy, judging by the look of it. Solid wood. Brass hardware. It's painted white, and in places the paint is yellowed with age. However, though it's more white and grimy yellow than it is anything else, tonight this is neither a white nor a yellow door. A series of bloody handprints arcs from the area around the brass knob across the upper portion of the door, and their bright patterns render the color of the background unimportant. Eight, ten, twelve, or more impressions of a woman's hands. Palms and spread fingers. Each hand partially overlapping the one before it. Some smeared, some as clear as police-file prints. All glistening, wet. All fresh. Those scarlet images bring to mind the spread wings of a bird leaping into flight, fleeing to the sky, in a flutter of fear. Staring at them, I am mesmerized, unable to get my breath, my heart storming, because the handprints convey an unbearable sense of the woman's terror, desperation, and frantic resistance to the prospect of being forced beyond the gray concrete vestibule of this secret world.

I can't go forward. Can't. Won't. I'm just a boy, barefoot, unarmed, afraid, not ready for the truth.

I don't remember moving my right hand, but now it's on the brass knob. I open the red door.

PART TWO

TO THE SOURCE OF THE FLOW

▼

On the road that I have taken,
one day, walking, I awaken,
amazed to see where I have come,
where I'm going, where I'm from.

This is not the path I thought.
This is not the place I sought.
This is not the dream I bought,
just a fever of fate I've caught.

I'll change highways in a while,
at the crossroads, one more mile.
My path is lit by my own fire.
I'm going only where I desire.

On the road that I have taken,
one day, walking, I awaken.
One day, walking, I awaken,
on the road that I have taken.
—*The Book of Counted Sorrows*

ELEVEN

Friday afternoon, after discussing Spencer Grant's scar with Dr. Mondello, Roy Miro left Los Angeles International aboard an agency Learjet, with a glass of properly chilled Robert Mondavi chardonnay in one hand and a bowl of shelled pistachios in his lap. He was the only passenger, and he expected to be in Las Vegas in an hour.

A few minutes short of his destination, his flight was diverted to Flagstaff, Arizona. Flash floods, spawned by the worst storm to batter Nevada in a decade, had inundated lower areas of Las Vegas. Also, lightning had damaged vital electronic systems at the airport, McCarran International, forcing a suspension of service.

By the time the jet was on the ground in Flagstaff, the official word was that McCarran would resume operations in two hours or less. Roy remained aboard, so he would not waste precious minutes returning from the terminal when the pilot learned that McCarran was up and running again.

He passed the time, at first, by linking to Mama in Virginia and using her extensive data-bank connections to teach a lesson to Captain Harris Descoteaux, the Los Angeles police officer who had irritated him earlier in the day. Descoteaux had too little respect for higher authority. Soon, however, in addition to a Caribbean lilt, his voice would have a new note of humility.

Later, Roy watched a PBS documentary on one of three television sets that served the passenger compartment of the Lear. The program was about Dr. Jack Kevorkian—dubbed Dr. Death by the media—who had made it his mission in life to assist the terminally ill when they expressed a desire to commit suicide, though he was persecuted by the law for doing so.

Roy was enthralled by the documentary. More than once, he was moved to tears. By the middle of the program, he was compelled to lean forward from his chair and place one hand flat on the screen each time Jack Kevorkian appeared in closeup. With his palm against the blessed image of the doctor's face, Roy could *feel* the purity of the man, a saintly aura, a thrill of spiritual power.

In a fair world, in a society based on true justice, Kevorkian would have been left to do his work in peace. Roy was depressed to hear about the man's suffering at the hands of regressive forces.

He took solace, however, from the knowledge that the day was swiftly approaching when a man like Kevorkian would never again be treated as a pariah. He would be embraced by a grateful nation and provided with an office, facilities, and salary commensurate with his contribution to a better world.

The world was so full of suffering and injustice that *anyone* who wanted to be assisted in suicide, terminally ill or not, should have that assistance. Roy passionately believed that even those who were chronically but not terminally ill, including many of the elderly, should be granted eternal rest if they wished to have it.

Those who didn't see the wisdom of self-elimination should not be abandoned, either. They should be given free counseling, until they could perceive the immeasurable beauty of the gift that they were being offered.

Hand on the screen. Kevorkian in closeup. *Feel* the power.

The day would come when the disabled would suffer no more pain or indignities. No more wheelchairs or leg braces. No more Seeing Eye dogs. No more hearing aids, prosthetic limbs, no more grueling sessions with speech therapists. Only the peace of endless sleep.

Dr. Jack Kevorkian's face filled the screen. Smiling. Oh, that smile.

Roy put *both* hands to the warm glass. He opened his heart and permitted that fabulous smile to flow into him. He unchained his soul and allowed Kevorkian's spiritual power to lift him up.

Eventually the science of genetic engineering would ensure that none but healthy children were born, and eventually they would all be beautiful, as well as strong and sound. They would be *perfect*. Until that day came, however, Roy saw a need for an assisted-suicide program for infants born with less than the full use of their five senses and all four limbs. He was even ahead of Kevorkian on this.

In fact, when his hard work with the agency was done, when the country had the compassionate government that it deserved and was on the threshold of Utopia, he would like to spend the rest of his life serving in a suicide-assistance program for infants. He could not imagine anything more rewarding than holding a defective baby in his arms while a lethal injection was administered, comforting the child as it passed from imperfect flesh to a transcendent spiritual plane.

His heart swelled with love for those less fortunate than he. The halt and blind. The maimed and the ill and the elderly and the depressed and the learning impaired.

After two hours on the ground in Flagstaff, by the time McCarran reopened and the Learjet departed for a second try at Las Vegas, the documentary had ended. Kevorkian's smile was no longer to be seen. Nevertheless, Roy remained in a state of rapture that he was sure would last for at least several days.

The power was now in him. He would experience no more failure, no more setbacks.

In flight, he received a telephone call from the agent seeking Ethel and George Porth, the grandparents who had raised Spencer Grant after the death of his mother. According to county property records, the Porths had once owned the house at the San Francisco address in Grant's military records, but they had sold it ten years ago. The buyers had resold it seven years thereafter, and the new owners, in residence just three years, had never heard of the Porths and had no clue as to their whereabouts. The agent was continuing the search.

Roy had every confidence that they would find the Porths. The tide had turned in their favor. *Feel* the power.

By the time the Learjet landed in Las Vegas, night had fallen. Although the sky was overcast, the rain had stopped.

Roy was met at the debarkation gate by a driver who looked like a Spam loaf in a suit. He said only that his name was Prock and that the car was in front of the terminal. Glowering, he stalked away, expecting to be followed, clearly uninterested in small talk, as rude as the most arrogant maître d' in New York City.

Roy decided to be amused rather than insulted.

The nondescript Chevrolet was parked illegally in the loading zone. Although Prock seemed bigger than the car that he was driving, somehow he fit inside.

The air was chilly, but Roy found it invigorating.

Because Prock kept the heater turned up high, the interior of the Chevy was stuffy, but Roy chose to think of it as cozy.

He was in a brilliant mood.

They went downtown with illegal haste.

Though Prock stayed on secondary streets and kept away from the busy hotels and casinos, the glare of those neon-lined avenues was reflected on the bellies of the low clouds. The red-orange-green-yellow sky might have seemed like a vision of Hell to a gambler who had just lost next week's grocery money, but Roy found it festive.

After delivering Roy to the agency's downtown headquarters, Prock drove off to deliver his baggage to the hotel for him.

On the fifth floor of the high rise, Bobby Dubois was waiting. Dubois, the evening duty officer, was a tall, lanky Texan with mud-brown eyes and hair the color of range dust, on whom clothes hung like thrift-shop castaways on a stick-and-straw scarecrow. Although big-boned, rough-hewn, with a mottled complexion, with jug-handle ears, with teeth as crooked as the tombstones in a cow-town cemetery, with not a single feature that even the kindest critic could deem perfect, Dubois had a good-old-boy charm and an easy manner that distracted attention from the fact he was a biological tragedy.

Sometimes Roy was surprised that he could be around Dubois for long periods, yet resist the urge to commit a mercy killing.

"That boy, he's some cute sonofabitch, the way he drove out of that roadblock and into the amusement park," Dubois said as he led Roy down the hall from his office to the satellite-surveillance room. "And that dog of his, just bobbin' its head up and down, up and down, like one of them spring-necked novelties that people put on the rear-window shelves in their cars. That dog, he got palsy or what?"

"I don't know," Roy said.

"My granpap, he once had a dog with palsy. Name was Scooter, but we called him Boomer 'cause he could cut the godawfulest loud farts. I'm talkin' about the dog, you understand, not my granpap."

"Of course," Roy said as they reached the door at the end of the hall.

"Boomer got palsied his last year," Dubois said, hesitating with his hand on the door-knob. " 'Course he was older than dirt by then, so it wasn't any surprise. You should've seen that poor hound shake. Palsied up somethin' fierce. Let me tell you, Roy, when old Boomer lifted a hind leg and let go with his stream, all palsied like he was—you dived for cover or wished you was in another county."

"Sounds like someone should have put him to sleep," Roy said as Dubois opened the door.

The Texan followed Roy into the satellite-surveillance center. "Nah, Boomer was a good old dog. If the tables had been turned, that old hound wouldn't never have taken a gun and put granpap to sleep."

Roy really *was* in a good mood. He could have listened to Bobby Dubois for hours.

The satellite-surveillance center was forty feet by sixty feet. Only two of the twelve computer workstations in the middle of the room were manned, both by women wearing headsets and murmuring into mouthpieces as they studied the data streaming across their VDTs. A third technician was working at a light table, examining several large photographic negatives through a magnifying glass.

One of the two longer walls was largely occupied by an immense screen on which was projected a map of the world. Cloud formations were superimposed on it, along with green lettering that indicated weather conditions planetwide.

Red, blue, white, yellow, and green lights blinked steadily, revealing the current positions of scores of satellites. Many were electronic-communications packages handling microwave relays of telephone, television, and radio signals. Others were engaged in topographical mapping, oil exploration, meteorology, astronomy, international espionage, and domestic surveillance, among numerous other tasks.

The owners of those satellites ranged from public corporations to government agencies and military services. Some were the property of nations other than the United States or of businesses based beyond U.S. shores. Regardless of the ownership or origin, however, every satellite on that wall display could be accessed and used by the agency, and the legitimate operators usually remained unaware that their systems had been invaded.

At a U-shaped control console in front of the huge screen, Bobby Dubois said, "The sonofabitch rode straight out of Spaceport Vegas off into the desert, and our boys weren't equipped to chase around playin' Lawrence of Arabia."

"Did you put up a chopper to track him?"

"Weather turned bad too fast. A real toad-drowner, rain comin' down like every angel in Heaven was takin' a leak at the same time."

Dubois pushed a button on the console, and the map of the world faded from the wall. An actual satellite view of Oregon, Idaho, California, and Nevada appeared in its place. Seen from orbit, the boundaries of those four states would have been difficult to define, so borders were overlaid in orange lines.

Western and southern Oregon, southern Idaho, northern through central California, and all of Nevada were concealed below a dense layer of clouds.

"This here's a direct satellite feed. There's just a three-minute delay for transmission and then conversion of the digital code back into images again," said Dubois.

Along eastern Nevada and eastern Idaho, soft pulses of light rippled through the clouds. Roy knew that he was seeing lightning from above the storm. It was strangely beautiful.

"Right now, the only storm activity is out on the eastern edge of the front. 'Cept for an isolated patch of spit-thin rain here and there, things are pretty quiet all the way back to the ass-end of Oregon. But we can't just do a look-down for the sonofabitch, not even with infrared. It'd be like trying to see the bottom of a soup bowl through clam chowder."

"How long until clear skies?" Roy asked.

"There's a kick-ass wind at higher altitudes, pushing the front east-southeast, so we should have a clear look at the whole Mojave and surrounding territory before dawn."

A surveillance subject, sitting in bright sunshine and reading a newspaper, could be filmed from a satellite with sufficiently high resolution that the headlines on his paper would be legible. However, in clear weather, in an unpopulated wasteland that boasted no animals as large as a man, locating and identifying a moving object as large as a Ford Explorer would not be easy, because the territory to be examined was so vast. Nevertheless, it could be done.

Roy said, "He could leave the desert for one highway or another, put the pedal to the metal, and be long gone by morning."

"Damn few paved roads in this part of the state. We got lookout teams in every direction, on every serious highway and sorry strip of blacktop. Interstate Fifteen, Federal Highway Ninety-five, Federal Highway Ninety-three. Plus State Routes One-forty-six, One-fifty-six, One-fifty-eight, One-sixty, One-sixty-eight, and One-sixty-nine. Lookin' for a green Ford Explorer with some body damage fore and aft. Lookin' for a man with a dog in *any* vehicle. Lookin' for a man with a big facial scar. Hell, we got this whole part of the state locked down tighter than a mosquito's butt."

"Unless he already got off the desert and back onto a highway before you put your men in place."

"We moved quick. Anyway, in a storm as bad as that one, goin' overland, he made piss-poor time. Fact is, he's damn lucky if he didn't bog down somewhere, four-wheel drive or no four-wheel drive. We'll nail the sonofabitch tomorrow."

"I hope you're right," Roy said.

"I'd bet my pecker on it."

"And they say Las Vegas locals aren't big gamblers."

"How's he tied up with the woman anyway?"

"I wish I knew," Roy said, watching as lightning flowered softly under the clouds on the leading edge of the storm front. "What about this tape of the conversation between Grant and the old woman?"

"You want to hear that?"

"Yes."

"It starts from when he first says the name Hannah Rainey."

"Let's give it a listen," Roy said, turning away from the wall display.

All the way down the hall, into the elevator, and down to the deepest subterranean level of the building, Dubois talked about the best places to get good chili in Vegas, as though he had reason to believe that Roy cared. "There's this joint on Paradise Road, the chili's so hot some folks been known to spontaneously combust from eatin' it, *whoosh,* they just go up like torches."

The elevator reached the subbasement.

"We're talkin' chili that makes you sweat from your fingernails, makes your belly button pop out like a meat thermometer."

The doors slid open.

Roy stepped into a windowless concrete room.

Along the far wall were scores of recording machines.

In the middle of the room, rising from a computer workstation, was the most stunningly gorgeous woman Roy had ever seen, blond and green-eyed, so beautiful that she took his breath away, so beautiful that she set his heart to racing and sent his blood pressure soaring high into the stroke-risk zone, so achingly beautiful that no words could adequately describe her—nor could any music ever written be sweet enough to celebrate her—so beautiful and so incomparable that he couldn't breathe or speak, so radiant that she blinded him to the dreariness of that bunker and left him surrounded by her magnificent light.

The flood had disappeared over the cliff like bathwater down a tub drain. The arroyo was now merely an enormous ditch.

To a considerable depth, the soil was mostly sand, extremely porous, so the rain had not puddled on it. The downpour had filtered quickly into a deep aquifer. The surface had dried out and firmed up almost as rapidly as the empty channel had previously turned into a racing, spumous river.

Nevertheless, before she had risked taking the Range Rover into the channel, although the machine was as surefooted as a tank, she had walked the route from the eroded arroyo wall to the Explorer and checked the condition of the ground. Satisfied that the bed of the ghost river wasn't muddy or soft and that it would provide sufficient traction, she had driven the Rover into that declivity and had backed between the two columns of rock to the suspended Explorer.

Even now, after rescuing the dog and putting him in the back of the Rover, and after disentangling Grant from his safety harness, she was amazed by the precarious position in which the Explorer had come to rest. She was tempted to lean past the unconscious man and look through the gaping hole where the side window had been, but even if she could have seen much in the darkness, she knew that she wouldn't enjoy the view.

The flood tide had lifted the truck more than ten feet above the floor of the arroyo before wedging it in that pincer of stone, on the brink of the cliff. Now that the river had vanished beneath it, the Explorer hung up there, its four wheels in midair, as though gripped in a pair of tweezers that belonged to a giant.

When she'd first seen it, she'd stood in childlike wonder, mouth open and eyes wide. She was no less astonished than she would have been if she'd seen a flying saucer and its unearthly crew.

She'd been certain that Grant had been swept out of the truck and carried to his death. Or that he was dead inside.

To get up to his truck, she'd had to back her Rover under it, putting the rear wheels uncomfortably close to the edge of the cliff. Then she had stood on the roof, which brought her head just to the bottom of the Explorer's front passenger door. She had reached up to the handle and, in spite of the awkward angle, had managed to open the door.

Water poured out, but the dog was what startled her. Whimpering and miserable, huddled on the passenger seat, he had peered down at her with a mixture of alarm and yearning.

She didn't want him jumping onto the Rover. He might slip on that smooth surface and fracture a leg, or tumble and break his neck.

Although the pooch hadn't looked as if he would perform any canine stunts, she had warned him to stay where he was. She climbed down from the Rover, drove it forward five yards, turned it around to direct the headlights on the ground under the Explorer, got out again, and coaxed the dog to jump to the sandy riverbed.

He needed a *lot* of coaxing. Poised on the edge of the seat, he repeatedly built up the courage to jump. But each time, he turned his head away at the last moment and shrank back, as if he were facing a chasm instead of a ten- or twelve-foot drop.

Finally, she remembered how Theda Davidowitz had often talked to Sparkle, and she tried the same approach with this dog: "Come on, sweetums, come to mama, come on. Little sweetums, little pretty-eyed snookie-wookums."

In the truck above, the pooch pricked one ear and regarded her with acute interest.

"Come here, come on, snookums, little sweetums."

He began to quiver with excitement.

"Come to mama. Come on, little pretty eyes."

The dog crouched on the seat, muscles tensed, poised to leap.

"Come give mama a kissie, little cutie, little cutie baby."

She felt idiotic, but the dog jumped. He sprang out of the open door of the Explorer, sailed in a long graceful arc through the night air, and landed on all fours.

He was so startled by his own agility and bravery that he turned to look up at the truck and then sat down as if in shock. He flopped onto his side, breathing hard.

She had to carry him to the Rover and lay him in the cargo area directly behind the front seat. He repeatedly rolled his eyes at her, and he licked her hand once.

"You're a strange one," she said, and the dog sighed.

Then she had turned the Rover around again, backed it under the suspended Explorer, and climbed up to find Spencer Grant slumped behind the steering wheel, woozily conscious.

Now he was out cold again. He was murmuring to someone in a dream, and she wondered how she would get him out of the Explorer if he didn't revive soon.

She tried talking to him and shaking him gently, but she wasn't able to get a response from him. He was already damp and shivering, so there was no point in scooping a handful of water off the floor and splashing his face.

His injuries needed to be treated as soon as possible, but that was not the primary reason that she was anxious to get him into the Rover and away from there. Dangerous people were searching for him. With their resources, even hampered by weather and terrain, they would find him if she didn't quickly move him to a secure place.

Grant solved her dilemma not merely by regaining consciousness but by virtually *exploding* out of his unnatural sleep. With a gasp and a wordless cry, he bolted upright in his seat, bathed in a sudden sweat yet shuddering so furiously that his teeth chattered.

He was face-to-face with her, inches away, and even in the poor light, she saw the horror in his eyes. Worse, there was a bleakness that transmitted his chill deep into her own heart.

He spoke urgently, though exhaustion and thirst had reduced his voice to a coarse whisper: "*Nobody knows.*"

"It's all right," she said.

"*Nobody. Nobody knows.*"

"Easy. You'll be okay."

"*Nobody knows,*" he insisted, and he seemed to be caught between fear and grief, between terror and tears.

A terrible hopelessness informed his tortured voice and every aspect of his face to such an extent that she was struck speechless. It seemed foolish to continue to repeat meaningless reassurances to a man who appeared to have been granted a vision of the cankerous souls in Hades.

Though he looked into her eyes, Spencer seemed to be gazing at someone or something far away, and he was speaking in a rush of words, more to himself than to her: "*It's a chain, iron chain, it runs through me, through my brain, my heart, through my guts, a chain, no way to get loose, no escape."*

He was scaring her. She hadn't thought that she could be scared anymore, at least not easily, certainly not with mere words. But he was scaring her witless.

"Come on, Spencer," she said. "Let's go. Okay? Help me get you out of here."

When the slightly chubby, twinkly-eyed man stepped out of the elevator with Bobby Dubois into the windowless subbasement, he halted in his tracks and gazed at Eve as a starving man might have stared at a bowl of peaches and cream.

Eve Jammer was accustomed to having a powerful effect on men. When she had been a topless showgirl on the Las Vegas stage, she had been one beauty among many—yet the eyes of all the men had followed her nearly to the exclusion of the other women, as though something about her face and body was not just more appealing to the eye but so harmonious that it was like a secret siren's song. She drew men's eyes to herself as inevitably as a skillful hypnotist could capture a subject's mind by swinging a gold medallion on a chain or simply with the sinuous movements of his hands.

Even poor little Thurmon Stookey—the dentist who'd had the bad luck to be in the same hotel elevator with the two gorillas from whom Eve had taken the million in cash—had been vulnerable to her charms at a time when he should have been too terrified to entertain the slightest thought of sex. With the two goons dead on the elevator floor and the Korth .38 pointed at his face, Stookey had let his eyes drift from the bore of the revolver to the lush cleavage revealed by Eve's low-cut sweater. Judging by the glimmer that had come into his myopic eyes just as she'd squeezed the trigger, Eve figured that the dentist's final thought had not been *God help me* but *What a set.*

No man had ever affected Eve to even a small fraction of the extent to which she affected most men. Indeed, she could take or leave most men. Her interest was drawn only to those from whom she might extract money or from whom she might learn the tricks of obtaining and holding on to power. Her ultimate goal was to be extremely rich and feared, not loved. Being an object of fear, totally in control, having the power of life and death over others: *That* was infinitely more erotic than *any* man's body or lovemaking skills could ever be.

Still, when she was introduced to Roy Miro, she felt something unusual. A flutter of the heart. A mild disorientation that was not in the least unpleasant.

What she was feeling couldn't have been called desire. Eve's desires were all exhaustively mapped and labeled, and the periodic satisfaction of each was achieved with mathematical calculation, to a schedule as precise as that kept by a fascist train conductor. She had no time or patience for spontaneity in either business or personal affairs; the intrusion of unplanned passion would have been as repulsive to her as being forced to eat worms.

Undeniably, however, she felt *something* from the first moment she saw Roy Miro. And minute by minute, as they discussed the Grant-Davidowitz tape and then listened to it, her peculiar interest in him increased. An unfamiliar thrill of anticipation coursed through her as she wondered where events were leading.

For the life of her, she couldn't figure out what qualities of the man inspired her fascination. He was rather pleasant looking, with merry blue eyes, a choirboy face, and a sweet smile—but he was not handsome in the usual sense of the word. He was fifteen pounds overweight, somewhat pale, and he didn't appear to be rich. He dressed with less flair than any Nazarene passing out religious publications door-to-door.

Frequently Miro asked her to replay a passage of the Grant-Davidowitz recording, as though it contained a clue that required pondering, but she knew that he had become preoccupied with her and had missed something.

For both Eve and Miro, Bobby Dubois pretty much ceased to exist. In spite of his height and physical awkwardness, in spite of his colorful and ceaseless chatter, Dubois was of no more interest to either of them than were the bunker's plain concrete walls.

When everything on the recording had been played and replayed, Miro went through some shuffle and jive to the effect that he was unable to do anything about Grant for the time being, except wait: wait for him to surface; wait for the skies to clear so a satellite search could begin; wait for search teams already in the field to turn up something; wait for agents investigating other aspects of the case, in other cities, to get back to him. Then he asked Eve if she was free for dinner.

She accepted the invitation with an uncharacteristic lack of coyness. She had a growing sense that what she responded to in the man was some secret power that he possessed, a strength that was mostly hidden and that could be glimpsed only in the self-confidence of his easy smile and in those blue-blue eyes that never revealed anything but amusement, as if this man expected always to have the last laugh.

Although Miro had been assigned a car from the agency pool while he was in Vegas, he rode in her own Honda to a favorite restaurant of hers on Flamingo Road. Reflections of a sea of neon rolled in tidal patterns across low clouds, and the night seemed filled with magic.

She expected to get to know him better over dinner and a couple of glasses of wine— and to understand, by dessert, why he fascinated her. However, his skills as a conversationalist were equivalent to his looks: pleasant enough, but far from beguiling. Nothing that Miro said, nothing that he did, no gesture, no look brought Eve any closer to understanding the curious attraction that he held for her.

By the time they left the restaurant and crossed the parking lot toward her car, she was frustrated and confused. She didn't know whether she should invite him back to her place or not. She didn't want sex with him. It wasn't that kind of attraction, exactly. Of course, some men revealed their truest selves when they had sex: by what they liked to do, by how they did it, by what they said and how they acted both during and after. But she didn't want to take him home, do it with him, get all sweaty, go the whole disgusting route, and *still* not understand what it was about him that so intrigued her.

She was in a dilemma.

Then, as they drew near to her car, with the cold wind soughing in a nearby row of palm trees and the air scented with the aroma of charcoal-broiled steaks from the restaurant, Roy Miro did the most unexpected and outrageous thing that Eve had ever seen in thirty-three years of outrageous experience.

An immeasurable time after getting down from the Explorer and into the Range Rover— which could have been an hour or two minutes or thirty days and thirty nights, for all he knew—Spencer woke and saw a herd of tumbleweed pacing them. The shadows of mesquite and paddle-leaf cactus leaped through the headlights.

He rolled his head to the left, against the back of the seat, and saw Valerie behind the wheel. "Hi."

"Hi, there."

"How'd you get here?"

"That's too complicated for you right now."

"I'm a complicated guy."

"I don't doubt it."

"Where we going?"

"Away."

"Good."

"How're you feeling?"

"Woozy."

"Don't pee on the seat," she said with obvious amusement.

He said, "I'll try not to."

"Good."

"Where's my dog?"

"Who do you think's licking your ear?"

"Oh."

"He's right there behind you."

"Hi, pal."

"What's his name," she asked.

"Rocky."

"You've got to be kidding."

"About what?"

"The name. Doesn't fit."

"I named him that so he'd have more confidence."

"Isn't working," she said.

Strange rock formations loomed, like temples to gods forgotten before human beings had been capable of conceiving the idea of time and counting the passage of days. They awed him, and she drove among them with great expertise, whipping left and right, down a long hill, onto a vast, dark flatness.

"Never knew his real name," Spencer said.

"Real name?"

"Puppy name. Before the pound."

"Wasn't Rocky."

"Probably not."

"What was it before Spencer?"

"He was never named Spencer."

"So you're clearheaded enough to be evasive."

"Not really. Just habit. What's your name?"

"Valerie Keene."

"Liar."

He went away for a while. When he came around again, there was still desert: sand and stone, scrub and tumbleweed, darkness pierced by headlights.

"Valerie," he said.

"Yeah?"

"What's your real name?"

"Bess."

"Bess what?"

"Bess Baer."

"Spell it."

"B-A-E-R."

"Really?"

"Really. For now."

"What's that mean?"

"It means what it means."

"It means that's your name now, after Valerie."

"So?"

"What was your name before Valerie?"

"Hannah Rainey."

"Oh, yeah," he said, realizing that he was firing on only four of six cylinders. "Before that?"

"Gina Delucio."

"Was that real?"

"It felt real."

"Is that the name you were born with?"

"You mean my puppy name?"

"Yeah. That your puppy name?"

"Nobody's called me by my puppy name since before I was in the pound," she said.

"You're very funny."

"You like funny women?"

"I must."

" 'And then the funny woman,' " she said, as if reading from a printed page, " 'and the cowardly dog and the mysterious man rode off into the desert in search of their real names.' "

"In search of a place to puke."

"Oh, no."

"Oh, yes."

She applied the brakes, and he flung open the door.

Later, when he woke, still riding through the dark desert, he said, "I have the most god-awful taste in my mouth."

"I don't doubt it."

"What's your name?"

"Bess."

"Bullshit."

"No, Baer. Bess Baer. What's your name?"

"My faithful Indian sidekick calls me Kemosabe."

"How do you feel?"

"Like shit," he said.

"Well, that's what 'Kemosabe' means."

"Are we ever going to stop?"

"Not while we have cloud cover."

"What've clouds got to do with anything?"

"Satellites," she said.

"You are the strangest woman I've ever known."

"Just wait."

"How the *hell* did you find me?"

"Maybe I'm psychic."

"Are you psychic?"

"No."

He sighed and closed his eyes. He could almost imagine that he was on a merry-go-round. "*I* was supposed to find *you*."

"Surprise."

"I wanted to help you."

"Thanks."

He let go of his grip on the world of the waking. For a while all was silent and serene. Then he walked out of the darkness and opened the red door. There were rats in the catacombs.

Roy did a crazy thing. Even as he was doing it, he was amazed at the risk he was taking.

He decided that he should be himself in front of Eve Jammer. His real self. His deeply committed, compassionate, caring self that was never more than half revealed in the bland, bureaucratic functionary that he appeared to be to most people.

Roy was willing to take risks with this stunning woman, because he sensed that her mind was as marvelous as her ravishing face and body. The woman within, so close to emotional and intellectual perfection, would understand him as no one else ever had.

Over dinner, they had not found the key that would open the doors in their souls and let them merge, which was their destiny. As they were leaving the restaurant, Roy was concerned that their moment of opportunity would pass and that their destiny would be thwarted, so he tapped the power of Dr. Kevorkian, which he'd recently absorbed from the television in the Learjet. He found the courage to reveal his true heart to Eve and force the fulfillment of their destiny.

Behind the restaurant, a blue Dodge van was parked three spaces to the right of Eve's Honda, and a man and woman were getting out of it, on their way to dinner. They were in their forties, and the man was in a wheelchair. He was being lowered from a side door of the van on an electric lift, which he operated without assistance.

Otherwise, the parking lot was deserted.

To Eve, Roy said, "Come with me a minute. Come say hello."

"Huh?"

Roy walked directly to the Dodge. "Good evening," he said as he reached under his coat to his shoulder holster.

The couple looked up at him, and both said, "Good evening," with a thread of puzzlement sewn through their voices, as if trying to recall where they had met him before.

"I feel your pain," Roy said as he drew his pistol.

He shot the man in the head.

His second round hit the woman in the throat, but it didn't finish her. She fell to the ground, twitching grotesquely.

Roy stepped past the dead man in the wheelchair. To the woman on the ground, he said, "Sorry," and then he shot her again.

The new silencer on the Beretta worked well. With the February wind moaning through the palm fronds, none of the three shots would have been audible farther than ten feet away.

Roy turned to Eve Jammer.

She looked thunderstruck.

He wondered if he had been too impulsive for a first date.

"So sad," he said, "the quality of life that some people are forced to endure."

Eve looked up from the bodies and met Roy's eyes. She didn't scream or even speak. Of course, she might have been in shock. But he didn't think that was the case. She seemed to want to understand.

Maybe everything would be all right after all.

"Can't leave them like this." He holstered his gun and pulled on his gloves. "They have a right to be treated with dignity."

The remote-control unit that operated the wheelchair lift was attached to the arm of the chair. Roy pressed a button and sent the dead man back up from the parking lot.

He climbed into the van through the double-wide sliding door, which had been pushed to one side. When the wheelchair completed its ascent, he rolled it inside.

Assuming that the man and woman were husband and wife, Roy planned the tableau accordingly. The situation was so public that he didn't have time to be original. He would have to repeat what he had done with the Bettonfields on Wednesday evening in Beverly Hills.

Tall lampposts were spaced around the parking lot. Just enough bluish light came through the open door to allow him to do his work.

He lifted the dead man out of the chair and placed him faceup on the floor. The van was uncarpeted. Roy was remorseful about that, but he had no padding or blankets with which to make the couple's final rest more comfortable.

He pushed the chair into a corner, out of the way.

Outside again, while Eve watched, Roy lifted the dead woman and put her into the van. He climbed in after her and arranged her beside her husband. He folded her right hand around her husband's left.

Both of the woman's eyes were open, as was one of her husband's, and Roy was about to press them shut with his gloved fingers when a better idea occurred to him. He peeled up the husband's closed eyelid and waited to see if it would remain open. It did. He turned the man's head to the left and the woman's head to the right, so they were gazing into each other's eyes, into the eternity that they now shared in a far better realm than Las Vegas, Nevada, far better than any place in this dismal, imperfect world.

He crouched at the feet of the cadavers for a moment, admiring his work. The tenderness expressed by their positions was enormously pleasing to him. Obviously, they had been in love and were now together forever, as any lovers would wish to be.

Eve Jammer stood at the open door, staring at the dead couple. Even the desert wind seemed to be aware of her exceptional beauty and to treasure it, for her golden hair was shaped into exquisitely tapered streamers. She appeared not windblown but wind*adored*.

"It's so sad," Roy said. "What quality of life could they have had—with him imprisoned in a wheelchair, and with her tied to him by bonds of love? Their lives were so limited by his infirmities, their futures tethered to that damned chair. How much better now."

Without saying a word, Eve turned away and walked to the Honda.

Roy got out of the Dodge van and, after one last look at the loving couple, closed the sliding door.

Eve was waiting behind the wheel of her car, with the engine running. If she had been frightened of him, she would have tried to drive away without him or would have run back to the restaurant.

He got in the Honda and buckled his safety harness.

They sat in silence.

Clearly, she intuited that he was no murderer, that what he had done was a moral act, and that he operated on a higher plane than did the average man. Her silence was only indicative of her struggle to translate her intuition into intellectual concepts and thereby more fully understand him.

She drove out of the parking lot.

Roy took off his leather gloves and returned them to the inside coat pocket from which he had gotten them.

For a while, Eve followed a random route through a series of residential neighborhoods, just driving to drive, going nowhere yet.

To Roy, the lights in all the huddled houses no longer seemed to be either warm or mysterious, as they had seemed on other nights and in other neighborhoods, in other cities, when he had cruised similar streets alone. Now they were merely sad: terribly sad little lights that inadequately illuminated the sad little lives of people who would never enjoy a passionate commitment to an ideal, not of the sort that so enriched Roy's life, sad little people who would never rise above the herd as he had risen, who would never experience a transcendent relationship with anyone as exceptional as Eve Jammer.

When at last the time seemed right, he said, "I yearn for a better world. But more than better, Eve. Oh, much more."

She didn't reply.

"Perfection," he said quietly but with great conviction, "in all things. Perfect laws and perfect justice. Perfect beauty. I dream of a perfect society, where everyone enjoys perfect health, perfect equality, in which the economy hums always like a perfectly tuned machine, where everyone lives in harmony with everyone else and with nature. Where no offense is ever given or taken. Where all dreams are perfectly rational and considerate. Where *all* dreams come true."

He was so moved by his soliloquy that his voice became thick toward the end of it, and he had to blink back tears.

Still she said nothing.

Night streets. Lighted windows. Little houses, little lives. So much confusion, sadness, yearning, and alienation in those houses.

"I do what I can," he said, "to make an ideal world. I scrub away some of its imperfect elements and push it inch by grudging inch toward perfection. Oh, not that I think I can change the world. Not alone, not me, and not even a thousand or a hundred thousand like me. But I light a little candle whenever I can, one little candle after another, pushing back the darkness one small shadow at a time."

They were on the east side of town, almost at the city limits, cruising into higher land and less populated neighborhoods than they had traveled previously. At an intersection, she suddenly made a U-turn and headed back into the sea of lights from which they'd come.

"You may say I'm a dreamer," Roy admitted. "But I'm not the only one. I think you're a dreamer, too, Eve, in your own special way. If you can admit being a dreamer . . . maybe if all of us dreamers can admit it and join together, the world could someday live as one."

Her silence was now profound.

He dared to look at her, and she was more devastating than he had remembered. His heart thudded slow and heavy, weighed down by the sweet burden of her beauty.

When at last she spoke, her voice was quavery. "You didn't take anything from them."

It wasn't fear that made her words shimmer as they passed along her elegant throat and across her ripe lips but, rather, a tremendous excitement. And her tremulous voice in turn excited Roy. He said, "No. Nothing."

"Not even the money from her purse or his wallet."

"Of course not. I'm not a taker, Eve. I'm a giver."

"I've never seen . . ." She seemed unable to find the words even to describe what he had done.

"Yes, I know," he said, delighted to see how completely he had swept her away.

". . . never seen such . . ."

"Yes."

". . . never such . . ."

"I know, dear one. I know."

". . . such *power*," she said.

That was not the word he had thought that she was searching for. But she had pronounced it with such passion, imbued it with so much erotic energy, he could not be disappointed that she had yet to grasp the full meaning of what he had done.

"They're just going out for dinner," she said excitedly. She had begun to drive too fast, recklessly. "Just going out to dinner, an ordinary night, nothing special, and—*wham!*— you whack them! Just like that, Jesus, take them out, and not even to get anything that belongs to them, not even because they crossed you or anything like that. Just for me. Just for me, to show me who you really *are*."

"Well, yes, for you," he said. "But not only for you, Eve. Don't you see? I removed two imperfect lives from creation, inching the world closer to perfection. And at the same time, I relieved those two sad people of the burden of this cruel life, this imperfect world, where nothing could ever be as they hoped. I gave to the world, and I gave to those poor people, and there were no losers."

"You're like the wind," she said breathlessly, "like a fantastic storm wind, hurricane, tornado, except there's no weatherman to warn anyone you're coming. You've got the power of the storm, you're a force of nature—sweeping out of nowhere, for no reason. *Wham!*"

Worried that she was missing the point, Roy said, "Wait, wait a minute, Eve, listen to me."

She was so excited that she couldn't drive anymore. She angled the Honda to the curb, tramped the brakes so hard that Roy would have been pitched into the windshield if his harness hadn't been buckled.

Slamming the gearshift into park with nearly enough force to snap it off, she turned to him. "You're an earthquake, just like an earthquake. People can be walking along, carefree, sun shining, birds singing—and then the ground opens and just swallows them up."

She laughed with delight. Hers was a girlish, trilling, musical laugh, so infectious that he had difficulty not laughing with her.

He took her hands in his. They were elegant, long-fingered, as exquisitely shaped as the hands of Guinevere, and the touch of them was more than any man deserved.

Unfortunately, the radius and ulna, above the perfectly shaped carpals of her wrist, were not of the supreme caliber of the bones in her hands. He was careful not to look at them. Or touch them.

"Eve, listen. You must understand. It's extremely important that you understand."

She grew solemn at once, realizing that they had reached a most serious point in their relationship. She was even more beautiful when somber than when laughing.

He said, "You're right, this is a great power. The greatest of all powers, and that's why you've got to be clear about it."

Although the only light in the car came from the instrument panel, her green eyes blazed as if with the reflection of summer sun. They were perfect eyes, as flawless and compelling as those of the woman for whom he had been hunting this past year, whose photograph he carried in his wallet.

Eve's left *brow* was perfect too. But a slight irregularity marred her right superciliary arch, above her eye socket: It was regrettably too prominent, only fractionally more so than the left, formed with barely half a gram too much bone, but nevertheless out of balance and shy of the perfection on the left.

That was okay. He could live with that. He would just focus on her angelic eyes below her brow, and on each of her incomparable hands below her knobby radius and ulna. Though flawed, she was the only woman he'd ever seen with more than one perfect feature. Ever, ever, ever. And her treasures weren't limited to her hands and eyes.

"Unlike other power, Eve, this doesn't flow from anger," he explained, wanting this precious woman to understand his mission and his innermost self. "It doesn't come from hatred, either. It's not the power of rage, envy, bitterness, greed. It's not like the power some people find in courage or honor—or that they gain from a belief in God. It transcends those powers, Eve. Do you know what it is?"

She was rapt, unable to speak. She only shook her head: no.

"My power," he said, "is the power of compassion."

"Compassion," she whispered.

"Compassion. If you try to understand other people, to feel their pain, to really *know* the anguish of their lives, to love them in spite of their faults, you're overcome by such pity, such *intense* pity, it's intolerable. It must be relieved. So you tap into the immeasurable, inexhaustible power of compassion. You *act* to relieve suffering, to ease the world a hairsbreadth closer to perfection."

"Compassion," she whispered again, as if she had never heard the word before, or as if he had shown her a definition of it that she had never previously appreciated.

Roy could not look away from her mouth as she repeated the word twice again. Her lips were divine. He couldn't imagine why he had thought that Melissa Wicklun's lips were perfect, for Eve's lips made Melissa's seem less attractive than those of a leprous toad. These were lips beside which the ripest plum would look as withered as a prune, beside which the sweetest strawberry would look sour.

Playing Henry Higgins to her Eliza Doolittle, he continued her first lesson in moral refinement: "When you're motivated solely by compassion, when no personal gain is involved, then *any* act is moral, utterly moral, and you owe no explanations to anyone, ever. Acting from compassion, you're freed forever from doubt, and that is a power like no other."

"Any act," she said, so overcome by the concept that she could barely find enough breath to speak.

"Any," he assured her.

She licked her lips.

Oh, God, her tongue was so delicate, glistened so intriguingly, slipped so sensuously across her lips, was so *perfectly* tapered that a faint sigh of ecstasy escaped him before he was quite aware of it.

Perfect lips. Perfect tongue. If only her chin had not been tragically fleshy. Others might think it was the chin of a goddess, but Roy was cursed with a greater sensitivity to imperfection than were other men. He was acutely aware of the smidgin of excess fat that lent her chin a barely perceptible *puffy* look. He would just have to focus on her lips, on her tongue, and not allow his gaze to drift down from there.

"How many have you done?" she asked.

"Done? Oh. You mean, like back at the restaurant."

"Yes. How many?"

"Well, I don't count them. That would seem . . . I don't know . . . it would seem prideful. I don't want praise. No. My satisfaction is just in doing what I know is right. It's a very private satisfaction."

"How many?" she persisted. "A rough estimate."

"Oh, I don't know. Over the years . . . a couple of hundred, a few hundred, something like that."

She closed her eyes and shivered. "When you do them . . . just before you do them and they look in your eyes, are they afraid?"

"Yes, but I wish they weren't. I wish they could see that I know their anguish, that I'm acting from compassion, that it's going to be quick and painless."

With her own eyes closed, half swooning, she said, "They look into your eyes, and they see the power you have over them, the power of a *storm*, and they're afraid."

He released her right hand and pointed his forefinger at the flat section of bone immediately above the root of her perfect nose. It was a nose that made all the other fine noses seem as unformed as the "nose" on a coconut shell. Slowly, he moved his finger toward her face as he said, "You. Have. The. Most. Exquisite. Glabella. I. Have. Ever. Seen."

With the last word, he touched his finger to her glabella, the flat portion of the front skull bone between her unimpeachable left superciliary arch and her unfortunately bony right superciliary arch, directly above her nose.

Although her eyes were closed, Eve didn't flinch with surprise at his touch. She seemed to have developed such a closeness to him, so quickly, that she was aware of his every intention and slightest movement without the aid of vision—and without relying on any of the other five senses, for that matter.

He took his finger off her glabella. "Do you believe in fate?"

"Yes."

"We *are* fate."

She opened her eyes and said, "Let's go back to my place."

On the trip to her house, she broke traffic laws by the score. Roy didn't approve, but he withheld his criticism.

She lived in a small two-story house in a recently completed tract. It was nearly identical to the other houses on the street.

Roy had expected glamour. Disappointed, he reminded himself that Eve, though stunning, was but another woefully underpaid bureaucrat.

As they waited in the Honda, in the driveway, for the automatic garage door to finish lifting out of the way, he said, "How did a woman like you wind up working in the agency?"

"I wanted the job, and my father had the influence to make it happen," she said, driving into the garage.

"Who's your father?"

"He's a rotten sonofabitch," she said. "I hate him. Let's not go into all that, Roy, please. Don't ruin the mood."

The last thing that he wanted to do was ruin the mood.

Out of the car, at the door between the garage and the house, as Eve fumbled in her purse for keys, she was suddenly nervous and clumsy. She turned to him, leaned close. "Oh, God, I can't stop thinking about it, how you did them, how you just walked up and did them. Such *power* in the way you did it."

She was virtually smouldering with desire. He could feel the heat rolling off her, driving the February chill out of the garage.

"You have so much to teach me," she said.

A turning point in their relationship had arrived. Roy needed to explain one more thing about himself. He'd been delaying bringing it up, for fear she would not understand this one quirk as easily as she had absorbed and accepted what he'd had to say about the power of compassion. But he could delay no longer.

As Eve returned her attention to her purse and at last extracted the ring of keys from it, Roy said, "I want to see you undressed."

"Yes, darling, yes," she said, and the keys clinked noisily as she searched for the right one on the ring.

He said, "I want to see you entirely nude."

"Entirely, yes, all for you."

"I have to know how much of the rest of you is as perfect as the perfect parts that I can already see."

"You're so sweet," she said, hastily inserting the correct key into the dead-bolt lock.

"From the soles of your feet to the curve of your spine, to the backs of your ears, to the pores in the skin of your scalp. I want to see every inch of you, nothing hidden, nothing at all."

Throwing open the unlocked door, rushing inside, switching on a kitchen light, she said, "Oh, you are too much, you are so *strong*. Every crevice, darling, every inch and fold and crevice."

As she dropped her purse and keys on the kitchen table and began to strip out of her coat, he followed her inside and said, "But that doesn't mean *I* want to undress or . . . or anything."

That stopped her. She blinked at him.

He said, "I want to see. And touch you, but not much of that. Just a little touching, when something looks perfect, to feel if the skin is as smooth and silky as it appears, to test the resilience, to feel if the muscle tension is as wonderful as it looks. You don't have to touch me at all." He hurried on, afraid that he was losing her. "I want to make love to you, to the perfect parts of you, make passionate love with my eyes, with a few quick touches, perhaps, but with nothing else. I don't want to spoil it by doing . . . what other people do. Don't want to debase it. Don't need that sort of thing."

She stared at him so long that he almost turned and fled.

Suddenly Eve squealed shrilly, and Roy took a step back, more than half afraid of her. Offended and humiliated, she might fling herself at him and claw his face, tear at his eyes.

Then, to his astonishment, he realized that she was laughing, though not cruelly, not laughing at him. She was laughing with pure joy. She hugged herself and squealed as if she were a schoolgirl, and her sublime green eyes shone with delight.

"My God," she said tremulously, "you're even better than you seemed, even better than I thought, better than I could ever hope. You're perfect, Roy, you're perfect, perfect."

He smiled uncertainly. He was still not entirely free of the fear that she was going to claw him.

Eve grabbed his right hand, pulled him through the kitchen, across a dining room, snapping on lights and talking as she went: "I was willing . . . if you wanted *that*. But that's not what I want, either, all that pawing and squeezing, all that sweating, it *disgusts* me, having another person's sweat all over me, all slick and sticky with another person's sweat, I can't stand that, it *sickens* me."

"Fluids," he said with revulsion, "how can there be anything *sexy* about another person's fluids, exchanging fluids?"

With growing excitement, pulling him into a hallway, Eve said, "Fluids, my God, doesn't it make you want to die, just *die*, with all the fluids that have to be involved, so much that's *wet*. They all want to lick and suck my breasts, all that saliva, it's so hideous, and shoving their tongues in my mouth—"

"*Spittle!*" he said, grimacing. "What's so erotic about swapping spit, for God's sake?"

They had reached the threshold of her bedroom. He stopped her on the brink of the paradise that they were about to create together.

"If I ever kiss you," he promised, "it'll be a dry kiss, as dry as paper, dry as sand."

Eve was shaking with excitement.

"No tongue," he swore. "Even the lips mustn't be moist."

"And never lips to lips—"

"—because then even in a dry kiss—"

"—we'd be swapping—"

"—breath for breath—"

"—and there's moisture in breath—"

"—vapors from the lungs," he said.

With a gladdening of his heart almost too sweet to endure, Roy knew that this splendid woman was, indeed, more like him than he ever could have hoped when he first stepped out of that elevator and saw her. They were two voices in harmony, two hearts beating in unison, two souls soaring to the same song, emphatically simpatico.

"No man has ever been in this bedroom," she said, leading him across the threshold. "Only you. Only you."

The portion of the walls immediately to the left and right of the bed, as well as the area of the ceiling directly above it, was mirrored. Otherwise, the walls and ceiling were upholstered with midnight-blue satin the precise shade of the carpet. A single chair stood in a corner, upholstered in silvery silk. The two windows were covered with polished-nickel blinds. The bed was sleek and modern, with radius footboard, bookcase headboard, tall flanking cabinets, and a light bridge; it was finished with several coats of high-gloss, midnight-blue lacquer in which glimmered silvery speckles like stars. Above the headboard was another mirror. Instead of a bedspread, she had a silver-fox fur throw—"Just fake fur," she assured him when he expressed concern about the rights of helpless animals—which was the most lustrous and luxurious thing he had ever seen.

Here was the glamour for which Roy had yearned.

The computerized lighting was voice-activated. It offered six distinct moods through clever combinations of strategically placed halogen pin spots (with a variety of colored lenses), mirror-framing neon in three colors (that could be displayed singly or two or three at a time), and imaginative applications of fiber optics. Furthermore, each mood could be subtly adjusted by a voice-activated rheostat that responded to the commands "up" and "down."

When Eve touched a button on the headboard, the tambour doors on the tall bed-flanking cabinets hummed up, out of sight. Shelves were revealed, laden with bottles of lotions and scented oils, ten or twelve rubber phalluses in various sizes and colors, and a collection of battery-powered and hand-operated sex toys that were bewildering in their design and complexity.

Eve switched on a CD player with a hundred-disc carousel and set it for random play. "It's loaded with everything from Rod Stewart to Metallica, Elton John, Garth Brooks, the Beatles, the Bee Gees, Bruce Springsteen, Bob Seger, Screamin' Jay Hawkins, James Brown and the Famous Flames, and Bach's *Goldberg Variations*. Somehow it's more exciting when there's so many different kinds of music and when you never know what will be playing next."

After taking off his topcoat but not his suit jacket, Roy Miro moved the upholstered chair out of the corner. He positioned it to one side of the bed, near the footboard, to ensure a glorious view yet to avoid, as much as possible, casting his reflections in the mirrors and spoiling the multitudinous images of *her* perfection.

He sat in the chair and smiled.

She stood beside the bed, fully clothed, while Elton John sang about healing hands. "This is like a dream. To be here, doing exactly what I like to do, but with someone who can appreciate me—"

"I appreciate you, I do."

"—who can adore me—"

"I adore you."

"—who can surrender to me—"

"I'm yours."

"—without soiling the beauty of it."

"No fluids. No pawing."

"Suddenly," she said, "I'm as shy as a virgin."

"I could stare at you for hours, fully clothed."

She tore off her blouse so violently that buttons popped and the fabric ripped. In a minute she was completely nude, and more of what had been hidden proved to be perfect than imperfect.

Reveling in his gasp of pleased disbelief, she said, "You see why I don't like to make love in the usual way? When I have me, what do I need with anyone else?"

Thereafter, she turned from him and proceeded as she would have done if he'd not been there. Clearly, she took intense satisfaction from knowing that she could hold him totally in her power without ever having to touch him.

She stood before the mirror, examining herself from every angle, caressing herself tenderly, wonderingly, and her rapture at what she saw was so exciting to Roy that he could draw only shallow breaths.

When she finally went to the bed, with Bruce Springsteen singing about whiskey and cars, she cast off the silver-fox throw. For just a moment, Roy was disappointed, for he had wanted to see her writhing upon those lustrous pelts, whether faux or real. But she pulled back the top sheet and the lower sheet as well, revealing a black rubber mattress cover that instantly intrigued him.

From a shelf in one of the open cabinets, she removed a bottle of jewel-pure amber oil, unscrewed the cap, and poured a small pool of it in the center of the bed. A subtle and appealing fragrance, as light and fresh as a spring breeze, drifted to Roy: not a floral scent, but spices—cinnamon, ginger, and other, more exotic ingredients.

While James Brown sang about urgent desire, Eve rolled onto the big bed, straddling the puddle of oil. She anointed her hands and began working the amber essence into her flawless skin. For fifteen minutes, her hands moved knowingly over every curve and plane of her body, lingering at each lovely, yielding roundness and at each shadowy, mysterious cleft. More often than not, what Eve touched was perfect. But when she touched a part that was beneath Roy's standards and dismaying to him, he focused on her hands, for they themselves were without flaw—at least below the too-bony radii and ulnae.

The sight of Eve upon the glistening black rubber, her lush body all gold and pink, slick with a fluid that was satisfyingly pure and not of human origin, had elevated Roy Miro to a spiritual plane that he had never before attained, not even by the use of secret Eastern techniques of meditation, not even when a channeler had once brought forth the spirit of his dead mother at a séance in Pacific Heights, not even with peyote or vibrating crystals or high-colonic therapy administered by an innocent-looking twenty-year-old technician dressed accommodatingly as a Girl Scout. And judging by the lazy pace that she had set, Eve expected to spend hours in the exploration of her magnificent self.

Consequently, Roy did something that he had never done before. He took his pager from his pocket, and because there was no way to switch off the beeper on this particular model, he popped open the plastic plate on the back and removed the batteries.

For one night, his country would have to get along without him, and suffering humanity would have to make do without its champion.

Pain brought Spencer out of a black-and-white dream featuring surreal architecture and mutant biology, all the more disturbing for the lack of color. His entire body was a mass of chronic aches, dull and relentlessly throbbing, but a sharp pain in the top of his head was what broke the chains of his unnatural sleep.

It was still night. Or night again. He didn't know which.

He was lying on his back, on an air mattress, under a blanket. His shoulders and head were elevated by a pillow and by something under the pillow.

The soft hissing sound and characteristic eerie glow of a Coleman lantern identified the light source somewhere behind him.

The lambent light revealed weather-smoothed rock formations to the left and right. Directly ahead of him lay a slab of what he supposed was the Mojave with an icing of night, which the beams of the lantern couldn't melt. Overhead, stretched from one thrust of rock to the other, was a cover of desert-camouflage canvas.

Another sharp pain lanced across his scalp.

"Be still," she said.

He realized that his pillow rested on her crossed legs and that his head lay in her lap.

"What're you doing?" He was spooked by the weakness of his own voice.

She said, "Sewing up this laceration."

"You can't do that."

"It keeps breaking open and bleeding."

"I'm not a quilt."

"What's that supposed to mean?"

"You're not a doctor."

"Aren't I?"

"Are you?"

"No. *Be still.*"

"It hurts."

"Of course."

"It'll get infected," he worried.

"I shaved the area first, then sterilized it."

"You shaved my *head?*"

"Just one little spot, around the gash."

"Do you have *any* idea what you're doing?"

"You mean in terms of barbering or doctoring?"

"Either one."

"I've got a little basic knowledge."

"Ouch, damn it!"

"If you're going to be such a baby, I'll use a spritz of local anesthetic."

"You have that? Why didn't you use it?"

"You were already unconscious."

He closed his eyes, walked through a black-and-white place made of bones, under an arch of skulls, and then opened his eyes again and said, "Well, I'm not now."

"You're not what?"

"Unconscious," he said.

"You just were again. A few minutes passed between our last exchange and this one. And while you were out that time, I almost finished. Another stitch and I'm through."

"Why'd we stop?"

"You weren't traveling well."

"Sure, I was."

"You needed some treatment. Now you need rest. Besides, the cloud cover is breaking up fast."

"Got to go. Early bird gets the tomato."

"Tomato? That's interesting."

He frowned. "I say tomato? Why're you trying to confuse me?"

"Because it's so easy. There—the last suture."

Spencer closed his grainy eyes. In the somber black-and-white world, jackals with human faces were prowling the vine-tangled rubble of a once-great cathedral. He could hear children crying in rooms hidden beneath the ruins.

When he opened his eyes, he found that he was lying flat. His head was now elevated only a couple of inches on the pillow.

Valerie was sitting on the ground beside him, watching over him. Her dark hair fell softly along one side of her face, and she was pretty in the lamplight.

"You're pretty in the lamplight," he said.

"Next you'll be asking if I'm an Aquarius or a Capricorn."

"Nah, I don't give a shit."

She laughed.

"I like your laugh," he said.

She smiled, turned her head, and ruminated on the dark desert.

He said, "What do you like about me?"

"I like your dog."

"He's a great dog. What else?"

Looking at him again, she said, "You've got nice eyes."

"I do?"

"Honest eyes."

"Are they? Used to have nice hair, too. All shaved off now. I was butchered."

"Barbered. Just one small spot."

"Barbered and then butchered. What are you doing out here in the desert?"

She stared at him awhile, then looked away without answering.

He wouldn't let her off that easily. "What are you doing out here? I'll just keep asking until the repetition drives you insane. What are you doing out here?"

"Saving your ass."

"Tricky. I mean, what were you doing here in the first place?"

"Looking for you."

"Why?" he wondered.

"Because you've been looking for me."

"But how'd you find me, for God's sake?"

"Ouija board."

"I don't think I can believe anything you say."

"You're right. It was Tarot cards."

"Who're we running from?"

She shrugged. The desert engaged her attention again. At last she said, "History, I guess."

"There you go, trying to confuse me again."

"Specifically, the cockroach."

"We're running from a cockroach?"

"That's what I call him, 'cause it infuriates him."

His gaze rolled from Valerie to the tarp that hung ten feet above them. "Why the roof?"

"Blends with the terrain. It's a heat-dispersing fabric too, so we won't show up strong on any infrared look-down."

"Look-down?"

"Eyes in the sky."

"God?"

"No, the cockroach."

"The cockroach has eyes in the sky?"

"He and his people, yeah."

Spencer thought about that. Finally he said, "I'm not sure if I'm awake or dreaming."

"Some days," she said, "neither am I."

In the black-and-white world, the sky seethed with eyes, and a great white owl flew overhead, casting a moonshadow in the shape of an angel.

Eve's desire was insatiable, and her energy was inexhaustible, as though each protracted bout of ecstasy electrified rather than enervated her. At the end of an hour, she seemed more vital than ever, more beautiful, aglow.

Before Roy's adoring eyes, her incredible body seemed to be sculpted and pumped up by her ceaseless rhythmic flexing-contracting-flexing, by her writhing-thrashing-thrusting, just as a long session of lifting weights pumped up a bodybuilder. After years of exploring all the ways she could satisfy herself, she enjoyed a flexibility that Roy judged to be somewhere between that of a gold-medal Olympic gymnast and a carnival contortionist, combined with the endurance of an Alaskan dogsled team. There was no doubt whatsoever that a session in bed with herself provided a thorough workout for every muscle from her radiant head to her cute toes.

Regardless of the astounding knots into which she tied herself, regardless of the bizarre intimacies she took with herself, she never looked at all grotesque or absurd, but unfailingly beautiful, from any angle, in even the most unlikely acts. She was always milk and honey on that black rubber, peaches and cream, flowing and smooth, the most desirable creature ever to grace the earth.

Halfway through the second hour, Roy was convinced that sixty percent of this angel's features—body and face overall—were perfect by even the most stringent standards. Another thirty-five percent of her was not perfect but so *close* to perfect as to break his heart, and only five percent was plain.

Nothing about her—no slightest line or concavity or convexity—was ugly.

Roy was certain that Eve must soon stop pleasuring herself or otherwise collapse unconscious. But by the end of the second hour, she seemed to have more appetite and capacity than when she'd begun. The power of her sensuality was so great that every piece of music was changed by her horizontal dance, until it seemed that all of it, even the Bach, had been expressly composed as the score for a pornographic movie. From time to time she called out the number of a new lighting arrangement, said "up" or "down" to the rheostat, and her selection was always the most flattering for the next position into which she folded herself.

She was thrilled by watching herself in the mirrors. And by watching herself watch herself. And by watching herself as she watched herself watching herself. The infinity of images bounced back and forth between the mirrors on opposite walls, until she could believe that she had filled the universe with replications of herself. The mirrors seemed magical, transmitting all the energy of each reflection back into her own dynamic flesh, overloading her with power, until she was a runaway blond engine of eroticism.

Sometime during the third hour, batteries gave out in a few of her favorite toys, gears froze in others, and she surrendered herself once more to the expertise of her own bare hands. For a while, in fact, her hands seemed to be separate entities from her, each alive in its own right. They were in such a frenzy of lust that they couldn't occupy themselves with just one of her many treasures for any length of time; they kept sliding over her ample curves, up-around-down her oiled skin, massaging and tweaking and caressing and stroking one delight after another. They were like a pair of starving diners at a fabulous smorgasbord that had been prepared to celebrate the imminence of Armageddon, allowed only precious seconds to gorge themselves before all was obliterated by a sun gone nova.

But the sun did not go nova, of course, and eventually—if gradually—those matchless hands slowed, slowed, finally stopped, and were sated. As was their mistress.

For a while, after it was over, Roy couldn't get up from his chair. He couldn't even slump back from the edge of it. He was numb, paralyzed, tingling strangely in every extremity.

In time, Eve rose from the bed and stepped into the adjoining bathroom. When she returned, carrying two plush towels—one damp, one dry—she was no longer gleaming with oil. With the damp cloth, she removed the glistening residue from the rubber mattress cover, then carefully wiped it down with the dry towel. She replaced the bottom sheet that she had earlier cast off.

Roy joined her on the bed. Eve lay on her back, her head on a pillow. He stretched out beside her, on his back, his head on another pillow. She was still gloriously nude, and he remained fully clothed—though at some point during the night, he had loosened his necktie by an inch.

Neither of them made the mistake of trying to comment upon what had transpired. Mere words could not have done the experience justice and might have made a nearly religious odyssey seem somehow tawdry. Anyway, Roy already knew that it had been good for Eve; and as for himself, well, he had seen more physical human perfection in those few hours—and in *action*—than in his entire life theretofore.

After a while, gazing at his darling's reflection on the ceiling as she stared at his, Roy began to talk, and the night entered a new phase of communion that was nearly as intimate, intense, and life-changing as the more physical phase that had preceded it. He spoke further about the power of compassion, refining the concept for her. He told her that humankind always hungered for perfection. People would endure unendurable pain, accept awful deprivation, countenance savage brutalities, live in constant and abject terror—if only they were convinced that their sufferings were the tolls that must be paid on the highway to Utopia, to Heaven on earth. A person motivated by compassion—yet who was also aware of the masses' willingness to suffer—could change the world. Although he, Roy Miro of the merry blue eyes and Santa Claus smile, did not believe that he possessed the charisma to be that leader of leaders who would launch the next crusade for perfection, he hoped to be one who served that special person and served him well.

"I light my little candles," he said. "One at a time."

For hours Roy talked while Eve interjected numerous questions and perceptive comments. He was excited to see how she thrilled to his ideas almost as she had thrilled to her battery-powered toys and to her own practiced hands.

She was especially moved when he explained how an enlightened society ought to expand on the work of Dr. Kevorkian, compassionately assisting in the self-destruction not solely of suicidal people but also of those poor souls who were deeply depressed, offering easy exits not only to the terminally ill but to the chronically ill, the disabled, the maimed, the psychologically impaired.

And when Roy talked about his concept for a suicide-assistance program for infants, to bring a compassionate solution to the problem of babies born with even the slightest defects that might affect their lives, Eve made a few breathless sounds similar to those that had escaped her in the throes of passion. She pressed her hands to her breasts once more, though this time only in an attempt to quiet the fierce pounding of her heart.

As Eve filled her hands with her bosoms, Roy could not take his eyes off the reflection of her that hovered above him. For a moment he thought that he might weep at the sight of her sixty-percent-perfect face and form.

Sometime before dawn, intellectual orgasms sent them spiraling into sleep, as physical orgasms had not the power to do. Roy was so fulfilled that he didn't even dream.

Hours later, Eve woke him. She had already showered and dressed for the day.

"You've never been more radiant," he told her.

"You've changed my life," she said.

"And you mine."

Although she was late for work in her concrete bunker, she drove him to the Strip hotel at which Prock, his taciturn driver from the previous night, had left his luggage. It was Saturday, but Eve worked seven days a week. Roy admired her commitment.

The desert morning was bright. The sky was a cool, serene blue.

At the hotel, under the entrance portico, before Roy got out of the car, he and Eve made plans to see each other soon, to experience again the pleasures of the night just past.

He stood by the front entrance to watch her drive away. When she was gone, he went inside. He passed the front desk, crossed the raucous casino, and took an elevator to the thirty-sixth and highest floor in the main tower.

He didn't recall putting one foot in front of the other since getting out of her car. As far as he knew, he had floated into the elevator.

He had never imagined that his pursuit of the fugitive bitch and the scarred man would lead him to the most perfect woman in existence. Destiny was a funny thing.

When the doors opened at the thirty-sixth floor, Roy stepped into a long corridor with custom-sculpted, tone-on-tone, wall-to-wall Edward Fields carpet. Wide enough to be considered a gallery rather than a hallway, the space was furnished with early-nineteenth-century French antiques and paintings of some quality from the same period.

This was one of three floors originally designed to offer huge luxury suites, free of charge, to high rollers who were willing to wager fortunes at the games downstairs. The thirty-fifth and thirty-fourth floors still served that function. However, since the agency had purchased the resort for its moneymaking and money-laundering potential, the suites on the top floor had been set aside for the convenience of out-of-town operatives of a certain executive level.

The thirty-sixth floor was served by its own concierge, who was established in a cozy office across from the elevator. Roy picked up the key to his suite from the man on duty, Henri, who didn't so much as raise an eyebrow over the rumpled condition of his guest's suit.

Key in hand, on his way to his rooms, whistling softly, Roy looked forward to a hot shower, a shave, and a lavish room-service breakfast. But when he opened the gilded door and went into the suite, he found two local agents waiting for him. They were in a state of acute but respectful consternation, and only when Roy saw them did he remember that his pager was in one of his jacket pockets and the batteries in another.

"We've been looking everywhere for you since four o'clock this morning," said one of his visitors.

"We've located Grant's Explorer," said the second.

"Abandoned," said the first. "There's a ground search under way for him—"

"—though he might be dead—"

"—or rescued—"

"—because it looks like someone got there before us—"

"—anyway, there are other tire tracks—"

"—so we don't have much time; we've got to move."

In his mind's eye, Roy pictured Eve Jammer: golden and pink, oiled and limber, writhing on black rubber, more perfect than not. That would sustain him, no matter how bad the day proved to be.

Spencer woke in the purple shade under the camouflage tarp, but the desert beyond was bathed in harsh white sunshine.

The light stung his eyes, forcing him to squint, although that pain was as nothing compared with the headache that cleaved his brow from temple to temple, on a slight diagonal. Against the backs of his eyeballs, red lights spun with the abrasiveness of razor-blade pinwheels.

He was hot as well. Burning up. Though he suspected that the day was not especially warm.

Thirsty. His tongue felt swollen. It was stuck to the roof of his mouth. His throat was scratchy, raw.

He was still lying on an air mattress, with his head on a meager pillow, under a blanket in spite of the insufferable heat—but he was no longer lying alone. The woman was snuggled against his right side, exerting a sweet pressure against his flank, hip, thigh. Somehow he had gotten his right arm around her without meeting an objection—*Way to go, Spence, my man!*—and now he relished the feel of her under his hand: so warm, so soft, so sleek, so furry.

Uncommonly furry for a woman.

He turned his head and saw Rocky.

"Hi, pal."

Talking was painful. Each word was a spiny burr being torn out of his throat. His own speech echoed piercingly through his skull, as though it had been stepped up by amplifiers inside his sinus cavities.

The dog licked Spencer's right ear.

Whispering to spare his throat, he said, "Yeah, I love you too."

"Am I interrupting anything?" Valerie asked, dropping to her knees at his left side.

"Just a boy and his dog, hangin' out together."

"How're you feeling?"

"Lousy."

"Are you allergic to any drugs?"

"Hate the taste of Pepto-Bismol."

"Are you allergic to any antibiotics?"

"Everything's spinning."

"Are you allergic to any antibiotics?"

"Strawberries give me hives."

"Are you delirious or just difficult?"

"Both."

Maybe he drifted away for a while, because the next thing he knew, she was giving him an injection in his left arm. He smelled the alcohol with which she had swabbed the area over the vein.

"Antibiotic?" he whispered.

"Liquified strawberries."

The dog was no longer lying at Spencer's side. He was sitting next to the woman, watching with interest as she withdrew the needle from his master's arm.

Spencer said, "I have an infection?"

"Maybe secondary. I'm taking no chances."

"You a nurse?"

"Not a doctor, not a nurse."

"How do you know what to do?"

"He tells me," she said, indicating Rocky.

"Always joking. Must be a comedian."

"Yes, but licensed to give injections. Do you think you can hold down some water?"

"How about bacon and eggs?"

"Water seems hard enough. Last time, you spit it up."

"Disgusting."

"You apologized."

"I'm a gentleman."

Even with her assistance, he was tested to his limits merely by the effort required to sit up. He choked on the water a couple of times, but it tasted cool and sweet, and he thought he would be able to keep it in his stomach.

After she eased him flat onto his back again, he said, "Tell me the truth."

"If I know it."

"Am I dying?"

"No."

"We have one rule around here," he said.

"Which is?"

"Never lie to the dog."

She looked at Rocky.

The mutt wagged his tail.

"Lie to yourself. Lie to me. But never lie to the dog."

"As rules go, it seems pretty sensible," she said.

"So am I dying?"

"I don't know."

"That's better," Spencer said, and he passed out.

Roy Miro took fifteen minutes to shave, brush his teeth, and shower. He changed into chinos, a red cotton sweater, and a tan corduroy jacket. He had no time for the breakfast that he so badly wanted. The concierge, Henri, provided him with two chocolate-almond croissants in a white paper bag and two cups of the finest Colombian coffee in a disposable plastic thermos.

In a corner of the hotel parking lot, a Bell JetRanger executive helicopter was waiting for Roy. As on the jet from L.A., he was the only person in the plushly upholstered passenger cabin.

On the flight out to the discovery in the Mojave, Roy ate both croissants and drank the black coffee while using his attaché case computer to connect to Mama. He reviewed the overnight developments in the investigation.

Not much had happened. Back in southern California, John Kleck had not turned up any leads that might tell them where the woman had gone after abandoning her car at the airport in Orange County. Likewise, they had not succeeded in tracing the telephone number to which Grant's cleverly programmed system had faxed photos of Roy and his men from the Malibu cabin.

The biggest news, which wasn't much, came from San Francisco. The agent tracking down George and Ethel Porth—the grandparents who evidently had raised Spencer Grant following his mother's passing—now knew, from public records, that a death certificate had been issued for Ethel ten years ago. Evidently that was why her husband sold the house at that time. George Porth had died, too, just three years ago. Now that the agent couldn't hope to talk with the Porths about their grandson, he was pursuing other avenues of investigation.

Through Mama, Roy routed a message to the agent's E-mail number in San Francisco, suggesting that he check the records of the probate court to determine if the grandson had been an heir to either the estate of Ethel Porth or that of her husband. Maybe the Porths had not known their grandson as "Spencer Grant" and had used his real name in their wills. If for some inexplicable reason they had aided and abetted his use of that false identity for purposes including enlistment in the military, they nevertheless might have cited his real name when disposing of their estates.

It wasn't much of a lead, but it was worth checking out.

As Roy unplugged the computer and closed it, the pilot of the JetRanger alerted him, by way of the public-address system, that they were one minute from their destination. "Coming up on our right."

Roy leaned to the window beside his seat. They were paralleling a wide arroyo, heading almost due east across the desert.

The glare of sun on sand was intense. He took sunglasses from an inner jacket pocket and put them on.

Ahead, three Jeep wagons, all agency hardware, were clustered in the middle of the dry wash. Eight men were waiting around the vehicles, and most of them were watching the approaching helicopter.

The JetRanger swept over the Jeeps and agents, and suddenly the land below dropped a thousand feet as the chopper soared across the brink of a precipice. Roy's stomach dropped, too, because of the abrupt change in perspective and because of something that he had glimpsed but couldn't quite believe that he had really seen.

High over the valley floor, the pilot entered a wide starboard turn and brought Roy around for a better look at the place where the arroyo met the edge of the cliff. In fact, using the two towers of rock in the middle of the dry wash as a visual fulcrum, he flew a full three-hundred-sixty-degree circle. Roy had a chance to see the Explorer from every amazing angle.

He took off his sunglasses. The truck was still there in the full glare of daylight. He put the glasses on as the JetRanger brought him around again and landed in the arroyo, near the Jeeps.

Disembarking from the chopper, Roy was met by Ted Tavelov, the agent in charge at the site. Tavelov was shorter and twenty years older than Roy, lean and sun browned; he had leathery skin and a dry-as-beef-jerky look from having spent too many years outdoors in the desert. He was dressed in cowboy boots, jeans, a blue flannel shirt, and a Stetson. Although the day was cool, Tavelov wore no jacket, as if he had stored up so much Mojave heat in his sun-cured flesh that he would never again be cold.

As they walked toward the Explorer, the chopper engine fell silent behind them. The rotors wheezed more slowly to a halt.

Roy said, "There's no sign of either the man or the dog, so I hear."

"Nothing in there but a dead rat."

"Was the water really *that* high when it jammed the truck between those rocks?"

"Yep. Sometime yesterday afternoon, at the height of the storm."

"Then maybe he was washed out, went over the falls."

"Not if he stayed buckled up."

"Well, farther up the river, maybe he tried to swim for shore."

"Man would have to be a fool to try swimming in a flash flood, the water moving like an express train. This man a fool?"

"No."

"See these tracks here," Tavelov said, pointing to tire marks in the silt of the arroyo bed. "Even what little wind there's been since the storm has worn 'em down some. But you can still see where somebody drove down the south bank, under the Explorer, probably stood on the roof of his vehicle to get up there."

"When would the arroyo have dried up enough for that?"

"Water level drops fast when the rain stops. And this ground, deep sand—it dries out quick. Say . . . seven or eight last night."

Standing deep inside the rock-walled passage, gazing up at the Explorer, Roy said, "Grant could've climbed down and walked away before the other vehicle got here."

"Fact is, you'll see some vague footprints that *don't* belong to the first group of my hopeless asshole assistants who tramped up the scene. And judging by 'em, you might make a case that a woman drove in here and took him away. Him and the dog. And his luggage."

Roy frowned. "A woman?"

"One set of prints is of a size that you know it's got to be a man. Even big women don't often have feet as big as would be in proportion to the rest of 'em. The second set is small prints, which might be those of a boy, say ten to thirteen. But I doubt any boy was drivin' on his own out here. Some small men have feet might step into shoes that size. But not many. So most likely it was a woman."

If a woman had come to Grant's rescue, Roy was obliged to wonder if she was *the* woman, the fugitive. That raised anew the questions that had plagued him since Wednesday night: Who *was* Spencer Grant, what in the hell did the bastard have to do with the woman, what sort of wild card was he, was he likely to screw up their operations, and would he put them all at risk of exposure?

Yesterday, when Roy had stood in Eve's bunker, listening to the laser-disc recording, he'd been more baffled than enlightened by what he'd heard. Judging by the questions and the few comments that Grant managed to insert into Davidowitz's monologue, he knew little about "Hannah Rainey," but for mysterious reasons, he was busily learning everything he could. Until then, Roy had assumed that Grant and the woman already had some kind of close relationship; so the task had been to determine the nature of that relationship and to figure how much sensitive information the woman had shared with Grant. But if the guy didn't already know her, why had he been at her bungalow that rainy night, and why had he made it his personal crusade to find her?

Roy didn't want to believe that the woman had shown up here in the arroyo, because to believe it was to be even more confused. "So you're saying what—that he called someone on his cellular and she came right out to get him?"

Tavelov was not rattled by Roy's sarcasm. "Could've been some desert rat, likes living out where there aren't phones, electricity. There are some. Though none I know about for twenty miles. Or it could've been an off-roader, just having himself some fun."

"In a storm."

"Storm was over. Anyway, the world's full of fools."

"And whoever it is just happens to stumble across the Explorer. In this whole vast desert."

Tavelov shrugged. "We found the truck. It's your job, making sense of it."

Walking back to the entrance of the rock-walled sluiceway, staring at the far riverbank, Roy said, "Whoever she was, she drove into the arroyo from the south, then also drove out to the south. Can we follow those tire tracks?"

"Yep, you can—pretty clear for maybe four hundred yards, then spotty for another two hundred. Then they vanish. The wind wiped 'em out in some places. Other places, ground's too hard to take tracks."

"Well, let's search farther out, see if the tracks reappear."

"Already tried. While we were waiting."

Tavelov gave an edge to the word "waiting."

Roy said, "My damn pager was broken, and I didn't know it."

"By foot and chopper, we pretty much had a good look-around in every direction to the south bank of the wash. Went three miles east, three south, three west."

"Well," Roy said, "extend the search. Go out six miles and see if you can pick up the trail again."

"Just going to be a waste of time."

Roy thought of Eve as she had been last night, and that memory gave him the strength to remain calm, to smile, and to say, with characteristic pleasantness, "Probably is a waste of time, probably is. But I guess we've got to try anyway."

"Wind's picking up."

"Maybe it is."

"Definitely picking up. Going to erase everything."

Perfection on black rubber.

Roy said, "Then let's try to stay ahead of it. Bring in more men, another chopper, push out *ten* miles in each direction."

• • •

Spencer was not awake. But he wasn't asleep, either. He was taking a drunkard's walk along the thin line between.

He heard himself mumbling. He couldn't make much sense of what he was saying. Yet he was ever in the grip of a feverish urgency, certain there was something important that he must tell someone—although what that vital information was, and to whom he must impart it, eluded him.

Occasionally he opened his eyes. Blurry vision. He blinked. Squinted. Couldn't see well enough to be sure even if it was daytime or if the light came from the Coleman lantern.

Always, Valerie was there. Close enough for him to know, even with his vision so poor, that it was her. Sometimes she was wiping his face with a damp cloth, sometimes changing a cool compress on his forehead. Sometimes she was just watching, and he sensed that she was worried, though he couldn't clearly see her expression.

Once, when he swam up from his personal darkness and stared out through the distorting pools that shimmered in his eye sockets, Valerie was turned half away from him, busy at a hidden task. Behind him, farther back under the camouflage tarp, the Rover's engine was idling. He heard another familiar sound: the soft but unmistakable *tick-tickety-tick* of well-practiced fingers flying over a computer keyboard. Odd.

From time to time, she talked to him. Those were the moments when he was best able to focus his mind and to mumble something that was halfway comprehensible, though he still faded in and out.

Once he faded in to hear himself asking, ". . . how'd you find me . . . out here . . . way out here . . . between nothing and nowhere?"

"Bug on your Explorer."

"Cockroach?"

"The other kind of bug."

"Spider?"

"Electronic."

"Bug on my truck?"

"That's right. I put it there."

"Like . . . you mean . . . a transmitter thing?" he asked fuzzily.

"Just like a transmitter thing."

"Why?"

"Because you followed me home."

"When?"

"Tuesday night. No point denying it."

"Oh, yeah. Night we met."

"You make it sound almost romantic."

"Was for me."

Valerie was silent. Finally she said, "You're not kidding, are you?"

"Liked you right off."

After another silence, she said, "You come to The Red Door, chat me up, seem like just a nice customer, then you follow me home."

The full meaning of her revelations was sinking in gradually, and a slow-dawning amazement was overtaking him. "You knew?"

"You were good. But if I couldn't spot a tail, I'd have been dead a long time ago."

"The bug. How?"

"How did I plant it? Went out the back door while you were sitting across the street in your truck. Hot-wired somebody's car a block or so away, drove to my street, parked up the block from you, waited till you left, then followed you."

"Followed *me*?"

"What's good for the goose."

"Followed me . . . Malibu?"

"Followed you Malibu."

"And I never saw."

"Well, you weren't expecting to be followed."

"Jesus."

"I climbed your gate, waited till all the lights were out in your cabin."

"Jesus."

"Fixed the transmitter to the undercarriage of your truck, wired it to work off the battery."

"You just happened to have a transmitter."

"You'd be surprised what I just happen to have."

"Maybe not anymore."

Although Spencer didn't want to leave her, Valerie grew blurrier and faded into shadows. He drifted into his inner darkness once more.

Later he must have swum up again, because she was shimmering in front of him. He heard himself say, "Bug on my truck," with amazement.

"I had to know who you were, why you were following me. I knew you weren't one of *them*."

He said weakly, "Cockroach's people."

"That's right."

"Coulda been one of them."

"No, because you'd have blown my brains out the first time you were close enough to do it."

"They don't like you, huh?"

"Not much. So I wondered who you were."

"Now you know."

"Not really. You're a mystery, Spencer Grant."

"*Me* a mystery!" He laughed. Pain hammered across his entire head when he laughed, but he laughed anyway. "Least you have a name for me."

"Sure. But no more real than those you have for me."

"It's real."

"Sure."

"Legal name. Spencer Grant. Guaranteed."

"Maybe. But who were you before you were a cop, before you went to UCLA, way back before you were in the army?"

"You know all about me."

"Not all. Just what you've left on the records, just as much as you wanted anybody to find. Following me home, you spooked me, so I started checking you out."

"You moved out of the bungalow because of me."

"Didn't know who the hell you were. But I figured if you could find me, so could they. Again."

"And they did."

"The very next day."

"So when I spooked you . . . I saved you."

"You could look at it that way."

"Without me, you'd have been there."

"Maybe."

"When the SWAT team hit."

"Probably."

"Seems like it's all sort of . . . meant to be."

"But what were *you* doing there?" she asked.

"Well . . ."

"In my house."

"You were gone."

"So?"

"Wasn't your place anymore."

"Did you know it wasn't my place anymore when you went in?"

The full meaning of her revelations kept giving him delayed jolts. He blinked furiously, vainly trying to see her face clearly. "Jesus, if you bugged my truck . . . !"

"What?"

"Then were you following me Wednesday night?"

She said, "Yeah. Seeing what you were all about."

"From Malibu . . . ?"

"To The Red Door."

"Then back to your place in Santa Monica?"

"I wasn't *inside* like you were."

"But you saw it go down, the assault."

"From a distance. Don't change the subject."

"What subject?" he asked, genuinely confused.

"You were going to explain why you broke into my house Wednesday night," she reminded him. She wasn't angry. Her voice wasn't sharp. He would have felt better if she'd been flat-out angry with him.

"You . . . you didn't show up at work."

"So you break into my house?"

"Didn't break in."

"Have I forgotten that I sent you an invitation?"

"Door was unlocked."

"Every unlocked door is an invitation to you?"

"I was . . . worried."

"Yeah, worried. Come on, tell me the truth. What were you looking for in my house that night?"

"I was . . ."

"You were what?"

"I needed . . ."

"What? What did you need in my house?"

Spencer wasn't sure whether he was dying from his injuries or from embarrassment. Whatever the case, he lost consciousness.

The Bell JetRanger transported Roy Miro from the dry wash in the open desert straight to the landing pad on the roof of the agency's high rise in downtown Las Vegas. While a ground and air search was being conducted in the Mojave for the woman and the vehicle that had taken Spencer Grant away from the wreckage of his Explorer, Roy spent Saturday afternoon in the fifth-floor satellite-surveillance center.

While he worked, he ate a substantial lunch that he ordered from the commissary, to compensate for missing the lavish breakfast about which he'd fantasized. Besides, later he would need all the energy that he was able to muster, when he went home with Eve Jammer again.

The previous evening, when Bobby Dubois had brought Roy to that same room, it had been quiet, operating with a minimal staff. Now every computer and other piece of equipment was manned, and murmured conversations were being conducted throughout the large chamber.

Most likely, the vehicle they were seeking had traveled a considerable distance during the night, in spite of the inhospitable terrain. Grant and the woman might even have gotten far enough to pick up a highway beyond the surveillance posts that the agency had established on every route out of the southern half of the state, in which case they had slipped through the net again.

On the other hand, perhaps they hadn't gotten far at all. They might have bogged down. They might have had mechanical failure.

Perhaps Grant had been injured in the Explorer. According to Ted Tavelov, bloodstains discolored the driver's seat, and it didn't appear as if the blood had come from the dead rat. If Grant was in bad shape, maybe he'd been *unable* to travel far.

Roy was determined to think positively. The world was what you made it—or tried to make it. His entire life was committed to that philosophy.

Of the available satellites in geosynchronous orbits that kept them positioned over the western and southwestern United States at all times, three were capable of the intense degree of surveillance that Roy Miro wished to conduct of the state of Nevada and of all neighboring states. One of those three space-based observation posts was under the control of the Drug Enforcement Administration. One was owned by the Environmental Protection Agency. The third was a military venture officially shared by the army, navy, air force, marines, and coast guard—but it was, in fact, under the iron-fisted political control of the office of the Chairman of the Joint Chiefs of Staff.

No contest. The Environmental Protection Agency.

The Drug Enforcement Administration, in spite of the dedication of its agents and largely because of meddling politicians, had pretty much failed in its assigned mission. And the military services, at least in these years following the end of the Cold War, were confused as to their purpose, under-funded, and moribund.

By contrast, the Environmental Protection Agency was fulfilling its mission to an unprecedented degree for a government agency, in part because there was no well-organized criminal element or interest group opposed to it, and because many of its workers were motivated by a fierce desire to save the natural world. The EPA cooperated so successfully with the Department of Justice that a citizen who even inadvertently contaminated protected wetlands was at risk of spending more time in prison than would a doped-up gangsta dude who killed a 7-Eleven clerk, a pregnant mother, two nuns, and a kitten while he was stealing forty dollars and a Mars bar.

Consequently, because shining success bred increased budgets and the greatest access to additional off-budget funding, the EPA owned the finest of hardware, from office equipment to orbital surveillance satellites. If any federal bureaucracy were to obtain independent control of nuclear weapons, it would be the EPA, although it was the least likely to use them—except, perhaps, in a turf dispute with the Department of the Interior.

To find Spencer Grant and the woman, therefore, the agency was using the EPA surveillance satellite—Earthguard 3—which was in a geosynchronous orbit over the western United States. To seize complete and uncontested use of that asset, Mama infiltrated EPA computers and fed them false data to the effect that Earthguard 3 had experienced sudden, total systems failure. Scientists at EPA satellite-tracking facilities had immediately mounted a campaign to diagnose the ills of Earthguard 3 by long-distance telemechanical testing. However, Mama had secretly intercepted all commands sent to that eighty-million-dollar package of sophisticated electronics—and she would continue to do so until the agency no longer needed Earthguard 3, at which time she would allow it to go on-line again for the EPA.

From space, the agency could now conduct a supramagnified visual inspection of a multistate area. It could focus all the way down to a square-meter-by-square-meter search pattern if the need arose to get in that tight on a suspect vehicle or person.

Earthguard 3 also provided two methods of highly advanced night surveillance. Using profile-guided infrared, it could differentiate between a vehicle and stationary sources of radiant heat by the very fact of the target's mobility and by its distinct thermal signature. The system also could employ a variation on Star Tron night-vision technology to magnify ambient light by a factor of eighteen thousand, making a night scene appear nearly as bright as an overcast day—although with a monochromatic, eerie green cast.

All images were automatically processed through an enhancement program aboard the satellite prior to encoding and transmission. And upon receipt in the Vegas control center, an equally automated but more sophisticated enhancement program, run on the latest-generation Cray supercomputer, further clarified the high-definition video image before projecting it on the wall display. If additional clarification was desired, stills taken from the tape could be subjected to more enhancement procedures under the supervision of talented technicians.

The effectiveness of satellite surveillance—whether infrared, night-vision, or ordinary telescopic photography—varied according to the territory under scrutiny. Generally, the more populated an area, the less successful a space-based search for anything as small as a single individual or vehicle, because there were far too many objects in motion and too many heat sources to be sorted through and analyzed either accurately or on a timely basis. Towns were easier to observe than cities, rural areas easier than towns, and open highways could be monitored better than metropolitan streets.

If Spencer Grant and the woman had been delayed in their flight, as Roy hoped, they were still in ideal territory to be located and tracked by Earthguard 3. Barren, unpopulated desert.

Saturday afternoon through evening, as suspect vehicles were spotted, they were either studied and eliminated or maintained on an under-observation list until a determination could be made that their occupants didn't fit the fugitive-party profile: woman, man, and dog.

After watching the big wall display for hours, Roy was impressed by how *perfect* their part of the world appeared to be from orbit. All colors were soft and subdued, and all shapes appeared harmonious.

The illusion of perfection was more convincing when Earthguard was surveying larger rather than smaller areas and was, therefore, using the lowest magnification. It was *most* convincing when the image was in infrared. The less he was able to detect obvious signs of human civilization, the closer to perfection the planet appeared.

Perhaps those extremists who insisted that the population of the earth be expediently reduced by ninety percent, by any means, to save the ecology were onto something. What quality of life could anyone have in a world that civilization had utterly despoiled?

If such a program of population reduction was ever instituted, he would take deep personal satisfaction in helping to administer it, although the work would be exhausting and often thankless.

The day waned without either the ground or air search turning up a trace of the fugitives. At nightfall the hunt was called off until dawn. And Earthguard 3, with all its eyes and all its ways of seeing, was no more successful than the men on foot and the helicopter crews, though at least it could continue searching throughout the night.

Roy remained in the satellite-surveillance center until almost eight o'clock, when he left with Eve Jammer for dinner at an Armenian restaurant. Over a tasty fattoush salad and then superb rack of lamb, they discussed the concept of massive and rapid population reduction. They imagined ways in which it might be achieved without undesirable side effects, such as nuclear radiation and uncontrollable riots in the streets. And they conceived *several* fair methods of determining which ten percent of the population would survive to carry on a less chaotic and drastically perfected version of the human saga. They sketched possible symbols for the population-reduction movement, composed inspiring slogans, and debated what the uniforms ought to look like. They were in a state of high excitement by the time they left the restaurant to go to Eve's place. They might have killed any cop who had been foolish enough to stop them for doing seventy miles an hour through hospital and residential zones.

• • •

The stained and shadowed walls had faces. Strange, embedded faces. Half-seen, tortured expressions. Mouths open in cries for mercy that were never answered. Hands. Reaching hands. Silently beseeching. Ghostly white tableaux, streaked gray and rust-red in some places, mottled brown and yellow in others. Face by face and body beside body, some limbs overlapping, but always the posture of the supplicant, always the expressions of despairing beggars: pleading, imploring, praying.

"Nobody knows . . . nobody knows . . ."

"Spencer? Can you hear me, Spencer?"

Valerie's voice echoed down a long tunnel to him as he walked in a place between wakefulness and true sleep, between denial and acceptance, between one hell and another.

"Easy now, easy, don't be afraid, it's okay, you're dreaming."

"No. See? See? Here in the catacombs, here, the catacombs."

"Only a dream."

"Like in school, in the book, pictures, like in Rome, martyrs, down in the catacombs, but worse, worse, worse . . ."

"You can walk away from there. It's only a dream."

He heard his own voice diminishing from a shout to a withered, miserable cry: "Oh God, oh my God, *oh my God!*"

"Here, take my hand. Spencer, can you hear me? Hold my hand. I'm here. I'm with you."

"They were so afraid, afraid, all alone and afraid. See how afraid they are? Alone, no one to hear, no one, nobody ever knew, so afraid. Oh, Jesus, Jesus, help me, Jesus."

"Come on, hold my hand, that's it, that's good, hold tight. I'm right here with you. You aren't alone anymore, Spencer."

He held on to her warm hand, and somehow she led him away from the blind white faces, the silent cries.

By the power of her hand, Spencer drifted, lighter than air, up from the deep place, through darkness, through a red door. Not the door with wet handprints on the aged-white background. This door was entirely red, dry, with a film of dust. It opened into sapphire-blue light, black booths and chairs, polished-steel trim, mirrored walls. Deserted bandstand. A handful of people drinking quietly at tables. In jeans and a suede jacket instead of slit skirt and black sweater, she sat on a barstool beside him, because business was slow. He was lying on an air mattress, sweating yet chilled, and she was perched on a stool, yet they were at the same level, holding hands, talking easily, as though they were old friends, with the hiss of the Coleman lantern in the background.

He knew he was delirious. He didn't care. She was so pretty.

"Why did you go into my house Wednesday night?"

"Already told you?"

"No. You keep avoiding an answer."

"Needed to know about you."

"Why?"

"You hate me?"

"Of course not. I just want to understand."

"Went to your place, sting grenades coming through the windows."

"You could've walked away when you realized what trouble I was."

"No, can't let you end up in a ditch, eighty miles from home."

"What?"

"Or in catacombs."

"After you knew I was trouble, why'd you wade in deeper?"

"Told you. I liked you first time we met."

"That was just Tuesday night! I'm a stranger to you."

"I want . . ."

"What?"

"I want . . . a life."

"You don't have a life?"

"A life . . . with hope."

The cocktail lounge dissolved, and the blue light changed to sour yellow. The stained and shadowed walls had faces. White faces, death masks, mouths open in voiceless terror, silently beseeching.

A spider followed the electrical cord that hung in loops from the ceiling, and its exaggerated shadow scurried across the stained white faces of the innocent.

Later, in the cocktail lounge again, he said to her, "You're a good person."

"You can't know that."

"Theda."

"Theda thinks everyone's a good person."

"She was so sick. You took care of her."

"Only for a couple of weeks."

"Day and night."

"Wasn't that big a deal."

"Now me."

"I haven't pulled you through yet."

"More I learn about you, the better you are."

She said, "Hell, maybe I *am* a saint."

"No. Just a good person. Too sarcastic to be a saint."

She laughed. "I can't help liking you, Spencer Grant."

"This is nice. Getting to know each other."

"Is that what we're doing?"

Impulsively, he said, "I love you."

Valerie was silent for so long that Spencer thought he'd lost consciousness again.

At last she said, "You're delirious."

"Not about this."

"I'll change the compress on your forehead."

"I love you."

"You better be quiet, try to get some rest."

"I'll always love you."

"Be quiet, you strange man," she said with what he believed and hoped was affection. "Just be quiet and rest."

"Always," he repeated.

Having confessed that the hope he sought was her, Spencer was so greatly relieved that he sank into a darkness without catacombs.

A long time later, not certain if he was awake or asleep, in a half-light that might have been dawn, dusk, lamp glow, or the cold and sourceless luminosity of a dream, Spencer was surprised to hear himself say, "Michael."

"Ah, you're back," she said.

"Michael."

"No one here's named Michael."

"You need to know about him," Spencer warned.

"Okay. Tell me."

He wished he could see her. There was only light and shadow, not even a blurred shape anymore.

He said, "You need to know if . . . if you're going to be with me."

"Tell me," she encouraged.

"Don't hate me when you know."

"I'm not an easy hater. Trust me, Spencer. Trust me and talk to me. Who is Michael?"

His voice was fragile. "Died when he was fourteen."

"Michael was a friend?"

"He was me. Died fourteen . . . wasn't buried till he was sixteen."

"Michael was you?"

"Walking around dead two years, then I was Spencer."

"What was your . . . what was Michael's last name?"

He knew then that he must be awake, not dreaming, because he had never felt as bad in a dream as he felt at that moment. The need to reveal could no longer be repressed, yet revelation was agony. His heart beat hard and fast, though it was pierced by secrets as painful as needles. "His last name . . . was the devil's name."

"What was the devil's name?"

Spencer was silent, trying to speak but unable.

"What was the devil's name?" she asked again.

"Ackblom," he said, spitting out the hated syllables.

"Ackblom? Why do you say that's the name of the devil?"

"Don't you remember? Didn't you ever hear?"

"I guess you'll have to tell me."

"Before Michael was Spencer," said Spencer, "he had a dad. Like other boys . . . had a dad . . . but not like other dads. His f-father's name was . . . was . . . his name was Steven. Steven Ackblom. The artist."

"Oh, my God."

"Don't be afraid of me," he pleaded, his voice breaking apart, word by desperate word.

"You're the boy?"

"Don't hate me."

"You're that boy."

"Don't hate me."

"Why would I hate you?"

"Because . . . I'm the boy."

"The boy who was a hero," she said.

"No."

"Yes, you were."

"I couldn't save them."

"But you saved all those who might've come after them."

The sound of his own voice chilled him deeper than cold rain had chilled him earlier. "Couldn't save them."

"It's all right."

"Couldn't save them." He felt a hand upon his face. Upon his scar. Tracing the hot line of his cicatricial brand.

She said, "You poor bastard. You poor, sweet bastard."

Saturday night, perched on the edge of a chair in Eve Jammer's bedroom, Roy Miro saw examples of perfection that even the best-equipped surveillance satellite could not have shown him.

This time, Eve didn't pull the satin sheets back to reveal black rubber and didn't use scented oils. She had a new—and stranger—set of toys. And although Roy was surprised to discover that it was possible, Eve achieved greater heights of self-gratification and had a greater erotic impact on him than she had managed the night before.

After a night of cataloguing Eve's perfections, Roy required the greatest patience for the imperfect day that followed.

Through Sunday morning and afternoon, satellite surveillance, helicopters, and on-foot search teams had no more success locating the fugitives than they'd had on Saturday.

Operatives in Carmel, California—sent there following Theda Davidowitz's revelation to Grant that "Hannah Rainey" had thought it was the ideal place to live—were enjoying the natural beauty and the refreshing winter fog. Of the woman, however, they had seen no sign.

From Orange County, John Kleck issued another important-sounding report to the effect that he had come up with no leads whatsoever.

In San Francisco, the agent who had tracked down the Porths, only to discover that they had died years ago, had gained access to probate records. He'd learned that Ethel Porth's estate had passed entirely to George; George's estate had passed to their grandson—Spencer Grant of Malibu, California, sole issue of the Porths' only child, Jennifer. Nothing had been found to indicate that Grant had ever gone by another name or that his father's identity was known.

From a corner of the satellite-surveillance control center, Roy spoke by telephone with Thomas Summerton. Although it was Sunday, Summerton was in his office in Washington rather than at his estate in Virginia. As security conscious as ever, he treated Roy's call as a wrong number, then phoned back on a deep-cover line a while later, using a scrambling device matched to Roy's.

"Hell of a mess in Arizona," Summerton said. He was furious.

Roy didn't know what his boss was talking about.

Summerton said, "Rich asshole activist out there, thinks he can save the world. You see the news?"

"Too busy," Roy said.

"This asshole—he's gotten some evidence that would embarrass me on the Texas situation last year. He's been feeling out some people about how best to break the story. So we were going to hit him quick, make sure there was evidence of drug dealing on his property."

"The asset-forfeiture provision?"

"Yeah. Seize everything. When his family has nothing to live on and he doesn't have the assets to pay for a serious defense, he'll come around. They usually do. But then the operation went wrong."

They usually do, Roy thought wearily. But he didn't speak his mind. He knew Summerton wouldn't appreciate candor. Besides, that thought had been a prime example of shamefully negative thinking.

"Now," Summerton said dourly, "an FBI agent's dead, out there in Arizona."

"A real one or a floater like me?"

"A real one. The asshole activist's wife and boy are dead in the front yard too, and he's sniping from the house, so we can't hide the bodies from the TV cameras down the block. And anyway, a neighbor has it all on videotape!"

"Did the guy kill his own wife and kid?"

"I wish. But maybe it can still look that way."

"Even with videotape?"

"You've been around long enough to know photographic evidence rarely clinches anything. Look at the Rodney King video. Hell, look at the Zapruder film of the Kennedy hit." Summerton sighed. "So I hope you've got good news for me, Roy, something to cheer me up."

Being Summerton's right-hand man was getting to be dreary work. Roy wished that he could report *some* progress on his current case.

"Well," Summerton said, just before hanging up, "right now no news seems like good news to me."

Later, prior to leaving the Vegas offices on Sunday evening, Roy decided to ask Mama to use NEXIS and other data-search services to scan for "Jennifer Corrine Porth" in all media data banks that were offered on various information networks—and to report by morning. The past fifteen to twenty years' issues of many major newspapers and magazines, including the *New York Times,* were electronically stored and available for on-line research. In a previous perusal of those resources, Mama had turned up the name "Spencer Grant" only related to the killing of the two carjackers in Los Angeles a few years ago. But she might have more luck with the mother's name.

If Jennifer Corrine Porth had died in a colorful fashion—or if she'd had even a middle-level reputation in business, government, or the arts—her death would have made a few major newspapers. And if Mama located any stories about her or any long obituaries, a valuable reference to Jennifer's only surviving child might be buried in them.

Roy stubbornly clung to positive thinking. He was confident that Mama would find a reference to Jennifer and break the case wide open.

The woman. The boy. The barn in the background. The man in the shadows.

He didn't have to take the photographs out of the envelope in which he was keeping them to recall those images with total clarity. The pictures teased his memory, for he knew that he'd seen the people in them before. A long time ago. In some compelling context.

Sunday night, Eve helped to keep Roy's spirits high and his thoughts on a positive track. Aware that she was adored and that Roy's adoration gave her total power over him, she worked herself into a frenzy that exceeded anything he had seen before.

For part of their unforgettable third encounter, he sat on the closed lid of the toilet, watching, while she proved that a shower stall could be as conducive to erotic games as any fur-draped, satin-sheeted, or rubber-covered bed.

He was astounded that anyone would have thought to invent and manufacture many of the water toys in her collection. Those devices were cleverly designed, intriguingly flexible, glistening with such lifelike need, convincingly *biological* in their battery- or hand-powered throbbing, mysterious and thrilling in their serpentine-knobby-dimpled-rubbery complexity. Roy was able to identify with them as if they were extensions of the body—part human, part machine—that he sometimes inhabited in dreams. When Eve handled those toys, Roy felt as though her perfect hands were fondling portions of his own anatomy by remote control.

In the blurring steam, the hot water, and the lather of scented soap, Eve seemed to be ninety percent perfect rather than just sixty percent. She was as unreal as an idealized woman in a painting.

Nothing this side of death could have been more fulfilling for Roy than watching Eve methodically stimulate one exquisite anatomical feature at a time, in each case with a device that seemed to be the amputated but functioning organ of a superlover from the future. Roy was able to focus his observations so tightly that Eve herself ceased to exist for him, and each sensuous encounter in the large shower stall—with bench and grab bars—was between one perfect body part and its fleshless analogue: erotic geometry, prurient physics, a study in the fluid dynamics of insatiable lust. The experience was untainted by personality or by any other human trait or association. Roy was transported into extreme realms of voyeuristic pleasure so intense that he almost screamed with the pain of his joy.

Spencer woke when the sun was above the eastern mountains. The light was coppery, and long morning shadows spilled westward across the badlands from every thrust of rock and impertinence of gnarled vegetation.

His vision wasn't blurred. The sun no longer stung his eyes.

Out at the edge of the shade that was provided by the tarp, Valerie sat on the ground, her back to him. She was bent to a task that he couldn't see.

Rocky was sitting at Valerie's side, his back also to Spencer.

An engine was idling. Spencer had the strength to lift his head and turn toward the sound. The Range Rover. Behind him, deeper in the tarp-covered niche. An orange utility cord led from the open driver's door of the Rover to Valerie.

Spencer felt dreadful, but he was grateful for the improvement in his condition since his most recent bout of consciousness. His skull no longer seemed about to explode; his headache was down to a dull thump over his right eye. Dry mouth. Chapped lips. But his throat wasn't hot and achy anymore.

The morning was genuinely warm. The heat wasn't from a fever, because his forehead felt cool. He threw back the blanket.

He yawned, stretched—and groaned. His muscles ached, but after the battering he had taken, that was to be expected.

Alerted by Spencer's groan, Rocky hurried to him. The mutt was grinning, trembling, whipping his tail from side to side, in a frenzy of delight to see his master awake.

Spencer endured an enthusiastic face licking before he managed to get a grip on the dog's collar and hold him at tongue's length.

Looking over her shoulder, Valerie said, "Good morning."

She was as lovely in the early sun as she had been in lamplight.

He almost repeated that sentiment aloud but was disconcerted by a dim memory of having said too much already, when he had been out of his head. He suspected himself not merely of having revealed secrets that he would rather have kept but of having been artlessly candid about his feelings for her, as ingenuous as an infatuated puppy.

As he sat up, denying the dog another lick at his face, Spencer said, "No offense, pal, but you stink something fierce."

He got to his knees, rose to his feet, and swayed for a moment.

"Dizzy?" Valerie asked.

"No. That's gone."

"Good. I think you had a bad concussion. I'm no doctor—as you made clear. But I've got some reference books with me."

"Just a little weak now. Hungry. Starving, in fact."

"That's a good sign, I think."

Now that Rocky was no longer in his face, Spencer realized that the dog didn't stink. He himself was the offending party: the wet-mud fragrance of the river, the sourness of several fever sweats.

Valerie returned to her work.

Being careful to stay upwind of her, and trying not to let the playful mutt trip him, Spencer shuffled to the edge of the shaded enclosure to see what the woman was doing.

A computer sat on a black plastic mat on the ground. It wasn't a laptop but a full PC with a MasterPiece surge protector between the logic unit and the color monitor. The keyboard was on her lap.

It was remarkable to see such an elaborate high-tech workstation plunked down in the middle of a primitive landscape that had remained largely unchanged for hundreds of thousands if not millions of years.

"How many megabytes?" he asked.

"Not mega. Giga. Ten gigabytes."

"You need all that?"

"Some of the programs I use are pretty damn complex. They fill up a lot of hard disk."

The orange electrical cord from the Rover was plugged into the logic unit. Another orange cord led from the back of the logic unit to a peculiar device sitting in the sunlight ten feet beyond the shade line of their tarp-covered hideaway: It looked like an inverted Frisbee with a flared rather than inward-curling rim; underneath, at its center, it was fixed to a ball joint, which was in turn fixed to a four-inch flexible black metal arm, which disappeared into a gray box approximately a foot square and four inches deep.

Busy at the keyboard, Valerie answered his question before he could ask it. "Satellite up-link."

"You talking to aliens?" he asked, only half joking.

"Right now, to the dee-oh-dee computer," she said, pausing to study the data that scrolled up the screen.

"Dee-oh-dee?" he wondered.

"Department of Defense."

DOD.

He squatted on his haunches. "Are you a government agent?"

"I didn't say I was talking to the DOD computer with the DOD's permission. Or knowledge, for that matter. I up-linked to a phone-company satellite, accessed one of their lines reserved for systems testing, called in to the DOD deep computer in Arlington, Virginia."

"Deep," he mused.

"Heavily secured."

"I bet that's not a number you got from directory assistance."

"Phone number's not the hardest part. It's more difficult to get the operating codes that let you use their system once you're into it. Without them, being able to make the connection wouldn't matter."

"And you have those codes?"

"I've had full access to DOD for fourteen months." Her fingers flew over the keyboard again. "Hardest to get is the access code to the program with which they periodically change all the *other* access codes. But if you don't have *that* sucker, you can't stay current unless they send you a new invitation every once in a while."

"So fourteen months ago, you just happened to find all these numbers and whatnot scrawled on a rest room wall?"

"Three people I loved gave their lives for those codes."

That response, though delivered in no graver a tone of voice than anything else Valerie had said, carried an emotional weight that left Spencer silent and pondering for a while.

A foot-long lizard—mostly brown, flecked with black and gold—slithered from under a nearby rock into the sunshine and scampered across the warm sand. When it saw Valerie, it froze and watched her. Its silver-and-green eyes were protuberant, with pebbly lids.

Rocky saw the lizard too. He retreated behind his master.

Spencer found himself smiling at the reptile, although he was not sure why he should be so pleased by its sudden appearance. Then he realized that he was unconsciously fingering the carved soapstone medallion that hung against his chest, and he understood. Louis Lee. Pheasants and dragons. Prosperity and long life.

Three people I loved gave their lives for those codes.

Spencer's smile faded. To Valerie, he said, "What are you?"

Without looking up from the display screen, she said, "You mean, am I an international terrorist or a good patriotic American?"

"Well, I wouldn't put it like that."

Instead of answering him, she said, "Over the past five days, I tried to learn what I could about you. Not very damn much. You've just about erased yourself from official existence. So I think I've got a right to ask the same question: What are *you?*"

He shrugged. "Just someone who values his privacy."

"Sure. And what I am is a concerned and interested citizen—not a whole lot different from you."

"Except I don't know how to get into DOD."

"You fiddled with your military records."

"That's an easy-access database compared with the big muddy you're wading in right now. What the hell are you looking for?"

"The DOD tracks every satellite in orbit: civilian, government, military—both domestic and foreign. I'm one-stop shopping for all the satellites with the surveillance capabilities to look down into this little corner of the world and find us if we go out and about."

"I thought that was part of a dream," he said uneasily, "that talk about eyes in the sky."

"You'd be surprised what's up there. 'Surprised' is one word. As for surveillance, there are probably two to six satellites with that capability in orbit over the western and south-western states."

Rattled, he said, "What happens when you identify them?"

"The DOD will have their access codes. I'll use those to up-link to each satellite, poke around in its current programs, and see if it's looking for us."

"This awesome lady here pokes around in satellites," he said to Rocky, but the dog seemed less impressed than his master was, as if canines had been up to similar shenanigans for ages. To Valerie, Spencer said, "I don't think the word 'hacker' is adequate for you."

"So . . . what did they call people like me when you were on that computer-crime task force?"

"I don't think we even conceived there *were* people like you."

"Well, we're here."

"They'd really hunt us with satellites?" he asked doubtfully. "I mean, we're not that important—are we?"

"They think I am. And you've got them totally confused. They can't figure out how the hell you fit in. Until they get an idea what you're all about, they'll figure you're as dangerous to them as I am—maybe more so. The unknown—that's you, from their viewpoint— is always more frightening than the known."

He mulled that over. "Who're these people you're talking about?"

"Maybe you're safer if you don't know."

Spencer opened his mouth to respond, then held his silence. He didn't want to argue. Not yet, anyway. First, he needed to clean up and get something to eat.

Without pausing in her work, Valerie explained that plastic jugs of bottled water, a basin, liquid soap, sponges, and a clean towel were just inside the Rover's tailgate. "Don't use a lot of water. It's our drinking supply if we have to be out here a few more days."

Rocky followed his master to the truck, glancing back nervously at the lizard in the sun.

Spencer discovered that Valerie had salvaged his belongings from the Explorer. He was able to shave and change into clean clothes, in addition to taking a sponge bath. He felt refreshed, and he could no longer smell his own body odor. He couldn't get his hair quite as clean as he would have liked, however, because his scalp was tender, not just around the sutured laceration but across the entire crown of his head.

The Rover was a truck-style station wagon, like the Explorer, and it was packed solid with gear and supplies from the tailgate to within two feet of the front seats. The food was just where a well-organized person would stow it: in boxes and coolers immediately be-hind the two-foot clear space, easily accessible from either the driver's or passenger's seat.

Most of the provisions were canned and bottled, except for boxes of crackers. Because Spencer was too hungry to take the time to cook, he selected two small tins of Vienna sausages, two snack-size packets of cheese crackers, and a single-serving lunch-box can of pears.

In one of the Styrofoam coolers, also within easy reach of the front seats, he found weapons. A SIG 9mm pistol. A Micro Uzi that appeared to have been illegally converted for full automatic fire. There were spare magazines of ammunition for both.

Spencer stared at the weapons, then turned to look through the windshield at the woman sitting with her computer, twenty feet away.

That Valerie was skilled at many things, Spencer had no doubt. She seemed so well pre-pared for every contingency that she could serve as the paradigm not only for all Girl Scouts but for doomsday survivalists. She was clever, intelligent, funny, daring, coura-geous, and easy to look at in lamplight, in sunlight, in any light at all. Undoubtedly she was also practiced in the use of both the pistol and the submachine gun, because other-wise she was too practical to be in possession of them: She simply wouldn't waste space on tools that she couldn't use, and she wouldn't risk the penalties for possession of a fully automatic Uzi unless she was able—and willing—to fire it.

Spencer wondered if she had ever been forced to shoot at another human being. He hoped not. And he hoped that she would never be driven to such an extreme. Sadly, however, life seemed to be handing her nothing but extremes.

He opened a tin of sausages with the ring tab on top. Resisting an urge to wolf down the contents in a single great mouthful, he ate one of the miniature frankfurters, then another. Nothing had ever tasted half as good. He popped the third in his mouth as he returned to Valerie.

Rocky danced and whimpered at his side, begging for his share.

"Mine," Spencer said.

Though he hunkered down beside Valerie, he didn't speak to her. She seemed especially focused on the cryptic data that filled the display screen.

The lizard was in the sun, alert and poised to flee, at the same spot where it had been almost half an hour earlier. Tiny dinosaur.

Spencer opened a second can of sausages, shared two with the dog, and was just finishing the last of the rest when Valerie jerked in surprise.

She gasped. *"Oh, shit!"*

The lizard vanished under the rock from which it had appeared.

Spencer glimpsed a word flashing on the display screen: LOCKON.

Valerie hit the power switch on the logic unit.

Just before the screen went dead, Spencer saw two more words flash under the first: TRACE BACK.

Valerie exploded to her feet, yanked both utility-cord plugs from the computer, and sprinted into the sun, to the microwave dish. "Load everything into the Rover!"

Getting to his feet, Spencer said, "What's happening?"

"They're using an EPA satellite." She had already retrieved the microwave dish and had turned toward him. "And they're running some sort of weird damned security program. Locks onto any invasive signal and traces back." Hurrying past him, she said, "Help me pack. Move, damn it, *move!*"

He balanced the keyboard on top of the monitor and picked up the entire workstation, including the rubber mat beneath it. Following Valerie to the Rover, his bruised muscles protesting at the demand for haste, he said, "They found us?"

"Bastards!" she fumed.

"Maybe you switched off in time."

"No."

"How can they be sure it's us?"

"They'll know."

"It was just a microwave signal, no fingerprints on it."

"They're coming," she insisted.

Sunday night, their third night together, Eve Jammer and Roy Miro had begun their passionate but contact-free lovemaking earlier in the evening than they had done previously. Therefore, although that session was the longest and most ardent to date, they concluded before midnight. Thereafter, they lay chastely side by side on her bed, in the soft blue glow of indirect neon, each of them guarded by the loving eyes of the other's reflection in the ceiling mirror. Eve was as naked as the day that she'd slipped into the world, and Roy was fully clothed. In time they enjoyed a deep and restful sleep.

Because he had brought an overnight bag, Roy was able to get ready for work in the morning without returning to his hotel suite on the Strip. He showered in the guest bath, rather than in Eve's, for he had no desire to undress and reveal his many imperfections, from his stubby toes to his knobby knees, to his paunch, to the spray of freckles and the two moles on his chest. Besides, neither of them wanted to follow the other's session in any shower stall. If he were to stand on tiles wet with her bathwater or vice versa . . . well, in a subtle but disturbing way, that act would violate the satisfyingly dry relationship, free of fluid exchanges, which they had established and on which they thrived.

He supposed some people would think them mad. But anyone who was truly in love would understand.

With no need to go to the hotel, Roy arrived at the satellite-communications room early Monday. When he walked through the door, he knew that something exciting had transpired only moments before. Several people were gathered down front, gazing up at the wall display, and the buzz of conversation had a positive sound.

Ken Hyckman, the morning duty officer, was smiling broadly. Clearly eager to be the first to impart the good news, he waved at Roy to come down to the U-shaped control console.

Hyckman was a tall, blandly handsome, blown-dry type. He looked as if he had joined the agency following an attempt at a career as a TV news anchorman.

According to Eve, Hyckman had made several passes at her, but she had put a chill on him each time. If Roy had thought that Ken Hyckman was in any way a threat to Eve, he would have blown the bastard's head off right there, and to hell with the consequences. He found considerable peace of mind, however, in the knowledge that he had fallen in love with a woman who could pretty much take care of herself.

"We found them!" Hyckman announced as Roy approached him at the control console. "She up-linked to Earthguard to see if we were using it for satellite surveillance."

"How do you know it's her?"

"It's her *style*."

"Admittedly, she's a bold one," Roy said. "But I hope you've got more to go on than sheer instinct."

"Well, hell, the up-link was from the middle of nowhere. Who else would it be?" Hyckman asked, pointing at the wall.

The orbital view currently on display was a simple, enhanced, telescopic look-down that included the southern halves of Nevada and Utah, plus the northern third of Arizona. Las Vegas was in the lower left corner. The three red and two white rings of a small, flashing bull's-eye marked the remote position from which the up-link had been initiated.

Hyckman said, "One hundred and fifteen miles north-northeast of Vegas, in desert flats northeast of Pahroc Summit and northwest of Oak Springs Summit. Middle of nowhere, like I told you."

"It's an EPA satellite we're using," Roy reminded him. "Could have been an EPA employee trying to up-link to get an aerial view of his work site beamed down to a computer there. Or a spectrographic analysis of the terrain. Or a hundred other things."

"EPA employee? But it's the middle of nowhere," Hyckman said. He seemed stuck on that phrase, as though repeating the haunting lyrics of an old song. "Middle of nowhere."

"Curiously enough," Roy said with a warm smile that took the sting out of his sarcasm, "a lot of environmental research is done in the field, right out there in the *environment*, and you'd be amazed if you knew how much of the planet is in the middle of nowhere."

"Yeah, maybe so. But if it was somebody legitimate, a scientist or something, why terminate contact so fast, before doing anything?"

"Now *that* is the first shred of meat you've provided," Roy said. "But it's not enough to nourish a certainty."

Hyckman looked bewildered. "What?"

Instead of explaining, Roy said, "What's with the bull's-eye? Targets are always marked with a white cross."

Grinning, pleased with himself, Hyckman said, "I thought this was more interesting, adds a little fun."

"Looks like a video game," Roy said.

"Thanks," Hyckman said, interpreting the slight as a compliment.

"Factoring in magnification," Roy said, "what altitude does this view represent?"

"Twenty thousand feet."

"Much too high. Bring us down to five thousand."

"We're in the process right now," Hyckman said, indicating some of the people working at the computers in the center of the room.

A cool, soft, female voice came from the control-center address system: *"Higher-magnification view coming up."*

The terrain was rugged, if not forbidding, but Valerie drove as she might have driven on a smooth ribbon of freeway blacktop. The tortured Rover leaped and plunged, rocked and swayed, bounced and shuddered across that inhospitable land, rattling and creaking as if at any moment it would explode like the overstressed springs and gearwheels of a clockwork toy.

Spencer occupied the passenger seat, with the SIG 9mm pistol in his right hand. The Micro Uzi was on the floor between his feet.

Rocky sat behind them, in the narrow clear space between the back of the front seat and the mass of gear that filled the rest of the cargo area all the way to the tailgate. The dog's good ear was pricked, because he was interested in their lurching progress, and his other ear flapped like a rag.

"Can't we slow down a little?" Spencer asked. He had to raise his voice to be heard above the tumult: the roaring engine, the tires stuttering across a washboard gully.

Valerie leaned over the steering wheel, looked up at the sky, craned her head left and right. "Wide and blue. No clouds anywhere, damn it. I was hoping we wouldn't have to make a run for it until we had clouds again."

"Does it matter? What about the infrared surveillance you were talking about, the way they can see through clouds?"

Looking ahead again as the Range Rover chewed its way up the gully wall, she said, "That's a threat when we're sitting still, in the middle of nowhere, the only unnatural heat source for miles. But it's not much good to them when we're on the move. Especially not if we were on a highway, with other cars, where they can't analyze the Rover's heat signature and distinguish it in traffic."

The top of the gully wall proved to be a low ridge, over which they shot with sufficient speed to be airborne for a second or two. They slammed front-tires-first onto a long, gradual slope of gray-black-pink shale.

Slivers of shale, spun up by the tires, showered against the undercarriage, and Valerie shouted to be heard above a hard clatter as loud as a hailstorm: "With a sky that blue, we have more to worry about than infrared. They have a clear, bare-eyed look-down at us."

"You think they've already seen us?"

"You can bet your ass they're already *looking* for us," she said, barely audible because of the machine-gun shatters of shale that volleyed beneath them.

"Eyes in the sky," he said, more to himself than to her.

The world seemed upside down: Blue heavens had become the place where demons lived.

Valerie shouted: "Yeah, they're looking. And for sure, it won't be much longer till we're spotted, considering we're the only moving thing, other than snakes and jackrabbits, for at least five miles in any direction."

The Rover roared off the shale onto softer soil, and the sudden diminution of noise was such a relief that the usual tumult, which had earlier been so annoying, now seemed by comparison like the music of a string quartet.

Valerie said, "Damn! I only up-linked to confirm that it was clear. I didn't really think they'd still be there, still tying up a satellite for a third day. And I sure as hell didn't think they'd be locking on incoming signals."

"Three days?"

"Yeah, they probably started surveillance before dawn Saturday, as soon as the storm passed and the sky cleared. Oh, man, they must want us even worse than I thought."

"What day is this?" he asked uneasily.

"Monday."

"I was sure this was Sunday."

"You were dead to the world a lot longer than you think. Since sometime Friday afternoon."

Even if unconsciousness had healed into ordinary sleep sometime during the previous night, he had been pretty much out of his head for forty-eight to sixty hours. Because he valued self-control so highly, the contemplation of such a lengthy delirium made him queasy.

He remembered some of what he'd said when he'd been out of his head. He wondered what else he had told her that he couldn't recall.

Looking at the sky again, Valerie said, "I *hate* these bastards!"

"Who are they?" he asked, not for the first time.

"You don't want to know," she said, as before. "As soon as you know, you're a dead man."

"Looks like there's a good chance I'm already a dead man. And I sure wouldn't want them to whack me and never know who they were."

She mulled that over as she accelerated up another hill, a long one this time. "Okay. You've got a point. But later. Right now, I've got to concentrate on getting us out of this mess."

"There's a way out?"

"Between slim and none—but a way."

"I thought, with that satellite, they were going to spot us any second now."

"They will. But the nearest place the bastards have any men is probably back in Vegas, a hundred and ten miles from here, maybe even a hundred twenty. That's how far I got Friday night, before I decided that staying on the move was making you worse. By the time they get a hit squad together and fly in here after us, we've got two hours minimum, two and a half max."

"To do what?"

"To lose them again," she said somewhat impatiently.

"How do we lose them if they're watching us from outer space, for God's sake?" he demanded.

"Boy, does *that* sound paranoid," she said.

"It's not paranoid, it's what they're *doing*."

"I know, I know. But it sure sounds crazy, doesn't it?" She adopted a voice not dissimilar from that of Goofy, the Disney cartoon character. "Watching us from outer space, funny little men in pointy hats, with ray guns, gonna steal our women, destroy the world."

Behind them, Rocky woofed softly, intrigued by the Goofy voice.

She dropped the funny voice. "Are we living in screwed-up times or what? God in Heaven, are we ever."

As they crested the top of the long hill, giving the springs another hard workout, Spencer said, "One minute I think I know you, and the next minute I don't know you at all."

"Good. Keeps you alert. We need to be alert."

"You suddenly seem to think this is funny."

"Oh, sometimes I can't *feel* the humor any more than you're able to right now. But we live in God's amusement park. Take it too seriously, you'll go nuts. On some level, everything's funny, even the blood and the dying. Don't you think so?"

"No. No, I don't."

"Then how do you ever get along?" she asked, but not in the least flippantly, with total seriousness now.

"It hasn't been easy."

The broad, flat top of the hill featured more brush than they had yet encountered. Valerie didn't let up on the accelerator, and the Rover smashed through everything in its way.

Spencer persisted: "How will we lose them if they're watching us from outer space?"

"Trick 'em."

"How?"

"With some clever moves."

"Such as?"

"I don't know yet."

He wouldn't relent: "When will you know?"

"I sure hope before our two hours are up." She frowned at the odometer. "Seems like we ought to've gone six miles."

"Seems like a hundred. Much more of this damn bouncing, and my headache's going to come back hard."

The broad top of the hill didn't drop off abruptly but melted into a long, descending slope that was covered with tall grass as dry, pale, and translucent as insect wings. At the bottom were two lanes of blacktop that led east and west.

"What's that?" he wondered.

"Old Federal Highway Ninety-three," she said.

"You knew it was there? How?"

"Either I studied a map while you were out of your head—or I'm just dead-on psychic."

"Probably both," he said, for again she had surprised him.

Because the view from five thousand feet didn't provide adequate resolution of car-size objects at ground level, Roy requested that the system focus down to one thousand feet.

For clarity, that extreme degree of magnification required more than the usual amount of image enhancement. The additional processing of the incoming Earthguard transmission required so much computer capacity that other agency work was halted to free the Cray for this urgent task. Otherwise, more minutes of delay would have occurred between receipt of an image and its projection in the control center.

Less than a minute passed before the cool, almost whispery, female voice again spoke softly from the public-address system: *"Suspect vehicle acquired."*

Ken Hyckman dashed away from the control console into the two rows of computers, all of which were manned. He returned within another minute, boyish and buoyant. "We've got her."

"We can't know yet," Roy cautioned.

"Oh, we've got her, all right," Hyckman said excitedly, turning to beam at the wall display. "What other vehicle would be out there, on the move, in the same area where somebody tried to up-link?"

"Could still be some EPA scientist."

"Suddenly on the run?"

"Maybe just moving around."

"Moving *real* fast for the terrain."

"Well, there aren't any speed limits out there."

"Too coincidental," said Hyckman. "It's her."

"We'll see."

With a ripple, beginning at the left and moving to the right across the wall display, the image changed. The new view shifted, blurred, shifted, cleared, shifted, blurred, cleared again—and they were looking down from one thousand feet onto rough terrain.

A vehicle of unidentifiable type and make, obviously with off-road capability, raced across a table of brush-covered land. It was still a woefully tiny object seen from that altitude.

"Focus down to five hundred feet," Roy ordered.

"Higher-magnification view coming up."

After a brief delay, the display rippled left to right again. The image blurred, shifted, blurred, cleared.

Earthguard 3 was not directly over the moving target but in a geosynchronous orbit to the east and north. Therefore, the target was observed at an angle, which required additional automated processing of the image to eliminate distortions caused by the perspective. The result, however, was a picture that included not only the rectangular forms of the roof and hood but a severe angular view of one flank of the vehicle.

Although Roy knew that an element of distortion still remained, he was half convinced that he could see a couple of brighter spots glimmering in that fleet shadow, which might have been driver's-side windows reflecting the morning sun.

As the suspect vehicle reached the brink of the hill and began to descend a long slope, Roy peered at the foremost of those possible windows and wondered if, indeed, the woman waited to be discovered on the other side of a pane of sun-bronzed glass. Had they found her at last?

The target was approaching a highway.

"What road is that?" Roy demanded. "Give us some overlays, let's identify this. Quickly."

Hyckman pressed a console key and spoke into the microphone.

On the wall, by the time the suspect turned east onto the two-lane highway, a multicolored overlay identified a few topographical features—as well as Federal Highway 93.

When Valerie didn't hesitate before turning east on the highway, Spencer said, "Why not west?"

"Because there's nothing in that direction but Nevada badlands. First town is over two hundred miles. Warm Springs, they call it, but it's so small it might as well be Warm *Spit*. We'd never get that far. Lonely, empty land. There's a thousand places they could hit us between here and there, and no one would ever see what happened. We'd just disappear off the face of the earth."

"So where are we headed?"

"It's several miles to Caliente, then ten more to Panaca—"

"They don't sound like metropolises, either."

"Then we cross the border into Utah. Modena, Newcastle—they aren't exactly cities that never sleep. But after Newcastle, there's Cedar City."

"Big time."

"Fourteen thousand people or thereabouts," she said. "Which is maybe all the bigger we need to give us a chance to slip surveillance long enough to get out of the Rover and into something else."

The two-lane blacktop featured frequent subsidence swales, lumpy patches, and unrepaired potholes. Along both shoulders, the pavement was deteriorating. As an obstacle course, it provided no challenge to the Rover—though after the jolting overland journey, Spencer wished the truck had cushier springs and shock absorbers.

Regardless of the road condition, Valerie kept the pedal down, maintaining a speed that was punishing if not reckless.

"I hope this pavement gets better soon," he said.

"Judging by the map, it probably gets worse after Panaca. From there on, all the way into Cedar City, it's just state routes."

"And how far to Cedar City?"

"About a hundred and twenty miles," she said, as though that was not bad news.

He gaped at her in disbelief. "You've got to be kidding. Even with luck, on roads like this—roads worse than this!—we'll need two hours to get there."

"We're doing seventy now."

"And it feels like a hundred and seventy!" His voice quavered as the tires jittered over a section of pavement that was as runneled as corduroy.

Her voice vibrating too, she said, "Boy, I hope you don't have hemorrhoids."

"You won't be able to keep up this speed all the way. We'll be getting into Cedar City with that hit squad right on our ass."

She shrugged. "Well, I'll bet people around there could use some excitement. Been a long time since last summer's Shakespeare Festival."

At Roy's request, the magnification had been increased again to provide a view equivalent to the one that they would have had if they really had been two hundred feet above the target. Image enhancement became more difficult with each incremental increase in magnification—but fortunately there was enough additional logic-unit capacity to avoid a further processing delay.

The scale of the wall display was so much larger than before that the target rapidly progressed across the width, vanishing off the right-hand edge. But it reappeared from the left as Earthguard projected a new segment of territory that lay immediately east of the one out of which the target had driven.

The truck was rushing east, instead of south as before, so the angle now revealed some of the windshield, across which played reflections of sunlight and shadow.

"Target profile identified as that of a late-model Range Rover."

Roy Miro stared at the wall display, trying to make up his mind whether to bet the bank that the suspect vehicle contained at least the woman, if not also the scarred man.

Occasionally he glimpsed dark figures within the Rover, but he couldn't identify them. He couldn't even see well enough to be sure how many people were in the damn thing or what sex they were.

Further magnification would require long, tedious enhancement sessions. By the time they were able to obtain a more detailed look inside that vehicle, the driver would have been able to reach—and get lost in—any of half a dozen major cities.

If he committed men and equipment to stopping the Range Rover, and if the occupants proved to be innocent people, he would forfeit any chance of nailing the woman. She might break cover while he was distracted, might slip down into Arizona or back into California.

"Target's speed is seventy-two miles per hour."

To justify going after the Rover, a lot of assumptions had to be made, with little or no supporting evidence. That Spencer Grant had survived when his Explorer had been swept away in a flash flood. That somehow he had been able to alert the woman to his whereabouts. That she had rendezvoused with him in the desert, and that they had driven away together in her vehicle. That the woman, realizing the agency might resort to orbital-surveillance resources to locate her, had gone to ground early Saturday, before the cloud cover dissipated. That this morning she had broken cover, had started up-linking with available surveillance satellites to determine if anyone was still looking specifically for her, had been surprised by the trace-back program, and had just minutes ago begun to run for her life.

That was a series of assumptions long enough to make Roy uneasy.

"Target's speed is seventy-four miles per hour."

"Too damn fast for the roads in that area," Ken Hyckman said. "It's her, and she's scared."

Saturday and Sunday, Earthguard had discovered two hundred sixteen suspect vehicles in the designated search zone, most of which had been engaged in off-road recreation of one kind or another. The drivers and passengers eventually had gotten out of their vehicles, been observed either by satellite or chopper overflight, and proved not to be Grant or the woman. This might be number two hundred seventeen on that list of false alarms.

"Target's speed is seventy-six miles per hour."

On the other hand, this was the best suspect they'd had in more than two days of searching.

And ever since Friday afternoon in Flagstaff, Arizona, the power of Kevorkian had been with him. It had brought him to Eve and had changed his life. He should trust in it to guide his decisions.

He closed his eyes, took several deep breaths, and said, "Let's put a team together and go after them."

"Yes!" Ken Hyckman said, punching one fist into the air in an annoying, adolescent expression of enthusiasm.

"Twelve men, full assault gear," Roy said, "leaving in fifteen minutes or less. Arrange transport from the roof here, so we don't waste time. Two large executive choppers."

"You got it," Hyckman promised.

"Make sure they understand to terminate the woman on sight."

"Of course."

"With extreme prejudice."

Hyckman nodded.

"Give her no chance—*no chance*—to slip loose again. But we have to take Grant alive, interrogate him, find out how he fits into all this, who the sonofabitch is working for."

"To give you the quality of satellite look-down you'll need in the field," Hyckman said, "we'll have to remote-program Earthguard to alter its orbit temporarily, nail it specifically to that Rover."

"Do it," Roy said.

TWELVE

By that Monday morning in February, Captain Harris Descoteaux, of the Los Angeles Police Department, would not have been surprised to discover that he had died the previous Friday and had been in Hell ever since. The outrages perpetrated upon him would have occupied the time and energies of numerous clever, malicious, industrious demons.

At eleven-thirty Friday night, as Harris was making love to his wife, Jessica, and as their daughters—Willa and Ondine—were asleep or watching television in other bedrooms, an FBI special-weapons-and-tactics team, in a joint operation between the FBI and the Drug Enforcement Administration, raided the Descoteaux house on a quiet street in Burbank. The assault was executed with the stalwart commitment and merciless force exhibited by any platoon of United States Marines in any battle in any war in the country's history.

On all sides of the house, with a synchronization that would have been envied by the most demanding symphony-orchestra conductor, stun grenades were launched through windows. The blasts of sound instantly disoriented Harris, Jessica, and their daughters, and also temporarily impaired their motor-nerve functions.

Even as porcelain figurines toppled and paintings clattered against walls in response to those shock waves, the front and back doors were battered down. Heavily armed men in black helmets and bullet-resistant vests swarmed into the Descoteaux residence and dispersed like a doomsday tide through its rooms.

One moment, in romantically soft amber lamplight, Harris was in the arms of his wife, gliding back and forth on the sweet dissolving edge of bliss. The next moment, passion having turned to terror, he was staggering around in the infuriatingly *dim* lamplight, naked and confused. His limbs twitched, his knees repeatedly buckled, and the room seemed to tumble like a giant barrel in a carnival fun house.

Though his ears were ringing, he heard men shouting elsewhere in the house: "FBI! FBI! FBI!" The booming voices weren't reassuring. Addled by a stun grenade, he couldn't think what those letters meant.

He remembered the nightstand. His revolver. Loaded.

He couldn't recall how to open a drawer. Suddenly it seemed to require superhuman intelligence, the dexterity of a torch juggler.

Then the bedroom was crowded with men as big as professional football players, all shouting at once. They forced Harris to lie facedown on the floor, with his hands behind his head.

His mind cleared. He remembered the meaning of FBI. Terror and confusion didn't evaporate, but diminished to fear and bafflement.

A helicopter roared into position above the house. Searchlights swept the yard. Over the furious pounding of the rotors, Harris heard a sound so cold that he felt as if ice had formed in his blood: his daughters, screaming as the doors to their rooms crashed open.

Being required to lie naked on the floor while Jessica was rousted from bed, equally naked, was deeply humiliating. They made her stand in a corner, with only her hands to cover herself, while they searched the bed for weapons. After an eternity, they tossed a blanket to her, and she wrapped herself in it.

Harris was eventually permitted to sit on the edge of the bed, still naked, burning with humiliation. They presented the search warrant, and he was surprised to find his name and address. He had assumed that they had invaded the wrong house. He explained that he was an LAPD captain, but they already knew and were unmoved.

At last Harris was permitted to dress in gray exercise sweats. He and Jessica were taken into the living room.

Ondine and Willa were huddled on the sofa, hugging each other for emotional support. The girls tried to rush to their parents but were restrained by officers who ordered them to remain seated.

Ondine was thirteen, and Willa was fourteen. Both girls had their mother's beauty. Ondine was dressed for bed in panties and a T-shirt that featured the face of a rap singer. Willa was wearing a cut-off T-shirt, cut-off pajama bottoms, and yellow knee socks.

Some officers were looking at the girls in a way they had no right to look. Harris asked that his daughters be allowed to put on robes, but he was ignored. While Jessica was taken to an armchair, Harris was flanked by two men who tried to lead him out of the room.

When he again requested that the girls be given robes and was ignored, he pulled away from his escorts, indignant. His indignation was interpreted as resistance. He was hit in the stomach with the butt of an assault rifle, driven to his knees, and handcuffed.

In the garage, a man who identified himself as "Agent Gurland" was at the workbench, examining a hundred plastic-wrapped kilos of cocaine, worth millions. Harris stared in disbelief, with a growing chill, as he was told that the coke had been found in his garage.

"I'm innocent. I'm a cop. I've been set up. This is nuts!"

Gurland perfunctorily recited a list of constitutional rights.

Harris was infuriated by their indifference to everything he said. His anger and frustration earned him more rough handling as he was escorted out of the house to a car at the curb. Along the street, neighbors had come onto their lawns and porches to watch.

He was taken to a federal detention facility. There he was permitted to call his attorney— who was his brother, Darius.

By virtue of being a policeman, and therefore endangered if confined with cop-hating felons, he expected to be segregated in the lockup. Instead, he was put into a holding cell with six men waiting to be charged on offenses ranging from interstate transportation of illegal drugs to the hatchet murder of a federal marshal.

All claimed that they were being railroaded. Although a few were *obviously* bad pieces of work, the captain found himself more than half believing their protestations of innocence.

At two-thirty Saturday morning, sitting across from Harris at a scarred Formica-topped table in a lawyer-client conference room, Darius said, "This is total bullshit, total, it stinks, it really *reeks*. You're the most honest man I've ever known, a straight arrow since you were a kid. You made it *hell* for a brother to measure up. You're an annoying goddamned *saint*, is what you are! Anyone who says you're a cocaine dealer is a moron or a liar. Listen, don't worry about this, don't worry for a minute, a second, a nanosecond. You have an exemplary past, not a stain, the record of an annoying goddamned saint. We'll get low bail, and eventually we'll convince them it's a mistake or a conspiracy. Listen, I swear to you, it's never going to go to trial, on our mother's grave, I swear to you."

Darius was five years younger than Harris but resembled him to such an extent that they seemed to be twins. He was also as brilliant as he was hyperkinetic, a fine criminal trial attorney. If Darius said there was no reason to worry, Harris would try not to worry.

"Listen, if it's a conspiracy," Darius said, "who's behind it? What walking slime would do this? Why? What enemies have you made?"

"I can't think of any. Not any who're capable of this."

"It's total bullshit. We'll have them crawling on their bellies to apologize, the bastards, the morons, the ignorant geeks. This *burns* me. Even saints make enemies, Harris."

"I can't point a finger," Harris insisted.

"Maybe saints *especially* make enemies."

Less than eight hours later, shortly after ten o'clock Saturday morning, with his brother at his side, Harris was brought before a judge. He was ordered held for trial. The federal prosecutor wanted a ten-million-dollar bail, but Darius argued for Harris's release on his own recognizance. Bail was set at five hundred thousand, which Darius considered acceptable because Harris would be free upon posting ten percent to a bondsman's ninety.

Harris and Jessica had seventy-three thousand in stocks and savings accounts. Since Harris didn't intend to flee prosecution, they would get their money back when he went to court.

The situation wasn't ideal. But before they could proceed to structure a legal counteroffensive and get the charges dismissed, Harris had to regain his freedom and escape the extraordinary danger faced by a police officer in jail. At least events were finally moving in the right direction.

Seven hours later, at five o'clock Saturday afternoon, Harris was taken from the holding cell to the lawyer-client conference room, where Darius was waiting for him again—with bad news. The FBI had persuaded a judge that probable cause existed to conclude that the Descoteaux house had been used for illegal purposes, thus permitting immediate application of federal property-forfeiture statutes. The FBI and DEA then acquired liens against the house and its contents.

To protect the government's interests, federal marshals had evicted Jessica, Willa, and Ondine, permitting them to pack only a few articles of clothing. The locks had been changed. At least for the time being, guards were posted at the property.

Darius said, "This is crap. Okay, maybe it doesn't technically violate the recent Supreme Court decision on forfeiture, but it sure as hell violates the *spirit*. For one thing, the court said they now have to give the property owner a notice of intent to seize."

"Intent to seize?" Harris said, bewildered.

"Of course, they'll say they served that notice at the same time as the eviction order, which they did. But the court clearly meant there should be a decent interval between notice and eviction."

Harris didn't understand. "Evicted Jessica and the girls?"

"Don't worry about them," Darius said. "They're staying with Bonnie and me. They're all right."

"How can they evict them?"

"Until the Supreme Court rules on other aspects of forfeiture laws, if it ever does, eviction can still take place prior to the hearing, which is unfair. Unfair? Jesus, it's worse than unfair, it's totalitarian. At least these days you get a hearing, which wasn't required till recently. You'll go before a judge in ten days, and he'll listen to your argument against forfeiture."

"It's my house."

"That's no argument. We'll do better than that."

"But it's my house."

"I have to tell you, the hearing doesn't mean much. The feds will pull every trick in the book to be sure it's assigned to a judge with a strong history of endorsing the forfeiture laws. I'll try to prevent that, try to get you a judge who still remembers this is supposed to be a democracy. But the reality is, ninety-nine percent of the time, the feds get the judge they want. We'll have a hearing, but the ruling is almost certain to be against us and in favor of forfeiture."

Harris was having difficulty absorbing the horror of what his brother had told him. Shaking his head, he said, "They can't put my family out of the house. I haven't been convicted of anything."

"You're a cop. You must know how the forfeiture laws work. They've been on the books ten years, growing broader every year."

"I'm a cop, yes, not a prosecutor. I get the bad guys, and the district attorney's office decides under what laws to prosecute."

"Then this will be an unpleasant lesson. See . . . to lose your property under forfeiture statutes, you don't have to be convicted."

"They can take my property even if I'm found innocent?" Harris said, and he was sure that he was having a nightmare based on some Kafka short story he'd read in college.

"Harris, listen very closely here. Forget about conviction or acquittal. *They can take your property and not even charge you with a crime.* Without taking you to court. Of course, you *have* been charged, which gives them an even stronger hand."

"Wait, wait. How did this happen?"

"If there's evidence of any nature that the property was used for an illegal purpose, *even one of which you have no knowledge,* that's sufficient probable cause for forfeiture. Isn't that a cute touch? You don't even have to know about it, to lose your property."

"No, I mean, *how did this happen in America?*"

"The war against drugs. That's what the forfeiture laws were written for. To come down hard on drug dealers, break them."

Darius was more subdued than on his previous visit that morning. His hyperkinetic nature was expressed not primarily in his usual, voluble flow of words as much as in his ceaseless fidgeting.

Harris was as alarmed by the change in his brother as by what he was learning. "This evidence, the cocaine, was *planted.*"

"You know that, I know that. But the court has to see you prove it before it'll reverse a forfeiture."

"You mean, I'm guilty till proven innocent."

"That's the way the forfeiture laws work. But at least you've been charged with a crime. You'll have your day in court. By proving you're innocent in a criminal trial, you'll indirectly have a chance to prove forfeiture was unjustified. Now, I hope to God they don't drop the charges."

Harris blinked in surprise. "You hope they *don't* drop them?"

"If they drop the charges, no criminal trial. Then the best chance you'll ever have to get your house back is at the upcoming hearing I mentioned."

"My *best* chance? At this rigged hearing?"

"Not rigged exactly. Just in front of *their* judge."

"What's the difference?"

Darius nodded wearily. "Not much. And once forfeiture is approved in that hearing, if you didn't have a criminal trial in which to state your case, you'd have to initiate legal action, sue the FBI and the DEA, to get the forfeiture overturned. That would be an uphill battle. Government attorneys would repeatedly attempt to have your suit dismissed—until they found a sympathetic court. Even if you got a jury or panel of judges to overturn the forfeiture, the government would appeal and appeal, trying to exhaust you."

"But if they dropped the charges against me, how could they still keep my house?" He understood what his brother had told him. He just didn't understand the logic or the justice of it.

"Like I explained," Darius said patiently, "all they have to show is evidence the *property* was used for illegal purposes. Not that you or any member of your family was involved in that activity."

"But then who would they claim was stashing cocaine there?"

Darius sighed. "They don't have to name anyone."

Astonished, reluctantly accepting the full monstrousness of it at last, Harris said, "They can seize my house by claiming someone was dealing drugs out of it—but not have to name a suspect?"

"As long as they have evidence, yes."

"The evidence was planted!"

"Like I explained already, you'd have to prove that to a court."

"But if they don't charge me with a crime, I might never get *into* a court with a suit of my own."

"Right." Darius smiled humorlessly. "Now you see why I hope to God they don't drop the charges. Now you understand the rules."

"Rules?" Harris said. "These aren't rules. This is *madness.*"

He needed to pace, work off a sudden dark energy that filled him. His anger and outrage were so great that his knees were weak when he tried to stand. Halfway to his feet, he was forced to sit again, as if suffering the effects of another stun grenade.

"You okay?" Darius worried.

"But these laws were only supposed to target major drug dealers, racketeers, Mafia."

"Sure. People who might liquidate property, flee the country before they went to trial. That was the original intent when the laws were passed. But now there are two hundred federal offenses, not just drug offenses, that allow property forfeiture without trial, and they were used fifty thousand times last year."

"Fifty thousand!"

"It's becoming a major source of funding for law enforcement. Once liquidated, eighty percent of seized assets goes to the police agencies in the case, twenty percent to the prosecutor."

They sat in silence. The old-fashioned wall clock ticked softly. The sound brought to mind the image of a time bomb, and Harris felt as though he were, in fact, sitting on just such an explosive device.

No less angry than he had been but more in control of his anger, he said at last, "They're going to sell my house, aren't they?"

"Well, at least this is a federal seizure. If it was under the California forfeiture law, it'd be gone ten days after the hearing. Feds give us more time."

"They'll sell it."

"Listen, we'll do everything we can to overturn before then. . . ." Darius's voice trailed away. He was no longer able to look his brother in the eyes. Finally he said, "And even after assets are liquidated, if you can overturn, then you can get compensation—though not for any costs you incurred related to the forfeiture."

"But I can kiss my house good-bye. I might get money back but not my house. And I can't get back all the *time* this will take."

"There's legislation in Congress to reform these laws."

"Reform? Not toss them out completely?"

"No. The government likes the laws too much. Even the proposed reforms don't go far enough and don't have wide support yet."

"Evicted my family," Harris said, still gripped by disbelief.

"Harris, I feel rotten. I'll do everything I can, I'll be a tiger on their ass, I swear, but I ought to be able to do *more*."

Harris's hands were fisted again on the table. "None of this is your fault, little brother. You didn't write the laws. We'll . . . just cope. Somehow, we'll cope. The important thing now is to post bail, so I can get out of here."

Darius put the heels of his coal-black hands to his eyes and pressed gently, as if trying to banish his weariness. Like Harris, he hadn't slept the previous night. "That's going to take until Monday. I'll go to my bank first thing Monday morning—"

"No, no. You don't have to put up your money for bail. We've got it. Didn't Jessica tell you? And our bank's open Saturdays."

"She told me. But—"

"Not open now, but it was earlier. God, I wanted out today."

Lowering his hands from his face, Darius met his brother's eyes with reluctance. "Harris, they've impounded your bank accounts too."

"They can't do that," he said angrily, but no longer with any conviction. "Can they?"

"Savings, checking, all of it, whether it was a joint account with Jessie, in your name, or just in her name. They're calling it all illegal drug profits, even the Christmas-club account."

Harris felt as if he'd been hit in the face. A strange numbness began to spread through him. "Darius, I can't . . . I can't let you put up all the bail. Not fifty thousand. We have some stocks—"

"Your brokerage account's impounded too, pending forfeiture."

Harris stared at the clock. The second hand twitched around the face. The time-bomb sound seemed louder, louder.

Reaching across the conference-room table, putting his hands over Harris's fists, Darius said, "Big brother, I swear, we'll get through this together."

"With everything impounded . . . we have nothing but the cash in my wallet and Jessica's purse. Jesus. Maybe just her purse. My wallet is in the nightstand drawer at home, if she didn't think to bring it when . . . when they made her and the girls leave."

"So Bonnie and I are putting up bail, and we don't want any argument about it," Darius said.

Tick . . . tick . . . tick . . .

Harris's entire face was numb. The back of his neck was numb, pebbled with gooseflesh. Numb and cold.

Darius squeezed his brother's hands reassuringly once more, and then finally let go.

Harris said, "How are Jessica and I going to rent a place if we can't put together first month, last month, and security deposit?"

"You'll move in with Bonnie and me for the duration. That's already been settled."

"Your house isn't that big. You don't have room for four more."

"Jessie and the girls are already with us. You're just one more. Sure, it'll be tight, but we'll be fine. Nobody'll mind if it's a bit of a squeeze. We're family. We're in this together."

"But this might take months to get resolved. My God, it could take *years*, couldn't it?"

Tick . . . tick . . . tick . . .

Later, as Darius was about to leave, he said, "I want you to think hard about enemies, Harris. This isn't all just a big mistake. This took planning, cunning, and contacts. Somewhere, you've got a smart and powerful enemy, whether you realize it or not. Think about it. If you come up with any names, that might help me."

Saturday night, Harris shared a windowless four-bed cell with two alleged murderers and with a rapist who bragged about assaulting women in ten states. He slept only fitfully.

Sunday night, he slept much better, only because he was by then utterly exhausted. Dreams tormented him. All were nightmares, and in each, sooner or later, there was a clock ticking, ticking.

Monday, he was up at dawn, eager to be free. He was loath to let Darius and Bonnie tie up so much money to make his bail. Of course, he had no intention of fleeing jurisdiction, so they wouldn't lose their funds. And he had developed a prison claustrophobia that, if it continued to worsen, would soon be intolerable.

Though his situation was dreadful, unthinkable, he nevertheless took some solace from the certainty that the worst was behind him. Everything had been taken away—or soon would be taken. He was at the bottom, and in spite of the long fight ahead, he had nowhere to go but up.

That was Monday morning. Early.

At Caliente, Nevada, the federal highway angled north, but at Panaca they left it for a state route that turned east toward the Utah border. The rural highway carried them into higher land that had a stark, cauldron-of-creation quality, almost pre-Mesozoic, even though it was forested with pine and spruce.

As crazy as it sounded, Spencer was nevertheless completely convinced by Valerie's fear of satellite surveillance. All was blue above, with no monstrous mechanical presences hovering like something out of *Star Wars*, but he was uncomfortably aware of being watched, mile by lonely mile.

Regardless of the eye in the sky and the professional killers who might be en route to Utah to intercept them, Spencer was ravenous. Two small cans of Vienna sausages had not satisfied his hunger. He ate cheese crackers and washed them down with a Coke.

Behind the front seats, sitting erect in his narrow quarters, Rocky was so enthusiastic about Valerie's way with a Rover that he expressed no interest in the cheese crackers. He grinned broadly. His head bobbed up and down, up and down.

"What's with the dog?" she asked.

"He likes the way you drive. He has a need for speed."

"Really? He's such a frightened little guy most of the time."

"I just found out about this speed thing myself," Spencer said.

"Why's he so afraid of everything?"

"He was abused before he wound up in the pound, before I brought him home. I don't know what's in his past."

"Well, it's nice to see him enjoying himself so much."

Rocky's head bobbed enthusiastically.

As tree shadows flickered across the roadway, Spencer said, "I don't know what's in your past, either." Instead of responding, she eased down on the accelerator, but Spencer persisted: "Who are you running from? Now they're my enemies too. I have a right to know."

She stared intently at the road. "They don't have a name."

"What—a secret society of fanatical assassins, like in an old Fu Manchu novel?"

"More or less." She was serious. "It's a nameless government agency, financed by misdirected appropriations intended for lots of other programs. Also by hundreds of millions of dollars a year from cases involving the asset-forfeiture laws. Originally it was intended to be used to conceal the illegal actions and botched operations of government bureaus and agencies ranging from the post office to the FBI. A political pressure-release valve."

"An independent cover-up squad."

"Then if a reporter or anybody discovered evidence of a cover-up in a case that, say, the FBI had investigated, that cover-up couldn't be traced to anyone in the FBI itself. This independent group covers the Bureau's ass, so the Bureau never has to destroy evidence, bribe judges, intimidate witnesses, all that nasty stuff. The perpetrators are mysterious, nameless. No proof they're government employees."

The sky was still blue and cloudless, but the day seemed darker than it had been before.

Spencer said, "There's enough paranoia in this concept for half a dozen Oliver Stone movies."

"Stone sees the shadow of the oppressor but doesn't understand who casts it," she said. "Hell, even the average FBI or ATF agent is unaware this agency exists. It operates at a very high level."

"How high?" he wondered.

"Its top officers answer to Thomas Summerton."

Spencer frowned. "Is that name supposed to mean something?"

"He's independently wealthy, a major political fund-raiser and wheeler-dealer. And currently the first deputy attorney general."

"Of what?"

"Of the Kingdom of Oz—what do you think?" she said impatiently. "First Deputy Attorney General of the United States!"

"You've got to be putting me on."

"Look it up in an almanac, read a newspaper."

"I don't mean you're kidding about him being the first deputy. I mean, about him being involved in a conspiracy like this."

"I know it for a fact. I know *him*. Personally."

"But in that position, he's the second most powerful person in the Department of Justice. The next link up the chain from him . . ."

"Curdles your blood, doesn't it?"

"Are you saying the attorney general knows about this?"

She shook her head. "I don't know. I hope not. I've never seen any evidence. But I don't rule out anything anymore."

Ahead, in the westbound lane, a gray Chevrolet van topped a hill and came toward them. Spencer didn't like the looks of it. According to Valerie's schedule, they weren't likely to be in immediate danger for the better part of two hours yet. But she might be wrong. Maybe the agency didn't have to fly in thugs from Vegas. Maybe it already had operatives in the area.

He wanted to tell her to turn off the road at once. They had to put trees between themselves and any fusillade of machine-gun fire directed at them. But there was nowhere to go: no connecting road in sight and a six-foot drop beyond the narrow shoulder.

He put his hand on the SIG 9mm pistol that lay in his lap.

As the oncoming Chevy passed the Rover, the driver gave them a look of astonished recognition. He was big. About forty. A broad, hard face. His eyes widened, and his mouth opened as he spoke to another man in the van with him, and then he was gone.

Spencer turned in his seat to look after the Chevy, but because of Rocky and half a ton of gear, he wasn't able to see through the tailgate window. He peered in his side mirror and watched the van as it dwindled westward behind them. No brake lights. It wasn't turning to follow the Rover.

Belatedly, he realized that the driver's look of astonishment had nothing to do with recognition. The man simply had been amazed by how fast they were going. According to the speedometer, Valerie was pressing eighty-five miles per hour, thirty over the legal speed limit and fifteen or twenty too fast for the condition of the road.

Spencer's heart was thudding. Not because of her driving.

Valerie met his eyes again. She was clearly aware of the fear that had gripped him. "I warned you that you didn't really want to know who they are." She turned her attention to the highway. "Kind of gives you the heebie-jeebies, doesn't it?"

"Heebie-jeebies doesn't quite describe it. I feel as if . . ."

"You've been given an ice-water enema?" she suggested.

"You find even *this* funny?"

"On one level."

"Not me. Jesus. If the attorney general knows," he said, "then the *next* link up the chain—"

"The President of the United States."

"I don't know what's worse: that maybe the president and the attorney general sanction an agency like you described . . . or that it operates at such a high level *without* their knowledge. Because if they don't know, and they stumble across its existence—"

"They're dead meat."

"And if they don't know, then the people who're running this country aren't the people we elected."

"I can't say it goes as high as the attorney general. And I don't have a clue about Oval Office involvement. I hope not. But—"

"But you don't rule out anything anymore," he finished for her.

"Not after what I've been through. These days, I don't really trust anyone but God and myself. Lately I'm not so sure about God."

Down in the concrete aural cavity, where the agency listened to Las Vegas with a multitude of secret ears, Roy Miro said good-bye to Eve Jammer.

There were no tears, no qualms at being separated and possibly never seeing each other again. They were confident of being together soon. Roy was still energized by the spiritual power of Kevorkian, felt all but immortal. For her part, Eve seemed never to have realized that she *could* die or that anything she truly wanted—such as Roy—could be denied her.

They stood close. He put down his attaché case to be able to hold her flawless hands, and he said, "I'll try to be back here this evening, but there's no guarantee."

"I'll miss you," she said huskily. "But if you can't make it, I'll do something to remember you by, something that will remind me how exciting you are and make me even more eager to have you back."

"What? Tell me what you're going to do, so I can carry the image in my mind, an image of you to make the time away pass faster."

He was surprised at how good he was at this love talk. He had always known that he was a shameless romantic, but he had never been sure that he would know how to act when and if he ever found a woman who measured up to his standards.

"I don't want to tell you now," she said playfully. "I want you to dream, wonder, imagine. Because when you get back and I tell you—*then* we'll have the most thrilling night we've had yet."

The heat pouring off Eve was incredible. Roy wanted nothing more than to close his eyes and melt in her radiance.

He kissed her on the cheek. His lips were chapped from the desert air, and her skin was hot. It was a deliciously dry kiss.

Turning away from her was agony. At the elevator, as the doors slid open, he looked back. She was poised on one foot, the other raised. On the concrete floor was a black spider.

"Darling, no!" he said.

She looked up at him, baffled.

"A spider is a *perfect* little creation, Mother Nature at her best. A spinner of beautiful webs. A perfectly engineered killing machine. Its kind have been here since before the first man ever walked the earth. It deserves to live in peace."

"I don't like them much," she said with the cutest little pout that Roy had ever seen.

"When I get back, we'll examine one together, under a magnifying glass," he promised. "You'll see how perfect it is, how compact and efficient and functional. Once I show you how perfect arachnids are, they'll never seem the same to you again. You'll cherish them."

"Well," she said reluctantly, "all right," and she carefully stepped over the spider instead of tramping on it.

Full of love, Roy rode the elevator to the top floor of the high rise. He climbed a service staircase to the roof.

Eight of the twelve men in the strike force had already boarded the first of the two customized executive helicopters. With a hard clatter of rotors, the craft lifted into the sky, up and away.

The second—and identical—chopper was hovering at the north side of the building. When the landing pad was clear, the helicopter descended to pick up the four other men, all of whom were in civilian clothes but were carrying duffel bags full of weapons and gear.

Roy boarded last and sat at the back of the cabin. The seat across the aisle and the two in the forward row were empty.

As the craft took off, he opened his attaché case and plugged the computer power and transmission cables into outlets in the back wall of the cabin. He divorced the cellular telephone from the workstation and put it on the seat across the aisle. He no longer needed it. Instead, he was using the chopper's communications system. A phone keypad appeared right on the display screen. After putting a call through to Mama in Virginia, he identified himself as "Pooh," provided a thumbprint, and accessed the satellite-surveillance center in the Las Vegas branch of the agency.

A miniature version of the scene on the surveillance-center wall screen appeared on Roy's VDT. The Range Rover was moving at reckless speeds, which strongly indicated that the woman was behind the wheel. It was past Panaca, Nevada, bulleting toward the Utah border.

"Something like this agency was bound to come along sooner or later," she said as they approached the Utah border. "By insisting on a perfect world, we've opened the door to fascism."

"I'm not sure I follow that." He wasn't certain that he wanted to follow it, either. She spoke with unsettling conviction.

"There've been so many laws written by so many idealists with competing visions of Utopia that nobody can get through a single day without inadvertently and unknowingly breaking a score of them."

"Cops are asked to enforce tens of thousands of laws," Spencer agreed, "more than they can keep track of."

"So they tend to lose a true sense of their mission. They lose focus. You saw it happening when you were a cop, didn't you?"

"Sure. There's been some controversy, several times, about LAPD intelligence operations that targeted legitimate citizens' groups."

"Because those particular groups at that particular time were on the 'wrong' side of sensitive issues. Government has politicized every aspect of life, including law-enforcement agencies, and all of us are going to suffer for it, regardless of our political views."

"Most cops are good guys."

"I know that. But tell me something: These days, the cops who rise to the top in the system . . . are they usually the best, or are they more often the ones who're politically astute, the great schmoozers. Are they ass kissers who know how to handle a senator, a congressman, a mayor, a city councilman, and political activists of all stripes?"

"Maybe it's always been that way."

"No. We'll probably never again see men like Elliot Ness in charge of anything—but there used to be a lot like him. Cops used to respect the brass they served. Is it always that way now?"

Spencer didn't even have to answer that one.

Valerie said, "Now it's the politicized cops who set agendas, allocate resources. It's worst at the federal level. Fortunes are spent chasing violators of vaguely written laws against hate crimes, pornography, pollution, product mislabeling, sexual harassment. Don't get me wrong. I'd love to see the world rid of every bigot, pornographer, polluter, snake-oil peddler, every jerk who harasses a woman. But at the same time, we're living with the highest rates of murder, rape, and robbery of any society in history."

The more passionately Valerie spoke, the faster she drove.

Spencer winced every time he looked away from her face to the road over which they hurtled. If she lost control, if they spun out and flew off the blacktop into those towering spruces, they wouldn't have to worry about hit squads coming in from Las Vegas.

Behind them, however, Rocky was exuberant.

She said, "The streets aren't safe. Some places, people aren't even safe in their own homes. Federal law-enforcement agencies have lost focus. When they lose focus, they make mistakes and need to be bailed out of scandals to save politicians' hides—cop politicians, as well as the appointed and elected kind."

"Which is where this agency without a name comes in."

"To sweep up the dirt, hide it under the rug—so no politicians have to put their fingerprints on the broom," she said bitterly.

They crossed into Utah.

They were still over the outskirts of North Las Vegas, only a few minutes into the flight, when the copilot came to the rear of the passenger compartment. He was carrying a security phone with a built-in scrambler, which he plugged in and handed to Roy.

The phone had a headset, leaving Roy's hands free. The cabin was heavily insulated, and the saucer-size earphones were of such high quality that he could hear no engine or rotor noise, although he could feel the separate vibrations of both through his seat.

Gary Duvall—the agent in northern California who had been assigned to look into the matter of Ethel and George Porth—was calling. But not from California. He was now in Denver, Colorado.

The assumption had been made that the Porths had already been living in San Francisco when their daughter had died and when their grandson had first come to live with them. That assumption had turned out to be false.

Duvall had finally located one of the Porths' former neighbors in San Francisco, who had remembered that Ethel and George had moved there from Denver. By then their daughter had been dead a long time, and their grandson, Spencer, was sixteen.

"A long time?" Roy said doubtfully. "But I thought the boy lost his mother when he was fourteen, in the same car accident where he got his scar. That's just two years earlier."

"No. Not just two years. Not a car accident."

Duvall had unearthed a secret, and he was clearly one of those people who relished being in possession of secrets. The childish I-know-something-that-you-don't-know tone of his voice indicated that he would parcel out his treasured information in order to savor each little revelation.

Sighing, Roy leaned back in his seat. "Tell me."

"I flew to Denver," Duvall said, "to see if maybe the Porths had sold a house here the same year they bought one in San Francisco. They had. So I tried to find some Denver neighbors who remembered them. No problem. I found several. People don't move as often here as in California. And they recalled the Porths and the boy because it was such sensational stuff, what happened to them."

Sighing again, Roy opened the manila envelope in which he was still carrying some of the photographs that he had found in the shoe box in Spencer Grant's Malibu cabin.

"The mother, Jennifer, she died when the boy was eight," Duvall said. "And it wasn't in any accident."

Roy slid the four photos out of the envelope. The topmost was the snapshot taken when the woman was perhaps twenty. She was wearing a simple summer dress, dappled in sun and shadow, standing by a tree that was dripping clusters of white flowers.

"Jenny was a horsewoman," Duvall said, and Roy remembered the other pictures with horses. "Rode them, bred them. The night she died, she went to a meeting of the county breeder's association."

"This was in Denver, somewhere around Denver?"

"No, that's where her parents lived. Jenny's home was in Vail, on a small ranch just outside Vail, Colorado. She showed up at that meeting of the breeder's association, but she never came home again."

The second photograph was of Jennifer and her son at the picnic table. She was hugging the boy. His baseball cap was askew.

Duvall said, "Her car was found abandoned. There was a manhunt for her. But she wasn't anywhere near home. A week later, someone finally discovered her body in a ditch, eighty miles from Vail."

As when he'd sat at the kitchen table in the Malibu cabin on Friday morning and had sorted through the photographs for the first time, Roy was overcome by a haunting sense that the woman's face was familiar. Every word that Duvall spoke brought Roy closer to the enlightenment that had eluded him three mornings ago.

Duvall's voice now came through the headphones with a strange, seductive softness: "She was found naked. Tortured, molested. Back then, it was the most savage murder anyone had ever seen. Even these days, when we've seen it all, the details would give you nightmares."

The third snapshot showed Jennifer and the boy at poolside. She held one hand behind her son's head, making horns with two fingers. The barn loomed in the background.

"Every indication was . . . she'd fallen victim to some transient," said Duvall, pouring out the details in ever smaller drops as his flask of secrets slowly emptied. "A sociopath. Some guy with a car but no permanent address, roaming the interstate highways. It was a relatively new syndrome then, twenty-two years ago, but police had started to see it often enough to recognize it: the footloose serial killer, no ties to family or community, a shark out of his school."

The woman. The boy. The barn in the background

"The crime wasn't solved for a while. For six years, in fact."

The vibrations from the helicopter engine and rotors traveled through the frame of the craft, up Roy's seat, into his bones, and carried with them a chill. A not unpleasant chill.

"The boy and his father continued to live on the ranch," Duvall said. "There *was* a father."

The woman. The boy. The barn in the background.

Roy turned up the fourth and final photograph.

The man in the shadows. That piercing stare.

"The boy's name wasn't Spencer. Michael," Gary Duvall revealed.

The black-and-white studio photograph of the man in his middle thirties was moody: a fine study in contrasts, sunlight and darkness. Peculiar shadows, cast by unidentifiable objects beyond the frame, appeared to swarm across the wall, drawn by the subject, as if this were a man who commanded the night and all its powers.

"The boy's name was Michael—"

"Ackblom." Roy was at last able to recognize the subject in spite of the shadows that hid at least half the face. "Michael Ackblom. His father was Steven Ackblom, the painter. The murderer."

"That's right," Duvall said, sounding disappointed that he had not been able to hold off that secret for another second or two.

"Refresh my memory. How many bodies did they eventually find?"

"Forty-one," Duvall said. "And they've always thought there were more somewhere else."

" 'They were all so beautiful in their pain, and all like angels when they died,' " Roy quoted.

"You remember that?" Duvall said in surprise.

"It's the only thing Ackblom said in court."

"It's just about the only thing he said to the cops or his lawyer or anyone. He didn't feel that he'd done anything so wrong, but he acknowledged as how he understood why society thought he had. So he pleaded guilty, confessed, and accepted sentencing."

" 'They were all so beautiful in their pain, and all like angels when they died,' " Roy whispered.

As the Rover raced through the Utah morning, sunshine angled among the needled branches of the evergreens, flaring and flickering across the windshield. To Spencer, the swift play of bright light and shadow was as frenetic and disorienting as the pulsing of a stroboscopic lamp in a dark nightclub.

Even as he closed his eyes against that assault, he realized that he was bothered more by the association that each white flare triggered in his memory than he was by the sunshine itself. To his mind's eye, every lambent glint and glimmer was the flash of hard, cold steel out of catacomb gloom.

He never ceased to be amazed and distressed by how completely the past remained alive in the present and by how the struggle to forget was an inducement to memory.

Tracing his scar with the fingertips of his right hand, he said, "Give me an example. Tell me about one of the scandals this nameless agency smoothed over."

She hesitated. "David Koresh. The Branch Davidian compound. Waco, Texas."

Her words startled him into opening his eyes even in the bright steel blades of sunshine and the dark-blood shadows. He stared at her in disbelief. "Koresh was a maniac!"

"No argument from me. He was four different kinds of maniac, as far as I know, and I sure wouldn't disagree that the world is better off with him out of it."

"Me neither."

"But if the Bureau of Alcohol, Tobacco and Firearms wanted him on weapons charges, they could've collared him at a bar in Waco, where he often went to hear a band he liked—and *then* they could've entered the compound, with him out of the way. Instead of storming his place with a SWAT team. There were children in there, for God's sake."

"Endangered children," he reminded her.

"They sure were. They were burned to death."

"Low blow," he said accusingly, playing devil's advocate.

"The government never produced any illegal weapons. At the trial they claimed to've found guns converted to full automatic fire, but there are lots of discrepancies. The Texas Rangers recovered only two guns for each sect member—all legal. Texas is a big gun state. Seventeen million people, over sixty million guns—four per resident. People in the sect had half the guns in the *average* Texas household."

"Okay, this was in the newspapers. And the child-abuse stories turned out to have no apparent substance. That's been reported—even if not widely. It's a tragedy, for those dead kids *and* for the ATF. But what exactly did this nameless agency cover up? It was an ugly, very public mess for the government. Seems like they did a bad job making the ATF look good in this."

"Oh, but they were brilliant at concealing the most explosive aspect of the case. An element in ATF loyal to Tom Summerton instead of to the current director intended to use Koresh as a test case for applying asset-forfeiture laws to religious organizations."

As Utah rolled under their wheels and they drew nearer to Modena, Spencer continued to finger his scar while he thought about what she had revealed.

The trees had thinned out. The pines and spruces were too far from the highway to cast shadows across the pavement, and the sword dance of sunlight had ended. Yet Spencer noted that Valerie squinted at the road ahead and flinched slightly from time to time, as though she was threatened by her own blades of memory.

Behind them, Rocky seemed oblivious of the sobering weight of their conversation. Whatever its drawbacks, there were also many advantages to the canine condition.

At last Spencer said, "Targeting religious groups for asset seizure, even fringe figures like Koresh—that's a major bombshell if it's true. It shows utter contempt for the Constitution."

"There are lots of cults and splinter sects these days, with millions in assets. That Korean minister—Reverend Moon? I'll bet his church has hundreds of millions on U.S. soil. If any religious organization is involved in criminal activity, its tax-free status is revoked. Then if the ATF or FBI has a lien for asset forfeiture, it'll be first in line, even ahead of the IRS, to grab everything."

"A steady cash flow to buy more toys and better office furniture for the bureaus involved," he said ruminatively. "And help to keep this nameless agency afloat. Even make it grow. While lots of local police forces—the guys who have to deal with real hard-core crime, street gangs, murder, rape—they're all so starved for funds they can't have pay raises or buy new equipment."

As Modena passed by in four blinks of an eye, Valerie said, "And the accountability provisions of federal and state forfeiture laws are dismal. Seized assets are inadequately tracked—so a percentage just vanishes into the pockets of some of the officials involved."

"Legalized theft."

"No one's ever caught, so it might as well be legal. Anyway, Summerton's element in ATF planned to plant drugs, phony records of major drug sales, and lots of illegal weapons in the Mount Carmel Center—Koresh's compound—after the success of the initial assault."

"But the initial assault failed."

"Koresh was more unstable than they realized. So innocent ATF agents were killed. And innocent children. It became a media circus. With everyone watching, Summerton's goons couldn't plant the drugs and guns. The operation was abandoned. But by then there was a paper trail inside ATF: secret memos, reports, files. All that had to be eliminated quickly. A couple of *people* were also eliminated, people who knew too much and might squeal."

"And you're saying this nameless agency cleaned up that mess."

"I'm not *saying* they did. They really *did*."

"How do you fit into all this? How do you know Summerton?"

She chewed on her lower lip and seemed to be thinking hard about how much she should reveal.

He said, "Who *are* you, Valerie Keene? Who are you, Hannah Rainey? Who are you, Bess Baer?"

"Who are *you*, Spencer Grant?" she asked angrily, but her anger was false.

"Unless I'm mistaken, I told you a name, a real and true name, when I was out of my head, last night or the night before."

She hesitated, nodded, but kept her eyes on the road.

He found his voice diminishing to a softness barely louder than a murmur, and though he was unable to force himself to speak louder, he knew that she heard every word he said. "Michael Ackblom. It's a name I've hated for more than half my life. It hasn't even been my legal name for fourteen years, not since my grandparents helped me apply to a court to have it changed. And since the day the judge granted that change, it's a name I've never spoken, not once in all that time. Until I told you."

He fell into a silence.

She didn't speak, as though in spite of the silence, she knew that he wasn't finished.

The things that Spencer needed to say to her were more easily said in a liberating delirium like the one in which he'd made his previous revelations. Now he was inhibited by a reserve that resulted less from shyness than from an acute awareness that he was a damaged man and that she deserved someone finer than he could ever be.

"And even if I hadn't been delirious," he continued, "I would've told you anyway, sooner or later. Because I don't want to keep any secrets from you."

How difficult it sometimes could be to say the things that most deeply and urgently needed to be said. If given a choice, he wouldn't have selected either that time or that place to say any of it: on a lonely Utah highway, watched and pursued, hurtling toward likely death or toward an unexpected gift of freedom—and in either case toward the unknown. Life chose its consequential moments, however, without the consultation of those who lived them. And the pain of speaking from the heart was always, in the end, more endurable than the suffering that was the price of silence.

He took a deep breath. "What I'm trying to say to you . . . it's so presumptuous. Worse than that. Foolish, ridiculous. For God's sake, I can't even describe what I feel for you because I don't have the words. There might not even be words for it. All I know is that what I feel is wonderful, strange, different from anything I ever expected to feel, different from anything people are *supposed* to feel."

She kept her attention on the highway, which allowed Spencer to look at her as he spoke. The sheen of her dark hair, the delicacy of her profile, and the strength of her beautiful sun-browned hands on the steering wheel encouraged him to continue. If she had met his eyes at that moment, however, he might have been too intimidated to express the rest of what he longed to say.

"Crazier still, I can't tell you *why* I feel this way about you. It's just there. Inside me. It's a feeling that just sprang up. Not there one moment . . . but there the next, as if it had always been there. As if *you'd* always been there, or as if I'd spent my life waiting for you to be there."

The more words that tumbled from him and the faster they came, the more he feared that he would never be able to find the *right* words. At least she seemed to know that she should not respond or, worse, encourage him. He was balanced so precariously on the high wire of revelation that the slightest blow, although unintended, would knock him off.

"I don't know. I'm so awkward at this. The problem is I'm just fourteen years old when it comes to this, when it comes to emotion, frozen back there in adolescence, as inarticulate as a boy about this sort of thing. And if I can't explain what I feel or why I feel it—then how can I expect you ever to feel anything in return? Jesus. I was right: 'Presumptuous' is the wrong word. 'Foolish' is better."

He retreated to the safety of silence again. But he didn't dare linger in silence, because he would soon lose the will to break it.

"Foolish or not, I've got hope now, and I'm going to hold onto it until you tell me to let go. I'll tell you all about Michael Ackblom, the boy who used to be. I'll tell you everything you want to know, everything you can bear to hear. But I want the same thing from you. I want to know all there is to know. No secrets. This is an end to secrets. Here, now, from this moment on, no secrets. Whatever we can have together—if we can have anything at all—has to be honest, true, clean, shining, like nothing I've known before."

The speed of the Rover had fallen while he talked.

His latest silence was not just another pause between painful attempts to express himself, and she seemed to be aware of its new quality. She looked at him. Her lovely, dark eyes shone with the warmth and kindness to which he had responded in The Red Door less than a week ago, when he'd first met her.

When the warmth threatened to well into tears, she turned her attention to the road once more.

Since encountering her again in the arroyo on Friday night, he had not until now seen quite that same exceptionally kind and open spirit; of necessity, it had been masked by doubt, by caution. She hadn't trusted him anymore, after he'd followed her home from work. Her life had taught her to be cynical and suspicious of others, as surely as his life had taught him to be afraid of what he might one day find crouched and waiting within himself.

She became aware that she'd let their speed fall. She tramped on the accelerator, and the Rover surged forward.

Spencer waited.

Trees crowded close to the highway again. Filleting blades of light flashed across the glass, spattering quick sprays of shadows behind them.

"My name," she said, "is Eleanor. People used to call me Ellie. Ellie Summerton."

"Not . . . his daughter?"

"No. Thank God, no. His daughter-in-law. My maiden name was Golding. Eleanor Golding. I was married to Tom's son, only child. Danny Summerton. Danny's dead now. Been dead for fourteen months." Her voice was pulled between anger and sadness, and often the balance in the contest shifted in the middle of a word, stretching it and distorting it. "Some days it seems he's only been gone a week or so, and some days it feels like he's been gone forever. Danny knew too much. And he was going to talk. He was killed to shut him up."

"Summerton . . . killed his own son?"

Her voice became so cold that anger seemed to have won forever against the insistent pull of sadness. "He's even worse than that. He ordered someone else to do it. My mom and dad were killed too . . . just because they happened to be in the way when the agency men came for Danny."

Her voice was colder than ever, and she was whiter than pale. During his days as a policeman, Spencer had seen a few faces as white as Ellie's was at that moment—but they had all been faces in one morgue or another.

"I was there. I escaped," she said. "I was lucky. That's what I've been telling myself ever since. Lucky."

". . . but Michael had no peace, even once he'd gone to Denver to live with his grandparents, the Porths," Gary Duvall said. "Every kid in school knew the name Ackblom. An unusual name. And the father was a famous artist even before he became a famous murderer, killed his wife and forty-one others. Besides, the kid's picture had been in all the papers. Boy hero. He was an object of unending curiosity. Everyone stared. And every time it seemed the media would leave him alone, there would be another flare-up of interest, and they'd be hounding him again, even though he was just a kid, for God's sake."

"Journalists," Roy said scornfully. "You know what they're like. Cold bastards. Only the story matters. They have no compassion."

"The kid had been through a similar hell, unwanted notoriety, when he'd been eight years old, after his mother's body was found in that ditch. This time it was tearing him apart. The grandparents were retired, could live anywhere, so after almost two years they decided to get Michael out of Colorado altogether. A new city, new state, new start. That's what they told neighbors—but they wouldn't tell anyone where they were going. They uprooted themselves and left their friends for the sake of the boy. They must've figured that was the only way he'd have a chance to make a normal life for himself."

"New city, new state, new start—and even a new name," Roy said. "They legally changed it, didn't they?"

"Right here in Denver, before they moved away. Given the circumstances, the court record of the change is sealed, of course."

"Of course."

"But I've reviewed it. Michael Steven Ackblom became Spencer Grant, no middle name or even initial. An odd choice. It seems to have been a name the boy came up with himself, but I don't know where he got it."

"From old movies he liked."

"Huh?"

"Good work. Thanks, Gary."

Roy disconnected with the touch of a button, but he didn't take off the telephone headset.

He stared at the photograph of Steven Ackblom. The man in the shadows.

Engines, rotors, powerful desires, and sympathy for the devil vibrated in Roy's bones. He shivered with a not unpleasant chill.

They were all so beautiful in their pain, and all like angels when they died.

Here and there in the gloom beneath the trees, where shadows held back the sun through most or all of the day, patches of white snow shone like bone in the carcass of the earth.

The true desert was behind them. Winter had come to this area, had been driven back by an early thaw, and would no doubt come again before true spring. But now the sky was blue, on a day when Spencer would have welcomed bitterly cold wind and dense swirls of snow to blind all eyes above.

"Danny was a brilliant software designer," Ellie said. "He'd been a computer nerd since junior high. Me too. Since the eighth grade, I've lived and breathed computers. We met in college. My being a hacker, deep into that world, which is mostly guys—that's what drew Danny to me."

Spencer remembered how Ellie had looked as she'd sat on desert sand; at the edge of the morning sun, bent over a computer, up-linking to satellites, dazzling in her expertise, her limpid eyes alight with the pleasure that she got from being so skillful at the task, with a curve of hair like a raven's wing against her cheek.

Whatever she might believe, her status as a hacker had not been the only thing that had drawn Danny to her. She was compelling for many reasons, but most of all because she seemed, at all times, more *alive* than most other people.

Her attention was on the highway, but she was clearly having difficulty treating the past with detachment and was struggling not to become lost in it. "After graduate school, Danny had job offers, but his father was relentless about him coming to work at the Bureau of Alcohol, Tobacco and Firearms. Back then, years before he went to the Department of Justice, Tom Summerton was Director of the ATF."

"But that was in a different administration."

"Oh, in Tom's case, it doesn't matter much who's in power in Washington, either party, left or right. He's always appointed to an important position in what they laughingly call 'public service.' Twenty years ago, he inherited over one billion dollars, which is now probably two, and he gives huge amounts to both parties. He's clever enough to position himself as nonpartisan, a statesman rather than a politician, a man who knows how to get things done, no ideological axe to grind, only wants to make a better world."

"That's a hard act to pull off," Spencer said.

"Easy for him. Because he believes in nothing. Except himself. And power. Power is his food, drink, love, sex. *Using* power is the thrill, not forwarding the ideals it serves. In Washington, a lust for power keeps the devil busy buying souls, but Tom is so ambitious he must have collected a record price for his."

Responding to the simmering fury in the undertone of her voice, Spencer said, "Did you always hate him?"

"Yes," Ellie said forthrightly. "Quietly despised the stinking sonofabitch. I didn't want Danny to work at ATF, because he was too innocent, naive, too easily taken in by his old man."

"What did he do there?"

"Developed Mama. The computer system, the software to run it—which they later called Mama. It was supposed to be the biggest, baddest anticrime data resource in the world, a system that could process billions of bytes at record speeds, link together federal and state and local law enforcement with ease, eliminate duplication of effort, and finally give the good guys an edge."

"Very stirring."

"Isn't it? And Mama turned out awesome. But Tom never intended her to serve any legit branch of government. He used ATF resources to develop her, yeah, but his intention all along was to make Mama the core of this nameless agency."

"So Danny realized it had gone sour?"

"Maybe he knew but didn't want to admit. He stayed with it."

"How long?"

"Too long," she said sadly. "Until his dad had left the ATF and moved to the Department of Justice, a full year after Mama and the agency were in place. But eventually he accepted that Mama's entire purpose was to make it possible for the government to *commit* crimes and not be caught. He was eaten alive with anger, self-disgust."

"And when he wanted out, they wouldn't let him go."

"We didn't realize there was no leaving. I mean, Tom is a piece of walking shit, but he was still Danny's *father*. And Danny was his only child. Danny's mother died when he was young. Cancer. So it seemed like Danny was all Tom had."

Following the violent death of his own mother, Spencer and his father also were drawn closer in the aftermath. Or so it had seemed. Until a certain night in July.

Ellie said, "Then it became obvious—this work with the agency was mandatory lifetime employment."

"Like being the personal attorney to a Mafia don."

"The only way out was to go public, blow the whole dirty business wide open. Secretly Danny prepared his own file of Mama's software and a history of the cover-ups the agency was involved with."

"You realized the danger?"

"On one level. But deep down inside, I think both of us, to different degrees, had trouble believing Tom would have Danny killed. We were twenty-eight, for God's sake. Death was an abstract concept to us. At twenty-eight, who really believes he's ever going to die?"

"And then the hit men showed up."

"No SWAT team. More subtle. Three men on Thanksgiving evening. The year before last. My folks' place in Connecticut. My dad is . . . was a doctor. A doctor's life, especially in a small town, isn't his own. Even on Thanksgiving. So . . . near the end of dinner, I was in the kitchen . . . getting the pumpkin pie . . . when the doorbell rang. . . ."

For once, Spencer didn't want to look at her lovely face. He closed his eyes.

Ellie took a deep breath and went on: "The kitchen was at the end of the hall from the foyer. I pushed the swinging door aside to see who our visitor was, just as my mother opened . . . just as she opened the front door."

Spencer waited for her to tell it at her own pace. If he had made the correct assumptions about the sequence of events since that door had been opened, fourteen months in the past, this was the first time that she had described those murders to anyone. Between then and now, she had been on the run, unable to fully trust another human being and unwilling to risk the lives of innocent people by involving them in her personal tragedy.

"Two men at the front door. Nothing special about them. Could have been Dad's patients, for all I knew. First one was wearing a red-plaid hunting jacket. He said something to Mom, then came inside, pushing her back, a gun in his hand. Never heard a shot. Silencer. But I saw . . . a spray of blood . . . the back of her head blowing out."

With his eyes closed against the sight of Ellie's face, Spencer could clearly visualize that Connecticut foyer and the horror that she described.

"Dad and Danny were in the dining room. I screamed, 'Run, get away.' I knew it was the agency. I didn't go out the rear door. Instinct, maybe. I'd have been killed on the back porch. Ran into the laundry room off the kitchen, then into the garage and out the side garage door. The house is on two acres, lots of lawn, but I got to the fence between our place and the Doyle house. I was going over it, almost over it, when a bullet ricocheted off the wrought iron. Somebody shooting from behind our house. Another silencer. No sound but the slug smacking iron. I was frantic, ran across the Doyles' yard. Nobody home, away at their kids' place for the holiday, windows dark. I ran through a gate, into St. George's Wood. Presbyterian church sits on six or eight acres, surrounded by woods— mostly pines, sycamores. Ran a ways. Stopped in the trees. Looked back. Thought one of them would be after me. But I was alone. I guess I'd been too fast or maybe they didn't want to chase me in public, waving guns. And just then snow started falling, just *then*, big fat flakes. . . ."

Behind his closed eyes, Spencer could see her on that distant night, in that faraway place: alone in darkness, without a coat, shivering, breathless, terrified. Abruptly, torrents of white flakes spiraled through the bare limbs of the sycamores, and the timing made the snow seem more than merely a sudden change of weather, gave it the significance of an omen.

"There was something uncanny about it . . . sort of eerie . . . ," Ellie said, confirming what Spencer sensed that she had felt and what he himself might have felt under those circumstances. "I don't know . . . can't explain it . . . the snow was like a curtain coming down, a stage curtain, the end of an act, end of *something*. I knew then they were all dead. Not just my mother. Dad and Danny too."

Her voice trembled with grief. Talking for the first time about those killings, she had reopened the scabs that had formed over her raw pain, as he had known she would.

Reluctantly he opened his eyes and looked at her.

She was beyond pale now. Ashen. Tears shimmered in her eyes, but her cheeks were still dry.

"Want me to drive?" he asked.

"No. Better if I do. Keeps me focused here and now . . . instead of too much back then."

A roadside sign indicated that they were eight miles from the town of Newcastle.

Spencer stared out the side window at a landscape that seemed barren in spite of the many trees and murky in spite of the sunshine.

Ellie said, "Then in the street, beyond the trees, a car roared by, really moving. It went under a streetlamp, and I was close enough to see the man in the front passenger seat. Red hunting jacket. The driver, one more in the backseat—three altogether. After they went past, I ran through the trees, toward the street, going to shout for help, for the police, but I stopped before I got there. I knew who'd done it . . . the agency, Tom. But no proof."

"What about Danny's files?"

"Back in Washington. A set of diskettes hidden in our apartment, another set in a bank safe-deposit box. And I knew Tom must already have both sets, or he wouldn't have been so . . . bold. If I went to the cops, if I surfaced anywhere, Tom would get me. Sooner or later. It would look like an accident or suicide. So I went back to the house. Back through St. George's Wood, the gate at the Doyle house, over the iron fence. At our house, I almost couldn't force myself through the kitchen . . . the hall . . . to Mom in the foyer. Even after all this time, when I try to picture my mother's face, I can't see it without the wound, the blood, the bone structure distorted by the bullets. Those bastards haven't even left me with a clean memory of my mother's face . . . just that awful, bloody *thing*."

For a while she couldn't go on.

Aware of Ellie's anguish, Rocky mewled softly. He was no longer bobbing and grinning. He huddled in his narrow space, head down, both ears limp. His love of speed was outweighed by his sensitivity to the woman's pain.

Two miles from Newcastle, Ellie at last continued: "And in the dining room, Danny and Dad were dead, shot repeatedly in the head, not to be sure they were dead . . . just for the sheer savagery. I had to . . . to touch the bodies, take the money out of their wallets. I was going to need every dollar I could get. Raided Mom's purse, jewelry box. Opened the safe in Dad's den, took his coin collection. Jesus, I felt like a thief, worse than a thief . . . a grave robber. I didn't pack my suitcase, just left with what I was wearing, partly because I started to get spooked that the killers would come back. But also because . . . it was so silent in that house, just me and the bodies and the snow falling past the windows, so *quiet*, as if not only Mom and Dad and Danny were dead, but as if the whole world had died, the end of everything, and I was the last one left, alone."

Newcastle was a repeat of Modena. Small. Isolated. It offered no place to hide from people who could look down on the whole world as if they were gods.

Ellie said, "I left the house in our Honda, Danny's and mine, but I knew I had to get rid of it in a few hours. When Tom realized I hadn't gone to the cops, the whole agency would be looking for me, and they'd have a description of the car, the plate number."

He looked at her again. Her eyes were no longer watery. She had repressed her grief with a fierce weight of anger.

He said, "What do the police think happened in that house, to Danny and your folks? Where do they think you are? Not Summerton's people. I mean the *real* police."

"I suspect Tom intended to make it look as if a well-organized group of terrorists wasted us as a way of punishing him. Oh, he could've milked that for sympathy! And used the sympathy to weasel more power for himself inside the Department of Justice."

"But with you gone, they couldn't plant their phony evidence, because you might show up to refute it."

"Yeah. Later, the media decided that Danny and my folks . . . well, you know, it was one of those deplorable acts of senseless violence we see so often, blah-blah-blah. Terrible, sick, blah-blah-blah, but only a three-day story. As for me . . . obviously I'd been taken away, raped and murdered, my body left where it might never be found."

"That was fourteen months ago?" he asked. "And the agency's still this hot to get you?"

"I have some significant codes they don't know I have, things Danny and I memorized . . . a lot of knowledge. I don't have hard proof against them. But I *know* everything about them, which makes me dangerous enough. Tom will never stop looking, as long as he lives."

Like a great black wasp, the helicopter droned across the Nevada badlands.

Roy was still wearing the telephone headset with the saucer-size earphones, blocking out the engine and rotor noise to concentrate on the photograph of Steven Ackblom. The loudest sound in his private realm was the slow, heavy thudding of his heart.

When Ackblom's secret work had been exposed, Roy had been only sixteen years old and still confused about the meaning of life and about his own place in the world. He was drawn to beautiful things: the paintings of Childe Hassam and so many others, classical music, antique French furniture, Chinese porcelain, lyrical poetry. He was always a happy boy when alone in his room, with Beethoven or Bach on the stereo, gazing at the color photographs in a book about Fabergé eggs, Paul Storr silver, or Sung Dynasty porcelains. Likewise, he was happy when he was wandering alone through an art museum. He was seldom happy around people, however, although he wanted desperately to have friends and to be liked. In his expansive but guarded heart, young Roy was convinced that he had been born to make an important contribution to the world, and he knew that when he discovered what his contribution would be, he then would become widely admired and loved. Nevertheless, at sixteen and bedeviled by the impatience of youth, he was enormously frustrated by the need to wait for his purpose and his destiny to be revealed to him.

He had been fascinated by the newspaper accounts of the Ackblom tragedy, because in the mystery of the artist's double life, he had sensed a resolution to his own deep confusion. He acquired two books with color plates of Ackblom's art—and responded powerfully to the work. Though Ackblom's pictures were beautiful, even ennobling, Roy's enthusiasm wasn't aroused only by the paintings themselves. He was also affected by the artist's inner struggle, which he inferred from the paintings and which he believed to be similar to his own.

Basically, Steven Ackblom was preoccupied with two subjects and produced two types of paintings.

Although only in his mid-thirties, he had been obsessed enough to produce an enormous body of work, consisting half of exceptionally beautiful still lifes. Fruit, vegetables, stones, flowers, pebbles, the contents of a sewing box, buttons, tools, plates, a collection of old bottles, bottle caps—humble and exalted objects alike were rendered in remarkable detail, so realistic that they seemed three-dimensional. In fact, each item attained a hyper-reality, appeared to be more real than the object that had served as the model for it, and possessed an eerie beauty. Ackblom never resorted to the forced beauty of sentimentality or unrestrained romanticism; his vision was always convincing, moving, and sometimes breathtaking.

The subjects of the remainder of the paintings were people: portraits of individuals and of groups containing three to seven subjects. More frequently, they were faces rather than full figures, but when they were figures, they were invariably nudes. Sometimes Ackblom's men, women, and children were ethereally beautiful on the surface, though their comeliness was always tainted by a subtle but terrible pressure within them, as if some monstrous possessing spirit might explode from their fragile flesh at any moment. This pressure distorted a feature here and there, not dramatically but just enough to rob them of perfect beauty. And sometimes the artist portrayed ugly—even grotesque—individuals, within whom there was also fearful pressure, though its effect was to force a feature here and there to conform to an ideal of beauty. Their malformed countenances were all the more chilling for being, in some aspects, lightly touched by grace. As a consequence of the conflict between inner and outer realities, the people in both types of portraits were enormously expressive, although their expressions were more mysterious and haunting than any that enlivened the faces of real human beings.

Seizing on those portraits, the news media had been quick to make the most obvious interpretation. They claimed that the artist—himself a handsome man—had been painting his own demon within, crying out for help or issuing a warning regarding his true nature.

Although he was only sixteen, Roy Miro understood that Ackblom's paintings were not about the artist himself, but about the world as he perceived it. Ackblom had no need to cry out for help or to warn anyone, for he didn't see himself as demonic. Taken as a whole, what his art said was that no human being could ever achieve the perfect beauty of even the humblest object in the inanimate world.

Ackblom's great paintings helped young Roy to understand why he was delighted to be alone with the artistic works of human beings, yet was often unhappy in the company of human beings themselves. No work of art could be flawless, because an imperfect human being had created it. Yet art was the distillation of the best in humanity. Therefore, works of art were closer to perfection than those who created them.

Favoring the inanimate over the animate was all right. It was acceptable to value art above people.

That was the first lesson he learned from Steven Ackblom.

Wanting to know more about the man, Roy had discovered that the artist was, not surprisingly, extremely private and seldom spoke to anyone for publication. Roy managed to find two interviews. In one, Ackblom held forth with great feeling and compassion about the misery of the human condition. One quotation seemed to leap from the text: "Love is the most human of all emotions because love is messy. And of all the things we can feel with our minds and bodies, severe pain is the purest, for it drives everything else from our awareness and focuses us as perfectly as we can ever be focused."

Ackblom had pleaded guilty to the murders of his wife and forty-one others, rather than face a lengthy trial that he couldn't win. In the courtroom, entering his plea, the painter had disgusted and angered the judge by saying, of his forty-two victims: "They were all so beautiful in their pain, and all like angels when they died."

Roy began to understand what Ackblom had been doing in those rooms under the barn. In subjecting his victims to torture, the artist was trying to focus them toward a moment of perfection, when they would briefly shine—even though still alive—with a beauty equal to that of inanimate objects.

Purity and beauty were the same thing. Pure lines, pure forms, pure light, pure color, pure sound, pure emotion, pure thought, pure faith, pure ideals. However, human beings were capable of achieving purity, in any thought or endeavor, only rarely and only in extreme circumstances—which made the human condition pitiable.

That was the second lesson he learned from Steven Ackblom.

For a few years, Roy's heartfelt pity for humanity intensified and matured. One day shortly after his twentieth birthday, as a bud suddenly blossoms into a full-blown rose, his pity became compassion. He considered the latter to be a purer emotion than the former. Pity often entailed a subtle element of disgust for the object of pity or a sense of superiority on the part of the person who felt pity for another. But compassion was an unpolluted, crystalline, piercing empathy for other people, a perfect understanding of their suffering.

Guided by compassion, acting on frequent opportunities to make the world a better place, confident of the purity of his motivation, Roy had then become a more enlightened man than Steven Ackblom. He had found his destiny.

Now, thirteen years later, sitting in the back of the executive helicopter as it carried him toward Utah, Roy smiled at the photograph of the artist in swarming shadows.

Funny how everything in life seemed connected to everything else. A forgotten moment or half-remembered face from the past could suddenly become important again.

The artist had never been so central a figure in Roy's life that he could have been called a mentor or even an inspiration. Roy had never believed that Ackblom was a madman—as the media had portrayed him—but saw him as merely misguided. The best answer to the hopelessness of the human condition was not to grant one moment of pure beauty to each imperfect soul by the elevating effect of severe pain. That was a pathetically transient triumph. The better answer was to identify those most in need of release—then, with dignity and compassion and merciful speed, set them free of their imperfect human condition.

Nevertheless, at a crucial time, the artist had unknowingly taught a few vital truths to a confused boy. Though Steven Ackblom was a misguided and tragic figure, Roy owed him a debt.

It was ironic—and an intriguing example of cosmic justice—that Roy should be the one to rid the world of the troubled and thankless son who had betrayed Ackblom. The artist's quest for human perfection had been misguided but, in Roy's view, well meaning. Their sorry world would inch closer to an ideal state with Michael (now Spencer) removed from it. And pure justice seemed to require that Spencer be removed only subsequent to being subjected to prolonged and severe pain, in a manner that would adequately honor his visionary father.

As Roy took off the telephone headset, he heard the pilot making an announcement on the public-address system. ". . . according to Vegas control, allowing for the target's current speed, we're approximately sixteen minutes from rendezvous. Sixteen minutes to the target."

A sky like blue glass.

Seventeen miles to Cedar City.

They began to encounter more traffic on the two-lane highway. Ellie used the horn to encourage slow vehicles to get out of her way. When the drivers were stubborn, she took nail-biting risks to get around them in no-passing zones or even passed them to the right when the shoulder of the highway was wide enough.

Their speed dropped because of the interference that the traffic posed, but the need for increased recklessness made it seem as though they were actually going faster than ever. Spencer held on to one edge of his seat. In the back, Rocky was bobbing his head again.

"Even without proof," Spencer suggested, "you could go to the press. You could point them in the right direction, put Summerton on the defensive—"

"Tried that twice. First a *New York Times* reporter. Contacted her on her office computer, had an on-line dialogue and set up a meeting at an Indian restaurant. Made it clear if she told anyone, anyone at all, my life *and* hers wouldn't be worth spit. I got there four hours early, watched the place with binoculars from the roof of a building across the street, to be sure she came alone and there wasn't any obvious stakeout. I figured I'd make her wait, go in half an hour late, take the extra time to watch the street. But fifteen minutes after she arrived . . . the restaurant blew up. Gas explosion, so the police said."

"The reporter?"

"Dead. Along with fourteen other people in there."

"Dear God."

"Then, a week later, a guy from the *Washington Post* was supposed to meet me in a public park. I actually set it up with a cellular phone from another rooftop overlooking that site, but not obvious enough to be seen. Made it for six hours later. About an hour and a half go by, and then a water department truck pulls up near the park. The work crew opens a manhole, sets out some safety cones and sawhorses with flashers on them."

"But they weren't really city workers."

"I had a battery-powered multiband scanner with me on that roof. Picked up the frequency they were using to coordinate the phony work crew with a phony lunch wagon on the other side of the park."

"You are something else," he said admiringly.

"Three agents in the park, too, one pretending he's a panhandler, two pretending to be park-service employees doing maintenance. Then the time comes and the reporter shows up, walks to the monument where I told him we'd meet—and the sonofabitch is wired too! I hear him muttering to them that he doesn't see me anywhere, what should he do. And they're calming him, telling him it's cool, he should just wait. The little weasel must've been in Tom Summerton's pocket, called him up right after talking to me."

Ten miles west of Cedar City, they pulled behind a Dodge pickup that was doing ten miles per hour under the legal limit. At the rear window of the cab, two rifles hung in a rack.

The pickup driver let Ellie pound on the horn for a while, mule-stubborn about pulling over to let her by.

"What's wrong with this jerk?" she fumed. She gave him more horn, but he played deaf. "As far as he knows, we have someone dying in here, needs a doctor fast."

"Hell, these days, we could be a couple of lunatic dopers just spoiling for a shootout."

The man in the pickup was moved by neither compassion nor fear. Finally he responded to the horn by putting his arm out the window and flipping Ellie the finger.

Passing to the left was impossible at the moment. Visibility was limited, and what highway they *could* see was occupied by a steady stream of oncoming traffic.

Spencer looked at his watch. They had only fifteen minutes left from the two-hour safety margin that Ellie had estimated.

The man in the pickup, however, seemed to have all the time in the world.

"Jackass," she said, and whipped the Rover to the right, trying to get around the slow vehicle by using the shoulder of the highway.

When she pulled even with the Dodge, it accelerated to match her speed. Twice Ellie pumped more juice to the Rover, twice it leaped forward, and twice the pickup matched her new pace.

The other driver repeatedly glanced away from the road to glare at them. He was in his forties. Under a baseball cap, his face revealed all the intelligence of a shovel.

Clearly, he intended to pace Ellie until the shoulder narrowed and she was forced to fall in behind him again.

Shovelface didn't know what kind of woman he was dealing with, of course, but Ellie promptly showed him. She pulled the Rover to the left, bashing the pickup hard enough to startle the driver into shifting his foot off the accelerator. The pickup lost speed. The Rover shot ahead. Shovelface jammed the pedal again, but he was too late: Ellie swung the Rover onto the pavement, in front of the Dodge.

As the Rover lurched left then right, Rocky yelped with surprise and fell onto his side. He scrambled into a sitting position again and snorted in what might have been either embarrassment or delight.

Spencer looked at his watch. "You think they'll hook up with local cops before they come after us?"

"No. They'll try to keep locals out of it."

"Then what should we be looking for?"

"If they fly in from Vegas—or anywhere else—I think they'll be in a chopper. More maneuverability, flexibility. With satellite tracking, they can pinpoint the Rover, come right in over us, and blow us off the highway, if they get a chance."

Leaning forward, Spencer peered through the windshield at the threatening blue sky.

A horn blared behind them.

"Damn," Ellie said, glancing at her side mirror.

Checking the mirror on his side, Spencer saw that the Dodge had caught up with them. The angry driver was pounding his horn as Ellie had pounded hers earlier.

"We don't need this right now," she worried.

"Okay," Spencer said, "so let's see if he'll take a rain check on a shootout. If we survive the agency, then we'll come back and give him a fair whack at us."

"Think he'd go for that?"

"Seems like a reasonable man."

Pressing the Rover as hard as ever, Ellie managed to glance at Spencer and smile. "You're getting the attitude."

"It's contagious."

Here and there, scattered along both sides of the highway, were businesses, houses. This wasn't quite yet Cedar City, but they were definitely back in civilization.

The slug in the Dodge pickup pounded on the horn with such enthusiasm that every blast must have been sending a thrill through his groin.

On the display screen in the open attaché case, relayed from Las Vegas, was the view from Earthguard, enormously magnified and enhanced, looking down on the state highway just west of Cedar City.

The Range Rover was pulling one reckless stunt after another. Sitting in the back of the chopper, with the open case on his lap, Roy was riveted by the performance, which was like something out of an action movie, though seen from one monotonous angle.

No one drove that fast, weaving lane to lane, sometimes facing down oncoming traffic, unless he was drunk or being pursued. This driver wasn't drunk. There was nothing sloppy about the way the Rover was being handled. It was rash, daredevil driving, but it was also skillful. And from all appearances, the Rover was not being chased.

Roy was finally convinced that the woman was behind the wheel of that vehicle. After being alarmed by the satellite trace-back to her computer, she would never take comfort from the fact that no pursuit car was racing up her tailpipe. She knew that they either would be waiting ahead for her at a roadblock or would take her out from the air. Before either of those things happened, she was trying to get into a town, where she could blend into a busy flow of traffic and use whatever architecture of the urban landscape might help her to escape their eyes.

Cedar City wasn't nearly large enough, of course, to provide her with the opportunities she needed. Evidently she underestimated the power and clarity of surveillance from orbit.

At the front of the chopper's passenger compartment, the four strike force officers were checking their weapons. They distributed spare magazines of ammunition in their pockets.

Civilian clothing was the uniform for this mission. They wanted to get in, nail the woman, capture Grant, and get out before Cedar City law enforcement showed up. If they became involved with the locals, they would only have to deceive them, and deception involved the risk of making mistakes and being unmasked—especially when they had no idea how much Grant knew and what he might say if the cops insisted on talking to him. Besides, dealing with locals also took too much damn time. Both choppers were marked with phony registration numbers to mislead observers. As long as the men wore no identifying clothing or gear, witnesses would have little or nothing useful to tell the police later.

Every member of the strike force, including Roy, was protected by a bullet-resistant body vest under his clothes and was carrying Drug Enforcement Administration ID that could be produced quickly to placate the local authorities if necessary. If they were lucky, however, they would be back in the air three minutes after touching down, with Spencer Grant in custody, with the woman's body, but with no wounded of their own.

The woman was finished. She was still breathing, still had a heartbeat, but in fact she was already stone dead.

On the computer in Roy's lap, Earthguard 3 showed the target drastically slowing. Then the Rover passed another vehicle, perhaps a pickup, on the shoulder of the highway. The pickup increased its speed, too, and suddenly a drag race seemed to be under way.

Frowning, Roy squinted at the display screen.

The pilot announced that they were five minutes from the target.

Cedar City.

There was too much traffic to facilitate their escape, and too little to allow them to blend in and confuse Earthguard. She was also hindered by being on streets with gutters instead of on open highways with wide shoulders. And traffic lights. And that stupid pickup jockey insistently pounding, pounding, pounding his horn.

Ellie turned right at an intersection, frantically surveying both sides of the street. Fast-food restaurants. Service stations. Convenience stores. She had no idea exactly what she was looking for. She only knew that she would recognize it when she saw it: a place or situation that they could turn to their advantage.

She had hoped for time to scout the territory and find a way to get the Rover under cover: a grove of evergreens with a dense canopy of branches, a large parking garage, any place in which they might evade the eyes in the sky and leave the Rover without being spotted. Then they could either buy or heist new wheels, and from orbit they would again be indistinguishable from other vehicles on the highway.

She supposed she would earn a bed of nails in Hades for sure if she killed the creep in the Dodge pickup—but the satisfaction might be worth the price. He hammered on the horn as if he were a confused and angry ape determined to beat the damned thing until it stopped bleating at him.

He also tried to get around them during every break in oncoming traffic, but Ellie swerved to block him. The passenger side of the pickup was badly scraped and crumpled from when she had bashed into it with the Rover, so the guy probably figured that he had nothing to lose by pulling alongside and forcing her to the curb.

She couldn't let him do that. They were quickly running out of time. Having to deal with the ape would consume precious minutes.

"Tell me it's not," Spencer shouted above the blaring horn.

"Not what?"

Then she realized that he was pointing through the windshield. Something in the sky. To the southwest. Two large executive-style helicopters. One behind and to the left of the other. Both black. The polished hulls and windows glistened as if sheathed with ice, and the morning sun shimmered off the whirling rotors. The two craft were like huge insects out of an apocalyptic 1950s science fiction movie about the dangers of nuclear radiation. Less than two miles away.

She saw a U-shaped strip shopping center ahead on the left. Skating on the fragile ice of instinct, she accelerated, hung a hard left through a gap in traffic, and drove into a short access road that served the big parking lot.

Near her right ear, the dog was panting with excitement, and it sounded uncannily like soft laughter: *Heh-heh-heh-heh-heh-heh!*

Spencer still had to shout, because the horn-blower remained close behind them: "What're we doing?"

"Got to get new wheels."

"Out in the open?"

"Only choice."

"They'll see us make the switch."

"Create a diversion."

"How?"

"I'm thinking," she said.

"I was afraid of that."

With only the lightest application of the brakes, she turned right and then sped southward across the blacktop lot, instead of approaching the stores to the east.

The pickup stayed close behind them.

In the southwest sky, the two helicopters were no more than one mile away. They had altered course to follow the Range Rover. They were descending as they approached.

The anchor store in the U-shaped complex was a supermarket in the center of the middle wing. Beyond the glass front and glass doors, the cavernous interior was filled with hard fluorescent light. Flanking that store were smaller businesses, selling clothing and books and records and health foods. Other small stores filled the two end wings.

The hour was still so early that most of the shops had just opened. Only the supermarket had been doing business for any length of time, and there were few parked cars other than the twenty or thirty clustered in front of that central enterprise.

"Gimme the pistol," she said urgently. "Put it on my lap."

Spencer gave the SIG to her, and then he picked up the Micro Uzi from the floor between his feet.

No obvious opportunity for creating a diversion awaited her toward the south. She did a hard, fishtailing U-turn and headed back north toward the center of the parking lot.

That maneuver so surprised the ape that he put his pickup into a slide and almost rolled it in his eagerness to stay behind her. While regaining control, at least, he stopped blowing his horn.

The dog was still panting: *Heh-heh-heh-heh-heh!*

She continued to parallel the street on which they had been traveling when she had spotted the shopping center, staying away from the stores.

She said, "Anything you want to take with you?"

"Just my suitcase."

"You don't need it. I already took the money out."

"You what?"

"The fifty thousand in the false bottom," she said.

"You found my money?" He seemed astonished.

"I found it."

"You took it out of the case?"

"It's right there in the canvas bag behind my seat. With my laptop and some other stuff."

"You found my money?" he repeated disbelievingly.

"We'll talk about it later."

"Bet on it."

The ape in the Dodge was on her case again, blowing his horn, but he was not as close as he had been.

To the southwest, the choppers were less than half a mile away and only about a hundred feet off the ground, angling down.

She said, "You see the bag I mean?"

He looked behind her seat. "Yeah. There past Rocky."

After clashing with the Dodge, she wasn't sure if her door would open easily. She didn't want to have to wrestle with the bag and the door at the same time. "Take it with you when we come to a stop."

"Are we coming to a stop?" he asked.

"Oh, yeah."

A final turn. Hard right. She swung into one of the center aisles in the parking lot. It led directly east, to the front of the supermarket. As she approached the building, she put her hand on the horn and held it there, making even more noise than the ape was making behind her.

"Oh, no," Spencer said, with dawning awareness.

"Diversion!" Ellie shouted.

"This is nuts!"

"No choice!"

"It's still nuts!"

Across the face of the market, sales banners were taped to the big sections of plate glass, advertising Coke and potatoes and toilet tissue and rock salt for home water softeners. Most were along the top half of those tall panes; through the glass, below and between the signs, Ellie could see the checkout stations. In the fluorescent light, a few clerks and customers were looking out, alerted by the strident horns. As she shot toward them, the small ovals of their faces were as luminously white as the painted masks of harlequins. One woman ran, which startled the others into scattering for safety.

She hoped to God they would all manage to get out of the way in time. She didn't want to hurt any innocent bystanders. But she didn't want to be gunned down by the men who would pour out of those helicopters, either.

Do or die.

The Rover was moving fast but not flat-out. The trick was to have enough speed to jump the curb onto the wide promenade in front of the market and get through the glass wall and all the merchandise that was stacked waist-high beyond it. But at too high a speed, she would crash into the checkout stations with deadly impact.

"Gonna make it!" Then she remembered never to lie to the dog. "Probably!"

Over the horns and the sound of the engines, she suddenly heard the *chuda-chuda-chuda* of the choppers. Or maybe she felt more than heard the pressure waves cast off by their rotors. They must be directly over the parking lot.

The front tires rammed the curb, the Range Rover leaped, Rocky yelped, and Ellie simultaneously released the horn and took her foot off the accelerator. She tramped on the brakes as the tires slammed into the concrete. The promenade didn't seem so wide when the Rover was skidding across it at thirty or forty miles an hour, with the scared-pig squeal of hot rubber on pavement, not so very wide at all, hell, not nearly wide *enough*. Her sudden awareness of the Rover's oncoming reflection was followed instantly by cascades of glass, ringing down like shattered icicles. They plowed through big wooden pallets, on which were stacked fifty-pound bags of potatoes or some damn thing, and finally took a header into the end of a checkout station. Panels of fiberboard popped apart, the stainless steel grocery chute buckled like gift-wrapping foil, the rubber conveyor belt snapped in two and spun off its rollers and rippled into the air as if it were a giant black flatworm, and the cash register almost toppled to the floor. The impact wasn't as hard as Ellie had feared, and as if to celebrate their safe landing, gay foulards of translucent plastic bags blossomed briefly, with a flourish, in midair, from the pockets of an invisible magician.

"Okay?" she asked, releasing the buckle on her safety harness.

He said, "Next time, I drive."

She tried her door. It protested, screeching and grinding, but neither the brush with the Dodge nor the explosive entry into the market had jammed the latch. Grabbing the SIG 9mm that was trapped between her thighs, she clambered out of the Range Rover.

Spencer had already gotten out of the other side.

The morning was filled with the clatter of helicopters.

The two choppers appeared on the computer screen because they had entered the boundaries of Earthguard's two-hundred-foot look-down. Roy sat in the second of the craft, studying the top of that very machine as it was photographed from orbit, marveling at the strange possibilities of the modern world.

Because the pilot was making a straight-on approach to the target, neither the porthole on the left nor the one on the right gave Roy any view. He stayed with the computer to watch the Range Rover as it strove to elude the pickup truck by weaving back and forth across the shopping-center parking lot. As the pickup tried to get back up to speed after making a bad U-turn, the Rover swung toward the central building in the complex—which was, judging by its size, a supermarket or a discount store like Wal-Mart or Target.

Only at the last moment did Roy realize that the Rover was going to ram the place. When it hit, he expected to see it rebound in a mass of flattened and tangled metal. But it disappeared, merged with the building. With horror, he realized that it had driven through an entrance or a glass wall and that the occupants had survived.

He lifted the open attaché case off his lap, put it on the cabin deck, in the aisle beside his seat, and bolted to his feet in alarm. He did not pause to go through the back-out security procedures with Mama, didn't disconnect, didn't unplug, but stepped over the computer and hurried toward the pilot's cabin.

From what he'd seen on the display, he knew that both choppers had crossed over the power lines at the street. They were above the parking lot, easing toward touchdown, making a forward speed of only two or three miles an hour, all but hovering. They were so *close* to the damn woman, but now she was out of sight.

Once out of sight, she might quickly be out of reach as well. Gone again. No. Intolerable.

Armed and ready for action, the four strike force agents had gotten to their feet and were blocking the aisle near the exit.

"Clear the way, clear the way!"

Roy struggled through the assembled hulks to the head of the aisle, jerked open a door, and leaned into the cramped cockpit.

The pilot's attention was focused on avoiding the parking lot lampposts and the parked cars as he gentled the JetRanger toward the blacktop. But the second man, who was both copilot and navigator, turned in his seat to look at Roy as the door opened.

"She drove into the damned building," Roy said, looking out through the windshield at the shattered glass along the front of the supermarket.

"Wild, huh?" the copilot agreed, grinning.

Too many cars were spread out across the blacktop to allow either chopper to put down directly in front of the market. They were angling toward opposite ends of the building, one to the north and the other to the south.

Pointing at the first craft, with its full complement of eight strike force agents, Roy said, "No, no. Tell him I want him over the building, in back, not here, in back, all eight of his men deployed in back, stopping everyone on foot."

Their pilot was already in radio contact with the pilot of the other craft. While he hovered twenty feet over the parking lot, he repeated Roy's orders into the mouthpiece of his headset.

"They'll try to go through the market and out the back," Roy said, striving to rein in his anger and remain calm. Deep breaths. In with the pale-peach vapor of blessed tranquility. Out with the bile-green mist of anger, tension, stress.

Their chopper was hovering too low for Roy to be able to see over the roof of the market. From the Earthguard look-down on his computer, however, he remembered what lay behind the shopping center: a wide service alley, a concrete-block wall, and then a housing development with numerous trees. Houses and trees. Too many places to hide, too many vehicles to steal.

North of them, just as the first JetRanger was about to touch down on the parking lot and disgorge its men, the pilot got Roy's message. Rotor speed picked up, and the craft began to lift into the air again.

Peach in. Green out.

A carpet of brown nuggets had spilled from some of the torn fifty-pound bags, and they crunched under Spencer's shoes as he got out of the Rover and ran between two checkout stations. He carried the canvas bag by its straps. In the other hand, he clutched the Uzi.

He glanced to his left. Ellie was paralleling him in the next checkout lane. The shopping aisles were long and ran front to back of the store. He met Ellie at the head of the nearest aisle.

"Out the back." She hurried toward the rear of the supermarket.

Starting after her, he remembered Rocky. The mutt had gotten out of the Rover behind him. Where was Mr. Rocky Dog?

He stopped, spun around, ran back two steps, and saw the hapless canine in the checkout lane that he himself had used. Rocky was eating some of the brown nuggets that hadn't been crushed under his master's shoes. Dry dog food. Fifty pounds or more of it.

"Rocky!"

The mutt looked up and wagged his tail.

"Come on!"

Rocky didn't even consider the command. He snatched up a few more nuggets, crunching them with delight.

"Rocky!"

The dog regarded him again, one ear up and one down, bushy tail banging against the side of the cashier's counter.

In his sternest voice, Spencer said, *"Mine!"*

Regretful but obedient, a little ashamed, Rocky trotted away from the food. When he saw Ellie, who had stopped halfway down the long aisle to wait for them, he broke into a sprint. Ellie resumed her flight, and Rocky dashed exuberantly past her, unaware that they were running for their lives.

At the end of the aisle, three men rushed into sight from the left and halted when they saw Ellie, Spencer, the dog, the guns. Two were in white uniforms: names stitched on their shirt pockets, employees of the market. The third—in street clothes, with a loaf of French bread in one hand—must have been a customer.

With an alacrity and sinuosity more like that of a cat, Rocky transformed his headlong plunge into an immediate retreat. Eeling around on himself, tail between his legs, almost on his belly, he waddled back toward his master for protection.

The men were startled, not aggressive. But they froze, blocking the way.

"*Back off!*" Spencer shouted.

Aiming at the ceiling, he punctuated his demand with a short burst from the Uzi, blowing out a fluorescent strip and precipitating a shower of lightbulb glass and chopped-up acoustic tiles.

Terrified, the three men scattered.

A pair of swinging doors at the back of the market was recessed between dairy cases to the left and lunch-meat-and-cheese coolers to the right. Ellie slammed through the doors. Spencer followed with Rocky. They were in a short hallway, with rooms to both sides.

The sound of the helicopters was muffled there.

At the end of the hallway, they burst into a cavernous room that extended the width of the building: bare concrete walls, fluorescent lights, open rafters instead of a suspended ceiling. An area in the center of the chamber was open, but merchandise in shipping cartons was stacked sixteen feet high in aisles on both sides—additional stock of products from shampoo to fresh produce.

Spencer spotted a few stockroom employees watching warily from between the storage aisles.

Directly ahead, beyond the open work area, was an enormous metal roll-up door through which big trucks could be backed inside and unloaded. To the right of the shipping entrance was a man-size door. They ran to it, opened it, and went outside into the fifty-foot-wide service alley.

No one in sight.

A twenty-foot-deep overhang sprouted from the wall above the roll-up. It extended the length of the market, jutting nearly halfway across the alley, to allow additional trucks to pull under it and unload while protected from the elements. It was also protection from eyes in the sky.

The morning was surprisingly chilly. Though the market and stockroom had been cool, Spencer wasn't prepared for the briskness of the outside air. The temperature must have been in the mid-forties. In more than two hours of breakneck travel, they had come from the edge of a desert into higher altitudes and a different climate.

He saw no point in following the service alley left or right. Both ways, they would only be going around the U-shaped structure to the parking lot out front.

On three sides of the shopping center, a nine-foot-high privacy wall separated it from its neighbors: concrete blocks, painted white, capped with bricks. If it had been six feet, they might have scaled it fast enough to escape. Nine feet, no way in hell. They could throw the canvas bag across, easy enough, but they couldn't simply heave a seventy-pound dog to the other side and hope he landed well.

Out at the front of the supermarket, the pitch of engines from at least one of the helicopters changed. The clatter of its props grew louder. It was coming to the rear of the building.

Ellie dashed to the right, along the shaded back of the market. Spencer knew what she intended. They had one hope. He followed her.

She stopped at the limit of the overhang, which marked the end of the supermarket. Beyond was that portion of the back wall of the shopping center belonging to neighboring businesses.

Ellie glowered at Rocky. "Stay close to the building, tight against it," she told him, as if he could understand.

Maybe he could. Ellie hurried out into the sunshine, heeding her own advice, and Rocky trotted between her and Spencer, staying close to the back wall of the shopping center.

Spencer didn't know if satellite surveillance was acute enough to differentiate between them and the structure. He didn't know if the two-foot overhang on the main roof, high above, provided cover. But even if Ellie's strategy was smart, Spencer still *felt* watched.

The stuttering thunder of the chopper grew louder. Judging by the sound, it was up and out of the front parking lot, starting across the roof.

South of the supermarket, the first business was a dry cleaner. A small sign bearing the name of the shop was posted on the employee entrance. Locked.

The sky was full of apocalyptic sound.

Beyond the dry cleaner was a Hallmark card shop. The service door was unlocked. Ellie yanked it open.

Roy Miro leaned through the cockpit door to watch as the other chopper rose higher than the building, hovered for a moment, then angled across the roof toward the back of the supermarket.

Pointing to a clear area of blacktop just south of the market, for the benefit of his own pilot, Roy said, "There, smack in front of Hallmark, put us down right there."

As the pilot took them down the last twenty feet and maneuvered to the desired landing point, Roy joined the four agents at the door in the passenger cabin. Breathing deeply. Peach in. Green out.

He pulled the Beretta from his shoulder holster. The silencer was still fitted to the weapon. He removed it and dropped it in an inside jacket pocket. This wasn't a clandestine operation that required silencers, not with all the attention they were attracting. And the pistol would allow more accuracy without the trajectory distortion caused by a silencer.

They touched down.

One of the strike team agents slid the door out of the way, and they exited rapidly, one after the other, into the battering downdraft from the rotor blades.

As Spencer followed Ellie and Rocky through the door into the back room of the card shop, he glanced up into cannonades of sound. Silhouetted against the icy-blue sky, straight overhead, the outer edges of the rotors appeared first, chopping through the dry Utah air. Then the glide-slope antenna on the nose of the craft eased into view. As the leading edge of the downdraft hit him, he stepped inside and pulled the door shut, barely in time to avoid being seen.

The deadbolt had a brass thumb turn on the inside of the door. Although the hit squad would focus first on the back of the market, Spencer engaged the lock.

They were in a narrow, windowless storeroom that smelled of rose-scented air freshener. Ellie opened the next door before Spencer had closed the first. Beyond the storeroom was a small office with overhead fluorescents. Two desks. A computer. Files.

Two more doors led out of there. One stood half open to a tiny bathroom: toilet and sink. The other connected the office to the shop itself.

The long, narrow store was crowded with pyramidal island displays of cards, carousels of more cards, giftwrap, puzzles, stuffed toys, decorative candles, and novelties. The current promotion was for Valentine's Day, and there was an abundance of overhead banners and decorative wall hangings, all hearts and flowers.

The festiveness of the place was an unsettling reminder that regardless of what happened to him and Ellie and Rocky in the next few minutes, the world would spin on, unheeding. If they were shot dead in Hallmark, their bodies would be hauled away, the blood would be expunged from the carpet, a rose-scented air freshener would be employed in generous sprays, a few more potpourri might be set out for sale, and the stream of lovers coming in to buy cards would continue all but unabated.

Two women, evidently employees, were at the glass storefront, backs turned. They stared out at the activity in the parking lot.

Ellie started toward them.

Following her, Spencer suddenly wondered if she intended to take hostages. He didn't like that idea. Not at all. Jesus, no. These agency people, as she had described them and as he had seen them in action, wouldn't hesitate to blow away a hostage, even a woman or a child, to get at their target—especially not early in an operation, when witnesses were the most confused and no reporters were yet on the scene with cameras.

He didn't want innocent blood on his hands.

Of course, they couldn't merely wait in Hallmark until the agency went away. When they weren't found in the supermarket, the search would surely spread to adjacent stores.

Their best chance to escape was to slip out the front door of the card shop while the hit team's attention remained focused on the supermarket, try to get to a parked car, and hot-wire it. Not much of a chance. As thin as paper, as thin as hope itself. But it was all they had, better than hostages, so he clung to it.

With the chopper landing virtually at the back door, the card shop was so hammered by the screaming of engines and the pounding of rotor blades that it couldn't have been noisier if it had been under an amusement-park roller coaster. The Valentine banners trembled overhead. Hundreds of novelty key rings jangled from the hooks of a display stand. A collection of small ornate picture frames rattled against the glass shelf on which they stood. Even the walls of the store seemed to thrum like drumheads.

The racket was so ungodly that he wondered about the shopping center. It must be cheapjack construction, the worst crap, if one chopper could set up such reverberations in its walls.

They were almost to the front of the store, fifteen feet from the women at the window, when the reason for the fearful tumult became obvious: The second helicopter settled down in front of the shop, beyond the covered promenade, in the parking lot. The store was bracketed by the machines, shaken by cross-vibrations.

Ellie halted at the sight of the chopper.

Rocky seemed less worried by the cacophony than by an unfurled poster of Beethoven—the movie-star Saint Bernard, not the composer of symphonies—and he shied from it, taking refuge behind Ellie's legs.

The two women at the window were still unaware that they had company. They were side by side, chattering excitedly, and though their voices were raised above the clamor of the machines, their words were unintelligible to Spencer.

As he stepped to Ellie's side, gazing at the chopper with dread, he saw a door slide open on the fuselage. Armed men jumped to the blacktop, one after the other. The first was carrying a submachine gun larger than Spencer's Micro Uzi. The second had an automatic rifle. The third toted a pair of grenade-launching rifles, no doubt equipped with stun, sting, or gas payloads. The fourth man was armed with a submachine gun, and the fifth had only a pistol.

The fifth man was the last, and he was different from the four hulks who preceded him. Shorter, somewhat pudgy. He held his pistol to one side, aimed at the ground, and ran with less athletic grace than his companions.

None of the five approached the card shop. They raced toward the front of the supermarket, moving quickly out of view.

The chopper's engine was idling. The blades were still turning, though at a slower speed. The hit team hoped to be in and out fast.

"Ladies," Ellie said.

The women didn't hear her over the still considerable noise of the helicopters and of their own excited conversation.

Ellie raised her voice: *"Ladies, damn it!"*

Startled, exclaiming, wide-eyed, they turned.

Ellie didn't point the SIG 9mm at them, but she made sure they got a good look at it. "Get away from those windows, come here."

They hesitated, glanced at each other, at the pistol.

"I don't want to hurt you." Ellie was unmistakably sincere. "But I'll do what I have to do if you don't *come here right now*!"

The women stepped away from the storefront windows, one of them moving slower than the other. The slowpoke cast a furtive glance at the nearby entrance door.

"Don't even think about it," Ellie told her. "I'll shoot you in the back, so help me God, and if you aren't killed, you'll be in a wheelchair forever. Okay, yeah, that's better, come here."

Spencer stepped aside—and Rocky hid behind him—as Ellie guided the frightened women along the aisle. Halfway through the store, she made them lie facedown, one behind the other, with their heads toward the back wall.

"If either of you looks up anytime in the next fifteen minutes, I'll kill you both," Ellie told them.

Spencer didn't know if she was as sincere this time as when she had told them that she didn't *want* to hurt them, but she sounded as though she were. If he had been one of the women, he wouldn't have raised his head to look around until at least Easter.

Returning to him, Ellie said, "Pilot's still in the chopper."

He moved a few steps closer to the front of the store. Through the side window of the cockpit, one of the crew was visible, probably the copilot. "Two of them, I'm sure."

"They don't take part in the assault?" Ellie asked.

"No, of course not, they're flyers, not gunmen."

She went to the door and looked north toward the front of the supermarket. "Have to do it. No time to think about it. We just have to do it."

Spencer didn't even need to ask her what she was talking about. She was an instinctive survivor with fourteen hard months of combat experience under her belt, and *he* remembered most of what the United States Army Rangers had taught him about strategy and about thinking on his feet. They couldn't go back the way they'd come. Couldn't stay in the card shop, either. Eventually it would be searched. They could no longer hope to reach a car in the parking lot and hot-wire it, behind the backs of the gunmen, because all the cars were parked to the front of the chopper, requiring them to pass in full view of its crew. They were left with one option. One terrible, desperate option. It required boldness, courage—and either a dash of fatalism or an enormous measure of brainless self-confidence. They were both ready to do it.

"Take this," he said, handing her the canvas bag, "this too," and then gave her the Uzi.

As he took the SIG from her and tucked it under the waistband of his jeans, against his belly, she said, "I guess you have to."

"It's a three-second dash, at most, even less for him, but we can't risk him freezing up."

Spencer squatted, scooped up Rocky, and stood with the dog cradled like a child in his arms.

Rocky didn't know whether to wag his tail or be afraid, whether they were having fun or were in big trouble. He was clearly on the brink of sensory overload. In that condition he customarily either went all limp and quivery—or flew into a frenzy of terror.

Ellie eased open the door to check the front of the supermarket.

Glancing at the two women on the floor, Spencer saw that they were obeying the instructions they'd been given.

"Now," Ellie said, stepping outside, holding the door for him.

He went through sideways, so as not to bash Rocky's head into the door frame. Stepping onto the covered shopping promenade, he glanced toward the market. All but one of the gunmen had gone inside. A thug with submachine guns remained outside, facing away from them.

In the chopper, the copilot was looking down at something on his lap, not out the side window of the cockpit.

Half convinced that Rocky weighed seven hundred rather than seventy pounds, Spencer sprinted to the open door in the helicopter fuselage. It was only a thirty-foot dash, even counting the ten-foot width of the promenade, but those were the longest thirty feet in the universe, a quirk of physics, an eerie scientific anomaly, a bizarre distortion in the fabric of creation, stretching ever longer in front of him as he ran—and then he was there, pushing the dog inside, scrambling up and into the craft himself.

Ellie was so close behind him that she might as well have been his backpack. She dropped the canvas bag the moment she was up and across the threshold, but she held on to the Uzi.

Unless someone was crouched behind one of the ten seats, the passenger compartment was deserted. Just to be safe, Ellie moved back down the aisle, checking left and right.

Spencer stepped to the nearby cockpit door, opened it. He was just in time to jam the muzzle of the pistol in the face of the copilot, who was starting to get up from his seat.

"Take us up," Spencer told the pilot.

The two men appeared even more surprised than the women in the card shop.

"Take us up now—*now!*—or I'll blow this asshole's brains out through that window, then *yours!*" Spencer shouted so forcefully that he sprayed the crewmen with spittle and felt the veins in his temples popping up like those in a weight lifter's biceps.

He thought he sounded every bit as frightening as Ellie.

Just inside the shattered glass wall of the supermarket, beside the wrecked Range Rover, in a drift of dog food, Roy and three agents stood with their weapons aimed at a tall man with a flat face, yellow teeth, and coal-black eyes as cold as a viper's. The guy clutched a semiautomatic rifle in both hands, and although he wasn't aiming it at anyone, he looked mean enough and angry enough to use it on the baby Jesus Himself.

He was the driver of the pickup. His Dodge stood abandoned in the parking lot, one door hanging wide open. He had come inside either to seek vengeance for whatever had happened on the highway or to play the hero.

"Drop the gun!" Roy repeated for the third time.

"Says who?"

"Says who?"

"That's right."

"Are you a moron? Am I talking to a blithering *idiot* here? You see four guys holding heavy weapons on you, and you don't understand the logic of dropping that rifle?"

"You cops or what?" asked the viper-eyed man.

Roy wanted to kill him. No more formalities. The guy was too damn stupid to live. He'd be better off dead. A sad case. Society would be better off without him too. Cut him down, right there, right now, and then find the woman and Grant.

The only problem was that Roy's dream of a three-minute mission, in and out and away before the nosy locals showed up, was no longer achievable. The operation had gone sour when the hateful woman had driven into the market, and it was getting more sour by the moment. Hell, it was past sour into bitter. They were going to have to deal with Cedar City cops, and that was going to be more difficult if one of the residents they were sworn to protect was lying dead on a mound of Purina Dog Chow.

If they were going to have to work with locals, he might as well show a badge to this fool. From an inner jacket pocket, he withdrew an ID wallet, flipped it open, and flashed his phony credentials. "Drug Enforcement Administration."

"Well, sure," the man said. "Now, that's all right."

He lowered the gun to the floor, let go of it. Then he actually put one hand to the bill of his baseball cap and tipped it at Roy with what seemed to be sincere respect.

Roy said, "You go sit in the back of your truck. Not inside. In the open, behind the cab. You wait there. You try to leave, that guy outside with a machine gun will cut your legs off at the knees."

"Yes, sir." With convincing solemnity, he tipped his cap again, and then he walked out through the damaged front wall of the store.

Roy almost turned and shot him in the back.

Peach in. Green out.

"Spread out across the front of the store," he told his men, "and wait, keep alert."

The team coming in from the back would search the supermarket exhaustively, flushing out Grant and the woman if they tried to hide anywhere inside. The fugitives would be driven forward and forced either to surrender or to die in a barrage of gunfire.

The woman, of course, would be shot to death whether she tried to surrender or not. They were taking no more chances with her.

"There'll be employees and customers coming through," he called out to his three men as they deployed across the store to both sides of him. "Don't let *anybody* leave. Herd them over near the manager's office. Even if you think they have *no* resemblance to the pair we're looking for, hold them. Even if it's the Pope, you *hold* him."

Outside, the helicopter engine went from a low idle to a loud roar. The pilot revved it. Revved it again.

What the hell?

Frowning, Roy clambered through the debris and went outside to see what was happening.

The agent posted in front of the market was looking toward the Hallmark shop, where the chopper was lifting off.

"What's he doing?" Roy asked.

"Taking off."

"Why?"

"Must be going somewhere."

Another moron. Stay calm. Peach in. Green out.

"Who told him to leave his position, who told him to take off?" Roy demanded.

As soon as the question was put, he knew the answer. He didn't know *how* it was possible, but he knew why the chopper was taking off and who was in it.

He jammed the Beretta into his shoulder holster, wrenched the submachine gun out of the surprised agent's hands, and charged toward the ascending aircraft. He intended to rupture its fuel tanks and bring it to the ground.

Raising the weapon, finger on the trigger, Roy realized there was no way he was ever going to be able to explain his actions to the satisfaction of a straight-arrow Utah cop with no appreciation for the moral ambiguity of federal law enforcement. Shooting at his own helicopter. Jeopardizing his pilot and copilot. Destroying a hugely expensive piece of government machinery. Perhaps causing it to crash into occupied stores. Great, fiery gouts of aviation fuel splashing everything and anyone in their path. Respected Cedar City merchants transformed into human torches, running in circles through the February morning, blazing and shrieking. It would all be colorful and exciting, and nailing the woman would be worth the lives of any number of bystanders, but explaining the catastrophe would be as hopeless as trying to explain the fine points of nuclear physics to the idiot sitting in the back of the Dodge pickup.

And there was at least a fifty-fifty chance that the chief of police would be a clean-cut Mormon who had never tasted an alcoholic drink in his life, who had never smoked, and who would not be tuned in properly to the concepts of untaxable hush money and police-agency collusion. Bet on it. A Mormon.

Reluctantly, Roy lowered the submachine gun.

The chopper rose swiftly.

"Why Utah?" he shouted furiously at the fugitives that he could not see but that he *knew* were frustratingly close.

Peach in. Green out.

He had to calm down. Think cosmically.

The situation would be resolved in his favor. He still had the second chopper to use as a pursuit vehicle. And Earthguard 3 would find it easier to track the JetRanger than the Rover, because the chopper was larger than the truck and because it traveled above all sheltering vegetation and above the distracting movement of ground-level traffic.

Overhead, the hijacked aircraft swung east, across the roof of the card store.

In the passenger cabin, Ellie crouched beside the opening in the fuselage, leaned against the door frame, and looked down at the shopping center roof that passed under her. God, her heart was booming as loud as the rotor blades. She was terrified that the chopper would tip or lurch and that she would fall out.

During the past fourteen months, she had learned more about herself than in the entire previous twenty-eight years. For one thing, her love of life, her sheer joy in *being* alive, was greater than she had ever realized until the three people she had loved most had been taken from her in one brutal, bloody night. In the face of so much death, with her own existence in constant jeopardy, she now savored both the warmth of every sun-filled day and the chill wind of every raging storm, weeds as much as flowers, the bitter and the sweet. She had never been a fraction as aware of her love of freedom—her *need* for freedom—as when she had been forced to fight to keep it. And in those fourteen months, she had been amazed to learn that she had the guts to walk precipices, leap chasms, and grin in the devil's face; amazed to discover that she was not capable of losing hope; amazed to find that she was but one of many fugitives from an imploding world, all of them perpetually on the rim of a black hole and resisting its God-crushing gravity; amazed by how much fear she could tolerate and still thrive.

One day, of course, she would amaze herself straight into a sudden death. Maybe today. Leaning against the frame of the open door in the fuselage. Finished by a bullet or by a long, hard fall.

They traversed the building and moved over the fifty-foot-wide service alley. The other helicopter was down there, parked behind Hallmark. No gunmen were in the immediate vicinity of the craft. Evidently, they had already bailed out and had moved in on the back of the supermarket, under the twenty-foot overhang.

With Spencer giving orders to their own pilot, they hovered in position long enough for Ellie to use the Micro Uzi on the tail assembly of the craft on the ground. The weapon had two magazines, welded at right angles to each other, with a capacity of forty rounds—minus the few that Spencer had fired into the supermarket ceiling. She emptied both magazines, slapped in spares, emptied those too. The bullets destroyed the horizontal stabilizer, damaged the tail rotor, and punched holes in the tail pylon, disabling the aircraft.

If her assault was answered by any return fire, she was unaware of it. The gunmen who had moved off to cover the back of the market were probably too surprised and confused to be sure what to do.

Besides, the entire attack on the grounded chopper had taken only twenty seconds. Then she put the Uzi on the cabin deck and slid the door shut. The pilot, at Spencer's direction, immediately took them due north at high speed.

Rocky was crouched between two of the passenger seats, watching her intently. He was not as exuberant as he had been since they'd fled their camp in Nevada shortly after dawn. He had slipped into his more familiar suit of fretfulness and timidity.

"It's okay, pooch."

His disbelief was unconcealed.

"Well, it sure could be worse," she said.

He whimpered.

"Poor baby."

With both ears drooping, racked by shivers, Rocky was the essence of misery.

"How can I say anything that'll make you feel better," she asked the dog, "if I'm not allowed to lie to you."

From the nearby cockpit door, Spencer said, "That's a pretty grim assessment of our situation, considering we just slipped loose of a damned tight knot."

"We're not out of this mess yet."

"Well, there's something I tell Mr. Rocky Dog now and then, when he's down in the dumps. It's something that helps me a little, though I can't say whether it works for him."

"What?" Ellie asked.

"You've got to remember, whatever happens—it's only life, we all get through it."

THIRTEEN

Monday morning, after his bail had been posted, crossing the parking lot to his brother's BMW, Harris Descoteaux stopped twice to turn his face to the sun. He basked in its warmth. He had once read that black people, even those as midnight-dark as he was, could get skin cancer from too much sun. Being black was no absolute guarantee against melanoma. Being black, of course, was no guarantee against any misfortune, quite the opposite, so melanoma would have to wait in line with all the other horrors that might befall him. After spending fifty-eight hours in jail, where direct sunlight was more difficult to get than a hit of heroin, he felt as if he wanted to stand in the sun until his skin blistered, until his bones melted, until he became one giant pulsing melanoma. *Anything* was better than being locked away in a sunless prison. He inhaled deeply, too, because the smog-tainted air of Los Angeles smelled so sweet. Like the juice of an exotic fruit. The scent of freedom. He wanted to stretch, run, leap, twirl, whoop, and holler—but there were some things that a man of forty-four simply did not do, regardless of how giddy with freedom he might be.

In the car, as Darius started the engine, Harris put a hand on his arm, staying him for a moment. "Darius, I'll never forget this—what you've done for me, what you're still doing."

"Hey, it's nothing."

"The hell it isn't."

"Well, you'd have done the same for me."

"I think I would've. I hope I would've."

"There you go again, working on sainthood, putting on those robes of modesty. Man, whatever I know about doing the right thing, I learned from you. So what I did here, it's what you would do."

Harris grinned and lightly punched Darius on the shoulder. "I love you, little brother."

"Love you, big brother."

Darius lived in Westwood, and from downtown, the drive could take as little as thirty minutes on a Monday morning, after the rush hour, or more than twice that long. It was always a crapshoot. They had a choice between using Wilshire Boulevard, all the way across the city, or the Santa Monica Freeway. Darius chose Wilshire, because some days the rush hour never ended and the freeway became Hell with talk radio.

For a while, Harris was all right, enjoying his freedom if not the thought of the legal nightmare that lay ahead; however, as they were approaching Fairfax Boulevard, he began to feel ill. The first symptom was a mild but disturbing dizziness, a strange conviction that the city was ever so slowly revolving around them even as they drove through it. The sensation came and went, but each time that it gripped him, he suffered a spell of tachycardia more frantic than the one before it. When his heart fluttered through more beats in a half-minute seizure than the heart of a frightened hummingbird, he was overcome by the peculiar worry that he wasn't getting enough oxygen. When he tried to breathe deeply, he found he could barely breathe at all.

At first he thought that the air in the car was stale. Stuffy, too warm. He didn't want to reveal his distress to his brother—who was on the car phone, taking care of business—so he casually fiddled with the vent controls, until he got a draft of cool air directed at his face. Ventilation didn't help. The air wasn't stuffy but *thick*, like the heavy vapors of something odorless but toxic.

He endured the city revolving around the BMW, his heart bursting into fits of tachycardia, the air so syrup-thick that he could inhale only an inadequate drizzle, the oppressive intensity of light that forced him to squint against the sunshine that he had so recently enjoyed, the feeling that a crushing weight was hovering over him—but then he was enveloped by nausea so intense that he cried out for his brother to pull to the curb. They were crossing Robertson Boulevard. Darius engaged the emergency flashers, swung out of traffic just past the intersection, and stopped in a no-parking zone.

Harris flung open his door, leaned out, regurgitated violently. He had eaten none of the jailhouse breakfast that he'd been offered, so he was racked only by the dry heaves, although they were no less distressing or less exhausting because of that.

The siege passed. He slumped back in his seat, pulled the door shut, and closed his eyes. Shaking.

"Are you all right?" Darius asked worriedly. "Harris? Harris, what's wrong?"

With the spell past, Harris knew he'd been stricken by nothing more—and nothing less—than an attack of prison claustrophobia. It had been infinitely worse, however, than any panic attacks that had plagued him when he had actually been behind bars.

"Harris? Talk to me."

"I'm in prison, little brother."

"We're standing together on this, remember. Together, we're stronger than anybody, always were and always will be."

"I'm in prison," Harris repeated.

"Listen, these charges are bullshit. You were set up. None of this will stick. You're a Teflon defendant. You're not going to spend another day in jail."

Harris opened his eyes. The sunshine was no longer painfully bright. In fact, the February day seemed to have darkened with his mood.

He said, "Never stole a dime in my life. Never cheated on my taxes. Never cheated on my wife. Paid back every loan I ever took. Worked overtime most weeks since I've been a cop. Walked the straight and narrow—and let me tell you, little brother, it hasn't always been easy. Sometimes I get tired, fed up, tempted to take an easier way. I've had bribe money in my hand, and it felt good, but I just couldn't make my hand put it into my pocket. Close. Oh, yes, a lot closer than you ever want to know. And there've been some women . . . they would've been there for me, and I could've put Jessica way back in my mind while I was with them, and maybe I would've cheated on her if the opportunities had been just the littlest bit easier. I know it's in me to do it—"

"Harris—"

"I'm telling you, I've got evil in me as much as anyone, some desires that scare me. Even if I don't give in to them, just *having* them scares the living bejesus out of me sometimes. I'm no saint, the way you kid about. But I've always walked the line, walked that goddamned line. It's a mean mother of a line, straight and narrow, sharp as a razor, cuts right into you when you walk it long enough. You're always bleeding on that line, and sometimes you wonder why you don't just step off and walk in the cool grass. But I've always wanted to be a man our mother could be proud of. I wanted to shine in your eyes too, little brother, in the eyes of my wife and kids. I love you all so damned much, I never wanted any of you to know about any of the ugliness in me."

"The same ugliness that's in all of us, Harris. All of us. So why are you going on like this, doing this to yourself?"

"If I've walked that line, hard as it is, and something like this can happen to *me*, then it can happen to anyone."

Darius regarded him with stubborn perplexity. He was obviously struggling to understand Harris's anguish but was only halfway there.

"Little brother, I'm sure you'll clear me of the charges. No more nights in jail. But you explained the asset-forfeiture laws, and you did a damned good job, made it *too* clear. They have to *prove* I'm a drug dealer to put me back in jail, and they'll never be able to do that because it's all trumped up. But they don't have to prove a damn thing to keep my house, my bank accounts. They only have to show 'reasonable cause' that maybe the house was the site of illegal activity, and they'll say the planted drugs are reasonable cause even if the drugs don't *prove* anything."

"There's that reform law in Congress—"

"Moving slowly."

"Well, you never know. If some sort of reform passes, maybe it'll even tie forfeiture to conviction."

"Can you guarantee I'll get my house back?"

"With your clean record, your years of service—"

Harris gently interrupted: "Darius, under the current law, can you *guarantee* I'll get my house back?"

Darius stared at him in silence. A shimmer of tears blurred his eyes, and he looked away. He was an attorney, and it was his job to obtain justice for his big brother, and he was overwhelmed by the truth that he was all but powerless to assure even minimal fairness.

"If it can happen to me, it can happen to anyone," Harris said. "It could happen to you next. It could happen to my kids someday. Darius . . . maybe I get *something* back from the bastards, say as much as eighty cents on the dollar once all my costs are deducted. And maybe I get my life on track, start to rebuild. But how do I know it won't happen to me again, somewhere down the road?"

Having held back the tears, Darius looked at him again, shocked. "No, that's not possible. This is outrageous, unusual—"

"Why can't it happen again?" Harris persisted. "If it happened once, why not twice?"

Darius had no answer.

"If my house isn't really *my* house, if my bank accounts aren't really mine, if they can take what they want without proving a thing, what's to keep them from coming back? Do you see? I'm in prison, little brother. Maybe I'll never be behind bars again, but I'm in another kind of prison and never going to get free. The prison of expectations. The prison of fear. The prison of doubt, distrust."

Darius put one hand to his forehead, pressed and pulled at his brow, as if he would like to extract from his mind the awareness that Harris had forced upon him.

The car's emergency-flasher indicator blinked rhythmically, in time with a soft but penetrating sound, as if warning of the crisis in Harris Descoteaux's life.

"When the realization began to hit me," Harris said, "back there a few blocks ago, when I began to see what a box I'm in, what a box anyone could be in under these rules, I just was . . . overwhelmed . . . felt so claustrophobic that it made me sick to my stomach."

Darius lowered the hand from his brow. He looked lost. "I don't know what to say."

"I don't think there's anything anyone can say."

For a while they just sat there, with Wilshire Boulevard traffic whizzing by them, with the city so bright and busy all around, with the true darkness of modern life not to be glimpsed in mere palm shadows and awning-shaded shop entrances.

"Let's go home," Harris said.

They drove the rest of the way to Westwood in silence.

Darius's house was a handsome brick-and-clapboard Colonial with a columned portico. The spacious lot featured huge old ficus trees. The limbs were massive yet gracious in their all-encompassing spread, and the roots went back to the Los Angeles of Jean Harlow and Mae West and W. C. Fields, if not further.

It was a major achievement for Darius and Bonnie to have earned such a place in the world, considering how far down the ladder they had started their climb. Of the two Descoteaux brothers, Darius had enjoyed the greater financial success.

As the BMW pulled into the brick driveway, Harris was overcome by regret that his own troubles would inevitably taint the pride and well-earned pleasure that Darius took from that Westwood house and from everything else that he and Bonnie had acquired or achieved. What pride in their struggles and what pleasure in their attainments could survive, undiminished, after the realization that their position was maintained only at the sufferance of mad kings who might confiscate all for a royal purpose or dispatch a deputation of blackguards, under the protective heraldry of the monarch, to lay waste and burn? This beautiful house was only ashes waiting for the fire, and when Darius and Bonnie regarded their handsome residence henceforth, they would be troubled by the faintest scent of smoke, the bitter taste of burnt dreams.

Jessica met them at the door, hugged Harris fiercely, and wept against his shoulder. To have held her any tighter, he would have had to hurt her. She, the girls, his brother, and his sister-in-law were all that he had now. He was not merely without possessions but without his once strong belief in the system of law and justice that had inspired and sustained him during his entire adult life. From that moment on, he would trust in nothing except himself and the few people who were closest to him. Security, if it existed at all, could not be bought, but was a gift to be given only by family and friends.

Bonnie had taken Ondine and Willa to the mall to buy some new clothes for them.

"I should've gone along, but I just couldn't," Jessica said, wiping at the tears in the corners of her eyes. She seemed fragile in a way she had never been before. "I'm still . . . I'm shaking from all this. Harris, when they came on Saturday with . . . with the seizure notice, when they made us move out, we were only allowed to take one suitcase each, clothes and personal stuff, no jewelry, no . . . no anything."

"It's an outrageous abuse of legal process," Darius said angrily and with palpable frustration.

"And they stood over us, watching what we packed," Jessica told Harris. "Those men . . . just standing there, while the girls opened dresser drawers to get their underwear, bras . . ." That memory brought a snarl of outrage to her voice and, for the time being, chased off the emotional fragility that dismayed Harris and that was so unlike her. "It was *disgusting*! They were so arrogant, such bastards about it. I was just waiting for one of the sonsofbitches to touch me, to try to hurry me along with a little hand on the arm, anything like that, because I'd have kicked him in the balls so hard he'd have been wearing dresses and high heels the rest of his life."

He was surprised to hear himself laugh.

Darius laughed too.

Jessica said, "Well, I would have."

"I know," Harris said. "I know you would."

"I don't see what's so funny."

"I don't either, honey, but it is."

"Maybe you've got to have balls to see the humor," Darius said.

That made Harris laugh again.

Shaking her head in amazement at the inexplicable behavior of men in general and these two in particular, Jessica went to the kitchen, where she was preparing the ingredients for a pair of her justly renowned walnut-apple pies. They followed her.

Harris watched her peel an apple. Her hands were trembling.

He said, "Shouldn't the girls be in school? They can wait till the weekend to buy clothes."

Jessica and Darius exchanged a look, and Darius said, "We all felt it was better they stay out of school for a week. Until the press coverage isn't so . . . fresh."

That was something Harris hadn't really thought about: his name and photograph in the newspapers, headlines about a drug-dealing cop, the television anchorpersons conducting their happy talk around lurid accounts of his alleged secret life of crime. Ondine and Willa would have to endure heavy humiliation whenever they returned to school, whether it was tomorrow or next week or a month from now. *Hey, can your dad sell me an ounce of pure white? How much does your old man charge to fix a speeding ticket? Does your daddy just deal in drugs, or can he get a hooker for me?* Dear God. This wound was separate from all others.

Whoever his mysterious enemies were, whoever had done this to him, they must have been aware that they were destroying not only him but his family as well. Though Harris knew nothing else about them, he knew they were utterly without pity and as merciless as snakes.

From the wall phone in the kitchen, he made a call that he had been dreading—to Carl Falkenberg, his boss at Parker Center. He was prepared to use accumulated personal days and vacation, in order not to return to work for three weeks, in the hope that the conspiracy against him would miraculously collapse during that time. But, as he had feared, they were suspending him from duty indefinitely, although with pay. Carl was supportive but uncharacteristically reserved, as if he were responding to every question by reading from a carefully worded selection of answers. Even if the charges against Harris were eventually dropped or if a trial resulted in a verdict of innocence, there would be a parallel investigation by the LAPD Internal Affairs Division, and if its findings discredited him, he would be discharged from duty regardless of the outcome in federal court. Consequently, Carl was keeping a safe professional distance.

Harris hung up, sat at the kitchen table, and quietly conveyed the essence of the conversation to Jessica and Darius. He was aware of an unnerving hollowness in his voice, but he couldn't get rid of it.

"At least it's suspension with pay," Jessica said.

"They have to keep paying me or get in trouble with the union," Harris explained. "It's no gift."

Darius brewed a pot of coffee, and while Jessica continued with her pie-making, he and Harris remained in the kitchen, so the three of them could discuss legal options and strategies. Although the situation was grim, it felt good to be talking about taking action, striking back.

But the hits just kept on coming.

Not even half an hour passed before Carl Falkenberg called to inform Harris that the Internal Revenue Service had served the LAPD with a legal order to garnishee his wages against "possible unpaid taxes from trafficking in illegal drugs." Although his suspension was with pay, his weekly salary would have to be held in trust until the issue of his guilt or innocence was determined in court.

Walking back to the table and sitting opposite his brother again, Harris told them the latest. His voice was now as flat and emotionless as that of a talking machine.

Darius exploded off his chair, furious. "Damn it, this is not right, this does not wash, no way, I'll be damned if it does! Nobody has proved *anything*. We'll get this garnishment withdrawn. We'll start on it right now. It might take a few days, but we'll make them eat that piece of paper, Harris, I swear to you that we'll make the bastards eat it." He hurried out of the kitchen, evidently to his study and the telephone there.

For a long spiral of seconds, Harris and Jessica stared at each other. Neither of them spoke. They had been married so long that sometimes they didn't have to speak to know what they would have said to each other.

She returned her attention to the dough in the pie pan, which she had been crimping along the edge with her thumb and forefinger. Ever since Harris had come home, Jessica's hands had been trembling noticeably. Now the tremors were gone. Her hands were steady. He had the terrible feeling that her steadiness was the result of a bleak resignation to the unbeatable superiority of the unknown forces arrayed against them.

He looked out the window beside the table. Sunshine streamed through ficus branches. The flowers in the beds of English primrose were almost Day-Glo bright. The backyard was expansive, well and lushly landscaped, with a swimming pool in the center of a used-brick patio. To every dreamer living in deprivation, that backyard was a perfect symbol of success. A highly motivating image. But Harris Descoteaux knew what it really was. Just another room in the prison.

While the JetRanger flew due north, Ellie sat in one of the two seats in the last row of the passenger cabin. She held the open attaché case on her lap and worked with the computer that was built into it.

She was still marveling over her good fortune. When she had first boarded the chopper and had searched the cabin to be sure no agency men were hiding there, before they had even taken off, she had discovered the computer on the deck at the end of the aisle. She recognized it immediately as hardware developed for the agency, because she'd actually looked over Danny's shoulder when he had been designing some of the critical software for it. She realized that it was plugged in and on-line, but she was too busy to check it out closely until after they got off the ground and disabled the second JetRanger. Safely in the air, northbound toward Salt Lake City, she returned to the computer and was astonished when she realized that the image on the display screen was the satellite look-down of the very shopping center from which they had just escaped. If the agency had temporarily hijacked Earthguard 3 from the EPA to search for her and Spencer, they could only have done so through their omnipotent home-office computer system in Virginia. Mama. Only Mama had such power. The workstation that had been abandoned in the chopper was on-line with Mama, the megabitch herself.

If she had found the computer unplugged, she wouldn't have been able to get into Mama. A thumbprint was required to get on-line. Danny hadn't designed the software, but he had seen a demonstration of it and had told her about it, as excited as a child who had been shown one of the best toys ever. Because her thumbprint was not one of the approved, the hardware would have been useless to her.

Spencer came back down the aisle, with Rocky padding along behind him, and Ellie glanced up from the VDT in surprise. "Shouldn't you be keeping a gun on the crew?"

"I took their headsets away from them, so they can't use the radio. They don't have any weapons up there, and even if they had an arsenal, they might not use it. They're flyboys, not murderous thugs. But they think we *are* murderous thugs, *insane* murderous thugs, and they're nicely respectful."

"Yeah, well, they also know we need them to fly this crate."

As Ellie returned to her work on the computer, Spencer picked up the cellular phone that someone had abandoned on the last seat in the port-side row. He sat across the aisle from her.

"Well, see," he said, "they think I can fly this eggbeater if anything happens to them."

"Can you?" she asked, without shifting her attention from the video display, keeping her fingers busy on the keys.

"No. But when I was a Ranger, I learned a lot about choppers—mostly related to how you sabotage them, boobytrap them, and blow them up. I recognize all the flight instruments, know the names of them. I was real convincing. Fact is, they probably think the only reason I haven't already killed them is because I don't want to have to haul their bodies out of the cockpit and sit in their blood."

"What if they lock the cockpit door?"

"I broke the lock. And they don't have anything in there to wedge the door shut with."

She said, "You're pretty good at this."

"Aw, shucks, not really. What've you got there?"

While Ellie worked, she told him about their good fortune.

"Everything's coming up roses," he said with only a half-note of sarcasm. "What're you doing?"

"Through Mama, I've up-linked to Earthguard, the EPA satellite they've been using to track us. I've gotten into the core of its operating program. All the way to the program-management level."

He whistled in appreciation. "Look, even Mr. Rocky Dog is impressed."

She glanced up and saw that Rocky was grinning. His tail swished back and forth on the deck, thumping into the seats on both sides of the aisle.

"You're going to screw up a hundred-million-dollar satellite, turn it into space junk?" Spencer asked.

"Only for a while. Freeze it up for six hours. By then they won't have a clue where to look for us."

"Ah, go ahead, have fun, screw it up permanently."

"When the agency isn't using it for crap like this, it might actually do some beneficial work."

"So you're a civic-minded individual after all."

"Well, I was a Girl Scout once. It gets in your blood, like a disease."

"Then you probably wouldn't want to go out with me tonight, spraypaint some graffiti on highway overpasses."

"There!" she said, and tapped the ENTER key. She studied the data that came up on the screen and smiled. "Earthguard just shut down for a six-hour nap. They've lost us— except for radar tracking. Are you sure we're keeping due north and high enough for radar to pick us up, like I asked?"

"The boys up front promised me."

"Perfect."

"What did you do before all this?" he asked.

"Freelance software designer, specializing in video games."

"You created video games?"

"Yeah."

"Well, of course, you did."

"I'm serious. I did."

"No, you missed my inflection," he said. "I meant, *of course* you did. It's obvious. And now you're in a real-life video game."

"The way the world's going, everyone'll be living in one big video game eventually, and it's sure as hell not going to be a nice one, not 'Super Mario Brothers' or anything that gentle. More like 'Mortal Kombat.' "

"Now that you've disabled a hundred-million-dollar satellite, what next?"

As they had talked, Ellie had been focused on the VDT. She had retreated from Earthguard, back into Mama. She was calling up menus, one after the other, speed-reading them. "I'm looking around, seeing what's the best damage I can do."

"Mind doing something for me first?"

"Tell me what, while I nose around here."

He told her about the trap that he had set for anyone who might break into his cabin while he was gone.

It was her turn to whistle appreciatively. "God, I'd like to've seen their faces when they figured out what was going down. And what happened to the digitized photographs when they left Malibu?"

"They were transmitted to the Pacific Bell central computer, preceded by a code that activated a program I'd previously designed and secretly buried there. That program allowed them to be received and then retransmitted to the Illinois Bell central computer, where I buried another little hidden program that came to life in response to the special access code, and it received them from Pacific Bell."

"You think the agency didn't track them that far?"

"Well, to Pacific Bell, sure. But after my little program sent them to Chicago, it erased all record of that call. Then it self-destructed."

"Sometimes a self-destruct can be rebuilt and examined. Then they'd see the instructions about erasing the call to Illinois Bell."

"Not in this case. This was a beautiful little self-destructed program that stayed beautifully self-destructed, I guarantee you. When it dismantled itself, it also took out a reasonably large block of the Pacific Bell system."

Ellie interrupted her urgent search of Mama's programs to look at him. "How large is reasonably large?"

"About thirty thousand people must've been without telephone service for two to three hours before they got backup systems on-line."

"You were never a Girl Scout," she said.

"Well, I was never given a chance."

"You learned a lot in that computer-crime task force."

"I was a diligent employee," he admitted.

"More than you learned about helicopters, for sure. So you think those photos are still waiting in the Chicago Bell computer?"

"I'll walk you through the routine, and we'll find out. Might be useful to get a good look at the faces of some of these thugs—for future reference. Don't you think?"

"I think. Tell me what to do."

Three minutes later, the first of the photographs appeared on the video display of the computer in her lap. Spencer leaned across the narrow aisle from his seat, and she angled the attaché case so they both could see the screen.

"That's my living room," he said.

"You're not deeply interested in decor, are you?"

"My favorite period style is Early Neat."

"More like Late Monastery."

Two men in riot gear were moving through the room quickly enough to be blurred in the still shot.

"Hit the space bar," Spencer said.

She hit the bar, and the next photograph appeared on the screen. They went through the first ten shots in less than a minute. A few provided a clear image of a face or two. But it was difficult to get a sense of what a man looked like when he was wearing a riot helmet with a chin strap.

"Just shuffle through them until we see something new," he said.

Ellie rapidly, repeatedly tapped the space bar, flipping through the photos, until they came to shot number thirty-one. A new man appeared, and he was not in riot gear.

"Sonofabitch," Spencer said.

"I think so," she agreed.

"Let's see thirty-two."

She tapped the space bar.

"Well."

"Yeah."

"Thirty-three."

Tap.

"No doubt about it," she said.

Tap. Thirty-four.

Tap. Thirty-five.

Tap. Thirty-six.

The same man was in shot after shot, moving around the living room of the cabin in Malibu. And he was the last of the five men they had seen getting out of this very helicopter in front of the Hallmark card store a short while ago.

"Weirdest thing of all," Ellie said, "I'll bet we're looking at his picture on *his* computer."

"You're probably sitting in his seat."

"In his helicopter."

Spencer said, "My God, he must be pissed."

Quickly they went through the rest of the photographs. That pudgy-faced, rather jolly-looking fellow was in every shot until he apparently spit on a piece of paper and pasted it to the camera lens.

"I won't forget what he looks like," Spencer said, "but I wish we had a printer, could get a copy of that."

"There's a printer built in," she said, indicating a slot on the side of the attaché case. "I think there's a supply of maybe fifty sheets of eight-and-a-half-by-eleven bond paper. I sort of remember that's what Danny told me about it."

"All I need is one."

"Two. One for me."

They picked the clearest shot of their benign-looking enemy, and Ellie printed out twice.

"You've never seen him before, huh?" Spencer asked.

"Never."

"Well, I suspect we'll be seeing him again."

Ellie closed out Illinois Bell and returned to Mama's seemingly endless series of menus. The depth and breadth of the megabitch's abilities really did make her seem omnipotent and omniscient.

Settling back into his seat, Spencer said, "Think you can give Mama a terminal stroke?"

She shook her head. "No. Too many redundancies built into her for that."

"A bloody nose, then?"

"At least that much."

She was aware of him staring at her for the better part of a minute, while she worked. Finally he said, "Have you broken many?"

"Noses? Me?"

"Hearts."

She was amazed to feel a blush rising in her cheeks. "Not me."

"You could. Easy."

She said nothing.

"The dog's listening," he said.

"What?"

"I can only speak the truth."

"I'm no cover girl."

"I love the way you look."

"I'd like a better nose."

"I'll buy you a different one if you want."

"I'll think about it."

"But it's only going to be different. Not any better."

"You're a strange man."

"Besides, I wasn't talking about looks."

She didn't respond, just kept poring through Mama.

He said, "If I was blind, if I'd never seen your face, I already know you well enough that you could still break my heart."

When she was finally able to take a breath, she said, "As soon as they give up on Earth-guard, they'll try to get control of another satellite and find us again. So it's time to drop below radar and change course. Better tell the flyboys."

After a hesitation, which might have indicated disappointment in her failure to respond in any expected fashion to the way he had bared his feelings, he said, "Where are we going?"

"As near the Colorado border as this bucket will take us."

"I'll find out how much fuel we have. But why Colorado?"

"Because Denver is the nearest really major city. And if we can get to a major city, I can make contact with people who can help us."

"Do we need help?"

"Haven't you been paying attention?"

"I've got a history with Colorado," he said, and an uneasiness marked his voice.

"I'm aware of that."

"Quite a history."

"Does it matter?"

"Maybe," he said, and he was no longer romancing her. "I guess it shouldn't. It's just a place. . . ."

She met his eyes. "The heat's on us too high right now. We need to get to some people who can hide us out, let things cool off."

"You know people like that?"

"Not until recently. I've always been on my own before. But lately . . . things have changed."

"Who are they?"

"Good people. That's all you need to know for now."

"Then I guess we're going to Denver," he said.

Mormons, Mormons were everywhere, a plague of Mormons, Mormons in neatly pressed uniforms, clean-shaven, clear-eyed, too soft-spoken for cops, so excessively polite that Roy Miro wondered if it was all an act, Mormons to the left of him, Mormons to the right of him, both local and county authorities, and all of them too efficient and by-the-book either to flub their investigation or to let this whole mess be covered over with a wink and a slap on the back. What bothered Roy the most about these particular Mormons was that they robbed him of his usual advantage, because in their company, his affable manner was nothing unusual. His politeness paled in comparison to theirs. His quick and easy smile was only one in a blizzard of smiles full of teeth remarkably whiter than his own. They swarmed through the shopping center and the supermarket, these Mormons, asking their oh-so-polite questions, armed with their small notebooks and Bic pens and direct Mormon stares, and Roy could never be sure that they were buying any part of his cover story or that they were convinced by his impeccable phony credentials.

Hard as he tried, he couldn't figure out how to schmooze with Mormon cops. He wondered if they would respond well and open up to him if he told them how very much he liked their tabernacle choir. He didn't actually like or dislike their choir, however, and he had a feeling that they would know he was lying just to warm them up. The same was true of the Osmonds, the premier Mormon show-business family. He neither liked nor disliked their singing and dancing; they were undeniably talented, but they just weren't to his taste. Marie Osmond had *perfect* legs, legs that he could have spent hours kissing and stroking, legs against which he wished that he could crush handfuls of soft red roses—but he was pretty sure that these Mormons were not the type of cops who would enthusiastically join in on a conversation about that sort of thing.

He was certain that not all of the cops were Mormons. The equal-opportunity laws ensured a diverse police force. If he could find those who weren't Mormons, he might be able to establish the degree of rapport necessary to grease the wheels of their investigation, one way or another, and get the hell out of there. But the non-Mormons were indistinguishable from the Mormons because they'd adopted Mormon ways, manners, and mannerisms. The non-Mormons—whoever the cunning bastards might be—were all polite, pressed, well groomed, sober, with infuriatingly well-scrubbed teeth that were free of all telltale nicotine stains. One of the officers was a black man named Hargrave, and Roy was positive that he'd found at least one cop to whom the teachings of Brigham Young were no more important than those of Kali, the malevolent form of the Hindu Mother Goddess, but Hargrave turned out to be perhaps the most Mormon of all Mormons who had ever walked the Mormon Way. Hargrave had a walletful of pictures of his wife and nine children, including two sons who were currently on religious missions in squalid corners of Brazil and Tonga.

Eventually the situation spooked Roy as much as it frustrated him. He felt as if he were in *Invasion of the Body Snatchers*.

Before the city and county patrol cars had begun to arrive—all well polished and in excellent repair—Roy had used the secure phone in the disabled helicopter to order two more customized JetRangers out of Las Vegas, but the agency had only one more at that office to send him. "Jesus," Ken Hyckman had said, "you're going through choppers like they're Kleenex." Roy would be continuing the pursuit of the woman and Grant with only nine of his twelve men, which was the maximum number that could be packed into the one new craft.

Although the disabled JetRanger wouldn't be repaired and able to take off from behind the Hallmark store for at least thirty-six hours, the new chopper was already out of Vegas and on its way to Cedar City. Earthguard was being retargeted to track the stolen aircraft. They had suffered a setback, no argument about that, but the situation was by no means an unmitigated disaster. One battle lost—even one *more* battle lost—didn't mean they would lose the war.

He wasn't calmed by inhaling the pale-peach vapor of tranquility and exhaling the bile-green vapor of rage and frustration. He found no comfort in any of the other meditative techniques that for years had worked so reliably. Only one thing kept his counterproductive anger in check: thinking about Eve Jammer in all her glorious sixty-percent perfection. Nude. Oiled. Writhing. Blond splendor on black rubber.

The new helicopter wouldn't reach Cedar City until past noon, but Roy was confident of being able to tough out the Mormons until then. Under their watchful eyes, he wandered among them, answered their questions again and again, examined the contents of the Rover, tagged everything in the vehicle for impoundment, and all the while his head was filled with images of Eve pleasuring herself with her perfect hands and with a variety of devices that had been designed by sexually obsessed inventors whose creative genius exceeded that of Thomas Edison and Albert Einstein combined.

As he was standing at a supermarket checkout counter, examining the computer and the file box of twenty software diskettes that had been removed from the back of the Range Rover, Roy remembered Mama. For one frantic moment of denial, he tried to delude himself into remembering that he had switched off or unplugged the attaché case computer before he had departed the chopper. No good. He could see the video display as it had been when he'd put the workstation on the deck beside his seat before he had hurried to the cockpit: the satellite look-down on the shopping center.

"Holy *shit*!" he exclaimed, and every Mormon cop within hearing twitched as one.

Roy raced to the back of the supermarket, through the stockroom, out the rear door, through the milling strike force agents and cops, to the damaged helicopter, where he could use the secure phone with its scrambling device.

He called Las Vegas and reached Ken Hyckman in the satellite-surveillance center. "We've got trouble—"

Even as Roy started to explain, Hyckman talked over him with pompous ex-anchorman solemnity: "We have trouble here. Earthguard's onboard computer crashed. It inexplicably went off the air. We're working on it, but we—"

Roy interrupted, because he knew the woman must have used his VDT to take out Earthguard. "Ken, listen, my field computer was in that stolen chopper, and it was on-line with Mama."

"Holy shit!" Ken Hyckman said, but in the satellite-surveillance center, there were no Mormon cops to twitch.

"Get on with Mama, have her cut off my unit and block it from ever reaccessing her. *Ever.*"

The JetRanger chattered eastward across Utah, flying as low as one hundred feet above ground level where possible, to avoid radar detection.

Rocky remained with Ellie after Spencer went forward to oversee the crew again. She was too intensely focused on learning as much as she could about Mama's capabilities to be able to pet the pooch or even talk at him a little. His unrewarded company seemed to be a touching and welcome indication that he had come to trust and approve of her.

She might as well have smashed the VDT and spent the time giving the dog a good scratch behind the ears, because before she was able to accomplish anything, the data on the video display vanished and was replaced by a blue field. A question flashed at her in red letters against the blue: WHO GOES THERE?

This development was no surprise. She had expected to be cut off long before she could do any damage to Mama. The system was designed with elaborate redundancies, protections against hacker penetrations, and virus vaccines. Finding a route into Mama's deep program-management level, where major destruction could be wrought, would require not merely hours of diligent probing but days. Ellie had been fortunate to have the time necessary to take out Earthguard, for she could never have achieved such total control of the satellite without Mama's assistance. To attempt not merely to use Mama but to bloody her nose had been overreaching. Nevertheless, doomed as the effort was, Ellie had been obliged to try.

When she had no answer for the red-letter question, the screen went blank and changed from blue to gray. It looked dead. She knew there was no point in trying to reacquire Mama.

She unplugged the computer, put it in the aisle beside her seat, and reached for the dog. He wiggled to her, lashing his tail. As she bent forward to pet him, she noticed a manila envelope on the deck, half under her seat.

After petting and scratching the pooch for a minute or two, Ellie retrieved the envelope from under the seat. It contained four photographs.

She recognized Spencer in spite of how very young he was in the snapshots. Although the man was visible in the boy, he had lost more than youth since the days when those pictures had been taken. More than innocence. More than the effervescent spirit that seemed evident in the smile and body language of the child. Life also had stolen an ineffable quality from him, and the loss was no less apparent for being inexpressible.

Ellie studied the woman's face in the two pictures that showed her with Spencer, and was convinced that they were mother and son. If appearances didn't deceive—and in this instance she sensed that they did not—Spencer's mother had been gentle, kind, soft-spoken, with a girlish sense of fun.

In a third photo, the mother was younger than in the two with Spencer, perhaps twenty, standing alone in front of a tree laden with white flowers. She appeared to be radiantly innocent, not naive but unspoiled and without cynicism. Maybe Ellie was reading too much into a photo, but she perceived in Spencer's mother a vulnerability so poignant that suddenly tears welled in her eyes.

Squinting, biting her lower lip, determined not to weep, she was at last forced to wipe her eyes with the heel of her hand. She wasn't moved solely by Spencer's loss. Staring at the woman in the summer dress, she thought of her own mother, taken from her so brutally.

Ellie stood on the shore of a warm sea of memories, but she couldn't bathe in the comfort of them. Every wave of recollection, regardless of how innocent it seemed, broke on the same dark beach. Her mother's face, in every recaptured moment of the past, was as it had been in death: bloodied, bullet-shattered, with a fixed gaze so full of horror that it seemed as if, at the penultimate moment, the dear woman had glimpsed what lay beyond this world and had seen only a cold, vast emptiness.

Shivering, Ellie turned her eyes away from the snapshot to the starboard porthole beside her seat. The blue sky was as forbidding as an icy sea, and close beneath the low-flying craft passed a meaningless blur of rock, vegetation, and human endeavor.

When she was certain that she was in control of her emotions, Ellie looked again at the woman in the summer dress—and then at the final of the four photographs. She had noted aspects of the mother in the son, but she saw a much greater resemblance between Spencer and the shadow-shrouded man in the fourth picture. She knew this had to be his father, even though she didn't recognize the infamous artist.

The resemblance, however, was limited to the dark hair, darker eyes, the shape of the chin, and a few other features. In Spencer's face, there was none of the arrogance and potential for cruelty that made his father appear to be so cold and forbidding.

Or perhaps she saw those things in Steven Ackblom only because she knew that she was gazing at a monster. If she had come upon the photo without reason to suspect who the man was—or if she had met him in life, at a party or on the street—she might have seen nothing about him that made him more ominous than Spencer or other men.

Ellie was immediately sorry that such a thought had occurred to her, for it encouraged her to wonder if the kind, good man she saw in Spencer was an illusion or, at best, only part of the truth. She realized, somewhat to her surprise, that she did not want to doubt Spencer Grant. Instead, she was eager to believe in him, as she had not believed in anything or anyone for a long time.

If I was blind, if I'd never seen your face, I already know you well enough that you could still break my heart.

Those words had been so sincere, such an uncalculated revelation of his feelings and his vulnerability, that she had been left briefly speechless. Yet she hadn't possessed the courage to give him any reason to believe that she might be capable of reciprocating his feelings for her.

Danny had been dead only fourteen months, and that was, by her standards, far too short a time to grieve. To touch another man this soon, to care, to love—that seemed to be a betrayal of the man whom she had *first* loved and whom she would still love, to the exclusion of all others, were he alive.

On the other hand, fourteen months of loneliness was, by any measure, an eternity.

To be honest with herself, she had to admit that her reticence sprang from more than a concern about the propriety or impropriety of a fourteen-month period of mourning. As fine and loving as Danny had been, he never would have found it possible to bare his heart as directly or as completely as Spencer had done repeatedly since she'd driven him out of that dry wash in the desert. Danny had not been unromantic, but he had expressed his feelings less directly, with thoughtful gifts and kindnesses, rather than with words, as if to say "I love you" would have been to cast a curse upon their relationship. She was unaccustomed to the rough poetry of a man like Spencer, when he spoke from his heart, and she was not sure what she thought of it.

That was a lie. She liked it. More than liked it. In her hardened heart, she was surprised to find a tender place that wasn't merely responsive to Spencer's forthright expressions of love but that longed for more. That longing was like the profound thirst of a desert traveler, and she now realized it was a thirst that had been in need of slaking all her life.

She was reluctant to respond to Spencer not primarily because she might have grieved too short a time for Danny but because she sensed that the first love of her life might eventually prove not to be the greatest. Finding the capacity to love again seemed like a betrayal of Danny. But it was far worse—cruel rejection—to love another *more* than she had loved her murdered husband.

Perhaps that would never happen. If she opened herself to this still mysterious man, perhaps she would ultimately discover that the room he occupied in her heart would never be as large or warm as the one in which Danny had lived and would always live.

In carrying her loyalty to Danny's memory so far, she supposed that she was allowing honest sentiment to degenerate into a sugary pudding of sentimentality. Surely no one was born to love but once and never again, even if fate carried that first love to an early grave. If creation operated on rules that stern, God had built a cold, bleak universe. Surely love—and all emotions—were in one regard like muscles: growing stronger with exercise, withering when not used. Loving Danny might have given her the emotional strength, in the wake of his passing, to love Spencer more.

And to be fair to Danny, he had been raised by a soulless father—and a brittle, socialite mother—in whose icy embrace he'd learned to be self-contained and guarded. He had given her all that he could give, and she had been fortunate and happy in his arms. So happy, in fact, that suddenly she could no longer imagine going through the rest of her life without seeking, from someone else, the gift that Danny had been the first to give her.

How many women had ever affected a man so strongly that he had, after one evening of conversation, given up a comfortable existence and put his life in extreme jeopardy to be with her? She was more than merely mystified and flattered by Spencer's commitment. She felt special, foolish, girlish, reckless. She was reluctantly enchanted.

Frowning, she studied Steven Ackblom's photograph again.

She knew that Spencer's commitment to her—and all that he had done to find her—might be seen as less the result of love than of obsession. In the son of a savage serial killer, any sign of obsession might reasonably be viewed as a cause for alarm, as a reflection of the father's madness.

Ellie returned all four photographs to the envelope. She closed it with its small metal clasp.

She believed Spencer was, in all ways that mattered, *not* his father's son. He was no more dangerous to her than was Mr. Rocky Dog. For three nights in the desert, as she had listened to him murmuring in delirium, between his periodic ascensions to a shaky state of consciousness, she had heard nothing to make her suspect that he was the bad seed of a bad seed.

In reality, even if Spencer was a danger to her, he was no match for the agency when it came to being a threat. The agency was still out there, hunting for them.

What Ellie really needed to worry about was whether she could avoid the agency's goons long enough to discover and enjoy whatever emotional connections might evolve between her and this complex and enigmatic man. By Spencer's own admission, he had secrets that were still unrevealed. More for his sake than hers, those secrets would have to be aired before any future they might have together could be discussed or even discerned; because until he settled his debts with the past, he would never know the peace of mind or the self-respect needed for love to flourish.

She looked out at the sky again.

They flew across Utah in their sleek black machine, strangers in their own land, putting the sun behind them, heading eastward toward the horizon from which, several hours hence, the night would come.

. . .

Harris Descoteaux showered in the gray and maroon guest bathroom of his brother's Westwood home, but the scent of the jailhouse, which he believed he could detect on himself, was ineradicable. Jessica had packed three changes of clothes for him on Saturday, prior to being evicted from their house in Burbank. From that meager wardrobe, he selected Nikes, gray cords, and a long-sleeve, dark-green knit shirt.

When he told his wife that he was going for a walk, she wanted him to wait until the pies could be taken from the oven, so she could go with him. Darius, busy on the telephone in his study, suggested that he delay leaving for half an hour, so they could walk together. Harris sensed that they were concerned about his despondency. They felt he should not be alone.

He reassured them that he had no intention of throwing himself in front of a truck, that he needed to exercise after a weekend in a cell, and that he wanted to be alone to think. He borrowed one of Darius's leather jackets from the foyer closet and went into the cool February morning.

The residential streets of Westwood were hilly. Within a few blocks, he realized that a weekend spent sitting in a cell actually *had* left his muscles cramped and in need of stretching.

He hadn't been telling the truth when he had said that he wanted to be alone to think. Actually, he wanted to *stop* thinking. Ever since the assault on his house on Friday night, his mind had been spinning ceaselessly. And thinking had gotten him nowhere but into bleaker places within himself.

Even what little sleep he had gotten had been no surcease from worry, for he had dreamed about faceless men in black uniforms and shiny black jackboots. In the nightmares, they buckled Ondine, Willa, and Jessica into collars and leashes, as if dealing with dogs instead of with people, and led them away, leaving Harris alone.

As there was no escape from worry in his sleep, there was none in the company of Jessica or Darius. His brother was ceaselessly working on the case or brooding aloud about offensive and defensive legal strategies. And Jessica was—as Ondine and Willa would be, when they returned from the mall—a constant reminder that he had failed his family. None of them would say anything of that kind, of course, and he knew that the thought would never actually cross their minds. He had done nothing to earn the catastrophe that had befallen them. Yet, though he was blameless, he blamed himself. Somewhere, sometime, someplace, he'd made an enemy whose retribution was psychotically in excess of whatever offense Harris unwittingly had committed. If only he had done one thing differently, avoided one offending statement or act, perhaps none of this would have happened. Every time he thought of Jessica or his daughters, his inadvertent and unavoidable culpability seemed to be a greater sin.

The men in jackboots, though only creatures from his dream, had in a very real sense begun to deny him the comfort of his family without the need to buckle them in leashes and lead them away. His anger and frustration at his powerlessness and his self-inflicted guilt, as surely as bricks and mortar, had become the components of a wall between him and those he loved; and this barrier was likely to become wider and higher with time.

Alone, therefore, he walked the winding streets and the hills of Westwood. Many palms, ficuses, and pines kept the neighborhood California-green in February, but there were also numerous sycamores and maples and birches that were bare-limbed in winter. Harris focused largely on the interesting patterns of sunlight and tree shadows that alternately swagged and filigreed the sidewalk ahead. He tried to use them to induce a state of self-imposed hypnosis, in which all thought was banished except for an awareness of the need to keep putting one foot in front of the other.

He had some success at that game. In a half trance, he was only peripherally aware of the sapphire-blue Toyota that passed him and, abruptly chugging and stalling out, pulled to the curb and stopped nearly a block ahead. A man got out of the car and opened the hood, but Harris remained focused on the tapestry of sun and shade on which he trod.

As Harris passed the front of the Toyota, the stranger turned from his examination of the engine and said, "Sir, may I give you something to think about?"

Harris continued a couple of steps before he realized that the man was speaking to him. Halting, turning, rising from his self-induced hypnosis, he said, "Excuse me?"

The stranger was a tall black man in his late twenties. He was as skinny as a fourteen-year-old, with the somber and intense manner of an elderly man who had seen too much and carried too great a grief all his life. Dressed in black slacks, a black turtleneck sweater, and a black jacket, he seemed to want to project an ominous image. But if that was his intention, it was defeated by his large, bottle-thick glasses, his thinness, and a voice which, while deep, was as velvety and appealing as that of Mel Torme.

"May I give you something to think about?" he asked again, and then he continued without waiting for a response. "What's happened to you couldn't happen to a United States Representative or Senator."

The street was uncannily quiet for being in such a metropolitan area. The sunlight seemed different from what it had been a moment ago. The glimmer that it laid along the curved surfaces of the blue Toyota struck Harris as unnatural.

"Most people are unaware of it," said the stranger, "but for decades, politicians have exempted current and future members of the U.S. Congress from most of the laws they pass. Asset forfeiture, for one. If cops nail a senator peddling cocaine out of his Cadillac by a schoolyard, his car can't be seized the way your house was."

Harris had the peculiar feeling that he had hypnotized himself so well that this tall man in black was an apparition in a trance-state dream.

"You might be able to prosecute him for drug dealing and get a conviction—unless his fellow politicians just censor him or expel him from Congress and, at the same time, arrange his immunity from prosecution. But you couldn't seize his assets for drug dealing or any of the other two hundred offenses for which they seize yours."

Harris said, "Who are you?"

Ignoring the question, the stranger went on in that soft voice: "Politicians pay no Social Security taxes. They have their own retirement fund. And they don't rob it to finance other programs, the way they drain Social Security. *Their* pensions are safe."

Harris looked anxiously around the street to see who might be watching, what other vehicles and men might have accompanied this man. Although the stranger wasn't threatening, the situation itself suddenly seemed ominous. He felt that he was being set up, as if the point of the encounter was to tease from him some seditious statement for which he could be arrested, prosecuted, and imprisoned.

That was an absurd fear. Free speech was still well guaranteed. No citizens of the world were as openly and heatedly opinionated as his countrymen. Recent events obviously had inspired a paranoia over which he needed to gain control.

Yet he remained afraid to speak.

The stranger said, "They exempt themselves from health-care plans they intend to force on you, so someday you'll have to wait months for things like gallbladder surgery, but they'll get the care they need on demand. Somehow we've allowed ourselves to be ruled by the greediest and most envious among us."

Harris found the nerve to speak again, but only to repeat the question he had already asked and to add another. "Who are you? What do you want?"

"I only want to give you something to think about until the next time," said the stranger. Then he turned and slammed shut the hood of the blue Toyota.

Emboldened when the other's back was to him, Harris stepped off the curb and grabbed the man by the arm. "Look here—"

"I have to go," the stranger said. "As far as I know, we're not being watched. The chances are a thousand to one. But with today's technology, you can't be a hundred percent sure anymore. Until now, to anyone observing us, you just seem to've struck up a conversation with a guy who has car trouble, offered some assistance. But if we stand here talking any longer, and if someone *is* watching, they'll come in for a closer look and turn on their directional microphones."

He went to the driver's door of his Toyota.

Bewildered, Harris said, "But what was this all about?"

"Be patient, Mr. Descoteaux. Just go with the flow, just ride the wave, and you'll find out."

"What wave?"

Opening the driver's door, the stranger cracked his first smile since he had spoken. "Well, I guess . . . the microwave, the light wave, the waves of the future."

He got in the car, started the engine, and drove away, leaving Harris more bewildered than ever.

The microwave. The light wave. The waves of the future.

What the *hell* had just happened?

Harris Descoteaux turned in a circle, studying the neighborhood, and for the most part it seemed unremarkable. Sky and earth. Houses and trees. Lawns and sidewalks. Sunlight and shadows. But in the fabric of the day, glimmering darkly in the deep warp and woof, were threads of mystery that had not been there earlier.

He walked on. Periodically, however, as he had not done before, he glanced over his shoulder.

Roy Miro in the Empire of the Mormons. After dealing with the Cedar City Police and the county sheriff's deputies for nearly two hours, Roy had experienced enough niceness to last him until at least the first of July. He understood the value of a smile, courtesy, and unfailing friendliness, because he used a disarming approach in his own work. But these Mormon cops carried it to extremes. He began to long for the cool indifference of Los Angeles, the hard selfishness of Las Vegas, even the surliness and insanity of New York.

His mood was not enhanced by the news of Earthguard's shutdown. He had been further rattled by subsequently learning that the stolen helicopter had descended to such a low altitude that two military facilities tracking it (in response to urgent agency requests that they believed had come from the Drug Enforcement Administration) had lost the craft. They hadn't been able to reacquire it. The fugitives were gone, and only God and a couple of kidnapped pilots knew where.

Roy dreaded having to make his report to Tom Summerton.

The replacement JetRanger was due from Las Vegas in less than twenty minutes, but he didn't know what he was going to do with it. Park it in the shopping-center lot and sit in it, waiting for someone to sight the fugitives? He might still be there when the time rolled around to do Christmas shopping again. Besides, these Mormon cops would undoubtedly keep bringing him coffee and doughnuts, and they would hang around to help him pass the time.

He was spared all the horrors of continued niceness when Gary Duvall telephoned again from Colorado and put the investigation back on track. The call came through on the scrambler-equipped security phone in the disabled chopper.

Roy sat in the back of the cabin and put on the headset.

"You're not easy to track down," Duvall told him.

"Complications here," Roy said succinctly. "You're still in Colorado? I thought you'd be on your way back to San Francisco by this time."

"I got interested in this Ackblom angle. Always been fascinated by these serial killers. Dahmer, Bundy, that Ed Gein fellow a lot of years ago. Weird stuff. Got me to wondering what in hell the son of a serial killer is doing mixed up with this woman."

"We're all wondering," Roy assured him.

As before, Duvall was going to pay out whatever he had learned in small installments.

"While I was so close, I decide to hop over from Denver to Vail, have a look at the ranch where it happened. It's a quick flight. Almost took longer to board and disembark than it took to get there."

"You're there now?"

"At the ranch? No. I just got back from there. But I'm still in Vail. And wait'll you hear what I discovered."

"I guess I'll have to."

"Huh?"

"Wait," Roy said.

Either missing the sarcasm or ignoring it, Duvall said, "I've got two tasty enchiladas of information to feed you. Enchilada number one—what do you think happened to the ranch after they took all of the bodies out of there and Ackblom went to prison for life?"

"It became a retreat for Carmelite nuns," Roy said.

"Where'd you hear that?" Duvall asked, unaware that Roy's answer had been intended to be humorous. "Aren't any nuns anywhere around the place. There's this couple lives on the ranch, Paul and Anita Dresmund. Been there for years. Fifteen years. Everyone around Vail thinks they own the place, and they don't let on any different. They're only about fifty-five now, but they have the look and style of people who might've been able to retire at forty—which is what they claimed—or never worked at all, lived on inheritance. They're perfect for the job."

"What job?"

"Caretakers."

"Who does own it?"

"That's the creepy part."

"I'm sure it is."

"Part of the Dresmunds' job is to pretend ownership and not reveal they're paid care-takers. They like to ski, live the easy life, and it doesn't bother them to be living in a place with that reputation, so keeping their mouths shut has been easy."

"But they opened up to you?"

"Well, you know, people take FBI credentials and a few threats of criminal charges a lot more seriously than they should," Duvall said. "Anyway, until about a year and a half ago, they were paid by an attorney in Denver."

"You've got his name?"

"Bentley Lingerhold. But I don't think we'll need to bother with him. Until a year and a half ago, the Dresmunds' checks were issued from a trust fund, the Vail Memorial Trust, overseen by this attorney. I had my field computer with me, got on-line with Mama, had her track it down. It's a defunct entity, but there's still a record of it. Actually, it was managed by another trust that still exists—the Spencer Grant Living Trust."

"Good God," Roy said.

"Stunning, huh?"

"The son still owns that property?"

"Yeah, through other entities he controls. A year and a half ago, ownership was trans-ferred from the Vail Memorial Trust, which was essentially owned by the son, to an offshore corporation on Grand Cayman Island. That's a tax-shelter haven in the Caribbean that—"

"Yes, I know. Go on."

"Since then, the Dresmunds have been getting their checks from something called Van-ishment International. Through Mama, I got into the Grand Cayman bank where the ac-count is located. I wasn't able to learn its value or call up any transaction records, but I *was* able to find out that Vanishment is controlled by a Swiss-based holding company: Amelia Earhart Enterprises."

Roy fidgeted in his seat, wishing that he'd brought a pen and notebook to keep all these details straight.

Duvall said, "The grandparents, George and Ethel Porth, formed the Vail Memorial Trust well over fifteen years ago, about six months after the Ackblom story exploded. They used it to manage the property at a one-step remove, to keep their names disassociated from it."

"Why didn't they sell the place?"

"Haven't a clue. Anyway, a year later they set up the Spencer Grant Living Trust for the boy, here in Denver, through this Bentley Lingerhold, just after the kid had his name legally changed. At the same time they put *that* trust in charge of the Vail Memorial Trust. But Vanishment International came into existence just a year and a half ago, long after both grandparents were dead, so you've got to figure that Grant himself set it up and that he's moved most of his assets out of the United States."

"Starting at about the same time he began to eliminate his name from most public records," Roy mused. "Okay, tell me something . . . when you're talking trusts and off-shore corporations, you're talking about big money, aren't you?"

"Big," Duvall confirmed.

"Where'd it come from? I mean, I know the father was famous. . . ."

"After the old man pleaded guilty to all those murders, you know what happened to him?"

"Tell me."

"He accepted a sentence of life imprisonment in an institution for the criminally insane. No possibility of parole. He made no arguments, no appeals. The guy was absolutely serene from the moment he was arrested, all the way through the final proceeding. Not one outburst, no expressions of regret."

"No point. He knew he didn't have any defense. He wasn't crazy."

"He wasn't?" Duvall said, surprised.

"Well, not irrational, not babbling or raving or anything like that. He knew he couldn't get off. He was just being realistic."

"I guess so. Anyway, then the grandparents moved to have the son declared the legal owner of Ackblom's assets. In fact, at the Porths' request, the court ultimately divided the liquidated assets—minus the ranch—between the boy and the immediate families of the victims, in those cases where any spouses or children survived them. Want to guess how much they split?"

"No," Roy said. He glanced out the porthole and saw a pair of local cops walking alongside the aircraft, looking it over.

Duvall didn't even hesitate at Roy's "no," but poured out more details: "Well, the money came from selling paintings from Ackblom's personal collection of other artists' work, but mainly from the sale of some of his own paintings that he'd never been willing to put on the market. It totaled a little more than twenty-nine million dollars."

"*After* taxes?"

"See, the value of his paintings *soared* with the notoriety. Seems funny, doesn't it, that anyone would want to hang his work in their homes, knowing what the artist did. You'd think the value of his stuff would just collapse. But there was a frenzy in the art market. Values went through the roof."

Roy remembered the color plates of Ackblom's work that he had studied as a boy, at the time the story broke, and he couldn't quite understand Duvall's point. Ackblom's art was exquisite. If Roy could have afforded to buy them, he would have decorated his own home with dozens of the artist's canvases.

Duvall said, "Prices have continued to climb all these years, though more slowly than in the first year after. The family would have been better off holding onto some of the art. Anyway, the boy ended up with fourteen and a half million after taxes. Unless he lives high on the hog, that ought to have grown into an even more substantial fortune over all these years."

Roy thought of the cabin in Malibu, the cheap furniture and walls without any art-work. "No high living."

"Really? Well, you know, his old man didn't live nearly as high as he could have, either. He refused to have a bigger house, didn't want any live-in servants. Just a day maid and a property foreman who went home at five o'clock. Ackblom said he needed to keep his life as simple as possible to preserve his creative energy." Gary Duvall laughed. "Of course he really just didn't want anyone around at night to catch him at his games under the barn."

Wandering back along the side of the chopper again, the Mormon cops looked up at Roy, where he was watching them from the porthole.

He waved.

They waved and smiled.

"Still," Duvall said, "it's a wonder the wife didn't tumble to it sooner. He'd been ex-perimenting with his 'performance' art for four years before she got wise."

"She wasn't an artist."

"What?"

"She didn't have the vision to anticipate. Without the vision to anticipate . . . she wouldn't become suspicious without good reason."

"Can't say I follow you. Four years, for heaven's sake."

Then six more until the boy had found out. Ten years, forty-two victims, slightly more than four a year.

The numbers, Roy decided, weren't particularly impressive. The factors that made Steven Ackblom one for the record books were his fame *before* his secret life was discov-ered, his position of respect in his community, his status as a family man (most classic ser-ial killers were loners), and his desire to apply his exceptional talent to the art of torture in order to help his subjects achieve a moment of perfect beauty.

"But why," Roy wondered again, "would the son want to hold on to that property? With all its associations. He wanted to change his name. Why not rid himself of the ranch too?"

"Strange, huh?"

"And if not the son, why not the grandparents? Why didn't they sell it off when they were his legal guardians, make that decision for him? After their daughter was killed there . . . why would they want to have anything to do with the place?"

"There's something there," Duvall said.

"What do you mean?"

"Some explanation. Some reason. Whatever it is, it's weird."

"This caretaker couple—"

"Paul and Anita Dresmund."

"—did they say whether Grant ever comes around?"

"He doesn't. At least, they've never seen anybody with a scar like he's got."

"So who oversees them?"

"Until a year and a half ago, they only ever saw two people related to the Vail Memo-rial Trust. This lawyer, Lingerhold, or one of his partners would come by twice a year, just to check that the ranch was being maintained, that the Dresmunds were earning their salary and spending the upkeep fund on genuinely needed maintenance."

"And for the past year and a half?"

"Since Vanishment International has owned the place, nobody's come around at all," Duvall said. "God, I'd love to find out how much he's got stashed away in Amelia Earhart Enterprises, but you know we're never going to pry that out of the Swiss."

In recent years, Switzerland had grown alarmed by the large number of cases in which U.S. authorities had sought to seize the Swiss accounts of American citizens by invoking asset-forfeiture statutes without proof of criminal activity. The Swiss increasingly viewed such laws as blunt tools of political repression. Every month they retreated further from their traditional cooperation in criminal cases.

"What's the other taco?" Roy asked.

"Huh?"

"The second taco. You said you had two tacos to feed me."

"Enchiladas," Duvall said. "Two enchiladas of information."

"Well, I'm hungry," Roy said pleasantly. He was proud of his patience, after all the tests to which the Mormon cops had put it. "So why don't you heat up that second enchilada?"

Gary Duvall served it to him, and it was as tasty as promised.

The moment he hung up on Duvall, Roy called the Vegas office and spoke to Ken Hyckman, who would soon conclude his shift as the morning duty officer. "Ken, where's that JetRanger?"

"Ten minutes from you."

"I'm going to send it back with most of the men here."

"You're giving up?"

"You know we've lost radar contact on them."

"Right."

"They're gone, and we're not going to reconnect with them that way. But I have another lead, a good one, and I'm jumping on it. I need a jet."

"Jesus."

"I didn't say I needed to hear a little profanity."

"Sorry."

"What about the Lear I came in on Friday night?"

"It's still here. Serviced and ready."

"Is there anywhere in my vicinity it can land, any military base where I could meet it?"

"Let me check," Hyckman said, and he put Roy on hold.

While he waited, Roy thought about Eve Jammer. He would not be able to return to Las Vegas that evening. He wondered what his blond sweetness would do to remember him and to keep him in her heart. She had said that it would be something special. He assumed she would practice new positions, if there were any, and try out erotic aids that she had never used before, in order to prepare an experience for him that, a night or two hence, would leave him shuddering and breathless as never before. When he attempted to imagine what those erotic aids might be, his mind spun. And his mouth went as dry as sand—which was perfect.

Ken Hyckman came back on the line. "We can put the Lear down right there in Cedar City."

"This burg can take a Lear?"

"Brian Head is just twenty-nine miles east of there."

"Who?"

"Not who. What. First-rate ski resort, lots of pricey homes up on the mountain. Lots of rich people and corporations own condos in Brian Head, bring their jets in to Cedar City and drive up from there. It doesn't have anything like O'Hare or LAX, no bars and newsstands and baggage carousels, but the airfield can handle long landing requirements."

"Is a crew standing by with the Lear?"

"Absolutely. We can get them out of McCarran and to you by one o'clock."

"Terrific. I'll ask one of the grinning gendarmes to drive me to the airfield."

"Who?"

"One of the courteous constables," Roy said. He was in a fine mood again.

"I'm not sure this scrambler is giving me what you're saying."

"One of the Mormon marshals."

Either getting the point or deciding that he didn't need to understand, Hyckman said, "They'll have to file a flight plan here. Where are you going from Cedar City?"

"Denver," Roy said.

Slumped in the last seat in the starboard aisle, Ellie dozed on and off for a couple of hours. In fourteen months as a fugitive, she had learned to put aside her fears and worries, sleeping whenever she had a chance.

Shortly after she woke, while she was stretching and yawning, Spencer returned from an extended visit with the two-man crew. He sat across from her.

As Rocky curled up in the aisle at his feet, Spencer said, "More good news. According to the boys, this is an extensively customized eggbeater. For one thing, they have jumped-up engines on this baby, so we can carry an extra-heavy load, which allows them to saddle her with big auxiliary fuel tanks. She's got a lot more range than the standard model. They're sure they can get us all the way across the border and past Grand Junction before there's any danger of the tanks running dry, if we want to go that far."

"The farther the better," she said. "But not right in or around Grand Junction. We don't want to be seen by a lot of curious people. Better out somewhere, but not so far out that we can't find wheels nearby."

"We won't make it to the Grand Junction area until half an hour or so before twilight. Right now it's only ten past two o'clock. Well, three o'clock in the Mountain Time Zone. Still plenty of time to look at a map and pick a general area to put down."

She pointed to the canvas duffel bag on the seat in front of hers. "Listen, about your fifty thousand dollars—"

He held up one hand to silence her. "I was just startled that you found it, that's all. You had every right and reason to search my luggage after you located me in the desert. You didn't know why the hell I was trying to track you down. In fact, I wouldn't be surprised if you still weren't entirely clear on that."

"You always carry that kind of pocket change?"

"About a year and a half ago," he said, "I started salting cash and gold coins in safe-deposit boxes in California, Nevada, Arizona. Also opened savings accounts in various cities, under false names and Social Security numbers. Shifted everything else out of the country."

"Why?"

"So I could move fast."

"You expected to be on the run like this?"

"No. I just didn't like what I saw happening on that computer-crime task force. They taught me all about computers, including that access to information is the essence of freedom. And yet what they ultimately wanted to do was restrict that access in as many instances as possible and to the greatest extent possible."

Playing devil's advocate, Ellie said, "I thought the idea was just to prevent criminal hackers from using computers to steal and maybe to stop them from vandalizing data banks."

"And I'm all for that kind of crime control. But they want to keep a thumb on *everybody*. Most authorities these days . . . they violate privacy all the time, fishing both openly and secretly in data banks. Everyone from the IRS to the Immigration and Naturalization Service. Even the Bureau of Land Management, for God's sake. They were all helping to fund this regional task force with grants, and they all gave me the creeps."

"You see a new world coming—"

"—like a runaway freight train—"

"—and you don't like the shape of it—"

"—don't think I want to be a part of it."

"Do you see yourself as a cyberpunk, an on-line outlaw?"

"No. Just a survivor."

"Is that why you've been erasing yourself from public record—a little survival insurance?"

No shadow fell across him, but his features seemed to darken. He had looked haggard to begin with, which was understandable after the ordeal of the past few days. But now he was sunken-eyed, gaunt, and older than his years.

He said, "At first I was just . . . getting ready to go away." He sighed and wiped a hand across his face. "This sounds strange maybe. But changing my name from Michael Ackblom to Spencer Grant wasn't enough. Moving from Colorado, starting a new life . . . none of it was ever enough. I couldn't forget who I was . . . whose son I was. So I decided to wipe myself out of existence, painstakingly, methodically, until there was no record in the world that I existed under *any* name. What I'd been learning about computers gave me that power."

"And then? When you were erased?"

"That's what I could never figure out. And then? What next? Wipe myself out for real? Suicide?"

"That's not you." She found her heart sinking at the thought.

"No, not me," he agreed. "I never brooded about eating a shotgun barrel or anything like that. And I had an obligation to Rocky, to be here for him."

Sprawled on the deck, the dog raised his head at the sound of his name. He swished his tail.

"Then, after a while," he continued, "even though I didn't know what I was going to do, I decided there was still virtue in becoming invisible. Just because, as you say, of this new world coming, this brave new high-tech world with all its blessings—and curses."

"Why did you leave your DMV file and your military records partly intact? You could've wiped them out completely, long ago."

He smiled. "Being too clever, maybe. I thought I'd just change my address on them, a few salient details, so they weren't much use to anyone. But by leaving them in place, I could always go back to look at them and see if somebody was searching for me."

"You booby-trapped them?"

"Sort of, yeah. I buried little programs in those computers, very deep, very subtle. Each time anyone goes into my DMV or military files without using a little code I implanted, the system adds one asterisk to the end of the last sentence in the file. The idea was that I'd check once or twice a week, and if I saw asterisks, saw that someone was investigating me . . . well, then maybe it would be time to walk away from the cabin in Malibu and just move on."

"Move on where?"

"Anywhere. Just move on and keep moving."

"Paranoid," she said.

"Damned paranoid."

She laughed quietly. So did he.

He said, "By the time I left that task force, I knew that the way the world's changing, everybody's going to have somebody looking for him sooner or later. And most people, most of the time, are going to wish they hadn't been findable."

Ellie checked her wristwatch. "Maybe we should take a look at that map now."

"They have a slew of maps up front," he said.

She watched him walk forward to the cockpit door. His shoulders were slumped. He moved with evident weariness, and he still appeared to be somewhat stiff from his days of immobility.

Suddenly Ellie was chilled by a feeling that Spencer Grant was not going to make it through this with her, that he was going to die somewhere in the night ahead. The foreboding was perhaps not strong enough to be called an explicit premonition, but it was more powerful than a mere hunch.

The possibility of losing him left her half sick with dread. She knew then that she cared for him even more than she had been able to admit.

When he returned with the map, he said, "What's wrong?"

"Nothing. Why?"

"You look like you've seen a ghost."

"Just tired," she lied. "And starved."

"I can do something about the starved part." As he sat in the seat across the aisle again, he produced four candy bars from the pockets of his fleece-lined denim jacket.

"Where'd you get these?"

"The boys up front have a snack box. They were happy to share. They're really a couple of swell guys."

"Especially with a gun to their heads."

"Especially then," he agreed.

Rocky sat up and cocked his good ear with keen interest when he smelled the candy bars.

"Ours," Spencer said firmly. "When we're out of the air and on the road again, we'll stop and get some real food for you, something healthier than this."

The dog licked his chops.

"Look, pal," Spencer said, "I didn't stop in the supermarket to graze on the wreckage, like you did. I need every bite of these, or I'll collapse on my face. Now you just lie down and forget it. Okay?"

Rocky yawned, looked around with pretended disinterest, and stretched out on the deck again.

"You two have an incredible rapport," she said.

"Yeah, we're Siamese twins, separated at birth. You couldn't know that, of course, because he's had a lot of plastic surgery."

She could not take her eyes off his face. More than weariness was visible in it. She could see the certain shadow of death.

Disconcertingly perceptive and alert to her mood, Spencer said, "What?"

"Thanks for the candy."

"It would've been filet mignon if I could've swung it."

He unfolded the map. They held it between their seats, studying the territory around Grand Junction, Colorado.

Twice she dared to look at him, and each glimpse made her heart race with fear. She could too clearly see the skull beneath the skin, the promise of the grave that was usually so well concealed by the mask of life.

She felt ignorant, silly, superstitious, like a foolish child. There were other explanations besides omens and portents and psychic images of tragedy to come. Perhaps, after the Thanksgiving night when Danny and her parents had been snatched away forever, this fear would plague her every time that she crossed the line between caring for people and loving them.

Roy landed at Stapleton International Airport in Denver, aboard the Learjet, after twenty-five minutes in a holding pattern. The local office of the agency had assigned two operatives to work with him, as he had requested on the scrambler phone while in flight. Both men—Burt Rink and Oliver Fordyce—were waiting in the parking bay as the Lear taxied into it. They were in their early thirties, tall, clean-shaven. They wore black topcoats, dark-blue suits, dark ties, white shirts, and black Oxfords with rubber rather than leather-soles. All that was also as Roy had requested.

Rink and Fordyce had new clothes for Roy that were virtually identical to their own outfits. Having shaved and showered aboard the jet during the trip from Cedar City, Roy needed only to change clothes before they could switch from the plane to the black Chrysler super-stretch limousine that was waiting at the foot of the portable stairs.

The day was bone-freezing. The sky was as clear as an arctic sea and deeper than time. Icicles hung along the eaves of building roofs, and banks of snow marked the far limits of runways.

Stapleton was on the northeastern edge of the city, and their appointment with Dr. Sabrina Palma was beyond the *southwest* suburbs. Roy would have insisted on a police escort, under one pretense or another, except that he didn't want to call any more attention to themselves than absolutely necessary.

"It's a four-thirty appointment," Fordyce said as he and Rink settled into the back of the limousine, facing to the rear, where Roy sat facing forward. "We'll make it with a few minutes to spare."

The driver had been instructed not to dawdle. They accelerated away from the Learjet as if they *did* have a police escort.

Rink passed a nine-by-twelve white envelope to Roy. "These are all the documents you required."

"You have your Secret Service credentials?" Roy asked.

From suit-coat pockets, Rink and Fordyce withdrew their ID wallets and flipped them open to reveal holographic identification cards with their photographs and authentic SS badges. Rink's name for the upcoming meeting was Sidney Eugene Tarkenton. Fordyce was Lawrence Albert Olmeyer.

Roy extracted his own ID wallet from among the documents in the white envelope. He was J. Robert Cotter.

"Let's all remember who we are. Be sure to call one another by these names," Roy said. "I don't expect you'll need to say much—or even anything at all. I'll do the talking. You're there primarily to lend the whole thing an air of realism. You'll enter Dr. Palma's office behind me and post yourselves to the left and the right of the door. Stand with your feet about eighteen inches apart, arms down in front of you, one hand clasped over the other. When I introduce you to her, you'll say 'Doctor' and nod or 'Pleased to meet you' and nod. Stoic at all times. About as expressionless as a Buckingham Palace guard. Eyes straight ahead. No fidgeting. If you're asked to sit down, you'll politely say 'No, thank you, Doctor.' Yes, I know, it's ridiculous, but this is how people are used to seeing Secret Service agents in the movies, so any indication that you're a real human being will ring false to her. Is that understood, Sidney?"

"Yes, sir."

"Is that understood, Lawrence?"

"I prefer Larry," said Oliver Fordyce.

"Is that understood, Larry?"

"Yes, sir."

"Good."

Roy withdrew the other documents from the envelope, examined them, and was satisfied.

He was taking one of the greatest risks of his career, but he was remarkably calm. He was not even assigning agents to seek the fugitives in Salt Lake City or anywhere else directly north of Cedar City, because he was confident that their flight in that direction had been a ruse. They had altered course immediately after dropping under the radar floor. He doubted that they would go west, back into Nevada, because that state's empty vastness provided too little cover. Which left south and east. After the two enchiladas of information from Gary Duvall, Roy had reviewed everything he knew about Spencer Grant and had decided that he could accurately predict in which direction the man—and, with luck, the woman—would proceed. East-northeast. Moreover, he had divined *exactly* where Grant would impact at the end of that east-northeast trajectory, even more confidently than he could have plotted the line of a bullet from the barrel of a rifle. Roy was calm not solely because he trusted in his well-exercised powers of deductive reasoning but also because, in this special instance, destiny walked with him as surely as blood flowed in his veins.

"Can I assume that the team I asked for earlier today is on its way to Vail?" he asked.

"Twelve men," said Fordyce.

Glancing at his watch, Rink said, "They should be meeting Duvall there just about now."

For sixteen years, Michael Ackblom—aka "Spencer Grant"—had been denying the deep desire to return to that place, repressing the need, resisting the powerful magnet of the past. Nevertheless, either consciously or unconsciously, he had always known that he must pay a visit to those old haunts sooner or later. Otherwise, he would have sold the property to be rid of that tangible reminder of a time he wanted to forget, just as he had sloughed off his old name for a new one. He retained ownership for the same reason that he'd never sought surgery to have his facial scar minimized. *He's punishing himself with the scar,* Dr. Nero Mondello had said, in his white-on-white office in Beverly Hills. *Reminding himself of something he would like to forget but feels obligated to remember.* As long as Grant had lived in California and had followed a pressure-free daily routine, perhaps he could have indefinitely resisted the call of that killing ground in Colorado. But now he was running for his life and under tremendous pressure, and he had come near enough to his old home to ensure that the siren song of the past would be irresistible. Roy was betting everything that the son of the serial killer would return to the marrow of the nightmare, from which all the blood had sprung.

Spencer Grant had unfinished business at the ranch outside Vail. And only two people in the world knew what it was.

Beyond the heavily tinted windows of the speeding limousine, in the rapidly dwindling winter afternoon, the modern city of Denver appeared to be smoky and as vaguely defined at the edges as piles of ancient ruins entwined with ivy and shrouded with moss.

West of Grand Junction, inside the Colorado National Monument, the JetRanger landed in an eroded basin between one parenthesis of red rock formations and another of low hills mantled with junipers and pinyon pines. A skin of dry snow, less than half an inch thick, was flayed into crystalline clouds by the downdraft.

A hundred feet away, a green-black screen of trees served as backdrop to the bright silhouette of a white Ford Bronco. A man in a green ski suit stood at the open tailgate, watching the helicopter.

Spencer stayed with the crew while Ellie went outside to have a word with the man at the truck. With the JetRanger engine off and the rotor blades dead, the rock- and tree-rimmed basin was as silent as a deserted cathedral. She could hear nothing but the squeak and crunch of her own footsteps on the snow-filmed, frozen earth.

As she drew close to the Bronco, she saw a tripod with a camera on it. Related gear was spread across the lowered tailgate.

The photographer, bearded and furious, was spouting steam from his nostrils as if about to explode. "You ruined my shot. That pristine swath of snow curving up to that thrusting, fiery rock. Such contrast, such drama. And now *ruined.*"

She glanced back at the rock formations beyond the helicopter. They were still fiery, a luminous stained-glass red in the beams of the westering sun, and they were still thrusting. But he was right about the snow: It wasn't pristine any longer.

"Sorry."

"Sorry doesn't cut it," he said sharply.

She studied the snow in the vicinity of the Bronco. As far as she could tell, his were the only footprints in it. He was alone.

"What the hell are you doing out here anyway?" the photographer demanded. "There are sound restrictions here, nothing as noisy as that allowed. This is a wildlife preserve."

"Then cooperate and preserve your own," she said, drawing the SIG 9mm from under her leather jacket.

In the JetRanger again, while Ellie held the pistol and the Micro Uzi, Spencer cut strips out of the upholstery. He used those lengths of leather to bind the wrists of each of the three men to the arms of the passenger seats in which he'd made them sit.

"I won't gag you," he told them. "Nobody's likely to hear you shouting anyway."

"We'll freeze to death," the pilot fretted.

"You'll work your arms loose in half an hour at most. Another half an hour or forty-five minutes to walk out to the highway we crossed over when we flew in. Not nearly enough time to freeze."

"Just to be safe," Ellie assured them, "as soon as we get to a town, we'll call the police and tell them where you are."

Twilight had arrived. Stars were beginning to appear in the deep purple of the eastern sky as it curved down to the horizon.

While Spencer drove the Bronco, Rocky panted in Ellie's ear from the cargo area behind her seat. They found the way overland toward the highway with no difficulty. The route was clearly marked by the tire tracks in the snow that the truck had made on its trip into the picturesque basin.

"Why'd you tell them we'd call the police?" Spencer wondered.

"You want them to freeze?"

"I don't think there's much chance of that."

"I won't risk it."

"Yeah, but these days, it's possible—maybe not likely, but possible—that any call you make to a police department is going to be received on a caller-ID line, not just if you punch nine-one-one. Fact is, a smaller city like Grand Junction, with not so much street crime or so many demands on resources, is a lot more likely to have money to spend on fancy communications systems with all the bells and whistles. You call them, then they know right away the address you're phoning from. It comes up on the screen in front of the police operator. And then they'll know what direction we went, what road we left Grand Junction on."

"I know. But we're not going to make it that simple for them," she said, and explained what she had in mind.

"I like it," he said.

The Rocky Mountain Prison for the Criminally Insane had been constructed in the Great Depression, under the auspices of the Work Projects Administration, and it looked as solid and formidable as the Rockies themselves. It was a squat, rambling building with small, deep-set, barred windows even in the administration wing. The walls were faced with iron-gray granite. An even darker granite had been used for lintels, window stools, door and window surrounds, coins, and carved cornices. The whole pile slumped under a gabled attic and a black slate roof.

The general effect, Roy Miro felt, was as depressing as it was ominous. Without hyperbole, the structure could be said to brood high upon its hillside, as if it were a living creature. In the late-afternoon shadows of the steep slopes that rose behind the prison, its windows were filled with a sour-yellow light that might have been reflected through connecting corridors from the dungeons of some mountain demon who lived deeper in the Rockies.

Approaching the prison in the limousine, standing before it, and walking its public corridors to Dr. Palma's office, Roy was overcome with compassion for the poor souls locked away in that heap of stone. He grieved as well for the equally suffering warders who, in looking after the deranged, were forced to spend so much of their lives in such circumstances. If it had been within his authority to do so, he would have sealed up every last window and vent, with all the inmates and attendants inside, and put them out of their misery with a gentle-acting but lethal gas.

Dr. Sabrina Palma's reception lounge and office were so warmly and luxuriously furnished that, by contrast with the building that surrounded them, they seemed to belong not only in another and more exalted place—a New York penthouse, a Palm Beach bay-side mansion—but in another age than the 1930s, a time warp in which the rest of the prison seemed still to exist. Sofas and chairs were recognizably by J. Robert Scott, uphol-stered in platinum and gold silks. Tables and mirror frames and side chairs were also by J. Robert Scott, done in a variety of exotic woods with bold grains, all either bleached or whitewashed. The deeply sculpted, beige-on-beige carpet might have been from Edward Fields. At the center of the inner office was a massive Monteverde & Young desk, in a crescent-moon shape, that must have cost forty thousand dollars.

Roy had never seen an office of any public official to equal those two rooms, not even in the highest circles of official Washington. He knew at once what to make of it, and he knew that he had a sword to hold over Dr. Palma if she gave him any resistance.

Sabrina Palma was the director of the prison medical staff. By virtue of its being as much hospital as prison, she was also the equivalent of a warden in any ordinary correc-tional facility. And she was as striking as her office. Raven-black hair. Green eyes. Skin as pale and smooth as pooled milk. Early forties, tall, svelte but shapely. She wore a black knit suit with a white silk blouse.

After identifying himself, Roy introduced her to Agent Olmeyer—

"Pleased to meet you, Doctor."

—and Agent Tarkenton.

"Doctor."

She invited them all to sit down.

"No, thank you, Doctor," said Olmeyer, and took up a position to the right of the door that connected the inner and outer offices.

"No, thank you, Doctor," said Tarkenton, and took up a position to the left of the same door.

Roy proceeded to one of three exquisite chairs in front of Dr. Palma's desk as she cir-cled to the plush leather throne behind it. She sat in a cascade of indirect, amber light that made her pale skin glow as if with inner fire.

"I'm here on a matter of the utmost importance," Roy told her in as gracious a tone as he could command. "We believe—no, we are certain—that the son of one of your inmates is currently stalking the President of the United States and intends to assassinate him."

When she heard the name of the would-be assassin and knew the identity of his father, Sabrina Palma raised her eyebrows. After she examined the documents that Roy withdrew from the white envelope and after she learned what he expected of her, she excused herself and went to the outer office to make several urgent telephone calls.

Roy waited in his chair.

Beyond the three narrow windows, spread out across the night below the prison, the lights of Denver gleamed and glittered.

He looked at his watch. By now, on the far side of the Rockies, Duvall and his twelve men ought to have settled inconspicuously into the creeping night. They wanted to be ready, in case the travelers arrived far earlier than anticipated.

The hood of night had fully covered the face of twilight by the time they reached the out-skirts of Grand Junction.

With a population of over thirty-five thousand, the city was big enough to delay them. But Ellie had a penlight and the map that she had taken from the helicopter, and she found the simplest route.

Two-thirds of the way around the city, at a multiplex cinema, they stopped to go shop-ping for a new vehicle. Apparently, none of the shows was either letting out or about to begin, for no moviegoers were arriving or leaving. The sprawling parking lot was full of cars but devoid of people.

"Get an Explorer or a Jeep if you can," she said as he opened the door of the Bronco, letting in a frigid draft. "Something like that. It's more convenient."

"Thieves can't be choosers," he said.

"They have to be." As he got out, she shifted over behind the steering wheel. "Hey, if you're not choosy, then you're not a thief, you're a trash collector."

While Ellie drifted along one aisle, pacing him, Spencer moved boldly from vehicle to vehicle, trying the doors. Each time that he found one unlocked, he leaned inside long enough to check for keys in the ignition, behind the sun visor, and under the driver's seat.

Watching his master through the side windows of the Bronco, Rocky whined as though with concern.

"Dangerous, yes," Ellie said. "I can't lie to the dog. But not half as dangerous as driving through the front of a supermarket with helicopters full of thugs on your tail. You've just got to keep this in perspective."

The fourteenth set of wheels that Spencer tried was a big black Chevy pickup with an extended cab that provided both front and back seats. He climbed into it, pulled the door shut, started the engine, and reversed out of the parking slot.

Ellie parked the Bronco in the space that the Chevy had vacated. They needed only fifteen seconds to transfer the guns, the duffel bag, and the dog to the pickup. Then they were on their way again.

On the east side of the city, they started looking for any motel that appeared to have been recently constructed. The rooms in most older establishments were not computer friendly.

At a self-described "motor lodge" that looked new enough to have held its ribbon-cutting ceremony just hours ago, Ellie left Spencer and Rocky in the pickup while she went into the front office to ask the desk clerk if their accommodations would allow her to use her modem. "I have a report due at my office in Cleveland by morning." In fact, all rooms were properly wired for her needs. Using her Bess Baer ID for the first time, she took a double with a queen-size bed and paid cash in advance.

"How soon can we be on the road again?" Spencer asked as they parked in front of their unit.

"Forty-five minutes tops, probably half an hour," she promised.

"We're miles from where we took the pickup, but I have a bad feeling about hanging around here too long."

"You aren't the only one."

She couldn't help but notice the decor of the room even as she took Spencer's laptop computer out of the duffel bag, put it on the desk next to an arrangement of accessible plugs and phone jacks, and concentrated on getting it ready for business. Blue-and-black-speckled carpet. Blue-and-yellow-striped draperies. Green-and-blue-checkered bedspread. Blue and gold and silver wallpaper in a pale ameboid pattern. It looked like army camouflage for an alien planet.

"While you're working on that," Spencer said, "I'll take Rocky out to do his business. He must be ready to burst."

"Doesn't seem in distress."

"He'd be too embarrassed to let on." At the door, he turned to her again and said, "I saw fast-food places across the street. I'll walk over there and get us some burgers and stuff too, if that sounds like it would hit the spot."

"Just buy plenty," she said.

While Spencer and the pooch were gone, Ellie accessed the AT&T central computer, which she had penetrated a long time ago and had explored in depth. Through AT&T's nationwide linkages, she had been able, in the past, to finesse her way into the computers of several regional phone companies at all ends of the country, although she'd never before tried to slide into the Colorado system. For a hacker as for a concert pianist or an

Olympic gymnast, however, training and practice were the keys to success, and she was extremely well trained and well practiced.

When Spencer and Rocky returned after only twenty-five minutes, Ellie was already deep inside the regional system, scrolling rapidly down a dauntingly long list of pay-phone numbers with corresponding addresses that were arranged county by county. She settled on a phone at a service station in Montrose, Colorado, sixty-six miles south of Grand Junction.

Manipulating the main switching system in the regional phone company, she rang the Grand Junction Police while routing the call from their motel room through the service-station pay phone down in Montrose. She called the emergency number, rather than the main police number, just to be sure that the source address would appear onscreen in front of the operator.

"Grand Junction Police."

Ellie began without any preamble: "We hijacked a Bell JetRanger helicopter in Cedar City, Utah, earlier today—" When the police operator attempted to interrupt with questions that would encourage a standard-format report, Ellie shouted the woman down: "Shut up, shut up! I'm only going to say this once, so you better listen, or people will die!" She grinned at Spencer, who was opening bags of wonderfully fragrant food on the dinette table. "The chopper is now on the ground in the Colorado National Monument, with the crew aboard. They're unhurt but tied up. If they have to spend the night out there, they'll freeze to death. I'll describe the landing site just once, and you better get the details right if you want to save their lives."

She gave succinct directions and disconnected.

Two things had been achieved. The three men in the JetRanger would be found soon. And the Grand Junction Police Department had an address in Montrose, sixty-six miles to the south, from which the emergency call had been made, indicating that Ellie and Spencer were either about to flee east on Federal Highway 50, toward Pueblo, or continue south on Federal Highway 550 toward Durango. Several state routes branched off those main arteries as well, providing enough possibilities to keep agency search teams fully occupied. Meanwhile, she and Spencer and Mr. Rocky Dog would be headed to Denver on Interstate 70.

Dr. Sabrina Palma was being difficult, which was no surprise to Roy. Before arriving at the prison, he had expected objections to his plans, based on medical, security, and political grounds. The moment he had seen her office, he had known that vital financial considerations would weigh more heavily against him than all the genuinely ethical arguments that she might have pursued.

"I can't conceive of any circumstances, related to the threat against the President, that would require Steven Ackblom's removal from this facility," she said crisply. Though she had returned to the formidable leather chair, she no longer relaxed in it but sat forward on the edge, arms on her crescent desk. Her manicured hands were alternately fisted on her blotter or busy with various pieces of Lalique crystal—small animals, colorful fishes—that were arranged to one side of her blotter. "He's an extremely dangerous individual, an arrogant and utterly selfish man who would never cooperate with you even if there *was* something he could do to help you find his son—though I can't imagine what that would be."

As pleasant as he ever was, Roy said, "Dr. Palma, with all due respect, it isn't for you to imagine or be told how he could help us or how we expect to win his cooperation. This is an urgent matter of national security. I am not permitted to share any details with you, regardless of how much I might want to."

"This man is evil, Mr. Cotter."

"Yes, I'm aware of his history."

"You aren't understanding me—"

Roy gently interrupted, pointing to one of the documents on her desk. "You have read the judicial order, signed by a justice of the Colorado Supreme Court, conveying Steven Ackblom into my temporary custody."

"Yes, but—"

"I assume that when you left the room to make telephone calls, one of them was to confirm that signature?"

"Yes, and it's legitimate. He was still in his office, and he confirmed it personally."

In fact, it was a real signature. That particular justice lived in the agency's pocket.

Sabrina Palma was not satisfied. "But what does your judge know about evil like this? What experience does he have with this particular man?"

Pointing to another document on the desk, Roy said, "And may I assume that you've confirmed the genuineness of the letter from my boss, the secretary of the Treasury? You called Washington?"

"I didn't speak with him, no, of course not."

"He's a busy man. But there must have been an assistant. . . ."

"Yes," the doctor admitted grudgingly. "I spoke with one of his assistants, who verified the request."

The signature of the secretary of the Treasury had been forged. The assistant, one of a swarm of minions, was an agency sympathizer. He was no doubt still standing by in the secretary's office, after hours, to field another call on the private number that Roy had given to Sabrina Palma, just in case she called again.

Pointing to a third document on her desk, Roy said, "And this request from the first deputy attorney general?"

"Yes, I called him."

"I understand you've actually met Mr. Summerton."

"Yes, at a conference on the insanity plea and its effect on the health of the judicial system. About six months ago."

"I trust Mr. Summerton was persuasive."

"Quite. Look, Mr. Cotter, I have a call in to the governor's office, and if we can just wait until—"

"I'm afraid we've no time to wait. As I've told you, the life of the President of the United States is at stake."

"This is a prisoner of exceptional—"

"Dr. Palma," Roy said. His voice now had a steely edge, though he continued to smile. "You do not have to worry about losing your golden goose. I swear to you that he will be back in your care within twenty-four hours."

Her green eyes fixed him with an angry stare, but she did not respond.

"I hadn't heard that Steven Ackblom has continued to paint since his incarceration," Roy said.

Dr. Palma's gaze flicked to the two men at the door, who were in convincingly rigid Secret Service postures, then returned to Roy. "He produces a little work, yes. Not much. Two or three pieces a year."

"Worth millions at the current rate."

"There is nothing unethical going on here, Mr. Cotter."

"I didn't imagine there was," Roy said innocently.

"Of his own free will, without coercion of any sort, Mr. Ackblom assigns all rights to each of his new paintings to this institution—after he tires of it hanging in his cell. The proceeds from their sale are used entirely to supplement the funds that are budgeted to us by the State of Colorado. And these days, in this economy, the state generally underfunds prison operations of all kinds, as if the institutionalized don't deserve adequate care."

Roy slid one hand lightly, appreciatively, *lovingly* along the glass-smooth, radius edge of the forty-thousand-dollar desk. "Yes, I'm sure that without the lagniappe of Ackblom's art, things here would be grim indeed."

She was silent again.

"Tell me, Doctor, in addition to the two or three major pieces that Ackblom produces each year, as he just sort of dabbles in his art to pass his entombed days, are there perhaps sketches, pencil studies, scraps of scrawlings that aren't worth the bother for him to assign to this institution? You know what I mean: insignificant doodlings, preliminaries, worth hardly ten or twenty thousand each, which one might take home to hang on one's bathroom walls? Or even simply incinerate along with the rest of the garbage?"

Her hatred for him was so intense that he would not have been surprised if the blush that rose in her face had been hot enough to make her cotton-white skin explode into flames, as if it were not skin at all but magicians' flashpaper.

"I adore your watch," he said, indicating the Piaget on her slender wrist. The rim of the face was enhanced by alternating diamonds and emeralds.

The fourth document on the desk was a transferral order that acknowledged Roy's legal authority—by direction of the Colorado Supreme Court—to receive Ackblom into his temporary custody. Roy had already signed it in the limousine. Now Dr. Palma signed it too.

Delighted, Roy said, "Is Ackblom on any medications, any antipsychotics, that we should continue to give him?"

She met his eyes again, and her anger was watered down with concern. "No antipsychotics. He doesn't need them. He isn't psychotic by any current psychological definition of the term. Mr. Cotter, I'm trying my best to make you understand this man exhibits none of the classic signs of psychosis. He is that most imprecisely defined creature—a sociopath, yes. But a sociopath by his actions only, by what we know him to have done, not by anything that he says or can be shown to believe. Administer any psychological test you want, and he comes through with flying colors, a perfectly normal guy, well adjusted, balanced, not even markedly neurotic—"

"I understand he's been a model prisoner these sixteen years."

"That means nothing. That's what I'm trying to tell you. Look, I'm a medical doctor and a psychiatrist. But over the years, from observation and experience, I've lost all faith in psychiatry. Freud and Jung—they were both full of shit." That crude word had shocking power, coming from a woman as elegant as she. "Their theories of how the human mind works are worthless, exercises in self-justification, philosophies devised only to excuse their own desires. No one knows how the mind works. Even when we can administer a drug and correct a mental condition, we only know *that* the drug is effective, not *why*. And in Ackblom's case, his behavior isn't based in a physiological problem any more than it is in a psychological problem."

"You have no compassion for him?"

She leaned across her desk, focusing intently on him. "I tell you, Mr. Cotter, there *is* evil in the world. Evil that exists without cause, without rationalization. Evil that doesn't arise from trauma or abuse or deprivation. Steven Ackblom is, in my judgment, a prime example of evil. He is sane, utterly sane. He clearly knows the difference between right and wrong. He chose to do monstrous things, knowing they were monstrous, and even though he felt no psychological compulsion to do them."

"You have no compassion for your patient?" Roy asked again.

"He isn't my patient, Mr. Cotter. He's my prisoner."

"However you choose to look at him, doesn't he deserve some compassion—a man who's fallen from such heights?"

"He deserves to be shot in the head and buried in an unmarked grave," she said bluntly. She was not attractive anymore. She looked like a witch, raven-haired and pale, with eyes as green as those of certain cats. "But because Mr. Ackblom entered a guilty plea, and because it was easiest to commit him to this facility, the state supported the fiction that he was a sick man."

Of all the people Roy had met in his busy life, he had disliked few and had hated fewer still. For nearly everyone that he had ever met, he had found compassion in his heart, regardless of their shortcomings or personalities. But he flatly despised Dr. Sabrina Palma.

When he found time in his busy schedule, he would give her a comeuppance that would make what he'd done to Harris Descoteaux seem merciful.

"Even if you can't find some compassion for the Steven Ackblom who killed those people," Roy said, rising from his chair, "I would think you could find some for the Steven Ackblom who has been so generous to you."

"He is evil." She was unrelenting. "He deserves no compassion. Just use him however you must, then return him."

"Well, maybe you *do* know a thing or two about evil, Doctor."

"The advantage I've taken of the arrangement here," she said coolly, "is a sin, Mr. Cotter. I know that. And one way or another, I'll pay for the sin. But there's a difference between a sinful act, which springs from weakness, and one that's pure evil. I am able to recognize that difference."

"How handy for you," he said, and began to gather up the papers from her desk.

They sat on the motel bed, chowing down on Burger King burgers, french fries, and chocolate-chip cookies. Rocky ate off a torn paper bag on the floor.

That morning in the desert, now hardly twelve hours behind them, seemed to be an eternity in the past. Ellie and Spencer had learned so much about each other that they could eat in silence, enjoying the food, without feeling the least awkward together.

He surprised her, however, when, toward the end of their hurried meal, he expressed the desire to stop at the ranch outside Vail, on their way to Denver. And "surprised" was not the word for it when he told her that he still owned the place.

"Maybe I've always known that I'd have to go back eventually," he said, unable to look at her.

He put the last of his dinner aside, appetite lost. Sitting lotus-fashion on the bed, he folded his hands on his right knee and stared at them as if they were more mysterious than artifacts from lost Atlantis.

"In the beginning," he continued, "my grandparents held on to the place because they didn't want anyone to buy it and maybe make some god-awful tourist attraction out of it. Or let the news media into those underground rooms for more morbid stories. The bodies had been removed, everything cleaned out, but it was still the *place*, could still attract media interest. After I went into therapy, which I stayed with for about a year, the therapist felt we should keep the property until I was ready to go back."

"Why?" Ellie wondered. "Why ever go back?"

He hesitated. Then: "Because part of that night is a blank to me. I've never been able to remember what happened toward the end, after I shot him. . . ."

"What do you mean? You shot him, and you ran for help, and that was the end of it."

"No."

"What?"

He shook his head. Still staring at his hands. Very still hands. Like hands of carved marble, resting on his knee.

Finally he said, "That's what I've got to find out. I've got to go back there, back down there, and find out. Because if I don't, I'm never going to be . . . right with myself . . . or any good for you."

"You can't go back there, not with the agency after you."

"They wouldn't look for us there. They can't have found out who I was. Who I really am. Michael. They can't know that."

"They might," she said.

She went to the duffel bag and got the envelope of photographs that she had found on the deck of the JetRanger, half under her seat. She presented them to him.

"They found these in a shoe box in my cabin," he said. "They probably just took them for reference. You wouldn't recognize . . . my father. No one would. Not from this shot."

"You can't be sure."

"Anyway, I don't own the property under any identity they would associate with me, even if somehow they got into sealed court records and found out I'd changed my name from Ackblom. I hold it through an offshore corporation."

"The agency is damned resourceful, Spencer."

Looking up from his hands, he met her eyes. "All right, I'm willing to believe they're resourceful enough to uncover all of it—given enough time. But surely not this quickly. That just means I've got more reason than ever to go there tonight. When am I going to have a chance again, after we go to Denver and to wherever we'll go after that? By the time I can return to Vail again, maybe they *will* have discovered I still own the ranch. Then I'll never be able to go back and finish this. We pass right by Vail on the way to Denver. It's off Interstate Seventy."

"I know," she said shakily, remembering that moment in the helicopter, somewhere over Utah, when she had sensed that he might not live through the night to share the morning with her.

He said, "If you don't want to go there with me, we can work that out too. But . . . even if I could be sure the agency would never learn about the place, I'd have to go back tonight. Ellie, if I don't go back now, when I have the guts to face it, I might never work up the courage later. It's taken sixteen years this time."

She sat for a while, staring at her own hands. Then she got up and went to the laptop, which was still plugged in and connected to the modem. She switched it on.

He followed her to the desk. "What're you doing?"

"What's the address of the ranch?" she asked.

It was a rural address, rather than a street number. He gave it to her, then again after she asked him to repeat it. "But why? What's this about?"

"What's the name of the offshore company?"

"Vanishment International."

"You're kidding."

"No."

"And that's the name on the deed now—Vanishment International? That's how it would show on the tax records?"

"Yeah." Spencer pulled up another chair beside hers and sat on it as Rocky came sniffing around to see if they had more food. "Ellie, will you open up?"

"I'm going to try to crack into public land records out there," she said. "I need to call up a parcel map if I can get one. I've got to figure out the exact geographic coordinates of the place."

"Is all that supposed to mean something?"

"By God, if we're going in there, if we're taking a risk like that, then we're going to be as heavily armed as possible." She was talking to herself more than to him. "We're going to be ready to defend ourselves against anything."

"What're you talking about?"

"Too complicated. Later. Now I need some silence."

Her quick hands worked magic on the keyboard. Spencer watched the screen as Ellie moved from Grand Junction to the courthouse computer in Vail. Then she peeled the county's data-system onion one layer at a time.

• • •

Wearing a slightly large suit of clothes provided by the agency and a top-coat identical to those of his three companions, in shackles and handcuffs, the famous and infamous Steven Ackblom sat beside Roy in the back of the limousine.

The artist was fifty-three but appeared to be only a few years older than when he had been on the front pages of newspapers, where the sensation mongers had variously dubbed him the Vampire of Vail, the Madman of the Mountains, and the Psycho Michelangelo. Although a trace of gray had appeared at his temples, his hair was otherwise black and glossy and not in the least receding. His handsome face was remarkably smooth and youthful, and his brow was unmarked. A soft smile line curved downward from the outer flare of each nostril, and fans of fine crinkles spread at the outer corners of his eyes: None of that aged him whatsoever; in fact, it gave the impression that he suffered few troubles but enjoyed many sources of amusement.

As in the photograph that Roy had found in the Malibu cabin and as in all the pictures that had appeared in newspapers and magazines sixteen years ago, Steven Ackblom's eyes were his most commanding feature. Nevertheless, the arrogance that Roy had perceived even in the shadowy publicity still was not there now, if it ever had been; in its place was a quiet self-confidence. Likewise, the menace that could be read into any photograph, when one knew the accomplishments of the man, was not in the least visible in person. His gaze was direct and clear, but not threatening. Roy had been surprised and not displeased to discover an uncommon gentleness in Ackblom's eyes, and a poignant empathy as well, from which it was easy to infer that he was a person of considerable wisdom, whose understanding of the human condition was deep, complete.

Even in the limousine's odd and inadequate illumination, which came from the recessed lights under the heel-kicks of the car seats and from the low-wattage sconces in the doorposts, Ackblom was a presence to be reckoned with—although in no way that the press, in its sensation seeking, had begun to touch upon. He was quiet, but his taciturnity had no quality of inarticulateness or distraction. Quite the opposite: His silences spoke more than other men's most polished flights of oratory, and he was always and unmistakably observant and alert. He moved little, never fidgeted. Occasionally, when he accompanied a comment with a gesture, the movement of his cuffed hands was so economical that the chain between his wrists clinked softly if at all. His stillness was not rigid but relaxed, not limp but full of quiescent power. It was impossible to sit at his side and be unaware that he possessed tremendous intelligence: He all but hummed with it, as if his mind was a dynamic machine of such omnipotence that it could move worlds and alter the cosmos.

In his entire thirty-three years, Roy Miro had met only two people whose mere physical presence had engendered in him an approximation of love. The first had been Eve Marie Jammer. The second was Steven Ackblom. Both in the same week. In this wondrous February, destiny had become, indeed, his cloak and his companion. He sat at Steven Ackblom's side, discreetly enthralled. He wanted desperately to make the artist aware that he, Roy Miro, was a person of profound insights and exceptional accomplishments.

Rink and Fordyce (Tarkenton and Olmeyer had ceased to exist upon leaving Dr. Palma's office) seemed not to be as charmed by Ackblom as Roy was—or charmed at all. Sitting in the rear-facing seats, they appeared uninterested in what the artist had to say. Fordyce closed his eyes for long periods of time, as though meditating. Rink stared out the window, although he could have seen nothing whatsoever of the night through the darkly tinted glass. On those rare occasions when a gesture of Ackblom's rang a soft clink from his cuffs, and on those even rarer occasions when he shifted his feet enough to rattle the shackles that connected his ankles, Fordyce's eyes popped open like the counterbalanced eyes of a doll, and Rink's head snapped from the unseen night to the artist. Otherwise they seemed to pay no attention to him.

Depressingly, Rink and Fordyce clearly had formed their opinions of Ackblom based on what drivel they had gleaned from the media, not from what they could observe for themselves. Their denseness was no surprise, of course. Rink and Fordyce were men not of ideas but of action, not of passion but of crude desire. The agency had need of their type, although they were sadly without vision, pitiable creatures of woeful limitations who would one day inch the world closer to perfection by departing it.

"At the time, I was quite young, only two years older than your son," Roy said, "but I understood what you were trying to achieve."

"And what was that?" Ackblom asked. His voice was in the lower tenor range, mellow, with a timbre that suggested he might have had a career as a singer if he'd wished.

Roy explained his theories about the artist's work: that those eerie and compelling portraits weren't about people's hateful desires building like boiler pressure beneath their beautiful surfaces, but were meant to be viewed *with* the still lifes and, together, were a statement about the human desire—and struggle—for perfection. "And if your work with living subjects resulted in their attainment of a perfect beauty, even for a brief time before they died, then your crimes weren't crimes at all but acts of charity, acts of profound compassion, because too few people in this world will ever know any moment of perfection in their entire lives. Through torture, you gave those forty-one—your wife as well, I assume— a transcendent experience. Had they lived, they might eventually have thanked you."

Roy was speaking sincerely, although previously he had believed that Ackblom had been misguided in the means by which he had pursued the grail of perfection. That was before he had met the man. Now, he felt ashamed of his woeful underestimation of the artist's talent and keen perception.

In the rear-facing seats, neither Rink nor Fordyce evinced any surprise or interest in anything that Roy said. In their service with the agency, they had heard so many outrageous lies, all so well and sincerely delivered, that they undoubtedly believed their boss was only playing with Ackblom, cleverly manipulating a madman into the degree of cooperation required from him to ensure the success of the current operation. Roy was in the singular and thrilling position of being able to express his deepest feelings, with the knowledge that Ackblom would fully comprehend him even while Rink and Fordyce would think he was engaged only in Machiavellian games.

Roy did not go so far as to reveal his personal commitment to compassionate treatment of the sadder cases that he met in his many travels. Stories like those about the Bettonfields in Beverly Hills, Chester and Guinevere in Burbank, and the paraplegic and his wife outside the restaurant in Vegas might strike even Rink and Fordyce as too specific in detail to be impromptu fabrications invented to win the artist's confidence.

"The world would be an infinitely better place," Roy opined, restricting his observations to safely general concepts, "if the breeding stock of humanity was thinned out. Eliminate the most imperfect specimens first. Always working up from the bottom. Until those permitted to survive are the people who most closely meet the standards for the ideal citizens needed to build a gentler and more enlightened society. Don't you agree?"

"The process would certainly be fascinating," Ackblom replied.

Roy took the comment to be approving. "Yes, wouldn't it?"

"Always supposing that one was on the committee of eliminators," the artist said, "and not among those to be judged."

"Well, of course, that's a given."

Ackblom favored him with a smile. "Then what fun."

They were driving over the mountains on Interstate 70, rather than flying to Vail. The trip would require less than two hours by car. Returning across Denver from the prison to Stapleton, waiting for flight clearance, and making the journey by air would actually have taken longer. Besides, the limousine was more intimate and quieter than the jet. Roy was able to spend more quality time with the artist than he would have been able to enjoy in the Lear.

Gradually, mile by mile, Roy Miro came to understand why Steven Ackblom affected him as powerfully as Eve had affected him. Although the artist was a handsome man, nothing about his physical appearance could qualify as a perfect feature. Yet in some way, he *was* perfect. Roy sensed it. A radiance. A subtle harmony. Soothing vibrations. In some aspect of his being, Ackblom was without the slightest flaw. For the time being, the artist's perfect quality or virtue remained tantalizingly mysterious, but Roy was confident of discovering it by the time they arrived at the ranch outside Vail.

The limousine cruised into ever higher mountains, through vast primeval forests encrusted with snow, upward into silvery moonlight—all of which the tinted windows reduced to a smoky blur. The tires hummed.

While Spencer drove the stolen black pickup east on Interstate 70 out of Grand Junction, Ellie slumped in her seat and worked feverishly on the laptop, which she had plugged into the cigarette lighter. The computer was elevated on a pillow that they had filched from the motel. Periodically she consulted a printout of the parcel map and other information that she had obtained about the ranch.

"What're you doing?" he asked again.

"Calculations."

"What calculations?"

"Ssshhhhh. Rocky's sleeping on the backseat."

From her duffel bag, she had produced diskettes of software which she'd installed in the machine. Evidently they were programs of her own design, adapted to his laptop while he had lingered in delirium for more than two days in the Mojave. When he had asked her why she had backed up her own computer—now gone with the Rover—with his quite different system, she had said, "Former Girl Scout. Remember? We always like to be prepared."

He had no idea what her software allowed her to do. Across the screen flickered formulas and graphs. Holographic globes of the earth revolved at her command, and from them she extracted areas for enlargement and closer examination.

Vail was only three hours away. Spencer wished that they could use the time to talk, to discover more about each other. Three hours was such a short time—especially if it proved to be the last three hours they ever had together.

FOURTEEN

When he returned to his brother's house from his walk through the hilly streets of Westwood, Harris Descoteaux did not mention the encounter with the tall man in the blue Toyota. For one thing, it seemed half like a dream. Improbable. Besides, he hadn't been able to make up his mind whether that stranger had been a friend or an enemy. He didn't want to alarm Darius or Jessica.

Late that afternoon, after Ondine and Willa returned from the mall with their aunt and after Darius and Bonnie's son, Martin, came home from school, Darius decided that they needed to have a little fun. He insisted on packing everyone—the seven of them—into the VW Microbus, which he had so lovingly restored with his own hands, to go to a movie and then to dinner at Hamlet Gardens.

Neither Harris nor Jessica wanted to go to movies and dinners in restaurants when every dollar spent was a dollar that they were mooching. Not even Ondine and Willa, as resilient as any teenagers, had yet bounced back from the trauma of the SWAT attack on Friday or from having been put out of their own home by federal marshals.

Darius was adamant that a movie and dinner at Hamlet Gardens were precisely the right medicines for what ailed them. And his persistence was one of the qualities that made him an exceptional attorney.

That was how, at six-fifteen Monday evening, Harris came to be in a theater with a boisterous crowd, unable to grasp the humor in scenes that everyone else found hilarious, and succumbing to another attack of claustrophobia. The darkness. So many people in one room. The body heat of the crowd. He was afflicted, first, by an inability to draw a deep breath and then by a mild dizziness. He feared that worse would swiftly follow. He whispered to Jessica that he had to use the bathroom. When worry crossed her face, he patted her arm and smiled reassuringly, and then he got the hell out of there.

The men's room was deserted. At one of the four sinks, Harris turned on the cold water. He bent over the bowl and splashed his face repeatedly, trying to cool down from the overheated theater and chase away the dizziness.

The noise of the running water prevented him from hearing the other man enter. When he looked up, he was no longer alone.

About thirty, Asian, wearing loafers and jeans and a dark-blue sweater with prancing red reindeer, the stranger stood two sinks away. He was combing his hair. He met Harris's eyes in the mirror, and he smiled. "Sir, may I give you something to think about?"

Harris recognized the question as the very one with which the tall man in the blue Toyota had initially addressed him. Startled, he backed away from the sink so fast that he crashed against the swinging door at one of the toilet stalls. He tottered, almost fell, but caught the hingeless side of the jamb to keep his balance.

"For a while the Japanese economy was so hot that it gave the world the idea that maybe big government and big business must work hand in glove."

"Who are you?" Harris asked, quicker off the mark with this man than he had been with the first.

Ignoring the question, the smiling stranger said, "So now we hear about national industrial policies. Big business and government strike deals every day. Push my social programs and enhance my power, says the politician, and I'll guarantee your profit."

"What does any of this matter to me?"

"Be patient, Mr. Descoteaux."

"But—"

"Union members get screwed because government conspires with their bosses. Small businessmen get screwed, everyone too little to play in the hundred-billion-dollar league. Now the secretary of defense wants to use the military as an arm of economic policy."

Harris returned to the sink, where he had left the cold water running. He turned it off.

"A business-government alliance, enforced by the military and domestic police—once, this was called fascism. Will we see fascism in our time, Mr. Descoteaux? Or is this something new, not to worry?"

Harris was trembling. He realized that his face and hands were dripping, and he yanked paper towels from the dispenser.

"And if it's something new, Mr. Descoteaux, is it going to be something good? Maybe. Maybe we'll go through a time of adjustment, and thereafter everything will be delightful." He nodded, smiling, as if considering that possibility. "Or maybe this new thing will turn out to be a new kind of hell."

"I don't care about any of this," Harris said angrily. "I'm not political."

"You don't need to be. To protect yourself, you need only to be informed."

"Look, whoever you are, I just want my house back. I want my life like it was. I want to go on just the way everything was."

"That will never transpire, Mr. Descoteaux."

"Why is this happening to me?"

"Have you read the novels of Philip K. Dick, Mr. Descoteaux?"

"Who? No."

Harris felt more than ever as if he had crossed into White Rabbit and Cheshire Cat territory.

The stranger shook his head with dismay. "The futuristic world Mr. Dick wrote about is the world we're sliding into. It's a scary place, this Dicksian world. More than ever, a person needs friends."

"Are you a friend?" Harris demanded. "Who are you people?"

"Be patient and consider what I've said."

The man started for the door.

Harris reached out to stop him but decided against it. A moment later he was alone.

His bowels were suddenly in turmoil. He hadn't lied to Jessica after all: He really did need to use the bathroom.

Approaching Vail, high in the western Rockies, Roy Miro used the phone in the limousine to call the number of the cellular unit that Gary Duvall had given him earlier.

"Clear?" he asked.

"No sign of them yet," Duvall said.

"We're almost there."

"You really think they're going to show?"

The stolen JetRanger and its crew had been found in the Colorado National Monument. A call from the woman to the Grand Junction police had been traced to Montrose, indicating that she and Spencer Grant were fleeing south toward Durango. Roy didn't believe it. He knew that telephone calls could be deceptively routed with the assistance of a computer. He trusted not in a traced call but in the power of the past; where the past and the present met, he would find the fugitives.

"They'll show," Roy said. "Cosmic forces are with us tonight."

"Cosmic forces?" Duvall said, as if playing into a joke, waiting for the punch line.

"They'll show," Roy repeated, and he disconnected.

Beside Roy, Steven Ackblom sat silent and serene.

"We'll be there in just a few minutes," Roy told him.

Ackblom smiled. "There's no place like home."

Spencer had been driving for nearly an hour and a half before Ellie switched off the computer and unplugged it from the cigarette lighter. A dew of perspiration beaded her forehead, although the interior of the truck was not overheated.

"God knows if I'm mounting a good defense or planning a double suicide," she said. "Could go either way. But now it's there for us to use if we have to."

"Use what?"

"I'm not going to tell you," she said bluntly. "It'll take too much time. Besides, you'd try to talk me out of it. Which would be a waste of time. I know the arguments against it, and I've already rejected them."

"And this makes an argument so much easier—when you handle both sides of it."

She remained somber. "If worse comes to worst, I'll have no choice but to use it, no matter how insane that seems."

Rocky had awakened in the backseat a short while ago, and to him, Spencer said, "Pal, you're not confused back there, are you?"

"Ask me anything else but not about *that*," Ellie said. "If I talk about it, if I even think too much about it, then I'll be too damn scared to do it when the time comes, *if* the time comes. I hope to God we don't need it."

Spencer had never heard her babble before. She usually kept tight control of herself. Now she was spooking him.

Panting, Rocky poked his head between the front seats. One ear up, one down: refreshed and interested.

"I didn't think you were confused," Spencer told him. "Me, I'm twice as befuddled as a lightning bug bashing itself to bits to get out of an old mayonnaise jar. But I suppose that higher forms of intelligence, like the canine species, would have no trouble figuring out what she's ranting about."

Ellie stared at the road ahead, rubbing absentmindedly at her chin with the knuckles of her right hand.

She had said that he could ask her about anything except *that*, whatever *that* might be, so he took her up on it. "Where was 'Bess Baer' going to settle down before I mucked things up? Where were you going to take that Rover and make a new life?"

"Wasn't going to settle again," she said, proving that she was listening. "I gave up on that. Sooner or later, they find me if I stay in one place too long. I spent a lot of the money I had . . . and some from friends . . . to buy that Rover and the gear in it. With that, I figured I could keep moving and go just about anywhere."

"I'll pay for the Rover."

"That's not what I was after."

"I know. But what's mine is yours anyway."

"Oh? When did that happen?"

"No strings attached," he said.

"I like to pay my own way."

"No point discussing it."

"What you say is final, huh?"

"No. What the dog says is final."

"This was Rocky's decision?"

"He takes care of all my finances."

Rocky grinned. He liked hearing his name.

"Because it's Rocky's idea," she said, "I'll keep an open mind."

Spencer said, "Why do you call Summerton a cockroach? Why does that annoy him particularly?"

"Tom's got a phobia about insects. All kinds of insects. Even a housefly can make him squirm. But he's especially uptight about cockroaches. When he sees one—and they used to have an infestation at the ATF when he was there—he goes off the deep end. It's almost comic. Like in a cartoon when an elephant spots a mouse. Anyway, a few weeks after . . . after Danny and my folks were killed, and after I gave up trying to approach reporters with what I knew, I called old Tom at his office in the Department of Justice, just rang him up from a pay phone in midtown Chicago."

"Good grief."

"The most private of his private lines, the one he picks up himself. Surprised him. He tried to play innocent, keep me talking until he could have me whacked right at that pay phone. I told him he shouldn't be so afraid of cockroaches, since he was one himself. Told him that someday I'll stomp him flat, kill him. And I meant what I said. Someday, somehow, I'll send him straight to Hell."

Spencer glanced at her. She was staring at the night ahead, still brooding. Slender, so pleasing to the eye, in some ways as delicate as any flower, she was nevertheless as fierce and tough as any special-forces soldier that Spencer had ever known.

He loved her beyond all reason, without reservation, without qualification, with a passion immeasurable, loved every aspect of her face, loved the sound of her voice, loved her singular vitality, loved the kindness of her heart and the agility of her mind, loved her so purely and intensely that sometimes when he looked at her, a hush seemed to fall across the world. He prayed that she was a favored child of fate, destined to have a long life, because if she died before he did, there would be no hope for him, no hope at all.

He drove east into the night, past Rifle and Silt and New Castle and Glenwood Springs. The interstate highway frequently followed the bottoms of deep, narrow canyons with sheer walls of seamed stone. In daylight, it was some of the most breathtaking scenery on the planet. In February darkness, those soaring ramparts of rock pressed close, black monoliths that denied him the choice of going left or right and that funneled him toward higher places, toward dire confrontations so inevitable that they seemed to have been waiting to unfold since before the universe had exploded into existence. From the floor of that crevasse, only a ribbon of sky was visible, sprinkled with a meagerness of stars, as though Heaven could accommodate no more souls and would soon close its gates forever.

Roy touched a button in the armrest. Beside him, the car window purred down. "Is it as you remember?" he asked the artist.

As they turned off the two-lane country road, Ackblom leaned past Roy to look outside.

Toward the front of the property, untrammeled snow mantled the paddocks that surrounded the stables. No horses had been boarded there in twenty-two years, since Jennifer's death, because horses had been her love, not her husband's. The fencing was well maintained and so white that it was only dimly visible against the frosted fields.

The bare driveway was flanked by waist-high walls of snow that had been pushed there by a plow. Its course was serpentine.

At Steven Ackblom's request, the driver stopped at the house rather than proceeding directly to the barn.

Roy put up the window while Fordyce removed the shackles from the artist's ankles. Then the handcuffs. Roy did not want his guest to suffer the further indignity of those bonds.

In their journey across the mountains, he and the artist had achieved a rapport deeper than he would have thought possible in such a short acquaintance. More than handcuffs and shackles, the mutual respect between them was certain to guarantee Ackblom's fullest cooperation.

He and the artist got out of the limousine, leaving Rink and Fordyce and the driver to wait for them. No wind carved the night, but the air was frigid.

As the fenced fields had been, the lawns were white and softly luminous in the platinum light of the partial moon. The evergreen shrubs were encrusted with snow. Its limbs jacketed in ice, a winter-shorn maple cast a faint moonshadow upon the yard.

The two-story Victorian farmhouse was white with green shutters. A deep front porch extended from corner to corner, and the embracing balustrade had white balusters under a green handrail. A gingerbread cornice marked the transition from the walls to the dormered roof, and a fringe of small icicles overhung the eaves.

The windows were all dark. The Dresmunds had cooperated with Duvall. For the night, they were staying in Vail, perhaps curious about events at the ranch but selling their forgetfulness for the price of dinner in a four-star restaurant, champagne, hot-house strawberries dipped in chocolate, and a restful night in a luxury hotel suite. Later, with Grant dead and no caretaker job to be filled, they would regret making such a bad bargain.

Duvall and the twelve men under his supervision were scattered with utmost discretion across the property. Roy couldn't discern where a single man was concealed.

"It's lovely here in the spring," said Steven Ackblom, speaking not with audible regret but as if remembering May mornings full of sun, mild evenings full of stars and cricket songs.

"It's lovely now too," Roy said.

"Yes, isn't it?" With a smile that might have been melancholy, Ackblom turned to survey the entire property. "I was happy here."

"It's easy to see why," Roy said.

The artist sighed. " 'Pleasure is oft a visitant, but pain clings cruelly to us.' "

"Excuse me?"

"Keats," Ackblom explained.

"Ah. I'm sorry if being here depresses you."

"No, no. Don't trouble yourself about that. It doesn't in the least depress me. By nature, I'm depression-proof. And seeing this place again . . . it's a sweet pain, one well worth experiencing."

They got into the limousine and were driven to the barn behind the house.

In the small town of Eagle, west of Vail, they stopped for gasoline. In a minimart adjacent to the service station, Ellie was able to purchase two tubes of Super Glue, the store's entire supply.

"Why Super Glue?" Spencer asked when she returned to the pumps, where he was counting out cash to the attendant.

"Because it's a lot harder to find welding tools and supplies."

"Well, of course it is," he said, as though he knew what she was talking about.

She remained solemn. Her fund of smiles had been depleted. "I hope it's not too cold for this stuff to bond."

"What're you going to do with your Super Glue, if I may ask?"

"Glue something."

"Well, of course you are."

Ellie got into the backseat with Rocky.

At her direction, Spencer drove the pickup past the service bays of the repair garage to the edge of the station property. He parked beside a ten-foot-high ridge of plowed snow.

Fending off the mutt's friendly tongue, Ellie unlatched the small sliding window between the cab and the cargo bed. She slid the movable half open only an inch.

From the canvas duffel bag, she removed the last of the major items that she had chosen to salvage when the signal trace-back from Earthguard had made it necessary to abandon the Range Rover. A long orange utility cord. An adapter that transformed any car or truck cigarette lighter into two electrical sockets from which current could be drawn when the engine was running. Finally, there was the compact satellite up-link with automated tracking arm and collapsible Frisbee-like receiving dish.

Outside again, Spencer put down the tailgate, and they climbed into the empty bed of the pickup. Ellie used most of the Super Glue to fix the microwave transceiver to the painted metal cargo bed.

"You know," he said, "a drop or two usually does the trick."

"Got to be sure it doesn't pop loose at the worst moment and start sliding around. It has to remain stationary."

"After that much glue, you'll probably need a small nuclear device to get it off."

Head cocked in curiosity, Rocky watched them through the back window of the cab.

The adhesive required longer than usual to bond, either because Ellie used too much or because of the cold. In ten minutes, however, the microwave transceiver was fixed securely to the truck bed.

She opened the collapsible receiving dish to its full eighteen-inch extension. She plugged one end of the utility cord into the base of the transceiver. Then she hooked her fingers into the narrow gap that she had left in the rear window of the cab, slid the pane farther open, and fed the electrical cord into the backseat.

Rocky pushed his snout through the window and licked Ellie's hands as she worked.

When the cord between the transceiver and the window was taut but not stretched tight, she pushed Rocky's snout out of the way and slid the window as tightly shut as the cord would allow.

"We're going to track somebody by satellite?" Spencer asked as they jumped off the back of the truck.

"Information is power," she said.

Putting up the tailgate, he said, "Well, of course it is."

"And I have some heavy-duty knowledge."

"I wouldn't dispute that for a moment."

They returned to the cab of the pickup.

She pulled the utility cord from the backseat and plugged it into one of the two sockets in the cigarette-lighter adapter. She plugged the laptop into the second socket.

"All right," she said grimly, "next stop—Vail."

He started the engine.

Almost too excited to drive, Eve Jammer cruised the Vegas night, searching for an opportunity to become the completely fulfilled woman that Roy had shown her how to be.

Cruising past a seedy bar where flashing neon signs advertised topless dancers, Eve saw a sorry-looking, middle-aged guy step out the front door. He was bald, maybe forty pounds overweight, with facial skin folds to rival those of any Shar-Pei. His shoulders were slumped under a yoke of weariness. Hands in his coat pockets, head hung low, he schlepped toward the half-full parking lot beside the bar.

She drove past him into the lot and parked in an empty stall. Through her side window, she watched him approaching. He shuffled as if too beaten down by the world to fight gravity any more than he absolutely had to.

She could imagine how it was for him. Too old, too unattractive, too fat, too socially awkward, too poor to win the favors of a girl like those he so much desired. He was on his way home after a few beers, bound for a lonely bed, having passed a few hours watching gorgeous, big-breasted, long-legged, firm-bodied young women whom he could never possess. Frustrated, depressed. Achingly lonely.

Eve felt so sorry for that man, to whom life had been grossly unfair.

She got out of her car and approached him as he reached his ten-year-old, unwashed Pontiac. "Excuse me," she said.

He turned, and his eyes widened at the sight of her.

"You were here the other night," she guessed, making it sound like a statement.

"Well . . . yeah, last week," he said. He couldn't restrain himself from looking her over. He was probably unaware of licking his lips.

"I saw you then," she said, pretending shyness. "I . . . I didn't have the nerve to say hello."

He gaped at her in disbelief. And he was slightly wary, unable to believe a woman like her would be coming on to him.

"The thing is," she said, "you look exactly like my dad." Which was a lie.

"I do?"

He was less wary now that she had mentioned her dad, but there was also less pathetic hope in his eyes.

"Oh, exactly like him," she said. "And . . . and the thing is . . . the thing is that . . . I hope you won't think I'm weird . . . but the thing is . . . the only men I can do it with, go to bed with and be really wild with . . . are men who look like my father."

As he realized that he had stumbled into a bed of good fortune more exciting than any in his most testosterone-flooded fantasies, the jowled and dewlapped Romeo straightened his shoulders. His chest lifted. A smile of sheer delight made him look ten years younger, though no less like a Shar-Pei.

In that transcendent moment, when the poor man no doubt felt more alive and happier than he'd been in weeks, months, perhaps even years, Eve drew the silencer-fitted Beretta from her big handbag and shot him three times.

She also had a Polaroid in the handbag. Although worried that a car might pull into the lot and that other patrons might leave the bar momentarily, she took three snapshots of the dead man as he lay on the black-top beside his Pontiac.

Driving home, she thought about what a fine thing she had done: helping that dear man to find a way out of his imperfect life, giving him his freedom from rejection, depression, loneliness, and despair. Tears melted from her eyes. She didn't sob or become too emotional to be dangerous behind the wheel. She wept quietly, quietly, though the compassion in her heart was powerful and profound.

She wept all the way home, into the garage, through the house, into her bedroom, where she arranged the Polaroids on the nightstand for Roy to see when he returned from Colorado in a day or two—and then a funny thing happened. As deeply moved as she was by what she had done, as copious and genuine as her tears had been, nevertheless, she was abruptly dry-eyed and incredibly *horny*.

At the window with the artist, Roy watched the limousine as it headed back to the county road and away. It would return for them after the drama of the night had been played out.

They were standing in the front room of the converted barn. The darkness was relieved only by the moonlight that sifted through the windows and by the green glow of the security-panel readout next to the front door. With numbers that Gary Duvall had obtained from the Dresmunds, Roy had disengaged the alarm when they'd come in, then had reset it. There were no motion detectors, only magnetic contacts at each door and window, so he and the artist could move about freely without triggering the system.

This large first-floor room had once been a private gallery where Steven had exhibited the paintings that he favored among all those that he had produced. Now the chamber was vacant, and every faint sound echoed hollowly off the cold walls. Sixteen years had passed since the great man's art had adorned the place.

Roy knew this was a moment he would remember with exceptional clarity for the rest of his life, as he would remember the *precise* expression of wonder on Eve's face when he had granted peace to that man and woman in the restaurant parking lot. Although the degree of humanity's imperfection ensured that the ongoing human drama would always be a tragedy, there were moments of transcendent experience, like this, that made life worth living.

Sadly, most people were too timid to seize the day and discover what such transcendence felt like. Timidity, however, had never been one of Roy's shortcomings.

Revelation of his compassionate crusade had earned Roy all the glories of Eve's bedroom, and he had decided that revelation was called for again. Journeying across the mountains, he had realized that Steven was perfect in some way few people ever were—although the nature of his perfection was more subtle than Eve's devastating beauty, more sensed than seen, intriguing, mysterious. Instinctively Roy knew that Steven and he were simpatico to an even greater extent than were he and Eve. True friendship might be forged between them if he revealed himself to the artist as forthrightly as he'd revealed himself to the dear heart in Las Vegas.

Standing by the moonlit window, in the dark and empty gallery, Roy Miro began to explain, with tasteful humility, how he had put his ideals into practice in ways that even the agency, for all its willingness to be bold, would have been too timid to endorse. As the artist listened, Roy almost hoped that the fugitives would not come that night or the next, not until he and Steven were granted sufficient time together to build a foundation for the friendship that surely was destined to enrich their lives.

Outside Hamlet Gardens in Westwood, the uniformed valet brought Darius's VW Microbus from the narrow lot beside the building, drove it into the street, and swung it to the curb at the front entrance, where the two Descoteaux families waited, fresh from dinner.

Harris was at the rear of their group, and as he was about to step into the Microbus, a woman touched his shoulder. "Sir, may I give you something to think about?"

He wasn't surprised. He didn't back off, as he had done in the men's room at the theater. Turning, he saw an attractive redhead in high heels, an ankle-length coat in a shade of green complementary to her complexion, and a stylishly wide-brimmed hat worn at a rakish angle. She appeared to be on her way to a party or a nightclub.

"If the new world order turns out to be peace, prosperity, and democracy, how wonderful for us all," she said. "But perhaps it will be less appealing, more like the Dark Ages if the Dark Ages had had all these wonderful new forms of high-tech entertainment to make them tolerable. But I think you'd agree . . . being able to get the latest movies on video doesn't fully compensate for enslavement."

"What do you want from me?"

"To help you," she said. "But you have to want the help, have to know you need it, and have to be ready to do what needs done."

From inside the Microbus, his family was staring at him with curiosity and concern.

"I'm no bomb-throwing revolutionary," he told the woman in the green coat.

"Nor are we," she said. "Bombs and guns are the instruments of last resort. Knowledge should be the first and foremost weapon in any resistance."

"What knowledge do I have that you could want?"

"To begin with," she said, "the knowledge of how fragile your freedom is in the current scheme of things. That gives you a degree of commitment that we value."

The valet, though standing just out of earshot, was staring at them oddly.

From a coat pocket, the woman extracted a piece of paper and showed it to Harris. He saw a telephone number and three words.

When he tried to take the paper from her, she held it tightly. "No, Mr. Descoteaux. I would prefer that you memorize it."

The number was designed to be memorable, and the three words gave him no difficulty, either.

As Harris stared at the paper, the woman said, "The man who has done this to you is named Roy Miro."

He remembered the name but not where he had heard it before.

"He came to you pretending to be an FBI agent," she said.

"The guy asking about Spence!" he said, looking up from the paper. He was suddenly furious, now that he had a face to put on the enemy who had thus far been faceless. "But what in the hell did I do to him? We had the mildest disagreement over an officer who once served under me. That's all!" Then he heard the other part of what she had said, and he frowned. "*Pretended* to be with the FBI? But he was. I checked him out between the time he made the appointment and when he came to the office."

"They are seldom what they seem to be," the redhead said.

"They? Who are *they*?"

"Who they have always been, through the ages," she said, and smiled. "Sorry. No time to be other than inscrutable."

"I'm going to get my house back," he said adamantly, although he did not feel as confident as he sounded.

"But you won't. And even if the public outcry was loud enough to have these laws rescinded, they'd just pass new laws giving them other ways to ruin people they want to ruin. The problem's not one law. These are power fanatics who want to tell everyone how they should live, what they should think, read, say, feel."

"How do I get at Miro?"

"You can't. He's too deep-cover to be easily exposed."

"But—"

"I'm not here to tell you how to get Roy Miro. I'm here to warn you that you must not go back to your brother's tonight."

A chill shimmered through the chambers of fluid in his spine, working up his back to the base of his neck with a queer, methodical progression like no chill he had ever felt before.

He said, "What's going to happen now?"

"Your ordeal isn't over. It isn't ever going to be over if you let them have their way. You'll be arrested for the murder of two drug dealers, the wife of one, the girlfriend of the other, and three young children. Your fingerprints have been found on objects in the house where they were shot to death."

"I never killed anyone!"

The valet heard enough of that exclamation to scowl.

Darius was getting out of the Microbus to see what was wrong.

"The objects with your prints on them were taken from your home and planted at the scene of the murders. The story will probably be that you disposed of two competitors who tried to muscle in on your territory, and you wiped out the wife, girlfriend, and kids just to teach other dealers a hard lesson."

Harris's heart was pounding so fiercely that he would not have been surprised to see his breast shuddering visibly with each hard beat. Instead of pumping warm blood, it seemed to be circulating liquid Freon through his body. He was colder than a dead man.

Fear regressed him to the vulnerability and helplessness of childhood. He heard himself seeking solace in the faith of his beloved, gospel-singing mother, a faith from which he had slipped away through the years but to which he now suddenly reached out with a sincerity that surprised him: "Jesus, dear sweet Jesus, help me."

"Perhaps He will," the woman said as Darius approached them. "But in the meantime, we're ready to help as well. If you're smart, you'll call that number, use those passwords, and get on with your life—instead of getting on with your death."

As Darius joined them, he said, "What's up, Harris?"

The redhead returned the slip of paper to her coat pocket.

Harris said, "But that's just it. How can I ever get on with my life after what's happened to me?"

"You can," she said, "though you won't be Harris Descoteaux anymore."

She smiled and nodded at Darius, and she walked away.

Harris watched her go, overcome by that here-we-are-in-the-magic-kingdom-of-Oz feeling again.

Long ago those acres had been beautiful. As a boy with another name, Spencer had been especially fond of the ranch in wintertime, swaddled in white. By day, it was a bright empire of snow forts, tunnels, and sled runs that had been tamped down with great care and patience. On clear nights, the Rocky Mountain sky was deeper than eternity, deeper even than the mind could imagine, and starlight sparkled in the icicles.

Returning after his own eternity in exile, he found nothing that was pleasing to the eye. Each slope and curve of land, each building, each tree was the same as it had been in that distant age, but for the fact that the pines and maples and birches were taller than before. Changeless though it might be, the ranch now impressed him as the ugliest place that he had ever seen, even when flattered by its winter dress. They were harsh acres, and the stark geometry of those fields and hills was designed, at every turn, to offend the eye, like the architecture of Hell. The trees were only ordinary specimens, but they looked to him as though they were malformed and gnarled by disease, nurtured on horrors that had leached into the soil and into their roots from the nearby catacombs. The buildings—stables, house, barn—were all graceless hulks, looming and haunted, the windows as black and menacing as open graves.

Spencer parked at the house. His heart was pounding. His mouth was so dry and his throat was so tight that he could hardly swallow. The door of the pickup opened with the resistance of a massive portal on a bank vault.

Ellie remained in the truck, with the computer on her lap. If trouble came, she was on-line and ready for whatever strange purpose she had prepared. Through the microwave transceiver, she had linked to a satellite and from there into a computer system that she hadn't identified to Spencer and that could be anywhere on the surface of the earth. Information might be power, as she had said, but Spencer couldn't imagine how information would shield them from bullets, if the agency was nearby and lying in wait for them.

As though he were a deep-sea diver, encased in a cumbersome pressure suit and steel helmet, burdened by an incalculable tonnage of water, he walked to the front steps, crossed the porch, and stood at the door. He rang the bell.

He heard the chimes inside, the same five notes that had marked a visitor's arrival when he'd lived there as a boy, and even as they rang out, he had to struggle against an urge to turn and run. He was a grown man, and the hobgoblins that terrorized children should have had no power over him. Irrationally, however, he was afraid that the chimes would be answered by his mother, dead but walking, as naked as she'd been found in that ditch, all her wounds revealed.

He found the willpower to censor the mental image of the corpse. He rang the bell again.

The night was so hushed that he felt as though he would be able to hear the earthworms deep in the ground, below the frost line, if only he could clear his mind and listen for their telltale writhing.

When no one responded to the bell the second time, Spencer retrieved the spare key from the hiding place atop the door head. The Dresmunds had been instructed to leave it there, in the event that it was ever needed by the owner. The dead-bolt locks of the house and barn were keyed the same. With that freezing bit of brass half sticking to his fingers, he hurried back to the black pickup.

The driveway forked. One lane led past the front of the barn and the other behind it. He took the second route.

"I should go inside the same way I went that night," he told Ellie. "By the back door. Re-create the moment."

They parked where the van with the rainbow mural had stood in a long-ago darkness. That vehicle had been his father's. He'd seen it for the first time that night because it had always been garaged off the property and registered under a false name. It was the hunting wagon in which Steven Ackblom had traveled to various distant places to stalk and capture the women and the girls who were destined to become permanent residents of his catacombs. For the most part, he'd driven it onto the property only when his wife and son had been away, visiting her parents or at horse shows—though also on rare occasions when his darker desires became stronger than his caution.

Ellie wanted to stay in the pickup truck, leave the engine running, and keep the computer on her lap, with her fingers poised over the keys, ready to respond to any provocation.

Spencer couldn't imagine anything that she could possibly do, while actually under attack, to force a call-back of the agency thugs. But she was dead serious, and he knew her well enough to trust that her plan, however peculiar, was not frivolous.

"They're not here," he told her. "No one's waiting for us. If they were here, they'd have been all over us by now."

"I don't know. . . ."

"To remember what happened in those missing minutes, I'm going to have to go down . . . into that place. Rocky isn't company enough. I don't have the courage to go alone, and I'm not ashamed to say so."

Ellie nodded. "You shouldn't be. If I were you, I'd never have been able to come this far. I'd have driven by, never looked back." She surveyed the moon-dappled fields and hills behind the barn.

"No one," he said.

"All right." Her fingers tapped across the laptop keyboard, and she pulled back from whatever computer she had invaded. The display screen went dark. "Let's go."

Spencer doused the headlights. He switched off the engine.

He took the pistol. Ellie had the Micro Uzi.

When they got out of the truck, Rocky insisted on scrambling out with them. He was shaking, saturated by his master's mood, afraid to go with them but equally afraid to stay behind.

Shivering more violently than the dog. Spencer peered into the sky. It was as clear and star-spattered as it had been on that July night. This time, however, the cataracts of moonlight revealed neither an owl nor an angel.

In the dark gallery, where Roy had spoken of many things and the artist had listened with increasing interest and gratifying respect, the grumble of the approaching truck brought a temporary halt to the sharing of intimacies.

To avoid the risk of being seen, they took one step back from the window. They still had a view of the driveway.

Instead of stopping in front of the barn, the pickup continued around to the back of the building.

"I brought you here," Roy said, "because I have to know how your son's involved with this woman. He's a wild card. We can't figure him. There's a feeling of organization about his involvement. That disturbs us. For some time, we've suspected there may be a loosely woven organization out to undo our work or, failing that, cause us as many headaches as it can. He might be involved with such a group. If it exists. Maybe they're assisting the woman. Anyway, considering Spencer's . . . I'm sorry. Considering *Michael's* military training and his obvious Spartan mind-set, I don't think he'll crack under the usual methods of interrogation, no matter how much pain is involved."

"He's a strong-willed boy," Steven acknowledged.

"But if *you* interrogate him, he'll break wide open."

"You might be right," Steven said. "Quite perceptive."

"And this also gives me a chance to help right a wrong."

"What wrong would that be?"

"Well, of course, it's wrong for a son to betray his father."

"Ah. And in addition to being able to avenge that betrayal, may I have the woman?" Steven asked.

Roy thought of those lovely eyes, so direct and challenging. He had coveted them for fourteen months. He would be willing to relinquish his claim, however, in return for the opportunity to witness what a creative genius of Steven Ackblom's stature could achieve when permitted to work in the medium of living flesh.

In anticipation of visitors, they now spoke in whispers:

"Yes, that seems only fair," Roy said. "But I want to watch."

"You understand that what I'll do to her will be . . . extreme."

"The timid never know transcendence."

"That's very true," Steven agreed.

" 'They were all so beautiful in their pain, and all like angels when they died,' " Roy quoted.

"And you want to see that brief, perfect beauty," Ackblom said.

"Yes."

From the far end of the building came the scrape and clack of a lock bolt. A hesitation. Then the faint creak of door hinges.

Darius braked at the stop sign. He was traveling east, and he lived two and a half blocks north of where he had stopped, but he didn't put on the turn signal.

Facing the Microbus from across the intersection were four television-news vans with elaborate microwave dishes on the roofs. Two were parked to the left, two to the right, bathed in the sodium-yellow light-fall from the streetlamps. One was from KNBC, the local affiliate of the national network, and another was marked KTLA, which was Channel 5, the independent station with the highest news ratings in the Los Angeles market. Harris couldn't make out the call letters on the other vans, but he figured they would be from the ABC and CBS affiliate stations in Los Angeles. Behind them were a few cars, and in addition to the people in all those vehicles, half a dozen others were milling around, talking.

Darius's voice was colored by both heavy sarcasm and anger: "Must be a breaking story."

"Not quite yet," Harris said grimly. "Best to drive straight through, right by them, and not so fast that they pay any attention to us."

Instead of turning left, toward home, Darius did as his brother asked.

Passing the media, Harris leaned forward, as if fiddling with the radio, averting his face from the windows. "They've been tipped off, asked to stay a few blocks away until it goes down. Somebody wants to ensure there'll be plenty of film of me being taken out of the house in handcuffs. If they go as far as using a SWAT team, then just before the bastards break down the door, these TV vans will get the word to come on up."

Behind Harris, from the middle of three rows of seats, Ondine leaned forward. "Daddy, you mean they're all here to film *you?*"

"I'd bet on it, honey."

"The bastards," she fumed.

"Just newsmen doing their job."

Willa, more emotionally fragile than her sister, began to cry again.

"Ondine's right," Bonnie agreed. "Stinking bastards."

From the very back of the Microbus, Martin said, "Man, this is wild. Uncle Harris, they're going after you like you were Michael Jackson or someone."

"Okay, we're past them," Darius said, so Harris could sit up straight again.

Bonnie said, "The police must think we're home, 'cause of the way the security system handles the lights when no one's there."

"It's programmed with a dozen scenarios," Darius explained. "It cycles through a different one every night no one's there, switching off lamps in one room, on in another, switching radios and TVs on and off, imitating realistic patterns of activity. Supposed to convince burglars. Never expected I'd be happy about it convincing cops."

Bonnie asked, "What now?"

"Let's just drive for a while." Harris put his hands in front of the heater vents, in the jets of hot air. He couldn't get warm. "Just drive while I think about this."

Already they had spent fifteen minutes cruising through Bel Air while he'd told them about the man who had approached him during his walk, the second stranger in the theater men's room, and the redhead in the green coat. Even before seeing the TV-news vans, they had all regarded the woman's warning as seriously as the events of the past few days argued that they should. But it had seemed feasible to drive by the house, quickly leave off Bonnie and Martin, then return ten minutes later and pick them up, along with the clothes that Ondine and Willa had gotten at the mall and with the pathetically few belongings that Jessica and the girls had been able to remove from their own home during the eviction on Saturday. However, their aimless cruising had resulted in an indirect approach to the house, a chance encounter with the TV-news vans, and the realization that the warning had been even more urgent than they had thought.

Darius drove to Wilshire Boulevard and headed west, toward Santa Monica and the sea.

"When I'm charged with the premeditated murder of seven people, including three children," Harris thought aloud, "the prosecutor is going to go for 'first-degree murder, special circumstances,' sure as God made little green apples."

Darius said, "Bail's out of the question. Won't be any. They'll say you're a flight risk."

From her seat at the back, beside Martin, Jessica said, "Even if there was bail, we have no way to raise the money to post it."

"Court calendars are clogged," Darius noted. "So many laws these days, seventy thousand pages out of Congress last year. All those defendants, all those appeals. Most cases move like glaciers. Jesus, Harris, you'll be in jail a year, maybe two, just waiting for a day in court, getting through the trial—"

"That's time lost forever," Jessica said angrily, "even if the jury finds him innocent."

Ondine began to cry again, with Willa.

Harris vividly recalled each of his incapacitating attacks of jailhouse claustrophobia. "I'd never make it six months, not a chance, maybe not even a month."

Circling through the city, where the millions of bright lights were inadequate to hold back the darkness, they discussed options. In the end, they realized that there *were* no options. He had no choice but to run. Yet without money or ID, he wouldn't get far before he was chased down and apprehended. His only hope, therefore, was the mysterious group to which the redhead in the green coat and the other two strangers belonged, although Harris knew too little about them to feel comfortable putting his future in their hands.

Jessica, Ondine, and Willa were adamantly opposed to being separated from him. They feared that any separation was going to be permanent, so they ruled out the option of his going on the run alone. He was sure they were right. Besides, he didn't want to be apart from them, because he suspected that they would remain targets in his absence.

Looking back through the shadow-filled Microbus, past the dark faces of his children and his sister-in-law, Harris met the eyes of his wife, where she sat next to Martin. "It can't have come to this."

"All that matters is that we're together."

"Everything we've worked so hard for—"

"Gone already."

"—to start over at forty-four—"

"Better than dying at forty-four," said Jessica.

"You're a trooper," he said lovingly.

Jessica smiled. "Well, it could've been an earthquake, the house gone, and all of us besides."

Harris turned his attention to Ondine and Willa. They were done with tears, shaky but with a new light of defiance in their eyes.

He said, "All the friends you've made in school—"

"Oh, they're just kids." Ondine strove to be airy about losing all her pals and confidants, which to a teenager would be the hardest thing about such an abrupt change. "Just a bunch of kids, silly kids, that's all."

"And," Willa said, "you're our dad."

For the first time since the nightmare had begun, Harris was moved to quiet tears of his own.

"It's settled then," Jessica announced. "Darius, start looking for a pay phone."

They found one at the end of a strip shopping center, in front of a pizza parlor.

Harris had to ask Darius for change. Then he got out of the Microbus and went to the telephone alone.

Through the windows of the pizza parlor, he saw people eating, drinking beer, talking. A group at one large table was having an especially good time; he could hear their laughter above the music from the jukebox. None of them seemed to be aware that the world had recently turned upside down and inside out.

Harris was gripped by an envy so intense that he wanted to smash the windows, burst into the restaurant, overturn the tables, knock the food and the mugs of beer out of those people's hands, shout at them and shake them until their illusions of safety and normalcy were shattered into as many pieces as his own had been. He was so bitter that he might have done it—*would* have done it—if he hadn't had a wife and two daughters to think about, if he had been facing his frightening new life alone. It wasn't even their happiness that he envied; it was their blessed ignorance that he longed to regain for himself, though he knew that no knowledge could ever be unlearned.

He lifted the handset from the pay phone and deposited coins. For a blood-freezing moment, he listened to the dial tone, unable to remember the number that had been on the paper in the redhead's hand. Then it came to him, and he punched the buttons on the keypad, his hand shaking so badly that he half expected to discover that he had not entered the number correctly.

On the third ring, a man answered with a simple, "Hello?"

"I need help," Harris said, and realized that he hadn't even identified himself. "I'm sorry. I'm . . . my name is . . . Descoteaux. Harris Descoteaux. One of your people, whoever you are, she said to call this number, that you could help me, that you were ready to help."

After a hesitation, the man at the other end of the line said, "If you had this number, and if you got it legitimately, then you must be aware there's a certain protocol."

"Protocol?"

There was no response.

For a moment, Harris panicked that the man was going to hang up and walk away from that phone and be forever thereafter unreachable. He couldn't understand what was expected of him—until he remembered the three passwords that had been printed on the piece of paper below the telephone number. The redhead had told him that he must memorize those too. He said, "Pheasants and dragons."

At the security keypad, in the short hallway at the back of the barn, Spencer entered the series of numbers that disarmed the alarm. The Dresmunds had been instructed not to alter the codes, in order to make access easy for the owner if he ever returned when they were gone. When Spencer punched in the last digit, the luminous readout changed from ARMED AND SECURE to the less bright READY TO ARM.

He had brought a flashlight from the pickup. He directed the beam along the left-hand wall. "Half bath, just a toilet and sink," he told Ellie. Beyond the first door, a second: "That's a small storage room." At the end of the hall, the light found a third door. "He had a gallery that way, open only to the wealthiest collectors. And from the gallery, there's a staircase up to what used to be his studio on the second floor." He swung the beam to the right side of the corridor, where only one door waited. It was ajar. "That used to be the file room."

He could have switched on the overhead fluorescent panels. Sixteen years ago, however, he had entered in gloom, guided only by the radiance of the green letters on the security-system readout. Intuitively, he knew that his best hope of remembering what he had repressed for so long was to re-create the circumstances of that night insofar as he was able. The barn had been air-conditioned then, and now the heat was turned low, so the February chill in the air was nearly right. The harsh glare of overhead fluorescent bulbs would too drastically alter the mood. If he were striving for a roughly authentic re-creation, even a flashlight was too reassuring, but he didn't have the nerve to proceed in the same depth of darkness into which he had gone when he was fourteen.

Rocky whined and scratched at the back door, which Ellie had closed behind them. He was shivering and miserable.

For the most part and for reasons that Spencer would never be able to determine, Rocky's argument with darkness was limited to that in the outside world. He usually functioned well enough indoors, in the dark, although sometimes he required a night-light to banish an especially bad case of the willies.

"Poor thing," Ellie said.

The flashlight was brighter than any night-light. Rocky should have been sufficiently comforted by it. Instead, he quaked so hard that it seemed as if his ribs ought to make xylophone music against one another.

"It's okay, pal," Spencer told the dog. "What you sense is something in the past, over and done with a long time ago. Nothing here and now is worth being scared of."

The dog scratched at the door, unconvinced.

"Should I let him out?" Ellie wondered.

"No. He'll just realize it's night outside and start scratching to get back in."

Again directing the flashlight at the file-room door, Spencer knew that his own inner turmoil must be the source of the dog's fear. Rocky was always acutely sensitive to his moods. Spencer strove to calm himself. After all, what he had said to the dog was true: The aura of evil that clung to these walls was the residue of a horror from the past, and there was nothing here and now to fear.

On the other hand, what was true for the dog was not as true for Spencer. He still *lived* partly in the past, held fast by the dark asphalt of memory. In fact, he was gripped even more fiercely by what he could not quite remember than by what he could recall so clearly; his self-denied recollections formed the deepest tar pit of all. The events of sixteen years ago could not harm Rocky, but for Spencer, they had the real potential to snare, engulf, and destroy him.

He began to tell Ellie about the night of the owl, the rainbow, and the knife. The sound of his own voice scared him. Each word seemed like a link in one of those chain drives by which any roller coaster was hauled inexorably up the first hill on its track and by which a gondola with a gargoyle masthead was pulled into the ghost-filled darkness of a fun house. Chain drives worked only in one direction, and once the journey had begun, even if a section of track had collapsed ahead or an all-consuming fire had broken out in the deepest chamber of the fun house, there was no backing up.

"That summer, and for many summers before it, I slept without air-conditioning in my bedroom. The house had a hot-water, radiant-heat system that was quiet in the winter, and that was okay. But I was bothered by the hiss and whistle of cold air being forced through the vanes in the vent grille, the hum of the compressor echoing along the ductwork. . . . No, 'bothered' isn't the word. It scared me. I was afraid that the noise of the air conditioner would mask some sound in the night . . . a sound that I'd better be able to hear and respond to . . . or die."

"What sound?" Ellie asked.

"I didn't know. It was just a fear, a childish thing. Or so I thought at the time. I was embarrassed by it. But that's why my window was open, why I heard the cry. I tried to tell myself it was only an owl or an owl's prey, far off in the night. But . . . it was so desperate, so thin and full of fear . . . so human . . ."

More swiftly than when he had been confessing to strangers in barrooms and to the dog, he recounted his journey on that July night: out of the silent house, across the summer lawn with its faux frost of moonlight, to the corner of the barn and the visitation of the owl, to the van where the stench of urine rose from the open back door, and into the hall where they now stood together.

"And then I opened the door to the file room," he said.

He opened it once more and crossed the threshold.

Ellie followed him.

In the dark hallway from which the two of them had come, Rocky still whined and scratched at the back door, trying to get out.

Spencer played the beam of the flashlight around the file room. The long worktable was gone, as were the two chairs. The row of file cabinets had been removed as well.

The knotty-pine cupboards still filled the far end of the room from floor to ceiling and corner to corner. They featured three pairs of tall, narrow doors.

He pointed the beam of light at the center doors and said, "They were standing open, and a strange faint light was coming out of them from inside the cabinet, where there weren't any lights." He heard a new note of strain in his voice. "My heart was knocking so hard it shook my arms. I fisted my hands and held them at my sides, struggling to control myself. I wanted to run, just turn and run back to bed and forget it all."

He was talking about how he had felt then, in the long ago, but he could as easily have been speaking of the present.

He opened the center pair of knotty-pine doors. The unused hinges squeaked. He shone the light into the cabinet and panned it across empty shelves.

"Four latches hold the back wall in place," he told her.

His father had concealed the latches behind clever strips of flip-up molding. Spencer found all four: one to the left at the back of the bottom shelf, one to the right; one to the left at the back of the second-highest shelf, one to the right.

Behind him, Rocky padded into the file room, claws ticking on the polished-pine floor. Ellie said, "That's right, pooch, you stay with us."

After handing the flashlight to Ellie, Spencer pushed on the shelves. The guts of the cabinet rolled backward into darkness. Small wheels creaked along old metal tracks.

He stepped over the base frame of the unit, into the space that had been vacated by the shelves. Standing inside the cupboard, he pushed the back wall all the way into the hidden vestibule beyond.

His palms were damp. He blotted them on his jeans.

Retrieving the flashlight from Ellie, he went into the six-foot-square room behind the cupboard. A chain dangled from the bare bulb in the ceiling socket. He tugged on it and was rewarded with light as sulfurous as he remembered it from that night.

Concrete floor. Concrete-block walls. As in his dreams.

After Ellie shut the knotty-pine doors, closing herself in the cabinet, she and Rocky followed him into the cramped room beyond.

"That night, I stood out there in the file room, looking in through the back of the cupboard, toward this yellow light, and I wanted to run away so badly. I thought I *had* started to run . . . but the next thing I knew, I was in the cupboard. I said to myself, 'Run, run, get the hell out of here.' But then I was all the way through the cupboard and in this vestibule, without any awareness of having taken a step. It was like . . . like I was drawn . . . in a trance . . . couldn't go back no matter how much I wanted to."

"It's a yellow bug light," she said, "like you use outdoors during the summer." She seemed to find that curious.

"Sure. To keep mosquitoes away. They never work that well. And I don't know why he used it here, instead of an ordinary bulb."

"Well, maybe it was the only one handy at the time."

"No. Never. Not him. He must have felt there was something more aesthetic about the yellow light, more suited to his purpose. He lived a carefully considered life. Everything he did was done with the aesthetics well worked out in his mind. From the clothes he wore to the way he prepared a sandwich. That's one thing that makes what he did under this place so horrible . . . the long and careful consideration."

He realized that he was tracing his scar with the fingertips of his right hand while holding the flashlight in his left. He lowered his hand to the SIG 9mm pistol that was still jammed under his belt, against his belly, but he didn't draw it.

"How could your mother not know about this place?" Ellie asked, gazing up and around at the vestibule.

"He owned the ranch before they were married. Remodeled the barn before she saw it. This used to be part of the area that became the file room. He added those pine cabinets out there himself, to close off this space, after the contractors left, so they wouldn't know he'd concealed the access to the basement. Last of all, he brought in a guy to lay pine floors through the rest of the place."

The Micro Uzi was equipped with a carrying strap. Ellie slung it over her shoulder, apparently so she could hug herself with both arms. "He was planning what he did . . . planning it before he even married your mother, before you were born?"

Her disgust was as heavy as the chill in the air. Spencer only hoped that she was able to absorb all the revelations that lay ahead without letting her repulsion transfer in any degree from the father to the son. He desperately prayed that he would remain clean in her eyes, untainted.

In his own eyes he regarded himself with disgust every time he saw even an innocent aspect of his father in himself. Sometimes, meeting his reflection in a mirror, Spencer would remember his father's equally dark eyes, and he would look away, shuddering and sick to his stomach.

He said, "Maybe he didn't know exactly why he wanted a secret place then. I hope that's true. I hope he married my mother and conceived me with her before he'd ever had any desires like . . . like those he satisfied here. However, I suspect he knew why he needed the rooms below. He just wasn't ready to use them. Like when he was struck by an idea for a painting, sometimes he'd think about it for years before the work began."

She looked yellow in the glow of the bug light, but he sensed that she was as pale as bleached bone. She stared at the closed door that led from the vestibule to the basement stairs. Nodding at it, she said, "He considered that, down there, to be part of his work?"

"Nobody knows for sure. That's what he seemed to imply. But he might have been playing games with the cops, the psychiatrists, just having his fun. He was an extremely intelligent man. He was able to manipulate people so easily. He enjoyed doing that. Who knows what was going through his mind . . . really?"

"But when did he start this . . . this work?"

"Five years after they married. When I was only four years old. And it was another four years before she discovered it . . . and had to die. The police figured it out by identifying the . . . remains of the earliest victims."

Rocky had slipped around them to the basement entrance. He was sniffing pensively and unhappily along the narrow crack between the door and the threshold.

"Sometimes," Spencer said, "in the middle of the night, when I can't sleep, I think of how he held me on his lap, wrestled with me on the floor when I was five or six, smoothed my hair. . . ." His voice choked with emotion. He took a deep breath and forced himself to continue, for he had come here to continue to the end, to be finished with it at last. "Touching me . . . with those hands, those hands, after those same hands had . . . under the barn . . . doing those terrible things."

"Oh," Ellie said softly, as if stricken by a small stab of pain.

Spencer hoped that what he saw in her eyes was an understanding of what he'd carried with him all these years and a compassion for him—not a deepening of her revulsion.

He said, "Makes me sick . . . that my own father ever touched me. Worse . . . I think about how he might have left a fresh corpse down in the darkness, a dead woman, how he might have come out of his catacombs with the scent of her blood still in his memory, up from that place and into the house . . . upstairs into my mother's bed . . . into her arms . . . touching her. . . ."

"Oh, my God," Ellie said.

She closed her eyes as though she couldn't bear to look at him.

He knew he was part of the horror, even if he had been innocent. He was so inextrica-bly associated with the monstrous brutality of his father that others couldn't know his name and look at him without seeing, in their mind's eye, young Michael himself standing in the corruption of the slaughterhouse. Through the chambers of his heart, despair and blood were pumped in equal measure.

Then she opened her eyes. Tears glimmered in her lashes. She put her hand to his scar, touching him as tenderly as he had ever been touched. With five words she made clear to him that in her eyes he was free of all stain: "Oh, God, I'm so sorry."

Even if he were to live one hundred years, Spencer knew he could never love her more than he loved her then. Her caring touch, at that moment of all moments, was the greatest act of kindness that he had ever known.

He only wished that he was as sure of his utter innocence as Ellie was. He must recap-ture the missing moments of memory that he had come there again to find. But he prayed to God and to his own lost mother for mercy, because he was afraid he would discover that he was, in all ways, the son of his father.

Ellie had given him the strength for whatever waited ahead. Before that courage could fade, he turned to the basement door.

Rocky looked up at him and whimpered. He reached down, stroked the dog's head.

The door was streaked with more grime than it had been when last he'd seen it. Paint had peeled off in places.

"It was closed, but it was different from this," he said, going back to that far July. "Someone must have scrubbed away the stains, the hands."

"Hands?"

He raised his hand from the dog to the door. "Arcing from the knob across the upper part . . . ten or twelve overlapping prints made by a woman's hands, fingers spread . . . like the wings of birds . . . in fresh blood, still wet, so red."

As Spencer moved his own hand across the cold wood, he saw the bloody prints reap-pear, glistening. They seemed as real as they had been on the long-ago night, but he knew that they were only birds of memory taking flight again in his own mind, visible to him but not to Ellie.

"I'm hypnotized by them, can't take my eyes off them, because they convey an unbear-able sense of the woman's terror . . . desperation . . . frantic resistance to being forced out of this vestibule and into the secret . . . the secret world below."

He realized that he had placed his hand on the doorknob. It was cold against his palm.

A tremor shook years off his voice, until he sounded younger to himself: "Staring at the blood . . . knowing that she needs help . . . needs my help . . . but I can't go forward. Can't. Jesus. Won't. I'm just a boy, for God's sake. Barefoot, unarmed, afraid, not ready for the truth. But somehow, standing here as scared as I am . . . somehow I finally open the red door. . . ."

Ellie gasped. "Spencer."

Her sound of surprise and the weight she gave to his name caused Spencer to pull back from the past and turn to her, alarmed, but they were still alone.

"Last Tuesday night," she said, "when you were looking for a bar . . . why did you happen to stop in the place where I worked?"

"It was the first one I noticed."

"That's all?"

"And I'd never been there before. It always has to be a new place."

"But the name."

He stared at her, uncomprehending.

She said, "The Red Door."

"Good God."

The connection had escaped him until she made it.

"You called this the red door," she said.

"Because . . . all the blood, the bloody handprints."

For sixteen years, he had been seeking the courage to return to the living nightmare beyond the red door. When he had seen the cocktail lounge on that rainy night in Santa Monica, with the red-painted entrance and the name spelled out above it in neon—THE RED DOOR—he could not possibly have driven past. The opportunity to open a symbolic door, at a time when he had not yet found the strength to return to Colorado and open the other—and only important—red door, had been irresistible to his subconscious mind even while he remained safely oblivious to the implications on a conscious level. And by passing through that symbolic door, he'd arrived in this vestibule behind the pine cabinet, where he must turn the cold brass knob that remained unwarmed by his hand, open the real door, and descend into the catacombs, where he had left a part of himself more than sixteen years ago.

His life was a speeding train on parallel rails of free choice and destiny. Though destiny seemed to have bent the rail of choice to bring him to this place at this time, he needed to believe that choice would bend the rail of destiny tonight and carry him off to a future not in a rigorous line with his past. Otherwise, he would discover that he was fundamentally the son of his father. And that was a fate with which he could not live: end of the line.

He turned the knob.

Rocky edged back, out of the way.

Spencer opened the door.

The yellow light from the vestibule revealed the first few treads of concrete stairs that led down into darkness.

Reaching through the doorway and to the right, he found the switch and clicked on the cellar light. It was blue. He didn't know why blue had been chosen. His inability to think in harmony with his father and to understand such curious details seemed to confirm that he was not like that hateful man in any way that mattered.

Going down the steep stairs to the cellar, he switched off the flashlight. From now on, the way would be lighted as it had been on a certain July and in all the July-spawned dreams that he had since endured.

Rocky followed, then Ellie.

That subterranean chamber was not the full size of the barn above, only about twelve by twenty feet. The furnace and hot-water heater were in a closet upstairs, and the room was utterly vacant. In the blue light, the concrete walls and floor looked strangely like steel.

"Here?" Ellie asked.

"No. Here he kept files of photographs and videotapes."

"Not . . ."

"Yes. Of them . . . of the way they died. Of what he did to them, step by step."

"Dear God."

Spencer moved around the cellar, seeing it as he had seen it on that night of the red door. "The files and a compact photographer's development lab were behind a black curtain at that end of the room. There was a TV set on a plain black metal stand. And a VCR. Facing the television was a single chair. Right here. Not comfortable. All straight lines, wood, painted sour-apple green, unpadded. And a small round table stood beside the chair, where he could put a glass of whatever he was drinking. Table was painted purple. The chair was a flat green, but the table was glossy, highly lacquered. The glass that he drank from was actually a piece of fine cut-crystal, and the blue light sparkled in all its bevels."

"Where did he . . ." Ellie spotted the door, which was flush with the wall and painted to match. It reflected the blue light precisely as the concrete reflected it, becoming all but invisible. "There?"

"Yes." His voice was even softer and more distant than the cry that had awakened him from July sleep.

Half a minute didn't so much pass as crumble away like unstable ground beneath him.

Ellie came to his side. She took his right hand and held it tightly. "Let's do what you've come to do, then get the hell out of this place."

He nodded. He didn't trust himself to speak.

He let go of her hand and opened the heavy gray door. There was no lock on their side of it, only on the far side.

That July night, when Spencer had reached this point, his father had not yet returned from chaining the woman in the abattoir, so the door had been unlocked. No doubt, once the victim had been secured, the artist would have retraced his path to the vestibule above, to close the knotty-pine doors from within the cabinet; then from the secret vestibule, he would have rolled the back of the cupboard into place; he would have locked the upper door from the cellar stairs, would have locked this gray door from inside. Then he would have returned to his captive in the abattoir, confident that no screams, regardless of how piercing, could penetrate to the barn above or to the world beyond.

Spencer crossed the raised concrete sill. An exposed switch box was fixed to the rough masonry of a brick-and-plaster wall. A length of flexible metal conduit rose from it into shadows. He snapped the switch, and a series of small lights winked on. They were suspended from a looped cord along the center of the ceiling, leading out of sight around a curved passageway.

Ellie whispered, *"Spencer, wait!"*

When he looked back into the first basement, he saw that Rocky had returned to the foot of the stairs. The dog trembled visibly, gazing up toward the vestibule behind the file-room cupboards. One ear drooped, as always, but the other stood straight up. His tail was not tucked between his legs, but held low to the floor, and it wasn't wagging.

Spencer stepped back into the cellar. He pulled the pistol from under his belt.

Shrugging the Micro Uzi off her shoulder, taking a two-hand grip on the weapon, Ellie eased past the dog, onto the steep stairs. She climbed slowly, listening.

Spencer moved with equal care to Rocky's side.

In the vestibule, the artist had stood to the side of the open door, and Roy had stood next to him, both with their backs pressed to the wall, listening to the couple in the cellar below. The stairwell added a hollow note to the voices as it funneled them upward, but the words were nonetheless clear.

Roy had hoped to hear something that would explain the man's connection with the woman, at least a crumb of information about the suspected conspiracy against the agency and the shadowy organization that he had mentioned to Steven in the gallery a few minutes ago. But they spoke only of the famous night sixteen years in the past.

Steven seemed amused to be eavesdropping on that of all possible conversations. He turned his head twice to smile at Roy, and once he raised one finger to his lips as if warning Roy to be quiet.

There was something of an imp in the artist, a playfulness that made him a good companion. Roy wished he didn't have to return Steven to prison. But he could think of no way, in the currently delicate political climate of the country, to free the artist either openly or clandestinely. Dr. Sabrina Palma would again have her benefactor. The best Roy could hope for was that he would find other credible reasons to visit Steven from time to time or even to obtain temporary custody again for consultation in other field operations.

When the woman had whispered urgently to Grant—*"Spencer, wait!"*—Roy had known that the dog must have sensed their presence. They had made no telltale noise, so it could only be the damned dog.

Roy considered easing past the artist to the edge of the open door. He could try a shot to the head of the first person who came out of the stairwell.

But it might be Grant. He didn't want to waste Grant until he had some answers from

him. And if it was the woman who was shot dead on the spot, Steven wouldn't be as motivated to help extract information from his son as he would be if he knew that he could
look forward to bringing her to a state of angelic beauty.

Peach in. Green out.

Worse: Assuming that the pair below were still armed with the submachine gun they
had used to destroy the stabilizer of the chopper in Cedar City, and assuming that the first
one across the threshold would be armed with that piece, the risk of a confrontation at
this juncture was too great. If Roy missed with his attempted head shot, the burst of return fire from the Micro Uzi would chop him and Steven to pieces.

Discretion seemed wise.

Roy touched the artist on the shoulder and gestured for him to follow. They could not
quickly reach the open back of the cupboard and then slip through the pine cabinet doors
into the room beyond, because to get there they would have to cross in front of the cellar
stairs. Even if neither of the pair below was far enough up the stairs to see them, their passage through the center of the room, directly under the yellow light, would ensure that
their darting shadows betrayed them. Instead, staying flat against the concrete blocks to
avoid casting shadows into the room, they sidled away from the door to the wall directly
opposite the entrance from the cupboard. They squeezed into the narrow space behind the
displaced back wall of the cupboard, which Grant or the woman had rolled into the
vestibule on a set of sliding-door tracks. That movable section was seven feet high and
more than four feet wide. There was an eighteen-inch-wide hiding space between it and
the concrete wall. Standing at an angle between them and the cellar door, it provided just
enough cover.

If Grant or the woman or both of them came into the vestibule and crept to the gaping
hole in the back wall of the cupboard, Roy could lean out from concealment and shoot
one or both of them in the back, disabling rather than killing them.

If they came instead to look into the narrow space behind the dislocated guts of the
cabinet, he would still have to try for a head shot before they opened fire.

Peach in. Green out.

He listened intently. Pistol in his right hand. Muzzle aimed at the ceiling.

He heard the stealthy scrape of a shoe on concrete. Someone had reached the top of
the stairs.

Spencer remained at the bottom of the stairs. He wished that Ellie had given him a chance
to go up there in her place.

Three steps from the top, she paused for perhaps half a minute, listening, then proceeded to the landing at the head of the stairs. She stood for a moment, silhouetted in the
rectangle of yellow light from the upper room, framed in the blue light of the lower room,
like a stark figure in a modernistic painting.

Spencer realized that Rocky had lost interest in the room above and had slipped away
from his side. The dog was at the other side of the cellar, at the open gray door.

Above, Ellie crossed the threshold and stopped just inside the vestibule. She looked left
and right, listening.

In the cellar, Spencer glanced at Rocky again. One ear pricked, head cocked, trembling,
the dog peered warily into the passageway that led to the catacombs and on to the heart
of the horror.

Speaking to Ellie, Spencer said, "Looks like fur face is just having a bad case of the
heebie-jeebies."

From the vestibule, she glanced down at him.

Behind him, Rocky whined.

"Now he's at the other door, ready to make a puddle if I don't keep looking at him."

"Seems to be okay up here," she said, and she descended the stairs again.

"The whole place spooks him, that's all," Spencer said. "My friend here is easily frightened by most new places. This time, of course, it's with damned good reason."

He engaged the safety on the pistol and again tucked it under the waistband of his jeans.

"He's not the only one spooked," Ellie said, shouldering the Uzi. "Let's finish this."

Spencer crossed the threshold again, from the cellar into the world beyond. With each step forward, he moved backward in time.

They left the VW Microbus on the street to which the man on the phone had directed Harris. Darius, Bonnie, and Martin walked with Harris, Jessica, and the girls across the adjacent park toward the beach a hundred and fifty yards away.

No one could be seen within the discs of light beneath the tall lampposts, but bursts of eerie laughter issued from the surrounding darkness. Above the rumble and slosh of the surf, Harris heard voices, fragmentary and strange, on all sides, near and far. A woman who sounded blitzed on something: "You're a real catman, baby, really a catman, you are." A man's high-pitched laughter trilled through the night, from a place far to the north of the unseen woman. To the south, another man, old by the sound of him, sobbed with grief. Yet another unspottable man, with a pure young voice, kept repeating the same three words, as if chanting a mantra: "Eyes in tongues, eyes in tongues, eyes in tongues . . ." It seemed to Harris that he was shepherding his family across an open-air Bedlam, through a madhouse with no roof other than palm fronds and night sky.

Homeless winos and crackheads lived in some of the lusher stands of shrubbery, in concealed cardboard boxes insulated with newspapers and old blankets. In the sunlight, the beach crowd moved in and the day was filled with well-tanned skaters and surfers and seekers of false dreams. Then the true residents wandered to the streets to make the rounds of trash bins, to panhandle, and to shamble on quests that only they could understand. But at night, the park belonged to them again, and the green lawns and the benches and the handball courts were as dangerous as any places on earth. In darkness, the deranged souls then ventured forth from the undergrowth to prey on one another. They were likely to prey, as well, on unwary visitors who incorrectly assumed that a park was public domain at any hour of the day.

It was no place for women and girls—unsafe for armed men, in fact—but it was the only quick route to the sand and to the foot of the old pier. At the pier stairs, they were to be met by someone who would take them on from there to the new life that they were so blindly embracing.

They had expected to wait. But even as they approached the dark structure, a man walked out of the shadows between those pilings that were still above the tide line. He joined them at the foot of the stairs.

Even with no lamppost nearby, with only the ambient light of the great city that hugged the shoreline, Harris recognized the man who had come for them. It was the Asian in the reindeer sweater, whom he had first encountered in the theater men's room in Westwood earlier in the evening.

"Pheasants and dragons," the man said, as though he was not sure that Harris could tell one Asian from another.

"Yes, I know you," Harris said.

"You were told to come alone," the contact admonished, but not angrily.

"We wanted to say good-bye," Darius told him. "And we didn't know . . . We wanted to know—how will we contact them where they're going?"

"You won't," said the man in the reindeer sweater. "Hard as it may be, you've got to accept that you will probably never see them again."

In the Microbus, both before Harris had made the phone call from the pizza parlor and after, as they had found their way to the park, they had discussed the likelihood of a permanent separation. For a moment, no one could speak. They stared at one another, in a state of denial that approached paralysis.

The man in the reindeer sweater backed off a few yards to give them privacy, but he said, "We have little time."

Although Harris had lost his house, his bank accounts, his job, and everything but the clothes on his back, those losses now seemed inconsequential. Property rights, he had learned from bitter experience, were the essence of all civil rights, but the theft of every dime of his property did not have one tenth—not one *hundredth*—the impact of losing these beloved people. The theft of their home and savings was a blow, but this loss was an inner wound, as if a piece of his heart had been cut out. The pain was of an immeasurably greater magnitude and of a quality inexpressible.

They said good-bye with fewer words than Harris would ever have imagined possible— because no words were adequate. They hugged one another fiercely, acknowledging that they were most likely parting until they met again on whatever shore lay beyond the grave. Their mother had believed in that far and better shore. Since childhood they had drifted away from the belief that she had instilled in them, but they were for this terrible moment, in this place, fully in the faith again. Harris held Bonnie tightly, then Martin, and came at last to his brother, who was separating tearfully from Jessica. He hugged Darius and kissed his cheek. He had not kissed his brother for more years than he could recall, because for so long they had both been too adult for that. Now he wondered at the silly rules that had constituted his sense of mature behavior, for in a single kiss, all was said that needed to be said.

The incoming waves crashed through the pier pilings behind them with a roar hardly louder than the pounding of Harris's own heart, as at last he stepped back from Darius. Wishing there were more light in the gloom, he studied his brother's face for the last time in this life, desperate to freeze it in memory, for he was leaving without even a photograph.

"Must go," said the man in the reindeer sweater.

"Maybe everything won't fall over the brink," Darius said.

"We can hope."

"Maybe the world will come to its senses."

"You be careful going back through that park," Harris said.

"We're safe," Darius said. "Nobody back there's more dangerous than me. I'm an attorney, remember?"

Harris's laugh was perilously close to a sob.

Instead of good-bye, he simply said, "Little brother."

Darius nodded. For a moment it seemed that he wouldn't be able to say anything more. But then: "Big brother."

Jessica and Bonnie turned away from each other, both of them with Kleenex pressed to their eyes.

The girls and Martin parted.

The man in the reindeer sweater led one Descoteaux family south along the beach while the other Descoteaux family stood by the foot of the pier, watching. The sward was as pale as a path in a dream. The phosphorescent foam from the breakers dissolved on the sand with a whispery sizzle like urgent voices delivering incomprehensible warnings from out of the shadows in a nightmare.

Three times, Harris glanced at the other Descoteaux family over his shoulder, but then he could not bear to look back again.

They continued south on the beach, even after they reached the end of the park. They passed a few restaurants, all closed on that Monday night, then a hotel, a few condominiums, and warmly lighted beachfront houses in which lives were still lived without awareness of the hovering darkness.

After a mile and a half, perhaps even two miles, they came to another restaurant. Lights were on in that establishment, but the big windows were too high above the beach for Harris to see any diners at the view tables. The man in the reindeer sweater led them off the sward, alongside the restaurant, into the parking lot in front of the place. They went to a green-and-white motor home that dwarfed the cars around it.

"Why couldn't my brother have brought us directly here?" Harris asked.

Their escort said, "It wouldn't be a good idea for him to know this vehicle or its license number. For his own sake."

They followed the stranger into the motor home through a side door, just aft of the open cockpit, and into the kitchen. He stepped aside and directed them farther back into the vehicle.

An Asian woman in her early or middle fifties, in a black pants suit and a Chinese-red blouse, was standing at the dining table, beyond the kitchen, waiting for them. Her face was uncommonly gentle, and her smile was warm.

"So pleased that you could come," she said, as if they were paying her a social visit. "The dining nook seats seven altogether, plenty of room for the five of us. We'll be able to talk on the way, and we've so much to discuss."

They slid around the horseshoe-shaped booth, until the five of them encircled the table.

The man in the reindeer sweater had gotten behind the steering wheel. He started the engine.

"You may call me Mary," said the Asian woman, "because it's best that you don't know my name."

Harris considered keeping his silence, but he had no talent for deception. "I'm afraid that I recognize you, and I'm sure that my wife does as well."

"Yes," Jessica confirmed.

"We've eaten in your restaurant several times," Harris said, "up in West Hollywood. On most of those occasions, either you or your husband was greeting guests at the front door."

She nodded and smiled. "I'm flattered that you would recognize me out of . . . shall we say, out of context."

"You and your husband are so charming," Jessica said. "Not easy to forget."

"How was dinner when you had it with us?"

"Always wonderful."

"Thank you. So kind of you to say so. We do try. But now I haven't had the pleasure of meeting your lovely daughters," said the restaurateur, "although I know their names." She reached across the table to take each girl's hand. "Ondine, Willa, my name is Mae Lee. It's a pleasure to meet you both, and I want you to be unafraid. You are in good hands now."

The motor home pulled out of the restaurant parking lot, into the street, and away.

"Where are we going?" Willa asked.

"First, out of California," said Mae Lee. "To Las Vegas. Many motor homes crowd the highway between here and Vegas. We're just one more. At that point, I leave you, and you go on with someone else. Your father's picture will be all over the news for a time, and while they're telling their lies about him, you will all be in a safe and quiet place. You will change your looks as much as possible and learn what you will be able to do to help others like yourselves. You will have new names, first and middle and last. New hairstyles. Mr. Descoteaux, you might grow a beard, and you will certainly work with a good voice coach to lose your Caribbean accent, pleasant as it is to the ear. Oh, there will be many changes, and more fun than you imagine there could be now. And meaningful work. The world has not ended, Ondine. It has not ended, Willa. It's only passing through one edge of a dark cloud. There are things to be done to be sure that the cloud does not swallow us entirely. Which, I promise you, it will not. Now, before we begin, may I serve anyone tea, coffee, wine, beer, or a soft drink perhaps?"

. . . bare-chested and barefoot, colder even than I was in the hot July night, I stand in the room of blue light, past the green chair and purple table, before the open door, deter-

mined to abandon this strange quest and race back up into the summer night, where a boy might become a boy again, where the truth which I don't know that I know can remain unknown forever.

Between one blink and another, however, as though transported by the power of a magical incantation, I've left the blue room and have arrived in what must be the basement of an earlier barn that stood on a site adjacent to that which the current barn occupies. While the old barn aboveground was torn down and the land was smoothed over and planted with grass, the cellars were left intact and were connected to the deepest chamber of the new barn.

I'm again being drawn forward against my will. Or think that I am. But although I shudder in fear of some dark force that draws me, it's my own deeper need to know, my true will, that draws me. I've repressed it since the night my mother died.

I'm in a curving corridor, six feet wide. A looping electrical cord runs along the center of the rounded ceiling. Low-wattage bulbs, like those on a Christmas tree, are spaced a foot apart. The walls are rough red-black brick, sloppily mortared. The bricks are overlaid in places with patches and veins of stained white plaster as smooth and greasy as the marbling fat in a slab of meat.

I pause in the curved passage, listening to my rampaging heart, listening to the unseen rooms ahead for a clue as to what might lie in wait for me, listening to the rooms behind for a voice to call me back to the safe world above. But there's no sound ahead or behind, only my heart, and even though I don't want to listen to the things it tells me, I sense that my heart has all the answers. In my heart I know that the truth about my precious mother lies ahead and that what lies behind is a world which will never be the same for me again, a world which changed forever and for the worse when I walked out of it.

The floor is stone. It might as well be ice beneath my feet. It slopes steeply but in a wide loop that would make it possible to push a wheelbarrow up without becoming exhausted or roll one down without losing control of it.

Across that icy stone, I walk barefoot and afraid, around the curve and into a room that's thirty feet long and twelve wide. The floor is flat here, the descent complete. A low, flat ceiling. The frosted-white, low-wattage Christmas bulbs on the looping cord continue to provide the only light. This might have been a fruit cellar in the days before electrical service was brought to the ranch, stacked full of August potatoes and September apples, deep enough to be cool in summer and above freezing in winter. There might have been shelves of home-canned fruits and vegetables stored here as well, enough to last three seasons, although the shelves are long gone.

Whatever the room might once have been, it is something very different now, and I am suddenly frozen to the floor, unable to move. One entire long wall and half the other are occupied by tableaux of life-size human figures carved in white plaster and surrounded by plaster, forming out of a plaster background, as if trying to force their way out of the wall. Grown women but also girls as young as ten or twelve. Twenty, thirty, maybe even forty of them. All naked. Some in their own niches, others in groups of two and three, face beside face, here and there with arms overlapping. He has mockingly arranged a few so they are holding hands for comfort in their terror. Their expressions are unbearable to look upon. Screaming, pleading, agonized, wrenched and suffering, warped by fear beyond measure and by unimaginable pain. Without exception, their bodies are humbled. Often their hands are raised defensively or extended beseechingly or crossed over breasts, over genitals. Here a woman peers between the spread fingers of hands that she's clasped defensively across her face. Imploring, praying, they would be a horror unendurable if they were only what they seem to be at first glance, only sculpture, only the twisted expression of a deranged mind. But they're worse, and even in the cloistering shadows, their blank white stares transfix me, freeze me to the stone floor. The face of the Medusa was so hideous it transformed those who saw it to stone, but these faces aren't like that. These are petrifying because they are all women who might have been mothers like my mother, *young girls who might have been my sisters if I'd been fortunate enough to have sisters, all people who were loved by someone and who loved, who had felt the sun on their faces and the coolness of rain, who'd laughed and dreamed of the future and worried and hoped. They turn me to stone because of the common humanity that I share with them, because I can feel their terror and be moved by it. Their tortured expressions are so poignant that their pain is my pain, their deaths my death. And their sense of being abandoned and fearfully alone in their final hours is the abandonment and isolation that I feel now.*

The sight of them is unendurable. Yet I'm compelled to look, because even though I am only fourteen, only fourteen, I know that what they've suffered demands witnessing and pity and anger, these mothers who might have been mine, these sisters who might have been my sisters, these victims like me.

The medium appears to be molded, sculpted plaster. But the plaster is only the preserving material that records their tormented expressions and beseeching postures—which aren't their true postures and expressions at death but cruel arrangements he made after. Even in the merciful shadows and cold arcs of frosty light, I see places where the plaster has been discolored by unthinkable substances seeping from within: gray and rust and yellowish green, a biological patina by which it's possible to date the figures in the tableaux.

The smell is indescribable, less because of its vileness than because of its complexity, though it is repulsive enough to make me ill. Later, it became known that he had used a sorcerer's brew of chemicals in an attempt to preserve the bodies within the plaster sarcophaguses. To a considerable extent he had been successful, though some decomposition occurred. The underlying stink is that of the world below cemetery lawns. The ghastliness of caskets long after living people have looked into them and closed the lids. But it is masked by scents as pungent as that of ammonia and as fresh as that of lemons. It is bitter and sour and sweet—and so strange that the cloying stench alone, without the ghostly figures, could make my heart pound and my blood run as icy as January rivers.

In the unfinished wall, there's a niche already prepared for a new body. He has chiseled out the bricks and stacked them to one side of the hole. He has scooped out a cavity in the earth beyond the wall and has carried that soil away. Lined up near the cavity are fifty-pound bags of dry plaster mix, a long wooden mixing trough lined with steel, two cans of tar-based sealant, both the tools of a mason and those of a sculptor, a stack of wooden pegs, coils of wire, and other items that I can't quite see.

He is ready. He needs only the woman who will become the next figure in the tableau. But he has her too, of course, for it is she who lost control of her bladder in the back of the rainbow van. Her hands have made the flock of bloody birds across the vestibule door.

Something moves, quick and furtive, out of the new hole in the wall, among the tools and supplies, through shadows and patches of light as pale as snow. It freezes at the sight of me as I have frozen before the martyred women in the walls. It's a rat, but no rat like any other. Its skull is deformed, one eye lower than the other, mouth twisted in a permanent lopsided grin. Another scurries after the first and also goes rigid when it sees me, though not before it rises on hind feet. It too is a creature like no other, encumbered by strange excrescences of bone or cartilage different from anything the first rat exhibits, and with a nose that spreads too wide across its narrow face. These are members of the small family of vermin that survives within the catacombs, tunneling behind the tableaux, nourished in part on that which has been saturated with toxic chemical preservatives. Each year a new generation of their kind produces more mutant forms than was produced the year before. Now they break their paralysis, as I can't yet break mine, and they scurry back into the hole from which they came.

Sixteen years later, that long chamber was not entirely as it had been on the night of owls and rats. The plaster had been torn down and hauled away. The victims had been removed from the niches in the walls. Between the columns of red-black brick that Spencer's father had left as supports, the dark earth was exposed. Police and forensic pathologists, who labored for weeks within that room, had added vertical four-by-four beams between some brick columns, as if they hadn't trusted solely to the supports that Steven Ackblom had thought sufficient.

The cool, dry air now smelled faintly of stone and earth, but it was a clean smell. The pungent miasma of chemicals and the stink of biological decay were gone.

Standing in that low-ceilinged space again, with Ellie and the dog, Spencer vividly recalled the fright that had nearly crippled him when he was fourteen. However, fear was the least of what he felt—which surprised him. Horror and disgust were part of it, but not as great as a diamond-hard anger. Sorrow for the dead. Compassion for those who had loved them. Guilt for having failed to save anyone.

He knew regret, as well, for the life he might have had but had never known. And now never could.

Above all, what overcame him was an unexpected reverence, as he might have felt at any place where the innocent had perished: from Calvary to Dachau, to Babi Yar, to the unnamed fields where Stalin buried millions, to rooms where Jeffrey Dahmer dwelt, to the torture chambers of the Inquisition.

The soil of any killing ground isn't sanctified by the murderers who practice there. Though they often think themselves exalted, they are as the maggots that live in dung, and no maggots can transform one square centimeter of earth into holy ground.

Sacred, instead, are the victims, for each dies in the place of someone whom fate allows to live. And though many may unwittingly or unwillingly die in the place of others, the sacrifice is no less sacred for the fact that fate chose those who would make it.

If there had been votive candles in those cleansed catacombs, Spencer would have wanted to light them and gaze into their flames until they blinded him. Had there been an altar, he would have prayed at the foot of it. If by offering his own life he could have brought back the forty-one and his mother, or any one of them, he would not have hesitated to rid himself of this world in hope of waking in another.

All he could do, however, was quietly honor the dead by never forgetting the details of their final passage through this place. His duty was to be witness. By shunning memory, he would dishonor those who had died here in his place. The price of forgetfulness would be his soul.

Describing those catacombs as they had been in that long-ago time, coming at last to the woman's cry that had roused him from his paralytic terror, he was suddenly unable to go on. He continued to speak, or thought he did, but then he realized that no more words would come. His mouth worked, but his voice was only a silence that he cast into the silence of the room.

Finally a thin, high, brief, childlike cry of anguish came from him. It was not unlike the one cry that had jolted him from his bed on that July night or the one that, later, had broken his paralysis. He buried his face in his hands and stood, shaking with grief too intense for tears or sobbing, waiting for the seizure to pass.

Ellie was aware that no word or touch could console him.

In glorious canine innocence, Rocky believed any sadness could be relieved by a wagging tail, a cuddle, an affectionate warm lick. He rubbed his flank against his master's legs and swished his tail—and padded away in confusion when none of his tricks worked.

Spencer found himself speaking again almost as unexpectedly as he had found himself *unable* to speak a minute or two ago. "I heard the woman's cry again. From down there at the end of the catacombs. Hardly loud enough to be a scream. More a wail to God."

He started toward the last door, at the end of the catacombs. Ellie and Rocky stayed with him.

"Even as I moved past the dead women in these walls, I was remembering something from six years before, when I'd been eight years old—another cry. My mother's. That spring night, I woke hungry, got out of bed for a snack. There were fresh chocolate-chip cookies in the kitchen jar. I'd been dreaming about them. Went downstairs. The lights were on in some rooms. I thought I'd find my mom or dad along the way. But I didn't see them."

Spencer stopped at the painted black door at the end of the catacombs. Catacombs they were and always would be to him, even with the bodies all disinterred and taken away.

Ellie and Rocky stopped at his side.

"The kitchen was dark. I was going to take as many cookies as I could carry, more than I would ever be allowed to have at one time. I was opening the jar when I heard a scream. Outside. Behind the house. Went to the window by the table. Parted the curtain. My mom was on the lawn. Running back to the house from the barn. He . . . he was be-hind her. He caught her on the patio. Beside the pool. Swung her around. Hit her. In the face. She screamed again. He hit her. Hit and hit. And again. So fast. My mom. Hitting her with his fist. She fell. He kicked her in the head. He kicked my mom in the head. She was quiet. So fast. All over so fast. He looked toward the house. He couldn't see me in the dark kitchen, at the narrow gap in the curtains. He picked her up. Carried her to the barn. I stood at the window awhile. Then I put the cookies back in the jar. Put the lid on. Went back upstairs. Got into bed. Pulled up the covers."

"And didn't remember any of it for six years?" Ellie asked.

Spencer shook his head. "Buried it. That's why I couldn't sleep with the air conditioner running. Deep down where I didn't realize it, I was afraid he would come for me in the night, and I wouldn't hear him because of the air conditioner."

"And then that night, all those years later, your window open, another cry—"

"It reached me deeper than I could understand, drew me out of bed, out to the barn, down here. And when I was walking toward this black door, toward the scream . . ."

Ellie reached to the lever-action knob on the door, to open it, but he stayed her hand.

"Not yet," he said. "I'm not ready to go in there again yet."

. . . barefoot on icy stone, I approach the black door, filled with the fear of what I have seen tonight but also with the fear of what I saw on that spring night when I was eight, which has been repressed since then but all at once comes bursting up from within me. I'm in a state beyond mere terror. No word is adequate for what I feel. I'm at the black door, touching the black door, so black, glossy, like a moonless night sky reflected in the blind face of a pond. I'm nearly as confused as I am terrified, for it seems to me that I'm both eight and fourteen, that I'm opening the door to save not merely the woman who made bloody birds on the vestibule door but to save my mother as well. Time past and time present melt together, and all is one, and I enter the slaughterhouse.

I step into deep space, infinite night around me. The ceiling is ink-black to match the walls, the walls to match the floor, the floor like a chute to Hell. A naked woman, half conscious, lips split and bleeding, rolling her head in listless denial, is manacled to a burnished-steel slab, which seems to float in blackness because its supports also are black. A single light. Directly over the table. In a black fixture. It floats in the void, pin-spotting the steel, like a celestial object or the cruel beam of a godlike inquisitor. My father's wear-ing black. Only his face and hands are visible, as if severed but alive in their own right, as if he's an apparition struggling toward completion. He's extracting a gleaming hypoder-mic syringe from thin air—actually from a drawer beneath the steel slab, a drawer invisi-ble in its blackness-upon-blackness.

I shout, "No, no, no," as I plunge at him, surprising him, so the syringe drops back into the thin air from which it came, and I drive him backward, backward, past the table, out of the focused light, into blackest infinity, until we crash into the wall at the end of the universe. I'm screaming, punching, but I'm fourteen and slender, and he's in his prime, muscular, powerful. I kick him, but I'm barefoot. He lifts me effortlessly, turns with me, floating in space, slams me back-first into the hard blackness, knocking the wind out of me, slams me again. Pain along my spine. Another blackness rises inside me, deeper than the abyss all around. But the woman cries out again, and her voice helps me resist the inner darkness, even if I can't resist my father's far greater strength.

Then he presses me to the wall with his body, holding me off the floor with his hands, his face looming before mine, locks of black hair falling across his forehead, eyes so dark that they seem to be holes through which I'm seeing the blackness behind him. "Don't be afraid, don't, don't be afraid, boy. Baby boy, I won't hurt you. You're my blood, my seed, my creation, my baby. I'd never hurt you. Okay? You understand? You hear me, son, sweet boy, my sweet little Mikey, you hear me? I'm glad you're here. It had to happen sooner or later. Sooner the better. Sweet boy, my boy. I know why you're here, I know why you've come."

I'm dazed and disoriented because of the perfect blackness of that room, because of the horrors in the catacombs, because of being lifted bodily and pounded against the wall. In my condition, his voice is as lulling as fearsome, strangely seductive, and I'm nearly convinced he won't harm me. Somehow I must have misunderstood the things I've seen. He continues speaking in that hypnotic way, words pouring out, giving me no chance to think, Jesus, my mind spinning, him pressing me to the wall, face like a great moon over me.

"I know why you've come. I know what you are. I know why you're here. You're my blood, my seed, my son, no different from me than my reflection in a mirror. Do you hear me, Mikey, sweet baby boy, hear me? I know what you are, why you've come, why you're here, what you need. What you need. I know, I know. You know it too. You knew it when you came through the door and saw her on the table, saw her breasts, saw between her spread legs. You knew, oh, yes, oh, you knew, you wanted it, you knew, you knew what you wanted, what you need, what you are. And it's all right, Mikey, it's all right, baby boy. It's all right what you are, what I am. It's how we were born, each of us, it's what we were meant to be."

Then we're standing at the table, and I'm not sure how we got there, the woman lying in front of me and my father pressing against my back, pinning me to the table. He has a vicious grip on my right wrist, pushes my hand onto her breasts, slides it along her naked body. She's half conscious. Opens her eyes. I'm staring into her eyes, begging her to understand, as he forces my hand everywhere, all the time talking, talking, telling me that I can do anything to her I want, it's right, it's what I was born to do, she's only here to be what I need her to be.

I come far enough out of a daze to struggle briefly, fiercely. Too brief, not fierce enough. His arm's around my throat, choking me, jamming me against the table with his body, choking with his left arm, choking, the taste of blood in my mouth, until I'm weak again. He knows when to release the pressure, before I pass out, because he doesn't want me to pass out. He has other plans. I sag against him, crying now, tears dropping onto the bare skin of the manacled woman.

He lets go of my right hand. I hardly have strength to lift it from the woman. Clink and rattle. Down at my side. I look. One of his disembodied hands. Sorting through the silvery instruments that are floating in the void. He plucks a scalpel from the weightless array of clamps and forceps and needles and blades. Seizes my hand, presses the scalpel into it, folds his hand over mine, grinding my knuckles, forcing me to grip the blade. Below us the woman sees our hands and the shining steel, and she begs us not to hurt her.

"I know what you are," he says, "I know what you are, sweet boy, my baby boy. Just be what you are, just let go and be what you are. You think she's beautiful now? You think she's the most beautiful thing you've ever seen? Oh, just wait until we've shown her how to be more beautiful. Let Daddy show you what you are, what you need, what you

like. Let me show you what fun it is to be what you are. Listen, Mikey, listen now, the same dark river runs through your heart and mine. Listen, and you can hear it, that deep dark river, roaring along, swift and powerful, roaring along. With me now, with me, just let the river carry you along. Be with me now and lift the blade high. See how it shines? Let her see it, see how she sees it, how she has eyes for nothing else. Shining and high in your hand and mine. Feel the power we have over her, over all the weak and foolish ones who can never understand. Be with me, lift it high—"

He has one arm loosely around my throat, my right hand gripped by his, so my left arm is free. Instead of reaching back for him or trying to jam my elbow into him, which won't work, I plant my hand against the stainless steel. Unendurable horror and desperation empower me. With that hand and my whole body, I shove away from the table. Then with my legs. Then my feet. Kicking against the table with both feet. Raging backward into the bastard, unbalancing him. He stumbles, still grinding the hand in which I've got the scalpel, trying to tighten the arm at my throat. But then he falls backward, me atop him. The scalpel clinks away in darkness. My falling weight drives the breath out of him. I'm free. Free. Scramble across the black floor. The door. My right hand aching. No hope of helping the woman. But I can bring help. Police. Someone. She can still be saved. Through the door, onto my feet, tottering, flailing to keep my balance, out into the catacombs, running, running past all the frozen white women, trying to shout. Throat bleeding inside. Raw and raspy. Voice a whisper. No one on the ranch to hear me anyway. Just me, him, the naked woman. But I'm running, running, screaming in a whisper when there's no one to hear.

The expression on Ellie's face cut through Spencer's heart.

He said, "I shouldn't have brought you here, shouldn't have put you through this."

She was gray in the light of the frost-white bulbs. "No, it's what you had to do. If I had any doubts, I have none now. You can't have gone on forever . . . with all of this."

"But that's what I'll have to do. Go on forever with it. And I don't know now why I thought I could find a life. I don't have any right to make you carry this weight with me."

"You can go on with it and have a life . . . as long as you remember it all. And I think now I know what it is you can't remember, where those lost minutes come in."

Spencer couldn't bear to meet her eyes. He looked at Rocky, where the dog sat in deep despondency: head lowered, ears drooping, shivering.

Then he turned his eyes to the black door. Whatever he found beyond it would decide whether he had a future with or without Ellie. He might have neither.

"I didn't try to run back to the house," he said, returning in his mind to that distant night. "He would have caught me before I'd gotten there, before I could use a telephone. Instead, I went up to the vestibule, out of the cupboard, through the file room, and turned right toward the front of the building, into the gallery. By the time I was on the stairs to his studio, I could hear him coming through the darkness behind me. I knew he kept a gun in the lower left-hand drawer of his desk. I'd seen it once when he'd sent me there to get something. Entering the studio, I hit the light switch, ran past his easels, supply cabinets, to the far corner. The desk was L-shaped. I vaulted over it, crashed into the chair, clawed at the drawer, got it open. The gun was there. I didn't know how to use it, whether it had a safety. My right hand was throbbing. I could hardly hold the damn thing, even in both hands. He was off the stairs, into the studio, coming for me, so I pointed and pulled the trigger. It was a revolver. No safety. The recoil about knocked me on my ass."

"And you shot him."

"Not yet. I must've pulled up hard on it when I squeezed the trigger, pulled off target, so the bullet took a chunk out of the ceiling. But I held on to the gun, and he stopped coming. At least he didn't come as fast, not pell-mell anymore. But he was so calm, Ellie, so calm. As if nothing had happened, just my dad, good old dad, a little perturbed with me, you know, but telling me everything was going to be all right, romancing me with that sweet talk like in the black room. So sincere. So hypnotic. And so *sure* that he could make it work if I only gave him time."

Ellie said, "But he didn't know that you'd seen him beat your mother and carry her back to the barn six years before. He might have thought you would put together her death and his secret rooms when you came down from your panic—but until then he thought he had time to bring you around."

Spencer stared at the black door.

"Yeah, maybe that's what he thought. I don't know. He told me that to be like him was to know what life was all about, the true fullness of life without limits or rules. He said I'd enjoy what he could show me how to do. He said I'd already started to enjoy it back in that black room, that I'd been afraid of enjoying it, but that I'd learn it was all right to have that kind of fun."

"But you didn't enjoy it. You were repulsed."

"He said that I did, that he could see I did. His genes ran through me like a river, he said again, through my heart just like a river. Our shared river of destiny, the dark river of our hearts. When he got to the desk, so close I couldn't miss again, I shot him. He *flew* backward from the impact. The spray of blood was horrible. It seemed for sure that I'd killed him, but then I hadn't seen much blood until that night, and a little looked like a lot. He hit the floor, rolled facedown, and lay there, very still. I ran out of the studio, back down here. . . ."

The black door waited.

She didn't speak for a while. He couldn't.

Then Ellie said, "And in that room with the woman . . . those are the minutes you can't remember."

The door. He should have had the old cellars collapsed with explosives. Filled in with dirt. Sealed forever. He shouldn't have left that black door to be opened again.

"Coming back here," he said with difficulty, "I had to carry the revolver in my left hand because of how he'd clenched my right so hard in his, grinding my knuckles together. It was throbbing, full of pain. But the thing is . . . it wasn't just pain I felt in it."

He looked at that hand now. He could see it smaller, younger, the hand of a fourteen-year-old boy.

"I could still feel . . . the smoothness of the woman's skin, from when he'd forced my hand over her body. Feel the roundness of her breasts. The resiliency and fullness of them. The flatness of her belly. The crispness of pubic hair . . . the heat of her. All those feelings were in my hand, *still* in my hand, as real as the pain."

"You were only a boy," she said without any evidence of disgust. "It was the first time you'd ever seen a woman undressed, the first time you'd ever touched a woman. My God, Spencer, in supercharged circumstances like that, not just terrifying but so emotional in every way, so confusing, such a damned *primal* moment—touching her was bound to reach you on every level, all at the same time. Your father knew that. He was a clever sonofabitch. He tried to use your turmoil to manipulate you. But it didn't *mean* anything."

She was too understanding and forgiving. In this blighted world, those who were too forgiving paid a cruel price for a Christian bent.

"So, I came back through the catacombs, with the dead all around me in the walls, with the memory of my father's blood, and *still* with the feel of her breasts in my hand. The vivid memory of how rubbery her nipples had felt against my palm—"

"Don't do this to yourself."

"Never lie to the dog," Spencer said, with no humor this time, but with a bitterness and rage that frightened him.

A fury welled in his heart, blacker than the door before him. He was no more able to shake it off than he had been able, that July, to shake from his hand the remembered warmth and shapes and sensuous textures of the naked woman. His rage was undirected, and that was why it had been intensifying in his deep unconscious for sixteen years. He'd never been sure if it should be turned against his father or against himself. Lacking a target, he had denied the existence of that rage, repressed it. Now, condensed into a distillate of purest wrath, it was eating through him as corrosively as any acid.

". . . with the vivid memory of how her nipples had felt against my palm," he continued, but in a voice that shook equally with anger and with fear, "I came back here. To this door. Opened it. Went into the black room. . . . And the next thing I remember is walking *away* from here, the door falling shut behind me. . . ."

. . . barefoot, walking back through the catacombs, with a void in my memory more perfectly black than the room behind me, not sure where I've just been, what's just happened. Passing the women in the walls. Women. Girls. Mothers. Sisters. Their silent screams. Perpetual screams. Where is God? What does God care? Why has He abandoned them all here? Why has He abandoned me? A magnified spider shadow scurries across their plaster faces, along the looping shadow of the light cord. As I'm passing the new niche in the wall, the niche prepared for the woman in the black room, my father comes out of that hole, out of the dark earth, splattered with blood, staggering, wheezing in agony, but so fast, so fast, as fast as the spider. The hot flash of steel out of shadows. Knife. He sometimes paints still lifes of knives, making them glow as if they were holy relics. Flashing steel, flashing pain across my face. Drop the gun. Hands to my face. Flap of cheek hanging off my chin. My bare teeth against my fingers, a grin of teeth exposed along the whole side of my face. Tongue leaping against my fingers in the open side of my face. And he slashes again. Misses. Falls. He's too weak to get up. Backing away from him, I pull my cheek in place, blood streaming between my fingers, running down my throat. I'm trying to hold my face together. Oh, God, trying to hold my face together and running, running. Behind me, he's too weak to get off the floor but not too weak to call after me: "Did you kill her, did you kill her, baby boy, did you like it, did you kill her?"

Spencer still could not look directly at Ellie and might never be able to look directly at her again, not eye-to-eye. He could see her peripherally, and he knew that she was crying quietly. Crying for him, eyes flooded, face glistening.

He couldn't cry for himself. He had never been able to let go and fully purge his pain, because he didn't know if he was worthy of tears, of hers or his own or anyone's tears.

All he could feel now was that rage, which was still without a target.

"The police found the woman dead in the black room," he said.

"Spencer, *he* killed her." Her voice trembled. "It must have been him. The police said it was him. You were the boy hero."

Staring at the black door, he shook his head. "When did he kill her, Ellie? *When?* He dropped the scalpel when we both fell to the floor. Then I ran, and he ran after me."

"But there were other scalpels, other sharp instruments in the drawer. You said so yourself. He grabbed one and killed her. It would only have taken seconds. Only a few seconds, Spencer. The bastard knew you couldn't get far, that he'd catch up with you. And he was so *excited* after his struggle with you that he couldn't wait, *shaking* with excitement, so he had to kill her then, hard and fast and brutally."

"Later, he's on the floor, after he slashed me, and I'm running away, and he's calling after me, asking if I killed her, if I liked killing her."

"Oh, he knew. He *knew* she was dead before you ever came back here to free her. Maybe he was insane and maybe he wasn't, but he was sure as hell the purest evil that ever walked. Don't you see? He hadn't converted you to his way, and he hadn't been able to kill you, either, so all that was left for him was to ruin your life if he could, to plant that seed of doubt in your mind. You were a boy, half blind with panic and terror, confused, and he knew your turmoil. He understood, and he used it against you, just for the sheer, sick *fun* of it."

For more than half his lifetime, Spencer had tried to convince himself of the scenario that she had just painted for him. But the void in his memory remained. The continued amnesia seemed to argue that the truth was different from what he desperately wished had happened.

"Go," he said thickly. "Run for the truck, drive away from here, go to Denver. I shouldn't have brought you here. I can't ask you to come any farther with me."

"I'm here. I'm not leaving."

"I mean it. Get out."

"No way."

"Get out. Take the dog."

"No."

Rocky was whining, shaking, huddling against a column of blood-dark brick, in torment as racking as any Spencer had ever seen.

"Take him. He likes you."

"I'm not going." Through tears, she said, "This is *my* decision, damn it, and you can't make it for me!"

He turned on her, seized handfuls of her leather jacket, all but lifted her off the floor, frantically trying to force her to understand. In his rage and fear and self-loathing, he had managed, after all, to look her in the eyes one more time. "For Christ's sake, after all you've seen and heard, don't you get it? I left part of myself in that room, that abattoir where he did his butchering, left something there I couldn't live with. What in the name of God could that be, huh? Something *worse* than the catacombs, *worse* than all the rest of it. It has to be worse because I remembered all the rest of it! If I go back in there and remember what I did to her, there'll be no forgetting ever again, no hiding from it anymore. And this is a memory . . . like fire. It's going to burn through me. Whatever's left, whatever isn't burned away, it won't be *me* anymore, Ellie, not after I know what I did to her. And then who're you going to be down here with, down here in this godforsaken place *alone* with?"

She raised one hand to his face and traced the line of his scar, though he tried to flinch away from her. She said, "If I was blind, if I'd never seen your face, I already know you well enough that you could still break my heart."

"Oh, Ellie, don't."

"I'm not leaving."

"Ellie, please."

"No."

He couldn't direct his rage at her, either, especially not at her. He let go of her. Stood with his hands at his sides. Fourteen again. Weak with his outrage. Afraid. Lost.

She put her hand on the lever-action door handle.

"Wait." He withdrew the SIG 9mm pistol from under the waistband of his blue jeans, disengaged the safety, jacked a bullet into the chamber, and held the piece out to her. "You should have both guns." She started to object, but he cut her off. "Keep the pistol in your hand. Don't get too close to me in there."

"Spencer, whatever you remember, it's not going to turn you into your father, not in an instant, no matter how terrible it is."

"How do you know that? I've spent sixteen years picking at it, prying and poking, trying to dig it out of the darkness, but it won't come. Now if it comes . . ."

She engaged the safety on the pistol.

"Ellie—"

"I don't want it to go off accidentally."

"My father wrestled on the floor with me and tickled me and made funny faces for me when I was little. Played ball with me. And when I wanted to develop my drawing ability, he patiently taught technique to me. But before and after . . . he came down here, that same man, and he tortured women, girls, hour after hour, for days in some cases. He moved with ease between this world and the one above."

"I'm not going to keep a gun ready, point a gun at you, like I'm afraid you're some kind of monster, when I know you're not. Please, Spencer. Please don't ask me to do that. Let's just finish this."

In the deep quiet at the end of the catacombs, he took a moment to prepare himself. Nothing moved anywhere in that long room. No rats, misshapen or otherwise, dwelt there anymore. The Dresmunds had been instructed to eradicate them with poison.

Spencer opened the black door.

He switched on the light.

He hesitated on the threshold, then went inside.

Miserable though the dog was, he padded into that room as well. Maybe he was afraid to be alone in the catacombs. Or maybe this time his misery *was* entirely a reaction to his master's state of mind, in which case he knew that his company was needed. He stayed close to Spencer.

Ellie entered last, and the weighted door closed behind her.

The abattoir was nearly as disorienting now as it had been on that night of scalpels and knives. The stainless steel table was gone. The chamber was empty. The unrelieved blackness allowed no point of reference, so one moment the room appeared to be hardly larger than a casket, but in the next moment it seemed infinitely larger than it actually was. The only light was still the tightly focused bulb in the black ceiling fixture.

The Dresmunds had been instructed to keep all lights functional. They had not been told to clean the abattoir, yet only the thinnest film of dust veiled the walls, no doubt because the room was not ventilated and was always shut up tight.

It was a time capsule, sealed for sixteen years, containing not the memorabilia of bygone days but lost memories.

The place affected Spencer even more powerfully than he had expected. He could see the glimmer of the scalpel as if it hung in the air even now.

. . . barefoot, carrying the revolver in my left hand, I hurry down from the studio where I shot my father, through the back of the cupboard into a world not anything like the one behind the wardrobe in those books by C. S. Lewis, through the catacombs, not daring to look left or right, because those dead women seem to be straining to break out of their plaster. I have the crazy fear that they might pull loose as if the plaster is still wet, come for me, take me into one of the walls with them. I'm my father's son and I deserve to choke on cold wet plaster, have it squeezed into my nostrils and poured down my throat, until I'm as one with the figures in the tableaux, unbreathing, a harbor for the rats. My heart's knocking so hard that each beat makes my vision darken slightly, briefly, as if the surges in blood pressure will burst vessels in my eyes. I feel each beat in my right hand too. The pain in my knuckles throbs, lub-dub, three small hearts in every finger. But I love the pain. I want more pain. Back in the vestibule and descending the stairs into the room of blue light, I repeatedly rapped the swollen knuckles of that hand with the revolver that I held in the other. Now I rap them hard again in the catacombs, to drive out all feeling but pain. Because . . . because equal to the pain, dear Jesus God Almighty, I still have it on my hand, like a stain on my hand: the smoothness of the woman's skin. The full curves and warm resiliency of her breasts, turgid nipples rubbing my palm. The flatness of belly, the tautness of muscles as she strains against the manacles. The lubricious heat into which he forces my fingers against all my resistance, against her terrible half-dazed protest. Her eyes were locked with mine. Pleading with her eyes. The misery of her eyes. But the traitor hand has its own sense memory, unshakable, and it makes me sick. All the feelings in my hand make me sick, and some of the feelings in my heart. I have such disgust, loathing, such fear of myself. But other feelings too—unclean emotions in harmony with the excitement of the hateful hand. And at the door to the black room I stop, lean against the wall, and vomit. Sweating. Shuddering with chills. When I turn away from the mess, with only

my stomach purged, I force myself to grab the lever-action handle with my injured hand, making pain shoot up my forearm as I violently jerk open the door. And then I'm inside, into the black room again.

Don't look at her. Don't. Don't! Don't look at her naked. No right to look at her naked. This can be done with my eyes averted, edging to the table, aware of her only as a flesh-colored form out of the corner of my eye, floating in the darkness over there. "It's okay," I tell her, my voice so hoarse from the choking, "it's okay, lady, he's dead, lady, I shot him. I'll let you loose, get you out of here, don't be afraid." And then I realize I haven't any idea where to find the keys to the manacles. "Lady, I don't have a key, no key, got to go for help, call the cops. But it's okay, he's dead." No sound from her there, out of the corner of my eye. She'd been dazed from the blows to her head, only half conscious, and now she's passed out. But I don't want her to wake up after I've gone and be alone and afraid. I remember the look in her eyes—was it the same look in my mother's eyes at the very end?—and I don't want her to be so afraid when she wakes and thinks he's coming back for her. That's all, that's all. I just don't want her to be afraid, so I'm going to have to bring her around, shake her, wake her up, make her understand that he's dead and that I'll be back with help. I edge to the table, trying not to look at her body, going to look only at her face. A smell hits me. Terrible. Nauseating. The blackness is dizzying again. I put one hand out. Against the table. To steady myself. It's the right hand, still remembering the curve of her breasts; and I put it down in a warm, viscous, slippery mass that wasn't there before. I look at her face. Mouth open. Eyes. Dead blank eyes. He's been at her. Two slashes. Vicious. Brutal. All of his great strength behind the blade. Her throat. Her abdomen. I spin away from the table, away from the woman, collide with the wall. Wiping my right hand on the black wall, calling for Jesus and for my mother, and saying "lady please lady please," as if she could mend herself by an act of will if only she'd listen to my pleas. Wiping wiping wiping the hand, front and back, on the wall, not only wiping off what I've pressed it into but wiping off the way she felt when she was alive, wiping hard, harder, angrily, furiously, until my hand seems on fire, until there's nothing in my hand but pain. And then I stand there awhile. Not quite sure where I am any longer. I know there's a door. I go to it. Through it. Oh, yes. The catacombs.

Spencer stood in the center of the black room, his right hand in front of his face, staring at it in the hard projected light, as though it was not at all the same hand that had been at the end of his wrist for the past sixteen years.

Almost wonderingly, he said, "I would've saved her."

"I know that," Ellie said.

"But I couldn't save anyone."

"And that's not your fault, either."

For the first time since that ancient July, he thought he might have the capacity to accept, not soon but eventually, that he had no greater weight of guilt to carry than any other man. Darker memories, a more intimate experience of the human capacity for evil, knowledge that other people would never want forced on them as it had been forced on him—all of that, yes, but not a greater weight of guilt.

Rocky barked. Twice. Loud.

Startled, Spencer said, "He never barks."

Slipping off the safety on the SIG, Ellie swung toward the door as it flew open. She wasn't quick enough.

The genial-looking man—the same who had broken into the Malibu cabin—burst into the black room. He had a silencer-fitted Beretta in his right hand, and he was smiling and squeezing off a shot as he came.

Ellie took the round in her right shoulder, squealed in pain. Her hand spasmed and released the pistol, and she was slammed into the wall. She sagged against the blackness, gasping with the shock of being shot, realized the Micro Uzi was sliding off her shoulder, and made a grab for it with her left hand. It slipped through her fingers, hit the floor, and spun away from her.

The pistol was gone, clattering beyond reach across the floor toward the man with the Beretta. But Spencer went for the Uzi even as it was falling.

The smiling man fired again. The bullet sparked off the stone inches from Spencer's reaching hand, forcing him to pull back, and it ricocheted around the room.

The shooter seemed unfazed by the whine of the bouncing slug, as if he led such a charmed life that his safety was a foregone conclusion.

"I'd prefer not to shoot you," he said. "I didn't want to shoot Ellie, either. I've other plans for both of you. But one more wrong move—and you'll take away all my choices. Now kick the Uzi over here."

Instead of doing what he had been told, Spencer went to Ellie. He touched her face and looked at her shoulder. "How bad?"

She was clutching her wound, trying not to reveal the extent of her pain, but the truth was in her eyes. "Okay, I'm okay, it's nothing," she said, yet Spencer saw her glance at the whimpering dog when she lied.

The heavy door to the abattoir hadn't fallen shut. Someone was holding it open. The shooter stepped aside to let him enter. The second man was Steven Ackblom.

Roy was certain that this would be one of the most interesting nights of his life. It might even be as singular as the first night that he had spent with Eve, although he wouldn't betray her even by hoping that it might be better. This was an incredible confluence of events: the capture of the woman at last; the chance to learn what Grant might know about any organized opposition to the agency, then the pleasure of putting that troubled man out of his misery; a unique opportunity to be with one of the great artists of the century as he turned his hand to the medium that had made him famous; and when it was done, perhaps even Eleanor's perfect eyes would be salvageable. Cosmic forces were at work in the design of such a night.

When Steven entered the room, the expression on Spencer Grant's face was worth the loss of at least two helicopters and a satellite. Anger darkened his face, twisted his features. It was a rage so pure that it possessed a fascinating beauty all its own. Enraged, Grant nonetheless shrank back with the woman.

"Hello, Mikey," Steven said. "How've you been?"

The son—once Mikey, now Spencer—was unable to speak.

"I've been well but . . . in boring circumstances," said the artist.

Spencer Grant remained silent. Roy was chilled by the expression in the ex-cop's eyes.

Steven looked around at the black ceiling, walls, floor. "They blamed me for the woman you did here that night. I took the fall on that one too. For you, baby boy."

"He never touched her," Ellie Summerton said.

"Didn't he?" the artist asked.

"We know he didn't."

Steven sighed with regret. "Well, no, he didn't. But he was *that* close to doing her." He held up his thumb and forefinger, only a quarter of an inch apart. "That close."

"He was never close at all," she said, but Grant remained unable to speak.

"Wasn't he?" Steven said. "Well, I think he was. I think if I'd been a little smarter, if I'd encouraged him to drop his pants and climb on top of her first, then he would have been happy to take the scalpel afterward. He'd have been more in the spirit of things then, you see."

"You're not my father," Grant said emptily.

"You're wrong about that, my sweet boy. Your mother was a firm believer in marital vows. There was only ever me with her. I'm sure of that. In the end, here in this room, she was able to keep not the slightest secret from me."

Roy thought that Grant was going to come across the room with all the fury of a bull, heedless of bullets.

"What a pathetic little dog," Steven said. "Look at him shaking, hanging his head. Perfect pet for you, Mikey. He reminds me of the way you acted here that night. When I gave you the chance to transcend, you were too much of a pussy to seize it."

The woman appeared to be furious too, perhaps even angrier than she was afraid, though both. Her eyes had never been more beautiful.

"How long ago that was, Mikey, and what a new world this is," Steven said, taking a couple of steps toward his son and the woman, forcing them to shrink back farther. "I was so ahead of my time, so much deeper into the avant-garde than I ever fully realized. The newspapers called me insane. I ought to demand a retraction, don't you think? Now, the streets are crawling with men more violent than I ever was. Gangs have gunfights anywhere they please, and babies get shot down on kindergarten playgrounds—and nobody does anything about it. The enlightened are too busy worrying that you're going to eat a food additive that'll shave three and a half days off your lifespan. Did you read about the FBI agents up in Idaho, where they shot an unarmed woman while she was *holding* her baby, and shot her fourteen-year-old son in the back when he tried to run from them? Killed them both. You see that in the papers, Mikey? And now men like Roy here hold very responsible positions in government. Why, I could be a fabulously successful politician these days. I've got everything it takes. I'm not insane, Mikey. Daddy's not insane and never was. Evil, yes, I embrace that. From earliest childhood, I had it all in that regard. I've always liked to have fun. But I'm not crazy, baby boy. Roy here, guardian of public safety, protector of the republic—why, Mikey, *he's* a raving lunatic."

Roy smiled at Steven, wondering what joke he was setting up. The artist was endlessly amusing. But Steven had moved so far into the room that Roy couldn't see his face, only the back of his head.

"Mikey, you should hear Roy rant on about compassion, about the poor quality of life that so many people live and shouldn't have to, about reducing population by ninety percent to save the environment. He loves everybody. He understands their suffering. He weeps for them. And when he has a chance, he'll blow them to kingdom come to make society a little nicer. It's a hoot, Mikey. And they give him helicopters and limousines and all the cash he needs and flunkies with big guns in shoulder holsters. They let him run around making a better world. And this man, Mikey, I'm telling you, he's got worms in his brain."

Playing along with it, Roy said, "Worms in my brain, big old slimy worms in my brain."

"See," Steven said. "He's a funny guy, Roy is. Only wants to be liked. Most people do like him too. Don't they, Roy?"

Roy sensed that they were coming to the punch line. "Well, now, Steven, I don't want to be bragging about myself—"

"See!" Steven said. "He's a modest man too. Modest and kind and compassionate. Doesn't everybody like you, Roy? Come on. Don't be so bashful."

"Well, yeah, most people like me," Roy admitted, "but that's because I treat everyone with respect."

"That's right!" Steven said. He laughed. "Roy treats everyone with the same solemn respect. Why, he's an equal-opportunity killer. Evenhanded treatment for everyone from a presidential aide wasted in a Washington park and then made to look like a suicide . . . to an ordinary paraplegic shot down to spare him the daily struggle. Roy doesn't understand that these things have to be done for *fun*. Only for fun. Otherwise, it's insane, it really is, to do it for some noble *purpose*. He's so solemn about it, thinks of himself as a dreamer, a

man of ideals. But he does uphold his ideals—I'll give him that much. He plays no fa-
vorites. He's the least prejudiced, most egalitarian, foaming-at-the-mouth lunatic who
ever lived. Don't you agree, Mr. Rink?"

Rink? Roy didn't want Rink or Fordyce hearing any of this, for God's sake, seeing any
of this. They were muscle, not true insiders. He turned to the door, wondering why he
hadn't heard it open—and saw that no one was there. Then he heard the scrape of the Micro Uzi against concrete as Steven Ackblom plucked it off the floor, and he knew what was
happening.

Too late.

The Uzi chattered in Steven's hands. Bullets tore into Roy. He fell, rolled, and tried to
fire back. Though he was still holding the gun, he couldn't make his finger squeeze the
trigger. Paralyzed. He was paralyzed.

Over the zinging-whining ricochets, something snarled viciously: a sound out of a horror movie, echoing off the black walls with more blood-curdling effect than the bullets.
For a second Roy couldn't understand what it was, where it was coming from. He almost
thought that it was Grant because of the fury in the scarred man's face, but then he saw
the beast exploding through the air toward Steven. The artist tried to swing around, away
from Roy, and cut down the attack dog. But the hellish thing was already on him, driving
him backward into the wall. It tore at his hands. He dropped the Uzi. Then it was climbing him, snapping at his face, at his throat.

Steven was screaming.

Roy wanted to tell him that the most dangerous people of all—and evidently the most
dangerous dogs as well—were those who had been beaten down the hardest. When even
their pride and hope had been taken from them, when they were driven into the last of all
corners, then they had nothing to lose. To avoid producing such desperate men, applying
compassion to the suffering as early as possible was the right thing to do for them, the
moral thing to do—but also the *wisest* thing to do. He couldn't tell the artist any of that,
however, because in addition to being paralyzed, he found that he couldn't speak either.

"Rocky, no! Off! Rocky, off!"

Spencer pulled the dog by the collar and struggled with him until at last Rocky obeyed.

The artist was sitting on the floor. His legs were drawn up defensively. His arms
crossed over his face, and he was bleeding from his hands.

Ellie had picked up the Uzi. Spencer took it from her.

He saw that her left ear was bleeding. "You've been hit again."

"Ricochet. Grazed," she said, and this time she could have met the dog's eyes
forthrightly.

Spencer looked down at the thing that was his father.

The murderous bastard had lowered his arms from his face. He was infuriatingly calm.
"They've got men posted from one end of the property to the other. Nobody here in the
building, but once you step outside, you won't get far. You can't get away, Mikey."

Ellie said, "They won't have heard the gunfire. Not if no one above-ground ever heard
the screams from this place. We still have a chance."

The wife-killer shook his head. "Not unless you take me and the amazing Mr. Miro
here."

"He's dead," Ellie said.

"Doesn't matter. He's more useful dead. Never know what a man like him might do, so
I'd be edgy if we had to carry him out of here while he was alive. We take him between us,
baby boy, you and me. They'll see he's hurt, but they won't know how badly. Maybe they
value him highly enough to hold back."

"I don't want your help," Spencer said.

"Of course you don't, but you need it," his father said. "They won't have moved your truck. Their instructions were to stay back, at a distance, just maintain surveillance, until they heard from Roy. So we can move him to the truck, between us, and they won't be sure what's going on." He rose painfully to his feet.

Spencer backed away from him, as he would have backed away from something that had appeared in a chalk pentagram in response to the summons of a sorcerer. Rocky retreated as well, growling.

Ellie was in the doorway, leaning against the jamb. She was out of the way, reasonably safe.

Spencer had the dog—what a dog!—and he had the gun. His father had no weapon, and he was hampered by his bitten hands. Yet Spencer was as afraid of him as he had ever been on that July night or since.

"Do we need him?" he asked Ellie.

"Hell, no."

"You're sure whatever you were doing with the computer, it's going to work?"

"More sure of that than we could ever be sure of him."

To his father, Spencer said, "What happens to you if I leave you to them?"

The artist examined his bitten hands with interest, studying the punctures not as though concerned about the damage but as though inspecting a flower or another beautiful object that he had never seen before. "What happens to me, Mikey? You mean when I go back to prison? I do a little reading to pass the time. I still paint some—did you know? I think I'll paint a portrait of your little bitch there in the doorway, as I imagine she'd look with no clothes, and as I *know* she'd look if I'd ever had the chance to put her on a table here and make her realize her true potential. I see that disgusts you, baby boy. But really, it's such a small pleasure to allow me, considering she'll never have been more beautiful than on my canvas. My way of sharing in her with you." He sighed and looked up from his hands, as if unperturbed by the pain. "What happens if you leave me to them, Mikey? You'll be condemning me to a life that's a waste of my talent and joie de vivre, a barren and tiny existence behind gray walls. That's what happens to me, you ungrateful little snot."

"You said they were worse than you."

"Well, I know what I am."

"What's that mean?"

"Self-awareness is a virtue in which they're lacking."

"They let you out."

"Temporarily. A consultation."

"They'll let you out again, won't they?"

"Let's hope it doesn't take another sixteen years." He smiled, as if his bleeding hands had suffered only paper cuts. "But, yes, we're in an age that's giving birth to a new breed of fascists, and I would hope that from time to time they might find my expertise useful to them."

"You're figuring you won't even go back," Spencer said. "You think you'll get away from them tonight, don't you?"

"Too many of them, Mikey. Big men with big guns in shoulder holsters. Big black Chrysler limousines. Helicopters whenever they want them. No, no, I'll probably have to bide my time until another consultation."

"Lying, mother-killing sonofabitch," Spencer said.

"Oh, don't try to frighten me," his father said. "I remember sixteen years ago, this room. You were a little pussy then, Mikey, and you're a little pussy now. That's some scar you've got there, baby boy. How long did you have to recuperate before you could eat solid foods?"

"I saw you beat her to the ground by the swimming pool."

"If confession makes you feel good, go right ahead."

"I was in the kitchen for cookies, heard her scream."

"Did you get your cookies?"

"When she was down, you kicked her in the head."

"Don't be tedious, Mikey. You were never the son I might have wished to have, but you were never tedious before."

The man was unshakably calm, self-possessed. He had an aura of power that was daunting—but no look of madness whatsoever in his eyes. He could preach a sermon and be thought a priest. He claimed that he wasn't mad, but evil.

Spencer wondered if that could be true.

"Mikey, you really owe me, you know. Without me, you wouldn't exist. No matter what you think of me, I *am* your father."

"Without you, I wouldn't exist. Yeah. And that would be okay. That would be fine. But without my mother—I might have been exactly like you. It's her I owe. Only her. She's the one who gave me whatever salvation I can ever have."

"Mikey, Mikey, you simply can't make me feel guilty. You want me to put on a big sad face? Okay, I'll put on a big sad face. But your mother was nothing to me. Nothing but useful cover for a while, a helpful deceit with nice knockers. But she was too curious. And when I had to bring her down here, she was just like all the others—although less exciting than most."

"Well, just the same," Spencer said, "this is for her." He fired a short burst from the Uzi, blowing his father to Hell.

There were no ricochets to worry about. Every bullet found its mark, and the dead man carried them down to the floor with him, in a pool of the darkest blood that Spencer had ever seen.

Rocky leaped in surprise at the gunfire, then cocked his head and studied Steven Ackblom. He sniffed him as if the scent was far different from any he had encountered before. As Spencer stared down at his dead father, he was aware of Rocky gazing up curiously at him. Then the dog joined Ellie at the door.

When at last he went to the door too, Spencer was afraid to look at Ellie.

"I wondered if you would actually be able to do it," she said. "If you hadn't, I'd have had to, and the recoil would have hurt like hell with this arm."

He met her eyes. She wasn't trying to make him feel better about what he had done. She had meant what she'd said.

"I didn't enjoy it," he said.

"I would have."

"I don't think so."

"Immensely."

"I didn't hate doing it, either."

"Why should you? You have to stomp a cockroach when you get a chance."

"How's your shoulder?"

"Hurts like hell, but it's not bleeding all that much." She flexed her right hand, wincing. "I'll still be able to work the computer keyboard with both hands. I just hope to God I can work it fast enough."

The three of them hurried through the depopulated catacombs, toward the blue room, the yellow vestibule, and the strange world above.

Roy had no pain. In fact, he could feel nothing at all. Which made it easier for him to play dead. He feared that they would finish him off if they realized he was alive. Spencer Grant, aka Michael Ackblom, was indisputably as insane as his father and capable of any atrocity. Therefore, Roy closed his eyes and used his paralysis to his advantage.

After the singular opportunity that he had given the artist, Roy was disappointed in the man. Such blithe treachery.

More to the point, Roy was disappointed in himself. He had badly misjudged Steven Ackblom. The brilliance and sensitivity that he had perceived in the artist had been no illusion; however, he had allowed himself to be deceived into believing that what he saw was the whole story. He had never glimpsed the dark side.

Of course he was always so quick to *like* people, just as the artist had said. And he was acutely aware of everyone's suffering, within moments of having met them. That was one of his virtues, and he would not have wanted to be a less tenderhearted person. He had been deeply moved by Ackblom's plight: such a witty and talented man, locked in a cell for the rest of his life. Compassion had blinded Roy to the full truth.

He still had hope of coming out of this alive and seeing Eve again. He didn't *feel* as though he were dying. Of course, he was unable to feel much of anything at all, below the neck.

He took comfort from the knowledge that if he were to die, he would go to the great cosmic party and be welcomed by so many friends whom he'd sent ahead of him with great tenderness. For Eve's sake, he wanted to live, but to some extent he longed for that higher plane where there was a single sex, where everyone had the same radiant-blue skin color, where every person was perfectly beautiful in an androgynous blue way, where no one was dumb, no one too smart, where everyone had identical living quarters and wardrobes and footwear, where there was high-quality mineral water and fresh fruit for the asking. He would have to be introduced to everyone he had known in this world, because he wouldn't recognize them in their new perfect, identical blue bodies. That seemed sad: not to see people as they had been. On the other hand, he wouldn't want to spend eternity with his dear mother if he had to look at her face all bashed in as it had been just after he had sent her on to that better place.

He tried speaking and found that his voice had returned. "Are you dead, Steven, or are you faking?"

Across the black room, slumped against a black wall, the artist didn't answer.

"I think they're gone and won't be coming back. So if you're faking, it's all clear now."

No reply.

"Well, then you've gone over, and all the bad in you was left here. I'm sure you're full of remorse now and wish you'd been more compassionate toward me. So if you could exert a little of your cosmic power, reach through the veil, and work a little miracle so I can walk again, I believe that would be appropriate."

The room remained silent.

He still couldn't feel anything below his neck.

"I hope I don't need the services of a spirit channeler to get your attention," Roy said. "That would be inconvenient."

Silence. Stillness. Cold white light in a tight cone, blazing down through the center of that encapsulating blackness.

"I'll just wait. I'm sure that reaching through the veil takes a lot of effort."

Any moment now, a miracle.

Opening the driver's door of the pickup, Spencer was suddenly afraid that he had lost the keys. They were in his jacket pocket.

By the time Spencer got behind the wheel and started the engine, Rocky was in the backseat, and Ellie was already in the other front seat. The motel pillow was across her thighs, the laptop was on the pillow, and she was waiting to power up the computer.

When the engine turned over and Ellie switched on the laptop, she said, "Don't go anywhere yet."

"We're sitting ducks here."

"I've got to get back into Godzilla."

"Godzilla."

"The system I was in before we got out of the truck."

"What's Godzilla?"

"As long as we're just sitting here, they probably won't do anything except watch us and wait. But as soon as we start to move, they'll have to act, and I don't want them coming at us until we're ready for them."

"What's Godzilla?"

"Ssshhh. I have to concentrate."

Spencer looked out his side window at the fields and hills. The snow didn't glow as brightly as it had earlier, because the moon was waning. He had been trained to spot clandestine surveillance in both urban and rural settings, but he could see no signs of the agency observers, though he knew they were out there.

Ellie's fingers were busy. Keys clicked. Data and diagrams played across the screen.

Focusing on the winterscape once more, Spencer remembered snow forts, castles, tunnels, carefully tamped sled runs. More important: In addition to the physical details of old playgrounds in the snow, he faintly recalled the joy of laboring on those projects and of setting out on those boyhood adventures. Recollections of innocent times. Childhood fantasies. Happiness. They were faint memories. Faint but perhaps recoverable with practice. For a long time, he hadn't been able to remember even a single moment of his childhood with fondness. The events in that July not only had changed his life forever thereafter but had changed his perception of what his life had been like before the owl, the rats, the scalpel, and the knife.

Sometimes his mother had helped him build castles of snow. He remembered times when she'd gone sledding with him. They especially enjoyed going out after dusk. The night was so crisp, the world so mysterious in black and white. With billions of stars above, you could pretend that the sled was a rocket and you were off to other worlds.

He thought of his mother's grave in Denver, and he suddenly wanted to go there for the first time since his grandparents had moved him to San Francisco. He wanted to sit on the ground beside her and reminisce about nights when they had gone sledding under a billion stars, when her laughter had carried like music across the white fields.

Rocky stood on the floor in back, paws planted on the front seat, and craned his head forward to lick affectionately at the side of Spencer's face.

He turned and stroked the dog's head and neck. "Mr. Rocky Dog, more powerful than a locomotive, faster than a speeding bullet, able to leap tall buildings in a single bound, terror of all cats and Dobermans. Where did *that* come from, hmmm?" He scratched behind the dog's ears. Then with his fingertips, he gently explored the crushed cartilage that ensured the left ear would always droop. "Way back in the bad old days, did the person who did this to you look anything like the man back there in the black room? Or did you recognize a scent? Do the evil ones smell alike, pal?" Rocky luxuriated in the attention. "Mr. Rocky Dog, furry hero, ought to have his own comic book. Show us some teeth, give us a thrill." Rocky just panted. "Come on, show us some teeth," Spencer said, growling and skinning his lips back from his own teeth. Rocky liked the game, bared his own teeth, and they went *grrrrrr* at each other, muzzle to muzzle.

"Ready," Ellie said.

"Thank God," he said, "I just ran out of things to do to keep from going nuts."

"You've got to help me spot them," she said. "I'll be looking too, but I might not see one of them."

Indicating the screen, he said, "That's Godzilla?"

"No. This is the gameboard that Godzilla and I are both going to play with. It's a grid of the five acres immediately around the house and barn. Each of these tiny grid blocks is six meters on a side. I just hope to God my entry data, those property maps and county records, were accurate enough. I know they're not dead-on, not by a long shot, but let's pray they're close. See this green shape? That's the house. See this? The barn. Here are the stables down toward the end of the driveway. This blinking dot—that's us. See this line—that's the county road, where we want to be."

"Is this based on one of the video games you invented?"

"No, this is nasty reality," she said. "And whatever happens, Spencer . . . I love you. I can't imagine anything better than spending the rest of my life with you. I just hope it's going to be more than five minutes."

He had started to put the truck in gear. Her frank expression of her feelings made him hesitate, because he wanted to kiss her now, here, for the first time, in case it was the last time too.

Then he froze and stared at her in amazement as comprehension came. "Godzilla's looking straight down at us right now, isn't he?"

"Yeah."

"It's a satellite? And you've hijacked it?"

"Been saving these codes for a day when I was in a really tight corner, no other way out, because I'll never get a chance to use them again. When we're out of here, when I let go of Godzilla, they'll shut it down and reprogram."

"What does it do besides look down?"

"Remember the movies?"

"Godzilla movies?"

"His white-hot, glowing breath?"

"You're making this up."

"He had halitosis that melted tanks."

"Oh, my God."

"Now or never," she said.

"Now," he said, putting the truck into reverse, wanting to get it over with before he had any more time to think about it.

He switched on the headlights, backed away from the barn, and headed around the building, retracing the route that they had taken from the county road.

"Not too fast," she said. "It'll pay to tiptoe out of here, believe me."

Spencer let up on the accelerator.

Drifting along now. Easing past the front of the barn. The other branch of the driveway over there. The backyard to the right. The swimming pool.

A brilliant white searchlight fixed them from an open second-floor window of the house, sixty yards to their right and forty yards ahead. Spencer was blinded when he looked in that direction, and he could not see whether there were sharpshooters with rifles at any of the other windows.

Ellie's fingers rattled the keys.

He glanced over and saw a yellow indicator line on the display screen. It represented a swath about two meters wide and twenty-four meters long, between them and the house.

Ellie pressed ENTER.

"Squint!" she said, and in the same moment Spencer shouted, "Rocky, down!"

Out of the stars came a blue-white incandescence. It was not as fierce as he had expected, marginally brighter than the spotlight from the house, but it was infinitely stranger than anything he had ever seen—above-ground. The beam was crisply defined along the edges, and it seemed not to be radiating light as much as *containing* it, holding an atomic fire within a skin as thin as the surface tension on a pond. A bone-vibrating hum accompanied it, like electronic feedback from huge stadium speakers, and a sudden turbulence of air. As the light moved on a course that Ellie had laid out for it (two meters wide, twenty-four meters long, between them and the house but approaching neither), a roar arose similar to the subterranean grumble of the few grinding-type earthquakes that Spencer had ridden out over the years, although this was far louder. The earth shook hard enough to rock the truck. In that two-meter-wide swath, the snow and the ground beneath it leaped into flames, turned molten in an instant, to what depth he didn't know. The beam moved along, and the center of a big sycamore vanished in a flash; it didn't merely burst into flame but *disappeared* as if it had never existed. The tree was instantly converted into light and into heat that was detectable even inside the truck with the windows closed, almost thirty yards from the beam itself. Numerous splintered branches, which had hung beyond the sharply defined edge of the beam, fell to the ground on both sides of the light, and they were on fire at the points of severance. The blue-white blade burned past the pickup, across the backyard, diagonally between them and the house, across one edge of the patio, vaporizing concrete, all the way to the end of the path that Ellie had set it upon—and then it winked out.

A two-meter-wide, twenty-four-meter length of earth glowed white-hot, boiling like a lava flow at its freshest, on the high slopes of a volcano. The magma churned brightly in the trench that contained it, bubbling and popping and spitting showers of red and white sparks into the air, casting a glow that reached even to the truck and colored the surviving snow red-orange.

During the event, if they had not been too stunned to speak, they would have had to shout at each other to be heard. Now the silence seemed as profound as that in the vacuum of deep space.

At the house, the agency men switched off the searchlight.

"Keep moving," Ellie said urgently.

Spencer hadn't realized that he'd braked to a complete stop.

They drifted forward again. Easy. Moving cautiously through the lion's den. Easy. He risked a little more speed than before, because the lions had to be scared shitless right now.

"God bless America," Spencer said shakily.

"Oh, Godzilla isn't one of ours."

"It isn't?"

"Japanese."

"The Japanese have a death-ray satellite?"

"Enhanced-laser technology. And they have eight satellites in the system."

"I thought they were busy making better televisions."

She was working diligently on the keyboard again, getting ready for the worst. "Damn it, my right hand's cramping."

He saw that she had targeted the house.

She said, "The U.S. has something similar, but I don't have any codes that'll get me into our system. The fools on our side call it the Hyperspace Hammer, which has nothing to do with what it is. It's just a name they liked from a video game."

"You invent the game?"

"Actually, yes."

"They make an amusement park ride out of it?"

"Yes."

"I saw one."

Moving past the house now. Not even looking up at the windows. Not tempting fate.

"You can commandeer a secret Japanese defense satellite?"

"Through the DOD," she said.

"Department of Defense."

"The Japanese don't know it, but the DOD can grab Godzilla's brain any time they want. I'm just using the doorways that the DOD has already installed."

He remembered something that she had said in the desert only that morning, when he had expressed surprise about the possibility of satellite surveillance. He quoted it back to her: " 'You'd be surprised what's up there. "Surprised" is one word.' "

"The Israelis have their own system."

"The *Israelis*!"

"Yeah, little Israel. They worry me less than anyone else who's got it. Chinese. Think about that. Maybe the French. No more jokes about Paris cabdrivers. God knows who else has it."

They were almost past the house.

A small round hole was punched through the side window behind Ellie, even as the sound of the shot cracked the night, and Spencer felt the round thud into the back of his seat. The velocity of the bullet was so great that the tempered glass crazed slightly but did not collapse inward. Thank God, Rocky was barking energetically instead of squealing in agony.

"Stupid bastards," Ellie said as she pressed ENTER again.

Out of airless space, a lambent column of blue-white light shot down into the two-story Victorian farmhouse, instantly vaporizing a core two meters in diameter. The rest of the structure exploded. Flames filled the night. If anyone was left alive in that crumbling house, they would have to get out too fast to worry about holding on to their weapons and taking additional potshots at the pickup.

Ellie was shaken. "I couldn't risk them hitting the up-link behind us. If that goes, we're in deep trouble."

"The Russians have this?"

"This and weirder stuff."

"Weirder stuff?"

"That's why most everyone else is desperate to get their version of Godzilla. Zhirinovsky. Heard of him?"

"Russian politician."

Bending her head again to the VDT, entering new instructions, she said, "Him and the people associated with him, the whole network of them even after he's gone—they're old-fashioned communists who want to rule the world. Except this time they're actually willing to blow it up if they don't get their way. No more graceful defeats. And even if someone's smart enough to wipe out the Zhirinovsky faction, there's always some new power freak, somewhere, calling himself a politician."

Forty yards ahead, on the right, a Ford Bronco erupted from concealment in a stand of trees and bushes. It pulled across the driveway, blocking their escape.

Spencer halted the pickup.

Though the driver of the Bronco stayed behind the wheel, two men with high-power rifles jumped out of the back and dropped into sharpshooter positions. They raised their weapons.

"Down!" Spencer said, and pushed Ellie's head below window level even as he slid down in his seat.

"They aren't," she said in disbelief.

"They are."

"Blocking the driveway?"

"Two sharpshooters and a Bronco."

"Haven't they been paying attention?"

"Stay down, Rocky," he said.

The dog was standing again with his forepaws on the front seat, bobbing his head excitedly.

"Rocky, *down*!" Spencer said fiercely.

The dog whimpered as though his feelings had been hurt, but he dropped to the floor in back.

Ellie said, "How far are they?"

Spencer risked a quick peek, slid down again, and a bullet rang off the window post without shattering the windshield. "I'd say forty yards."

She typed. On the screen appeared a yellow line to the right of the driveway. It was twelve meters long, angling over an open field toward the Bronco, but it stopped a meter or two from the edge of the pavement.

"Don't want to score the driveway," she said. "Tires would dissolve when we tried to get across the molten ground."

"Can I press ENTER?" he asked.

"Be my guest."

He pressed it and sat up, squinting, as the breath of Godzilla streamed down through the night again, scoring the land. The ground shook, and an apocalyptic thunder rose under them as if the planet was coming apart. The night air hummed deafeningly, and the merciless beam dazzled along the course that she'd assigned to it.

Before Godzilla had turned the earth into white-hot sludge along even half those twelve meters, the pair of sharpshooters dropped their weapons and leaped for the vehicle behind them. As they hung on to the sides of the Bronco, the driver careened off the blacktop, churned across a frozen field beyond, smashed through a white board fence, crossed a paddock, rammed through another fence, and passed the first of the stables. When Godzilla stopped short of the driveway and the night was suddenly dark and quiet again, the Bronco was still going, fast dwindling into the gloom, as though the driver might head overland until he ran out of gasoline.

Spencer drove to the county road. He stopped and looked both ways. No traffic. He turned right, toward Denver.

For a few miles, neither of them spoke.

Rocky stood with his forepaws on the back of the front seat, gazing ahead at the highway. In the two years that Spencer had known him, the dog had never liked to look back.

Ellie sat with her hand clamped to her wound. Spencer hoped that the people she knew in Denver could get her medical attention. The medications that she had finessed, by computer, out of various drug companies had been lost with the Range Rover.

Eventually, she said, "We'd better stop in Copper Mountain, see if we can find new wheels. This truck's too recognizable."

"Okay."

She switched off the computer. Unplugged it.

The mountains were dark with evergreens and pale with snow.

The moon was setting behind the truck, and the night sky ahead was ablaze with stars.

FIFTEEN

Eve Jammer hated Washington, D.C., in August. Actually, she hated Washington through all seasons with equal passion. Admittedly, the city was pleasant for a short while, when the cherry blossoms were in bloom; during the rest of the year it sucked. Humid, crowded, noisy, dirty, crime-ridden. Full of boring, stupid, greedy politicians whose ideals were either in their pants or in their pants pockets. It was an inconvenient place for a capital, and sometimes she dreamed about moving the government elsewhere, when the time was right. Maybe to Las Vegas.

As she drove through the sweltering August heat, she had the air conditioner in her Chrysler Town Car turned nearly to its highest setting, with the fans on maximum blow. Freezing air blasted across her face and body and up her skirt, but she was still hot. Part of the heat, of course, had nothing to do with the day: She was so horny she could have won a head-butting duel with a ram.

She hated the Chrysler almost as much as she hated Washington. With all her money and position, she ought to have been able to drive a Mercedes, if not a Rolls-Royce. But a politician's wife had to be careful of appearances—at least for a while yet. It was impolitic to drive a foreign-made car.

Eighteen months had passed since Eve Jammer had met Roy Miro and had learned the nature of her true destiny. For sixteen months, she had been married to the widely admired Senator E. Jackson Haynes, who would head the party's national ticket in next year's election. That wasn't speculation. It had already been arranged, and all his rivals would screw up one way or another in the primaries, leaving him standing alone, a giant of a man on the world scene.

Personally, she loathed E. Jackson Haynes and wouldn't let him touch her, except in public. Even then, there were several pages of rules that he'd been required to memorize, defining the acceptable limits relating to affectionate hugs, kisses on the cheek, and hand holding. The recordings that she had of him in his Vegas hideaway, engaged in sex with several different little girls and boys below the age of twelve, had ensured his prompt acceptance of her proposal of marriage and the strict terms of convenience under which their relationship would be conducted.

Jackson didn't pout too much or too often about the arrangement. He was keen on the idea of being president. And without the library of recordings that Eve possessed, which incriminated all of his most serious political rivals, he wouldn't have had a chance in hell of getting close to the White House.

For a while, she had worried that a few of the politicians and power brokers whose enmity she had earned would be too thickheaded to realize that the boxes in which she'd put them were inescapable. If they terminated her, they would all fall in the biggest, dirtiest series of political scandals in history. More than scandals. Many of these servants of the people had committed outrages appalling enough to cause riots in the streets, even if federal agents were dispatched with machine guns to quell them.

Some of the worst hard-asses hadn't been convinced that she'd secreted copies of her recordings all over the world or that the contents of those laser discs were destined for the airwaves within hours of her death, from multiple—and, in many cases, automated—sources. The last of them had come around, however, when she had accessed their home television sets through satellite and cable facilities—while blocking all other customers—and had played for them, one by one, fragments of their recorded crimes. Sitting in their own bedrooms and dens, they had listened with astonishment, terrified that she was broadcasting those fragments to the world.

Computer technology was wonderful.

Many of the hard-asses had been with wives or mistresses when those unexpected, intensely personal broadcasts had appeared on their television screens. In most cases, their significant others were as guilty or as power mad as they were themselves, and eager to keep their mouths shut. However, one influential senator and a member of the president's cabinet had been married to women who exhibited bizarre moral codes and who refused to keep secret what they had learned. Before divorce proceedings and public revelations could begin, both had been shot to death at different automatic-teller machines on the same night. That tragedy resulted in the lowering of the nation's flag at all government buildings, citywide, for twenty-four hours—and in the introduction of a bill in Congress to require the posting of health warnings on all automated tellers.

Eve turned the air conditioner control to the highest setting. Just thinking about those women's expressions when she'd put the gun to their heads made her hotter than ever.

She was still two miles from Cloverfield, and the Washington traffic was terrible. She wanted to blow her horn and flip a stiff finger at some of the insufferable morons who were causing the snarls at the intersections, but she had to be discreet. The next First Lady of the United States could not be seen flipping off anyone. Besides, she had learned from Roy that anger was a weakness. Anger should be controlled and transformed into that only truly ennobling emotion—compassion. These bad drivers didn't *want* to tie up traffic; they were simply lacking in sufficient intellect to drive well. Their lives were probably blighted in many ways. They deserved not anger but compassionate release to a better world, whenever that release could be privately given.

She considered jotting down license numbers, to make it possible to find some of these poor souls later and, at her leisure, give them that gift of gifts. She was in too great a hurry, however, to be as compassionate as she would have liked.

She couldn't wait to get to Cloverfield and share the good news about Daddy's generosity. Through a complex chain of international trusts and corporations, her father—Thomas Summerton, First Deputy Attorney General of the United States—had transferred three hundred million dollars of his holdings to her, which provided her with as much freedom as did the laser-disc recordings from two years in that spider-infested Vegas bunker.

The smartest thing she had ever done, in a life of smart moves, was not to squeeze Daddy for money years ago, when she'd first gotten the goods on him. She had asked, instead, for a job with the agency. Daddy had believed that she'd wanted the bunker job because it was so easy: nothing to do down there but sit, read magazines, and collect a hundred thousand a year in salary. He'd made the mistake of thinking that she was a not-too-bright, small-time hustler.

Some men never seemed to stop thinking with their pants long enough to get wise. Tom Summerton was one of them.

Ages ago, when Eve's mother had been Daddy's mistress, he would have been wise to treat her better. But when she got pregnant and refused to abort the baby, he had dumped her. Hard. Even in those days, Daddy had been a rich young man and heir to even more, and although he hadn't achieved much political power yet, he'd had great ambition. He easily could have afforded to treat Mama well. When she threatened to go public and ruin his reputation, however, he'd sent a couple of goons to beat her up, and she'd nearly had a miscarriage. Thereafter, poor Mama had been a bitter, frightened woman until the day she died.

Daddy had been thinking with his pants when he'd been stupid enough to keep a fifteen-year-old mistress like Mama. And later he'd been thinking with his pants *pockets* when he should have been thinking with his head or his heart.

He was thinking with his pants again when he'd allowed Eve to seduce him—though, of course, he hadn't ever seen her before and hadn't known that she was his daughter. By then, he had forgotten poor Mama as if she'd been a one-night stand, although he had been putting it to her for two years before he dumped her. And if Mama barely existed in his memory, the possibility of having fathered a child had been wiped off his mental slate completely.

Eve had not simply seduced him but had *reduced* him to a state of animal lust that, over a period of weeks, made him the easiest of marks. When she eventually suggested a little fantasy role-playing, wherein they would act like father and violated daughter in bed, he had been excited. Her pretend-resistance and pitiful cries of rape excited him to new feats of endurance. Preserved on high-resolution videotape. From four angles. Recorded on the finest audio equipment. She'd saved some of his ejaculate in order to have a genetic match done with a sample of her own blood, to convince him that she was, indeed, his darling child. The tape of their role-playing would unquestionably be viewed by authorities as nothing less than forcible incest.

Upon being presented with that package, Daddy had for once in his life thought with his brain. He was convinced that killing her would not save him, so he had been willing to pay whatever was necessary to buy her silence. He'd been surprised and pleased when she'd asked not for any of his money but for a secure, well-paid government job. He'd been less pleased when she'd wanted to know a lot more about the agency and the secret derring-do about which he'd bragged once or twice in bed. After a few difficult days, however, he had seen the wisdom of bringing her into the agency fold.

"You're a cunning little bitch," he said when they had reached agreement. He'd put an arm around her with genuine affection.

He had been disappointed, after giving her the job, to learn that they would not continue sleeping together, but he had gotten over that loss in time. He really had thought that "cunning" was the best word to describe her. Her ability to use her position in the bunker for her own ends didn't become clear to him until he learned that she had married E. Jackson Haynes, after a whirlwind courtship of two days, and had managed to put most of the powerful politicians in the city under her thumb. *Then* she had gone to him to begin discussions regarding an inheritance—and Daddy had discovered that "cunning" might not be a sufficiently descriptive word.

Now she reached the end of the entrance drive to Cloverfield and parked at a red curb near the front door, beside a sign that stated NO PARKING ANYTIME. She put one of Jackson's "Member of Congress" cards on the dashboard, relished the icy air of the Chrysler for one more moment, then stepped out into the August heat and humidity.

Cloverfield—all white columns and stately walls—was one of the finest institutions of its kind in the continental United States. A liveried doorman greeted her. The concierge at the main desk in the lounge was a distinguished-looking British gentleman named Danfield, though she didn't know if that was his first or last name.

After Danfield signed her in and chatted pleasantly with her, Eve walked the familiar route through the hushed halls. Original paintings by famous American artists of previous centuries were well complemented by antique Persian runners on wine-dark mahogany floors polished to a watery sheen.

When she entered Roy's suite, she found the dear man shuffling around in his walker, getting some exercise. With the attention of the finest specialists and therapists in the world, he had regained full use of his arms. Increasingly, he seemed certain to be able to walk on his own again within a few months—though with a limp.

She gave him a dry kiss on the cheek. He favored her with one even dryer.

"You're more beautiful every time you visit," he said.

"Well, men's heads still turn," she said, "but not like they used to, not when I have to wear clothes like these."

A future First Lady of the United States couldn't dress as would a former Las Vegas showgirl who'd gotten a thrill out of driving men insane. These days she even wore a bra that spread her breasts out and restrained them, to make her appear less amply endowed than she really was.

She had never been a showgirl anyway, and her surname had not been Jammer but Lincoln, as in Abraham. She had attended school in five different states and West Germany, because her father had been a career military man who'd been transferred from base to base. She had graduated from the Sorbonne in Paris and had spent a number of years teaching poor children in the Kingdom of Tonga, in the South Pacific. At least, that was what every data record would reveal to even the most industrious reporter armed with the most powerful computer and the cleverest mind.

She and Roy sat side by side on a settee. Pots of hot tea, an array of pastries, clotted cream, and jam had been provided on a charming little Chippendale table.

While they sipped and munched, she told him about the three hundred million that her father had transferred to her. Roy was so happy for her that tears came to his eyes. He was a dear man.

They talked about the future.

The time when they could be together again, every night, without any subterfuge, seemed depressingly distant. E. Jackson Haynes would assume the office of president on January twentieth, seventeen months hence. He and the vice-president would be assassinated the

following year—though Jackson was unaware of that detail. With the approval of constitutional scholars and the advice of the Supreme Court of the United States, both houses of
Congress would take the unprecedented step of calling for a special election. Eve Marie
Lincoln Haynes, widow of the martyred president, would run for the office, be elected by
a landslide, and begin serving her first term.

"A year after *that*, I'll have mourned a decent length of time," she told Roy. "Don't
you think a year?"

"More than decent. Especially as the public will love you so much and want happiness
for you."

"And then I can marry the heroic FBI agent who tracked down and killed that escaped
maniac, Steven Ackblom."

"Four years until we're together forever," Roy said. "Not so long, really. I promise
you, Eve, I'll make you happy and do honor to my position as First Gentleman."

"I know you will, darling," she said.

"And by then, anyone who doesn't like *anything* you do—"

"—we shall treat with utmost compassion."

"Exactly."

"Now let's not talk anymore about how long we have to wait. Let's discuss more of
your wonderful ideas. Let's make *plans*."

For a long time they talked about uniforms for a variety of new federal organizations
they wished to create, with a special focus on whether metal snaps and zippers were more
exciting than traditional bone buttons.

SIXTEEN

In the broiling sun, hard-bodied young men and legions of strikingly attractive women in
the briefest of bikinis soaked up the rays and casually struck poses for one another. Children built sand castles. Retirees sat under umbrellas, wearing straw hats, soaking up the
shade. They were all happily oblivious of eyes in the sky and of the possibility that they
could be instantaneously vaporized at the whim of politicians of various nationalities—or
even by a demented-genius computer hacker, living in a cyberpunk fantasy, in Cleveland
or London or Cape Town or Pittsburgh.

As he walked along the shore, near the tide line, with the huge hotels piled one beside
the other to his right, he rubbed lightly at his face. His beard itched. He'd had it for
six months, and it wasn't a scruffy-looking beard. On the contrary, it was soft and full,
and Ellie insisted that he was even more handsome with it than without it. Nevertheless,
on a hot August day in Miami Beach, it itched as if he had fleas, and he longed to be
clean-shaven.

Besides, he liked the appearance of his beardless face. During the eighteen months since
the night on which Godzilla had attacked the ranch in Vail, a superb plastic surgeon in the
private-pay sector of the British medical establishment had performed three separate procedures on the cicatrix. It had been reduced to a hairline scar that was virtually invisible
even when he was tanned. Additional work had been done on his nose and chin.

He used scores of names these days, but neither Spencer Grant nor Michael Ackblom
was one of them. Among his closest friends in the resistance, he was known as Phil
Richards. Ellie had chosen to keep her first name and adopt Richards as her last. Rocky
responded as well to "Killer" as he had to his previous name.

Phil turned his back to the ocean, made his way between the ranks of sunbathers, and entered the lushly landscaped grounds of one of the newer hotels. In sandals, white shorts, and a flamboyant Hawaiian shirt, he resembled countless other tourists.

The hotel swimming pool was bigger than a football field and as freeform as any tropical lagoon. Artificial-rock perimeter. Artificial-rock sunning islands in the center. A two-story waterfall spilling into one palm-shaded end.

In a grotto behind the cascading water, the poolside bar could be reached either on foot or by swimmers. It was a Polynesian-style pavilion with plenty of bamboo, dry palm fronds, and conch shells. The cocktail waitresses wore thongs, wraparound skirts made from a bright orchid-patterned fabric, and matching bikini tops; each had a fresh flower pinned in her hair.

The Padrakian family—Bob, Jean, and their eight-year-old son, Mark—were sitting at a small table near the grotto wall. Bob was drinking rum and Coke, Mark was having a root beer, and Jean was nervously shredding a cocktail napkin and chewing on her lower lip.

Phil approached the table and startled Jean—to whom he was a stranger—by loudly saying, "Hey, Sally, you look fabulous," and by giving her a hug and a kiss on the cheek. He ruffled Mark's hair: "How you doing, Pete? I'm going to take you snorkeling later— what do you think of that?" Vigorously shaking hands with Bob, he said, "Better watch that gut, buddy, or you're going to wind up looking like Uncle Morty." Then he sat down with them and quietly said, "Pheasants and dragons."

A few minutes later, after he had finished a piña colada and surreptitiously studied the other customers in the bar to be sure that none of them was unusually interested in the Padrakians, Phil paid for all their drinks with cash. He walked with them into the hotel, chatting about nonexistent mutual relatives. Through the frigid lobby. Out under the porte cochere, into the stifling heat and humidity. As far as he could tell, no one was trailing or watching them.

The Padrakians had followed telephone instructions well. They were dressed as sun-worshipping tourists from New Jersey, although Bob was pushing the disguise too far by wearing black loafers and black socks with Bermuda shorts.

A sightseeing van with large windows along the sides approached on the hotel entrance drive and stopped at the curb in front of them, under the porte cochere. The current magnetic-mat signs on each of its front doors declared CAPTAIN BLACKBEARD'S WATER ADVENTURES. Under that, above a picture of a grinning pirate, less bold letters explained GUIDED SCUBA TOURS, JET-SKI RENTALS, WATER-SKIING, DEEP-SEA FISHING.

The driver got out and came around the front of the van to open the sliding side door for them. He wore a stylishly wrinkled white linen shirt, lightweight white ducks, and bright pink canvas shoes with green laces. Even with dreadlocks and one silver earring, he managed to look as intellectual and dignified as he had ever been in a three-piece suit or in a police captain's uniform, in the days when Phil had served under him in the West Los Angeles Division of the LAPD. His ink-black skin seemed even darker and glossier in the tropical heat of Miami than it had been in Los Angeles.

The Padrakians climbed into the back of the van, and Phil sat up front with the driver, who was now known to his friends as Ronald—Ron, for short—Truman. "Love the shoes," Phil said.

"My daughters picked them out for me."

"Yeah, but you like 'em."

"Can't lie. They're cool gear."

"You were half dancing, the way you came around the van, showing them off."

Flashing a grin as he drove away from the hotel, Ron said, "You white men always envy our moves."

Ron was speaking with a British accent so convincing that Phil could close his eyes and see Big Ben. In the course of losing his Caribbean lilt, Ron had discovered a talent for accents and dialects. He was now their man of a thousand voices.

"I gotta tell you," Bob Padrakian said nervously from the seat behind them, "we're scared out of our wits about this."

"You're all right now," Phil said. He turned around in his seat to smile reassuringly at the three refugees.

"Nobody following us, unless it's a look-down," Ron said, though the Padrakians probably didn't know what he meant. "And that's not very likely."

"I mean," Padrakian said, "we don't even know who the hell you people are."

"We're your friends," Phil assured him. "In fact, if things work out for you folks anything like the way they worked out for me and for Ron and his family, then we're going to be the best friends you've ever had."

"More than friends, really," Ron said. "Family."

Bob and Jean looked dubious and scared. Mark was young enough to be unconcerned.

"Just sit tight for a little while and don't worry," Phil told them. "Everything'll be explained real soon."

At a huge shopping mall, they parked and went inside. They passed dozens of stores, entered one of the less busy wings, went through a door marked with international symbols for rest rooms and telephones, and were in a long service hallway. They passed the phones and the public facilities. A stairway at the end of the corridor led down to one of the mall's big communal shipping rooms, where some smaller shops, without exterior truck docks, received incoming merchandise.

Two of the four roll-up, truck-bay doors were open, and delivery vehicles were backed up to them. Three uniformed employees from a store that sold cheese, cured meats, and gourmet foods were rapidly unloading the truck at bay number four. As they stacked cartons on handcarts and wheeled them to a freight elevator, they showed no interest in Phil, Ron, and the Padrakians. Many of the boxes were labeled PERISHABLE, KEEP REFRIGERATED, and time was of the essence.

At the truck in bay number one—a small model compared with the eighteen-wheeler in bay four—the driver appeared from out of the dark, sixteen-foot-deep cargo hold. As they approached, he jumped down to the floor. The five of them climbed inside, as though going for a ride in the back of a delivery truck was unremarkable. The driver closed the door after them, and a moment later they were on the road.

The cargo hold was empty except for piles of quilted shipping pads of the kind used by furniture movers. They sat on the pads in pitch blackness. They were unable to talk because of the engine noise and the hollow rattle of the metal walls around them.

Twenty minutes later, the truck stopped. The engine died. After five minutes, the rear door opened. The driver appeared in dazzling sunshine. "Quickly. Nobody's in sight right now."

When they disembarked from the truck, they were in a corner of a parking lot at a public beach. Sunlight flared off the windshields and chrome trim of the parked cars, and white gulls kited through the sky. Phil could smell sea salt in the air.

"Only a short walk now," Ron told the Padrakians.

The campgrounds were less than a quarter of a mile from where they left the truck. The tan-and-black Road King motor home was large, but it was only one of many its size that were parked at utility hookups among the palms.

The trees lazily stirred in the humid on-shore breeze. A hundred yards away, at the edge of the breaking surf, two pelicans stalked stiffly back and forth through the fringe of foaming water, as if engaged in an ancient Egyptian dance.

Inside the Road King, Ellie was one of three people working at video-display terminals in the living room. She rose, smiling, to receive Phil's embrace and kiss.

Rubbing her belly affectionately, he said, "Ron has new shoes."

"I saw them earlier."

"Tell him he really has nice moves in those shoes. Makes him feel good."

"It does, huh?"

"Makes him feel black."

"He is black."

"Well, of course, he is."

She and Phil joined Ron and the Padrakians in the horseshoe-shaped dining nook that seated seven.

Sitting beside Jean Padrakian, welcoming her to this new life, Ellie took the woman's hand and held it, as if Jean were a sister whom she hadn't seen for a while and whose touch was a comfort to her. She had a singular warmth that quickly put new people at ease.

Phil watched her with pride and love—and with not a little envy of her easy sociability.

Eventually, still clinging to a dim hope that he could someday return to his old life, unable to fully accept the new one that they were offering him, Bob Padrakian said, "But we've lost everything. Everything. Fine, okay, I get a new name and brand-new ID, a past history that no one can shake. But where do we go from here? How do I make a living?"

"We'd like you to work with us," Phil said. "If you don't want that . . . then we can set you up in a new place, with start-up capital to get you back on your feet. You can live entirely outside of the resistance. We can even see that you get a decent job."

"But you'll never know peace again," Ron said, "because now you're aware that no one's safe in this brave new world order."

"It was your—and Jean's—terrific computer skills that got you into trouble with them," Phil said. "And skills like yours are what we can never get enough of."

Bob frowned. "What would we be doing—exactly?"

"Harassing them at every turn. Infiltrating their computers to learn who's on their hit lists. Pull those targeted people out of harm's way *before* the axe falls, whenever possible. Destroy illegal police files on innocent citizens who're guilty of nothing more than having strong opinions. There's a lot to do."

Bob glanced around at the motor home, at the two people working at VDTs in the living room. "You seem to be well organized and well financed. Is foreign money involved here?" He looked meaningfully at Ron Truman. "No matter what's happening in this country right now or for the foreseeable future, I still think of myself as an American, and I always will."

Dropping the British accent in favor of a Louisiana bayou drawl, Ron said, "I'm as American as crawfish pie, Bob." He switched to a heart-of-Virginia accent, "I can quote you any passage from the writings of Thomas Jefferson. I've memorized them all. A year and a half ago, I couldn't have quoted one sentence. Now his collected works are my bible."

"We get our financing by stealing from the thieves," Ellie told Bob. "Manipulate their computer records, transfer funds from them to us in a lot of ways you'll probably find ingenious. There's so much unaccounted slush in their bookkeeping that half the time they aren't even aware anything's been stolen from them."

"Stealing from thieves," Bob said. "What thieves?"

"Politicians. Government agencies with 'black funds' that they spend on secret projects."

The quick patter of four small feet signaled Killer's arrival from the back bedroom, where he had been napping. He squirmed under the table, startling Jean Padrakian, lashing everyone's legs with his tail. He pushed between the table and the booth, planting his forepaws on young Mark's lap.

The boy giggled delightedly as he was subjected to a vigorous face licking. "What's his name?"

"Killer," Ellie said.

Jean was worried. "He's not dangerous, is he?"

Phil and Ellie exchanged glances and smiles. He said, "Killer's our ambassador of goodwill. We've never had a diplomatic crisis since he graciously accepted the post."

For the past eighteen months, Killer had not looked himself. He wasn't tan and brown and white and black, as in the days when he had been Rocky, but entirely black. An incognito canine. Rover on the run. A mutt in masquerade. Fugitive furball. Phil had already decided that when he shaved off his beard (soon), they would also allow Killer's coat to change gradually back to its natural colors.

"Bob," Ron said, returning to the issue at hand, "we're living in a time when the highest of high technology makes it possible for a relative handful of totalitarians to subvert a democratic society and control large sections of its government, economy, and culture—with great subtlety. If they control too much of it for too long, unopposed, they'll get bolder. They'll want to control it all, every aspect of people's lives. And by the time the general public wakes up to what's happened, their ability to resist will have been leached away. The forces marshaled against them will be unchallengeable."

"Then subtle control might be traded for the blatant exercise of raw power," Ellie said. "That's when they open the 'reeducation' camps to help us wayward souls learn the right path."

Bob stared at her in shock. "You don't really think it could ever happen here, something that extreme."

Instead of replying, Ellie met his eyes, until he had time to think about what outrageous injustices had already been committed against him and his family to bring them to this place at this time in their lives.

"Jesus," he whispered, and he gazed down thoughtfully at his folded hands on the table.

Jean looked at her son as the boy happily petted and scratched Killer, then glanced at Ellie's swollen stomach. "Bob, this is where we belong. This is our future. It's right. These people have hope, and we need hope badly." She turned to Ellie. "When's the baby due?"

"Two months."

"Boy or girl?"

"We're having a little girl."

"You picked a name for her yet?"

"Jennifer Corrine."

"That's pretty," Jean said.

Ellie smiled. "For Phil's mother and mine."

To Bob Padrakian, Phil said, "We *do* have hope. More than enough hope to have children and to get on with life even in the resistance. Because modern technology has its good side too. You know that. You love high technology as much as we do. The benefits to humanity far outweigh the problems. But there are always would-be Hitlers. So it's fallen to us to fight a new kind of war, one that more often uses knowledge than guns to fight battles."

"Though guns," Ron said, "sometimes have their place."

Bob considered Ellie's swollen belly, then turned to his wife. "You're sure?"

"They have hope," Jean said simply.

Her husband nodded. "Then this is the future."

Later, on the brink of twilight, Phil and Ellie and Killer went for a walk on the beach.

The sun was huge, low, and red. It quickly sank out of sight beyond the western horizon.

To the east, over the Atlantic, the sky became deep and vast and purple-black, and the stars came out to allow sailors to chart courses on the otherwise strange sea.

Phil and Ellie talked of Jennifer Corrine and of all the hopes that they had for her, of shoes and ships and sealing wax, of cabbages and kings. They took turns throwing a ball, but Killer allowed no one to take turns chasing it.

Phil, who once had been Michael and the son of evil, who once had been Spencer and for so long imprisoned in one moment of a July night, put his arm around his wife's shoulders. Staring at the ever-shining stars, he knew that human lives were free of the chains of fate except in one regard: It was the human destiny to be free.

It darkles, (tinct, tint) all this our funanimal world.
—James Joyce, *Finnegans Wake*

INTENSITY

▼

This book is for Florence Koontz.
My mother. Long lost. My guardian.

Hope is the destination that we seek.
Love is the road that leads to hope.
Courage is the motor that drives us.
We travel out of darkness into faith.

—*The Book of Counted Sorrows*

ONE

The red sun balances on the highest ramparts of the mountains, and in its waning light, the foothills appear to be ablaze. A cool breeze blows down out of the sun and fans through the tall dry grass, which streams like waves of golden fire along the slopes toward the rich and shadowed valley.

In the knee-high grass, he stands with his hands in the pockets of his denim jacket, studying the vineyards below. The vines were pruned during the winter. The new growing season has just begun. The colorful wild mustard that flourished between the rows during the colder months has been chopped back and the stubble plowed under. The earth is dark and fertile.

The vineyards encircle a barn, outbuildings, and a bungalow for the caretaker. Except for the barn, the largest structure is the owners' Victorian house with its gables, dormers, decorative millwork under the eaves, and carved pediment over the front porch steps.

Paul and Sarah Templeton live in the house year-round, and their daughter, Laura, visits occasionally from San Francisco, where she attends university. She is supposed to be in residence throughout this weekend.

He dreamily contemplates a mental image of Laura's face, as detailed as a photograph. Curiously, the girl's perfect features engender thoughts of succulent, sugar-laden bunches of pinot noir and grenache with translucent purple skin. He can actually taste the phantom grapes as he imagines them bursting between his teeth.

As it slowly sinks behind the mountains, the sun sprays light so warmly colored and so mordant that, where touched, the darkening land appears to be wet with it and dyed forever. The grass grows red as well, no longer like a fireless burning but, instead, a red tide washing around his knees.

He turns his back on the house and the vineyards. Savoring the steadily intensifying taste of grapes, he walks westward into the shadows cast by the high forested ridges.

He can smell the small animals of the open meadows cowering in their burrows. He hears the whisper of feathers carving the wind as a hunting hawk circles hundreds of feet overhead, and he feels the cold glimmer of stars that are not yet visible.

In the strange sea of shimmering red light, the black shadows of overhanging trees flickered shark-swift across the windshield.

On the winding two-lane blacktop, Laura Templeton handled the Mustang with an expertise that Chyna admired, but she drove too fast. "You've got a heavy foot," Chyna said.

Laura grinned. "Better than a big butt."

"You'll get us killed."

"Mom has rules about being late for dinner."

"Being late is better than being *dead* for dinner."

"You've never met my mom. She's hell on rules."

"So is the highway patrol."

Laura laughed. "Sometimes you sound just like her."

"Who?"

"My mom."

Bracing herself as Laura took a curve too fast, Chyna said, "Well, one of us has to be a responsible adult."

"Sometimes I can't believe you're only three years older than me," Laura said affectionately. "Twenty-six, huh? You sure you're not a *hundred* and twenty-six?"

"I'm ancient," Chyna said.

They had left San Francisco under a hard blue sky, taking a four-day break from classes at the University of California, where, in the spring, they would earn master's degrees in psychology. Laura hadn't been delayed in her education by the need to earn her tuition and living expenses, but Chyna had spent the past ten years attending classes part time while working full time as a waitress, first in a Denny's, then in a unit of the Olive Garden chain, and most recently in an upscale restaurant with white tablecloths and cloth napkins and fresh flowers on the tables and customers—bless them—who routinely tipped fifteen or twenty percent. This visit to the Templetons' house in the Napa Valley would be the closest thing to a vacation that she'd had in a decade.

From San Francisco, Laura had followed Interstate 80 through Berkeley and across the eastern end of San Pablo Bay. Blue heron had stalked the shallows and leaped gracefully into flight: enormous, eerily prehistoric, beautiful against the cloudless heavens.

Now, in the gold-and-crimson sunset, scattered clouds burned in the sky, and the Napa Valley unrolled like a radiant tapestry. Laura had departed the main road in favor of a scenic route; however, she drove so fast that Chyna was seldom able to take her eyes off the highway to enjoy the scenery.

"Man, I love speed," Laura said.

"I hate it."

"I like to move, streak, *fly*. Hey, maybe I was a gazelle in a previous life. You think?"

Chyna looked at the speedometer and grimaced. "Yeah, maybe a gazelle—or a mad-woman locked away in Bedlam."

"Or a cheetah. Cheetahs are really fast."

"Yeah, a cheetah, and one day you were chasing your prey and ran straight off the edge of a cliff at full tilt. You were the Wile E. Coyote of cheetahs."

"I'm a good driver, Chyna."

"I know."

"Then relax."

"I can't."

Laura sighed with fake exasperation. "Ever?"

"When I sleep," Chyna said, and she nearly jammed her feet through the floorboards as the Mustang took a wide curve at high speed.

Beyond the narrow graveled shoulder of the two-lane, the land sloped down through wild mustard and looping brambles to a row of tall black alders fringed with early-spring buds. Beyond the alders lay vineyards drenched with fierce red light, and Chyna was convinced that the car would slide off the blacktop, roll down the embankment, and crash into the trees, and that her blood would fertilize the nearest of the vines.

Instead, Laura effortlessly held the Mustang to the pavement. The car swept out of the curve and up a long incline.

Laura said, "I bet you even worry in your sleep."

"Well, sooner or later, in every dream there's a boogeyman. You've got to be on the lookout for him."

"I have lots of dreams without boogeymen," Laura said. "I have wonderful dreams."

"Getting shot out of a cannon?"

"That would be fun. No, but sometimes I dream that I can fly. I'm always naked and just floating or swooping along fifty feet above the ground, over telephone lines, across fields of bright flowers, over treetops. So free. People look up and smile and wave. They're so delighted to see that I can fly, so happy for me. And sometimes I'm with this beautiful guy, lean and muscular, with a mane of golden hair and lovely green eyes that look all the way *through* me to my soul, and we're making love in midair, drifting up there, and I'm having spectacular orgasms, one after another, floating through sunshine with flowers below and birds swooping overhead, birds with these gorgeous iridescent-blue wings and singing the most fantastic birdsongs you ever heard, and I feel as if I'm full of dazzling light, just a creature of light, and like I'm going to explode, such an energy, explode and form a whole new universe and *be* the universe and live forever. You ever have a dream like that?"

Chyna had finally taken her eyes off the onrushing blacktop. She stared in blank-faced astonishment at Laura. Finally she said, "No."

Glancing away from the two-lane, Laura said, "Really? You never had a dream like that?"

"Never."

"I have lots of dreams like that."

"Could you keep your eyes on the road, kiddo?"

Laura looked at the highway and said, "Don't you ever dream about sex?"

"Sometimes."

"And?"

"What?"

"*And?*"

Chyna shrugged. "It's bad."

Frowning, Laura said, "You dream about having bad sex? Listen, Chyna, you don't have to *dream* about that—there are lots of guys who can provide all the bad sex you want."

"Ho, ho. I mean these are nightmares, very threatening."

"Sex is threatening?"

"Because I'm always a little girl in the dreams—six or seven or eight—and I'm always hiding from this man, not quite sure what he wants, why he's looking for me, but I know he wants something from me that he shouldn't have, something terrible, and it's going to be like dying."

"Who's the man?"

"Different men."

"Some of the creeps your mother used to hang out with?"

Chyna had told Laura a great deal about her mother. She had never told anyone else. "Yeah. Them. I always got away from them in real life. They never touched me. And they never touch me in the dreams. But there's always a threat, always a possibility. . . ."

"So these aren't just dreams. They're memories too."

"I wish they *were* just dreams."

"What about when you're awake?" Laura asked.

"What do you mean?"

"Do you just turn all warm and fuzzy and let yourself go when a man makes love to you . . . or is the past always there?"

"What is this—analysis at eighty miles an hour?"

"Dodging the question?"

"You're a snoop."

"It's called friendship."

"It's called snoopery."

"Dodging the question?"

Chyna sighed. "All right. I like being with a man. I'm not inhibited. I'll admit that I've never felt as though I'm a creature of light going to explode into a new universe, but I've been fully satisfied, always had fun."

"Fully?"

"Fully."

Chyna had never actually been with a man until she was twenty-one; and her intimate relationships now totaled exactly two. Both had been gentle, kind, and decent men, and in each case Chyna had greatly enjoyed the lovemaking. One affair had lasted eleven months, the other thirteen, and neither lover had left her a single troubling memory. Nevertheless, neither man had helped her banish the vicious dreams, which continued to plague her periodically, and she'd been unable to achieve an emotional bond equal to the physical intimacy. To a man whom she loved, Chyna could give her body, but even for love, she could not entirely give her mind and heart. She was afraid to commit herself, to trust without reservation. No one in her life, with the possible exception of Laura Templeton—stunt driver and dream flier—had ever earned total trust.

Wind shrieked along the sides of the car. In the flickering shadows and fiery light, the long incline ahead of them seemed to be a ramp, as if they were going to be launched into space when they reached the top, vaulting across a dozen burning buses while a stadium full of thrill-seekers cheered.

"What if a tire blows?" Chyna asked.

"The tires won't blow," Laura said confidently.

"What if one does?"

Wrenching her face into an exaggerated, demonic grin, Laura said, "Then we're just girl jelly in a can. They won't even be able to separate the remains into two distinct bodies. A total amorphous mess. They won't even need coffins for us. They'll just pour our remains in a jug and put us in one grave, and the headstone will read: *Laura Chyna Templeton Shepherd. Only a Cuisinart Would Have Been More Thorough.*"

Chyna had hair so dark that it was virtually black, and Laura was a blue-eyed blonde, yet they were enough alike to be sisters. Both were five feet four and slender; they wore the same dress size. Each had high cheekbones and delicate features. Chyna had always felt that her mouth was too wide, but Laura, whose mouth was as wide as Chyna's, said it wasn't wide at all but merely "generous" enough to ensure an especially winning smile.

As Laura's love of speed proved, however, they were in some ways profoundly different people. The differences, perhaps more than the similarities, were what drew them to each other.

"You think your mom and dad will like me?" Chyna asked.

"I thought you were worried about a blown tire."

"I'm a multichannel worrier. Will they like me?"

"Of course they'll like you. You know what *I* worry about?" Laura asked as they raced toward the top of the incline.

"Apparently, not death."

"You. I worry about you," Laura said. She glanced at Chyna, and her expression was uncharacteristically serious.

"I can take care of myself," Chyna assured her.

"I don't doubt *that*. I know you too well to doubt *that*. But life isn't just about taking care of yourself, keeping your head down, getting through."

"Laura Templeton, girl philosopher."

"Life is about *living*."

"Deep," Chyna said sarcastically.

"Deeper than you think."

The Mustang crested the long hill, and there were no burning buses or cheering multitudes, but ahead of them was an older-model Buick, cruising well below the posted limit. Laura cut their speed by more than half, and they pulled behind the other car. Even in the fading light, Chyna could see that the round-shouldered driver was a white-haired, elderly man.

They were in a no-passing zone. The road rose and fell, turned left and right, rose again, and they could not see far ahead.

Laura switched on the Mustang headlights, hoping to encourage the driver of the Buick either to increase his speed or to ease over where the shoulder widened to let them pass.

"Take your own advice—relax, kiddo," Chyna said.

"Hate to be late for dinner."

"From everything you've said about her, I don't think your mom's the type to beat us with wire coat hangers."

"Mom's the best."

"So relax," Chyna said.

"But she has this disappointed look she gives you that's *worse* than wire coat hangers. Most people don't know this, but Mom is the reason the Cold War ended. Several years ago, the Pentagon sent her off to Moscow so she could give the whole damn Politburo the *Look*, and all those Soviet thugs just collapsed with remorse."

Ahead of them, the old man in the Buick checked his rearview mirror.

The white hair in the headlight beams, the angle of the man's head, and the mere suggestion of his eyes reflected in the mirror suddenly engendered in Chyna a powerful sense of déjà vu. For a moment, she didn't understand why a chill came over her—but then she was cast back in memory to an incident that she had long tried unsuccessfully to forget: another twilight, nineteen years ago, a lonely Florida highway.

"Oh, Jesus," she said.

Laura glanced at her. "What's wrong?"

Chyna closed her eyes.

"Chyna, you're as white as a ghost. What is it?"

"A long time ago . . . when I was just a little girl, seven years old . . . Maybe we were in the Everglades, maybe not . . . but the land was swampy like the 'glades. There weren't many trees, and the few you could see were hung with Spanish moss. Everything was flat as far as you could see, lots of sky and flatness, the sunlight red and fading like now, a back road somewhere, far away from anything, very rural, two narrow lanes, so damn empty and lonely. . . ."

Chyna had been with her mother and Jim Woltz, a Key West drug dealer and gunrunner with whom they had lived now and then, for a month or two at a time, during her childhood. They had been on a business trip and had been returning to the Keys in Woltz's vintage red Cadillac, one of those models with massive tailfins and with what seemed to be five tons of chrome grillwork. Woltz was driving fast on that straight highway, exceeding a hundred miles an hour at times. They hadn't encountered another car for almost fifteen minutes before they roared up behind the elderly couple in the tan Mercedes. The woman was driving. Birdlike. Close-cropped silver hair. Seventy-five if she was a day. She was doing forty miles an hour. Woltz could have pulled around the Mercedes; they were in a passing zone, and no traffic was in sight for miles on that dead-flat highway.

"But he was high on something," Chyna told Laura, eyes still closed, watching the memory with growing dread as it played like a movie on a screen behind her eyes. "He was most of the time high on something. Maybe it was cocaine that day. I don't know. Don't remember. He was drinking too. They were both drinking, him and my mother. They had a cooler full of ice. Bottles of grapefruit juice and vodka. The old lady in the Mercedes was driving really slow, and that incensed Woltz. He wasn't rational. What did it matter to him? He could've pulled around her. But the sight of her driving so slow on the wide-open highway infuriated him. Drugs and booze, that's all. So irrational. When he was angry . . . red-faced, arteries throbbing in his neck, jaw muscles bulging. No one could get angry quite as *totally* as Jim Woltz. His rage excited my mother. Always excited her. So she teased him, encouraged him. I was in the backseat, hanging on tight, pleading with her to stop, but she kept at him."

For a while, Woltz had hung close behind the other car, blowing his horn at the elderly couple, trying to force them to go faster. A few times he had nudged the rear bumper of the Mercedes with the front bumper of the Cadillac, metal kissing metal with a squeal. Eventually the old woman got rattled and began to swerve erratically, afraid to go faster with Woltz so close behind her but too frightened of him to pull off the road and let him pass by.

"Of course," Chyna said, "he wouldn't have gone past and left her alone. By then he was too psychotic. He would have stopped when she stopped. It still would have ended badly."

Woltz had pulled alongside the Mercedes a few times, driving in the wrong lane, shouting and shaking his fist at the white-haired couple, who first tried to ignore him and then stared back wide-eyed and fearful. Each time, rather than drive by and leave them in his dust, he had dropped behind again to play tag with their rear bumper. To Woltz, in his drug fever and alcoholic haze, this harassment was deadly serious business, with an importance and a meaning that could never be understood by anyone who was clean and sober. To Chyna's mother, Anne, it was all a game, an adventure, and it was she, in her ceaseless search for excitement, who said, *Why don't we give her a driving test?* Woltz said, *Test? I don't need to give the old bitch a test to see she can't drive for shit.* This time, as Woltz pulled beside the Mercedes, matching speeds with it, Anne said, *I mean, see if she can keep it on the road. Make it a challenge for her.*

To Laura, Chyna recalled, "There was a canal parallel to the road, one of those drainage channels you see along some Florida highways. Not deep but deep enough. Woltz used the Cadillac to crowd the Mercedes onto the shoulder of the road. The woman should have crowded him back, forced him the other way. She should have tramped the pedal to the floor and pegged the speedometer and gotten the hell out of there. The Mercedes would've outrun the Cadillac, no problem. But she was old and scared, and she'd never encountered anyone like this. I think she was just disbelieving, so unable to understand the kind of people she was up against, unable to grasp how far they'd go *even though she and her husband had done nothing to them.* Woltz forced her off the road. The Mercedes rolled into the canal."

Woltz had stopped, shifted the Cadillac into reverse, and backed up to where the Mercedes was swiftly sinking. He and Anne had gotten out of the car to watch. Chyna's mother had insisted that she watch too: *Come on, you little chicken. You don't want to miss this, baby. This is one to remember.* The passenger's side of the Mercedes was flat against the muddy bottom of the canal, and the driver's side was revealed to them as they stood on the embankment in the humid evening air. They were being bitten by hordes of mosquitoes but were hardly aware of them, mesmerized by the sight below them, gazing through the driver-side windows of the submerged vehicle.

"It was twilight," Chyna told Laura, putting into words the images behind her closed eyes, "so the headlights were on, still on even after the Mercedes sank, and there were lights inside the car. They had air-conditioning, so all the windows were closed, and neither the windshield nor the driver-side window had shattered when the car rolled. We could see inside, 'cause the windows were only a few inches under water. There was no sign of the husband. Maybe he was knocked unconscious when they rolled. But the old woman . . . her face was at the window. The car was flooded, but there was a big bubble of air against the inside of the glass, and she pressed her face into it so she could breathe. We stood there looking down at her. Woltz could have helped. My mother could have helped. But they just watched. The old woman couldn't seem to get the window open, and the door must have been jammed, or maybe she was just too scared and too weak."

Chyna had tried to pull away, but her mother had held her, speaking urgently to her, the whispered words borne on a tide of breath sour with vodka and grapefruit juice. *We're different than other people, baby. No rules apply to us. You'll never understand what freedom really means if you don't watch this.* Chyna had closed her eyes, but she had still been able to hear the old woman screaming into the big air bubble inside the submerged car. Muffled screaming.

"Then gradually the screaming faded . . . finally stopped," Chyna told Laura. "When I opened my eyes, twilight had gone and night had come. There was still light in the Mercedes, and the woman's face was still pressed to the glass, but a breeze had risen, rippling the water in the canal, and her features were a blur. I knew she was dead. She and her husband. I started to cry. Woltz didn't like that. He threatened to drag me into the canal, open a door on the Mercedes, and shove me inside with the dead people. My mother made me drink some grapefruit juice with vodka. I was only seven. The rest of the way back to Key West, I lay on the backseat, dizzy from the vodka, half drunk and a little sick, still crying but quietly, so I wouldn't make Woltz angry, crying quietly until I fell asleep."

In Laura's Mustang, the only sounds were the soft rumble of the engine and the singing of the tires on the blacktop.

Chyna finally opened her eyes and came back from the memory of Florida, from the long-ago humid twilight to the Napa Valley, where most of the red light had gone out of the sky and darkness encroached on all sides.

The old man in the Buick was no longer in front of them. They were not driving as fast as before, and evidently he had gotten far ahead of them.

Laura said softly, "Dear God."

Chyna was shaking uncontrollably. She plucked a few Kleenex from the console box between the seats, blew her nose, and blotted her eyes. Over the past two years, she had shared part of her childhood with Laura, but every new revelation—and there was much still to reveal—was as difficult as the one before it. When she spoke of the past, she always burned with shame, as though she had been as guilty as her mother, as if every criminal act and spell of madness could be blamed on her, though she had been only a helpless child trapped in the insanity of others.

"Will you ever see her again?" Laura asked.

Recollection had left Chyna half numb with horror. "I don't know."

"Would you want to?"

Chyna hesitated. Her hands were curled into fists, the damp Kleenex wadded in the right one. "Maybe."

"For God's sake why?"

"To ask her why. To try to understand. To settle some things. But . . . maybe not."

"Do you even know where she is?"

"No. But it wouldn't surprise me if she was in jail. Or dead. You can't live like that and hope to grow old."

They drove down out of the foothills into the valley.

Eventually Chyna said, "I can still see her standing in the steamy darkness on the banks of that canal, greasy with sweat, her hair hanging damp and all tangled, covered with mosquito bites, eyes bleary from vodka. Laura, even then she was *still* the most beautiful woman you've ever seen. She was always so beautiful, so perfect on the outside, like someone out of a dream, like an angel . . . but she was never half as beautiful as when she was excited, when there'd been violence. I can see her standing there, only visible because of the greenish glow from the headlights of the Mercedes rising through the murky canal water, so ravishing in that green light, glorious, the most beautiful person you've ever seen, like a goddess from another world."

Gradually Chyna's trembling subsided. The heat of shame faded from her face, but slowly.

She was immeasurably grateful for Laura's concern and support. A friend. Until Laura, Chyna had lived secretly with her past, unable to speak of it to anyone. Now, having unburdened herself of another hateful corrupting memory, she couldn't begin to put her gratitude into words.

"It's okay," Laura said, as if reading Chyna's mind.

They rode in silence.

They were late for dinner.

To Chyna, the Templeton house looked inviting at first glimpse: Victorian, gabled, roomy, with deep porches front and rear. It stood a half mile off the county road, at the end of a gravel driveway, surrounded by one hundred twenty acres of vineyards.

For three generations, the Templetons had grown grapes, but they had never made wine. They were under contract to one of the finest vintners in the valley, and because they owned fertile land with the highest-quality vines, they received an excellent price for their crop.

Sarah Templeton appeared on the front porch when she heard the Mustang in the driveway, and she came quickly down the steps to the stone walkway to greet Laura and Chyna. She was a lovely, girlishly slim woman in her early or mid forties, with stylishly short blond hair, wearing tan jeans and a long-sleeved emerald-green blouse with green embroidery on the collar, simultaneously chic and motherly. When Sarah hugged Laura and kissed her and held her with such evident and fierce love, Chyna was struck by a pang of envy and by a shiver of misery at never having known a mother's love.

She was surprised again when Sarah turned to her, embraced her, kissed her on the cheek, and, still holding her close, said, "Laura tells me you're the sister she never had, so I want you to feel at home here, sweetheart. When you're here with us, this is your place as much as ours."

Chyna stood stiffly at first, so unfamiliar with the rituals of family affection that she didn't know quite how to respond. Then she returned the embrace awkwardly and murmured an inadequate thank-you. Her throat was suddenly so tight that she was amazed to be able to speak at all.

Putting her arms around both Laura and Chyna, guiding them to the broad flight of porch steps, Sarah said, "We'll get your luggage later. Dinner's ready now. Come along. Laura's told me so much about you, Chyna."

"Well, Mom," said Laura, "I didn't tell you about Chyna being into voodoo. I sort of hid that part. She'll need to sacrifice a live chicken every night at midnight while she's staying with us."

"We only grow grapes. We don't have any chickens, dear," Sarah said. "But after dinner we can drive to one of the farms in the area and buy a few."

Chyna laughed and looked at Laura as if to say, *Where's the infamous Look?*

Laura understood. "In your honor, Chyna, all wire coat hangers and equivalent devices have been put away."

"Whatever are you talking about?" Sarah asked.

"You know me, Mom—a babbling ditz. Sometimes not even I know what I'm talking about."

Paul Templeton, Laura's father, was in the big kitchen, taking a potato-and-cheese casserole out of the oven. He was a neat, compact man, five feet ten, with thick dark hair and a ruddy complexion. He set the steaming dish aside, stripped off a pair of oven mitts, and greeted Laura as warmly as Sarah had done. After being introduced to Chyna, he took one of her hands in both of his, which were rough and work worn, and with feigned solemnity he said, "We prayed you'd make the trip in one piece. Does my little girl still handle that Mustang as if she thinks it's the Batmobile?"

"Hey, Dad," Laura said, "I guess you've forgotten who taught me to drive."

"I was instructing you in the basic techniques," Paul said. "I didn't expect you to acquire my *style.*"

Sarah said, "I refuse to think about Laura's driving. I'd just be worried sick all the time."

"Face it, Mom, there's an Indianapolis 500 gene on Dad's side of the family, and he passed it to me."

"She's an excellent driver," Chyna said. "I always feel safe with Laura."

Laura grinned at her and gave a thumbs-up sign.

Dinner was a long, leisurely affair because the Templetons liked to talk to one another, *thrived* on talking to one another. They were careful to include Chyna and seemed genuinely interested in what she had to say, but even when the conversation wandered to family matters of which Chyna had little knowledge, she somehow felt a part of it, as though she was, by a magical osmosis, actually being absorbed into the Templeton clan.

Laura's thirtyish brother, Jack, and his wife, Nina, lived in the caretaker's bungalow elsewhere in the vineyard, but a previous obligation had prevented them from joining the family for dinner. Chyna was assured that she would see them in the morning, and she felt no trepidation about meeting them, as she'd felt before she'd met Sarah and Paul. Throughout her troubled life, there had been no place where she had truly felt at home; while she might never feel entirely at home in this place either, at least she felt welcome here.

After dinner, Chyna and Laura went for a walk in the moonlit vineyards, between the rows of low pruned vines that had not yet begun to sprout either leafy trailers or fruit. The cool air was redolent with the pleasant fecund smell of freshly plowed earth, and there was a sense of mystery in the dark fields that she found intriguing, enchanting—but at times disconcerting, as if they were among unseen presences, ancient spirits that were not all benign.

When they had strolled deep into the vines and then turned back toward the house, Chyna said, "You're the best friend I've ever had."

"Me too," Laura said.

"More than that . . ." Chyna's voice trailed away. She had been about to say, *You're the* only *friend I've ever had,* but that made her seem so lame and, besides, was still an inadequate expression of what she felt for this girl. They were, indeed, in one sense sisters.

Laura linked arms with her and merely said, "I know."

"When you have babies, I want them to call me Aunt Chyna."

"Listen, Shepherd, don't you think I should find a guy and get married before I start pumping out the babies?"

"Whoever he is, he better be the best husband in the world to you, or I promise I'll cut his *cojones* off."

"Do me a favor, okay?" Laura said. "Don't tell him about this promise until after the wedding. Some guys might be put off by it."

From elsewhere in the vineyards came a disquieting sound that stopped Chyna. A protracted creaking.

"It's just the breeze working at a loose barn door, rusty hinges," Laura said.

It sounded as if someone were opening a giant door in the wall of night itself and stepping in from another world.

Chyna Shepherd could not sleep comfortably in strange houses. Throughout her childhood and adolescence, her mother had dragged her from one end of the country to the other, staying nowhere longer than a month or two. So many terrible things had happened to them in so many places that Chyna eventually learned to view each new house not as a new beginning, not with hope for stability and happiness, but with suspicion and quiet dread.

Now she was long rid of her troubled mother and free to stay only where she wished. These days, her life was almost as stable as that of a cloistered nun, as meticulously planned as any bomb squad's procedures for disarming an explosive device, and without any of the turmoil on which her mother had thrived.

Nevertheless, this first night in the Templetons' house, Chyna was reluctant to undress and go to bed. She sat in the darkness in a medallion-back armchair at one of the two windows in the guest room, gazing out at the moonlit vineyards, fields, and hills of the Napa Valley.

Laura was in another room, at the far end of the second-floor hall, no doubt sound asleep, at peace because this house was not at all strange to her.

From the guest-room window, the early-spring vineyards were barely visible. Vague geometric patterns.

Beyond the cultivated rows were gentle hills mantled in long dry grass, silver in the moonlight. An inconstant breeze stirred through the valley, and sometimes the wild grass seemed to roll like ocean waves across the slopes, softly aglimmer with lambent lunar light.

Above the hills was the Coast Range, and above those peaks were cascades of stars and a full white moon. Storm clouds coming across the mountains from the northwest would soon darken the night, turning the silver hills first to pewter and then to blackest iron.

When she heard the first scream, Chyna was gazing at the stars, drawn by their cold light as she had been since childhood, fascinated by the thought of distant worlds that might be barren and clean, free of pestilence. At first the muffled cry seemed to be only a memory, a fragment of a shrill argument from another strange house in the past, echoing across time. Often, as a child, eager to hide from her mother and her mother's friends when they were drunk or high, she climbed onto porch roofs or into backyard trees, slipped through windows onto fire escapes, away to secret places far from the fray, where she could study the stars and where voices raised in argument or sexual excitement or shrill drug-induced giddiness came to her as though from out of a radio, from faraway places and people who had no connection whatsoever with her life.

The second cry, though also brief and only slightly louder than the first, was indisputably of the moment, not a memory, and Chyna sat forward on her chair. Tense. Head cocked. Listening.

She wanted to believe that the voice had come from outside, so she continued to stare into the night, surveying the vineyards and the hills beyond. Breeze-driven waves swelled through the dry grass on the moon-washed slopes: a water mirage like the ghost tides of an ancient sea.

From elsewhere in the large house came a soft thump, as though a heavy object had fallen to a carpeted floor.

Chyna immediately rose from the chair and stood utterly still, expectant.

Trouble often followed voices raised in one kind of passion or another. Sometimes, however, the worst offenses were preceded by calculated silences and stealth.

She had difficulty reconciling the idea of domestic violence with Paul and Sarah Templeton, who had seemed kind and loving toward each other as toward their daughter. Nevertheless, appearances and realities were seldom the same, and the human talent for deception was far greater than that of the chameleon, the mockingbird, or the praying mantis, which masked its ferocious cannibalism with a serene and devout posture.

Following the stifled cries and the soft thump, silence sifted down like a snowfall. The hush was eerily deep, as unnatural as that in which the deaf lived. This was the stillness before the pounce, the quietude of the coiled snake.

In another part of the house, someone was standing as motionless as she herself was standing, as alert as she was, intently listening. Someone dangerous. She could sense the predatory presence, a subtle new pressure in the air, not dissimilar to that preceding a violent thunderstorm.

On one level, six years of psychology classes caused her to question her immediate fearful interpretation of those night sounds, which conceivably could be insignificant, after all. Any well-trained psychoanalyst would have a wealth of labels to pin on someone who leaped first to a negative conclusion, who lived in expectation of sudden violence.

But she had to trust her instinct. It had been honed by many years of hard experience.

Intuitively certain that safety lay in movement, she stepped quietly away from the chair at the window, toward the hall door. In spite of the moonglow, her eyes had adjusted to darkness during the two hours that she had sat in the lightless room, and now she eased through the gloom with no fear of blundering into furniture.

She was only halfway to the door when she heard approaching footsteps in the second-floor hall. The heavy, urgent tread was alien to this house.

Unhampered by the interminable second-guessing that accompanied an education in psychology, reverting to the intuition and defenses of childhood, Chyna quickly retreated to the bed. She dropped to her knees.

Farther along the hall, the footsteps stopped. A door opened.

She was aware of the absurdity of attributing rage to the mere opening of a door. The rattle of the knob being turned, the rasp of the unsecured latch, the spike-sharp squeak of an unoiled hinge—they were only sounds, neither meek nor furious, guilty nor innocent, and could have been made as easily by a priest as by a burglar. Yet she *knew* that rage was at work in the night.

Flat on her stomach, she wriggled under the bed, feet toward the headboard. It was a graceful piece of furniture with sturdy galbe legs, and fortunately it didn't sit as close to the floor as did most beds. One inch less of clearance would have prevented her from hiding under it.

Footsteps sounded in the hall again.

Another door opened. The guest-room door. Directly opposite the foot of the bed.

Someone switched on the lights.

Chyna lay with her head turned to one side, her right ear pressed to the carpet. Staring out from under the footboard, she could see a man's black boots and the legs of his blue jeans below mid-calf.

He stood just inside the threshold, evidently surveying the room. He would see a bed still neatly made at one o'clock in the morning, with four decorative needlepoint pillows arranged against the headboard.

She had left nothing on the nightstands. No clothes tossed on chairs. The paperback novel that she had brought with her for bedtime reading was in a bureau drawer.

She preferred spaces that were clean and uncluttered to the point of monastic sterility. Her preference might now save her life.

Again a faint doubt, the acquired propensity for self-analysis that plagued all psychology students, flickered through her. If the man in the doorway was someone with a right to be in the house—Paul Templeton or Laura's brother, Jack, who lived with his wife in the vineyard manager's bungalow elsewhere on the property—and if some crisis was unfolding that explained why he would burst into her room without knocking, she was going to appear to be a prime fool, if not a hysteric, when she crawled out from under the bed.

Then, directly in front of the black boots, a fat red droplet—another, and a third—fell to the wheat-gold carpet. *Plop-plop-plop.* Blood. The first two soaked into the thick nylon pile. The third held its surface tension, shimmering like a ruby.

Chyna knew the blood wasn't that of the intruder. She tried not to think about the sharp instrument from which it might have fallen.

He moved off to her right, deeper into the room, and she rolled her eyes to follow him.

The bed had carved side rails into which the spread was tightly tucked. No overhanging fabric obstructed her view of his boots.

Obversely, without a spread draped to the floor, the space under the bed was more visible to him. From certain angles, he might even be able to look down and see a swatch of *her* blue jeans, the toe of one of her Rockports, the cranberry-red sleeve of her cotton sweater where it stretched over her bent elbow.

She was thankful that the bed was queen-size, offering more cover than a single or double.

If he was breathing hard, either with excitement or with the rage that she had sensed in his approach, Chyna couldn't hear him. With one ear pressed tightly to the plush carpet, she was half deaf. Wood slats and box springs weighed on her back, and her chest barely had room to expand to accommodate her own shallow, cautious, open-mouth inhalations. The hammering of her compressed heart against her breastbone echoed tympanically within her, and it seemed to fill the claustrophobic confines of her hiding place to such an extent that the intruder was certain to hear.

He went to the bathroom, pushed open the door, and flicked on the lights.

She had put away all her toiletries in the medicine cabinet. Even her toothbrush. Nothing lay out that might alert him to her presence.

But was the sink dry?

On retiring to her room at eleven o'clock, she had used the toilet and then had washed her hands. That was two hours ago. Any residual water in the bowl surely would have drained away or evaporated.

Lemon-scented liquid soap in a pump dispenser was provided at the sink. Fortunately, there was no damp bar of soap to betray her.

She worried about the hand towel. She doubted that it could still be damp two hours after the little use she had made of it. Nonetheless, in spite of a propensity for neatness and order, she might have left it hanging ever so slightly askew or with one telltale wrinkle.

He seemed to stand on the bathroom threshold for an eternity. Then he switched off the fluorescent light and returned to the bedroom.

Occasionally, as a little girl—and then not so little—Chyna had taken refuge under beds. Sometimes they looked for her there; sometimes, though it was the most obvious of all hidey-holes, they never thought to look. Of those who found her, a few had checked under the bed first—but most had left it for last.

Another red droplet fell to the carpet, as though the beast might be shedding slow tears of blood.

He moved toward the closet door.

Chyna had to turn her head slightly, straining her neck, to keep track of him.

The closet was deep, a walk-in with a chain-pull light in the center. She heard the distinctive snap of the tugged switch, then the clinking of the metal beads in the chain as they rattled against the light bulb.

The Templetons stored their own luggage at the back of that closet. Stacked with the other suitcases, Chyna's single bag and train case were not obviously those of a guest in residence.

She had brought several changes of clothes: two dresses, two skirts, another pair of jeans, a pair of chinos, a leather jacket. Because Chyna was the same size as Laura, the intruder might conclude that the few garments on the rod were just spillovers from the packed closet in Laura's room rather than evidence of a houseguest.

If he had been in Laura's bedroom, however, and had seen the condition of her closet—then what had happened to Laura?

She must not think about that. Not now. Not yet. For the moment, she needed to focus all her thoughts, all her wits, on staying alive.

Eighteen years ago, on the night of her eighth birthday, in a seaside cottage on Key West, Chyna had squirmed under her bed to hide from Jim Woltz, her mother's friend. A storm had been raging from the Gulf of Mexico, and the sky-blistering lightning had made her fearful of escaping to the sanctuary of the beach where she'd retreated on other nights. After committing herself to the cramped space under that iron bed, which had been lower slung than this one, she had discovered that she was sharing it with a palmetto beetle. Palmettos were not as exotic or as pretty as their name. In fact, they were nothing more than enormous tropical cockroaches. This one had been as large as her little-girl hand. Ordinarily the hateful bug would have scurried away from her. But it had seemed less alarmed by her than by the thundering Woltz, who had crashed around her small room in a drunken fury, rebounding tirelessly from the furniture and the walls, like an enraged animal throwing itself against the bars of its cage. Chyna had been barefoot, dressed in blue shorts and a white tube top, and the palmetto beetle had raced in a frenzy over all that exposed skin, between her toes, up and down her legs and up again, across her back, along her neck, into her hair, over her shoulder, the length of her slender arm. She hadn't dared to squeal in revulsion, afraid of drawing Woltz's attention. He had been wild that night, like a monster from a dream, and she had been convinced that, like all monsters, he possessed supernaturally keen sight and hearing, the better to hunt children. She hadn't even found the courage to strike out at the beetle or knock it away, for fear that Woltz would hear the smallest sound even over the shriek of the storm and the incessant crashing of thunder. She had endured the palmetto's attentions in order to avoid those of Woltz, clenching her teeth to bite off a scream, praying desperately for God to save her, then praying harder for God to take her, praying for an end to the torment even if by a bolt of lightning, an end to the torment, an end, dear God, an end.

Now, although she wasn't sharing the space under this galhe-leg bed with any cockroach, Chyna could feel one crawling over her toes as if she were that barefoot girl again, scurrying up her legs as if she were wearing not jeans but cotton shorts. She had never again worn her hair long since the night of her eighth birthday, when the bug had burrowed through her tresses, but now she felt the ghost of that palmetto in her closely cropped hair.

The man in the closet, perhaps capable of atrocities infinitely worse than the wickedest dreams of Woltz, tugged on the chain-pull. The light went out with a click followed by a tinkle of metal beads.

The booted feet reappeared and approached the bed. A fresh tear of blood glistened on the curve of black leather.

He was going to drop to one knee beside the bed.

Dear God, he'll find me cowering like a child, choking on my own stifled scream, in a cold sweat, all dignity lost in the desperate struggle to stay alive, untouched and alive, untouched and alive.

She had the crazy feeling that when he peered under the side rail, face-to-face with her, he would be not a man but an enormous palmetto with multifaceted black eyes.

She had been reduced to the helplessness of childhood, to the primal fear that she had hoped never to know again. He had stolen from her the self-respect that she had earned from years of endurance—that she had *earned*, God damn him—and the injustice of it filled her eyes with bitter tears.

But then his blurred boots turned away from her and kept moving. He walked past the bed to the open door.

Whatever he'd thought about the clothes hanging in the closet, apparently he had not inferred from them that the guest room was occupied.

She blinked furiously, clearing her tear-blurred vision.

He stopped and turned, evidently studying the bedroom one last time.

Lest he hear her child-shallow exhalations, Chyna held her breath.

She was glad that she wore no perfume. She was certain that he would have smelled her.

He switched off the light, stepped into the hall, and pulled the door shut as he went.

His footsteps moved off the way he had come, for her room was the last on the second floor. His tread swiftly faded, cloaked by the fierce pounding of her heart.

Her first inclination was to remain in that narrow haven between the carpet and the box springs, wait until daybreak or even longer, wait until there came a long silence that ceased to seem like the stillness of a crouched predator.

But she didn't know what had happened to Laura, Paul, or Sarah. Any of them—all of them—might be alive, grievously wounded but drawing breath. The intruder might even be keeping them alive to torture them at his leisure. Any newspaper regularly reported stories of cruelty no worse than the possible scenarios that now unreeled vividly in her mind. And if any of the Templetons still lived, Chyna might be their only hope of survival.

She had crawled out of all the many hideaways of her childhood with less fear than she felt when she hesitantly slid out from under this bed. Of course she had more to lose now than before she had walked out on her mother, ten years ago: a decent life built on a decade of ceaseless struggle and hard-won self-respect. It seemed madness to take this risk when safety was assured simply by her staying put. But personal safety at the expense of others was cowardice, and cowardice was a right only of small children who lacked the strength and experience to defend themselves.

She couldn't simply retreat into the defensive detachment of her childhood. Doing so would mean the end of all self-respect. Slow-motion suicide. It's not possible to retreat into a bottomless pit—one can only plunge.

In the open once more, she rose into a crouch beside the bed. For a while that was as far as she got. She was frozen by the expectation that the door would crash open and that the intruder would burst in again.

The house was as echo-free as any airless moon.

Chyna rose to her feet and silently crossed the dark guest room. Unable to see the trio of blood drops, she tried to step around the place where they had fallen earlier.

She pressed her left ear to the crack between the door and the jamb, listening for movement or breathing in the hall. She heard nothing, yet she remained suspicious.

He could be on the other side of the door. Smiling. Deeply amused to think that she was listening. Biding his time. Patient because he knew that eventually she would open the door and step into his arms.

Screw it.

She put her hand on the knob, turned it cautiously, and winced as the spring latch scraped softly out of its notch. At least the hinges were lubricated and silent.

Even in the inkiness to which her vision had not totally readapted, she could see that no one was waiting for her. She stepped out of her room and soundlessly pulled the door shut.

The guest quarters were off the shorter arm of the L-shaped upstairs hall. To her right were the back stairs, which led down to the kitchen. To her left lay the turn into the longer arm of the L.

She ruled out the back stairs. She had descended them earlier in the evening, when she and Laura went out to walk the vineyards. They were wooden and worn. They creaked and popped. The stairwell acted as an amplifier, as hollow and efficient as a steel drum. With the house so preternaturally silent, it would be impossible to creep down the back stairs undetected.

The second-floor hall and the front stairs, on the other hand, were plushly carpeted.

From around the corner, somewhere along the main hallway, came a soft amber glow. In the wallpaper, the delicate pattern of faded roses appeared to absorb the light rather than reflect it, acquiring an enigmatic depth that it had not previously possessed.

If the intruder had been standing anywhere between the junction of the hallways and the source of the light, he would have cast a distorted shadow across that luminous paper garden or on the wheat-gold carpet. There was no shadow.

Keeping her back close to the wall, Chyna edged to the corner, hesitated, and leaned out to scout the way ahead. The main hallway was deserted.

Two sources of faint amber light relieved the gloom. The first came from a half-open door on the right: Paul and Sarah's suite. The second was much farther down the hallway, past the front stairs, on the left: Laura's room.

The other doors all seemed to be closed. She didn't know what lay beyond them. Perhaps other bedrooms, a bath, an upstairs study, closets. Although Chyna was most drawn to—and most afraid of—the lighted rooms, every closed door was also a danger.

The unplumbable silence tempted her to believe that the intruder had gone. This was a temptation best resisted.

Forward, then, through the paper arbor of printed roses to the half-open door of the master suite. Hesitating there. On the brink.

When she found whatever waited to be found, all her illusions of order and stability might dissolve. The truth of life might then reassert itself, after ten years during which she had diligently denied it: chaos, like the flow of a stream of mercury, its course unpredictable.

The man in the blue jeans and black boots might have returned to the master suite after leaving the guest room, but more likely not. Other amusements in the house would no doubt be more appealing to him.

Fearful of lingering too long in the hall, she sidled across the threshold, without pushing the door open wider.

Paul and Sarah's room was spacious. A sitting area included a pair of armchairs and footstools facing a fireplace. Bookshelves crammed with hardcovers flanked the mantel, their titles lost in shadows.

The nightstand lamps were colorfully patterned ginger jars with pleated shades. One of them was aglow; crimson streaks and blots stained its shade.

Chyna stopped well short of the foot of the bed, already close enough to see too much. Neither Paul nor Sarah was there, but the sheets and blankets were in tangled disarray, trailing onto the floor on the right side of the bed. On the left, the linens were soaked with blood, and a wet spray glistened on the headboard and in an arc across the wall.

She closed her eyes. Heard something. Spun around, crouching in expectation of an assault. She was alone.

The noise had always been there, a background hiss-patter-splash of falling water. She hadn't heard it on entering the room, because she had been deafened by bloodstains as loud as the angry shouting of a maddened mob.

Synesthesia. The word had stuck with her from a psychology text, more because she thought it was a beautiful arrangement of syllables than because she expected ever to experience it herself. Synesthesia: a confusion of the senses in which a scent might register as a flash of color, a sound actually might be perceived as a scent, and the texture of a surface under the hand might seem to be a trilling laugh or a scream.

Closing her eyes had blocked out the roar of the bloodstains, whereupon she had heard the falling water. Now she recognized it as the sound of the shower in the adjoining bathroom.

That door was ajar half an inch. For the first time since she had entered from the hallway, Chyna noticed the thin band of fluorescent light along the bathroom jamb.

When she looked away from that door, reluctant to confront what might wait beyond it, she spotted the telephone on the right-hand nightstand. That was the side of the bed without blood, which made it more approachable for her.

She lifted the handset from the cradle. No dial tone. She had not expected to hear one. Nothing was ever that easy.

She opened the single drawer on the nightstand, hoping to find a handgun. No luck.

Still certain that her only hope of safety lay in movement, that crawling into a hole and hiding should always be the strategy of last resort, Chyna had gone around to the other side of the king-size bed before she quite realized that she had taken a first step. In front of the bathroom door, the carpet was badly stained.

Grimacing, she went to the second nightstand and eased open the drawer. In the mortal fall of light, she discovered a pair of reading glasses with yellow reflections in the half-moon lenses, a paperback men's adventure novel, a box of Kleenex, a tube of lip balm, but no weapon.

As she closed the drawer, she smelled burned gunpowder underlying the hot-copper stench of fresh blood.

She was familiar with that odor. Over the years, more than a few of her mother's friends either had used guns to get what they wanted or had been at least fascinated by them.

Chyna had heard no shots. The intruder evidently had a weapon with a sound suppressor.

Water continued to cascade into the shower beyond the door. That susurrous splash, though soft and soothing under other circumstances, now abraded her nerves as effectively as the whine of a dentist's drill.

She was sure that the intruder wasn't in the bathroom. His work here was done. He was busy elsewhere in the house.

Right this minute she was not as frightened of the man himself as she was of discovering exactly what he had done. But the choice before her was the essence of the entire human agony: not knowing was ultimately worse than knowing.

At last she pushed open the door. Squinting, she entered the fluorescent glare.

The roomy bath featured yellow and white ceramic tile. On the walls at chair-rail height and around the edges of the vanity and lavatory counters ran a decorative tile band of daffodils and green leaves. She had expected more blood.

Paul Templeton was propped on the toilet in his blue pajamas. Lengths of wide strapping tape across his lap fixed him to the bowl. More tape encircled both his chest and the toilet tank, holding him upright.

Through the semitransparent bands of tape, three separate bullet wounds were visible in his chest. There might have been more than three. She didn't care to look for them and had no need to know. He appeared to have died instantly, most likely in his sleep, and to have been dead before he was brought into the bathroom.

Grief welled in her, black and cold. Survival meant repressing it at all costs, and surviving was the thing that she did best.

A collar of strapping tape around Paul's neck became a leash that tethered him to a hand-towel rack on the wall behind the toilet. The purpose was to prevent his head from falling forward onto his chest—and to direct his dead gaze toward the shower. His eyelids were taped open, and in his right eye was a starburst hemorrhage.

Shuddering, Chyna looked away from him.

Although the intruder had needed to kill Paul in his sleep to establish control of the house quickly, here he had been fantasizing that the husband was being forced to watch the atrocities committed against the wife.

This was a classic tableau, a favorite of those sociopaths who took delight in performing for their victims. They actually seemed to believe that for a while the recently dead could still see, still hear, and were thus capable of admiring the bold antics and posing of a tormentor who feared neither man nor God. Textbooks described the delusion. In one of her aberrant-psychology classes at UCSF, a speaker from the FBI's Behavioral Science Section had given them more graphic descriptions of such scenes than any textbooks could provide.

Firsthand, however, the impact of this brutality was worse than words could convey. Almost paralyzing. Chyna's legs felt heavy and stiff. The tingling in her hands was incipient numbness.

Sarah Templeton was in the stall shower, which was separate from the tub. Although the glass door was closed—and frosted—Chyna was able to see a faint, vaguely pinkish shape huddled on the shower floor.

On the face of the soffit above the glass door, the killer had printed two words. The black letters appeared to have been made with multiple strokes of an eyebrow pencil: DIRTY BITCH.

Chyna had never wanted anything as much as she wanted to be free of the obligation to look into this shower stall. Surely Sarah could not be alive.

Yet if she turned away without being certain that the woman was beyond all help, ineradicable guilt would ensure that her own survival would become a kind of walking death.

Besides, she had committed her life to trying to understand this very aspect of human cruelty, and no published case study would ever bring her closer to comprehension than might the things that she saw here. In this house, on this night, the bleak landscape of the sociopathic mind had been externalized.

Echoing off the tile walls, the sizzle-splash of the falling water sounded like the hissing of serpents and the brittle laughter of strange children.

The water must be cold. Otherwise, steam would have been seething over the top of the shower enclosure.

Chyna held her breath, gripped the anodized aluminum handle, and opened the stall door.

Sarah Templeton had been wearing a pale-green teddy and matching panties. Her garments were in a sodden ball in one corner of the shower.

After her husband had been shot, the woman had evidently been hammered unconscious, perhaps with the butt of the gun. Then she had been gagged; her cheeks bulged with whatever rag had been forced into her mouth. Strips of strapping tape had sealed her lips, but in the relentless icy spray, the edges of the tape had begun to peel away from her skin.

With Sarah, the killer had used a knife. She was not alive.

Chyna quietly closed the stall door.

If there was such a thing as mercy, then Sarah Templeton had never regained any awareness after being knocked unconscious.

She remembered the hug that Sarah had given her on the front walk when she had first arrived with Laura. Repressing tears, she wished that she herself were dead instead of the precious woman in the shower stall. Indeed, she *was* half dead and less alive by the minute, because a piece of her heart died with each of these people.

Chyna returned to the bedroom. She moved away from the bed but didn't go immediately toward the hall door. Instead, she stood in the darkest corner, shaking uncontrollably.

Her stomach rolled. An acidic burning rose in her chest, and a bitter taste filled the back of her mouth. She suppressed an urge to vomit. The killer might hear her retching, and then he would come to get her.

Although she'd met Laura's parents only the previous afternoon, Chyna had known them also from her friend's numerous anecdotes and colorful stories of family adventures. She should have felt even more grief than she did, but she had only a limited capacity for it right now. Later it would hit her harder. Grief thrived in a quiet heart, and right now hers thundered with terror and revulsion.

She was shocked that the killer had done so much damage while she had sat, unknowing, at the guest-room window, brooding on the stars and thinking of other nights when she had gazed at them from rooftops, backyard trees, and beaches. From what she'd seen, he had taken at least ten or fifteen minutes with Paul and Sarah before searching the rest of the large house to locate and overpower the remaining occupants.

Sometimes a man like this got a special thrill from risking interruption, even apprehension. Perhaps a half-asleep, bewildered child would be drawn into the parents' room by some commotion and then would have to be pursued and dragged down before escaping the house. Such possibilities heightened the pleasure that the creep took from his activities in the bedroom and the bath.

This *was* a pleasure to him. A compulsion, but not one over which he despaired. Fun. His recreation. No guilt—therefore, no anguish. Savagery gladdened him.

Somewhere in the house, he was either at play or resting until he was ready to begin the game again.

As her shakes subsided to shivers, Chyna grew increasingly afraid for Laura. Those two muffled cries, minutes ago, had surely come after Sarah was already dead, so Laura must have been surprised in her sleep by a man smelling of her mother's blood. As soon as he had overpowered and secured her, he had hurried to search the rest of the second floor, concerned that another member of the family might have been alerted by her stifled screams.

He might not have returned immediately to Laura. Having found no one in any of the other rooms, confident that the house was firmly under his reign, he most likely had gone exploring. If the textbooks were correct, he would probably wish to violate every private space. Pore through the contents of his host's and hostess's closets and desk drawers. Eat food from their refrigerator. Read their mail. Perhaps finger and smell the soiled clothing in the laundry-room hamper. If he could locate collections of family photographs, he might even sit in the den for an hour or longer, amusing himself with those albums.

Sooner or later, however, he would return to Laura.

Sarah Templeton had been an extremely attractive woman, but night visitors like this man were drawn toward youth; they fed on innocence. Laura was his meat of choice, as irresistible as birds' eggs to certain tree-climbing serpents.

When at last Chyna overcame her racking nausea and was certain that she wouldn't betray herself by being suddenly and violently sick, she crept out of the corner and silently crossed the room.

She wouldn't have been safe in the master suite anyway. Before the visitor left, he was likely to return here for one last look at poor Sarah in the shower with her slender arms crossed in a pathetic and ineffective posture of defense.

At the half-open door, Chyna paused to listen.

Directly across the hall, the faded roses on the wallpaper seemed more mysterious than ever. The pattern had such enigmatic depth that she was almost convinced she might be able to part the thorny vines and step out of that paper arbor into a sunny realm where, when she looked back, this house would not exist.

With the light from the nightstand lamp behind her, she could not ease cautiously into the doorway and take her time peeking left and right, because when she moved onto the threshold, she would cast a shadow on those faded roses across the hall. Dawdling behind that unavoidable announcement of herself would be dangerous.

Seduced by a long silence that seemed to promise safety, she finally sidled between the half-open door and the jamb, into the hallway—and he was *there*. Ten feet away. Near the head of the front stairs, which lay to the right. His back was to her.

She froze. Half in the hallway. Half on the threshold to the master suite. If he turned, she would not be able to slip away before he glimpsed her from the corner of his eye—yet she was unable to move now while there was still a chance to avoid him. She was afraid that if she made any sound whatsoever, he would hear it and spin toward her. Even the microwhispers of carpet fibers compressing under her shoe, if she moved, seemed certain to draw his attention.

The visitor was doing something so bizarre that Chyna was as transfixed by his activity as by her fear. His hands were raised in front of him, stretched as high as he could reach, and his spread fingers languorously combed the air. He seemed to be in a trance, as though trying to seine psychic impressions from the ether.

He was a big man. Six feet two, maybe even taller. Muscular. Narrow waist, enormous shoulders. His denim jacket stretched tautly across his broad back.

His hair was thick and brown, neatly barbered against the nape of his bull neck, but Chyna could not see his face. She hoped never to see it.

His seining fingers, stained with blood, looked crushingly strong. He would be able to choke the life out of her with a single-hand grip.

"Come to me," he murmured.

Even in a whisper, his rough voice had a timbre and a power that were magnetic.

"Come to me."

He seemed to be speaking not to a vision that only he could see but to *Chyna*, as if his senses were so acute that he had been able to detect her merely from the movement of the air that she had displaced when she'd stepped soundlessly through the doorway.

Then she saw the spider. It dangled from the ceiling on a gossamer filament a foot above the killer's reaching hands.

"Please."

As if responding to the man's supplications, the spider spun out its thread, descending. The killer stopped reaching, turned his hand palm-up. "Little one," he breathed.

Fat and black, the obedient spider reeled itself down into the big open palm.

The killer brought his hand to his mouth and tipped his head back slightly. He either crushed the spider and ate it—or ate it alive.

He stood motionless, savoring.

Finally, without looking back, he went to the head of the stairs on the right, at the midpoint of the hallway, and descended spider-quick and almost spider-silent to the first floor.

Chyna shuddered, stunned to be alive.

TWO

The house held a drowning depth of stillness as a dam held water, with tremendous pent-up power and pressure on the breast.

When Chyna found the courage to move, she cautiously approached the head of the stairs. She feared that the visitor had not fully descended to the first floor, that he was toying with her, standing just out of sight, waiting, smiling. He would reach for her, palms up, and say, *Come to me.*

She held her breath, risked exposure, and looked down. The stairs curved through gradients of gloom to the foyer below. She could see just well enough to be sure that he wasn't there.

As far as Chyna could discern, no lamps were on downstairs. She wondered what he was doing in that darkness, guided only by the pale moonglow at the windows. Perhaps he was in a corner, crouched like a spider, sensitive to the faintest changes in the patterns of the air, dreaming of silent stalkings and the frenzied rending of prey.

She went quickly past the head of the stairs, into the last length of hallway, to the next open door and the second source of amber light, dreading what she might find. But she could cope with both the dread and the finding. It was always *not* knowing, turning away from truth, that caused night sweats and bad dreams.

This room was smaller than the master suite, with no sitting area. A corner desk. A double bed. One nightstand with a brass lamp, a dresser, a vanity with a padded bench.

On the wall above the bed was a poster-size portrait of Freud. Chyna loathed Freud. But Laura, dear of heart and idealistic, clung to a belief in many aspects of Freudian theory; she embraced the dream of a guiltless world, with everyone a victim of his troubled past and yearning for rehabilitation.

Laura was lying facedown on the bed, atop the sheets and the blankets. Her wrists were handcuffed behind her. A second pair of handcuffs secured her ankles. Linking both of those shiny steel restraints was a shackling chain.

She had been violated. The pants of her baggy blue pajamas had been cut off with a neatness worthy of a conscientious tailor; the blue panels of cloth had been smoothed across the blankets to both sides of her. The pajama shirt had been shoved up her back; now it was gathered in rumpled folds across her shoulders and the nape of her neck.

Chyna moved deeper into the room, her fear equaled now by a swelling sorrow that seemed to enlarge her heart yet leave it cold and empty. When she caught a faint odor of spilled semen, her fear and sorrow were matched by anger. As she stooped beside the bed, her hands curled into such hard fists that her fingernails pressed painfully into her palms.

Sweat-damp blond hair was pasted to the side of Laura's face. Her delicate features were salt-pale and clenched in anxiety, and her eyes were squeezed tightly shut.

She was not dead. Not dead. It seemed impossible.

The girl—terror had reduced her to the condition of a girl—was murmuring so softly that the words couldn't be heard even from a distance of inches, yet so urgently that the meaning was harrowingly clear. It was a prayer, one that Chyna had recited on numerous nights long ago, in far places: a prayer for mercy, a plea to be delivered from this horror untouched and alive, dear God, please, untouched and alive.

On those other nights, Chyna had been spared both violation and death. Already, half of Laura's petition had gone unanswered.

Chyna's throat tightened with anguish, and she could barely speak: "It's me."

Laura's eyelids sprang open, and her blue eyes rolled like those of a terrified horse, wide with disbelief. "All dead."

"Ssshhh," Chyna whispered.

"Blood. His hands."

"Ssshhh. I'll get you out of here."

"Stank like blood. Jack's dead. Nina. Everyone."

Jack, her brother, whom Chyna had not met. Nina, her sister-in-law. Evidently the killer had been to the vineyard manager's bungalow before coming to the main house. Four dead. There was no help to be found anywhere on the sprawling property.

Chyna glanced worriedly at the open door, then quickly rose to test the handcuffs on Laura's wrists. Securely locked.

With fettered hands and fettered ankles linked by a chain, Laura was thoroughly hobbled. She wouldn't be able to stand, let alone walk.

Chyna wasn't strong enough to carry her.

She saw her reflection in the vanity mirror across the room, and she realized with a shock how nakedly her terror was revealed in her wrenched face.

Trying to look more composed for Laura's sake, Chyna stopped beside the bed again and murmured almost as softly as her friend had been praying: "Is there a gun?"

"What?"

"A gun in the house?"

"No."

"Nowhere in the house?"

"No, no."

"Shit."

"Jack."

"What?"

"Has one."

"A gun? At the bungalow?" Chyna asked.

"Jack has a gun."

Chyna didn't have time to get to the bungalow and back before the killer returned to Laura's room. Anyway, more likely than not, he had already found the gun and confiscated it.

"Do you know who he is?"

"No." Laura's sky-blue eyes appeared to darken with despair. "Get out."

"I'll find a weapon."

"*Get out,*" Laura whispered more urgently, cold sweat glistening on her brow.

"A knife," Chyna said.

"Don't die for me." Then, *sotto voce,* tremulously but fiercely, fiercely she said: "Run, Chyna. Oh, God, please *run!*"

"I'll be back."

"*Run.*"

From outside, a sound arose. A truck engine. Approaching.

Astonished, Chyna shot to her feet. "Someone's coming. Help's coming."

Laura's bedroom was toward the front of the house. Chyna stepped to the nearer of two windows, which provided a view of the half-mile driveway leading in from the two-lane county road.

A quarter of a mile away, bright headlights pierced the night. Judging by the height of the lights from the ground, Chyna concluded that the truck was big.

How miraculous that anyone would show up at this hour, in this lonely place.

As a thrill of hope swept through Chyna, she realized that the killer would have heard the engine too. The man or men in the truck wouldn't know what trouble they were getting into. When they stopped in front of the house, they would be dead men breathing.

"Hold on," she said, touched Laura's damp forehead to reassure her, and then crossed the room to the door, leaving her friend under the smug and somber gaze of Sigmund Freud.

The hallway was deserted.

Chyna hurried to the head of the curved stairs, hesitated to commit herself to the tenebrous lair below, but then realized that she had nowhere else to go. She went down as fast as she dared without the support of the handrail. Staying clear of the balustrade. Too exposed there. Close to the wall was better.

She quickly passed a series of large landscape paintings in ornate frames, which seemed almost to be windows on actual pastoral vistas. Earlier, they had been bright and cheerful scenes. Now they were ominous: goblin forests, black rivers, killing fields.

The foyer. An oval area rug on polished oak. Through a closed door to the right was Paul Templeton's study. Through the archway on the left was the dark living room.

The killer could be anywhere.

Outside, the roar of the truck grew louder. It was almost to the house. The driver would be shot through the windshield the moment that he braked to a stop. Or gunned down when he stepped out from behind the steering wheel.

Chyna had to warn him, not solely for his sake but for her own, for Laura's. He was their only hope.

Certain that the spider-eating intruder was nearby, she expected a savage attack and, abandoning caution, *flew* at the front door. The oval rug rucked beneath her feet, twisted, and nearly spun out from under her. She stumbled, reached out to break her fall, and slammed both palms flat against the front door.

Such a noise, hellacious noise, booming through the house, had surely drawn the killer's attention away from the approaching truck.

Chyna fumbled, found the knob, and twisted it. The door was unlocked. Gasping, she pulled it open.

A cool breeze out of the northwest, faintly scented by freshly turned vineyard earth and fungicide, whistled through the bare limbs of the maple trees that flanked the front walkway. Snuffling like a pack of hounds, it rushed past her into the foyer as she stepped out onto the front porch.

The truck had already passed the house and was heading away from her. It would come around for a second approach on the end-loop of the driveway, which was wide enough to accommodate produce haulers in the harvest season, and park facing out toward the county road. But it wasn't a truck after all. A motor home. An older model with rounded lines, well kept, forty feet long, either blue or green. Its chrome glimmered like quicksilver under the late-winter moon.

Amazed that she had not yet been stabbed or shot or struck from behind, glancing back at the open front door where the killer hadn't yet appeared, Chyna headed for the porch steps.

The motor home rounded the end of the loop, beginning to turn toward her. Its twin beams swept across the Templetons' barn and other outbuildings.

Larch and maple and evergreen shadows fled before the arcing headlights. They flickered darkly through the trellis at the end of the porch, along the white balustrade, across the lawn and the stone walkway, stretching impossibly, swooping into the night as if trying frantically to tear free of the trees that cast them.

The deep quiet in the house, the lack of lights downstairs, the killer's failure to attack her as she escaped, the timely arrival of the motor home—suddenly all of those things made chilling sense. The killer was driving the motor home.

"*No.*"

Chyna swiftly retreated from the porch steps and scrambled back into the foyer.

At her heels, the headlights came all the way around the end of the driveway loop. They pierced the trellis grid, projecting geometric patterns across the porch floor and the front wall of the house.

She closed the door and fumbled for the big lock above the knob. Found the thumb-turn. Engaged the heavy deadbolt.

Then she realized her mistake. The front door had been unlocked because the killer had gone out that way. If he found it locked now, he would know that Laura wasn't the only person alive in the house, and the hunt would begin.

Her sweaty fingers slipped on the brass thumb-turn, but the bolt snapped open with a hard *clack*.

Earlier, he must have parked the vehicle near the end of the half-mile-long driveway, out toward the county road, and must have walked to the house.

Now tires crunched through gravel. Air brakes issued a soft whoosh and a softer whine, and the motor home came to a full stop in front of the house.

Remembering the oval rug that had turned under her feet and had nearly sent her sprawling, Chyna dropped to her knees. She crawled across the wool, smoothing the rumples with her hands. If the killer tripped over the disarranged rug, he would know that it hadn't been in that condition when he'd left.

Footsteps arose outside: boot heels ringing off the flagstone walkway.

Chyna came to her feet and turned toward the study. No good. She couldn't know for sure where he would go when he reentered the house, and if he stepped into the study, she would be trapped in there with him.

His tread echoed hollowly from the wooden porch steps.

Chyna lunged across the foyer, through the archway, into the dark living room—and immediately came to a halt, afraid of stumbling into furniture and knocking it over. She edged forward, feeling her way with both hands, vision hampered by the muddy-red ghost images of the motor-home headlights, which still floated faintly across her retinas.

The front door opened.

Less than halfway across the living room, Chyna squatted beside an armchair. If the killer entered and switched on the lights, he would see her.

Without closing the door behind him, the man appeared in the foyer, beyond the arch. He was dimly limned by the glow from the second-floor hallway. He passed the living room and went directly to the stairs.

Laura.

Chyna still had no weapon.

She thought of the fireplace poker. Not good enough. Unless she caved in his skull on the first blow or broke his arm, he would wrest the poker away from her. She had the strength of terror, but maybe that wouldn't be enough.

Rather than rise to her feet and blunder blindly across the living room, she stayed down and crawled because it was safer and quicker. She reached the dining-room archway and angled toward where she thought she'd find the kitchen door.

She thumped into a chair. It rattled against a table leg. On the table, something shifted with a *clink-clink*, and she remembered seeing carefully arranged ceramic fruit in a copper bowl.

She didn't think that he could have heard these sounds all the way upstairs, so she kept going. There was nothing to do but keep going anyway, whether he had heard or not.

When she reached the swinging door sooner than she had expected, she got to her feet.

Though the infiltrating moonlight was already dim, it suddenly faded away, causing the flesh on the nape of her neck to crawl with a dire expectation. She turned, pressing her back against the doorframe, certain that the killer was close behind her, silhouetted in front of a window, blocking the lunar glow, but he wasn't there. The silver radiance no longer painted the glass. Evidently the storm clouds, rolling out of the northwest since before midnight, had finally shrouded the moon.

Pushing on the swinging door, she went into the kitchen.

She wouldn't need to switch on the overhead fluorescent panels. The upper of the double ovens featured a digital clock with green numerals that emitted a surprising amount of light, enough to allow her to find her way around the room.

She recalled having seen a section of butcher-block countertop to one side of the stainless-steel sinks. The sinks were in front of the wider of the two windows. She slid her hand along the cold granite counters until she located the remembered wooden surface.

The house above her seemed filled with a higher order of silence than ever before.

What's the bastard doing up there in all that silence, up there in all that silence with Laura?

Under the butcher block was a drawer where she expected to find knives. Found them. Neatly slotted in a holder.

She withdrew one. Too short. Another. This one was a bread knife with a blunt round end. The third that she selected proved to be a butcher knife. She carefully tested the cutting edge against the ball of her thumb and found it satisfyingly sharp.

Upstairs, Laura screamed.

Chyna started toward the dining-room door but sensed intuitively that she dared not go that way. She rushed instead to the back stairs, even though they couldn't be climbed without making noise.

She switched on the light in the stairwell. The killer could not see her here.

From the second floor, Laura cried out again—a terrible wail of despair, pain, horror, like a cry that might have been heard in the poison-gas chambers at Dachau or in the windowless interrogation rooms of Siberian prisons during the era of the gulags. It was not a scream for help or even a begging for mercy, but a plea for release at any cost, even death.

Chyna clambered up the stairs into that scream, which presented her with real resistance, as if she were a swimmer struggling toward the surface of a sea, against a great weight of water. As cold as an Arctic current, the cry chilled her, numbed her, throbbed icily in the hollows of her bones. She was overcome by a compulsion to scream *with* Laura as a dog wails in sympathy when it hears another dog suffering, a primal need to howl in misery at the sheer helplessness of human existence in a universe full of dead stars, and she had to fight that urge.

Laura's scream spiraled into a bawling for her mother, though she must know that her mother was dead. "Mommy, Mommy, *Mommeeeeee.*" She was reduced to the dependency of an infant, too terrified of life itself to find solace anywhere but in the familiar succoring breast and in the sound of that same heartbeat remembered from the womb.

And then sudden quiet.

Bleak silence.

On the landing, halfway to the second floor, Chyna was surprised to realize that the thousand-fathom weight of the scream had brought her to a standstill. Her legs were weak; her calf and thigh muscles quivered as if she had run a marathon. She seemed on the brink of collapse.

Because it might signify the end of hope, the silence was now as oppressive as the scream. She bent her head under a hush as heavy as an iron crown, hunched her shoulders, and huddled miserably upon herself.

It would be so easy to lean against the wall, slide down to the floor, put the knife aside, and curl defensively. Just wait until he had gone away. Wait until a relative or a friend of the family arrived, discovered the bodies, went for the police, and took care of everything.

Instead, after pausing only a few seconds on the landing, Chyna forced herself to continue the climb, heart pounding so hard that it seemed as if each blow might knock her down.

Her arms shook uncontrollably. In her white-knuckle grip, the butcher knife carved wobbly patterns in the air in front of her, and she wondered if she would have the strength, in any confrontation, to thrust and slash effectively.

That was the thinking of a loser, and she hated herself for it. During the past ten years she had transformed herself into a winner, and she was determined not to backslide.

The old wooden stairs protested under her, but she moved fast, heedless of the noise. Whether Laura was alive or dead, the killer would be at play, distracted by his games, unlikely to hear anything other than the thunderous rush of his own blood in his ears and over whatever urgent inner voices spoke to him at that very moment when he held a life in his hands.

She stepped into the upstairs hall. Propelled by her fear for Laura and by a rage born from self-disgust at her moment of weakness on the landing, she hurried past the closed door of the guest room to the turn in the L-shaped corridor, around the corner, past the half-open door of the master suite and through the amber light that spilled from it. She dashed along the arbor of faded roses, rage swelling into fury as she went, shocked by her own boldness, seeming to glide along the carpet, as swift as if sliding down an icy slope, straight to the open door of Laura's room, without hesitation, knife raised high, her arm no longer shaking, steady and sure, crazy with terror and despair and righteousness, across the threshold and into the bedroom, where Freud was unshaken by what had happened under his gaze—and where the rumpled bed was empty.

Chyna whirled around in disbelief. Laura was gone. The room was deserted.

Over the rush of her breathing and the booming of her heart, she heard the rattle-clink of a shackle chain. Not in the room. Elsewhere.

Careless of danger, she returned to the hall, to the balustrade that overlooked the foyer.

Below, barely illuminated by the pale light from the upstairs hallway, the killer went through the open front door onto the porch. He was carrying Laura in his arms. She was wrapped in a bedsheet, one pale arm trailing limply, head lolling to the side, and face concealed by her golden hair: unconscious, offering no resistance.

He must have been descending the shadowy stairs when Chyna had passed them. She had been so focused on getting to Laura's room, so pumped for the attack, that she hadn't been aware of him, even though the chain and the cuffs must have been rattling then as well.

Evidently, he'd been making enough noise that he hadn't heard Chyna either.

Instinct had told her to take the back stairs, and she'd been wise to listen. If she'd been ascending the front stairs, she'd have met him as he'd been coming down. He would have thrown Laura at her, followed the two of them as they tumbled into the foyer, kicked the knife out of Chyna's hand if she hadn't lost it already, and savaged her where she'd fallen.

She couldn't let him take Laura away.

Afraid that thinking about the situation would paralyze her again, Chyna recklessly descended the stairs. If she could take him by surprise and plunge the knife into his back, Laura might yet have a chance.

She could do it too. She wasn't squeamish. She could slam the blade deep, try for his heart from the back, puncture a lung, yank the knife out of him and ram it in again, stab the son of a bitch and listen to him squealing for mercy and stab stab stab him until he was silent forever. Never had she done anything like that; never had she hurt anyone. But she could do it now, waste him, because she was terrified for Laura, because she was sick at the thought of failing her friend—and because she was a natural-born vengeance machine, a human being.

At the bottom of the stairs, the oval rug didn't spin out from under her as it had done before, and she went straight toward the open door.

She no longer held the knife high but held it low, at her side. If he heard her coming, he would turn, and then she could swing the knife up in an arc, under the girl that he held in his arms, and into his belly. That was better than trying to plunge it into his back, where the point might be deflected by a shoulder blade or rib, or might skid off his spine. Go for the softest part of him. She'd be face-to-face with him that way. Looking straight into his eyes. Would that make her hesitate? He had it coming. The bastard. She thought of Sarah on the floor of the shower stall, huddled naked in the cold drizzle. She could do it. She could do it.

Into the doorway, across the threshold, onto the porch, she was not only ready to kill but prepared to die in the attempt to get him. Yet as swift as she had been, she hadn't been swift enough, because he was not just that moment going down the porch steps, as she had hoped, but was *already* nearing the motor home. The burden of Laura hadn't slowed him at all. He was inhumanly quick.

She landed on only one stair tread from the front porch to the walkway, and the rubber soles of her shoes slapped the flagstones loud enough to carry even over the moaning of the wind. The moon was gone, and half the stars as well, displaced by towering palisades of clouds, but if the killer heard her and turned, he would be able to see her clearly.

Evidently, he didn't hear, for he didn't glance back, and Chyna angled off the walkway, onto the quieter grass, determinedly going after him.

Two doors were open on the motor home: one at the driver's side of the cockpit, the other on that same flank of the vehicle but two-thirds of the way toward the back. The killer chose the rear door.

With Laura in his arms, he was forced to turn sideways, pulling her tightly to him as he squeezed through the open door and crabbed up the two interior steps, but he was as agile as he was strong. He disappeared into the vehicle before Chyna could reach him.

She considered going inside after him. But all the windows were curtained, so she didn't know if he had turned left or right. And if he had put Laura down immediately upon entering, he would now be better able to defend himself against an attack. That was his turf, beyond the door, and she wasn't sufficiently reckless with vengeance to want to confront him there.

She pressed her back to the wall of the motor home, beside the open door, waiting for him. If he came outside again, she'd go at him even as his foot was reaching for the ground. The element of surprise was still working for her, maybe better than ever—because the killer was close to a clean getaway and feeling so good about himself that he might be careless.

Maybe he wouldn't come outside again, but at least he would have to reach out to pull the door shut. Standing on the step, leaning to grab at the handle, he would not be well balanced, and she would have the knife deep into him before he had a chance to jerk back.

Movement inside. A thump.

She tensed.

He didn't appear.

Silence again.

The scent of blood was suddenly heavy out of the northwest, as though a slaughter-house lay upwind of her. Then it passed, and she realized that she hadn't actually smelled blood but had flashed back on the smell of the sodden sheets in the Templetons' master suite.

The aluminum wall of the motor home was cold against her spine, and she shivered because it seemed that some of the coldness of the man inside was seeping through to her.

Waiting, she began to lose her nerve. Resurgent fear tempered her rage, shifting the balance from vengeance to survival. But she could still do it. She could do it. She struggled to hold on to her crazy-hot anger.

Then the killer came out of the motor home, but he didn't use the exit beside her. He stepped from the open cab door at the front of the vehicle.

Chyna's breath caught in her throat, and the chill wind from the oncoming storm seemed bitter with the scent of failure.

He was too far away. No longer distracted by the weight of Laura in his arms and the rattling of her shackles, he would hear Chyna coming. She no longer had the element of surprise to even the odds.

He stood just outside the cab door, thirty feet from her, stretching almost lazily. He rolled his big shoulders as if to shake weariness from them, and he massaged the back of his neck.

If he turned his head to the left, he would see her at once. If she didn't remain absolutely still, he would surely spot her slightest movement even from the corner of his eye.

He was downwind of her, and she was half afraid that he would smell her fear. He seemed more animal than human, even in the fluid grace with which he moved, and she had no trouble believing that he was gifted with wild talents and preternatural senses.

Although he wasn't holding the silencer-fitted gun with which he had killed Paul Templeton, it might be tucked under his belt. If she tried to flee, he could draw the weapon and shoot her dead before she got far.

But he *wouldn't* shoot her dead. Nothing that easy. He'd pop her in the leg, bring her down, and take her captive. Load her into the motor home with Laura. He'd want to play with her later.

Finished stretching, he moved briskly toward the house. Up the walkway. Onto the porch. Inside.

He never looked back.

Chyna's pent-up breath stuttered from her in a tattoo of fear, and she inhaled with a shudder.

Before her courage faded further, she hurried forward to the cab door and climbed behind the steering wheel. Her best hope was to find keys in the ignition, in which case she would be able to start the engine and drive away with Laura, go into Napa to the police.

No keys.

She glanced at the house, wondering how long he would be gone. Maybe he was searching for valuables now that the killing was done. Or selecting souvenirs. That could take five minutes, ten minutes, even longer. Which might be enough time to get Laura out of the motor home and hide her somewhere. Somehow.

She still had the knife. And now that she was in the killer's domain without his knowledge, she had regained the precious element of surprise.

Nevertheless, her heart raced, and her dry mouth was filled with the slightly metallic taste of feverish anxiety.

The seat swiveled, clearing the console. She was able to step from behind the steering wheel into the lounge area, which featured built-in sofas upholstered in a hunter-plaid fabric.

The steel floor was carpeted, of course, but after long years of hard travel, it creaked softly under her feet.

She had expected the place to smell like a Grand Guignol theater where the sadistic plays involved no make-believe, but instead the air was redolent of recently brewed coffee and cinnamon rolls. How odd—and somehow profoundly disturbing—that a man like this should find any satisfaction at all in innocent pleasures.

"Laura," she whispered, as though the killer might hear her all the way from the house. Then more fiercely than ever, yet in a whisper: "*Laura!*"

Beyond the lounge and open to it were a kitchenette and a cozy dining alcove with a booth upholstered in red vinyl. Running off the battery, a lamp hung aglow over the dining-nook table.

Laura was not to be seen anywhere.

Moving swiftly out of the dining area, Chyna came to the rear door standing open on the right, through which the killer had entered with the unconscious girl in his arms.

"Laura."

Aft of the outer door, a short cramped hall led along the driver's side of the vehicle, illuminated by a low-voltage safety fixture. There was also a skylight, now black. On the left were two closed doors, and at the end a third stood ajar.

The first door opened into a tiny bath. The space was a marvel of efficient design: a toilet, a sink, a medicine cabinet, and a corner shower stall.

Behind the second door was a closet. A few changes of clothes hung from a chrome rod.

At the end of the hall was a small bedroom with imitation-wood paneling and a closet with an accordion-style vinyl door. The meager light from the hall didn't brighten the place much, but Chyna could see well enough to identify Laura; the girl was lying face-down on the narrow bed, swaddled in a sheet, with only her small bare feet and her golden hair revealed.

Urgently whispering her friend's name, Chyna stepped to the bed and dropped to her knees.

Laura didn't respond. Still unconscious.

Chyna couldn't lift the girl, couldn't carry her as the killer had done, so she had to try to rouse her instead. She pulled aside a flap of sheet and was eye-to-eye with her friend.

They were sapphire-blue eyes now, not pale-sky blue, perhaps because the light in the room was so poor or perhaps because they were occluded with death. Her mouth was open, and blood moistened her lips.

The crazy fucking hateful bastard had taken her with him even though she was dead, for God-knew-what purposes, maybe because she was something he could touch and look at and talk to for a few days to remind him of the glory. A souvenir.

Chyna's stomach cramped painfully, not with revulsion or disgust but with guilt, with failure and futility and sheer black despair.

"Oh, baby," she said to the dead girl. "Oh, baby, sweetie, I'm so sorry, I'm so sorry."

Not that she could have done anything more than she had tried to do. What could she have done? She couldn't have attacked the bastard bare-handed when she had stood behind him in the upstairs hall, when he had been cooing to the dangling spider. What could she have done? She couldn't have gotten to the kitchen any sooner, found the knife any faster, climbed the back stairs any quicker.

"I'm so sorry."

This beautiful girl, this dear heart, would never find the husband about whom she had fantasized, never have the children who would have been a betterment to the world by the simple virtue of having been *her* children. Twenty-three years of getting ready to make a contribution, to make a difference in the lives of others, so full of ideals and hope: But now her gift would never be given, and the world would be immeasurably poorer for it.

"I love you, Laura. We all love you."

Any words, any sentiment, any expression of grief was horribly inadequate; worse than inadequate—meaningless. Laura was gone, all that warmth and kindness gone forever, and even the most heartfelt words were only words.

Chyna's stomach cramped with a sense of loss, clenched tight and pulled her relentlessly into a black hole within herself.

At the same time she felt her breast swelling with a sob that, if voiced, would be explosive. A single tear would loose a flood. Even one soft sob would bring on an uncontrollable wail.

She couldn't risk grief. Not while she was in the motor home. The killer would be returning at any minute, and she couldn't mourn Laura until she was safely out of there and until he was gone. She no longer had any reason to stay, for Laura was indisputably dead and irretrievable.

Nearby a door slammed hard, shaking the thin metal walls around Chyna.

The killer was back.

Something rattled. Rattled.

With the butcher knife in hand, Chyna swiftly backed away from Laura to the wall next to the open door. Unexpressed grief was a high-octane fuel for rage, and in an instant she was burning with fury, afire with the need to hurt him, slash him, spill his guts, hear him scream, and bring the haunting awareness of mortality to his eyes as he had brought it to Laura's.

He'll come into the room. I'll cut him. He'll come and I'll cut him. It was a prayer, not a plan. *He'll come. I'll cut him. He'll come. I'll cut him.*

The shadowy room darkened. He was at the door, blocking the meager light from the hall.

Silently, the knife in her hand jittered furiously up and down like the needle on a sewing machine, stitching the pattern of her fear in the air.

He was at the threshold. Right there. Right *there.* He would come in for one more look at the pretty blond dead girl, for one more feel of her cool skin, and Chyna would get him when he crossed the threshold, cut him.

Instead, he closed the door and went away.

Aghast, she listened to his retreating footsteps, the creaking as the carpeted steel floor torqued under his boots, and she wondered what to do now.

The driver's door slammed. The engine started. The brakes released with a brief faint shriek.

They were on the move.

THREE

Dead girls lie as troubled in the dark as in the light. As the motor home sped along the runneled driveway, Laura's shackles clinked ceaselessly, only half muffled by the sheet in which she was loosely wrapped.

Blinded, still pressed to the fiberboard wall beside the bedroom door, Chyna Shepherd could almost believe that even in death Laura struggled against the injustice of her murder. *Clink-clink.*

Periodic sprays of gravel spurted from beneath the tires and rattled against the undercarriage. Shortly the motor home would reach the county road, smooth blacktop.

If Chyna tried to bail out now, the killer was sure to hear the back door bang open when the wind tore it out of her grasp, or spot it in his sideview mirror. In these winter-dormant grape fields, where the nearest houses were inhabited only by the dead, he would certainly risk stopping and giving chase, and she would not get far before he brought her down.

Better to wait. Give him a few miles on the county road, even until they reached a more major route, until they were likely to be passing through a town or traveling in at least sparse traffic. He wouldn't be as quick to come after her if people were nearby to respond to her cries for help.

She felt along the wall for a switch. The door was tightly shut; no light would spill into the hallway. She found the toggle, flicked it up, but nothing happened. The overhead bulb must have burned out.

She remembered seeing a pharmacy-style reading lamp bolted to the side of the built-in nightstand. By the time she felt her way across the small room, the motor home began to slow.

She hesitated with the lamp switch between thumb and forefinger, heart suddenly racing again because she was afraid that he was going to brake to a full stop, get out from behind the wheel, and come back to the little bedroom. Now that a confrontation could no longer save Laura, now that Chyna's molten rage had cooled to anger, she hoped only to avoid him, escape, and give the authorities the information that they would need to find him.

The vehicle didn't come to a full stop, after all, but hung a wide left turn onto a paved surface and picked up speed once more. The county road.

As far as Chyna could recall, the next intersection would be State Highway 29, which she and Laura had driven the previous afternoon. Between here and there, the only turnoffs were to other vineyards, small farms, and houses. He wasn't likely to pay a visit to any of those places or slaughter any more innocently sleeping families. The night was waning.

She clicked the lamp switch, and a circle of muddy light fell on the bed.

She tried not to look at the body, even though it was mostly concealed by the enwrapping linens. If she thought too much about Laura right now, she'd be sucked into a slough of black despondency. She needed to remain energized and clearheaded if she hoped to survive.

Although she wasn't likely to find any weapon better than the butcher knife, she had nothing to lose by searching for one. Since the killer was armed with a silencer-equipped pistol, he might keep other guns in the motor home.

The single nightstand had two drawers. The upper contained a package of gauze pads, a few green and yellow sponges of the size used to wash dishes, a small plastic squeeze bottle of some clear fluid, a roll of cloth tape, a comb, a hairbrush with a tortoiseshell handle, a half-empty tube of K-Y jelly, a full bottle of skin lotion with aloe vera, a pair of needle-nose pliers with yellow rubber-clad handles, and a pair of scissors.

She could imagine the uses to which he had put some of those items, and she didn't want to think about the others. Sometimes, no doubt, the women he brought into this room were alive when he put them on the bed.

She considered the scissors. But the butcher knife would be more effective if she needed to use it.

In the lower, deeper drawer was a hard-plastic container rather like a fishing-tackle box. When she opened it, she found a complete sewing kit, with numerous spools of thread in a variety of colors, a pincushion, packets of needles, a needle threader, an extensive selection of buttons, and other paraphernalia. None of that was helpful to her, and she put it away.

As she got up from her knees, she noticed that the window over the bed had been covered with a sheet of plywood that had been bolted to the wall. A couple of folded swatches of blue fabric were trapped between the plywood and the window frame: the edge of an underlying drapery panel.

From outside, the window would appear to be merely curtained. Anyone inside, even if clever and fortunate enough to struggle free of her bonds, would never be able to open the window and signal to passing motorists for help.

As there was no other furniture in the cramped bedroom, the closet was the only remaining place where Chyna could hope to find a gun or anything that might be used as a weapon. She circled the bed to the accordion-style vinyl door, which hung from an overhead track.

When she pulled the folding door aside, it compressed into pleats that stacked to the left, and in the closet was a dead man.

Shock threw Chyna back against the bed. The mattress caught her behind the knees. She almost fell backward atop Laura, kept her balance, but dropped the knife.

The rear of the closet appeared to have been retrofitted with welded steel plates fixed to the vehicle frame for added strength. Two ringbolts, widely separated and high-set, were welded to the steel. Wrists manacled to the ringbolts, the dead man hung with his arms spread in cruciform. His feet were together like the feet of Christ on the cross—not nailed, however, but shackled to another ringbolt in the closet floor.

He was young—seventeen, eighteen, surely not twenty. Clad in only a pair of white cotton briefs, his lean pale body was badly battered. His head didn't hang forward on his chest but was tipped to one side, and his left temple rested against the biceps of his raised left arm. He had thick curly black hair. His eyelids had been sewn tightly shut with green thread. With yellow thread, two buttons above his upper lip were secured to a pair of matching buttons just under his lower lip.

Chyna heard herself talking to God. An incoherent, beseeching babble. She clenched her teeth and choked on the words, though it was unlikely that her voice could have carried to the front of the motor home over the rumble of the engine and the droning of the big tires.

She pulled shut the pleated-vinyl panel. Though flimsy, it moved as ponderously as a vault door. The magnetic latch clicked into place with a sound like snapping bone.

In all the textbooks she had ever read, no case study of sociopathic violence had ever contained a description of a crime sufficiently vivid to make her want to retreat to a corner and sit on the floor and pull her knees against her chest and hug herself. That was precisely what she did now—choosing the corner farthest from the closet.

She had to get control of herself, quickly, starting with her manic breathing. She was gasping, sucking in great lungfuls, yet she couldn't seem to get enough air. The deeper and faster she inhaled, the dizzier she became. Her peripheral vision surrendered to an encroaching darkness until she seemed to be peering down a long black tunnel toward the dingy motor-home bedroom at the far end.

She told herself that the young man in the closet had been dead when the killer had gone to work with the sewing kit. And if he'd not been dead, at least he'd been mercifully unconscious. Then she told herself not to think about it at all, because thinking about it only made the tunnel longer and narrower, made the bedroom more distant and the lights dimmer than ever.

She put her face in her hands, and her hands were cold but her face seemed colder. For no reason that Chyna could understand, she thought of her mother's face, as clear as a photograph in her mind's eye. And then she *did* understand.

To Chyna's mother, the prospect of violence had been romantic, even glamorous. For a while they had lived in a commune in Oakland, where everyone talked of making a better world and where, more nights than not, the adults gathered around the kitchen table, drinking wine and smoking pot, discussing how best to tear down the hated system, sometimes also playing pinochle or Trivial Pursuit as they discussed the strategies that might bring utopia at last, sometimes far too enraptured by revolution to be interested in any lesser games. There were bridges and tunnels that could all be blown up with absurd ease, disrupting transportation; telephone-company installations could be targeted to throw communications into chaos; meat-packing plants must be burned to put an end to the brutal exploitation of animals. They planned intricate bank robberies and bold assaults on armored cars to finance their operations. The route they would have taken to peace, freedom, and justice was always cratered by explosions, littered with uncountable bodies. After Oakland, Chyna and her mother had hit the road for a few weeks and had wound up again in Key West with their old friend Jim Woltz, the enthusiastic nihilist who was deep in the drug trade, with a sideline in illegal weapons. Under his oceanfront cottage, he had carved out a bunker in which he stored a personal collection of two hundred firearms. Chyna's mother was a beautiful woman, even on bad days when depression plagued her, when her green eyes were gray and sad with miseries that she could not explain. But at that kitchen table in Oakland and in that cool bunker beneath the cottage in Key West— in fact, whenever she was at the side of a man like Woltz—her porcelain skin was even clearer than usual, almost translucent; excitement enlivened her exquisite features; she became magically more graceful, appeared more lithe and supple, was quicker to smile. The prospect of violence, playing at being Bonnie to any man's Clyde, filled her stunning face with a light as glorious as a Florida sunset, and her jewel-green eyes were, at those times, as compelling and mysterious as the Gulf of Mexico darkening toward twilight.

Although the prospect of violence might be romantic, the reality was blood, bone, decomposition, dust. The reality was Laura on the bed and the unknown young man sewn into silence behind the pleated vinyl door.

Chyna sat with her cold hands covering her colder face, aware that she would never be as strangely beautiful as her mother.

Eventually she regained control of her breathing.

The motor home rolled on, and she was reminded of nights when, as a child, she had dozed on trains, on buses, in the backseats of cars, lulled by the motion and the hum of wheels, unsure where her mother was taking her, dreaming of being part of a family like one of those on television—with befuddled but loving parents, an amusing next-door neighbor who might be frustrating but never malicious, and a dog that knew a few tricks. But good dreams never lasted, and she woke repeatedly from nightmares, gazing out windows at strange landscapes, wishing that she could travel forever without stopping. The road was a promise of peace, but destinations were always hell.

This time would be no different from all those others. Wherever they were bound, Chyna didn't want to go there. She intended to get off between destinations and hoped to find her way back to the better life that she had struggled so hard to build these past ten years.

She left the corner of the bedroom to retrieve the butcher knife, which she had dropped when she'd been rocked backward by the sight of the dead man in the closet. Then she went around the bed to the nightstand and switched off the pharmacy lamp.

Being in the dark with dead people didn't frighten her. Only the living were a danger.

The motor home slowed again and then turned left. Chyna leaned against the tilt of the vehicle to keep her balance.

They must be on State Highway 29. A right turn would have taken them down the Napa Valley, south into the town of Napa. She wasn't sure what communities lay to the north, other than St. Helena and Calistoga.

Even between the towns, however, there would be vineyards, farms, houses, and rural businesses. Wherever she got out of the motor home, she should be able to find help within a reasonable distance.

She sidled blindly to the door and stood with one hand on the knob, waiting for instinct to guide her once more. Much of her life had been lived like a balancing act on a spearpoint fence, and on a particularly difficult night when she was twelve, she had decided that instinct was, in fact, the quiet voice of God. Prayers *did* receive replies, but you had to listen closely and believe in the answer. At twelve, she wrote in her diary: "God doesn't shout; He whispers, and in the whisper is the way."

Waiting for the whisper, she thought about the battered body in the closet, which appeared to have been dead for less than a day, and about Laura, still warm on the sagging bed. Sarah, Paul, Laura's brother Jack, Jack's wife, Nina: six people murdered in twenty-four hours. The eater of spiders was not an ordinary homicidal sociopath. In the language of the cops and the criminologists who specialized in searching for and stopping men like this, he was *hot*, going through a *hot phase*, burning up with desire, need. But Chyna, who intended to follow her master's in psychology with a doctorate in criminology, even if she had to work six years waiting tables to get there, sensed that this guy was not just hot. He was a singularity, conforming only in part to standard profiles in aberrant psychology, as purely alien as something from the stars, a runaway killing machine, merciless and irresistible. She had no hope of eluding him if she didn't wait for the murmuring voice of instinct.

She remembered seeing a large rearview mirror when she'd briefly occupied the driver's seat earlier. The vehicle had no rear window, so the mirror was there to provide the driver with a view of the lounge and the dining area behind him. He would be able to see all the way into the end hall that served the bath and bedroom, and if the devil's luck was with him, he would glance up just when Chyna opened the door, stepped out, and was exposed.

When the moment felt right, Chyna opened the door.

A small blessing, a good omen: The ceiling light in the hall was out.

Standing in gloom, she quietly pulled shut the bedroom door.

The lamp above the dining table was on as before. At the front of the vehicle was the green glow of the instrument panel—and beyond the windshield, the headlights were silver swords.

After moving forward past the bathroom and out of the welcome shadows, she crouched behind the paneled side of the dining nook. She peered across the crescent booth to the back of the driver's head, about twenty feet away.

He seemed so close—and, for the first time, vulnerable.

Nevertheless, Chyna wasn't foolish enough to creep forward and attack him while he was driving. If he heard her coming or glanced at the rearview mirror and spotted her, he could wrench the steering wheel or slam on the brakes, sending her sprawling. Then he might be able to stop the vehicle and get to her before she could reach the rear door— or he might swivel in his chair and shoot her down.

The entrance through which he had carried Laura was immediately to Chyna's left. She sat on the floor with her feet in the step well, facing this door, concealed from the driver by the dining nook.

She put the butcher knife aside. When she leaped out, she would probably fall and roll—and she might easily stab herself with the knife if she tried to take it with her.

She didn't intend to jump until the driver either stopped at an intersection or entered a turn sharp enough to require him to cut his speed dramatically. She couldn't risk breaking a leg or being knocked unconscious in a fall, because then she wouldn't be able to get away from the road and safely into hiding.

She didn't doubt that he would be aware of her escape even as it began. He would hear the door open or the wind whistling at it, and he would see her either in his rearview or in his side-mounted mirror as she made her break for freedom. Even in the unlikely event that she was not seen, the wind would slam the door hard behind her the instant she was gone; the killer would suspect that he hadn't been alone with his collection of corpses, and he'd pull off the highway and come back along the pavement, panicky, to have a look.

Or perhaps not panicky. Not panicky at all. More likely, he would search with grim, methodical, machine efficiency. This guy was all about control and power, and Chyna found it difficult to imagine him *ever* succumbing to panic.

The motor home slowed, and Chyna's heart quickened. As the driver reduced speed further, Chyna rose into a crouch in the step well and put a hand on the lever-action door handle.

They came to a full stop, and she pressed down on the handle, but the door was locked. Quietly but insistently she pressed up, down, up—to no avail.

She couldn't find any latch button. Just a keyhole.

She remembered the rattling that she'd heard when she'd been in the bedroom and the spider eater had come back inside and closed this door. *Rattle, rattle.* The rattle of a key, perhaps.

Maybe this was a safety feature to prevent kids from tumbling out into traffic. Or maybe the crazy bastard had modified the door lock to enhance security, to make it more difficult for a burglar or casual intruder to stumble upon any lip-sewn or shackled cadavers that might just happen to be aboard. Can't be too careful when you have dead bodies stacked in the bedroom. Prudence requires certain security measures.

The motor home pulled forward through the intersection and began to pick up speed again.

She should have known that escape wouldn't be easy. *Nothing* was easy. Ever.

She sat down, leaning against the breakfast-nook paneling, still facing the door, thinking furiously.

Earlier, on her way back through the vehicle from the driver's seat, she'd seen a door on the other side, toward the front, behind the copilot's chair. Most motor homes had two doors, but this was a rare older model with three. She was reluctant to go forward to escape, however, and for the same reason that she didn't want to attack him: He might see her coming, rock her off her feet, and shoot her before she could get up.

All right, she had one advantage. He didn't know that she was aboard.

If she couldn't just open a door and jump out, if she was going to have to kill him, she could lie in wait here past the dining nook, surprise the bastard, gut him, step over him, and leave by the front. Just minutes ago she had been ready to kill him, and she could make herself be ready again.

The engine vibrations rose through the floor, half numbing her butt. Total numbing would have been welcome; the carpet soon proved to be inadequate padding, and her tailbone began to ache. She shifted her weight from cheek to cheek, leaned forward and then leaned back; nothing provided more than a few seconds of relief. The ache spread to the small of her back, and mild discomfort escalated into serious pain.

Twenty minutes, half an hour, forty minutes, an hour, longer, she endured the agony by striving to imagine all the ways that her escape might unfold once the motor home stopped and the killer got out from behind the wheel. Concentrating. Thinking it through. Planning for myriad eventualities. Finally, however, she couldn't think about anything but the pain.

The motor home was cool, and down in the step well, there was no heat at all. The engine and road vibrations penetrated her shoes, beating relentlessly on her heels and soles. She flexed her toes, afraid that her cold, achy feet and stiffening calf muscles would develop cramps and hobble her when the time came for action.

With a strange hilarity unnervingly close to despair, she thought, *Forget about grief. Forget about justice. Right now just give me a comfortable chair to pamper my ass, just let me sit for a while until my feet are warm again, and later you can have my life if you want it.*

The prolonged inactivity not only took a physical toll but soon began to depress her. Back at the house when she'd first heard the intruder, before he had even come to the guest room, Chyna had known that safety lay in movement. Now *emotional* safety lay in movement, distraction. But circumstances required her to be still and wait. She had too much time to think—and too many disturbing thoughts on which to dwell.

She worked herself into such a state of distress that tears welled—which was when she realized that she was not suffering unduly from butt ache or back pain or the cold throbbing in her feet. The real pain was in her heart, the anguish that she had been forced to repress since she'd found Paul and Sarah, since she'd detected the vague ammoniacal scent of semen in Laura's bedroom and had seen the dimly gleaming links of the shackling chain. Her physical pain was only a lame excuse for tears.

If she dared weep in self-pity, however, then a *flood* would come for Paul, for Sarah, for Laura, for the whole sorry damn screwed-up human race, and in useless resentment at the fact that hard-won hope so often spiraled into nightmare. She would bury her face in her hands, uselessly wailing the question that had been asked of God more often than any other: *Why, why, why, why, why?*

Surrendering to tears would be so easy, *satisfying*. These were selfish tears of defeat; they would not only purge the heart of grief but also wash out the need to care about anyone, anything. Blessed relief could be hers if she simply admitted that the long struggle to understand wasn't worth the pain of experience. Her sobbing would bring the motor home to a sudden halt, and the driver would come back to find her huddled at the step well. He would club her, drag her into the bedroom, rape her beside the body of her friend; there would be terror beyond anything that she had ever known before, but it would be brief. And this time it would be final. He would free her forever from the need to ask *why*, from the torment of repeatedly falling through the fragile floor of hope into this too familiar desolation.

For a long time, maybe even since the stormy night of her eighth birthday and the frenzied palmetto beetle, she'd known that being a victim was often a *choice* people made. As a child, she hadn't been able to put this insight into words, and she hadn't known why so many people chose suffering; when older, she had recognized their self-hatred, masochism, weakness.

Not all or even most suffering is at the hands of fate; it befalls us at our invitation.

She'd always chosen not to be victimized, to resist and fight back, to hold on to hope and dignity and faith in the future. But victimhood was seductive, a release from responsibility and caring: Fear would be transmuted into weary resignation; failure would no longer generate guilt but, instead, would spawn a comforting self-pity.

Now she trembled on an emotional high wire, not sure whether she would be able to keep her balance or would allow herself to fail and fall.

The motor home slowed again. They were angling to the right. Slowing. Maybe pulling off the highway and stopping.

She tried the door. She knew that it was locked, but she quietly worked the lever-action handle anyway, because she wasn't capable, after all, of simply giving up.

As they climbed a slight incline, their speed continued to drop.

Wincing at the pain in her calves and thighs as she moved, yet relieved to be off her butt, she rose just far enough to look across the dining nook.

The back of the killer's head was the most hateful thing that Chyna had ever seen, and it aroused fresh anger in her. The brain beneath that curve of bone hummed with vicious fantasies. It was infuriating that he should be alive and Laura dead. That he should be sitting here so smug, so content with all his memories of blood, recalling the pleas for mercy that must be like music to him. That he should ever see a sunset again and take pleasure from it, or taste a peach, or smell a flower. To Chyna, the back of this man's skull seemed like the smooth chitinous helmet of an insect, and she believed that if she ever touched him, he would be as cold as a squirming beetle under her hand.

Beyond the driver, beyond the windshield, at the top of the low rise toward which they were headed, a structure appeared, indistinct and unidentifiable. A few tall sodium-vapor arc lamps cast a sour, sulfurous light.

She squatted below the back of the dining nook again.

She picked up the knife.

They had reached the top of the rise. They were on level ground once more. Steadily slowing.

Turning around, facing away from the exit, she eased into the step well. Left foot on the lower step, right foot on the higher. Back pressed to the locked door, crouching in shadows beyond the reach of the nook lamp, she was ready to launch herself up and at him if he came back through the motor home and gave her a chance.

With a final sigh of air brakes, the vehicle stopped.

Wherever they were, people might be nearby. People who could help her.

But if she screamed, would those outside be near enough to hear?

Even if they heard, they would never reach her in time. The killer would get to her first, gun in hand.

Besides, maybe this was a roadside rest area: nothing more than a parking lot, some picnic tables, a poster warning about the dangers of campfires, and rest rooms. He might have taken a break to use the public facilities or the john in the trailer. At this dead hour, after three o'clock in the morning, they were likely to be the only vehicle on site, in which case she could scream until she was hoarse, and no one would come to her assistance.

The engine cut off.

Quiet. No vibrations in the floor.

Now that the motor home was still, Chyna was shaking. No longer depressed. Stomach muscles fluttering. Scared again. Because she wanted to live.

She would have preferred that he go outside and give her a chance to escape, but she expected him to use the trailer facilities instead of the public rest room. He would come right past her. If she couldn't escape, then she was hot to finish this.

Crazily, she wondered if what came out of him when he was cut would be blood—or the stuff that oozed from a fat beetle when it was crushed.

She expected to hear the bastard moving, heavy footfalls and the hollow *spong* when he stepped on a weak seam in the floor, but there was silence. Maybe he was taking a moment to stretch his arms, roll his achy shoulders, massage the back of his bull neck, and shrug off the weariness of travel.

Or perhaps he *had* glimpsed her in the rearview mirror, her face moon-bright in the light from the dining-table lamp. He could ease out of his seat and creep toward her, avoiding all the creaks in the floor because he knew where they were. Slide into the dining nook. Lean over the back of the booth. Shoot her point-blank where she crouched in the step well. Shoot her in the face.

Chyna looked up and to her left, across the back of the booth. Too low to see the lamp hanging over the center of the table, she saw only the glow of it. She wondered if the angle of his approach would give her a warning or if he would just be a sudden silhouette popping up from the booth as he opened fire on her.

FOUR

Intensity.

He believes in living with intensity.

Sitting at the steering wheel, he closes his eyes and massages the back of his neck.

He isn't trying to get rid of the pain. It came on its own, and it will leave him naturally in time. He never takes Tylenol and other crap like that.

What he's trying to do is *enjoy* the pain as fully as possible. With his fingertips he finds an especially sore spot just to the left of the third cervical vertebra, and he presses on it until the pain causes faint sprays of twinkly white and gray lights in the blackness behind his eyelids, like distant fireworks in a world without color.

Very nice.

Pain is merely a part of life. By embracing it, one can find surprising satisfaction in suffering. More important, getting in touch with his own pain makes it easier for him to take pleasure in the pain of others.

Two vertebrae farther down, he locates an even more sensitive point of inflamed tendon or muscle, a wonderful little button buried in the flesh which, when pressed, causes pain to shoot all the way across his shoulder and down his trapezius. At first he works the spot with a lover's tender touch, groaning softly, then he attacks it vigorously until the sweet agony makes him suck air between his clenched teeth.

Intensity.

He does not expect to live forever. His time in this body is finite and precious—and therefore must not be wasted.

He does not believe in reincarnation or in any of the standard promises of an afterlife that are sold by the world's great religions—although at times he senses that he is approaching a revelation of tremendous importance. He *is* willing to contemplate the possibility that the immortal soul exists, and that his own spirit may one day be exalted. But if he is to undergo an apotheosis, it will be brought about by his own bold actions, not by divine grace; if he, in fact, becomes a god, the transformation will occur because he has already chosen to *live* like a god—without fear, without remorse, without limits, with all his senses fiercely sharpened.

Anyone can smell a rose and enjoy the scent. But he has long been training himself to *feel* the destruction of its beauty when he crushes the flower in his fist. If he were to have a rose now, and if he were to chew the petals, he would be able to *taste* not merely the rose itself but the redness of it; likewise, he could taste the yellowness of buttercups, the blue of hyacinths. He could taste the bee that had crawled across the blossom on its eternal buzzing task of pollination, the soil out of which the flower had grown, and the wind that had caressed it through the summer of its growing.

He has never met anyone who can understand the intensity with which he experiences the world or the greater intensity for which he strives. With his help, perhaps Ariel will understand one day. Now, of course, she is too immature to achieve the insight.

One last squeeze of his neck. The pain. He sighs.

From the copilot's seat, he picks up a folded raincoat. No rain is yet falling, but he needs to cover his blood-spattered clothing before going inside.

He could have changed into clean clothes prior to leaving the Templeton house, but he enjoys wearing these. The patina excites him.

He gets out of the driver's seat, stands behind it, and pulls on the coat.

He washed his hands in the kitchen sink at the Templeton house, though he would have preferred to leave them stained too. While he can conceal his clothes under a raincoat, hiding his hands is not as easy.

He never wears gloves. To do so would be to concede that he fears apprehension, which he does not.

Although his fingerprints are on file with federal and state agencies, the prints he leaves at the scene will never match those that bear his name in the records. Like the rest of the world, police organizations are hell-bent on computerization; by now most fingerprint-image reference banks are in the form of digitized data, to facilitate high-speed scanning and processing. Even more easily than hard files, electronic files can be manipulated, because the work can be done at a great distance; there is no need to burglarize highly secure facilities, when instead he can be a ghost haunting their machines from across a continent. Because of his intelligence, talents, and connections, he has been able to meddle with the data.

Wearing gloves, even thin surgical latex gloves, would be an intolerable barrier to sensation. He likes to let his hand glide lightly over the fine golden hairs on a woman's thigh, take time to appreciate the texture of pebbled gooseflesh against his palm, to relish the fierce heat of skin and then, after, the warmth all fading, fading. When he kills, he finds it absolutely essential to feel the wetness.

The prints under his name in the various files are, in fact, those of a young marine named Bernard Petain, who died tragically during training maneuvers at Camp Pendleton many years ago. And the prints that he leaves at the scene, often etched in blood, cannot be matched to any on file with the military, the FBI, the Department of Motor Vehicles, or anywhere else.

He finishes buttoning the raincoat, turns up the collar, and looks at his hands. Stains under three fingernails. It might be grease or soil. No one will be suspicious of it.

He himself can smell the blood on his clothes even through the black nylon raincoat and insulated liner, but others are not sufficiently sensitive to detect it.

Staring at the residue under his nails, however, he can hear the screams again, that lovely music in the night, the Templeton house as reverberant as a concert hall, and no one to hear except him and the deaf vineyards.

If he is ever caught in the act, the authorities will print him again, discover his deception with the computers, and eventually link him to a long list of unsolved murders. But he isn't concerned about that. He'll never be taken alive, never be put on trial. Whatever they learn about his activities after his death will only add to the glory of his name.

He is Edgler Foreman Vess. From the letters of his name, one can extract a long list of power words: GOD, FEAR, DEMON, SAVE, RAGE, ANGER, DRAGON, FORGE, SEED, SEMEN, FREE, and others. Also words with a mystical quality: DREAM, VESSEL, LORE, FOREVER, MARVEL. Sometimes the last thing that he whispers to a victim is a sentence composed from this list of words. One that he especially likes and uses often is GOD FEARS ME.

Anyway, all questions of fingerprints and other evidence are moot, because he will never be caught. He is thirty-three years old. He has been enjoying himself in this fashion for a long time, and he has never had a close call.

Now he takes the pistol out of the open console between the pilot's and copilot's chairs. A Heckler & Koch P7.

Earlier, he had reloaded the thirteen-round magazine. Now he unscrews the sound suppressor, because he has no plans to visit other houses this night. Besides, the baffles are probably damaged from the shots that he has fired, diminishing both the effect of the silencer and the accuracy of the weapon.

Occasionally he daydreams about what it would be like if the impossible happened, if he were interrupted at play and surrounded by a SWAT team. With his experience and knowledge, the ensuing showdown would be thrillingly *intense*.

If there is a single secret behind the success of Edgler Vess, it is his belief that no twist of fate is either good or bad, that no experience is qualitatively better than another. Winning twenty million dollars in the lottery is no more to be desired than being trapped by a SWAT team, and a shootout with the authorities is no more to be dreaded than winning all that money. The value of any experience isn't in its positive or negative effect on his life but in the sheer luminous power of it, the vividness, the ferocity, the amount and degree of pure sensation that it provides. Intensity.

Vess puts the sound suppressor in the console between the seats.

He drops the pistol into the right-hand pocket of his raincoat.

He is not expecting trouble. Nevertheless, he goes nowhere unarmed. One can never be too careful. Besides, opportunities often arise unexpectedly.

In the driver's seat again, he takes the keys from the ignition and checks that the brake is firmly set. He opens the door and gets out of the motor home.

All eight gasoline pumps are self-service. He is parked at the outer of the two service islands. He needs to go to the cashier in the associated convenience store to pay in advance and to identify the pump that he'll be using so it can be turned on.

The night breathes. At higher altitudes, a strong gale drives masses of clouds out of the northwest toward the southeast. Here at ground level, a lesser exhalation of cold wind huffs between the pumps, whistles alongside the motor home, and flaps the raincoat against Vess's legs. The convenience store—buff brick below, white aluminum siding above, big windows full of merchandise—stands in front of rising hills that are covered with huge evergreens; the wind soughs through their branches with a hollow, ancient, lonely voice.

Out on Highway 101, there is little traffic at this hour. When a truck passes, it cleaves the wind with a cry that seems strangely Jurassic.

A Pontiac with Washington State license plates is parked at the inner service island, under the yellow sodium-vapor lamps. Other than the motor home, it is the only vehicle in sight. A bumper sticker on the back announces that ELECTRICIANS KNOW HOW TO PLUG IT IN.

On the roof of the building, positioned for maximum visibility from 101, is a red neon sign that announces OPEN 24 HOURS. Red is the quality of the sound each passing truck makes out there on the highway. In the glow, his hands look as if he never washed them.

As Vess approaches the entrance, the glass door swings open, and a man comes out carrying a family-size bag of potato chips and a six-pack of Coke in cans. He is a chubby guy with long sideburns and a walrus mustache.

Gesturing at the sky, he says, "Storm's coming," as he hurries past Vess.

"Good," Vess says. He likes storms. He enjoys driving in them. The more torrential the rain, the better. With lightning flashing and trees cracking in the wind and pavement as slick as ice.

The guy with the walrus mustache goes to the Pontiac.

Vess enters the convenience store, wondering what an electrician from Washington is doing on the road in northern California at this ungodly hour of the night.

He's fascinated by the way in which lives connect briefly, with a potential for drama that is sometimes fulfilled and sometimes not. A man stops for gasoline, lingers to buy potato chips and Coke, makes a comment on the weather to a stranger—and continues on his journey. The stranger could as easily follow the man to the car and blow his brains out. There would be risks for the shooter, but not serious risks; it could be managed with surprising discretion. The man's survival is either full of mysterious meaning or utterly meaningless; Vess is unable to decide which.

If fate doesn't actually exist, it ought to.

The small store is warm, clean, and brightly lighted. Three narrow aisles extend to the left of the door, offering the usual roadside merchandise: every imaginable snack food, the basic patent medicines, magazines, paperback books, postcards, novelty items designed to hang from rearview mirrors, and selected canned goods that sell to campers and to people, like Vess, who travel in homes on wheels. Along the back wall are tall coolers full of beer and soft drinks, as well as a couple of freezers containing ice cream treats. To the right of the door is the service counter that separates the two cashiers' stations and the clerical area from the public part of the store.

Two employees are on duty, both men. These days, no one works alone in such places at night—and with good reason.

The guy at the cash register is a redhead in his thirties with freckles and a two-inch-diameter birthmark, as pink as uncooked salmon, on his pale forehead. The mark is uncannily like the image of a fetus curled in a womb, as if a gestating twin had died early in the mother's pregnancy and left its fossilized image on the surviving brother's brow.

The redheaded cashier is reading a paperback. He looks up at Vess, and his eyes are as gray as ashes but clear and piercing. "What can I do for you, sir?"

"I'm at pump seven," Vess says.

The radio is tuned to a country station. Alan Jackson sings about midnight in Montgomery, the wind, a whippoorwill, a lonesome chill, and the ghost of Hank Williams.

"How you want to pay?" asks the cashier.

"If I put any more on the credit cards, the Bank of America's going to send someone around to break my legs," says Vess, and he slaps down a hundred-dollar bill. "Figure I'll need about sixty bucks' worth."

The combination of the song, the birthmark, and the cashier's haunting gray eyes generates in Vess an eerie sense of expectancy. Something exceptional is about to happen.

"Paying off Christmas like the rest of us, huh?" says the cashier as he rings up the sale.

"Hell, I'll still be payin' off Christmas *next* Christmas."

The second clerk sits on a stool farther along the counter. He's not at a cash register but is laboring on the bookkeeping or checking inventory sheets—anyway, doing some kind of paperwork.

Vess has not previously looked directly at the second man, and now he discovers that this is the exceptional thing he felt looming.

"Storm coming," he says to the second clerk.

The man looks up from the papers spread on the counter. He is in his twenties, at least half Asian, and strikingly handsome. No. More than handsome. Jet-black hair, golden complexion, eyes as liquid as oil and as deep as wells. There is a gentle quality to his good looks that almost gives him an effeminate aspect—but not quite.

Ariel would love him. He is just her type.

"Might be cold enough for snow in some of the mountain passes," says the Asian, "if you're going that way."

He has a pleasant—almost musical—voice that would charm Ariel. He is really quite breathtaking.

To the cashier who is counting out change, Vess says, "Just hold on to that. I need a supply of munchies too. I'll be back as soon as I fill up the tank."

He leaves quickly, afraid that they might sense his excitement and become alarmed.

Although he's been in the store no more than a minute, the night seems markedly colder than it was when he went inside. Invigorating. He catches the fragrance of pine trees and spruce—even fir from far to the north—inhales the sweet *greenness* of the heavily timbered hills behind him, detects the crisp scent of oncoming rain, smells the ozone of lightning bolts not yet hurled, breathes in the pungent fear of small animals that already quake in the fields and forests in anticipation of the storm.

After she was certain that he had left the motor home, Chyna crept forward through the vehicle, holding the butcher knife in front of her.

The windows in the dining area and the lounge were curtained, so she was not able to see what lay outside. At the front, however, the windshield revealed that they had stopped at a service station.

She had no idea where the killer was. He had left no more than a minute earlier. He might be outside, within a few feet of the door.

She hadn't heard him removing the gas cap or jacking the pump nozzle into the tank. But from the way they were parked, fuel was evidently taken on board from the starboard side, so that was most likely where he would be.

Afraid to proceed without knowing his exact whereabouts, but even more afraid to remain in the motor home, she slipped into the driver's seat. The headlights were off, and the instrument panel was dark, but there was enough backglow from the dining-nook lamp to make her supremely visible from outside.

At the next island, a Pontiac pulled away from the pumps. Its red taillights swiftly dwindled.

As far as she could see, the motor home was now the only vehicle at the station.

The keys weren't in the ignition. She wouldn't have tried to drive off anyway. That had been an option back in the vineyard, when there had been no help nearby. Here, there must be employees—and whoever pulled off the highway next.

She cracked the door, wincing at the hard sound, jumped out, and stumbled when she hit the ground. The butcher knife popped from her hand as if greased, clattered against the pavement, and spun away.

Certain that she had drawn the killer's attention and that he was already bearing down on her, Chyna scrambled to her feet. She spun left, then right, with her hands out in front of her in pathetic defense. But the eater of spiders was nowhere to be seen on the brightly lighted blacktop.

She pressed the door shut, searched the surrounding pavement for the knife, couldn't immediately spot it—and froze when a man came out of the station about fifty or sixty feet away. He was wearing a long coat, so at first Chyna was sure that he couldn't be the killer, but then immediately she recalled the inexplicable rustling of fabric to which she had listened before he had left the motor home, and she *knew*.

The only place to hide was behind one of the pumps at the next service island, but that was thirty feet away, between her and the store, with a lot of bright exposed pavement to cross. Besides, he was approaching the same island from the other side, and he would reach it first, catching her in the open.

If she tried to get around the motor home, he would spot her and wonder where she

had come from. His psychosis probably included a measure of paranoia, and he would assume that she had been in his vehicle. He would pursue her. Relentlessly.

Instead, even as she saw him leaving the store, Chyna dropped flat to the pavement.
Counting on the obstructing pumps at the first island to mask any movement close to the
ground, she crawled on her belly under the motor home.

The killer didn't cry out, didn't pick up his pace. He hadn't seen her.

From her hiding place, she watched him approach. As he drew close, the sulfurous
light was so bright that she could recognize his black leather boots as the same pair that
she had studied from beneath the guest-room bed a couple of hours before.

She turned her head to follow him as he went around the back of the motor home to
the starboard side, where he stopped at one of the pumps.

The blacktop was cold against her thighs, belly, and breasts. It leached the body heat
out of her through her jeans and cotton sweater, and she began to shiver.

She listened as the killer disengaged the hose spout from the nozzle boot, opened the
fuel port on the side of the motor home, and removed the tank cap. She figured it would
take a few minutes to fill the behemoth, so she began to ease out of her hiding place even
as she heard the spout thunk into the tank.

Still flat at ground level, she suddenly saw the butcher knife. Out on the blacktop. Ten
feet from the front bumper. The yellow light glimmered along the cutting edge.

Even as she was sliding into the open, however, before she could push to her feet, she
heard boot heels on blacktop. She glanced back under the motor home and saw that the
killer evidently had fixed the nozzle trigger in place with the regulator clip, because he was
on the move again.

Frantically and as silently as possible, she retreated beneath the vehicle once more. She
could hear gasoline sloshing into the fuel tank.

The killer walked forward along the starboard side, around the front, to the driver's
door. But he didn't open the door. He paused. Very still. Then he walked to the butcher
knife, stooped, and picked it up.

Chyna held her breath, though it seemed impossible that the killer could intuit the
meaning of the knife. He'd never seen it before. He couldn't know that it had come from
the Templeton house. Although it was indisputably odd to find a butcher knife lying on a
service-station approach lane, it might have fallen out of any vehicle that had passed
through.

With the knife, he returned to the motor home and climbed inside, leaving the driver's
door open behind him.

Over Chyna's head, the footsteps on the steel floor were as hollow as voodoo drums.
As best she could tell, he stopped in the dining area.

Vess isn't prone to see omens and portents everywhere he looks. A single hawk flying
across the face of the full moon, glimpsed at midnight, will not fill him with expectations
of either disaster or good fortune. A black cat crossing his path, a mirror shattering while
his reflection is captured in it, a news story about the birth of a two-headed calf—none of
these things will rattle him. He is convinced that he makes his own fate and that spiritual
transcendence—if such a thing can happen—ensues merely from one's acting boldly and
living with intensity.

Nevertheless, the large butcher knife makes him wonder. It has a totemic quality, an almost magical aura. He carefully places it on the counter in the kitchen, where the light
lays a wet sheen along the weapon's cutting edge.

When he picked it off the blacktop, the blade had been cold but the handle had been
vaguely warm, as if with the anticipatory heat of his grip.

Eventually he will experiment with this strangely discarded blade to determine if anything special happens when he cuts someone with it. At the moment, however, it doesn't provide him with the advantage that he needs for the work at hand.

He has the Heckler & Koch P7 snug in the right-hand pocket of his raincoat, but he doesn't feel that even it is adequate to the situation.

The two lads behind the cashiers' counter are not in the war zone of a big-city 7-Eleven market, but they are smart enough to take precautions. Not even Beverly Hills and Bel Air, peopled by wealthy actors and retired football stars, are any longer safe at night either for or *from* their citizens. These fellows will have a firearm for self-protection and will know how to use it. Dealing with them will require an intimidating weapon with formidable stopping power.

He opens a cabinet to the left of the oven. A Mossberg short-barreled, pistol-grip, pump-action, 12-gauge shotgun is mounted in a pair of spring clamps on the shelf. He pops it loose of the clamps and lays it on the countertop.

The magazine tube of the 12-gauge is already loaded. Although he doesn't belong to the American Automobile Association, Edgler Vess is otherwise always prepared for any eventuality when he travels.

In the cabinet is a box of shotgun shells, open for easy access. He takes a few and puts them on the counter next to the Mossberg, though he is not likely to need them.

He quickly unbuttons the raincoat but doesn't take it off. He transfers the pistol from his right-hand exterior pocket to an interior, right-hand breast pocket in the lining. This is also where he places the spare shells.

From a kitchen drawer, he withdraws a compact Polaroid camera. He tucks it into the pocket from which he just removed the Heckler & Koch P7. From his wallet, he removes a trimmed Polaroid snapshot of his special girl, Ariel, and he slips it into the same pocket that contains the camera.

With his seven-inch switchblade, which is tacky from all the work for which it was used at the Templeton house, he slashes the lining of the left coat pocket. Then he rips away these tattered fragments of fabric. Now, if he were to drop coins into this pocket, they would fall straight to the floor.

He puts the shotgun under his open coat and holds it with his left hand, through the ruined pocket. The concealment is effective. He does not believe that he looks at all suspicious.

He quickly paces back to the bedroom, then forward, practicing his walk. He is able to move freely without banging the shotgun against his legs.

After all, he can draw upon the nimbleness and the grace of the spider from the Templeton house.

Although he doesn't care what damage he does to the birthmarked cashier with the ashen eyes, he'll have to be careful not to destroy the face of the young Asian gentleman. He must have good photographs for Ariel.

Overhead, the killer seemed to be occupied in the dining area. The floor creaked under him as he shifted his weight.

Unless he had drawn open the curtains, he couldn't see outside from where he was. With luck, Chyna could make a break for freedom.

She considered remaining under the vehicle, letting him tank up and drive away, and only then going inside to call the police.

But he had found the butcher knife; he would be thinking about it. Though she could see no way that he could grasp the significance of the knife, by now she had an almost superstitious dread of him and was irrationally convinced that he would find her if she remained where she was.

She crawled out from under the motor home, rose into a crouch, glanced at the open door, and then looked back and up at the windows along the side. The curtains were closed.

Emboldened, she got to her feet, crossed to the inner service island, and stepped between the pumps. She glanced back, but the killer remained inside the vehicle.

She went out of the night into bright fluorescent light and the twang of country music. Two employees were behind the counter on the right, and she intended to say *Call the police*, but then she glanced through the glass door that had just closed behind her, and she saw the killer getting out of the motor home and coming toward the store, even though he hadn't finished filling the fuel tank.

He was looking down. He hadn't seen her.

She moved away from the door.

The two men stared at her expectantly.

If she told them to call the police, they would want to know why, and there was no time for a discussion, not even enough time for the telephone call. Instead, she said, "Please don't let him know I'm here," and before they could reply, she walked away from them, along an aisle with goods shelved six feet high on both sides, to the far end of the store.

As she stepped out of the aisle to hide at the end of a row of display cases, Chyna heard the door open and the killer enter. A growl of wind came with him, and then the door swung shut.

The redheaded cashier and the young Asian gentleman with the liquid-night eyes are staring at him strangely, as if they know something they shouldn't, and he almost pulls the shotgun from under his coat the moment that he walks through the door, almost blows them away without preamble. But he tells himself that he is misreading them, that they are merely intrigued by him, because he is, after all, a striking figure. Often people sense his exceptional power and are aware that he lives a larger life than they do. He is a popular man at parties, and women are frequently attracted to him. These men are merely drawn to him as are so many others. Besides, if he whacks them immediately, without a word, he will be denying himself the pleasure of foreplay.

Alan Jackson is no longer singing on the radio, and cocking one ear appreciatively, Vess says, "Man, I like that Emmylou Harris, don't you? Was there ever anyone could sing this stuff so it got to you that way?"

"She's good," says the redhead. Previously he was outgoing. Now he seems reserved.

The Asian says nothing, inscrutable in this Zen temple of Twinkies, Hershey bars, beer nuts, snack crackers, and Doritos.

"I love a song about home fires and family," Vess says.

"You on vacation?" asks the redhead.

"Hell, friend, I'm always on vacation."

"Too young to be retired."

"I mean," says Vess, "life itself is a vacation if you look at it the right way. Been doing some hunting."

"Around these parts? What game's in season?" the redhead asks.

The Asian remains silent but attentive. He takes a Slim Jim sausage off a display rack and skins open the plastic wrapper without letting his gaze flicker from Vess.

They don't suspect for a second that they're both going to be dead in a minute, and their cow-stupid lack of awareness delights Vess. It is quite funny, really. How dramatically their eyes will widen in the instant that the shotgun roars.

Instead of answering the cashier's question, Vess says, "Are you a hunter?"

"Fishing's my sport," the redhead says.

"Never cared for it," says Vess.

"Great way to get in touch with nature—little boat on the lake, peaceful water."

Vess shakes his head. "You can't see anything in their eyes."

The redhead blinks, confused. "In whose eyes?"

"I mean, they're just *fish*. They just have these flat, glassy eyes. Jesus."

"Well, I never said they're pretty. But nothing tastes better than your own-caught salmon or a mess of trout."

Edgler Vess listens to the music for a moment, letting the two men watch him. The song genuinely affects him. He feels the piercing loneliness of the road, the longing of a lover far from home. He is a sensitive man.

The Asian bites off a piece of the Slim Jim. He chews daintily, his jaw muscles hardly moving.

Vess decides that he will take the unfinished sausage back to Ariel. She can put her mouth where the Asian had his. This intimacy with the beautiful young man will be Vess's gift to the girl.

He says, "Sure will be glad to get home to my Ariel. Isn't that a pretty name?"

"Sure is," says the redhead.

"Fits her too."

"She the missus?" asks the redhead. His friendliness is not as natural as when Vess spoke with him about turning on pump number seven. He is definitely uncomfortable and trying not to show it.

Time to startle them, see how they react. Will either of them begin to realize just how much trouble is coming?

"Nope," Vess says. "No ball and chain for me. Maybe one day. Anyway, Ariel's only sixteen, not ready yet."

They are not sure what to say. Sixteen is half his age. Sixteen is still a child. Jailbait.

The risk he's taking is enormous and titillating. Another customer might pull off the highway at any moment, raising the stakes.

"Prettiest thing you'll ever see this side of paradise," says Vess, and he licks his lips. "Ariel, I mean."

He takes the Polaroid snapshot from his coat pocket and drops it onto the counter. The clerks stare at it.

"She's pure angel," says Vess. "Porcelain skin. Breathtaking. Makes your scrotum twang like a bass fiddle."

With barely disguised distaste, the cashier looks at the pump-monitor board to the left of the cash register and says, "Your sixty bucks just finished going in the tank."

Vess says, "Don't get me wrong. I never touched her—that way. She's been locked in the basement the past year, where I can look at her anytime I want to. Waiting for my little doll to ripen, get just a little sweeter."

As glassy-eyed as fish, they gaze at him. He relishes their expressions.

Then he smiles, laughs, and says, "Hey, had you going there, didn't I?"

Neither man smiles back at him, and the redhead says tightly, "You still going to make some other purchases, or do you just want your change?"

Vess puts on his most sincere face. He can almost manage a blush. "Listen, sorry if I offended. I'm a joker. Can't help puttin' people on."

"Well," says the redhead, "I have a sixteen-year-old daughter, so I don't see what's funny."

Speaking to the Asian, Vess says, "When I go hunting, I take trophies. You know—like a matador gets the bull's tail and ears? Sometimes it's just a picture. Gifts for Ariel. She'll really like you."

As he speaks, he raises the Mossberg, draped with the raincoat as if with black funeral bunting, seizes it in both hands, blows the redheaded cashier off his stool, and pumps another shell into the breech.

The Asian. Oh, how his eyes widen. The expression in them is like nothing ever to be seen in the eyes of fish.

Even as the redhead crashes to the floor, this young Asian gentleman with the fabulous eyes has one hand under the counter, going for a weapon.

Vess says, "Don't, or I'll shove the bullets up your ass."

But the Asian brings up the revolver anyway, a Smith & Wesson .38 Chief's Special, so Vess thrusts the shotgun across the counter and fires point-blank at his chest, loath to mess up that perfect face. The young man is airborne off the stool, the revolver spinning from his hand even before he has a chance to squeeze off one round.

The redhead is screaming.

Vess walks to the gate in the counter and passes through to the work area.

The redheaded cashier with the sixteen-year-old daughter waiting at home is curled as if imitating the fetus-like pink birthmark on his forehead, hugging himself, holding himself together. On the radio, Garth Brooks sings "Thunder Rolls." Now the cashier is screaming and crying at the same time. The screams reverberate in the plate-glass windows, and the echo of the shotgun still roars in Vess's ears, and a new customer could walk into the store at any second. The moment is achingly intense.

One more round finishes the cashier.

The Asian is unconscious and going fast. Happily, his face is unmarked.

Like a pilgrim genuflecting before a shrine, Vess drops onto one knee as a final gasp rattles from the dying young man. A sound like the brittle flutter of insect wings. He leans close to inhale the other's exhalation, breathes deeply. Now small measures of the Asian's grace and beauty are a part of him, conveyed on the scent of the Slim Jim.

The Brooks song is followed by that old Johnny Cash number "A Boy Named Sue," which is silly enough to spoil the mood. Vess turns off the radio.

As he reloads, he surveys the area behind the counter and spots a row of wall switches. They are labeled with the locations of the lights that they control. He shuts down all the exterior lighting, including the OPEN 24 HOURS of red neon on the roof.

When he also switches off the fluorescent ceiling panels, the store is not plunged into total darkness. The display lights in the long row of coolers glow eerily behind the insulated glass doors. A lighted clock advertising Coors beer hangs on one wall, and at the counter, a gooseneck lamp illuminates the papers on which the Asian gentleman was working.

Nevertheless, the shadows are deep, and the place appears to be closed. It's unlikely that a customer will pull in from the highway.

Of course a county sheriff's deputy or highway patrol officer, curious about why this establishment that never closes is, in fact, suddenly closed, might investigate. Consequently, Vess doesn't dawdle over the tasks that remain.

Huddled with her back against the end panel of the shelves, as far as she could get from the cashiers' counter, Chyna felt exposed by the display-case light to her right and threatened by the shadows to her left. In the silence following the gunfire and the cessation of the music, she became convinced that the killer could hear her ragged, shuddery breathing. But she couldn't quiet herself, and she couldn't stop shaking any more than a rabbit could cease shivering in the shadow of a wolf.

Maybe the rumble of the compressors for the coolers and freezers would provide enough covering sound to save her. She wanted to lean out to one side and then the other to check the flanking aisles, but she could not summon the courage to look. She was crazily certain that, leaning out, she'd come face-to-face with the eater of spiders.

She had thought that nothing could be more devastating than finding the bodies of Paul and Sarah—and later Laura—but this had been worse. This time she had been in the same room when murder happened, close enough not merely to hear the screams but to feel them like punches in the chest.

She supposed the killer was robbing the place, but he didn't need to kill the clerks just to get the money. Necessity, of course, was not a deciding factor with him. He had killed them simply because he enjoyed doing so. He was on a roll. He was *hot*.

She seemed trapped in an endless night. A breakdown in the cosmic machinery, gears jammed. Stars locked in place. No sunrise ever rising. And coming down through the frozen sky, a terrible coldness.

A light flashed, and Chyna brought her hands up defensively in front of her face. Then she realized that the flash had come from the other end of the store. And again.

Edgler Vess is not a hunter, as he had told the redheaded cashier, but a connoisseur who collects exquisite images, recording most of them with the camera of his mind's eye but once in a while with the Polaroid camera. Memories of great beauty enliven his thoughts every day and form the basis of his gratifying dreams.

Each camera flash seems to linger in the huge eyes of the Asian clerk, glimmering as if it were his spirit trapped behind his corneas and seeking egress from the cooling mortal coil.

Once, in Nevada, Vess had killed an incomparable twenty-year-old brunette, whose face had made Claudia Schiffer and Kate Moss look like hags. Before meticulously destroying her, he had taken six photographs. With threats, he had even managed to make her smile in three of the shots; she had a radiant smile. Once every thirty days during the three months following that memorable episode, he had cut up and eaten one of the photos in which she'd been smiling, and with the consumption of each, he had been fiercely aroused by the destruction of her beauty. He had felt her smile in his belly, a warming radiance, and knew that he himself was more beautiful because he contained it.

He can't remember the brunette's name. Names are never of any importance to him.

Knowing the name of the young Asian gentleman, however, will be helpful when he describes this episode to Ariel. He puts aside the Polaroid, rolls the dead man over, and takes his wallet from his hip pocket.

Holding the driver's license in the light from the gooseneck lamp, he sees that the name is Thomas Fujimoto.

Vess decides to call him Fuji. Like the mountain.

He returns the license to the wallet and tucks the wallet in the pocket. He takes none of the dead man's money. He won't touch the cash in the register either—except to extract the forty dollars in change that is due him. He isn't a thief.

With three photographs taken, he needs only to keep his promise to Fuji and prove that he is a man of his word. It is an awkward bit of business, but he finds it amusing.

Now he must deal with the security system, which has recorded everything that he's done. A video camera is mounted over the front door and focused on the cashiers' counter.

Edgler Foreman Vess has no desire to see himself on television news. Living with intensity is virtually impossible when one is in prison.

Chyna was in control of her breathing again, but her heart knocked so hard that her vision pulsed, and the carotid arteries thumped in her throat as though jolts of electricity were slamming through them.

Again convinced that safety lay in movement, she leaned into the light and looked around the corner into the aisle in front of the coolers. The killer was not in sight, although she could hear him moving at the other end of the store: crisp furtive rustlings like a rat in a drift of autumn leaves.

On her hands and knees, stomach clenched in terror, she crawled into the spill of cooler light far enough to look along the narrow aisle, seeking something on the shelves to the right that might serve as a weapon. Without the butcher knife, she felt helpless.

No knives were conveniently for sale. Nearest to her were hanging displays of novelty key chains, fingernail clippers, pocket combs, styptic pencils, packets of moistened towelettes, eyeglass-cleaning papers, decks of playing cards, and disposable cigarette lighters.

She reached up and took one of the lighters off the rack. She wasn't sure how she could use it to defend herself, but in the absence of a satisfyingly sharp length of steel, fire was the only weapon available to her.

The overhead fluorescent panels blinked on. The brightness froze her.

She looked toward the far end of the store. The killer wasn't in sight, but across one wall his slouched shadow swelled huge and then shrank and then glided away like that of a moth swooping past a floodlamp.

Vess switches the lights on only to look at the video camera mounted above the front door.

Of course the incriminating tape is not contained in the camera. If access were that easy, even some of the dimwit thugs who make a living sticking up service stations and convenience stores would be smart enough to climb on a stool and eject the cassette to take it with them or otherwise destroy the evidence. The camera is sending the image to a video recorder elsewhere in the building.

The system is an add-on, so the transmission cable isn't buried in the wall. This is fortunate for Vess, because if the cable were hidden, the search would be more time-consuming. The line isn't even tucked up above the suspended acoustic-tile ceiling. Bracketed to the Sheetrock, it leads openly to the back partition behind the cashiers' counter and through a half-inch-diameter hole in that wall to another room.

There's a door to that room as well. He finds an office with one desk, gray metal filing cabinets, a small safe with a combination lock, and wood-pattern Formica storage cabinets.

Fortunately, the recorder isn't in the safe. The transmission cable comes through the wall from the store, continues through two more brackets for a distance of about seven feet, then drops down through the top of one of the storage cabinets. No attempt at concealment whatsoever.

He opens the upper doors to the cabinet, doesn't find what he seeks, and checks below. Three machines are stacked atop one another.

Tape whispers through the bottom machine, and the indicator light shines above the word RECORD. He presses the STOP button, then EJECT, and he drops the cassette into his raincoat pocket.

He might play it for Ariel. The quality will not be first-rate, because this is an old system, outdated technology. But the precious girl will be impressed by his bold performance even in too brightly lit scenes on black-and-white tape that has been re-recorded too often.

A telephone stands on the desk. He uncouples it from the cord that leads to the wall jack and uses the butt of the shotgun to smash the keypad.

A new shift of clerks will come on duty, probably at eight or nine o'clock, in four or five hours. By then Vess will be long gone. But there's no point in making it easy for them to call the police. Something might go wrong with his plans, delaying him here or on the highway, and then he will be glad that he bought himself an extra half hour by destroying the telephones.

Beside the door is a pegboard on which hang eight keys, each with its own tag. With the exception of the current regrettable interruption in service, this establishment is open twenty-four hours a day—yet there's a key to lock the front door. He slips it off its peg.

In the work area behind the cashiers' counter once more, after closing the office door behind him, Vess snaps down a switch, and the overhead fluorescents wink out.

He stands in the dim light that remains, breathing through his mouth, licking his lips, rolling his tongue over his gums, tasting the lingering acrid scent of gunfire. The gloom feels good against his face and the backs of his hands; the shadows are as erotic as slender, trembling hands.

Stepping around the bodies, he goes to the counter and takes only his forty dollars from the cash register drawer.

The young Asian's Smith & Wesson .38 Chief's Special lies on the counter, in the cone of light from the gooseneck lamp, where Vess carefully placed it minutes ago. He is no more capable of stealing the gun than he is of taking money that doesn't belong to him.

The Slim Jim, from which the Asian took a large bite, is also on the counter. Unfortunately, the wrapper was *peeled* off; therefore, it is useless.

Vess plucks another sausage from the display rack, neatly chews off the end of the plastic wrapper, and slides the tube of meat out of the package. He inserts the shorter sausage (missing the Asian's bite) into the wrapper and twists the end shut. He puts this in his pocket with the videotape—for Ariel.

He pays for the sausage that he threw away, making change from the open register drawer.

On the counter is a telephone. He unplugs it from the jack and smashes the keypad with the butt of the shotgun.

Now he goes shopping.

Chyna was relieved when the lights went off, frightened by the hammering, and then alert in the subsequent silence.

She had crept out of the cooler-lighted aisle and returned to her shelter at the end of the shelf row, where she had quietly peeled open the cardboard-and-plastic package that contained the disposable cigarette lighter. While the overhead fluorescents had been on and the flickering flame couldn't betray her, she had tested the lighter, and it had worked.

Now she clutched this pathetic weapon and prayed that the killer would finish whatever he was doing—maybe looting the cash register—and just, for God's sake, get out of here. She didn't want to have to go up against him with a Bic butane. If he stumbled onto her, she might be able to take advantage of his surprise, thrust the lighter in his face, and give him a nasty little burn—or even set his hair on fire—before he recoiled. More likely, his reflexes would be uncannily quick; he'd knock the lighter out of her hand before she could do any damage.

Even if she burned him, she would gain only precious seconds to turn and flee. Hurting, he would come after her, and with his long legs, he would be swift. Then the outcome of the race would depend on whether her terror or his insane rage was the greater motivating force.

She heard movement, the creak of the counter gate, footsteps. Half nauseated from protracted fear, she was gloriously heartened when it seemed that he was leaving.

Then she realized that the footsteps were not crossing toward the door at the front of the store. They were approaching her.

She was squatting on her haunches, back pressed to the end panel of the shelf row, not immediately sure where he was. In the first of the three aisles, toward the front of the store? In the center aisle immediately to her left?

No.

The third aisle.

To her right.

He was coming past the coolers. Not fast. Not as if he knew that she was here and intended to whack her.

Rising into a crouch but staying low, Chyna eased to the left, into the middle of the three passages. Here the glow from the coolers, one row removed, bounced off the acoustic-tile ceiling but provided little illumination. All the merchandise was shelved with shadows.

She started forward toward the cashiers' counter, thankful for her soft-soled shoes—and then she remembered the packaging from which she had extracted the Bic lighter. She'd left it on the floor where she'd been squatting at the end of the shelf row.

He would see it, probably even step on it. Maybe he would think that earlier in the night some shoplifter had slipped the lighter out of the packaging to conceal it more easily in a pocket. Or maybe he would *know*.

Intuition might serve him as well as it sometimes served Chyna. If intuition was the whisper of God, then perhaps another and less benevolent god spoke with equal subtleness to a man like this.

She turned back, leaned around the corner, and snatched up the empty package. The stiff plastic crinkled in her shaky grip, but the sound was faint and, luckily, masked by his footsteps.

He was at least halfway down the third aisle by the time she started forward along the second. But he was taking his time while she was scuttling as fast as she could, and she reached the head of her aisle before he arrived at the end of his.

At the terminus of the shelf row, instead of a flat panel like the one at the far end, there was a freestanding wire carousel rack holding paperback books, and Chyna nearly collided with it when she turned the corner. She caught herself just in time, slipped around the rack, and sheltered against it, between aisles once more.

On the floor lay a Polaroid photograph: a close-up of a strikingly beautiful girl of about sixteen, with long platinum-blond hair. The teenager's features were composed but not relaxed, frozen in a studied blandness, as though her true feelings were so explosive that she would self-destruct if she acknowledged them. Her eyes subtly belied her calm demeanor; they were slightly wide, watchful, achingly expressive, windows on a soul in torment, full of anger and fear and desperation.

This must be the photograph that he had shown to the clerks. Ariel. The girl in the cellar.

Although she and Ariel bore no resemblance to each other, Chyna felt as though she were staring into a mirror rather than looking at a picture. In Ariel, she recognized a terror akin to the fear that had suffused her own childhood, a familiar desperation, loneliness as deep as a cold polar ocean.

The killer's footsteps brought her back to the moment. Judging by the sound of them, he was no longer in the third aisle. He had turned the corner at the back of the store and was now in the middle passage.

He was coming forward, leisurely covering the same territory over which Chyna had just scuttled.

What the hell is he doing?

She wanted to take the photograph but didn't dare. She put it on the floor where she had found it.

She went around the paperback carousel into the third aisle, which the killer had just left, and she headed toward the end of the shelf row again. She stayed close to the merchandise on the left, away from the glass doors of the lighted coolers on the right, to avoid throwing a shadow on the ceiling tiles, which he might see.

When she was moving, she could still hear his heavy footsteps, but unless she stopped to listen, she couldn't tell in which direction he was headed. Yet she didn't dare stop to take a bearing on him, lest he circle again into this aisle and catch her in the open. When she reached the end of the row and turned the corner, she half expected to discover that he had changed directions, to collide with him, and to be caught.

But he wasn't there.

Sitting on her haunches, Chyna leaned back against the end panel of the shelf row, the very spot from which she'd started. Gingerly she put the empty Bic lighter package on the floor between her feet, in the same place from which she had retrieved it less than a minute before.

She listened. No footsteps. Other than the noise made by the coolers, only silence.

Thumb poised, she clutched the lighter in her fist, prepared to strike the flame.

• • •

Vess stuffs two snack packages of cheese-and-peanut-butter crackers, one Planters peanut bar, and two Hershey bars with almonds into his raincoat pockets, in which he's already carrying the pistol, the Polaroid, and the videotape.

He totals the cost in his head. Because he doesn't want to waste time going behind the register to make change, he rounds the figure to the nearest dollar and leaves the payment on the counter.

After picking up the fallen photograph of Ariel, he hesitates, soaking up the atmosphere of aftermath. There is a special quality to a room in which people have recently perished: like the hush in a theater during that instant between when the final curtain falls on a perfect performance and when the wild applause begins; a sense of triumph but also a solemn awareness of eternity suspended like a cold droplet at the point of a melting icicle. With the screaming done and the blood pooled in stillness, Edgler Vess is better able to appreciate the effects of his bold actions and to relish the quiet intensity of death.

Finally he leaves the store. Using the tagged key that he took from the pegboard, he locks the door.

At the corner of the building is one public telephone. With its armored cord, the handset isn't easily torn loose, so he hammers it against the phone box five, ten, twenty times, until the plastic cracks, revealing the microphone. He tears the mike out of the broken mouthpiece, drops it on the pavement, and methodically crushes it under his boot heel. Then he hangs the useless handset on the switch hook again.

His work here is done. Although satisfying, this interlude was unexpected; it has put him behind schedule.

He has much driving to do. He is not tired. He had slept all the previous afternoon and well into the evening, before visiting the Templetons. Nevertheless, he is loath to waste more time. He longs to be home.

Far to the north, sheets of lightning flutter softly between dense layers of clouds, pulses rather than bolts. Vess is pleased by the prospect of a big storm. Here at ground level, where life is lived, tumult and turmoil are fundamental elements of the human climate, and for reasons that he cannot understand, he is unfailingly reassured by the sight of violence in higher realms as well. Though he fears nothing, he is sometimes inexplicably disturbed by the sight of *serene* skies—whether blue or overcast—and often on a clear night when the sky is deep with stars, he prefers not to gaze into that immensity.

Now no stars are visible. Above lie only sullen masses of clouds harried by a cold wind, briefly veined with lightning, pregnant with a deluge.

Vess hurries across the blacktop toward the motor home, eager to resume his journey northward, to meet the promised storm, to find that best place in the night where the lightning will come in great shattering bolts, where a harder wind will crack trees, where rain will fall in destructive floods.

Crouching at the end of the shelf row, Chyna had listened to the door open and close, not daring to believe that the killer had left at last and that her ordeal might be over. Breath held, she'd waited for the sound of the door opening again and for his footsteps as he reentered.

When she had heard, instead, the key scraping-clicking in the lock and the deadbolt snapping into place, she had gone forward along the middle of the three aisles, staying low, cat-quiet because she expected, superstitiously, that he might hear the slightest sound even from outside.

A violent hammering, reverberating through the building walls, had brought her to a sudden halt at the head of the aisle. He was pounding furiously on something, but she couldn't imagine what it might be.

When the hammering stopped, Chyna hesitated, then rose from her crouch and leaned around the end of the shelves. She looked to the right, past the first aisle, toward the glass door and the windows at the front of the store.

With the outside lights off, the service islands lay in murk as deep as that on any river bottom.

She could not at first see the killer, who was at one with the night in his black raincoat. But then he moved, wading through the darkness toward the motor home.

Even if he glanced back, he wouldn't be able to see her in the dimly lighted store. Her heart thundered anyway as she stepped into the open area between the heads of the three aisles and the cashiers' counter.

The photograph of Ariel was no longer on the floor. She wished that she could believe it had never existed.

At the moment, the two employees who had kept the secret of her presence were more important than Ariel or the killer. The roar of the shotgun and the sudden cessation of the soul-shriveling screams had convinced her that they were dead. But she must be sure. If one of them clung miraculously to life, and if she could get help for him—police and paramedics—she would partially redeem herself.

She had been unable to do anything to stop the blood-loving bastard; she had only cowered out of his sight, praying frantically for invisibility. Now nausea rolled like a slop of chilled oysters in her stomach—and at the same time she was lifted by a sickening exhilaration that she had lived when so many others had died. Understandable though it was, the exhilaration shamed her, and for herself as well as for the two clerks, she hoped that she could still save them.

She pushed through the gate in the counter, and the piercing creak of a hinge scraped the hollows of her bones.

A gooseneck lamp provided some light.

The two men were on the floor.

"Ah," she said. And then: "God."

They were beyond her help, and immediately she turned away from them, her vision blurring.

On the counter, directly under the lamp, lay a revolver. She stared at it in disbelief, blinking back tears.

Evidently it had belonged to one of the clerks. She'd overheard the conversation between the killer and the two men; and she vaguely recalled a harsh admonition that might have been a warning to drop a gun. This gun.

She grabbed it, held it in both hands—a weight that buoyed her.

If the killer returned, she was ready, no longer helpless, for she knew how to use guns. Some of her mother's craziest friends had been expert with weaponry, hate-filled people with a queer brightness in the eyes that was a sign of drug use in some cases but that was visible in others only when they spoke passionately about their deep commitment to truth and justice. On an isolated farm in Montana, when Chyna was only twelve, a woman named Doreen and a man named Kirk had instructed her in the use of a pistol, although her slender arms had jumped wildly with the recoil. Patiently teaching her control, they had said that someday she would be a true soldier and a credit to the movement.

Chyna had wanted to learn about firearms not to use them in one noble cause or another but to protect herself from those people in her mother's strange circles who succumbed to drug-enhanced rages—or who stared at her with a sick desire. She had been too young to want their attention, too self-respecting to encourage them—but thanks to her mother, she had not been too innocent to understand what some of them wanted to do with her.

Now, with the dead clerk's revolver in hand, she turned and saw the shattered telephone.

"Shit."

She hurried back through the gate, into the public part of the store, directly to the front door.

The motor home was still parked on this side of the farther of the two service islands. The headlights were off.

The killer was not in sight at first—but then he walked into view around the back of the motor home, his unbuttoned coat flaring like a cape in the wind.

Although the man was about sixty feet away, surely he couldn't see her at the door. He wasn't even looking in her direction, but Chyna took a step backward.

Apparently he had been racking the hose at the gasoline pump and capping the fuel tank. He walked alongside the vehicle toward the driver's door.

She had planned to telephone the police and tell them that the killer was headed north on Highway 101. Now, by the time she got to a phone, called the cops, and made them understand the situation, he might have as much as an hour's lead. Within an hour, he would have several choices of other routes that branched off 101. He might continue north toward Oregon, turn east toward Nevada—or even angle west to the coast, thereafter turning south again along the Pacific and into San Francisco, vanishing in the urban maze. The more miles he traveled before an all-points bulletin went out for him, the harder he would be to find. He would soon be in another police agency's jurisdiction, first a different county and perhaps eventually a different state, complicating the search for him.

And now that she thought about it, Chyna realized that she had precious little information that would be helpful to the cops. The motor home might be blue or green; she wasn't sure which—or even if it was either—because she'd seen it only in the darkness and then in the color-distorting yellow glow of the service station's sodium-vapor lights. She didn't know the make of it either, and she hadn't seen the license plate.

He was getting away.

Unhurried, clearly confident that he was in no imminent danger of discovery, he climbed into the motor home and pulled shut the driver's door.

He's going to get away. Jesus. No, intolerable, unthinkable. He can't be allowed to get away, never pay for what he did to Laura, to all of them—even worse, have a chance to do it again. No, God, please, let me drop the hateful rotten fucking bastard with a shot in the head.

She stepped close to the door again. It could be unlocked only with a key. She didn't have a key.

She heard the motor-home engine turn over.

If she shot out the glass, he would hear. Even over the roar of the engine and from a distance, he would hear.

Once through the door, she would be too far away to shoot him. Fifty or sixty feet, at night, with a handgun, the gasoline pumps intervening. No way. She had to get close, right up against the motor home, put the muzzle to the window.

But if he heard her shoot her way through the locked door and saw her coming out of the store, she wouldn't have a chance to get close to him, not in a million years, and then *he* would be stalking *her* again, across the service-station property, wherever she went, and his shotgun was better armament than her revolver.

Out at the motor home, he switched on the headlights.

"No."

She ran to the gate in the counter, shoved through it, stepped around the dead men, and went to the door in the back wall.

There had to be a rear entrance. Both practical function and fire codes would require it.

The door opened onto blackness. As far as she could tell, there were no windows ahead of her. Maybe it was only a supply closet or a bathroom. She stepped across the threshold, closed the door behind her to prevent light from leaking into the store, felt along the wall to her left, found a switch, and risked turning on the lights.

She was in a cramped office. On the desk was another shattered telephone.

Directly across the room from the door that she had just used was another door. No obvious lock. That *would* be a bathroom.

To her left, in the back wall of the building, a metal door featured a pair of over-and-under deadbolts with thumb-turns. She disengaged the locks and opened the door, and a flood tide of cold wind washed into the office.

Behind the store spread a twenty-foot-wide paved area, and then a steep hillside rose with serried trees that were black in the night and restless in the wind. A security light in a wire cage revealed two parked cars, which probably belonged to the clerks.

Cursing the killer, Chyna turned to the right and sprinted along the shorter length of the building, around the corner, past public rest rooms. She had never caused anyone physical harm, not once in her life, but she was ready to kill now, and she knew that she could do it without hesitation, with no thought of mercy, with a vengeance, because *he* had empowered her to do it. This was what he had reduced her to—this blind, animal fury—and the worst thing was that it felt *good*, this rage, so good in comparison to the fear and helplessness she had endured, a sweet singing of rushing blood in the veins and an exhilarating sense of savage strength. She should have been appalled at the lust for blood that seized her, but she *liked* it, and she knew that she would like it even more when she caught up with the motor home and shot him through the driver's-side window, pulled open the door and shot him again where he sat bleeding, dragged him out and let him sprawl on the pavement and emptied the revolver into him until he could never again go hunting.

She rounded the second corner and reached the front of the building.

The motor home was pulling away from the pumps.

She raced after it, faster than she had ever run in her life, cleaving a resistant wind that stung new tears from her eyes, shoes pounding noisily on the blacktop.

Now it was *Dear Lord, let me catch him* instead of *Dear Lord, let me get away from him*, and now it was *Dear Lord, let me kill him* instead of *Dear Lord, don't let him kill me*.

The motor home picked up speed. It was already out of the service area, entering the eighth-of-a-mile lane that would take it back onto the highway.

She would never be able to catch it.

He was getting away.

She halted and planted her feet wide apart. The revolver was in her right hand. She raised it, gripped it with both hands, arms extended, elbows locked. Shooter's stance. Every good girl should know it, come the revolution.

Her heart didn't merely beat, it crashed, and every explosive pump shook her arms, so she couldn't hold the revolver on target. The motor home was too distant anyway. She'd miss it by yards. And even if she got lucky and put one round in the back wall, it would be nowhere near the driver. He was out of her reach, beyond harm, cruising away.

It was over. She could go for help, find the nearest working phone, call the local police, and try to cut his lead time as short as possible—but for now and here, it was over.

Except that it wasn't over, and she knew it wasn't, no matter how much she wanted to be finished with it, because she said aloud, "Ariel."

Sixteen. Prettiest thing this side of paradise. Pure angel. Porcelain skin. Breathtaking. Locked in the basement for a year. Never touched her—that way. Waiting for her to ripen, get just a little sweeter.

In Chyna's mind's eye, the Polaroid photograph of Ariel was as clear and detailed as it had been when she'd held it in her hand. That bland expression, maintained with obvious effort. Those eyes, brimming with anguish.

Earlier, listening to the conversation between the killer and the two clerks, Chyna had *known* that he was not merely playing games with them, that he was telling the truth. The creep was letting them in on his secrets, admitting his perverse crimes, getting a kick out of revealing his guilt because he knew that they were going to die and that they would never have a chance to repeat his admissions to anyone. Even if she'd never seen the photograph, she would have *known*.

Ariel. Those eyes. The anguish.

While she had been concentrating on her own survival, Chyna had blocked all thoughts of the captive girl from her mind. And when she had found the revolver, she had at once convinced herself that all she wanted was to kill this son of a bitch, blow his brains out, because the truth was something that she hadn't quite been able to face.

The truth had been that she didn't dare kill him, because when he was dead, they might never find Ariel—or find her days too late, after she had died of starvation or thirst in her basement cell. He might have the girl locked under his house, which they would probably be able to locate from whatever identification he was carrying, but he might have stashed her elsewhere, in a place remote, to which he and only he could lead them. Chyna had pursued the killer to disable him, so the cops would be able to wrench from him the location at which Ariel was being held. If she could have caught up with the motor home, she would have tried to yank open the driver's door, shoot the vicious bastard in the leg as she ran alongside, wound him badly enough that he would have to stop the vehicle. But she'd had to hide that truth from herself because trying to wound him was a lot riskier than going for a head shot through the window, and she might not have had the courage to run so fast and try so hard if she had admitted to herself what, in fact, had needed to be done.

With its burden of corpses, with its driver whose name might well be Legion, the big motor home dwindled down the service road toward Highway 101, quite literally Hell on wheels.

Somewhere he had a house, and under the house was a basement, and in the basement was a sixteen-year-old girl named Ariel, held prisoner for a year, untouched but soon to be violated, alive but not for long.

"She's real," Chyna whispered to the wind.

The taillights receded into the night.

She frantically surveyed the lonely stretch of countryside. She was unable to see help in any direction. No house lights in the immediate vicinity. Just trees and darkness. Something glowed faintly to the north, beyond a hill or two, but she didn't know the source, and anyway she couldn't get that far quickly on foot.

On the highway, a truck appeared from the south behind a blaze of headlights, but it didn't pull off to tank up at the shuttered service station. It shrieked past, the driver oblivious of Chyna.

The lumbering motor home was almost to the far end of the connecting road.

Sobbing with frustration, with anger, with fear for the girl whom she had never met, and with despair for her own culpability if that girl died, Chyna turned away from the motor home. Hurried past the gasoline pumps. Around the building, back the way she had come.

Throughout her own childhood, no one had ever held out a hand to her. No one had ever cared that she was trapped, frightened, and helpless.

Now, when she thought of the Polaroid snapshot, the image was like one of those holograms that changed depending on the angle at which it was viewed. Sometimes it was Ariel's face, but sometimes it was Chyna's own.

As she ran, she prayed that she wouldn't have to go inside again. And search the bodies.

Distant lightning flickered, and faraway thunder clattered like boot heels on hollow basement stairs. On the steep hills behind the building, black trees thrashed in the escalating wind.

The first car was a white Chevrolet. Ten years old. Unlocked.

When she scrambled in behind the steering wheel, the worn-out seat springs creaked, and a candy-bar wrapper or something crackled underfoot. The interior stank of stale cigarette smoke.

The keys were not in the ignition. She checked behind the sun visor. Under the driver's seat. Nothing.

The second car was a Honda, newer than the Chevy. It smelled of a lemon-scented air freshener, and the keys were in a coin tray on the console.

She placed the revolver on the passenger seat, within easy reach, reluctant to let it out of her hand. As an adult, she had always relied on prudence and caution to stay out of harm's way. She hadn't held a gun since she'd walked out on her mother at the age of sixteen. Now she could not imagine living without a weapon at her side, and she doubted that she ever would do so again—which was a development that dismayed her.

The engine turned over at once. The tires shrieked, and she peeled rubber getting started. Smoke bloomed from the spinning wheels, but then she shot out from behind the building and rocketed past the service islands.

The connecting road to the freeway was deserted. The motor home was out of sight.

At this point, 101 was a four-lane divided highway, so the motor home couldn't have gotten across the median to turn south. The killer had to have gone north, and he couldn't have traveled far in the little lead time that he had.

Chyna went after him.

FIVE

At four o'clock in the morning, oncoming traffic is sparse, but each set of headlights purls through the fine hairs in Edgler Vess's ears. This is a pleasant sound, separate from the passing roar of engines and the Doppler-shift whine of other vehicles' tires on the pavement.

As he drives, he eats one of the Hershey bars. The silkiness of melting chocolate on his tongue reminds him of the music of Angelo Badalamenti, and the music of Badalamenti brings to mind the waxy surface of a scarlet anthurium, and the anthurium sparks an intensely sensual recollection of the cool taste and crispness of cornichons, which for several seconds completely overwhelms the actual taste of the chocolate.

Listening to the murmur of oncoming headlights, engaged in this free association of sensory input and memory, Vess is a happy man. He experiences life far more intensely than do other people; he is a singularity. Because his mind is not cluttered with foolishness and false emotions, he is able to perceive what others cannot. He understands the nature of the world, the purpose of existence, and the truth behind the Big Lie; because of these insights, he is free, and because he is free, he is always happy.

The nature of the world is sensation. We drift in an ocean of sensory stimuli: motion, color, texture, shape, heat, cold, natural symphonies of sound, an infinite number of scents, tastes beyond the human ability to catalogue. Nothing but sensation endures. Living things all die. Great cities do not last. Metal corrodes and stone crumbles. Over eons, continents are reshaped, whole mountain ranges vanish, and seas run dry. The planet itself will be vaporized when the sun self-destructs. But even in the void of deep space, between solar systems, in that profound vacuum that will not transmit sound, there is nevertheless light and darkness, cold, motion, shape, and the awful panorama of eternity.

The sole purpose of existence is to open oneself to sensation and to satisfy all appetites as they arise. Edgler Vess knows that there is no such thing as a good or bad sensation— only raw sensation itself—and that every sensory experience is worthwhile. Negative and positive values are merely human interpretations of value-neutral stimuli and, therefore, are only as enduring—which is to say, as meaningless—as human beings themselves. He enjoys the most bitter taste as much as he relishes the sweetness of a ripe peach; in fact, he occasionally chews a few aspirin not to relieve a headache but to savor the incomparable flavor of the medication. When he accidentally cuts himself, he is never afraid, because he finds pain fascinating and welcomes it as merely another form of pleasure; even the taste of his own blood intrigues him.

Mr. Vess is not sure if there is such a thing as the immortal soul, but he is unshakably certain that if souls exist, we are not born with them in the same way that we are born with eyes and ears. He believes that the soul, if real, *accretes* in the same manner as a coral reef grows from the deposit of countless millions of calcareous skeletons secreted by marine polyps. We build the reef of the soul, however, not from dead polyps but from steadily accreted sensations through the course of a lifetime. In Vess's considered opinion, if one wishes to have a formidable soul—or any soul at all—one must open oneself to every possible sensation, plunge into the bottomless ocean of sensory stimuli that is our world, and *experience* with no consideration of good or bad, right or wrong, with no fear but only fortitude. If his belief is correct, then he himself is building what may be the most intricate, elaborated—if not to say baroque—and *important* soul that has ever transcended this level of existence.

The Big Lie is that such concepts as love, guilt, and hate are real. Put Mr. Vess into a room with any priest, show them a pencil, and they will agree on its color, size, and shape. Blindfold them, hold cinnamon under their noses, and they will both identify it from the smell. But bring before them a mother cuddling her baby, and the priest will see love where Mr. Vess will see only a woman who enjoys the sensations provided by the infant— the scrubbed smell of it, the softness of its pink skin, the undeniably pleasing roundness of its simply-formed face, the musicality of its giggle; its apparent helplessness and dependence deeply satisfy her. The greatest curse of humanity's high intelligence is that, in most members of the species, it leads to a yearning to be more than they are. All men and women, in Vess's view, are fundamentally nothing other than animals—smart animals, indeed, but animals nonetheless; reptiles, in fact, evolved from whatever fish with legs first crawled out of the primordial sea. They are, he knows, motivated and formed solely by sensory stimuli, yet unable to admit to the primacy of physical sensation over intellect and emotion. They are even frightened of the reptile consciousness within, its needs and hungers, and they attempt to restrict its sensation seeking by using lies such as love, guilt, hate, courage, loyalty, and honor.

This is the philosophy of Mr. Edgler Vess. He embraces his reptilian nature. The glory of him is to be found in his unmatched accretion of sensations. This is a functional philosophy, requiring its adherent to endorse neither the black-and-white values that so hamper religious persons nor the embarrassing contradictions of the situational ethics that characterize both the modern atheist and those whose religion is politics.

Life *is*. Vess lives. That is the sum of it.

Driving north on Highway 101, finishing the second of his two Hershey bars, Vess considers, not for the first time, that there is a similarity between the texture of melting chocolate and that of thickening blood.

He recalls the restful silence of the blood pooled around Mrs. Templeton in the shower stall before he disturbed it by turning on the cold water.

The memory of the hollow drumming in that shower makes him aware of the coldness of all the rain as yet unleashed by the pending storm toward which he is driving.

He sees a quick blush of lightning along the face of the clouds, and he knows that it tastes like ozone.

Above the monotonous rumble of the motor-home engine, he hears a peal of thunder, and that sound is also a vivid image in his mind: the young Asian's eyes opening wide, wide, wide with the first crash of the shotgun.

Even in the airless void between galaxies: the light and the darkness, color, texture, motion, shape, and pain.

• • •

The highway rose, and the forests crowded close. On a wide curve, the headlights of the Honda swept across the flanking hills, revealing that some of the looming trees were immense spruces and pines. Soon, perhaps, redwoods.

Chyna kept her foot down hard on the accelerator. To the best of her recollection, this was the first time she had ever broken a speed limit. She'd never been fined for a traffic violation; but she would be grateful now if a cop pulled her over.

Her unblemished driving record resulted from her preference for moderation in all things, including the pace at which she ordinarily drove. Judging by the catastrophes that she had seen befall others, survival was closely related to moderation, and her whole life was about survival, as any nun's life might be defined by the word *faith* or any politician's by *power*. She seldom drank more than one glass of wine, never used drugs, engaged in no dangerous sports, ate a diet low in fat and salt and sugar, stayed out of neighborhoods reputed to be dangerous, never expressed strong opinions, and in general was safely inconspicuous—all in the interest of getting by, hanging on, surviving.

Against the odds, she had already survived the events of the past few hours. *The killer didn't even know that she existed.* She had made it. She was free. It was over. The smart thing, the wise thing, the sane thing—the *Chyna* thing—to do was to let him go, just let him get away, pull off to the side of the road, stop, surrender to the shakes that she was strenuously repressing, and thank God that she was untouched and alive.

As she drove, Chyna argued against her previous conviction, insisting that the teenage girl in the cellar, Ariel of the angelic face, wasn't real. The photo might be of a girl whom he had already killed. The story of her incarceration might be only a sick fantasy, a psychotic's version of a Brothers Grimm tale, Rapunzel underground, merely a mind game that he'd been playing with the two clerks.

"Liar," she called herself.

The girl in the photo was alive somewhere, imprisoned. Ariel was no fantasy. Indeed, she was Chyna; they were one and the same, because all lost girls are the same girl, united by their suffering.

She kept her foot pressed firmly on the accelerator, and the Honda crested a hill, and the aged motor home was on the long gradual downslope ahead, five hundred feet away. Her breath caught in her throat, and then she exhaled with a whispered, "*Oh, Jesus.*"

She was approaching him at too great a speed. She eased off the accelerator.

By the time she was two hundred feet from the motor home, she had matched speeds with it. She fell back farther, hoping that he hadn't noticed her initial haste.

He was driving between fifty and fifty-five miles per hour, a prudent pace on that highway, especially as they were now traveling on a stretch without a median strip and with somewhat narrower lanes than previously. He wouldn't necessarily expect her to pass him, and he shouldn't be suspicious when she remained behind; after all, at this sleepy hour, not every driver in California was in a blistering hurry or suicidally reckless.

At this more reasonable speed, she didn't have to concentrate as intently as before on the road ahead, and she quickly searched the immediate interior of the car in hopes of finding a cellular telephone. She was pessimistic about the chances that a night clerk at a service station would have a portable phone, but on the other hand, half the world seemed to have them now, not just salesmen and Realtors and lawyers. She checked the console box. Then the glove box. Under the driver's seat. Unfortunately, her pessimism proved well founded.

Southbound traffic passed in the oncoming lanes: a big rig with a lead-footed driver, a Mercedes close in its wake—then, following a long gap, a Ford. Chyna paid special attention to the cars, hoping that one of them would be a police cruiser.

If she spotted a cop, she intended to get his attention with the car horn and by making a weaving spectacle of herself in his rearview mirror. If she was too late with the horn and if the cop didn't look back and catch a glimpse of her reckless slalom, she would turn and pursue him, reluctantly letting the motor home out of her sight.

She wasn't hopeful about finding a cop anytime soon.

All the luck seemed to be with the killer. He conducted himself with a confidence that unnerved Chyna. Perhaps that confidence was the only guarantor of his good luck— although even for one as rooted in reality as Chyna, it was easy to let superstition overwhelm her, attributing to him powers dark and supernatural.

No. He was only a man.

And now she had a revolver. She was no longer helpless.

The worst was past.

Lightning traveled the northern sky again, but this time it was not pale or diffused through cloud layers. The bolts were as bright as though the naked sun were breaking through from the other side of the night.

In those stroboscopic flashes, the motor home seemed to vibrate, as if divine wrath would shatter it and its driver.

In this world, however, retribution was left to mortal men and women. God was content to wait for the next life to mete out punishment; in Chyna's view, this was His only cruel aspect, but in this was cruelty enough.

Explosions of thunder followed the lightning. Although something above should have broken, nothing did, and the rain remained bottled higher in the night.

She hoped to spot a sign for a highway patrol depot, where she could seek help, but none appeared. The nearest town of appreciable size, where she might be fortunate enough to find a police station or a cruising squad car, was Eureka, which was hardly a metropolis. And even Eureka was at least an hour away.

As a child, flat under beds and curled in the backs of closets, perched on rooftops and balanced in the upper reaches of trees, in winter barns and on warm night beaches, she had hidden and waited out the passions and the rages of adults, always with dread but also with patience and with a Zen-like disconnection from the realities of time. Now impatience plagued her as never before. She wanted to see this man caught, manacled, harried to justice, *hurt*. Desperately she wanted this and without a single additional minute of delay, *before he could kill again*. Her own survival wasn't currently at stake but that of a teenage girl whom she had never met, and she was surprised—and made uneasy—to discover that she could care so ferociously about a stranger.

Perhaps she had always possessed that capacity and simply had never been in a situation that required recognition of it. But no. That was self deception. Ten years ago, she would never have followed the motor home. Nor five years ago. Nor last year. Perhaps not even yesterday.

Something had profoundly changed her, and it hadn't been the brutality that she'd seen a few hours earlier at the Templeton house. Viscerally she was aware that this unsettling metamorphosis had been a long time coming, like the slow alteration in a river's course— by imperceptible fractions of a degree, day after day. Then suddenly mere survival was not enough for her any longer; the final palisade of soil crumbled, the last stone shifted, and the destination of the river changed.

She frightened herself. This reckless caring.

More lightning, more ferocious than before, revealed redwood trees so massive that they reminded her of cathedral spires. The steeple-shattering light was followed by quakes of thunder as violent as any shift in the San Andreas. The sky fissured, and rain fell.

In the first instant, the drops were fat and milky white in the headlights, as if the night were an extinguished chandelier in which were suspended an infinite number of rock-crystal pendants. They shattered into the windshield, against the hood, across the blacktop.

On the highway ahead, the motor home began to disappear into the downpour.

In seconds the drops dwindled drastically in size even as they increased in number. They became silver gray in the headlamps, and fell not straight down as before but at an angle in the punishing wind.

Chyna switched the windshield wipers to their highest setting, but the motor home continued to slip rapidly away into the storm as visibility declined. The killer was not lowering his speed in respect of the worsening weather; he was accelerating.

Afraid to let him out of her sight for as much as a second, Chyna closed the gap between them to about two hundred feet. She was worried that he would attach the correct significance to her maneuver and realize that somehow she was onto him.

Southbound traffic had been sparse to begin with, but now it declined in direct proportion to the power of the escalating storm, as though most motorists had been washed off the highway.

No headlights appeared in the rearview mirror either. The psychotic in the motor home had set a pace that no one but Chyna was likely to match.

She felt almost as alone with him here in the open as she had been inside his abattoir on wheels.

Then, as enough time passed to make the lonely lanes of blacktop and the dreary cataracts of rain less threatening than monotonous, the killer suddenly surprised her. With a quick touch of his brakes, without bothering to use a turn signal, he angled to the right onto an exit lane.

Chyna fell back somewhat, again concerned that he would become suspicious, seeing her take the same exit. Because theirs were the only two vehicles in sight, she could not be inconspicuous. But she had no choice other than to follow him.

By the time she reached the end of the ramp, the motor home had vanished into the rain and thin mist, but from the ramp entrance, she had seen it turn left. In fact, the two-lane road led only west, and a sign indicated that she was already within the boundaries of Humboldt Redwood State Park.

In addition, three communities lay ahead: Honeydew, Petrolia, and Capetown. She'd never heard of any of them, and she was sure that they were little more than wide places in the road, where she would find no police.

Leaning forward over the steering wheel, squinting through the rain-smeared windshield, she drove into the park, eager to catch up with the killer again, because he might live in or near one of those three small towns. She was wise to let him out of sight for a minute, so he wouldn't think that she was too eager to stay on his tail. But soon she would need to reestablish visual contact before he reached the far side of the park and, perhaps thereafter, turned off the county road onto a driveway or a private lane.

The deeper the road wound among the heaven-reaching trees, the less forcefully the rain beat against the Honda. The storm was not diminishing at all, but the huge ramparts of redwoods sheltered the pavement from the worst of the deluge.

On this narrower, twisting route, it wasn't possible to maintain the pace they had kept on Highway 101. Furthermore, the killer apparently had decided that he no longer needed to make good time, perhaps because he'd put what seemed a safe distance between himself and the dead men at the service station, and when Chyna caught up with him in hardly more than a minute, he was driving under the posted speed limit.

Now, closer than she'd been before, she noticed that the motor home didn't have license plates. California—and some other states, for all she knew—didn't issue temporary plates for a newly purchased vehicle, and it was legal to drive without the tags until they came in the mail from the Department of Motor Vehicles. Or perhaps before going to the Templetons' house, the killer had removed his plates rather than risk a witness with a good memory.

Easing off the accelerator, Chyna glanced at the speedometer—and spotted a red warning light. The fuel-gauge needle was below the EMPTY mark.

She had no idea how long the warning light had been burning, because she'd been concentrating intently on the motor home and the dangers of the slick pavement. The car might have a gallon or two in the tank—or even now be running on its last pint.

Trailing the killer to his home base was no longer an option.

. . .

The meaning of redwoods is not grandeur, beauty, peace, or the timelessness of nature. The meaning of redwoods is power.

As he drives, Edgler Vess rolls down the window beside him and draws deep breaths of the cold air, which is rich with the fragrance of redwoods, which is a scent of power. This power flows into him with the fragrance, and his own power is thus enhanced.

Redwoods are power because their great size is unmatched by any other trees, because they are ancient—many of these very specimens dating back centuries before the birth of Jesus Christ—because their extraordinary bark, as thick as armor and high in tannin, makes them all but impervious to insects, disease, and fire. They are power because they endure while all around them dies; men and animals pass among them and pass forever away; birds alight in their high branches and seem freer than anything rooted in rock and soil, but eventually, in a sudden quietness of the heart, the birds swoon off the sturdy limbs and thump to the ground or plummet from the sky, and the trees still soar; on the shadowed floors of these groves, sun-shy ferns and rhododendrons flourish season after season, but their immortality is illusory, for they too die, and new generations of their species rise in the decomposing remains of the old. Christ expired on a cross of dogwood, the prince of peace and prophet of love, but in the span of His life, not one of these trees had been brought down by any storm; though they cared not about peace and knew nothing of love, they had endured. Busily engaged on his endless harvests, Death casts frenetic shadows among the indifferent redwoods, a ceaseless flickering that dances across their massive trunks with no effect, like the dark equivalent of leaping firelight on hearthstones.

Power is living while others inevitably perish. Power is cool indifference to their suffering. Power is taking nourishment from the deaths of others, just as the mighty redwoods draw sustenance from the perpetual decomposition of what once lived, but lived only briefly, around them. This is also part of the philosophy of Edgler Foreman Vess.

Through the open window, he breathes in the scent of redwoods, and the molecules of their fragrance adhere to the surface cells of his lungs, and the power of millennia is conveyed therefrom into his freshly oxygenated blood, pumps through his heart, reaches to every extremity of him, filling him with strength and energy.

Power is God, God is nature, nature is power, and the power is in him.

His power is ever increasing.

If he worshiped, he would be an ardent pantheist, committed to the belief that all things are sacred, every tree and every flower and every blade of grass, every bird and every beetle. The world is full of pantheists these days; he would be at home among them if he were to join their ranks. When everything is sacred, *nothing* is. For him, that is the beauty of pantheism. If the life of a child is equal to the life of a bluegill or a barn owl, then Vess may kill attractive little girls as casually as he might crush a scorpion underfoot, with no greater moral offense though with considerably more pleasure.

But he worships nothing.

As he rounds a curve into a straightaway flanked by redwoods of even greater girth than any he has previously seen, stark white bones of lightning crack through the black skin of the sky. A roar of thunder like a bellow of rage shudders the air.

Rain washes the smell of lightning down through the night. Two scents of power, lightning and redwoods—electricity and time, fierce heat and stolid endurance—are offered to him now, and he inhales deeply with pleasure.

Taking this county road through the redwoods, along the coast, and reconnecting with Highway 101 south of Eureka will add between half an hour and an hour to his travel time, depending on the pace he sets and the strength of the storm. But as eager as he is to get home to Ariel, he could not have resisted the power of the redwoods.

Headlights appear behind him, visible in the angled side mirror. A car. For nearly an hour, one followed him on the freeway, hanging at a distance. This must be a different vehicle, because this driver is more aggressive than the one on the freeway, closing the distance between them at high speed.

Recklessly, the car—a Honda—pulls around the motor home, into the lane reserved for oncoming traffic, though this is not a passing zone. There is no other traffic, and they are on a straightaway, but the Honda has insufficient distance to complete the maneuver before the next blind turn in the road, especially on the treacherous rain-slick blacktop.

Vess reduces speed.

The racing Honda pulls alongside him.

Looking down through the windshield of the car, Vess has barely a glimpse of the person behind the steering wheel, because the rain and the high-speed windshield wipers inhibit his view. Nothing more than a suggestion of a deep-red shirt or sweater. A pale hand on the wheel. The wrist is slender enough to indicate that the driver is most likely a woman. She appears to be alone. Then the car moves far enough forward so that Vess is looking down on the roof, and the windshield is out of sight.

They are rapidly approaching the curve.

Vess further reduces his speed.

Through his open window, he listens to the shriek of the Honda as the driver accelerates. All the formidable power of that engine seems pathetically weak in these majestic groves, like the angry buzz of a gnat among a herd of elephants.

With so little effort that he would not increase his heartbeat, Vess could pull the wheel to the left, slam the motor home into the Honda, and force the car off the road. It would either roll and then explode—or shatter head-on into one of the twenty-foot-diameter redwood trunks.

He is tempted.

The spectacle would be gratifying.

He spares the woman in the Honda only because he's in a mood for subtle—rather than explosive—sensation. This gratifying expedition has brought him not merely the Napa Valley family that he originally set out to destroy, but the hitchhiker now hanging in the bedroom closet like Poe's lover of Amontillado in the stone wall of a wine cellar, as well as the two clerks at the service station. This is already a satiating richness. The reef of the soul is built from varied experience, not from repetitive sensation. Right now he doesn't need the somber music of blood and the spurting warmth of screams; instead, he needs to smell the wetness of the rain, feel the towering mass of the trees, and listen to the cool pendulousness of the night-hidden ferns.

He applies the brakes, cutting his speed.

The Honda streaks past him, kicking up a high spray of dirty water. It enters the curve ahead with a flash of brake lights: red in the black storm, red glimmering off the damp gray bark of the big conifers, apocalyptic tracers of red rippling across the pavement. Then gone.

Edgler Vess is alone again, behind the wheel of his ark, in a colorless world of gray rain, black shadows, and sparkling white headlight beams, at peace to commune with the redwoods and draw from them a measure of their power.

He thinks of Christ on the vertical bed of dogwood, and the idea of the meek inheriting the earth makes him smile. He doesn't wish to inherit anything. He is a raging fire, powerful and hot; he will burn all the color out of this world, consume every scintilla of sensation that it has to offer, and he will leave behind a realm of ashes. Let the meek inherit ashes.

Passing the motor home, going too fast to prevent the Honda from straddling the double yellow line all the way around the curve, Chyna had been afraid that the parched engine would cough and choke and fail. Now that she had seen the red warning light, she was aware of it—a peripheral radiance—even when she wasn't looking at the instrument panel. But the Honda ran confidently on dregs, on fumes, on some strange grace.

She needed to put distance between herself and the killer, and gain time to set her plan in motion. She pushed the car as hard as she dared on the storm-greased pavement.

The narrow road rounded another bend, straightened out, entered a gradual descent, took another curve, rose on a gentle slope, but descended again, and in spite of the intermittent interruptions of these extremely low inclines, the land was generally monotonous in its contours, making its way steadily down toward the Pacific, not many miles to the west. Now low ramparts of soft earth flanked the blacktop just beyond both shoulders, and this wasn't suitable for her purposes. But then the road returned to the same level as the surrounding forest, and she entered another almost imperceptibly declining straightaway and found the ideal circumstances she required.

She figured that she had gained a full minute on him, maybe a minute and a half, depending on whether he had appreciably increased his speed after she passed him. Anyway, a minute should be long enough.

She slowed to thirty miles an hour and nonetheless seemed to be *hurtling* through the woods. She let the speed decrease to twenty-five, wondering again about her headlong rush to heroism but still unable to fully understand it. Then she drove off the roadway, flew across the right shoulder, thumped through a shallow drainage swale, and rammed into the fortress base of one of the biggest of the redwoods. The left headlight burst, the impact-absorbing bumper cracked and crumpled and collapsed as it had been designed to do, and metal shrieked briefly.

Because she was wearing a safety harness, she wasn't thrown into the steering wheel or through the windshield. But the diagonal strap tightened so hard across her breasts that she grunted with shock and pain.

The engine was still running.

With no time to get out and inspect the front of the car, Chyna was afraid that the damage wasn't sufficiently impressive to convince the killer that someone could have been injured in the crash. When he came upon this scene a few seconds from now, he must take everything at face value without hesitation. Otherwise, if he was suspicious, nothing would work as she had planned.

Immediately she shifted the Honda into reverse and backed away from the tree, which stood inviolate. The ground was carpeted with wet redwood needles on which the tires spun before gripping, but not enough rain had fallen to churn the earth into mud. Rattling and clinking, the car bounced across the shallow drainage swale, which ran with only an inch or two of muddy water, and backed onto the pavement again.

Chyna glanced toward the top of the gently ascending slope down which she had just driven. As yet there was not even a faint glow of approaching headlights from beyond the curve.

He was coming. No doubt about that.

Soon.

She didn't have time to reverse even part of the way up the slope. But she needed to build a little speed.

With her left foot, she tramped the brake pedal as far toward the floorboards as it would go, and with her right foot she eased down on the accelerator. The engine whined, then shrieked. The car strained like a spurred horse pressing against the gate of a rodeo chute. She could feel it wanting to surge forward, as if it were a living thing, and she wondered how much acceleration would be too much, enough to kill her or trap her in wreckage. Then she gave it a little more juice, smelled something burning, and raised her left foot from the brake pedal.

The tires spun furiously on the glistering blacktop, and then with a shudder the Honda shot forward, rattled and splashed across the ditch, and slammed into the trunk of the redwood. The right headlight burst, metal squealed, the hood crumpled and tweaked and popped open with a sound oddly like a hard strum on a banjo, but the windshield didn't shatter.

The engine stuttered. Either the fuel had been exhausted at last or the crash had done severe mechanical damage.

Gasping for breath after the cinching punishment of the shoulder harness, praying that the engine wouldn't fail just yet, Chyna popped the car into reverse again.

Ideally, the Honda would be blocking the road when the killer came around the bend. She had to force him to stop—and to get out of his motor home.

The battered car wheezed, almost stalled, then unexpectedly revved, and Chyna said gratefully, "Jesus," as it rolled backward onto the pavement.

She pulled across both lanes but swung around a little, angling the car uphill so the killer would be able to see the damaged front end as soon as he negotiated the curve.

The engine clunked twice and died, but that was all right. She was in position.

Without the engine noise for competition, the rain seemed to be falling more forcefully than before, rattling on the roof and snapping against the glass.

At the upper curve, darkness still held.

She put the Honda in park, so it would not coast backward when she took her foot off the brake.

The headlights were both broken out, but the windshield wipers continued to thump back and forth, operating on battery power. She didn't switch them off.

She opened the driver's door and, feeling horribly exposed in the dome light, started to get out. She needed to be away from the car and in hiding by the time the motor home appeared—which would be in maybe twenty seconds, maybe ten, hard to say because she had lost track of how much time had passed since she herself had driven around the bend.

The gun.

Before she fully escaped the car, Chyna remembered the revolver. She swung back inside, reached for the weapon—but it was no longer on the seat.

In the first or second crash, the gun must have been thrown onto the floor. Leaning across the console between the front seats, she felt frantically in the darkness, found cold steel, the barrel, her finger actually slipping into the smooth muzzle. With a wordless murmur of relief, she fished the gun from the foot space and reversed her grip on it.

With the weapon firmly in hand, she scrambled out of the Honda. She left the driver's door standing open.

Rain chilled her, and wind.

In the direction from which she had come, the night brightened faintly, and the redwood trunks near the shoulder of the curve began to glow as if in the radiance of a sudden moon.

Chyna sprinted off the slippery blacktop and splashed through another shallow drainage ditch, shuddering as the icy water poured over the tops of her shoes. On this side of the pavement, the trees were set back twenty or thirty feet from the shoulder. She headed for the colossal woods at a point directly across the highway from the behemoth into which she had driven the Honda.

Long before she reached the nearest tree, she skidded on the spongy mat of wet needles, fell, and landed on a cluster of redwood cones. The cones crumbled slightly—a hard crunching sound against the small of her back—although judging by the flash of pain, it almost seemed as though her spine was the source of the cracking.

She would have preferred to crawl on her hands and knees to concealment, but she had to hold on to the revolver, and she was concerned that, crawling, she would inadvertently plug the barrel with dirt or wet needles. She was up and moving at once, therefore, as the highway behind her flared with light and an engine quarreled noisily with the storm.

The motor home had turned the bend.

She was only fifteen feet or so from the highway, which wasn't far enough, because there was little underbrush to provide cover beneath the giant redwoods—largely ferns, and more of them in the gloom ahead than in the area immediately around her. He must not see her. All was lost if he glimpsed her as she dashed for cover.

Fortunately, her blue jeans were dark, not stone-washed and highly reflective, and her sweater was cranberry red, which was not as bad as if it had been white or yellow, and her hair was not blond but dark. Yet she could have felt no more visible if she had been trying to run to cover in a wedding dress.

He would be focused on the Honda, surprised to see it angled across both lanes. He wouldn't immediately glance to either side of the highway, and when his attention did flicker away from the car, he was likely to look to the right, where the Honda had run off the road and struck the tree, not to the left, where Chyna was seeking shelter.

Telling herself that she was safe and had not been seen, but not actually believing herself, she reached the first phalanx of massive redwoods. They grew astonishingly close to one another, considering their daunting size. She slipped around the deeply corrugated trunk of a fifteen-foot-diameter giant that thrived in such intimacy with an even larger specimen that the passageway between the towering pair was less than two feet.

The lowest branches above her were a hundred fifty to a hundred eighty feet off the ground, visible only when lightning backlit them. Standing between these trunks was rather like standing between the nave columns of a cathedral too large ever to be built this side of Heaven; the bristled boughs formed majestic vaults fifteen stories overhead.

From her damp and cloistered retreat, she peered out warily at the highway.

Beyond the lacy screen of low ferns, silver plating the rain and growing brighter by the second, came the headlights of the motor home. They were accompanied by the soft pule of air brakes.

Mr. Vess stops on the pavement, as the shoulder is neither wide enough nor firm enough to accommodate his motor home. Although this scenic highway is obviously little used in these hours before dawn and in such foul weather as this, he is loath to block traffic any longer than is absolutely necessary. He well knows the California Vehicle Code.

He pushes the gearshift into park, engages the emergency brake, but leaves the engine running and the headlights on. He doesn't bother to slip into his raincoat, and when he gets out of the motor home, he leaves the door standing open.

The rain on the pavement is a drumming, and on the metal of the vehicles a singing, and on the foliage of the trees a chorus chanting wordlessly. The rain sounds please him, as does the chill, as does the fecund smell of ferns and loamy soil.

This is the same Honda that passed him a few minutes earlier. He is not surprised to see it in this sorry condition, considering the reckless speed at which it had been traveling.

Evidently, the car had skidded off the road and into the tree. Then the driver had backed it onto the pavement again before the engine failed.

But where is the driver?

Another motorist might have come along from the west and taken any injured person to get medical treatment. But that seems too fortuitous and too timely. After all, the accident can't have happened more than a minute or two ago.

The driver's door is open, and when Vess leans inside, he sees that the keys are in the ignition. The windshield wipers sweep the glass. The taillights, the interior ceiling light, and the gauges in the instrument panel are all aglow.

He steps away from the car and looks at the tree toward which the tire tracks lead. The bark is scarred from the impact but only superficially.

Intrigued, he surveys the rest of the grove on that side of the highway.

Quite possibly, the driver climbed out of the wrecked car, dazed from a blow to the head, and wandered into the redwoods. Even now she might be traveling farther into the primeval grove, lost and confused—or maybe, having collapsed from injuries, she lies unconscious in a fern glade.

The closely grown trees form a maze of narrow corridors, more wood than open space. Even at high noon on a cloudless day, sunshine would penetrate to the forest floor only in a few thin bright blades, and stubborn darkness would impose itself in most of these deep reaches, as though each of the many hundreds of thousands of nights since the grove's beginning had left its residue of shadows. Now, still on the witching side of dawn, that blackness is so pure that it seems almost like a thing alive, crouching and predatory and yet welcoming.

This special darkness stirs Mr. Vess and makes him yearn for experiences that he senses are available to him but that he cannot imagine, experiences that are mysterious and transforming, yet which he cannot even dimly envision. Far into the redwoods, down corridors of fissured bark, in some secret citadel of bestial passion, where shadows dwell that are older than human history, a mystical adventure awaits.

If the woman, in fact, is wandering in the woods, he could park the motor home and search for her. Perhaps the knife that he found at the service station is an omen, after all, and hers may be the blood that he is meant to draw with that blade.

He imagines what it would be like to take off his clothes and enter the grove naked with the knife, relying solely on his primitive instincts to stalk her and bring her down, the rain and mist cold on his skin, the air steaming once he has breathed it, unchilled by the rain but imparting his heat to the night, tearing ferociously at the woman's clothes as he drags her to the forest floor. He is already erect with the dream of it, but he wonders if he would attack her first with knife or phallus—or perhaps with his teeth. That decision would be made in the moment of capture, and much would depend on how attractive she was; but he is convinced that whatever might happen between them would be unprecedented and mysterious—and inexpressibly *intense*.

Dawn is coming in an hour or so, however, and he would be wise to be on his way. He must put more distance between himself and the places where he took his entertainment during the night.

Being good at being Edgler Vess requires, among other qualities, the ability to repress his most ardent passions when indulgence in them is dangerous. If he instantly gratified every desire, he would be less a man than an animal—and either long dead or imprisoned. Being Edgler Vess means being free but not reckless, being quick but not impulsive. He must have a sense of proportion. And good timing. Hell, he needs the timing of a tap-dance master. And a nice smile. A truly nice smile combined with self-control can take a person a long way.

He smiles at the forest.

The motor home stood on the pavement, approximately twenty feet from the battered Honda, shrunken in appearance because the redwoods dwarfed it.

As the killer had walked down the roadway to the abandoned car through the headlight beams from the motor home, Chyna had crept upslope through the dark forest, moving parallel to him but in the opposite direction. She had circled behind the tree to the right of her, gripping the revolver in her right hand, with her left hand flat against the trunk for balance in case she stumbled over a root or other obstruction. Under her palm, she had felt the deep pattern of repetitive Gothic arches formed by the fissures in the thick bark. With each uncertain step that she had taken around this great easy curve, she had felt that the tree was less like a tree than like a building, a windowless fortress erected against all the rage of the world.

After navigating a hemisphere of the trunk to the shoulder-wide gap between this tree and the next, she peered out once more. The killer stood near the open door of the Honda, gazing into the forest on the far side of the highway.

She was worried that another motorist would come along before she could carry out her plan.

She moved on, circling the next tree. It was even larger than the previous behemoth. The bark featured the familiar Gothic patterns.

In spite of the shrill wind keening high above and collected drizzles of rain spattering down from the lofty branches, the grove impressed her as a good safe place, dark but not in spirit, cold but not forbidding. She was still alone in her troubles—but curiously, for the first time all night, she didn't *feel* alone.

At the next trunk-framed gap in the forest wall, Chyna looked out again and saw the killer getting into the Honda. He would have to move the disabled car out of the way, because there wasn't room to drive around it.

She glanced at the motor home. Perhaps because she knew what lay within it—a dead man closeted in chains, a dead woman swaddled in a white shroud—the vehicle seemed as ominous as any war machine.

She could just wait in the grove. Forget about her plan. He would leave, and life would go on.

So easy to wait. Survive.

The police would find the girl. Ariel. Somehow. In time. Without the need for heroics.

Chyna leaned against the tree, suddenly weak. Weak and shaking. Shaking and almost physically ill with despair, with fear.

The taillights and interior lights of the Honda dimmed with the grinding of the starter, as the killer tried to get the engine to turn over.

Then another noise came to Chyna. Much closer than the car. Behind her. A rustle, a snap, a soft snort like a startled horse exhaling.

Frightened, she turned.

In the backwash of light from the motor home out on the highway, Chyna saw angels in the redwood grove. Or so it seemed for a moment. Regarding her were gentle faces, pale in the darkness, eyes luminous and inquisitive and kind.

But even in that meager moonlike glow, she was unable to sustain a hope of angels. After a brief initial confusion, she realized that these creatures were a breed of coastal elk without antlers.

Six stood together in a fifteen-foot-wide space between this outer row of trees and the deeper growth, so close that Chyna could have been among them in three steps. Their noble heads were lifted, ears pricked, gazes fixed intently on her.

The elk were curious, but although timid by nature, they seemed oddly unafraid of her.

Once, for two months, she and her mother had stayed on a ranch in Mendocino County, where a group of well-armed survivalists waited for the race wars that they believed would soon destroy the nation, and in that doomsday atmosphere, Chyna had spent as much time as possible exploring the surrounding countryside, hills and vales of singular beauty, groves of pines, golden fields where scattered oaks stood—each alone and huge and black-limbed against the sky—and where small herds of coastal elk appeared from time to time, always keeping at a distance from human beings and their works. She had stalked them not as a hunter but with awkward girlish guile, as shy as the elk themselves but irresistibly attracted to the tranquillity and the peace that they radiated in a world otherwise saturated with violence.

In those two months, she had never managed to get closer than eighty or ninety feet to the elk herds before they had reacted to her nonchalant approach, whidding to farther fields and ridges.

Now *they* had approached *her*, vigilant but not frightened, as if they were the same elk of her childhood, at long last willing to believe in her peaceable intentions.

Coastal elk should have been somewhat closer to the sea, in the open meadows beyond the redwoods, where the grass was lush and green from the winter rains, where the grazing was good. Although they were not strangers to the forest, their presence here, in the rainy predawn darkness, was remarkable.

Then she saw others in addition to the herd of six—one here, one there, and there a third, and still more—between trees, at a greater distance than the initial group. Some were barely visible in the bosky grove, at the extreme reach of the backwash from the motor-home headlights, but she thought that there were as many as a dozen altogether, all standing at attention, as though transfixed by woodland music beyond human hearing.

Lightning spread branches across the sky, put down jagged roots toward the earth, and briefly brightened the grove sufficiently for Chyna to see all the elk more clearly than before. More of them than she had thought. In mist and ferns, among flowering red rhododendron, revealed by fluttering leaves of light. Heads lifted, their breath steaming from black nostrils. Their eyes fixed on her.

She looked out at the highway.

The killer had given up trying to start the engine. He put the Honda in gear, and it began to roll backward on the slightly sloped pavement.

After one last glance at the elk, Chyna stepped out from between the two redwoods.

The killer pulled the steering wheel hard to the right, letting the momentum of the car carry it backward in an arc until it was facing downhill.

Through sparse ferns and scattered clumps of bunch grass, Chyna approached the highway. The weakness in her legs was gone, and her spasm of irresolution had passed.

Under the killer's guidance, the Honda coasted downhill and onto the right shoulder.

She could go after him, shoot him in the car or as he got out of the car. But he was fifty yards away now, sixty, and he would surely see her coming. She would have no hope of keeping the advantage of surprise, so she would have to shoot to kill, which would do Ariel no good at all, because with this bastard dead they would still have to search for the girl wherever she was hidden. And they might never find her. Besides, the creep probably had a gun on him, and if this turned into a shooting match, he would win, because he was far more practiced than she was—and bolder.

She had no one to whom she could turn. As in childhood.

So now get out of sight quickly. Don't be rash. Wait for the ideal situation. Pick the moment of the confrontation and control the showdown when it comes.

Fierce lightning again, and a long hard crash of thunder like vast structures collapsing high in the night.

She reached the motor home.

Oh, God.

The driver's door stood open.

Oh, Jesus. Oh, God.

She couldn't do it.

She *had* to do it.

Downhill, on the shoulder, with a rattle of twisted steel, the Honda was coasting to a stop.

She had the revolver. That made all the difference. She was safe with the gun.

Who will save this girl hidden in a cellar, this girl ripening for this sonofabitch bastard freak, this girl like me? Who is ever there for frightened girls hiding in the backs of closets or under beds, who is ever there but twitching palmetto beetles? Who will be there if not me, where will I be if not there, why is this the only choice—and when the answer is so obvious, why even ask why?

Downslope, the Honda came to a full stop.

With the revolver heavy in her hand, Chyna climbed into the cockpit and behind the steering wheel. She swung around in the driver's seat, got up, and hurried back through the motor home, murmuring, "Jesus, Jesus," telling herself that it was all right, this crazy thing she was doing, all right because this time she had the revolver.

But she wondered if even the gun would give her enough of an edge when the time arrived to go face-to-face with this man.

Of course a direct confrontation might never have to take place. Chyna intended to hide until they arrived at his house and then find out where the girl was being held. With that information, she would be able to go to the police, and they could nail this creep and free Ariel and—

And what?

And in saving the girl, she would save herself. From what, she was not sure. From a life of merely surviving? From the endless and fruitless struggle to understand?

Crazy, crazy, but there was no turning back now. And in her heart she knew that risking all was less crazy than living a life that had no higher goal than survival.

As if thrown forward by the hard knocking of her heart, Chyna reached the rear of the motor home. The closed door to the only bedroom.

Jesus.

She didn't want to go in there. With Laura dead. The man in the closet. The sewing kit waiting to be used again.

Jesus.

But it was the best place to hide, so she opened the door and went in and closed the door behind her and eased to the left through the palpable darkness and put her back against the wall.

Maybe he wouldn't drive straight home. He might stop at some point between here and there to come to the back of the motor home and have a look at his trophies.

Then she would kill him the instant that he stepped through the door. Empty the revolver into him. Take no chances.

With him dead, they might never find Ariel. Or they might find her only after she had perished of starvation, an excruciatingly painful way to die.

Nevertheless, if the killer entered this bedroom, Chyna wouldn't rely on half measures. She would not attempt to wound him and keep him alive for police interrogation, not in this tight space with him looming over her and with so many ways that things could go wrong.

Lights off, windshield wipers off, Edgler Vess sits in the dead car by the side of the road. Thinking.

There are numerous ways that he can proceed from here. Life is always a laden buffet of treats, a vast smorgasbord groaning with infinite choices of sensations and experiences to thrill the heart—but never more so than now. He wishes to exploit the opportunity to the fullest possible extent, to extract from it the greatest possible excitement and the most poignant sensations, and he must, therefore, not act precipitously.

Luck had given him a glimpse of her in the rearview mirror: as fleet as a deer across the blacktop, hesitating at the open door of the motor home, and then up and inside and out of sight.

She must be the woman from the Honda. When she passed him earlier, he had looked down through the windshield of her car and had seen her red sweater.

In the accident, she might have received a hard blow to the head. Now perhaps she is dazed, confused, frightened. This would explain why she doesn't approach him directly and ask for help or for a ride to the nearest service station. If her thoughts are addled, the irrational decision to become a stowaway aboard the motor home might seem perfectly reasonable to her.

She did not appear to be suffering from a head injury, however, or any injury at all. She hadn't staggered or stumbled across the highway but had been swift and surefooted. At this distance and in the rearview mirror, Vess wouldn't have been able to see blood even if she had been bleeding; but he knows intuitively that there was no blood.

The longer he considers the situation, the more it seems to him that the accident was staged.

But *why?*

If the motive had been robbery, she would have accosted him the moment that he stepped onto the highway.

Besides, he isn't driving one of those elaborate three-hundred-thousand-dollar land yachts that, by their very flashiness, advertise their contents to thieves. His vehicle is seventeen years old and, though well maintained, worth considerably less than fifty thousand bucks. It seems pointless to wreck a relatively new Honda for the purpose of looting the contents of an aging vehicle that promises no treasures.

He has left his keys in the ignition, the engine running. She already could have driven away in the motor home if that had been her intention.

And a woman alone on a lonely highway at night is not likely to be planning a robbery. Such behavior doesn't fit any criminal profile.

He is baffled.

Deeply.

Mr. Vess's simple life is not often touched by mystery. There are things that can be killed and things that can't. Some things are harder to kill than others, and some are more fun to kill than others. Some scream, some weep, some do both, some only tremble silently and wait for the end as if having spent their whole lives in anticipation of this awful pain. Thus the days go by—pleasantly straightforward, a river of raw sensation upon which enigma seldom sets sail.

But this woman in a red sweater is an enigma, all right, as mysterious and intriguing as anyone Mr. Vess has ever known. What experiences he will have with her are difficult to imagine, and he is excited by the prospect of such novelty.

He gets out of the Honda and closes the door.

For a moment he stands staring at the forest in the cold rain, hoping to appear unsuspecting if the woman should be watching him from inside the motor home. Maybe he is wondering what happened to the driver of the Honda. Maybe he is a good citizen, concerned about her and considering a search of the woods.

Multiple bolts of lightning chase across the sky, as white and jagged as running skeletons. The subsequent blasts of thunder are so powerful that they rattle through Mr. Vess's bones, a vibration that he finds most agreeable.

Unfazed by the storm, several elk suddenly appear from out of the forest, drifting between the trees and into the bordering sward of ferns. They move with stately grace, in a silence that is ethereal behind the fading echo of thunder, eyes shining in the backwash of the headlight beams. They seem almost to be apparitions rather than real animals.

Two, five, seven, and yet more of them appear. Some stop as though posing, and others move farther but then stop as well, until now a dozen or more are revealed and standing still, and every one of them is staring at Mr. Vess.

Their beauty is unearthly, and killing them would be enormously satisfying. If he had one of his guns at hand, he would shoot as many of them as he could manage before they bolted beyond range.

As a young boy, he began his work with animals. Actually, he'd begun with insects, but soon he had moved on to turtles and lizards, and then to cats and larger species. As a teenager, as soon as he had gotten a driver's license, he had roamed back roads some nights and in the early mornings before school, shooting deer if he spotted any, stray dogs, cows in fields, and horses in corrals if he was certain that he could get away with it.

He is flushed with nostalgia at the thought of killing these elk. The sight of their blood would intensify the redness of his own and make his arteries sing.

Though usually reticent and easily spooked, the elk stare boldly at him. They do not seem to be watching with alarm, are not in the least skittish or poised to flee. Indeed, their directness strikes him as strange; uncharacteristically, he feels uneasy.

Anyway, the woman in the red sweater awaits him, and she is more interesting than any number of elk. He is a grown man now, no longer a boy, and his quest for intense experiences cannot be satisfactorily conducted along the byways of the past. Edgler Vess has long ago put aside childish things.

He returns to the motor home.

At the door, he sees that the woman is in neither the pilot's nor the copilot's position.

Swinging in behind the steering wheel, he glances back but can see no sign of her in the lounge or the dining area. The short and shadowy hall at the end appears deserted as well.

Facing forward but keeping his eyes on the rearview mirror, he opens the tambour-top console between the seats. His pistol is still there, where he left it, sans silencer.

Pistol in hand, he swivels in his chair, gets up, and moves back through the motor home to the kitchen and dining area. The butcher knife, found on the service-station blacktop, lies on the counter as before. He opens the cabinet to the left of the oven and discovers that the 12-gauge Mossberg is securely in its spring clamps, to which he returned it after killing the two clerks.

He doesn't know if she is armed with a weapon of her own. From the distance at which he'd seen her, he hadn't been able to discern whether she was empty-handed or, equally important, whether she was attractive enough to be a fun kill.

Farther back, then, through his narrow domain, with special caution at the end of the dining nook, behind which lies the step well. She's not crouched here either.

Into the hall.

The sound of the rain. The idling engine.

He opens the bathroom door, quickly and noisily, aware that stealth isn't possible in this reverberant tin can on wheels. The cramped bathroom is as it should be, no stowaway on the pot or in the shower stall.

Next the shallow wardrobe with its sliding door. But she isn't in there either.

The only place remaining to be searched is the bedroom.

Vess stands before this last closed door, positively enchanted by the thought of the woman huddled in there, unaware of those with whom she shares her hiding place.

No thread of light is visible along the threshold or the jamb, so she no doubt entered in darkness. Evidently she has not yet sat upon the bed and found the sleeping beauty.

Perhaps she has edged warily around the small room and, by blind exploration, has discovered the folding door to the closet. Perhaps if Vess opens this bedroom door, she will simultaneously pull aside those vinyl panels and attempt to slip swiftly and quietly into the closet, only to feel a strange cold form hanging there instead of sport shirts.

Mr. Vess is amused.

The temptation to throw open the door is almost irresistible, to see her carom off the body in the closet, then to the bed, then away from the dead girl, screaming first at the sewn-shut face of the boy and then at the manacled girl and then at Vess himself, in a comic pinball spin of terror.

Following that spectacle, however, they will have to get down to issues at once. He will quickly learn who she is and what she thinks she is doing here.

Mr. Vess realizes that he doesn't want this rare experience with mystery to end. He finds it more pleasing to prolong the suspense and chew on the puzzle for a while.

He was beginning to feel weary from his recent activities. Now he is energized by these unexpected developments.

Certain risks are involved, of course, in playing it this way. But it is impossible to live with intensity and avoid risk. Risk is at the heart of an intense existence.

He backs quietly away from the bedroom door.

Noisily, he steps into the bathroom, takes a piss, and flushes the toilet, so the woman will think that he came to the back of the motor home not in search of her but to answer the call of nature. If she continues to believe that her presence is unknown, she will proceed on whatever course of action brought her here in the first place, and it will be interesting to see what she does.

He goes forward again, pausing in the kitchen to pump a cup of hot coffee from the two-quart thermos on the counter by the cooktop. He also switches on a couple of lights so he will be able to see the interior clearly in the rearview mirror.

Behind the steering wheel once more, he sips the coffee. It is hot, black, and bitter, just the way he likes it. He secures the cup in a holder bracketed to the dashboard.

He tucks the pistol in the open console box between the seats, with the safeties off and the butt up. He can put his hand on it in a second, turn in his seat, shoot the woman before she can get near him, and still maintain control of the motor home.

But he doesn't think that she will try to harm him, at least not soon. If harming him was her primary intention, she would have gone after him already.

Strange.

"Why? What now?" he says aloud, enjoying the drama of his peculiar situation. "What now? What next? What ho? Surprise, surprise."

He drinks more coffee. The aroma reminds him of the crisp texture of burned toast.

Outside, the elk are gone.

A night of mysteries.

The mounting wind lashes the long fronds of the ferns. Like evidence of violence, bright wet rhododendron blossoms spray through the night.

The forest stands untouched. The power of time is stored in those massive, dark, vertical forms.

Mr. Vess shifts the motor home out of park and releases the emergency brake. Onward.

After he cruises past the damaged Honda, he glances at the rearview mirror. The bedroom door remains closed. The woman is in hiding.

With the motor home rolling again, perhaps the stowaway will risk turning on a light and will take this opportunity to meet her roommates.

Mr. Vess smiles.

Of all the expeditions that he has conducted, this is the most interesting and exciting. And it isn't over yet.

Chyna sat on the floor in the darkness. Her back was against the wall. The revolver lay at her side.

She was untouched and alive.

"Chyna Shepherd, untouched and alive," she whispered, and this was both a prayer and a joke.

Throughout her childhood, she frequently prayed earnestly for that double blessing—her virtue and her life—and her prayers were often as rambling and incoherent as they were frantic. Eventually she had worried that God was growing weary of her endless desperate pleas for deliverance, that He was sick of her inability to take care of herself and stay out of trouble, and that He might decide that she had used up all of the divine mercy allotted to her. God was busy, after all, running the entire universe, watching over so many drunks and fools, with the devil working mischief everywhere, volcanoes erupting, sailors lost in storms, sparrows falling. By the time Chyna was ten or eleven, in consideration of God's hectic schedule, she had condensed her rambling pleas, in times of terror, to this: "God, this is Chyna Shepherd, here in"—fill the blank with the name of the current place—"and I'm begging you, please, please, please, just let me get through this untouched and alive." Soon, realizing that God, being God, would know precisely where she was, she reduced her entreaty further to: "God, this is Chyna Shepherd. Please get me through this untouched and alive." Finally, certain that God was exasperatedly familiar with her panicky presumptions on His time and grace, she had shortened her plea to a telegraphic minimum: "Chyna Shepherd, untouched and alive." In crises—under beds or lost in closets behind concealing clothes or in cobwebbed attics smelling of dust and raw wood or, once, flattened against the ground in a mire of rat shit in the crawl space under a moldering old house—she had whispered those five words or chanted them silently, over and over, indefatigably, *Chyna-Shepherd-untouched-and-alive,* ceaselessly reciting them not because she was afraid that God might be distracted by other business and fail to hear her but to remind herself that He was out there, had received her message, and would take care of her if she was patient. And when each crisis passed, when the black flood of terror receded, when her stuttering heart finally began to speak each beat clearly and calmly again, she had repeated the five words once more but with a different inflection than she had used previously, not as a plea for deliverance this time but as a dutiful report, *Chyna-Shepherd-untouched-and-alive*, much as a sailor in wartime might report to his captain after the ship had survived a vigorous strafing by enemy planes—"All present and accounted for, sir." She was present; she was accounted for; and she let God know of her gratitude with the same five words, figuring that He would hear the difference in her inflection and would understand. It had become a little joke with young Chyna, and sometimes she had even accompanied the report with a salute, which seemed all right because she had figured that God, being God, must have a sense of humor.

"Chyna Shepherd, untouched and alive."

This time, from the motor-home bedroom, it was simultaneously a report on her survival and a fervent prayer to be spared from whatever brutality might be coming next.

"Chyna Shepherd, untouched and alive."

As a little girl, she had loathed her name—except when she had been praying to survive. It was frivolous, a stupid misspelling of a real word, and when other kids teased her about it, she wasn't able to mount a defense. Considering that her mother was called Anne, such a simple name, the choice of *Chyna* seemed not merely frivolous but thoughtless and even mean. During most of the time that Anne was pregnant, she had lived in a commune of radical environmentalists—a cell of the infamous Earth Army—who believed that any degree of violence was justifiable in defense of nature. They had spiked trees with the hope that loggers would lose hands in accidents with power saws. They had burned down two meat-packing plants and the hapless night watchmen in them, sabotaged the construction equipment at new housing tracts that encroached upon the wilds, and killed a scientist at Stanford because they disapproved of his use of animals in his laboratory experiments. Influenced by these friends, Anne Shepherd had considered many names for her daughter: Hyacinth, Meadow, Ocean, Sky, Snow, Rain, Leaf, Butterfly. . . . By the time she had given birth, however, she had moved on from the Earth Army, and she had named Chyna after China because, as she had once explained, "Honey, I just suddenly realized one day that China is the only just society on earth, and it seemed like a beautiful name." She had never been able to recall why she had changed the *i* to *y*, though by then she had been a working partner in a methamphetamine lab, packaging speed in affordable five-dollar hits and sampling the merchandise often enough to have been left with a few blank days in her memory. Only when praying for deliverance had young Chyna *liked* her name, because she had figured that God would remember her more easily for it, would not get her confused with the millions of Marys and Carolines and Lindas and Heathers and Tracys and Janes.

Now her name no longer dismayed or pleased her. It was just a name like any other.

She had learned that who she was—the true *person* she was—had nothing whatsoever to do with her name, and little to do with the life that she'd led with her mother for sixteen years. She couldn't be blamed for the dreadful hates and lusts she had seen, for the obscenities heard, for the crimes witnessed, or for the things that some of her mother's male friends had wanted from her. She was not defined either by a name or by shameful experience; instead, she was formed by dreams and hopes, by aspirations, by self-respect and perseverance. She wasn't clay in the hands of others; she was rock, and with her own determined hands, she could sculpt the person that she wanted to be.

She hadn't reached this realization until a year ago, when she was twenty-five. The wisdom had come to her not in a dazzling flash but slowly, in the way that a plot of bare earth is covered gradually by creeping ajuga until one day, as if miraculously, the brown dirt is gone and everywhere are emerald-green leaves and tiny blue flowers. Worthwhile knowledge always seemed hard-won while the winning was in progress—but seemed easily acquired in retrospect.

The old motor home lumbered through the night, creaking like a long-sealed door, ticking like a rusted clock too corroded to register every second faithfully, toward dawn.

Crazy. Crazy to be taking this trip.

But nowhere else to go.

This was where her entire life had been leading. Reckless courage wasn't restricted to the battlefield—or to men.

She was wet and cold and frightened—and strangely, for the first time in her entire life, she was at peace with herself.

"Ariel," Chyna said softly, one girl in the darkness speaking reassuringly to another.

S I X

Mr. Vess drives out of the redwoods into a drizzling dawn, first iron gray and then somewhat paler, through coastal meadows the same drear shades of metal as the sky, back onto Highway 101, into forests again, but of pine and spruce this time, out of Humboldt County into Del Norte County, ever more isolated terrain, eventually leaving 101 for a route that leads north-northeast.

For the first part of the journey, he glances frequently at the rearview mirror, but the bedroom door remains closed, and the woman seems comfortable with the cadavers or, perhaps, with her ignorance of them. In her retreat, the window is sealed off with plywood, and the light of dawn doesn't penetrate.

Vess is a superb driver, and he makes excellent time, even in bad weather. We do best those things that we enjoy doing, which is why Mr. Vess is such a success at killing and why he combines that enthusiasm with his love of driving rather than restrict himself to prey within a reasonable radius of his home.

Being on the open road with landscapes ever changing, Edgler Vess is the recipient of a constant influx of fresh visual sensation. And of course, to one with his exquisitely refined senses and his ability to use them in a hologrammatic manner, a beautiful sight can also be a musical sound. A scent caught through the open window can be not solely an olfactory experience but tactile too, the sweet fragrance of lilac like a woman's warm breath against his skin. Ensconced in the driver's seat of his motor home, he travels through a rich sea of sensation that washes him the way water ceaselessly washes the hull of a deeply submerged submarine.

Now he crosses into Oregon. The mountains come to him and pull him up into their fastnesses.

The thickening stands of trees on the steep slopes are more gray than green in the stubborn rain, and the sight of them is like biting on a piece of ice, hard between his teeth, a slight but pleasant metallic taste, and a shattering coldness against his lips.

He seldom glances at the rearview mirror any more. The woman is a mystery, and mysteries of this nature can't be resolved by the sheer desire to resolve them. Ultimately she will reveal herself, and the intensity of the experience will depend upon whatever purpose she has and what secrets she possesses.

The waiting is delicious.

Throughout the last few hours of the journey, Vess leaves the radio off, although not because he is afraid that music will mask the sounds of the woman stalking forward through the motor home. In fact, he rarely listens to the radio while driving. In his memory is a vast library of recordings of the music that he likes best: the cries and squeals, the prayerful whispers, the shrieks as thin as paper cuts, the pulsatory sobbings for mercy, and the erotic inducements of final desperations.

As he leaves the state highway for the county route, he recalls specifically Sarah Templeton in her shower stall, her screams and her frantic gagging muffled by the green dishwashing sponge that he'd stuffed into her mouth and by the two strips of strapping tape that sealed her lips. Nothing on the radio, from Elton John to Garth Brooks to Pearl Jam to Sheryl Crow—to Mozart or Beethoven, for that matter—can compare to this interior entertainment.

He follows the rain-swept, two-lane county route to his private driveway. The entrance is securely gated and flanked by thickets of pines and brambly underbrush.

The gate is made of tubular steel and barbed wire, set between stainless-steel posts in concrete footings. It features an electric motor with remote operation, and when Mr. Vess pushes a button on the hand-held control that he fishes from the console box, the barrier swings inward to the left, in a satisfying stately manner.

After driving the motor home onto his property, he brakes to a stop once more, rolls down his window, holds out the control unit, with the signal-transmission window reversed in his grip. In his sideview mirror, he watches as the gate closes.

The driveway is nearly as long as that at the Templeton family's vineyards, as his property encompasses fifty-four acres that back up to a government-owned wilderness, which measures many miles on a side. He is not as well to do as the Templetons; land here is far cheaper than in the Napa Valley.

In spite of the lack of paving, there is little mud and no real danger of the motor home bogging down. The topsoil is shallow; the lane was graded down to the underlying shale. The way is a bit rough, but this is not, after all, New York City, New York.

Vess drives up a modest incline, between looming ranks of tall pines, spruces, scattered firs, and then the trees recede a little, and he crosses the bald hilltop. The road descends easily, in a graceful curve, into a small vale, with the house at the end and the hills rising behind in the sheeting rain and morning fog.

His heart swells at the sight of home. Home is where his Ariel patiently awaits.

The two-story house is small but solidly built of logs mortared with cement. The old logs are nearly black with layers of pitch; and time has darkened the cement to a tobacco brown, except for the tan and gray mottling of recent repairs.

The house was constructed in the late 1920s by the owner of a family logging business, long before small operators were regulated out of such work and before the government declared the surrounding public lands off-limits to timber harvesters. Electricity was brought in sometime during the forties.

Edgler Vess has owned the house for six years. Upon purchasing the place, he rewired it, improved the plumbing, enlarged the second-floor bathroom. And, entirely on his own, of course, he undertook extensive and secret remodeling work in the basement.

To some, the property may seem isolated, inconveniently far from a 7-Eleven or a multiplex cinema. But for Mr. Vess, whose pleasures would never be understood by most neighbors, relative isolation is *the* fundamental requirement when he is shopping for real estate.

On a summer afternoon or evening, however, sitting in a bentwood rocker on the front porch, gazing out at the deep yard and the acres of wildflowers in the fields cleared by the logger and his sons, or staring at the great spread of stars, even the most meek and citified man would agree that isolation has its appeal.

In good weather, Mr. Vess likes to take his dinner and a couple of beers on the porch. When the mountain silences become boring, he allows himself to hear the voices of those who are buried in the field: their groveling and lamentations, the music that he prefers to any on the radio.

In addition to the house, there is a small barn, not because the original owner of the property farmed any of the land that he cleared of trees but because he kept horses. This second building is of traditional wood-frame construction on a concrete footing and field-stone stem wall; wind, rain, and sun long ago laid down a silver patina on the durable cedar siding, which Vess finds lovely.

Since he owns no horses, he uses the barn as a garage.

Now, however, he pulls to a stop beside the house, rather than continuing to the barn. The woman is in the motor home, and he will soon need to deal with her. He prefers to park here, where he can watch her from the house and wait for developments.

He glances at the rearview mirror.

Still no sign of her.

Switching off the engine but not the windshield wipers, Vess waits for his guards to appear. The late-March morning is animate with slanting rain and wind-shaken things, but nothing moves of its own deliberation.

They have been trained not to charge willy-nilly at approaching vehicles and even to bide their time with intruders who are on foot, the better to lure them into a zone from which escape is impossible. These guards know that stealth is as important as savage fury, that the most successful assaults are preceded by calculated stillnesses to lull the quarry into a false confidence.

Finally the first black head appears, bullet sleek but for its pricked ears, low to the ground at the rear corner of the house. The dog hesitates to reveal more of himself, surveying the scene to make sure that he understands what is happening.

"Good fella," Vess whispers.

At the nearest corner of the barn, between the cedar siding and the trunk of a winter-bare maple, another dog appears. It is little more than a shadow of a shadow in the rain.

Vess wouldn't have noticed these sentries if he hadn't known to look for them. Their self-control is remarkable, a testament to his abilities as a trainer.

Two more dogs lurk somewhere, perhaps behind the motor home or belly crawling through shrubbery where he can't see them. They are all Dobermans, five and six years old, in their prime.

Vess has not cropped their ears or bobbed their tails, as is usually done with Dobermans, for he has an affinity for nature's predators. He is able to perceive the world to a degree as he believes that animals perceive it—the elemental nature of their view, their needs, the importance of raw sensation. They have a kinship.

The dog by the corner of the house slinks into the open, and the dog at the barn emerges from beneath the black-limbed maple. A third Doberman rises from behind the massive and half-petrified stump of a long-vanquished cedar in the side yard, around which has grown a tangled mass of holly.

The motor home is familiar to them. Their vision, while not their strongest suit, is probably sufficient to allow them to recognize him through the windshield. With a sense of smell twenty thousand times more acute than that of the average human being, they no doubt detect his scent even through the rain and even though he is inside the motor home. Yet they don't wag their tails or in any way exhibit pleasure, because they are still on duty.

The fourth dog remains hidden, but these three drift warily toward him through the rain and the mist. Their heads are lifted, pointy ears flicked up and forward.

In their disciplined silence and indifference to the storm, they remind him of the herd of elk in the redwood grove the previous night, eerily intent. The big difference, of course, is that these creatures, if confronted by anyone other than their beloved master, would not respond with the timidity of elk but would tear the throat out of that luckless person.

Although she would not have believed it possible, Chyna had been lulled into sleep by the hum of the tires and the motion of the motor home. Her dreams were of strange houses in which the geometry of the rooms was ever changing and bizarre; something eager and hungry lived within the walls, and at night it spoke to her through vent grilles and electrical outlets, whispering its needs.

The brakes woke her. Immediately she realized that the motor home had come to a full halt once before and then had started up again, only moments ago; she had dozed through that first stop, disturbed in her sleep but not fully awakened. Now, although they were on the move again and the killer was obviously still behind the steering wheel, Chyna grabbed the revolver from the floor beside her, scrambled to her feet, and stood with her back to the wall, tense and alert.

From the tilt of the floor and the laboring sound of the engine, she knew that they were climbing a hill. Then they reached the top and headed downward. Soon they stopped again, and at last the engine cut out.

The rain was the only sound.

She waited for footsteps.

Although she knew that she was awake, she seemed to be in a dream, rigid in darkness, with the susurrant rain like whispering in the walls.

Mr. Vess takes the time to put on his raincoat and to slip his Heckler & Koch P7 into one pocket. He removes the Mossberg shotgun from the cabinet in the kitchenette, in case the woman searches the place after he leaves. He switches off the lights.

When he descends from the motor home, heedless of the cold rain, the three big dogs come to him, and then the fourth from behind the vehicle. All are quivering with excitement at his return but still holding themselves in check, not wanting to be thought derelict in their duty.

Just before departing on this expedition, Mr. Vess had placed the Dobermans on attack status by speaking the name *Nietzsche*. They will remain primed to kill anyone who walks onto the property until he speaks the name *Seuss*, whereupon they will be as affable as any other group of sociable mutts—except, of course, if anyone unwisely threatens their master.

After propping his shotgun against the side of the motor home, he holds his hands out to the dogs. They eagerly crowd around to sniff his fingers. Sniffing, panting, licking, licking, yes, yes, they have missed him so very much.

He squats on his haunches, coming down to their level, and now their delight is uncontainable. Their ears twitch, and shivers of pure pleasure pass visibly along their lean flanks, and they whine softly with sheer happiness, jealously pressing all at once at him, to be touched, patted, scratched.

They live in an enormous kennel against the back of the barn, which they can enter and leave at will. It is electrically heated during cold weather to ensure their comfort and their continued good health.

"Hi there, Muenster. How you doing, Liederkranz? Tilsiter, boy, you look like one mean sonofabitch. Hey, Limburger, are you a good boy, are you my good boy?"

Each, at the mention of his name, is filled with such joy that he would roll on his back and bare his belly and paw the air and grin at death—if he weren't still on duty. Part of the fun for Vess is watching the struggle between training and nature in each animal, a sweet agony that makes two of them pee in nervous frustration.

Mr. Vess has rigged electrically operated dispensers inside the kennel, which in his absence automatically pay out measured portions of food for each Doberman. The system clock has a backup battery to continue timing meals even during a power failure of short duration. In the event of a long-term loss of power, the dogs can always resort to hunting for their sustenance; the surrounding meadows are full of field mice and rabbits and squirrels, and the Dobermans are fierce predators. Their communal water trough is fed by a drip line, but if it should ever cease to function, they can find their way to a nearby spring that runs through the property.

Most of Mr. Vess's expeditions are three-day weekends, rarely as long as five days, and the dogs have a ten-day food supply without counting rabbits, mice, and squirrels. They constitute an efficient and reliable security system: never a short in any circuit, never a failed motion detector, never a corroded magnetic contact—and never a false alarm.

Oh, and how these dogs love him, how unreservedly and loyally, as no memory chips and wires and cameras and infrared heat sensors ever could. They smell the bloodstains on his jeans and denim jacket, and they push their sleek heads under his open raincoat, ears laid back, sniffing eagerly now, detecting not merely the blood but the lingering stench of terror that his victims exuded when in his hands, their pain, their helplessness, the sex that he had with the one named Laura. This mélange of pungent odors not only excites the dogs but increases their respect for Vess. They have been taught to kill not merely in self-defense, not just for food; with a degree of iron self-control, they have been taught to kill for the sheer savage pleasure of it, to please their master. They are acutely aware that their master can match their savagery. And unlike them, he has never needed to be taught. Their high regard for Edgler Vess soars higher, and they mewl softly and quiver and roll their soulful eyes at him in worshipful awe.

Mr. Vess gets to his feet. He picks up the shotgun and slams the door of the motor home.

The dogs spring to his side, jostling one another to be close to him, alertly surveying the rain-shrouded day for any threat to their master.

Quietly, so the woman inside cannot possibly hear the word, he says, "Seuss."

The dogs freeze, looking up at him, heads cocked.

"Seuss," he repeats.

The four Dobermans are no longer on attack status and will not automatically tear to pieces anyone who enters the property. They shake themselves, as if casting off tension, then pad around in a vaguely bewildered fashion, sniffing at the grass and at the front tires of the motor home.

They are like Mafia hit men who, following their own executions, have now regained a baffled self-awareness after being reincarnated, only to discover that they are accountants in this new life.

If any visitor were to attempt to harm their master, of course, they would leap to his defense, whether or not he had time to shout the word *Nietzsche*. The result wouldn't be pretty.

They are trained first to tear out the throat. Then they will bite the face to effect maximum terror and pain—go for the eyes, the nose, the lips. Then the crotch. Then the belly. They won't kill and turn at once away; they will be busy for a while with their quarry, after they have brought it down, until no doubt exists that they have done their job.

Even a man with a shotgun could not take out all of them before at least one managed to sink its teeth into his throat. Gunfire will not drive them away or even make them flinch. Nothing can frighten them. Most likely, the hypothetical man with the shotgun would be able to wipe out only two before the remaining pair overwhelmed him.

"Crib," says Mr. Vess.

This single word instructs the dogs to go to their kennel, and they take off as one, sprinting toward the barn. Still, they do not bark, for he has schooled them in silence.

Ordinarily he would allow them to stay with him and enjoy his company and spend the day in his house with him and even pile up like a black and tan quilt with him as he sleeps away the afternoon. He would cuddle them and coo to them; for they have been, after all, such good dogs. They deserve their reward.

The woman in the red sweater, however, prevents Mr. Vess from dealing with the dogs as he usually would. If they are a visible presence, they will inhibit her, and she may cower inside the motor home, afraid to exit.

The woman must be given enough freedom to act. Or at least the illusion of freedom.

He is curious to see what she will do.

She must have a purpose, some motivation for the strange things that she has done thus far. Everyone has a purpose.

Mr. Vess's purpose is to satisfy all appetites as they arise, to seek ever more outrageous experience, to immerse himself deeply in sensation.

Whatever the woman *believes* her purpose to be, Vess knows that in the end, her true purpose will be to serve his. She is a glorious variety of powerful and exquisite sensations in human skin, packaged solely for his enjoyment—rather like a Hershey bar in its brown and silver wrapper or a Slim Jim sausage snug in its plastic tube.

The last of the racing Dobermans vanishes behind the barn, to the kennel.

Mr. Vess walks through the soggy grass to the old log house and climbs a set of field-stone steps to the front porch. Although he carries the pistol-grip 12-gauge Mossberg, he makes an effort to appear otherwise nonchalant, in case the woman has come forward from the bedroom at the rear of the motor home to watch him through a window.

The bentwood rocker has been stored away until spring.

Trailing silvery slime across the wet floorboards of the porch, several early-spring snails test the air with their semitransparent, gelatinous feelers, hauling their spiral shells on strange quests. Mr. Vess is careful to step around them.

A mobile hangs at one corner of the porch, from the fascia board at the edge of the shake-shingle roof. It is made of twenty-eight white seashells, all quite small, some with lovely pink interiors; most are spiral in form, and all are relatively exotic.

The mobile does not make a good wind chime, because most of the notes that it strikes are flat. It greets him with a flurry of atonal clinking, but he smiles because it has . . . well, not sentimental but at least nostalgic value to him.

This fine piece of folk craft once belonged to a young woman who lived in a suburb of Seattle, Washington. She had been an attorney, about thirty-two, sufficiently successful to live alone in her own house in an upscale neighborhood. For a person tough enough to thrive in the combative legal profession, this woman had kept a surprisingly frilly—in fact, downright girlish—bedroom: a four-poster bed with a pink canopy trimmed with lace and fringe, rose-patterned bedspread, and starched dust ruffles; a big collection of teddy bears; paintings of English cottages hung with morning-glory vines and surrounded by lush primrose gardens; and several seashell mobiles.

He had done exciting things to her in that bedroom. Then he had taken her away in the motor home to places remote enough to allow him to perform other acts even more exciting. She had asked *why?*—and he had answered, *Because this is what I do.* That was all the truth and all the reason of him.

Mr. Vess can't recall her name, though he fondly remembers many things about her. Parts of her were as pink and smooth and lovely as the insides of some of these dangling seashells. He has an especially vivid mental image of her small hands, almost as slender and delicate as those of a child.

He had been fascinated by her hands. Enchanted. He had never sensed anyone's vulnerability so intensely as he'd sensed hers when he held her small, trembling, but strong hands in his. Oh, he had been like a swooning schoolboy with her hands.

When he had hung the mobile on the porch, as a memento of the attorney, he had added one item. It dangles, now, on a piece of green string: her slender index finger, reduced to bare bones but still undeniably elegant, the three phalanges from tip to the base knuckle, clinking against the little conch shells and miniature bivalve fans and trumpet shells and tiny spirals similar to the whorled homes of snails.

Clink-clink.

Clink-clink.

He unlocks the front door and enters the house. He closes but does not lock the door behind him, allowing the woman to have access if she chooses to take it.

Who knows what she will choose to do?

Already her behavior is as astonishing as it is mysterious.

She excites him.

Vess turns from the shadowy front room to the narrow enclosed stairs immediately to his left. He quickly climbs the steps two at a time, one hand on the oak banister, to the second floor. A short hallway serves two bedrooms and a bath. His room is to the left.

In his private chamber, he drops the Mossberg on the bed and crosses to the south-facing window, which is covered by a blue drape with blackout lining. He doesn't need to draw the drape aside to see the motor home on the driveway below. The two pleated panels of fabric don't quite meet, and when he puts his eye to the two-inch gap, he has a clear view of the entire vehicle.

Unless she slipped out of the motor home immediately behind him, which is highly doubtful, the woman is still inside. He can see down through the windshield at an angle into the pilot's and copilot's seats, and she has not advanced to either.

He takes the pistol from his pocket and puts it on the dresser. He shrugs out of the raincoat and tosses it atop the chenille spread on the neatly made bed.

When he checks at the window again, there is as yet no sign of the mystery woman at the motor home below.

He hurries into the hallway to the bathroom. White tile, white paint, white tub, white sink, white toilet, polished brass fixtures with white ceramic knobs. Everything gleams. Not a single smudge mars the mirror.

Mr. Vess likes a bright, clean bathroom. For a while, lifetimes ago, he lived with his grandmother in Chicago, and she was incapable of keeping a bathroom clean enough to meet his standards. Finally, exasperated beyond endurance, he had killed the old bitch. He'd been eleven when he put the knife in her.

Now he reaches behind the shower curtain and cranks the COLD faucet all the way open. He isn't actually going to take a shower, so there's no point in wasting hot water.

He quickly adjusts the shower head until the spray is as heavy as it gets. The water pounds down into the fiberglass tub, filling the bathroom with thunder. He knows from experience that the sound carries throughout the small house; even with rain on the roof, this is much louder than the sound of the shower in Sarah Templeton's bedroom, and it will be heard downstairs.

On a wall shelf above the toilet is a clock radio. He switches it on and adjusts the volume.

The radio is set to a Portland station featuring twenty-four-hour-a-day news. Ordinarily, when bathing and attending to his toilet, Mr. Vess likes to listen to the news, not because he has any interest in the latest political or cultural developments but because these days the news is largely about people maiming and killing one another—war, terrorism, rape, assault, murder. And when people can't kill one another in sufficient numbers to keep the reporters busy, nature always saves the day with a tornado, a hurricane, a big earthquake, or an outbreak of flesh-eating bacteria.

Sometimes, listening to the news and letting the various reports spark fond memories of his own homicidal exploits, he realizes that he himself is also a force of nature: a hurricane, a lightning storm, a planet-smashing asteroid hurtling through the void, the distillate of all human ferocity in a single body. Elemental power. The thought pleases him.

Now, however, news will not set the stage properly. Hastily he turns the tuning knob until he finds a station playing music. "Take the A Train" by Duke Ellington.

Perfect.

The big-band sound brings to his mind's eye an image of light flaring off cut crystal and luminous bubbles rising in a champagne glass, and it reminds him of the smell of fresh-cut limes, lemons. He can *feel* the notes in the air, some shimmering-bursting like bubbles and others bouncing off him like hundreds of little rubber balls and some like windblown leaves crisp with autumn: a very *tactile* music, exuberant and exhilarating.

The woman will be subtly lulled by the swing beat. It will be difficult for her to believe, really believe, that anything bad can happen to her with such music as background.

Perfect.

He hurries back to his bedroom, to the window, having been away from it no more than a minute.

Rain snaps against the glass, streams.

On the driveway below, the motor home stands as before.

The woman still must be inside. She probably won't just burst out of the vehicle and run pell-mell; she's likely to exit warily, hesitant on both sides of the door. Although there might have been time for her to get out of the motor home while Mr. Vess was in the bathroom, she would almost certainly be huddling against it, getting her bearings, assessing the situation. From this high vantage point, he can see around most of the vehicle, with the exception of blind spots toward the rear on the port side and at the very back, and the woman is not in sight.

"Ready when you are, Miss Desmond," he says, referring to the Gloria Swanson character in *Sunset Boulevard*.

That movie had had a great effect on him when he'd first seen it on television. He'd been thirteen, a year out of counseling for the murder of his grandmother. On one level, he had known that Norma Desmond was supposed to be the tragic villain of the piece, that the writer and director *intended* for her to fulfill that role—but he had admired her, *loved* her. Her selfishness was thrilling, her self-absorption heroic. She was the truest character he had ever seen in a movie. *This* was what people were actually like, under the pretense and hypocrisy, under all the crap about love, compassion, altruism; they were all like Norma Desmond but couldn't admit it to themselves. Norma didn't give a *shit* about the rest of the world, and she bent everyone to her iron will even when she was no longer young or beautiful or famous, and when she couldn't bend William Holden's character as far as she wanted, she just boldly picked up a gun and *shot* him, which was *so* powerful, *so* audacious, that young Edgler had been too excited to sleep that night. He had lain awake wondering what it would be like to encounter a woman as superior and genuine as Norma Desmond—and then to break her, kill her, take all the strength of her selfishness and make it his own.

Maybe this mystery woman is a little bit like Norma Desmond. She's bold, sure enough. He can't figure what the hell she's doing, what she's after; and when he understands her motivation, maybe she won't be anything like Norma Desmond. But at least she is already something new and interesting in his experience.

The rain.

The wind.

The motor home.

"Take the A Train" has given way to "String of Pearls."

Murmuring softly against the blue drapes, Mr. Vess says, "Ready when you are."

After the killer had gotten out of the motor home and slammed the door, Chyna had waited in the dark bedroom for a long while in the one-note lullaby of rain.

She had told herself that she was being prudent. Listen. Wait. Be sure. Absolutely sure.

But then she'd been forced to admit that she had lost her nerve. Although she had mostly dried out during the ride north from Humboldt County, she was still cold, and the source of her chills was the ice of doubt in her guts.

The eater of spiders was gone, and to Chyna, even remaining in blackness with two dead bodies was far preferable to going outside where she might encounter him again. She knew that he would be back, that this bedroom was not, in fact, a safe place, but for a while, what she *knew* was overruled by what she *felt*.

When at last she broke her paralysis, she moved with reckless abandon, as though any hesitation would result in another and worse paralysis, which she would be unable to overcome. She yanked open the bedroom door, plunged into the hall, with the revolver held in front of her because maybe the murderous bastard hadn't gotten out after all, and she went all the way forward past the bathroom and through the dining area and into the lounge, where she stopped a few feet back from the driver's seat.

The only light was a bleak gray haze that came through the skylight in the hall behind her and through the windshield ahead, but she could see that the killer wasn't here. She was alone.

Outside, directly ahead of the motor home, lay a sodden yard, a few dripping trees, and a rough driveway leading to a weathered barn.

Chyna moved to a starboard window, cautiously peeled back one corner of the greasy drape, and saw a log house about twenty feet away. Mottled with time and many coats of creosote, streaming with rain, the walls glistened like dark snakeskin.

Although she had no way of being certain, she assumed that it was the killer's house. He had told the men in the service station that he was going home after his "hunting" trip, and everything he had told them had sounded to her like the truth, including—and especially—the taunts about young Ariel.

The killer must be inside.

Chyna went forward again and leaned over the driver's seat to look at the ignition. The keys weren't there. They weren't in the console box either.

She slipped into the copilot's seat, feeling frightfully exposed in spite of the blurring rain that washed down the windows. She could find nothing in the console box, in the shallow glove box, in either door pouch, or under either front seat that revealed the name of the owner or anything else about him.

He would be returning soon. For some demented reason, he had gone to a lot of trouble and taken risks to bring the cadavers, and most likely he would not leave them in the motor home for long.

The obscuring rain made it difficult for her to be sure, but she thought that the drapes were drawn at the first-floor windows on this side of the house. Consequently, the killer would not casually glance out and spot her when she stepped from the motor home. She couldn't see the pair of second-floor windows half as well as those lower down, but they also might be draped.

She cracked open the door, and a cold knife of wind thrust at her through the gap. She got out and closed the door behind her as quietly as possible.

The sky was low and turbulent.

Forested hills rose rank after rank behind the house, vanishing into the pearly mist. Chyna sensed mountains looming above the hills in the overcast; they would still be capped with snow this early in the spring.

She hurried to the flagstone steps and went up onto the porch, out of the rain, but it was coming down so hard that already she was soaked again. She stood with her back to the rough wall.

Windows flanked the front door, and the drapes were drawn behind the nearer of the two.

Music inside.

Swing music.

She stared out at the meadows, along the lane that led from the house to the top of a low hill and thence out of sight. Perhaps, beyond the hill, other houses stood along that unpaved track, where she would find people who could help her.

But who had ever helped her before, all these long years?

She remembered the two brief stops that had awakened her, and she suspected that the motor home had passed through a gate. Nevertheless, even if this was a private driveway, it would lead sooner or later to a public road, where she would find assistance from residents or passing motorists.

The top of the hill was approximately a quarter of a mile from the house. This was a lot of open ground to cover before she would be out of sight. If he saw her, he would probably be able to chase her down before she got away.

And she still didn't know that this was his house. Even if it *was* his house, she couldn't be sure that this was where he kept Ariel. If Chyna brought back the authorities and Ariel wasn't here, then the killer might never tell them where to find the girl.

She had to be sure that Ariel was in the basement.

But if the girl *was* here, then when Chyna came back with the cops, the killer might barricade himself in the house. It would take a SWAT team to pry him out of the place—and before they got to him, he might kill Ariel and commit suicide.

In fact, that was almost certainly how it would play out as soon as any cops showed up. He would know that his freedom was at an end, that his games were over, that he would have no more *fun,* and all he would see available to him was one last, apocalyptic celebration of madness.

Chyna couldn't bear to lose this imperiled girl so soon after losing Laura, failing Laura. Intolerable. She couldn't keep failing people as, all her life, others had failed her. Meaning wasn't to be found in psychology classes and textbooks but in caring, in hard sacrifice, in faith, in *action*. She didn't want to take these risks. She wanted to live—but for someone other than herself.

At least now she had a gun.

And the advantage of surprise.

Earlier, at the Templeton house and in the motor home and then at the service station, she'd also had the advantage of surprise, but she hadn't been in possession of the revolver.

She realized that she was arguing herself into taking the most dangerous course of action open to her, making excuses for going into the house. Going into the house was obviously crazy, Jesus, a totally crazy move, Jesus, but she was striving hard to rationalize it, because she had already made up her mind that this was what she was going to do.

Coming out of the motor home, the woman has a gun in her right hand. It looks as if it might be a .38—perhaps a Chief's Special.

This is a popular weapon with some cops. But this woman doesn't move like a cop, doesn't handle the weapon as a cop would—although clearly she is somewhat comfortable with a gun.

No, she's definitely not an officer of the law. Something else. Something weird.

Mr. Vess has never been so intrigued by anyone as he is by this spunky little lady, this mysterious adventurer. She's a real treat.

The moment she sprints from the motor home to the house and out of sight, Vess moves from the window on the south wall of his bedroom to the window on the east wall. It is also covered by a blue drape, which he parts.

No sign of her.

He waits, holding his breath, but she doesn't head east along the lane. After half a minute or so, he knows that she isn't going to run.

If she had taken off, she would have sorely disappointed him. He doesn't think of her as a person who would run. She is bold. He wants her to be bold.

Had she run, he would have sent the dogs after her, not with instructions to kill but merely to detain. Then he would have retrieved her to question her at his leisure.

But *she* is coming to *him*. For whatever unimaginable reason, she will follow him into the house. With her revolver.

He will need to be cautious. But oh, what fun he is having. Her gun only makes the game more intense.

The front porch is immediately below this window, but he isn't able to see it because of the overhanging roof. The mystery woman is somewhere on the porch. He can *feel* her close, perhaps directly under him.

He retrieves his pistol from the nightstand and glides quietly across the wall-to-wall carpet into the open doorway. He steps into the hall and quickly to the head of the enclosed stairs, where he stops. He can see only the landing below, not the living room, but he listens.

If she opens the front door, he will know, because one of the hinges makes a dry ratcheting sound. It's not a loud noise, but it is distinctive. Because he's listening specifically for that corroded hinge, not even the drumming of the rain on the roof, the pounding of the shower into the bathtub, and "In the Mood" on the radio can entirely mask the sound.

Crazy. But she was going to do it. For Ariel. For Laura. But also for herself. Maybe most of all for herself.

After all these years under beds, in closets, in attic shadows—no more hiding. After all these years of getting by, keeping her head down, drawing no attention to herself—suddenly she had to *do* something or explode. She'd been living in a prison since the day she'd been born, even after leaving her mother, a prison of fear and shame and lowered expectations, and she'd been so accustomed to her circumscribed life that she had not recognized the bars. Now righteous rage released her, and she was crazy with freedom.

The chilly wind kicked up, and shatters of rain blasted under the porch roof.

Seashell wind chimes clattered, an irritation of flat notes.

Chyna eased past the window, trying to avoid several snails on the porch floor. The drapes remained tightly shut.

The front door was closed but unlocked. She slowly pushed it inward. One hinge rasped.

The big-band tune finished with a flourish, and at once two voices arose from deeper in the house. Chyna froze on the threshold, but then she realized that she was listening to an advertisement. The music had been coming from a radio.

It was possible that the killer shared the house with someone other than Ariel, and other than the procession of victims or dead bodies brought back from his road trips. Chyna couldn't conceive of his having a family, a wife and children, a psychotic Brady Bunch waiting for him; but there were rare cases on record of homicidal sociopaths working together, like the two men who proved to be the Hillside Strangler in Los Angeles a couple of decades ago.

Voices on a radio, however, were no threat.

With the revolver held in front of her, she went inside. The incoming wind whistled into the house, rattling a wobbly lampshade and threatening to betray her, so she closed the door.

The radio voices came down an enclosed stairwell to her left. She kept one eye on the doorless opening at the foot of those steps, in case more than voices descended.

The front room on the ground floor ran the entire width of the small house, and although it was illuminated only by the gray light from the windows, it was nothing like what she had expected to find. There were hunter-green leather armchairs with footstools, a tartan-plaid sofa on large ball feet, rustic oak end tables, and a section of bookshelves that held perhaps three hundred volumes. On the hearth of the big river-rock fireplace were gleaming brass andirons, and on the mantel was an old clock with two bronze stags rearing up on their hind legs. The decor was thoroughly but not aggressively masculine—no glassily staring deer or bear heads on the walls, no hunting prints, no rifles on display, just cozy and comfortable. Where she had been expecting pervasive clutter as evidence of his seriously disordered mind, there was neatness. Instead of filth, cleanliness; even in the shadows, Chyna could see that the room was well dusted and swept. Rather than being burdened with the stench of death, the house was redolent of lemon-oil furniture polish and a subtle pine-scented air freshener, as well as the faint and pleasant smell of char from the fireplace.

Selling H & R Block tax services and then doughnuts, the radio voices bounced with enthusiasm down the stairs. The killer had it cranked up too loud; the volume level seemed wrong to Chyna, as if he was trying to mask other sounds.

There *was* another sound, similar to but different from the rain, and after a moment she recognized it. A shower.

That was why he had set the radio so loud. He was listening to the music while taking a shower.

She was in luck. As long as the killer was in the shower, she could search for Ariel without the risk of being discovered.

Chyna hurriedly crossed the front room to a half-open door, went through, and found a kitchen. Canary-yellow ceramic tile with knotty-pine cabinets. On the floor, gray vinyl tile speckled with yellow and green and red. Well scrubbed. Everything in its place.

She was soaked, rain dripping off her hair and still seeping from her jeans onto the clean floor.

Taped to the side of the refrigerator was a calendar already turned forward to April, with a color photograph that showed one white and one black kitten—both with dazzling green eyes—peering out from a huge spray of lilies.

The normality of the house terrified her: the gleaming surfaces, the tidiness, the homey touches, the sense that a person lived here who might walk in daylight on any street and pass for human in spite of the atrocities that he had committed.

Don't think about it.

Keep moving. Safety in movement.

She went past the rear door. Through the four glass panes in the upper half, she saw a back porch, a green yard, a couple of big trees, and the barn.

Without any architectural division, the kitchen opened into the dining area, and the combined space was probably two-thirds the width of the house. The round dinette table was dark pine, supported by a thick central drum rather than legs; the four heavy pine captain's chairs featured tie on back and seat cushions.

Upstairs, the music started again, but it was softer in the kitchen than in the front room. If she had been an aficionado of big-band music, however, she would have been able to recognize the tune from here.

The noise of the running shower was more apparent in the kitchen than in the living room, because the pipes were channeled through the rear wall of the old house. Water being drawn upward to the bathroom made an urgent, hollow rushing sound through copper. Furthermore, the pipe wasn't tied down and insulated as well as it ought to have been, and at some point along its course, it vibrated against a wall stud: rapid knocking behind plasterboard, *tatta-tatta-tatta-tatta-tatta.*

If that noise abruptly stopped, she would know that her safe time in the house was limited. In the subsequent silence, she could count on no more than a minute or two of grace while he toweled off. Thereafter he might show up anywhere.

Chyna looked around for a telephone but saw only a wall jack into which one could be plugged. If there had been a phone, she might have paused to call 911, supposing there *was* 911 service out here in . . . well, wherever the hell they were—these boondocks. Knowing that help was on the way would have made the remainder of the search less nerve-racking.

At the north end of the dining area was another door. Although the killer was in the shower upstairs, she turned the knob as quietly as she could and crossed the threshold with caution.

Beyond lay a combination laundry and storage room. A washer. An electric dryer. Boxes and bottles of laundry supplies were stored in an orderly fashion on two open shelves, and the air smelled like detergent and bleach.

The rush of water and the knocking pipe were even louder here than they had been in the kitchen.

To the left, past the washer and dryer, was another door—rough pine, painted lime green. She opened it and saw stairs leading down to a black cellar, and her heart began to beat faster.

"Ariel," she said softly, but there was no answer, because she had spoken more to herself than to the girl.

No windows at all below. Not even a turbid leak of gray storm light seeping through narrow casements or screened ventilation cutouts. Dungeon dark.

But if the bastard was keeping a girl down there, how odd that he wouldn't have added a lock to this upper door. It offered only the spring latch that retracted with a twist of the knob, not a real lock of any kind.

The captive might be sealed in a windowless room deep below, of course, or even manacled. Ariel might have no hope of reaching these stairs and this upper door, even if left alone for days to worry at her restraints, which would explain why the killer was confident that one more barrier to her flight wasn't necessary even when he was away from home.

Nevertheless, it seemed peculiar that he wouldn't be concerned about a thief breaking into the house when he was gone, descending to the cellar, and inadvertently discovering the imprisoned girl. Considering the obvious age of the structure, its rusticity, and the lack of any apparent alarm keypads, Chyna doubted that the house had a security system. The killer, with all his secrets, ought to have installed a steel door to the cellar, with locks as impregnable as those on a bank vault.

The lack of special security might mean that the girl, Ariel, was not here.

Chyna didn't want to dwell on that possibility. She *had* to find Ariel.

Leaning through the doorway, she felt along the stairwell wall for the switch, and snapped it up. Lights came on both at the upper landing and in the basement.

The bare concrete steps—a single flight—were steep. They appeared to be much newer than the house itself, perhaps even a relatively recent addition.

The high-velocity surge of water through plumbing and the hard rapping of the loose pipe in the wall told her that the killer was still busy in the bathroom above, scrubbing away all traces of his crimes. *Tatta-tatta-tatta . . .*

Louder than before but still in a whisper, she said: "Ariel."

Out of the still air below, no response.

Louder. "Ariel."

Nothing.

Chyna didn't want to go down into this windowless pit, with no way out except the stairs, even with a lockless door above. But she couldn't think of any way to avoid the descent, not if she was to learn for sure whether Ariel was here.

Tatta-tatta-tatta-tatta-tatta . . .

It always came to this, even with childhood long past and being grown up and everything supposedly in control, everything supposedly all right; even then it *still* came to this: alone, dizzy with fear, alone, down into a bleak-dark-cramped place, no exits, sustained only by mad hope, with the world indifferent, no one to wonder about her or care where she might have gone.

Listening intently for the slightest change in the sound of the rushing water and the vibrating pipe, Chyna went down one step at a time, her left hand on the iron railing. The gun was extended in her right hand; she was clenching it so fiercely that her knuckles ached.

"Chyna Shepherd, untouched and alive," she said shakily. "Chyna Shepherd, untouched and alive."

Halfway down the stairs, she glanced back and up. At the end of a trail of her wet shoeprints, the landing seemed a quarter of a mile above her, as far away as the top of the knoll had seemed from the front porch of the house.

Alice down the rabbit hole into a madness without tea parties.

. . .

At the open doorway between the in-kitchen dining area and the laundry room, Mr. Edg-ler Vess hears the mystery woman call to Ariel. She is only a few feet away from him, around the corner, past the washer and the dryer, so there can be no mistake about what name she speaks.

Ariel.

Stupefied, he stands blinking and open-mouthed in the fragrance of laundry detergent and in the wall-muffled rattle of copper pipes, with her voice echoing in memory.

There is no way for her to know about Ariel.

Yet she calls to the girl again, louder than before.

Mr. Vess suddenly feels terribly violated, oppressed, observed. He glances back at the windows in the dining area and the kitchen, expecting to discover the radiant faces of ac-cusing strangers pressed to those panes. He sees only the rain and the drowned gray light, but he is still anguished.

This is not fun any longer. Not fun at all.

The mystery is *too* deep. And alarming.

It is as if this woman didn't come to him out of that Honda but came through an in-visible barrier between dimensions, out of some world beyond this one, from which she has been secretly watching him. The flavor is distinctly supernatural, the texture other-worldly, and now the laundry detergent smells like burning incense, and the cloying air seems thick with unseen presences.

Fearful and plagued by doubt, unaccustomed to both of those emotions, Mr. Vess steps into the laundry room, raising the Heckler & Koch P7. His finger wraps the trigger, al-ready beginning to squeeze off a shot.

The cellar door stands open. The stairwell light is on.

The woman is not in sight.

He eases off the trigger without firing.

On those infrequent occasions when he has guests to the house to dinner or for a busi-ness meeting, he always leaves a Doberman in the laundry room. The dog lies in here, silent and dozing. But if anyone other than Vess were to enter, the dog would bark and snarl and drive him backward.

When the master is away, Dobermans vigilantly patrol the entire property, and no one has a hope of getting into the house itself, let alone into the cellar.

Mr. Vess has never put a lock on the door to the cellar steps because he is concerned that it might accidentally trip, imprisoning him down there when he is at play and un-awares. With a key-operated deadbolt, of course, this catastrophe could never happen. He himself is incapable of imagining how any such mechanism could malfunction and trap him; nevertheless, he's too concerned about the prospect to take the risk.

Over the years, he has seen coincidence at work in the world, and people perishing be-cause of it. One late-June afternoon near dusk, as Mr. Vess was driving to Reno, Nevada, on Interstate 80, a young blonde in a Mustang convertible had passed his motor home. She was wearing white shorts and a white blouse, and her long hair streamed red-gold in the twilight wind. Filled with an instant and powerful need to smash her beautiful face, he had pressed the motor home to its limits to keep her swifter Mustang in sight, but his quest had seemed doomed. As the highway rose into the Sierras, the speed of the motor home had fallen, and the Mustang had pulled away. Even if he had been able to draw close to the woman, the traffic had been too heavy—too many witnesses—for him to try anything as bold as forcing her off the highway. Then one of the tires on the Mustang had blown. Traveling at such high speed, she nearly spun out, nearly rolled, swerved from lane to lane, blue smoke pouring off the tires, but then she got control and pulled the car off the road onto the shoulder. Mr. Vess had stopped to assist her. She had been grateful for his offer of help, smiling and pleasantly shy, a nice girl with a one-inch gold cross on a chain around her neck, and later she had wept so bitterly and struggled so excitingly to re-sist surrendering her beauty, to turn her face away from his various sharp instruments, just a high-spirited young woman full of life and on the way to Reno until coincidence gave her to him.

And if a blown tire, why not a malfunctioning lock?

If coincidence can give, it can take.

Mr. Vess lives with intensity but not without caution.

Now this woman, calling for Ariel, has come into his life, like a blown tire, and sud-denly he's not sure if she is a gift to him or he to her.

Remembering her revolver and wishing for Dobermans, he glides across the laundry room to the cellar door.

The woman's voice rises from the stairs below: "China Shepherd untouched and alive."

The words are so strange—the meaning so mysterious—that they seem to be an incan-tation, encoded and cryptic.

Confirming that perception, the woman repeats herself, as though she is chanting: "China Shepherd untouched and alive."

Though Vess is not usually superstitious, he experiences a heightened sense of the supernatural, beyond anything he's felt thus far. His scalp prickles, and the flesh on the nape of his neck crawls, and his hand tightens on the pistol.

After a hesitation, he leans through the open door and looks down the cellar stairs.

The woman is only a few steps from the bottom. She's got one hand on the railing, the revolver held out in front of her in the other hand.

Not a cop. An amateur.

Nonetheless, she might be Mr. Vess's blown tire, and he's jumpy, twitchy, still ex-tremely curious about her but prepared to put his safety ahead of his curiosity.

He eases through the doorway onto the upper landing.

As close as she is, she does not hear him because all is concrete, nothing to creak.

He aims his pistol at the center of her back. The first shot will catapult her off her feet, send her flying with her arms spread toward the basement below, and the second shot will take her as she is in flight. Then he'll race down the stairs behind her, firing the third and fourth rounds, hitting her in the legs if possible. He'll drop on top of her, press the muzzle into the back of her head, and then, then, then when he's totally in control of her, domi-nant, he can decide whether she's still a threat or not, whether he can risk questioning her or whether she's so dangerous that nothing will do but to put a couple of rounds in her brain.

As the woman passes under the light near the foot of the stairs, Mr. Vess gets a better look at her revolver. It is indeed a Smith & Wesson .38 Chief's Special, as he had thought earlier, when he had seen it from the second-floor bedroom window, but suddenly the make and model of the weapon have electrifying meaning for him.

He smells a Slim Jim sausage. He remembers liquid-night eyes widening in shock, ter-ror, and despair.

He has seen two of these guns in the past several hours. The first belonged to the young Asian gentleman at the service station, who drew it from under the counter in self-defense but never had the opportunity to fire.

Although the Chief's Special is a popular revolver, it is not so universally admired that one sees it everywhere in use. Edgler Vess *knows*, with the certainty of a fox on the scent of a rabbit in the weeds, that this is the same gun.

Although there are still many mysteries about the woman on the stairs below him, though her presence here is no less astonishing to him than it was before, there is nothing supernatural about her. She knows the name *Ariel* not because she has been watching from some world beyond this one, not because she is in the dutiful service of some higher force, but simply because she must have been *there*, in the service station, when Vess was chatting up the two clerks and when, moments later, he killed them.

Where she could have been hiding, how he could have overlooked her, why she would feel the need to pursue him, where she got all the courage for this reckless adventure— these are things he can't discern through intuition alone. But now he will have the opportunity to put these questions to her.

Lowering his pistol, he steps back into the laundry room, lest she glance up the stairs and see him.

His uncharacteristic fear, his eerie perception of oppressive supernatural forces, lifts like a fog from him, and he is amazed by his own brief spasm of gullibility. He, who has no illusions about the nature of existence. He, who is so clear-seeing. He, who knows the primacy of pure sensation. Even he, the most rational of all men, has spooked.

He almost laughs at his foolishness—and at once puts it out of his mind.

The woman must be to the bottom of the stairs by now.

He will allow her to explore. After all, for whatever bizarre reasons, this is what she has come here to do, and Vess is curious about her reactions to the things that she discovers.

He is having fun again.

Once more, the game is on.

Chyna reached the bottom of the stairs.

The outer wall of mortared stone was to her right. There was nowhere to go in that direction.

To her left was a chamber about ten feet from front to back, and as wide as the house. She moved away from the foot of the stairs, into this new space.

At one end stood an oil-fired furnace and a large electric water heater. At the other end were tall metal storage cabinets with vent slits in the doors, a workbench, and a tool chest on wheels.

Directly ahead, in a concrete-block wall, a strange door waited.

Click-whoosh.

Chyna swung to the right and almost squeezed off a shot before she realized that the sound had come from the furnace: the electric pilot light clicking on, fuel taking flame.

Over the sound of the furnace, she was still able to hear the vibrating pipe. *Tatta-tatta-tatta.* It was fainter here than on the stairs, but still audible.

She could barely make out the music from the second-floor bathroom, an inconstant thread of melody, primarily the passages in brass or wailing clarinet.

Evidently for soundproofing, the door in the back wall was padded like a theater door, in leather-grain maroon vinyl divided into quiltlike squares by eight upholstery nails with large round heads covered in matching vinyl. The frame was upholstered in the same material.

No lock, not even a spring latch, prevented her from proceeding.

Putting her hand on the vinyl, Chyna discovered that the padding was even more plush than it appeared to be. As much as two inches of foam covered the underlying wood.

She gripped the long stainless-steel, U-shaped handle. When she pulled, the vinyl-encased door softly scraped and squeaked across the upholstery on the jamb. The fit was snug: When the door swung all the way free of the jamb and the seal was broken, there was a faint sound similar to that made when one opened a jar of vacuum-packed peanuts.

The door was upholstered on the inside as well. The overall thickness was in excess of five inches.

Beyond this new threshold lay a six-foot-square chamber with a low ceiling, which reminded her of an elevator, except that every surface other than the floor was upholstered. The floor was covered with a rubber mat of the kind used in many restaurant kitchens for the comfort of cooks who worked on their feet for hours at a time. In the dim light from the recessed overhead bulb, she saw that the fabric here wasn't vinyl but gray cotton with a nubbly texture.

The strangeness of the place sharpened her fear, yet at the same time she was so sure she understood the purpose of the padded vestibule that her stomach rolled with faint nausea.

Directly opposite the door that Chyna held open was one more door. It was also padded and set in an upholstered frame.

Finally, here were locks. The gray upholstery plumped around two heavy-duty brass lock cylinders. She couldn't proceed without keys.

Then she noticed a small padded panel overlying the door itself—at eye level, perhaps six by ten inches with a knob attached. It was like the sliding panel over the view port in the solid door of a maximum-security prison cell.

Tatta-tatta-tatta . . .

The killer seemed to be taking an unusually long shower. On the other hand, Chyna hadn't been in the house more than three minutes; it just seemed longer. If he was having a leisurely scrub, he might not be half done.

Tatta-tatta . . .

She would have preferred to hold open the outer door while she stepped into the vestibule and slid aside the panel on the inner view port, but the distance was too great. She had to let the door fall shut behind her.

The moment that the upholstered door met the upholstered jamb with a whisper-squeak of softly abraded vinyl, Chyna could no longer hear the vibrating water pipe. The quiet was so profound that even her ragged breathing was barely audible. Under the padding, the walls must have been covered with layers of sound-attenuating insulation.

Or perhaps the killer had shut off the shower just as the door had fallen shut. And was now toweling dry. Or pulling on a robe without bothering to towel off. On his way downstairs.

Fearful, unable to breathe, she opened the door again.

Tatta-tatta-tatta and the rush of water moving at high velocity, under pressure.

She exhaled explosively with relief.

She was still safe.

All right, okay, be cool, keep moving, find out if the girl is here and then do what has to be done.

Reluctantly she allowed the door to fall shut. The rattling of the pipe was again sealed out.

She felt as though she was suffocating. Perhaps ventilation in the vestibule was inadequate, but it was the sound-deadening effect of the padded walls, at least as much as poor airflow, that made the atmosphere seem as thick as smoke and unbreathable.

Chyna slid aside the padded panel on the inner door.

Beyond was rose-colored light.

The port was fitted with a sturdy screen to protect the viewer from assault by whoever or whatever was within.

Chyna put her face to the port and saw a large chamber nearly the size of the living room under which it was situated. In portions of the space, shadows were pooled deep, and the only light came from three lamps with fringed fabric shades and pink bulbs that were each putting out about forty watts.

At two places along the back wall were panels of red and gold brocade that hung from brass rods as if covering windows, but there could be no windows underground; the brocade was just set dressing to make the room more comfortable. On the wall to the left, barely touched by light, was a large tattered tapestry: a scene of women in long dresses and cloche hats riding horses sidesaddle through spring grass and flowers, past a verdant forest.

The furnishings included a plump armchair with antimacassars, a double bed with a white headboard painted with a scene not quite discernible in the rose light, bookcases with acanthus-leaf molding, cabinets with mullioned doors, a small dining table with a heavily carved apron, two Directoire chairs with flower-pattern upholstery flanking the table, and a refrigerator. An immense dark-stained armoire, featuring crackle-glazed flower appliqués on all the door panels, was old but probably not a genuine antique, battered but handsome. A padded vanity bench sat before a makeup table with a triptych mirror in a gilded, fluted frame. In a far corner was a toilet and a sink.

As weird as this subterranean room was, like a storage vault for the stage furniture from a production of *Arsenic and Old Lace*, the collection of dolls was by far the strangest thing about it. Kewpie dolls, Cabbage Patch Kids, Raggedy Ann, and numerous other varieties, both old and new, some more than three feet tall, some smaller than a milk carton, were dressed in diapers, snowsuits, elaborate bridal dresses, checkered rompers, cowboy outfits, tennis togs, pajamas, hula skirts, kimonos, clown suits, overalls, nighties, and sailor suits. They filled the bookshelves, peered out through the glass doors of some of the cabinets, perched on the armoire, sat atop the refrigerator, stood and sat on the floor along the walls. Others were piled atop one another in a corner and at the foot of the bed, legs and arms jutting at odd stiff angles, heads cocked as on broken necks, like stacks of gaily attired corpses awaiting transport to a crematorium. Two hundred, or three hundred, or more small faces either glowed in the gentle light or were ghost-pale in the shadows, some of bisque and some of china and some of cloth, some wood and some plastic. Their glass, tin, button, cloth, and painted-ceramic eyes reflected the light, shone brightly where the dolls were placed near any of the three lamps, glowed as moodily as banked coals where they were consigned to the darker corners.

For a moment, Chyna was half convinced that these dolls could actually see, except for a few individuals who appeared to be blind behind cataracts of rose light, and that *awareness* glimmered in their terrible eyes. Although none of them moved—or even shifted their gaze—they had an aura of life about them. Their power was uncanny, as though the killer were also a warlock who stole the souls of those he murdered and imprisoned them in these figures.

Then quiet movement in the room, a shadow coming out of gloom, proved to be the captive, and when she stepped into sight, the dolls lost their eerie magic. She was the most beautiful child that Chyna had ever seen, more beautiful even than in the Polaroid snapshot, with straight lustrous hair that was an enchanting shade of auburn in the peculiar light though platinum blond in reality. Fine-boned, slender, graceful, she possessed a beauty that was ethereal, angelic, and she seemed to be not a real girl but an apparition bearing a message about redemption, a manger, hope, and a guiding star.

She was dressed in black penny loafers, white knee socks, a blue or black skirt, and a short-sleeved white blouse with dark piping on the collar and across the pocket flap, as though she was in the uniform of a parochial school.

No doubt the killer provided the girl with the clothes that he wished her to wear, and Chyna saw at once why he would favor outfits like this. Though physically she was undoubtedly sixteen, she seemed younger when dressed in this fashion; with her slender arms, with her delicate wrists and hands, in this blushing light, the demure uniform made her seem like a child of eleven, shy of her confirmation Sunday, naive and innocent.

Sociopaths like this man were drawn to beauty and to innocence, because they were compelled to defile it. When innocence was stripped away, when beauty was cut and crushed, the malformed beast could at last feel superior to this person he had coveted. After the innocent and the beautiful were left dead and rotting, the world was to some degree made to more closely resemble the killer's interior landscape.

The girl sat in the armchair.

She was holding a book. She opened it, turned a few pages, and appeared to read.

Although she had surely heard the panel sliding back from the view port in the door, she did not look up. Apparently she assumed that her visitor was, as always, the eater of spiders.

With a rush of emotion that pinched her heart and surprised her with its intensity, Chyna said, "Ariel."

The name fell through the port as into an airless void, having carried no distance whatsoever, creating no echo.

The girl's cell obviously had been lined with numerous layers of soundproofing, perhaps with even more layers than the vestibule, and all this attention to the containment of her shouts and screams seemed to indicate that from time to time the killer invited people into his home. Perhaps to dinner. Or to have a few beers and watch a football game. That he would dare such a thing was only one more proof of his outrageous boldness.

But that he would have friends at all chilled Chyna, friends not demented like him, who would be horrified to discover the girl in his cellar and to know that their host slaughtered whole families for his entertainment. He passed for human in the workaday world. People laughed at his jokes. Sought his advice. Shared their joys and sorrows with him. Perhaps he attended church. On some Saturday nights, did he go dancing, smoothly two-stepping around the floor with a smiling woman in his arms, keeping time to the same music everyone else heard?

Chyna raised her voice: "Ariel."

The girl failed to look up.

Louder still, all but shouting it through the screened port in the padded door: *"Ariel!"*

In the chair, knees primly together, the book in her lap, head bowed to the page, wings of hair hiding most of her face, Ariel sat as if deaf—or as if she were a girl in the back of a closet, tuning out the shouted arguments of drunk and drug-sodden adults, tuning out further and further until she was in a great deep silent place of her own, untouchable.

Chyna recalled times, as a young girl, when simply hiding from her mother and her mother's more dangerous friends had not provided her with a sufficient sense of security. Sometimes the arguments or the celebrations became too violent or too boisterous; the chaos of noise and crazy laughter and cursing spun like a tornado around her even where she had concealed herself, and her fear spiraled out of control, until she thought that her heart would burst or her head explode. Then she went away to more welcoming places in her mind, through the back of the old wardrobe into the land of Narnia, which she had read about in the wonderful books of Mr. C. S. Lewis, or to visit Toad Hall and the Wild Wood from *The Wind in the Willows*, or into realms that she herself invented.

She had always been able to come back from those escapements. But on occasion, she had thought about how wonderful it would be to stay in that faraway place, where neither her mother nor her mother's kind would ever be able to find her again, no matter how hard they looked. In those exotic kingdoms, there was often danger, but there were also true and faithful friends like none found on *this* side of magical wardrobes.

Now, peering through the screened port at the girl in the chair, Chyna was sure that Ariel had sought refuge in just such a far place and was detached from this sorry world in every way that counted. After a year in this dismal hole, from time to time suffering the attentions of the sociopath upstairs, perhaps she had wandered so far along the road of inner adventure that she could not easily—or ever— return.

In fact, the girl raised her gaze from the book and sat staring neither at Chyna's face in the door port nor apparently at anything in the room, but at something in a world twice removed from this one. Even in the inadequate rose light, Chyna could see that Ariel's eyes were out of focus and as strange as the eyes of any of the dolls that surrounded her.

The killer had told the men at the service station that he had not yet touched Ariel in "that way," and Chyna believed him. Because once he had taken her innocence, he would need to smash her beauty; and when that was done, he would kill her. The fact that she was alive argued that she was still untouched.

Yet day after day, month after dreadful month, she had lived in exhausting suspense, waiting for the hateful son of a bitch to decide that she was "ripe," waiting for his brutal assault, his sour breath on her face, his hot and insistent hands, the terrible irresistible weight of him, every indignity and humiliation. In her single room, there had been nowhere to hide; she could not escape to the rooftop, to the beach, to the attic, to the crawlspace, to the upper limbs of the tree in the backyard.

"Ariel."

The refuge to which she had escaped might be in the pages of the book that she now held. She functioned in this world, grooming and feeding and bathing and dressing herself, but she *lived* in some other dimension.

Chyna's heart rolled in a sea of sorrow in a storm of rage, and through the port in the upholstered door, she said, "I'm here, Ariel. I'm here. You aren't alone any more."

Ariel's gaze didn't shift out of dreams, and she was as still as any of the dolls.

"I am your guardian, Ariel. I'll keep you safe."

As the girl followed a long and winding road farther into her private Elsewhere, her hands relaxed, and the book slipped out of them. It slid off the edge of the chair and thumped to the floor, and all except a whisper of the sound was absorbed by the special walls and ceiling. She was not aware of having dropped the volume, and she sat unmoving.

"I'm your guardian," Chyna repeated, and wondered vaguely at her choice of words.

She was more afraid for Ariel than for herself, and her heart was racing faster than ever before.

"Your guardian."

Hot tears blurred Chyna's vision, disabling tears, an indulgence she could not afford. She blinked furiously until her eyes were dry and her vision was clear.

She turned from the locked inner door and angrily pushed open the outer one.

Tatta-tatta-tatta-tatta-tatta . . .

As she stepped out of the heavy sound-baffling of the vestibule and into the first room in the basement, the rattling pipe seemed louder than she remembered.

Tatta-tatta-tatta . . .

Perhaps a minute had passed since she'd slid aside the padded panel on the view port.

The son of a bitch bastard freak was still in his shower, naked and defenseless. And now that Chyna knew where Ariel was, she didn't have to worry that the cops would need him to lead them to the girl.

The gun felt good in her hand.

It felt wonderful in her hand.

If she could have freed Ariel and gotten her out of there, she would have done that rather than take the violent option. But she didn't possess a key, and that inner door was not going to be easy to break down.

Tatta-tatta-tatta . . .

She had only one choice. She went to the cellar stairs.

Blue steel gleaming in her hand.

Even if he finished showering and shut off the water before Chyna was able to reach him, he'd still be naked and defenseless, toweling off, so she would go in there, into the bathroom, and open fire on him point-blank, shoot him down, empty the revolver into him, the first shot right through his fucking heart, then put at least one round in his face, to be sure that he was really done for. Take no chances. No chances at all. Use every round, squeeze the trigger until the hammer click-click-clicked on the expended cartridges in a totally empty cylinder. She could do it. Kill the crazy freak, kill him over and over again, kill him until he stayed killed. She could do it, *would* do it.

She climbed the steep stairs, treading on wet footprints that she'd left in her descent: Chyna Shepherd no longer hiding, up and out of that hole, untouched, alive, coming out of Narnia forever.

Tatta-tatta-tatta . . .

Thinking ahead as she moved, Chyna wondered if she should shoot him through the shower curtain—if it was, in fact, a curtain instead of a glass door—because if she *didn't* shoot him through it, then she would have to hold the revolver in just one hand while she yanked the curtain or the door aside. That would be risky, because a strange and dismaying weakness was creeping into her fingers and into her wrists. Her arms were shaking so badly that already she had to grip the weapon with both hands to prevent herself from dropping it.

Her heart rattling like the copper pipe, scared about the coming confrontation even if the crazy geek *was* naked and defenseless, Chyna reached the upper landing and entered the laundry room.

She couldn't shoot him through the curtain, because she wouldn't know whether she'd hit him or not. She'd be shooting blind, unable to aim for his chest or head.

Past the dryer and the washer, through the fragrance of laundry detergent, she reached the open door to the kitchen. Crossing the threshold, she belatedly registered the important thing that she had seen on the landing at the head of the cellar stairs: wet shoeprints larger than her own, among her prints, overlapping her prints, where he had stood only a short while ago.

She was already rushing into the kitchen, with too much momentum to halt, and the killer came at her from the right, past the dinette set. He was big, strong, a juggernaut, neither naked nor defenseless, the shower having been a ruse all along.

He was fast, but she was marginally faster. He tried to drive her backward and slam her against the cabinets, but she slid out of the way, raising the revolver, with the muzzle three feet from his face, and she pulled the trigger, and the hammer made a dry, stick-breaking sound as it fell on an empty chamber.

She backed hard into the side of the refrigerator, dislodging the kittens-and-lilies calendar, which clattered to the floor at her feet.

The killer was still rushing at her.

She squeezed the trigger, and the revolver clicked again, which made no sense—*shit*—because the clerk in the service station never had a chance to fire it before he had been blown away by the shotgun. No cartridges should be missing.

This was the first time that she had seen the killer's face. Always before, she'd glimpsed just the back of his head, the top of his skull, the side of his face but from a distance. He was not what she had expected, not moon-faced and pale-lipped and heavy-jawed. He was handsome, with blue eyes that were a beautiful contrast with his dark hair—nothing crazy in his clear eyes—broad clean features, and a nice smile.

Smiling, he continued to come straight at her as she squeezed the trigger a third time, and the hammer fell yet again on an empty chamber. Smiling, he tore the revolver out of her hand with such force that she thought her finger broke before it slipped through the trigger guard, and she squealed in pain.

The killer backed away from her, holding the weapon, his eyes sparkling with excitement. "What a kick *that* was."

Chyna huddled against the side of the refrigerator, tramping on kitten faces.

"I knew it was the same gun," he said, "but what if I'd been wrong? I'd have one big hole in my face right now, wouldn't I, little lady?"

Weak and dizzy with terror, she looked around desperately for anything that could be used as a weapon, but there was nothing close at hand.

"One big hole in my face," he repeated, as if he found that prospect amusing.

One of the cabinets might contain knives, but she had no way of knowing which drawer to check.

"Intense," he said, smiling at the revolver in his hand.

A pistol lay on the counter across the kitchen, beside the sink, well out of her reach. Chyna couldn't believe this: He had brought a gun of his own, but he hadn't used it, had set it aside, and had gone for her bare-handed instead.

"You're an attractive woman."

She looked away from the pistol, hoping he hadn't noticed that she'd seen it. But she was fooling herself, and she knew it, because he saw everything, everything.

He pointed the revolver at her. "You were back there in the service station last night."

She was gasping for breath, but she didn't seem to be drawing any air. She was breathing too fast and too shallowly, in danger of hyperventilating, and she was furious with herself, *furious*, because he was so calm.

He said, "I know you were there, somehow, somewhere, and I know you found this Chief's Special after I left, but for the life of me, I can't figure why you're *here*."

Maybe she would be able to get to the pistol before he could stop her. It was a million-to-one chance. Two million, three. Hell, face it, impossible.

From five feet away, aiming the revolver at the bridge of her nose, his voice bubbly with exhilaration, the killer said, "But even though it was the Asian's piece, I was walking into the mouth of the dragon here. I was lucky just now. Are you?"

Although reaching the pistol was probably impossible, she didn't have any alternatives. Nothing to lose.

With a note of impatience, he said, "Honey, listen to me, please, I'm talking to you. Do you feel lucky right now? As lucky as I've been?"

Trying not to stare at the pistol, reluctant to look into his too-normal eyes, she gazed down the bore of the revolver and managed to say, "No," and she half believed that she heard that single word echoing back to her out of the barrel, *No*.

"Let's see if you are."

"No."

"Oh, be adventurous, sweetheart. Let's see if you're lucky," he said, and he pulled the trigger.

Although the weapon had failed to fire three times, she expected it to explode in her face, because that seemed to be the way luck was running for her, and she flinched.

Click.

"You *are* lucky, even more so than I am."

Chyna didn't know what he was talking about. She couldn't focus her thoughts on anything but the pistol by the sink, this last miraculous chance.

"When Fuji started to pull this piece on me," the killer said, "didn't you hear what I promised him?"

All this talking and the bastard's calm demeanor unnerved Chyna even further. She expected him to shoot her, cut her, beat her, and probably rape her, torture answers from her before or after, but she didn't expect to have to *chat* with him, for God's sake, as if what they had been through was only a pleasant little road trip, a shared vacation that had taken a couple of interesting twists.

Still pointing the revolver at her, he said, "What I told Fuji was, 'Don't, or I'll shove the bullets up your ass.' I always keep my promises. Don't you?"

His patter finally captured her undivided attention.

"In such poor light, and with all that blood everywhere, not wanting to look, squeamish, you probably didn't see that Fuji's pants were pulled down."

He was right. After a glance showed her that the clerks were both dead, she had averted her eyes and stepped around their bodies.

He said, "I managed to insert four rounds in him."

Now she closed her eyes. Opened them at once. She didn't want to see him, looming and handsome with his nice smile, dry bloodstains on his clothes and nothing disturbing in his eyes. But she didn't dare look away.

Chyna Shepherd, untouched and alive.

"I put four bullets in," he said, "but then they started popping back out. A little post-mortem gas release. It was ridiculous, quite funny, really, but I was pressed for time, as you might understand, and finally it was just too much trouble to do the fifth."

Maybe this was best. Maybe one more round of Russian roulette, and then peace at long last, no more trying to understand why there was so much cruelty in the world when kindness was the easier choice.

He said, "This is a five-shot weapon."

The empty socket of the muzzle stared blindly at her, and she wondered if she would see the flash and hear the roar or whether the blackness in the barrel would become her own blackness, without any awareness of the exchange.

Then the killer turned the revolver away from her and pulled the trigger. The blast rattled windows, and the slug tore through a cabinet door along the nearest wall, spraying splinters of pine and shattering dishes inside.

Bits of wood were still flying when Chyna grabbed a drawer and yanked it out of the cabinet. It was so heavy that it almost pulled out of her hand, but she was suddenly strong with desperation, and she slung it upward at the killer's head, the contents spilling from it as it arced high toward his brow.

Spoons, forks, butter knives dueling in the air, flashing with cold fluorescent reflections, ringing down on him and across the tile floor, startled him backward into the dinette table.

Even as the killer stumbled away in surprise, Chyna was moving toward the sink. An instant after she heard the empty drawer crash against something, she put her hand on the grip of the pistol. She saw a red dot on the steel frame, which was probably exposed when the safety was off, as on other pistols with which she was familiar, and she didn't have to worry about empty chambers, as with the revolver, because if there was even one bullet in the magazine, just one, it would be in the breech, *please*, and at this close range one round might be all that she needed.

But her trigger finger was already stiffening and swelling, and when she tried to hook it through the guard, the flare of pain rocked her. She bobbled on a black tide of nausea, swayed, fumbling at the trigger guard with her middle finger.

Skating across the littered floor with an ice-brittle clatter-clink of scattering tableware, the killer reached Chyna before she could bring the gun up and turn. He slammed his arm down on hers and trapped her hand against the countertop.

Reflexively her finger pulled the trigger. A bullet smashed the backsplash. Chips of yellow ceramic tile sprayed in her face, and she might have been blinded if she hadn't squeezed her eyes shut in time.

He slammed the heel of his hand against the side of her head, sending a spray of darkness across the backs of her eyes, like shards of exploding black glass, and then he clubbed his fist against the nape of her neck.

With no memory of having fallen, Chyna was lying on the kitchen floor, with a bug's-eye view across the vinyl tile, gazing through a cataclysmic tumble of eating utensils. Interesting. Spoons were the size of shovels. Forks as big as pitchforks. Knives were lances.

The killer's boots. Black boots. Moving around.

For a moment she became confused, thinking that she was back in the Templeton house in the Napa Valley, hiding under the bed in the guest room. But there hadn't been flatware scattered across that bedroom floor, and when she focused on the stainless-steel utensils again, her thoughts cleared.

"Now I'm going to have to wash all these," the killer said, "before I put them away."

He was circling through the kitchen, picking up the flatware and being methodical about it, keeping spoons with spoons, knives with knives.

Chyna was surprised that she could move her arm, which was as heavy as a great tree limb, a petrified tree once wood but now stone. Nevertheless, she managed to point at the killer and even curl her throbbing trigger finger, swallowing her pain and the bitter taste that came with it.

The gun didn't fire.

She squeezed the trigger again, and still there was no boom, and then she realized that her hand was empty. She wasn't holding the pistol.

Strange.

One of the knives was near her hand. It was a table knife with a finely serrated edge, suitable for spreading butter or for slicing well-cooked chicken or for cutting green beans into bite-size pieces, but not ideal for stabbing someone to death. A knife was a knife, however, better than no weapon at all, and she quietly closed her hand around it.

Now all she had to do was find the strength to get off the floor. Curiously, she couldn't even lift her head. She had never before felt so *tired*.

She had been hit hard on the back of the neck. She wondered about spinal injury.

She refused to weep. She had the knife.

The killer came to her, stooped, and extracted the knife from her hand. She was amazed at how easily it *slipped* from her fingers, even though she clutched it ferociously, as if it hadn't been a knife at all but a sliver of melting ice.

"Bad girl," he said, and rapped the flat of the blade against the top of her skull.

He continued with the cleanup.

While trying not to think about spinal injuries, Chyna managed to get her hand around a fork.

He returned and took that away from her too. "No," he said, as though he were training a recalcitrant puppy. "No."

"Bastard," she said, dismayed to hear a slur in her voice.

"Sticks and stones."

"Fucking bastard."

"Oh, very pretty," he said scornfully.

"Shithead."

"I should wash your mouth out with soap."

"Asshole."

"Your mother never taught you words like that."

"You don't know my mother," she said thickly.

He hit her again, a hard chop to the side of the neck this time.

Then Chyna lay in darkness, listening worriedly to her mother's distant gay laughter and strange men's voices. Shattering glass. Cursing. Thunder and wind. Palm trees thrashing in the night over Key West. The quality of the laughter changed. Mocking now. Crashes that weren't thunder. And the skittery palmetto beetle over her bare legs and across her back. Other times. Other places. In the vapory realm of dreams, the iron fist of memory.

SEVEN

Shortly after nine o'clock in the morning, after dealing with the woman and washing the flatware, Mr. Vess sets loose the dogs.

At the back door, at the front door, and in his bedroom, there are call buttons that, when pushed, sound a soft buzzer in the kennel behind the barn. When the Dobermans have been sent there with the word *crib*, as they were sent earlier, the buzzer is a command that at once returns them to active patrol.

He uses the call button by the kitchen door and then steps to the large window by the dinette to watch the backyard.

The sky is low and gray, still shrouding the Siskiyou Mountains, but rain is no longer falling. The drooping boughs of the evergreens drip steadily. The bark on the deciduous trees is a sodden black; their limbs—some with the first fragile green buds of spring, others still barren—are so coaly that they appear to have been stripped by fire.

Some people might think that the scene is passive now, with the thunder spent and the lightning extinguished, but Mr. Vess knows that a storm is as powerful in its aftermath as in its raging. He is in harmony with this new kind of power, the quiescent power of growth that water bestows on the land.

From the back of the barn come the Dobermans. They pad side by side for a distance, but then split up and proceed each in his own direction.

They are not on attack status at this time. They will chase down and detain any intruder, but they will not kill him. To prime them for blood, Mr. Vess must speak the name *Nietzsche.*

One of the dogs—Liederkranz—comes onto the back porch, where he stares at the window, adoring his master. His tail wags once, and then once again, but he is on duty, and this brief and measured display of affection is all that he will allow himself.

Liederkranz returns to the backyard. He stands tall, vigilant. He gazes first to the south, then west, and then east. He lowers his head, smells the wet grass, and at last he moves off across the lawn, sniffing industriously. His ears flatten against his skull as he concentrates on a scent, tracking something that he imagines might be a threat to his master.

On a few occasions, as a reward to the Dobermans and to keep them sharp, Mr. Vess has turned loose a captive and has allowed the dogs to stalk her, forgoing the pleasure of the kill himself. It is an entertaining spectacle.

Secure behind the screen of his four-legged Praetorian Guard, Mr. Vess goes upstairs to the bathroom and adjusts the water in the shower until it is luxuriously hot. He lowers the volume of the radio but leaves it tuned to the swing-music program.

As he strips off his soiled clothing, clouds of steam pour over the top of the shower curtain. This humidity enhances the fragrance of the dark stains in his garments. Naked, he stands for a couple of minutes with his face buried in the blue jeans, the T-shirt, the denim jacket, breathing deeply at first but then delicately sniffing one exquisite nuance of odor after another, wishing that his sense of smell were twenty thousand times more intense than it is, like that of a Doberman.

Nevertheless, these aromas transport him into the night just past. He hears once more the soft popping of the sound suppressor on the pistol, the muffled cries of terror and the thin pleas for mercy in the night calm of the Templeton house. He smells Mrs. Templeton's lilac-scented body lotion, which she'd applied to her skin before retiring, the fragrance of the sachet in the daughter's underwear drawer. He tastes, in memory, the spider.

Regretfully, he puts the clothes aside for laundering, because by this evening he must pass for the ordinary man that he is not, and this reverse lycanthropy requires time if the transformation is to be convincing.

Therefore, as Benny Goodman plays "One O'clock Jump," Mr. Vess plunges into the stinging-hot water, being especially vigorous with the washcloth and lavish with a bar of Irish Spring, scrubbing away the too pungent scents of sex and death, which might alarm the sheep. They must never suspect the shepherd of having a snaggle-toothed snout and a bushy tail inside his herdsman's disguise. Taking his time, bopping to song after song, he shampoos his thick hair twice and then treats it with a penetrating conditioner. He uses a small brush to scrub under his fingernails. He is a perfectly proportioned man, lean but muscular. As always, he takes great pleasure in soaping himself, enjoying the sculpted contours of his body under his slippery hands; he feels like the music sounds, like the soap smells, like the taste of sweetened whipping cream.

Life *is.* Vess lives.

Chyna came out of Key West darkness and tropical thunder into a fluorescent glare that stung her bleary eyes. At first she mistook the fear that drove her pounding heart for the fear of Jim Woltz, her mother's friend; she thought that her face was pressed to the floor under the bed in his seaside cottage. But then she remembered the killer and the captive girl.

She was sitting forward in a chair, slumped over the round table in the dining area off the knotty-pine kitchen. Her head was turned to her right, and she was looking through a window at the back porch, the backyard.

The killer had removed a seat cushion from one of the other chairs and had placed it under her head, so her face wouldn't press uncomfortably against the wood. She shuddered at his thoughtfulness.

As she tried to lift her head, pain shot up the back of her neck and throbbed in the right side of her face. She almost blacked out, and decided not to be in a rush about getting up.

When she shifted in the chair, the clink of chains indicated that getting up might not be a choice either now or later. Her hands were in her lap, and when she tried to lift one, she lifted both, for her wrists were cuffed.

She tried to pull her feet apart—and discovered that her ankles were shackled. Judging by the noisy rattling and clinking that her small movements generated, there were other encumbrances as well.

Outside, something as black as soot bounded across the green lawn, scampered up the steps, and crossed the porch. It came to the window, jumped up, put its paws on the window stool, and peered in at her. A Doberman pinscher.

Against her breasts, Ariel holds an open book as if it is a shield, hands splayed across the binding. She is in the enormous armchair, legs drawn up beneath her, the only perfect doll of all those in the room.

Mr. Vess sits on a footstool before her.

He cleans up well. Showered, shampooed, shaved, and combed, he is presentable in any company, and any mother, seeing him on the arm of her daughter, would think that he was a prize. He is wearing loafers without socks, beige cotton Dockers, a braided leather belt, and a pale-green chambray shirt.

In her schoolgirl uniform, Ariel looks good too. Vess is pleased to see that she has regularly groomed herself in his absence, as she was instructed. It is not easy for her, taking only sponge baths and shampooing her glorious hair in the sink.

He constructed this room for others, who came before her, none of whom was in residence longer than two months. Until he'd met his Ariel, and learned what an engagingly independent spirit she was, he'd never imagined that he would insist on anyone staying this long. Consequently, a shower had seemed unnecessary.

He had first seen the girl in a newspaper photograph. Though only a tenth-grader, she had been something of a prodigy and had led her Sacramento high school team to victory in a statewide California academic decathlon. She had looked so tender. The newspaper had trembled in his hands when he had seen her, and he had known at once that he must drive to Sacramento and meet her. He'd shot the father. The mother had owned an enormous collection of dolls and had made dolls of her own as a hobby. Vess had beaten her to death with a ventriloquist dummy that had a large, carved-maple head as effective as a baseball bat.

"You're more beautiful than ever," he tells Ariel, and his voice is muffled by the soundproofing, as if he were speaking from inside a coffin, buried alive.

She does not reply or even acknowledge his presence. She is in her silent mode, as she has been without interruption for more than six months.

"I missed you."

These days, she never looks at him but stares at a point above his head and off to one side. If he were to stand up from the footstool and move into her line of sight, she would *still* be looking over his head and to one side, though he would never quite be able to see her eyes shift in avoidance.

"I brought a few things to show you."

From a shoe box on the floor beside the footstool, he extracts two Polaroid photographs. She will not accept them or turn her eyes to them, but Vess knows that she will examine these mementos after he leaves.

She is not as lost to this world as she pretends to be. They are engaged in a complicated game with high stakes, and she is a good player.

"This first is a picture of a lady named Sarah Templeton, the way she looked before I had her. She was in her forties but very attractive. A lovely woman."

The armchair is so deep that the seat cushion provides a ledge in front of Ariel on which Vess can place the photograph.

"Lovely," he repeats.

Ariel doesn't blink. She is capable of staring fixedly without blinking for surprisingly long periods. Now and then Mr. Vess worries that she will damage her striking blue eyes; corneas require frequent lubrication. Of course, if she goes too long without blinking and her eyes become dangerously dry, the irritation will cause tears to spring up involuntarily.

"This is a second photograph of Sarah, after I was finished with her," Mr. Vess says, and he also places this picture on the chair. "As you can see if you choose to look, the word *lovely* doesn't apply any more. Beauty never lasts. Things change."

From the shoe box he takes two more photographs.

"This is Sarah's daughter, Laura. Before. And after. You can see she was beautiful. Like a butterfly. But there's a worm in every butterfly, you know."

He places these snapshots on the chair and reaches into the box again.

"This was Laura's father. Oh, and here's her brother . . . and the brother's wife. They were incidental."

Finally he brings out the three Polaroids of the young Asian gentleman and the Slim Jim with the bite missing.

"His name is Fuji. Like the mountain in Japan."

Vess puts two of the three photos on the chair.

"I'll keep one for myself. To eat. And then I'll be Fuji, with the power of the East and the power of the mountain, and when the time comes for me to do you, you'll feel both the boy and the mountain in me, and so many other people, all their power. It'll be very exciting for you, Ariel, so exciting that when it's over, you won't even care that you're dead."

This is a long speech for Mr. Vess. He is for the most part not a garrulous man. The girl's beauty, however, moves him now and then to speeches.

He holds up the Slim Jim.

"The missing bite was taken by Fuji just before I killed him. His saliva will have dried on the meat. You can taste a little of his quiet power, his inscrutable nature."

He puts the wrapped sausage on the chair.

"I'll be back after midnight," Mr. Vess promises. "We'll go out to the motor home, so you can see Laura, the real Laura, not just the picture of her. I brought her back so you could see what becomes of all pretty things. And there's a young man too, a hitchhiker that I picked up along the way. I showed him a photograph of you, and I just didn't like the way he looked at it. He wasn't respectful. He leered. I didn't like something he said about you, so I sewed his mouth shut, and I sewed his eyes shut because of the way he looked at your picture. You'll be excited to see what I did to him. You can touch him . . . and Laura."

Vess watches her closely for any tic, shudder, flinch, or subtle change in the eyes that will indicate that she hears him. He *knows* that she hears, but she is clever at maintaining a solemn face and a pretense of catatonic detachment.

If he can force one faint flinch from her, one tic, then he will soon shatter her completely and have her howling like a goggle-eyed patient in the deepest wards of Bedlam. That collapse into ranting insanity is always fascinating to watch.

But she is tough, this girl, with surprising inner resources. Good. The challenge thrills him.

"And from the motor home we'll go out to the meadow with the dogs, Ariel, and you can watch while I bury Laura and the hitchhiker. Maybe the sky will clear by that time, and maybe there'll be stars or even moonlight."

Ariel huddles on the chair with her book, eyes distant, lips slightly parted, a deeply still girl.

"Hey, you know, I bought another doll for you. An interesting little shop in Napa, California, a place that sells the work of local craftsmen. It's a clever rag doll. You'll like it. I'll give it to you later."

Mr. Vess gets up from the footstool and takes a casual inventory of the contents of the refrigerator and the cabinet that serves as the girl's pantry. She has enough supplies to carry her three more days, and he will restock her shelves tomorrow.

"You're not eating quite as much as you should," he admonishes. "That's ungrateful of you. I've given you a refrigerator, a microwave, hot and cold running water. You've got everything you need to take care of yourself. You should eat."

The dolls are no less responsive than the girl.

"You've lost two or three pounds. It hasn't affected your looks yet, but you can't lose any more."

She gazes into thin air, as if waiting for her voice-box string to be pulled before she recites recorded messages.

"Don't think you can starve yourself until you're haggard and unattractive. You can't escape me that way, Ariel. I'll strap you down and force-feed you if I have to. I'll make you swallow a rubber tube and pump baby food into your stomach. In fact, I'd enjoy it. Do you like pureed peas? Carrots? Applesauce? I guess it doesn't matter, since you won't taste them—unless you regurgitate."

He gazes at her silken hair, which is red blond in the filtered light. This sight translates through all five of Vess's extraordinary senses, and he is bathed in the sensory splendor of her hair, in all the sounds and smells and textures that the look of it conveys to him. One stimulus has so many associations for him that he could lose himself for hours in the contemplation of a single hair or one drop of rain, if he chose, because that item would become an entire world of sensation to him.

He moves to the armchair and stands over the girl.

She doesn't acknowledge him, and although he has entered her line of sight, her gaze has somehow shifted above and to one side of him without his being aware of the moment when it happened.

She is magically evasive.

"Maybe I could get a word or two out of you if I set you on fire. What do you think? Hmmm? A little lighter fluid on that golden hair—and *whoosh!*"

She does not blink.

"Or I'll give you to the dogs, see if that unties your tongue."

No flinch, no tic, no shudder. What a girl.

Mr. Vess stoops, lowering his face toward Ariel's, until they are nose-to-nose.

Her eyes are now directly aligned with his—yet she is still not looking at him. She seems to peer *through* him, as if he is not a man of flesh and blood but a haunting spirit that she can't quite detect. This isn't merely the old trick of letting her eyes swim out of focus; it's a ruse infinitely more clever than that, which he can't understand at all.

Nose-to-nose with her, Vess whispers, "We'll go to the meadow after midnight. I'll bury Laura and the hitchhiker. Maybe I'll put you into the ground with them and cover you up, three in one grave. Them dead and you alive. Would you speak then, Ariel? Would you say *please?*"

No answer.

He waits.

Her breathing is low and even. He is so close to her that her exhalations are warm and steady against his lips, like promises of kisses to come.

She must feel his breath too.

She may be frightened of him and even repulsed by him, but she also finds him alluring. He has no doubt about this. Everyone is fascinated by bad boys.

He says, "Maybe there'll be stars."

Such a blueness in her eyes, such sparkling depths.

"Or even moonlight," he whispers.

The steel cuffs on Chyna's ankles were linked by a sturdy chain. A second and far longer chain, connected by a carabiner to the first, wound around the thick legs of the chair and around the stretcher bars between the legs, returned between her feet, encircled the big barrel that supported the round table, and connected again to the carabiner. The chains didn't contain enough play to allow her to stand. Even if she'd been able to stand, she would have had to carry the chair on her back, and the restricting shape and the weight of it would have forced her to bend forward like a hunchbacked troll. And once standing, she could not have moved from the table to which she was tethered.

Her hands were cuffed in front of her. A chain was hooked into the shackle that encircled her right wrist. From there it led around her, wound between the back rails of the chair behind the tie-on pad, then to the shackle on her left wrist. This chain contained enough slack to allow her to rest her arms on the table if she wished.

She sat with her hands folded, leaning forward, staring at the red and swollen index finger on her right hand, waiting.

Her finger throbbed, and she had a headache, but her neck pain had subsided. She knew that it would return worse than ever in another twenty-four hours, like the delayed agony of severe whiplash.

Of course, if she was still alive in another twenty-four hours, neck pain would be the least of her worries.

The Doberman was no longer at the window. She had seen two at once on the lawn, padding back and forth, sniffing the grass and the air, pausing occasionally to prick their ears and listen intently, then padding away again, obviously on guard duty.

During the previous night, Chyna had used rage to overcome her terror before it had incapacitated her, but now she discovered that humiliation was even more effective at quelling fear. Having been unable to protect herself, having wound up in bondage—that was not the source of her humiliation; what mortified worse was her failure to fulfill her promise to the girl in the cellar.

I am your guardian. I'll keep you safe.

She kept returning, in memory, to the upholstered vestibule and the view port on the inner door. The girl among the dolls had given no indication that she had heard the promise. But Chyna was sick with the certainty that she had raised false hopes, that the girl would feel betrayed and more abandoned than ever, and that she would withdraw even further into her private Elsewhere.

I am your guardian.

In retrospect, Chyna found her arrogance not merely astonishing but perverse, delusional. In twenty-six years of living, she'd never saved anyone, in any sense whatsoever. She was no heroine, no mystery-novel-series character with just a colorful dash of angst and a soupçon of endearing character flaws and, otherwise, the competence of Sherlock Holmes and James Bond combined. Keeping herself alive, mentally stable, and emotionally intact had been enough of a struggle for her. She was still a lost girl herself, fumbling blindly through the years for some insight or resolution that probably wasn't even out there to be found, yet she'd stood at that view port and promised deliverance.

I am your guardian.

She opened her folded hands. She flattened her hands on the table and slid them across the wood as if smoothing away wrinkles in a tablecloth, and as she moved, her chains rattled.

She wasn't a fighter, after all, no one's paladin; she worked as a waitress. She was good at it, piling up tips, because sixteen years in her mother's bent world had taught her that one way to ensure survival was to be ingratiating. With her customers, she was indefatigably charming, relentlessly agreeable, and always eager to please. The relationship between a diner and a waitress was, to her way of thinking, the *ideal* relationship, because it was brief, formal, generally conducted with a high degree of politeness, and required no baring of the heart.

I am your guardian.

In her obsessive determination to protect herself at all costs, she was always friendly with the other waitresses where she worked, but she never made friends with any of them. Friendships involved commitment, risks. She had learned not to make herself vulnerable to the hurt and betrayal that ensued from commitments.

Over the years, she'd had affairs with only two men. She had liked both and had loved the second, but the first relationship had lasted eleven months and the second only thirteen. Lovers, if they were worthwhile, required more than simple commitment; they needed revelation, sharing, the bond of emotional intimacy. She found it difficult to reveal much about her childhood or her mother, in part because her utter helplessness during those years embarrassed her. More to the point, she had come to the hard realization that her mother had never really loved her, perhaps had never been capable of loving her or anyone. And how could she expect to be cherished by any man who knew that she'd been unloved even by her mother?

She was aware that this attitude was irrational, but awareness didn't free her. She understood that she was not responsible for what her mother had done to her, but regardless of what so many therapists claimed in their books and on their radio talk shows, understanding alone didn't lead to healing. Even after a decade beyond her mother's control, Chyna was at times convinced that all the dark events of all those troubled years could have been avoided if only she, Chyna, had been a better girl, more worthy.

I am your guardian.

She folded her hands on the table again. She leaned forward until her forehead was pressed to the backs of her thumbs, and she closed her eyes.

The only close friend she'd ever had was Laura Templeton. Their relationship was something that she had wanted badly but had never sought, desperately needed but did little to nurture; it was purely a testament to Laura's vivaciousness, perseverance, and selflessness in the face of Chyna's caution and reserve, a result of Laura's dear heart and her singular capacity to love. And now Laura was dead.

I am your guardian.

In Laura's room, under the dead gaze of Freud, Chyna had knelt beside the bed and whispered to her shackled friend, *I'll get you out of here.* God, how it hurt to think of it. *I'll get you out of here.* Her stomach knotted excruciatingly with self-disgust. *I'll find a weapon,* she had promised. Laura, selfless to the end, had urged her to run, to get out. *Don't die for me,* Laura had said. But Chyna had answered, *I'll be back.*

Now here came grief again, swooping like a great dark bird into her heart, and she almost let its wings enfold her, too eager for the strange solace of those battering pinions— until she realized that she was using grief to knock humiliation from its perch. Grieving, she would have no room for self-loathing.

I am your guardian.

Although the clerk had never fired the revolver, she should have checked it. She should have known. Somehow. Some way. Though she could not possibly have known what Vess had done with the bullets, she should have *known.*

Laura had always told her that she was too hard on herself, that she would never heal if she kept inflicting new bruises on the old in endless self-flagellation.

But Laura was dead.

I am your guardian.

Chyna's humiliation festered into shame.

And if humiliation was a good tool for repressing terror, shame was even better. Steeping in shame, she knew no fear at all, even though she was in shackles in the house of a sadistic murderer, with no one in the world looking for her. Justice seemed served by her being there.

Then she heard footsteps approaching.

She raised her head and opened her eyes.

The killer entered from the laundry room, evidently returning from the girl in the cellar.

Without speaking to Chyna, without glancing at her, as if she didn't exist, he went to the refrigerator, removed a carton of eggs, and put it on the counter beside the sink. He deftly broke eight eggs into a bowl and threw the shells in the trash. He set the bowl in the refrigerator and proceeded to peel and chop a Bermuda onion.

Chyna hadn't eaten in more than twelve hours; nonetheless, she was dismayed to discover that she was suddenly ravenous. The onion was the sweetest scent that she had ever known, and her mouth began to water. After so much blood, after losing the only close friend she'd ever had, it seemed heartless to have an appetite so soon.

The killer put the chopped onion into a Tupperware container, snapped the lid tight, and placed it in the refrigerator beside the bowl of eggs. Next he grated half a wedge of cheddar cheese into another Tupperware container.

He was brisk and efficient in the kitchen, and he seemed to be enjoying himself. He kept his work area neat. He also washed his hands thoroughly between each task and dried them on a hand towel, not on the dish towel.

Finally the killer came to the dinette table. He sat across from Chyna, relaxed and self-confident and college-boy casual in his Dockers, braided belt, and soft chambray shirt.

Shame, which had seemed on the verge of consuming her, instead had burned itself out for the time being. A strange combination of smoldering anger and bitter despondency had replaced it.

"Now," he said, "I'm sure you're hungry, and as soon as we have a little chat, I'll make cheese omelets with stacks of toast. But to earn your breakfast, you have to tell me who you are, where you were hiding at that service station, and why you're here."

She glared at him.

With a smile, he said, "Don't think you can hold out on me."

She would be damned rather than tell him anything.

"Here's how it is," he said. "I'll kill you anyway. I'm not sure how yet. Probably in front of Ariel. She's seen bodies before, but she's never been there at the moment itself, to hear that last scream, in the sudden wetness of it all."

Chyna tried to keep her eyes on him, show no weakness.

He said, "However I choose to do you, I'll make it a lot harder for you if you don't talk to me willingly. There are things I enjoy that can be done before or after you're dead. Cooperate, and I'll do them after."

Chyna tried unsuccessfully to see some sign of madness in his eyes. Such a merry shade of blue.

"Well?"

"You're a sick sonofabitch."

Smiling again, he said, "The last thing I expected you to be was tedious."

"I know why you sewed shut his eyes and mouth," she said.

"Ah, so you found him in the closet."

"You raped him before you killed him or while you killed him. You sewed his eyes shut because he'd seen, sewed his mouth shut because you're ashamed of what you did and you're afraid that, even dead, he might tell someone."

Unfazed, he said, "Actually, I didn't have sex with him."

"Liar."

"But if I had, I wouldn't have been embarrassed. You think I'm that unsophisticated?

We're all bisexual, don't you think? I have the urge for a man, sometimes, and with some of them I've indulged it. It's all sensation. Just sensation."

"Maggot."

"I know what you're trying to do," he said amiably, clearly amused by her, "but it just won't work. You're hoping one insult or another will set me off. As if I'm some hair-trigger psychopath who'll just explode if you call me the right name, push the right button, maybe insult my mother or say nasty things about the Lord. Then you hope I'll kill you fast, in a wild rage, and get it over with."

Chyna realized that he was right, although she had not been consciously aware of her own intentions. Failure, shame, and the helplessness of being shackled had reduced her to a despair that she had preferred not to consider. Now she was sickened less by him than by herself, wondering if she was a quitter and a loser, after all, just like her mother.

"But I'm not a psychopath," he said.

"Then what are you?"

"Oh . . . call me a homicidal adventurer. Or perhaps the only clear-thinking person you've ever met."

" 'Maggot' works better for me."

He leaned forward in his chair. "Here's the thing—either you tell me all about yourself, everything I want to know, or I'll work on your face with a knife while you sit there. For every question you refuse to answer, I'll take off a piece—the lobe of an ear, the tip of your pretty nose. Carve you like scrimshaw."

He said this not threateningly but matter-of-factly, and she knew that he had the stomach for it.

"I'll take all day," he said, "and you'll be insane long before you're dead."

"All right."

"All right what—conversation or scrimshaw?"

"Conversation."

"Good girl."

She was prepared to die if it came to that, but she saw no point in suffering needlessly.

"What's your name?" he asked.

"Shepherd. Chyna Shepherd. C-h-y-n-a."

"Ah, not a cryptic chant, after all."

"What?"

"Odd name."

"Is it?"

"Don't spar with me, Chyna. Go on."

"All right. But first, may I have something to drink? I'm dehydrated."

At the sink, he drew a glass of water. He put three ice cubes in it. He started to bring it to her, then halted and said, "I could add a slice of lemon."

She knew he wasn't joking. Home from the hunt, he was working now to recast himself from the role of savage stalker into that of accountant or clerk or real estate agent or car mechanic or whatever it was that he did when he was passing for normal. Some sociopaths could put on a false persona that was more convincing than the best performances of the finest actors who had ever lived, and this man was probably one of those, although after immersion in wanton slaughter, he needed this period of adjustment to remind himself of the manners and courtesies of civilized society.

"No, thanks," she said to the offer of lemon.

"It's no trouble," he graciously assured her.

"Just the water."

When he put the glass down, he slipped a cork-lined ceramic coaster under it. Then he sat across the table from her again.

Chyna was repelled by the prospect of drinking from a glass that he had handled, but she really was dehydrated. Her mouth was dry, and her throat was vaguely sore.

Because of the cuffs, she picked up the glass in both hands.

She knew that he was watching her for signs of fear.

The water didn't slop around in the tumbler. The rim of the glass didn't chatter against her teeth.

She truly wasn't afraid of him any more, at least not for the moment, although maybe later. Certainly later. Now her interior landscape was a desert under sullen skies: numbing desolation, with the angry flicker of lightning toward a far horizon.

She drank half of the water before she put the glass down.

"When I entered the room a moment ago," the killer said, "you were sitting with your hands folded, your head bowed against your hands. Were you praying?"

She thought about it. "No."

"There's no point in lying to me."

"I'm not lying. I wasn't praying just then."

"But you do pray?"

"Sometimes."

"God fears me."

She waited.

He said, "*God fears me*—those are words that can be made from the letters of my name."

"I see."

"Dragon seed."

"From the letters of your name," she said.

"Yes. And . . . forge of rage."

"It's an interesting game."

"Names are interesting. Yours is passive. A place name for a first name. And Shepherd—bucolic, fuzzily Christian. When I think of your name, I see an Asian peasant on a hillside with sheep . . . or a slant-eyed Christ making converts among the heathens." He smiled, amused by his banter. "But clearly, your name doesn't define you well. You're not a passive person."

"I have been," she said, "most of my life."

"Really? Well, you weren't passive last night."

"Not last night," she agreed. "But until then."

"My name, on the other hand, is a power name. Edgler Foreman Vess." He spelled it for her. "Not Edgar. Edge-ler. Like 'on the edge.' And Vess . . . if you draw it out, it's like a serpent hissing."

"Demon."

"Yes, that's right. It's there in my name—*demon*."

"Anger."

He seemed pleased by her willingness to play. "You're good at this, especially considering that you don't have pen and paper."

"Vessel," she said. "That's in your name too."

"An easy one. But also *semen*. Vessel and semen, female and male. Would you like to craft an insult out of that, Chyna?"

Instead of replying, she picked up the glass and drank half of the remaining water. The ice cubes were cold against her teeth.

"Now that you've wet your whistle," Vess said, "I want to know all about you. Remember—scrimshaw."

Chyna told him everything, beginning with the moment that she had heard a scream while sitting at the guest-bedroom window in the Templeton house. She delivered her account in a monotone, not by calculation but because suddenly she could speak no other way. She tried to vary her inflection, put life into her words—but failed.

The sound of her voice, droning through the events of the night, scared her as Edgler

Vess no longer did. Her account came to her as if she were listening to someone else speak, and it was the voice of a lost and defeated person.

She told herself that she was not defeated, that she still had hope, that she would get the best of this murderous bastard one way or another. But her inner voice lacked all conviction.

In spite of Chyna's spiritless recitation of events, Vess was a rapt listener. He began in a relaxed slouch, lounging back in his chair, but by the time Chyna finished, he was leaning forward with his arms on the table, hunched toward her.

He interrupted her several times to ask questions. At the end, he sat for a while in contemplative silence.

She could not bear to look at him. She folded her hands on the table, closed her eyes, and put her forehead against the backs of her church-door thumbs, as she had been when Vess had come out of the laundry room.

She wasn't praying this time either. She lacked the hope needed for prayer.

After a few minutes, she heard Vess's chair slide back from the table. He got up. She heard him moving around, and then the familiar clatter of any cook being busy in any kitchen.

She smelled butter heating in a pan, then browning onions.

In the telling of her story, Chyna had lost her appetite, and it didn't return with the aroma of the onions.

Finally Vess said, "Funny that I didn't smell you right away at the Templetons'."

"You can do that?" she asked, without raising her head from her hands. "You can just smell people out, as if you were a damn dog?"

"Usually," he said, taking no offense, and with what seemed to be utmost seriousness. "And you must have made a sound more than once through the night. You surely can't be *that* stealthy. Even your breathing I should have heard."

Then came the sound of a wire whisk vigorously beating eggs in a bowl.

She smelled bread toasting.

"In a still house, with everyone dead, your movement should have made currents in the air, like a cool breath on the back of my neck, shivering the fine hairs on my hands. Your *every* movement should have been a different texture against my eyes. And when I walked through a space where you'd just been, I should have sensed the displacement of air caused by your passage."

He was stone crazy. So cute in his chambray shirt, with his beautiful blue eyes, his thick dark hair combed straight back from his forehead, and the dimple in his left cheek— but pustulant and canker-riddled inside.

"My senses, you see, are unusually acute."

He ran the water in the sink. Without looking, she knew that he was rinsing the whisk. He wouldn't put it aside dirty.

He said, "My senses are so sharp because I've given myself to sensation. Sensation is my religion, you might say."

A sizzling arose, much louder than the cooking sound of onions, and a new aroma.

"But you were invisible to me," he said. "Like a spirit. What makes you special?"

Bitter, she murmured against the tabletop, "If I was special, would I be here in chains?"

Although Chyna hadn't actually spoken to him and wouldn't have thought that he could hear her above the crisp sputtering of eggs and onions, Vess said, "I suppose you're right."

Later, when he put the plates on the table, she raised her head and moved her hands.

"Rather than make you eat with your hands, I'm going to give you a fork," he said, "because I assume you see the pointlessness of throwing it and trying to stick me in the eye."

She nodded.

"Good girl."

On her plate was a plump four-egg omelet oozing cheddar cheese and stippled with sautéed onions. On top were three slices of a firm tomato and a sprinkling of chopped parsley. Two pieces of buttered toast, each neatly sliced on the diagonal, were arranged to bracket the omelet.

He refilled her water glass and added two more cubes of ice.

Famished only a short while ago, Chyna now could hardly tolerate the sight of food. She knew that she must eat, so she picked at the eggs and nibbled the toast. But she would never be able to finish all that he had given her.

Vess ate with gusto but not noisily or sloppily. His table manners were beyond reproach, and he used his napkin frequently to blot his lips.

Chyna was deep in her private grayness, and the more Vess appeared to enjoy his breakfast, the more her own omelet began to taste like ashes.

"You'd be quite attractive if you weren't so rumpled and sweaty, your face smudged with dirt, your hair straggly from the rain. Very attractive, I think. A real charmer under that grime. Maybe later I'll bathe you."

Chyna Shepherd, untouched and alive.

Uncannily, after a further silence, Edgler Vess said, "Untouched and alive."

She *knew* that she had not spoken the prayer aloud.

"Untouched and alive," he repeated. "Is that what you said . . . on the stairs earlier, on your way down to Ariel?"

She stared at him, speechless.

"Is it?"

Finally: "Yes."

"I've been wondering about it. You said your name and then those three words, though none of it made sense when I didn't know that Chyna Shepherd was your name."

She looked away from him, at the window. A Doberman roamed the backyard.

"Was it a prayer?" he asked.

In her desolation, Chyna hadn't thought that he could scare her any more, but she had been wrong. His intuitiveness was frightening—and not entirely for reasons that she could understand.

She looked away from the Doberman and met Vess's eyes. For one brief moment, she saw the dog within, a dark and merciless aspect.

"Was it a prayer?" he asked again.

"Yes."

"In your heart, Chyna, deep in your heart, do you truly believe that God really exists? Be truthful now, not just with me but with yourself."

At one time—not long ago—she had been just barely sure enough of what she believed to answer *Yes.* Now she was silent.

"Even if God exists," Vess said, "does He know that *you* do?"

She took another bite of the omelet. It seemed greasier than before. The eggs and butter and cheese, too rich, cloyed in her mouth, and she could hardly swallow.

She put down her fork. She was finished. She'd eaten no more than a third of her meal.

Vess finished the food on his plate, washing it down with coffee that he didn't offer her—no doubt because he thought that she would try to throw the hot brew in his eyes.

"You look so glum," Vess said.

She didn't reply.

"You're feeling like such a failure, aren't you? You've failed poor Ariel, yourself, and God too, if He exists."

"What do you want with me?" she asked. She meant, *Why put me through this, why not kill me and get it over with?*

"I haven't figured that out yet," Vess said. "Whatever I do with you, it's got to be special. I feel you're special, whether you think you are or not, and whatever we do together should be . . . intense."

She closed her eyes and wondered if she could find Narnia again after all these years.

He said, "I can't answer your question as to what I want with you—but I have no doubts about what I want with Ariel. Would you like to hear what I intend to do with her?"

Most likely, she was too old to believe in anything, even just a magic wardrobe.

Vess's voice came out of her internal grayness, as if he lived there as well as in the real world: "I asked you a question, Chyna. Remember our bargain? You can either answer it—or I'll slice off a piece of your face. Would you like to hear what I intend to do with Ariel?"

"I'm sure I know."

"Yes, some of it. Sex, that's obvious. She's a luscious piece. I haven't touched her yet, but I will. And I believe she's a virgin. At least, in the days when she still talked, she said she was, and she didn't seem like the kind of girl who would lie."

Or there was the Wild Wood beyond the River, Ratty and Mole and Mr. Badger, green boughs hanging full in the summer sun and Pan piping in the cool shadows under the trees.

"And I want to hear her crying, lost and crying. I want to smell the purity of her tears. I want to feel the exquisite texture of her screams, know the clean smell of them, and the taste of her terror. There's always that. Always that."

Neither the languid river nor the Wild Wood materialized, though Chyna strained to see them. Ratty, Mole, Mr. Badger, and Mr. Toad were gone forever into the hateful death that claims all things. And the sadness of this, in its way, was as great as the sadness of what had happened to Laura and what would soon happen to Chyna herself.

Vess said, "Once in a while, I bring one of them back to the room in the cellar—and always for the same purpose."

She didn't want to hear this. The handcuffs made it difficult to cover her ears. And if she had tried, he would have shackled her wrists to her ankles. He would insist that she listen.

"The most intense experiences of my life have all taken place in that room, Chyna. Not the sex. Not the beating or the cutting. That all comes later, and it's a lagniappe. First, I break them down, and *that* is when it gets intense."

Her chest was tight. She could breathe only shallowly.

He said, "The first day or two, they all think they'll go out of their minds with fear, but they're wrong. It takes longer than a day or two to drive someone insane, truly and irrevocably insane. Ariel is my seventh captive, and the others all held on to their sanity for weeks. One of them cracked on the eighteenth day, but three of them lasted a full two months."

Chyna gave up on the elusive Wild Wood and met his gaze across the table.

"Psychological torture is so much more interesting and difficult to undertake than the physical variety, although the latter can be undeniably thrilling," Vess said. "The mind is so much tougher than the body, a greater challenge by far. And when the mind goes, I swear that I can hear the *crack*, a harder sound than bone splitting—and oh, how it reverberates."

She tried to see the animal consciousness in his eyes, which she had glimpsed unexpectedly before. She *needed* to see it.

"When they crack, some of them writhe on the floor, thrash, rend their clothes. They tear at their hair, Chyna, and claw their faces, and some of them bite themselves hard enough to draw blood. They maim themselves in so many inventive ways. They sob and sob, can't stop for hours, sometimes for days, sobbing in their sleep. They bark like dogs, Chyna, and screech and flail their arms as if they're convinced that they can fly. They hallucinate and see things more frightening than I am to them. Some speak in tongues. It's called *glossolalia*. Do you know the condition? Quite fascinating. Convincingly like a language yet meaningless, a ranting or pleading babble. Some lose control of their bodily functions and wallow in their filth. Messy but riveting to watch—the true base condition of humanity, to which most people can only admit in madness."

As hard as she tried, Chyna could see no beast in his eyes, only a placid blueness and the watchful darkness of the pupil, and she was no longer sure that she had ever seen it. He wasn't half man and half wolf, not a creature that fell to all fours in the light of the full moon. Worse, he was nothing but a man—living at one extreme end of the spectrum of human cruelty, but nonetheless only a man.

"Some take refuge in catatonic silences," Vess continued, "as Ariel has done. But I always break them out of that. Ariel is by far the most stubborn, but that only makes her interesting. I'll break her too, and when her *crack* comes, Chyna, it'll be like no other. Glorious. Intense."

"The most intense experience of all is showing mercy," Chyna said, and had no idea whatsoever where she had found those words. They sounded like a plea, and she didn't want him to think that she was begging for her life. Even in her despair, she would not be reduced to groveling.

A sudden smile made Vess look almost like a boy, one given to puns and pranks, collector of baseball cards, rider of bikes, builder of model airplanes, and altar boy on Sundays. She thought that he was smiling at what she'd said, amused by her naiveté, but this was not the case, as he made clear with his next words.

"Maybe . . . what I want from you," Vess said, "is to be with me when I finally make Ariel snap. Instead of killing you in front of her to drive her over the edge, I'll drive her some other way. And you can watch."

Oh, God.

"You're a psychology student, after all, almost a genuine *master* of psychology. Right? Sitting there in such stern judgment of me, so certain that my mind is 'aberrant' and that you know exactly how I think. Well, then, how interesting it would be to see if any of the modern theories of the working of the mind are undone by this little experiment. Don't you think so? After I break Ariel, you could write a paper about it, Chyna, for my eyes only. I'd enjoy reading your considered observations."

Dear God, it would never come to that. She'd never be a witness to such a thing. Though in shackles, she would find a way to commit suicide before she would let him take her down to that room to watch that lovely girl . . . to watch her dissolve. Chyna would bite open her own wrists, swallow her tongue, contrive to fall down the steps and break her neck, something. Something.

Evidently aware that he had jolted her out of gray despair into stark horror, Vess smiled again—and then turned his attention to her breakfast plate. "Do you intend to eat the rest of that?"

"No."

"Then I'll have it."

He slid his empty plate aside and pulled hers in front of him. Using her fork, he cut a bite-size piece of the cold omelet, put it in his mouth, and moaned softly in delight. Slowly, sensuously, Vess extracted the tines from his mouth, pressing his lips firmly around them as they slid loose, then reaching with his tongue for one last lick.

After he swallowed the bite of eggs, he said, "I could taste you on the fork. Your saliva has a lovely flavor—except for a faint bitterness. No doubt that's not a usual component, just the result of a sour stomach."

She could find no escape by closing her eyes, so she watched as he devoured the remains of her breakfast.

When he finished, she had a question of her own. "Last night . . . why did you eat the spider?"

"Why not?"

"That's no answer."

"It's the best answer to any question."

"Then give me second-best."

"You think it was disgusting?"

"I'm just curious."

"No doubt, you see it as a negative experience—eating an icky, squirmy spider."

"No doubt."

"But there are no negative experiences, Chyna. Only sensations. No values can be attached to pure sensation."

"Of course they can."

"If you think so, then you're in the wrong century. Anyway, the spider had an interesting flavor, and now I understand spiders better for having absorbed one. Do you know about flatworm learning?"

"Flatworm?"

"You should have encountered it in a basic biology course along the way to becoming such a highly educated woman. You see, certain flatworms can gradually learn to negotiate a maze—"

She did remember, and interrupted: "Then if you grind them up and feed them to another batch of flatworms, batch number two can run the same maze on the first try."

"Good. Yes." Vess nodded happily. "They absorb the knowledge with the flesh."

She didn't need to consider how to phrase her next question, for Vess could be neither insulted nor flattered. "Jesus, you don't actually believe you now know what it's like to be a spider, have all the knowledge of a spider, because you've eaten one?"

"Of course not, Chyna. If I were that literal-minded, I'd be crazy. Wouldn't I? In an institution somewhere, talking to a crowd of imaginary friends. But because of my sharp senses, I *did* absorb from the spider an ineffable quality of spiderness that you'll never be able to understand. I heightened my awareness of the spider as a marvelously engineered little hunter, a creature of power. *Spider* is a power word, you know, though it can't be formed from the letters of my name." He hesitated, pondering, and then continued: "It *can* be formed from the letters of your name."

She didn't bother to remind him about her mother's precious spelling. Only *spyder* could be found in *Chyna Shepherd*.

"And it was risky, eating a spider, which added considerably to the appeal," Vess continued. "Unless you're an entomologist, you can't be sure if any particular specimen is poisonous or not. Some, like the brown recluse, are extremely dangerous. A bite on the hand is one thing . . . but I had to be sure that I was quick and crushed it against the roof of my mouth before it could bite my tongue."

"You like taking risks."

He shrugged. "I'm just that kind of guy."

"On edge."

"Words in my name," he acknowledged.

"And if you'd been bitten on the tongue?"

"Pain is the same as pleasure, just different. Learn to enjoy it, and you're happier with life."

"Even pain is value neutral?"

"Sure. Just sensation. It helps grow the reef of the soul—if there is a soul."

She didn't know what the hell he was talking about—the reef of the soul—and she didn't ask. She was weary of him. Weary of fearing him, even weary of hating him. With her questions, she was striving to *understand,* as she had striven all her life, and she was tired to death of this search for meaning. She would never know why some people committed countless little cruelties—or bigger ones—and the struggle to understand had only exhausted her and left her empty, cold, and gray inside.

Pointing to her red and swollen index finger, Vess said, "That must hurt. And your neck."

"The headache's the worst of it. And none of it's anything like pleasure."

"Well, I can't easily show you the way to enlightenment and prove you're wrong. It takes time. But there's a smaller lesson, quick to learn. . . ."

He got up from his chair and went to a spice rack at the end of the kitchen cabinets. Among the small bottles and tins of thyme, cloves, dill, nutmeg, chili pepper, ginger, marjoram, and cinnamon was a bottle of aspirin.

"I don't take this for headaches, because I like to savor the pain. But I keep aspirin on hand because, once in a while, I like to chew on them for the taste."

"They're vile."

"Just bitter. Bitterness can be as pleasing as sweetness when you learn that every experience, every sensation, is worthwhile."

He returned to the table with the bottle of aspirin. He put it in front of her—and took away her glass of water.

"No, thanks," she said.

"Bitterness has its place."

She ignored the bottle.

"Suit yourself," Vess said, clearing the plates off the table.

Although Chyna needed relief from her various pains, she refused to touch the aspirin. Perhaps irrationally—but nonetheless strongly—she felt that by chewing a few of the tablets, even strictly for the medicinal effect, she would be stepping into the strange rooms of Edgler Vess's madness. This was a threshold that she didn't care to cross for any purpose, even with one foot solidly anchored in the real world.

He hand-washed the breakfast plates, bowls, pans, and utensils. He was efficient and fastidious, using steaming hot water and lots of lemon-scented dishwashing liquid.

Chyna had one more question that could not go unasked, and at last she said, "Why the Templetons? Why choose them of all people? It wasn't random, was it, not just the place you happened to stop in the night?"

"Not just random," he agreed, scrubbing the omelet pan with a plastic scouring pad. "A few weeks back, Paul Templeton was up this way on business, and when—"

"You *knew* him?"

"Not really. He was in town, the county seat, on business like I said, and as he was taking something from his wallet to show me, a set of those little hinged plastic windows fell out, you know, with little wallet-size photographs, and I picked them up for him. One of the pictures was his wife. Another was Laura. She looked so . . . fresh, unspoiled. I said something like 'That's a pretty girl,' and Paul was off and running about her, every inch the proud papa. Told me she was soon going to have her master's degree in psychology, three-point-eight grade average and everything. He told me how he really missed her away at school, even after six years of getting used to it, and how he couldn't wait for the end of the month, because Laura was coming home for a three-day weekend. He didn't mention she was bringing along a friend."

An accident. Photos dropped. A casual exchange, mere idle conversation.

The arbitrariness of it was breathtaking and almost more than Chyna could bear.

Then, as she watched Vess thoroughly wiping off the counters and rinsing the dishpan and scrubbing the sink, Chyna began to feel that what had happened to the Templeton family was worse than merely arbitrary. All this violent death began to seem fated, an inexorable spiral into lasting darkness, as if they had been born and had lived only for Edgler Vess.

It was as if she too had been born and had struggled this far only for the purpose of bringing one moment of sick satisfaction to this soulless predator.

The worst horror of his rampages was not the pain and fear that he inflicted, not the blood, not the mutilated cadavers. The pain and the fear were comparatively brief, considering all the routine pain and anxiety of life. The blood and bodies were merely aftermath. The worst horror was that he stole meaning from the unfinished lives of those people he killed, made *himself* the primary purpose of their existence, robbed them not of time but of fulfillment.

His base sins were envy—of beauty, of happiness—and pride, bending the whole world to his view of creation, and these were the greatest sins of all, the same transgressions over which the devil himself, once an archangel, had stumbled and fallen a long way out of Heaven.

Hand-drying the plates, pans, and flatware in the drainage rack, returning each piece to the proper shelf or drawer, Edgler Vess looked as pink-clean as a freshly bathed baby and as innocent as the stillborn. He smelled of soap, a good bracing aftershave, and lemon-scented dishwashing liquid. But in spite of all this, Chyna found herself superstitiously expecting to detect a whiff of brimstone.

Every life led to a series of quiet epiphanies—or at least to opportunities for epiphanies—and Chyna was washed by a poignant new grief when she thought about this grim aspect of the Templeton family's interrupted journeys. The kindnesses they might have done for others. The love they might have given. The things they might have come to understand in their hearts.

Vess finished the breakfast clean-up and returned to the table. "I have a few things to do upstairs, outside—and then I'll have to sleep four or five hours if I can. I've got to go to work this evening. I need my rest."

She wondered what work he did, but she didn't ask. He might be talking about a job—or about his dogged assault on Ariel's sanity. If the latter, Chyna didn't want to know what was coming.

"When you shift around in the chair, do it easy. Those chains will scrape the wood if you're not careful."

"I'd hate to mar the furniture," she said.

He stared at her for perhaps half a minute and then said, "If you're stupid enough to think you can get free, I'll hear the chains rattling, and I'll have to come back in here to quiet you. If that's necessary, you won't like what I'll do."

She said nothing. She was hopelessly hobbled and chained down. She couldn't possibly escape.

"Even if you somehow get free of the table and chairs, you can't move fast. And attack dogs patrol the grounds."

"I've seen them," she assured him.

"If you weren't chained, they'd still drag you down and kill you before you'd gone ten steps from the door."

She believed him—but she didn't understand why he felt the need to press the point so hard.

"I once turned a young man loose in the yard," Vess said. "He raced straight to the nearest tree and got up and out of harm's way with only one bad bite in his right calf and a nip on the left ankle. He braced himself in the branches and thought he would be safe for a little while, with the dogs circling below and watching him, but I got a twenty-two rifle and went out on the back porch and shot him in the leg from there. He fell out of the tree, and then it was all over in maybe a minute."

Chyna said nothing. There were moments when communicating with this hateful thing seemed no more possible than discussing the merits of Mozart with a shark. This was one of those moments.

"You were invisible to me last night," he said.

She waited.

His gaze traveled over her, and he seemed to be looking for a loose link in one of the chains or a handcuff left open and unnoticed until now. "Like a spirit."

She was not sure that it was ever possible to discern what this thing was thinking—but right now, by God, it seemed to be vaguely uneasy about leaving her alone. She couldn't for the life of her imagine *why*.

"Stay?" he said.

She nodded.

"Good girl."

He went to the door between the kitchen and the living room.

Realizing that they had one more issue to discuss, she said, "Before you go . . ."

He turned to look at her.

"Could you take me to a bathroom?" she asked.

"It's too much trouble to undo the chains just now," he said. "Piss in your pants if you have to. I'm going to clean you up later anyway. And I can buy new chair cushions."

He pushed through the door into the living room and was gone.

Chyna was determined not to endure the humiliation of sitting in her own waste. She had a faint urge to pee, but it wasn't insistent yet. Later she would be in trouble.

How odd—that she could still care about avoiding humiliation or think about the future.

Halfway across the living room, Mr. Vess stops to listen to the woman in the kitchen. He hears no clink of chains. He waits. And still no sound. The silence troubles him.

He's not sure what to make of her. He knows so much about her now—yet she still contains mysteries.

Shackled and in his complete control, surely she cannot be his blown tire. She smells of despair and defeat. In the beaten tone of her voice, he sees the gray of ashes and feels the texture of a coffin blanket. She is as good as dead, and she is resigned to it. Yet . . .

From the kitchen comes the clink of chains. Not loud, not a vigorous assault on her bonds. Just a quiet rattle as she shifts position—perhaps to clasp her thighs tightly together to repress the urge to urinate.

Mr. Vess smiles.

He goes upstairs to his room. From the top shelf at the back of his walk-in closet, he takes down a telephone. In the bedroom, he plugs it into a wall jack and makes two calls, letting people know that he has returned from his three-day vacation and will be back in harness by this evening.

Although he is confident that the Dobermans, in his absence, will never allow anyone to get into the house, Vess keeps only two phones and secretes them in closets when he is not at home. In the extremely unlikely event that an intruder should manage to sprint through the attacking dogs and get into the house alive, he will not be able to call for help.

The danger of cellular phones has been on Mr. Vess's mind in recent days. It's difficult to imagine a would-be burglar carrying a portable phone or using it to call the police for help from a house in which he's become trapped by guard dogs, but stranger things have happened. If Chyna Shepherd had found a cellular phone in the clerk's Honda the previous night, she would not be the one now languishing in shackles.

The technological revolution here at the end of the millennium offers numerous conveniences and great opportunities, but it also has dangerous aspects. Thanks to his expertise with computers, he has cleverly altered his fingerprint files with various agencies and can go without gloves at places like the Templeton house, enjoying the full sensuality of the experience without fear. But one cellular phone in the wrong hands at the wrong time could lead suddenly to the most intense experience of his life—and the final one. He sometimes longs for the simpler age of Jack the Ripper, or the splendid Ed Gein, who inspired *Psycho*, or Richard Speck; he dreams wistfully of the less complicated world of earlier decades and of killing fields that were less trampled, then, by such as he.

By feverishly pursuing high ratings, by hyping every story steeped in blood, by making celebrities out of killers, and by fawning over celebrity killers, the electronic news media happily may have inspired more of his clear-thinking kind. But they have also alarmed the sheep too much. Too many in the herd are walleyed with alertness and quick to run at the first perception of danger.

Still, he manages to have his fun.

After making his calls, Mr. Vess goes out to the motor home. The license plates, the blunt-end screws and the nuts to attach them to the vehicle, and a screwdriver are in a drawer in the kitchenette.

By various means, usually two or three weeks prior to one of his expeditions, Mr. Vess carefully selects his primary targets, like the Templeton family. And though he sometimes brings back a living prize for the cellar room, he nearly always travels well beyond the borders of Oregon to minimize the chances that his two lives—good citizen and homicidal adventurer—will cross at the most inconvenient moment. (Though he didn't employ this method to get Laura Templeton, he has found that clandestine browsing, via computer, through the huge Department of Motor Vehicles' records in neighboring California is an excellent method of locating attractive women. Their driver's license photographs—head shots only—are now on file with the DMV. Provided with each picture are the woman's age, height, and weight—statistics that assist Vess in identifying unacceptable candidates, so he can avoid grandmothers who photograph well and plump women with thin faces. And though some people list post office boxes only, most use their street addresses; thereafter, Mr. Vess needs only a series of good maps.) Upon nearing the end of his drive, when he gets within fifty miles of the target residence, he removes the license plates from the motor home. Later, because he makes a point of being far away from the scene of his games by the time anyone finds the aftermath, he could be tracked down only if someone in the victim's neighborhood happened to see the motor home and, though it looked perfectly innocent, happened to glance at the plates and—that damn blown tire again—happened to have a photographic memory. Therefore, he leaves the tags off his vehicle until he is safely back in Oregon.

If he were stopped by a police officer for speeding or for some other traffic violation, he would express surprise when asked about his missing license plates and would say that, for God knows what reason, they must have been stolen. He is a good actor; he could sell his bafflement. If the chance arose to do so without putting himself in serious jeopardy, he would kill the cop. And if no such opportunity presented itself, he would most likely be able to count on a swift resolution of the problem by calling upon professional courtesy.

Now he squats on his haunches and attaches one of the tags to the frame in the front license-plate niche.

One by one the dogs come to him, sniffing at his hands and his clothes, perhaps disappointed to find only the scents of aftershave and dishwashing soap. They are starved for attention, but they are on duty. None of them lingers long, each returning to its patrol after one pat on the head, a scratch behind the ears, and a word of affection.

"Good dog," Mr. Vess says to each. "Good dog."

When he finishes with the front plate, he stands, stretches, and yawns while surveying his domain.

At ground level, anyway, the wind has died. The air is still and moist. It smells of wet grass, earth, moldering dead leaves, and pine forests.

With the rain finished, the mist is lifting off the foothills and off the lower flanks of the mountains behind the house. He can't see the peaks of the western range yet or even the blanket of snow lingering on the higher slopes. But directly overhead and to the east, where the mist doesn't intervene, the clouds are more gray than thunderhead black, a soft moleskin gray, and they are moving rapidly southeast in front of a high-altitude wind. By midnight, as he promised Ariel, there might be stars and even a moon to light the tall grass in the meadow and to shine in the milky eyes of the dead Laura.

Mr. Vess goes to the back of the motor home to attach the second license plate—and discovers odd tracks on the driveway. As he stands staring at them, a frown pools and deepens on his face.

The driveway is shale, but during a heavy rain, mud washes out from the surrounding yard. Here and there it forms a thin skin atop the stone, not soupy but dark and dense.

In this skin of mud are hoof impressions, perhaps those of a deer. A sizable deer. It has crossed the driveway more than once.

He sees a place where it stood for a while, pawing the ground.

No tire tracks mar the mud, because they were erased by the rain that had been falling when he'd come home. Evidently the deer spoor date from after the storm.

He crouches beside the tracks and puts his fingers to the cold mud. He can feel the hardness and smoothness of the hooves that stamped the marks.

A variety of deer thrive in the nearby foothills and mountains. They rarely venture onto Mr. Vess's property, however, because they are frightened of the Dobermans.

This is the most peculiar thing about the deer tracks: that among them are no paw prints from the dogs.

The Dobermans have been trained to focus on human intruders and, as much as possible, to ignore wildlife. Otherwise, they might be distracted at a moment crucial to their master's safety. They will never attack rabbits or squirrels or possums—or deer—unless severe hunger eventually drives them to it. They won't even give playful chase.

Nevertheless, the dogs will take notice of other animals that cross their path. They indulge their curiosity within the limits of their training.

They would have approached this deer and circled ever closer as it stood here, either paralyzing it with fright or spooking it off. And after it had gone, they would have padded back and forth across the driveway, sniffing its spoor.

But not one paw print is visible among the hoof impressions.

Rubbing his muddy fingertips together, Mr. Vess rises to his full height and slowly turns in a circle, studying the surrounding land. The meadows to the north and the distant piney woods beyond. The driveway leading east to the bald knoll. The yard to the south, more meadows beyond, and woods again. Finally the backyard, past the barn, to the foothills. The deer—if it was a deer—is gone.

Edgler Vess stands motionless. Listening. Watchful. Breathing deeply, seeking scents. Then for a while he inhales through his open mouth, catching what he can upon his tongue. He feels the moist air like the clammy skin of a cadaver against his face. All his senses are open wide, irised to the max, and the freshly washed world drains into them.

Finally he can detect no harm in the morning.

As Vess is putting the license plate on the back of the motor home, Tilsiter pads to him. The dog nuzzles his master's neck.

Vess encourages the Doberman to stay. When he is finished with the plate, he points Tilsiter to the nearby deer spoor.

The dog seems not to see the tracks. Or, seeing them, he does not have any interest.

Vess leads him to the spoor, right in among the prints. Once more he points to them.

Because Tilsiter appears to be confused, Vess places his hand on the back of the dog's head and presses his muzzle into one of the tracks.

The Doberman catches a scent at last, sniffs eagerly, whimpers with excitement—then decides that he doesn't like what he smells. He squirms out from under his master's hand and backs off, looking sheepish.

"What?" says Vess.

The dog licks his chops. He looks away from Vess, surveys the meadows, the lane, the yard. He glances at Vess again, but then he trots off to the south, returning to patrol.

The trees still dripping. The mists rising. The spent clouds scudding fast toward the southeast.

Mr. Vess decides to kill Chyna Shepherd immediately.

He will haul her into the yard, make her lie facedown on the grass, and put a couple of bullets in the back of her skull. He has to go to work this evening, and before that he has to get some sleep, so he won't have time to enjoy a slow kill.

Later, when he gets home, he can bury her in the meadow with the four dogs watching, insects singing and feeding on one another in the tall grass, and Ariel forced to kiss each of the corpses before it goes forever into the ground—all this in moonlight if there is any.

Quickly now, finish her and sleep.

As he hurries toward the house, he realizes that the screwdriver is still in his hand, which might be more interesting than using the pistol, yet just as quick.

Up the flagstone steps, onto the front porch, where the finger of the Seattle attorney hangs silent among the seashells in the cool windless air.

He doesn't bother to wipe his feet, a rare breach of compulsive procedure.

The ratcheting hinge is matched by the sound of his own ragged breathing as he opens the door and steps into the house. When he closes the door, he is startled to hear his thudding heartbeats chasing one another.

He is never afraid, never. With this woman, however, he has been *unsettled* more than once.

A few steps into the room, he halts, getting a grip on himself. Now that he is inside again, he doesn't understand why killing her seemed to be such an urgent priority.

Intuition.

But never has his intuition delivered such a clamorous message that has left him this conflicted. The woman is special, and he so badly wants to use her in special ways. Merely pumping two shots into the back of her head or sticking the screwdriver into her a few times would be such a waste of her potential.

He is never afraid. Never.

Even being unsettled like this is a challenge to his dearest image of himself. The poet Sylvia Plath, whose work leaves Mr. Vess uncharacteristically ambivalent, once said that the world was ruled by panic, "panic with a dog-face, devil-face, hag-face, whore-face, panic in capital letters with no face at all—the same Johnny Panic, awake or asleep." But Johnny Panic does not rule Edgler Vess and never will, because Mr. Vess has no illusions about the nature of existence, no doubts about his purpose, and no moments of his life that ever require reinterpretation when he has the time for quiet reflection.

Sensation.

Intensity.

He cannot live with intensity if he is afraid, because Johnny Panic inhibits spontaneity and experimentation. Therefore, he will not allow this woman of mysteries to spook him.

As both his breathing and his heartbeat subside to normal rates, he turns the rubberized handle of the screwdriver around and around in his hand, staring at the short blunt blade at the end of the long steel shank.

The moment Vess entered the kitchen, before he spoke, Chyna sensed he had changed from the man that she had known thus far. He was in a different mood from any that had previously possessed him, although the precise difference was so subtle that she was not able to define it.

He approached the table as if to sit down, then stopped short of his chair. Frowning and silent, he stared at her.

In his right hand was a screwdriver. Ceaselessly he rolled the handle through his fingers, as if tightening an imaginary screw.

On the floor behind him were crumbling chunks of mud. He had come inside with dirty shoes.

She knew that she must not speak first. They were at a strange juncture where words might not mean what they had meant before, where the most innocent statement might be an incitement to violence.

A short while ago, she had half preferred to be killed quickly, and she had tried to trigger one of his homicidal impulses. She had also considered ways that, although shackled, she might be able to commit suicide. Now she held her tongue to avoid inadvertently enraging him.

Evidently, even in her desolation, she continued to harbor a small but stubborn hope that was camouflaged in the grayness where she could not see it. A stupid denial. A pathetic longing for one more chance. Hope, which had always seemed ennobling to her, now seemed as dehumanizing as feverish greed, as squalid as lust, just an animal hunger for more life at any cost.

She was in a deep, bleak place.

Finally Vess said, "Last night."

She waited.

"In the redwoods."

"Yes?"

"Did you see anything?" he asked.

"See what?"

"Anything odd?"

"No."

"You must have."

She shook her head.

"The elk," he said.

"Oh. Yes, the elk."

"A herd of them."

"Yes."

"You didn't think they were peculiar?"

"Coastal elk. They thrive in that area."

"These seemed almost tame."

"Maybe because tourists drive through there all the time."

Slowly turning and turning the screwdriver, he considered her explanation. "Maybe."

Chyna saw that the fingers of his right hand were covered with a film of dry mud.

He said, "I can smell the musk of them now, the texture of their eyes, hear the greenness of the ferns swaying around them, and it's a cold dark oil in my blood."

No reply was possible, and she didn't try to make one.

Vess lowered his gaze from Chyna's eyes to the turning point of the screwdriver—and then to his shoes. He looked over his shoulder and saw the mud on the floor.

"This won't do," he said.

He put the screwdriver on a nearby counter.

He took off his shoes and carried them into the laundry room, where he left them to be cleaned later.

He returned in his bare feet and, using paper towels and a bottle of Windex, cleaned every crumb of mud from the tiles. In the living room, he used a vacuum cleaner to sweep the mud out of the carpet.

These domestic chores occupied him for almost fifteen minutes, and by the time he finished, he was no longer in the mood that had possessed him when he'd entered the kitchen. Housework seemed to scrub away his blues.

"I'm going to go upstairs and sleep now," he said. "You'll be quiet and not rattle your chains much."

She said nothing.

"You'll be quiet, or I'll come down and shove five feet of the chain up your ass."

She nodded.

"Good girl."

He left the room.

The difference between Vess's usual demeanor and his recent mood no longer eluded Chyna. For a few minutes, he had lacked his usual self-confidence. Now he had it back.

Mr. Vess always sleeps in the nude to facilitate his dreams.

In slumberland, all the people whom he encounters are naked, whether they are being torn asunder beneath him in glorious wetness or are running in a pack with him through high shadowed places and down into moonlight. There is a heat in his dreams that not only makes clothes superfluous but burns from him the very concept of clothes, so going naked is more natural in the dreamworld than in the real one.

He never suffers from nightmares. This is because, in his daily life, he confronts the sources of his tensions and deals with them. He is never dragged down by guilt. He is not judgmental of others and is never affected by what they think of him. He knows that if something he wishes to do *feels* right, then it *is* right. He always looks out for number one, because to be a successful human being, he must first like himself. Consequently, he always goes to his bed with a clear mind and an untroubled heart.

Now, within seconds of resting his head on his pillow, Mr. Vess is asleep. From time to time his legs cycle beneath the covers, as if he is chasing something.

Once, in his sleep, he says, "Father," almost reverentially, and the word hangs like a bubble on the air—which is odd, because when Edgler Vess was nine years old, he burned his father to death.

Chains rattling, Chyna leaned down and picked up the spare cushion from the floor beside her chair. She put it on the table, slumped forward, and rested her head on it.

According to the kitchen clock, it was a quarter till twelve. She had been awake well over twenty-four hours, except when she had dozed in the motor home and when she had sat here unconscious after Vess clubbed her.

Although exhausted, and numb with despair, she did not expect to be able to sleep. But she hoped that by keeping her eyes closed and letting her thoughts drift to more pleasant times, she might be able to take her mind off her mild but gradually increasing urge to pee and off the pain in her neck and trigger finger.

She was walking in a wind full of torn red blossoms, curiously unafraid of the darkness and of the lightning that sometimes split it, when she was awakened not by thunder but by the sound of scissors clipping through paper.

She lifted her head from the pillow and sat up straight. The fluorescent light stung her eyes.

Edgler Vess was standing at the sink, cutting open a large bag of potato chips.

He said, "Ah, you're awake, you sleepyhead."

Chyna looked at the clock. Twenty minutes till five.

He said, "I thought it might take a brass band to bring you around."

She had been asleep almost five hours. Her eyes were grainy. Her mouth was sour. She could smell her body odor, and she felt greasy.

She had not wet herself in her sleep, and she was briefly lifted by an absurd sense of triumph that she had not yet been reduced to that lower level of humiliation. Then she realized how pathetic she was, priding herself on her continence, and her internal grayness darkened by a degree or two.

Vess was wearing black boots, khaki slacks, a black belt, and a white T-shirt.

His arms were muscular, enormous. She would never be able to struggle successfully against those arms.

He brought a plate to the table. He had made a sandwich for her. "Ham and cheese with mustard."

A ruffle of lettuce showed at the edges of the bread. He had placed two dill pickle spears beside the sandwich.

As Vess put the bag of potato chips on the table, Chyna said, "I don't want it."

"You have to eat," he said.

She looked out the window at the deep yard in late-afternoon light.

"If you don't eat," he said, "I'll eventually have to force-feed you." He picked up the bottle of aspirin and shook it to get her attention. "Tasty?"

"I didn't take any," she said.

"Ah, then you're learning to enjoy your pain."

He seemed to win either way.

He took away the aspirin and returned with a glass of water. Smiling, he said, "You've got to keep those kidneys functioning or they'll atrophy."

As Vess cleaned the counter where he'd made the sandwich, Chyna said, "Were you abused as a child?" and hated herself for asking the question, for *still* trying to understand.

Vess laughed and shook his head. "This isn't a textbook, Chyna. This is real life."

"Were you?"

"No. My father was a Chicago accountant. My mom sold women's wear at a department store. They loved me. Bought me too many toys, more than I could use, especially since I preferred playing with . . . other things."

"Animals," she said.

"That's right."

"And before animals—insects or very little things like goldfish or turtles."

"Is that in your textbooks?"

"It's the earliest and worst sign. Torturing animals."

He shrugged. "It was fun . . . watching the stupid thing crawl on fire inside its shell. Really, Chyna, you have to learn to get beyond these petty value judgments."

She closed her eyes, hoping he would go to work.

"Anyway, my folks loved me, all caught up in *that* delusion. When I was nine, I set a fire. Lighter fluid in their bed while they were sleeping, then a cigarette."

"My God."

"There you go again."

"Why?"

He mocked: "Why not?"

"Jesus."

"Want the second-best answer?"

"Yes," she said.

"Then look at me when I talk to you."

She opened her eyes.

His gaze cleaved her. "I set them on fire because I thought maybe they were beginning to catch on."

"To what?"

"To the fact that I was something special."

"They caught you with the turtle," she guessed.

"No. A neighbor's kitten. We lived in a nice suburb. There were so many pets in the neighborhood. Anyway, when they caught me, there was talk of doctors. Even at nine, I knew I couldn't allow that. Doctors might be harder to fool. So we had a little fire."

"And nothing was done to you?"

Finished with his cleaning, he sat down at the table. "No one suspected. Dad was smoking in bed, the firemen said. It happens all the time. The whole house went. I barely got out alive, and Mommy was screaming, and I couldn't get to her, couldn't help my mommy, and I was *so* scared." He winked at her. "After that, I went to live with my grandma. She was an annoying old biddy, full of rules, regulations, standards of conduct, manners, and courtesies I had to learn. But she couldn't keep a clean house. Her bathroom was just disgusting. She led me into my second and last mistake. I killed her while she was standing in the kitchen, just like this, preparing dinner. It was an impulsive thing, a knife twice in each kidney."

"How old?"

Slyly playing with her, he said, "Grandma or me?"

"You."

"Eleven. Too young to be put on trial. Too young for anyone to *really* believe that I knew what I was doing."

"They had to do *something* to you."

"Fourteen months in a caring facility. Lots of therapy, lots of counseling, lots and lots of attention and hugs. Because, you see, I must have offed poor Grandma because of my unexpressed grief over the accidental deaths of my parents in that awful, awful fire. One day I realized what they were trying to tell me, and I just broke down and cried and cried. Oh, Chyna, how I cried, and wallowed in remorse for poor Grandma. The therapists and social workers were so appreciative of the wallowing."

"Where did you go from the facility?"

"I was adopted."

Speechless, she stared at him.

"I know what you're thinking," he said. "Not many twelve-year-old orphans get adopted. People are usually looking for infants to mold in their own image. But I was such a *beautiful* boy, Chyna, an almost ethereally beautiful boy. Can you believe that?"

"Yes."

"People want beautiful children. Beautiful children with nice smiles. I was sweet tempered and charming. By then I'd learned to hide better among all you hypocrites. I'd never again be caught with a bloody kitten or a dead grandmother."

"But who . . . who would adopt you after what you did?"

"What I did was expunged from my record, of course. I was just the littlest boy, after all. Chyna, you wouldn't expect my whole life to be ruined just because of one mistake? Psychiatrists and social workers were the grease in my wheels, and I will always be beholden to them for their sweet, earnest desire to believe."

"Your adoptive parents didn't know?"

"They knew that I'd been traumatized by the death of my parents in a fire, that the trauma had led to counseling, and that I needed to be watched for signs of depression. They wanted so badly to make my life better, to prevent depression from ever touching me again."

"What happened to them?"

"We lived there in Chicago two years, and then we moved here to Oregon. I let them live for quite a while, and I let them pretend to love me. Why not? They enjoyed their delusions so much. But then, after I graduated from college, I was twenty years old and needed more money than I had, so there had to be another dreadful accident, another fire in the night. But it was eleven long years since the fire that took my real mom and dad, and half a continent away. No social workers had seen me in years, and there were no files about my horrible mistake with Grandma, so no connections were ever made."

They sat in silence.

After a while he tapped the plate in front of her. "Eat, eat," he cajoled. "I'll be eating at a diner myself. Sorry I can't keep you company."

"I believe you," she said.

"What?"

"That you were never abused."

"Though that runs against everything you've been taught. Good girl, Chyna. You know the truth when you hear it. Maybe there's hope for you yet."

"There's no understanding you," she said, though she was talking more to herself than to him.

"Of course there is. I'm just in touch with my reptilian nature, Chyna. It's in all of us. We all evolved from that slimy, legged fish that first crawled out of the sea. The reptile consciousness . . . it's still in all of us, but most of you struggle so hard to hide it from yourselves, to convince yourselves that you're something cleaner and better than what you really are. The irony is, if you'd just for once acknowledge your reptile nature, you'd find the freedom and the happiness that you're all so frantic to achieve and never do."

He tapped the plate again, and then the glass of water. He got up and tucked his chair under the table.

"That conversation wasn't quite as you expected, was it, Chyna?"

"No."

"You were expecting me to equivocate, to whine on about being a victim, to indulge in elaborately structured self-delusions, to spit up some tale of warping incest. You wanted to believe your clever probing might expose a secret religious fanaticism, bring revelations that I hear godly voices in my head. You didn't expect it to be this straightforward. This *honest.*"

He went to the door between the kitchen and the living room, and then turned to look at her. "I'm not unique, Chyna. The world is filled with the likes of me—most are just less free. You know where I think a lot of my type wind up?"

In spite of herself, she asked, "Where?"

"In politics. Imagine having the power to start wars, Chyna. How gratifying that would be. Of course, in public life, one would generally have to forgo the pleasure of getting right down in the wet of it, hands dirty with all the wonderful fluids. One would have to be satisfied with the thrill of sending thousands to their deaths, remote destruction. But I believe I could adapt to that. And there would always be photos from the war zone, reports, all as graphic as one requested. *And never a danger of apprehension.* More amazing—they build monuments to you. You can bomb a small country into oblivion, and dinners are given in your honor. You can kill thirty-four children in a religious community, crush them with tanks, burn them alive, claim they were dangerous cultists—then sit back to the sound of applause. Such power. Intensity."

He glanced at the clock.

A few minutes past five.

He said, "I'll finish dressing and be gone. Back as soon after midnight as I can be." He shook his head as if saddened by the sight of her. "Untouched and alive. What kind of existence is that, Chyna? Not one worth having. Get in touch with your reptile consciousness. Embrace the cold and the dark. That's what we are."

He left her in chains as twilight entered the world and the light withdrew.

EIGHT

Mr. Vess steps onto the porch, locks the front door, and then whistles for the dogs.

The day is growing cooler as it wanes, and the air is bracing. He zips up his jacket.

From different points of the compass, the four Dobermans sprint out of the twilight and race to the porch. As they scamper to Vess and jostle one another to be the closest to him, their big paws thump on the boards in a fandango of canine delight.

He kneels among them, generously doling out affection once more.

Oddly like people, these Dobermans appear to be unable to detect the insincerity of

Mr. Vess's love. They are only tools to him, not treasured pets, and the attention he gives them is like the 3-In-One oil with which he occasionally lubricates his power drill, hand-held belt sander, and chain saw. In the movies, it is always a dog that senses the werewolf potential in the moon-fearing man and greets him with a growl, always a dog that shies away from the character who is secretly harboring the alien parasite in his body. But movies are not life.

The dogs are no doubt deceiving him just as he deceives them. Their love is nothing but respect—or sublimated fear of him.

He stands, and the dogs look up expectantly. Earlier, they had been summoned from their kennel by the buzzer; therefore, they are now merely on an apprehend-and-detain status.

"Nietzsche," he says.

As one, the four Dobermans twitch and then become rigid. Their ears first prick at the command word but then flatten.

Their black eyes shine in the dusk.

Abruptly they depart the porch, scattering across the property, having been elevated to attack status.

Putting on his hat, Mr. Vess walks toward the barn, where he keeps his car.

He leaves the motor home parked beside the house. Later, to minimize the distance that the two bodies will have to be carried, he will back the vehicle along the lane, closer to the meadow of unmarked graves.

As he walks, Mr. Vess draws slow, deep breaths and clears his mind, preparing himself for reentry into the workaday world.

He enjoys the charade of his second life, passing for one of the repressed and deluded who, in uncountable multitudes, rule the earth with lies, who pass their lives in denial, anxiety, and hypocrisy. He is like a fox in a pen of mentally deficient chickens that are unable to distinguish between a predator and one of their own, and this is a fine game for a fox with a sense of humor.

Every day, all day long, Vess weighs other people with his eyes, furtively tests their firmness with a friendly touch, breathes the enticing scents of their flesh, selecting among them as if choosing packaged poultry at a market. He does not often kill those whom he meets in his public persona—only if he is absolutely certain that he can get away with it and if the particular chicken promises to be tasty.

If Chyna Shepherd hadn't disturbed his usual routine, Vess would have spent more time reacclimating himself to his role as an ordinary guy. He might have watched a game show on television, read a couple of chapters in a romance novel by Robert James Waller, and skimmed an issue of *People* to remind himself of those things that the desperate ruck of humanity uses to anesthetize itself against the awareness of its true animal nature and the inevitability of death. He might have stood before a mirror for a while, practicing his smile, studying his eyes.

Nevertheless, by the time he reaches the silvered-cedar barn, he is confident that he will slide back into his second life without a ripple and that all those who look into his pond will be comforted to see their own faces reflected. Most people have expended so much effort and time in the denial of their predatory nature that they cannot easily recognize it in others.

He opens the man-size door beside the larger roll-up, pauses, and glances toward the back of the house. He left the woman in the dark, so he can't even vaguely discern her form through the distant window.

The sunless, somber twilight is still bright enough, however, for Ms. Shepherd, the eminent psychologist, to have seen him as he walked to the barn. She could be watching now.

Mr. Vess wonders what she thinks of him in this surprising new guise. She must be shocked. More illusions shattered. Seeing him on his way to his second life, realizing that indeed he passes for a stand-up citizen, she must be plunged into a despair deeper than any she has yet known.

He has such a way with women.

After Vess turned off the lights and left the kitchen, Chyna leaned back in the pine captain's chair, away from the table, because the smell of the ham sandwich sickened her. It wasn't spoiled; it smelled like a ham sandwich ought to smell. But the very idea of food made her gag.

About twenty-one hours had passed since she'd finished her most recent full meal, dinner at the Templeton house. The few bites of cheese omelet that she'd had at breakfast weren't enough to sustain her, especially considering all of the physical activity of the previous night; she should have been famished.

Eating was an admission of hope, however, and she didn't want to hope any more. She had spent her life hoping, a fool intoxicated with optimistic expectations. But every hope proved to be as empty as a bubble. Every dream was glass waiting to be shattered.

Until last night, she had thought that she'd climbed far out of childhood misery, up a greased ladder toward phenomenal heights of understanding, and she had been quietly proud of herself and of her accomplishments. Now it seemed that she had not been climbing after all, that her ascent had been an illusion, and that for years her feet had been slipping over the same two well-lubricated rungs, as if she'd been on one of those exercise machines, a StairMaster, expending enormous energy—but not one inch higher when she stopped than she had been when she'd started. The long years of waitressing, the sore legs and the stubborn pain in the small of her back from being on her feet for hours, taking the toughest classes she could find at the University of California, studying late into the night after she returned home from work, the countless sacrifices, the loneliness, the ceaseless striving, striving—all of that had led *here*, to this dismal place, to these chains, into this deepening twilight.

She had hoped one day to understand her mother, to find good reason to forgive. She had even, God help her, secretly hoped that they might reach a truce. They could never have a healthy mother-daughter relationship, and they could never be friends; but it had seemed possible, at least, that she and Anne might one day have lunch together at any café with a view of the sea, alfresco on the patio under a huge umbrella, where they would never speak of the past but would make pleasant small talk about movies, the weather, the way the seagulls wheeled across the sapphire sky, perhaps with no healing affection but without any hatred between them. Now she knew that even if by some miracle she escaped untouched and alive from this imprisonment, she would never reach that dreamed-of degree of understanding; rapprochement between her and her mother could not be achieved.

Human cruelty and treachery surpassed all understanding. There were no answers. Only excuses.

Chyna felt lost. She was in a stranger place than Edgler Vess's kitchen and in a more forbidding darkness.

In all her years, she had never before felt lost, not truly lost. Frightened, yes. Sometimes confused and bleak. But always she had held a map in her mind, with a route marked if only vaguely, and she had believed that in her heart was a compass that couldn't fail her. She had been in the wrong place many times, but she'd always been sure that there was a way out—just as in any fun-house mirror maze there is always a safe path through the infinite images of oneself, through more fearful reflections, and through all of the enigmatic silver shadows.

No map this time.

No compass.

Life itself was the ultimate fun-house mirror maze, and she was lost in its nautilus chambers, with no one to turn to for comfort, no hand to hold.

Finally admitting that she had been essentially motherless since birth and always would be motherless, and with her only close friend lying dead in Edgler Vess's motor home, Chyna wished that she knew her father's name, that she had at least once seen his face. Her mother's maiden name was Shepherd; she had never been married. "Be glad you're illegitimate, baby," Anne had said, "because that means you're *free*. Little bastard children don't have as many relatives clinging like psychic leeches and sucking away their souls." Over the years, when Chyna had asked about her father, Anne had said only that he was dead, and she had been able to say it dry-eyed, even lightheartedly. She wouldn't provide details of his appearance, discuss what work he'd done, reveal where he'd lived, or acknowledge that he'd had a name. "By the time I was pregnant with you," Anne once said, "I wasn't seeing him any more. He was history. I never told him about you. He never knew."

Chyna liked to daydream about him sometimes: She imagined that her mother had lied about this, as about so many things, and that her dad was alive. He would be a lot like Gregory Peck in *To Kill a Mockingbird*, a big man with gentle eyes, soft-spoken, kind, quietly humorous, with a keen sense of justice, certain of who he was and of what he believed. He would be a man who was admired and respected by other people but who thought himself no more special than anyone else. He would love her.

If she had known his name, either first or last, she would have spoken it now, aloud. The mere sound of her father's name would have comforted her.

She was crying. Through the many hours since she had come under Vess's thrall, she had felt tears welling more than once, and she had repressed them. But she couldn't dam this hot flood. She despised herself for crying—but only briefly. These bitter tears were a welcome admission that there was no hope for her. They washed her free of hope, and that was what she wanted now, because hope led only to disappointment and pain. All her troubled life, since at least her eighth birthday, she had refused to weep freely, really let loose with tears. Being tough and dry-eyed was the only way to get respect from those people who, on seeing the smallest weakness in another, got a fearful muddy light in their eyes and closed in like jackals around a gazelle with a broken leg. But withholding tears wouldn't fend off the jackal who had promised to be back after midnight, and a lifetime of grief and hurt burst from her. Great wet sobs shook Chyna so hard that her chest began to ache worse than her neck or her sprained finger. Her throat soon felt hot and raw. She sagged in her clinking chains, in her imprisoning chair, face clenched and streaming and hot, stomach clenched and cold, the taste of salt in her mouth, gasping, groaning in despair, choking on the smothering awareness of her terrible solitude. She shuddered uncontrollably, and her hands spasmed into frail fists but then opened and grasped at the air around her head as if her anguish were a cowl that might be torn off and cast aside. Profoundly alone, unloved and lost, she spiraled down into a mental mirror maze without even her father's name for comfort.

After a while, an engine roared. She heard the brassy toot of a horn: two short blasts and then two more.

Chyna lifted her head, looked through the nearby window, and saw the headlights of a car leaving the barn. Her vision was blurred by tears. She couldn't see the car itself as it sped past the house in the gray dusk, but it must be driven by Vess, of course. Then it was gone.

The jaunty toot of the horn mocked her, but that mockery wasn't enough to rekindle her anger.

She stared out at the gloaming and didn't care that it might be the last twilight she ever saw. She cared only that she had spent too much of her twenty-six years alone, with no one at her side to share the sunsets, the starry skies, the turbulent beauty of storm clouds. She wished that she had reached out to people more, instead of retreating inward, wished that she had not made her heart into a sheltering closet. Now, when nothing mattered any more, when the insight couldn't do her any damn good at all, she realized that there was less hope of survival alone than with others. She'd been acutely aware that terror, betrayal, and cruelty had a human face, but she had not sufficiently appreciated that courage, kindness, and love had a human face as well. Hope wasn't a cottage industry; it was neither a product that she could manufacture like needlepoint samplers nor a substance she could secrete, in her cautious solitude, like a maple tree producing the essence of syrup. Hope was to be found in other people, by reaching out, by taking risks, by opening her fortress heart.

This insight seemed so obvious, the simplest of wisdom, yet she had not been able to arrive at it until *in extremis.*

And the chance had long ago passed to act upon it. She would die as she had lived—alone. This further realization might have wrung greater rivers of tears from her but, instead, drove her into a bleaker place than she'd been before, an interior garden of stone and ashes.

Then, as she was still gazing out the window, she saw something moving in the last of the dusk. Though it was blurred by her tears, she could see that it was too large to be a Doberman.

But if Vess had gone, how could it be a man?

Chyna blotted her eyes on the sleeve of her sweater, and she blinked until the mysterious shape resolved out of tears and twilight shadows. It was an elk. A female, without antlers.

It ambled across the backyard, from the forested foothills to the west, pausing twice to tear up a mouthful of the succulent grass. As Chyna knew from her months on the ranch in Mendocino County many years ago, these animals were highly sociable and always traveled in herds, but this one seemed to be alone.

The Dobermans should have been after this intruder, barking and snarling and excited by the prospect of blood. Surely the dogs would be able to smell it even from the farthest corners of the property. Yet no Dobermans were in sight.

Likewise, the elk should have caught the scent of the dogs and galloped at once for safety, wild-eyed and snorting. Nature had made its kind prey to mountain lions and wolves and packs of coyotes; as dinner-on-the-hoof to so many predators, elk were always watchful and cautious.

But this specimen seemed utterly unconcerned that dogs were in the immediate neighborhood. Except for the two brief pauses to graze on the lush grass, it came directly to the back porch, with no sign of skittishness.

Although Chyna was not a wildlife expert, this seemed to her to be a *coastal* elk, the same type she had encountered in the grove of redwoods. Its coat was gray-brown, and it had the familiar white and black markings on the body and face.

Yet she was sure that this place was too far from the sea to be a suitable home for coastal elk or to provide the ideal vegetation for their diet. When she'd gotten out of the motor home, she'd had an impression of mountains all around. Now the rain had stopped and the mist had lifted; in the west, where the dregs of daylight swiftly drained away, the black silhouettes of high peaks pressed against tattered clouds and electric-purple sky. With a mountain range of such formidable size between here and the Pacific Ocean, coastal elk could not have found their way so far inland, for they were basically a lowland breed partial to plains and gentle hills. This must be a different type of elk—although with coloration strikingly similar to that of the animals she had seen the previous night.

The imposing creature stood outside the wooden balustrade of the shallow porch, no more than eight feet away, staring directly at the window. At Chyna.

She found it difficult to believe that the elk could see her. With the lights off, the kitchen was currently darker than the dusk in which the animal stood. From its perspective, the interior of the house should have been unrelievedly black.

Yet she couldn't deny that its eyes met hers. Large dark eyes, shining softly.

She remembered Vess's sudden return to the kitchen this morning. He'd been inexplicably tense, ceaselessly turning the screwdriver in his hand, an odd light in his eyes. And he'd been full of questions about the elk in the redwood grove.

Chyna didn't know why the elk mattered to Vess any more than she could imagine why this one stood here, now, unchallenged by the dogs, studying her intently through the window. She didn't puzzle long over this mystery. She was in a mood to accept, to experience, to admit that understanding was not always achievable.

As the deep-purple sky turned to indigo and then to India ink, the eyes of the elk grew gradually more luminous. They were not red like the eyes of some animals at night, but golden.

Pale plumes of breath streamed rhythmically from its wet black nostrils.

Without breaking eye contact with the animal, Chyna pressed the insides of her wrists together as best she could with the handcuffs intervening. The steel chains rattled: all the lengths between her and the chair on which she sat, between her and the table, between her and the past.

She remembered her solemn pledge, earlier in the day, to kill herself rather than be a witness to the complete mental destruction of the young girl in the cellar. She had believed that she would be able to find the courage to bite open the veins in her wrists and bleed to death. The pain would be sharp but relatively brief . . . and then she would fade sleepily from this blackness into another, which would be eternal.

She had stopped crying. Her eyes were dry.

Her heartbeat was surprisingly slow, like that of a sleeper in the dreamless rest provided by a powerful sedative.

She raised her hands in front of her face, bending them backward as severely as possible and spreading her fingers wide so she could still gaze into the eyes of the elk.

She brought her mouth to the place on her left wrist where she would have to bite. Her breath was warm on her cool skin.

The light was entirely gone from the day. The mountains and the heavens were like one great black looming swell on a night sea, a drowning weight coming down.

The elk's heart-shaped face was barely visible from a distance of only eight feet. Its eyes, however, shone.

Chyna put her lips against her left wrist. In the kiss, she felt her dangerously steady pulse.

Through the gloom, she and the sentinel elk watched each other, and she didn't know whether this creature had mesmerized her or she had mesmerized it.

Then she pressed her lips to her right wrist. The same coolness of skin, the same ponderous pulse.

She parted her lips and used her teeth to pinch a thickness of flesh. There seemed to be enough tissue gathered between her incisors to make a mortal tear. Certainly she would be successful if she bit a second time, a third.

On the brink of the bite, she understood that it required no courage whatsoever. Precisely the opposite was true. *Not* biting was an act of valor.

But she didn't care about valor, didn't give a rat's ass about courage. Or about anything. All she cared about was putting an end to the loneliness, the pain, the achingly empty sense of futility.

And the girl. Ariel. Down in the hateful silent dark.

For a while she remained poised for the fatal nip.

Between its solemn measured beats, her heart was filled with the stillness of deep water.

Then, without being aware of releasing the pinch of flesh from between her teeth, Chyna realized that her lips were pressed to her unbitten wrist again. She could feel her slow pulse in this kiss of life.

The elk was gone.

Gone.

Chyna was surprised to see only darkness where the creature had stood. She didn't believe that she had closed her eyes or even blinked. Yet she must have been in a blinding trance, because the stately elk had vanished into the night as mysteriously as a stage magician's assistant dematerializes beneath an artfully draped black shroud.

Suddenly her heart began to pound hard and fast.

"No," she whispered in the dark kitchen, and the word was both a promise and a prayer.

Her heart like a wheel—spinning, racing—drove her out of that internal grayness in which she had been lost, out of that bleakness into a brighter landscape.

"No." There was defiance in her voice this time, and she did not whisper. "No."

She shook her chains as if she were a spirited horse trying to throw off its traces.

"No, no, no. Shit, no." Her protests were loud enough for her voice to echo off the hard surface of the refrigerator, the glass in the oven door, the ceramic-tile counters.

She tried to pull away from the table to stand up. But a loop of chain secured her chair to the barrel that supported the tabletop, limiting its movement.

If she dug her heels into the vinyl-tile floor and attempted to scoot backward, she would probably not be able to move at all. At best she would only drag the heavy table with her inch by inch. And in a lifetime of trying, she would not be able to put enough tension on the chain to snap it.

She was still adamant in her rejection of surrender—"No, damn it, no way, *no*"—pressing the words through clenched teeth.

She reached forward, pulling taut the chain that led around her back from the left handcuff to the right. It was wound between the spindles of the rail-back chair, behind the tie-on pad. She strained, hoping to hear the crack of dry wood, jerked hard, harder, and sharp pain sewed a hot seam in her neck; the agony of the clubbing was renewed in her neck and in the right side of her face, but she would not let pain stop her. She jerked harder than ever, scarring the nice furniture for damn sure, and again—*pull, pull*—firmly holding the chair down with her body while simultaneously half lifting it off the floor as she yanked furiously at the back rails, and yanked again, until her biceps quivered. *Pull.* As she grunted with effort and frustration, needles of pain stitched down the back of her neck, across both shoulders, and into her arms. *Pull!* Putting everything she had into the effort, straining longer than before, clenching her teeth so hard that tics developed in her jaw muscles, she pulled once more until she felt the arteries throbbing in her temples and saw red and silver pinwheels of light spinning behind her eyelids. But she wasn't rewarded with any breaking sounds. The chair was solid, the spindles were thick, and every joint was well made.

Her heart *boomed*, partly because of her struggles but largely because she was brimming with an exhilarating sense of liberation. Which was crazy, crazy, because she was still shackled, no closer to breaking her bonds than she had been at any moment since she'd awakened in this chair. Yet she felt as if she had already escaped and was only waiting for reality to catch up with the freedom that she had *willed* for herself.

She sat gasping, thinking.

Sweat beaded her brow.

Forget the chair for now. To get loose from it, she would have to be able to stand and move. She couldn't deal with the chair until she was free of the table.

She was unable to reach down far enough to unscrew the carabiner that joined the shorter chain between her ankles to the longer chain that entwined the chair and the table. Otherwise, she might easily have freed her legs from both pieces of furniture.

If she could overturn the table, the loop of chain that wrapped the supporting pedestal and connected with her leg irons would then slide free as the bottom of that barrel tipped up and off the floor. Wouldn't it? Sitting in the dark, she couldn't quite visualize the mechanics of what she was proposing, but she thought that turning the table on its side would work.

Unfortunately, the chair across from hers, the one in which Vess had sat, was an obstruction that would most likely prevent the table from tipping over. She had to get rid of it, clear the way. Shackled as she was, however, and with the barrel pedestal intervening, she couldn't extend her legs far enough to kick at the other chair and knock it aside. Hobbled and tethered, she was also unable to stand and reach across the big round table and simply push the obstruction out of the way.

Finally she tried scooting backward in her chair, hoping to drag the table with her, away from Vess's chair. The chain encircling the pedestal drew taut. As she strained backward, digging her heels into the floor, it seemed that the piece was too heavy to be dragged, and she wondered if the barrel was filled with a bag of sand to keep the table from wobbling. But then it creaked and stuttered a few inches across the vinyl tiles, rattling the sandwich plate and the glass of water that stood on it.

This was harder work than she had anticipated. She felt as though she were on one of those television shows devoted to stunts and stupid physical challenges, pulling a railroad car. A loaded railroad car. Nevertheless, the table moved grudgingly. In a couple of minutes, after pausing twice to get her breath, she stopped because she was concerned that she might back against the wall between the kitchen and the laundry room; she needed to leave herself some maneuvering space. Although it was difficult to estimate distance in the dark, she believed that she had dragged the table about three feet, far enough to be clear of Vess's chair.

Trying to favor her sprained finger, she placed her cuffed hands under the table and lifted. It weighed considerably more than she did—a two-inch pine top, the thick staves in the supporting barrel, the black iron hoops around the staves, perhaps that bag of sand—and she couldn't get much leverage while she was forced to remain seated. The bottom of the barrel tipped up an inch, then two inches. The water glass toppled, spilling its contents, rolled away from her, dropped off the table, and shattered on the floor. All the noise made it seem as if her plan was working—she hissed, "Yes!"—but then because she had underestimated the weight and the effort required to move it, she had to relent, and the barrel slammed down.

Chyna flexed her muscles, took a deep breath, and immediately returned to the task. This time she planted her feet as far apart as her shackles would allow. On the underside of the table, she flattened her upturned palms against the pine, thumbs hooked toward herself over the smooth bull-nose edge. She tensed her legs as well as her arms, and when she shoved up on the table, she pushed with her legs too, getting to her feet an inch at a time, one hard-won inch for each inch that the table tipped up and backward. She did not have enough slack in the various tethering chains to be able to get all the way—or halfway—erect, so she rose haltingly in a stiff and awkward crouch, cramped under the weight of the table. She put enormous strain on her knees and thighs, wheezing, shuddering with the effort, but she persevered because each precious inch that she was able to gain improved her leverage; she was using her entire body to lift, lift, lift.

The sandwich plate and the bag of potato chips slid off the table. China cracked and chips scattered across the floor with a sound unnervingly like scurrying rodents.

The pain in her neck was excruciating, and someone seemed to be twisting a corkscrew into her right clavicle. But pain couldn't stop her. It *motivated*. The greater her pain, the more she identified with Laura and the whole Templeton family, with the young man hanging in the motor-home closet, with the service-station clerks, and with all the people who might be buried down in the meadow; and the more she identified with them, the more she wanted Edgler Vess to suffer a world of hurt. She was in an Old Testament mood, unwilling to turn the other cheek just now. She wanted Vess screaming on a rack, stretched until his joints popped apart and his tendons tore. She didn't want to see him confined to a state hospital for the criminally insane, there to be analyzed and counseled and instructed as to how best to increase his self-esteem, treated with a panoply of anti-psychotic drugs, given a private room and television, booked in card tournaments with his fellow patients, and treated to a turkey dinner on Christmas. Instead of having him consigned to the mercies of psychiatrists and social workers, Chyna wanted to condemn him to the skilled hands of an imaginative torturer, and then *see* how long the sonofabitch bastard freak remained faithful to his philosophy about all experiences being value neutral, all sensations equally worthwhile. This ardent desire, refined from her pain, was not noble in the least, but it was pure, a high-octane fuel that burned with an intense light, and it kept her motor running.

This side of the barrel pedestal was off the floor perhaps three inches—she could only guess—approximately as high as she had gotten it before, but she still had plenty of steam left. Bent in a backward Z, as hunched as a God-cursed troll, she muscled the table up, knees aching, thighs *quivering* with the strain, her butt clenched tighter than a politician's fist around a cash bribe. She encouraged herself aloud by talking to the table as if it possessed awareness: *"Come on, come on, come on, move, shit, shit, move, you sonofabitch, higher, come on, damn you, damn it, come on."*

A ludicrous mental image of herself flashed through her mind: She must resemble a character in one of those movie scenes where the deceived cowboy cottons to the truth and overturns the poker table on the dishonest itinerant cardshark, except that she was playing the drama in slow motion, as in a Western underwater.

Initially the chair remained exactly where it had been when her butt parted company with it, but as her arms lifted higher and stretched farther in front of her, the heavy chair was hoisted off the floor by the tightening chain that circled behind her from wrist to wrist and wound through the vertical spindles behind the tie-on pad. Now she was lifting the table in front and the chair at her back. The hard edge of the seat jammed against her thighs, and the curved pine headpiece of the railed back pressed cruelly below her shoulder blades, as the chair began to act like a V-clamp to prevent her from rising much further.

Nevertheless, Chyna squeezed against the table as she lifted it, separating herself from the confining chair enough to be able to rise out of her crouch just one more inch, then one more. At the extreme limits of strength and endurance, she grunted loudly, rhythmically: *"Uh, uh, uh, uh!"* Sweat glazed her face, stung her eyes, but there was no light in the kitchen anyway, no reason she had to see what she was doing in order to get it done. Her burning eyes didn't bother her; this was small-time pain; but she felt as though she was about to burst a blood vessel from the straining—or throw a clot off an artery wall and recapture it deep in her brain.

Fear was with her again, for the first time in hours, because even as she strained against the table, she couldn't help thinking about what Edgler Vess would do with her if he returned home to find her on the floor, dazed and incoherent from a stroke. With her mind reduced to hasty pudding, she would no longer be the sophisticated toy she had been; she'd be insufficiently responsive to provide him with the requisite thrills when he tortured her. Then perhaps Vess would revert to the crude turtle games of his youth. Maybe he would drag her into the backyard to set her on fire for the pleasure of watching her crawl jerkily in circles on crippled, blazing limbs.

The table crashed onto its side hard enough to jar the dishes in the kitchen cabinets and rattle a loose pane in a window.

Though she had been striving fiercely for precisely this result, she was so surprised by her abrupt success that she didn't cry out in triumph. She leaned against the curve of the tilted table and gasped for breath.

Half a minute later, when she tried to pull away, she discovered that the chain was still wrapped tightly around the barrel pedestal and that she remained encumbered.

She attempted to tug it loose. No luck.

Dropping to her hands and knees, carrying the chair on her back, she reached under the canted table, as though she were at the seashore and seeking shade beneath a giant beach umbrella. In the darkness she felt around the bottom of the barrel that served as the pedestal, and she discovered that this part of the job was not yet finished.

The table was tipped on its side—like a mushroom with a large cap, stem meeting the floor at an angle. Given the position from which she'd had to work, she had not been able to tip it completely over, with the pedestal straight up in the air. The bottom of the barrel, recessed inside a chime hoop, was fully exposed; however, the tethering chain was trapped in the angle between the floor and the *side* of the barrel.

Lifting the chair with her, Chyna struggled to her feet but rose only to a crouch. She reached down with both hands, hooked her fingers around the chime hoop, paused to gather her strength, and pulled upward.

Although she tried to hold her injured trigger finger out of the way, her sweaty hands slipped on the painted iron hoop. She stubbed the fingertips of her right hand hard against the rough bottom of the barrel, and such a brilliant pain flashed through her swollen index finger that she cried out in dazzled agony.

For a while she hunched over, protectively holding her injured hand against her breast, waiting for the pain to subside. Eventually it faded somewhat.

After blotting her hands on her jeans, she hooked her fingers around the chime hoop once more, hesitated, heaved, and the barrel pedestal came off the floor half an inch, an inch. With her left foot, she pawed at the loop of chain until she thought it was free, and then she let the pedestal drop to the floor again.

She scooted backward in her chair, and this time nothing impeded her. The loop of chain rattled across the floor, no longer anchoring her to the table.

Her chair bumped into the wall that separated the kitchen from the laundry room. She hitched sideways, out from behind the table, toward the window, which was but a faint gray rectangle between the blackness of the unlighted kitchen and the slightly less dark night.

Although Chyna was far from being free, farther still from being safe, she was exhilarated, because at least she had *done* something. A headache like an endless incoming tide throbbed in waves across her brow and along her right temple, and the pain in her neck was savage. Her swollen index finger was a world of misery in itself. In spite of her thick socks, her ankles felt as though they had been bruised and abraded by the shackles, and her left wrist stung where she had skinned it while trying to yank the spindles out of the back of the chair. Her joints ached and her muscles burned from the demands she had put on them, and she had a stitch in her left side that was pulling like a needle threaded with hot wire—yet she was grinning and exhilarated.

When she was beside the window, she let the legs of her chair touch the floor. She sat down.

As her heartbeat slowed from its frenzied hammering, Chyna leaned back against the cushion, still breathing hard, and surprised herself by laughing. Musical, unexpectedly girlish laughter burst from her, an astonishing giggle, part delight, part nervous relief.

She blotted her sweat-stung eyes on one sleeve of her cotton sweater, and then on the other sleeve. With her cuffed hands, she awkwardly smoothed her short hair back from her brow, across which it had fallen in damp licks.

As a softer, more subdued trill of laughter bubbled from her, Chyna detected movement out of the corner of her right eye. She turned to the window, happily thinking, *The elk.*

A Doberman was staring at her.

Few stars and, as yet, no moon shone between the torn clouds, and the dog was oil black. Yet it was clearly visible, because its pointed face was only inches from hers, with nothing between them except the glass. Its inky eyes were cold and merciless, sharklike in their steadiness and glassy concentration. Inquisitively, it pressed its wet nose against the pane.

A thin whine escaped the Doberman, audible even through the glass: neither a whimper of fear nor a plea for attention, but a needful keening that perfectly expressed the killing passion in its eyes.

Chyna was no longer laughing.

The dog dropped from the window, out of sight.

She heard its paws thumping hollowly against the boards as it paced rapidly back and forth across the porch. Between urgent whines, it made a low quarrelsome sound.

Then the dog jumped into view, planting its broad forepaws on the window stool, eye-to-eye with her once more. Agitated, it bared its long teeth threateningly, but it didn't bark or snarl.

Perhaps the sound of the water glass shattering on the floor or the crash of the table tipping onto its side had carried into the backyard, and this Doberman had been close enough to hear. The dog might have been standing at this window for a while, listening to Chyna alternately cursing her bonds and encouraging herself as she had struggled to be free of the table; and certainly it had heard her laughter. Dogs had lousy eyesight, and this one would not be able to see more than her face, nothing of the wreckage. They had a phenomenal sense of smell, however, so maybe the beast was able to detect the scent of her sudden exuberance through the barrier of glass—and was alarmed by that.

The window was about five or six feet long and four feet high, divided into two sliding panels. Obviously not part of the original architecture, it appeared to have been installed during a relatively recent remodel. If there had been numerous smaller panes separated by wide sturdy mullions of wood, Chyna would have been a lot more confident. But either of the two sheets of glass was large enough to admit the agitated Doberman if it tried to smash through at her.

Surely that wouldn't happen. The dogs had been trained to patrol the grounds, not to assault the house.

The bared teeth were pearly, vaguely luminous, gray-white in the gloom: a wide but humorless smile.

Rather than make any sudden provocative movements, Chyna waited until the Doberman dropped from the window again before she reached to the floor and picked up the loop of excess chain to avoid tripping over it. Listening to the dog padding back and forth on the porch, she rose into the Rumpelstiltskin crouch that the burdening chair imposed. She edged around the kitchen, staying close to the walls and cabinets, feeling her way as best she could while cuffed and holding the loop of chain in one hand. She shuffled her feet more than her shackles required, hoping to shove the broken drinking glass and the fragments of the plate aside rather than step on them.

When she reached the doorway between the kitchen and the front room, she found the light switches but was reluctant to flip them up. Glancing back and seeing the Doberman at the window again, she wished that she could leave the kitchen dark.

She needed to search the drawers, however, so she snapped on the overhead lights. At the window, the Doberman twitched, flattened its ears to its skull, immediately pricked them again, found her with its eyes, and fixed her with its gaze.

Ignoring the Doberman, Chyna bent forward as far as her fetters would allow, hoisting the chair on her back. She strove to reach the carabiner that linked the shorter chain between her leg irons with the longer chain that had encircled the table pedestal and that still wrapped the stretcher bars of the chair. But even free of the table, she was trammeled in such a way that she could not put her fingers on this coupling.

She retraced her path along the cabinets. She opened one drawer after another and studied the contents.

When she passed the telephone jack in the wall, she paused to stare at it, frustrated. If Edgler Vess had a life other than that of a "homicidal adventurer," actually held a job and maintained any social life whatsoever as a cover for his true nature, he would have a telephone; the jack wasn't merely a dead plug left by the previous owners of the house. He must have hidden the phone.

For a psychotic killer, raging out of control on one level, Vess was surprisingly careful and methodical when it came to covering his ass. An agent of chaos, leaving behind rubble in the lives of others, he nevertheless kept his own affairs tidy and avoided mistakes.

She opened a few of the cupboard doors and peered into cabinets, but she found only pots, pans, dishes, and glasses. She soon gave up on the phone when she realized that Vess, having taken the trouble to unplug and conceal it, would have hidden it outside the kitchen and in a place where she was unlikely to find it even if she'd had hours to devote to the search.

She continued opening drawers. In the fourth, she discovered a compartmentalized plastic tray containing a collection of small culinary tools and gadgets.

She parked the chair beside the open drawer and sat down.

Outside, the Doberman was pacing again, paws thumping faster than before, all but *running* back and forth on the porch, back and forth, and whining louder as well. Chyna couldn't understand why it was still so agitated. She wasn't breaking dishes or overturning furniture any longer. She was quietly looking in drawers, minimizing the clatter of her chains, doing nothing to alarm the dog. It seemed to realize that she was escaping, but that was impossible; it was only an animal; it couldn't understand the complexities of her situation. Only an animal. Yet it raced worriedly from end to end of the porch, jumped to peer in the window again, fixed her with its fierce black eyes, and seemed to be saying, *Get away from the drawer, bitch!*

She plucked a wooden-handled corkscrew from the drawer, examined the spiraling point, and discarded it. A bottle opener. No. Potato peeler. Lemon-rind shaver. No. She found an eight-inch-long pair of heavy-duty tweezers, which Vess probably used to extract olives and pickles and similar items from tightly packed jars. The gripping blades of the tweezers proved too large to be inserted into the tight keyholes on her handcuffs, so she discarded them as well.

Then she located the ideal item: a five-inch long steel pin, which she believed was called a poultry strut. A dozen were fixed together by a tightly wound rubber band, and she pulled one loose. The pin was rigid, about a sixteenth of an inch in diameter, with a point at the end of the shank and a half-inch-wide eye loop at the top. Smaller struts were made for pinning shut roasting chickens, but this one was for turkeys.

The thought of succulent roasted turkey brought the smell of it immediately to mind. Chyna's mouth watered, and her stomach growled, and she wished that she'd eaten some of the ham and cheese sandwich Vess had made for her.

She held the strut between the thumb and the middle digit of her right hand, sparing her swollen index finger, and slipped the point into the keyway on the left handcuff. Probing experimentally, she produced a lot of small ticking and scraping sounds, trying to feel the lock mechanism in the gateway of the cuff.

She remembered a movie in which the greatest psychotic killer and criminal genius of his age fashioned a handcuff key out of the metal ink tube from a ballpoint pen and an ordinary paper clip. He sprang one cuff and then the other in about fifteen seconds, maybe ten, after which he overpowered his two guards, killed them, and cut the face off one to wear as a disguise, although he used a penknife for the surgery, not the homemade handcuff key. Over the years, she had seen many other movies in which prisoners picked open cuffs and leg irons, and none of them had any more training for it than she did.

Ten minutes later, with her left cuff still securely locked, Chyna said, "Movies are full of shit."

She was so frustrated that her hand trembled and she couldn't control the strut. It jittered uselessly in the tight keyway.

On the porch, the dog wasn't pacing as fast as it had paced earlier, but it was still disturbed. Twice it clawed at the back door, once with considerable fervor, as if it thought it might be able to dig its way through the wood.

Chyna switched the strut to her left hand and worked on the right cuff for a while.

Ticks, clicks, scrapes, and squeaks. She was concentrating so intently on picking the tiny lock that she was sweating as copiously as when she had been struggling to overturn the heavy table.

Finally she threw the turkey strut on the floor, and it bounced *ping-ping-ping* across the tiles, across a piece of the broken plate, and off a shard of the water glass.

Perhaps she could have freed herself in a wink if she had been the greatest psychotic killer and criminal genius of her age. But she was only a waitress and a psychology student.

Even as inconveniently sane and law-abiding as she was, she might be able to pop the handcuffs off her wrists and the larger shackles off her ankles with a more suitable tool than the turkey strut, but she would probably need hours to do it. She couldn't dedicate hours solely to the job of freeing herself from the chair and chains, because once she was unfettered, there were many other urgent tasks to be done before Vess returned.

She slammed the drawer shut. Holding the chain out of her way and hauling the chair with her, she got to her feet.

With a jangle worthy of the Ghost of Christmas Past, Chyna went to the door between the kitchen and the living room.

Behind her, at the window in the dining area, a weird screeching arose. She looked back and saw that the big Doberman was scratching frantically at the glass with both forepaws. Its claws squeaked down the pane with a sound as unsettling as fingernails dragged across a chalkboard.

She had intended to find her way into the dark living room by the light spilling through the open door, but the dog spooked her. While she'd picked at the cuff locks, the Doberman had grown slightly calmer, but now it was as disturbed as ever. Hoping to calm it before it decided to spring through the window, she turned off the overhead fluorescent panels.

Squeak-squeak-squeak.

Claws, glass.

Squeak-squeak.

She eased across the threshold, leaving the kitchen, and pushed the door shut behind her, blocking out the squeaking. Blocking out the damn dog as well, in case it proved to be crazed enough to burst through the glass.

She felt along the wall. Evidently the only switches were on the other side of the room, by the front door.

The living room seemed to be blacker than the kitchen. The drapes were drawn over one of the two expansive windows that faced onto the front porch. The other window was a barely defined gray rectangle that admitted no more light than had the double-pane slider in the kitchen.

Chyna stood motionless, taking time to orient herself, trying to recall the furnishings. She had been in the room only once before, briefly, and the space had been clotted with shadows. When she had entered from the front porch this morning, the kitchen door had been somewhat to her left in the back wall. The handsome sofa with ball feet, covered in a tartan-plaid fabric, had been to the right, which would put it, now, to her left as she faced toward the front of the house. Rustic oak end tables had flanked the large sofa—and on each end table had been a lamp.

Trying to hold this clear image of the room in her mind, she hobbled warily through the darkness, afraid of falling over a chair or a footstool or a magazine rack. Swaddled in chains and under the weight of the chair, she would be unable to check her fall in a natural manner and might be so twisted by her shackles that she would break an ankle or even a leg.

Whereupon, Edgler Vess would come home, dismayed by the mess and disappointed that she had damaged herself before he'd had a chance to play with her. Then either there would be turtle games or he would experiment with her fractured limb to teach her to enjoy pain.

The first thing she bumped into was the sofa, and she did not fall. Sliding her hand along the upholstered back, she sidled to the left until she came to the end table. She reached out and found the lamp shade, the wire ribs beneath the taut cloth.

She fumbled around the shell of the socket and then around the base of the lamp itself. As her fingers finally pinched the rotary switch, she was suddenly certain that a strong hand was going to come out of the darkness and cover hers, that Vess had crept back into the house, that he was sitting on the sofa only *inches* from her. With amusement, he had been listening to her struggles, sitting like a fat, patient spider in his tartan-plaid web, anticipating the pleasure of shattering her hopes when at last she hobbled this far. The light would blink on, and Vess would smile and wink at her and say, *Intense.*

The switch was a nub of ice between thumb and finger. Frozen to her skin.

Heart drumming like the wings of a frantic fettered bird, the beats so hard that they prevented her lungs from expanding, the pulse in her throat swelling so large that she was unable to swallow, Chyna broke her paralysis and clicked the switch. Soft light washed the room. Edgler Vess was not on the sofa. Not in an armchair. Not anywhere in the room. She exhaled explosively, with a shudder that rattled her chains, and leaned against the sofa, and gradually her fluttering heart grew calmer.

After those gray hours of depression during which she had been emotionally dead, she was energized by this siege of terror. If she ever suffered a killing bout of cardiac arrhythmia, the mere thought of Vess would be more effective at jump-starting her heart than the electrical paddles of a defibrillation machine. Fear proved that she had come back to life and that she had found hope again.

She shambled to the gray river-rock fireplace that extended from floor to ceiling across the entire north wall of the room. The deep hearth in the center wasn't raised, which would make her work easier.

She had considered going down to the cellar, where earlier she had seen a workbench, to examine the saws that were surely in Vess's tool collection. But she had quickly ruled out that solution.

Descending the steep cellar steps while hobbled, festooned with steel chains, and carrying the heavy pine chair on her back would be a stunt not quite equivalent to leaping the Snake River Gorge on a rocket-powered motorcycle, perhaps, but undeniably risky. She was moderately confident of making her way to the bottom without pitching forward and cracking her skull like an eggshell on the concrete or breaking a leg in thirty-six places—but far from *entirely* confident. Her strength wasn't what it ought to have been, because she hadn't eaten much in the past twenty-four hours and because she had already been through an exhausting physical ordeal. Furthermore, all her separate pains made her shaky. A trip to the cellar seemed simple enough, but under these circumstances, it would be equivalent to an acrobat slugging down four double martinis before walking the high wire.

Besides, even if she could find a sharp-toothed saw small enough to be easily handled, she wouldn't be able to use it at an angle that would allow her to bear down with effective force. To free the lower chain from the chair, she would have to cut through all three of the horizontal stretcher bars between the chair legs, each of which was an inch or an inch and a half in diameter, around which the links were wound. To accomplish this, she would have to sit, bend forward, and saw *backward* under the chair. Even if the upper chain had sufficient slack to allow her to reach down far enough for the task, which she doubted, she would only be able to scrape feebly at the wood. With luck, she'd whittle through the third stretcher sometime in the late spring. Then she would have to turn her attention to the five sturdy spindles in the back of the chair to free the upper chain, and not even a carnival contortionist born with rubber bones could get at them with a saw while pinioned as Chyna was.

Hacking through the steel chains was impossible. She would be able to get at them from an angle better than that from which she could approach the stretcher bars between the chair legs. But Vess wasn't likely to own saw blades that could carve through steel, and Chyna definitely didn't have the necessary strength.

She was resigned to more primitive measures than saws. And she was worried about the potential for injury and about how painful the process of liberation might be.

On the mantel, the bronze stags leaped perpetually, antlers to antlers, over the round white face of the clock.

Eight minutes past seven.

She had almost five hours until Vess returned.

Or maybe not.

He had said that he would be back as soon *after* midnight as possible, but Chyna had no reason to suppose that he'd been telling the truth. He might return at ten o'clock. Or eight o'clock. Or ten minutes from now.

She shuffled onto the floor-level flagstone hearth and then to the right, past the firebox and the brass andiron, past the deep mantel. The entire wall flanking the fireplace was smooth gray river rock—just the hard surface that she needed.

Chyna stood with her left side toward the rock, twisted her upper body to the left as far as possible without turning her feet, in the manner of an Olympic athlete preparing to toss a discus, and then swung sharply and forcefully to the right. This maneuver threw the chair—on her back—in the opposite direction from her body and slammed it into the wall. It clattered against the rock, rebounded with a ringing of chains, and thudded against her hard enough to hurt her shoulder, ribs, and hip. She tried the same trick again, putting even more energy into it, but after the second time, she was able to judge by the sound that she would, at best, scar the finish and chip a few slivers out of the pine. Hundreds of these lame blows might demolish the chair in time, turn it into kindling; but before she hammered it against the rock that often, suffering the recoil each time, she would be a bruised and bloodied mess, and her bones would splinter, and her joints would separate like the links in a pop-bead necklace.

By swinging the chair as though she were a dog wagging its tail, she couldn't get the requisite force behind it. She had been afraid of this. As far as she could determine, there was only one other approach that might work—but she didn't like it.

Chyna looked at the mantel clock. Only two minutes had passed since the last time she'd glanced at it.

Two minutes was nothing if she had until midnight, but it was a disastrous waste of time if Vess was on his way home right now. He might be turning off the public road, through the gate, into his long private driveway this very moment, the lying bastard, having set her up to believe that he would be gone until after midnight, then sneaking back early to—

She was baking a nourishing loaf of panic, plump and yeasty, and if she allowed herself to eat a single slice, then she'd gorge on it. This was an appetite she didn't dare indulge. Panic wasted time and energy.

She must remain calm.

To free herself from the chair, she needed to use her body as if it were a pneumatic ram, and she would have to endure serious pain. She was already in severe pain, but what was coming would be worse—devastating—and it scared her.

Surely there was another way.

She stood listening to her heart and to the hollow ticking of the mantel clock.

If she went upstairs first, maybe she would find a telephone and be able to call the police. They would know how to deal with the Dobermans. They would have the keys to get her out of the shackles and manacles. They would free Ariel too. With that one phone call, all burdens would be lifted from her.

But she knew in her heart—the old friend intuition—that she was not going to find any telephones upstairs either. Edgler Vess was unfailingly thorough. A phone would be in service in the house whenever he was home—but not when he was away. He might actually unplug the unit and take it with him each time he left.

Trammeled, unbalanced by the chair and therefore dangerously clumsy, Chyna would be risking a crippling fall if she climbed the stairs. She would face an even greater risk when, after finding no telephone, she had to come back down again. And in the process, she would have wasted precious time.

Turning her back to the river-rock wall, she shuffled six feet from it, stopped, closed her eyes, and gathered her courage.

Possibly one of the spindles in the rail-back chair would crack apart and be driven forward. The splintered end would puncture the tie-on cushion or slip past it and then skewer her, back to front, straight through her guts.

More likely, she'd sustain a spinal injury. With all the force of the impact directed against the lower half of the chair, the legs of it would be driven into *her* legs; the upper half would first pull away from her—then recoil and snap hard against her upper back or neck. The spindles were fixed between the seat and the wide slab of radius-cut pine that served as the headrail, and the headrail was so solid that it would do major damage if it cracked into her cervical vertebrae with sufficient force. She might wind up on the living-room floor, under the chair and chains, paralyzed from the neck down.

Sometimes she brooded about possibilities too much, dwelt beyond reason on all the myriad ways that any situation or any relationship could go terribly wrong. This was also a result of having spent her childhood hiding on the wrong side of bedsprings, waiting for either the fighting or the partying to stop.

For a while when Chyna was seven, she and her mother had stayed with a man named Zack and a woman named Memphis in a ramshackle old farmhouse not far from New Orleans, and one night two men had come to visit, carrying a Styrofoam cooler, and Memphis had killed them less than five minutes after they arrived. The visitors had been in the kitchen, sitting at the table. One of them had been talking to Chyna and the other had been twisting the cap off a bottle of beer—when Memphis withdrew a gun from the refrigerator and shot both men in the head, one after the other, so fast that the second one didn't even have time to dive for cover before she put a round in his face. As slippery and quick as a skink, Chyna fled, certain that Memphis had gone crazy and would kill them all. She hid in a drift of loose hay in the barn loft. During the hour that the adults took to find her, she so often visualized her own face dissolving with the impact of a bullet that every image in her mind's eye—even fleeting glimpses of the Wild Wood to which she could not quite escape—was entirely in shades of red, wet red.

But she had survived that night.

She had been surviving for a long time. Eternity.

And she would survive this too—or die trying.

Without opening her eyes, Chyna hurtled backward as fast as her leg irons would allow, and in spite of her fear, she figured that she must be at least a somewhat comic sight, because she had to shuffle frantically to build speed, had to throw herself toward spinal injury in quick little baby steps. But then she slammed into the rocks, and there was nothing whatsoever funny about *that*.

She'd been bent forward slightly to lift the legs of the chair behind her and to ensure that they, rather than another part of it, would strike first and take the hard initial blow. With her entire weight behind the assault, there was a satisfyingly splintery *thwack* on impact—and the pine legs were jammed painfully into the backs of her legs. Chyna stumbled forward, and the upper part of the chair whiplashed into her neck, as she had expected, and she was knocked off balance. She dropped to her knees on the flagstone hearth and fell forward with the chair still on her back, hurting in too many places to bother taking an inventory.

Hobbled, she couldn't get to her feet unless she was gripping something. She crawled to the nearest armchair and pulled herself up, grunting with effort and pain.

She didn't *like* pain the way Vess claimed to like it, but she wasn't going to bitch about it either. At least she could still crawl and stand. No spinal injury yet. Better to feel pain than nothing at all.

The legs of the chair and the stretcher bars between the legs seemed to be intact. But judging by the sound of the impact, she had weakened them.

Starting eight feet from the wall this time, Chyna shuffled backward as fast as she could, trying to ram the chair legs into the rock at the same angle as before. She was rewarded with a distinctive *crack*—the sound of splintering wood, though it felt like shattering bone.

A dam of pain burst inside her. Cold currents dragged her down, but she resisted the undertow with the desperate determination of a swimmer struggling against a drowning darkness.

She hadn't been knocked off her feet this time. She shuffled forward. Not pausing to catch her breath, still hunched to ensure that the chair legs would take the brunt of the impact, she charged backward into the rock wall.

Chyna woke facedown on the floor in front of the hearth, aware that she must have been unconscious for a minute or two.

The carpet was as cold and undulant as moving water. She wasn't floating in it but glimmering along the rippled surface, as though she were coppery spangles of sunlight or the dark reflection of a cloud.

The worst pain was in the back of her head. She must have struck it against something.

She felt so much better when she didn't think about her pain or her problems, when she simply accepted that she was nothing more than a cloud shadow riding on the mirrored surface of a rolling river, as insubstantial as the purling patterns on moving water, gliding away, liquid and cool, away, away.

Ariel. In the cellar. Among the watchful dolls.

I am my sister's keeper.

Somehow she got to her hands and knees.

She heard the hollow thump of paws on the front porch floor.

When she pulled herself to her feet against an armchair, she looked at the window that wasn't covered by drapes. Two Dobermans were standing with their forepaws on the windowsill, staring at her, their eyes radiant yellow with reflections of the soft amber light from the lamp on the end table.

At the base of the stone wall was one of the rear legs of the chair. That length of turned pine was all jagged splinters at the thicker end, where it had been fixed to the underside of the seat. Bristling from the side of it at a ninety-degree angle was the one-inch stretcher bar that had connected it to the other rear leg.

The lower chain was more than half free.

On the porch, one dog paced. The other still watched Chyna.

She worked the upper chain to the left through the spindles at her back, drawing her right hand behind her head, to provide as much slack as possible for her left hand. Then she reached down to her left, under the chair arm and then under the thick slab seat, feeling for the legs. The left rear leg was gone, obviously the one on the floor by the wall. The side stretcher still extended from the left front leg, but with the rear leg gone, it no longer connected to anything, and the chain had slipped off it.

When she worked the upper chain to the right, to be able to feel under the chair with that hand, she discovered that the other rear leg was slightly loose. She pulled, pushed, and twisted, trying to break it off. But she couldn't get adequate leverage, and the leg was still too firmly attached to succumb to her efforts.

No stretcher bar had ever linked the two front legs. Now the lower chain was prevented from slipping entirely free only by the stretcher bar between the legs on the right side.

Once more she charged backward hard, into the rock. Blazing pain exploded through her entire body, and she was almost blown away. But when the right rear leg didn't snap loose, she said, "Hell, no," refusing to surrender to hurt, to exhaustion, to anything, anything, and she hobbled forward and then launched herself backward once more. Wood split with a dry crackle, broken turnings of pine clattered off flagstones, and with a bright ringing, the lower chain fell free of the chair.

Bending forward, dizzy, filled with a whirling darkness, shaking violently, she leaned with both hands on the back of the big leather armchair. She was half sick with pain and with fear of what damage she might have done to her body, wondering about fractured vertebrae and internal bleeding.

Squeak-squeak-squeak.

One of the dogs clawed at the window glass.

Squeak-squeak.

Chyna wasn't free yet. She was still chained to the upper half of the chair.

The four spindles between the headrail and the seat were thinner than the stretcher bars between the legs, so they ought to break more easily than those bars had broken. She hadn't been able to keep the chair legs from mercilessly hammering the backs of her knees and her thighs, but for this part of the operation, the tie-on foam cushion between her and the spindles should provide her with some protection.

A pair of floor-to-ceiling rock pilasters flanked the firebox and supported the six-inch slab of laminated maple that served as the mantel. They were curved, and it seemed to Chyna that the radius would help focus the impact on one or two spindles at a time instead of spreading it across the four.

She moved the heavy andiron out of the way. She pushed aside a brass rack of fireplace tools. The lifting and shoving made her head spin and her stomach churn, and a hundred agonies assailed her.

She no longer dared to think about what she was doing. She just did it, past courage now, past consideration and calculation, driven by a blind animal determination to be free.

This time, she didn't hunch over; as far as she was able, she stood straight and rammed backward into the pilaster. The cushion did provide protection, but not enough. She was suffering so many contusions, wrenched muscles, and battered bones that the jarring blow would have been devastating even if it had been twice as well padded, like the tap of a dentist's rubber hammer on a rotten tooth in need of a root-canal job. Right now every joint in her body seemed to be a rotten tooth. She didn't pause, because she was afraid that all of those pains, pulsing at once, would soon shake her to the floor, shake her apart, so she would never be able to pull herself together and get up. She was rapidly running out of resources, and with a black tide lapping at the edges of her vision, she was also running out of time. Howling with misery in expectation of the pain, she rammed backward and screamed when the blow rattled her bones like dice in a cup. Agony. But immediately she threw herself into the pilaster again, chains jangling, and again, wood splintering, and again, screaming, *Jesus,* unable to stop screaming and frightened by her own cries, while the vigilant dogs made that needful keening at the window, and yet once more backward, *hammering* herself into the rock.

Then she was again facedown on the floor without remembering how she had gotten there, racked by dry heaves because there was nothing in her stomach to throw up, gagging on a vile taste in the back of her mouth, hands clenched against the very thought of defeat, feeling small and weak and pitiful, shuddering, shuddering.

The shudders gradually diminished, however, and the carpet began to undulate, pleasantly cool beneath her, and she was a cloud shadow on fast-moving waters. The sun-haloed shadow and the fathomless water moved in the same direction, always in the same direction, onward and forever, swift and silken, toward the edge of the world and then off into a void, flowing still, so dark.

NINE

Expecting dogs, Chyna woke from red dreams of refrigerator-chilled guns and exploding heads, but there were no dogs. She was alone in the living room, and all was quiet. The Dobermans were not padding back and forth on the porch, and when she was finally able to lift her head, she saw no dogs at the undraped window.

They were outside, calmer now because they realized that their time would come. Watching the door and windows. Waiting to see her face. Alert for the *snick* of a latch, the rasp of a hinge.

She was in so much pain that she was surprised to have regained consciousness. She was more surprised that her head was clear.

One pain was separate from and more urgent than all her other distresses. Unlike the agonies of tortured bones and muscles, this painful pressure could be relieved easily, and she wouldn't even have to put herself through the gruesome ordeal of moving from where she lay.

"Hell no," she mumbled, and slowly she sat up.

Getting to her feet, she disturbed deep hurts that had slept as long as she had been lying on the floor but woke as soon as she began to rise: grindings in her bones and hot flares in her muscles. Some were intense enough, at least initially, to make her freeze and gasp for breath, but by the time she was standing tall, she knew there was no single pain so terrible that it would cripple her; and while the burden of her combined agonies was daunting, she was going to be able to carry it.

She *didn't* have to carry the heavy chair any longer. It lay on the floor around her in fragments and splinters, and none of her chains was encumbered by it.

According to the mantel clock, the time was three minutes till eight, which unsettled her. The last she remembered, it had been ten minutes past seven. She wasn't sure how long she had taken to break free from the chair, but she suspected that she had lain unconscious for half an hour, perhaps longer. The sweat had dried on her body, and her hair was only slightly damp at the nape of her neck, so half an hour was probably correct. This realization made her feel weak and uncertain again.

If Vess could be believed, Chyna still had four hours until he returned. But there was much to be done, and four hours might not be time enough.

Chyna sat on the edge of the sofa. Freed from the pine dining chair, she was at last able to reach the carabiner on the short chain between her ankles. This steel coupling connected the shorter chain to the longer one that had wrapped the chair and the table pedestal. After screwing open the metal sleeve to reveal the gate in the carabiner, she disconnected herself from the longer chain.

Her ankles remained cuffed, and on her way to the stairs to the second floor, she still had to shuffle.

She switched on the stairwell light and laboriously climbed the narrow stairs, moving first her left foot and then her right onto each tread. Because of the hobbling chain, she was unable to ascend one foot per tread, step over step, as she normally would have done, and her progress was slow.

She kept a two-hand grip on the handrail. With the heavy chair gone from her back, she was no longer precariously balanced, but she remained wary of tripping in her fetters.

Past the landing, halfway up the second flight, all of her pains and the fear of falling and the hot pressure in her bladder combined to double her over with severe stomach cramps. She leaned against the wall of the stairwell, clutching the handrail, suddenly sheathed in sour sweat, moaning low and wordlessly in misery. She was certain that she was going to pass out, tumble backward, and break her neck.

But the cramps passed, and she continued climbing. Soon she reached the second floor.

She switched on the hall light and found three doors. Those to the left and right were closed, but the one at the end of the hallway stood open, revealing a bathroom.

In the bathroom, although her hands were manacled and trembling badly, she managed to unbuckle her belt, unbutton her jeans, unzip, and skin down jeans and panties. Sitting, she was hit by more waves of cramps, and these were markedly more vicious than those she had endured on the stairs. She had refused to wet herself at the kitchen table, as Vess had wanted her to do, refused to be reduced to that degree of helplessness. Now she couldn't make water, though she desperately wanted to do that—*needed* to do it to stop the cramps—and she wondered if she had held out so long that a bladder spasm was pinching off the flow. Such a thing was possible, and abruptly the cramps grew more severe, as if confirming her diagnosis. She felt as if her guts were being rolled through a wringer—but then the cramps passed and relief came.

With the sudden flood, she was surprised to hear herself say, "Chyna Shepherd, untouched and alive and able to pee." Then she was simultaneously laughing and sobbing, not with relief but with a weird sense of triumph.

Getting free of the table, shattering and shaking off the chair, and *not* wetting her pants seemed, together, to be an act of endurance and of courage equivalent to setting foot on the moon with the first astronauts to land there, slogging through blinding blizzards to the Pole with Admiral Peary, or storming the beaches of Normandy against the might of the German army. She laughed at herself, laughed until tears spilled down her face; nevertheless, she still felt *that* degree of triumph. She knew how small—even pathetic—her triumph was, but she felt that it was big.

"Rot in Hell," she said to Edgler Vess, and she hoped that someday she would have the chance to say it to his face just before she pulled a trigger and blew him out of this world.

She had so much pain in her back from the battering that she'd endured, especially low around her kidneys, that when she was done, she checked in the toilet bowl for blood. She was relieved to see that her urine was clear.

Glancing in the mirror above the sink, however, she was shocked by her reflection. Her short hair was tangled and lank with sweat. The right side of her face along the jaw seemed to be smeared with a purple ink, but when she touched it, she discovered that this was the trailing edge of a bruise that mottled that entire side of her neck. Where it wasn't bruised or smeared with dirt, her skin was gray and grainy, as if she had been suffering through a long and difficult illness. Her right eye was fiery, no white visible any more: just the dark iris and the darker pupil floating in an elliptical pool of blood. Both the bloodied eye and the clear left eye gazed back at her with a haunted expression so unnerving that she turned away from her own reflection in confusion and fear.

The face in the mirror was that of a woman who had already *lost* some battle. It wasn't the face of a winner.

Chyna tried to press that dispiriting thought out of her mind at once. What she had seen was the face of a fighter—no longer the face of a mere survivor, but a *fighter*. Every fighter sustained some punishment, both physical and emotional. Without anguish and agony, there was no hope of winning.

She shuffled from the bathroom to the door on the right side of the upstairs hall, which opened onto Vess's bedroom. Simple furniture and a minimum of it. A neatly made bed with a beige chenille spread. No paintings. No bibelots or decorative accessories. No books or magazines, or any newspapers folded open to crossword puzzles. This was nothing more than a place to sleep, not a room where he lingered or lived.

Where he truly lived was in the pain of others, in a storm of death, in the calm eye of the storm where all was orderly but where the wind howled on every side.

Chyna checked the nightstand drawers for a gun but didn't find one. She found no phone either.

The large walk-in closet was ten feet deep and as wide as the bedroom, essentially a room of its own. At a glance, the closet held nothing useful to her. She was sure to discover something worthwhile if she searched, maybe even a well-hidden gun. But there were built-in cabinets with laden shelves and packed drawers, and boxes were stacked on boxes; she would need hours to pore through everything. More urgent tasks awaited her.

She emptied the dresser drawers on the floor, but they contained only socks, underwear, sweaters, sweatshirts, and a few rolled belts. No guns.

Across the hall from Vess's bedroom was a Spartan study. Bare walls. Blackout blinds instead of drapes. On two long worktables stood two computers, each with its own laser printer. Of the numerous items of computer-related equipment, she could identify some but was mystified by others.

Between the long tables was an office chair. The floor was not carpeted; the bare wood was exposed, evidently to make it easier for Vess to roll between tables.

The drab, utilitarian room intrigued her. She sensed that it was an important place. Time was precious, but there was something here worth pausing to examine.

She sat in the chair and looked around, bewildered. She knew that the world was wired these days, even into the hinterlands, but it seemed odd to find all this high-tech equipment in such a remote and rustic house.

Chyna suspected that Vess was set up to enter the Internet, but there was no phone or modem in sight. She spotted two unused phone jacks in the baseboard. His meticulous security procedures had served him well again; she was stymied.

What did he do here?

On one of the tables were six or eight ring-bound notebooks with colorful covers, and she opened the nearest. The binder was divided into five sections, each with the name of an agency of the federal government. The first was the Social Security Administration. The pages were filled with what seemed to be notes from Vess to himself regarding the trial-and-error method by which he had hacked his way into the administration's data files and had learned to manipulate them. The second divider was labeled U.S. DEPT OF STATE (PASSPORT AGENCY), and judging by the following notes, Vess was engaged in an incomplete experiment to determine if, by a byzantine route, he might be able to enter and control the Passport Agency's computerized records without being detected.

Part of what he was doing, evidently, was preparing for the day when he slipped up in his "homicidal adventuring" and required new identities.

Chyna didn't believe, however, that Vess's only projects were the altering of his public records and the obtaining of fake ID. She was troubled by the feeling that this room contained information about Vess that could be of vital importance to her own survival if only she knew where to look for it.

She put down the notebook and swiveled in the chair to face the second computer. Under one end of this table stood a two-drawer file cabinet. She opened the top drawer and saw Pendaflex hanging files with blue tags; each tag featured a person's name, with the surname first.

Each folder contained a two-sheet dossier on a different law-enforcement officer, and after a couple of minutes of investigation, Chyna decided that they were deputies with the sheriff's department in the very county in which Vess's house was located. These dossiers provided all vital statistics on the officers plus information about their families and their personal lives. A Xerox of each deputy's official ID photo was also attached.

Did the freak see some advantage in collecting information on all the local cops as insurance against the day when he might find himself in a standoff with them? This effort seemed excessive even for one as meticulous as Edgler Vess; on the other hand, excess was his philosophy.

The lower drawer of the filing cabinet contained manila folders as well. The tabs of these also featured names, like those in the upper drawer, but only surnames.

In the first folder, labeled ALMES, Chyna found a full-page enlargement of the California driver's license of an attractive young blonde named Mia Lorinda Almes. Judging by the exceptional clarity, it wasn't a Xerox blow-up of the original license but a digitized data transmission received on a phone line, through a computer, and reproduced on a high-quality laser printer.

The only other items in the folder were six Polaroid photographs of Mia Lorinda Almes. The first two were close-ups from different angles. She was beautiful. And terrified.

This file drawer was Edgler Vess's equivalent of a scrapbook.

Four more Polaroids of Mia Almes.

Don't look.

The next two were full-body shots. The young woman was naked in both. Manacled.

Chyna closed her eyes. But opened them. She was compelled to look, perhaps because she was determined not to hide from anything any more.

In the fifth and sixth photos, the young woman was dead, and in the last her beautiful face was gone as if it had been blown off or sheared away.

The folder and the photographs fluttered from Chyna's hands to the floor, where they clicked against the wood and spun and were still. She hid her face in her hands.

She wasn't trying to block from her mind the gruesome image on the snapshot. Instead, she was striving to repress a nineteen-year-old memory of a farmhouse outside New Orleans, two visitors with a Styrofoam cooler, a gun taken from the refrigerator, and the cold accuracy with which a woman named Memphis had fired two rounds.

Memory, however, always has its way.

The visitors, who'd done business with Zack and Memphis before, had been there to make a drug purchase. The cooler had been filled with packets of hundred-dollar bills. Maybe Zack didn't have the promised shipment, or maybe he and Memphis just needed more money than they could get from a sale; whatever the reason, they had decided to rip off the two men.

After the gunfire, Chyna had hidden in the barn loft, certain that Memphis would kill them all. When Memphis and Anne found her, she fought them bitterly. But she was only seven years old and no match for them. With owls hooting in alarm and taking flight from the rafters, the women dragged Chyna out of the mice-infested hay and carried her to the house.

Zack had been gone by then, having taken the bodies elsewhere, and Memphis had cleaned up the blood in the kitchen while Anne had forced Chyna to drink a shot of whiskey. Chyna didn't want the whiskey, sealed her lips against it, but Anne said, "You're a wreck, for Christ's sake, you can't stop blubbering, and one shot isn't going to hurt you. This is what you need, kiddo, trust Mama, this is what you need. A shot of good whiskey will break a fever, you know, and what you've got now is a kind of fever. Come on, you little wuss, it's not poison. Jesus, you can be a whiny little shit sometimes. Either you drink it quick, or I'll hold you down and pinch your nose shut, and Memphis will pour it in when you open your mouth to breathe. That how you want it?" So Chyna drank the whiskey, and then took a second shot with a few ounces of milk when her mother decided that she needed it. The booze made her dizzy and strange but did not calm her.

She had appeared calmer to *them* because, good little fisher that she was, she'd caught her fear and reeled it inside, where they could not see it. Even by the age of seven, she had begun to understand that a show of fear was dangerous, because others interpreted it as weakness, and there was no place in this world for the weak.

Later that night, Zack had returned with whiskey on *his* breath too. He was exuberant, in a raucous and celebratory mood. He came straight to Chyna and hugged her, kissed her on the cheek, took her by the hands and tried to make her dance with him. "That bastard

Bobby, the last time he was here, I *knew* by the way he couldn't take his eyes off Chyna that he was hot for little girls, a genuine sicko, so tonight he walks in and his tongue just about uncurls to his knees when he sees her! You could've shot the geek half a dozen times, Memphis, before he might've noticed!" Bobby had been the man sitting at the kitchen table, talking to Chyna, his beautiful gray eyes fixed intently on her, speaking *directly* to her in a way that few adults ever spoke to kids, asking whether she liked kittens or puppies best and did she want to grow up to be a famous movie star or a nurse or a doctor or what, when Memphis shot him in the head. "The way our Chyna girl was dressed," Zack said excitedly, "Bobby just about totally forgot anyone else was here." The night was hot and swamp-humid, and before the visitors arrived, Chyna's mother made her change out of her shorts and T-shirt into a brief yellow bikini swimsuit: "But only the bottoms because, child, you're going to get heatstroke in this weather." Although only seven, Chyna was old enough to feel peculiar about going bare-chested, even if she didn't quite know why she felt that way. She'd gone bare-chested when she was younger, even just the previous summer, when she was six; and it *was* an awfully hot, sticky night. When Zack said that the way she was dressed had something to do with Bobby's forgetting that anyone else was in the room, Chyna didn't understand what he meant. Years later, when she *did* understand, she had confronted her mother with it. Anne had laughed and said, "Oh, baby, don't get self-righteous on me. We get along by using what we've got, and one sure thing we girls have is our bodies. You were the perfect distraction. Anyway, poor dumb old Bobby never touched you, did he? He just got to gawk at you a little, that's all, while Memphis went for the gun. Don't forget, sweetie, we were cut in for a piece of that pie and lived well on it for a while." And Chyna had wanted to say, *But you used me, you put me right there in front of him where I'd see his head come apart, and I was only seven!*

All these years later, in Edgler Vess's study, she could still hear the crash of the shot and see Bobby's face explode; the memory was as vivid as ever it had been. She didn't know what gun Memphis used, but the ammunition must have been high-caliber hollow-point lead wadcutters that expanded on impact, because the damage they inflicted had been tremendous.

She lowered her hands from her face and looked at the open file cabinet. Vess had used three formats of folders, with staggered tab placement, so it was easy for Chyna to see all the names along the length of the drawer. Much farther back from the Almes file was one labeled TEMPLETON.

She pushed the drawer shut with her foot.

She'd found too much in this study—yet nothing helpful.

Before leaving the second floor, she turned off all the lights. If Vess came home early, before Chyna could get away with Ariel, the lights would warn him that something was amiss. He would be lulled by darkness, however, and as he crossed the threshold, she might have one last chance to kill him.

She hoped it wouldn't come to that. In spite of her fantasies of pulling the trigger on Vess, Chyna didn't want to have to confront him again, even if she found a shotgun and loaded it herself and had an opportunity to test fire it before he arrived. She was a survivor, and she was a fighter, but Vess was more than either: as unreachable as stars, something come down from a high darkness. She was no match for him, and she didn't want another chance to prove it.

One tread at a time, balanced against the handrail, as fast as she dared, Chyna went down to the living room. None of the Dobermans was at the undraped window.

The mantel clock put the time at twenty-two minutes past eight, and suddenly the night seemed to be a sled on a slope of ice, picking up speed.

She extinguished the lamp and shuffled through darkness to the kitchen. There she turned on the fluorescent lights, only to avoid tripping in the debris, falling, and cutting herself on broken glass.

No Dobermans were on the back porch either. At the window, only the night waited.

Entering the windowless laundry room, she shut off the kitchen lights behind her and pulled the door shut.

Down to the cellar, then, to the workbench and cabinets that she had seen earlier.

In the tall metal cabinets with the vent slits in the doors, she found cans of paint and lacquer, paintbrushes, and drop cloths folded as precisely as fine linen sheets. One entire cabinet was filled with thick pads from which dangled black leather straps with chrome-plated buckles; she didn't have any idea what they were, and she left them undisturbed. In the final cabinet, Vess stored several power tools, including an electric drill.

In one of the drawers on the big wheeled tool chest, she located an extensive collection of drill bits in three clear plastic boxes. She also found a pair of Plexiglas safety goggles.

A power strip with eight outlets was attached to the wall behind the workbench, but a duplex receptacle was also available low on the wall beside the bench. She needed the lower outlet, because it allowed her to sit on the floor.

Although the drill bits weren't labeled except as to size, Chyna figured that they were all meant for woodworking and would not bore easily—if at all—through steel. She didn't want to pierce the steel anyway; she wanted only to screw up the lock mechanisms on her leg irons enough to spring them open.

She chose a bit approximately the size of the leg-iron keyway, fitted it into the chuck, and tightened it. When she held the drill in both hands and squeezed the trigger, it issued a shrill whine. The spiral throat of the slender bit spun so fast that it blurred until it seemed as smooth and harmless as the shank.

Chyna released the trigger, set the silent drill aside on the floor, and put on the protective goggles. She was disconcerted by the thought that Vess had worn these goggles. Strangely, she expected that everything she saw through them would be distorted, as if the molecules of the lenses had been transformed by the magnetic power with which Vess drew all the sights of his world to his eyes.

But what she saw through the goggles was no different from what she saw without them, although her field of vision was circumscribed by the frames.

She picked up the drill with both hands again and inserted the tip of the bit into the keyway on the shackle that encircled her left ankle. When she pressed the trigger, steel spun against steel with a hellish shriek. The bit stuttered violently, jumped out of the keyway, and skipped across the two-inch-wide shackle, spitting tiny sparks. If her reflexes hadn't been good, the whirling auger would have bored through her foot, but she released the trigger and jerked up on the drill just in time to avoid disaster.

The lock might have been damaged. She couldn't be sure. But it was still engaged, and the shackle was secure.

She inserted the bit into the keyway again. She gripped the drill tighter than before and bore down with more effort to keep the bit from kicking out of the hole. Steel shrieked, shrieked, and blue wisps of foul-smelling smoke rose from the grinding point, and the vibrating shackle pressed painfully into her ankle in spite of the intervening sock. The drill shook in her hands, which were suddenly damp with cold sweat from the strain of controlling it. A spray of metal slivers swirled up from the keyway, spattered her face. The bit snapped, and the broken-off end *zinged* past her head, rang off the concrete-block wall hard enough to take a chip out of it, and clinked like a half-spent bullet across the cellar floor.

Her left cheek stung, and she found a splinter of steel embedded in her flesh. It was about a quarter of an inch long and as thin as a sliver of glass. She was able to grasp it between her fingernails and pluck it free. The tiny puncture was bleeding; she had blood on her fingertips and felt a thin warm trickle making its way down her face to the corner of her mouth.

She freed the shank of the broken bit from the drill and threw it aside. She selected a slightly larger bit and tightened it into the jaws of the chuck.

Again, she drilled the keyway. The shackle around her left ankle popped open. Not more than a minute later, the lock on the other shackle cracked too.

Chyna put the drill aside and rose shakily to her feet, every muscle in her legs trembling. She was shaky not because of her many pains, not because of her hunger and weakness, but because she had freed herself from the shackles after having been in despair only a couple of hours before. She had freed *herself*.

She was still handcuffed, however, and she could not hold the drill one-handed while she bored out the lock on each manacle. But she already had an idea about how she might extricate her hands.

Although other challenges faced her in addition to the manacles, although escape was by no means assured, jubilation swelled in Chyna as she climbed the cellar steps. She went tread over tread, not one step at a time as the shackles had required, *bounding* up the stairs in spite of her weakness and the tremors in her muscles, without even using the handrail, to the landing, into the laundry room, past the washer and dryer. And there she abruptly halted with her hands on the knob of the closed door, remembering how she had raced along this same route and into the kitchen this morning, reassured by the *tatta-tatta-tatta* of the vibrating water pipe in the wall, only to be blindsided by Vess.

She stood at the threshold until her breathing quieted, but she was unable to quiet her heart, which had been thundering with excitement and with the steepness of the stairs but now pounded with fear of Edgler Vess. She listened at the door for a while, heard nothing over the thudding in her breast, and turned the knob as stealthily as possible.

The hinges operated smoothly, soundlessly, and the door opened into the kitchen, which was as dark as she had left it. She found the light switch, hesitated, flipped it up— and Vess was not waiting for her.

As long as she lived, would she ever again be able to go through a doorway without flinching?

From a drawer where earlier Chyna had seen a set of cutlery, she extracted a butcher knife with a well-worn walnut handle. She put it on the counter near the sink.

She got a drinking glass from another cabinet, filled it from the cold-water tap, and drank the entire glassful in long swallows before lowering it from her lips. Nothing she had ever drunk had been half as delicious as those eight ounces.

In the refrigerator, she found an unopened coffeecake with white icing, cinnamon, walnuts. She ripped open the wrapper and tore off a chunk of the cake. She stood over the sink, eating voraciously, stuffing her mouth until her cheeks bulged, greedily licking icing from her lips, crumbs and chunks of walnuts dropping into the sink.

She was in an uncommon state of mind as she ate: now moaning with delight, now half choking with laughter, now gagging and on the verge of tears, now laughing again. In a storm of emotions. But that was okay. Storms always passed sooner or later, and they were cleansing.

She had come so far. Yet she had so far to go. That was the nature of the journey.

From the spice rack she removed the bottle of aspirin. She shook two tablets into the palm of her hand, but she didn't chew them. She drew another glass of water and took the aspirin, then took two more.

She sang, "I did it my way," from Sinatra's standard, and then added, "took the fucking aspirin my way." She laughed and ate more coffeecake, and for a moment she felt crazy with accomplishment.

Dogs out there in the night, she reminded herself, *Dobermans in the darkness, rotten bastard Nazi dogs with big teeth and eyes black like sharks' eyes.*

At a key organizer next to the spice rack, the keys to the motor home hung from one of the four pegs; the other pegs were empty. Vess would be careful with the keys to the soundproofed cell and would no doubt keep them on him at all times.

She picked up the butcher knife and the half-eaten coffee cake and went to the cellar, turning off the kitchen lights behind her.

• • •

Pintle and gudgeon.

Chyna knew these two exotic words, as she knew so many others, because, as a girl, she had encountered them in books written by C. S. Lewis and Madeleine L'Engle and Robert Louis Stevenson and Kenneth Grahame. And every time that she'd come across a word she had not known, she'd looked it up in a tattered paperback dictionary, a prized possession that she took with her wherever her restless mother chose to drag her, year after year, until it was held together with so much age-brittled Scotch tape that she could barely read some of the definitions through the strips of yellowing cellophane.

Pintle. That was the name of the pin in a hinge, which pivoted when a door opened or closed.

Gudgeon. That was the sleeve—or barrel—in which the pintle moved.

The thick inner door of the soundproofed vestibule was equipped with three hinges. The pintle in each hinge had a slightly rounded head that overhung the gudgeon by about a sixteenth of an inch all the way around.

From the tools in the wheeled cabinet, Chyna selected a hammer and a screwdriver.

With the workbench stool and a scrap of wood for a wedge, she propped open the outer padded door of the vestibule. Then she placed the butcher knife on the rubber mat on the vestibule floor, within easy reach.

She slid aside the cover on the view port in the inner door and saw the gathering of dolls in pinkish lamplight. Some had eyes as radiant as the eyes of lizards, and some had eyes as dark as those of certain Dobermans.

In the enormous armchair, Ariel sat with her legs drawn up on the seat cushion, head tipped forward, face obscured by a fall of hair. She might have been asleep—except that her hands were balled tightly in her lap. If her eyes were open, she would be staring at her fists.

"It's only me," Chyna said.

The girl didn't respond.

"Don't be afraid."

Ariel was so motionless that even her veil of hair did not stir.

"It's only me."

This time, deeply humbled, Chyna made no claim to being anyone's guardian or salvation.

She started with the lowest hinge. The length of chain between her manacles was barely long enough to allow her to use the tools. She held the screwdriver in her left hand, with the tip of the blade angled under the pintle cap. Without sufficient play in the manacle chain, she couldn't grasp the hammer by its handle, so she gripped it instead by the head and tapped the bottom of the screwdriver as forcefully as possible considering the limitations on movement. Fortunately, the hinge was well lubricated, and with each tap, the pintle rose farther out of the gudgeon. Five minutes later, in spite of some resistance from the third pin, she popped it out of the uppermost hinge.

The gudgeons were formed of interleaving knuckles that were part of the hinge leaf on the doorframe and that on the inner edge of the door itself. These knuckles separated slightly, because the pintles were no longer present to hold them together in a single barrel.

Now the door was kept in place only by the pair of locks on the right side, but one-inch deadbolts wouldn't swing like hinges. Chyna pulled the padded door by the knuckles of the gudgeons. At first only one inch of its five-inch width came out of the jamb on the left, vinyl squeaking against vinyl. She hooked her fingers around this exposed edge, yanked hard, and her vision clouded with a crimson tint as the pain in her swollen finger flared again. But she was rewarded with the shrill metallic *skreek* of the brass deadbolts working in the striker plates and then with a faint crack of wood as the whole lock assembly put heavy strain on the jamb. Redoubling her efforts, she pulled rhythmically, prying open the door in tiny increments, until she was gasping so hard that she was no longer able to curse with frustration.

The weight of the door and the position of the two deadbolts began to work to her advantage. The locks were close together, one set directly over the other, not evenly spaced like hinges, so the heavy slab tried to twist on them as if they were a single pivot point. Because a greater length of the door lay above the locks than below, the top tipped outward, induced by gravity. Chyna took advantage of these inevitable forces, yanked harder, and grunted with satisfaction when wood splintered again. The entire five-inch width of the padded slab swung free of the jamb on the side that had been hinged. With the frame no longer in the way, she pulled the door to the left, and on the right side, the deadbolts slid out of the striker plates.

Suddenly the door came toward her, free of all restraint, and it was too heavy to be lowered slowly out of its frame. She backed rapidly into the cellar, letting the slab thud to the floor of the vestibule just as she vacated it.

Chyna waited, catching her breath, listening to the house for any indication that Vess had returned.

Finally she reentered the vestibule. She crossed the fallen door as if it were a bridge, and she went into the cell.

The dolls watched, unmoving and sly.

Ariel was sitting in the armchair, head lowered, hands fisted in her lap, exactly as she had been when Chyna had spoken to her through the port in the door. If she had heard the hammering and subsequent commotion, she had not been disturbed by it.

"Ariel?" Chyna said.

The girl didn't reply or raise her head.

Chyna sat on the footstool in front of the armchair. "Honey, it's time to go."

When she received no response, Chyna leaned forward, lowered her head, and looked up at the girl's shadowed face. Ariel's eyes were open, and her gaze was fixed on her white-knuckled fists. Her lips were moving, as though she were whispering confidences to someone, but no sound escaped her.

Chyna put her cuffed hands under Ariel's chin and lifted her head. The girl didn't try to pull away, didn't flinch, but was revealed when her veil of hair slid away from her face. Although they were eye-to-eye, Ariel stared through Chyna, as if all in this world were transparent, and in her eyes was a chilling bleakness, as if the landscape of her other world was lifeless, daunting.

"We have to go. Before he comes home."

Bright-eyed and attentive, perhaps the dolls listened. Ariel apparently did not.

With both hands, Chyna enfolded one of the girl's fists. The bones were sharp and the skin was cold, clenched as fiercely as if she had been suspended from rocks at a precipice.

Chyna tried to pry the fingers apart. The sculpted digits of a marble fist would have been hardly more resistant.

Finally Chyna lifted the hand and kissed it more tenderly than she had ever kissed anyone before, more tenderly than she had ever been kissed, and she said softly, "I want to help you. I *need* to help you, honey. If I can't leave here with you, there's no point in my leaving at all."

Ariel didn't respond.

"Please let me help you." Softer still: "*Please.*"

Chyna kissed the hand once more, and at last she felt the girl's fingers stir. They opened partway, cold and stiff, but would not relax entirely, as hooked and rigid as a skeleton's fingers in which the joints had calcified.

Ariel's desire to reach out for help, tempered by her paralyzing fear of commitment, was achingly familiar to Chyna. It struck in her a chord of sympathy and pity for this girl, for all lost girls, and her throat tightened so severely that for a moment she was unable to swallow or breathe.

Then she slipped one cuffed hand into Ariel's and the other over it, got up from the footstool, and said, "Come on, child. Come with me. Out of here."

Though Ariel's face remained as expressionless as an egg, though she continued to look through Chyna with the otherworldly detachment of a novitiate in the thrall of a holy visitation, her head spinning with visions, she got up from the armchair. After taking only two steps toward the door, however, she stopped and would not go farther in spite of Chyna's pleas. The girl might be able to envision an imaginary world in which she could find a fragile peace, a Wild Wood of her own, but perhaps she was no longer able to imagine that *this* world extended beyond the walls of her cell and, failing to visualize it, could not cross the threshold into it.

Chyna released Ariel's hand. She selected a doll—a bisque charmer with golden ringlets and painted green eyes, wearing a white eyelet pinafore over a blue dress. She pressed it against the girl's breast and encouraged her to embrace it. She wasn't sure why the collection was here, but perhaps Ariel liked the dolls, in which case she might come along more readily if given one for comfort.

Initially, Ariel was unresponsive, standing with one hand still fisted at her side and the other like a half-open crab claw. Then, without shifting her gaze from faraway things, she took the doll in both hands, gripping it by the legs. Like the shadow of a bird in flight, a fierce expression crossed her face and was gone before it could be clearly read. She turned, swung the doll as if it were a sledgehammer, and smashed its head into the top of the dinette table, shattering the unglazed-china face.

Startled, Chyna said, "Honey, no," and gripped the girl by the shoulder.

Ariel wrenched away from Chyna and slammed the doll into the table again, harder than before, and Chyna stepped backward, not in fear but in respect of the girl's fury. And fury it was, a righteous anger, not merely an autistic spasm, in spite of the fact that she remained expressionless.

She pounded the doll against the table repeatedly, until its smashed head broke and spun across the room and bounced off a wall, until both its arms cracked and fell away, until it was ruined beyond repair. Then she dropped it and stood trembling, arms hanging at her sides. She was still staring into the Elsewhere and was no more with Chyna than she had ever been.

From the bookcases, from atop the cabinets, from the shadowed corners of the room, the dolls watched intently, as if they were thrilled by her outburst and in some strange way feeding on it as Vess himself would have fed if he'd been there to see.

Chyna wanted to put her arms around the girl, but the handcuffs made it impossible to embrace her. Instead, she touched Ariel's face and kissed her on the forehead. "Ariel, untouched and alive."

Rigid, shaking, Ariel neither pulled away from Chyna nor leaned toward her. Gradually the girl's trembling subsided.

"I need your help," Chyna pleaded. "I need you."

This time, as if sleepwalking, Ariel allowed herself to be led from the cell.

They crossed the fallen door through the vestibule. In the cellar, Chyna picked up the drill from the floor, plugged it into the power strip on the wall, and put it on the workbench.

She had no timepiece for reference, but she was sure that nine o'clock had come and gone. In the night were dogs waiting and Edgler Vess somewhere at work, bemused by waking dreams of returning home to his pair of captives.

Trying unsuccessfully to get the girl's eyes to focus on her, Chyna explained what they needed to do. She might be able to drive the motor home while handcuffed, though not without some difficulty, as she would have to let go of the steering wheel to shift gears. Dealing with the dogs while cuffed would be a lot harder. Perhaps impossible. If they were to make the best use of the time remaining before Vess's return, and if they were to have the best chance of getting away, Ariel was going to have to drill out the locks on the manacles.

The girl gave no indication that she heard a word of what Chyna told her. Indeed, before Chyna finished, Ariel's lips were moving again in a silent conversation with some phantom; she didn't "speak" ceaselessly but paused from time to time as if receiving a response from an imaginary friend.

Nevertheless, Chyna showed her how to hold the drill and press the trigger. The girl didn't blink at the sudden shriek of the motor and the air-cutting whistle of the whirling bit.

"Now you hold it," Chyna said.

Oblivious, Ariel stood with her arms at her sides, hands half open and fingers hooked as they had been since she had dropped the ruined doll.

"We don't have much time, honey."

In her clockless Elsewhere, time meant nothing to Ariel.

Chyna put the drill on the workbench. She drew the girl in front of the tool and placed her hands on it.

Ariel didn't pull away or let her hands slide off the drill, but she didn't lift it either.

Chyna *knew* that the girl heard her, understood the situation, and, on some level, yearned to help.

"Our hopes are in your hands, honey. You can do it."

She retrieved the workbench stool from the outer vestibule door, which it had been propping open, and sat down. She put her hands on the workbench, wrists turned to expose the tiny keyhole on the left manacle.

Staring at the concrete-block wall, *through* the wall, speaking soundlessly to a psychic friend beyond all walls, Ariel seemed to be unaware of the drill. Or to her it might have been not a drill but another object altogether, one that filled her either with hope or with fear, the thing of which she spoke to her phantom friend.

Even if the girl picked up the drill and focused her eyes on the manacle, the chance that she would be able to perform this task seemed slim. The chance that she would avoid boring through Chyna's palm or wrist seemed slimmer still.

On the other hand, although the likelihood of salvation from any trouble or enemy in this life was always slim, Chyna had survived uncounted nights of blood rage and questing lust. Survival was far different from salvation, of course, but it was a prerequisite.

Anyway, she was ready to do now what she had never been able to do before, not even with Laura Templeton: *trust*. Trust without reservation. And if this girl tried and failed, let the drill slip and damaged flesh rather than steel, Chyna wasn't going to blame her for the failure. Sometimes, just *trying* was a triumph.

And she knew Ariel wanted to try.

She *knew*.

For a minute or so, Chyna encouraged the girl to begin, and when that didn't work, she tried waiting in silence. But silence led her thoughts to the bronze stags and the clock over which they leaped on the living room mantel, and in her mind's eye the clock acquired the face of the young man who hung in the motor home closet, eyelids tightly stitched and lips sewn shut in a silence even deeper than that in the cellar.

With no calculation, surprised to hear what she was doing but relying on instinct, Chyna began to tell Ariel what had happened on the long-ago night of her eighth birthday: the cottage in Key West, the storm, Jim Woltz, the frantic palmetto beetle under the low-slung iron bed . . .

Drunk on Dos Equis and high on a pair of small white pills that he had popped with the first bottle of beer, Woltz had teased Chyna because she had failed to blow out all the candles on her birthday cake in a single breath, leaving one aflame. "This is bad luck, kid. Oh, man, this brings a world of grief down on us. If you don't get all the candles out, you invite gremlins and trolls into your life, all sorts of bad characters after your stash and cash." Just then the night sky had convulsed with white light, and the shadows of palm fronds had leaped across the kitchen windows. The cottage rattled in the shock waves of thunderclaps as hard as bomb blasts, and the storm broke. "See?" Woltz said. "If we don't rectify this situation right away, then some bad guys will get the best of us and chop us up into bloody chunks and put us in bait buckets and go out on some deep-sea boat, trolling for sharks, using us as chum. Do you want to be shark chum, kid?" This speech frightened Chyna, but her mother found it amusing. Her mother had been drinking vodka with lemonade since late afternoon.

Woltz relit the candles and insisted that Chyna try once more. When she failed again to extinguish more than seven with one breath, Woltz seized her hand, licked her thumb and index finger, his tongue lingering in a way that disgusted her, and then forced her to snuff the remaining flame by pinching the candlewick. Although there was a brief hotness against her skin, she had not been burned; however, her fingers had been marked with black smudges from the smoking wick, and the sight of them had terrified her.

When Chyna began to cry, Woltz held her by one arm, keeping her in her chair, while Anne relit the eight, insisting that she try again. The third time, Chyna was able to extinguish only six candles with her first shuddery breath. When Woltz attempted to make her pinch both flames with her fingers, she pulled loose and ran out of the kitchen, intending to flee to the beach, but lightning had shattered like bright mirrors around the cottage, the night flashing with sharp silver fragments, and thunder as fierce as the cannonades of warships boomed out of the Gulf of Mexico, so she had fled instead to the small room in which she slept, crawled under the sagging bed, into those secret shadows where the palmetto beetle waited.

"Woltz, the stinking sonofabitch, came through the house after me," Chyna told Ariel, "shouting my name, knocking over furniture, slamming doors, saying he was going to chop me up for chum and then scatter me in the sea. Later I realized it was an act. He'd been trying to scare the crap out of me. He always liked to scare me, make me cry, 'cause I didn't cry easily . . . never easily. . . ."

Chyna stopped, unable to go on.

Ariel stared not toward the wall, as before, but down at the power drill on which her hands were placed. Whether she saw the drill was another matter; her eyes were still far away.

The girl might not be listening, yet Chyna felt compelled to tell the rest of what had happened that night in Key West.

This was the first time she had ever revealed to anyone, other than Laura, any of the things that had happened to her when she was a child. Shame had always silenced her, which was inexplicable because none of the degradation she endured had resulted from her own actions. She had been a victim, small and defenseless; yet she was burdened with the shame that all her tormentors, including her mother, were incapable of feeling.

She had hidden some of the worst details of her past even from Laura Templeton, her only good friend. Often, on the brink of a revelation to Laura, she would pull back from disclosure and speak not about the events that she had endured and not about the people who had tormented her but about places—Key West, Mendocino County, New Orleans, San Francisco, Wyoming—where she had lived. She was lyrical when the subject was the natural beauty of mountains, plains, bayous, or low moonlit breakers rolling in from the Gulf of Mexico, but she could feel anger tightening her face and shame coloring it when she told the harder truths about the friends of Anne who had populated her childhood.

Now her throat was tight. She was curiously aware of the weight of her heart, like a stone in her chest, heavy with the past.

Sick with shame and anger, she nevertheless sensed that she must finish telling Ariel what had happened during that Florida night of unextinguished candles. Revelation might be a door out of darkness.

"Oh, God, how I hated him, the greasy bastard, stinking of beer and sweat, crashing around my room, drunk and screaming, going to cut me up for bait, Anne laughing out in the living room and then at the doorway, that drunken laugh of hers, hooting and shrill, thinking he was so funny, Jesus, and all the time it was my birthday, my special day, my *birthday."* Tears might have come now if she had not spent a lifetime learning to repress them. "And the palmetto all over me, frantic, scurrying, up my back and into my hair . . ."

In the sticky, suffocating Key West heat, thunder had rattled in the window and sung in the bedsprings, and cold blue reflections of lightning had fluttered like a dream fire across the painted wood floor. Chyna almost screamed when the tropical cockroach, as big as her little-girl hand, burrowed through her long hair, but fear of Woltz kept her silent. She endured, as well, when the beetle scuttled out of her hair, across her shoulder, down her slender arm, to the floor, hoping that it would flee into the room, not daring to fling it away for fear that any movement she made would be heard by Woltz in spite of the thunder, in spite of his shouted threats and curses, even over her mother's laughter. But the palmetto scurried along her side to one of her bare feet and began to explore that end of her again, foot and ankle, calf and thigh. Then it crawled under one leg of her shorts, into the cleft of her butt, antennae quivering. She had lain in a paralysis of terror, wanting only for the torment to end, for lightning to strike her, for God to take her away to somewhere better than this hateful world.

Laughing, her mother had entered the room: "Jimmy, you nut, she's not here. She's gone outside, along the beach somewhere, like always." And Woltz said, "Well, if she comes back, I'm going to cut her up for chum, I swear I am." Then he laughed and said, "Man, did you see her *eyes?* Christ! She was scared shitless." "Yeah," Anne said, "she's a gutless little wuss. She'll be hiding out there for hours. I don't know when the hell she'll ever grow up." Woltz said, "Sure doesn't take after her mother. You were *born* grown up, weren't you, baby?" "Listen, asshole," Anne said, "you pull any crap like that with me, I'm sure not going to run like she did. I'll kick your balls so hard you'll have to change your name to Nancy." Woltz roared with laughter, and from under the bed Chyna saw her mother's bare feet approach Woltz's feet, and then her mother was giggling.

Fat and obscene and agitated, the palmetto had crawled out from under the waistband of Chyna's shorts and into the small of her back, moving toward her neck, and she had been unable to bear the thought of it in her hair again. Regardless of the consequence, she reached back as the beetle crossed her tube top, and seized it. The thing twitched, squirmed in her hand, but she tightened her fist.

Head turned to the side, peering from under the bed, Chyna had still been gazing at her mother's bare feet. As flashes of lightning strobed the small room, a cloth swirled to the floor, a soft drift of yellow linen around Anne's slender ankles. Her blouse. She giggled drunkenly as her shorts slid down her tanned legs, and she stepped out of them.

In Chyna's clenched hand, the angry beetle's legs had churned. Antennae quivered, ceaselessly seeking. Woltz kicked off his sandals, and one of them clattered to the edge of the bed, in front of Chyna's face, and she heard a zipper. Hard and cool and oily, the palmetto's small head rolled between two of Chyna's fingers. Woltz's tattered jeans fell in a heap, with a soft *clink* of the belt buckle.

He and Anne had dropped onto the narrow bed, and the springs had twanged, and the weight had made the frame slats sag against Chyna's shoulders and back, pinning her to the floor. Sighs, murmurs, urgent encouragements, groans, breathless gasps, and coarse animal grunting—Chyna had heard it on other nights in Key West and elsewhere but always before through walls, from rooms next door. She didn't really know what it meant, and she didn't *want* to know, because she sensed that this knowledge would bring new dangers, with which she wasn't equipped to deal. Whatever her mother and Woltz were doing above her was both frightening and deeply sad, full of terrible meaning, no less strange or less powerful than the thunder breaking up the sky above the Gulf and the lightning thrown out of Heaven into the earth.

Chyna had closed her eyes against the lightning and the sight of the discarded clothes. She strove to shut out the smell of dust and mildew and beer and sweat and her mother's scented bath soap, and she imagined that her ears were packed full of wax that muffled the thunder and the drumming of the rain on the roof and the sounds of Anne with Woltz.

As fiercely clenched as she was, she ought to have been able to squeeze herself into a safe state of insensate patience or even through a magical portal into the Wild Wood.

She had been less than half successful, however, because Woltz had rocked the narrow bed so forcefully that Chyna consciously had to time her breathing to the rhythm he established. When the frame slats swagged down with the full thrust of his weight, they pressed Chyna so hard against the bare wood floor that her chest ached and her lungs couldn't expand. She could inhale only when he lifted up, and when he bore down, he virtually forced her to exhale. It went on for what seemed to be a long time, and when at last it was over, Chyna lay shivering and sweat-soaked, numb with terror and desperate to forget what she had heard, surprised that the breath hadn't been crushed out of her forever and that her heart had not burst. In her hand was what remained of the large palmetto beetle, which she had unwittingly crushed; ichor oozed between her fingers, a disgusting slime that might have been vaguely warm when first it had gushed from the beetle but was now cool, and her stomach rolled with nausea at the alien texture of the stuff.

After a while, following a spate of murmurs and soft laughter, Anne had gotten off the bed, snatched up her clothes, and gone down the hall to the bathroom. As the bathroom door closed, Woltz switched on a small nightstand lamp, shifted his weight on the bed, and leaned over the side. His face appeared upside down in front of Chyna. The light was behind him and his face was shadowed but for a dark glitter in his eyes. He smiled at her and said, "How's the birthday girl?" Chyna was unable to speak or move, and she half believed that the wetness in her hand was a bloody hunk of chum. She knew that Woltz would chop her up for having heard him with her mother, chop her to pieces and put her in bait buckets and take her out to sea for the sharks. Instead, he'd gotten out of bed and—from her perspective once more just a pair of feet—he had squirmed into his jeans, put on his sandals, and left the room.

In Edgler Vess's cellar, thousands of miles and eighteen years from that night in Key West, Chyna saw that Ariel at last seemed to be staring *at* the power drill rather than through it.

"I don't know how long I stayed under the bed," she continued. "Maybe a few minutes, maybe an hour. I heard him and my mother in the kitchen again, getting another bottle of beer, fixing another vodka with lemonade for her, talking and laughing. And there was something in her laugh—a dirty little snicker . . . I'm not sure—but something that made me think she knew I'd been hiding under there, knew it but went along with Woltz when he unbuttoned her blouse."

She stared at her cuffed hands on the workbench.

She could feel the beetle's ichor as if it were even now oozing between her fingers. When she had crushed the insect, she had also crushed what remained of her own fragile innocence and all hope of being a daughter to her mother; though after that night, she had still needed years to understand as much.

"I've no memory at all of how I left the cottage, maybe through the front door, maybe through a window, but the next thing I knew, I was on the beach in the storm. I went to the edge of the water and washed my hands in the surf. The breakers weren't huge. They seldom are, there, except in a hurricane, and this was only a tropical storm, almost windless, the heavy rain coming straight down. Still, the waves were bigger than usual, and I thought about swimming out into the black water until I found an undertow. I tried to persuade myself that it would be all right, just swimming in the dark until I got tired, told myself I would just be going to God."

Ariel's hands appeared to tighten on the drill.

"But for the first time in my life, I was afraid of the sea—of how the breaking waves sounded like a giant heart, of how the nearby water was as shiny black as a beetle's shell and seemed to curve up, in the near distance, to meet a black sky that didn't shine at all. It was the endlessness and seamlessness of the dark that scared me—the *continuity*—although that wasn't a word I knew back then. So I stretched out on the beach, flat on my back in the sand, with the rain beating down on me so hard that I couldn't keep my eyes open. Even behind my eyelids, I could see the lightning, a bright ghost of it, and because I was too scared to swim out to God, I waited for God to come to me, blazing bright. But He didn't come, didn't come, and eventually I fell asleep. Shortly after dawn, when I woke, the storm had passed. The sky was red in the east, sapphire in the west, the ocean flat and green. I went inside, and Anne and Woltz were still asleep in his room. My birthday cake was on the kitchen table where it had been the night before. The pink and white icing was soft and beaded with yellowish oil in the heat, and the eight candles were all cockeyed. No one had cut a slice from it, and I didn't touch it either. . . . Two days later, my mother pulled up stakes and carted me off to Tupelo, Mississippi, or Santa Fe, or maybe Boston. I don't remember where, exactly, but I was relieved to be leaving—and afraid of who we would settle in with next. Happy only in the traveling, gone from one thing but not yet arrived at the next, the peace of the road or the rails. I could have traveled forever without a destination."

Above them, the house of Edgler Vess remained silent.

A spiky shadow moved across the cellar floor.

Looking up, Chyna saw a busy spider spinning a web between one of the ceiling joists and one of the lighting fixtures.

Maybe she'd have to deal with the Dobermans while handcuffed. Time was running out.

Ariel picked up the power drill.

Chyna opened her mouth to speak a few words of encouragement but then was afraid that she might say the wrong thing and send the girl deeper into her trance.

Instead, she spotted the safety goggles and, making no comment, got up and put them on the girl. Ariel submitted without objection.

Chyna returned to the stool and waited.

A frown surfaced in the placid pool of Ariel's face. It didn't subside again but floated there.

The girl pressed the trigger of the drill experimentally. The motor shrieked, and the bit whirled. She released the trigger and watched the bit spin to a stop.

Chyna realized that she was holding her breath. She let it out, inhaled deeply, and the air was sweeter than before. She adjusted the position of her hands on the workbench to present Ariel with the left cuff.

Behind the goggles, Ariel's eyes slowly shifted from the point of the drill bit to the keyhole. She was definitely looking *at* things now, but she still appeared detached.

Trust.

Chyna closed her eyes.

As she waited, the silence grew so deep that she began to hear distant imaginary noises, analogue to the phantom lights that play faintly behind closed eyelids: the soft solemn tick of the mantel clock upstairs, the restless movement of vigilant Dobermans in the night outside.

Something pressed against the left manacle.

Chyna opened her eyes.

The bit was in the keyway.

She didn't look up at the girl but closed her eyes again, more tightly this time than previously, to protect them from flying metal shavings. She turned her head to one side.

Ariel bore down on the drill to prevent it from popping out of the keyway, just as Chyna had instructed. The steel manacle pressed hard against Chyna's wrist.

Silence. Stillness. Gathering courage.

Suddenly the drill motor whined. Steel squealed against steel, and the sound was followed by the thin, acrid odor of hot metal. Vibrations in Chyna's wrist bones spread up her arm, exacerbating all the aches and pains in her muscles. A clatter, a hard *ping*, and the left manacle fell open.

She could have functioned reasonably well with the pair of cuffs dangling from her right hand. Perhaps it didn't make sense to risk injury for the relatively small additional advantage of being free of the manacles altogether. But this wasn't about logic. It wasn't about a rational comparison of risks and advantages. It was about faith.

The bit clicked against the keyway as it was inserted into the right manacle. The drill shrieked, and steel jittered-spun against steel. A spray of tiny shavings spattered across the side of Chyna's face, and the lock cracked.

Ariel released the trigger and lifted the drill away.

With a laugh of relief and delight, Chyna shook off the manacles and raised her hands, gazing at them in wonder. Both of her wrists were abraded—actually raw and seeping in places. But that pain was less severe than many others that afflicted her, and no pain could diminish the exhilaration of being free at last.

As if not sure what to do next, Ariel stood with the drill in both hands.

Chyna took the tool and set it aside on the workbench. "Thank you, honey. That was terrific. You did great, really great, you were perfect."

The girl's arms hung at her sides again, and her delicate pale hands were no longer hooked like claws but were as slack as those of a sleeper.

Chyna slipped the goggles off Ariel's head, and they made eye contact, *real* contact. Chyna saw the girl who lived behind the lovely face, the true girl inside the safe fortress of the skull, where Edgler Vess could get at her only with tremendous effort if ever.

Then, in an instant, Ariel's gaze traveled from this world to the sanctuary of her Elsewhere.

Chyna said, "Nooooo," because she didn't want to lose the girl whom she had so briefly glimpsed. She put her arms around Ariel and held her tight and said, "Come back, honey. It's okay. Come back to me, talk to me."

But Ariel did not come back. After pulling herself completely into the world of Edgler Vess long enough to drill out the locks on the manacles, she had exhausted her courage.

"Okay, I don't blame you. We're not out of here yet," Chyna said. "But now we only have the dogs to worry about."

Though still living in a far realm, Ariel allowed Chyna to take her hand and lead her to the stairs.

"We can handle a bunch of damn dogs, kid. Better believe it," Chyna said, though she was not sure if she believed it herself.

Free of manacles and shackles, no longer carrying a chair on her back, with a stomach full of coffeecake, and with a gloriously empty bladder, she had nothing to think about except the dogs. Halfway up the stairs toward the laundry room, she remembered something that she had seen earlier; it had been puzzling then, but it was clear now—and vitally important.

"Wait. Wait here," she told Ariel, and pressed the girl's limp hand around the railing.

She plunged back down the stairs, went to the metal cabinets, and pulled open the door behind which she had seen the strange pads trailing black leather straps with chrome-plated buckles. She pulled them out, scattering them on the floor around her, until the cabinet was empty.

They weren't pads. They were heavily padded garments. A jacket with a dense foam outer layer under a man-made fabric that appeared to be a lot tougher than leather. Especially thick padding around both arms. A pair of bulky chaps featured hard plastic under the padding, body-armor quality; the plastic was segmented and hinged at the knees to allow the wearer flexibility. Another pair of chaps protected the backs of the legs and came with a hard-plastic butt shield, a waist belt, and buckles that connected them to the front chaps.

Behind the garments were gloves and an odd padded helmet with a clear Plexiglas face shield. She also found a vest that was labeled KEVLAR, which looked exactly like the bulletproof garments worn by members of police SWAT teams.

A few small tears marred the garments—and in many places other rips had been sewn shut with black thread as heavy as fishing line. She recognized the same neat stitches that she had seen in the young hitchhiker's lips and eyelids. Here and there in the padding were unrepaired punctures. Tooth marks.

This was the protective gear that Vess wore when he worked with the Dobermans.

Apparently he layered on enough padding and armor to walk safely through a pride of hungry lions. For a man who liked to take risks, who believed in living life on the edge, he seemed to take excessive precautions when putting his pack of Dobermans through their training sessions.

Vess's extraordinary safeguards told Chyna everything that she needed to know about the savagery of the dogs.

T E N

Less than twenty-two hours since the first cry in the Templeton house in Napa. A lifetime. And now toward another midnight and into whatever lay beyond.

Two lamps were aglow in the living room. Chyna no longer cared about keeping the house dark. As soon as she went out the front door and confronted the dogs, there would be no hope of lulling Vess into a false sense of security if he came home early.

According to the mantel clock, it was ten-thirty.

Ariel sat in one of the armchairs. She was hugging herself and rocking slowly back and forth, as if suffering from a stomachache, although she made no sound and remained expressionless.

Protective gear designed for Vess was huge on Chyna, and she vacillated between feeling ridiculous and worrying that she would be dangerously impeded by the bulky garb. She had rolled up the bottoms of the chaps and fixed them in place with large safety pins that she'd found in a sewing kit in the laundry room. The belts of the chaps featured loops and long Velcro closures, so she was able to cinch them tight enough to keep them from sliding down over her hips. The cuffs of the padded sleeves were folded back and pinned too, and the Kevlar vest helped to bulk her up, so she wasn't quite swimming in the jacket. She wore a segmented plastic-armor collar that encircled her neck and prevented the dogs from tearing out her throat. She couldn't have been more cumbersomely dressed if she'd been cleaning up nuclear waste in a post-meltdown reactor.

Nevertheless, she was vulnerable in places, especially at her feet and ankles. Vess's training togs included a pair of leather combat boots with steel toes, but they were much too big for her. As protection against attack dogs, her soft Rockports were hardly more effective than bedroom slippers. In order to get to the motor home without being severely bitten, she would have to be quick and aggressive.

She had considered carrying a club of some kind. But with her agility impaired by the layers of protective gear, she couldn't use it effectively enough to hurt any of the Dobermans or even dissuade them from attacking.

Instead, Chyna was equipped with two lever-action spray bottles that she'd found in a laundry-room cabinet. One had been filled with a liquid glass cleaner and the other with a spot remover for use on carpets and upholstery. She had emptied both bottles into the kitchen sink, rinsed them out, considered filling them with bleach, but chose pure ammonia, of which the fastidious Vess, the keeper of a spotless house, possessed two one-quart containers. Now the plastic spray bottles stood beside the front door. The nozzle on each could be adjusted to produce a spray or a stream, and both were set at STREAM.

In the armchair, Ariel continued to hug herself and to rock back and forth in silence, gazing down at the carpet.

Although it was unlikely that the catatonic girl would get up from the chair and go anywhere on her own, Chyna said, "Now, you stay right where you are, honey. Don't move, okay? I'll be back for you soon."

Ariel didn't reply.

"Don't move."

Chyna's layers of protective clothing were beginning to weigh painfully on her bruised muscles and sore joints. Minute by minute, the discomfort was going to make her slower mentally and physically. She had to act while she was still reasonably sharp.

She put on the visored helmet. She had lined the interior with a folded towel so it wouldn't sit loosely on her head, and the chin strap helped to keep it secure. The curved shield of Plexiglas came two inches below her chin, but the underside was open to allow air to flow in freely—and there were six small holes across the center of the pane for additional ventilation.

She stepped to one front window and then to the other, looking onto the porch, which was visible in the light that spilled out from the living-room lamps. There were no Dobermans in sight.

The yard beyond the porch was dark, and the meadow beyond the yard seemed as black as the far side of the moon. The dogs might be standing out there, watching her silhouette in the lighted windows. In fact, they might be waiting just beyond the porch balustrade, crouched and ready to spring.

She glanced at the clock.

Ten thirty-eight.

"Oh, God, I don't want to do this," she murmured.

Curiously, she remembered a cocoon that she'd found when she and her mother had been staying with some people in Pennsylvania fourteen or fifteen years before. The chrysalis had been hanging from a twig on a birch tree, semitransparent and backlit by a beam of sunlight, so she had been able to see the insect within. It was a butterfly that had passed all the way through the pupa stage, a fully mature imago. Its metamorphosis complete, it had been quivering frantically within the cocoon, its wirelike legs twitching ceaselessly, as if it was eager to be free but frightened of the hostile world into which it would be born. Now, in her padding and hard-plastic armor, Chyna quivered like that butterfly, although she was not eager to burst free into the night world that awaited her but wanted to withdraw even deeper into her chrysalis.

She went to the front door.

She pulled on the stained leather gloves, which were heavy but surprisingly flexible. They were too large but had adjustable Velcro bands at the wrists to hold them in place.

She had sewn a brass key to the thumb of the right-hand glove, running the thread through the hole in the key bow. The entire blade, with all its tumbler-activating serrations, extended beyond the tip of the thumb, so it could be inserted easily into the keyway on the door of the motor home. She didn't want to have to fumble the key from a pocket with the dogs attacking from all sides—and she sure as hell didn't want to risk dropping it.

Of course, the vehicle might not be locked. But she wasn't taking any chances.

From the floor, she picked up the spray bottles. One in each hand. Again, she checked to be sure that they were set on STREAM.

She quietly disengaged the deadbolt lock, listened for the hollow thump of paws on the board floor, and finally cracked the door.

The porch looked clear.

Chyna crossed the threshold and quickly pulled the door shut behind her, fumbling at the knob because she was hampered by the plastic bottles in her hands.

She hooked her fingers around the levers on the bottles. The effectiveness of these weapons would depend on how fast the dogs came at her and whether she could aim well in the brief window of opportunity that they would give her.

In a night as windless as it was deep, the seashell mobile hung motionless. Not even a single leaf stirred on the tree at the north end of the porch.

The night seemed to be soundless. With her ears under the padded helmet, however, she wasn't able to hear small noises.

She had the weird feeling that the entire world was but a highly detailed diorama sealed inside a glass paperweight.

Without even the faintest breeze to carry her scent to the dogs, maybe they would not be aware that she had come outside.

Yeah, and maybe pigs can fly but just don't want us to know.

The fieldstone steps were at the south end of the porch. The motor home stood in the driveway, twenty feet from the bottom of the steps.

Keeping her back to the wall of the house, she edged to her right. As she moved, she glanced repeatedly to her left at the railed north side of the porch, and out past the balustrade into the front yard directly ahead of her. No dogs.

The night was so chilly that her breath formed a faint fog on the inside of her visor. Each flare of condensation faded quickly—but each seemed to fan out across the Plexiglas farther than the one before it. In spite of the ventilation from under her chin and through the six penny-size holes across the center of the pane, she began to worry that her own hot exhalations were gradually going to leave her effectively blind. She was breathing hard and fast, and she was hardly more able to slow her rate of respiration than quiet the rapid pounding of her heart.

If she *blew* each breath out, angling it toward the open bottom of the face shield, she would be able to minimize the problem. This resulted in a faint, hollow whistling characterized by a vibrato that revealed the depth of her fear.

Two small sliding steps, three, four: She eased sideways past the living-room window. She was uncomfortably aware of the light at her back. Silhouetted again.

She should have turned all the lights out, but she hadn't wanted Ariel to be alone in the dark. In her current condition, perhaps the girl would not have known if the lights were on or off, but it had felt wrong to leave her in blackness.

Having crossed half the distance from the door to the south end of the porch without incident, Chyna grew bolder. Instead of edging sideways, she turned directly toward the steps and shuffled forward as fast as the hampering gear would allow.

As black as the night out of which it came, as silent as the high patchy clouds sailing slowly across fields of stars, the first Doberman sprinted toward her from the front of the motor home. It didn't bark or growl.

She almost failed to see it in time. Because she forgot to exhale with calculation, a wave of condensation spread across the inside of the visor. At once, the pale film of moisture retreated like an ebbing surf, but the dog was already *there*, leaping toward the steps, ears flattened against its tapered skull, lips skinned back from its teeth.

She squeezed the lever of the spray bottle that she clutched in her right hand. Ammonia shot six or seven feet in the still air.

The dog wasn't within range when the first stream spattered onto the porch floor, but it was closing fast.

She felt stupid, like a kid with a water pistol. This wasn't going to work. Wasn't going to work. But oh, Jesus, it *had* to work or she was dog chow.

Immediately she pumped the lever again, and the dog was on the steps, where the stream fell short of it, and she wished that she had a sprayer with more pressure, one with at least a twenty-foot range, so she could stop the beast before it got near her, but she squeezed the trigger again even as the previous stream was still falling, and this one got the dog as it came up onto the porch. She was aiming for its eyes, but the ammonia splashed its muzzle, spattering its nose and its bared teeth.

The effect was instantaneous. The Doberman lost its footing and tumbled toward Chyna, squealing, and would have crashed into her if she hadn't jumped aside.

With caustic ammonia slathering its tongue and fumes filling its lungs, unable to draw a breath of clean air, the dog rolled onto its back, pawing frantically at its snout. It wheezed and hacked and made shrill sounds of distress.

Chyna turned from it. She kept moving.

She was surprised to hear herself speaking aloud: "Shit, shit, shit . . ."

Onward, then, to the head of the porch steps, where she glanced back warily and saw that the big dog was on its feet, wobbling in circles, shaking its head. Between sharp squeals of pain, it was sneezing violently.

The second dog virtually *flew* out of the darkness, attacking as Chyna descended the bottom step. From the corner of her eye, she detected movement to her left, turned her head, and saw an airborne Doberman—*oh, God*—like an incoming mortar round. Though she raised her left arm and started to swing toward the dog, she wasn't quick enough, and before she could loose a stream of ammonia, she was hit so hard that she was nearly bowled off her feet. She stumbled sideways but somehow maintained her balance.

The Doberman's teeth were sunk into the thick sleeve on her left arm. It wasn't merely holding her as a police dog would have done but was working at the padding as if chewing on meat, trying to rip off a chunk and severely disable her, tear open an artery so she would bleed to death, but fortunately its teeth hadn't penetrated to her flesh.

After coming at her in disciplined silence, the dog still wasn't snarling. But from low in its throat issued a sound halfway between a growl and a hungry keening, an eerie and needful cry that Chyna heard too clearly in spite of her padded helmet.

Point-blank, reaching across her body with her right hand, she squirted a stream of ammonia into the Doberman's fierce black eyes.

The dog's jaws flew open as if they were part of a mechanical device that had popped a tension spring, and it spun away from her, silvery strings of saliva trailing from its black lips, howling in agony.

She remembered the words of warning on the ammonia label: *Causes substantial but temporary eye injury.*

Squealing like an injured child, the dog rolled in the grass, pawing at its eyes as the first animal had pawed at its snout, but with even greater urgency.

The manufacturer recommended rinsing contaminated eyes with plenty of water for fifteen minutes. The dog had no water, unless it instinctively made its way to a stream or pond, so it would not be a problem to her for *at least* a quarter of an hour, most likely far longer.

The Doberman sprang to its feet and chased its tail, snapping its teeth. It stumbled and fell again, scrambled erect, and streaked away into the night, temporarily blinded, in considerable pain.

Incredibly, listening to the poor thing's screams as she hurried toward the motor home, Chyna winced with remorse. It would have torn her apart without hesitation if it could have gotten at her, but it was a mindless killer only by training, not by nature. In a way, the dogs were just other victims of Edgler Vess, their lives bent to his purpose. She would have spared them suffering if she had been able to rely solely on the protective clothing.

How many more dogs?

Vess had implied there was a pack. Hadn't he said *four?* Of course, he might be lying. There might be only two.

Move, move, move.

At the passenger-side cockpit door of the motor home, she tried the handle. Locked.

No more dogs, just five seconds without dogs, please.

She dropped the spray bottle from her right hand, so she could pinch the bow of the key between her thumb and finger. She was barely able to feel it through the thick gloves.

Her hand was shaking. The key missed the keyhole and chattered against the chrome face of the lock cylinder. She would have dropped it if it hadn't been sewn to the glove.

From behind this time, just as she was about to slip the key into the door on her second try, a Doberman hit her, leaping onto her back, biting at the nape of her neck.

She was slammed forward against the vehicle. The face shield on her helmet smacked hard against the door.

The dog's teeth were sunk into the thick rolled collar of the trainer's jacket, no doubt also into the padding on the segmented plastic collar that she wore under the jacket to protect her neck. It was holding on to her by its teeth, tearing at her ineffectively with its claws, like a demon lover in a nightmare.

As the dog's impact had pitched her forward against the motor home, now the weight of it and its furious squirming dragged her away from the vehicle. She almost toppled backward, but she knew that the advantage would go to the dog if it managed to drag her to the ground.

Stay up. Stay tall.

Lurching around a hundred eighty degrees as she struggled to keep her balance, she saw that the first Doberman was no longer on the porch. Astonishingly, the creature hanging from her neck must be the small one that she had squirted on the muzzle. Now it was able to get its breath again, back in service, undaunted by her chemical arsenal, giving its all for Edgler Vess.

On the plus side, maybe there *were* only two dogs.

She still had the spray bottle in her left hand. She squeezed the trigger, aiming several squirts over her shoulder. But the heavy padding in the jacket sleeves didn't allow her to bend her arms much, and she wasn't able to fire at an angle that could splash the ammonia in the dog's eyes.

She threw herself backward against the side of the motor home, much as she had hurtled into the fireplace earlier. The Doberman was trapped between her and the vehicle as the chair had been between her and the river-rock wall, and it took the brunt of the impact.

Letting go of her, falling away, the dog squealed, a pitiful sound that sickened her, but also a good sound—*oh, yes*—a good sound as sweet as any music.

Buckles jangling, padded chaps slapping together, Chyna scuttled sideways, trying to get out of the animal's reach, worried about her ankles, her vulnerable ankles.

But suddenly the Doberman no longer seemed to be in a fighting mood. It slunk away from her, tail tucked between its legs, rolling its eyes to keep a watch on her peripherally, shaking and wheezing as though it had damaged a lung, and favoring its hind leg on the right side.

She squeezed the trigger on the spray bottle. The creature was out of range, and the stream of ammonia arced into the grass.

Two dogs down.

Move, move.

Chyna turned to the motor home again—and cried out as a third dog, weighing more than she did, leaped at her throat, bit through the jacket, and staggered her backward.

Going down. *Shit.* And as she went, the dog was on top of her, chewing frenziedly at the collar of the jacket.

When Chyna hit the ground, her breath was knocked from her in spite of all the padding, and the spray bottle popped out of her left hand, spun into the air. She grabbed at it as it tumbled away, but she missed.

The dog ripped loose a strip of padding from around the jacket collar and shook its head, casting the scrap aside, spraying her face shield with gobs of foamy saliva. It bore in at her again, tearing more fiercely at the same spot, burrowing deeper, seeking meat, blood, triumph.

She pounded its sleek head with both fists, trying to smash its ears, hoping that they would be sensitive, vulnerable. "Get off, damn it, off! Off!"

The Doberman snapped at her right hand, missed, teeth clashing audibly, snapped again, and connected. Its incisors didn't instantly penetrate the tough leather glove, but it shook her hand viciously, as though it had hold of a rat and meant to snap its spine. Though her skin hadn't been broken, the grinding pressure of the bite was so painful that Chyna screamed.

In an instant, the dog released her hand and was at her throat again. Past the torn jacket. Teeth slashing at the Kevlar vest.

Howling in pain, Chyna stretched her throbbing right hand toward the spray bottle lying in the grass. The weapon was a foot beyond her reach.

When turning her head to look at the bottle, she inadvertently caused the bottom of her face shield to lift, giving the Doberman better access to her throat, and it thrust its muzzle under the curve of Plexiglas, above the Kevlar vest, biting into the thick padding on the exterior of the segmented hard-plastic collar, which was her last defense. Intent on tearing this band of body armor away, the dog jerked back so hard that Chyna's head was lifted off the ground, and pain flared across the nape of her neck.

She tried to heave the Doberman off her. It was heavy, bearing down stubbornly, paws digging frantically at her.

As the dog wrenched at Chyna's protective collar, she could feel its hot breath against the underside of her chin. If it could get its snout under the shield at a slightly better angle, it might be able to bite her chin, *would* be able to bite her chin, and at any moment it was going to realize this.

She heaved with all her strength, and the dog clung, but she was able to hitch a few inches closer to the spray bottle. She heaved again, and now the bottle was just six inches beyond her grasping fingertips.

She saw the other Doberman limping toward her, ready to rejoin the fray. She hadn't damaged its lungs, after all, when she slammed it between her and the motor home.

Two of them. She couldn't handle two of them at once, both on top of her.

She heaved, desperately hitching sideways on her back, dragging the clinging Doberman with her.

Its hot tongue licked the underside of her chin, licked, tasting her sweat. It was making that horrible, needful sound deep in its throat.

Heave.

Spotting her point of greatest vulnerability, the limping dog scuttled toward her right foot. She kicked at it, and the dog dodged back, but then it darted in again. She kicked, and the Doberman bit the heel of her Rockport.

Her frantic breathing fogged the inside of the visor. In fact, the breath of the clinging Doberman fogged it too, because its muzzle was under the Plexiglas. She was effectively blind.

Kicking with both feet to ward off the limping dog. Kicking, heaving sideways.

The other's hot tongue slathered her chin. Its sour breath. Teeth gnashing an inch short of her flesh. The tongue again.

Chyna touched the spray bottle. Closed her fingers around it.

Though the bite hadn't penetrated the glove, her hand was still throbbing with such crippling pain that she was afraid she wouldn't be able to hold on to the bottle or find the right grip, wouldn't be able to work the lever-action trigger, but then she blindly squeezed off a stream of ammonia. Unthinking, she had used her swollen trigger finger, and the flash of pain made her dizzy. She shifted her middle finger onto the lever and squeezed off another blast.

In spite of her kicking, the injured dog bit through her shoe. Teeth pierced her right foot.

Chyna triggered another thick stream of ammonia toward her feet, yet another, and abruptly that Doberman let go of her. Both she and the dog were shrieking, blind and shaking and living now in the same commonwealth of pain.

Snapping teeth. The remaining dog. Pressing toward her chin, under the visor. *Snap-snap-snap*. And the eager hungry whine.

She jammed the bottle in its face, pulled the trigger, pulled, and the dog scrambled off her, screaming.

A few drops of ammonia penetrated the visor through the series of small holes across the center of the pane. She wasn't able to see through the fogged Plexiglas, and the acrid fumes made breathing difficult.

Gasping, eyes watering, she dropped the spray bottle and crawled on her hands and knees toward where she thought the motor home stood. She bumped into the side of it and pulled herself to her feet. Her bitten foot felt hot, perhaps because it was soaking in the bath of blood contained in her shoe, but she could put her weight on it.

Three dogs so far.

If three, then surely four.

The fourth would be coming.

As the ammonia evaporated from the face shield and less rapidly from the front of her torn jacket, the quantity of fumes decreased but not quickly enough. She was eager to remove the helmet and draw an unobstructed breath. She didn't dare take it off, however, not until she was inside the motor home.

Choking on ammonia fumes, trying to remember to exhale downward under the Plexiglas visor but half blinded because her eyes wouldn't stop watering, Chyna felt along the side of the motor home until she found the cockpit door again. She was surprised that she could walk on her bitten foot with only tolerable twinges of pain.

The key was still sewn securely to her right glove. She pinched it between her thumb and forefinger.

A dog was wailing in the distance, probably the first one that she had squirted in the eyes. Nearby, another was crying pitifully and howling. A third whimpered, sneezed, gagged on fumes.

But where was the fourth?

Fumbling at the lock cylinder, she found the keyhole by trial and error. She opened the door. She hauled herself up into the copilot's seat.

As she pulled the door shut, something slammed into the outside of it. The fourth dog. She took off the helmet, the gloves. She stripped out of the padded jacket.

Teeth bared, the fourth Doberman leaped at the side window. Its claws rattled briefly against the glass, and then it dropped back to the lawn, glaring at her.

Revealed by the light from the narrow hallway, Laura Templeton's body still lay on the bed in a tangle of manacles and chains, wrapped in a sheet.

Chyna's chest tightened with emotion, and her throat swelled so that she had trouble swallowing. She told herself that the corpse on the bed was not really Laura. The essence of Laura was gone, and this was only the husk, merely flesh and bone on a long journey to dust. Laura's spirit had traveled in the night to a brighter and warmer home, and there was no point shedding tears for her, because she had transcended.

The closet door was closed. Chyna was sure that the dead man still hung in there.

In the fourteen hours or longer since she had been in the motor-home bedroom, the stuffy air had acquired a faint but repulsive scent of corruption. She had expected worse. Nevertheless, she breathed through her mouth, trying to avoid the smell.

She switched on the reading lamp and opened the top drawer of the nightstand. The items that she had discovered the previous night were still there, rattling softly against one another as the engine vibrations translated through the floor.

She was nervous about leaving the engine running, because the sound of it would mask the approach of another vehicle in case Vess came home earlier. But she needed lights, and she didn't want to risk depleting the battery.

From the drawer, she withdrew the package of gauze pads, the roll of cloth tape, and the scissors.

In the lounge area behind the cockpit, she sat in one of the armchairs. Earlier, she had stripped out of all the protective gear. Now she removed her right shoe. Her sock was sodden with blood, and she peeled it off.

From two punctures in the top of her foot, blood welled dark and thick. It was seeping, however, not spurting, and she wasn't going to die from the wound itself anytime soon.

She quickly pressed a double thickness of gauze pads over the seeping holes and fixed them in place with a length of cloth tape. By tightening the tape to apply a little pressure, she might be able to make the bleeding slow or stop.

She would have preferred to saturate the punctures with Bactine or iodine, but she didn't have anything like that. Anyway, infection wouldn't set in for a few hours, and by then she would have gotten away from here and obtained medical attention. Or she'd be dead of other causes.

The chance of rabies seemed small to nil. Edgler Vess would be solicitous of the health of his dogs. They would have received all their vaccinations.

Her sock was cold and slimy with blood, and she didn't even try to pull it on again. She slipped her bandaged foot into her shoe and tied the lace slightly looser than usual.

A folding metal stepstool was stored in a narrow slot between the kitchen cabinetry and the refrigerator. She carried it into the short hallway at the end of the vehicle and opened it under the skylight, which was a flat panel of frosted plastic about three feet long and perhaps twenty inches wide.

She climbed onto the stool to inspect the skylight, hoping that it either tilted open to admit fresh air or was attached to the roof from the interior. Unfortunately, the panel was fixed, with no louver function, and the mounting flange was on the exterior, so she could not get at any screws or rivets from the inside.

Under her padded clothing, she had worn a tool belt that she'd found in one of the drawers of Vess's workbench. She had taken it off with the rest of the gear. Now it was on the table in the dining nook.

Unable to be certain what tools she would need, she'd brought a pair of standard pliers, a pair of needle-nose pliers, both flat and rat-tail files, and several sizes of screwdrivers with standard blades and Phillips heads. There was also a hammer, which was the only thing that she could use.

When she stood on the first step of the two-step stool, the top of her head was only ten inches from the skylight. Averting her face, she swung the hammer with her left hand, and the flat steel head met the plastic with a horrendous bang and clatter.

The skylight was undamaged.

Chyna swung the hammer relentlessly. Each blow reverberated in the plastic overhead but also through all of her strained and weary muscles, through her aching bones.

The motor home was at least fifteen years old, and this appeared to be the original factory-installed skylight. It wasn't Plexiglas but some less formidable material; over many years of sunshine and bad weather, the plastic had grown brittle. Finally the rectangular panel cracked along one edge of the frame. Chyna hammered at the leading point of the fissure, making it grow all the way to the corner, then along the narrow end, and then along the other three-foot length.

She had to pause several times to catch her breath and to change the hammer from hand to hand. At last the panel rattled loosely in its frame; it now seemed to be secured only by splinters of material along the fissures and by the uncracked fourth edge.

Chyna dropped the hammer, slowly flexed her hands a few times to work some of the stiffness out of them, and then put both palms flat against the plastic. Grunting with the effort, she pushed upward as she climbed onto the second step of the stool.

With a brittle splintering of plastic, the panel lifted an inch, jagged edges squeaking against each other. Then it bent backward at its fourth side, creaking, resisting her . . .

resisting . . . until she cried out wordlessly in frustration and, finding new strength, pushed even harder. Abruptly the fourth side cracked all the way through, with a *bang!* as loud as a gunshot.

She pushed the panel out through the ceiling. It rattled across the roof and dropped to the driveway.

Through the hole above her head, Chyna saw clouds suddenly slide away from the moon. Cold light bathed her upturned face, and in the bottomless sky was the clean white fire of stars.

Chyna backed the motor home off the driveway and alongside the front of the house, parallel to the porch and as close to it as she could get. She let the big vehicle roll slowly, anxious not to tear up the thick grass, because under it the ground might be muddy even half a day after the rain had stopped. She didn't dare bog down.

When she was in position, she put the vehicle in park and set the emergency brake. She left the engine running.

In the short hall at the back of the motor home, the stepstool had fallen over. She put it upright, climbed the two steps, and stood with her head in the night air, above the open frame of the broken-out skylight.

She wished the stool had a third step. She needed to muscle herself out of the hallway, and she was at a less advantageous angle than she would have liked.

She placed her hands flat on the roof on opposite sides of the twenty-inch-wide rectangular opening and struggled to lever her body out of the motor home. She strained so hard that she could feel the tendons flaring between her neck and shoulders, her pulse pounding like doomsday drums in her temples and carotid arteries, every muscle in her arms and across her back quivering with the effort.

Pain and exhaustion seemed certain to thwart her. But then she thought of Ariel in the living-room armchair: rocking back and forth, hugging herself, a faraway look in her eyes, her lips parted in what might have been a silent scream. That image of the girl empowered Chyna, put her in touch with hitherto unknown resources. Her shaking arms slowly straightened, pulling her body out of the hallway, and inch by inch she kicked her feet as if she were a swimmer ascending from the depths. At last her elbows locked with her arms at full extension, and she heaved forward, out through the skylight, onto the roof.

On the way, her sweater caught on small fragments of plastic that bristled from the skylight frame. A few jagged points pierced the knit material and stung her belly, but she broke loose of them.

She crawled forward, rolled onto her back, hiked her sweater, and felt her stomach to see how badly she had been cut. Blood wept from a couple of shallow punctures, but she wasn't hurt seriously.

From far off in the night came the howls of at least two injured dogs. Their pathetic cries were so filled with fear, vulnerability, misery, and loneliness that Chyna could hardly bear to listen.

She eased to the edge of the roof and looked down at the yard to the east of the house.

The uninjured Doberman trotted around the front of the motor home and spotted her at once. It stood directly under her, gazing up, teeth bared. It seemed unfazed by the suffering of its three comrades.

Chyna moved away from the edge and got to her feet. The metal surface was somewhat slippery with dew, and she was thankful for the rubber tread on her Rockports. If she lost her footing and fell off into the yard, with no weapons and no protective clothing, the one remaining Doberman would overwhelm her and tear out her throat in ten seconds flat.

The motor home was only a few inches below the edge of the porch roof. She had parked so close that the distance between the vehicle and the house was less than a foot.

She stepped up and across that gap, onto the sloped roof of the porch. The asphalt shingles had a sandy texture and weren't nearly as treacherous as the top of the motor home.

The slope wasn't steep either, and she climbed easily to the front wall of the house. The recent rain had liberated a tarry scent from the numerous coats of creosote with which the logs had been treated over the years.

The double-hung window of Vess's second-story bedroom was open three inches, as she had left it before departing the house. She slipped her aching hands through the opening and, groaning, shoved up on the bottom panel. In this wet weather, the wood had swollen, but although it stuck a couple of times, she got it all the way open.

She climbed through the window into Vess's bedroom, where she had left a lamp burning.

In the upstairs hall, she glanced at the open door across from the bedroom. The dark study lay beyond, and she was still troubled by the feeling that there was something in it that she had missed, something vital she should know about Edgler Vess.

But she had no time for additional detective work. She hurried downstairs to the living room.

Ariel was huddled in the armchair where she had been left. She was still hugging herself and rocking, lost.

According to the mantel clock, the time was four minutes past eleven.

"You stay right there," Chyna instructed. "Just a minute more, honey."

She went through the kitchen to the laundry room, in search of a broom. She found both a broom and a sponge mop. The mop had the longer handle of the two, so she took it instead of the broom.

As she entered the living room again, she heard a familiar and dreaded sound. *Squeak-squeak. Squeak-squeak-squeak.*

She glanced at the nearest window and saw the uninjured Doberman clawing the glass. Its pointy ears were pricked, but they flattened against its skull when Chyna made eye contact with the creature. The Doberman issued the now-familiar needful keening that caused the fine hairs to stiffen on the nape of Chyna's neck.

Squeak-squeak-squeak.

Turning away from the dog, Chyna started toward Ariel—and then had her attention drawn to the other living-room window. A Doberman stood with its forepaws at the base of that pane too.

This had to be the first one she had encountered when she'd gone out of the house, the same animal that she had sprayed in the muzzle. It had recovered quickly and had bitten her foot when she'd been pinned on the ground by the third dog.

She was sure that she'd blinded the second dog, which had shot at her like a mortar round from out of the darkness, and the third as well. Until now she had assumed that her second chance at *this* animal had also resulted in a disabling eye shot.

She'd been wrong.

At the time, of course, she herself had been all but blinded by her fogged visor—and frantic, because the third dog had been holding her down and chewing through the padding at her throat, licking at her chin. All she had known was that this animal had shrieked when she'd squirted it and that it had stopped biting her foot.

The stream of ammonia must have splashed the dog's muzzle the second time, just as it had during their first encounter.

"Lucky bastard," she whispered.

The twice-injured Doberman didn't scratch at the window glass. It just watched her. Intently. Ears standing straight up. Missing nothing.

Or perhaps it wasn't the same dog at all. Perhaps there were *five* of them. Or six.

At the other window: *Squeak-squeak. Squeak-squeak.*

Crouching in front of Ariel, Chyna said, "Honey, we're ready to go."

The girl rocked.

Chyna took hold of one of Ariel's hands. This time, she didn't have to pry the fingers out of a marble-hard fist, and at her urging, the girl got up from the chair.

Carrying the sponge mop in one hand, leading the girl with the other, Chyna crossed the living room, past the two big front windows. She moved slowly and didn't look directly at the Dobermans, because she was afraid that either haste or another moment of confrontational eye contact might spur them to smash through the glass.

She and Ariel stepped through a doorless opening to the stairs.

Behind them, one of the dogs began to bark.

Chyna didn't like that. Didn't like that at all. None of them had barked before. Their disciplined stealth had been chilling—but now the barking was worse than their silence.

Climbing the stairs, pulling the girl after her, Chyna felt a hundred years old, weak and depleted. She wanted to sit and catch her breath and let her aching legs rest. To keep moving, Ariel needed constant tension on her arm; without it, she stopped and stood murmuring soundlessly. Each riser seemed higher than the one below it, as though Chyna were the storybook Alice in the wake of the white rabbit, her stomach full of exotic mushrooms, ascending an enchanted staircase in some dark wonderland.

Then, as they turned at the landing and started up the second flight, glass shattered into the living room below. In an instant, that sound made Chyna young again, able to bound like a gazelle up stairs made for giants.

"Hurry!" she urged Ariel, pulling her along.

The girl picked up her pace but still seemed to be plodding.

Leaping, desperate, to the top of the second flight, Chyna said, *"Hurry!"*

Vicious barking rose in the stairwell below.

Chyna entered the upstairs hall, holding tightly to the girl's hand. She could hear the galloping thunder of ascending dogs louder even than her own heart.

To the door on the left. Into Vess's bedroom.

She dragged Ariel after her, across the threshold, and slammed the door. There was no lock, just the spring latch activated by the knob.

They're dogs, for God's sake, just dogs, mean as hell, but they can't operate a doorknob.

A dog threw itself against the door, which rattled in its frame but seemed secure.

Chyna led Ariel to the open window, where she propped the mop against the wall.

Barking, barking, the dogs clawed at the door.

With both hands, Chyna clasped the girl's face, leaned close, and peered hopefully into her beautiful blue but vacant eyes. "Honey, please, I need you again, like I needed you with the power drill and the handcuffs. I need you a lot worse now, Ariel, because we don't have much time, not much time at all, and we're so close, we really are, so damn *close.*"

Though their eyes were at most three inches apart, Ariel seemed not to see Chyna.

"Listen to me, listen, honey, wherever you are, wherever you're hiding out there in the Wild Wood or beyond the wardrobe door there in Narnia—is that where you are, baby?—or maybe Oz, but wherever you are, *please* listen to me and do what I tell you. We've got to go out on the porch roof. It's not steep, you can do it, but you have to be careful. I want you to go out the window and then take a couple of steps to the left. Not to the right. There's not much roof to the right, you'll fall off. Take a couple steps to the left and stop and just wait there for me. I'll be right behind you, just wait, and I'll take you on from there."

She let go of the girl's face and hugged her fiercely, loving her as she would have loved a sister if she'd had one, as she wished she had been able to love her mother, loving her for what she had been through, for having suffered and survived.

"I am your guardian, honey. *I'm your guardian.* Vess is never going to touch you again, the freak, the hateful bastard. He's never going to touch you again. I'm going to get you out of this stinking place, and away from him forever, but you have to work with me, you have to help and listen and be careful, so careful."

She let go of the girl and met her eyes again.

Ariel was still Elsewhere. There was no flicker of recognition as there had been for a split second in the cellar, after the girl had used the drill.

The barking had stopped.

From the far side of the room came a new and disturbing sound. Not the clatter of the door shaking in its frame. A harder rattling noise. Metallic.

The knob was jiggling back and forth. One of the dogs must be pawing industriously at it.

The door wasn't well fitted. Chyna could see a half-inch gap between the edge of it and the jamb. In the gap was a gleam of shiny brass: the tongue of the simple latch. If the latch was not seated deeply in the jamb, even the dog's fumbling might, by purest chance, spring it open.

"Wait," she told Ariel.

She crossed the room and tried to pull the dresser in front of the door.

The dogs must have sensed that she'd drawn nearer, because they began barking again. The old black iron knob rattled more furiously than before.

The dresser was heavy. But there was no straight-backed chair that she could wedge under the knob, and the nightstand didn't seem bulky enough to prevent the dogs from shoving the door open if, in fact, the spring latch popped out of the jamb.

Heavy as it was, she nevertheless dragged the dresser halfway across the bedroom door. That seemed good enough.

The Dobermans were going crazy, barking more ferociously than ever, as if they knew that she had foiled them.

When Chyna turned to Ariel again, the girl was gone.

"No."

Panicked, she ran to the window and looked outside.

Radiant in moonlight, hair silver now instead of blond, Ariel waited on the porch roof exactly two short steps to the left of the window, where she'd been told to go. Her back was pressed to the log wall of the house, and she was staring at the sky, though she was probably still focused on something infinitely farther away than mere stars.

Chyna pushed the sponge mop onto the roof and then went out through the window while the infuriated Dobermans raged in the house behind her.

Outside, blinded dogs were no longer wailing miserably in the distance.

Chyna reached for the girl. Ariel's hand was not stiff and clawlike as it had been before. It was still cold but now limp.

"That was good, honey, that was good. You did just what I said. But always wait for me, okay? Stay with me."

She picked up the mop with her free hand and led Ariel to the edge of the porch roof. The gap between them and the motor home was less than a foot wide, but it was potentially dangerous for someone in Ariel's condition.

"Let's step across together. Okay, honey?"

Ariel was still gazing at the sky. In her eyes were cataracts of moonlight that made her look like a milky-eyed corpse.

Chilled as if the dead moonlight eyes were an omen, Chyna let go of her companion's hand and gently forced her to tilt her head down until she was looking at the gap between the porch roof and the motor home.

"Together. Here, give me your hand. Be careful to step across. It's not wide, you don't even have to jump it, no strain. But if you step into it, you might fall through to the ground, where the dogs could get you. And even if you don't fall through, you're sure to be hurt."

Chyna stepped across, but Ariel didn't follow.

Turning to the girl, still holding her slack hand, Chyna tugged gently. "Come on, baby, let's go, let's get out of here. We'll turn him in to the cops, and he'll never be able to hurt anybody again, not ever, not you or me or *anyone.*"

After a hesitation, Ariel stepped across the gap onto the roof of the motor home—and slipped on the dew-wet metal. Chyna dropped the mop, grabbed the girl, and kept her from falling.

"Almost there, baby."

She picked up the mop again and led Ariel to the open skylight, where she encouraged her to kneel.

"That's good. Now wait. Almost there."

Chyna stretched out on her stomach, leaned into the skylight, and used the mop to push the stepstool toward the back of the hall and out of the way. Dropping down onto it, one of them might have broken a leg.

They were so close to escape. They couldn't take any chances.

Chyna got to her feet and threw the mop into the yard.

Bending down, putting one hand on the girl's shoulder, she said, "Okay, now slide along here and put your legs through the skylight. Come on, honey. Sit on the edge, watch the sharp pieces of plastic, yeah, that's it, let your legs dangle. Okay, now just drop to the floor inside, and then go forward. Okay? Do you understand? Go forward toward the cockpit, honey, so I won't fall on you when I come through."

Chyna gave the girl a gentle push, which was all she required. Ariel dropped into the motor home, landed on her feet, stumbled on the hammer that Chyna had discarded earlier, and put one hand against the wall to steady herself.

"Go forward," Chyna urged.

Behind her, a second-story window shattered onto the porch roof. One of the two study windows. The door to Vess's office had not been closed, and the dogs had gotten into it from the upstairs hall after the bedroom door had frustrated them.

She turned and saw a Doberman coming straight at her across the roof, *leaping* toward her with such velocity that, when it hit her, it would carry her off the top of the motor home and into the yard.

She twisted aside, but the dog was a lot quicker than she was, correcting its trajectory even as it bounded onto the vehicle. When it landed, however, it slipped on the dewy surface, skidded, claws screeching on the metal, and to Chyna's astonishment, it tumbled past her, slid off the roof, and left her untouched.

Howling, the dog fell into the yard, squealed when it hit the ground, and tried to scramble to its feet. Something was wrong with its hindquarters. It couldn't stand up. Perhaps it had broken its pelvis. It was in pain but still so furious that it remained focused on Chyna rather than itself. The dog sat barking up at her, its hind legs twisted to one side at an unnatural angle.

Not barking, wary and watchful, the other Doberman also had come through the broken study window onto the porch roof. This was the one that she'd squirted *twice* with ammonia, hitting the muzzle both times, for even now it shook its head and snorted as if plagued by lingering fumes. It had learned to respect her, and it wasn't going to rush at her as rashly as the other dog had done.

Sooner or later, of course, it would realize that she no longer had the spray bottle, that she was holding nothing that might be used as a weapon. Then it would regain its courage.

What to do?

She wished that she hadn't thrown the sponge mop into the yard. She could have jabbed at the Doberman with the wooden handle when it attacked. She might even have been able to hurt it if she poked hard enough. But the mop was beyond reach.

Think.

Instead of approaching her across the porch roof, the Doberman slunk along the front wall of the house, its shoulders hunched and its head low, away from her but glancing back. It reached the open window of Vess's bedroom, and then it slowly returned, alternately looking down at the shards of moonlight-silvered glass among which it carefully placed its feet and glaring at her from under its brow.

Chyna tried to think of something in the motor home that could be used as a weapon. The girl could pass it up to her.

She said softly, "Ariel."

The dog halted at the sound of her voice.

"Ariel."

But the girl didn't reply.

Hopeless. Ariel could not be coaxed into action fast enough to be of any help.

When finally the Doberman attacked, Chyna wouldn't be lucky again, either. This one would not hurtle across the porch roof and slide off the motor home without getting its teeth in her. When it leaped at her, she would have nothing to fight with except her bare hands.

The dog stopped pacing. It raised its tapered black head and stared at her, ears pricked, panting.

Chyna's mind raced. She had never before been able to think quite this clearly and quickly.

Although loath to take her eyes off the Doberman, she glanced down through the skylight.

Ariel was not in the short hallway below. She'd gone forward as she'd been instructed. Good girl.

The dog was no longer panting. It stood rigid and vigilant. As Chyna watched, its ears twitched and then flattened against its skull.

Chyna said, "Screw it," and she jumped through the broken-out skylight into the motor home. Pain exploded through her bitten foot.

The stepstool, which she had pushed aside with the sponge mop, was against the closed bedroom door. She grabbed it and dragged it forward, out from under the skylight.

Paws thumped on the metal roof.

Chyna snatched the hammer from the floor and slipped the handle under the waistband of her blue jeans. Even through her red cotton sweater, the steel head was cold against her belly.

The dog appeared in the opening above, a predatory silhouette in the moonlight.

Chyna picked up the stepstool, which had a tubular metal handle that served as a backrail when the top step was used as a chair. She eased backward to the bathroom door, realizing just *how* narrow the hall was. She didn't have enough room to swing the stool like a club, but it was still useful. She held it in front of her in the manner of a lion tamer with a chair.

"Come on, you bastard," she said to the looming dog, dismayed to hear how shaky her voice was. "Come on."

The animal hesitated warily at the brink of the opening above.

She didn't dare turn away. The moment she turned, it would come in after her.

She raised her voice, shouting angrily at the Doberman, taunting it: "Come on! What're you waiting for? What the hell are you scared of, you chickenshit?"

The dog growled.

"Come on, come on, damn you, come down here and get it! *Come and get it!*"

Snarling, the Doberman jumped. The instant that it landed in the hallway, it seemed to ricochet off the floor and straight toward Chyna without any hesitation.

She didn't take a defensive position. That would be death. She had one chance. One slim chance. Aggressive action. Go for it. She immediately rushed the dog, meeting its attack head-on, jamming the legs of the stool at it as though they were four swords.

The impact of the dog rocked her, almost knocked her down, but then the animal rebounded from her, yelping in pain, perhaps having taken one of the stool legs in an eye or hard against the tip of its snout. It tumbled toward the back of the short hall.

As the Doberman sprang to its feet, it seemed a little wobbly. Chyna was on top of it, jabbing mercilessly with the metal legs of the stool, pressing the dog backward, keeping it off balance so it couldn't get around the stool and at her side, or under the stool and at her ankles, or over the stool and at her face. In spite of its injuries, the dog was quick, strong, dear God, hugely strong, and as lithe as a cat. The muscles in her arms burned with the effort, and her heart hammered so hard that her vision brightened then dimmed with each hard pulse, but she dared not relent even for a second. When the stool began to fold shut, pinching two of her fingers, she popped it open at once, jabbed the legs into the dog, jabbed, jabbed, until she drove the animal against the bedroom door, where she caged it between that panel of Masonite and the legs of the stool. The Doberman squirmed, snarled, snapped at the stool, clawed at the floor, clawed at the door, kicked, frantic to escape its trap. It was Chyna's weight and all muscle, not containable for long. She leaned her body against the stool, pressing it into the dog, then let go of the stool with one hand so she could extract the hammer from her waistband. She couldn't control the stool as well with one hand as with two, and the dog eeled up the bedroom door and came over the top of its cage, straining its head forward, snapping savagely at her, its teeth huge, slobber flying from its chops, eyes black and bloody and protuberant with rage. Still leaning against the stool, Chyna swung the big hammer. It struck with a *pock* on bone, and the dog screamed. Chyna swung the hammer again, landing a second blow on the skull, and the dog stopped screaming, slumped.

She stepped back.

The stool clattered to the floor.

The dog was still breathing. It made a pitiful sound. Then it tried to get up.

She swung the hammer a third time. That was the end of it.

Breathing raggedly, dripping cold sweat, Chyna dropped the hammer and stumbled into the bathroom. She threw up in the toilet, purging herself of Vess's coffeecake.

She did not feel triumphant.

In her entire life, she had never killed anything larger than a palmetto beetle—until now. Self-defense justified the killing but didn't make it easier.

Acutely aware of how little time they had left, she nevertheless paused at the sink to splash handfuls of cold water in her face and to rinse out her mouth.

Her reflection in the mirror scared her. Such a face. Bruised and bloodied. Eyes sunken, encircled by dark rings. Hair dirty and tangled. She looked crazed.

In a way, she *was* crazy. Crazy with a love of freedom, with an urgent thirst for it. Finally, finally. Freedom from Vess and from her mother. From the past. From the need to understand. She was crazy with the hope that she could save Ariel and at last do more than merely survive.

The girl was on a sofa in the lounge, hugging herself, rocking back and forth. She was making her first sound since Chyna had seen her through the view port in the padded door the previous morning: a wretched, rhythmic moaning.

"It's okay, honey. Hush now. Everything's going to be all right. You'll see."

The girl continued moaning and would not be soothed.

Chyna led her forward, settled her into the copilot's seat, and engaged her safety harness. "We're getting out of here, baby. It's all over now."

She swung into the driver's seat. The engine was running and not overheated. According to the fuel gauge, they had plenty of gasoline. Good oil pressure. No warning lights were aglow.

The instrument panel included a clock. Maybe it didn't keep time well. The motor home was old, after all. The clock read ten minutes till midnight.

Chyna switched on the headlights, disengaged the emergency brake, and put the motor home in gear.

She remembered that she must not risk spinning the wheels and digging tire-clutching holes in the lawn. Instead of accelerating, she allowed the vehicle to drift slowly forward, off the grass, and then she turned left onto the driveway, heading east.

She wasn't accustomed to driving anything as large as the motor home, but she handled it well enough. After what she'd been through in the past twenty-four hours, there wasn't a vehicle in the world that would be too much for her to handle. If the only thing available had been an army tank, she would have figured out how to work the controls and how to wrestle with the steering, and she would have driven it out of here.

Glancing at the side mirror, she watched the log house dwindling into the moonlit night behind them. The place was full of light and appeared as welcoming as any home that she had ever seen.

Ariel had fallen silent. She was bent forward in her harness. Her hands were buried in her hair, and she was clutching her head as if she felt it would explode.

"We're on our way," Chyna assured her. "Not far now, not far."

The girl's face was no longer placid, as it had been since Chyna first glimpsed her in the lamplight in the doll-crowded room, and it was not lovely either. Her features were contorted in an expression of wrenching anguish, and she appeared to be sobbing, although she produced no sound and no tears.

It was impossible to know what torments the girl was suffering. Perhaps she was terrified that they would encounter Edgler Vess and be stopped only a few feet short of escape. Or perhaps she wasn't reacting to anything here, now, but was lost in a terrible moment of the past, or was responding to imaginary events in the fantasy Elsewhere into which Vess had driven her.

They topped the bald rise and started down a long gradual slope where trees crowded close to the driveway. Chyna was sure that Vess had paused on both sides of a gate the previous morning, when he had driven onto the property, and she figured it couldn't be much farther ahead.

Vess hadn't gotten out of the motor home to deal with the gate. It must be electrically operated.

Gripping the steering wheel with one hand, Chyna slid open the tambour top on the console box between the seats. She fumbled through the contents and found a remote-control device just as the gate appeared in the headlights.

The barrier was formidable. Steel posts. Tubular steel rails and crossbars. Barbed wire. She hoped to God that she wouldn't have to ram it, because even the big motor home might not be able to break it down.

She pointed the remote control at the windshield, pressed the button, and jubilantly said, "*Yes,*" when the gate began to swing inward.

She let up on the accelerator and tapped the brake pedal, giving the heavy barrier time to come all the way open before she got close enough to obstruct it. The gate moved ponderously.

Fear beat through her, like the frantic wings of a dark bird, and she was suddenly *sure* that Vess was going to pull his car into the end of the driveway, blocking them, just as the gate finished opening.

But she drove between the posts to a two-lane blacktop highway that led left and right. No car was visible in either direction.

To the north, left, the highway climbed into a forested night, toward ragged moon-frosted clouds and stars, as if it were a ramp that would carry them right off the planet and up into deepest space.

To the south, the lanes descended, curving out of sight through fields and woods. In the distance, perhaps five or six miles away, a faint golden radiance lay against the night, like a Japanese fan on black velvet, as if a small town waited in that direction.

Chyna turned south, leaving Edgler Vess's gate wide open. She accelerated. Twenty miles an hour. Thirty. She held the motor home at forty miles an hour, but she found it easy to imagine that she was going faster than any jet plane. Flying, free.

Although she was suffering uncounted pains and was plagued by a degree of bone-deep exhaustion that she'd never before experienced, her spirit soared.

"Chyna Shepherd, untouched and alive," she said, not as a prayer but as a report to God.

They were in a rural stretch of countryside, with no houses or businesses to either the east or the west of the road, no lights except the glow in the distance, but Chyna felt *bathed* in light.

Ariel continued to clutch her head, and her sweet face remained tormented.

"Ariel, untouched and alive," Chyna told her. "Untouched and alive. Alive. It's okay, honey. Everything's going to be okay." She checked the odometer. "It's three miles behind us and getting farther behind every minute, every second."

They crested a low hill, and Chyna squinted in the sudden flare of oncoming headlights. A single car was approaching uphill in the northbound lane.

She tensed, because it might be Vess.

The clock showed three minutes to midnight.

Even if it was Vess, and though he would be certain to recognize his own vehicle, Chyna felt secure. The motor home was a lot bigger than his car, so he wouldn't be able to run her off the highway. In fact, she'd be able to smash the hell out of him, if it came to that, and she wouldn't hesitate to use the motor home as a battering ram if she couldn't outrun him.

But it wasn't Vess. As the car drew nearer, she saw something on the roof, first thought that it was a ski rack, but then realized that it was an array of unlit emergency beacons and a siren-bullhorn. Last night, as she had followed Vess north on Highway 101 toward redwood country, she had hoped to encounter a police car—and now she had found one.

She pounded the horn, flashed the headlights, and braked the motor home.

"Cops!" she told Ariel. "Honey, see, everything's going to be all right. We found ourselves some cops!"

The girl huddled forward, snared in her harness.

In response to her horn and the flashing lights, the police officer switched on his emergency beacons, although he didn't use his siren.

Chyna pulled to the side of the road and stopped. "They can get Vess before he discovers we're gone and tries to run."

The cruiser had already passed her. She had glimpsed the words SHERIFF'S DEPART-MENT in the crest on the driver's door, and they were the two most glorious words in the English language.

In the sideview mirror, she watched the car as it hung a wide U-turn in the middle of the road. It came past her in the southbound lane now, and it coasted to a stop thirty feet ahead, on the graveled shoulder.

Relieved and exhilarated, Chyna opened her door and jumped down from the driver's seat. She headed toward the cruiser.

She could see that only one officer was in the car. He was wearing a trooper's hat with a wide brim. He didn't seem to be in any hurry to get out.

The revolving emergency beacons cast off gouts of red light that streamed across the moonlit pavement, and splashes of blue light as in a turbulent dream, while the tall trees by the side of the road appeared to leap close and then away, close and then away. A wind came out of nowhere to harry dead leaves and clouds of grit across the blacktop as though the strobing beacons themselves had disturbed the stillness.

Almost halfway to the car, where the policeman still sat behind the steering wheel, Chyna remembered the files in Vess's study, and suddenly they meant something far different from what they had meant before, as did the handcuffs.

She stopped.

"Oh, Jesus."

She *knew.*

Chyna spun away from the black-and-white and sprinted back to the motor home. In the flashing blue and red light, weighed down by the fat moon, she felt as if she were running slow motion in a dream, through air as thick as custard.

When she reached the open door she glanced toward the patrol car. The cop was getting out.

Gasping, Chyna climbed up into the driver's seat, pulling the door shut behind her.

The officer had gotten out of the cruiser. Edgler Vess.

Chyna released the emergency brake.

Vess opened fire.

ELEVEN

Sheriff Edgler Foreman Vess, youngest sheriff in the county's history, watches the side mirror as Chyna Shepherd hurries along the shoulder of the highway toward his patrol car, and he wonders if this woman is, after all, his blown tire, the destroyer of his bright future. When she abruptly stops, whips around, and races back through the flashing lights toward the motor home, Mr. Vess's alarm increases.

At the same time, he is enormously taken with her and is not entirely sorry that they met. He says aloud, "What a clever bitch you are."

Getting out of the black-and-white, he draws his revolver, intending to put a round in one of her legs. He still has some hope of salvaging the situation. If he can disable her and get her into the motor home before another motorist comes along, all will be well. What fun he will have when he wraps her in chains again. Ariel won't lift a hand to help this woman, and if she tries, he'll pistol-whip the little bitch into submission; that will spoil the plans he has for her, but he's been looking at her beautiful face for a year, wanting to smash it, and the smashing will be enormously satisfying even in these circumstances.

Although Vess is quick getting out of the car, Chyna is faster. By the time he raises the revolver, she is behind the wheel of the motor home, drawing the door shut.

He can't take any chances now, can't risk merely wounding her to have fun with her later. She has to be wasted. He pumps six rounds through the windshield.

When Chyna saw the gun coming up, she shouted, "Get down!" She pushed Ariel's head below the windshield, throwing herself sideways, half out of her seat, across the open console. She covered the girl as best she could, squeezing her eyes tightly shut and shouting at the girl to close hers too.

Gunshots cracked, one right after the other, as fast as Vess could squeeze them off, and the windshield imploded. Sheets of gummy safety glass crashed into the front seats, spilling over Chyna and the girl, and things split and shattered farther back in the motor home as the slugs found stopping points.

She tried to count the shots. She thought she heard six. Maybe only five. She wasn't sure. *Damn.* Then she realized that it didn't matter how many rounds he'd fired, because she hadn't gotten a good look at the weapon. She didn't know for sure that it was a revolver. A pistol wouldn't have just six rounds; it could have ten or more, a *lot* more if it had an expanded magazine.

Risking a bullet in the face, Chyna sat up, shaking off cascades of gummy-prickly glass, and looked out through the empty windshield frame. She saw Edgler Vess by the patrol car, thirty feet away. He was tipping the expended cartridges out of his piece, so it had to be a revolver.

Already she had released the emergency brake. Now she shifted the motor home out of park.

Standing tall, appearing cool and unhurried but nevertheless nimble-fingered, Vess plucked a speedloader from the dump pouch on his gun belt.

Thanks to her mother's criminal friends, Chyna knew all about speedloaders. Before Vess could reload, she took her foot off the brake pedal and stomped the accelerator.

Move, move, move.

Slipping the speedloader into the revolver and twisting it, Vess looked up almost casually when he heard the roar of the motor-home engine.

Chyna drove onto the pavement as though she intended to sweep past the patrol car and away, but she was going to run the freak into the ground.

Vess dropped the speedloader, snapped the cylinder shut.

Afraid that Ariel might look up, Chyna shouted, "Stay down, stay down!" She ducked her own head just as a slug smacked off the window frame and ricocheted back through the vehicle.

She raised her head at once, because the motor home was on the move, and she needed to see what she was doing. She swung the wheel to the right, heading for Vess at the open door of the patrol car.

He fired again, and she seemed to be looking straight down the bore of the barrel when the quick flame flared. She heard a strange hissing-throbbing-buzzing, not unlike the lightning-quick passage of a fat bumblebee on a summer afternoon, and she smelled something hot, like singed hair.

Vess dived into the car to get out of her way. The motor home smashed into the open door, ripping it away, maybe taking off one or both of the hateful bastard's legs as well.

The fragrance of gunfire always reminds Sheriff Vess of the stink of sex, maybe because it smells hot or maybe because there's a trace of the same ammonia odor in gunpowder that is stronger in semen, but no matter what the reason, gunfire excites him and gives him an instant erection, and when he leaps into the car, he lets out an exuberant whoop. The roar of the motor home is all around him, bearing down on him, the headlights blazing, as much tumult as if he were in the middle of a close encounter of the third kind. As he dives for safety, he yanks his legs in after himself, knowing that this is going to be close, damn close, which is what makes it *fun*. Something raps hard against his right foot, cold wind rushes in around him, the driver's door tears off and clatters end over end along the blacktop as the motor home shrieks past.

The sheriff's right foot is numb, and although he feels no pain yet, he believes that it might have been crushed or even torn off. When he sits up in the driver's seat, holsters his revolver, and reaches down with one hand to feel for the expected stump and the warm gush of blood, he discovers that he is intact. The heel was torn off his boot. Just that. No worse. The rubber heel.

His foot is numb, and his calf tingles all the way to the knee, but the sheriff laughs. "You'll pay for the shoe repair, you bitch."

The motor home is two hundred feet from him, heading south.

Because he never switched off the engine when he pulled onto the shoulder of the highway, he needs only to release the hand brake and shift into drive. The tires kick up a storm of gravel that thunders against the undercarriage. The black-and-white lurches forward. Hot rubber shrieks like babies in pain, bites into the blacktop, and Vess rockets after the motor home.

Too late, distracted by his numb foot and recklessly eager to get his hands on the woman, he realizes that the big vehicle is no longer heading south. It's reversing toward him at maybe thirty miles an hour, even faster.

He slams his foot down on the brake pedal, but before he can pull the wheel to the left to get out of the way, the motor home crashes into him with a horrendous sound, and it's like hitting a rock wall. His head snaps back, and then he pitches forward against the steering wheel so hard that all the breath is knocked out of him, while a dizzying darkness swirls at the edges of his vision.

The hood buckles and pops open, and he can't see a damn thing through the windshield. But he hears his tires spinning and smells burning rubber. The patrol car is being pushed backward, and though the collision dramatically slowed the motor home for a moment, it's picking up speed again.

He tries to shift the black-and-white into reverse, figuring that he can back away from the motor home even as it's pushing at him, but the stick first stutters stubbornly in his hand, clunks into neutral, and then freezes. The transmission is shot.

As bad: He suspects that the smashed front end of the car is hung up on the back of the motor home.

She's going to push him off the highway. In some places the drop-off from the shoulder is eight or ten feet and steep enough virtually to ensure that the patrol car will tumble ass-over-teakettle if it goes over the edge. Worse, if they *are* hung up on each other, and if the woman doesn't have full control of the motor home, she'll most likely roll it off the road on top of the black-and-white, crushing him.

Hell, maybe that's what she's *trying* to do.

She's a damn singularity, all right, in her own way just like him. He admires her for it.

He smells gasoline. This is not a good place to be.

To the right of the center console and the police radio (which he switched off when he first saw the motor home and realized that it was his own), a pump-action 20-gauge shotgun is mounted barrel-up in spring clips attached to the dashboard. It has a five-shell magazine, which Sheriff Vess always keeps loaded.

He grabs the shotgun, wrenches it out of the clips, holds it in both hands, and slides left from behind the steering wheel. He bails out through the missing door.

They're reversing at twenty or twenty-five miles an hour, rapidly gaining speed because the car is in neutral and no longer resisting the backward rush. The pavement comes up to meet him as though he's a parachutist with huge holes in his silks. He hits and rolls, keeping his arms tucked in against his body in the hope that he won't break any bones, fiercely clutching the shotgun, tumbling diagonally across the blacktop to the shoulder beyond the northbound lane. He tries to keep his head up, but he takes a bad knock, and another. He welcomes the pain, shouting with delight, reveling in the incredible *intensity* of this adventure.

Chyna was watching the side mirror when Edgler Vess sprang out of the patrol car, slammed into the blacktop, and rolled across the highway.

"Shit."

By the time that Chyna braked to a full stop, crying out at the flash of pain in her bitten foot, Vess was sprawled facedown on the far shoulder of the roadway, three hundred feet to the south. He lay perfectly still. Though she didn't believe that the tumble had killed him, she was sure that he must be unconscious or at least dazed.

She wasn't capable of running over him while he lay insensate. But she wasn't going to wait around to give him a sporting chance either.

She buckled into the combination shoulder and lap belt. She suspected that she was going to need it.

As she shifted into drive and started forward, she became aware of a sharp stinging along the right side of her head, and when she put a hand to her scalp, she discovered that she was bleeding. The passing bumblebee buzz had been a grazing bullet, which had burned a shallow furrow about three inches long and a sixteenth of an inch deep. Any closer, it would have taken off the side of her skull. This also explained the faint smell of burning that she'd briefly detected: hot lead, a few singed hairs.

Ariel was sitting up in a sparkling mantilla and shawl of gummy glass. She gazed out through the missing windshield toward Vess, but she was blank-eyed.

The girl's hands were bleeding. Chyna's heart leaped at the sight of the wet blood, but she realized that the wounds were only tiny cuts, nothing serious. The safety glass couldn't cause mortal injury, but it was prickly enough to nick the skin.

When Chyna looked at Vess again, he was on his hands and knees, two hundred feet away. Beside him lay a shotgun.

She tramped on the accelerator.

A hard *clunk* at the back of the motor home. The vehicle shook. Another *clunk*. Then a scraping noise arose, and a hellacious clatter-jangle, but they gained speed.

Glancing at the side mirror, she saw showers of sparks as ragged steel scraped across blacktop.

The damaged patrol car was behind her, rumbling along in her wake. She was dragging it.

Sheriff Vess's right ear is badly abraded, torn, and the smell of his blood is like January wind rushing across snowfields high on a mountain slope. A brassy ringing in *both* ears reminds him of the bitter metallic taste of the spider in the Templeton house, and he savors it.

As he gets to his feet, all bones intact, choking down the interestingly sour insistence of vomit, he picks up the shotgun. He's happy to see that it seems to have come through in fine shape.

The motor home is angling toward him across the two-lane, about a hundred fifty feet away but closing fast, a juggernaut.

Instead of running off the road into the woods and away from the oncoming vehicle, he sprints toward it in a rightward-leading loop that will bring him alongside as it races past. He's limping—not because he has injured his leg but simply because he is missing the heel on his right boot.

Even with one boot heel too few, Vess is more agile than the lumbering vehicle, and the woman sees that she's not going to be able to run him down. She also sees the shotgun, no doubt, and she pulls the steering wheel to her right, away from him, ready to settle for escape instead of vengeance.

He has no intention of trying to blast her head off through the already shattered windshield or through the side window, partly because he's beginning to be spooked by her resilience and doesn't think he'll be able to do enough damage to stop her as she sails past like a skeet disk. Also, it's far easier to halt and shoot from the hip than to raise the gun and aim, and shooting from the hip means shooting low.

The recoil from the first three rounds, fired as quickly as he can work the pump action, nearly pounds the sheriff off his feet, but he takes out the front tire on the driver's side.

Hardly six feet from him, the motor home starts to slide. Snakes of rubber uncoil into the air from the ruined tire. As the behemoth streaks past, Vess uses his last two rounds to blow out the rear tire on the driver's side.

Now Ms. Chyna Shepherd, untouched and alive, has big trouble.

The steering wheel spun back and forth in Chyna's hands, burning her palms as she tried determinedly to hold on to it.

She tapped the brakes, and that seemed to be the absolute wrong thing to do because the vehicle yawed dangerously to the left, but when she let up on the brakes, that also seemed to be wrong because it yawed even more wildly to the right. The trailing black-and-white stuttered against the back bumper, and the motor home shuddered even as it swayed more violently side to side, and Chyna knew that they were going to tip over.

Half drunk on the deliciously complex smell of his own blood and the pure-sex stink of the shotgun fire, Sheriff Vess tosses the 20-gauge aside when the magazine is empty. With shining-eyed glee, he watches as the aged motor home rises inevitably off its starboard tires, tilting along the night highway on its port-side wheel rims. Virtually all of the rubber has shredded away; strips and chunks of it litter both lanes. The steel rims carve into the blacktop with a grinding sound that reminds him of the texture of crinoline crisp with dried blood, which brings to mind the taste of a certain young lady's mouth in the very moment that she died. Then the vehicle crashes onto its side hard enough for Vess to feel vibrations in the pavement beneath his feet. The flat boom echoes back and forth between the road-flanking trees, like the devil's own shotgun fire.

Hung up on the back of the motor home, the black-and-white is hauled onto its side by the larger vehicle. Then it finally tears loose, flips onto its roof, spins three hundred and sixty degrees, and comes to rest in the northbound lane.

The motor home is far past the car, three hundred feet away from the sheriff and still sliding, but it is slowing and will soon stop.

Everything is screwed up big time: the mess scattered all over the highway, which he will be hard-pressed to explain; the ruination of his plan to deal with Ariel in the methodical manner that has kept him so excited for the past year; and the incriminating bodies in the bedroom of his motor home.

Yet Sheriff Vess has never felt half as buoyant as he does now. He is so *alive*, all of his senses enhanced by the ferocity of the moment. He feels giddy, silly. He wants to caper under the moon and twirl with his arms out like a child making himself dizzy with the sight of spinning stars.

But there are two deaths to be dealt, a lovely young face to be disfigured, and that is fun too.

He reaches to his holster for his revolver. Evidently it fell out when he leaped from the car and tumbled across the highway. He looks around for it.

When the motor home slid to a stop, Chyna wasted no time being astonished to be alive. Instantly she disengaged her safety harness and then the girl's.

The starboard flank of the tipped-over motor home had become its ceiling in this new orientation. Ariel clung to the door handle up there to avoid dropping down on top of Chyna. The port flank, where Chyna lay, was now essentially the floor. The window in the driver's door at her side provided a close-up view only of blacktop.

She struggled out of her seat, turned around, and perched on the dashboard with her back to the windshield and her feet on the console box. She leaned her right side against the steering wheel.

The air was thick with gasoline fumes. Breathing was difficult.

She reached to Ariel and said, "Come on, baby, out through the windshield, quickly now."

When the girl failed to look at her but clung to the door and stared out the side window at the night sky, Chyna took her by the shoulder and pulled.

"Come on, honey, come on, come on, come on," she urged. "It's damn stupid if we die now, after getting this far. If you die now, won't the dolls laugh? Won't they laugh and *laugh*?"

• • •

Here, now, comes Sheriff Edgler Vess, battered and bleeding but sprightly in his step, past the roof of the motor home, which is now essentially the vehicle's port flank as it lies half capsized on this sea of blacktop and spilled gasoline. He glances curiously at the broken-out skylight but proceeds without hesitation to the front of the vehicle—where he discovers Chyna and Ariel, naughty girls, who have just come out through the windshield.

Their backs are to him, and they are moving away, heading toward the west side of the highway, where a sheltering grove of pines stands not far beyond the pavement, surely hoping to scuttle out of sight before he finds them. The woman is hobbling, urging the girl along with a hand in the small of her back.

Though the sheriff was unable to find his revolver, he has the 20-gauge, which he holds in both hands by the barrel. He comes in fast behind them. The woman hears the odd squish that he makes limping on one bad boot heel across the reeking wet pavement, but she doesn't have a chance to turn fully and confront him. Vess swings the shotgun like a club, putting everything he has into it, smashing the flat of the stock across her shoulder blades.

The woman is knocked off her feet, the breath hammered from her, unable to cry out. She pitches forward and sprawls facedown on the pavement, perhaps unconscious but certainly stunned immobile.

Ariel totters forward in the direction that she was headed, as though she knows nothing of what happened to Chyna, and perhaps she doesn't. Maybe she is desperate for freedom, but more likely she is stumbling across the blacktop with no more awareness than a wind-up doll.

The woman rolls onto her back, looking up at him, not dazed but white and wild-eyed with rage.

"God fears me," he says, which are words that can be formed from the letters of his name.

But the woman seems unimpressed. Wheezing, because of either the fumes or the blow to the back, she says, "Fuck you."

When he kills her, he will have to eat a piece of her, as he ate the spider, because in the difficult days ahead, he may need a measure of her extraordinary strength.

Ariel is fifty or sixty feet away, and the sheriff considers going after her. He decides to finish the woman first, because the girl can't get far in her condition.

When Vess looks down again, the woman is withdrawing a small object from a pocket of her jeans.

Chyna held the butane lighter that she'd been carrying since the service station where Vess had murdered the clerks. She released the childproof lock on the gas lever and slid her thumb onto the striker wheel. She was terrified to ignite it. She lay in gasoline, and her clothes, her hair, were soaked with it. She could barely draw breath through the suffocating fumes. Her trembling hand was damp with gasoline too, and she figured that the flame would leap immediately to her thumb, travel down her hand, her arm, enshrouding her entire body in only seconds.

But she had to trust that there was justice in the universe and meaning in the redwood mists, for without that trust, she would be no better than Edgler Vess, no better than a mindlessly seeking palmetto beetle.

She was lying at Vess's feet. Even if the worst happened, she would take him with her.

"Forever," she said, because that was another word that could be formed from the letters of his name, and she thumbed the striker wheel.

A pure flame spurted from the Bic but didn't instantly leap to her thumb, so she thrust the lighter against Vess's boot, dropped it, and the flame went out at once but not before igniting the gasoline-soaked leather.

Even as Chyna let go of the lighter, she rolled away from Vess, arms tucked against her breast, *spinning* across the blacktop, shocked by how quickly fire exploded high into the night behind her with a *whoosh* and a sudden wave of heat. Ethereally beautiful blue flames must be streaking toward her across the saturated pavement, and she steeled herself for the killing rapture of fire—but then she was out of the gasoline, rolling across dry highway.

Gasping for air, she shoved onto her feet, backing farther from the burning pavement and from the beast in the conflagration.

Edgler Vess was wearing boots of fire, screaming and stamping his feet as great sheets of flame were flung up from the blacktop around him.

Chyna saw his hair ignite, and she looked away.

Ariel was well beyond the gasoline-wet pavement and out of danger, though she seemed oblivious of the blaze. She was stopped with her back to the fire, gazing up at the stars.

Chyna hurried to the girl and led her another twenty feet south on the highway, just to be safe.

Vess's screaming was shrill and terrible and louder now, louder because, as Chyna discovered when she turned to look back, the freak was coming after them, a pillar of fire, totally engulfed. Yet he was on his feet, slogging through the boiling tar that bubbled out of the softening blacktop. His bright arms stretched in front of him, blue-white tongues of fire seething off his fingertips. A tornado of blood-red fire whirled in his open mouth, dragon fire spouted from his nostrils, his face vanished behind an orange mask of flames, yet he came onward, stubborn as a sunset, screaming.

Chyna pushed the girl behind her, but then Vess abruptly veered away from them, and it became clear to her that he hadn't seen them. He was seared blind, chasing neither her nor Ariel but an undeserved mercy.

In the middle of the highway, he fell across the yellow lines and lay there, jerking and twitching, writhing and kicking, gradually turning on his side, pulling his knees up to his chest, folding his blackened hands under his chin. His head curled down to his hands as though his neck were melting and unable to support it. Soon he was silent in his burning.

On one level, Vess knew the fading scream was his own, but his suffering was so intense that bizarre thoughts flared through his mind in a blaze of delirium. On another level, he believed that this eerie cry was not his own, after all, but issued from the unborn twin of the service-station clerk, which had left its image as a raw pink birthmark on the forehead of its brother. At the end, Vess was very afraid in the strangeness of the consuming fire, and then he was not a man any more but only an enduring darkness.

Pulling Ariel with her, Chyna backed farther from the fire, but at last she was unable to stand one moment longer. She sat on the highway, shaking uncontrollably, pain-racked, sick with relief. She began to cry, sobbing like a child, like an eight-year-old girl, loosing all of the tears never spent under beds or in mice-infested barn lofts or on lightning-scorched beaches.

In time, headlights appeared in the distance. Chyna watched as they approached, while beside her the girl mutely studied the moon.

TWELVE

From her hospital bed, Chyna gave detailed statements to the police but none to the reporters who strove so arduously to reach her. From the cops, in a spirit of reciprocity, she learned a great many things about Edgler Vess and the extent of his crimes, although none of it explained him.

Two things were of personal interest to her:

First, Paul Templeton, Laura's father, had been visiting Oregon on a business trip, weeks before Vess's assault on his family, when he had been stopped for speeding. The officer who wrote the citation was the young sheriff himself. It must have been on this occasion that the photographs had accidentally dropped out of Paul's wallet as he had been hunting for his driver's license, giving Vess a chance to see Laura's striking face.

Second, Ariel's complete name was Ariel Beth Delane. Until one year ago, she had lived with her parents and her nine-year-old brother in a quiet suburb of Sacramento, California. The mother and father had been shot in their beds. The boy had been tortured to death with the tools from a kit that Mrs. Delane had used in her doll-making hobby, and there was reason to believe that Ariel had been forced to watch before Vess had taken her away.

Besides policemen, Chyna saw numerous physicians. In addition to the necessary treatment for her physical injuries, she was more than once urged to discuss her experiences with a psychiatrist. The most persistent of these was a pleasant man named Dr. Kevin Lofglun, a boyish fifty-year-old with a musical laugh and a nervous habit of pulling on his right earlobe until it was cherry red. "I don't need therapy," she told him, "because *life* is therapy." He didn't quite understand this, and he wanted her to tell him about her codependent relationship with her mother, though it hadn't been codependent for at least ten years, since she had walked out. He wanted to help her learn to cope with grief, but she told him, "I don't want to learn to cope with it, Doctor. I want to *feel* it." When he spoke of post-traumatic stress syndrome, she spoke of hope; when he spoke of self-fulfillment, she spoke of responsibility; when he spoke of mechanisms for improving self-esteem, she spoke of faith and trust; and after a while he seemed to decide that he could do nothing for someone who was speaking a language so different from his own.

The doctors and nurses were worried that she would be unable to sleep, but she slept soundly. They were certain that she would have nightmares, but she only dreamed of a cathedral forest where she was never alone and always safe.

On April eleventh, just twelve days after being admitted to the hospital, she was discharged, and when she went out the front doors, there were over a hundred newspaper, radio, and television reporters waiting for her, including those from the sleazy tabloid shows that had sent her contracts, by Federal Express, offering large sums to tell her story. She made her way through them without answering any of their shouted questions but without being impolite. As she reached the taxi that was waiting for her, one of them pushed a microphone in her face and said inanely, "Ms. Shepherd, what does it feel like to be such a famous hero?" She stopped then and turned and said, "I'm no hero. I'm just passing through like all of you, wondering why it has to be so hard, hoping I never have to hurt anyone again." Those close enough to hear what she said fell silent, but the others shrieked at her again. She got into the taxi and rode away.

• • •

The Delane family had been heavily mortgaged and addicted to easy credit from Visa and MasterCard before Edgler Vess had freed them from their debts, so there was no estate to which Ariel was heir. Her paternal grandparents were alive but in poor health and with only limited financial resources.

Even if there had been any relatives financially comfortable enough to assume the burden of raising a teenage girl with Ariel's singular problems, they would not have felt adequate to the task. The girl was made a ward of the court, remanded to the care of a psychiatric hospital operated by the State of California.

No family member objected.

Through that summer and autumn, Chyna traveled weekly from San Francisco to Sacramento, petitioning the court to be declared Ariel Beth Delane's sole legal guardian, visiting the girl, and working patiently—some claimed stubbornly—through the byzantine legal and social-services systems. Otherwise, they would have condemned the girl to a life in asylums that were called "care facilities."

Although Chyna truly didn't see herself as a hero, many others did. The admiration with which certain influential people regarded her was at last the key that unlocked the bureaucratic heart and got her the permanent custody that she wanted. On a morning late in January, ten months after she had freed the girl from the doll-guarded cellar, she drove out of Sacramento with Ariel beside her.

They went home to the apartment in San Francisco.

Chyna never finished her master's degree in psychology, which she had been so close to earning. She continued her studies at the University of California at San Francisco, but she changed her major to literature. She had always liked to read, and though she didn't believe she possessed any writing talent, she thought she might enjoy being a book editor one day, working with writers. There was more truth in fiction than in science. She could also see herself as a teacher. If she spent the rest of her life waiting tables, that was all right as well, because she was good at it and found dignity in the labor.

The following summer, while Chyna was working the dinner shift, she and Ariel began spending many mornings and early afternoons at the beach. The girl liked to stare out at the bay from behind dark sunglasses, and sometimes she could be induced to stand at water's edge with the surf breaking around her ankles.

One day in June, not realizing quite what she was doing, Chyna used her index finger to write a word in the sand: PEACE. She stared at it for a minute, and to her surprise, she said to Ariel, "That's a word that can be made from the letters of my name."

On the first of July, while Ariel sat on their blanket, gazing out at the sun-spangled water, Chyna tried to read a newspaper, but every story distressed her. War, rape, murder, robbery, politicians spewing hatred from all ends of the political spectrum. She read a movie review full of vicious ipse dixit criticism of the director and screenwriter, questioning their very right to create, and then turned to a woman columnist's equally vitriolic attack on a novelist, none of it genuine criticism, merely venom, and she threw the paper in a trash can. Any more, such little hatreds and indirect assaults seemed to her uncomfortably clear reflections of stronger homicidal impulses that infected the human spirit; symbolic killings were different only in degree, not in kind, from genuine murder, and the sickness in the assailants' hearts was the same.

There are no explanations for human evil. Only excuses.

Also in early July, she noticed a man of about thirty who came to the beach a few mornings a week with his eight-year-old son and a laptop computer on which he worked in the deep shade of an umbrella. Eventually, they struck up a conversation. The father's name was Ned Barnes, and his boy was Jamie. Ned was a widower and, of all things, a freelance writer with several modestly successful novels to his credit. Jamie developed a crush on Ariel and brought her things that he found special—a handful of wildflowers, an interesting seashell, a picture of a comical-looking dog torn from a magazine—and put them beside her on the blanket without asking that she be mindful of them.

On August twelfth, Chyna cooked a spaghetti-and-meatball dinner for the four of them, at the apartment. Later she and Ned played Go Fish and other games with Jamie while Ariel sat staring placidly at her hands. Since the night in the motor home, that terrible anguished expression and silent scream had not crossed the girl's face. She had also stopped hugging herself and rocking anxiously.

Later in August, the four of them went to a movie together, and they continued to see one another at the beach, where they took up tenancy side by side. Their relationship was very relaxed, with no pressure or expectations. None of them wanted anything more than to be less alone.

In September, just after Labor Day, when there would not be many more days warm enough to recommend the beach, Ned looked up from his laptop next door and said, "Chyna."

She was reading a novel and only replied, "Hmmm," without taking her eyes off the page.

He insisted, "Look. Look at Ariel."

The girl wore cut-off blue jeans and a long-sleeve blouse, because the day was already a touch cool for sunbathing. She was barefoot at the edge of the water, surf breaking around her ankles, but she was not standing zombie-like and staring bayward, as usual. Instead, her arms were stretched over her head, and she was waving her hands in the air while quietly dancing in place.

"She loves the bay so," Ned said.

Chyna was unable to speak.

"She loves life," he said.

Choking on emotion, Chyna prayed that it was true.

The girl didn't dance long, and when later she returned to the blanket, her gaze was as faraway as ever.

By December of that year, more than twenty months after fleeing the house of Edgler Vess, Ariel was eighteen years old, no longer a girl but a lovely young woman. Frequently, however, she called for her mother and father in her sleep, for her brother, and her voice—the only time it was heard—was young, frail, and lost.

Then, on Christmas morning, among the gifts for Ariel, Ned, and Jamie that were stacked under the tree in the apartment living room, Chyna was surprised to find a small package for herself. It had been wrapped with great care, though as if by a child with more enthusiasm than skill. Her name was printed in uneven block letters on a snowman gift tag. When she opened the box, a slip of blue paper lay within. On the paper were four words that appeared to have been set down with considerable effort, much hesitation, and lots of stops and starts: *I want to live.*

Heart pounding, tongue thick, she took both of the girl's hands. For a while she didn't know what to say, and she couldn't have said it if she had known.

Finally words came haltingly: "This . . . this is the best . . . the best gift I've ever had, honey. This is the best there could ever be. This is all I want . . . for you to try."

She read the four words again, through tears.

I want to live.

Chyna said, "But you don't know how to get back, do you?"

The girl was very still. Then she blinked. Both of her hands tightened on Chyna's hands.

"There's a way," Chyna assured her.

The girl's hands gripped Chyna's even tighter.

"There's hope, baby. There's always hope. There's a way, and no one can ever find it alone, but we can find it together. We can find it together. You just have to believe."

The girl could not make eye contact, but her hands continued to grip Chyna's.

"I want to tell you a story about a redwood forest and something I saw there one night, and something I saw later, too, when I needed to see it. Maybe it won't mean as much to you, and maybe it wouldn't mean anything at all to other people, but it means the world to me, even if I don't fully understand it."

I want to live.

Over the next few years, the road back from the Wild Wood to the beauties and wonders of this world was not an easy one for Ariel. There were times of despair when she seemed to make no progress at all, or even slid backward.

Eventually, however, a day came when they traveled with Ned and Jamie to that redwood grove.

They walked through the ferns and the rhododendrons in the solemn shadows under the massive trees, and Ariel said, "Show me where."

Chyna led her by the hand to the very place, and said, "Here."

How scared Chyna had been that night, risking so much for a girl she had never seen. Scared less of Vess than of this new thing that she had found in herself. This reckless caring. And now she knows it is nothing that should have frightened her. It is the purpose for which we exist. This reckless caring.

SOLE
SURVIVOR

▼

TO THE MEMORY OF RAY MOCK,

my uncle, who long ago moved on to a better world.
In my childhood, when I was troubled and despairing,
your decency and kindness and good humor
taught me everything I ever needed to know
about what a man should be.

The sky is deep, the sky is dark.
The light of stars is so damn stark.
When I look up, I fill with fear.
If all we have is what lies here,
this lonely world, this troubled place,
then cold dead stars and empty space . . .
Well, I see no reason to persevere,
no reason to laugh or shed a tear,
no reason to sleep or ever to wake,
no promises to keep, and none to make.
And so at night I still raise my eyes
to study the clear but mysterious skies
that arch above us, as cold as stone.
Are you there, God? Are we alone?
                    —*The Book of Counted Sorrows*

PART ONE

LOST FOREVER

▼

ONE

At two-thirty Saturday morning, in Los Angeles, Joe Carpenter woke, clutching a pillow to his chest, calling his lost wife's name in the darkness. The anguished and haunted quality of his own voice had shaken him from sleep. Dreams fell from him not all at once but in trembling veils, as attic dust falls off rafters when a house rolls with an earthquake.

When he realized that he did not have Michelle in his arms, he held fast to the pillow anyway. He had come out of the dream with the scent of her hair. Now he was afraid that any movement he made would cause that memory to fade and leave him with only the sour smell of his night sweat.

Inevitably, no weight of stillness could hold the memory in all its vividness. The scent of her hair receded like a balloon rising, and soon it was beyond his grasp.

Bereft, he got up and went to the nearest of two windows. His bed, which consisted of nothing but a mattress on the floor, was the only furniture, so he did not have to be concerned about stumbling over obstructions in the gloom.

The studio apartment consisted of one large room with a kitchenette, a closet, and a cramped bathroom, all over a two-car detached garage in upper Laurel Canyon. After selling the house in Studio City, he had brought no furniture with him, because dead men needed no such comforts. He had come here to die.

For ten months he had been paying the rent, waiting for the morning when he would fail to wake.

The window faced the rising canyon wall, the ragged black shapes of evergreens and eucalyptuses. To the west was a fat moon glimpsed through the trees, a silvery promise beyond the bleak urban woods.

He was surprised that he was still not dead after all this time. He was not alive, either. Somewhere between. Half-way in the journey. He had to find an ending, because for him there could never be any going back.

After fetching an icy bottle of beer from the refrigerator in the kitchenette, Joe returned to the mattress. He sat with his back against the wall.

Beer at two-thirty in the morning. A sliding-down life.

He wished that he were capable of drinking himself to death. If he could drift out of this world in a numbing alcoholic haze, he might not care how long his departure required. Too much booze would irrevocably blur his memories, however, and his memories were sacred to him. He allowed himself only a few beers or glasses of wine at a time.

Other than the faint tree-filtered glimmer of moonlight on the window glass, the only light in the room came from the backlit buttons on the telephone keypad beside the mattress.

He knew only one person to whom he could talk frankly about his despair in the middle of the night—or in broad daylight. Though he was only thirty-seven, his mom and dad were long gone. He had no brothers or sisters. Friends had tried to comfort him after the catastrophe, but he had been too pained to talk about what had happened, and he had kept them at a distance so aggressively that he had offended most of them.

Now he picked up the phone, put it in his lap, and called Michelle's mother, Beth McKay.

In Virginia, nearly three thousand miles away, she picked up the phone on the first ring. "Joe?"

"Did I wake you?"

"You know me, dear—early to bed and up before dawn."

"Henry?" he asked, referring to Michelle's father.

"Oh, the old beast could sleep through Armageddon," she said affectionately.

She was a kind and gentle woman, full of compassion for Joe even as she coped with her own loss. She possessed an uncommon strength.

At the funeral, both Joe and Henry had needed to lean on Beth, and she had been a rock for them. Hours later, however, well after midnight, Joe had discovered her on the patio behind the Studio City house, sitting in a glider in her pajamas, hunched like an ancient crone, tortured by grief, muffling her sobs in a pillow that she had carried with her from the spare room, trying not to burden her husband or her son-in-law with her own pain. Joe sat beside her, but she didn't want her hand held or an arm around her shoulders. She flinched at his touch. Her anguish was so intense that it had scraped her nerves raw, until a murmur of commiseration was like a scream to her, until a loving hand scorched like a branding iron. Reluctant to leave her alone, he had picked up the long-handled net and skimmed the swimming pool: circling the water, scooping gnats and leaves off the black surface at two o'clock in the morning, not even able to see what he was doing, just grimly circling, circling, skimming, skimming, while Beth wept into the pillow, circling and circling until there was nothing to strain from the clear water except the reflections of cold uncaring stars. Eventually, having wrung all the tears from herself, Beth rose from the glider, came to him, and pried the net out of his hands. She had led him upstairs and tucked him in bed as though he were a child, and he had slept deeply for the first time in days.

Now, on the phone with her at a lamentable distance, Joe set aside his half-finished beer. "Is it dawn there yet, Beth?"

"Just a breath ago."

"Are you sitting at the kitchen table, watching it through the big window? Is the sky pretty?"

"Still black in the west, indigo overhead, and out to the east, a fan of pink and coral and sapphire like Japanese silk."

As strong as Beth was, Joe called her regularly not just for the strength she could offer but because he liked to listen to her talk. The particular timbre of her voice and her soft Virginia accent were the same as Michelle's had been.

He said, "You answered the phone with my name."

"Who else would it have been, dear?"

"Am I the only one who ever calls this early?"

"Rarely others. But this morning . . . it could only be you."

The worst had happened one year ago to the day, changing their lives forever. This was the first anniversary of their loss.

She said, "I hope you're eating better, Joe. Are you still losing weight?"

"No," he lied.

Gradually during the past year, he had become so indifferent to food that three months ago he began dropping weight. He had dropped twenty pounds to date.

"Is it going to be a hot day there?" he asked.

"Stifling hot and humid. There are some clouds, but we're not supposed to get rain, no relief. The clouds in the east are fringed with gold and full of pink. The sun's all the way out of bed now."

"It doesn't seem like a year already, does it, Beth?"

"Mostly not. But sometimes it seems ages ago."

"I miss them so much," he said. "I'm so lost without them."

"Oh, Joe. Honey, Henry and I love you. You're like a son to us. You *are* a son to us."

"I know, and I love you too, very much. But it's not enough, Beth, it's not enough." He took a deep breath. "This year, getting through, it's been hell. I can't handle another year like this."

"It'll get better with time."

"I'm afraid it won't. I'm scared. I'm no good alone, Beth."

"Have you thought some more about going back to work, Joe?"

Before the accident, he had been a crime reporter at the *Los Angeles Post*. His days as a journalist were over.

"I can't bear the sight of the bodies, Beth."

He was unable to look upon a victim of a drive-by shooting or a car-jacking, regardless of age or sex, without seeing Michelle or Chrissie or Nina lying bloody and battered before him.

"You could do other kinds of reporting. You're a good writer, Joe. Write some human interest stories. You need to be working, doing something that'll make you feel useful again."

Instead of answering her, he said, "I don't *function* alone. I just want to be with Michelle. I want to be with Chrissie and Nina."

"Someday you will be," she said, for in spite of everything, she remained a woman of faith.

"I want to be with them now." His voice broke, and he paused to put it back together. "I'm finished here, but I don't have the guts to move on."

"Don't talk like that, Joe."

He didn't have the courage to end his life, because he had no convictions about what came after this world. He did not truly believe that he would find his wife and daughters again in a realm of light and loving spirits. Lately, when he gazed at a night sky, he saw only distant suns in a meaningless void, but he couldn't bear to voice his doubt, because to do so would be to imply that Michelle's and the girls' lives had been meaningless as well.

Beth said, "We're all here for a purpose."

"They were my purpose. They're gone."

"Then there's another purpose you're meant for. It's your job now to find it. There's a reason you're still here."

"No reason," he disagreed. "Tell me about the sky, Beth."

After a hesitation, she said, "The clouds to the east aren't gilded anymore. The pink is gone too. They're white clouds, no rain in them, and not dense but like a filigree against the blue."

He listened to her describe the morning at the other end of the continent. Then they talked about fireflies, which she and Henry had enjoyed watching from their back porch the previous night. Southern California had no fireflies, but Joe remembered them from his boyhood in Pennsylvania. They talked about Henry's garden too, in which strawberries were ripening, and in time Joe grew sleepy.

Beth's last words to him were: "It's full daylight here now. Morning's going past us and heading your way, Joey. You give it a chance, morning's going to bring you the reason you need, some purpose, because that's what the morning does."

After he hung up, Joe lay on his side, staring at the window from which the silvery lunar light had faded. The moon had set. He was in the blackest depths of the night.

When he returned to sleep, he dreamed not of any glorious approaching purpose but of an unseen, indefinable, looming menace. Like a great weight falling through the sky above him.

Later Saturday morning, driving to Santa Monica, Joe Carpenter suffered an anxiety attack. His chest tightened, and he was able to draw breath only with effort. When he lifted one hand from the wheel, his fingers quivered like those of a palsied old man.

He was overcome by a sense of falling, as from a great height, as though his Honda had driven off the freeway into an inexplicable and bottomless abyss. The pavement stretched unbroken ahead of him, and the tires sang against the blacktop, but he could not reason himself back to a perception of stability.

Indeed, the plummeting sensation grew so severe and terrifying that he took his foot off the accelerator and tapped the brake pedal.

Horns blared and skidding tires squealed as traffic adjusted to his sudden deceleration. As cars and trucks swept past the Honda, the drivers glared murderously at Joe or mouthed offensive words or made obscene gestures. This was Greater Los Angeles in an age of change, crackling with the energy of doom, yearning for the Apocalypse, where an unintended slight or an inadvertent trespass on someone else's turf might result in a thermonuclear response.

His sense of falling did not abate. His stomach turned over as if he were aboard a roller coaster, plunging along a precipitous length of track. Although he was alone in the car, he heard the screams of passengers, faint at first and then louder, not the good-humored shrieks of thrill seekers at an amusement park, but cries of genuine anguish.

As though from a distance, he listened to himself whispering, "No, no, no, no."

A brief gap in traffic allowed him to angle the Honda off the pavement. The shoulder of the freeway was narrow. He stopped as close as possible to the guardrail, over which lush oleander bushes loomed like a great cresting green tide.

He put the car in Park but didn't switch off the engine. Even though he was sheathed in cold sweat, he needed the chill blasts of air conditioning to be able to breathe. The pressure on his chest increased. Each stuttering inhalation was a struggle, and each hot exhalation burst from him with an explosive wheeze.

Although the air in the Honda was clear, Joe smelled smoke. He tasted it too: the acrid mélange of burning oil, melting plastic, smoldering vinyl, scorched metal.

When he glanced at the dense clusters of leaves and the deep-red flowers of the oleander pressing against the windows on the passenger side, his imagination morphed them into billowing clouds of greasy smoke. The window became a rectangular porthole with rounded corners and thick dual-pane glass.

Joe might have thought he was losing his mind—if he hadn't suffered similar anxiety attacks during the past year. Although sometimes as much as two weeks passed between episodes, he often endured as many as three in one day, each lasting between ten minutes and half an hour.

He had seen a therapist. The counseling had not helped.

His doctor recommended anti-anxiety medication. He rejected the prescription. He wanted to feel the pain. It was all he had.

Closing his eyes, covering his face with his icy hands, he strove to regain control of himself, but the catastrophe continued to unfold around him. The sense of falling intensified. The smell of smoke thickened. The screams of phantom passengers grew louder.

Everything shook. The floor beneath his feet. The cabin walls. The ceiling. Horrendous rattling and twanging and banging and gong-like clanging accompanied the shaking, shaking, shaking.

"Please," he pleaded.

Without opening his eyes, he lowered his hands from his face. They lay fisted at his sides.

After a moment, the small hands of frightened children clutched at his hands, and he held them tightly.

The children were not in the car, of course, but in their seats in the doomed airliner. Joe was flashing back to the crash of Flight 353. For the duration of this seizure, he would be in two places at once: in the real world of the Honda and in the Nationwide Air 747 as it found its way down from the serenity of the stratosphere, through an overcast night sky, into a meadow as unforgiving as iron.

Michelle had been sitting between the kids. Her hands, not Joe's, were those that Chrissie and Nina gripped in their last long minutes of unimaginable dread.

As the shaking grew worse, the air was filled with projectiles. Paperback books, laptop computers, pocket calculators, flatware and dishes—because a few passengers had not yet finished dinner when disaster struck—plastic drinking glasses, single-serving bottles of liquor, pencils, and pens ricocheted through the cabin.

Coughing because of the smoke, Michelle would have urged the girls to keep their heads down. *Heads down. Protect your faces.*

Such faces. Beloved faces. Seven-year-old Chrissie had her mother's high cheekbones and clear green eyes. Joe would never forget the flush of joy that suffused Chrissie's face when she was taking a ballet lesson, or the squint-eyed concentration with which she approached home plate to take her turn at bat in Little League baseball games. Nina, only four, the pug-nosed munchkin with gray-violet eyes, had a way of crinkling her sweet face in pure delight at the sight of a dog or cat. Animals were drawn to her—and she to them— as though she were the reincarnation of St. Francis of Assisi, which was not a far-fetched idea when one saw her gazing with wonder and love upon even an ugly garden lizard cupped in her small, careful hands.

Heads down. Protect your faces.

In that advice was hope, the implication that they would all survive and that the worst thing that might happen to them would be a face-disfiguring encounter with a hurtling laptop or broken glass.

The fearsome turbulence increased. The angle of descent grew more severe, pinning Joe to his seat, so that he couldn't easily bend forward and protect his face.

Maybe the oxygen masks dropped from overhead, or maybe damage to the craft had resulted in a systems failure, with the consequence that masks had not been deployed at every seat. He didn't know if Michelle, Chrissie, and Nina had been able to breathe or if, choking on the billowing soot, they had struggled futilely to find fresh air.

Smoke surged more thickly through the passenger compartment. The cabin became as claustrophobic as any coal mine deep beneath the surface of the earth.

In the blinding blackdamp, hidden sinuosities of fire uncoiled like snakes. The wrenching terror of the aircraft's uncontrolled descent was equaled by the terror of not knowing where those flames were or when they might flash with greater vigor through the 747.

As the stress on the airliner increased to all but intolerable levels, thunderous vibrations shuddered through the fuselage. The giant wings thrummed as though they would tear loose. The steel frame groaned like a living beast in mortal agony, and perhaps minor welds broke with sounds as loud and sharp as gunshots. A few rivets sheered off, each with a piercing *screeeeek*.

To Michelle and Chrissie and little Nina, perhaps it seemed that the plane would disintegrate in flight and that they would be cast into the black sky, be spun away from one another, plummeting in their separate seats to three separate deaths, each abjectly alone at the instant of impact.

The huge 747-400, however, was a marvel of design and a triumph of engineering, brilliantly conceived and soundly constructed. In spite of the mysterious hydraulics failure that rendered the aircraft uncontrollable, the wings did not tear loose, and the fuselage did not disintegrate. Its powerful Pratt and Whitney engines screaming as if in defiance of gravity, Nationwide Flight 353 held together throughout its final descent.

At some point Michelle would have realized that all hope was lost, that they were in a dying plunge. With characteristic courage and selflessness, she would have thought only of the children then, would have concentrated on comforting them, distracting them as much as possible from thoughts of death. No doubt she leaned toward Nina, pulled her close, and in spite of the breath-stealing fumes, spoke into the girl's ear to be heard above the clamor: *It's okay, baby, we're together, I love you, hold on to Mommy, I love you, you're the best little girl who ever was.* Shaking down, down, down through the Colorado night, her voice full of emotion but devoid of panic, she had surely sought out Chrissie too: *It's all right, I'm with you, honey, hold my hand, I love you so much, I'm so very proud of you, we're together, it's all right, we'll always be together.*

In the Honda alongside the freeway, Joe could hear Michelle's voice almost as if from memory, as though he had been with her as she had comforted the children. He wanted desperately to believe that his daughters had been able to draw upon the strength of the exceptional woman who had been their mother. He needed to know that the last thing the girls heard in this world was Michelle telling them how very precious they were, how cherished.

The airliner met the meadow with such devastating impact that the sound was heard more than twenty miles away in the rural Colorado vastness, stirring hawks and owls and eagles out of trees and into flight, startling weary ranchers from their armchairs and early beds.

In the Honda, Joe Carpenter let out a muffled cry. He doubled over as if he had been struck hard in the chest.

The crash was catastrophic. Flight 353 exploded on impact and tumbled across the meadow, disintegrating into thousands of scorched and twisted fragments, spewing orange gouts of burning jet fuel that set fire to evergreens at the edge of the field. Three hundred and thirty people, including passengers and crew, perished instantly.

Michelle, who had taught Joe Carpenter most of what he knew about love and compassion, was snuffed out in that merciless moment. Chrissie, seven-year-old ballerina and baseball player, would never again pirouette on point or run the bases. And if animals felt the same psychic connection with Nina that she felt with them, then in that chilly Colorado night, the meadows and the wooded hills had been filled with small creatures that cowered miserably in their burrows.

Of his family, Joe Carpenter was the sole survivor.

He had not been with them on Flight 353. Every soul aboard had been hammered into ruin against the anvil of the earth. If he had been with them, then he too would have been identifiable only by his dental records and a printable finger or two.

His flashbacks to the crash were not memories but exhausting fevers of imagination, frequently expressed in dreams and sometimes in anxiety attacks like this one. Racked by guilt because he had not perished with his wife and daughters, Joe tortured himself with these attempts to share the horror that they must have experienced.

Inevitably, his imaginary journeys on the earthbound airplane failed to bring him the healing acceptance for which he longed. Instead, each nightmare and each waking seizure salted his wounds.

He opened his eyes and stared at the traffic speeding past him. If he chose the right moment, he could open the door, step out of the car, walk onto the freeway, and be struck dead by a truck.

He remained safely in the Honda, not because he was afraid to die, but for reasons unclear even to him. Perhaps, for the time being at least, he felt the need to punish himself with more life.

Against the passenger-side windows, the overgrown oleander bushes stirred ceaselessly in the wind from the passing traffic. The friction of the greenery against the glass raised an eerie whispering like lost and forlorn voices.

He was not shaking anymore.

The sweat on his face began to dry in the cold air gushing from the dashboard vents.

He was no longer plagued by a sensation of falling. He had reached bottom.

Through the August heat and a thin haze of smog, passing cars and trucks shimmered like mirages, trembling westward toward cleaner air and the cooling sea. Joe waited for a break in traffic and then headed once more for the edge of the continent.

THREE

The sand was bone white in the glare of the August sun. Cool and green and rolling came the sea, scattering the tiny shells of dead and dying creatures on the shore.

The beach at Santa Monica was crowded with people tanning, playing games, and eating picnic lunches on blankets and big towels. Although the day was a scorcher farther inland, here it was merely pleasantly warm, with a breeze coming off the Pacific.

A few sunbathers glanced curiously at Joe as he walked north through the coconut-oiled throng, because he was not dressed for the beach. He wore a white T-shirt, tan chinos, and running shoes without socks. He had not come to swim or sunbathe.

As lifeguards watched the swimmers, strolling young women in bikinis watched the lifeguards. Their rhythmic rituals distracted them entirely from the architects of shells cast on the foaming shore near their feet.

Children played in the surf, but Joe could not bear to watch them. Their laughter, shouts, and squeals of delight abraded his nerves and sparked in him an irrational anger.

Carrying a Styrofoam cooler and a towel, he continued north, gazing at the seared hills of Malibu beyond the curve of Santa Monica Bay. At last he found a less populated stretch of sand. He unrolled the towel, sat facing the sea, and took a bottle of beer from its bed of ice in the cooler.

If ocean-view property had been within his means, he would have finished out his life at the water's edge. The ceaseless susurration of surf, the sun-gilded and moonsilvered relentlessness of incoming breakers, and the smooth liquid curve to the far horizon brought him not any sense of peace, not serenity, but a welcome numbness.

The rhythms of the sea were all he ever expected to know of eternity and of God.

If he drank a few beers and let the therapeutic vistas of the Pacific wash through him, he might then be calm enough to go to the cemetery. To stand upon the earth that blanketed his wife and his daughters. To touch the stone that bore their names.

This day, of all days, he had an obligation to the dead.

Two teenage boys, improbably thin, wearing baggy swim trunks slung low on their narrow hips, ambled along the beach from the north and stopped near Joe's towel. One wore his long hair in a ponytail, the other in a buzz cut. Both were deeply browned by the sun. They turned to gaze at the ocean, their backs to him, blocking his view.

As Joe was about to ask them to move out of his way, the kid with the ponytail said, "You holding anything, man?"

Joe didn't answer because he thought, at first, that the boy was talking to his buzz-cut friend.

"You holding anything?" the kid asked again, still staring at the ocean. "Looking to make a score or move some merchandise?"

"I've got nothing but beer," Joe said impatiently, tipping up his sunglasses to get a better look at them, "and it's not for sale."

"Well," said the kid with the buzz cut, "if you ain't a candy store, there's a couple guys watching sure think you are."

"Where?"

"Don't look now," said the boy with the ponytail. "Wait till we get some distance. We been watching them watch you. They stink of cop so bad, I'm surprised you can't smell 'em."

The other said, "Fifty feet south, near the lifeguard tower. Two dinks in Hawaiian shirts, look like preachers on vacation."

"One's got binoculars. One's got a walkie-talkie."

Bewildered, Joe lowered his sunglasses and said, "Thanks."

"Hey," said the boy with the ponytail, "just doing the friendly thing, man. We hate those self-righteous assholes."

With nihilistic bitterness that sounded absurd coming from anyone so young, the kid with the buzz cut said, "Screw the system."

As arrogant as young male tigers, the boys continued south along the beach, checking out the girls. Joe had never gotten a good look at their faces.

A few minutes later, when he finished his first beer, he turned, opened the lid of the cooler, put away the empty can, and looked nonchalantly back along the strand. Two men in Hawaiian shirts were standing in the shadow of the lifeguard tower.

The taller of the two, in a predominantly green shirt and white cotton slacks, was studying Joe through a pair of binoculars. Alert to the possibility that he'd been spotted, he calmly turned with the binoculars to the south, as if interested not in Joe but in a group of bikini-clad teenagers.

The shorter man wore a shirt that was mostly red and orange. His tan slacks were rolled at the cuffs. He was barefoot in the sand, holding his shoes and socks in his left hand.

In his right hand, held down at his side, was another object, which might have been a small radio or a CD player. It might also have been a walkie-talkie.

The tall guy was cancerously tanned, with sun-bleached blond hair, but the smaller man was pale, a stranger to beaches.

Popping the tab on another beer and inhaling the fragrant foamy mist that sprayed from the can, Joe turned to the sea once more.

Although neither of the men looked as if he'd left home this morning with the intention of going to the shore, they appeared no more out of place than Joe did. The kids had said that the watchers stank of cop, but even though he'd been a crime reporter for fourteen years, Joe couldn't catch the scent.

Anyway, there was no reason for the police to be interested in him. With the murder rate soaring, rape almost as common as romance, and robbery so prevalent that half the populace seemed to be stealing from the other half, the cops would not waste time harassing him for drinking an alcoholic beverage on a public beach.

High on silent pinions, shining white, three sea gulls flew northward from the distant pier, at first paralleling the shoreline. Then they soared over the shimmering bay and wheeled across the sky.

Eventually Joe glanced back toward the lifeguard tower. The two men were no longer there.

He faced the sea again.

Incoming breakers broke, spilling shatters of foam on the sand. He watched the waves as a willing subject might watch a hypnotist's pendant swinging on a silver chain.

This time, however, the tides did not mesmerize, and he was unable to guide his troubled mind into calmer currents. Like the effect of a planet on its moon, the calendar pulled Joe into its orbit, and he couldn't stop his thoughts from revolving around the date: August 15, August 15, August 15. This first anniversary of the crash had an overwhelming gravity that crushed him down into memories of his loss.

When the remains of his wife and children had been conveyed to him, after the investigation of the crash and the meticulous cataloguing of both the organic and the inorganic debris, Joe was given only fragments of their bodies. The sealed caskets were the size usually reserved for the burial of infants. He received them as if he were taking possession of the sacred bones of saints nestled in reliquaries.

Although he understood the devastating effects of the airliner's impact, and though he knew that an unsparing fire had flashed through the debris, how strange it had seemed to Joe that Michelle's and the girls' physical remains should be so small. They had been such enormous presences in his life.

Without them, the world seemed to be an alien place. He didn't feel as if he belonged here until he was at least two hours out of bed. Some days the planet turned twenty-four hours without rotating Joe into an accommodation with life. Clearly this was one of them.

After he finished the second Coors, he put the empty can in the cooler. He wasn't ready to drive to the cemetery yet, but he needed to visit the nearest public rest room.

Joe rose to his feet, turned, and glimpsed the tall blond guy in the green Hawaiian shirt. The man, without binoculars for the moment, was not south near the lifeguard tower but north, about sixty feet away, sitting alone in the sand. To screen himself from Joe, he had taken a position beyond two young couples on blankets and a Mexican family that had staked their territory with folding chairs and two big yellow-striped beach umbrellas.

Casually Joe scanned the surrounding beach. The shorter of the two possible cops, the one wearing the predominantly red shirt, was not in sight.

The guy in the green shirt studiously avoided looking directly at Joe. He cupped one hand to his right ear, as if he were wearing a bad hearing aid and needed to block the music from the sunbathers' radios in order to focus on something else that he wanted to hear.

At this distance, Joe could not be certain, but he thought the man's lips were moving. He appeared to be engaged in a conversation with his missing companion.

Leaving his towel and cooler, Joe walked south toward the public rest rooms. He didn't need to glance back to know that the guy in the green Hawaiian shirt was watching him.

On reconsideration, he decided that getting soused on the sand probably *was* still against the law, even these days. After all, a society with such an enlightened tolerance of corruption and savagery needed to bear down hard on minor offenses to convince itself that it still had standards.

Nearer the pier, the crowds had grown since Joe's arrival. In the amusement center, the roller coaster clattered. Riders squealed.

He took off his sunglasses as he entered the busy public rest rooms.

The men's lavatory stank of urine and disinfectant. In the middle of the floor between the toilet stalls and the sinks, a large cockroach, half crushed but still alive, hitched around and around in a circle, having lost all sense of direction and purpose. Everyone avoided it—some with amusement, some with disgust or indifference.

After he had used a urinal, as he washed his hands, Joe studied the other men in the mirror, seeking a conspirator. He settled on a long-haired fourteen-year-old in swim trunks and sandals.

When the boy went to the paper-towel dispenser, Joe followed, took a few towels immediately after him, and said, "Outside, there might be a couple of cop types hanging out, waiting for me."

The boy met his eyes but didn't say anything, just kept drying his hands on the paper towels.

Joe said, "I'll give you twenty bucks to reconnoiter for me, then come back and tell me where they are."

The kid's eyes were the purple-blue shade of a fresh bruise, and his stare was as direct as a punch. "Thirty bucks."

Joe could not remember having been able to look so boldly and challengingly into an adult's eyes when he himself had been fourteen. Approached by a stranger with an offer like this, he would have shaken his head and left quickly.

"Fifteen now and fifteen when I come back," said the kid.

Wadding his paper towels and tossing them in the trash can, Joe said, "Ten now, twenty when you come back."

"Deal."

As he took his wallet from his pocket, Joe said, "One is about six two, tan, blond, in a green Hawaiian shirt. The other is maybe five ten, brown hair, balding, pale, in a red and orange Hawaiian."

The kid took the ten-dollar bill without breaking eye contact. "Maybe this is jive, there's nobody like that outside, and when I come back, you want me to go into one of those stalls with you to get the other twenty."

Joe was embarrassed not for being suspected of pedophilia but for the kid, who had grown up in a time and a place that required him to be so knowledgeable and street smart at such a young age. "No jive."

"'Cause I don't jump that way."

"Understood."

At least a few of the men present must have heard the exchange, but none appeared to be interested. This was a live-and-let-live age.

As the kid turned to leave, Joe said, "They won't be waiting right outside, easy to spot. They'll be at a distance, where they can see the place but aren't easily seen themselves."

Without responding, the boy went to the door, sandals clacking against the floor tiles.

"You take my ten bucks and don't come back," Joe warned, "I'll find you and kick your ass."

"Yeah, right," the kid said scornfully, and then he was gone.

Returning to one of the rust-stained sinks, Joe washed his hands again so he wouldn't appear to be loitering.

Three men in their twenties had gathered to watch the crippled cockroach, which was still chasing itself around one small portion of the lavatory floor. The bug's track was a circle twelve inches in diameter. It twitched brokenly along that circumference with such insectile single-mindedness that the men, hands full of dollar bills, were placing bets on how fast it would complete each lap.

Bending over the sink, Joe splashed handfuls of cold water on his face. The astringent taste and smell of chlorine was in the water, but any sense of cleanliness that it provided was more than countered by a stale, briny stink wafting out of the open drain.

The building wasn't well ventilated. The still air was hotter than the day outside, reeking of urine and sweat and disinfectant, so noxiously thick that breathing it was beginning to sicken him.

The kid seemed to be taking a long time.

Joe splashed more water in his face and then studied his beaded, dripping reflection in the streaked mirror. In spite of his tan and the new pinkness from the sun that he had absorbed in the past hour, he didn't look healthy. His eyes were gray, as they had been all his life. Once, however, it had been the bright gray of polished iron or wet induline; now it was the soft dead gray of ashes, and the whites were bloodshot.

A fourth man had joined the cockroach handicappers. He was in his mid-fifties, thirty years older than the other three but trying to be one of them by matching their enthusiasm for pointless cruelty. The gamblers had become an obstruction to the rest room traffic. They were getting rowdy, laughing at the spasmodic progress of the insect, urging it on as though it were a thoroughbred pounding across turf toward a finish line. "*Go, go, go, go, go!*" They noisily debated whether its pair of quivering antennae were part of its guidance system or the instruments with which it detected the scents of food and other roaches eager to copulate.

Striving to block out the voices of the raucous group, Joe searched his ashen eyes in the mirror, wondering what his motives had been when he sent the boy to scope out the men in the Hawaiian shirts. If they were conducting a surveillance, they must have mistaken him for someone else. They would realize their error soon, and he would never see them again. There was no good reason to confront them or to gather intelligence about them.

He had come to the beach to prepare himself for the visit to the graveyard. He needed to submit himself to the ancient rhythms of the eternal sea, which wore at him as waves wore at rock, smoothing the sharp edges of anxiety in his mind, polishing away the splinters in his heart. The sea delivered the message that life was nothing more than meaningless mechanics and cold tidal forces, a bleak message of hopelessness that was tranquilizing precisely because it was brutally humbling. He also needed another beer or even two to further numb his senses, so the lesson of the sea would remain with him as he crossed the city to the cemetery.

He *didn't* need distractions. He didn't need action. He didn't need mystery. For him, life had lost all mystery the same night that it had lost all meaning, in a silent Colorado meadow blasted with sudden thunder and fire.

Sandals slapping on the tiles, the boy returned to collect the remaining twenty of his thirty dollars. "Didn't see any big guy in a green shirt, but the other one's out there, sure enough, getting a sunburn on his bald spot."

Behind Joe, some of the gamblers whooped in triumph. Others groaned as the dying cockroach completed another circuit either a few seconds quicker or a few slower than its time for the previous lap.

Curious, the boy craned his neck to see what was happening.

"Where?" Joe asked, withdrawing a twenty from his wallet.

Still trying to see between the bodies of the circled gamblers, the boy said, "There's a palm tree, a couple of folding tables in the sand where this geeky bunch of Korean guys are playing chess, maybe sixty, eighty feet down the beach from here."

Although high frosted windows let in hard white sunshine and grimy fluorescent tubes shed bluish light overhead, the air seemed yellow, like an acidic mist.

"Look at me," Joe said.

Distracted by the cockroach race, the boy said, "Huh?"

"*Look at me.*"

Surprised by the quiet fury in Joe's voice, the kid briefly met his gaze. Then those troubling eyes, the color of contusions, refocused on the twenty-dollar bill.

"The guy you saw was wearing a red Hawaiian shirt?" Joe asked.

"Other colors in it, but mostly red and orange, yeah."

"What pants was he wearing?"

"Pants?"

"To keep you honest, I didn't tell you what else he was wearing. So if you saw him, now you tell me."

"Hey, man, I don't know. Was he wearing shorts or trunks or pants—how am I supposed to know?"

"You tell me."

"White? Tan? I'm not sure. Didn't know I was supposed to do a damn fashion report. He was just standing there, you know, looking out of place, holding his shoes in one hand, socks rolled up in them."

It was the same man whom Joe had seen with the walkie-talkie near the lifeguard station.

From the gamblers came noisy encouragements to the cockroach, laughter, curses, shouted offers of odds, the making of bets. They were so loud now that their voices echoed harshly off the concrete-block walls and seemed to reverberate in the mirrors with such force that Joe half expected those silvery surfaces to disintegrate.

"Was he actually watching the Koreans play chess or pretending?" Joe asked.

"He was watching this place and talking to the cream pies."

"Cream pies?"

"Couple of stone-gorgeous bitches in thong bikinis. Man, you should see the redhead bitch in the green thong. On a scale of one to ten, she's a twelve. Bring you all the way to attention, man."

"He was coming on to them?"

"Don't know what he thinks he's doing," said the kid. "Loser like him, neither of those bitches will give him a shot."

"Don't call them bitches," Joe said.

"What?"

"They're women."

In the kid's angry eyes, something flickered like visions of switchblades. "Hey, who the hell are you—the pope?"

The acidic yellow air seemed to thicken, and Joe imagined that he could feel it eating away his skin.

The swirling sound of flushing toilets inspired a spiraling sensation in his stomach. He struggled to repress sudden nausea.

To the boy, he said, "Describe the women."

With more challenge in his stare than ever, the kid said, "Totally stacked. Especially the redhead. But the brunette is just about as nice. I'd crawl on broken glass to get a whack at her, even if she is deaf."

"Deaf?"

"Must be deaf or something," said the boy. "She was putting a hearing aid kind of thing in her ear, taking it out and putting it in like she couldn't get it to fit right. Real sweet-looking bitch."

Even though he was six inches taller and forty pounds heavier than the boy, Joe wanted to seize the kid by the throat and choke him. Choke him until he promised never to use that word again without thinking. Until he understood how hateful it was and how it soiled him when he used it as casually as a conjunction.

Joe was frightened by the barely throttled violence of his reaction: teeth clenched, arteries throbbing in neck and temples, field of vision abruptly constricted by a blood-dark pressure at the periphery. His nausea grew worse, and he took a deep breath, another, calming himself.

Evidently the boy saw something in Joe's eyes that gave him pause. He became less confrontational, turning his gaze once more to the shouting gamblers. "Give me the twenty. I earned it."

Joe didn't relinquish the bill. "Where's your dad?"

"Say what?"

"Where's your mother?"

"What's it to you?"

"Where are they?"

"They got their own lives."

Joe's anger sagged into despair. "What's your name, kid?"

"What do you need to know for? You think I'm a baby, can't come to the beach alone? Screw you, I go where I want."

"You go where you want, but you don't have anywhere to be."

The kid made eye contact again. In his bruised stare was a glimpse of hurt and loneliness so deep Joe was shocked that anyone should have descended to it by the tender age of fourteen. "Anywhere to be? What's that supposed to mean?"

Joe sensed that they had made a connection on a profound level, that a door had opened unexpectedly for him and for this troubled boy, and that both of their futures could be changed for the better if he could just understand where they might be able to go after they crossed that threshold. But his own life was as hollow—his store of philosophy as empty—as any abandoned shell washed up on the nearby shore. He had no belief to share, no wisdom to impart, no hope to offer, insufficient substance to sustain himself, let alone another.

He was one of the lost, and the lost cannot lead.

The moment passed, and the kid plucked the twenty-dollar bill out of Joe's hand. His expression was more of a sneer than a smile when he mockingly repeated Joe's words, " 'They're women.' " Backing away, he said, "You get them hot, they're all just bitches."

"And are we all just dogs?" Joe asked, but the kid slipped out of the lavatory before he could hear the question.

Although Joe had washed his hands twice, he felt dirty.

He turned to the sinks again, but he could not easily reach them. Six men were now gathered immediately around the cockroach, and a few others were hanging back, watching.

The crowded lavatory was sweltering, Joe was streaming sweat, and the yellow air burned in his nostrils, corroded his lungs with each inhalation, stung his eyes. It was condensing on the mirrors, blurring the reflections of the agitated men until they seemed not to be creatures of flesh and blood but tortured spirits glimpsed through an abattoir window, wet with sulfurous steam, in the deepest kingdom of the damned. The fevered gamblers shouted at the roach, shaking fistfuls of dollars at it. Their voices blended into a single shrill ululation, seemingly senseless, a mad gibbering that rose in intensity and pitch until it sounded, to Joe, like a crystal-shattering squeal, piercing to the center of his brain and setting off dangerous vibrations in the core of him.

He pushed between two of the men and stamped on the crippled cockroach, killing it.

In the instant of stunned silence that followed his intrusion, Joe turned away from the men, shaking, shaking, the shattering sound still tremulant in his memory, still vibrating in his bones. He headed toward the exit, eager to get out of there before he exploded.

As one, the gamblers broke the paralytic grip of their surprise. They shouted angrily, as righteous in their outrage as churchgoers might be outraged at a filthy and drunken denizen of the streets who staggered into their service to sag against the chancel rail and vomit on the sanctuary floor.

One of the men, with a face as sun red as a slab of greasy ham, heat-cracked lips peeled back from snuff-stained teeth, seized Joe by one arm and spun him around. "What the shit you think you're doing, pal?"

"Let go of me."

"I was winning money here, pal."

The stranger's hand was damp on Joe's arm, dirty fingernails blunt but digging in to secure the slippery grip.

"Let go."

"I was winning money here," the guy repeated. His mouth twisted into such a wrathful grimace that his chapped lips split, and threads of blood unraveled from the cracks.

Grabbing the angry gambler by the wrist, Joe bent one of the dirty fingers back to break the bastard's grip. Even as the guy's eyes widened with surprise and alarm, even as he started to cry out in pain, Joe wrenched his arm up behind his back, twisted him around, and ran him forward, giving him the bum's rush, facefirst into the closed door of a toilet stall.

Joe had thought his strange rage had been vented earlier, as he had talked to the teenage boy, leaving only despair, but here it was again, disproportionate to the offense that seemed to have caused it, as hot and explosive as ever. He wasn't sure why he was doing this, why these men's callousness mattered to him, but before he quite realized the enormity of his overreaction, he battered the door with the guy's face, battered it again, and then a third time.

The rage didn't dissipate, but with the blood-dark pressure constricting his field of vision, filled with a primitive frenzy that leaped through him like a thousand monkeys skirling through a jungle of trees and vines, Joe was nevertheless able to recognize that he was out of control. He let go of the gambler, and the man fell to the floor in front of the toilet stall.

Shuddering with anger and with fear of his anger, Joe moved backward until the sinks prevented him from going any farther.

The other men in the lavatory had eased away from him. All were silent.

On the floor, the gambler lay on his back in scattered one- and five-dollar bills, his winnings. His chin was bearded with blood from his cracked lips. He pressed one hand to the left side of his face, which had taken the impact with the door. "It was just a cockroach, Christ's sake, just a lousy cockroach."

Joe tried to say that he was sorry. He couldn't speak.

"You almost broke my nose. You could've broke my nose. For a cockroach? Broke my nose for a cockroach?"

Sorry not for what he had done to this man, who had no doubt done worse to others, but sorry for himself, sorry for the miserable walking wreckage that he had become and for the dishonor that his inexcusable behavior brought to the memory of his wife and daughters, Joe nonetheless remained unable to express any regret. Choking on self-loathing as much as on the fetid air, he walked out of the reeking building into an ocean breeze that didn't refresh, a world as foul as the lavatory behind him.

In spite of the sun, he was shivering, because a cold coil of remorse was unwinding in his chest.

Halfway back to his beach towel and his cooler of beer, all but oblivious of the sunning multitudes through which he weaved, he remembered the pale-faced man in the red and orange Hawaiian shirt. He didn't halt, didn't even look back, but slogged onward through the sand.

He was no longer interested in learning who was conducting a surveillance of him—if that was what they were doing. He couldn't imagine why he had *ever* been intrigued by them. If they were police, they were bumblers, having mistaken him for someone else. They were not genuinely part of his life. He wouldn't even have noticed them if the kid with the ponytail hadn't drawn his attention to them. Soon they would realize their mistake and find their real quarry. In the meantime, to hell with them.

More people were gravitating to the portion of the beach where Joe had established camp. He considered packing and leaving, but he wasn't ready to go to the cemetery. The incident in the lavatory had opened the stopcock on his supply of adrenaline, canceling the effects of the lulling surf and the two beers that he had drunk.

Therefore, onto the beach towel again, one hand into the cooler, extracting not a beer but a half-moon of ice, pressing the ice to his forehead, he gazed out to sea. The gray-green chop seemed to be an infinite array of turning gears in a vast mechanism, and across it, bright silver flickers of sunlight jittered like electric current across a power grid. Waves approached and receded as monotonously as connecting rods pumping back and forth in an engine. The sea was a perpetually laboring machine with no purpose but the continuation of its own existence, romanticized and cherished by countless poets but incapable of knowing human passion, pain, and promise.

He believed that he must learn to accept the cold mechanics of Creation, because it made no sense to rail at a mindless machine. After all, a clock could not be held responsible for the too-swift passage of time. A loom could not be blamed for weaving the cloth that later was sewn into an executioner's hood. He hoped that if he came to terms with the mechanistic indifference of the universe, with the meaningless nature of life and death, he would find peace.

Such acceptance would be cold comfort, indeed, and deadening to the heart. But all he wanted now was an end to anguish, nights without nightmares, and release from the need to care.

Two newcomers arrived and spread a white beach blanket on the sand about twenty feet north of him. One was a stunning redhead in a green thong bikini skimpy enough to make a stripper blush. The other was a brunette, nearly as attractive as her friend.

The redhead wore her hair in a short, pixie cut. The brunette's hair was long, the better to conceal the communications device that she was no doubt wearing in one ear.

For women in their twenties, they were too giggly and girlish, high-spirited enough to call attention to themselves even if they had not been stunning. They lazily oiled themselves with tanning lotion, took turns greasing each other's back, touching with languorous pleasure, as if they were in the opening scene of an adult video, drawing the interest of every heterosexual male on the beach.

The strategy was clear. No one would suspect that he was under surveillance by operatives who concealed so little of themselves and concealed themselves so poorly. They were meant to be as unlikely as the men in the Hawaiian shirts had been obvious. But for thirty dollars' worth of reconnaissance and the libidinous observations of a horny fourteen-year-old, their strategy would have been effective.

With long tan legs and deep cleavage and tight round rumps, maybe they were also meant to engage Joe's interest and seduce him into conversation with them. If this was part of their assignment, they failed. Their charms didn't affect him.

During the past year, any erotic image or thought had the power to stir him only for a moment, whereupon he was overcome by poignant memories of Michelle, her precious body and her wholesome enthusiasm for pleasure. Inevitably, he thought also of the terrible long fall from stars to Colorado, the smoke, the fire, then death. Desire dissolved quickly in the solvent of loss.

These two women distracted Joe only to the extent that he was annoyed about their incompetent misidentification of him. He considered approaching them to inform them of their mistake, just to be rid of them. After the violence in the lavatory, however, the prospect of confrontation made him uneasy. He was drained of anger now, but he no longer trusted his self-control.

One year to the day.

Memories and gravestones.

He would get through it.

Surf broke, gathered the foamy fragments of itself, stole away, and broke again. In the patient study of that endless breaking, Joe Carpenter gradually grew calm.

Half an hour later, without the benefit of another beer, he was ready to visit the cemetery.

He shook the sand out of his towel. He folded the towel in half lengthwise, rolled it tight, and picked up the cooler.

As silken as the sea breeze, as buttery as sunlight, the lithe young women in the thong bikinis pretended to be enthralled by the monosyllabic repartee of two steroid-thickened suitors, the latest in a string of beach-boy Casanovas to take their shot.

The direction of his gaze masked by his sunglasses, Joe could see that the beauties' interest in the beefcake was pretense. They were *not* wearing sunglasses, and while they chattered and laughed and encouraged their admirers, they glanced surreptitiously at Joe.

He walked away and did not look back.

As he took some of the beach with him in his shoes, so he strove to take the indifference of the ocean with him in his heart.

Nevertheless, he could not help but wonder what police agency could boast such astonishingly beautiful women on its force. He had known some female cops who were as lovely and sexy as any movie star, but the redhead and her friend exceeded even celluloid standards.

In the parking lot, he half expected the men in the Hawaiian shirts to be watching his Honda. If they had it staked out, their surveillance post was well concealed.

Joe drove out of the lot and turned right on Pacific Coast Highway, checking his rearview mirror. He was not being followed.

Perhaps they had realized their error and were frantically looking for the right man.

• • •

From Wilshire Boulevard to the San Diego Freeway, north to the Ventura Freeway and then east, he drove out of the cooling influence of the sea breezes into the furnace heat of the San Fernando Valley. In the August glare, these suburbs looked as hot and hard-baked as kiln-fired pottery.

Three hundred acres of low rolling hills and shallow vales and broad lawns comprised the memorial park, a city of the deceased, Los Angeles of the dead, divided into neighborhoods by gracefully winding service roads. Famous actors and ordinary salesmen were buried here, rock-'n'-roll stars and reporters' families, side by side in the intimate democracy of death.

Joe drove past two small burial services in progress: cars parked along the curb, ranks of folding chairs set up on the grass, mounds of grave earth covered with soft green tarps. At each site, the mourners sat hunched, stifled in their black dresses and black suits, oppressed by heat as well as by grief and by a sense of their own mortality.

The cemetery included a few elaborate crypts and low-walled family garden plots, but there were no granite forests of vertical monuments and headstones. Some had chosen to entomb the remains of their loved ones in niches in the walls of communal mausoleums. Others preferred the bosom of the earth, where graves were marked only with bronze plaques in flat stone tablets flush with the ground, so as not to disturb the park-like setting.

Joe had put Michelle and the girls to rest on a gently rising hillside shaded by a scattering of stone pines and Indian laurels. Squirrels scampered across the grass on milder days than this, and rabbits came out at twilight. He believed that his three treasured women would have preferred this to the hardscape of a mausoleum, where there would not be the sound of wind-stirred trees on breezy evenings.

Far beyond the second of the two burial services, he parked at the curb, switched off the engine, and got out of the Honda. He stood beside the car in the hundred-degree heat, gathering his courage.

When he started up the gentle slope, he didn't look toward their graves. If he were to see the site from a distance, the approach to it would be daunting, and he would turn back. Even after an entire year, each visit was as disturbing to him as if he had come here to view not their burial plots but their battered bodies in a morgue. Wondering how many years would pass before his pain diminished, he ascended the rise with his head down, eyes on the ground, slump-shouldered in the heat, like an old dray horse following a long-familiar route, going home.

Consequently, he didn't see the woman at the graves until he was only ten or fifteen feet from her. Surprised, he halted.

She stood just out of the sun, in pine shadows. Her back was half to him. With a Polaroid camera, she was snapping photographs of the flush-set markers.

"Who are you?" he asked.

She didn't hear him, perhaps because he had spoken softly, perhaps because she was so intent upon her photography.

Stepping closer, he said, "What are you doing?"

Startled, she turned to face him.

Petite but athletic-looking, about five feet two, she had an immediate impact far greater than her size or her appearance could explain, as though she were clothed not merely in blue jeans and a yellow cotton blouse but in some powerful magnetic field that bent the world to her. Skin the shade of milk chocolate. Huge eyes as dark as the silt at the bottom of a cup of Armenian espresso, harder to read than the portents in tea leaves, with a distinct almond shape suggesting a touch of Asian blood in the family line. Hair not Afro-kinky or in cornrows but feather-cut, thick and naturally straight and so glossy black that it almost looked blue, which seemed Asian too. Her bone structure was all out of Africa: smooth broad brow, high cheekbones, finely carved but powerful, proud but beautiful. She was maybe five years older than Joe, in her early forties, but a quality of inno-cence in her knowing eyes and a faint aspect of child-like vulnerability in her otherwise strong face made her seem younger than he was.

"Who are you, what're you doing?" he repeated.

Lips parted as if to speak, speechless with surprise, she gazed at him as though he were an apparition. She raised one hand to his face and touched his cheek, and Joe did not flinch from her.

At first he thought he saw amazement in her eyes. The extreme tenderness of her touch caused him to look again, and he realized that what he saw was not wonderment but sad-ness and pity.

"I'm not ready to talk to you yet." Her soft voice was musical.

"Why're you taking pictures . . . why pictures of their graves?"

Clutching the camera with two hands, she said, "Soon. I'll be back when it's time. Don't despair. You'll see, like the others."

An almost supernatural quality to the moment half convinced Joe that *she* was an ap-parition, that her touch had been so achingly gentle precisely because it was barely real, an ectoplasmic caress.

The woman herself, however, was too powerfully present to be a ghost or a heatstroke illusion. Diminutive but dynamic. More real than anything in the day. More real than sky and trees and August sun, than granite and bronze. She had such a compelling presence that she seemed to be coming at him though she was standing still, to loom over him though she was ten inches shorter than he. She was more brightly lighted in the pine shad-ows than he was in the direct glare of the sun.

"How are you coping?" she asked.

Disoriented, he answered only by shaking his head.

"Not well," she whispered.

Joe looked past her, down at the granite and bronze markers. As if from very far away, he heard himself say, "Lost forever," speaking as much about himself as about his wife and daughters.

When he returned his attention to the woman, she was gazing past him, into the dis-tance. As the sound of a racing engine rose, concern crinkled the corners of her eyes and creased her forehead.

Joe turned to see what was troubling her. Along the road that he had traveled, a white Ford van was approaching at a far higher speed than the posted limit.

"Bastards," she said.

When Joe turned to the woman again, she was already running from him, angling across the slope toward the brow of the low hill.

"Hey, wait," he said.

She didn't pause or look back.

He started after her, but his physical condition wasn't as good as hers. She seemed to be an experienced runner. After a few steps, Joe halted. Defeated by the suffocating heat, he wouldn't be able to catch up with her.

Sunlight mirroring the windshield and flaring off the headlight lenses, the white van shot past Joe. It paralleled the woman as she sprinted across the grave rows.

Joe started back down the hill toward his car, not sure what he was going to do. Maybe he should give chase. What the hell was going on here?

Fifty or sixty yards beyond the parked Honda, brakes shrieking, leaving twin smears of rubber on the pavement behind it, the van slid to a stop at the curb. Both front doors flew open, and the men in Hawaiian shirts leaped out. They bolted after the woman.

Surprise halted Joe. He hadn't been followed from Santa Monica, not by the white van, not by any vehicle. He was sure of that.

Somehow they had known that he would come to the cemetery. And since neither of the men showed any interest in Joe, but went after the woman as if they were attack dogs, they must have been watching him at the beach not because they were interested in him, per se, but because they hoped that she would make contact with him at some point during the day.

The woman was their only quarry.

Hell, they must have been watching his apartment too, must have followed him from there to the beach.

As far as he knew, they had been keeping him under surveillance for days. Maybe weeks. He had been in such a daze of desolation for so long, walking through life like a sleeper drifting through a dream, that he would not have noticed these people slinking at the periphery of his vision.

Who is she, who are they, why was she photographing the graves?

Uphill and at least a hundred yards to the east, the woman fled under the generously spreading boughs of stone pines clustered along the perimeter of the burial grounds, across shaded grass only lightly dappled with sunshine. Her dusky skin blended with the shadows, but her yellow blouse betrayed her.

She was heading toward a particular point on the crest, as if familiar with the terrain. Considering that no cars were parked along this section of the cemetery road, except for Joe's Honda and the white van, she might have entered the memorial park by that route, on foot.

The men from the van had a lot of ground to make up if they were going to catch her. The tall one in the green shirt seemed in better shape than his partner, and his legs were considerably longer than the woman's, so he was gaining on her. Nevertheless, the smaller guy didn't relent even as he fell steadily behind. Sprinting frantically up the long sun-seared slope, stumbling over a grave marker, then over another, regaining his balance, he charged on, as though in an animal frenzy, in a blood fever, gripped by the *need* to be there when the woman was brought down.

Beyond the manicured hills of the cemetery were other hills in a natural condition: pale sandy soil, banks of shale, brown grass, stinkweed, mesquite, stunted manzanita, tumbleweed, scattered and gnarled dwarf oaks. Arid ravines led down into the undeveloped land above Griffith Observatory and east of the Los Angeles Zoo, a rattlesnake-infested plot of desert scrub in the heart of the urban sprawl.

If the woman got into the scrub before being caught, and if she knew her way, she could lose her pursuers by zigging and zagging from one narrow declivity to another.

Joe headed toward the abandoned white van. He might be able to learn something from it.

He wanted the woman to escape, though he wasn't entirely sure why his sympathies were with her.

As far as he knew, she might be a felon with a list of heinous crimes on her rap sheet. She hadn't looked like a criminal, hadn't sounded like one. This was Los Angeles, however, where clean-cut young men brutally shotgunned their parents and then, as orphans, tearfully begged the jury to pity them and show mercy. No one was what he seemed.

Yet . . . the gentleness of her fingertips against his cheek, the sorrow in her eyes, the tenderness in her voice, all marked her as a woman of compassion, whether she was a fugitive from the law or not. He could not wish her ill.

A vicious sound, hard and flat, cracked across the cemetery, leaving a brief throbbing wound in the hot stillness. Another crack followed.

The woman had nearly reached the brow of the hill. Visible between the last two bristling pines. Blue jeans. Yellow blouse. Stretching her legs with each stride. Brown arms pumping close to her sides.

The smaller man, in the red and orange Hawaiian shirt, had run wide of his companion, whom he was still trailing, to get a clear line of sight on the woman. He had stopped and raised his arms, holding something in both hands. A handgun. The son of a bitch was *shooting* at her.

Cops didn't try to shoot unarmed fugitives in the back. Not righteous cops.

Joe wanted to help her. He couldn't think of anything to do. If they were cops, he had no right to second-guess them. If they *weren't* cops, and even if he could catch up with them, they would probably shoot him down rather than let him interfere.

Crack.

The woman reached the crest.

"Go," Joe urged her in a hoarse whisper. "Go."

He didn't have a cellular phone in his own car, so he couldn't call 911. He had carried a mobile unit as a reporter, but these days he seldom called anyone even from his home phone.

The keening crack of another shot pierced the leaden heat.

If these men weren't police officers, they were desperate or crazy, or both, resorting to gunplay in such a public place, even though this part of the cemetery was currently deserted. The sound of the shots would travel, drawing the attention of the maintenance personnel who, merely by closing the formidable iron gate at the entrance to the park, could prevent the gunmen from driving out.

Apparently unhit, the woman disappeared over the top of the hill, into the scrub beyond. Both of the men in Hawaiian shirts went after her.

FOUR

Heart knocking so fiercely that his vision blurred with each hard-driven surge of blood, Joe Carpenter sprinted to the white van.

The Ford was not a recreational vehicle but a paneled van of the type commonly used by businesses to make small deliveries. Neither the back nor the side of the vehicle featured the name or logo of any enterprise.

The engine was running. Both front doors stood open.

He ran to the passenger side, skidded in a soggy patch of grass around a leaking sprinkler head, and leaned into the cab, hoping to find a cellular phone. If there was one, it wasn't in plain sight.

Maybe in the glove box. He popped it open.

Someone in the cargo hold behind the front seats, mistaking Joe for one of the men in the Hawaiian shirts, said, "Did you get Rose?"

Damn.

The glove box contained a few rolls of Life Savers that spilled onto the floor—and a window envelope from the Department of Motor Vehicles.

By law, every vehicle in California was required to carry a valid registration and proof of insurance.

"Hey, who the hell are you?" the guy in the cargo hold demanded.

Clutching the envelope, Joe turned away from the van.

He saw no point in trying to run. This man might be as quick to shoot people in the back as were the other two.

With a clatter and a *skreeeek* of hinges, the single door at the rear of the vehicle was flung open.

Joe walked directly toward the sound. A sledge-faced specimen with Popeye forearms, neck sufficiently thick to support a small car, came around the side of the van, and Joe opted for the surprise of instant and unreasonable aggression, driving one knee hard into his crotch.

Retching, wheezing for air, the guy started to bend forward, and Joe head-butted him in the face. He hit the ground unconscious, breathing noisily through his open mouth because his broken nose was streaming blood.

Although, as a kid, Joe had been a fighter and something of a troublemaker, he had not raised a fist against anyone since he met and married Michelle. Until today. Now, twice in the past two hours, he had resorted to violence, astonishing himself.

More than astonished, he was sickened by this primitive rage. He had never known such wrath before, not even during his troubled youth, yet here he was struggling to control it again as he had struggled in the public lavatory in Santa Monica. For the past year, the fall of Flight 353 had filled him with terrible despondency and grief, but he was beginning to realize that those feelings were like layers of oil atop another—darker—emotion that he had been denying; what filled the chambers of his heart to the brim was anger.

If the universe was a cold mechanism, if life was a journey from one empty blackness to another, he could not rant at God, because to do so was no more effective than screaming for help in the vacuum of deep space, where sound could not travel, or like trying to draw breath underwater. But now, given any excuse to vent his fury on *people*, he had seized the opportunity with disturbing enthusiasm.

Rubbing the top of his head, which hurt from butting the guy in the face, looking down at the unconscious hulk with the bleeding nose, Joe felt a satisfaction that he did not want to feel. A wild glee simultaneously thrilled and repulsed him.

Dressed in a T-shirt promoting the videogame Quake, baggy black pants, and red sneakers, the fallen man appeared to be in his late twenties, at least a decade younger than his two associates. His hands were massive enough to juggle cantaloupes, and a single letter was tattooed on the base phalange of each finger, thumbs excluded, to spell out ANABOLIC, as in anabolic steroid.

This was no stranger to violence.

Nevertheless, although self-defense justified a preemptive strike, Joe was disturbed by the savage pleasure he took from such swift brutality.

The guy sure didn't look like an officer of the law. Regardless of his appearance, he might be a cop, in which case assaulting him ensured serious consequences.

To Joe's surprise, even the prospect of jail didn't diminish his twisted satisfaction in the ferocity with which he had acted. He felt half nauseated, half out of his mind—but more alive than he had been in a year.

Exhilarated yet fearful of the moral depths into which this new empowering anger might take him, he glanced in both directions along the cemetery road. There was no oncoming traffic. He knelt beside his victim.

Breath whistled wetly through the man's throat, and he issued a soft childlike sigh. His eyelids fluttered, but he did not regain consciousness while his pockets were searched.

Joe found nothing but a few coins, a nail clipper, a set of house keys, and a wallet that contained the standard ID and credit cards. The guy's name was Wallace Morton Blick. He was carrying no police-agency badge or identification. Joe kept only the driver's license and returned the wallet to the pocket from which he had extracted it.

The two gunmen had not reappeared from the rugged scrub land beyond the cemetery hill. They had scrambled over the crest, after the woman, little more than a minute ago; even if she quickly slipped away from them, they weren't likely to give up on her and return after only a brief search.

Wondering at his boldness, Joe quickly dragged Wallace Blick away from the rear corner of the white van. He tucked him close to the flank of the vehicle, where he was less likely to be seen by anyone who came along the roadway. He rolled him onto his side so he would not choke on the blood that might be draining from his nasal passages down the back of his throat.

Joe went to the open rear door. He climbed into the back of the van. The low rumble of the idling engine vibrated in the floorboard.

The cramped cargo hold was lined on both sides with electronic communications, eavesdropping, and tracking equipment. A pair of compact command chairs, bolted to the floor, could be swiveled to face the arrayed devices on each side.

Squeezing past the first chair, Joe settled into the second, in front of an active computer. The interior of the van was air-conditioned, but the seat was still warm because Blick had vacated it less than a minute ago.

On the computer screen was a map. The streets had names meant to evoke feelings of peace and tranquillity, and Joe recognized them as the service roads through the cemetery.

A small blinking light on the map drew his attention. It was green, stationary, and located approximately where the van itself was parked.

A second blinking light, this one red and also stationary, was on the same road but some distance behind the van. He was sure that it represented his Honda.

The tracking system no doubt utilized a CD-ROM with exhaustive maps of Los Angeles County and environs, maybe of the entire state of California or of the country coast to coast. A single compact disc had sufficient capacity to contain detailed street maps for all of the contiguous states and Canada.

Someone had fixed a powerful transponder to his car. It emitted a microwave signal that could be followed from quite a distance. The computer utilized surveillance-satellite uplinks to triangulate the signal, then placed the Honda on the map relative to the position of the van, so they could track him without maintaining visual contact.

Leaving Santa Monica, all the way into the San Fernando Valley, Joe had seen no suspicious vehicle in his rearview mirror. This van had been able to stalk him while streets away or miles behind, out of sight.

As a reporter, he had once gone on a mobile surveillance with federal agents, a group of high-spirited cowboys from the Bureau of Alcohol, Tobacco and Firearms, who had used a similar but less sophisticated system than this.

Acutely aware that the battered Blick or one of the other two men might trap him here if he delayed too long, Joe swiveled in his chair, surveying the back of the van for some indication of the agency involved in this operation. They were tidy. He couldn't spot a single clue.

Two publications lay beside the computer station at which Blick had been working: one issue each of *Wired*, featuring yet another major article about the visionary splendiferousness of Bill Gates, and a magazine aimed at former Special Forces officers who wished to make horizontal career moves from military service into jobs as paid mercenaries. The latter was folded open to an article about belt-buckle knives sharp enough to eviscerate an adversary or cut through bone. Evidently this was Blick's reading matter during lulls in the surveillance operation, as when he had been waiting for Joe to grow weary of contemplating the sea from Santa Monica Beach.

Mr. Wallace Blick, of the ANABOLIC tattoo, was a techno geek with an edge.

When Joe climbed out of the van, Blick was groaning but not yet conscious. His legs pumped, a flurry of kicks, as if he were a dog dreaming of chasing rabbits, and his cool red sneakers tore divots from the grass.

Neither of the men in Hawaiian shirts had returned from the desert scrub beyond the hill.

Joe hadn't heard any more gunshots, although the terrain might have muffled them.

He hurried to his car. The door handle was bright with the kiss of the sun, and he hissed with pain when he touched it.

The interior of the car was so hot that it seemed on the verge of spontaneous combustion. He cranked down the window.

As he started the Honda, he glanced at the rearview mirror and saw a flatbed truck with board sides approaching from farther east in the cemetery. It was probably a groundskeeper's vehicle, either coming to investigate the gunfire or engaged in routine maintenance.

Joe could have followed the road to the west end of the memorial park and then looped all the way around to the entrance at the east perimeter, but he was in a hurry and wanted to go directly back the way he had come. Overwhelmed by a feeling that he had stretched his luck too far, he could almost hear a ticking like a time-bomb clock. Pulling away from the curb, he tried to hang a U-turn but couldn't quite manage it in one clean sweep.

He shifted into Reverse and tramped on the accelerator hard enough to make the tires squeal against the hot pavement. The Honda shot backward. He braked and shifted into Drive again.

Tick, tick, tick.

Instinct proved reliable. Just as he accelerated toward the approaching groundskeeper's truck, the rear window on the driver's side of the car, immediately behind his head, exploded, spraying glass across the backseat.

He didn't have to hear the shot to know what had happened.

Glancing to the left, he saw the man in the red Hawaiian shirt, stopped halfway down the hillside, in a shooter's stance. The guy, pale as a risen corpse, was dressed for a margarita party.

Someone shouted hoarse, slurred curses. Blick. Crawling away from the van on his hands and knees, dazedly shaking his blocky head, like a pit bull wounded in a dogfight, spraying bloody foam from his mouth: Blick.

Another round slammed into the body of the car with a hard thud, followed by a brief trailing twang.

With a rush of hot gibbering wind at the open and the shattered windows, the Honda spirited Joe out of range. He rocketed past the groundskeeper's truck at such high speed that it swerved to avoid him, though he was not in the least danger of colliding with it.

Past one burial service, where black-garbed mourners drifted like forlorn spirits away from the open grave, past another burial service, where the grieving huddled on chairs as if prepared to stay forever with whomever they had lost, past an Asian family putting a plate of fruit and cake on a fresh grave, Joe fled. He passed an unusual white church—a steeple atop a Palladian-arch cupola on columns atop a clock tower—which cast a stunted shadow in the early-afternoon sun. Past a white Southern Colonial mortuary that blazed like alabaster in the California aridity but begged for bayous. He drove recklessly, with the expectation of relentless pursuit, which didn't occur. He was also certain that his way would be blocked by the sudden arrival of swarms of police cars, but they still were not in sight when he raced between the open gates and out of the memorial park.

He drove under the Ventura Freeway, escaping into the suburban hive of the San Fernando Valley.

At a stoplight, quaking with tension, he watched a procession of a dozen street rods pass through the intersection, driven by the members of a car club on a Saturday outing: an era-perfect '41 Buick Roadmaster, a '47 Ford Sportsman Woodie with honey-maple paneling and black-cherry maroon paint, a '32 Ford Roadster in Art Deco style with full road pants and chrome speed lines. Each of the twelve was a testament to the car as art: chopped, channeled, sectioned, grafted, some on dropped spindles, with custom grilles, reconfigured hoods, frenched headlights, raised and flared wheel wells, hand-formed fender skirts. Painted, pinstriped, polished passion rolling on rubber.

Watching the street rods, he felt a curious sensation in his chest, a loosening, a stretching, both painful and exhilarating.

A block later he passed a park where, in spite of the heat, a young family—with three laughing children—was playing Frisbee with an exuberant Golden Retriever.

Heart pounding, Joe slowed the Honda. He almost pulled to the curb to watch.

At a corner, two lovely blond college girls, apparently twins, in white shorts and crisp white blouses, waited to cross the street, holding hands, as cool as spring water in the furnace heat. Mirage girls. Ethereal in the smog-stained concrete landscape. As clean and smooth and radiant as angels.

Past the girls was a massive display of zauschneria alongside a Spanish-style apartment building, laden with gorgeous clusters of tubular scarlet flowers. Michelle had loved zauschneria. She had planted it in the backyard of their Studio City house.

The day had changed. Indefinably but unquestionably changed.

No. No, not the day, not the city. Joe himself had changed, was changing, felt change rolling through him, as irresistible as an ocean tide.

His grief was as great as it had been in the awful loneliness of the night, his despair as deep as he had ever known it, but though he had begun the day sunk in melancholy, yearning for death, he now wanted desperately to live. He *needed* to live.

The engine that drove this change wasn't his close brush with death. Being shot at and nearly hit had not opened his eyes to the wonder and beauty of life. Nothing as simple as that.

Anger was the engine of change for him. He was bitterly angry not so much for what he had lost but angry for Michelle's sake, angry that Michelle had not been able to see the parade of street rods with him, or the masses of red flowers on the zauschneria, or now, here, this colorful riot of purple and red bougainvillea cascading across the roof of a Craftsman-style bungalow. He was furiously, wrenchingly angry that Chrissie and Nina would never play Frisbee with a dog of their own, would never grow up to grace the world with their beauty, would never know the thrill of accomplishment in whatever careers they might have chosen or the joy of a good marriage—or the love of their own children. Rage changed Joe, gnashed at him, bit deep enough to wake him from his long trance of self-pity and despair.

How are you coping? asked the woman photographing the graves.

I'm not ready to talk to you yet, she said.

Soon. I'll be back when it's time, she promised, as though she had revelations to make, truths to reveal.

The men in Hawaiian shirts. The computer-nerd thug in the Quake T-shirt. The redhead and the brunette in the thong bikinis. *Teams* of operatives keeping Joe under surveillance, evidently waiting for the woman to contact him. A van packed solid with satellite-assisted tracking gear, directional microphones, computers, high-resolution cameras. Gunmen willing to shoot him in cold blood because . . .

Why?

Because they thought the black woman at the graves had told him something he wasn't supposed to know? Because even being aware of her existence made him dangerous to them? Because they thought he might have come out of their van with enough information to learn their identities and intentions?

Of course he knew almost nothing about them, not who they were or what they wanted with the woman. Nevertheless, he could reach one inescapable conclusion: What he thought he knew about the deaths of his wife and daughters was either wrong or incomplete. Something wasn't kosher about the story of Nationwide Flight 353.

He didn't even need journalistic instinct to arrive at this chilling insight. On one level, he had known it from the moment that he saw the woman at the graves. Watching her snap photographs of the plot markers, meeting her compelling eyes, hearing the compassion in her soft voice, racked by the mystery of her words—*I'm not ready to talk to you yet*—he had known, by virtue of sheer common sense, that something was rotten.

Now, driving through placid Burbank, he seethed with a sense of injustice, treachery. There was a hateful wrongness with the world beyond the mere mechanical cruelty of it. Deception. Deceit. Lies. Conspiracy.

He had argued with himself that being angry with Creation was pointless, that only resignation and indifference offered him relief from his anguish. And he had been right. Raging at the imagined occupant of some celestial throne was wasted effort, as ineffective as throwing stones to extinguish the light of a star.

People, however, were a worthy target of his rage. The people who had concealed or distorted the exact circumstances of the crash of Flight 353.

Michelle, Chrissie, and Nina could never be brought back. Joe's life could never be made whole again. The wounds in his heart could not be healed. Whatever hidden truth waited to be uncovered, learning it would not give him a future. His life was over, and nothing could ever change that, nothing, but he had a right to know precisely how and exactly why Michelle and Chrissie and Nina had died. He had a sacred *obligation* to them to learn what had really happened to that doomed 747.

His bitterness was a fulcrum and his rage was a long lever with which he would move the world, the whole damn world, to learn the truth, no matter what damage he caused or whom he destroyed in the process.

On a tree-lined residential street, he pulled to the curb. He switched off the engine and got out of the car. He might not have much time before Blick and the others caught up with him.

The queen palms hung dead-limp and whisperless in the heat, which currently seemed to be as effective an embalming medium as a block of fly-trapping amber.

Joe looked under the hood first, but the transponder wasn't there. He squatted in front of the car and felt along the underside of the bumper. Nothing.

The clatter of a helicopter swelled in the distance, rapidly growing louder.

Groping blindly inside the front wheel well on the passenger side and then along the rocker panel, Joe found only road dirt and grease. Nothing was concealed inside the rear wheel well, either.

The chopper shot out of the north, passing directly overhead at extremely low altitude, no more than fifty feet above the houses. The long graceful fronds of the queen palms shook and whipped in the downdraft.

Joe looked up, alarmed, wondering if the crew of the chopper was looking for him, but his fear was pure paranoia and unjustified. Southbound, the aircraft roared away across the neighborhood without a pause.

He hadn't seen any police seal, any lettering or insignia.

The palms shuddered, shivered, then trembled into stillness once more.

Groping again, Joe found the transponder expansion-clamped to the energy absorber behind the Honda's rear bumper. With batteries, the entire package was the size of a pack of cigarettes. The signal that it sent was inaudible.

It looked harmless.

He placed the device on the pavement, intending to hammer it to pieces with his tire iron. When a gardener's truck approached along the street, hauling a fragrant load of shrub prunings and burlap-bundled grass, he decided to toss the still-functioning transponder among the clippings.

Maybe the bastards would waste some time and manpower following the truck to the dump.

In the car again, on the move, he spotted the helicopter a few miles to the south. It was flying in tight circles. Then hovering. Then flying in circles again.

His fear of it had not been groundless. The craft was either over the cemetery or, more likely, above the desert scrub north of the Griffith Observatory, searching for the fugitive woman.

Their resources were impressive.

PART TWO
SEARCHING BEHAVIOR

▼

F I V E

The *Los Angeles Times* booked more advertising than any newspaper in the United States, churning out fortunes for its owners even in an age when most print media were in decline. It was quartered downtown, in an entire high-rise, which it owned and which covered one city block.

Strictly speaking, the *Los Angeles Post* was not even in Los Angeles. It occupied an aging four-story building in Sun Valley, near the Burbank Airport, within the metroplex but not within the L.A. city limits.

Instead of a multiple-level underground garage, the *Post* provided an open lot surrounded by a chain-link fence topped with spirals of razor wire. Rather than a uniformed attendant with a name tag and a welcoming smile, a sullen young man, about nineteen, watched over the ungated entrance from a folding chair under a dirty café umbrella emblazoned with the Cinzano logo. He was listening to rap music on a radio. Head shaved, left nostril pierced by a gold ring, fingernails painted black, dressed in baggy black jeans with one carefully torn knee and a loose black T-shirt with the words FEAR NADA in red across his chest, he looked as if he were assessing the parts value of each arriving car to determine which would bring the most cash if stolen and delivered to a chop shop. In fact, he was checking for an employee sticker on the windshield, ready to direct visitors to on-street parking.

The stickers were replaced every two years, and Joe's was still valid. Two months after the fall of Flight 353, he had tendered his resignation, but his editor, Caesar Santos, had refused to accept it and had put him on an unpaid leave of absence, guaranteeing him a job when he was ready to return.

He was not ready. He would never be ready. But right now he needed to use the newspaper's computers and connections.

No money had been spent on the reception lounge: institutional-beige paint, steel chairs with blue vinyl pads, a steel-legged coffee table with a faux-granite Formica top, and two copies of that day's edition of the *Post*.

On the walls were simple framed black-and-white photographs by Bill Hannett, the paper's legendary prize-winning press photographer. Shots of riots, a city in flames, grinning looters running in the streets. Earthquake-cracked avenues, buildings in rubble. A young Hispanic woman jumping to her death from the sixth floor of a burning building. A brooding sky and a Pacific-facing mansion teetering on the edge of ruin on a rain-soaked, sliding hillside. In general, no journalistic enterprise, whether electronic or print, built its reputation or revenues on good news.

Behind the reception counter was Dewey Beemis, the combination receptionist and security guard, who had worked at the *Post* for over twenty years, since an insanely egotistical billionaire had founded it with the naive and hopeless intention of toppling the politically connected *Times* from its perch of power and prestige. Originally the paper had been quartered in a new building in Century City, with its public spaces conceived and furnished by the *uber*designer Steven Chase, at which time Dewey had been only one of several guards and not a receptionist. Even a megalomaniacal billionaire, determined to prevent the dehydration of his pride, grows weary of pouring away money with the tap open wide. Thus the grand offices were traded for more humble space in the valley. The staff had been pared down, and Dewey had hung on by virtue of being the only six-feet-four, bull-necked, plank-shouldered security guard who could type eighty words a minute and claim awesome computer skills.

With the passage of time, the *Post* had begun to break even. The brilliant and visionary Mr. Chase subsequently designed numerous striking interiors, which were celebrated in *Architectural Digest* and elsewhere, and then died in spite of his genius and talent, just as the billionaire would one day die in spite of his vast fortune, just as Dewey Beemis would die in spite of his commendable variety of skills and his infectious smile.

"Joe!" Dewey said, grinning, rising from his chair, a bearish presence, extending his big hand across the counter.

Joe shook hands. "How're you doing, Dewey?"

"Carver and Martin both graduated *summa cum laude* from UCLA in June, one going to law school now, the other medical," Dewey gushed, as if this news were only hours old and about to hit the front page of the next day's *Post*. Unlike the billionaire who employed him, Dewey's pride was not in his own accomplishments but in those of his children. "My Julie, she finished her second year on scholarship at Yale with a three-point-eight average, and this fall she takes over as editor of the student literary magazine, wants to be a novelist like this Annie Proulx she's always reading over and over again—"

With the sudden memory of Flight 353 passing through his eyes as obviously as a dimming cloud across a bright moon, Dewey silenced himself, ashamed to have been boasting about his sons and daughter to a man whose children were lost forever.

"How's Lena?" Joe asked, inquiring about Dewey's wife.

"She's good . . . she's okay, yeah, doing okay." Dewey smiled and nodded to cover his uneasiness, editing his natural enthusiasm for his family.

Joe hated this awkwardness in his friends, their pity. Even after an entire year, here it was. This was one reason he avoided everyone from his old life. The pity in their eyes was genuine compassion, but to Joe, although he knew that he was being unfair, they also seemed to be passing a sad judgment on him for being unable to put his life back together.

"I need to go upstairs, Dewey, put in a little time, do some research, if that's okay."

Dewey's expression brightened. "You coming back, Joe?"

"Maybe," Joe lied.

"Back on staff?"

"Thinking about it."

"Mr. Santos would love to hear that."

"Is he here today?"

"No. On vacation, actually, fishing up in Vancouver."

Relieved that he wouldn't have to lie to Caesar about his true motives, Joe said, "There's just something I've gotten interested in, a quirky human interest story, not my usual thing. Thought I'd come do some background."

"Mr. Santos would want you to feel like you're home. You go on up."

"Thanks, Dewey."

Joe pushed through a swinging door into a long hallway with a worn and stained green carpet, age-mottled paint, and a discolored acoustic-tile ceiling. Following the abandonment of the fat-city trappings that had characterized the *Post*'s years in Century City, the preferred image was guerrilla journalism, hardscrabble but righteous.

To the left was an elevator alcove. The doors at both shafts were scraped and dented.

The ground floor—largely given over to file rooms, clerical offices, classified ad sales, and the circulation department—was full of Saturday silence. In the quiet, Joe felt like an intruder. He imagined that anyone he encountered would perceive at once that he had returned under false pretenses.

While he was waiting for an elevator to open, he was surprised by Dewey, who had hurried from the reception lounge to give him a sealed white envelope. "Almost forgot this. Lady came by few days ago, said she had some information on a story just right for you."

"What story?"

"She didn't say. Just that you'd understand this."

Joe accepted the envelope as the elevator doors opened.

Dewey said, "Told her you hadn't worked here ten months, and she wanted your phone number. Of course I said I couldn't give it out. Or your address."

Stepping into the elevator, Joe said, "Thanks, Dewey."

"Told her I'd send it on or call you about it. Then I discovered you moved and got a new phone, unlisted, and we didn't have it."

"Can't be important," Joe assured him, indicating the envelope. After all, he was not actually returning to journalism.

As the elevator doors started to close, Dewey blocked them. Frowning, he said, "Wasn't just personnel records not up to speed with you, Joe. Nobody here, none of your friends, knew how to reach you."

"I know."

Dewey hesitated before he said, "You've been way down, huh?"

"Pretty far," Joe acknowledged. "But I'm climbing back up."

"Friends can hold the ladder steady, make it easier."

Touched, Joe nodded.

"Just remember," Dewey said.

"Thanks."

Dewey stepped back, and the doors closed.

The elevator rose, taking Joe with it.

The third floor was largely devoted to the newsroom, which had been subdivided into a maze of somewhat claustrophobic modular workstations, so that the entire space could not be seen at once. Every workstation had a computer, telephone, ergonomic chair, and other fundamentals of the trade.

This was very similar to the much larger newsroom at the *Times*. The only differences were that the furniture and the reconfigurable walls at the *Times* were newer and more stylish than those at the *Post*, the environment there was no doubt purged of the asbestos and formaldehyde that lent the air here its special astringent quality, and even on a Saturday afternoon the *Times* would be busier per square foot of floor space than the *Post* was now.

Twice over the years, Joe had been offered a job at the *Times*, but he had declined. Although the Gray Lady, as the competition was known in some circles, was a great newspaper, it was also the ad-fat voice of the status quo. He believed he'd be allowed and encouraged to do better and more aggressive reporting at the *Post*, which was like an asylum at times, but also heavy on ballsy attitude and gonzo style, with a reputation for never treating a politician's handout as real news and for assuming that every public official was either corrupt or incompetent, sex crazed or power mad.

A few years ago, after the Northridge earthquake, seismologists had discovered unsuspected links between a fault that ran under the heart of L.A. and one that lay beneath a series of communities in the San Fernando Valley. A joke swept the newsroom regarding what losses the city would suffer if one temblor destroyed the *Times* downtown and the *Post* in Sun Valley. Without the *Post*, according to the joke, Angelenos wouldn't know which politicians and other public servants were stealing them blind, accepting bribes from known drug dealers, and having sex with animals. The greater tragedy, however, would be the loss of the six-pound Sunday edition of the *Times*, without which no one would know what stores were conducting sales.

If the *Post* was as obstinate and relentless as a rat terrier crazed by the scent of rodents—which it was—it was redeemed, for Joe, by the nonpartisan nature of its fury. Furthermore, a high percentage of its targets were at least as corrupt as it wanted to believe they were.

Also, Michelle had been a featured columnist and editorial writer for the *Post*. He met her here, courted her here, and enjoyed their shared sense of being part of an underdog enterprise. She had carried their two babies in her belly through so many days of work in this place.

Now he found this building haunted by memories of her. In the unlikely event that he could eventually regain emotional stability and con himself into believing life had a purpose worth the struggle, the face of that one dear ghost would rock him every time he saw it. He would never be able to work at the *Post* again.

He went directly to his former workstation in the Metro section, grateful that no old friends saw him. His place had been assigned to Randy Colway, a good man, who wouldn't feel invaded if he found Joe in his chair.

Tacked to the noteboard were photographs of Randy's wife, their nine-year-old son, Ben, and six-year-old Lisbeth. Joe looked at them for a long moment—and then not again.

After switching on the computer, he reached into his pocket and withdrew the Department of Motor Vehicles envelope that he'd filched from the glove box of the white van at the cemetery. It contained the validated registration card. To his surprise, the registered owner wasn't a government body or a law-enforcement agency; it was something called Medsped, Inc.

He had not been expecting a corporate operation, for God's sake. Wallace Blick and his trigger-happy associates in the Hawaiian shirts didn't seem entirely like cops or federal agents, but they smelled a lot more like the law than they did like any corporate executives Joe had ever encountered.

Next he accessed the *Post*'s vast file of digitized back issues. Included was every word of every edition the newspaper had published since its inception—minus only the cartoons, horoscopes, crossword puzzles, and the like. Photographs were included.

He initiated a search for *Medsped* and found six mentions. They were small items from the business pages. He read them complete.

Medsped, a New Jersey corporation, had begun as an air ambulance service in several major cities. Later, it had expanded to specialize in the nationwide express delivery of emergency medical supplies, refrigerated or otherwise delicately preserved blood and tissue samples, as well as expensive and frangible scientific instruments. The company even undertook to carry samples of highly contagious bacteria and viruses between cooperating research laboratories in both the public and the military sectors. For these tasks, it maintained a modest fleet of aircraft and helicopters.

Helicopters.

And unmarked white vans?

Eight years ago, Medsped had been bought by Teknologik, Inc., a Delaware corporation with a score of wholly owned subsidiaries in the medical and computer industry. Its computer-related holdings were all companies developing products, mostly software, for the medical and medical-research communities.

When Joe ran a search on Teknologik, he was rewarded with forty-one stories, mostly from the business pages. The first two articles were so dry, however, so full of investment and accounting jargon, that the reward quickly began to seem like punishment.

He ordered copies of the four longest articles for review later.

While those were sliding into the printer tray, he asked for a list of stories the *Post* had published about the crash of Nationwide Flight 353. A series of headlines, with accompanying dates, appeared on the screen.

Joe had to steel himself to scan this story file. He sat for a minute or two with his eyes closed, breathing deeply, trying to conjure, in his mind's eye, an image of surf breaking on the beach at Santa Monica.

Finally, with teeth clenched so tightly that his jaw muscles twitched continuously, he called up story after story, scanning the contents. He wanted the one that, as a sidebar, would provide him with a complete passenger manifest.

He skipped quickly past photographs of the crash scene, which revealed debris chopped into such small chunks and tangled in such surreal shapes that the baffled eye could not begin to reconstruct the aircraft from its ruins. In the bleak dawn caught by these pictures, through the gray drizzle that had begun to fall about two hours after the disaster, National Transportation Safety Board investigators in biologically secure bodysuits with visored hoods prowled the blasted meadow. Looming in the background were scorched trees, gnarled black limbs clawing at the low sky.

He searched for and found the name of the NTSB Go-Team leader in charge of the investigation—Barbara Christman—and the fourteen specialists working under her.

A couple of the articles included photos of some of the crew and passengers. Not all of the three hundred and thirty souls aboard were pictured. The tendency was to focus on those victims who were Southern Californians returning home rather than on Easterners who had been coming to visit. Being part of the *Post* family, Michelle and the girls were prominently featured.

Eight months ago, upon moving into the apartment, in reaction to a morbid and obsessive preoccupation with family albums and loose snapshots, Joe had packed all the photos in a large cardboard box, reasoning that rubbing a wound retarded healing. He had taped the box shut and put it at the back of his only closet.

Now, in the course of his scanning, when their faces appeared on the screen, he was unable to breathe, though he had thought he would be prepared. Michelle's publicity shot, taken by one of the *Post*'s staff photographers, captured her beauty but not her tenderness, not her intelligence, not her charm, not her laughter. A mere picture was so inadequate, but still it was Michelle. Still. Chrissie's photo had been snapped at a *Post* Christmas party for children of the paper's employees. She was caught in a grin, eyes shining. How they shone. And little Nina, who sometimes wanted it pronounced *neen-ah* and other times *nine-ah*, was smiling that slightly lopsided smile that seemed to say she knew magical secrets.

Her smile reminded Joe of a silly song he sometimes sang to her when he put her to bed. Before he realized what he was doing, he found his breath again and heard himself whispering the words. *"Nine-ah, neen-ah, have you seen her? Neen-ah, nine-ah, no one finah."*

A breaking inside him threatened his self-control.

He clicked the mouse to get their images off the screen. But that didn't take their faces out of his mind, clearer than he had seen them since packing their photos away.

Bending forward in the chair, covering his face, shuddering, he muffled his voice in his cold hands. "Oh, shit. Oh, shit."

Surf breaking on a beach, now as before, tomorrow as today. Clocks and looms. Sunrises, sunsets, phases of the moon. Machines clicking, ticking. Eternal rhythms, meaningless motions.

The only sane response is indifference.

He lowered his hands from his face. Sat up straight again. Tried to focus on the computer screen.

He was concerned that he would draw attention to himself. If an old acquaintance looked into this three-walled cubicle to see what was wrong, Joe might have to explain what he was doing here, might even have to summon the strength to be sociable.

He found the passenger manifest for which he had been searching. The *Post* had saved him time and effort by listing separately those among the dead who had lived in Southern California. He printed out all their names, each of which was followed by the name of the town in which the deceased resided.

I'm not ready to talk to you yet, the photographer of graves had said to him, from which he had inferred that she would have things to tell him later.

Don't despair. You'll see, like the others.

See what? He had no idea.

What could she possibly tell him that would alleviate his despair? Nothing. Nothing.

. . . like the others. You'll see, like the others.

What others?

Only one answer satisfied him: other people who had lost loved ones on Flight 353, who had been as desolate as he was, people to whom she had already spoken.

He wasn't going to wait for her to return to him. With Wallace Blick and associates after her, she might not live long enough to pay him a visit and quench his curiosity.

When Joe finished sorting and stapling the printouts, he noticed the white envelope that Dewey Beemis had given him at the elevator downstairs. Joe had propped it against a box of Kleenex to the right of the computer and promptly forgotten about it.

As a crime reporter with a frequently seen byline, he had from time to time received story tips from newspaper readers who, to put it charitably, were not well glued together. They earnestly claimed to be the terrified victims of vicious harassment by a secret cult of Satanists operating in the city's parks department, or to know of sinister tobacco-industry executives who were plotting to lace baby formula with nicotine, or to be living across the street from a nest of spider-like extraterrestrials trying to pass as a nice family of Korean immigrants.

Once, when cornered by a pinwheel-eyed man who insisted that the mayor of Los Angeles was not human but a robot controlled by the audioanimatronics department at Disneyland, Joe had lowered his voice and said, with nervous sincerity, "Yes, we've known about that for years. But if we print a word of it, the people at Disney will kill us all." He had spoken with such conviction that the nutball had exploded backward and fled.

Consequently, he was expecting a crayon-scrawled message about evil psychic Martians living among us as Mormons—or the equivalent. He tore open the envelope. It contained a single sheet of white paper folded in thirds.

The three neatly typed sentences initially impressed him as a singularly cruel variation on the usual paranoid shriek: *I have been trying to reach you, Joe. My life depends on your discretion. I was aboard Flight 353.*

Everyone aboard the airliner had perished. He didn't believe in ghost mail from the Other Side, which probably made him unique among his contemporaries in this New Age City of Angels.

At the bottom of the page was a name: Rose Tucker. Under the name was a phone number with a Los Angeles area code. No address was provided.

Lightly flushed by the same anger that had burned so hotly in him earlier, and which could easily become a blaze again, Joe almost snatched up the phone to call Ms. Tucker. He wanted to tell her what a disturbed and vicious piece of garbage she was, wallowing in her schizophrenic fantasies, psychic vampire sucking on the misery of others to feed some sick need of her own—

And then he heard, in memory, the words that Wallace Blick first said to him in the cemetery. Unaware that anyone was in the white van, Joe had leaned through the open passenger door and popped the glove box in search of a cellular phone. Blick, briefly mistaking him for one of the men in the Hawaiian shirts, had said, *Did you get Rose?*

Rose.

Because Joe had been frightened by the gunmen, afraid for the woman they were pursuing, and startled to discover someone in the van, the importance of what Blick said had failed to register with him. Everything happened so fast after that. He had forgotten Blick's words until now.

Rose Tucker must have been the woman with the Polaroid camera, photographing the graves.

If she was nothing more than a whacked-out loser living in some schizophrenic fantasy, Medsped or Teknologik—or whoever the hell they were—wouldn't be throwing so much manpower and money into a search for her.

He remembered the exceptional presence of the woman in the cemetery. Her directness. Her self-possession and preternatural calm. The power of her unwavering stare.

She hadn't seemed like a flake. Quite the opposite.

I have been trying to reach you, Joe. My life depends on your discretion. I was aboard Flight 353.

Without realizing that he had gotten off the chair, Joe was standing, heart pounding, electrified. The sheet of paper rattled in his hands.

He stepped into the aisle behind the modular workstation and surveyed what he could see of the subdivided newsroom, seeking someone with whom he could share this development.

Look here. Read this, read it. Something's terribly wrong, Jesus, all wrong, not what we were told. Somebody walked away from the crash, lived through it. We have to do something about this, find the truth. No survivors, they said, no survivors, catastrophic crash, total wipeout catastrophic crash. What else have they told us that isn't true? How did the people on that plane really die? Why did they die? Why did they die?

Before anyone saw him standing there in furious distress, before he went in search of a familiar face, Joe had second thoughts about sharing anything he had learned. Rose Tucker's note said that her life depended on his discretion.

Besides, he had the crazy notion, somehow more powerfully convincing *because* of its irrationality, that if he shared the note with others, it would prove to be blank, that if he pressed Blick's driver's license into their hands, it would turn out to be his own license, that if he took someone with him to the cemetery, there would be no spent cartridges in the grass and no skid marks from the tires of the white van and no one there who had ever seen the vehicle or heard the gunshots.

This was a mystery delivered to him, to no one else but him, and he suddenly perceived that pursuing answers was not merely his duty but his *sacred* duty. In the resolution of this mystery was his mission, his purpose, and perhaps an unknowable redemption.

He didn't even understand precisely what he meant by any of that. He simply felt the truth of it bone-deep.

Trembling, he returned to the chair.

He wondered if he was entirely sane.

SIX

Joe called downstairs to the reception desk and asked Dewey Beemis about the woman who had left the envelope.

"Little bit of a lady," said Dewey.

He was a giant, however, and even a six-foot-tall Amazon might seem petite to him.

"Would you say five six, shorter?" Joe asked.

"Maybe five one, five two. But mighty. One of those ladies looks like a girl all her life but been a mountain-mover since she graduated grade school."

"Black woman?" Joe asked.

"Yeah, she was a sister."

"How old?"

"Maybe early forties. Pretty. Hair like raven wings. You upset about something, Joe?"

"No. No, I'm okay."

"You sound upset. This lady some kind of trouble?"

"No, she's okay, she's legit. Thanks, Dewey."

Joe put down the phone.

The nape of his neck was acrawl with gooseflesh. He rubbed it with one hand.

His palms were clammy. He blotted them on his jeans.

Nervously, he picked up the printout of the passenger manifest from Flight 353. Using a ruler to keep his place, he went down the list of the deceased, line by line, until he came to *Dr. Rose Marie Tucker.*

Doctor.

She might be a doctor of medicine or of literature, biologist or sociologist, musicologist or dentist, but in Joe's eyes, her credibility was enhanced by the mere fact that she had earned the honorific. The troubled people who believed the mayor to be a robot were more likely to be patients than doctors of any kind.

According to the manifest, Rose Tucker was forty-three years old, and her home was in Manassas, Virginia. Joe had never been in Manassas, but he had driven past it a few times, because it was an outer suburb of Washington, near the town where Michelle's parents lived.

Swiveling to the computer once more, he scrolled through the crash stories, seeking the thirty or more photographs of passengers, hoping hers would be among them. It was not.

Judging by Dewey's description, the woman who had written this note and the woman in the cemetery—whom Blick had called *Rose*—were the same person. If this Rose was truly Dr. Rose Marie Tucker of Manassas, Virginia—which couldn't be confirmed without a photo—then she had indeed been aboard Flight 353.

And had survived.

Reluctantly, Joe returned to the two largest accident-scene photographs. The first was the eerie shot with the stormy sky, the scorched-black trees, the debris pulverized and twisted into surreal sculpture, where the NTSB investigators, faceless in biohazard suits and hoods, seemed to drift like praying monks or like ominous spirits in a cold and flameless chamber in some forgotten level of Hell. The second was an aerial shot revealing wreckage so shattered and so widely strewn that the term "catastrophic accident" was a woefully inadequate description.

No one could have survived this disaster.

Yet Rose Tucker, if she was the *same* Rose Tucker who had boarded the plane that night, had evidently not only survived but walked away under her own power. Without serious injury. She had not been scarred or crippled.

Impossible. Dropping four miles in the clutch of planetary gravity, four long *miles*, accelerating unchecked into hard earth and rock, the 747 had not just smashed but splattered like an egg thrown at a brick wall, and then exploded, and then tumbled in seething furies of flame. To escape unmarked from the God-rattled ruins of Gomorrah, to step as unburnt as Shadrach from the fiery furnace of Nebuchadnezzar, to arise like Lazarus after four days in the grave, would have been less miraculous than to walk away untouched from the fall of Flight 353.

If he genuinely believed it was impossible, however, his mind would not have been roiled with anger and anxiety, with a strange awe, and with urgent curiosity. In him was a crazy yearning to embrace incredibilities, walk with wonder.

He called directory assistance in Manassas, seeking a telephone number for Dr. Rose Marie Tucker. He expected to be told that there was no such listing or that her service had been disconnected. After all, officially she was dead.

Instead, he was given a number.

She could not have walked away from the crash and gone home and picked up her life without causing a sensation. Besides, dangerous people were hunting her. They would have found her if she had ever returned to Manassas.

Perhaps family still lived in the house. For whatever reasons, they might have kept the phone in her name.

Joe punched in the number.

The call was answered on the second ring. "Yes?"

"Is this the Tucker residence?" Joe asked.

The voice was that of a man, crisp and without a regional accent: "Yes, it is."

"Could I speak to Dr. Tucker, please?"

"Who's calling?"

Intuition advised Joe to guard his own name. "Wally Blick."

"Excuse me. Who?"

"Wallace Blick."

The man at the other end of the line was silent. Then: "What is this in regard to?" His voice had barely changed, but a new alertness colored it, a shade of wariness.

Sensing that he had been too clever for his own good, Joe put down the phone.

He blotted his palms on his jeans again.

A reporter, passing behind Joe, reviewing the scribblings on a note pad as he went, greeted him without looking up: "Yo, Randy."

Consulting the typewritten message from Rose, Joe called the Los Angeles number that she had provided.

On the fifth ring, a woman answered. "Hello?"

"Could I speak to Rose Tucker, please?"

"Nobody here by that name," she said in an accent out of the deep South. "You got yourself a wrong number."

In spite of what she'd said, she didn't hang up.

"She gave me this number herself," Joe persisted.

"Sugar, let me guess—this was a lady you met at a party. She was just makin' nice to get you out of her hair."

"I don't think she'd do that."

"Oh, don't mean you're ugly, honey," she said in a voice that brought to mind magnolia blossoms and mint juleps and humid nights heavy with the scent of jasmine. "Just means you weren't the lady's type. Happens to the best."

"My name's Joe Carpenter."

"Nice name. Good solid name."

"What's *your* name?"

Teasingly, she said, "What kind of name do I sound like?"

"Sound like?"

"Maybe an Octavia or a Juliette?"

"More like a Demi."

"Like in Demi Moore the movie star?" she said disbelievingly.

"You have that sexy, smoky quality in your voice."

"Honey, my voice is pure grits and collard greens."

"Under the grits and collard greens, there's smoke."

She had a wonderful fulsome laugh. "Mister Joe Carpenter, middle name 'Slick.' Okay, I like Demi."

"Listen, Demi, I'd sure like to talk to Rose."

"Forget this old Rose person. Don't you pine away for her, Joe, not after she gives you a fake number. Big sea, lots of fish."

Joe was certain that this woman knew Rose and that she had been expecting him to call. Considering the viciousness of the enemies pursuing the enigmatic Dr. Tucker, however, Demi's circumspection was understandable.

She said, "What do you look like when you're bein' honest with yourself, sugar?"

"Six feet tall, brown hair, gray eyes."

"Handsome?"

"Just presentable."

"How old are you, Presentable Joe?"

"Older than you. Thirty-seven."

"You have a sweet voice. You ever go on blind dates?"

Demi was going to set up a meeting, after all.

He said, "Blind dates? Nothing against them."

"So how about with sexy-smoky little me?" she suggested with a laugh.

"Sure. When?"

"You free tomorrow evenin'?"

"I was hoping sooner."

"Don't be so eager, Presentable Joe. Takes time to set these things up right, so there's a chance it'll work, so no one gets hurt, so there's no broken hearts."

By Joe's interpretation, Demi was telling him that she was going to make damned sure the meeting was put together carefully, that the site needed to be scouted and secured in order for Rose's safety to be guaranteed. And maybe she couldn't get in touch with Rose with less than a twenty-four-hour notice.

"Besides, sugar, a girl starts to wonder why you're so pitiful desperate if you're really presentable."

"All right. Where tomorrow evening?"

"I'm goin' to give you the address of a gourmet coffee shop in Westwood. We'll meet out front at six, go in and have a cup, see do we like each other. If I think you really are presentable and you think I'm as sexy-smoky as my voice . . . why, then it could be a shinin' night of golden memories. You have a pen and paper?"

"Yes," he said, and he wrote down the name and address of the coffee shop as she gave it to him.

"Now do me one favor, sugar. You have a paper there with this phone number on. Tear it to bitty pieces and flush it down a john." When Joe hesitated, Demi said, "Won't be no good ever again, anyway," and she hung up.

The three typed sentences would not prove that Dr. Tucker had survived Flight 353 or that something about the crash was not kosher. He could have composed them himself. Dr. Tucker's name was typed as well, so there was no evidentiary signature.

Nevertheless, he was loath to dispose of the message. Although it would never prove anything to anyone else, it made these fantastic events seem more real to *him*.

He called Demi's number again to see if she would answer it in spite of what she had said.

To his surprise, he got a recorded message from the telephone company informing him that the number he had called was no longer in service. He was advised to make sure that he had entered the number correctly and then to call 411 for directory assistance. He tried the number again, with the same result.

Neat trick. He wondered how it had been done. Demi clearly was more sophisticated than her grits-and-collard-greens voice.

As Joe returned the handset to the cradle, the telephone rang, startling him so much that he let go of it as if he had burned his fingers. Embarrassed by his edginess, he picked it up on the third ring. "Hello?"

"*Los Angeles Post?*" a man asked.

"Yes."

"Is this Randy Colway's direct line?"

"That's right."

"Are you Mr. Colway?"

Startlement and the interlude with Demi had left Joe slow on the uptake. Now he recognized the uninflected voice as that of the man who had answered the phone at Rose Marie Tucker's house in Manassas, Virginia.

"Are you Mr. Colway?" the caller asked again.

"I'm Wallace Blick," Joe said.

"Mr. Carpenter?"

Chills climbed the ladder of his spine, vertebra to vertebra, and Joe slammed down the phone.

They knew where he was.

The dozens of modular workstations no longer seemed like a series of comfortably anonymous nooks. They were a maze with too many blind corners.

Quickly he gathered the printouts and the message that Rose Tucker had left for him.

As he was getting up from the chair, the phone rang again. He didn't answer it.

On his way out of the newsroom, he encountered Dan Shavers, who was returning from the photocopying center with a sheaf of papers in his left hand and his unlit pipe in the right. Shavers, utterly bald, with a luxuriant black beard, wore pleated black dress slacks, red-and-black checkered suspenders over a gray-and-white pinstriped shirt, and a yellow bow tie. His half-lens reading glasses dangled from his neck on a loop of black ribbon.

A reporter and columnist on the business desk, Shavers was as pompous and as awkward at small talk as he thought he was charming; however, he was benign in his self-delusion and touching in his mistaken conviction that he was a spellbinding raconteur. He said without preamble, "Joseph, dear boy, opened a case of '74 Mondavi Cabernet last week, one of twenty I bought as an investment when it was first released, even though at the time I was in Napa not to scout the vintners but to shop for an antique clock, and let me tell you, this wine has matured so well that—" He broke off, realizing that Joe had not worked at the newspaper for the better part of a year. Fumblingly, he tried to offer his condolences regarding "that terrible thing, that awful thing, all those poor people, your wife and the children."

Aware that Randy Colway's telephone was ringing again farther back in the newsroom, Joe interrupted Shavers, intending to brush him off, but then he said, "Listen, Dan, do you know a company called Teknologik?"

"Do I know them?" Shavers wiggled his eyebrows. "Very amusing, Joseph."

"You do know them? What's the story, Dan? Are they a pretty large conglomerate? I mean, are they powerful?"

"Oh, very profitable, Joseph, absolutely uncanny at recognizing cutting-edge technology in start-up companies and then acquiring them—or backing entrepreneurs who need cash to develop their ideas. Generally medically related technology but not always. Their top executives are infamous self-aggrandizers, think of themselves as some kind of business royalty, but they are no better than us. They, too, answer to He Who Must Be Obeyed."

Confused, Joe said, "He Who Must Be Obeyed?"

"As do we all, as do we all," said Shavers, smiling and nodding, raising his pipe to bite the stem.

Colway's phone stopped ringing. The silence made Joe more nervous than the insistent trilling tone had done.

They knew where he was.

"Got to go," he said, walking away as Shavers began to tell him about the advantages of owning Teknologik corporate bonds.

He proceeded directly to the nearest men's room. Fortunately, no one else was in the lavatory, no old acquaintances to delay him.

In one of the stalls, Joe tore Rose's message into small pieces. He flushed it down the toilet, as Demi had requested, waiting to confirm that every scrap vanished, flushing a second time to be sure that nothing was caught in the drain.

Medsped. Teknologik. Corporations conducting what appeared to be a police operation. Their long reach, from Los Angeles to Manassas, and their unnerving omniscience, argued that these were corporations with powerful connections beyond the business world, perhaps to the military.

Nevertheless, regardless of the stakes, it made no sense for a corporation to protect its interests with hit men brazen enough to shoot at people in public places—or anywhere else, for that matter. Regardless of how profitable Teknologik might be, big black numbers at the bottom of the balance sheet did not exempt corporate officers and executives from the law, not even here in Los Angeles, where the *lack* of money was known to be the root of all evil.

Considering the impunity with which they seemed to think they could use guns, the men whom he had encountered *must* be military personnel or federal agents. Joe had too little information to allow him even to conjecture what role Medsped and Teknologik played in the operation.

All the way along the third-floor hall to the elevators, he expected someone to call his name and order him to stop. Perhaps one of the men in Hawaiian shirts. Or Wallace Blick. Or a police officer.

If the people seeking Rose Tucker were federal agents, they would be able to obtain help from local police. For the time being, Joe would have to regard every man in uniform as a potential enemy.

As the elevator doors opened, he tensed, half expecting to be apprehended here in the alcove. The cab was empty.

On the way down to the first floor, he waited for the power to be cut off. When the doors opened on the lower alcove, he was surprised to find it deserted.

In all his life, he had never previously been in the grip of paranoia such as this. He was overreacting to the events of the early afternoon and to what he had learned since arriving at the offices of the *Post*.

He wondered if his exaggerated reactions—spells of extreme rage, spiraling fear—were a response to the past year of emotional deprivation. He had allowed himself to feel nothing whatsoever but grief, self-pity, and the terrible hollowness of incomprehensible loss. In fact, he'd striven hard not to feel even that much. He had tried to shed his pain, to rise from the ashes like a drab phoenix with no hope except the cold peace of indifference. Now that events forced him to open himself to the world again, he was swamped by emotion as a novice surfer was overwhelmed by each cresting wave.

In the reception lounge, as Joe entered, Dewey Beemis was on the telephone. He was listening so intently that his usually smooth dark face was furrowed. He murmured, "Yes, uh-huh, uh-huh, yes."

Heading toward the outer door, Joe waved good-bye.

Dewey said, "Joe, wait, wait a second."

Joe stopped and turned.

Though Dewey was listening to the caller again, his eyes were on Joe.

To indicate that he was in a hurry, Joe tapped one finger against his wristwatch.

"Hold on," Dewey said into the phone, and then to Joe, he said, "There's a man here calling about you."

Joe shook his head adamantly.

"Wants to talk to you," Dewey said.

Joe started toward the door again.

"Wait, Joe, man says he's FBI."

At the door, Joe hesitated and looked back at Dewey. The FBI couldn't be associated with the men in the Hawaiian shirts, not with men who shot at innocent people without bothering to ask questions, not with men like Wallace Blick. Could they? Wasn't he letting his fear run away with him again, succumbing to paranoia? He might get answers and protection from the FBI.

Of course, the man on the phone could be lying. He might not be with the Bureau. Possibly he was hoping to delay Joe until Blick and his friends—or others aligned with them—could get here.

With a shake of his head, Joe turned away from Dewey. He pushed through the door and into the August heat.

Behind him, Dewey said, "Joe?"

Joe walked toward his car. He resisted the urge to break into a run.

At the far end of the parking lot, by the open gate, the young attendant with the shaved head and the gold nose ring was watching. In this city where sometimes money mattered more than fidelity or honor or merit, style mattered more than money; fashions came and went even more frequently than principles and convictions, leaving only the unchanging signal colors of youth gangs as a sartorial tradition. This kid's look, punk-grunge-neopunk-whatever, was already as dated as spats, making him look less threatening than he thought and more pathetic than he would ever be able to comprehend. Yet under these circumstances, his interest in Joe seemed ominous.

Even at low volume, the hard beat of rap music thumped through the blistering air.

The interior of the Honda was hot but not intolerable. The side window, shattered by a bullet at the cemetery, provided just enough ventilation to prevent suffocation.

The attendant had probably noticed the broken-out window when Joe had driven in. Maybe he'd been thinking about it.

What does it matter if he has *been thinking? It's only a broken window.*

He was certain the engine wouldn't start, but it did.

As Joe backed out of the parking slot, Dewey Beemis opened the reception-lounge door and stepped outside onto the small concrete stoop under the awning that bore the logo of the *Post*. The big man looked not alarmed but puzzled.

Dewey wouldn't try to stop him. They were friends, after all, or had once been friends, and the man on the phone was just a voice.

Joe shifted the Honda into Drive.

Coming down the steps, Dewey shouted something. He didn't sound alarmed. He sounded confused, concerned.

Ignoring him nonetheless, Joe drove toward the exit.

Under the dirty Cinzano umbrella, the attendant rose from the folding chair. He was only two steps from the rolling gate that would close off the lot.

Atop the chain-link fence, the coils of razor wire flared with silver reflections of late-afternoon sunlight.

Joe glanced at the rearview mirror. Back there, Dewey was standing with his hands on his hips.

As Joe went past the Cinzano umbrella, the attendant didn't even come forth out of the shade. Watching with heavy-lidded eyes, as expressionless as an iguana, he wiped sweat off his brow with one hand, black fingernails glistening.

Through the open gate and turning right into the street, Joe was driving too fast. The tires squealed and sucked wetly at the sun-softened blacktop, but he didn't slow down.

He went west on Strathern Street and heard sirens by the time that he turned south on Lankershim Boulevard. Sirens were part of the music of the city, day and night; they didn't necessarily have anything to do with him.

Nevertheless, all the way to the Ventura Freeway, under it, and then west on Moorpark, he repeatedly checked the rearview mirror for pursuing vehicles, either marked or unmarked.

He was not a criminal. He should have felt safe going to the authorities to report the men in the cemetery, to tell them about the message from Rose Marie Tucker, and to report his suspicions about Flight 353.

On the other hand, in spite of being on the run for her life, Rose apparently hadn't sought protection from the cops, perhaps because there was no protection to be had. *My life depends on your discretion.*

He had been a crime reporter long enough to have seen more than a few cases in which the victim had been targeted not because of anything he had done, not because of money or other possessions that his assailant desired, but merely because of what he had known. A man with too much knowledge could be more dangerous than a man with a gun.

What knowledge Joe had about Flight 353 seemed, however, to be pathetically inadequate. If he was a target merely because he knew that Rose Tucker existed and that she claimed to have survived the crash, then the secrets *she* possessed must be so explosive that the power of them could be measured only in megatonnage.

As he drove west toward Studio City, he thought of the red letters emblazoned on the black T-shirt worn by the attendant at the *Post* parking lot: FEAR NADA. "Fear nothing" was a philosophy Joe could never embrace. He feared so much.

More than anything, he was tormented by the possibility that the crash had not been an accident, that Michelle and Chrissie and Nina died not at the whim of fate but by the hand of man. Although the National Transportation Safety Board hadn't been able to settle on a probable cause, hydraulic control systems failure complicated by human error was one possible scenario—and one with which he had been able to live because it was so impersonal, as mechanical and cold as the universe itself. He would find it intolerable, however, if they had perished from a cowardly act of terrorism or because of some more personal crime, their lives sacrificed to human greed or envy or hatred.

He feared what such a discovery would do to him. He feared what he might become, his potential for savagery, the hideous ease with which he might embrace vengeance and call it justice.

SEVEN

In the current atmosphere of fierce competitiveness that marked their industry, California bankers were keeping their offices open on Saturdays, some as late as five o'clock. Joe arrived at the Studio City branch of his bank twenty minutes before the doors closed.

When he sold the house here, he had not bothered to switch his account to a branch nearer his one-room apartment in Laurel Canyon. Convenience wasn't a consideration when time no longer mattered.

He went to a window where a woman named Heather was tending to paperwork as she waited for last-minute business. She had worked at this bank since Joe had first opened an account a decade ago.

"I need to make a cash withdrawal," he said, after the requisite small talk, "but I don't have my checkbook with me."

"That's no problem," she assured him.

It became a small problem, however, when Joe asked for twenty thousand dollars in hundred-dollar bills. Heather went to the other end of the bank and huddled in conversation with the head teller, who then consulted the assistant manager. This was a young man no less handsome than the current hottest movie hero; perhaps he was one of the legion of would-be stars who labored in the real world to survive while waiting for the fantasy of fame. They glanced at Joe as if his identity was now in doubt.

Taking in money, banks were like industrial vacuum cleaners. Giving it out, they were clogged faucets.

Heather returned with a guarded expression and the news that they were happy to accommodate him, though there were, of course, procedures that must be followed.

At the other end of the bank, the assistant manager was talking on his phone, and Joe suspected that he himself was the subject of the conversation. He knew he was letting his paranoia get the better of him again, but his mouth went dry, and his heartbeat increased.

The money was his. He needed it.

That Heather had known Joe for years—in fact, attended the same Lutheran church where Michelle had taken Chrissie and Nina to Sunday school and services—did not obviate her need to see his driver's license. The days of common trust and common sense were so far in America's past that they seemed not merely to be ancient history but to be part of the history of another country altogether.

He remained patient. Everything he owned was on deposit here, including nearly sixty thousand dollars in equity from the sale of the house, so he could not be denied the money, which he would need for living expenses. With the same people seeking him who were searching for Rose Tucker, he could not go back to the apartment and would have to live out of motels for the duration.

The assistant manager had concluded his call. He was staring at a note pad on his desk, tapping it with a pencil.

Joe had considered using his few credit cards to pay for things, supplemented by small sums withdrawn as needed from automated teller machines. But authorities could track a suspect through credit-card use and ATM activity—and be ever on his heels. They could even have his plastic seized by any merchant at the point of purchase.

A phone rang on the assistant manager's desk. He snatched it up, glanced at Joe, and turned away in his swivel chair, as if he worried that his lips might be read.

After procedures were followed and everyone was satisfied that Joe was neither his own evil twin nor a bold impersonator in a clever rubber mask, the assistant manager, his phone conversation concluded, slowly gathered the hundred-dollar bills from other tellers' drawers and from the vault. He brought the required sum to Heather and, with a fixed and uneasy smile, watched as she counted it for Joe.

Perhaps it was imagination, but Joe felt they disapproved of his carrying so much money, not because it put him in danger but because these days people who dealt in cash were stigmatized. The government required banks to report cash transactions of five thousand dollars or more, ostensibly to hamper attempts by drug lords to launder funds through legitimate financial institutions. In reality, no drug lord was ever inconvenienced by this law, but the financial activities of average citizens were now more easily monitored.

Throughout history, cash or the equivalent—diamonds, gold coins—had been the best guarantor of freedom and mobility. Cash meant the same things to Joe and nothing more. Yet from Heather and her bosses, he continued to endure a surreptitious scrutiny that seemed to be based on the assumption that he was engaged in some criminal enterprise or, at best, was on his way for a few days of unspeakable debauchery in Las Vegas.

As Heather put the twenty thousand in a manila envelope, the phone rang on the assistant manager's desk. Murmuring into the mouthpiece, he continued to find Joe of interest.

By the time Joe left the bank, five minutes past closing time, the last customer to depart, he was weak-kneed with apprehension.

The heat remained oppressive, and the five-o'clock sky was still cloudless and blue, although not the profound blue that it had been earlier. Now it was curiously depthless, a flat blue that reminded him of something he had seen before. The reference remained elusive until he had gotten into the car and started the engine—and then he recalled the dead-blue eyes of the last corpse that he had seen on a morgue gurney, the night he walked away from crime reporting forever.

When he drove out of the bank lot, he saw that the assistant manager was standing beyond the glass doors, all but hidden by the reflected bronze glare of the westering sun. Maybe he was storing away a description of the Honda and memorizing the license-plate number. Or maybe he was just locking the doors.

The metropolis shimmered under the blind blue stare of the dead sky.

...

Passing a small neighborhood shopping center, from across three lanes of traffic, Joe saw a woman with long auburn hair stepping out of a Ford Explorer. She was parked in front of a convenience store. From the passenger side jumped a little girl with a cap of tousled blond hair. Their faces were hidden from him.

Joe angled recklessly across traffic, nearly colliding with an elderly man in a gray Mercedes. At the intersection, as the light turned from yellow to red, he made an illegal U-turn.

He already regretted what he was about to do. But he could no more stop himself than he could hasten the day's end by commanding the sun to set. He was in the grip of a bizarre compulsion.

Shaken by his lack of self-control, he parked near the woman's Ford Explorer. He got out of the Honda. His legs were weak.

He stood staring at the convenience store. The woman and the child were in there, but he couldn't see them for the posters and merchandise displays in the big windows.

He turned away from the store and leaned against the Honda, trying to compose himself.

After the crash in Colorado, Beth McKay had referred him to a group called The Compassionate Friends, a nationwide organization for people who had lost children. Beth was slowly finding her way to acceptance through Compassionate Friends in Virginia, so Joe went to a few meetings of a local chapter, but he soon stopped attending. In that regard, he was like most other men in his situation; bereaved mothers went to the meetings faithfully and found comfort in talking with others whose children had been taken, but nearly all the fathers turned inward and held their pain close. Joe wanted to be one of the few who could find salvation by reaching out, but male biology or psychology—or pure stubbornness or self-pity—kept him aloof, alone.

At least, from The Compassionate Friends, he had discovered that this bizarre compulsion, by which he was now seized, was not unique to him. It was so common they had a name for it: *searching behavior.*

Everybody who lost a loved one engaged in a degree of searching behavior, although it was more intense for those who lost children. Some grievers suffered it worse than others. Joe had it bad.

Intellectually, he could accept that the dead were gone forever. Emotionally, on a primal level, he remained convinced that he would see them again. At times he expected his wife and daughters to walk through a door or to be on the phone when it rang. Driving, he was occasionally overcome by the certainty that Chrissie and Nina were behind him in the car, and he turned, breathless with excitement, more shocked by the emptiness of the backseat than he would have been to find that the girls were indeed alive again and with him.

Sometimes he saw them on a street. On a playground. In a park. On the beach. They were always at a distance, walking away from him. Sometimes he let them go, but sometimes he was compelled to follow, to see their faces, to say, "Wait for me, wait, I'm coming with you."

Now he turned away from the Honda. He went to the entrance of the convenience store.

Opening the door, he hesitated. He was torturing himself. The inevitable emotional implosion that would ensue when this woman and child proved not to be Michelle and Nina would be like taking a hammer to his own heart.

The events of the day—the encounter with Rose Tucker at the cemetery, her words to him, the shocking message waiting for him at the *Post*—had been so extraordinary that he discovered a gut-deep faith in uncanny possibilities that surprised him. If Rose could fall more than four miles, smash unchecked into Colorado rock, and walk away . . . Unreason overruled facts and logic. A brief, sweet madness stripped off the armor of indifference in which he'd clothed himself with so much struggle and determination, and into his heart surged something like hope.

He went into the store.

The cashier's counter was to his left. A pretty Korean woman in her thirties was clipping packages of Slim Jim sausages to a wire display rack. She smiled and nodded.

A Korean man, perhaps her husband, was at the cash register. He greeted Joe with a comment about the heat.

Ignoring them, Joe passed the first of four aisles, then the second. He saw the auburn-haired woman and the child at the end of the third aisle.

They were standing at a cooler full of soft drinks, their backs to him. He stood for a moment at the head of the aisle, waiting for them to turn toward him.

The woman was in white ankle-tie sandals, white cotton slacks, and a lime-green blouse. Michelle had owned similar sandals, similar slacks. Not the blouse. Not the blouse, that he could recall.

The little girl, Nina's age, Nina's size, was in white sandals like her mother's, pink shorts, and a white T-shirt. She stood with her head cocked to one side, swinging her slender arms, the way Nina sometimes stood.

Nine-ah, neen-ah, have you seen her?

Joe was halfway down the aisle before he realized that he was on the move.

He heard the little girl say, "Please, root beer, please?"

Then he heard himself say, "Nina," because Nina's favorite drink had been root beer. "Nina? Michelle?"

The woman and the child turned to him. They were not Nina and Michelle.

He had known they would not be the woman and the girl whom he had loved. He was operating not on reason but on a demented impulse of the heart. He had known, had *known*. Yet when he saw they were strangers, he felt as though he had been punched in the chest.

Stupidly, he said, "You . . . I thought . . . standing there . . ."

"Yes?" the woman said, puzzled and wary.

"Don't . . . don't let her go," he told the mother, surprised by the hoarseness of his own voice. "Don't let her go, out of your sight, on her own, they vanish, they're gone, unless you keep them close."

Alarm flickered across the woman's face.

With the innocent honesty of a four-year-old, piping up in a concerned and helpful tone, the little girl said, "Mister, you need to buy some soap. You sure smell. The soap's over that way, I'll show you."

The mother quickly took her daughter's hand, pulled her close.

Joe realized that he must, indeed, smell. He had been on the beach in the sun for a couple of hours, and later in the cemetery, and more than once he'd broken into a sweat of fear. He'd had nothing to eat during the day, so his breath must be sour with the beer that he had drunk at the shore.

"Thank you, sweetheart," he said. "You're right. I smell. I better get some soap."

Behind him, someone said, "Everything all right?"

Joe turned and saw the Korean proprietor. The man's previously placid face was now carved by worry.

"I thought they were people I knew," Joe explained. "People I knew . . . once."

He realized that he had left the apartment this morning without shaving. Stubbled, greasy with stale sweat, rumpled, breath sour and beery, eyes wild with blasted hope, he must be a daunting sight. Now he better understood the attitude of the people at the bank.

"Everything all right?" the proprietor asked the woman.

She was uncertain. "I guess so."

"I'm going," Joe said. He felt as if his internal organs were slip-sliding into new positions, his stomach rising and his heart dropping down into the pit of him. "It's okay, okay, just a mistake, I'm going."

He stepped past the owner and went quickly to the front of the store.

As he headed past the cashier's counter toward the door, the Korean woman worriedly said, "Everything all right?"

"Nothing, nothing," Joe said, and he hurried outside into the sedimentary heat of the settling day.

When he got into the Honda, he saw the manila envelope on the passenger's seat. He had left twenty thousand dollars unattended in an unlocked car. Although there had been no miracle in the convenience store, it was a miracle that the money was still here.

Tortured by severe stomach cramps, with a tightness in his chest that restricted his breathing, Joe wasn't confident of his ability to drive with adequate attention to traffic. But he didn't want the woman to think that he was waiting for her, stalking her. He started the Honda and left the shopping center.

Switching on the air conditioning, tilting the vents toward his face, he struggled for breath, as if his lungs had collapsed and he was striving to reinflate them with sheer willpower. What air he was able to inhale was heavy inside him, like a scalding liquid.

This was something else that he had learned from Compassionate Friends meetings: For most of those who lost children, not just for him, the pain was at times physical, stunning.

Wounded, he drove half hunched over the steering wheel, wheezing like an asthmatic.

He thought of the angry vow that he had made to destroy those who might be to blame for the fate of Flight 353, and he laughed briefly, sourly, at his foolishness, at the unlikely image of himself as an unstoppable engine of vengeance. He was walking wreckage. Dangerous to no one.

If he learned what had really happened to that 747, if treachery was indeed involved, and if he discovered who was responsible, the perpetrators would kill him before he could lift a hand against them. They were powerful, with apparently vast resources. He had no chance of bringing them to justice.

Nevertheless, he'd keep trying. The choice to turn away from the hunt was not his to make. Compulsion drove him. Searching behavior.

At a Kmart, Joe purchased an electric razor and a bottle of aftershave. He bought a toothbrush, toothpaste, and toiletries.

The glare of the fluorescent lights cut at his eyes. One wheel on his shopping cart wobbled noisily, louder in his imagination than in reality, exacerbating his headache.

Shopping quickly, he bought a suitcase, two pairs of blue jeans, a gray sports jacket—corduroy, because the fall lines were already on display in August—underwear, T-shirts, athletic socks, and a new pair of Nikes. He went strictly by the stated size, trying on nothing.

After leaving Kmart, he found a modest, clean motel in Malibu, on the ocean, where later he might be able to sleep to the rumble of the surf. He shaved, showered, and changed into clean clothes.

By seven-thirty, with an hour of sunlight left, he drove east to Culver City, where Thomas Lee Vadance's widow lived. Thomas had been listed on the passenger manifest for Flight 353, and his wife, Nora, had been quoted by the *Post*.

At a McDonald's, Joe bought two cheeseburgers and a cola. In the steel-tethered book at the restaurant's public phone, he found a number and an address for Nora Vadance.

From his previous life as a reporter, he had a *Thomas Brothers Guide*, the indispensable book of Los Angeles County street maps, but he thought he knew Mrs. Vadance's neighborhood.

While he drove, he ate both of the burgers and washed them down with the cola. He was surprised by his own sudden hunger.

The single-story house had a cedar-shingle roof, shingled walls, white trim, and white shutters. It was an odd mix of California ranch house and New England coastal cottage, but with its flagstone walkway and neatly tended beds of impatiens and agapanthus, it was charming.

The day was still warm. Heat shimmered off the flagstones.

With an orange-pink glow growing in the western sky and purple twilight just sliding into view in the east, Joe climbed two steps onto the porch and rang the bell.

The woman who answered the door was about thirty years old and pretty in a fresh-faced way. Although she was a brunette, she had the fair complexion of a redhead, with freckles and green eyes. She was in khaki shorts and a man's threadbare white shirt with the sleeves rolled up. Her hair was in disarray and damp with sweat, and on her left cheek was a smudge of dirt.

She looked as if she had been doing housework. And crying.

"Mrs. Vadance?" Joe asked.

"Yes."

Although he had always been smooth about ingratiating himself with an interviewee when he had been a reporter, he was awkward now. He felt too casually dressed for the serious questions that he had come to ask. His jeans were loose, the waistband gathered and cinched with a belt, and because the air was hot, he'd left the sports jacket in the Honda. He wished he'd bought a shirt instead of just T-shirts.

"Mrs. Vadance, I was wondering if I could speak with you—"

"I'm very busy right now—"

"My name's Joe Carpenter. My wife died on the plane. And my two little girls."

Her breath caught in her throat. Then: "One year ago."

"Yes. Tonight."

She stepped back from the door. "Come in."

He followed her into a cheery, predominantly white and yellow living room with chintz drapes and pillows. A dozen Lladró porcelains stood in a lighted corner display case.

She asked Joe to have a seat. As he settled in an armchair, she went to a doorway and called, "Bob? Bob, we have a visitor."

"I'm sorry to bother you on a Saturday night," Joe said.

Returning from the doorway and perching on the sofa, the woman said, "Not at all. But I'm afraid I'm not the Mrs. Vadance you came to see. I'm not Nora. My name's Clarise. It was my mother-in-law who lost her husband in the . . . in the accident."

From the back of the house, a man entered the living room, and Clarise introduced him as her husband. He was perhaps two years older than his wife, tall, lanky, crew-cut, with a pleasant and self-confident manner. His handshake was firm and his smile easy, but under his tan was a paleness, in his blue eyes a sorrow.

As Bob Vadance sat on the sofa beside his wife, Clarise explained that Joe's family had perished in the crash. To Joe, she said, "It was Bob's dad we lost, coming back from a business trip."

Of all the things that they might have said to one another, they established their bond by talking about how they had first heard the dreadful news out of Colorado.

Clarise and Bob, a fighter pilot assigned to Miramar Naval Air Station north of San Diego, had been out to dinner with two other pilots and their wives. They were at a cozy Italian restaurant and, after dinner, moved into the bar, where there was a television set. The baseball game was interrupted for a bulletin about Nationwide Flight 353. Bob had known his dad was flying that night from New York to L.A. and that he often traveled Nationwide, but he hadn't known the flight number. Using a bar phone to call Nationwide at LAX, he was quickly connected with a public-relations officer who confirmed that Thomas Lee Vadance was on the passenger manifest. Bob and Clarise had driven from Miramar to Culver City in record time, arriving shortly after eleven o'clock. They didn't call Nora, Bob's mother, because they didn't know if she had heard. If she was still unaware of the news, they wanted to tell her in person rather than over the phone. When they arrived just after midnight, the house was brightly lighted, the front door unlocked. Nora was in the kitchen, making corn chowder, a big pot of corn chowder, because Tom loved her corn chowder, and she was baking chocolate-chip cookies with pecans because

Bob loved those cookies too. She knew about the crash, knew that he was dead out there just east of the Rockies, but she needed to be doing something for him. They had been married when Nora was eighteen and Tom was twenty, had been married for thirty-five years, and she had needed to be doing something for him.

"In my case, I didn't know until I got to the airport to pick them up," Joe said. "They'd been to Virginia to visit Michelle's folks, and then three days in New York so the girls could meet their aunt Delia for the first time. I arrived early, of course, and first thing when I went into the terminal, I checked the monitors to see if their flight was on time. It was still shown as on time, but when I went up to the gate where it was supposed to arrive, airline personnel were greeting people as they approached the area, talking to them in low voices, leading some of them away to a private lounge. This young man came up to me, and before he opened his mouth, I knew what he was going to say. I wouldn't let him talk. I said, 'No, don't say it, don't you dare say it.' When he tried to speak anyway, I turned away from him, and when he put a hand on my arm, I knocked it off. I might have punched him to keep him from talking, except by then there were three of them, him and two women, around me, close around me. It was as if I didn't want to be told because being told was what made it real, that it wouldn't be real, you know, wouldn't actually have happened, if they didn't *say* it."

They were all silent, listening to the remembered voices of last year, the voices of strangers with terrible news.

"Mom took it so hard for a long time," Clarise said at last, speaking of her mother-in-law as fondly as if Nora had been her own mother. "She was only fifty-three, but she really didn't want to go on without Tom. They were—"

"—so close," Bob finished. "But then last week when we came to visit, she was way up, so much better. She'd been so bitter, depressed and bitter, but now she was full of life again. She'd always been cheerful before the crash, a real—"

"—people person, so outgoing," Clarise continued for him, as if their thoughts ran always on precisely the same track. "And suddenly here again last week was the woman we'd always known . . . and missed for the past year."

Dread washed through Joe when he realized they were speaking of Nora Vadance as one speaks of the dead. "What's happened?"

From a pocket of her khaki shorts, Clarise had taken a Kleenex. She was blotting her eyes. "Last week she said she knew now that Tom wasn't gone forever, that no one was ever gone forever. She seemed so *happy*. She was—"

"—radiant," Bob said, taking his wife's hand in his. "Joe, we don't know why really, with the depression gone and her being so full of plans for the first time in a year . . . but four days ago, my mom . . . she committed suicide."

The funeral had been held the previous day. Bob and Clarise didn't live here. They were staying only through Tuesday, packing Nora's clothes and personal effects for distribution to relatives and the Salvation Army Thrift Shop.

"It's so hard," Clarise said, unrolling and then rerolling the right sleeve on her white shirt as she talked. "She was such a sweet person."

"I shouldn't be here right now," Joe said, getting up from the armchair. "This isn't a good time."

Rising quickly, extending one hand almost pleadingly, Bob Vadance said, "No, please, sit down. Please. We need a break from the sorting . . . the packing. Talking to you . . . well . . ." He shrugged. He was all long arms and legs, graceful before but not now. "We all know what it's like. It's easier because—"

"—because we all know what it's like," Clarise finished.

After a hesitation, Joe sat in the armchair again. "I only have a few questions . . . and maybe only your mother could've answered them."

Having readjusted her right sleeve, Clarise unrolled and then rerolled the left. She needed to be doing something while she talked. Maybe she was afraid that her unoccupied hands would encourage her to express the grief that she was striving to control—perhaps by covering her face, by twisting and pulling her hair, or by curling into fists and striking something. "Joe . . . this heat . . . would you like something cold to drink?"

"No, thanks. Quick is better, and I'll go. What I wanted to ask your mother was if she'd been visited by anyone recently. By a woman who calls herself Rose."

Bob and Clarise exchanged a glance, and Bob said, "Would this be a black woman?"

A quiver passed through Joe. "Yes. Small, about five two, but with . . . real presence."

"Mom wouldn't say much about her," Clarise said, "but this Rose came once, and they talked, and it seemed as if something she told Mom was what made all the difference. We got the idea she was some sort of—"

"—spiritual adviser or something," Bob finished. "At first we didn't like the sound of it, thought it might be someone taking advantage of Mom, her being so down and vulnerable. We thought maybe this was some New Age crazy or—"

"—a con artist," Clarise continued, now leaning forward from the sofa to straighten the silk flowers in an arrangement on the coffee table. "Someone trying to rip her off or just mess with her mind."

"But when she talked about Rose, she was so—"

"—full of peace. It didn't seem this could be bad, not when it made Mom feel so much better. Anyway—"

"—she said this woman wasn't coming back," Bob finished. "Mom said, thanks to Rose, she knew Dad was somewhere safe. He hadn't just died and that was the end. He was somewhere safe and fine."

"She wouldn't tell us how she'd come around to this faith, when she'd never even been a churchgoer before," Clarise added. "Wouldn't say who Rose was or what Rose had told her."

"Wouldn't tell us much at all about the woman," Bob confirmed. "Just that it had to be a secret now, for a little while, but that eventually—"

"—everyone would know."

"Eventually everyone would know what?" Joe asked.

"That Dad was somewhere safe, I guess, somewhere safe and fine."

"No," Clarise said, finishing with the silk flowers, sitting back on the sofa, clasping her hands in her lap. "I think she meant more than that. I think she meant eventually everyone would know that none of us ever just dies, that we . . . go on somewhere safe."

Bob sighed. "I'll be frank with you, Joe. It made us a little nervous, hearing this superstitious stuff coming from my mother, who was always so down-to-earth. But it made her happy, and after the awfulness of the past year—"

"—we didn't see what harm it could do."

Spiritualism was not what Joe had expected. He was uneasy if not downright disappointed. He had thought that Dr. Rose Tucker knew what had really happened to Flight 353 and was prepared to finger those responsible. He had never imagined that what she had to offer was merely mysticism, spiritual counseling.

"Do you think she had an address for this Rose, a telephone number?"

Clarise said, "No. I don't think so. Mom was . . . mysterious about it." To her husband, she said, "Show him the picture."

"It's still in her bedroom," Bob said, rising from the sofa. "I'll get it."

"What picture?" Joe asked Clarise as Bob left the living room.

"Strange. It's one this Rose brought to Nora. It's kind of creepy, but Mom took comfort from it. It's a photo of Tom's grave."

• • •

The photograph was a standard color print taken with a Polaroid camera. The shot showed the headstone at Thomas Lee Vadance's grave: his name, the dates of his birth and death, the words "cherished husband and beloved father."

In memory, Joe could see Rose Marie Tucker in the cemetery: *I'm not ready to talk to you yet.*

Clarise said, "Mom went out and bought the frame. She wanted to keep the picture behind glass. It was important to her that it not get damaged."

"While we were staying here last week, three full days, she carried it with her everywhere," Bob said. "Cooking in the kitchen, sitting in the family room watching TV, outside on the patio when we were barbecuing, always with her."

"Even when we went out to dinner," Clarise said. "She put it in her purse."

"It's just a photograph," Joe said, puzzled.

"Just a photograph," Bob Vadance agreed. "She could've taken it herself—but for some reason it meant more to her because this Rose woman had taken it."

Joe slid a finger down the smooth silver-plated frame and across the glass, as if he were clairvoyant and able to read the meaning of the photograph by absorbing a lingering psychic energy from it.

"When she first showed it to us," said Clarise, "she watched us with such . . . expectation. As if she thought—"

"—we would have a bigger reaction to it," Bob concluded.

Putting the photograph on the coffee table, Joe frowned. "Bigger reaction? Like how?"

"We couldn't understand," Clarise said. She picked up the photo and began to polish the frame and glass on her shirttail. "When we didn't respond to it the way she hoped, then she asked us what we saw when we looked at it."

"A gravestone," Joe said.

"Dad's grave," Bob agreed.

Clarise shook her head. "Mom seemed to see more."

"More? Like what?"

"She wouldn't say, but she—"

"—told us the day would come when we would see it different," Bob finished.

In memory, Rose in the graveyard, clutching the camera in two hands, looking up at Joe: *You'll see, like the others.*

"Do you know who this Rose is? Why did you ask us about her?" Clarise wondered.

Joe told them about meeting the woman at the cemetery, but he said nothing about the men in the white van. In his edited version, Rose had left in a car, and he had been unable to detain her.

"But from what she said to me . . . I thought she might have visited the families of some other crash victims. She told me not to despair, told me that I'd see, like the others had seen, but she wasn't ready to talk yet. The trouble is, I couldn't wait for her to be ready. If she's talked to others, I want to know what she told them, what she helped them to see."

"Whatever it was," Clarise said, "it made Mom feel better."

"Or did it?" Bob wondered.

"For a week, it did," Clarise said. "For a week she was happy."

"But it led to this," Bob said.

If Joe hadn't been a reporter with so many years of experience asking hard questions of victims and their families, he might have found it difficult to push Bob and Clarise to contemplate another grim possibility that would expose them to fresh anguish. But when the events of this extraordinary day were considered, the question had to be asked: "Are you absolutely sure that it was suicide?"

Bob started to speak, faltered, and turned his head away to blink back tears.

Taking her husband's hand, Clarise said to Joe, "There's no question. Nora killed herself."

"Did she leave a note?"

"No," Clarise said. "Nothing to help us understand."

"She was so happy, you said. Radiant. If—"

"She left a videotape," Clarise said.

"You mean, saying good-bye?"

"No. It's this strange . . . this terrible . . ." She shook her head, face twisting with distaste, at a loss for words to describe the video. Then: "It's this *thing*."

Bob let go of his wife's hand and got to his feet. "I'm not much of a drinking man, Joe, but I need a drink for this."

Dismayed, Joe said, "I don't want to add to your suffering—"

"No, it's all right," Bob assured him. "We're all of us out of that crash together, survivors together, family of a sort, and there shouldn't be anything you can't talk about with family. You want a drink?"

"Sure."

"Clarise, don't tell him about the video until I'm back. I know you think it'll be easier on me if you talk about it when I'm not in the room, but it won't."

Bob Vadance regarded his wife with great tenderness, and when she replied, "I'll wait," her love for him was so evident that Joe had to look away. He was too sharply reminded of what he had lost.

When Bob was out of the room, Clarise started to adjust the arrangement of silk flowers again. Then she sat with her elbows on her bare knees, her face buried in her hands.

When finally she looked up at Joe, she said, "He's a good man."

"I like him."

"Good husband, good son. People don't know him—they see the fighter pilot, served in the Gulf War, tough guy. But he's gentle too. Sentimental streak a mile wide, like his dad."

Joe waited for what she really wanted to tell him.

After a pause, she said, "We've been slow to have children. I'm thirty, Bob's thirty-two. There seemed to be so much time, so much to do first. But now our kids will grow up without ever knowing Bob's dad or mom, and they were such *good* people."

"It's not your fault," Joe said. "It's all out of our hands. We're just passengers on this train, we don't drive it, no matter how much we like to think we do."

"Have you really reached that level of acceptance?"

"Trying."

"Are you even close?"

"Shit, no."

She laughed softly.

Joe hadn't made anyone laugh in a year—except Rose's friend on the phone earlier. Although pain and irony colored Clarise's brief laughter, there was also relief in it. Having affected her this way, Joe felt a connection with life that had eluded him for so long.

After a silence, Clarise said, "Joe, could this Rose be an evil person?"

"No. Just the opposite."

Her freckled face, so open and trusting by nature, now clouded with doubt. "You sound so sure."

"You would be too, if you met her."

Bob Vadance returned with three glasses, a bowl of cracked ice, a liter of 7UP, and a bottle of Seagram's 7 Crown. "I'm afraid there's no real choice to offer," he apologized. "Nobody in this family's much of a drinker—but when we do take a touch, we like it simple."

"This is fine," Joe said, and accepted his 7-and-7 when it was ready.

They tasted their drinks—Bob had mixed them strong—and for a moment the only sound was the clinking of ice.

Clarise said, "We know it was suicide, because she taped it."

Certain that he had misunderstood, Joe said, "Who taped it?"

"Nora, Bob's mother," Clarise said. "She videotaped her own suicide."

Twilight evaporated in a steam of crimson and purple light, and out of that neon vapor, night coalesced against the windows of the yellow and white living room.

Quickly and succinctly, with commendable self-control, Clarise revealed what she knew of her mother-in-law's horrible death. She spoke in a low voice, yet every word was bell-note clear and seemed to reverberate through Joe until he gradually began to tremble with the cumulative vibrations.

Bob Vadance finished none of his wife's sentences. He remained silent throughout, looking at neither Clarise nor Joe. He stared at his drink, to which he resorted frequently.

The compact Sanyo 8mm camcorder that had captured the death was Tom Vadance's toy. It had been stored in the closet in his study since before his death aboard Flight 353.

The camera was easy to use. Fuzzy-logic technology automatically adjusted the shutter speed and white balance. Though Nora had never had much experience with it, she could have learned the essentials of its operation in a few minutes.

The nicad battery had not contained much juice after a year in the closet. Therefore, Nora Vadance had taken time to recharge it, indicating a chilling degree of premeditation. The police found the AC adaptor and the battery charger plugged into an outlet on the kitchen counter.

Tuesday morning of this week, Nora went outside to the back of the house and set the camcorder on a patio table. She used two paperback books as shims to tilt the camera to the desired angle, and then she switched it on.

With the videotape rolling, she positioned a vinyl-strap patio chair ten feet from the lens. She revisited the camcorder to peer through the viewfinder, to be sure that the chair was in the center of the frame.

After returning to the chair and slightly repositioning it, she completely disrobed in view of the camcorder, neither in the manner of a performer nor with any hesitancy but simply as though she were getting ready for a bath. She neatly folded her blouse, her slacks, and her underwear, and she put them aside on the flagstone floor of the patio.

Naked, she walked out of camera range, apparently going into the house, to the kitchen. In forty seconds, when she returned, she was carrying a butcher knife. She sat in the chair, facing the camcorder.

According to the medical examiner's preliminary report, at approximately ten minutes past eight o'clock, Tuesday morning, Nora Vadance, in good health and previously thought to be of sound mind, having recently rebounded from depression over her husband's death, took her own life. Gripping the handle of the butcher knife in both hands, with savage force, she drove the blade deep into her abdomen. She extracted it and stabbed herself again. The third time, she pulled the blade left to right, eviscerating herself. Dropping the knife, she slumped in the chair, where she bled to death in less than one minute.

The camcorder continued to record the corpse to the end of the twenty-minute 8mm cassette.

Two hours later, at ten-thirty, Takashi Mishima, a sixty-six-year-old gardener on his scheduled rounds, discovered the body and immediately called the police.

When Clarise finished, Joe could say only, "Jesus."

Bob added whiskey to their drinks. His hands were shaking, and the bottle rattled against each glass.

Finally Joe said, "I gather the police have the tape."

"Yeah," Bob said. "Until the hearing or inquest or whatever it is they have to hold."

"So I hope this video is secondhand knowledge to you. I hope neither of you had to see it."

"I haven't," Bob said. "But Clarise did."

She was staring into her drink. "They told us what was in it . . . but neither Bob nor I could believe it, even though they were the police, even though they had no reason to lie to us. So I went into the station on Friday morning, before the funeral, and watched it. We had to know. And now we do. When they give us the tape back, I'll destroy it. Bob should never see it. Never."

Though Joe's respect for this woman was already high, she rose dramatically in his esteem.

"There are some things I'm wondering about," he said. "If you don't mind some questions."

"Go ahead," Bob said. "We have a lot of questions about it too, a thousand damn questions."

"First . . . it doesn't sound like there could be any possibility of duress."

Clarise shook her head. "It's not something you could force anyone to do to herself, is it? Not just with psychological pressure or threats. Besides, there wasn't anyone else in camera range—and no shadows of anyone. Her eyes didn't focus on anyone off camera. She was alone."

"When you described the tape, Clarise, it sounded as if Nora was going through this like a machine."

"That was the way she looked during most of it. No expression, her face just . . . slack."

"During *most* of it? So there was a moment she showed emotion?"

"Twice. After she'd almost completely undressed, she hesitated before taking off . . . her panties. She was a modest woman, Joe. That's one more weird thing about all of this."

Eyes closed, holding his cold glass of 7-and-7 against his forehead, Bob said, "Even if . . . even if we accept that she was so mentally disturbed she could do this to herself, it's hard to picture her videotaping herself naked . . . or wanting to be found that way."

Clarise said, "There's a high fence around the backyard. Thick bougainvillea on it. The neighbors couldn't have seen her. But Bob's right . . . she wouldn't want to be found like that. Anyway, as she was about to take off the panties, she hesitated. Finally that dead, slack look dissolved. Just for an instant, this terrible expression came across her face."

"Terrible how?" Joe asked.

Grimacing as she conjured the grisly video in her mind, Clarise described the moment as if she were seeing it again: "Her eyes are flat, blank, the lids a little heavy . . . then all of a sudden they go wide and there's depth to them, like normal eyes. Her face *wrenches*. First so expressionless but now *torn* with emotion. Shock. She looks so shocked, terrified. A lost expression that breaks your heart. But it lasts only a second or two, maybe three seconds, and now she shudders, and the look is gone, gone, and she's as calm as a machine again. She takes off her panties, folds them, and puts them aside."

"Was she on any medication?" Joe asked. "Any reason to believe she might have overdosed on something that induced a fugue state or a severe personality change?"

Clarise said, "Her doctor tells us he hadn't prescribed any medication for her. But because of her demeanor on the video, the police suspect drugs. The medical examiner is running toxicological tests."

"Which is ridiculous," Bob said forcefully. "My mother would never take illegal drugs. She didn't even like to take aspirin. She was such an *innocent* person, Joe, as if she wasn't even aware of all the changes for the worse in the world over the last thirty years, as if she was living decades behind the rest of us and happy to be there."

"There was an autopsy," Clarise said. "No brain tumor, brain lesions, no medical condition that might explain what she did."

"You mentioned a second time when she showed some emotion."

"Just before she . . . before she stabbed herself. It was just a flicker, even briefer than the first. Like a spasm. Her whole face wrenched as if she were going to scream. Then it was gone, and she remained expressionless to the end."

Jolted by a realization he had failed to reach when Clarise had first described the video, Joe said, "You mean she *never* screamed, cried out?"

"No. Never."

"But that's impossible."

"Right at the end, when she drops the knife . . . there's a soft sound that may be from her, hardly more than a sigh."

"The pain . . ." Joe couldn't bring himself to say that Nora Vadance's pain must have been excruciating.

"But she never screamed," Clarise insisted.

"Even involuntary response would have—"

"Silent. She was silent."

"The microphone was working?"

"Built-in, omnidirectional mike," Bob said.

"On the video," Clarise said, "you can hear other sounds. The scrape of the patio chair on the concrete when she repositions it. Bird songs. One sad-sounding dog barking in the distance. But nothing from her."

Stepping out of the front door, Joe searched the night, half expecting to see a white van or another suspicious-looking vehicle parked on the street in front of the Vadance place. From the house next door came the faint strains of Beethoven. The air was warm, but a soft breeze had sprung up from the west, bringing with it the fragrance of night-blooming jasmine. As far as Joe could discern, there was nothing menacing in this gracious night.

As Clarise and Bob followed him onto the porch, Joe said, "When they found Nora, was the photograph of Tom's grave with her?"

Bob said, "No. It was on the kitchen table. At the very end, she didn't carry it with her."

"We found it on the table when we arrived from San Diego," Clarise recalled. "Beside her breakfast plate."

Joe was surprised. "She'd eaten breakfast?"

"I know what you're thinking," Clarise said. "If she was going to kill herself, why bother with breakfast? It's even weirder than that, Joe. She'd made an omelet with Cheddar and chopped scallions and ham. Toast on the side. A glass of fresh-squeezed orange juice. She was halfway through eating it when she got up and went outside with the camcorder."

"The woman you described on the video was deeply depressed or in an altered state of some kind. How could she have had the mental clarity or the patience to make such a complicated breakfast?"

Clarise said, "And consider this—the *Los Angeles Times* was open beside her plate—"

"—and she was reading the comics," Bob finished.

For a moment they were silent, pondering the imponderable.

Then Bob said, "You see what I meant earlier when I said we have a thousand questions of our own."

As though they were friends of long acquaintance, Clarise put her arms around Joe and hugged him. "I hope this Rose is a good person, like you think. I hope you find her. And whatever she has to tell you, I hope it brings you some peace, Joe."

Moved, he returned her embrace. "Thanks, Clarise."

Bob had written their Miramar address and telephone number on a page from a note pad. He gave the folded slip of paper to Joe. "In case you have any more questions . . . or if you learn anything that might help us understand."

They shook hands. The handshake became a brotherly hug.

Clarise said, "What'll you do now, Joe?"

He checked the luminous dial of his watch. "It's only a few minutes past nine. I'm going to try to see another of the families tonight."

"Be careful," she said.

"I will."

"Something's wrong, Joe. Something's wrong big time."

"I know."

Bob and Clarise were still standing on the porch, side by side, watching Joe as he drove away.

Although he'd finished more than half of his second drink, Joe felt no effect from the 7-and-7. He had never seen a picture of Nora Vadance; nevertheless, the mental image he held of a faceless woman in a patio chair with a butcher knife was sufficiently sobering to counter twice the amount of whiskey that he had drunk.

The metropolis glowed, a luminous fungus festering along the coast. Like spore clouds, the sour-yellow radiance rose and smeared the sky. Only a few stars were visible: icy, distant light.

A minute ago, the night had seemed gracious, and he had seen nothing to fear in it. Now it *loomed*, and he repeatedly checked his rearview mirror.

EIGHT

Charles and Georgine Delmann lived in an enormous Georgian house on a half-acre lot in Hancock Park. A pair of magnolia trees framed the entrance to the front walk, which was flanked by knee-high box hedges so neatly groomed that they appeared to have been trimmed by legions of gardeners with cuticle scissors. The extremely rigid geometry of the house and grounds revealed a need for order, a faith in the superiority of human arrangement over the riot of nature.

The Delmanns were physicians. He was an internist specializing in cardiology, and she was both internist and ophthalmologist. They were prominent in the community, because in addition to their regular medical practices, they had founded and continued to oversee a free clinic for children in East Los Angeles and another in South Central.

When the 747-400 fell, the Delmanns lost their eighteen-year-old daughter, Angela, who had been returning from an invitation-only, six-week watercolor workshop at a university in New York, to prepare for her first year at art school in San Francisco. Apparently, she had been a talented painter with considerable promise.

Georgine Delmann herself answered the door. Joe recognized her from her photo in one of the *Post* articles about the crash. She was in her late forties, tall and slim, with richly glowing dusky skin, masses of curly dark hair, and lively eyes as purple-black as plums. Hers was a wild beauty, and she assiduously tamed it with steel-frame eyeglasses instead of contacts, no makeup, and gray slacks and white blouse that were manly in style.

When Joe told her his name, before he could say that his family had been on Flight 353, she exclaimed, to his surprise, "My God, we were just talking about you!"

"Me?"

Grabbing his hand, pulling him across the threshold into the marble-floored foyer, pushing the door shut with her hip, she didn't take her astonished gaze from him. "Lisa was telling us about your wife and daughters, about how you just dropped out, went away. But now here you are, here you are."

"Lisa?" he said, perplexed.

This night, at least, the sober-physician disguise of her severe clothes and steel-rimmed spectacles could not conceal the sparkling depths of Georgine Delmann's natural ebullience. She threw her arms around Joe and kissed him on the cheek so hard that he was rocked back on his heels. Then face-to-face with him, searching his eyes, she said excitedly, "She's been to see you too, hasn't she?"

"Lisa?"

"No, no, not Lisa. *Rose.*"

An inexplicable hope skipped like a thrown stone across the lake-dark surface of his heart. "Yes. But—"

"Come, come with me." Clutching his hand again, pulling him out of the foyer and along a hall toward the back of the house, she said, "We're back here, at the kitchen table—me and Charlie and Lisa."

At meetings of The Compassionate Friends, Joe had never seen any bereaved parent capable of this *effervescence.* He'd never heard of such a creature, either. Parents who lost young children spent five or six years—sometimes a decade or even more—striving, often fruitlessly, merely to overcome the conviction that they themselves should be dead instead of their offspring, that outliving their children was sinful or selfish—or even monstrously wicked. It wasn't much different for those who, like the Delmanns, had lost an eighteen-year-old. In fact, it was no different for a sixty-year-old parent who lost a thirty-year-old child. Age had nothing to do with it. The loss of a child at any stage of life is unnatural, so *wrong* that purpose is difficult to rediscover. Even when acceptance is achieved and a degree of happiness attained, joy often remains elusive forever, like a promise of water in a dry well once brimming but now holding only the deep, damp smell of past sustenance.

Yet here was Georgine Delmann, flushed and sparkling, girlishly excited, as she pulled Joe to the end of the hallway and through a swinging door. She seemed not merely to have recovered from the loss of her daughter in one short year but to have transcended it.

Joe's brief hope faded, for it seemed to him that Georgine Delmann must be either out of her mind or incomprehensibly shallow. Her apparent joy shocked him.

The lights were dimmed in the kitchen, but he could see that the space was cozy in spite of being large, with a maple floor, maple cabinetry, and sugar-brown granite counters. From overhead racks, in the low amber light, gleaming copper pots and pans and utensils dangled like festoons of temple bells waiting for the vespers hour.

Leading Joe across the kitchen to a breakfast table in a bay-window alcove, Georgine Delmann said, "Charlie, Lisa, look who's here! It's almost a miracle, isn't it?"

Beyond the beveled-glass windows was a backyard and pool, which outdoor lighting had transformed into a storybook scene full of sparkle and glister. On the oval table this side of the window were three decorative glass oil lamps with flames adance on floating wicks.

Beside the table stood a tall, good-looking man with thick silver hair: Dr. Charles Delmann.

As Georgine approached with Joe in tow, she said, "Charlie, it's Joe Carpenter. *The* Joe Carpenter."

Staring at Joe with something like wonder, Charlie Delmann came forward and vigorously shook his hand. "What's happening here, son?"

"I wish I knew," Joe said.

"Something strange and wonderful is happening," Delmann said, as transported by emotion as was his wife.

Rising from a chair at the table, blond hair further gilded by the lambent light of the oil lamps, was the Lisa to whom Georgine had referred. She was in her forties, with the smooth face of a college girl and faded-denim eyes that had seen more than one level of Hell.

Joe knew her well. Lisa Peccatone. She worked for the *Post.* A former colleague. An investigative reporter specializing in stories about particularly heinous criminals—serial killers, child abusers, rapists who mutilated their victims—she was driven by an obsession that Joe had never fully understood, prowling the bleakest chambers of the human heart, compelled to immerse herself in stories of blood and madness, seeking meaning in the most meaningless acts of human savagery. He sensed that a long time ago she had endured unspeakable offenses, had come out of childhood with a beast on her back, and could not shrive herself of the demon memory other than by struggling to *understand* what could never be understood. She was one of the kindest people he had ever known and one of the angriest, brilliant and deeply troubled, fearless but haunted, able to write prose so fine that it could lift the hearts of angels or strike terror into the hollow chests of devils. Joe admired the hell out of her. She was one of his best friends, yet he had abandoned her with all of his other friends when he had followed his lost family into a graveyard of the heart.

"Joey," she said, "you worthless sonofabitch, are you back on the job or are you here just because you're part of the story?"

"I'm on the job *because* I'm part of the story. But I'm not writing again. Don't have much faith in the power of words anymore."

"I don't have much faith in anything else."

"What're you doing here?" he asked.

"We called her just a few hours ago," said Georgine. "We asked her to come."

"No offense," Charlie said, clapping a hand on Joe's shoulder, "but Lisa's the only reporter we ever knew that we have a lot of respect for."

"Almost a decade now," Georgine said, "she's been doing eight hours a week of volunteer work at one of the free clinics we operate for disadvantaged kids."

Joe hadn't known this about Lisa and wouldn't have suspected it.

She could not repress a crooked, embarrassed smile. "Yeah, Joey, I'm a regular Mother Teresa. But listen, you shithead, don't you ruin my reputation by telling people at the *Post*."

"I want some wine. Who wants wine? A good Chardonnay, maybe a Cakebread or a Grgich Hills," Charlie enthused. He was infected with his wife's inappropriate good cheer, as if they were gathered on this solemn night of nights to *celebrate* the crash of Flight 353.

"Not for me," Joe said, increasingly disoriented.

"I'll have some," Lisa said.

"Me too," Georgine said. "I'll get the glasses."

"No, honey, sit, you sit here with Joe and Lisa," Charlie said. "I'll take care of everything."

As Joe and the women settled into chairs around the table, Charlie went to the far end of the kitchen.

Georgine's face was aglow with light from the oil lamps. "This is incredible, just incredible. Rose has been to see him too, Lisa."

Lisa Peccatone's face was half in lamplight but half in shadow. "When, Joe?"

"Today in the cemetery. Taking photographs of Michelle's and the girls' graves. She said she wasn't ready to talk to me yet . . . and went away."

Joe decided to reserve the rest of his story until he heard theirs, both in the interest of hastening their revelations and to ensure that their recitations were not colored too much by what he revealed.

"It can't have been her," Lisa said. "She died in the crash."

"That's the official story."

"Describe her," Lisa requested.

Joe went through the standard catalogue of physical details, but he spent as much time trying to convey the black woman's singular presence, the magnetism that almost seemed to bend her surroundings to her personal lines of force.

The eye in the shadowed side of Lisa's smooth face was dark and enigmatic, but the eye in the lamplit half revealed emotional turmoil as she responded to the description that Joe gave her. "Rosie always was charismatic, even in college."

Surprised, Joe said, "You know her?"

"We went to UCLA together too long ago to think about. We were roomies. We stayed reasonably close over the years."

"That's why Charlie and I decided to call Lisa a little while ago," said Georgine. "We knew she'd had a friend on Flight 353. But it was in the middle of the night, hours after Rose left here, that Charlie remembered Lisa's friend was also named Rose. We knew they must be one and the same, and we've been trying all day to decide what to do about Lisa."

"When was Rose here?" Joe asked.

"Yesterday evening," Georgine said. "She showed up just as we were on our way out to dinner. Made us promise to tell no one what she told us . . . not until she'd had a chance to see a few more of the victims' families here in L.A. But Lisa had been so depressed last year, with the news, and since she and Rose were such friends, we didn't see what harm it could do."

"I'm not here as a reporter," Lisa told Joe.

"You're always a reporter."

Georgine said, "Rose gave us this."

From her shirt pocket she withdrew a photograph and put it on the table. It was a shot of Angela Delmann's gravestone.

Eyes shining expectantly, Georgine said, "What do you see there, Joe?"

"I think the real question is what *you* see."

Elsewhere in the kitchen, Charlie Delmann opened drawers and sorted through the clattering contents, evidently searching for a corkscrew.

"We've already told Lisa." Georgine glanced across the room. "I'll wait until Charlie's here to tell you, Joe."

Lisa said, "It's damned weird, Joey, and I'm not sure what to make of what they've said. All I know is it scares the crap out of me."

"Scares you?" Georgine was astonished. "Lisa, dear, how on earth could it scare you?"

"You'll see," Lisa told Joe. This woman, usually blessed with the strength of stones, shivered like a reed. "But I guarantee you, Charlie and Georgine are two of the most level-headed people I know. Which you're sure going to need to keep in mind when they get started."

Picking up the Polaroid snapshot, Georgine gazed needfully at it, as though she wished not merely to burn it into her memory but to absorb the image and make it a physical part of her, leaving the film blank.

With a sigh, Lisa launched into a revelation: "I have my own weird piece to add to the puzzle, Joey. A year ago tonight, I was at LAX, waiting for Rosie's plane to land."

Georgine looked up from the photo. "You didn't tell us that."

"I was about to," Lisa said, "when Joey rang the doorbell."

At the far end of the kitchen, with a soft *pop*, a stubborn cork came free from a wine bottle, and Charlie Delmann grunted with satisfaction.

"I didn't see you at the airport that night, Lisa," Joe said.

"I was keeping a low profile. Torn up about Rosie but also . . . flat out scared."

"You were there to pick her up?"

"Rosie called me from New York and asked me to be at LAX with Bill Hannett."

Hannett was the photographer whose images of natural and man-made disasters hung on the walls of the reception lounge at the *Post*.

The pale-blue fabric of Lisa's eyes was worn now with worry. "Rosie desperately needed to talk to a reporter, and I was the only one she knew she could trust."

"Charlie," Georgine said, "you've got to come hear this."

"I can hear, I can hear," Charlie assured her. "Just pouring now. A minute."

"Rosie also gave me a list—six other people she wanted there," Lisa said. "Friends from years back. I managed to locate five of them on short notice and bring them with me that night. They were to be witnesses."

Rapt, Joe said, "Witnesses to what?"

"I don't know. She was so guarded. Excited, really *excited* about something, but also frightened. She said she was going to be getting off that plane with something that would change all of us forever, change the world."

"Change the world?" Joe said. "Every politician with a scheme and every actor with a rare thought thinks he can change the world these days."

"Oh, but in this case, Rose was right," Georgine said. Barely contained tears of excitement or joy shone in her eyes as she showed him the gravestone photo once more. "It's wonderful."

If he had fallen down the White Rabbit's hole, Joe didn't notice the plunge, but the territory in which he now found himself was increasingly surrealistic.

The flames in the oil lamps, which had been steady, flared and writhed in the tall glass chimneys, drawn upward by a draft that Joe could not feel.

Salamanders of yellow light wriggled across the previously dark side of Lisa's face. When she looked at the lamps, her eyes were as yellow as moons low on the horizon.

Quickly the flames subsided, and Lisa said, "Yeah, sure, it sounded melodramatic. But Rosie is no bullshit artist. And she *has* been working on something of enormous importance for six or seven years. I believed her."

Between the kitchen and the downstairs hall, the swinging door made its distinctive sound. Charlie Delmann had left the room without explanation.

"Charlie?" Georgine rose from her chair. "Now where's he gone? I can't believe he's missing this."

To Joe, Lisa said, "When I spoke to her on the phone a few hours before she boarded Flight 353, Rosie told me they were looking for her. She didn't think they would expect her to show up in L.A. But just in case they figured out what flight she was on, in case they were waiting for her, Rosie wanted *us* there too, so we could surround her the minute she got off the plane and prevent them from silencing her. She was going to give me the whole story right there at the debarkation gate."

"They?" Joe asked.

Georgine had started after Charlie to see where he'd gone, but interest in Lisa's story got the better of her, and she returned to her chair.

Lisa said, "Rosie was talking about the people she works for."

"Teknologik."

"You've been busy today, Joey."

"Busy trying to understand," he said, his mind now swimming through a swamp of hideous possibilities.

"You and me and Rosie all connected. Small world, huh?"

Sickened to think there were people murderous enough to kill three hundred and twenty-nine innocent bystanders merely to get at their true target, Joe said, "Lisa, dear God, tell me you don't think that plane was brought down just because Rose Tucker was on it."

Staring out at the shimmering blue light of the pool, Lisa thought about her answer before giving it. "That night I was sure of it. But then . . . the investigation showed no sign of a bomb. No probable cause really fixed. If anything, it was a combination of a minor mechanical error and human error on the part of the pilots."

"At least that's what we've been told."

"I spent time quietly looking into the National Transportation Safety Board, not on this crash so much as in general. They have an impeccable record, Joey. They're good people. No corruption. They're even pretty much above politics."

Georgine said, "But I believe Rose thinks she was responsible for what happened. She's convinced that her being there was the cause of it."

"But if she's even indirectly responsible for the death of your daughter," Joe said, "why do you find her so wonderful?"

Georgine's smile was surely no different from the one with which she had greeted—and charmed—him at the front door. To Joe, however, in his growing disorientation, her expression seemed to be as strange and unsettling as might be the smile on a clown encountered in a fog-threaded alley after midnight, alarming because it was so profoundly out of place. Through her disturbing smile, she said, "You want to know why, Joe? Because this is the end of the world as we know it."

To Lisa, Joe said exasperatedly, "Who *is* Rose Tucker, what does she do for Teknologik?"

"She's a geneticist, and a brilliant one."

"Specializing in recombinant DNA research." Georgine held up the Polaroid again, as if Joe should be able to grasp at once how the photo of a gravestone and genetic engineering were related.

"Exactly what she was doing for Teknologik," Lisa said, "I never knew. That's what she was going to tell me when she landed at LAX a year ago tonight. Now, because of what she told Georgine and Charlie yesterday . . . I can pretty much figure it out. I just don't know how to believe it."

Joe wondered about her odd locution: not *whether* to believe it, but *how* to believe it.

"What is Teknologik—besides what it appears to be?" he asked.

Lisa smiled thinly. "You have a good nose, Joe. A year off hasn't dulled your sense of smell. From things Rosie said over the years, vague references, I think you're looking at a singularity in a capitalist world—a company that can't fail."

"Can't fail?" Georgine asked.

"Because behind it there's a generous partner that covers all the losses."

"The military?" Joe wondered.

"Or some branch of government. Some organization with deeper pockets than any individual in the world. I got the sense, from Rosie, that this project wasn't funded with just a hundred million of research and development funds. We're talking major capital on the line here. There were billions behind this."

From upstairs came the boom of a gunshot.

Even muffled by intervening rooms, the nature of the sound was unmistakable.

The three of them came to their feet as one, and Georgine said, "Charlie?"

Perhaps because he had so recently sat with Bob and Clarise in that cheery yellow living room in Culver City, Joe immediately thought of Nora Vadance naked in the patio chair, the butcher knife grasped in both hands with the point toward her abdomen.

In the wake of the gunshot's echo, the silence settling down through the house seemed as deadly as the invisible and weightless rain of atomic radiation in the sepulchral stillness following nuclear thunder.

Alarm growing, Georgine shouted, "Charlie!"

As Georgine started away from the table, Joe restrained her. "No, wait, wait. I'll go. Call 911, and I'll go."

Lisa said, "Joey—"

"I know what this is," he said, sharply enough to forestall further discussion.

He hoped that he was wrong, that he didn't know what was happening here, that it had nothing to do with what Nora Vadance had done to herself. But if he was right, then he couldn't allow Georgine to be the first on the scene. In fact, she shouldn't have to see the aftermath at all, not now or later.

"I know what this is. Call 911," Joe repeated as he crossed the kitchen and pushed through the swinging door into the downstairs hall.

In the foyer, the chandelier dimmed and brightened, dimmed and brightened, like the flickering lights in one of those old prison movies when the governor's call came too late and the condemned man was fried in the electric chair.

Joe ran to the foot of the stairs but then was slowed by dread as he ascended toward the second floor, terrified that he would find what he expected.

A plague of suicide was as irrational a concept as any brewed in the stew-pot minds of those people who thought that the mayor was a robot and that evil aliens were watching them every moment of the day. Joe couldn't comprehend how Charlie Delmann could have gone from near euphoria to despair in the space of two minutes—as Nora Vadance had gone from a pleasant breakfast and the newspaper comics pages to self-evisceration without even pausing to leave a note of explanation.

If Joe was right about the meaning of the shot, however, there was a slim chance that the doctor was still alive. Maybe he hadn't done himself in with only one round. Maybe he could still be saved.

The prospect of saving a life, after so many had slipped like water through his hands, pushed Joe forward in spite of his dread. He climbed the rest of the stairs two at a time.

On the second floor, with barely a glance, he passed unlighted rooms and closed doors. At the end of the hallway, from behind a half-open door, came ruddy light.

The master suite was entered through a small foyer of its own. Beyond lay the bedroom, furnished with bone-colored contemporary upholstery. The graceful pale-green curves of Sung Dynasty pottery, displayed on glass shelves, imposed serenity on the chamber.

Dr. Charles Delmann was sprawled on a Chinese sleigh bed. Across him lay a Mossberg 12-gauge, pump-action, pistol-grip shotgun. Because of the short barrel, he had been able to put the muzzle between his teeth and easily reach the trigger. Even in the poor light, Joe could see there was no reason to check for a pulse.

The celadon lamp on the farther of the two nightstands provided the only illumination. The glow was ruddy because the shade was splashed with blood.

On a Saturday night ten months ago, in the course of covering a story, Joe had visited the city morgue, where the bagged bodies on the gurneys and the naked bodies on the autopsy tables waited for the attention of overworked pathologists. Abruptly he was gripped by the irrational conviction that the cadavers surrounding him were those of his wife and children; *all* of them were Michelle and the girls, as though Joe had wandered into a scene in a science fiction movie about clones. And from within the body-size drawers of the stainless-steel coolers, where more of the dead rested between destinations, arose the muffled voices of Michelle, Chrissie, little Nina, pleading with him to release them to the world of the living. Beside him, a coroner's assistant zipped open a body bag, and Joe looked down into the winter-white face of a dead woman, her painted mouth like a poinsettia leaf crumpled on snow, and he saw Michelle, Chrissie, Nina. The dead woman's blind blue eyes were mirrors of his own soaring madness. He had walked out of the morgue and submitted his resignation to Caesar Santos, his editor.

Now, he quickly turned away from the bed before any beloved faces materialized over that of the dead physician.

An eerie wheezing came to his attention, and for an instant he thought that Delmann was straining to draw breath through his shattered face. Then he realized that he was listening to his own ragged breathing.

On the nearer nightstand, the lighted green numbers on a digital clock were flashing. Time changes were occurring at a frantic pace: ten minutes with every flash, the hours reversing through the early evening and backward into the afternoon.

Joe had the crazy thought that the malfunctioning clock—which must have been hit by a stray shotgun pellet—might magically undo all that had happened, that Delmann might rise from death as the pellets rattled backward into the barrel and torn flesh reknit, that in a moment Joe himself might be on the Santa Monica beach once more, in the sun, and then back in his one-room apartment in the moon-deep night, on the telephone with Beth in Virginia, and backward, still backward, until Flight 353 had not yet gone down in Colorado.

From downstairs came a scream, imploding his desperate fantasy. Then another scream.

He thought it was Lisa. As tough as she was, she had probably never before screamed in her life, yet this was a cry of sheerest child-like terror.

He had been gone from the kitchen for at most a minute. What could have happened in a minute, so fast?

He reached toward the shotgun, intending to pluck it off the corpse. The magazine might contain other rounds.

No. Now it's a suicide scene. Move the weapon, and it looks like a murder scene. With me as the suspect.

He left the gun untouched.

Out of the thin blood-filtered light, into the hallway where a funerary stillness of shadows stood sentinel, toward the enormous chandelier that hung in a perpetual crystal rain above the foyer staircase, he ran.

The shotgun was useless. He wasn't capable of firing it at anyone. Besides, who was in the house but Georgine and Lisa? No one. No one.

Down the stairs two at a time, three at a time, under the crystal cascade of beveled teardrops, he grabbed at the banister to keep his balance. His palm, slick with cold sweat, slid across the mahogany.

Along the lower hall in a thunder of footsteps, he heard jangly music, and as he slammed through the swinging door, he saw pendulous copper pots and pans swinging on the racks overhead, gently clinking together.

The kitchen was as softly lit as it had been when he left. The overhead halogen downlights were dimmed so low as to be all but extinguished.

At the far end of the room, backlit by the quivering glow of the three decorative oil lamps on the table, Lisa stood with her fists pressed to her temples, as if struggling to contain a skull-cracking pressure. No longer screaming, she sobbed, groaned, shuddered out whispery words that might have been *Oh God, oh God.*

Georgine was not in sight.

As the copper chimes subsided like the soft dissonant music in a dream of trolls, Joe hurried toward Lisa, and from the corner of his eye, he glimpsed the open wine bottle where Charlie Delmann had left it on the island counter. Beside the bottle were three glasses of Chardonnay. The tremulous surface of each serving glimmered jewel-like, and Joe wondered fleetingly if something had been in the wine—poison, chemical, drug.

When Lisa saw Joe approaching, she lowered her hands from her temples and opened her fists, wet and red, rose-petal fingers adrip with dew. A stinging salt of sounds shook from her, pure animal emotion, more raw with grief and burning hotter with terror than any words could have.

At the end of the center island, on the floor in front of Lisa, Georgine Delmann was on her side in the fetal position, curled not in an unborn's anticipation of life but in an embrace of death, both hands still impossibly clenched on the handle of the knife that was her cold umbilical. Her mouth was twisted in a scream never voiced. Her eyes were wide, welling with terminal tears, but without depth.

The stink of evisceration hit Joe hard enough to knock him to the edge of an anxiety attack: the familiar sense of falling, falling as from a great height. If he succumbed to it, he would be of no use to anyone, no help to Lisa or to himself.

With little effort, he looked away from the horror on the floor. With a much greater effort, he willed himself back from the brink of emotional dissolution.

He turned toward Lisa to hold her, to comfort her, to move her away from the sight of her dead friend, but her back was now toward him.

Glass shattered, and Joe flinched. He thought wildly that some murderous adversary was breaking into the kitchen through the windows.

The breaking was not windows but glass oil lamps, which Lisa had grasped like bottles, by their tall chimneys. She had smashed the bulbous bases together, and a viscous spray of oil had burst from them.

Bright points of flame irised wider on the tabletop, became glaring pools of fire.

Joe grabbed her and tried to pull her away from the spreading blaze, but without a word, she wrenched loose of him and seized the third lamp.

"Lisa!"

Granite and bronze ignited in the Polaroid of Angela Delmann's grave, image and medium curling like a black burnt leaf.

Lisa tipped the third lamp, pouring the oil and the floating wick across the front of her dress.

For an instant Joe was immobilized by shock.

The oil washed Lisa, but somehow the slithering spot of flame slipped along the bodice and waist of her dress and was extinguished in the skirt.

On the table, the blazing pools overlapped, and molten streams flowed to all edges. Incandescent drizzle sizzled to the floor.

Joe reached for her again, but as if dipping into a wash basin, she scooped handfuls of flames off the table, splashing them against her breast. As Lisa's oil-soaked clothes exploded with fire, Joe snatched his hand back from her and cried, *"No!"*

Without a scream, which at least she had managed in reaction to Georgine's suicide, without a groan or even as much as a whimper, she raised her hands, in which balls of flame roiled. She stood briefly like the ancient goddess Diana with fiery moons balanced on her palms, and she brought her hands to her face, to her hair.

Joe reeled backward from the burning woman, from the sight that scorched his heart, from the hideous stench that withered him, from an insoluble mystery that left him empty of hope. He collided with cabinetry.

Remaining miraculously on her feet, as calm as though standing only in a cool rain, reflected in every angle of the big bay window, Lisa turned as if to look at Joe through her fuming veil. Mercifully, he could see nothing of her face.

Paralyzed by horror, he realized he was going to die next, not from the flames that licked the maple flooring around his shoes but by his own hand, in some fashion as monstrous as a self-inflicted shotgun wound, self-evisceration, self-immolation. The plague of suicide had not yet infected him, but it would claim him the moment that Lisa, entirely dead, crumpled in a heap on the floor—and yet he could not move.

Wrapped in a whirlwind of tempestuous flames, she flung off phantoms of light and ghosts of shadow, which crawled up the walls and swarmed across the ceiling, and some shadows were shadows, but some were unspooling ribbons of soot.

The bone-piercing shriek of the kitchen smoke alarm cracked the ice in Joe's marrow. He was jarred out of his trance.

He ran with the phantoms and the ghosts, out of that hell, past suspended copper pots like bright blank faces in a forge light, past three glasses of Chardonnay sparkling with images of flames and now the color of claret.

Through the swinging door, along the hallway, across the foyer, Joe felt closely pursued by something more than the blatting of the smoke alarm, as though a killer had been in the kitchen, after all, standing so still in a darkish corner that he had watched unnoticed. At the front door, as Joe grasped the knob, he expected a hand to drop upon his shoulder, expected to be spun around and confronted by a smiling assassin.

From behind him came not a hand and not, as he might have expected, a blast of heat, but a hissing cold that first prickled the nape of his neck and then seemed to drill into the summit of his spine, through the base of his skull. He was so panicked that he did not remember opening the door or leaving the house, but found himself crossing the porch, casting off the chill.

He hurried along the brick walk between the perfect box hedges. When he reached the pair of matched magnolias, where large flowers like the white faces of monkeys peered from among the glossy leaves, he glanced back. He was not, after all, being pursued by anyone.

The residential street was quiet but for the muffled blaring of the smoke alarms in the Delmann house: no traffic at the moment, no one out for a walk in the warm August night. On nearby porches and lawns, no one had yet been drawn outside by the commotion. Here the properties were so large and the stately houses so solidly built, with thick walls, that the screams might not have penetrated to the attention of the neighbors, and even the single gunshot might have been apprehended only as a car door slamming or a truck backfiring.

He considered waiting for the firemen and police, but he could not imagine how he would convincingly describe what had transpired in that house in a mere three or four hellish minutes. As he had lived those feverish events, they had seemed hallucinatory, from the sound of the shotgun to the moment when Lisa swathed herself in flames; and now they were like fragments of a deeper dream in the ongoing nightmare of his life.

The fire would destroy much of the evidence of suicide, and the police would detain him for questioning—then possibly on suspicion of murder. They would see a deeply troubled man who had lost his way after losing his family, who held no job, who lived in one room above a garage, who was gaunt from weight loss, whose eyes were haunted, who kept twenty thousand dollars in cash in the spare-tire well in the trunk of his car. His circumstances and his psychological profile would not dispose them to believe him even if his story had not been so far beyond the bounds of reason.

Before Joe could win his freedom, Teknologik and its associates would find him. They had tried to shoot him down merely because Rose *might* have told him something they didn't want known—and now he knew more than he'd known then, even if he didn't have any idea what the hell to make of it. Considering Teknologik's suspected connections to political and military power grids, Joe more likely than not would be killed in jail during a meticulously planned altercation with other prisoners well paid to waste him. If he survived jail, he would be followed on his release and eliminated at the first opportunity.

Trying not to break into a run and thereby draw attention to himself, he walked to the Honda across the street.

At the Delmann house, kitchen windows exploded. Following the brief ringing of falling glass, the shriek of the smoke alarm was considerably more audible than previously.

Joe glanced back and saw fire writhing out of the back of the house. The lamp oil served as an accelerant: Just inside the front door, which he had left standing open, tongues of fire already licked the walls of the downstairs hallway.

He got in the car. Pulled the door shut.

He had blood on his right hand. Not his own blood.

Shuddering, he popped open the console between the seats and tore a handful of tissues from a box of Kleenex. He scrubbed at his hand.

He stuffed the wadded tissues into the bag that had contained the burgers from McDonald's.

Evidence, he thought, although he was guilty of no crime.

The world had turned upside down. Lies were truth, truth was a lie, facts were fiction, the impossible was possible, and innocence was guilt.

He dug in his pockets for keys. Started the engine.

Through the broken-out window in the backseat, he heard not only the smoke alarms, several of them now, but neighbors shouting at one another, cries of fright in the summer night.

Trusting that their attention would be on the Delmann place and that they would not even notice him departing, Joe switched on the headlights. He swung the Honda into the street.

The lovely old Georgian house was now the domicile of dragons, where bright presences with incendiary breath prowled from room to room. While the dead lay in shrouds of fire, multiple sirens rose like lamentations in the distance.

Joe drove away into a night grown too strange to comprehend, into a world that no longer seemed to be the one into which he had been born.

PART THREE

ZERO POINT

NINE

This Halloween light in August, as orange as pumpkin lanterns but leaping high from pits in the sand, made even the innocent seem like debauched pagans in its glow.

On a stretch of beach where bonfires were permitted, ten blazed. Large families gathered at some, parties of teenagers and college students at others.

Joe walked among them. The beach was one he favored on nights when he came to the ocean for therapy, although usually he kept his distance from the bonfires.

Here the decibels of chatter were off the top of the scale, and barefoot couples danced in place to old tunes by the Beach Boys. But here a dozen listeners sat enthralled as a stocky man with a mane of white hair and a reverberant voice spun a ghost story.

The day's events had altered Joe's perception of everything, so it seemed he was looking at the world through a pair of peculiar glasses won in a game of chance on the midway of a mysterious carnival that traveled from venue to venue in whisper-quiet black trains, spectacles with the power not to distort the world but to reveal a secret dimension that was enigmatic, cold, and fearsome.

The dancers in bathing suits, bare limbs molten-bronze from the firelight, shook their shoulders and rolled their hips, dipped and swayed, beat their supple arms like wings or clawed at the radiant air, and to Joe each celebrant seemed to be two entities at the same time. Each was a real person, yes, but each was also a marionette, controlled by an unseen puppet master, string-tugged into postures of jubilation, winking glass eyes and cracking wooden smiles and laughing with the thrown voices of hidden ventriloquists, for the sole purpose of deceiving Joe into believing that this was a benign world that merited delight.

He passed a group of ten or twelve young men in swimming trunks. Their discarded wetsuits glistened like piles of sealskins or flayed eels or some other harvest of the sea. Their upended surfboards cast Stonehenge shadows across the sand. Testosterone levels were so high among them that the air virtually smelled of it, so high that it made them not rowdy but slow and murmurous, almost somnambulant with primal male fantasies.

The dancers, the storyteller and his audience, the surfers, and everyone else whom Joe passed watched him warily. This was not his imagination. Though their glances were mostly surreptitious, he was aware of their attention.

He wouldn't have been surprised if all of them worked for Teknologik or for whoever funded Teknologik.

On the other hand, although wading deep in paranoia, he was still sane enough to realize that he carried with him the unspeakable things he had seen at the Delmann house— and that these horrors were visible in him. The experience carved his face, painted a dull sheen of desolation in his eyes, and sculpted his body into angles of rage and dread. When he passed, the people on the beach saw a tormented man, and they were all city dwellers who understood the danger of tormented men.

He found a bonfire surrounded by twenty or more utterly silent young men and women with shaved heads. Each of them wore a sapphire-blue robe and white tennis shoes, and each had a gold ring in his or her left ear. The men were beardless. The women were without makeup. Many of both sexes were so strikingly attractive and so stylish in their raiment that he instantly thought of them as the Cult of the Beverly Hills Children.

He stood among them for a few minutes, watching them as they watched their fire in meditative silence. When they returned his attention, they had no fear of what they perceived in him. Their eyes were, without exception, calm pools in which he saw humbling depths of acceptance and a kindness like moonlight on water—but perhaps only because that was what he needed to see.

He was carrying the McDonald's bag that contained the wrappers of two cheeseburgers, an empty soft drink container, and the Kleenex with which he had scrubbed the blood off his hand. Evidence. He tossed the bag into the bonfire, and he watched the cultists as they watched the bag burst into flame, blacken, and vanish.

When he walked away, he wondered briefly what they believed the purpose of life to be. His fantasy was that in the mad spiral and plummet of modern life, these blue-robed faithful had learned a truth and achieved an enlightened state that gave meaning to existence. He didn't ask them, for fear their answer would be nothing other than one more version of the same sad longing and wishful thinking on which so many others based their hope.

A hundred yards up the beach from the bonfires, where the night ruled, he hunkered down at the purling edge of the surf and washed his hands in the inch-deep salty water. He picked up wet sand and scrubbed with it, scouring any lingering traces of blood from the creases in his knuckles and from under his fingernails.

After a final rinse of his hands, without bothering to take off his socks and Nikes or to roll up his jeans, he walked into the sea. He moved into the black tide and stopped after he passed the break line of the quiet surf, where the water was above his knees.

The gentle waves wore only thin frayed collars of phosphorescent foam. Curiously, though the night was clear and pierced by a moon, within a hundred yards the sea rolled naked, black, invisible.

Denied the pacifying vista that had drawn him to the shore, Joe found some solace in the surging tide that pressed against his legs and in the low, dumb grumble of the great watery machine. Eternal rhythms, meaningless motions, the peace of indifference.

He tried not to think about what had happened at the Delmann house. Those events were incomprehensible. Thinking about them would not lead to understanding.

He was dismayed to feel no grief and so little anguish about the Delmanns' and Lisa's deaths. At meetings of The Compassionate Friends, he had learned that following the loss of a child, parents often reported a disturbing inability to care about the suffering of others. Watching television news of freeway wrecks, apartment-building fires, and heinous murders, one sat numb and unaffected. Music that had once stirred the heart, art that had once touched the soul, now had no effect. Some people overcame this loss of sensitivity in a year or two, others in five years or ten, but others—never.

The Delmanns had seemed like fine people, but he had never really known them.

Lisa was a friend. Now she was dead. So what? Everyone died sooner or later. Your children. The woman who was the love of your life. Everyone.

The hardness of his heart frightened him. He felt loathsome. But he could not force himself to feel the pain of others. Only his own.

From the sea he sought the indifference to his losses that he already felt to the losses of others.

Yet he wondered what manner of beast he would become if even the deaths of Michelle and Chrissie and Nina no longer mattered to him. For the first time, he considered that utter indifference might inspire not inner peace but a limitless capacity for evil.

The busy service station and the adjacent twenty-four-hour convenience store were three blocks from his motel. Two public telephones were outside, near the rest rooms.

A few fat moths, white as snowflakes, circled under the cone-shaped downlights that were mounted along the building eaves. Vastly enlarged and distorted shadows of their wings swooped across the white stucco wall.

Joe had never bothered to cancel his phone-company credit card. With it, he placed several long-distance calls that he dared not make from his motel room if he hoped to remain safe there.

He wanted to speak to Barbara Christman, the IIC—Investigator in Charge—of the probe of Flight 353. It was eleven o'clock here on the West Coast and two o'clock Sunday morning in Washington, D.C. She would not be in her office, of course, and although Joe might be able to reach a duty officer at the National Transportation Safety Board even at this hour, he would never be given Christman's home number.

Nevertheless, he got the NTSB's main number from information and placed the call. The Board's new automated phone system gave him extensive options, including the opportunity to leave voice mail for any Board member, senior crash investigator, or executive-level civil servant. Supposedly, if he entered the first initial and first four letters of the surname of the party for whom he wished to leave a message, he would be connected. Though he carefully entered B-C-H-R-I, he was routed not to voice mail but to a recording that informed him no such extension existed. He tried again, with the same result.

Either Barbara Christman was no longer an employee or the voice-mail system wasn't functioning properly.

Although the IIC at any crash scene was a senior investigator operating out of the NTSB headquarters in Washington, other members of a Go-Team could be culled from specialists in field offices all over the country: Anchorage, Atlanta, Chicago, Denver, Fort Worth, Los Angeles, Miami, Kansas City, New York City, and Seattle. From the computer at the *Post*, Joe had obtained a list of most if not all of the team members, but he didn't know where even one of them was based.

Because the crash site was a little more than a hundred miles south of Denver, he assumed at least a few of the team had been drawn from that office. Using his list of eleven names, he sought phone numbers from directory assistance in Denver.

He obtained three listings. The other eight people were either unlisted or not Denver-area residents.

The ceaseless swelling and shrinking and swelling again of moth shadows across the stucco wall of the service station teased at Joe's memory. They reminded him of something, and increasingly he sensed that the recollection was as important as it was elusive. For a moment he stared intently at the swooping shadows, which were as amorphous as the molten forms in a Lava lamp, but he could not make the connection.

Though it was past midnight in Denver, Joe called all three men whose numbers he'd obtained. The first was the Go-Team meteorologist in charge of considering weather factors pertinent to the crash. His phone was picked up by an answering machine, and Joe didn't leave a message. The second was the man who had overseen the team division responsible for sifting the wreckage for metallurgical evidence. He was surly, possibly awakened by the phone, and uncooperative. The third man provided the link to Barbara Christman that Joe needed.

His name was Mario Oliveri. He had headed the human-performance division of the team, searching for errors possibly committed by the flight crew or air-traffic controllers.

In spite of the hour and the intrusion on his privacy, Oliveri was cordial, claiming to be a night owl who never went to bed before one o'clock. "But, Mr. Carpenter, I'm sure you'll understand that I do not speak to reporters about Board business, the details of any investigation. It's public record anyway."

"That's not why I've called, Mr. Oliveri. I'm having trouble reaching one of your senior investigators, whom I need to talk with urgently, and I'm hoping you can put me in touch. Something's wrong with her voice mail at your Washington offices."

"*Her* voice mail? We have no current senior investigators who are women. All six are men."

"Barbara Christman."

Oliveri said, "That had to be who it was. But she took early retirement months ago."

"Do you have a phone number for her?"

Oliveri hesitated. Then: "I'm afraid I don't."

"Maybe you know if she resides in D.C. itself or which suburb. If I knew where she lived, I might be able to get a phone—"

"I heard she came home to Colorado," Oliveri said. "She started out in the Denver field office a lot of years ago, was transferred out to Washington, and worked her way up to senior investigator."

"So she's in Denver now?"

Again Oliveri was silent, as if the very subject of Barbara Christman troubled him. At last he said, "I believe her actual home was Colorado Springs. That's about seventy miles south of Denver."

And it was less than forty miles from the meadow where the doomed 747 had come to a thunderous end.

"She's in Colorado Springs now?" Joe asked.

"I don't know."

"If she's married, the phone might be in a husband's name."

"She's been divorced for many years. Mr. Carpenter . . . I am wondering if . . ."

After long seconds during which Oliveri failed to complete his thought, Joe gently prodded: "Sir?"

"Is this related to Nationwide Flight 353?"

"Yes, sir. A year ago tonight."

Oliveri fell into silence once more.

Finally Joe said, "Is there something about what happened to Flight 353 . . . something unusual?"

"The investigation is public record, as I said."

"That's not what I asked."

The open line was filled with a silence so deep that Joe could half believe that he was connected not to Denver but to the far side of the moon.

"Mr. Oliveri?"

"I don't really have anything to tell you, Mr. Carpenter. But if I thought of something later . . . is there a number where I could reach you?"

Rather than explain his current circumstances, Joe said, "Sir, if you're an honest man, then you might be endangering yourself by calling me. There are some damned nasty people who would suddenly be interested in you if they knew we were in touch."

"What people?"

Ignoring the question, Joe said, "If something's on your mind—or on your conscience—take time to think about it. I'll get back to you in a day or two."

Joe hung up.

Moths swooped. Swooped. Batted against the floodlamps above. Clichés on the wing: moths to the flame.

The memory continued to elude Joe.

He called directory assistance in Colorado Springs. The operator provided him with a number for Barbara Christman.

She answered on the second ring. She did not sound as though she had been awakened.

Perhaps some of these investigators, who had walked through the unspeakable carnage of major air disasters, did not always find their way easily into sleep.

Joe told her his name and where his family had been one year ago this night, and he implied that he was still an active reporter with the *Post*.

Her initial silence had the cold, moon-far quality of Oliveri's. Then she said, "Are you here?"

"Excuse me?"

"Where are you calling from? Here in Colorado Springs?"

"No. Los Angeles."

"Oh," she said, and Joe thought he heard the faintest breath of regret when she exhaled that word.

He said, "Ms. Christman, I have some questions about Flight 353 that I would—"

"I'm sorry," she interrupted. "I know you've suffered terribly, Mr. Carpenter. I can't even conceive the depth of your anguish, and I know it's often difficult for family members to accept their losses in these horrible incidents, but there's nothing I could say to you that would help you find that acceptance or—"

"I'm not trying to learn acceptance, Ms. Christman. I'm trying to find out what *really* happened to that airliner."

"It's not unusual for people in your position to take refuge in conspiracy theories, Mr. Carpenter, because otherwise the loss seems so pointless, so random and inexplicable. Some people think we're covering up for airline incompetence or that we've been bought off by the Airline Pilots Association and that we've buried proof the flight crew was drunk or on drugs. This was just an accident, Mr. Carpenter. But if I were to spend a lot of time with you on the phone, trying to persuade you of that, I'd never convince you, and I'd be encouraging you in this denial fantasy. You have my deepest sympathy, you really do, but you need to be talking to a therapist, not to me."

Before Joe could reply, Barbara Christman hung up.

He called her again. Although he waited while the phone rang forty times, she did not answer it.

For the moment, he had accomplished all that was possible by telephone.

Halfway back to his Honda, he stopped. He turned and studied the side of the service station again, where the exaggerated and weirdly distorted shadows of moths washed across the white stucco, like nightmare phantoms gliding through the pale mists of a dream.

Moths to the flame. Three points of fire in three oil lamps. Tall glass chimneys.

In memory, he saw the three flames leap higher in the chimneys. Yellow lamplight glimmered across Lisa's somber face, and shadows swooped up the walls of the Delmanns' kitchen.

At the time, Joe had thought only that a vagrant draft had abruptly drawn the flames higher in the lamps, though the air in the kitchen had been still. Now, in retrospect, the serpentine fire, shimmering several inches upward from the three wicks, impressed him as possessing greater importance than he previously realized.

The incident had significance.

He watched the moths but pondered the oil wicks, standing beside the service station but seeing around him the kitchen with its maple cabinetry and sugar-brown granite counters.

Enlightenment did not rise in him as the flames had briefly risen in those lamps. Strive as he might, he could not identify the significance that he intuited.

He was weary, exhausted, battered from the trauma of the day. Until he was rested, he could not trust either his senses or his hunches.

On his back in the motel bed, head on a foam pillow, heart on a rock of hard memory, Joe ate a chocolate bar that he'd bought at the service station.

Until the final mouthful, he could discern no flavor whatsoever. With the last bite, the taste of blood flooded his mouth, as though he had bitten his tongue.

His tongue was not cut, however, and what plagued him was the familiar taste of guilt. Another day had ended, and he was still alive and unable to justify his survival.

Except for the light of the moon at the open balcony door and the green numerals of the digital alarm clock, the room was dark. He stared at the ceiling light fixture, which was vaguely visible—and only visible at all because the convex disk of glass was lightly frosted with moonglow. It floated like a ghostly visitant above him.

He thought of the luminous Chardonnay in the three glasses on the counter in the Delmanns' kitchen. No explanation there. Though Charlie might have tasted the wine before pouring it, Georgine and Lisa had never touched their glasses.

Thoughts like agitated moths swooped and fluttered through his mind, seeking light in his darkness.

He wished that he could talk with Beth in Virginia. But they might have her phone tapped and trace his call to find him. Besides, he was concerned that he would be putting Beth and Henry in jeopardy if he told them anything about what had happened to him since he'd found himself under surveillance at the beach.

Lulled by the maternal heart sound of the rhythmic surf, weighed down by weariness, wondering why he had escaped the plague of suicide at the Delmanns' house, he slipped into sleep with nightmares.

Later, he half woke in darkness, lying on his side, facing the alarm clock on the nightstand. The glowing green numbers reminded him of those on the clock in Charles Delmann's bloodied bedroom: time flashing backward in ten-minute increments.

Joe had supposed that a stray shotgun pellet must have struck the clock, damaging it. Now, in a swoon of sleep, he perceived that the explanation was different from what he had thought—something more mysterious and more significant than a mere bead of lead.

The clock and the oil lamps.

Numbers flashing, flames leaping.

Connections.

Significance.

Dreams reclaimed him briefly, but the alarm woke him long before dawn. He had been out less than three and a half hours, but after a year of restless nights, he was refreshed even by this much sleep.

Following a quick shower, as Joe dressed, he studied the digital clock. Revelation eluded him now as it had eluded him when he had been sotted with sleep.

Joe drove to LAX while the coast was still waiting for dawn.

He purchased a same-day, round-trip ticket to Denver. The return flight would bring him back to Los Angeles in time to keep the six-o'clock meeting with Demi—she of the sexy-smoky voice—at the coffeehouse in Westwood.

As he was on his way to the gate where his plane was already boarding, he saw two young men in blue robes at the check-in desk for a flight to Houston. Their shaved heads, the gold rings in their left ears, and their white tennis shoes identified them as members of the same cult as the group that he had encountered around the bonfire on the beach only hours earlier.

One of these men was black, the other was white, and both were carrying NEC laptops. The black man checked his wristwatch, which appeared to be a gold Rolex. Whatever their religious beliefs might be, they evidently didn't take vows of poverty or have much in common with the Hare Krishnas.

Although this was the first time Joe had been aboard an aircraft since receiving the news about Michelle and the girls a year earlier, he was not nervous during the trip to Denver. Initially he worried that he would have an anxiety attack and begin to relive the plunge of Flight 353 as he had so often imagined it, but after just a few minutes, he knew that he would be all right.

He wasn't apprehensive about dying in another crash. Perversely, if he perished in the same way that his wife and daughters had been taken, he would be calm and without fear on the long ride down into the earth, because such a fate would seem like a welcome return to balance in the universe, an open circle closed, a wrongness made right at last.

Of greater concern to him was what he might learn from Barbara Christman at the far end of his journey.

He was convinced that she didn't trust the privacy of telephone conversations but would talk with him face-to-face. He didn't think he had imagined the note of disappointment in her voice when she learned that he was not calling her from Colorado Springs. Likewise, her speech about the dangers of believing in conspiracy theories and the need for grief therapy, although compassionate and well stated, sounded to Joe as though it had been intended less for him than for the ears of eavesdroppers.

If Barbara Christman was carrying a burden that she longed to put down, the solution to the mystery of Flight 353 might be close at hand.

Joe wanted to know the whole truth, *needed* to know, but dreaded knowing. The peace of indifference would forever be beyond his reach if he learned that men, not fate, had been responsible for taking his family from him. The journey toward this particular truth was not an ascension toward a glorious light but a descent into darkness, chaos, the maelstrom.

He'd brought the printouts of four articles about Teknologik, which he had gotten from Randy Colway's computer at the *Post*. The business-section prose was so dry, however—and his attention span so short after only three and a half hours of sleep—that he wasn't able to concentrate.

He dozed fitfully across the Mojave Desert and the Rockies: two hours and fifteen minutes of half-formed dreams lit by oil lamps and the glow of digital clocks, in which understanding seemed about to wash over him but from which he woke still thirsty for answers.

In Denver, the humidity was unusually high and the sky overcast. To the west, the mountains lay buried under slow avalanches of early-morning fog.

In addition to his driver's license, he had to use a credit card as ID to obtain a rental car. He put down a cash deposit, however, trying to avoid the actual use of the card, which might leave a trail of plastic for anyone who was tracking him.

Though no one on the plane or in the terminal had seemed to be especially interested in him, Joe parked the car at a shopping center not far from the airport and searched it inside and out, under the hood and in the trunk, for a transponder like the one that he had found on his Honda the previous day. The rental Ford was clean.

From the shopping center, he wove a tangled course along surface streets, checking his rearview mirror for a tail. Convinced that he was not being followed, he finally picked up Interstate 25 and drove south.

Mile by mile, Joe pushed the Ford harder, eventually ignoring the speed limit, because he became increasingly convinced that if he didn't get to Barbara Christman's house in time, he would find her dead by her own hand. Eviscerated. Immolated. Or with the back of her head blown out.

TEN

In Colorado Springs, Joe found Barbara Christman's address in the telephone book. She lived in a diminutive jewel-box Victorian, Queen Anne style, exuberantly decorated with elaborate millwork.

When she came to the door in answer to the bell, she spoke before Joe had a chance to identify himself. "Even sooner than I expected you."

"Are you Barbara Christman?"

"Let's not do this here."

"I'm not sure you know who I—"

"Yes, I know. But not here."

"Where?"

"Is that your car at the curb?" she asked.

"The rental Ford."

"Park it in the next block. Two blocks. Wait there, and I'll pick you up."

She closed the door.

Joe stood on the porch a moment longer, considering whether he should ring the bell again. Then he decided that she wasn't likely to be planning to run out on him.

Two blocks south of Christman's house, he parked beside a grade-school playground. The swings, seesaws, and jungle gyms were unused on this Sunday morning. Otherwise, he would have parked elsewhere, to be safe from the silvery laughter of children.

He got out of the car and looked north. There was no sign of the woman yet.

Joe consulted his wristwatch. Ten minutes till ten o'clock, Pacific time, an hour later here. In eight hours, he would have to be back in Westwood to meet Demi—and Rose.

Along the sleepy street came a cat's paw of warm wind searching the boughs of the pine trees for hidden birds. It rustled the leaves on the branches of a nearby group of paper birches with trunks as luminous white as choirboys' surplices.

Under a sky gray-white with lowering mist to the west and drear with gunmetal thunderheads to the east, the day seemed to carry a heavy freight of dire portents. The flesh prickled on the nape of Joe's neck, and he began to feel as exposed as a red bull's-eye target on a shooting range.

When a Chevy sedan approached from the south and Joe saw three men in it, he moved casually around to the passenger's side of the rental car, using it for cover in the event that they opened fire on him. They passed without glancing in his direction.

A minute later, Barbara Christman arrived in an emerald-green Ford Explorer. She smelled faintly of bleach and soap, and he suspected she had been doing the laundry when he'd rung her bell.

As they headed south from the grade school, Joe said, "Ms. Christman, I'm wondering— where have you seen a photograph of me?"

"Never have," she said. "And call me Barbara."

"So, Barbara . . . when you opened your door a bit ago, how did you know who I was?"

"Hasn't been a stranger at my door in ages. Anyway, last night when you called back and I didn't answer, you let it ring more than thirty times."

"Forty."

"Even a persistent man would have given up after twenty. When it kept ringing and ringing, I knew you were more than persistent. Driven. I knew you'd come soon."

She was about fifty, dressed in Rockports, faded jeans, and a periwinkle-blue chambray shirt. Her thick white hair looked as if it had been cut by a good barber rather than styled by a beautician. Well tanned, with a broad face as open and inviting as a golden field of Kansas wheat, she appeared honest and trustworthy. Her stare was direct, and Joe liked her for the aura of efficiency that she projected and for the crisp self-assurance in her voice.

"Who are you afraid of, Barbara?"

"Don't know who they are."

"I'm going to get the answer somewhere," he warned.

"What I'm telling you is the truth, Joe. Never have known who they are. But they pulled strings I never thought could be pulled."

"To control the results of a Safety Board investigation?"

"The Board still has integrity, I think. But these people . . . they were able to make some evidence disappear."

"What evidence?"

Braking to a halt at a red traffic signal, she said, "What finally made you suspicious, Joe, after all this time? What about the story didn't ring true?"

"It all rang true—until I met the sole survivor."

She stared blankly at him, as though he had spoken in a foreign language of which she had no slightest knowledge.

"Rose Tucker," he said.

There seemed to be no deception in her hazel eyes but genuine puzzlement in her voice when she said, "Who's she?"

"She was aboard Flight 353. Yesterday she visited the graves of my wife and daughters while I was there."

"Impossible. No one survived. No one *could* have survived."

"She was on the passenger manifest."

Speechless, Barbara stared at him.

He said, "And some dangerous people are hunting for her—and now for me. Maybe the same people who made that evidence disappear."

A car horn blared behind them. The traffic signal had changed to green.

While she drove, Barbara reached to the dashboard controls and lowered the fan speed of the air conditioning, as though chilled. "No one could have survived," she insisted. "This was not your usual hit-and-skip crash, where there's a greater or lesser chance of any survivors depending on the angle of impact and lots of other factors. This was straight down, head-in, catastrophic."

"Head-in? I always thought it tumbled, broke apart."

"Didn't you read any newspaper accounts?"

He shook his head. "Couldn't. I just imagined . . ."

"Not a hit-and-skip, like most," she repeated. "Almost straight into the ground. Sort of similar to Hopewell, September '94. A USAir 737 went down in Hopewell Township, on its way to Pittsburgh, and was just . . . obliterated. Being aboard Flight 353 would have been . . . I'm sorry, Joe, but it would have been like standing in the middle of a bomb blast. A big bomb blast."

"There were some remains they were never able to identify."

"So little left *to* identify. The aftermath of something like this . . . it's more gruesome than you can imagine, Joe. Worse than you want to know, believe me."

He recalled the small caskets in which his family's remains had been conveyed to him, and the strength of the memory compressed his heart into a small stone.

Eventually, when he could speak again, he said, "My point is that there were a number of passengers for whom the pathologists were unable to find any remains. People who just . . . ceased to exist in an instant. Disappeared."

"A large majority of them," she said, turning onto State Highway 115 and heading south under a sky as hard as an iron kettle.

"Maybe this Rose Tucker didn't just . . . didn't just disintegrate on impact like the others. Maybe she disappeared because she walked away from the scene."

"*Walked?*"

"The woman I met wasn't disfigured or crippled. She appeared to have come through it without a scar."

Adamantly shaking her head, Barbara said, "She's lying to you, Joe. Flat out lying. She wasn't on that plane. She's playing some sort of sick game."

"I believe her."

"Why?"

"Because of things I've seen."

"What things?"

"I don't think I should tell you. Knowing . . . that might put you as deep in the hole as I am. I don't want to endanger you any more than I have to. Just by coming here, I might be causing you trouble." After a silence, she said, "You must have seen something pretty extraordinary to make you believe in a survivor."

"Stranger than you can imagine."

"Still . . . I don't believe it," she said.

"Good. That's safer."

They had driven out of Colorado Springs, through suburbs, into an area of ranches, traveling into increasingly rural territory. To the east, high plains dwindled into an arid flatness. To the west, the land rose gradually through fields and woods toward foothills half screened by gray mist.

He said, "You're not just driving aimlessly, are you?"

"If you want to fully understand what I'm going to tell you, it'll help to see." She glanced away from the road, and her concern for him was evident in her kind eyes. "Do you think you can handle it, Joe?"

"We're going . . . there."

"Yes. If you can handle it."

Joe closed his eyes and strove to suppress a welling anxiety. In his imagination, he could hear the screaming of the airliner's engines.

The crash scene was thirty to forty miles south and slightly west of Colorado Springs.

Barbara Christman was taking him to the meadow where the 747 had shattered like a vessel of glass.

"Only if you can handle it," she said gently.

The substance of his heart seemed to condense even further, until it was like a black hole in his chest.

The Explorer slowed. She was going to pull to the shoulder of the highway.

Joe opened his eyes. Even the thunderhead-filtered light seemed too bright. He willed himself to be deaf to the airplane-engine roar in his mind.

"No," he said. "Don't stop. Let's go. I'll be all right. I've got nothing to lose now."

They turned off the state highway onto an oiled-gravel road and soon off the gravel onto a dirt lane that led west through tall poplars with vertical branches streaming skyward like green fire. The poplars gave way to tamarack and birches, which surrendered the ground to white pines as the lane narrowed and the woods thickened.

Increasingly pitted and rutted, wandering among the trees as though weary and losing its way, the lane finally pulled a blanket of weeds across itself and curled up to rest under a canopy of evergreen boughs.

Parking and switching off the engine, Barbara said, "We'll walk from here. It's no more than half a mile, and the brush isn't especially thick."

Although the forest was not as dense and primeval as the vast stands of pine and spruce and fir on the fog-robed mountains looming to the west, civilization was so far removed that the soulful hush was reminiscent of a cathedral between services. Broken only by the snapping of twigs and the soft crunch of dry pine needles underfoot, this prayerful silence was, for Joe, as oppressive as the imagined roar of jet engines that sometimes shook him into an anxiety attack. It was a stillness full of eerie, disturbing expectation.

He trailed Barbara between columns of tall trees, under green vaults. Even in the late morning, the shadows were as deep as those in a monastery cloister.

The air was crisp with the aroma of pine. Musty with the scent of toadstools and natural mulch.

Step by step, a chill as damp as ice melt seeped from his bones and through his flesh, then out of his brow, his scalp, the nape of his neck, the curve of his spine. The day was warm, but he was not.

Eventually he could see an end to the ranks of trees, an open space past the last of the white pines. Though the forest had begun to seem claustrophobic, he was now reluctant to forsake the crowding greenery for the revelation that lay beyond.

Shivering, he followed Barbara through the last trees into the bottom of a gently rising meadow. The clearing was three hundred yards wide from north to south—and twice that long from the east, where they had entered it, to the wooded crest at the west end.

The wreckage was gone, but the meadow felt haunted.

The previous winter's melting snow and the heavy spring rains had spread a healing poultice of grass across the torn, burnt land. The grass and a scattering of yellow wild-flowers, however, could not conceal the most terrible wound in the earth: a ragged-edged, ovate depression approximately ninety yards by sixty yards. This enormous crater lay up-hill from them, in the northwest quadrant of the meadow.

"Impact point," Barbara Christman said.

They set out side by side, walking toward the precise place where three-quarters of a million pounds had come screaming out of the night sky into the earth, but Joe quickly fell behind Barbara and then came to a stop altogether. His soul was as gouged as this field, plowed by pain.

Barbara returned to Joe and, without a word, slipped her hand into his. He held tightly to her, and they set out again.

As they approached the impact point, he saw the fire-blackened trees along the north perimeter of the forest, which had served as backdrop to the crash-scene photograph in the *Post*. Some pines had been stripped bare of needles by the flames; their branches were charred stubs. A score of seared aspens, as brittle as charcoal, imprinted a stark geometry on the dismal sky.

They stopped at the eroded rim of the crater; the uneven floor below them was as deep as a two-story house in some places. Although patches of grass bristled from the sloping walls, it did not thrive on the bottom of the depression, where shattered slabs of gray stone showed through a thin skim of dirt and brown leaves deposited by the wind.

Barbara said, "It hit with enough force to blast away thousands of years of accumu-lated soil and still fracture the bedrock beneath."

Even more shaken by the power of the crash than he had expected to be, Joe turned his attention to the somber sky and struggled to breathe.

An eagle appeared out of the mountain mists to the west, flying eastward on a course as unwaveringly straight as a latitude line on a map. Silhouetted against the gray-white overcast, it was almost as dark as Poe's raven, but as it passed under that portion of sky that was blue-black with a still-brewing storm, it appeared to grow as pale as a spirit.

Joe turned to watch the bird as it passed overhead and away.

"Flight 353," Barbara said, "was tight on course and free of problems when it passed the Goodland navigational beacon, which is approximately a hundred and seventy air miles east of Colorado Springs. By the time it ended here, it was twenty-eight miles off course."

Encouraging Joe to stay with her on a slow walk around the crater rim, Barbara Christ-man summarized the known details of the doomed 747 from its takeoff until its pre-mature descent.

Out of John F. Kennedy International Airport in New York City, Flight 353, bound for Los Angeles, ordinarily would have followed a more southerly corridor than the one it traveled that August evening. Due to thunderstorms throughout the South and tornado warnings in the southern Midwest, another route was considered. More important, the headwinds on the northerly corridor were considerably less severe than those on the southern; by taking the path of least resistance, flight time and fuel consumption could be substantially reduced. Consequently, the Nationwide flight-route planning manager as-signed the aircraft to Jet Route 146.

Departing JFK only four minutes behind schedule, the nonstop to LAX sailed high over northern Pennsylvania, Cleveland, the southern curve of Lake Erie, and southern

Michigan. Routed south of Chicago, it crossed the Mississippi River from Illinois to Iowa at the city of Davenport. In Nebraska, passing the Lincoln navigational beacon, Flight 353 adjusted course southwest toward the next major forward beacon, at Goodland in the northwest corner of Kansas.

The battered flight-data recorder, salvaged from the wreckage, eventually revealed that the pilot made the proper course correction from Goodland toward the next major forward beacon, at Blue Mesa, Colorado. But about a hundred and ten miles past Goodland, something went wrong. Although it experienced no loss of altitude or airspeed, the 747 began to veer off its assigned flight path, now traveling west-southwest at a seven-degree deviation from Jet Route 146.

For two minutes, nothing more happened—and then the aircraft made a sudden three-degree heading change, nose right, as if the pilot had begun to recognize that he was off course. But just three seconds later, this was followed by an equally sudden four-degree heading change, nose left.

Analysis of all thirty parameters covered by this particular flight-data recorder seemed to confirm that the heading changes were either yawing of the craft or resulted in yawing. First the tail section had swung to the left—or port—while the nose had gone right—starboard—and then the tail had swung to the right and the nose to the left, skidding in midair almost as a car might fishtail on an icy highway.

Post-crash data analysis also gave rise to the suspicion that the pilot might have used the rudder to execute these abrupt changes of heading—which made no sense. Virtually all yaws result from movements of the rudder, the vertical panel in the tail, but pilots of commercial jets eschew use of the rudder out of consideration for their passengers. A severe yaw creates lateral acceleration, which can throw standing passengers to the floor, spill food and drinks, and induce a general state of alarm.

Captain Delroy Blane and his copilot, Victor Santorelli, were veterans with forty-two years of commercial piloting between them. For all heading changes, they would have used the ailerons—hinged panels on the trailing edge of each wing—which facilitate gentle banking turns. They would have resorted to the rudder only in the event of engine failure on takeoff or when landing in a strong crosswind.

The flight-data recorder had shown that eight seconds after the first yawing incident, Flight 353's heading again abruptly changed three degrees, nose left, followed two seconds later by a second and even more severe shift of seven degrees to the left. Both engines were at full performance and bore no responsibility for the heading change or the subsequent disaster.

As the front of the plane swung sharply to port, the starboard wing would have been moving faster through the air, rapidly gaining lift. When the starboard wing lifted, it forced the port wing down. During the next fateful twenty-two seconds, the banking angle grew to one hundred forty-six degrees, while the nose-down pitch reached eighty-four degrees.

In that incredibly short span of time, the 747 went from earth-parallel flight to a deadly roll while virtually standing on end.

Pilots with the experience of Blane and Santorelli should have been able to correct the yaw quickly, before it became a roll. Even then, they should have been able to pull the aircraft out of the roll before it became an inevitable plunge. Under any scenario that the human-performance experts could conceive, the captain would have turned the control wheel hard to the right and would have used the ailerons to bring the 747 back to level flight.

Instead, perhaps because of a singular hydraulic-systems failure that defeated the pilots' efforts, Nationwide Flight 353 rolled into a steepdive. With all jet engines still firing, it *rocketed* into this meadow, splashing millennia of accumulated soil as if it were water, boring to the bedrock with an impact powerful enough to crack the steel blades of the Pratt and Whitney power plants as though they were made of balsa wood, sufficiently

loud to shake all the winged residents out of the trees halfway up the slopes of distant
Pikes Peak.

Halfway around the impact crater, Barbara and Joe stopped, now facing east toward
beetling thunderheads, less concerned about the pending storm than about the brief thunder of that year-ago night.

Three hours after the crash, the headquarters contingent of the investigating team departed Washington from National Airport. They made the journey in a Gulfstream jet
owned by the Federal Aviation Administration.

During the night, Pueblo County fire and police officials had quickly ascertained that
there were no survivors. They pulled back so as not to disturb evidence that might help
the NTSB arrive at an understanding of the cause of the disaster, and they secured the
perimeter of the crash site.

By dawn, the Go-Team arrived in Pueblo, Colorado, which was closer to the incident
than Colorado Springs. They were met by regional FAA officials, who were already in
possession of the flight-data recorder and cockpit-voice recorder from Nationwide 353.
Both devices emitted signals by which they could be located; therefore, swift retrieval
from the wreckage had been possible even in darkness and even from the relative remote-
ness of the site.

"The recorders were put on the Gulfstream and flown back to the Safety Board's labs
in Washington," Barbara said. "The steel jackets were badly battered, even breached, but
we were hopeful the data could be extracted."

In a caravan of four-wheel-drive vehicles driven by county emergency-response personnel, the Safety Board team was conveyed to the crash site for its initial survey. The secured
perimeter extended to the gravel road that turned off State Highway 115, and gathered
along both sides of the paved highway in that vicinity were fire trucks, black-and-whites,
ambulances, drab sedans from federal and state agencies, coroners' vans, as well as scores
of cars and pickups belonging to the genuinely concerned, the curious, and the ghoulish.

"It's always chaos," Barbara said. "Lots of television vans with satellite dishes. Nearly
a hundred and fifty members of the press. They clamored for statements when they saw
us arrive, but we didn't have anything to say yet, and we came directly up here to the
site."

Her voice trailed away. She shoved her hands into the pockets of her jeans.

No wind was at play. No bees moved among the wildflowers. The surrounding woods
were full of motionless monk trees, which had taken vows of silence.

Joe lowered his gaze from the silent storm clouds, black with throttled thunder, to the
crater where the thunder of Flight 353 was now only a memory held deep in fractured
stone.

"I'm okay," he assured Barbara, though his voice was thick. "Go on. I need to know
what it was like."

After another half minute of silence, during which she gathered her thoughts and decided how much to tell him, Barbara said, "When you arrive with the Go-Team, the first
impression is always the same. Always. The smell. You never ever forget the stench. Jet
fuel. Smoldering vinyl and plastic—even the new blended thermoplastics and the phenolic
plastics burn under extreme conditions. There's the stink of seared insulation, melted rubber, and . . . roasted flesh, biological wastes from the ruptured lavatory holding tanks and
from the bodies."

Joe forced himself to continue looking into the pit, because he would need to go away
from this place with a new strength that would make it possible for him to seek justice
against all odds, regardless of the power of his adversaries.

"Ordinarily," Barbara said, "in even terribly violent crashes, you see some pieces of
wreckage large enough to allow you to envision the aircraft as it once was. A wing. The

empennage. A long section of fuselage. Depending on the angle of impact, you sometimes even have the nose and cockpit mostly intact."

"In the case of Flight 353?"

"The debris was so finely chopped, so gnarled, so compacted, that on first look it was impossible to see that it had been a plane. It seemed to us that a huge portion of the mass must be missing. But it was all here in the meadow and scattered some distance into the trees uphill, west and north. All here . . . but for the most part there was nothing bigger than a car door. All I saw that I could identify at first glance was a portion of an engine and a three-unit passenger-seat module."

"Was this the worst crash in your experience?" Joe asked.

"Never seen one worse. Only two others to equal it—including the Pennsylvania crash in '94, Hopewell, USAir Flight 427, en route to Pittsburgh. The one I mentioned earlier. I wasn't the IIC on that one, but I saw it."

"The bodies here. How were they when you arrived?"

"Joe . . ."

"You said no one could have survived. Why are you so sure?"

"You don't want to know the *why*." When he met her eyes, she looked away from him. "These are images that haunt your sleep, Joe. They wear away a part of your soul."

"The bodies?" he insisted.

With both hands, she pressed her white hair back from her face. She shook her head. She put her hands in her pockets again.

Joe drew a deep breath, exhaled with a shudder, and repeated his question. "The bodies? I need to know everything I can learn. Any detail about this might be helpful. And even if this isn't much help . . . it'll keep my anger high. Right now, Barbara, I need the anger to be able to go on."

"No bodies intact."

"None at all?"

"None even close to intact."

"How many of the three hundred and thirty were the pathologists finally able to identify . . . to find at least a few teeth from, body parts, something, anything, to tell who they were?"

Her voice was flat, studiedly emotionless, but almost a whisper. "I think slightly more than a hundred."

"Broken, severed, mangled," he said, hammering himself with the hard words.

"Far worse. All that immense hurtling energy released in an instant . . . you don't even recognize most of the biological debris as being human. The risk of infectious disease was high from blood and tissue contamination, so we had to pull out and revisit the site only in biologically secure gear. Every piece of wreckage had to be carted away and documented by the structural specialists, of course—so to protect them we had to set up four decontamination stations out along the gravel road. Most of the wreckage had to be processed there before it moved on to a hangar at Pueblo Airport."

Being brutal to prove to himself that his anguish would never again get the better of his anger until this quest was completed, Joe said, "It was pretty much like putting them through one of those tree-grinding machines."

"Enough, Joe. Knowing more details can't *ever* help you."

The meadow was so utterly soundless that it might have been the ignition point of all Creation, from which God's energies had long ago flowed toward the farthest ends of the universe, leaving only a mute vacuum.

A few fat bees, enervated by the August heat that was unable to penetrate Joe's chill, forsook their usual darting urgency and traveled languidly across the meadow from wildflower to wildflower, as though flying in their sleep and acting out a shared dream about collecting nectar. He could hear no buzzing as the torpid gatherers went about their work.

"And the cause," he asked, "was hydraulic-control failure—that stuff with the rudder, the yawing and then the roll?"

"You really haven't read about it, have you?"

"Couldn't."

She said, "The possibility of a bomb, anomalous weather, the wake vortex from another aircraft, and various other factors were eliminated pretty early. And the structures group, twenty-nine specialists in that division of the investigation alone, studied the wreckage in the hangar in Pueblo for eight months without being able to pin down a probable cause. They suspected lots of different things at one time or another. Malfunctioning yaw dampers, for one. Or an electronics-bay door failure. Engine-mount failure looked good to them for a while. And malfunctioning thrust reversers. But they eliminated each suspicion, and no official probable cause was found."

"How unusual is that?"

"Unusual. But sometimes we can't pin it down. Like Hopewell in '94. And, in fact, another 737 that went down on its approach to Colorado Springs in '91, killing everyone aboard. So it happens, we get stumped."

Joe realized there had been a disturbing qualifier in what she had said: no *official* probable cause.

Then a second realization struck him: "You took early retirement from the Safety Board about seven months ago. That's what Mario Oliveri told me."

"Mario. Good man. He headed the human-performance group in this investigation. But it's been almost nine months since I quit."

"If the structures group was still sifting the wreckage eight months after the crash . . . then you didn't stay to oversee the entire inquiry, even though you were the original IIC on it."

"Bailed out," she acknowledged. "When it all turned sour, when evidence disappeared, when I started to make some noise about it . . . they put the squeeze on me. At first I tried to stay on, but I just couldn't handle being part of a fraud. Couldn't do the *right* thing and spill the beans, either, so I bailed. Not proud of it. But I've got a hostage to fortune, Joe."

"Hostage to fortune. A child?"

"Denny. He's twenty-three now, not a baby anymore, but if I ever lost him . . ."

Joe knew too well how she would have finished that sentence. "They threatened your son?"

Although Barbara stared into the crater before her, she was seeing a potential disaster rather than the aftermath of a real one, a personal catastrophe rather than one involving three hundred and thirty deaths.

"It happened two weeks after the crash," she said. "I was in San Francisco, where Delroy Blane—the captain on Flight 353—had lived, overseeing a pretty intense investigation into his personal history, trying to discover any signs of psychological problems."

"Finding anything?"

"No. He seemed like a rock-solid guy. This was also at the time when I was pressing the hardest to go public with what had happened to certain evidence. I was staying in a hotel. I'm a reasonably sound sleeper. At two-thirty in the morning, someone switched on my nightstand lamp and put a gun in my face."

After years of waiting for Go-Team calls, Barbara had long ago overcome a tendency to shed sleep slowly. She woke to the click of the lamp switch and the flood of light as she would have awakened to the ringing telephone: instantly alert and clearheaded.

She might have cried out at the sight of the intruder, except that her shock pinched off her voice and her breath.

The gunman, about forty, had large sad eyes, hound-dog eyes, a nose bashed red by the slow blows of two decades of drink, and a sensuous mouth. His thick lips never quite closed, as though waiting for the next treat that couldn't be resisted—cigarette, whiskey, pastry, or breast.

His voice was as soft and sympathetic as a mortician's but with no unctuousness. He indicated that the pistol was fitted with a sound suppressor, and he assured her that if she tried to call for help, he would blow her brains out with no concern that anyone beyond the room would hear the shot.

She tried to ask who he was, what he wanted.

Hushing her, he sat on the edge of her bed.

He had nothing against her personally, he said, and it would depress him to have to kill her. Besides, if the IIC of the probe of Flight 353 were to be found murdered, inconvenient questions might be asked.

The sensualist's bosses, whoever they might be, could not afford inconvenient questions at this time, on this issue.

Barbara realized that a second man was in the room. He had been standing in the corner near the bathroom door, on the other side of the bed from the gunman.

This one was ten years younger than the first. His smooth pink face and choirboy eyes gave him an innocent demeanor that was belied by a disquietingly eager smile that came and went like the flickering of a serpent's tongue.

The older man pulled the covers off Barbara and politely asked her to get out of bed. They had a few things to explain to her, he said. And they wanted to be certain that she was alert and attentive throughout, because lives depended on her understanding and believing what they had come to tell her.

In her pajamas, she stood obediently while the younger man, with a flurry of brief smiles, went to the desk, withdrew the chair from the kneehole, and stood it opposite the foot of the bed. She sat as instructed.

She had been wondering how they had gotten in, as she'd engaged both the deadbolt and the security chain on the door to the corridor. Now she saw that both of the doors between this hotel room and the next—which could be connected to form a suite for those guests who required more space—stood open. The mystery remained, however, for she was certain that the door on this side had been securely locked with a deadbolt when she had gone to bed.

At the direction of the older man, the younger produced a roll of strapping tape and a pair of scissors. He secured Barbara's wrists tightly to the arms of the straight-back chair, wrapping the tape several times.

Frightened of being restrained and helpless, Barbara nonetheless submitted because she believed that the sad-eyed man would deliver on his threat to shoot her point-blank in the head if she resisted. With his sensuous mouth, as though sampling the contents of a bon-bon box, he had savored the words *blow your brains out.*

When the younger man cut a six-inch length of tape and pressed it firmly across Barbara's mouth, then secured that piece by winding a continuous length of tape twice around her head, she panicked for a moment but then regained control of herself. They were not going to pinch her nose shut and smother her. If they had come here to kill her, she would be dead already.

As the younger man retreated with his tremulous smiles to a shadowy corner, the sensualist sat on the foot of the bed, opposite Barbara. Their knees were no more than a few inches apart.

Putting his pistol aside on the rumpled sheets, he took a knife from a jacket pocket. A switchblade. He flicked it open.

Her fear soaring again, Barbara could manage to draw only quick, shallow breaths. The resultant whistling in her nose amused the man sitting with her.

From another jacket pocket, he withdrew a snack-size round of Gouda cheese. Using the knife, he removed the cellophane wrapper and then peeled off the red wax skin that prevented the Gouda from developing mold.

Carefully eating thin slivers of cheese off the wickedly sharp blade, he told Barbara that he knew where her son, Denny, lived and worked. He recited the addresses.

He also knew that Denny had been married to Rebekah for thirteen months, nine days, and—he consulted his watch, calculated—fifteen hours. He knew that Rebekah was six months pregnant with their first child, a girl, whom they were going to name Felicia.

To prevent harm from befalling Denny and his bride, Barbara was expected to accept the official story about what had happened to the tape from the cockpit-voice recorder on Flight 353—a story that she had rejected in discussions with her colleagues and that she had set out to disprove. She was also expected to forget what she had heard on the enhanced version of that tape.

If she continued to seek the truth of the situation or attempted to express her concerns to either the press or the public, Denny and Rebekah would disappear. In the deep basement of a private redoubt soundproofed and equipped for prolonged and difficult interrogations, the sensualist and his associates would shackle Denny, tape open his eyes, and force him to watch while they killed Rebekah and the unborn child.

Then they would surgically remove one of his fingers every day for ten days—taking elaborate measures to control bleeding, shock, and infection. They would keep him alive and alert, though steadily less whole. On the eleventh and twelfth days, they would remove his ears.

They had a full month of imaginative surgery planned.

Every day, as they took another piece of him, they would tell Denny that they would release him to his mother without further harm if she would only agree to cooperate with them in a conspiracy of silence that was, after all, in the national interest. Vitally important defense matters were involved here.

This would not be entirely true. The part about the national interest was true, from their point of view, at least, even though they could not, of course, explain to Barbara how the knowledge she possessed was a threat to her country. The part about her being able to earn Denny's release by cooperation would not be true, however, because once she failed to honor a pledge of silence, she would not be given a second chance, and her son would be forever lost to her. They would deceive Denny solely to ensure that he would spend the last month of his life desperately wondering why his mother had so stubbornly condemned him to such excruciating pain and' horrible disfigurement. By the end, half mad or worse, in deep spiritual misery, he would curse her vehemently and beg God to let her rot in Hell.

As he continued to carve the tiny wheel of Gouda and serve himself off the dangerous point of the blade, the sensualist assured Barbara that no one—not the police, not the admittedly clever FBI, not the mighty United States Army—could keep Denny and Rebekah safe forever. He claimed to be employed by an organization with such bottomless resources and extensive connections that it was capable of compromising and subverting any institution or agency of the federal or state governments.

He asked her to nod if she believed him.

She did believe him. Implicitly. Without reservation. His seductive voice, which seemed to lick each of his hideous threats to savor the texture and astringency of it, was filled with the quiet confidence and smug superiority of a megalomaniac who carries the badge of a secret authority, receives a comfortable salary with numerous fringe benefits, and knows that in his old age he will be able to rely upon the cushion of a generous civil-service pension.

He then asked her if she intended to cooperate.

With guilt and humiliation but also with utter sincerity, she nodded again. Yes. She would cooperate. Yes.

Studying a pale oval of cheese like a tiny filleted fish on the point of the blade, he said that he wanted her to be deeply impressed with his determination to ensure her cooperation, so impressed that she would be in no danger of forsaking the pledge she had just made to him. Therefore, on their way out of the hotel, he and his partner would select, at random, an employee or perhaps a guest—someone who just happened to cross their path— and would kill that person on the spot. Three shots: two in the chest, one in the head.

Stunned, Barbara protested from behind the gag, contorting her face in an effort to twist the tape and free her mouth. But it was pulled cruelly tight, and her lips were stuck firmly to the adhesive, and the only argument that she could get out was a pained, muffled, wordless pleading. She didn't want to be responsible for anyone's death. She was going to cooperate. There was no reason to impress her with their seriousness. No reason. She already *believed* in their seriousness.

Never taking his great sad eyes from her, without saying another word, he slowly finished his cheese.

His unwavering stare seemed to cause a power backflow, draining her of energy. Yet she could not look away.

When he had consumed the final morsel, he wiped the blade of his knife on the sheets. Then he folded it into the handle and returned the weapon to his pocket.

Sucking on his teeth and rolling his tongue slowly around his mouth, he gathered up the shredded cellophane and the peels of red wax. He rose from the bed and deposited the trash in the waste basket beside the desk.

The younger man stepped out of the shadowy corner. His thin but eager smile no longer fluttered uncertainly; it was fixed.

From behind the strapping tape, Barbara was still attempting to protest the murder of an innocent person when the older man returned to her and, with the edge of his right hand, chopped hard at the side of her neck.

As a scintillant darkness sprayed across her field of vision, she started to slump forward. She felt the chair tipping sideways. She was unconscious before her head hit the carpet.

For perhaps twenty minutes she dreamed of severed fingers in preserving sheaths of red wax. In shrimp-pink faces, fragile smiles broke like strings of pearls, the bright teeth bouncing and rolling across the floor, but in the black crescent between the curved pink lips, new pearls formed, and a choirboy eye blinked blue. There were hound-dog eyes too, as black and shiny as leeches, in which she saw not her reflection but images of Denny's screaming, earless face.

When she regained consciousness, she was slumped in the chair, which had been set upright again. Either the sensualist or his pearl-toothed companion had taken pity on her.

Her wrists were taped to the arms of the chair in such a fashion as to allow her to wrench loose if she applied herself diligently. She needed less than ten minutes to free her right hand, much less to slip the bonds on the left.

She used her own cuticle scissors to snip through the tape wound around her head. When she gingerly pulled it off her lips, it took far less skin than she expected.

Liberated and able to talk, she found herself at the telephone with the receiver in her hand. But she could think of no one whom she dared to call, and she put the phone down.

There was no point in warning the hotel's night manager that one of his employees or guests was in danger. If the gunman had kept his threat to impress her with a senseless, random killing, he had pulled the trigger already. He and his companion would have left the hotel at least half an hour ago.

Wincing at the throbbing pain in her neck, she went to the door that connected her room with theirs. She opened it and checked the inner face. Her privacy deadbolt latch was backed by a removable brass plate fixed in place with screws, which allowed access to the mechanism of her lock from the other side. The other room's door featured no such access plate.

The shiny brass looked new. She was certain that it had been installed shortly before she checked into the hotel—by the gunman and his companion acting either clandestinely or with the assistance of a hotel engineer. A clerk at the front desk was paid or coerced to put her in this room rather than any other.

Barbara was not much of a drinker, but she raided the honor bar for a two-shot miniature of vodka and a cold bottle of orange juice. Her hands were shaking so badly she could barely pour the ingredients into a glass. She drank the screwdriver straight down, opened another miniature, mixed a second drink, took a swallow of it—then went into the bathroom and threw up.

She felt unclean. With dawn less than an hour away, she took a long shower, scrubbing herself so hard and standing in water so hot that her skin grew red and stung unbearably.

Although she knew that it was pointless to change hotels, that they could find her again if they wanted her, she couldn't stay any longer in this place. She packed and, an hour after first light, went down to the front desk to pay her bill.

The ornate lobby was full of San Francisco policemen—uniformed officers and plain-clothes detectives.

From the wide-eyed cashier, Barbara learned that sometime after three o'clock in the morning, a young room-service waiter had been shot to death in a service corridor near the kitchen. Twice in the chest and once in the head.

The body had not been discovered immediately because, curiously, no one had heard gunfire.

Harried by fear that seemed to push her forward like a rude hand in the back, she checked out. She took a taxi to another hotel.

The day was high and blue. The city's famous fog was already pulling back across the bay into a towering palisade beyond the Golden Gate, of which she had a limited view from her new room.

She was an aeronautical engineer. A pilot. She held a master's degree in business administration from Columbia University. She had worked hard to become the only current female IIC working air crashes for the National Transportation Safety Board. When her husband had walked out on her seventeen years ago, she had raised Denny alone and raised him well. Now all that she had achieved seemed to have been gathered into the hand of the sad-eyed sensualist, wadded with the cellophane and the peels of red wax, and thrown into the trash can.

After canceling her appointments for the day, Barbara hung the *Do Not Disturb* sign on the door. She closed the draperies and curled on the bed in her new room.

Quaking fear became quaking grief. She wept uncontrollably for the dead room-service waiter whose name she didn't know, for Denny and Rebekah and unborn Felicia whose lives now seemed perpetually suspended on a slender thread, for her own loss of innocence and self-respect, for the three hundred and thirty people aboard Flight 353, for justice thwarted and hope lost.

A sudden wind groaned across the meadow, playing with old dry aspen leaves, like the devil counting souls and casting them away.

"I can't let you do this," Joe said. "I can't let you tell me what was on the cockpit-voice recorder if there's any chance it's going to put your son and his family in the hands of people like that."

"It's not for you to decide, Joe."

"The hell it's not."

"When you called from Los Angeles, I played dumb because I've got to assume my phone is permanently tapped, every word recorded. Actually, I don't think it is. I don't think they feel any *need* to tap it, because they know by now that they've got me muzzled."

"If there's even a chance—"

"And I know for certain I'm not being watched. My house isn't under observation. I'd have picked up on that long ago. When I walked out on the investigation, took early retirement, sold the house in Bethesda, and came back to Colorado Springs, they wrote me off, Joe. I was broken, and they knew it."

"You don't seem broken to me."

She patted his shoulder, grateful for the compliment. "I've rebuilt myself some. Anyway, if you weren't followed—"

"I wasn't. I lost them yesterday. No one could have followed me to LAX this morning."

"Then I figure there's no one to know we're here or to know what I tell you. All I ask is you never say you got it from me."

"I wouldn't do that to you. But there's still such a risk you'll be taking," he worried.

"I've had months to think about it, to live with it, and the way it seems to me is . . . They probably think I told Denny some of it, so he would know what danger he's in, so he'd be careful, watchful."

"Did you?"

"Not a word. What kind of a life could they have, knowing?"

"Not a normal one."

"But now Denny, Rebekah, Felicia, and I are going to be hanging by a thread as long as this cover-up continues. Our only hope is for someone else to blow it wide open, so then what little I know about it won't matter any more."

The storm clouds were not only in the east now. Like an armada of incoming starships in a film about futuristic warfare, ominous black thunderheads slowly resolved out of the white mists overhead.

"Otherwise," Barbara continued, "a year from now or two years from now, even though I've kept my mouth shut, they'll decide to tie up all the loose ends. Flight 353 will be such old news that no one will connect my death or Denny's or a handful of others to it. No suspicions will be raised if something happens to those of us with incriminating bits of information. These people, whoever the hell they are . . . they'll buy insurance with a car accident here, a fire there. A faked robbery to cover a murder. A suicide."

Through Joe's mind passed the waking-nightmare images of Lisa burning, Georgine dead on the kitchen floor, Charlie in the blood-tinted light.

He couldn't argue with Barbara's assessment. She probably had it figured right.

In a sky waiting to snarl and crackle, menacing faces formed in the clouds, blind and open-mouthed, choked with anger.

Taking her first fateful step toward revelation, Barbara said, "The flight-data recorder and the cockpit-voice recorder arrived in Washington on the Gulfstream and were in the labs by three o'clock Eastern Time the day after the crash."

"You were still just getting into the investigation here."

"That's right. Minh Tran—he's an electronics engineer with the Safety Board—and a few colleagues opened the Fairchild recorder. It's almost as large as a shoe box, jacketed in three-eighths of an inch of stainless steel. They cut it carefully, with a special saw. This particular unit had endured such violent impact that it was compressed four inches end to end—the steel just crunched up like cardboard—and one corner had been crushed, resulting in a small breach."

"And it still functioned?"

"No. The recorder was completely destroyed. But inside the larger box is the steel memory module. It contains the tape. It was also breached. A small amount of moisture had penetrated all the way into the memory module, but the tape wasn't entirely ruined. It had to be dried, processed, but that didn't take long, and then Minh and a few others gathered in a soundproof listening room to run it from the beginning. There were almost three hours of cockpit conversation leading up to the crash—"

Joe said, "They don't just run it fast forward to the last few minutes?"

"No. Something earlier in the flight, something that seemed to be of no importance to the pilots at the time, might provide clues that help us understand what we're hearing in the moments immediately before the plane went down."

Steadily rising, the warm wind was brisk enough now to foil the lethargic bees on their lazy quest from bloom to bloom. Surrendering the field to the oncoming storm, they departed for secret nests in the woods.

"Sometimes we get a cockpit tape that's all but useless to us," Barbara continued. "The recording quality's lousy for one reason or another. Maybe the tape's old and abraded. Maybe the microphone is the hand-held type or isn't functioning as well as it should, too much vibration. Maybe the recording head is worn and causing distortion."

"I would think there'd be daily maintenance, weekly replacement, when it's something as important as this."

"Remember, as a percentage of flights, planes rarely go down. There are costs and flight-time delays to be considered. Anyway, commercial aviation is a human enterprise, Joe. And what human enterprise ever operates to ideal standards?"

"Point taken."

"This time there was good and bad," she said. "Both Delroy Blane and Santorelli were wearing headsets with boom microphones, which is real damn good, much better than a hand-held. Those along with the overhead cockpit mike gave us three channels to study. On the bad side, the tape wasn't new. It had been recorded over a lot of times and was more deteriorated than we would have liked. Worse, whatever the nature of the moisture that reached the tape, it had caused some patchy corrosion to the recording surface."

From a back pocket of her jeans, she took a folded paper but didn't immediately hand it to Joe.

She said, "When Minh Tran and the others listened, they found that some portions of the tape were clearly audible and others were so full of scratchy static, so garbled, they could only discern one out of four or five words."

"What about the last minute?"

"That was one of the worst segments. It was decided that the tape would have to be cleaned and rehabilitated. Then the recording would be electronically enhanced to whatever extent possible. Bruce Laceroth, head of the Major Investigations Division, had been there to listen to the whole tape, and he called me in Pueblo, at a quarter past seven, Eastern Time, to tell me the status of the recording. They were stowing it for the night, going to start work with it again in the morning. It was depressing."

High above them, the eagle returned from the east, pale against the pregnant bellies of the clouds, still flying straight and true with the weight of the pending storm on its wings.

"Of course, that whole day had been depressing," Barbara said. "We'd brought in refrigerated trucks from Denver to collect all the human remains from the site, which had to be completed before we could begin to deal with the pieces of the plane itself. There was the usual organizational meeting, which is always exhausting, because so many interest groups—the airline, the manufacturer of the plane, the supplier of the power plants, the Airline Pilots Association, lots of others—all want to bend the proceedings to serve their interests as much as possible. Human nature—and not the prettier part of it. So you have to be reasonably diplomatic but also damn tough to keep the process truly impartial."

"And there was the media," he said, condemning his own kind so she wouldn't have to do it.

"Everywhere. Anyway, I'd only slept less than three hours the previous night, before I'd been awakened by the Go-Team call, and there was no chance even to doze on the

Gulfstream from National to Pueblo. I was like the walking dead when I hit the sheets a little before midnight—but back there in Washington, Minh Tran was still at it."

"The electronics engineer who cut open the recorder?"

Staring at the folded white paper that she had taken from her hip pocket, turning it over and over in her hands, Barbara said, "You have to understand about Minh. His family were Vietnamese boat people. Survived the communists after the fall of Saigon and then pirates at sea, even a typhoon. He was ten at the time, so he knew early that life was a struggle. To survive and prosper, he *expected* to give a hundred and ten percent."

"I have friends . . . had friends who were Vietnamese immigrants," Joe said. "Quite a culture. A lot of them have a work ethic that would break a plow horse."

"Exactly. When everyone else went home from the labs that night at a quarter past seven, they'd put in a long day. People at the Safety Board are pretty dedicated . . . but Minh more so. He didn't leave. He made a dinner of whatever he could get out of the vending machines, and he stayed to clean the tape and then to work on the last minute of it. Digitize the sound, load it in a computer, and then try to separate the static and other extraneous noises from the voices of the pilots and from the actual sounds that occurred aboard the aircraft. The layers of static proved to be so specifically patterned that the computer was able to help strip them away fairly quickly. Because the boom mikes had delivered strong signals to the recorder, Minh was able to clarify the pilots' voices under the junk noise. What he heard was extraordinary. Bizarre."

She handed the folded white paper to Joe.

He accepted but didn't open it. He was half afraid to see what it contained.

"At ten minutes till four in the morning Washington time, ten till two in Pueblo, Minh called me," Barbara said. "I'd told the hotel operator to hold all calls, I needed my sleep, but Minh talked his way through. He played the tape for me . . . and we discussed it. I always have a cassette recorder with me, because I like to tape all meetings myself and have my own transcripts prepared. So I got my machine and held it to the phone to make my own copy. I didn't want to wait until Minh got a clean tape to me by courier. After Minh hung up, I sat at the desk in my room and listened to the last exchanges between the pilots maybe ten or twelve times. Then I got out my notebook and made a handwritten transcript of it, because sometimes things appear different to you when you read them than when you listen. Occasionally the eye sees nuances that the ear misses."

Joe now knew what he held in his hand. He could tell by the thickness that there were three sheets of paper.

Barbara said, "Minh had called me first. He intended to call Bruce Laceroth, then the chairman and the vice chairman of the Board—if not all five Board members—so each of them could hear the tape himself. It wasn't standard protocol, but this was a strange and unprecedented situation. I'm sure Minh got to at least one of those people—though they all deny hearing from him. We'll never know for sure, because Minh Tran died in a fire at the labs shortly before six o'clock that same morning, approximately two hours after he called me in Pueblo."

"Jesus."

"A very intense fire. An impossibly intense fire."

Surveying the trees that surrounded the meadow, Joe expected to see the pale faces of watchers in the deep shadows of the woods. When he and Barbara had first arrived, the site had struck him as remote, but now he felt as exposed and vulnerable as if he had been standing in the middle of any intersection in L.A.

He said, "Let me guess—the original tape from the cockpit recorder was destroyed in the lab fire."

"Supposedly burned to powder, vanished, no trace, gone, good-bye," Barbara said.

"What about the computer that was processing the digitized version?"

"Scorched garbage. Nothing in it salvageable."

"But you still have your copy."

She shook her head. "I left the cassette in my hotel room while I went to a breakfast meeting. The contents of the cockpit tape were so explosive, I didn't intend to share it right away with everyone on the team. Until we'd had time to think it through, we needed to be careful about when and how we released it."

"Why?"

"The pilot was dead, but his reputation was at stake. His family would be devastated if he was blamed. We had to be absolutely sure. If the cause was laid in Captain Blane's lap, then tens of millions—even hundreds of millions—of dollars' worth of wrongful-death litigation would ensue. We had to act with due diligence. My plan was to bring Mario back to my room after breakfast to hear the tape, just the two of us."

"Mario Oliveri," Joe said, referring to the man in Denver who had told him last night that Barbara had retired and moved back to Colorado Springs.

"Yeah. As head of the human-performance group, Mario's thoughts were more important to me at that moment than anyone's. But just as we were finishing breakfast, we got word about the fire at the labs—about poor Minh. By the time I got back to my room with Mario, the copy of the tape I'd made over the phone was blank."

"Stolen and replaced."

"Or just erased on my own machine. I guess Minh told someone that I'd duped it long-distance."

"Right then you must have known."

She nodded. "Something was very wrong. Something stank."

Her mop of hair was as white as the feathers on the head of the eagle that had overflown them, but until this moment she had seemed younger than fifty. Now she suddenly seemed older.

"Something wrong," he said, "but you couldn't quite believe it."

"My life was the Safety Board. I was proud to be part of it. Still am, Joe. They're damn good people."

"Did you tell Mario what was on the tape?"

"Yeah."

"What was his reaction?"

"Amazement. Disbelief, I think."

"Did you show him the transcript you'd made?"

She was silent a moment. Then: "No."

"Why not?"

"My hackles were up."

"You didn't trust anyone."

"A fire that intense . . . there must have been an accelerant."

"Arson," Joe said.

"But no one ever raised the possibility. Except me. I don't have faith in the integrity of their investigation of that lab fire at all. Not at all."

"What did the autopsy on Minh reveal? If he was murdered and the fire set to cover it—"

"If he was, they couldn't prove it by what was left of the body. He was virtually cremated. The thing is . . . he was a really nice guy, Joe. He was sweet. He loved his job because he believed what he did would save lives, help to prevent other crashes. I hate these people, whoever they are."

Among the white pines at the foot of the meadow, near where Joe and Barbara had first entered the clearing, something moved: a shadow gliding through deeper shadows, dun against purple.

Joe held his breath. He squinted but could not identify what he had briefly glimpsed.

Barbara said, "I think it was just a deer."

"If it wasn't?"

"Then we're dead whether we finish this talk or not," she said in a matter-of-fact tone that revealed the bleak and paranoid new world order in which she lived following Flight 353.

He said, "The fact that your tape was erased—didn't that raise anyone's suspicions?"

"The consensus was that I'd been tired. Three hours' sleep the night of the crash—then only a few hours the next night before Minh called and woke me. Poor bleary-eyed Barbara. I'd sat listening to the tape over and over, over and over, and at the end I must have pressed the wrong button—you know?—and erased it without realizing what I'd done." Her face twisted with sarcasm. "You can see how it must have happened."

"Any chance of that?"

"None whatsoever."

Though Joe unfolded the three sheets of paper, he didn't yet begin to read them.

He said, "Why didn't they believe you when you told them what you'd heard on the tape? They were your colleagues. They knew you to be a responsible person."

"Maybe some of them did believe it—and didn't want to. Maybe some of them just chalked it up to my fatigue. I'd been fighting an ear infection for weeks, and it had worn me down even before Pueblo. Maybe they took that into account. I don't know. And there's one or two who just plain don't like me. Who among us is universally loved? Not me. Too pushy. Too opinionated. Anyway, it was all moot—because without a tape, there was no proof of the exchanges between Blane and Santorelli."

"When did you finally tell someone you'd made a transcript word for word?"

"I was saving that. I was trying to figure the right moment, the right context in which to mention it—preferably once the investigation turned up some detail that would support what I said had been on the tape."

"Because by itself your transcript isn't real proof."

"Exactly. Sure, it's better than nothing, better than memory alone, but I needed to augment it with something. Then those two creeps woke me in the hotel in San Francisco, and after that . . . Well, I just wasn't much of a crusader any more."

Out of the eastern forest, two deer leaped in tandem into the bottom of the meadow, a buck and a doe. They raced across the corner of the clearing, quickly disappearing into the trees on the northern perimeter.

Under the skin on the back of Joe's neck, ticks of apprehension still burrowed and twitched.

The movement he had glimpsed earlier must have been the two deer. From their volatile entrance into the meadow, however, he inferred that they had been flushed from the trees by something—or someone—that had frightened them.

He wondered if any corner of the world would ever feel safe to him again. But he knew the answer even as the question passed through his mind: no.

No corner. Not anywhere.

Not ever.

He said, "Who do you suspect—inside the Safety Board? Who did Minh call next after you? Because that person is probably the one who told him not to pass the word any further—and then arranged to have him killed and the evidence burned."

"It could have been any of them he was intending to call. They were all his superiors, and he would have obeyed their instructions. I'd like to think it can't be Bruce Laceroth, because he's a bedrock guy. He started out a grunt like the rest of us did, worked his way up. The five Board members, on the other hand, are presidential appointees, approved by the Senate for five-year terms."

"Political hacks."

"No, actually, the great majority of the board members over the years have been straight shooters, trying to do their best. Most of them are a credit to the agency, and others we just endure. Once in a while, yeah, one of them is slime in a suit."

"What about the current chairman and vice chairman? You said Minh Tran was going to call them—supposing he wasn't able to reach Laceroth first."

"They're not your ideal public servants. Maxine Wulce is the chairman. An attorney, young and politically ambitious, looking out for number one, a real piece of work. Wouldn't give you two cents for her."

"Vice chairman?"

"Hunter Parkman. Pure political patronage. He's old money, so he doesn't need the job, but he likes being a presidential appointee and talking crash lore at parties. Give you fifteen cents for him."

Although he had continued to study the woods at the foot of the meadow, Joe had seen no further movement among those trees.

Far to the east, a vein of lightning pulsed briefly through the dark muscle of the storm.

He counted the seconds between the silver flash and the rumble of thunder, translating time to distance, and judged that the rain was five or six miles from them.

Barbara said, "I've given you only a Xerox of the transcript I wrote down that night. I've hidden the original away. God knows why, since I'll never use it."

Joe was torn between a rage to know and a fear of knowing. He sensed that in the exchanges between Captain Blane and First Officer Santorelli, he would discover new dimensions to the terror that his wife and daughters had endured.

Finally Joe focused his attention on the first page, and Barbara watched over his shoulder as he followed the text with one finger to allow her to see where he was reading.

Sounds of First Officer Santorelli returning to his seat from the lavatory. His initial comments are captured by the overhead cockpit microphone before he puts on his headset with the boom mike.

SANTORELLI: Get to L.A. (unintelligible), I'm going to chow down on so much (unintelligible), hummus, tabbouleh, lebne with string cheese, big plateful of kibby till I bust. There's this Armenian place, it's the best. You like Middle East food?

Three seconds of silence.

SANTORELLI: Roy? Somethin' up?

Two seconds of silence.

SANTORELLI: What's this? What're we . . . Roy, you off the autopilot?

BLANE: One of their names is Dr. Louis Blom.

SANTORELLI: What?

BLANE: One of their names is Dr. Keith Ramlock.

SANTORELLI: (with audible concern) What's this on the McDoo? You been in the FMC, Roy?

When Joe inquired, Barbara said, "The 747-400s use digitized avionics. The instrument panel is dominated by six of the largest cathode-ray tubes made, for the display of data. And the McDoo means MCDU, the multifunction control and display unit. There's one beside each pilot's seat, and they're interconnected, so anything one pilot enters is updated on the other's unit. They control the Honeywell/Sperry FMC, the flight management computer. The pilots input the flight plan and the load sheet through the MCDU keyboards, and all en route flight-plan changes are also actuated with the McDoos."

"So Santorelli comes back from the john and sees that Blane has made changes to the flight plan. Is that unusual?"

"Depends on weather, turbulence, unexpected traffic, holding patterns because of airport problems at the destination . . ."

"But at this point in a coast-to-coast flight—little past the midpoint—in pretty good weather, with everything apparently ticking along routinely?"

Barbara nodded. "Yeah, Santorelli would wonder why they were making flight-plan changes under the circumstances. But I think the concern in his voice results more from Blane's unresponsiveness and from something unusual he saw on the McDoo, some plan change that didn't make sense."

"Which would be?"

"As I said earlier, they were seven degrees off course."

"Santorelli wouldn't have felt that happening when he was in the lavatory?"

"It started soon after he was off the flight deck, and it was a gradual, really gentle bank. He might have sensed something, but there's no reason he would have realized the change was so big."

"Who are these doctors—Blom and Ramlock?"

"I don't have a clue. But read on. It gets weirder."

BLANE: They're doing bad things to me.

SANTORELLI: Captain, what's wrong here?

BLANE: They're mean to me.

SANTORELLI: Hey, are you with me here?

BLANE: Make them stop.

Barbara said, "Blane's voice changes there. It's sort of odd all the way through this, but when he says, 'Make them stop,' there's a tremor in it, a fragility, as if he's actually in . . . not pain so much but emotional distress."

SANTORELLI: Captain . . . Roy, I'm taking over here now.

BLANE: Are we recording?

SANTORELLI: What?

BLANE: Make them stop hurting me.

SANTORELLI: (worriedly) Gonna be—

BLANE: Are we recording?

SANTORELLI: Gonna be all right now—

A hard sound like a punch. A grunt, apparently from Santorelli. Another punch. Santorelli falls silent.

BLANE: Are we recording?

As a timpani of thunder drummed an overture in the east, Joe said, "He suckerpunched his copilot?"

"Or hit him with some blunt object, maybe something he'd taken out of his flight bag and hidden beside his seat while Santorelli was in the lav, something he was ready with."

"Premeditation. What the hell?"

"Probably hit him in the face, because Santorelli went right out. He's silent for ten or twelve seconds, and then"—she pointed to the transcript—"we hear him groaning."

"Dear God."

"On the tape, Blane's voice now loses the tremor, the fragility. There's a bitterness that makes your skin crawl."

BLANE: Make them stop or when I get the chance . . . when I get the chance, I'll kill everybody. Everybody. I will. I'll do it. I'll kill everybody, and I'll like it.

The transcript rattled in Joe's hands.

He thought of the passengers on 353: some dozing in their seats, others reading books, working on laptops, leafing through magazines, knitting, watching a movie, having a drink, making plans for the future, all of them complacent, none aware of the terrifying events occurring in the cockpit.

Maybe Nina was at the window, gazing out at the stars or down at the top of the cloud cover below them; she liked the window seat. Michelle and Chrissie might have been playing a game of Go Fish or Old Maid; they traveled with decks for various games.

He was torturing himself. He was good at it because a part of him believed that he deserved to be tortured.

Forcing those thoughts out of his mind, Joe said, "What was going on with Blane, for God's sake? Drugs? Was his brain fried on something?"

"No. That was ruled out."

"How?"

"It's always a priority to find something of the pilots' remains to test for drugs and alcohol. It took some time in this case," she said, as with a sweep of one hand she indicated the scorched pines and aspens uphill, "because a lot of the organic debris was scattered as much as a hundred yards into the trees west and north of the impact."

An internal darkness encroached on Joe's field of vision, until he seemed to be looking at the world through a tunnel. He bit his tongue almost hard enough to draw blood, breathed slowly and deeply, and tried not to let Barbara see how shaken he was by these details.

She put her hands in her pockets. She kicked a stone into the crater. "Really need this stuff, Joe?"

"Yes."

She sighed. "We found a portion of a hand we suspected was Blane's because of a half-melted wedding band that was fused to the ring finger, a relatively unique gold band. There was some other tissue as well. With that we identified—"

"Fingerprints?"

"No, those were burned off. But his father's still alive, so the Armed Forces DNA Identification Laboratory was able to confirm it was Blane's tissue through a DNA match with a blood sample that his dad supplied."

"Reliable?"

"A hundred percent. Then the remains went to the toxicologists. There were minute amounts of ethanol in both Blane and Santorelli, but that was just the consequence of putrefaction. Blane's partial hand was in those woods more than seventy-two hours before we found it. Santorelli's remains—four days. Some ethanol related to tissue decay was to be expected. But otherwise, they both passed all the toxicologicals. They were clean and sober."

Joe tried to reconcile the words on the transcript with the toxicological findings. He couldn't.

He said, "What're the other possibilities? A stroke?"

"No, it just didn't sound that way on the tape I listened to," Barbara said. "Blane speaks clearly, with no slurring of the voice whatsoever. And although what he's saying is damn bizarre, it's nevertheless coherent—no transposition of words, no substitution of inappropriate words."

Frustrated, Joe said, "Then what the hell? A nervous breakdown, psychotic episode?"

Barbara's frustration was no less than Joe's: "But where the hell did it come from? Captain Delroy Michael Blane was the most rock-solid psychological specimen you'd ever want to meet. Totally stable guy."

"Not totally."

"Totally stable guy," she insisted. "Passed all the company psychological exams. Loyal family man. Faithful husband. A Mormon, active in his church. No drinking, no drugs, no gambling. Joe, you can't find *one person* out there who ever saw him in a single moment of aberrant behavior. By all accounts he wasn't just a good man, not just a solid man—but a *happy* man."

Lightning glimmered. Wheels of rolling thunder clattered along steel rails in the high east.

Pointing to the transcript, Barbara showed Joe where the 747 made the first sudden three-degree heading change, nose right, which precipitated a yaw. "At that point, Santorelli was groaning but not fully conscious yet. And just before the maneuver, Captain Blane said, 'This is fun.' There are these other sounds on the tape—here, the rattle and clink of small loose objects being flung around by the sudden lateral acceleration."

This is fun.

Joe couldn't take his eyes off those words.

Barbara turned the page for him. "Three seconds later, the aircraft made another violent heading change, of four degrees, nose left. In addition to the previous clatter, there were now sounds from the aircraft—a thump and a low shuddery noise. And Captain Blane is laughing."

"Laughing," Joe said with incomprehension. "He was going to go down with them, and he was laughing?"

"It wasn't anything you'd think of as a *mad* laugh, either. It was . . . a pleasant laugh, as if he were genuinely enjoying himself."

This is fun.

Eight seconds after the first yawing incident, there was another abrupt heading change of three degrees, nose left, followed just two seconds later by a severe shift of seven degrees, nose right. Blane laughed as he executed the first maneuver and, with the second, said, *Oh, wow!*

"This is where the starboard wing lifted, forcing the port wing down," Barbara said. "In twenty-two seconds the craft was banking at a hundred and forty-six degrees, with a downward nose pitch of eighty-four degrees."

"They were finished."

"It was deep trouble but not hopeless. There was still a chance they might have pulled out of it. Remember, they were above twenty thousand feet. Room for recovery."

Because he had never read about the crash or watched television reports of it, Joe had always pictured fire in the aircraft and smoke filling the cabin. A short while ago, when he had realized that the passengers were spared that particular terror, he'd hoped that the long journey down had been less terrifying than the imaginary plunge that he experienced in some of his anxiety attacks. Now, however, he wondered which would have been worse: the gush of smoke and the instant recognition of impending doom that would have come with it—or clean air and the hideously attenuated false hope of a last-minute correction, salvation.

The transcript indicated the sounding of alarms in the cockpit. An altitude alert tone. A recorded voice repeatedly warning *Traffic!* because they were descending through air corridors assigned to other craft.

Joe asked, "What's this reference to the 'stick-shaker alarm'?"

"It makes a loud rattling, a scary sound nobody's going to overlook, warning the pilots that the plane has lost lift. They're going into a stall."

Gripped in the fist of fate punching toward the earth, First Officer Victor Santorelli abruptly stopped mumbling. He regained consciousness. Perhaps he saw clouds whipping past the windshield. Or perhaps the 747 was already below the high overcast, affording him a ghostly panorama of onrushing Colorado landscape, faintly luminous in shades of gray from dusty pearl to charcoal, with the golden glow of Pueblo scintillant to the south. Or maybe the cacophony of alarms and the radical data flashing on the six big display screens told him in an instant all that he needed to know. He had said, *Oh, Jesus*.

"His voice was wet and nasal," Barbara said, "which might have meant that Blane broke his nose."

Even reading the transcript, Joe could hear Santorelli's terror and his frantic determination to survive.

SANTORELLI: Oh, Jesus. No, Jesus, no.

BLANE: (laughter) Whoooaaa. Here we go, Dr. Ramlock. Dr. Blom, here we go.

SANTORELLI: Pull!

BLANE: (laughter) Whoooaaa. (laughter) Are we recording?

SANTORELLI: Pull up!

Santorelli is breathing rapidly, wheezing. He's grunting, struggling with something, maybe with Blane, but it sounds more like he's fighting the control wheel. If Blane's respiration rate is elevated at all, it's not registering on the tape.

SANTORELLI: Shit, shit!

BLANE: Are we recording?

Baffled, Joe said, "Why does he keep asking about it being recorded?"
Barbara shook her head. "I don't know."
"He's a pilot for how long?"
"Over twenty years."
"He'd know the cockpit-voice recorder is always working. Right?"
"He should know. Yeah. But he's not exactly in his right mind, is he?"
Joe read the final words of the two men.

SANTORELLI: Pull!

BLANE: Oh, wow.

SANTORELLI: Mother of God . . .

BLANE: Oh, yeah.

SANTORELLI: No.

BLANE: (child-like excitement) Oh, yeah.

SANTORELLI: Susan.

BLANE: Now. Look.

Santorelli begins to scream.

BLANE: Cool.

Santorelli's scream is three and a half seconds long, lasting to the end of the recording, which is terminated by impact.

Wind swept the meadow grass. The sky was swollen with a waiting deluge. Nature was in a cleansing mood.

Joe folded the three sheets of paper. He tucked them into a jacket pocket.

For a while he couldn't speak.

Distant lightning. Thunder. Clouds in motion.

Finally, gazing into the crater, Joe said, "Santorelli's last word was a name."

"Susan."

"Who is she?"

"His wife."

"I thought so."

At the end, no more entreaties to God, no more pleas for divine mercy. At the end, a bleak acceptance. A name said lovingly, with regret and terrible longing but perhaps also with a measure of hope. And in the mind's eye not the cruel earth hurtling nearer or the darkness after, but a cherished face.

Again, for a while, Joe could not speak.

ELEVEN

From the impact crater, Barbara Christman led Joe farther up the sloping meadow and to the north, to a spot no more than twenty yards from the cluster of dead, charred aspens.

"Here somewhere, in this general area, if I remember right," she said. "But what does it matter?"

When Barbara first arrived in the meadow on the morning after the crash, the shredded and scattered debris of the 747-400 had not resembled the wreckage of an airliner. Only two pieces had been immediately recognizable: a portion of one engine and a three-unit passenger-seat module.

He said, "Three seats, side by side?"

"Yes."

"Upright?"

"Yes. What's your point?"

"Could you identify what part of the plane the seats were from?"

"Joe—"

"From what part of the plane?" he repeated patiently.

"Couldn't have been from first class, and not from business class on either the main deck or the upper, because those are all two-seat modules. The center rows in economy class have four seats, so it had to come from the port or starboard rows in economy."

"Damaged?"

"Of course."

"Badly?"

"Not as badly as you'd expect."

"Burned?"

"Not entirely."

"Burned at all?"

"As I remember . . . there were just a few small scorch marks, a little soot."

"In fact, wasn't the upholstery virtually intact?"

Her broad, clear face now clouded with concern. "Joe, no one survived this crash."

"Was the upholstery intact?" he pressed.

"As I remember . . . it was slightly torn. Nothing serious."

"Blood on the upholstery?"

"I don't recall."

"Any bodies in the seats?"

"No."

"Body parts?"

"No."

"Lap belts still attached?"

"I don't remember. I suppose so."

"If the lap belts were attached—"

"No, it's ridiculous to think—"

"Michelle and the girls were in economy," he said.

Barbara chewed on her lip, looked away from him, and stared toward the oncoming storm. "Joe, your family wasn't in those seats."

"I know that," he assured her. "I know."

But how he *wished*.

She met his eyes again.

He said, "They're dead. They're gone. I'm not in denial here, Barbara."

"So you're back to this Rose Tucker."

"If I can find out where she was sitting on the plane, and if it was either the port or starboard side in economy—that's at least some small corroboration."

"Of what?"

"Her story."

"Corroboration," Barbara said disbelievingly.

"That she survived."

Barbara shook her head.

"You didn't meet Rose," he said. "She's not a flake. I don't think she's a liar. She has such . . . power, presence."

On the wind came the ozone smell of the eastern lightning, that theater-curtain scent which always rises immediately before the rain makes its entrance.

In a tone of tender exasperation, Barbara said, "They came down four miles, straight in, nose in, no hit-and-skip, the whole damn plane *shattering* around Rose Tucker, unbelievable explosive force—"

"I understand that."

"God knows, I really don't mean to be cruel, Joe—but do you understand? After all you've heard, do you? Tremendous explosive force all around this Rose. Impact force great enough to pulverize stone. Other passengers and crew . . . in most cases the flesh is literally *stripped* off their bones in an instant, stripped away as clean as if boiled off. Shredded. Dissolved. Disintegrated. And the bones themselves splintered and crushed like breadsticks. Then in the second instant, even as the plane is still hammering into the meadow, a spray of jet fuel—a spray as fine as an aerosol mist—explodes. Everywhere fire. Geysers of fire, rivers of fire, rolling tides of inescapable fire. Rose Tucker didn't float down in her seat like a bit of dandelion fluff and just stroll away through the inferno."

Joe looked at the sky, and he looked at the land at his feet, and the land was the brighter of the two.

He said, "You've seen pictures, news film, of a town hit by a tornado, everything smashed flat and reduced to rubble so small that you could almost sift it through a colander—and right in the middle of the destruction is one house, untouched or nearly so."

"That's a weather phenomenon, a caprice of the wind. But this is simple physics, Joe. Laws of matter and motion. Caprice doesn't play a role in physics. If that whole damn town had been dropped four miles, then the one surviving house would have been rubble too."

"Some of the families of survivors . . . Rose has shown them something that lifts them up."

"What?"

"I don't know, Barbara. I want to see. I want her to show me too. But the point is . . . they believe her when she says she was aboard that airplane. It's more than mere belief." He remembered Georgine Delmann's shining eyes. "It's a profound conviction."

"Then she's a con artist without equal."

Joe only shrugged.

A few miles away, a tuning fork of lightning vibrated and broke the storm clouds. Shatters of gray rain fell to the east.

"For some reason," Barbara said, "you don't strike me as a devoutly religious man."

"I'm not. Michelle took the kids to Sunday school and church every week, but I didn't go. It was the one thing I didn't share with them."

"Hostile to religion?"

"No. Just no passion for it, no interest. I was always as indifferent to God as He seemed to be to me. After the crash . . . I took the one step left in my 'spiritual journey' from disinterest to disbelief. There's no way to reconcile the idea of a benign God with what happened to everyone on that plane . . . and to those of us who're going to spend the rest of our lives missing them."

"Then if you're such an atheist, why do you insist on believing in this miracle?"

"I'm not saying Rose Tucker's survival was a miracle."

"Damned if I can see what *else* it would be. Nothing but God Himself and a rescue team of angels could have pulled her out of that in one piece," Barbara insisted with a note of sarcasm.

"No divine intervention. There's another explanation, something amazing but logical."

"Impossible," she said stubbornly.

"Impossible? Yeah, well . . . so was everything that happened in the cockpit with Captain Blane."

She held his gaze while she searched for an answer in the deep and orderly files of her mind. She was not able to find one.

Instead, she said, "If you don't believe in anything—then what is it that you expect Rose to tell you? You say that what she tells them 'lifts them up.' Don't you imagine it's got to be something of a spiritual nature?"

"Not necessarily."

"What else would it be?"

"I don't know."

Repeating Joe's own words heavily colored with exasperation, she said, "'Something amazing but logical.'"

He looked away from her, toward the trees along the northern edge of the field, and he realized that in the fire-blasted aspen cluster was a sole survivor, reclothed in foliage. Instead of the characteristic smooth pale trunk, it had scaly black bark, which would provide a dazzling contrast when its leaves turned brilliant yellow in the autumn.

"Something amazing but logical," he agreed.

Closer than ever, lightning laddered down the sky, and the boom of thunder descended rung to rung.

"We better go," Barbara said. "There's nothing more here anyway."

Joe followed her down through the meadow, but he paused again at the rim of the impact crater.

The few times that he had gone to meetings of The Compassionate Friends, he had heard other grieving parents speak of the Zero Point. The Zero Point was the instant of the child's death, from which every future event would be dated, the eye blink during which crushing loss reset your internal gauges to zero. It was the moment at which your shabby box of hopes and wants—which had once seemed to be such a fabulous chest of bright dreams—was turned on end and emptied into an abyss, leaving you with zero expectations. In a clock tick, the future was no longer a kingdom of possibility and wonder, but a yoke of obligation—and only the unattainable past offered a hospitable place to live.

He had existed at the Zero Point for more than a year, with time receding from him in both directions, belonging to neither the days ahead nor those behind. It was as though he had been suspended in a tank of liquid nitrogen and lay deep in cryogenic slumber.

Now he stood at another Zero Point, the physical one, where his wife and daughters had perished. He wanted so badly to have them back that the wanting tore like eagle's claws at his viscera. But at last he wanted something else as well: justice for them, justice which could not give meaning to their deaths but which might give meaning to his.

He had to get all the way up from his cryogenic bed, shake the ice out of his bones and veins, and not lie down again until he had dug the truth out of the grave in which it had been buried. For his lost women, he would burn palaces, pull down empires, and waste the world if necessary for the truth to be found.

And now he understood the difference between justice and mere vengeance: genuine justice would bring him no relief of his pain, no sense of triumph; it would only allow him to step out of the Zero Point and, with his task completed, die in peace.

Down through the vaulted conifers came fluttering white wings of storm light, and again, and still more, as if the cracking sky were casting out a radiant multitude. Thunder and the rush of wind beat like pinions at Joe's ears, and by the many thousands, feathered shadows swooped and shuddered between the tree trunks and across the forest floor.

Just as he and Barbara reached her Ford Explorer, at the weedy end of the narrow dirt lane, a great fall of rain hissed and roared through the pines. They piled inside, their hair and faces jeweled, and her periwinkle-blue blouse was spattered with spots as dark as plum skin.

They didn't encounter whatever had frightened the deer from cover, but Joe was pretty sure now that the culprit had been another animal. In the run to beat the rain, he had sensed only wild things crouching—not the far deadlier threat of men.

Nevertheless, the crowding conifers seemed to provide ideal architecture for assassins. Secret bowers, blinds, ambushments, green-dark lairs.

As Barbara started the Explorer and drove back the way they had come, Joe was tense. Surveying the woods. Waiting for the bullet.

When they reached the gravel road, he said, "The two men that Blane named on the cockpit tape . . ."

"Dr. Blom and Dr. Ramlock."

"Have you tried to find out who they are, launched a search for them?"

"When I was in San Francisco, I was prying into Delroy Blane's background. Looking for any personal problems that might have put him in a precarious psychological condition. I asked his family and friends if they'd heard those names. No one had."

"You checked Blane's personal records, appointment calendars, his checkbook?"

"Yeah. Nothing. And Blane's family physician says he never referred his patient to any specialists with those names. There's no physician, psychiatrist, or psychologist in the San Francisco area by those names. That's as far as I carried it. Because then I was awakened by those bastards in my hotel room, a pistol in my face, and told to butt out."

To the end of the gravel road and onto the paved state route, where sizzling silver rain danced in a froth on the blacktop, Barbara fell into a troubled silence. Her brow was creased, but not—Joe sensed—because the inclement weather required that she concentrate on her driving.

The lightning and thunder had passed. Now the storm threw all its energy into wind and rain.

Joe listened to the monotonous thump of the windshield wipers.

He listened as well to the hard-driven drops snapping against the glass, which seemed at first to be a meaningless random rattle; but gradually he began to think that he perceived hidden patterns even in the rhythms of the rain.

Barbara found perhaps not a pattern but an intriguing puzzle piece that she had overlooked. "I'm remembering something peculiar, but . . ."

Joe waited.

". . . but I don't want to encourage you in this weird delusion of yours."

"Delusion?"

She glanced at him. "This idea that there might have been a survivor."

He said, "Encourage me. Encouragement isn't something I've had much of in the past year."

She hesitated but then sighed. "There was a rancher not far from here who was already asleep when Flight 353 went down. People who work the land go to bed early in these parts. The explosion woke him. And then someone came to his door."

"Who?"

"The next day, he called the county sheriff, and the sheriff's office put him in touch with the investigation command center. But it didn't seem to amount to much."

"Who came to his door in the middle of the night?"

"A witness," Barbara said.

"To the crash?"

"Supposedly."

She looked at him but then quickly returned her attention to the rain-swept highway.

In the context of what Joe had told her, this recollection seemed by the moment to grow more disturbing to Barbara. Her eyes pinched at the corners, as if she were straining to see not through the downpour but more clearly into the past, and her lips pressed together as she debated whether to say more.

"A witness to the crash," Joe prompted.

"I can't remember why, of all places, she went to this ranch house or what she wanted there."

"She?"

"The woman who claimed to have seen the plane go down."

"There's something more," Joe said.

"Yeah. As I recall . . . she was a black woman."

His breath went stale in his lungs, but at last he exhaled and said, "Did she give this rancher her name?"

"I don't know."

"If she did, I wonder if he'd remember it."

At the turnoff from the state route, the entrance road to the ranch was flanked by tall white posts that supported an overhead sign bearing graceful green letters on a white background: LOOSE CHANGE RANCH. Under those three words, in smaller letters and in script: *Jeff and Mercy Ealing*. The gate stood open.

The oiled-gravel lane was flanked by white ranch fencing that divided the fields into smaller pastures. They passed a big riding ring, exercise yards, and numerous white stables trimmed in green.

Barbara said, "I wasn't here last year, but one of my people gave me a report on it. Coming back to me now . . . It's a horse ranch. They breed and race quarter horses. Also breed and sell some show horses like Arabians, I think."

The pasture grass, alternately churned by wind and flattened by the pounding rain, was not currently home to any horses. The riding ring and the exercise yards were deserted.

In some of the stables, the top of the Dutch door at each stall was open. Here and there, from the safety of their quarters, horses peered out at the storm. Some were nearly as dark as the spaces in which they stood, but others were pale or dappled.

The large and handsome ranch house, white clapboard with green shutters, framed by groupings of aspens, had the deepest front porch that Joe had ever seen. Under the heavy cape of gloom thrown down by the thunderheads, a yellow glow as welcoming as hearth light filled some of the windows.

Barbara parked in the driveway turnaround. She and Joe ran through the rain—previously as warm as bath water but now cooler—to the screened porch. The door swung inward with a creak of hinges and the singing of a worn tension spring, sounds so rounded in tone that they were curiously pleasing; they spoke of time passed at a gentle pace, of gracious neglect rather than dilapidation.

The porch furniture was white wicker with green cushions, and ferns cascaded from wrought-iron stands.

The house door stood open, and a man of about sixty, in a black rain slicker, waited to one side on the porch. The weather-thickened skin of his sun-darkened face was well creased and patinaed like the leather of a long-used saddlebag. His blue eyes were as quick and friendly as his smile. He raised his voice to be heard above the drumming of the rain on the roof. "Mornin'. Good day for ducks."

"Are you Mr. Ealing?" Barbara asked.

"That would be me," said another man in a black slicker as he appeared in the open doorway.

He was six inches taller and twenty years younger than the man who had commented on the weather. But a life on horseback, in hot sun and dry wind and the nip of winter, had already begun to abrade the smooth, hard planes of youth and bless him with a pleasantly worn and appealing face that spoke of deep experience and rural wisdom.

Barbara introduced herself and Joe, implying that she still worked for the Safety Board and that Joe was her associate.

"You poking into that after a whole year?" Ealing asked.

"We weren't able to settle on a cause," Barbara said. "Never like to close a file until we know what happened. Why we're here is to ask about the woman who knocked on your door that night."

"Sure, I remember."

"Could you describe her?" Joe asked.

"Petite lady. About forty or so. Pretty."

"Black?"

"She was, yes. But also a touch of something else. Mexican maybe. Or more likely Chinese. Maybe Vietnamese."

Joe remembered the Asian quality of Rose Tucker's eyes. "Did she tell you her name?"

"Probably did," Ealing said. "But I don't recall it."

"How long after the crash did she show up here?" Barbara asked.

"Not too long." Ealing was carrying a leather satchel similar to a physician's bag. He shifted it from his right hand to his left. "The sound of the plane coming down woke me and Mercy before it hit. Louder than you ever hear a plane in these parts, but we knew what it had to be. I got out of bed, and Mercy turned on the light. I said, 'Oh, Lordy,' and then we heard it, like a big far-off quarry blast. The house even shook a little."

The older man was shifting impatiently from foot to foot.

Ealing said, "How is she, Ned?"

"Not good," Ned said. "Not good at all."

Looking out at the long driveway that dwindled through the lashing rain, Jeff Ealing said, "Where the hell's Doc Sheely?" He wiped one hand down his long face, which seemed to make it longer.

Barbara said, "If we've come at a bad time—"

"We've got a sick mare, but I can give you a minute," Ealing said. He returned to the night of the crash. "Mercy called Pueblo County Emergency Rescue, and I quick got dressed and drove the pickup out to the main road, headed south, trying to figure where it went down and could I help. You could see the fire in the sky—not direct but the glow. By the time I got oriented and into the vicinity, there was already a sheriff's car blocking the turnoff from the state route. Another pulled up behind me. They were setting up a barrier, waiting for the search-and-rescue teams, and they made it clear this wasn't a job for untrained do-gooders. So I came home."

"How long were you gone?" Joe asked.

"Couldn't have been more than forty-five minutes. Then I was in the kitchen here with Mercy for maybe half an hour, having some decaf with a shot of Bailey's, wide awake and listening to the news on the radio and wondering was it worth trying to get back to sleep, when we heard the knocking at the front door."

Joe said, "So she showed up an hour and fifteen minutes after the crash."

"Thereabouts."

Its engine noise masked by the heavy downpour and by the shivery chorus of wind-shaken aspens, the approaching vehicle didn't attract their attention until it was almost upon them. A Jeep Cherokee. As it swung into the turnaround in front of the house, its headlights, like silver swords, slashed at the chain-mail rain.

"Thank God!" Ned exclaimed, pulling up the hood on his slicker. The screen door sang as he pushed through it and into the storm.

"Doc Sheely's here," Jeff Ealing said. "Got to help him with the mare. But Mercy knows more about that woman than I do anyway. You go ahead and talk to her."

Mercy Ealing's graying blond hair was for the most part held away from her face and off her neck by three butterfly barrettes. She had been busy baking cookies, however, and a few curling locks had slipped loose, hanging in spirals along her flushed cheeks.

Wiping her hands on her apron and then, more thoroughly, on a dish towel, she insisted that Barbara and Joe sit at the breakfast table in the roomy kitchen while she poured coffee for them. She provided a plate heaped with freshly baked cookies.

The back door was ajar. An unscreened rear porch lay beyond. The cadenced rain was muffled here, like the drumming for a funeral cortege passing out on the highway.

The air was warm and redolent of oatmeal batter, chocolate, and roasting walnuts.

The coffee was good, and the cookies were better.

On the wall was a pictorial calendar with a Christian theme. The painting for August showed Jesus on the seashore, speaking to a pair of fishermen brothers, Peter and Andrew, who would cast aside their nets and follow Him to become fishers of men.

Joe felt as if he had fallen through a trapdoor into a different reality from the one in which he'd been living for a year, out of a cold strange place into the normal world with its little day-to-day crises, pleasantly routine tasks, and simple faith in the rightness of all things.

As she checked the cookies in the two ovens, Mercy recalled the night of the crash. "No, not Rose. Her name was Rachel Thomas."

Same initials, Joe realized. Maybe Rose walked out of the crash suspecting that somehow the plane had been brought down because she was aboard. She might be anxious to let her enemies think that she was dead. Keeping the same initials probably helped her remember the false name that she had given.

"She'd been driving from Colorado Springs to Pueblo when she saw the plane coming down, right over her," Mercy said. "The poor thing was so frightened, she jammed on the brakes, and the car spun out of control. Thank God for the seat belts. Went off the road, down an embankment, and turned over."

Barbara said, "She was injured?"

Spooning lumps of thick dough on greased baking sheets, Mercy said, "No, both fine and dandy, just shaken up some. It was only a little embankment. Rachel, she had dirt on her clothes, bits of grass and weeds stuck to her, but she was okay. Oh, shaky as a leaf in a gale but okay. She was such a sweet thing, I felt so sorry for her."

To Joe, Barbara said meaningfully, "So back then she was claiming to be a witness."

"Oh, I don't think she was making it up," Mercy said. "She was a witness, for sure. Very rattled by what she saw."

A timer buzzed. Diverted, Mercy slipped one hand into a baker's quilted mitten. From the oven, she withdrew a sheet filled with fragrant brown cookies.

"The woman came here that night for help?" Barbara asked.

Putting the hot aluminum tray on a wire cooling rack, Mercy said, "She wanted to call a taxi service in Pueblo, but I told her they never in a million years come way out here."

"She didn't want to get a tow truck for her car?" Joe asked.

"She didn't figure to be able to get it done at that hour of the night, all the way from Pueblo. She expected to come back the next day with the tow-truck driver."

Barbara said, "What did she do when you told her there was no way to get taxi service from out here?"

Sliding a sheet of raw dough drops into the oven, Mercy said, "Oh, then I drove them into Pueblo myself."

"All the way to Pueblo?" Barbara asked.

"Well, Jeff had to be up earlier than me. Rachel didn't want to stay over here, and it wasn't but an hour to get there, with my heavy foot on the pedal," Mercy said, closing the oven door.

"That was extraordinarily kind of you," Joe said.

"Was it? No, not really. The Lord wants us to be Samaritans. It's what we're here for. You see folks in trouble like this, you have to help them. And this was a real nice lady. All the way to Pueblo, she couldn't stop talking about the poor people on that plane. She was all torn up about it. Almost like it was her fault, what happened to them, just because she saw it a few seconds before it hit. Anyway, it was no big deal going to Pueblo . . . though coming back home that night was the devil's own trip, because there was so much traffic going to the crash site. Police cars, ambulances, fire trucks. Lots of lookie-loos too. Standing along the side of the road by their cars and pickups, hoping to see blood, I guess. Give me the creeps. Tragedy can bring out the best in people, but it also brings out the worst."

"On the way to Pueblo, did she show you where her car had gone off the highway?" Joe asked.

"She was too rattled to recognize the exact spot in the darkness and all. And we couldn't be stopping every half mile or whatever to see if maybe this was the right embankment, or then we'd never get the poor girl home to bed."

Another timer buzzed.

Putting on the quilted mitten again and opening the door on the second oven, Mercy said, "She was so pooped, all sleepy-eyed. She didn't care about tow trucks, just about getting home to bed."

Joe felt certain that there had been no car. Rose walked out of the burning meadow, into the woods, all but blind as she left the blaze for the dark, but desperately determined to get away before anyone discovered that she was alive, somehow sure that the 747 had been brought down because of her. Terrified, in a state of shock, horrified by the carnage, lost in the wilds, she had preferred to risk death from starvation and exposure rather than be found by a rescue team and perhaps fall into the hands of her eerily powerful enemies. Soon, by great good luck, she reached a ridge from which she was able to see, through the trees, the distant lights of the Loose Change Ranch.

Pushing aside her empty coffee cup, Barbara said, "Mercy, where did you take this woman in Pueblo? Do you remember the address?"

Holding the baking sheet half out of the oven to examine the cookies, Mercy said, "She never told me an address, just directed me street to street until we got to the house."

No doubt it was one that Rose had chosen at random, as it was unlikely that she knew anyone in Pueblo.

"Did you see her go inside?" Joe asked.

"I was going to wait until she unlocked the door and was inside. But she thanked me, said God bless, and I should scoot back home."

"Could you find the place again?" Barbara asked.

Deciding that the cookies needed an additional minute, Mercy slid the tray back into the oven, pulled off the mitten, and said, "Sure. Nice big house in a real nice neighborhood. But it wasn't Rachel's. It belonged to her partner in the medical practice. Did I say she was a doctor down in Pueblo?"

"But you didn't actually see her go into this place?" Joe asked. He assumed that Rose waited until Mercy was out of sight, then walked away from the house and found transportation out of Pueblo.

Mercy's face was red and dewy from the oven heat. Plucking two paper towels off a roll and blotting the sweat from her brow, she said, "No. Like I said, I dropped them off in front, and they went up the walk."

"Them?"

"The poor sleepy little thing. Such a dear. She was the daughter of Rachel's partner."

Startled, Barbara glanced at Joe, then leaned forward in her chair toward Mercy. "There was a child?"

"Such a little angel, sleepy but not cranky at all."

Joe flashed back to Mercy's mention of "seat belts," plural, and to other things she had said that suddenly required a more literal interpretation than he had given them. "You mean Rose . . . Rachel had a child with her?"

"Well, didn't I say?" Mercy looked puzzled, tossing the damp paper towel into a waste can.

"We didn't realize there was a child," Barbara said.

"I told you," Mercy said, perplexed by their confusion. "Back a year ago, when the fella came around from your Board, I told him all about Rachel and the little girl, about Rachel being a witness."

Looking at Joe, Barbara said, "I didn't remember that. I guess I did well even to remember this place at all."

Joe's heart turned over, turned like a wheel long stilled on a rusted axle.

Unaware of the tremendous impact that her revelation had on Joe, Mercy opened the oven door to check the cookies once more.

"How old was the girl?" he asked.

"Oh, about four or five," Mercy said.

Premonition weighed on Joe's eyes, and when he closed them, the darkness behind his lids swarmed with possibilities that he was terrified to consider.

"Can you . . . can you describe her?"

Mercy said, "She was just a little slip of a doll of a thing. Cute as a button—but then they're all pretty darn cute at that age, aren't they?"

When Joe opened his eyes, Barbara was staring at him, and her eyes brimmed with pity for him. She said, "Careful, Joe. It can't lead where you hope."

Mercy placed the hot baking sheet full of finished cookies on a second wire rack.

Joe said, "What color was her hair?"

"She was a little blonde."

He was moving around the table before he realized that he had risen from his chair.

Having picked up a spatula, Mercy was scooping the cookies off the cooler of the two baking sheets, transferring them to a large platter.

Joe went to her side. "Mercy, what color were this little girl's eyes?"

"Can't say I remember."

"Try."

"Blue, I guess," she said, sliding the spatula under another cookie.

"You guess?"

"Well, she was blond."

He surprised her by taking the spatula from her and putting it aside on the counter. "Look at me, Mercy. This is important."

From the table, Barbara warned him again. "Easy, Joe. Easy."

He knew that he should heed her warning. Indifference was his only defense. Indifference was his friend and his consolation. Hope is a bird that always flies, the light that always dies, a stone that crushes when it can't be carried any farther. Yet with a recklessness that frightened him, he felt himself shouldering that stone, stepping into the light, reaching toward those white wings.

"Mercy," he said, "not all blondes have blue eyes, do they?"

Face-to-face with him, captured by his intensity, Mercy Ealing said, "Well . . . I guess they don't."

"Some have green eyes, don't they?"

"Yes."

"If you think about it, I'm sure you've even seen blondes with brown eyes."

"Not many."

"But some," he said.

Premonition swelled in him again. His heart was a bucking horse now, iron-shod hooves kicking the stall boards of his ribs.

"This little girl," he said, "are you sure she had blue eyes?"

"No. Not sure at all."

"Could her eyes have been gray?"

"I don't know."

"Think. Try to remember."

Mercy's eyes swam out of focus as memory pulled her vision to the past, but after a moment, she shook her head. "I can't say they were gray, either."

"Look at my eyes, Mercy."

She was looking.

He said, "They're gray."

"Yes."

"An unusual shade of gray"

"Yes."

"With just the faintest touch of violet to them."

"I see it," she said.

"Could this girl . . . Mercy, could this child have had eyes like mine?"

She appeared to know what answer he needed to hear, even if she could not guess why. Being a goodhearted woman, she wanted to please him. At last, however, she said, "I don't really know. I can't say for sure."

A sinking sensation overcame Joe, but his heart continued to knock hard enough to shake him.

Keeping his voice calm, he said, "Picture the girl's face." He put his hands on Mercy's shoulders. "Close your eyes and try to see her again."

She closed her eyes.

"On her left cheek," Joe said. "Beside her earlobe. Only an inch in from her earlobe. A small mole."

Mercy's eyes twitched behind her smooth lids as she struggled to burnish her memory.

"It's more of a beauty mark than a mole," Joe said. "Not raised but flat. Roughly the shape of a crescent moon."

After a long hesitation, she said, "She might have had a mark like that, but I can't remember."

"Her smile. A little lopsided, a little crooked, turned up at the left corner of her mouth."

"She didn't smile that I remember. She was so sleepy . . . and a little dazed. Sweet but withdrawn."

Joe could not think of another distinguishing feature that might jar Mercy Ealing's memory. He could have regaled her for hours with stories about his daughter's grace, about her charm, about her humor and the musical quality of her laughter. He could have spoken at length of her beauty: the smooth sweep of her forehead, the coppery gold of her eyebrows and lashes, the pertness of her nose, her shell-like ears, the combination of fragility and stubborn strength in her face that sometimes made his heart ache when he watched her sleeping, the inquisitiveness and unmistakable intelligence that informed her every expression. Those were subjective impressions, however, and no matter how detailed such descriptions were, they could not lead Mercy to the answers that he had hoped to get from her.

He took his hands from her shoulders.

She opened her eyes.

Joe picked up the spatula he had taken from her. He put it down again. He didn't know what he was doing.

She said, "I'm sorry."

"It's okay. I was hoping . . . I thought . . . I don't know. I'm not sure what I was thinking."

Self-deceit was a suit that didn't fit him well, and even as he lied to Mercy Ealing, he stood naked to himself, excruciatingly aware of what he had been hoping, thinking. He'd been in a fit of searching behavior again, not chasing anyone into a convenience store this time, not stalking an imagined Michelle through a mall or department store, not rushing to a schoolyard fence for a closer glimpse of a Chrissie who was not Chrissie after all, but heart-deep in searching behavior nonetheless. The coincidence of this mystery child sharing his lost daughter's age and hair color had been all that he needed to send him racing pell-mell once more in pursuit of false hope.

"I'm sorry," Mercy said, clearly sensing the precipitous downward spiral of his mood. "Her eyes, the mole, the smile . . . just don't ring a bell. But I remember her name. Rachel called her Nina."

Behind Joe, at the table, Barbara got up so fast that she knocked over her chair.

TWELVE

At the corner of the back porch, the water falling through the downspout produced a gargle of phantom voices, eager and quarrelsome, guttural and whispery, spitting out questions in unknown tongues.

Joe's legs felt rubbery. He leaned with both hands on the wet railing. Rain blew under the porch eaves, spattering his face.

In answer to his question, Barbara pointed toward the low hills and the woods to the southwest. "The crash site was that way."

"How far?"

Mercy stood in the open kitchen door. "Maybe half a mile as the crow flies. Maybe a little farther."

Out of the torn meadow, into the forest where the fire died quickly because it had been a wet summer that year, farther into the darkness of the trees, thrashing through the thin underbrush, eyes adjusting grudgingly to the gloom, perhaps onto a deer trail that allowed easy passage, perhaps across another meadow, to the hilltop from which the ranch lights could be seen, Rose might have led—or mostly carried—the child. Half a mile as the crow flies, but twice or three times as far when one followed the contours of the land and the way of the deer.

"One and a half miles on foot," Joe said.

"Impossible," Barbara said.

"Very possible. She could have done it."

"I'm not talking about the hike." She turned to Mercy and said, "Mrs. Ealing, you have been an enormous help to us already, a really enormous help, but we've got a confidential matter to discuss here for a minute or two."

"Oh, of course, I understand. You just take all the time you want," said Mercy, hugely curious but still too polite to intrude. She backed off the threshold and closed the kitchen door.

"Only a mile and a half," Joe repeated.

"On the horizontal," Barbara said, moving close to him, putting a hand on his shoulder. "Only a mile and a half on the horizontal, but more than four miles on the vertical, straight down, sky to ground. *That's* the part I can't accept, Joe."

He was struggling with it himself. To believe in survivors required faith or something very like it, and he was without faith by choice and by necessity. To put faith in a God would require him to see meaning in the suffering that was the weft of human experience, and he could see no meaning to it. On the other hand, to believe that this miracle of survival resulted somehow from the scientific research in which Rose was engaged, to contemplate that humankind could reach successfully for god-like power—Shadrach saving Shadrach from the furnace, Lazarus raising Lazarus from the grave—required him to have faith in the transcendent spirit of humankind. Its goodness. Its beneficent genius. After fourteen years as a crime reporter, he knew men too well to bend his knee before the altar in the First Church of Humanity the Divine. Men had a genius for arranging their damnation, but few if any were capable of their own salvation.

With her hand still on Joe's shoulder, being tough with him but in the spirit of sisterly counseling, she said, "First you want me to believe there was one survivor of that holocaust. Now it's two. I stood in the smoking ruins, in the slaughterhouse, and I *know* that the odds against anyone walking out of there on her own two feet are billions to one."

"Granted."

"No—greater than billions to one. Astronomical, immeasurable."

"All right."

"So there simply are no odds whatsoever that *two* could have come through it, none, not even an infinitesimal chance."

He said, "There's a lot I haven't told you, and most of it I'm not going to tell you now, because you're probably safer not knowing. But one thing . . . this Rose Tucker is a scientist who's been working on something big for years, government or military financing behind it, something secret and very damn big."

"What?"

"I don't know. But before she boarded the flight in New York, she called a reporter out in Los Angeles, an old friend of hers, and set up an interview, with trusted witnesses, at the arrival gate at LAX. She said she was bringing something with her that would change the world forever."

Barbara searched his eyes, obviously seeking some sign that he was not serious about this change-the-world-overnight fantasy. She was a woman of logic and reason, impressed by facts and details, and experience had shown her that solutions were found at an inchworm's pace, in a journey of countless small steps. As an investigator, for years she'd dealt with puzzles that presented her with literally millions of pieces and that were hugely more complex than virtually any homicide case to which any police detective was ever assigned, mysteries of human action and machine failure that were solved not with miracles but with drudgery.

Joe understood the look in her eyes, because investigative journalism was not unlike her own work.

"Just what are you saying?" she pressed. "That when the plane rolls and plummets, Rose Tucker takes a squeeze bottle out of her purse, some fabulous new topical lotion that confers temporary invulnerability on the user, sort of like a sunscreen, and quickly coats herself?"

Joe almost laughed. This was the first time he'd felt like laughing in ages. "No, of course not."

"Then what?"

"I don't know. Something."

"Sounds like a big nothing."

"Something," he insisted.

With the forge fire of lightning now gone and with the crack of thunder silenced, the churning clouds had an iron-dark beauty.

In the distance the low, wooded hills were veiled in mists of enigma—the hills across which she had come that night, untouched out of fire and destruction.

Skirling wind made cottonwoods and aspens dance, and across the fields, billows of rain whirled like skirts in a tarantella.

He had hope again. It felt good. Exhilarating. Of course, that was why hope was dangerous. The glorious lifting up, the sweet sense of soaring, always too brief, and then the terrible fall that was more devastating because of the sublime heights from which it began.

But maybe it was worse never to hope at all.

He was filled with wonder and quickening expectation.

He was scared too.

"Something," he insisted.

He took his hands off the railing. His legs were sturdy again. He blotted his wet hands on his jeans. He wiped his rain-spattered face on the sleeve of his sportcoat.

Turning to Barbara, he said, "Somehow safe to the meadow, then a mile and a half to the ranch. A mile and a half in an hour and fifteen minutes, which might be just about right in the darkness, with a small child to carry or help along."

"I hate to be always the pin in the balloon—"

"Then don't be."

"—but there's one thing you have to consider."

"I'm listening."

Barbara hesitated. Then: "Just for the sake of argument, let's accept that there were survivors. That this woman was on the plane. Her name is Rose Tucker . . . but she told Mercy and Jeff that she was Rachel Thomas."

"So?"

"If she doesn't give them her real name, why does she give them Nina's real name?"

"These people who're after Rose . . . they're not after Nina, they don't care about Nina."

"If they find out Rose somehow saved the girl, and if she saved the girl because of this strange, radical news-truth-thing-whatever that she was bringing with her to the press interview in Los Angeles, then maybe somehow that makes the girl as big a danger to them as Rose herself seems to be."

"Maybe. I don't know. I don't care right now."

"My point is—she'd use another name for Nina."

"Not necessarily."

"She would," Barbara insisted.

"So what's the difference?"

"So maybe *Nina* is a false name."

He felt slapped. He didn't reply.

"Maybe the child who came to this house that night is really named Sarah or Mary or Jennifer . . ."

"No," Joe said firmly.

"Just like Rachel Thomas is a false name."

"If the child wasn't Nina, what an amazing coincidence it would be for Rose to pluck my daughter's name out of thin air. Talk about billion-to-one odds!"

"That plane could have been carrying more than one little blond girl going on five."

"Both of them named Nina? *Jesus*, Barbara."

"*If* there were survivors, and if one of them was a little blond girl," Barbara said, "you've at least got to prepare yourself for the possibility that she wasn't Nina."

"I know," he said, but he was angry with her for forcing him to say it. "I know."

"Do you?"

"Yes, of course."

"I'm worried for you, Joe."

"Thank you," he said sarcastically.

"Your soul's broken."

"I'm okay."

"You could fall apart so easy."

He shrugged.

"No," she said. "Look at yourself."

"I'm better than I was."

"She might not be Nina."

"She might not be Nina," he admitted, hating Barbara for this relentless insistence, even though he knew that she was genuinely concerned for him, that she was prescribing this pill of reality as a vaccine against the total collapse that he might experience if his hopes, in the end, were not realized. "I'm ready to face that she might turn out not to be Nina. Okay? Feel better? I can handle it if that's the case."

"You say it, but it's not true."

He glared at her. "It is true."

"Maybe a tiny piece of your heart knows she might not be Nina, a thin fiber, but the rest of your heart is right now pounding, *racing* with the conviction that she is."

He could feel his own eyes shining with—stinging with—the delirious expectation of a miraculous reunion.

Her eyes, however, were full of a sadness that infuriated him so much he was nearly capable of striking her.

Mercy making peanut-butter dough balls. A new curiosity—and wariness—in her eyes. Having seen, through the window, the emotional quality of the discussion on the porch. Perhaps catching a few words through the glass, even without attempting to eavesdrop.

Nevertheless, she was a Samaritan, with Jesus and Andrew and Simon Peter marking the month of August as a reminder for her, and she still wanted to do her best to help.

"No, actually, the girl never said her name. Rachel introduced her. The poor child never spoke two words. She was so tired, you see, so sleepy. And maybe in shock a little from the car rolling over. Not hurt, mind you. Not a mark on her. But her little face was as white and shiny as candle wax. Heavy-eyed and not really with us. Half in a sort of trance. I worried about her, but Rachel said she was okay, and Rachel was a doctor, after all, so then I didn't worry about it that much. The little doll slept in the car all the way to Pueblo."

Mercy rolled a ball of dough between her palms. She put the pale sphere on a baking sheet and flattened it slightly with the gentle pressure of her thumb.

"Rachel had been to Colorado Springs to visit family for the weekend, and she'd taken

Nina with her because Nina's dad and mom were on an anniversary cruise. At least that's how I understood it." Mercy began to fill a brown paper lunch bag with the cooled cookies that were stacked on the platter.

"Not the usual thing—I mean, a black doctor and a white doctor in practice together in these parts, and not usual, either, to see a black woman with a white child around here. But I take all that to mean the world's getting to be a better place at last, more tolerant, more loving."

She folded the top of the bag twice and handed it to Barbara.

"Thank you, Mercy."

To Joe, Mercy Ealing said, "I'm sure sorry I couldn't be more help to you."

"You've been a lot of help," he assured her. He smiled. "And there's cookies."

She looked toward the kitchen window that was on the side of the house rather than on the back of it. One of the stables was visible through the pall of rain.

She said, "A good cookie does lift the spirit, doesn't it? But I sure wish I could do more than make cookies for Jeff today. He dearly loves that mare."

Glancing at the calendar with the religious theme, Joe said, "How do you hold on to your faith, Mercy? How in a world with so much death, planes falling out of the sky and favorite mares being taken for no reason?"

She didn't seem surprised or offended by the question. "I don't know. Sometimes it's hard, isn't it? I used to be so angry that we couldn't have kids. I was working at some record for miscarriages, and then I just gave up. You want to scream at the sky sometimes. And there's nights you lie awake. But then I think . . . well, this life has its joys too. And, anyway, it's nothing but a place we have to pass through on our way to somewhere better. If we live forever, it doesn't matter so much what happens to us here."

Joe had been hoping for a more interesting answer. Insightful. Penetrating. Homespun wisdom. Something he could believe.

He said, "The mare will matter to Jeff. And it matters to you because it matters so much to him."

Picking up another lump of dough, rolling it into a pale moon, a tiny planet, she smiled and said, "Oh, if I understood it, Joe, then I wouldn't be me. I'd be God. And that's a job I sure wouldn't want."

"How so?"

"It's got to be even sadder than our end of things, don't you think? He knows our potential but has to watch us forever falling short, all the cruel things we do to one another, the hatred and the lies, the envy and greed and the endless coveting. We see only the ugliness people do to those around us, but He sees it all. The seat He's in has a sadder view than ours."

She put the ball of dough on the cookie sheet and impressed upon it the mark of her thumb: a moment of pleasure waiting to be baked, to be eaten, to lift the spirit.

The veterinarian's Jeep station wagon was still in the driveway, parked in front of the Explorer. A Weimaraner was lying in the back of the vehicle. As Joe and Barbara climbed into the Ford and slammed the doors, the dog raised its noble silver-gray head and stared at them through the rear window of the Jeep.

By the time that Barbara slipped the key into the ignition and started the Explorer, the humid air was filled with the aromas of oatmeal-chocolate-chip cookies and damp denim. The windshield quickly clouded with the condensation of their breath.

"If it's Nina, your Nina," Barbara said, waiting for the air conditioner to clear the glass, "then where has she been for this whole year?"

"With Rose Tucker somewhere."

"And why would Rose keep your daughter from you? Why such awful cruelty?"

"It's not cruelty. You hit on the answer yourself, out there on the back porch."

"Why do I suspect the only time you listen to me is when I'm full of shit?"

Joe said, "Somehow, since Nina survived with Rose, survived *because* of Rose, now Rose's enemies will want Nina too. If Nina had been sent home to me, she'd have been a target. Rose is just keeping her safe."

The pearly condensation retreated toward the edges of the windshield.

Barbara switched on the wipers.

From the rear window of the Jeep Cherokee, the Weimaraner still watched them without getting to its feet. Its eyes were luminous amber.

"Rose is keeping her safe," he repeated. "That's why I've got to learn everything I can about Flight 353 and stay alive long enough to find a way to break the story wide open. When it's exposed, when the bastards behind all of this are ruined and on their way to prison or the gas chamber, then Rose will be safe and Nina can . . . she can come back to me."

"If this Nina is your Nina," she reminded him.

"If she is, yes."

Under the somber yellow gaze of the dog, they swung past the Cherokee and circled the oval bed of blue and purple delphiniums around which the terminus of the driveway turned.

"You think we should have asked Mercy to help us find the house in Pueblo where she dropped Rose and the girl that night?" Barbara wondered.

"No point. Nothing there for us. They never went inside that house. As soon as Mercy drove out of sight, they moved on. Rose was just using Mercy to reach the nearest sizable town, where she could get transportation, maybe call a trusted friend in Los Angeles or somewhere. How large is Pueblo?"

"About a hundred thousand people."

"That's large enough. Plenty of ways in and out of a city that size. Bus, maybe train, rental car, even by air."

As they headed down the gravel driveway toward the paved road, Joe saw three men in hooded rain slickers exiting a stable stall beyond an exercise yard. Jeff Ealing, Ned, and the veterinarian.

They left both the lower and the upper halves of the Dutch door standing open. No horse followed them.

Huddled against the downpour, heads bowed as if they were a procession of monks, they moved toward the house. No clairvoyance was required to know that their shoulders were slumped not only under the weight of the storm but under the weight of defeat.

Now a call to the knackery. A beloved mare to be transported and rendered. Another summer afternoon on the Loose Change Ranch—never to be forgotten.

Joe hoped that the years, the toil, and the miscarriages had not caused any distance to open between Jeff and Mercy Ealing. He hoped that in the night they still held each other.

The gray storm light was so dim that Barbara switched on the headlights. In those twin beams, as they reached the paved highway, the silvery rain glittered like flensing knives.

In Colorado Springs, a network of shallow lakes had formed on the grammar-school playground next to which Joe had parked his rental car. In the gray-rinsed light, rising from the rain-dimpled water, the jungle gyms and the seesaws and the elaborate swing sets appeared strange to Joe, not at all like what they were, but like a steel-pipe Stonehenge more mysterious even than the ancient rock megaliths and trilithons on England's Salisbury Plain.

Everywhere he turned his eyes now, this world was different from the one that he had inhabited all his life. The change had begun the previous day, when he'd gone to the cemetery. Ever since, a *shift* seemed to be progressing with gathering power and speed, as though the world of Einsteinian laws had intersected with a universe where the rules of energy and matter were so different as to baffle the wisest mathematicians and the proudest physicists.

This new reality was both more piercingly beautiful and more fearsome than the one that it replaced. He knew the change was subjective and would never reverse itself. Nothing this side of death would ever again seem simple to him; the smoothest surface hid unknowable depths and complexities.

Barbara stopped in the street beside his rental car, two blocks from her house. "Well. I guess this is as far as we go."

"Thank you, Barbara. You've taken such risks—"

"I don't want you to worry about that. You hear me? It was my decision."

"If not for your kindness and your courage, I'd never have had a hope of getting to the bottom of this. Today you've opened a door for me."

"But a door to what?" she worried.

"Maybe to Nina."

Barbara looked weary and frightened and sad. She wiped one hand across her face, and then she looked only frightened and sad.

"Joe, you keep my voice in your head. Wherever you go from here, you remember to listen for me at the back of your mind. I'll be an old nag, telling you that even if two people somehow came out of that crash alive, it's damn unlikely that one of them is your Nina. Don't swing the sword on yourself, don't you be the one to cut yourself off at the knees."

He nodded.

"Promise me," she said.

"Promise."

"She's gone, Joe."

"Maybe."

"Armor your heart."

"We'll see."

"Better go," she said.

He opened the door and got out into the rain.

"Good luck," Barbara said.

"Thanks."

He slammed the door, and she drove away.

As he unlocked his rental car, Joe heard the Explorer's brakes bark less than half a block away. When he looked up, the Ford was reversing toward him, its red taillights shimmering on the slick blacktop.

She got out of the Explorer, came to him, put her arms around him, and held him tight. "You're a dear man, Joe Carpenter."

He embraced her too, but no words came to him. He remembered how badly he had wanted to strike her when she had pressed him to forsake the idea that Nina might be alive. He was ashamed by the hatred that he had felt for her then, ashamed and confused— but he was also touched by her friendship, which meant more to him now than he could have imagined when he first rang her doorbell.

"How can I have known you only a few short hours," she wondered, "and feel as if you're my son?"

She left him for the second time.

He got into his car as she drove away.

He watched the dwindling Explorer in the rearview mirror until it turned left into Barbara's driveway, two blocks behind him, and disappeared into her garage.

Across the street, the white trunks of the paper birches glowed like painted doorjambs, the deep moody shadows between like open doors to futures best left unvisited.

• • •

Soaked, he drove back to Denver with no regard for the speed limit, alternately using the heater and the air conditioner, trying to dry out his clothes.

He was electrified by the prospect of finding Nina.

In spite of what he had said to Barbara, in spite of what he had promised her, he knew that Nina was alive. One thing in this eerily altered world seemed absolutely right again at last: Nina alive, Nina out there somewhere. She was a warm light upon his skin, a spectrum of light beyond the ability of his eyes to detect, as were infrared and ultraviolet, but though he could not see her, he could feel her shining in the world.

This wasn't at all similar to the portentous feeling that had so often sent him spiraling into searching behavior, chasing after ghosts. This hope was rock under his hand, not mist.

He was as close to happiness as he had been in more than a year, but each time that his heart swelled too full with excitement, his mood was dampened by a pang of guilt. Even if he found Nina—*when* he found Nina—he would not also regain Michelle and Chrissie. They were gone forever, and it seemed callous of him to be too happy about reclaiming only one of three.

Nevertheless, the desire to learn the truth, which had motivated him to come to Colorado, was the tiniest fraction as powerful as the wrenching need to find his younger daughter, which now raged in him to a degree beyond the measurements used to define mere compulsion or obsession.

At Denver International Airport, he returned the car to the agency, paid the bill in cash, and retrieved his signed credit-card form. He was in the terminal again fifty minutes before his flight was scheduled to depart.

He was starving. But for two cookies in Mercy's kitchen, he had eaten nothing since the two cheeseburgers the previous evening on his way to the Vadance house and later a chocolate bar.

He found the nearest restaurant in the terminal. He ordered a club sandwich with french fries and a bottle of Heineken.

Bacon had never tasted half as good as it did now. He licked mayonnaise from his fingertips. The fries had a satisfying crunch, and the crisp dill pickle snapped with a spray of sour juice. For the first time since another August, he not only consumed his food but *relished* it.

On his way to the boarding gate, with twenty minutes to spare, he suddenly took a detour to the men's room. He thought he was going to be sick.

By the time he got into a stall and latched the door, his nausea passed. Instead of throwing up, he leaned his back against the door and wept.

He hadn't cried in many months, and he didn't know why he was crying now. Maybe because he was on the trembling edge of happiness with the thought of seeing Nina again. Or maybe because he was scared of never finding her or of losing her a second time. Maybe he was grieving anew for Michelle and Chrissie. Maybe he had learned too many dreadful details about what had happened to Flight 353 and to the people on it.

Maybe it was all those things.

He was on a runaway rocket of emotion, and he needed to regain control of himself. He wasn't going to be effective in his search for Rose and Nina if he swung wildly between euphoria and despair.

Red-eyed but recovered, he boarded the plane for Los Angeles as they issued the final call.

As the 737 took off, to Joe's surprise his heart made a hollow racket in his ears, like running footsteps descending stairs. He clutched the arms of his seat as though he might tumble forward and fall headlong.

He hadn't been afraid on the flight to Denver, but now he was in the lap of terror. Coming eastward, he would have welcomed death, for the wrongness of outliving his family had been heavy on his mind—but now, westward bound, he had a reason to live.

Even when they had reached cruising altitude and leveled off, he remained edgy. He could too easily imagine one of the pilots turning to the other and saying, *Are we recording?*

Since Joe could not get Captain Delroy Blane out of his mind anyway, he withdrew the three folded pages of the transcript from an inner jacket pocket. Reviewing it, he might see something that he had missed before—and he needed to keep his mind occupied, even if with this.

The flight wasn't heavily booked, a third of the seats empty. He had a window seat with no immediate neighbor, so he was afforded the privacy he needed.

In response to his request, a flight attendant brought a pen and note pad.

As he read through the transcript, he extracted Blane's dialogue and printed it on the note pad. Standing apart from First Officer Victor Santorelli's increasingly frantic statements and shorn of Barbara's descriptions of sounds and pauses, the captain's words might allow for the discovery of nuances otherwise not easy to spot.

When he was done, Joe folded the transcript and returned it to his coat pocket. Then he read from the note pad:

> *One of their names is Dr. Louis Blom.*
>
> *One of their names is Dr. Keith Ramlock.*
>
> *They're doing bad things to me.*
>
> *They're mean to me.*
>
> *Make them stop.*
>
> *Are we recording?*
>
> *Make them stop hurting me.*
>
> *Are we recording?*
>
> *Are we recording?*
>
> *Make them stop or when I get the chance . . . when I get the chance, I'll kill everybody. Everybody. I will. I'll do it. I'll kill everybody, and I'll like it.*
>
> *This is fun.*
>
> *Whoooaaa. Here we go, Dr. Ramlock. Dr. Blom, here we go.*
>
> *Whoooaaa. Are we recording?*
>
> *Are we recording?*
>
> *Oh, wow.*
>
> *Oh, yeah.*
>
> *Oh, yeah.*
>
> *Now. Look.*
>
> *Cool.*

Joe didn't see anything new in the material, but something he had noticed before was more obvious when Blane's dialogue was read in this extracted format. Although the captain was speaking in the voice of an adult, some of the things he was saying had a distinct childlike quality.

They're doing bad things to me. They're mean to me. Make them stop. Make them stop hurting me.

This was neither the phrasing nor the word choice most adults would use to accuse tormentors or to ask for help.

His longest speech, a threat to kill everybody *and like it*, was petulant and childish as well—especially when immediately followed by the observation *This is fun.*

Whoooaaa. Here we go . . . Whoooaaa. Oh, wow. Oh, yeah.

Blane's reaction to the roll and plunge of the 747 was like that of a boy thrilling to the arrival of a roller coaster at the crown of the first hill on the track and, then, to the first stomach-rolling drop. According to Barbara, the captain had sounded unafraid; and there was no more terror in his words than in his tone of voice.

Now. Look.

Those words were spoken three and a half seconds before impact, as Blane watched the nightscape bloom like a black rose beyond the windscreen. He seemed gripped not by fear but by a sense of wonder.

Cool.

Joe stared at that final word for a long time, until the shiver it caused had passed, until he could consider all the implications of it with a measure of detachment.

Cool.

To the end, Blane reacted like a boy on an amusement-park ride. He had exhibited no more concern for his passengers and crew than a thoughtless and arrogant child might exhibit for the insects that he tortured with matches.

Cool.

Even a thoughtless child, as selfish as only the very young and the incurably immature can be, would nonetheless have shown some fear for *himself*. Even a determinedly suicidal man, having leaped off a high ledge, would cry out in mortal fear if not regret as he hurtled toward the pavement. Yet this captain, in whatever altered state he occupied, watched oblivion approach with no apparent concern, even with delight, as though he recognized no physical threat to himself.

Cool.

Delroy Blane. Family man. Faithful husband. Devout Mormon. Stable, loving, kind, compassionate. Successful, happy, healthy. Everything to live for. Cleared by the toxicological tests.

What's wrong with this picture?

Cool.

A useless anger rose in Joe. It was not aimed at Blane, who surely was a victim too—though he didn't initially appear to be one. This was the simmering anger of his childhood and adolescence, undirected and therefore likely to swell like the ever-hotter steam in a boiler with no pressure-release valve.

He tucked the note pad into his jacket pocket.

His hands curled into fists. Unclenching them was difficult. He wanted to strike something. Anything. Until he broke it. Until his knuckles split and bled.

This blind anger always reminded Joe of his father.

Frank Carpenter had not been an angry person. The opposite. He never raised his voice in other than amusement and surprise and happy exclamation. He was a good man—inexplicably good and oddly optimistic, considering the suffering with which fate saddled him.

Joe, however, had been perpetually angry *for* him.

He could not remember his dad with two legs. Frank had lost the left one when his car was broadsided by a pickup truck driven by a nineteen-year-old drunk with lapsed insurance. Joe was not yet three years old at the time.

Frank and Donna, Joe's mother, had been married with little more than two paychecks and their work clothes. To save money, they carried only liability coverage with their car. The drunk driver had no assets, and they received no compensation from any insurance company for the loss of the limb.

The leg was amputated halfway between knee and hip. In those days there were no highly effective prostheses. Besides, a false leg with any sort of functioning knee was expensive. Frank became so agile and quick with one leg and a crutch that he joked about entering a marathon.

Joe had never been ashamed of his father's difference. He knew his dad not as a one-legged man with a peculiar lurching gait, but as a bedtime storyteller, an indefatigable player of Uncle Wiggly and other games, a patient softball coach.

The first serious fight he'd gotten into was when he was six, in first grade. A kid named Les Olner had referred to Frank as a "stupid cripple." Although Olner was a bully and bigger than Joe, his superior size was an insufficient advantage against the savage animal fury with which he was confronted. Joe beat the shit out of him. His intention was to put out Olner's right eye, so he would know what it was like to live with one of two, but a teacher pulled him off the battered kid before he could half blind him.

Afterward, he felt no remorse. He still felt none. He was not proud of this. It was just the way he felt.

Donna knew that her husband's heart would break a little if he learned his boy had gotten into trouble over him. She devised and enforced Joe's punishment herself, and together they concealed the incident from Frank.

That was the beginning of Joe's secret life of quiet rage and periodic violence. He grew up looking for a fight and usually finding one, but he chose the moment and the venue to ensure that his dad was unlikely to learn of it.

Frank was a roofer, but there was no scrambling up ladders and hustling from eaves to ridgeline with one leg. He was loath to take disability from the government, but he accepted it for a while, until he found a way to turn a talent for woodworking into an occupation.

He made jewelry boxes, lamp bases, and other items inlaid with exotic woods in intricate patterns, and he found shops that would carry his creations. For a while he cleared a few dollars more than the disability payments, which he relinquished.

A seamstress in a combination tailor's shop and dry cleaner, Donna came home from work every day with hair curled from the steam-press humidity and smelling of benzine and other liquid solvents. To this day, when Joe entered a dry-cleaning establishment, his first breath brought vividly to mind his mother's hair and her honey-brown eyes, which as a child he'd thought were faded from a darker brown by steam and chemicals.

Three years after losing the leg, Frank began suffering pain in his knuckles and then his wrists. The diagnosis was rheumatoid arthritis.

A vicious thing, this disease. And in Frank, it progressed with uncommon speed, a fire spreading through him: the spinal joints in his neck, his shoulders, hips, his one remaining knee.

He shut down his woodworking business. There were government programs providing assistance, though never enough and always with the measure of humiliation that bureaucrats dished out with a hateful—and often unconscious—generosity.

The Church helped too, and charity from the local parish was more compassionately provided and less humbling to receive. Frank and Donna were Catholics. Joe went to Mass with them faithfully but without faith.

In two years, already hampered by the loss of one leg, Frank was in a wheelchair.

Medical knowledge has advanced dramatically in thirty years, but in those days, treatments were less effective than they are now—especially in cases as severe as Frank's. Nonsteroidal anti-inflammatory drugs, injections of gold salts, and then much later penicillamine. Still the osteoporosis progressed. More cartilage and tendon tissue were lost from the chronic inflammation. Muscles continued to atrophy. Joints ached and swelled.

The immunosuppressant corticosteroids available at the time somewhat slowed but did not halt the deformation of joints, the frightening loss of function.

By the time Joe was thirteen, his daily routine included helping his dad dress and bathe when his mother was at work. From the first, he never resented any tasks that fell to him; to his surprise, he found within himself a tenderness that was a counterweight to the omnipresent anger that he directed at God but that he inadequately relieved on those unlucky boys with whom he periodically picked fights. For a long time Frank was mortified to have to rely on his son for such private matters, but eventually the shared challenge of bathing, grooming, and toilet brought them closer, deepened their feelings for each other.

By the time Joe was sixteen, Frank was suffering with fibrousankylosis. Huge rheumatoid nodules had formed at several joints, including one the size of a golf ball on his right wrist. His left elbow was deformed by a nodule almost as large as the softball that he had thrown so many hundreds of times in backyard practices when Joe had been six years old and getting into Little League.

His dad lived now for Joe's achievements, so Joe was an honor student in spite of a part-time job at McDonald's. He was a star quarterback on the high-school football team. Frank never put any pressure on him to excel. Love motivated Joe.

In the summer of that year, he joined the YMCA Youth Athletics Program: the boxing league. He was quick to learn, and the coach liked him, said he had talent. But in his first two practice matches, he continued hammering punches into opponents after they were sagging on the ropes, beaten and defenseless. He'd had to be pulled off. To them, boxing was recreation and self-defense, but to Joe it was savage therapy. He didn't want to hurt anyone, not any specific individual, but he *did* hurt people; consequently, he was not permitted to compete in the league.

Frank's chronic pericarditis, arising from the rheumatoid arthritis, led to a virulent infection of the pericardium, which ultimately led to heart failure. Frank died two days before Joe's eighteenth birthday.

The week following the funeral Mass, Joe visited the church after midnight, when it was deserted. He'd had too many beers. He sprayed black paint on all the stations of the cross. He overturned a cast-stone statue of Our Lady and smashed a score of the ruby-red glasses from the votive-candle rack.

He might have done considerably more damage if he had not quickly been overcome by a sense of futility. He could not teach remorse to God. He could not express his pain with sufficient power to penetrate the steel veil between this world and the next—if there was a next.

Slumping in the front pew, he wept.

He sat there less than a minute, however, because suddenly he felt that weeping in the church might seem to be an admission of his powerlessness. Ludicrously, he thought it important that his tears not be misconstrued as an acceptance of the cruelty with which the universe was ruled.

He left the church and was never apprehended for the vandalism. He felt no guilt about what he'd done—and, again, no pride.

For a while he was crazy, and then he went to college, where he fit in because half of the student body was crazy too, with youth, and the faculty with tenure.

His mother died just three years later, at the age of forty-seven. Lung cancer, spreading to the lymphatic system. She had never been a smoker. Neither had his father. Maybe it was the fumes of the benzine and other solvents in the dry cleaner's shop. Maybe it was weariness, loneliness, and a way out.

The night she died, Joe sat at her bedside in the hospital, holding her hand, putting cold compresses on her brow, and slipping slivers of ice into her parched mouth when she asked for them, while she spoke sporadically, half coherently, about a Knights of Columbus dinner dance to which Frank had taken her when Joe was only two, the year before the accident and amputation. There was a big band with eighteen fine musicians, playing genuine dance music, not just shake-in-place rock-'n'-roll. She and Frank were self-taught in the fox-trot, swing, and the cha-cha, but they weren't bad. They knew each other's moves. How they laughed. There were balloons, oh, hundreds of balloons, suspended in a net from the ceiling. The centerpiece on each table was a white plastic swan holding a fat candle surrounded by red chrysanthemums. Dessert was ice cream in a sugar swan. It was a night of swans. The balloons were red and white, hundreds of them. Holding her close in a slow dance, he whispered in her ear that she was the most beautiful woman in the room, and oh, how he loved her. A revolving ballroom chandelier cast off splinters of colored light, the balloons came down, red and white, and the sugar swan tasted of almonds when it crunched between the teeth. She was twenty-nine years old the night of the dance, and she relished this memory and no other through the final hour of her life, as though it had been the last good time she could recall.

Joe buried her from the same church that he had vandalized three years earlier. The stations of the cross had been restored. A new statue of the Holy Mother watched over a full complement of votive glasses on the tiered rack.

Later, he expressed his grief in a bar fight. His nose was broken, but he did worse damage to the other guy.

He stayed crazy until he met Michelle.

On their first date, as he had returned her to her apartment, she had told him that he had a wild streak a foot wide. When he'd taken that as a compliment, she had told him that only a moron, a hormone-crazed pubescent boy, or an ape in the zoo would be witless enough to take pride in it.

Thereafter, by her example, she taught him everything that was to shape his future. That love was worth the risk of loss. That anger harms no one more than he who harbors it. That both bitterness and true happiness are choices that we make, not conditions that fall upon us from the hands of fate. That peace is to be found in the acceptance of things that we are unable to change. That friends and family are the blood of life, and that the purpose of existence is caring, commitment.

Six days before their wedding, in the evening, Joe went alone to the church from which he'd buried his parents. Having calculated the cost of the damage he'd done years before, he stuffed a wad of hundred-dollar bills into the poor box.

He made the contribution neither because of guilt nor because his faith was regained. He did it for Michelle, though she would never know of the vandalism or of this act of restitution.

Thereafter, his life had begun.

And then ended one year ago.

Now Nina was in the world again, waiting to be found, waiting to be brought home.

With the hope of finding Nina as balm, Joe was able to take the heat out of his anger. To recover Nina, he must be totally in control of himself.

Anger harms no one more than he who harbors it.

He was ashamed by how quickly and absolutely he had turned away from all the lessons that Michelle had taught him. With the fall of Flight 353, he too had fallen, had plummeted out of the sky into which Michelle had lifted him with her love, and had returned to the mud of bitterness. His collapse was a dishonor to her, and now he felt a sting of guilt as sharp as he might have felt if he'd betrayed her with another woman.

Nina, mirror of her mother, offered him the reason and the chance to rebuild himself into a reflection of the person he had been before the crash. He could become again a man worthy of being her father.

Nine-ah, Neen-ah, have you seen her?

He leafed slowly through his treasure trove of mental images of Nina, and the effect was soothing. Gradually, his clenched hands relaxed.

He began the last hour of the flight by reading two of the four printouts of articles about Teknologik that he had retrieved from the *Post* computer the previous afternoon.

In the second, he came upon a piece of information that stunned him. Thirty-nine percent of Teknologik's stock, the largest single block, was owned by Nellor et Fils, a Swiss holding company with extensive and diverse interests in drug research, medical research, medical publishing, general publishing, and the film and broadcasting industries.

Nellor et Fils was the principal vehicle by which Horton Nellor and his son, Andrew, invested the family fortune, which was thought to be in excess of four billion dollars. Nellor was not Swiss, of course, but American. He had taken his base of operations offshore a long time ago. And more than twenty years ago, Horton Nellor had founded the *Los Angeles Post*. He still owned it.

For a while, Joe fingered his astonishment as though he were a whittler with an intriguingly shaped piece of driftwood, trying to decide how best to carve it. As in raw wood, something waited here to be discovered by the craftsman's hand; his knives were his mind and his journalistic instinct.

Horton Nellor's investments were widespread, so it might mean nothing whatsoever that he owned pieces of both Teknologik and the *Post*. Probably pure coincidence.

He owned the *Post* outright and was not an absentee publisher concerned only about profit; through his son, he exerted control over the editorial philosophy and the reportorial policies of the newspaper. He might not be so intimately involved, however, with Teknologik, Inc. His stake in that corporation was large but not in itself a controlling interest, so perhaps he was not engaged in the day-to-day operations, treating it only as a stock investment.

In that case, he was not necessarily personally aware of the top-secret research Rose Tucker and her associates had undertaken. And he was not necessarily carrying any degree of responsibility for the destruction of Flight 353.

Joe recalled his encounter the previous afternoon with Dan Shavers, the business-page columnist at the *Post*. Shavers pungently characterized the Teknologik executives: *infamous self-aggrandizers, think of themselves as some kind of business royalty, but they are no better than us. They, too, answer to He Who Must Be Obeyed.*

He Who Must Be Obeyed. Horton Nellor. Reviewing the rest of the brief conversation, Joe realized that Shavers had assumed that Joe knew of Nellor's interest in Teknologik. And the columnist seemed to have been implying that Nellor asserted his will at Teknologik no less than he did at the *Post*.

Joe also flashed back to something Lisa Peccatone had said in the kitchen at the Delmann house when the relationship between Rose Tucker and Teknologik was mentioned: *You and me and Rosie all connected. Small world, huh?*

At the time, he had thought she was referring to the fact that Flight 353 had become a spring point in the arcs of all their lives. Maybe what she really meant was that all of them worked for the same man.

Joe had never met Horton Nellor, who had become something of a recluse over the years. He'd seen photographs, of course. The billionaire, now in his late sixties, was silver-haired and round-faced, with pleasing if somewhat blurred features. He looked like a muffin on which, with icing, a baker had painted a grandfather face.

He did not appear to be a killer. He was known as a generous philanthropist. His reputation was not that of a man who would hire assassins or condone murder in the maintenance or expansion of his empire.

Human beings, however, were different from apples and oranges: The flavor of the peel did not reliably predict the taste of the pulp.

The fact remained that Joe and Michelle had worked for the same man as those who now wanted to kill Rose Tucker and who—in some as yet incomprehensible manner—had evidently destroyed Nationwide 353. The money that had long supported his family was the same money that had financed their murders.

His response to this revelation was so complexly tangled that he could not quickly unknot it, so dark that he could not easily see the entire shape of it.

Greasy fingers of nausea seined his guts.

Although he stared out the window for perhaps half an hour, he was not aware of the desert surrendering to the suburbs or the suburbs to the city. He was surprised when he realized that they were descending toward LAX.

On the ground, as they taxied to the assigned gate and as the telescoping mobile corridor was linked like an umbilical between the 737 and the terminal, Joe checked his wristwatch, considered the distance to Westwood, and calculated that he would be at least half an hour early for his meeting with Demi. Perfect. He wanted enough time to scope the meeting place from across the street and a block away before committing himself to it.

Demi should be reliable. She was Rose's friend. He had gotten her number from the message that Rose had left for him at the *Post*. But he wasn't in the mood to trust anyone.

After all, even if Rose Tucker's motives had been pure, even if she had kept Nina with her to prevent Teknologik from killing or kidnapping the girl, she had nevertheless withheld Joe's daughter from him for a year. Worse, she had allowed him to go on thinking that Nina—like Michelle and Chrissie—was dead. For reasons that he could not yet know, perhaps Rose would *never* want to return his little girl to him.

Trust no one.

As he got up from his seat and started forward toward the exit, he noticed a man in white slacks, white shirt, and white Panama hat rise from a seat farther forward in the cabin and glance back at him. The guy was about fifty, stockily built, with a thick mane of white hair that made him look like an aging rock star, especially under that hat.

This was no stranger.

For an instant, Joe thought that perhaps the man was, in fact, a lowercase celebrity—a musician in a famous band or a character actor from television. Then he was certain that he had seen him not on screen or stage but elsewhere, recently, and in significant circumstances.

Mr. Panama looked away from him after a fraction of a second of eye contact, stepped into the aisle, and moved forward. Like Joe, he was not burdened by any carry-on luggage, as though he had been on a day trip.

Eight or ten passengers were between the day-tripper and Joe. He was afraid he would lose track of his quarry before he figured out where he had previously seen him. He couldn't push along the narrow aisle past the intervening passengers without causing a commotion, however, and he preferred not to let Mr. Panama know that he had been spotted.

When Joe tried to use the distinctive hat as a prod to memory, he came up blank, but when he pictured the man without the hat and focused on the flowing white hair, he thought of the blue-robed cult members with the shaven heads. The connection eluded him, seemed absurd.

Then he thought of the bonfire around which the cultists had been standing last night on the beach, where he had disposed of the McDonald's bag that contained the Kleenex damp with Charlie Delmann's blood. And the lithe dancers in bathing suits around another bonfire. A third fire and the gathering of surfers inside the totemic ring of their upended boards. And still another fire, around which sat a dozen enthralled listeners as a stocky man with a broad charismatic face and a mane of white hair narrated a ghost story in a reverberant voice.

This man. The storyteller.

Joe had no doubt that they were one and the same.

He also knew there was no chance whatsoever that he had crossed this man's path on the beach last night and again here sheerly by chance. All is intimately interwoven in this most conspiratorial of all worlds.

They must have been conducting surveillance on him for weeks or months, waiting for Rose to contact him, when he had finally become aware of them on Santa Monica Beach, Saturday morning. During that time they had learned all his haunts, which were not numerous: the apartment, a couple of coffee shops, the cemetery, and a few favorite beaches where he went to learn indifference from the sea.

After he had disabled Wallace Blick, invaded their van, and then fled the cemetery, they had lost him. He had found the transponder on his car and thrown it into the passing gardener's truck, and they had lost him. They'd almost caught up with him again at the *Post*, but he'd slipped away minutes ahead of them.

So they had staked out his apartment, the coffee shops, the beaches—waiting for him to show up somewhere. The group being entertained by the ghost story had been ordinary civilians, but the storyteller who had insinuated himself into their gathering was not in the least ordinary.

They had picked Joe up once more the past night on the beach. He knew the correct surveillance jargon: They had *reacquired* him on the beach. Followed him to the convenience store from which he had telephoned Mario Oliveri in Denver and Barbara in Colorado Springs. Followed him to his motel.

They could have killed him there. Quietly. While he slept or after waking him with a gun to his head. They could have made it look like a drug overdose—or like suicide.

In the heat of the moment, they had been eager to shoot him down at the cemetery, but they were no longer in a hurry to see him dead. Because maybe, just maybe, he would lead them again to Rose Marie Tucker.

Evidently they weren't aware that he had been at the Delmann house, among other places, during the hours when they had lost contact with him. If they knew he'd seen what had happened to the Delmanns and to Lisa—even though he could not understand it— they probably would terminate him. Take no chances. Terminate him "with extreme prejudice," as their kind phrased it.

During the night, they had placed another tracking device on his car. In the hour before dawn, they followed him to LAX, always at a distance where they were in no danger of being spotted. Then to Denver and perhaps beyond.

Jesus.

What had frightened the deer in the woods?

Joe felt stupid and careless, although he knew that he was not either. He couldn't expect to be as good at this game as they were; he'd never played it before, but they played it every day.

He was getting better, though. He was getting better.

Farther up the aisle, the storyteller reached the exit door and disappeared into the debarkation umbilical.

Joe was afraid of losing his stalker, but it was imperative that they continue to believe that he was unaware of them.

Barbara Christman was in terrible danger. First thing, he had to find a phone and warn her.

Faking patience and boredom, he shuffled forward with the other passengers. In the umbilical, which was much wider than the aisle in the airplane, he finally slipped past them without appearing to be alarmed or in a hurry. He didn't realize that he was holding his breath until he exhaled hard with relief when he spotted his quarry ahead of him.

The huge terminal was busy. At the gates, the ranks of chairs were filled with passengers waiting to catch a late-afternoon flight in the fast-fading hours of the weekend. Chattering, laughing, arguing, brooding in silence, shuffling-striding-strolling-limping-ambling, arriving passengers poured out of other gates and along the concourse. There were singles, couples, entire families, blacks and whites and Asians and Latinos and four towering Samoan men, all with black porkpie hats, beautiful sloe-eyed women, willow graceful in their turquoise or ruby or sapphire saris, others in chadors and others in jeans, men in business suits, men in shorts and bright polo shirts, four young Hasidic Jews arguing (but joyfully) over the most mystical of all documents (a Los Angeles freeway map), uniformed soldiers, giggling children and shrieking children and two placid octogenarians in wheelchairs, a pair of tall Arab princes in akals and kaffiyehs and flowing djellabas, preceded by fierce bodyguards and trailed by retinues, beacon-red tourists drifting home-ward on the astringent fumes of medicated sunburn lotion, pale tourists arriving with the dampish smell of cloudy country clinging to them—and, like a white boat strangely serene in a typhoon, the man in the Panama hat, sailing imperiously through the polygenic sea.

As far as Joe was concerned, they might all be stage dressing, every one of them an agent of Teknologik or of institutions unknown, all watching him surreptitiously, snap-ping photographs of him with trick cameras concealed in their purses and attaché cases and tote bags, all conferring by hidden microphones as to whether he should be permitted to proceed or be gunned down on the spot.

He had never before felt so alone in a crowd.

Dreading what might happen—might even now *be* happening—to Barbara, he tried to keep the storyteller in sight while also searching for a telephone.

PART FOUR

PALE FIRE

▼

THIRTEEN

The public telephone, one in a cluster of four, was not in a booth, but the wings of a sound shield provided a small measure of privacy.

As he entered Barbara's Colorado Springs number on the keypad, Joe ground his teeth together as though he could bite off the noise of the crowded terminal and chew it into a silence that would allow him to concentrate. He needed to think through what he would say to her, but he had neither the time nor the solitude to craft the ideal speech, and he was afraid of committing a blunder that would pitch her deeper into trouble.

Even if her phone had not been tapped the previous evening, it was surely being monitored now, following his visit to her. His task was to warn her of the danger while simultaneously convincing the eavesdroppers that she had never broken the pledge of silence that would keep her and Denny safe.

As the telephone began to ring in Colorado, Joe glanced toward the storyteller, who had taken up a position farther along—and on the opposite side of—the concourse. He was standing outside the entrance to an airport newsstand and gift shop, nervously adjusting his Panama hat, and conversing with a Hispanic man in tan chinos, a green madras shirt, and a Dodgers cap.

Through the screen of passing travelers, Joe pretended not to watch the two men while they pretended, less convincingly, not to watch him. They were less circumspect than they should have been, because they were overconfident. Although they might give him credit for being industrious and clever, they thought that he was basically a jerk civilian in fast-running water way over his head.

He was exactly what they thought him to be, of course, but he hoped he was also more than they believed. A man driven by paternal love—and therefore dangerous. A man with a passion for justice that was alien to their world of situational ethics, in which the only morals were the morals of convenience.

Barbara answered the phone on the fifth ring, just as Joe was beginning to despair.

"It's me, Joe Carpenter," he said.

"I was just—"

Before Barbara could say anything that might reveal the extent of the revelations she'd made to him, Joe said, "Listen, I wanted to thank you again for taking me to the crash site. It wasn't easy, but it was something I had to do, had to see, if I was ever going to have any peace. I'm sorry if I badgered you about what *really* happened to that airplane. I was a little crazy, I guess. A couple of odd things have happened lately, and I just let my imagination run wild. You were right when you said most of the time things are exactly what they appear to be. It's just hard to accept that you can lose your family to anything as stupid as an accident, mechanical failure, human error, whatever. You feel like it just *has* to be a lot more significant than an accident because . . . well, because *they* were so significant to you. You know? You think there have to be villains somewhere, that it can't be just fate, because *God* wouldn't allow this to happen. But you started me thinking when you said the only place there's always villains is in the movies. If I'm going to get over this, I'm going to have to accept that these things just happen, that no one's to blame. Life is risk, right? God *does* let innocent people die, lets children die. It's that simple."

Joe was tense, waiting to hear what she would say, whether she had understood the urgent message that he was striving to convey so indirectly.

After a brief hesitation, Barbara said, "I hope you find peace, Joe, I really do. It took a lot of guts for you to go out there, right to the impact site. And it takes guts to face the fact that there's no one to blame in the end. As long as you're stuck in the idea that there's someone who's guilty of something, someone who's got to be brought to justice . . . well, then you're full of vengeance, and you're not healing."

She understood.

Joe closed his eyes and tried to gather his unraveled nerves into a tight bundle again.

He said, "It's just . . . we live in such weird times. It's easy to believe in vast conspiracies."

"Easier than facing hard truths. Your real argument isn't with the pilots or the maintenance crew. It isn't with the air-traffic controllers or with the people who built the airplane. Your real argument's with God."

"Which I can't win," he said, opening his eyes.

In front of the newsstand, the storyteller and the Dodgers fan finished their conversation. The storyteller departed.

"We're not supposed to understand why," Barbara said. "We just have to have faith that there's a reason. If you can learn to accept that, then you really might find peace. You're a very nice man, Joe. You don't deserve to be in such torment. I'll be praying for you."

"Thanks, Barbara. Thanks for everything."

"Good luck, Joe."

He almost wished her good luck as well, but those two words might be a tip-off to whoever was listening.

Instead, he said, "Good-bye."

Still hummingbird tense, he hung up.

Simply by going to Colorado and knocking on Barbara's door, he had put her, her son, and her son's entire family in terrible jeopardy—although he'd had no way of knowing this would be the consequence of his visit. Anything might happen to her now—or nothing—and Joe felt a chill of blame coil around his heart.

On the other hand, by going to Colorado, he had learned that Nina was miraculously alive. He was willing to take the moral responsibility for a hundred deaths in return for the mere hope of seeing her again.

He was aware of how monstrous it was to regard the life of his daughter as more precious than the lives of any hundred strangers—two hundred, a thousand. He didn't care. He would kill to save her, if that was the extreme to which he was driven. Kill anyone who got in his way. Any number.

Wasn't it the human dilemma to dream of being part of the larger community but, in the face of everlasting death, always to operate on personal and family imperatives? And he was, after all, too human.

Joe left the public telephones and followed the concourse toward the exit. As he reached the head of the escalators, he contrived to glance back.

The Dodgers fan followed at a discreet distance, well disguised by the ordinariness of his dress and demeanor. He wove himself into the crowd so skillfully that he was no more evident than any single thread in a coat of many colors.

Down the escalator and through the lower floor of the terminal, Joe did not look back again. Either the Dodgers fan would be there or he would have handed Joe over to another agent, as the storyteller had done.

Given their formidable resources, they would have a substantial contingent of operatives at the airport. He could never escape them here.

He had exactly an hour until he had to meet Demi, who he hoped would take him to Rose Tucker. If he didn't make the rendezvous in time, he had no way to reestablish contact with the woman.

His wristwatch seemed to be ticking as loudly as a grandfather clock.

• • •

Tortured faces melted into the mutant forms of strange animals and nightmare landscapes in the Rorschach stains on the walls of the vast, drab concrete parking structure. Engine noise from cars in other aisles, on other levels, echoed like a Grendel grumble through these man-made caverns.

His Honda was where he'd left it.

Although most of the vehicles in the garage were cars, three vans—none white—an old Volkswagen minibus with curtained windows, and a pickup truck with a camper shell were parked near enough to him to serve as surveillance posts. He didn't give any of them a second look.

He opened the car trunk, and using his body to block the view of any onlooker, he quickly checked the spare-tire well for the money. He had taken two thousand to Colorado, but he had left the bulk of his funds in the Honda. He was afraid the bank's manila envelope with the brass clasp would be gone, but it was where he'd left it.

He slipped the envelope under the waistband of his jeans. He considered taking the small suitcase as well, but if he transferred it to the front seat, the people watching him would not be suckered by the little drama he had planned for them.

In the driver's seat, he took the envelope out of his waistband, opened it, and tucked the packets of hundred-dollar bills in the various pockets of his corduroy jacket. He folded the empty envelope and put it in the console box.

When he backed out of the parking space and drove away, none of the suspect vehicles followed him immediately. They didn't need to be quick. Hidden somewhere on the Honda, another transponder was sending the surveillance team a signal that made constant visual contact unnecessary.

He drove down three levels to the exit. Departing vehicles were lined up at the cashiers' booths.

As he inched forward, he repeatedly checked his rearview mirror. Just as he reached the cashier, he saw the pickup with the camper shell pull into line six cars behind him.

Driving away from the airport, he held his speed slightly below the legal limit and made no effort to beat traffic lights as they turned yellow ahead of him. He didn't want to put too much distance between himself and his pursuers.

Preferring surface streets rather than the freeways, he headed toward the west side of the city. Block by block through a seedy commercial district, he searched for a setup that would serve his purposes.

The summer day was warm and clear, and the sunshine was diffused in matching parabolic rainbow arcs across the dirty windshield. The soapy washer spray and the wipers cleared the glass somewhat but not sufficiently.

Squinting through the glare, Joe almost failed to give the used-car dealership due consideration. Gem Fittich Auto Sales. Sunday was a car-shopping day, and the lot was open, though perhaps not for long. Realizing that this was precisely what he needed, he pulled to the right-hand curb and stopped half a block past the place.

He was in front of a transmission-repair shop. The business was housed in a badly maintained stucco and corrugated-steel building that appeared to have been blown *together* by a capricious tornado, using parts of several other structures that it had previously torn asunder. Fortunately, the shop was closed; he didn't want any good-Samaritan mechanics coming to his rescue.

He shut off the engine and got out of the Honda.

The pickup with the camper shell was not yet within sight on the street behind him.

He hurried to the front of the car and opened the hood.

The Honda was of no use to him anymore. This time they would have concealed the transponder so well that he would need hours to find it. He couldn't drive it to Westwood and lead them to Rose, but he couldn't simply abandon it, either, because then they would know that he was onto them.

He needed to disable the Honda in such a fashion that it would appear to be not sabotage but genuine mechanical failure. Eventually the people following him would open the hood, and if they spotted missing spark plugs or a disconnected distributor cap, they would know that they had been tricked.

Then Barbara Christman would be in deeper trouble than ever. They would realize that Joe had recognized the storyteller on the airplane, that he knew they'd been following him in Colorado—and that everything he'd said to Barbara on the phone had been designed to warn her and to convince them that she had not told him anything important when, in fact, she had told him everything.

He carefully unplugged the ignition control module but left it sitting loosely in its case. A casual inspection would not reveal that it was disengaged. Even if later they searched until they found the problem, they were more likely to assume that the ICM had worked loose on its own rather than that Joe had fiddled with it. At least they would be left with the element of doubt, affording Barbara some protection.

The pickup with the camper shell drove past him.

He didn't look directly at the truck but recognized it from the corner of his eye.

For a minute or two he pretended to study various things in the engine compartment. Poking this. Wiggling that. Scratching his head.

Leaving the hood up, he got behind the wheel again and tried to start the Honda, but of course he had no luck.

He got out of the car and went to look at the engine again.

Peripherally, he saw that the camper truck had turned off the street at the end of the block. It had stopped in the shallow parking area in front of an empty industrial building that featured a real-estate agency's large *For Sale* sign on the front.

He studied the engine another minute, cursing it with energy and color, just in case they had directional microphones trained on him.

Finally he slammed the hood and looked worriedly at his watch. He stood indecisively for a moment. Consulted his watch again. He said, "Shit."

He walked back the street in the direction he had come. When he arrived at the used-car lot, he hesitated for effect, then walked directly to the sales office.

Gem Fittich Auto Sales operated under numerous crisscrossing stringers of yellow and white and red plastic pennants faded by a summer of sun. In the breeze, they snapped like the flapping wings of a perpetually hovering flock of buzzards over more than thirty cars that ranged from good stock to steel carrion.

The office was in a small prefab building painted yellow with red trim. Through the large picture window, Joe could see a man lounging in a spring-back chair, watching a small television, loafer-clad feet propped on a desk.

As he climbed the two steps and went through the open doorway, he heard a sportscaster doing color commentary on a baseball game.

The building consisted of a single large room with a rest room in one corner, visible beyond the half-open door. The two desks, the four chairs, and the bank of metal file cabinets were cheap, but everything was clean and neatly kept.

Joe had been hoping for dust, clutter, and a sense of quiet desperation.

The fortyish salesman was cheery-looking, sandy-haired, wearing tan cotton slacks and a yellow polo shirt. He swung his feet off the desk, got up from his chair, and offered his hand. "Howdy! Didn't hear you drive up. I'm Gem Fittich."

Shaking his hand, Joe said, "Joe Carpenter. I need a car."

"You came to the right place." Fittich reached toward the portable television that stood on his desk.

"No, that's okay, leave it on," Joe said.

"You're a fan, you might not want to see this one. They're getting their butts kicked."

Right now the transmission-repair shop next door blocked them from the surveillance team. If the camper truck appeared across the street, however, as Joe more than half expected, and if directional microphones were trained on the big picture window, the audio from the baseball game might have to be turned up to foil the listeners.

Positioning himself so he could talk to Fittich and look past him to the sales lot and the street, Joe said, "What's the cheapest set of wheels you've got ready to roll?"

"Once you consider my prices, you're going to realize you can get plenty of value without having to settle for—"

"Here's the deal," Joe said, withdrawing packets of hundred-dollar bills from a jacket pocket. "Depending on how it performs on a test drive, I'll buy the cheapest car you have on the lot right now, one hundred percent cash money, no guarantee required."

Fittich liked the look of the cash. "Well, Joe, I've got this Subaru, she's a long road from the factory, but she's still got life in her. No air conditioning but radio and—"

"How much?"

"Well, now, I've done some work on her, have her tagged at twenty-one hundred fifty, but I'll let you have her for nineteen seventy-five. She—"

Joe considered offering less, but every minute counted, and considering what he was going to ask of Fittich, he decided that he wasn't in a position to bargain. He interrupted the salesman to say, "I'll take it."

After a disappointingly slow day in the iron-horse trade, Gem Fittich was clearly torn between pleasure at the prospect of a sale and uneasiness at the way in which they had arrived at terms. He smelled trouble. "You don't want to take a test drive?"

Putting two thousand in cash on Fittich's desk, Joe said, "That is exactly what I want to do. Alone."

Across the street, a tall man appeared on foot, coming from the direction in which the camper truck was parked. He stood in the shade of a bus-stop shelter. If he'd sat on the shelter bench, his view of the sales office would have been hampered by the merchandise parked in front of it.

"Alone?" Fittich asked, puzzled.

"You've got the whole purchase price there on the desk," Joe said. From his wallet, he withdrew his driver's license and handed it to Fittich. "I see you have a Xerox. Make a copy of my license."

The guy at the bus stop was wearing a short-sleeve shirt and slacks, and he wasn't carrying anything. Therefore, he wasn't equipped with a high-power, long-range listening device; he was just keeping watch.

Fittich followed the direction of Joe's gaze and said, "What trouble am I getting into here?"

Joe met the salesman's eyes. "None. You're clear. You're just doing business."

"Why's that fella at the bus stop interest you?"

"He doesn't. He's just a guy."

Fittich wasn't deceived. "If what's actually happening here is a *purchase*, not just a test drive, then there're state forms we have to fill out, sales tax to be collected, legal procedures."

"But it's just a test drive," Joe said.

He checked his wristwatch. He wasn't pretending to be worried about the hour now; he was genuinely concerned.

"All right, look, Mr. Fittich, no more bullshit. I don't have time. This is going to be even better for you than a sale, because here's what's going to happen. You take that money and stick it in the back of a desk drawer. Nobody ever has to know I gave it to you. I'll drive the Subaru to where I have to go, which is only someplace on the West Side. I'd take my own car, but they've got a tracking device on it, and I don't want to be followed. I'll abandon the Subaru in a safe area and call you by tomorrow to let you know where it is. You bring it back, and all that's happened is you've rented your cheapest car for one day for two thousand bucks tax free. The worst that happens is I don't call. You've still got the money—and a theft write-off."

Fittich turned the driver's license over and over in his hand. "Is somebody going to ask me why I'd let you make a test drive alone even with a copy of your license?"

"The guy looked honest to me," Joe said, feeding Fittich the lines he could use. "It was his picture on the license. And I just couldn't leave, 'cause I expected a call from a hot prospect who came in earlier and might buy the best piece of iron I have on the lot. Didn't want to risk missing that call."

"You got it all figured out," Fittich said.

His manner changed. The easygoing, smiley-faced salesman was a chrysalis from which another Gem Fittich was emerging, a version with more angles and harder edges.

He stepped to the Xerox and switched it on.

Nevertheless, Joe sensed that Fittich had not yet made up his mind. "The fact is, Mr. Fittich, even if they come in here and ask you some questions, there's nothing they could do to you—and nothing they'd want to bother doing."

"You in the drug trade?" Fittich asked bluntly.

"No."

"'Cause I hate people who sell drugs."

"I do too."

"Ruining our kids, ruining what's left of our country."

"I couldn't agree more."

"Not that there *is* much left." Fittich glanced through the window at the man at the bus stop. "They cops?"

"Not really."

"'Cause I support the cops. They got a hard job these days, trying to uphold the law when the biggest criminals are some of our own elected officials."

Joe shook his head. "These aren't any kind of cops you've ever heard of."

Fittich thought for a while, and then he said, "That was an honest answer."

"I'm being as truthful with you as I can be. But I'm in a hurry. They probably think I'm in here to call a mechanic or a tow truck or something. If I'm going to get that Subaru, I want it to be *now*, before they maybe tumble to what I'm really doing."

After glancing at the window and the bus stop across the street, Fittich said, "They government?"

"For all intents and purposes—yeah."

"You know why the drug problem just grows?" Fittich said. "It's because half this current group of politicians, they've been paid off to let it happen, and hell, a bunch of the bastards are even users themselves, so they don't care."

Joe said nothing, for fear that he would say the *wrong* thing. He didn't know the cause of Fittich's anger with authority. He could easily misspeak and be viewed suddenly as not a like thinker but as one of the enemy.

Frowning, Gem Fittich made a Xerox copy of the driver's license. He returned the laminated card to Joe, who put it away in his wallet.

At the desk again, Fittich stared at the money. He seemed to be disturbed about cooperating—not because he was worried about getting in trouble but because the moral dimension, in fact, was of concern to him. Finally he sighed, opened a drawer, and slid the two thousand into it.

From another drawer, he withdrew a set of keys and handed them to Joe.

Taking them gratefully, Joe said, "Where is it?"

Fittich pointed at the car through the window. "Half an hour, I probably got to call the cops and report it stolen, just to cover myself."

"I understand. With luck, I'll be where I'm going by then."

"Hell, don't worry, they won't even look for it anyway. You could use it a week and never get nailed."

"I *will* call you, Mr. Fittich, and tell you exactly where I left it."

"I expect you will." As Joe reached the open door, Fittich said, "Mr. Carpenter, do you believe in the end of all things?"

Joe paused on the threshold. "Excuse me?"

The Gem Fittich who had emerged from the chrysalis of the cheerful salesman was not merely harder edged and edgier; he also had peculiar eyes—eyes different from what they had been, full of not anger but an unnerving pensiveness. "The end of time in our time, the end of this mess of a world we've made, all of it just suddenly rolled up and put away like an old moth-eaten rug."

"I suppose it's got to end someday," Joe said.

"Not someday. Soon. Doesn't it seem to you that wrong and right have all got turned upside down, that we don't even half know the difference anymore?"

"Yes."

"Don't you wake up sometimes in the middle of the night and feel it coming? Like a tidal wave a thousand miles high, hanging over us, darker than the night and cold, going to crash over us and sweep us all away?"

"Yes," Joe said softly and truthfully. "Yes, I've often felt just that in the middle of the night."

The tsunami looming over Joe in dark hours was of an entirely personal nature, however: the loss of his family, towering so high that it blocked the stars and prevented him from seeing the future. He had often *longed* to be swept away by it.

He sensed that Fittich, sunk in some deep moral weariness, also longed for a delivering apocalypse. Joe was disquieted and surprised to discover he shared this melancholy with the car salesman.

The discovery disturbed him, because this expectation that the end of all things loomed was profoundly dysfunctional and antisocial, an illness from which he himself was only beginning to recover with great difficulty, and he feared for a society in which such gloom was widespread.

"Strange times," Fittich said, as Joe had said *weird times* to Barbara a short while ago. "They scare me." He went to his chair, put his feet on the desk, and stared at the ball game on television. "Better go now."

With the flesh on the nape of his neck as crinkled as crepe paper, Joe walked outside to the yellow Subaru.

Across the street, the man at the bus stop looked impatiently left and right, as though disgruntled about the unreliability of public transportation.

The engine of the Subaru turned over at once, but it sounded tinny. The steering wheel vibrated slightly. The upholstery was worn, and pine-fragrant solvents didn't quite mask the sour scent of cigarette smoke that over the years had saturated the vinyl and the carpet.

Without looking at the man in the bus-stop shelter, Joe drove out of the lot. He turned right and headed up the street past his abandoned Honda.

The pickup with the camper shell was still parked in front of the untenanted industrial building.

When Joe reached the intersection just past the camper truck, there was no cross-traffic. He slowed, did not come to a full stop, and instead put his foot down heavily on the accelerator.

In the rearview mirror, he saw the man from the bus stop hurrying toward the camper, which was already backing into the street. Without the transponder to guide them, they would have to maintain visual contact and risk following him close enough to blow their cover—which they thought they still enjoyed.

Within four miles Joe lost them at a major intersection when he sped through a yellow traffic signal that was changing to red. When the camper tried to follow him, it was thwarted by the surging cross-traffic. Even over the whine and rattle of the Subaru engine, he heard the sharp bark of their brakes as they slid to a halt inches short of a collision.

Twenty minutes later, he abandoned the Subaru on Hilgarde Street near the UCLA campus, as far as he dared from the address where he was to meet Demi. He walked fast to Westwood Boulevard, trying not to break into a run and draw attention to himself.

Not long ago Westwood Village had been an island of quaint charm in the more turbulent sea of the city around it, a mecca for shoppers and theatergoers. Amidst some of the most interesting small-scale architecture of any Los Angeles commercial district and along the tree-lined streets had thrived trendy clothing stores, galleries, restaurants, prosperous theaters featuring the latest cutting-edge dramas and comedies, and popular movie houses. It was a place to have fun, people-watch, and be seen.

Then, during a period when the city's ruling elite was in one of its periodic moods to view certain forms of sociopathic behavior as a legitimate protest, vagrancy increased, gang members began to loiter in groups, and open drug dealing commenced. A few shootings occurred in turf disputes, and many of the fun lovers and shoppers decided that the scene was *too* colorful and that to be seen here was to be marked as a victim.

Now Westwood was struggling back from the precipice. The streets were safer than they had been for a while. Many shops and galleries had closed, however, and new businesses had not moved into all of the empty storefronts. The lingering atmosphere of despair might take years to dissipate entirely. Built at the solemn pace of coral reefs, civilization could be destroyed with frightening swiftness, even by a blast of good intentions, and all that was lost could be regained, if ever, only with determination.

The gourmet coffeehouse was busy. From the open door came the delicious aromas of several exotic brews and the music of a lone guitarist playing a New Age tune that was mellow and relaxing though filled with tediously repetitive chords.

Joe intended to scout the meeting place from across the street and farther along the block, but he arrived too late to do so. At two minutes past six o'clock, he stood outside the coffeehouse as instructed, to the right of the entrance, and waited to be contacted.

Over the noise of the street traffic and the guitar, he heard a soft tuneless janglingtinkling. The sound instantly alarmed him, for reasons he could not explain, and he looked around nervously for the source.

Above the door were wind chimes crafted from at least twenty spoons of various sizes and materials. They clinked together in the light breeze.

Like a mischievous childhood playmate, memory taunted him from hiding place after hiding place in a deep garden of the past dappled by light and shadow. Then suddenly he recalled the ceiling-mounted rack of copper pots and pans in the Delmanns' kitchen.

Returning from Charlie Delmann's bedroom, in answer to Lisa's scream, Joe had heard the cookware clinking and softly clanging as he had hurried along the downstairs hall. Coming through the door into the kitchen, he saw the pots and pans swinging like pendulums from their hooks.

By the time he reached Lisa and saw Georgine's corpse on the floor, the cookware had settled into silence. But what set those items in motion in the first place? Lisa and Georgine were at the far end of the long room, nowhere near the dangling pots.

Like the flashing green numbers on the digital clock at Charlie Delmann's bedside, like the swelling of flames in the three oil lamps on the kitchen table, this coppery music was important.

He felt as though a hard rap of insight was about to crack the egg of his ignorance.

Holding his breath, mentally reaching for the elusive connection that would make sense of these things, Joe realized that the shell-cracking insight was receding. He strained to bring it back. Then, maddeningly, it was gone.

Perhaps *none* of these things was important: not the oil lamps, not the digital clock, not the jangling cookware. In a world viewed through lenses of paranoia—a pair of distorting spectacles that he had been wearing with good reason for the past day and a half—every falling leaf, every whisper of wind, and every fretwork of shadows was invested with a portentous meaning that, in reality, it did not possess. He was not merely a neutral observer, not merely a reporter this time, but a victim, central to his own story, so maybe he could not trust his journalistic instincts when he saw significance in these small, if admittedly strange, details.

Along the sidewalk came a tall black kid, college age, wearing shorts and a UCLA T-shirt, gliding on Roller-blades. Joe, puzzling over clues that might not be clues at all, paid little attention to the skater, until the kid spun to a stop in front of him and handed him a cellular phone.

"You'll need this," said the skater, in a bass voice that would have been pure gold to any fifties doo-wop group.

Before Joe could respond, the skater rolled away with powerful pushes of his muscular legs.

The phone rang in Joe's hand.

He surveyed the street, searching for the surveillance post from which he was being watched, but it was not obvious.

The phone rang again, and he answered it. "Yeah?"

"What's your name?" a man asked.

"Joe Carpenter."

"Who're you waiting for?"

"I don't know her name."

"What do you call her?"

"Demi."

"Walk a block and a half south. Turn right at the corner and keep going until you come to a bookstore. It's still open. Go in, find the biography section."

The caller hung up.

After all, there wasn't going to be a pleasant get-acquainted chat over coffee.

According to the business hours posted on the glass door, the bookstore closed on Sundays at six o'clock. It was a quarter past six. Through the big display windows, Joe saw that the fluorescent panels toward the front of the store were dark; only a few at the back were lighted, but when he tried the door, it was unlocked.

Inside, a single clerk waited at the cashiers' counter. He was black, in his late thirties, as small and wiry as a jockey, with a mustache and goatee. Behind the thick lenses of his horn-rimmed glasses, his eyes were as large as those of a persistent interrogator in a dream of inquisition.

"Biographies?" Joe asked.

Coming out from behind the counter, the clerk pointed to the right rear corner of the store, where light glowed beyond ranks of shadowed shelves.

As he headed deeper into the maze of books, Joe heard the front door being locked behind him.

In the biography aisle, another black man was waiting. He was a huge slab of ebony—and appeared capable of being an irresistible force or an immovable object, whichever was required. His face was as placid as that of Buddha.

He said, "Assume the position."

At once Joe knew he was dealing with a cop or former cop.

Obediently, he faced a wall of books, spread his legs wide, leaned forward with both hands against the shelves, and stared at the spines of the volumes in front of him. One in particular caught his attention: a massive biography of Henry James, the writer.

Henry James.

For some reason even that name seemed significant. Everything *seemed* significant, but nothing was. Least of all, the name of a long-dead writer.

The cop frisked him quickly and professionally, searching for a weapon or a transmitter. When he found neither, he said, "Show me some ID."

Joe turned away from the shelves and fished his driver's license from his wallet.

The cop compared the photo on the license with Joe's face, read his vital statistics and compared them to the reality, then returned the card. "See the cashier."

"What?"

"The guy when you came in."

The wiry man with the goatee was waiting by the front door. He unlocked it as Joe approached. "You still have the phone?"

Joe offered it to him.

"No, hold on to it," the cashier said. "There's a black Mustang parked at the curb. Drive it down to Wilshire and turn west. You'll be contacted."

As the cashier opened the door and held it, Joe stared at the car and said, "Whose is it?"

From behind the bottle-thick lenses, the magnified eyes studied him as though he were a bacterium at the lower end of a microscope. "What's it matter whose?"

"Doesn't, I guess."

Joe went outside and got into the Mustang. The keys were in the ignition.

At Wilshire Boulevard, he turned west. The car was almost as old as the Subaru that he had gotten from Gem Fittich. The engine sounded better, however, the interior was cleaner, and instead of pine-scented disinfectant masking the stink of stale cigarette smoke, the air held a faint tang of menthol aftershave.

Shortly after he drove through the underpass at the San Diego Freeway, the cellular phone rang. "Yeah?"

The man who had sent him to the bookstore now said, "You're going all the way to the ocean in Santa Monica. When you get there, I'll ring you with more directions."

"All right."

"Don't stop anywhere along the way. You understand?"

"Yes."

"We'll know if you do."

They were somewhere in the traffic around him, in front or behind—or both. He didn't bother to look for them.

The caller said, "Don't try to use your phone to call anyone. We'll know that too."

"I understand."

"Just one question. The car you're driving—why did you want to know whose it was?"

Joe said, "Some seriously unpleasant bastards are looking for me. If they find me, I don't want to get any innocent people in trouble just because I was using their car."

"Whole world's already in trouble, man. Haven't you noticed?" the caller asked, and then he disconnected.

With the exception of the cop—or former cop—in the bookstore, these people who were hiding Rose Tucker and providing security for her were amateurs with limited resources compared to the thugs who worked for Teknologik. But they were thoughtful and clever amateurs with undeniable talent for the game.

Joe was not halfway through Santa Monica, with the ocean still far ahead, when an image of the book spine rose in his mind—the name *Henry James.*

Henry James. So what?

Then the title of one of James's best-known works came to him. *The Turn of the Screw.* It would be on any short list of the most famous ghost stories ever written.

Ghost.

The inexplicable welling of the oil-lamp flames, the flashing of the numbers on the clock, the jangling pots and pans now seemed as if they might have been linked, after all. And as he recalled those images, it was easy in retrospect to discern a supernatural quality to them—although he was aware that his imagination might be enhancing the memories in that regard.

He remembered, as well, how the foyer chandelier had dimmed and brightened and dimmed repeatedly as he had hurried upstairs in response to the shotgun blast that killed Charlie Delmann. In the fearsome turmoil that followed, he'd forgotten that odd detail.

Now he was reminded of countless séance scenes in old movies and television programs, in which the opening of the door between this world and the realm of spirits was marked by the pulsing of electric lights or the guttering of candles without the presence of a draft.

Ghost.

This was absurd speculation. Worse than absurd. Insane. There were no such things as ghosts.

Yet now he recalled another disquieting incident that occurred as he'd fled the Delmann house.

Racing from the kitchen with the smoke alarm blaring behind him, along the hallway and across the foyer to the door. His hand on the knob. From behind comes a hissing cold, prickling his neck, drilling through the base of his skull. Then he is crossing the porch without any memory of having opened the door.

This seemed to be a meaningful incident as long as he considered it to be meaningful—but as soon as skepticism reasserted itself, the moment appeared to be utterly without import. Yes, if he had felt anything at the back of his neck, it should have been the heat of the fire, not a piercing chill. And, yes, this cold had been different from anything that he had ever felt before: not a spreading chill but like the tip of an icicle—indeed, more finely pointed yet, like a stiletto of steel taken from a freezer, a wire, a *needle*. A needle inserted into the summit of his spine. But this was a subjective perception of something that he had *felt*, not a journalist's measured observation of a concrete phenomenon. He'd been in a state of sheer panic, and he'd felt a lot of peculiar things; they were nothing but normal physiological responses to extreme stress. As for the few seconds of blank memory between the time when he'd put his hand on the doorknob and when he'd found himself most of the way across the porch . . . Well, that was also easily explained by panic, by stress, and by the blinding power of the overwhelming animal instinct to survive.

Not a ghost.

Rest in peace, Henry James.

As he progressed through Santa Monica toward the ocean, Joe's brief embrace of superstition loosened, lost all passion. Reason returned.

Nevertheless, something about the *concept* of a ghost continued to seem significant to him. He had a hunch that eventually he would arrive at a rational explanation derived from this consideration of the supernatural, a provable theory that would be as logical as the meticulously structured prose of Henry James.

A needle of ice. Piercing to the gray matter in the center of the spine. An injection, a quick cold squirt of . . . something.

Did Nora Vadance feel that ghost needle an instant before she got up from the breakfast table to fetch the camcorder?

Did the Delmanns feel it?

And Lisa?

Did Captain Delroy Blane feel it too, before he disengaged the autopilot, clubbed his first officer in the face, and calmly piloted Flight 353 straight into the earth?

Not a ghost, perhaps, but something fully as terrifying and as malevolent as any evil spirit returned from the abyss of the damned . . . something *akin* to a ghost.

• • •

When Joe was two blocks from the Pacific, the cell phone rang for the third time.

The caller said, "Okay, turn right on the Coast Highway and keep driving until you hear from us again."

To Joe's left, less than two hours of sunlight lay over the ocean, like lemon sauce cooking in a pan, gradually thickening to a deeper yellow.

In Malibu, the phone rang again. He was directed to a turnoff that would take him to Santa-Fe-by-the-Sea, a Southwest restaurant on a bluff overlooking the ocean.

"Leave the phone on the passenger's seat and give the car to the valet. He knows who you are. The reservation is in your name," said the caller, and he hung up for the last time.

The big restaurant looked like an adobe lodge transported from New Mexico, with turquoise window trim, turquoise doors, and walkways of red-clay tiles. The landscaping consisted of cactus gardens in beds of white pebbles—and two large sorrel trees with dark-green foliage and sprays of white flowers.

The Hispanic valet was more handsome by far than any current or past Latin movie star, affecting a moody and smoldering stare that he had surely practiced in front of a mirror for eventual use in front of a camera. As the man on the phone had promised, the valet was expecting Joe and didn't give him a claim check for the Mustang.

Inside, Santa-Fe-by-the-Sea featured massive lodgepole-pine ceiling beams, vanilla-colored plaster, and more red-clay pavers. The chairs and tables and other furnishings, which fortunately didn't push the Southwest theme to extremes, were J. Robert Scott knockoffs though not inexpensive, and the decorator's palette was restricted to pastels used to interpret classic Navajo motifs.

A fortune had been spent here; and Joe was acutely aware that by comparison to the decor, he was a scruffy specimen. He hadn't shaved since leaving for Colorado more than twelve hours ago. Because most contemporary male movie stars and directors indulged in a perpetually adolescent lifestyle, blue jeans were acceptable attire even at many tony establishments in Los Angeles. But his new corduroy jacket was wrinkled and baggy from having been rain-soaked earlier, and he had the rumpled look of a traveler—or a lush coming off a bender.

The young hostess, as beautiful as any famous actress and no doubt passing time in food service while waiting for the role that would win her an Oscar, seemed to find nothing about his appearance to disdain. She led him to a window table set for two.

Glass formed the entire west wall of the building. Tinted plastic blinds softened the power of the declining sun. The view of the coastline was spectacular as it curved outward to both the north and the south—and the sea was the sea.

"Your associate has been delayed," the hostess said, evidently referring to Demi. "She's asked that you have dinner without her, and she'll join you afterwards."

Joe didn't like this development. Didn't like it at all. He was eager to make the connection with Rose, eager to learn what she had to tell him—eager to find Nina.

He was playing by their rules, however. "All right. Thanks."

If Tom Cruise had undergone cosmetic surgery to improve his appearance, he might have been as handsome as Joe's waiter. His name was Gene, and he seemed to have had a twinkle surgically inserted in each of his gas-flame-blue eyes.

After ordering a Corona, Joe went to the men's room and winced at the mirror. With his beard stubble, he resembled one of the criminal Beagle Boys in old Scrooge McDuck comics. He washed his hands and face, combed his hair, and smoothed his jacket. He still looked like he should be seated at not a window table but a Dumpster.

Back at his table, sipping ice-cold beer, he surveyed the other patrons. Several were famous.

An action-movie hero three tables away was even more stubbled than Joe, and his hair was matted and tousled like that of a small boy just awakened from a nap. He was dressed in tattered black jeans and a pleated tuxedo shirt.

Nearer was an Oscar-nominated actor and well-known heroin addict in an eccentric outfit fumbled from the closet in a state of chemical bliss: black loafers without socks, green-plaid golf pants, a brown-checkered sports jacket, and a pale-blue denim shirt. In spite of his ensemble, the most colorful things about him were his bloodshot eyes and his swollen, flame-red eyelids.

Joe relaxed and enjoyed dinner. Puréed corn and black-bean soup were poured into the same dish in such a way as to form a yellow and black yin-and-yang pattern. The mesquite-grilled salmon was on a bed of mango-and-red-pepper salsa. Everything was delicious.

While he ate, he spent as much time watching the customers as he did staring at the sea. Even those who were not famous were colorful, frequently ravishing, and generally engaged in one sort of performance or another.

Los Angeles was the most glamorous, tackiest, most elegant, seediest, most clever, dumbest, most beautiful, ugliest, forward-looking, retro-thinking, altruistic, self-absorbed, deal-savvy, politically ignorant, artistic-minded, criminal-loving, meaning-obsessed, money-grubbing, laid-back, frantic city on the planet. And any two slices of it, as different as Bel Air and Watts, were nevertheless uncannily alike in essence: rich with the same crazy hungers, hopes, and despairs.

By the time he was finishing dinner with mango bread pudding and jalapeño ice cream, Joe was surprised to realize how much he enjoyed this people-watching. He and Michelle had spent afternoons strolling places as disparate as Rodeo Drive and City Walk, checking out the "two-footed entertainment," but he had not been interested in other people for the past year, interested only in himself and his pain.

The realization that Nina was alive and the prospect of finding her were slowly bringing Joe out of himself and back to life.

A heavyset black woman in a red and gold muumuu and two pounds of jewelry had been spelling the hostess. Now she escorted two men to a nearby table.

Both of these new patrons were dressed in black slacks, white silk shirts, and black leather jackets as supple as silk. The older of the two, approximately forty, had enormous sad eyes and a mouth sufficiently sensuous to assure him a contract to star in Revlon lipstick advertisements. He would have been handsome enough to be a waiter—except that his nose was red and misshapen from years of heavy drinking, and he never quite closed his mouth, which gave him a vacuous look. His blue-eyed companion, ten years younger, was as pink-faced as if he had been boiled—and plagued by a nervous smile that he couldn't control, as if chronically unsure of himself.

The willowy brunette having dinner with the movie star–slash–heroin addict developed an instant attraction for the guy with the Mick Jagger mouth, in spite of his rose-bloom nose. She stared at him so hard and so insistently that he responded to her as quickly as a trout would respond to a fat bug bobbing on the surface of a stream—though it was difficult to say which of these two was the trout and which the tender morsel.

The actor-addict became aware of his companion's infatuation, and he, too, began to stare at the man with the melancholy eyes—though he was glaring rather than flirting. Suddenly he rose from the table, almost knocking over his chair, and weaved across the restaurant, as if intending either to strike or regurgitate upon his rival. Instead, he curved away from the two men's table and disappeared into the hall that led to the rest rooms.

By this time, the sad-eyed man was eating baby shrimps on a bed of polenta. He speared each tiny crustacean on the point of his fork and studied it appreciatively before sucking it off the tines with obscene relish. As he leisurely savored each bite, he looked toward the brunette as if to say that if he ever got a chance to bed her, she could rest assured that she would wind up as thoroughly shelled and de-veined as the shrimps.

The brunette was aroused or repulsed. Hard to tell which. With some Angelenos, those two emotions were as inextricably entwined as the viscera of inoperable Siamese twins. Anyway, she departed the actor-addict's table and drew up a chair to sit with the two men in leather jackets.

Joe wondered how interesting things would get when the wasted actor returned—no doubt with a white dust glowing around the rims of his nostrils, since current heroin was sufficiently pure to snort. Before events could develop, the waiter, Gene of the twinkling eyes, stopped by to tell him there would be no charge for dinner and that Demi was waiting for him in the kitchen

Surprised, he left a tip and followed Gene's directions toward the hallway that served the rest rooms and the cookery.

The late-summer twilight had finally arrived. On the griddle-flat horizon, a sun like a bloody yolk cooked toward a darker hue.

As Joe crossed the restaurant, where all of the tables were now occupied, something about that three-person tableau—the brunette, the two men in leather jackets—teased his memory. By the time that he reached the hallway to the kitchen, he was puzzled by a full-blown case of déjà vu.

Before stepping into the hall, Joe turned for one look back. He saw the seducer with fork raised, savoring a speared shrimp with his sad eyes, while the brunette murmured something and the nervous pink-faced man watched.

Joe's puzzlement turned to alarm.

For an instant, he could not understand why his mouth went dry or why his heart began to race. Then in his mind's eye he saw the fork metamorphose into a stiletto, and the shrimp became a sliver of Gouda cheese.

Two men and a woman. Not in a restaurant but in a hotel room. Not this brunette but Barbara Christman. If not these two men, then two astonishingly similar to them.

Of course Joe had never seen them, only listened to Barbara's brief but vivid descriptions. The hound-dog eyes, the nose that was "bashed red by . . . decades of drink," the thick-lipped mouth. The younger of the two: pink-faced, with the ceaselessly flickering smile.

Joe was more than twenty-four hours past the ability ever to believe in coincidence again.

Impossibly, Teknologik was *here*.

He hurried along the hallway, through one of two swinging doors, and into a roomy antechamber used as a salad-prep area. Two white-uniformed men, artfully and rapidly arranging plates of greenery, never even glanced at him.

Beyond, in the main kitchen, the heavyset black woman in the voluminous muumuu was waiting for him. Even her bright dress and the cascades of glittering jewelry could not disguise her anxiety. Her big-mama, jazz-singer face was pretty and lively and made for mirth, but there was no song or laughter in her now.

"My name's Mahalia. Real sorry I couldn't have dinner with you, Presentable Joe. That would've been a treat." Her sexy-smoky voice pegged her as the woman whom he had named Demi. "But there's been a change of plans. Follow me, honey."

With the formidable majesty of a great ship leaving its dock, Mahalia set out across the busy and immaculate kitchen crowded with chefs, cooks, and assistants, past cooktops and ovens and griddles and grills, through steam and meat smoke and the eye-watering fragrance of sautéing onions.

Hurrying after her, Joe said, "Then you know about them?"

"Sure do. Been on the TV news today. The news people show you stuff to curl your hair, then try to sell you Fritos. This awful business changes everythin'."

He put an arm on her shoulder, halted her. "TV news?"

"Some people been murdered after she talks to them."

Even with the large culinary staff in white flurries of activity around them, they were afforded privacy for their conversation by the masking clang of pots, rattle of skillets, whir of mixers, swish of whisks, clatter of dishes, buzz, clink, tink, ping, pop, scrape, chop, sizzle.

"They call it somethin' else on the news," Mahalia said, "but it's murder sure enough."

"That's not what I mean," he said. "I'm talking about the men in the restaurant."

She frowned. "What men?"

"Two of them. Black slacks, white silk shirts, black leather jackets—"

"I walked 'em to their table."

"You did, yeah. I just recognized them a minute ago."

"Bad folks?"

"The worst."

Baffled, she shook her head. "But, sugar, we know you weren't followed."

"I wasn't, but maybe you were. Or maybe someone else who's protecting Rose was followed."

"Devil himself would have a hard time finding Rosie if he had to depend on getting to her through us."

"But somehow they've figured out who's been hiding her for a year, and now they're closing in."

Glowering, wrapped by bulletproof confidence, Mahalia said, "Nobody's gonna lay one little finger on Rosie."

"Is she here?"

"Waitin' for you."

A cold tide washed through his heart. "You don't understand—the two in the restaurant won't have come alone. There's sure to be more outside. Maybe a small army of them."

"Yeah, maybe, but they don't know what they're dealin' with, honey." Thunderheads of resolve massed in her dark face. "We're Baptists."

Certain that he could not have heard the woman correctly, Joe hurried after her as she continued through the kitchen.

At the far end of the big room, they went through an open door into a sparkling scullery where fruits and vegetables were cleaned and trimmed before being sent in to the main cookery. This late in the restaurant's day, no one was at work here.

Beyond the scullery was a concrete-floored receiving room that smelled of raw celery and peppers, damp wood and damp cardboard. On pallets along the right-hand wall, empty fruit and vegetable crates, boxes, and cases of empty beer bottles were stacked almost to the low ceiling.

Directly ahead, under a red Exit sign, was a wide steel exterior door, closed now, beyond which suppliers' trucks evidently parked to make deliveries. To the left was an elevator.

"Rose is down below." Mahalia pressed the call button, and the elevator doors slid open at once.

"What's under us?"

"Well, one time, this was the service elevator to a banquet room and deck, where you could have big parties right on the beach, but we can't use it like the joint did before us. Coastal Commission put a hard rule on us. Now it's just a storeroom. Once you go down, I'll have some boys come move the pallets and empty crates to this wall. We'll cover the elevator real nice. Nobody'll know it's even here."

Uneasy about being cornered, Joe said, "Yeah, but what if they come looking and they do find the elevator?"

"Gonna have to stop callin' you Presentable Joe. Better would be Worryin' Joe."

"After a while, they will come looking. They won't just wait till closing time and go home. So once I'm down there, do I have another way out?" he persisted.

"Never tore apart the front stairs, where the customers used to go down. Just covered the openin' with hinged panels so you don't really see it. You come up that way, though, you'll be right across from the hostess station, in the middle of plain view."

"No good."

"So if somethin' goes wrong, best to skedaddle out the lower door onto the deck. From there you have the beach, the whole coast."

"They could be covering that exit too."

"It's down at the base of the bluff. From the upper level, they can't know it's there. You should just try to relax, sugar. We're on the righteous side, which counts for somethin'."

"Not much."

"Worryin' Joe."

He stepped into the elevator but blocked the sliding door with his arm in case it tried to close. "How're you connected with this place, Mahalia?"

"Half owner."

"The food's great."

"You can look at me the way I am and think I don't *know*?" she asked good-naturedly.

"What're you to Rose?"

"Gonna call you Curious Joe pretty soon. Rosie married my brother Louis about twenty-two years ago. They met in college. Wasn't truly surprised when Louis turned out smart enough to go to college, but I was sure surprised he had the brains to fall for someone like Rosie. Then, of course, the man proved he was a pure fool, after all, when he up and divorced her four years later. Rosie couldn't have kids, and havin' kids was important to Louis—though with less air in his skull and any common sense at all, the man would've realized Rosie was more treasure than a houseful of babies."

"She hasn't been your sister-in-law for eighteen years, but you're willing to put yourself on the line for her?"

"Why not? You think Rosie turned into a vampire when Louis, the fool, divorced her? She's been the same sweet lady ever I met her. I love her like a sister. Now she's waitin', Curious Joe."

"One more thing. Earlier, when you told me these people don't know who they're dealing with . . . You didn't say 'We're Baptists'?"

"That's exactly what I did say. 'Tough' and 'Baptists' don't go together in your head— is that it?"

"Well—"

"Mama and Daddy stood up to the Klan down in Mississippi when the Klan had a whole lot more teeth than they do now, and so did my grandma and grandpap before them, and they never let fear weigh 'em down. When I was a little girl, we went through hurricanes off the Gulf of Mexico and Delta floods and encephalitis epidemics and poor times when we didn't know where tomorrow's food was comin' from, but we rode it out and still sung loud in the choir every Sunday. Maybe the United States Marines are some tougher than your average Southern black Baptist, Joe, but not by much."

"Rose is a lucky woman with a friend like you."

"I'm the lucky one," said Mahalia. "She lifts me up—now more than ever. Go on, Joe. And stay down there with her till we close this place and figure a way we can slip you two out. I'll come for you when it's time."

"Be ready for trouble long before that," he warned her.

"Go."

Joe let the doors slide shut.

The elevator descended.

FOURTEEN

Here now, at last and alone, at the far end of the long room, was Dr. Rose Marie Tucker, in one of four folding chairs at a scarred worktable, leaning forward, forearms on the table, hands clasped, waiting and silent, her eyes solemn and full of tenderness, this diminutive survivor, keeper of secrets that Joe had been desperate to learn but from which he suddenly shied.

Some of the recessed-can fixtures in the ceiling contained dead bulbs, and the live ones were haphazardly angled, so the floor that he slowly crossed was mottled with light and shadow as if it were an underwater realm. His own shadow preceded him, then fell behind, but again preceded him, flowed here into a pool of gloom and vanished like a soul into oblivion, only to swim into view three steps later. He felt as though he were a condemned man submerged in the concrete depths of an inescapable prison, on a long death-row walk toward lethal punishment—yet simultaneously he believed in the possibility of clemency and rebirth. As he approached the revelation that had lifted Georgine and Charlie Delmann from despair to euphoria, as he drew nearer the truth about Nina, his mind churned with conflicting currents, and hope like schools of bright koi darted through his internal darkness.

Against the left-hand wall were boxes of restaurant provisions, primarily paper towels for the rest rooms, candles for the tables, and janitorial supplies purchased in bulk. The right-hand wall, which faced the beach and the ocean beyond, featured two doors and a series of large windows, but the coast was not visible because the glass was protected by metal Rolladen security shutters. The banquet room felt like a bunker.

He pulled out a chair and sat across the table from Rose.

As in the cemetery the previous day, this woman radiated such extraordinary charismatic power that her petite stature was a source of continual surprise. She seemed more physically imposing than Joe—yet her wrists were as dainty as those of a twelve-year-old girl. Her magnetic eyes held him, touched him, and some knowledge in them humbled him in a way that no man twice his size could have humbled him—yet her features appeared so fragile, her throat so slender, her shoulders so delicate that she should have seemed as vulnerable as a child.

Joe reached across the table toward her.

She gripped his hand.

Dread fought with hope for his voice, and while the battle raged, he could not speak to ask about Nina.

More solemn now than she had been in the cemetery, Rose said, "It's all going so badly. They're killing everyone I talk to. They'll stop at nothing."

Relieved of the obligation to ask, first, the fateful question about his younger daughter, Joe found his voice. "I was there at the house in Hancock Park with the Delmanns . . . and Lisa."

Her eyes widened in alarm. "You don't mean . . . when it happened?"

"Yes."

Her small hand tightened on his. "You saw?"

He nodded. "They killed themselves. Such terrible . . . such violence, madness."

"Not madness. Not suicide. Murder. But how in the name of God did you survive?"

"I ran."

"While they were still being killed?"

"Charlie and Georgine were already dead. Lisa was still burning."

"So she wasn't dead yet when you ran?"

"No. Still on her feet and burning but not screaming, just quietly . . . quietly burning."

"Then you got out just in time. A miracle of your own."

"How, Rose? How was it done to them?"

Lowering her gaze from his eyes to their entwined hands, she didn't answer Joe's question. More to herself than to him, she said, "I thought this was the way to begin the work—by bringing the news to the families who'd lost loved ones on that airliner. But because of me . . . all this blood."

"You really were aboard Flight 353?" he asked.

She met his eyes again. "Economy class. Row sixteen, seat B, one away from the window."

The truth was in her voice as sure as rain and sunshine are in a green blade of grass.

Joe said, "You really walked away from the crash unharmed."

"Untouched," she said softly, emphasizing the miraculousness of her escape.

"And you weren't alone."

"Who told you?"

"Not the Delmanns. Not anyone else you've spoken with. They have all kept faith with you, held tight to whatever secrets you've told them. How I found out goes all the way back to that night. Do you remember Jeff and Mercy Ealing?"

A faint smile floated across her mouth and away as she said, "The Loose Change Ranch."

"I was there early this afternoon," he said.

"They're nice people."

"A lovely quiet life."

"And you're a good reporter."

"When the assignment matters to me."

Her eyes were midnight-dark but luminous lakes, and Joe could not tell whether the secrets sunk in them would drown or buoy him.

She said, "I'm so sorry about all the people on that plane. Sorry they went before their time. So sorry for their families . . . for you."

"You didn't realize that you were putting them in jeopardy—did you?"

"God, no."

"Then you've no guilt."

"I feel it, though."

"Tell me, Rose. Please. I've come a long, long way around to hear it. Tell me what you've told the others."

"But they're killing everyone I tell. Not just the Delmanns but others, half a dozen others."

"I don't care about the danger."

"But I care. Because now I *do* know the jeopardy I'm putting you in, and I've got to consider it."

"No jeopardy. None whatsoever. I'm dead anyway," he said. "Unless what you have to tell me is something that gives me a life again."

"You're a good man. In all the years you have left, you can contribute so much to this screwed-up world."

"Not in my condition."

Her eyes, those lakes, were sorrow given substance. Suddenly they scared him so profoundly that he wanted to look away from them—but could not.

Their conversation had given him time to approach the question from which at first he'd cringed, and now he knew that he must ask it before he lost his courage again. "Rose . . . Where is my daughter Nina?"

Rose Tucker hesitated. Finally, with her free hand, she reached into an inner pocket of her navy-blue blazer and withdrew a Polaroid photograph.

Joe could see that it was a picture of the flush-set headstone with the bronze plaque bearing the names of his wife and daughters—one of those she had taken the previous day.

With a squeeze of encouragement, she let go of his hand and pressed the photograph into it.

Staring at the Polaroid, he said, "She's not here. Not in the ground. Michelle and Chrissie, yes. But not Nina."

Almost in a whisper, she said, "Open your heart, Joe. Open your heart and your mind—and what do you see?"

At last she was bringing to him the transforming gift that she had brought to Nora Vadance, to the Delmanns, and to others.

He stared at the Polaroid.

"What do you see, Joe?"

"A gravestone."

"Open your mind."

With expectations that he could not put into words but that nevertheless caused his heart to race, Joe searched the image in his hand. "Granite, bronze . . . the grass around."

"Open your heart," she whispered.

"Their three names . . . the dates . . ."

"Keep looking."

" . . . sunshine . . . shadows . . ."

"Open your heart."

Although Rose's sincerity was evident and could not be doubted, her little mantra— *Open your mind, open your heart*—began to seem silly, as though she were not a scientist but a New Age guru.

"Open your mind," she persisted gently.

The granite. The bronze. The grass around.

She said, "Don't just look. *See.*"

The sweet milk of expectation began to curdle, and Joe felt his expression turning sour.

Rose said, "Does the photo feel strange to you? Not to your eyes . . . to your fingertips? Does it feel peculiar against your skin?"

He was about to tell her no, that it felt like nothing more than what it was, like a damned Polaroid, glossy and cool—but then it *did* feel peculiar.

First he became conscious of the elaborate texture of his own skin to an extent that he had never before experienced or imagined possible. He felt every arch, loop, and whorl as it pressed against the photo, and each tiny ridge and equally tiny trough of skin on each finger pad seemed to have its own exquisitely sensitive array of nerve endings.

More tactile data flowed to him from the Polaroid than he was able to process or understand. He was overwhelmed by the smoothness of the photograph, but also by the thousands of microscopic pits in the film surface that were invisible to the unassisted eye, and by the *feel* of the dyes and fixatives and other chemicals of which the graveyard image was composed.

Then to his touch, although not to his eye, the image on the Polaroid acquired depth, as if it were not merely a two-dimensional photograph but a window with a view of the grave, a window through which he was able to reach. He felt warm summer sun on his fingers, felt granite and bronze and a prickle of grass.

Weirder still: Now he *felt* a color, as if wires had crossed in his brain, jumbling his senses, and he said, "Blue," and immediately he *felt* a dazzling burst of light, and as if from a distance, he heard himself say, "Bright."

The feelings of blueness and light quickly became actual visual experiences: The banquet room began to fade into a bright blue haze.

Gasping, Joe dropped the photograph as if it had come alive in his hand.

The blue brightness *snapped* to a small point in the center of his field of vision, like the picture on a television screen when the Off switch is clicked. This point shrank until the final pixel of light hung starlike for an instant but then silently imploded and was gone.

Rose Tucker leaned across the table toward him.

Joe peered into her commanding eyes—and perceived something different from what he had seen before. The sorrow and the pity, yes. They remained. The compassion and the intelligence were still there, in as full measure as ever. But now he saw—or thought he saw—some part of her that rode a mad horse of obsession at a gallop toward a cliff over which she wanted him to follow.

As though reading his thoughts, she said, "Joe, what you're afraid of has nothing to do with me. What you're truly afraid of is *opening your mind* to something you've spent your life refusing to believe."

"Your voice," he said, "the whisper, the repetitive phrases—*Open your heart, open your mind*—like a hypnotist."

"You don't really believe that," she said as calmly as ever.

"Something on the Polaroid," he said, and heard the quiver of desperation in his voice.

"What do you mean?" she asked.

"A chemical substance."

"No."

"A hallucinogenic drug. Absorbed through the skin."

"No."

"Something I absorbed through the skin," he insisted, "put me in an altered state of consciousness." He rubbed his hands on his corduroy jacket.

"Nothing on the photograph could have entered your bloodstream through your skin *so quickly.* Nothing could have affected your mind in mere seconds."

"I don't know that to be true."

"I do."

"I'm no pharmacologist."

"Then consult one," she said without enmity.

"Shit." He was as irrationally angry with her as he had briefly been angry with Barbara Christman.

The more rattled he became, the deeper her equanimity. "What you experienced was synesthesia."

"What?"

All scientist now, Rose Tucker said, "Synesthesia. A sensation produced in one modality when a stimulus is applied in a different modality."

"Mumbo-jumbo."

"Not at all. For instance, a few bars of a familiar song are played—but instead of hearing them, you might see a certain color or smell an associated aroma. It's a rare condition in the general population, but it's what most people first feel with these photos—and it's common among mystics."

"Mystics!" He almost spat on the floor. "I'm no mystic, Dr. Tucker. I'm a crime reporter—or was. Only the facts matter to me."

"Synesthesia isn't simply the result of religious mania, if that's what you're thinking, Joe. It's a scientifically documented experience even among nonbelievers, and some well-grounded people think it's a glimpse of a higher state of consciousness."

Her eyes, such cool lakes before, seemed hot now, and when he peered into them, he looked at once away, afraid that her fire would spread to him. He was not sure if he saw evil in her or only wanted to see it, and he was thoroughly confused.

"If it was some skin-permeating drug on the photograph," she said, as maddeningly soft-spoken as any devil ever had been, "then the effect would have lingered after you dropped it."

He said nothing, spinning in his internal turmoil.

"But when you released the photo, the effect ceased. Because what you're confronted with here is nothing as comforting as mere illusion, Joe."

"Where's Nina?" he demanded.

Rose indicated the Polaroid, which now lay on the table where he had dropped it. "Look. See."

"No."

"Don't be afraid."

Anger surged in him, boiled. This was the savage anger that had frightened him before. It frightened him now, too, but he could not control it.

"Where's Nina, damn it?"

"Open your heart," she said quietly.

"This is bullshit."

"Open your mind."

"Open it how far? Until I've emptied out my head? Is that what you want me to be?"

She gave him time to get a grip on himself. Then: "I don't want you to be anything, Joe. You asked me where Nina is. You want to know about your family. I gave you the photograph so you could see. So you could see."

Her will was stronger than his, and after a while he found himself picking up the photograph.

"Remember the feeling," she encouraged him. "Let it come to you again."

It did not come to him again, however, although he turned the photograph over and over in his hands. He slid his fingertips in circles across the glossy image but could not feel the granite, the bronze, the grass. He summoned the blueness and the brightness, but they did not appear.

Tossing the photograph aside in disgust, he said, "I don't know what I'm doing with this."

Infuriatingly patient, she smiled compassionately and held out a hand to him.

He refused to take it.

Although he was frustrated by what he now perceived as her New Age proclivities, he also felt that somehow, by not being able to lose himself a second time in the phantasmal blue brightness, he had failed Michelle and Chrissie and Nina.

But if his experience had been only a hallucination, induced with chemicals or hypnosis, then it had no significance, and giving himself to the waking dream once again could not bring back those who were irretrievably lost.

A fusillade of confusions ricocheted through his mind.

Rose said, "It's okay. The imbued photograph is usually enough. But not always."

"Imbued?"

"It's okay, Joe. It's okay. Once in a while there's someone . . . someone like you . . . and then the only thing that convinces is galvanic contact."

"I don't know what you're talking about."

"The touch."

"What touch?"

Instead of answering him, Rose picked up the Polaroid snapshot and stared at it as though she could clearly see something that Joe could see not at all. If turmoil touched her heart and mind, she hid it well, for she seemed as tranquil as a country pond in a windless twilight.

Her serenity only inflamed Joe. "Where's Nina, damn it? Where is my little girl?"

Calmly she returned the photograph to her jacket pocket.

She said, "Joe, suppose that I was one of a group of scientists engaged in a revolutionary series of medical experiments, and then suppose we unexpectedly discovered something that could prove there was some kind of life after death."

"I might be a hell of a lot harder to convince than you."

Her softness was an irritating counterpoint to his sharpness: "It's not as outrageous an idea as you think. For the past couple of decades, discoveries in molecular biology and certain branches of physics have seemed ever more clearly to point toward a *created* universe."

"You're dodging my question. Where are you keeping Nina? Why have you let me go on thinking she's dead?"

Her face remained in an almost eerie repose. Her voice was still soft with a Zen-like sense of peace. "If science gave us a way to perceive the truth of an afterlife, would you really want to see this proof? Most people would say *yes* at once, without thinking how such knowledge would change them forever, change what they have always considered important, what they intend to do with their lives. And then . . . what if this were a revelation with an unnerving edge? Would you want to see this truth—even if it was as frightening as it was uplifting, as fearsome as it was joyous, as deeply and thoroughly strange as it was enlightening?"

"This is just a whole lot of babble to me, Dr. Tucker, a whole lot of nothing—like healing with crystals and channeling spirits and little gray men kidnapping people in flying saucers."

"Don't just look. See."

Through the red lenses of his defensive anger, Joe perceived her calmness as a tool of manipulation. He got up from his chair, hands fisted at his sides. "What were you bringing to L.A. on that plane, and why did Teknologik and its friends kill three hundred and thirty people to stop you?"

"I'm trying to tell you."

"Then *tell* me!"

She closed her eyes and folded her small brown hands, as though waiting for this storm in him to pass—but her serenity only fed the winds of his tempest.

"Horton Nellor. Once your boss, once mine. How does he figure in this?" Joe demanded. She said nothing.

"Why did the Delmanns and Lisa and Nora Vadance and Captain Blane commit suicide? And how can their suicides be murder, like you say? Who're those men upstairs? What the *hell* is this all about?" He was shaking. *"Where is Nina?"*

Rose opened her eyes and regarded him with sudden concern, her tranquillity at last disturbed. "What men upstairs?"

"Two thugs who work for Teknologik or some secret damn police agency, or someone."

She turned her gaze toward the restaurant. "You're sure?"

"I recognized them, having dinner."

Getting quickly to her feet, Rose stared at the low ceiling as though she were in a submarine sinking out of control into an abyss, furiously calculating the enormity of the crushing pressure, waiting for the first signs of failure in the hull.

"If two of them are inside, you can bet others are outside," Joe said.

"Dear God," she whispered.

"Mahalia's trying to figure a way to slip us past them after closing time."

"She doesn't understand. We've got to get out of here now."

"She's having boxes stacked in the receiving room to cover the entrance of the elevator—"

"I don't care about those men or their damn guns," Rose said, rounding the end of the table. "If they come down here after us, I can face that, handle that. I don't care about dying that way, Joe. But they don't really need to come after us. If they know we're somewhere in this building right now, they can remote us."

"What?"

"Remote us," she said fearfully, heading toward one of the doors that served the deck and the beach.

Following her, exasperated, Joe said, "What does that mean—remote us?"

The door was secured by a pair of thumb-turn deadbolts. She disengaged the upper one.

He clamped his hand over the lower lock, preventing her from opening it. "Where's Nina?"

"Get out of the way," she demanded.

"Where's Nina?"

"Joe, for God's sake—"

This was the first time that Rose Tucker had seemed vulnerable, and Joe was going to take advantage of the moment to get what he most wanted. "Where's Nina?"

"Later. I promise."

"*Now.*"

From upstairs came a loud clatter.

Rose gasped, turned from the door, and pressed her gaze upon the ceiling again as if it might crash down on them.

Joe heard voices raised in argument, filtered through the elevator shaft—Mahalia's and those of at least two or three men. He was sure that the clatter was the sound of empty packing crates and pallets being dragged and tossed away from the cab door.

When the men in the leather jackets discovered the elevator and knew there was a lower floor to the building, they might realize that they had left an escape gate open by not covering the beach. Indeed, others might even now be looking for a way down the sheer forty-foot bluff, with the hope of cutting off that route.

Nevertheless, face-to-face with Rose, recklessly determined to have an answer at any cost, fiercely insistent, Joe pressed his question: "Where's Nina?"

"Dead," she said, seeming to wrench the word from herself.

"Like hell she is."

"Please, Joe—"

He was furious with her for lying to him, as so many others had lied to him during the past year. "Like *hell* she is. No way. No damn way. I've talked to Mercy Ealing. Nina was alive that night and she's alive now, somewhere."

"If they know we're in this building," Rose repeated in a voice that now shook with urgency, "they can *remote* us. Like the Delmanns. Like Lisa. Like Captain Blane!"

"*Where is Nina?*"

The elevator motor rumbled to life, and the cab began to hum upward through the shaft.

"*Where is Nina?*"

Overhead, the banquet room lights dimmed, probably because the elevator drew power from their circuit.

At the dimming of the lights, Rose cried out in terror, threw her body against Joe, trying to knock him off his feet, and clawed frenziedly at the hand that he had clamped over the lower deadbolt.

Her nails gouged his flesh, and he hissed in pain and let go of the lock, and she pulled open the door. In came a breeze that smelled of the ocean, and out went Rose into the night.

Joe rushed after her, onto a twenty-foot-wide, eighty-foot-long, elevated wood deck overhung by the restaurant. It reverberated like a kettledrum with each footfall.

The scarlet sun had bled into a grave on the far side of Japan. The sky and the sea to the west were raven meeting crow, as feathery smooth and sensuous and inviting as death.

Rose was already at the head of the stairs.

Following her, Joe found two flights that led down fourteen or sixteen feet to the beach.

As dark as Rose was, and darkly dressed, she all but vanished in the black geometry of the steps below him. When she reached the pale sand, however, she regained some definition.

The strand was more than a hundred feet across at this point, and the phosphorescent tumble of surf churned out a low white noise that washed like a ghost sea around him. This was not a swimming or surfing beach, and there were no bonfires or even Coleman lanterns in sight in either direction.

To the east, the sky was a pustulant yellow overlaid on black, full of the glow of the city, as insistent as it was meaningless. Cast from high above, the pale-yellow rectangles of light from the restaurant windows quilted part of the beach.

Joe did not try to stop Rose or to slow her. Instead, when he caught up with her, he ran at her side, shortening his stride to avoid pulling ahead of her.

She was his only link to Nina. He was confused by her apparent mysticism, by her sudden transit from beatific calm to superstitious terror, and he was furious that she would lie to him about Nina now, after she had led him to believe, at the cemetery, that she would ultimately tell him the full truth. Yet his fate and hers were inextricably linked, because only she could ever lead him to his younger daughter.

As they ran north through the soft sand and passed the corner of the restaurant, someone rushed at them from ahead and to the right, from the bluff, a shadow in the night, quick and big, like the featureless beast that seeks us in nightmares, pursuer through corridors of dreams.

"Look out," Joe warned Rose, but she also saw the oncoming assailant and was already taking evasive action.

Joe attempted to intervene when the hurtling dark shape moved to cut Rose off—but he was blindsided by a second man, who came at him from the direction of the sea. This guy was as big as a professional football linebacker, and they both went down so hard that the breath should have been knocked out of Joe, but it wasn't, not entirely—he was wheezing but breathing—because the sand in which they landed was deep and soft, far above the highest lapping line of the compacting tide.

He kicked, flailed, ruthlessly used knees and elbows and feet, and rolled out from under his attacker, scrambling to his feet as he heard someone shout at Rose farther along the strand—"*Freeze, bitch!*"—after which he heard a shot, hard and flat. He didn't want to think about that shot, a whip of sound snapping across the beach to the growling sea, didn't want to think about Rose with a bullet in her head and his Nina lost again forever, but he couldn't avoid thinking about it, the possibility like a lash burn branded forever across the surface of his brain. His own assailant was cursing him and pushing up now from the sand, and as Joe spun around to deal with the threat, he was full of the meanness and fury that had gotten him thrown out of the youth boxing league twenty years ago, seething with church-vandalizing rage—he was an animal now, a heartless predator, cat-quick and savage—and he reacted as though this stranger were personally responsible for poor Frank's being crippled with rheumatoid arthritis, as if this son of a bitch had worked some hoodoo to make Frank's joints swell and deform, as if this wretched thug were the *sole perpetrator* who had somehow put a funnel in Captain Blane's ear and poured an elixir of madness into his head, so Joe kicked him in the crotch, and when the guy grunted and began to double over, Joe grabbed the bastard's head and at the same time drove a knee upward, shoving the face down into the knee and jamming the knee up hard into the face, a ballet of violence, and he actually heard the crunch of the man's nose disintegrating and felt the bite of teeth breaking against his kneecap. The guy collapsed backward on the beach, all at once choking and spitting blood and gasping for breath and crying like a small child, but this wasn't enough for Joe, because he was wild now, wilder than any animal, as wild as weather, a cyclone of anger and grief and frustration, and he kicked where he thought ribs would be, which hurt him almost as much as it hurt the broken man who received the blow, because Joe was only wearing Nikes, not hard-toed shoes, so he tried to stomp the guy's throat and crush his windpipe, but stomped his chest instead—and would have tried again, would have killed him, not quite realizing that he was doing so, but then he was rammed from behind by a third attacker.

Joe slammed facedown onto the beach, with the weight of this new assailant atop him, at least two hundred pounds pinning him down. Head to one side, spitting sand, he tried to heave the man off, but this time his breath *was* knocked out of him; he exhaled all of his strength with it, and he lay helpless.

Besides, as he gasped desperately for air, he felt his attacker thrust something cold and blunt against the side of his face, and he knew what it must be even before he heard the threat.

"You want me to blow your head off, I'll do it," the stranger said, and his reverberant voice had a ragged homicidal edge. "I'll do it, you asshole."

Joe believed him and stopped resisting. He struggled only for his breath.

Silent surrender wasn't good enough for the angry man atop him. "Answer me, you bastard. You want me to blow your damn head off? Do you?"

"No."

"Do you?"

"No."

"Going to behave?"

"Yes."

"I'm out of patience here."

"All right."

"Son of a bitch," the stranger said bitterly.

Joe said nothing more, just spit out sand and breathed deeply, getting his strength back with his wind, though trying to stave off the return of the brief madness that had seized him.

Where is Rose?

The man atop Joe was breathing hard too, expelling foul clouds of garlic breath, not only giving Joe time to calm down but getting his own strength back. He smelled of a lime-scented cologne and cigarette smoke.

What's happened to Rose?

"We're going to get up now," the guy said. "Me first. Getting up, I got this piece aimed at your head. You stay flat, dug right into the sand the way you are, just the way you are, until I step back and tell you it's okay to get up." For emphasis, he pressed the muzzle of the gun more deeply into Joe's face, twisting it back and forth; the inside of Joe's cheek pressed painfully against his teeth. "You understand, Carpenter?"

"Yes."

"I can waste you and walk away."

"I'm cool."

"Nobody can touch me."

"Not me anyway."

"I mean, I got a badge."

"Sure."

"You want to see it? I'll pin it to your damn lip."

Joe said nothing more.

They hadn't shouted *Police*, which didn't prove that they were phony cops, only that they didn't want to advertise. They hoped to do their business quickly, cleanly—and get out before they were required to explain their presence to the local authorities, which would at least tangle them in inter-jurisdictional paperwork and might result in troubling questions about what legitimate laws they were enforcing. If they weren't strictly employees of Teknologik, they had some measure of federal power behind them, but they hadn't shouted *FBI* or *DEA* or *ATF* when they had burst out of the night, so they were probably operatives with a clandestine agency paid for out of those many billions of dollars that the government dispensed off the accounting books, from the infamous Black Budget.

Finally the stranger eased off Joe, onto one knee, then stood and backed away a couple of steps. "Get up."

Rising from the sand, Joe was relieved to discover that his eyes were rapidly adapting to the darkness. When he had first come out of the banquet room and run north along the beach, hardly two minutes ago, the gloom had seemed deeper than it was now. The longer he remained night blind to any degree, the less likely he would be to see an advantage and to be able to seize it.

Although his rakish Panama hat was gone, and in spite of the darkness, the gunman was clearly recognizable: the storyteller. In his white slacks and white shirt, with his long white hair, he seemed to draw the meager ambient light to himself, glowing softly like an entity at a séance.

Joe glanced back and up at Santa-Fe-by-the-Sea. He saw the silhouettes of diners at their tables, but they probably couldn't see the action on the dark beach.

Crotch-kicked, face-slammed, the disabled agent still sprawled nearby on the sand, no longer choking but gagging, in pain, and still spitting blood. He was striving to squeeze off his flow of tears by wheezing out obscenities instead of sobs.

Joe shouted, "Rose!"

The white-clad gunman said, "Shut up."

"Rose!"

"Shut up and turn around."

Silent in the sand, a new man loomed behind the storyteller and, instead of proving to be another Teknologik drone, said, "I have a Desert Eagle .44 magnum just one inch from the back of your skull."

The storyteller seemed as surprised as Joe was, and Joe was *dizzied* by this turn of events.

The man with the Desert Eagle said, "You know how powerful this weapon is? You know what it'll do to your head?"

Still softly radiant but now also as powerless as a ghost, the astonished storyteller said, "Shit."

"Pulverize your skull, take your fat head right off your neck, is what it'll do," said the new arrival. "It's a doorbuster. Now toss your gun in the sand in front of Joe."

The storyteller hesitated.

"Now."

Managing to surrender with arrogance, the storyteller threw the gun as if disdaining it, and the weapon thudded into the sand at Joe's feet.

The savior with the .44 said, "Pick it up, Joe."

As Joe retrieved the pistol, he saw the new arrival use the Desert Eagle as a club. The storyteller dropped to his knees, then to his hands and knees, but did not go all the way out until struck with the pistol a second time, whereupon he plowed the sand with his face, planting his nose like a tuber. The stranger with the .44—a black man dressed entirely in black—stooped to turn the white-maned head gently to one side to ensure that the unconscious thug would not suffocate.

The agent with the knee-smashed face stopped cursing. Now that no witnesses of his own kind were able to hear, he sobbed miserably again.

The black man said, "Come on, Joe."

More impressed than ever with Mahalia and her odd collection of amateurs, Joe said, "Where's Rose?"

"This way. We've got her."

With the disabled agent's sobs purling eerily across the strand behind them, Joe hurried with the black man north, in the direction that he and Rose had been heading when they were assaulted.

He almost stumbled over another unconscious man lying in the sand. This was evidently the first one who had rushed them, the one who had fired a gun.

Rose was on the beach but in the inky shadow of the bluff. Joe could barely see her in the murk, but she seemed to be hugging herself as though she were shivering and cold on this mild summer night.

He was half surprised by the wave of relief that washed through him at the sight of her, not because she was his only link to Nina but because he was genuinely glad that she was alive and safe. For all that she had frustrated and angered and sorely confused him, she was still special, for he recalled, as well, the kindness in her eyes when she had encountered him in the cemetery, the tenderness and pity. Even in the darkness, small as she was, she had an imposing presence, an aura of mystery but also of consequence and prodigious wisdom, probably the same power with which great generals and holy women alike elicited sacrifice from their followers. And here, now, on the shore of the night sea, it was almost possible to believe that she had walked out of the deeps to the west, having breathed water as easily as she now breathed air, come to land with the wonderful secrets of another realm.

With her was a tall man in dark clothes. He was little more than a spectral form—except for masses of curly blond hair that shone faintly like sinuous strands of phosphorate seaweed.

Joe said, "Rose, are you all right?"

"Just got . . . battered around a little," she said in a voice taut with pain.

"I heard a shot," he worried. He wanted to touch her, but he wasn't sure that he should. Then he found himself with his arms around her, holding her.

She groaned in pain, and Joe started to let go of her, but she put one arm around him for a moment, embracing him to let him know that in spite of her injuries she was grateful for his expression of concern. "I'm fine, Joe. I'll be okay."

Shouting rose in the distance, from the bluff top beside the restaurant. And from the beach to the south, the disabled agent replied, calling feebly for help.

"Gotta get out of here," said the blond guy. "They're coming."

"Who are you people?" Rose asked.

Surprised, Joe said, "Aren't they Mahalia's crew?"

"No," Rose said. "Never saw them before."

"I'm Mark," said the man with the curly blond hair, "and he's Joshua."

The black man—Joshua—said something that sounded like: "We're both in finna face."

Rose said, "I'll be damned."

"Who, what? You're in what?" Joe asked.

"It's all right, Joe," Rose said. "I'm surprised, but I probably shouldn't be."

Joshua said, "We believe we're fighting on the same side, Dr. Tucker. Anyway, we have the same enemies."

Out of the distance, at first as soft as the murmur of a heart, but then like the approaching hooves of a headless horseman's steed, came the *whump-whump-whump* of helicopter rotors.

FIFTEEN

Having stolen nothing but their own freedom, they raced like fleeing thieves alongside the bluffs, which soared and then declined and then soared high again, almost as if mirroring Joe's adrenaline levels.

While they were on the move, with Mark in the lead and Rose at his heels, Joe heard Joshua talking urgently to someone. He glanced back and saw the black man with a cell phone. Hearing the word *car*, he realized that their escape was being planned and coordinated even as it was unfolding.

Just when they seemed to have gotten away, the thumping promise of the helicopter became a bright reality to the south. Like a beam from the jewel eye of a stone-temple god angered by desecration, a searchlight pierced the night and swept the beach. Its burning gaze arced from the sandy cliffs to the foaming surf and back again, moving relentlessly toward them.

Because the sand was soft near the base of the palisades, they left shapeless impressions in it. Their aerial pursuers, however, wouldn't be able to follow them by their footprints. Because this sand was never raked, as it might have been on a well-used public beach, it was disturbed by the tracks of many others who had come before them. If they had walked nearer the surf, in the area where higher tides had compacted the sand and left it smooth, their route would have been as clearly marked as if they'd left flares.

They passed several sets of switchback stairs leading to great houses on the bluffs above, some of masonry pinned to the cliff face with steel, some of wood bolted to deep pylons and vertical concrete beams. Joe glanced back once and saw the helicopter hovering by one staircase, the searchlight shimmering up the treads and across the railings.

He figured that a team of hunters might already have driven north from the restaurant and gone by foot to the beach to work methodically southward. Ultimately, if Mark kept them on the strand like this, they would be trapped between the northbound chopper and the southbound searchers.

Evidently the same thought occurred to Mark, because he suddenly led them to an unusual set of redwood stairs rising through a tall box frame. The structure was reminiscent of an early rocket gantry as built back when Cape Kennedy had been called Cape Canaveral, the spacecraft gone now and the architecture surrounding a curious void.

While they ascended, they were putting no additional distance between themselves and the chopper, but it continued to approach. Two, four, six, eight flights of steep stairs brought them to a landing where they seemed horribly exposed. The helicopter, after all, was hovering no more than a hundred feet above the beach—which put it perhaps forty feet above them as they stood atop the bluff—and hardly a hundred and fifty yards to the south. The house next door had no stairs to the shore, which made this platform even more prominent. If either the pilot or the copilot looked to the right and at the bluff top instead of at the searchlight-splashed sand below, discovery could not be avoided.

The upper landing was surrounded by a six-foot-tall, wrought-iron, gated security fence with a sharply inward-angled, spiked top to prevent unwanted visitors from gaining access by way of the beach below. It had been erected long ago, in the days when the Coastal Commission didn't control such things.

The helicopter was now little more than a hundred yards to the south, moving forward slowly, all but hovering. Its screaming engine and clattering rotors were so loud that Joe could not have made himself heard to his companions unless he shouted.

There was no easy way to climb the fence, not in the minute or two of grace they might have left. Joshua stepped forward with the doorbuster Desert Eagle, fired one round into the lock, and kicked the gate open.

The men in the helicopter could not have heard the gunshot, and it was unlikely that the sound was perceived in the house as anything more than additional racket caused by the aircraft. Indeed, every window was dark, and all was as still as though no one was home.

They passed through the gate into an expansive, estate-size property with low box hedges, formal rose gardens, bowl fountains currently dry, antique French terra-cotta walkways lit by bronze-tulip path lights, and multilevel terraces with limestone balustrades rising to a Mediterranean mansion. There were phoenix palms, ficus trees. Massive California live oaks were underlit by landscape spots: magisterial, frost-and-black, free-form scaffoldings of branches.

Because of the artfulness of the landscape lighting, no glare spoiled any corner. The romantic grounds cast off tangled shawls of shadow, intricate laces of soft light and hard darkness, in which the four of them surely could not be seen by the pilots even as the helicopter now drew almost even with the bluff on which the estate made its bed.

As he followed Rose and Mark up stone steps onto the lowest terrace, Joe hoped that security-system motion detectors were not installed on the exterior of the enormous house, only within its rooms. If their passage activated kleigs mounted high in the trees or atop the perimeter walls, the sudden dazzle would draw the pilots' attention.

He knew how difficult it could be even for a lone fugitive on foot to escape the bright eye of a police search chopper with a good and determined pilot—especially in comparatively open environs such as this neighborhood, which didn't offer the many hiding places of a city's mazes. The four of them would be altogether too easy to keep pinpointed once they had been spotted.

Earlier, an onshore breeze had come with the grace of gull wings from the sea; currently, the flow was offshore and stronger. This was one of those hot winds, called Santa Anas, born in the mountains to the east, out of the threshold of the Mojave, dry and blustery and curiously wearing on the nerves. Now a loud whispering rose from the oaks, and the great fronds of the phoenix palms hissed and rattled and creaked as though the trees were warning one another of gales that might soon descend.

Joe's fear of an outer security line seemed unwarranted as they hurriedly climbed another short flight of stone steps to the upper terrace. The grounds remained subtly lighted, heavily layered with sheltering shadows.

Out beyond the bluff's edge, the search chopper was parallel with them, moving slowly northward. The pilots' attention remained focused on the beach below.

Mark led them past an enormous swimming pool. The oil-black water glimmered with fluid arabesques of silver, as though schools of strange fish with luminous scales were swimming just beneath the surface.

They were still passing the pool when Rose stumbled. She almost fell but regained her balance. She halted, swaying.

"Are you all right?" Joe asked worriedly.

"Yes, fine, I'll be okay," she said, but her voice was thin, and she still appeared to be unsteady.

"How badly were you hurt back there?" Joe pressed as Mark and Joshua gathered around.

"Just knocked on my ass," she said. "Bruised a little."

"Rose—"

"I'm okay, Joe. It's just all this running, all those damn stairs up from the beach. I guess I'm not in as good a shape as I should be."

Joshua was talking sotto voce on the cell phone again.

"Let's go," Rose said. "Come on, come on, let's go."

Beyond the bluff, above the beach, the helicopter was almost past the estate.

Mark led the way again, and Rose followed with renewed energy. They dashed under the roof of the arched loggia against the rear wall, where they were no longer in any danger of being spotted by the chopper pilots, and then to the corner of the house.

As they moved single file along the side of the mansion on a walkway that serpentined through a small grove of shaggy-barked melaleucas, they were abruptly pinned in the bright beam of a big flashlight. Blocking the path ahead of them, a watchman said, "Hey, who the hell are—"

Acting without hesitation, Mark began to move even as the beam flicked on. The stranger was still speaking when Mark collided with him. The two men grunted from the impact.

The flashlight flew against the trunk of a melaleuca, rebounded onto the walkway, and spun on the stone, making shadows whirl like a pack of tail-chasing dogs.

Mark swiveled the startled watchman around, put a hammerlock on him, bum-rushed him off the sidewalk and through bordering flower beds, and slammed him against the side of the house so hard that the nearby windows rattled.

Scooping up the flashlight, Joshua directed it on the action, and Joe saw that they had been challenged by an overweight uniformed security guard of about fifty-five. Mark pressed him to his knees and kept a hand on the back of his head to force his face down and away from them, so he couldn't describe them later.

"He's not armed," Mark informed Joshua.

"Bastards," the watchman said bitterly.

"Ankle holster?" Joshua wondered.

"Not that, either."

The watchman said, "Stupid owners are pacifists or some damn thing. Won't have a gun on the place, even for me. So now here I am."

"We're not going to hurt you," Mark said, pulling him backward from the house and forcing him to sit on the ground with his back against the trunk of a melaleuca.

"You don't scare me," the watchman said, but he sounded scared.

"Dogs?" Mark demanded.

"Everywhere," the guard said. "Dobermans."

"He's lying," Mark said confidently.

Even Joe could hear the bluff in the watchman's voice.

Joshua gave the flashlight to Joe and said, "Keep it pointed at the ground." Then he produced handcuffs from a fanny pack.

Mark directed the guard to reach in back of himself and clasp his hands behind the tree. The trunk was only about ten inches in diameter, so the guard didn't have to contort himself, and Joshua snapped the cuffs on his wrists.

"The cops are on the way," the watchman gloated.

"No doubt riding Dobermans," Mark said.

"Bastard," said the watchman.

From his fanny pack, Mark withdrew a tightly rolled Ace bandage. "Bite on this," he told the guard.

"Bite on *this*," the guard said, indulging in one last bleat of hopeless bravado, and then he did as he was told.

Three times, Joshua wound electrician's tape around the guard's head and across his mouth, fixing the Ace bandage firmly in place.

From the watchman's belt, Mark unclipped what appeared to be a remote control. "This open the driveway gate?"

Through his gag, the watchman snarled something obscene, which issued as a meaningless mumble.

"Probably the gate."

To the guard, Joshua said, "Just relax. Don't chafe your wrists. We're not robbing the place. We're really not. We're only passing through."

Mark said, "When we've been gone half an hour, we'll call the cops so they can come and release you."

"Better get a dog," Joshua advised.

Taking the watchman's flashlight, Mark led them toward the front of the house.

Whoever these guys were, Joe was glad that they were on his side.

The estate occupied at least three acres. The huge house was set two hundred feet back from the front property wall at the street. In the eye of the wide, looping driveway was a four-tier marble fountain: four broad scalloped bowls, each supported by three leaping dolphins, bowls and dolphins diminishing in scale as they ascended. The bowls were full of water, but the pump was silent, and there were no spouts or cascades.

"We'll wait here," Mark said, leading them to the dolphins.

The dolphins and bowls rose out of a pool with a two-foot-high wall finished with a broad cap of limestone. Rose sat on the edge—and then so did Joe and Mark.

Taking the remote control they had gotten from the watchman, Joshua walked along the driveway toward the entrance gate, talking on the cellular phone as he went.

Dogs of warm Santa Ana wind chased cat-quick leaves and curls of papery melaleuca bark along the blacktop.

"How do you even know about me?" Rose asked Mark.

"When any enterprise is launched with a one-billion-dollar trust fund, like ours," Mark said, "it sure doesn't take long to get up to speed. Besides, computers and data technology are what we're about."

"What enterprise?" Joe asked.

The answer was the same mystifying response that Joshua had given on the beach, "In finna face."

"And what's that mean?"

"Later, Joe," Rose promised. "Go on, Mark."

"Well, so, from day one, we've had the funds to try to keep track of all promising research in every discipline, worldwide, that could conceivably lead to the epiphany we expect."

"Maybe so," Rose said, "but you people have been around two years, while the largest part of my research for the past *seven* years has been conducted under the tightest imaginable security."

"Doctor, you showed enormous promise in your field until you were about thirty-seven—and then suddenly your work appeared to come almost to a complete halt, except for a minor paper published here or there from time to time. You were a Niagara of creativity—and then went dry overnight."

"And that indicates what to you?"

"It's the signature pattern of a scientist who's been co-opted by the defense establishment or some other branch of government with sufficient power to enforce a total information blackout. So when we see something like that, we start trying to find out exactly where you're at work. Finally we located you at Teknologik, but not at any of their well-known and accessible facilities. A deep subterranean, biologically secure complex near Manassas, Virginia. Something called 'Project 99.'"

While he listened intently to the conversation, Joe watched as, out at the end of the long driveway, the ornate electric gate rolled aside.

"How much do you know about what we do on Project 99?" Rose asked.

"Not enough," Mark said.

"How can you know anything at all?"

"When I say we track ongoing research worldwide, I don't mean that we limit ourselves to the same publications and shared data banks that any science library has available to it."

With no animosity, Rose said, "That's a nice way of saying you try to penetrate computer security systems, hack your way in, break encryptions."

"Whatever. We don't do it for profit. We don't economically exploit the information we acquire. It's simply our mission, the search we were created to undertake."

Joe was surprised by his own patience. Although he was learning things by listening to them talk, the basic mystery only grew deeper. Yet he was prepared to wait for answers. The bizarre experience with the Polaroid snapshot in the banquet room had left him shaken. Now that he'd had time to think about what had happened, the synesthesia seemed to be but prelude to some revelation that was going to be more shattering and humbling than he had previously imagined. He remained committed to learning the truth, but now instinct warned him that he should allow the revelations to wash over him in small waves instead of in one devastating tsunami.

Joshua had gone through the open gate and was standing along the Pacific Coast Highway.

Over the eastern hills, the swollen moon ascended yellow-orange, and the warm wind seemed to blow down out of it.

Mark said, "You were one of thousands of researchers whose work we followed— though you were of somewhat special interest because of the extreme secrecy at Project 99. Then, a year ago, you left Manassas with something from the project, and overnight you were the most wanted person in the country. Even after you supposedly died aboard that airliner in Colorado. Even then . . . people were looking for you, lots of people, expending considerable resources, searching frantically for a dead woman—which seemed pretty weird to us."

Rose said nothing to encourage him. She seemed tired.

Joe took her hand. She was trembling, but she squeezed his hand as if to assure him that she was all right.

"Then we began to intercept reports from a certain clandestine police agency . . . reports that said you were alive and active in the L.A. area, that it involved families who'd lost loved ones on Flight 353. We set up some surveillance of our own. We're pretty good at it. Some of us are ex-military. Anyway, you could say we watched the watchers who were keeping tab on people like Joe here. And now . . . I guess it's a good thing we did."

"Yes. Thank you," she said. "But you don't know what you're getting into here. There's not just glory . . . there's terrible danger."

"Dr. Tucker," Mark persisted, "there are over nine thousand of us now, and we've committed our lives to what we do. We're not afraid. And now we believe that you may have found the interface—and that it's very different from anything we quite anticipated. If you've actually made that breakthrough . . . if humanity is at that pivot point in history when everything is going to change radically and forever . . . then *we* are your natural allies."

"I think you are," she agreed.

Gently but persistently selling her on this alliance, Mark said, "Doctor, we both have set ourselves against those forces of ignorance and fear and self-interest that want to keep the world in darkness."

"Remember, I once worked for them."

"But turned."

A car swung off Pacific Coast Highway and paused to pick up Joshua. It was followed through the gate and along the driveway by a second car.

Rose, Mark, and Joe got to their feet as the two vehicles—a Ford trailed by a Mercedes—circled the fountain and stopped in front of them.

Joshua stepped from the passenger door of the Ford, and a young brunette woman got out from behind the steering wheel. The Mercedes was driven by an Asian man of about thirty.

They all gathered before Rose Tucker, and for a moment everyone stood in silence.

The steadily escalating wind no longer spoke merely through the rustling foliage of the trees, through the cricket-rasping branches of the shrubbery, and through the hollow flute-like music issuing from the eaves of the mansion, for now it also enjoyed a voice of its own: a haunted keening that curled chillingly in listening ears, akin to the muted but frightful ululant crying of coyote packs chasing down prey in some far canyon of the night.

In the landscape lights, the shuddering greenery cast nervous shadows, and the gradually paling moon gazed at itself in the shiny surfaces of the automobiles.

Watching these four people as they watched Rose, Joe realized that they regarded the scientist not solely with curiosity but with wonder, perhaps even with awe, as though they stood in the presence of someone transcendent. Someone holy.

"I'm surprised to see every one of you in mufti," Rose said.

They smiled, and Joshua said, "Two years ago, when we first set out on this mission, we were reasonably quiet about it. Didn't want to excite a lot of media interest . . . because we thought we'd largely be misunderstood. What we didn't expect was that we'd have enemies. And enemies so violent."

"So powerful," Mark said.

"We thought everyone would want to know the answers we were seeking—if we ever found them. Now we know better."

"Ignorance is a bliss that some people will kill for," said the young woman.

"So a year ago," Joshua continued, "we adopted the robes as a distraction. People understand us as a cult—or think they do. We're more acceptable when we're viewed as fanatics, neatly labeled and confined to a box. We don't make people quite so nervous."

Robes.

Astonished, Joe said, "You wear blue robes, shave your heads."

Joshua said, "Some of us do, yes, as of a year ago—and those in the uniform pretend to be the entire membership. That's what I meant when I said the robes are a distraction—the robes, the shaved heads, the earrings, the visible communal enclaves. The rest of us have gone underground, where we can do the work without being spied on, subjected to harassment, and easily infiltrated."

"Come with us," the young woman said to Rose. "We know you may have found the way, and we want to help you bring it to the world—without interference."

Rose moved to her and put a hand against her cheek, much as she had touched Joe in the cemetery. "I might be with you soon, but not tonight. I need more time to think, to plan. And I'm in a hurry to see a young girl, a child, who is at the center of what is happening."

Nina, Joe thought, and his heart shuddered like the shadows of the wind-shaken trees.

Rose moved to the Asian man and touched him too. "I can tell you this much . . . we stand on the threshold you foresaw. We will go through that door, maybe not tomorrow or the day after tomorrow or next week, but in the years ahead."

She went to Joshua. "Together we will see the world change forever, bring the light of knowledge into the great dark loneliness of human existence. *In our time.*"

And finally she approached Mark. "I assume you brought two cars because you were prepared to give one to Joe and me."

"Yes. But we hoped—"

She put a hand on his arm. "Soon but not tonight. I've got urgent business, Mark. Everything we hope to achieve hangs in the balance right now, hangs so precariously—until I can reach the little girl I mentioned."

"Wherever she is, we can take you to her."

"No. Joe and I must do this alone—and quickly."

"You can take the Ford."

"Thank you."

Mark withdrew a folded one-dollar bill from his pocket and gave it to Rose. "There are just eight digits in the serial number on this bill. Ignore the fourth digit, and the other seven are a phone number in the 310 area code."

Rose tucked the bill into her jeans.

"When you're ready to join us," Mark said, "or if you're ever in trouble you can't get out of, ask for me at that number. We'll come for you no matter where you are."

She kissed him on the cheek. "We've got to go." She turned to Joe. "Will you drive?"

"Yes."

To Joshua, she said, "May I take your cell phone?"

He gave it to her.

Wings of furious wind beat around them as they got into the Ford. The keys were in the ignition.

As Rose pulled the car door shut, she said, "Oh, Jesus," and leaned forward, gasping for breath.

"You *are* hurt."

"Told you. I got knocked around."

"Where's it hurt?"

"We've got to get across the city," Rose said, "but I don't want to go back past Mahalia's."

"You could have a broken rib or two."

Ignoring him, she sat up straight, and her breathing improved as she said, "The creeps won't want to risk setting up a roadblock and a traffic check without cooperation from the local authorities, and they don't have time to get that. But you can bet your ass they'll be watching passing cars."

"If you've got a broken rib, it could puncture a lung."

"Joe, damn it, we don't have *time*. We've got to move if we're going to keep our girl alive."

He stared at her. "Nina?"

She met his eyes. She said, "Nina," but then a fearful look came into her face, and she turned from him.

"We can head north from here on PCH," he said, "then inland on Kanan-Dume Road. That's a county route up to Augora Hills. There we can get the 101 east to the 210."

"Go for it."

Faces powdered by moonlight, hair wind-tossed, the four who would leave in the Mercedes stood watching, backdropped by leaping stone dolphins and thrashing trees.

This tableau struck Joe as both exhilarating and ominous—and he could not identify the basis of either perception, other than to admit that the night was charged with an uncanny power that was beyond his understanding. Everything his gaze fell upon seemed to have monumental significance, as if he were in a state of heightened consciousness, and even the moon appeared different from any moon that he had ever seen before.

As Joe put the Ford in gear and began to pull away from the fountain, the young woman came forward to place her hand against the window beside Rose Tucker's face. On this side of the glass, Rose matched her palm to the other. The young woman was crying, her lovely face glimmering with moon-bright tears, and she moved with the car along the driveway, hurrying as it picked up speed, matching her hand to Rose's all the way to the gate before at last pulling back.

Joe felt almost as if somewhere earlier in the night he had stood before a mirror of madness and, closing his eyes, had passed through his own reflection into lunacy. Yet he did not want to return through the silvered surface to that old gray world. This was a lunacy that he found increasingly agreeable, perhaps because it offered him the one thing he desired most and could find only on this side of the looking glass—hope.

Slumped in the passenger seat beside him, Rose Tucker said, "Maybe all this is more than I can handle, Joe. I'm so tired—and so scared. I'm nobody special enough to do what needs doing, not nearly special enough to carry a weight like this."

"You seem pretty special to me," he said.

"I'm going to screw it up," she said as she entered a phone number on the keypad of the cellular phone. "I'm scared shitless that I'm not going to be strong enough to open that door and take us all through it." She pushed the Send button.

"Show me the door, tell me where it goes, and I'll help you," he said, wishing she would stop speaking in metaphors and give him the hard facts. "Why is Nina so important to whatever's happening? Where is she, Rose?"

Someone answered the cellular call, and Rose said, "It's me. Move Nina. Move her now."

Nina.

Rose listened for a moment but then said firmly, "No, now, move her right now, in the next five minutes, even sooner if you can. They linked Mahalia to me . . . yeah, and in spite of all the precautions we'd taken. It's only a matter of time now—and not very much time—until they make the connection to you."

Nina.

Joe turned off the Pacific Coast Highway onto the county road to Augora Hills, driving up through a rumpled bed of dark land from which the Santa Ana wind flung sheets of pale dust.

"Take her to Big Bear," Rose told the person on the phone.

Big Bear. Since Joe had talked to Mercy Ealing in Colorado—could it be less than nine hours ago?—Nina had been back in the world, miraculously returned, but in some corner where he could not find her. Soon, however, she would be in the town of Big Bear on the shores of Big Bear Lake, a resort in the nearby San Bernardino Mountains, a place he knew well. Her return was more real to him now that she was in a place that he could *name*, the byways of which he had walked, and he was flooded with such sweet anticipation that he wanted to shout to relieve the pressure of it. He kept his silence, however, and he rolled the name between the fingers of his mind, rolled it over and over as if it were a shiny coin: *Big Bear.*

Rose spoke into the phone: "If I can . . . I'm going to be there in a couple of hours. I love you. Go. Go *now*."

She terminated the call, put the phone on the seat between her legs, closed her eyes, and leaned against the door.

Joe realized that she was not making much use of her left hand. It was curled in her lap. Even in the dim light from the instrument panel, he could see that her hand was shaking uncontrollably.

"What's wrong with your arm?"

"Give it a rest, Joe. It's sweet of you to be concerned, but you're getting to be a nag. I'll be fine once we get to Nina."

He was silent for half a mile. Then: "Tell me everything. I deserve to know."

"You do, yes. It's not a long story . . . but where do I begin?"

SIXTEEN

Great bristling balls of tumbleweed, robbed of their green by the merciless Western sun, cracked from their roots by the withering dryness of the California summer, torn from their homes in the earth by the shrieking Santa Ana wind, now bounded out of the steep canyons and across the narrow highway, silver-gray in the headlights, a curiously melancholy sight, families of thistled skeletons like starved and harried refugees fleeing worse torment.

Joe said, "Start with those people back there. What kind of cult are they?"

She spelled it for him: *Infiniface.*

"It's a made word," she said, "shorthand for 'Interface with the Infinite.' And they're not a cult, not in any sense you mean it."

"Then what are they?"

Instead of answering immediately, she shifted in her seat, trying to get more comfortable. Checking her wristwatch, she said, "Can you drive faster?"

"Not on this road. In fact, better put on your safety belt."

"Not with my left side feeling like it does." Having adjusted her position, she said, "Do you know the name Loren Pollack?"

"The software genius. The poor man's Bill Gates."

"That's what the press sometimes calls him, yes. But I don't think the word *poor* should be associated with someone who started from scratch and made seven billion dollars by the age of forty-two."

"Maybe not."

She closed her eyes and slumped against the door, supporting her weight on her right side. Sweat beaded her brow, but her voice was strong. "Two years ago, Loren Pollack used a billion dollars of his money to form a charitable trust. Named it Infiniface. He believes many of the sciences, through research facilitated by new generations of superfast computers, are approaching discoveries that will bring us face-to-face with the reality of a Creator."

"Sounds like a cult to me."

"Oh, plenty of people think Pollack is a flake. But he's got a singular ability to grasp complex research from a wide variety of sciences—and he has vision. You know, there's a whole movement of modern physics that sees evidence of a created universe."

Frowning, Joe said, "What about chaos theory? I thought that was the big thing."

"Chaos theory doesn't say the universe is random and chaotic. It's an extremely broad theory that among many other things notes strangely complex relationships in *apparently* chaotic systems—like the weather. Look deeply enough in any chaos, and you find hidden regularities."

"Actually," he admitted, "I don't know a damn thing about it—just the way they use the term in the movies."

"Most movies are stupidity machines—like politicians. So . . . if Pollack was here, he'd tell you that just eighty years ago, science mocked religion's assertion that the universe was created *ex nihilo*, out of nothing. Everyone *knew* something couldn't be created from nothing—a violation of all the laws of physics. Now we understand more about molecular structure—and particle physicists create matter *ex nihilo* all the time." Inhaling with a hiss through clenched teeth, she leaned forward, popped open the glove box, and rummaged through its contents. "I was hoping for aspirin or Excedrin. I'd chew them dry."

"We could stop somewhere—"

"No. Drive. Just drive. Big Bear's so far . . ." She closed the glove box but remained sitting forward, as though that position gave her relief. "Anyway, physics and biology are the disciplines that most fascinate Pollack—especially molecular biology."

"Why molecular biology?"

"Because the more we understand living things on a molecular level, the clearer it becomes that everything is intelligently designed. You, me, mammals, fish, insects, plants, everything."

"Wait a second. Are you tossing away evolution here?"

"Not entirely. Wherever molecular biology takes us, there might still be a place for Darwin's theory of evolution—in some form."

"You're not one of those strict fundamentalists who believe we were created exactly five thousand years ago in the Garden of Eden."

"Hardly. But Darwin's theory was put forth in 1859, before we had any knowledge of atomic structure. He thought the smallest unit of a living creature was the cell—which he saw as just a lump of adaptable albumen."

"Albumen? You're losing me."

"The origin of this basic living matter, he thought, was most likely an accident of chemistry—and the origin of all species was explained through evolution. But we now know cells are enormously complex structures of such clockwork design that it's impossible to believe they are accidental in nature."

"We do? I guess I've been out of school a long time."

"Even in the matter of the species . . . Well, the two axioms of Darwinian theory—the continuity of nature and adaptable design—have never been validated by a single empirical discovery in nearly a hundred and fifty years."

"Now you *have* lost me."

"Let me put it another way." She still leaned forward, staring out at the dark hills and the steadily rising glow of the sprawling suburbs beyond. "Do you know who Francis Crick is?"

"No."

"He's a molecular biologist. In 1962, he shared the Nobel Prize in Medicine with Maurice Wilkins and James Watson for discovering the three-dimensional molecular structure of DNA—the double helix. Every advancement in genetics since then—and the countless revolutionary cures for diseases we're going to see over the next twenty years—spring directly from the work of Francis Crick and his colleagues. Crick is a scientist's scientist, Joe, to no degree a spiritualist or mystic. But do you know what he suggested a few years ago? That life on earth may well have been designed by an extra-terrestrial intelligence."

"Even highbrows read the *National Enquirer*, huh?"

"The point is—Crick was unable to square what we now know of molecular biology's complexity with the theory of natural selection, but he was unwilling to suggest a Creator in any spiritual sense."

"So . . . enter the ever-popular god-like aliens."

"But it totally begs the issue, you see? Even if every form of life on this planet was designed by extraterrestrials . . . who designed *them?*"

"It's the chicken or the egg all over again."

She laughed softly, but the laughter mutated into a cough that she couldn't easily suppress. She eased back, leaning against the door once more—and glared at him when he tried to suggest that she needed medical attention.

When she regained her breath, she said, "Loren Pollack believes the purpose of human intellectual striving—the purpose of science—is to increase our understanding of the universe, not just to give us better physical control of our environment or to satisfy curiosity, but to solve the puzzle of existence God has put before us."

"And by solving it to become like gods ourselves."

She smiled through her pain. "Now you're tuned to the Pollack frequency. Pollack thinks we're living in the time when some key scientific breakthrough will prove there is a Creator. Something that is . . . an interface with the infinite. This will bring the soul back to science—lifting humanity out of its fear and doubt, healing our divisions and hatreds, finally uniting our species on one quest that's both of the spirit and of the mind."

"Like *Star Trek*."

"Don't make me laugh again, Joe. It hurts too much."

Joe thought of Gem Fittich, the used-car dealer. Both Pollack and Fittich sensed an approaching end to the world as they knew it, but the oncoming tidal wave that Fittich perceived was dark and cold and obliterating, while Pollack foresaw a wave of purest light.

"So Pollack," she said, "founded Infiniface to facilitate this quest, to track research worldwide with an eye toward projects with . . . well, with metaphysical aspects that the scientists themselves might not recognize. To ensure that key discoveries were shared among researchers. To encourage specific projects that seemed to be leading to a breakthrough of the sort Pollack predicts."

"Infiniface isn't a religion at all."

"No. Pollack thinks all religions are valid to the extent that they recognize the existence of a created universe and a Creator—but that then they bog down in elaborate interpretations of what God expects of us. What's wanted of us, in Pollack's view, is to work together to learn, to understand, to peel the layers of the universe, to find God . . . and in the process to become His equals."

By now they were out of the dark hills and into suburbs again. Ahead was the entrance to the freeway that would take them east across the city.

As he drove up the ramp, heading toward Glendale and Pasadena, Joe said, "I don't believe in anything."

"I know."

"No loving god would allow such suffering."

"Pollack would say that the fallacy of your thinking lies in its narrow human perspective."

"Maybe Pollack is full of shit."

Whether Rose began to laugh again or fell directly victim to the cough, Joe couldn't tell, but she needed even longer than before to regain control of herself.

"You need to see a doctor," he insisted.

She was adamantly opposed. "Any delay . . . and Nina's dead."

"Don't make me choose between—"

"There *is* no choice. That's my point. If it's me or Nina . . . then she comes first. Because she's the future. She's the hope."

Orange-faced on first appearance, the moon had lost its blush and, stage fright behind it, had put on the stark white face of a smugly amused mime.

Sunday night traffic on the moon-mocked freeway was heavy as Angelenos returned from Vegas and other points in the desert, while desert dwellers streamed in the opposite direction, returning from the city and its beaches: ceaselessly restless, these multitudes, always seeking a greater happiness—and often finding it, but only for a weekend or an afternoon.

Joe drove as fast and as recklessly as he dared, weaving from lane to lane, but keeping in mind that they could not risk being stopped by the highway patrol. The car wasn't registered in either his name or Rose's. Even if they could prove it had been loaned to them, they would lose valuable time in the process.

"What is Project 99?" he asked her. "What the hell are they doing in that subterranean facility outside Manassas?"

"You've heard about the Human Genome Project."

"Yeah. Cover of *Newsweek*. As I understand it, they're figuring out what each human gene controls."

"The greatest scientific undertaking of our age," Rose said. "Mapping all one hundred thousand human genes and detailing the DNA alphabet of each. And they're making incredibly fast progress."

"Find out how to cure muscular dystrophy, multiple sclerosis—"

"Cancer, everything—given time."

"You're part of that?"

"No. Not directly. At Project 99 . . . we have a more exotic assignment. We're looking for those genes that seem to be associated with unusual talents."

"What—like Mozart or Rembrandt or Michael Jordan?"

"No. Not creative or athletic talents. Paranormal talents. Telepathy. Telekinesis. Pyrokinesis. It's a long strange list."

His immediate reaction was that of a crime reporter, not of a man who had recently seen the fantastic in action: "But there aren't such talents. That's science fiction."

"There are people who score far higher than chance on a variety of tests designed to disclose psychic abilities. Card prediction. Calling coin tosses. Thought-image transmission."

"That stuff they used to do at Duke University."

"That and more. When we find people who perform exceptionally well in these tests, we take blood samples from them. We study their genetic structure. Or children in poltergeist situations."

"Poltergeists?"

"Poltergeist phenomena—weeding out the hoaxes—aren't really ghosts. There's always one or more children in houses where this happens. We think the objects flying around the room and the ectoplasmic apparitions are caused by these children, by their unconscious exercise of powers they don't even know they have. We take samples from these kids when we can find them. We're building a library of unusual genetic profiles, looking for common patterns among people who have had all manner of paranormal experiences."

"And have you found something?"

She was silent, perhaps waiting for another spasm of pain to pass, though her face revealed more mental anguish than physical suffering. At last she said, "Quite a lot, yes."

If there had been enough light for Joe to see his reflection in the rearview mirror, he knew that he could have watched as his tan faded and his face turned as white as the moon, for he suddenly knew the essence of what Project 99 was all about. "You haven't just *studied* this."

"Not just. No."

"You've applied the research."

"Yes."

"How many work on Project 99?"

"Over two hundred of us."

"Making monsters," he said numbly.

"People," she said. "Making people in a lab."

"They may look like people, but some of them are monsters."

She was silent for perhaps a mile. Then she said, "Yes." And after another silence: "Though the true monsters are those of us who made them."

Fenced and patrolled, identified at the highway as a think tank called the Quartermass Institute, the property encompasses eighteen hundred acres in the Virginia countryside: meadowed hills where deer graze, hushed woods of birch and beeches where a plenitude of small game thrives beyond the rifle reach of hunters, ponds with ducks, and grassy fields with nesting plovers.

Although security appears to be minimal, no animal larger than a rabbit moves across these acres without being monitored by motion detectors, heat sensors, microphones, and cameras, which feed a continuous river of data to a Cray computer for continuous analysis. Unauthorized visitors are subject to immediate arrest, and on those rare occasions when hunters or adventurous teenagers scale the fence, they are halted and taken into custody within five hundred feet of the point of intrusion.

Near the geographical center of these peaceful acres is the orphanage, a cheerless three-story brick structure that resembles a hospital. Forty-eight children currently reside herein, every one below the age of six—though some appear older. They are all residents by virtue of having been born without mothers or fathers in any but the chemical sense. None of them was conceived in love, and none entered the world through a woman's womb. As fetuses, they were nurtured in mechanical wombs, adrift in amniotic fluid brewed in a laboratory.

As with laboratory rats and monkeys, as with dogs whose skulls are cut open and brains exposed for days during experiments related to the central nervous system, as with all animals that further the cause of knowledge, these orphans have no names. To name them would be to encourage their handlers to develop emotional attachments to them. The handlers—who include everyone from those security men who double as cooks to the scientists who bring these children into the world—must remain morally neutral and emotionally detached in order to do their work properly. Consequently, the children are known by letter and number codes that refer to the specific indices in Project 99's genetic-profile library from which their special abilities were selected.

Here on the third floor, southwest corner, in a room of her own, sits ATX-12-23. She is four years old, catatonic, and incontinent. She waits in her crib, in her own wastes until her nurse changes her, and she never complains. ATX-12-23 has never spoken a single word or uttered any sound whatsoever. As an infant, she never cried. She cannot walk. She sits motionlessly, staring into the middle distance, sometimes drooling. Her muscles are partially atrophied even though she is given manipulated exercise three times a week.

If her face were ever enlivened by expression, she might be beautiful, but the unrelieved slackness of her features gives her a chilling aspect. Cameras cover every inch of her room and record around the clock, which might seem to be a waste of videotape—except that from time to time, inanimate objects around ATX-12-23 become animated. Rubber balls of various colors levitate and spin in the air, float from wall to wall or circle the child's head for ten or twenty minutes at a time. Window blinds raise and lower without a hand touching them. Lights dim and flare, the digital clock speeds through the hours, and a teddy bear that she has never touched sometimes walks around the room on its stubby legs as if it contains the mechanical system that would allow it to do so.

Now come here, down to the second floor, to the third room east of the elevators, where lives a five-year-old male, KSB-22-09, who is neither physically nor mentally impaired. Indeed, he is an active redheaded boy with a genius-level IQ. He loves to learn, receives extensive tutoring daily, and is currently educated to a ninth-grade equivalent. He has numerous toys, books, and movies on video, and he participates in supervised play sessions with the other orphans, because it is deemed essential by the project architects that all subjects with normal mental faculties and full physical abilities be raised in as social an atmosphere as possible, given the limitations of the Institute. Sometimes when he tries hard (and sometimes when he is not trying at all), KSB-22-09 is able to make small objects—pencils, ball bearings, paper clips, thus far nothing larger than a glass of water—vanish. Simply vanish. He sends them elsewhere, into what he calls "The All Dark." He is not able to bring them back and cannot explain what The All Dark may be—though he does not like the place. He must be sedated to sleep, because he frequently suffers vivid nightmares in which he uncontrollably sends himself, piece by piece, into The All Dark—first a thumb, and then a toe, and then his left foot, a tooth and another tooth, one eye gone from a suddenly empty socket, and then an ear. Lately, KSB-22-09 is experiencing memory lapses and spells of paranoia, which are thought to be related to the long-term use of the sedative that he receives before bed each night.

Of the forty-eight orphans residing at the Institute, only seven exhibit any paranormal powers. The other forty-one, however, are not regarded as failures. Each of the seven successes first revealed his or her talent at a different age—one as young as eleven months, one as old as five. Consequently, the possibility remains that many of the forty-one will blossom in years to come—perhaps not until they experience the dramatic changes in body chemistry related to puberty. Eventually, of course, those subjects who age without revealing any valuable talent will have to be removed from the program, as even Project 99's resources are not infinite. The project's architects have not yet determined the optimum point of termination.

Although the steering wheel was hard under his hands and slick with his cold sweat, although the sound of the engine was familiar, although the freeway was solid under the spinning tires, Joe felt as if he had crossed into another dimension as treacherously amorphous and inimical to reason as the surreal landscapes in Salvador Dalí's paintings.

As his horror grew, he interrupted Rose: "This place you're describing is Hell. You . . . you couldn't have been part of anything like this. You're not that kind of person."

"Aren't I?"

"No."

Her voice grew thinner as she talked, as though the strength supporting her had been the secrets she kept, and as she revealed them one by one, her vitality ebbed as it had for Samson lock by lock. In her increasing weariness was a sweet relief like that dispensed in a confessional, a weakness that she seemed to embrace—but that was nonetheless colored by a gray wash of despair. "If I'm not that kind of person now . . . I must have been then."

"But how? Why? Why would you want to be involved with these . . . these atrocities?"

"Pride. To prove that I was as good as they thought I was, good enough to take on this unprecedented challenge. Excitement. The thrill of being involved with a program even better funded than the Manhattan Project. Why did the people who invented the atomic bomb work on it . . . knowing what they were making? Because others, elsewhere in the world, will do it if we don't . . . so maybe we have to do it to save ourselves from them?"

"Save ourselves by selling our souls?" he asked.

"There's no defense I can offer that should ever exonerate me," Rose said. "But it is true that when I signed on, there was no consensus that we would carry the experiments this far, that we would *apply* what we learned with such . . . zeal. We entered into the creation of the children in stages . . . down a slippery slope. We intended to monitor the first one just through the second trimester of the fetal stage—and, after all, we don't consider a fetus to be an actual human being. So it wasn't like we were experimenting on a *person*. And when we brought one of them to full term . . . there were intriguing anomalies in its EEG graphs, strangeness in its brainwave patterns that might have indicated heretofore unknown cerebral function. So we had to keep it alive to see . . . to see what we had achieved, to see if maybe we had moved evolution forward a giant step."

"Jesus."

Though he had first met this woman only thirty-six hours ago, his feelings for her had been rich and intense, ranging from virtual adoration to fear and now to repulsion. Yet from his repulsion came pity, because for the first time he saw in her one of the many cloves of human weakness that, in other forms, were so ripe in himself.

"Fairly early on," she said, "I *did* want out. So I was invited for a private chat with the project director, who made it clear to me that there was no quitting now. This had become a job with lifetime tenure. Even to attempt to leave Project 99 is to commit suicide—and to put the lives of your loved ones at risk as well."

"But couldn't you have gone to the press, broken the story wide open, shut them down?"

"Probably not without physical evidence, and all I had was what was in my head. Anyway, a couple of my colleagues had the idea that they could bring it all down, I think. One of them suffered a timely stroke. The other was shot three times in the head by a mugger—who was never caught. For a while . . . I was so depressed I considered killing myself and saving them the trouble. But then . . . along came CCY-21-21. . . ."

First, born a year ahead of CCY-21-21 was male subject SSW-89-58. He exhibits prodigious talents in every regard and his story is of importance to you because of your own recent experiences with people who eviscerate themselves and set themselves afire—and because of your losses in Colorado.

By the time he is forty-two months old, SSW-89-58 possesses the language skills of the average first-year college student and is able to read a three-hundred-page volume in one to three hours, depending on the complexity of the text. Higher math comes to him as easily as eating ice cream, as do foreign languages from French to Japanese. His physical development proceeds at an accelerated rate as well, and by the time he is four, he stands as tall and is as proportionately developed as the average seven-year-old. Paranormal talents are anticipated, but researchers are surprised by 89-58's great breadth of more ordinary genius—which includes the ability to play any piece of piano music after hearing it once—and by his physical precocity, for which no genetic selection has been made.

When 89-58 begins to exhibit paranormal abilities, he proves to be phenomenally endowed. His first startling achievement is remote viewing. As a game, he describes to researchers the rooms in their own homes, where he has never visited. He walks them through tours of museums to which he has never been admitted. When he is shown a photograph of a Wyoming mountain in which is buried a top-secret Strategic Air Command defense center, he describes in accurate detail the missile-status display boards in the war room. He is considered an espionage asset of incalculable value—until, fortunately by degrees, he discovers that he is able to step into a human mind as easily as he steps into distant rooms. He takes mental control of his primary handler, makes the man undress, and sends him through the halls of the orphanage, crowing like a rooster. When SSW-89-58 relinquishes control of the handler and what he's done is discovered, he is punished severely. He resents the punishment, resents it deeply. That night he conducts a remote viewing of the handler's home and enters the handler's mind at a distance of forty-six miles. Using the handler's body, he brutally murders the man's wife and daughter, and then he walks the handler through suicide.

Following this episode, SSW-89-58 is subdued by the use of a massive dose of tranquilizers administered by a dart gun. Two employees of Project 99 perish in the process.

Thereafter, for a period of eighteen days, he is maintained in a drug-induced coma while a team of scientists designs and oversees the urgent construction of a suitable habitat for their prize—one which will sustain his life but assure that he remains controlled. A faction of the staff suggests immediate termination of SSW-89-58, but this advice is considered and rejected. Every endeavor is at some point troubled by pessimists.

Here, now, come into the security room in the southeast corner of the first floor of the orphanage. In this place—if you were an employee—you must present yourself for the scrutiny of three guards, because this post is never manned by fewer, regardless of the hour. You must place your right hand on a scanner that will identify you by your fingerprints. You must peer into a retina scanner as well, which will compare your retinal patterns to those recorded in the scan taken when you first accepted employment.

From here you descend in an elevator past five subterranean levels, where much of the work of Project 99 is conducted. You are interested, however, in the sixth and lowest level, where you walk to the end of a long corridor and through a gray metal door. You stand in a plain room with simple institutional furnishings, with three security men, none of whom is interested in you. These men work six-hour shifts to ensure that they remain alert not only to what is happening in this room and the next but to nuances in one another's behavior.

One wall of this room features a large window that looks into the adjoining chamber. Frequently you will see Dr. Louis Blom or Dr. Keith Ramlock—or both—at work beyond this glass, for they are the designers of SSW-89-58 and oversee the exploration and the utilization of his gifts. When neither Dr. Blom nor Dr. Ramlock is present, at least three other members of their immediate staff are in attendance.

SSW-89-58 is never left unsupervised.

They were transitioning from Interstate 210 to Interstate 10 when Rose interrupted herself to say, "Joe, could you find an exit with a service station? I need to use a rest room."

"What's wrong?"

"Nothing. I just need . . . a rest room. I hate to waste the time. I want to get to Big Bear as quick as we can. But I don't want to wet my pants, either. No hurry. Just somewhere in the next few miles, okay?"

"All right."

She conducted him, once more, on her version of a remote viewing of Project 99 outside Manassas.

Onward, please, through the connecting door and into the final space, where stands the elaborate containment vessel in which 89-58 now lives and, barring any unforeseen and calamitous developments, in which he will spend the rest of his unnatural life. This is a tank that somewhat resembles the iron lungs which, in more primitive decades, were used to sustain victims of polio. Nestled like a pecan in its shell, 89-58 is entirely enclosed, pressed between the mattress-soft halves of a lubricated body mold that restricts all movement, including even the movement of each finger, limiting him to facial expressions and twitches—which no one can see anyway. He is supplied with bottled air directly through a nose clip from tanks outside the containment vessel. Likewise, he is pierced by redundant intravenous-drip lines, one in each arm and one in his left thigh, through which he receives life-sustaining nourishment, a balance of fluids, and a variety of drugs as his handlers see fit to administer them. He is permanently catheterized for the efficient elimination of waste. If any of these IV drips or other lifelines works loose or otherwise fails, an insistent alarm immediately alerts the handlers, and in spite of the existence of redundant systems, repairs are undertaken without delay.

The researchers and their assistants conduct conversations as necessary with 89-58 through a speakerphone. The clamshell body mold in which he lies inside the steel tank is equipped with audio feed to both of his ears and a microphone over his mouth. The staff is able to reduce 89-58's words to a background whisper whenever they wish, but he does not enjoy an equivalent privilege to tune them out. A clever video feed allows images to be transmitted by glass fiber to a pair of lenses fitted to 89-58's sockets; consequently, he can be shown photographs—and if necessary the geographical coordinates—of buildings and places in which he is required to conduct remote viewings. Sometimes he is shown photographs of individuals against whom it is desired that he take one form of action or another.

During a remote viewing, 89-58 describes in vivid detail what he sees in whatever far place they have sent him, and he dutifully answers questions that his handlers put to him. By monitoring his heart rate, blood pressure, respiratory rate, brainwaves, eyelid movements, and changes in the electrical conductivity of his skin, they are able to detect a lie with better than ninety-nine-percent accuracy. Furthermore, they test him from time to time by remoting him to places on which extensive, reliable intelligence has already been gathered; his answers are subsequently compared to the material currently in file.

He has been known to be a bad boy. He is not trusted.

When 89-58 is instructed to enter the mind of a specific person and either eliminate that individual or use him to eliminate another—which is most often a foreign national—the assignment is referred to as a "wet mission." This term is used partly because blood is spilled but largely because 89-58 is plunged not into the comparative dryness of faraway rooms but into the murky depths of a human mind. As he conducts a wet mission, 89-58 describes it to Dr. Blom or Dr. Ramlock, at least one of whom is always present during the event. After numerous such missions, Blom and Ramlock and their associates are adept at identifying deception even before the polygraph signals trouble.

For his handlers, video displays of electrical activity in 89-58's brain clearly define the activity in which he is engaged at every moment. When he is only remote viewing, the patterns are radically different from those that arise when he is engaged in wet work. If he is assigned only to observe some distant place and, while viewing, disobediently occupies the mind of someone in that remote location, either as an act of rebellion or sheerly for sport, this is known at once to his handlers.

If SSW-89-58 refuses an instruction, exceeds the parameters of an assignment, or exhibits any other signs of rebellion, he can be punished in numerous ways. Electrical contacts in the body mold—and in his catheter—can be activated to deliver painful shocks to selected tender points head to foot or over his entire skin surface. Piercing electronic squeals at excruciating volume may be blasted into his ears. Disgusting odors are easily introduced with his air supply. A variety of drugs are available to precipitate painful and terrifying physiological symptoms—such as violent muscle spasms and inflamed nerve sheaths—which pose no danger to the life of this valuable asset. Inducing claustrophobic panic by cutting off his air supply is also a simple but effective disciplinary technique.

If he is obedient, 89-58 can be rewarded in one of five ways. Although he receives his primary nutrients—carbohydrates, proteins, vitamins, minerals—through IV drips, a feeding tube can be extruded from the body mold and between his lips, to allow him to enjoy tasty liquids, from Coca-Cola to apple juice to chocolate milk. Second, because he is a piano prodigy and takes great pleasure from music, he can be rewarded with anything from the Beatles to Beethoven. Third, entire movies can be transmitted to the lenses over his eyes—and from such an intimate perspective, he seems to be virtually in the middle of the cinematic experience. Fourth, he can receive mood-elevating drugs that make him as happy, in some ways, as any boy in the world. Fifth, and best of all, he is sometimes allowed to go remote viewing in places that he would like to experience, and during these glorious expeditions, guided by his own interests, he knows freedom—or as much of it as he can imagine.

Routinely, no fewer than three staff monitor the containment vessel and its occupant, because 89-58 can control only one mind at a time. If any of the three were to turn suddenly violent or exhibit any unusual behavior, either of the other two could, with the flip of a switch, administer sufficient sedatives through the intravenous feeds to drop 89-58 into a virtually instant, deep, and powerless sleep. In the unlikely event that this should fail, a doomsday button follows the sedative with a lethal dose of nerve toxin that kills in three to five seconds.

The three guards on the other side of the observation window have similar buttons available for use at their discretion.

SSW-89-58 is not able to read minds. He is not a telepath. He can only repress the personality of the person he inhabits and take control of the physical plant. There is disagreement among the staff of Project 99 as to whether 89-58's lack of telepathic ability is a disappointment or a blessing.

Furthermore, when sent on a wet mission, he must know where his target is located before being able to invade its mind. He cannot search at will across the populations of the world but must be guided by his handlers, who first locate his prey. Once shown an image of the building or vehicle in which the target can be found—and when that place is geographically sited in his mind—he can act.

Thus far, he is also limited to the walls of that structure and cannot effectively pursue a wanted mind beyond the boundaries that are initially established. No one knows why this limitation should exist, though theories abound. Perhaps it is because the invisible psychic self, being only a wave energy of some type, responds to open spaces in much the manner of heat contained in a hot stone placed in a cold room: It radiates outward, dissipating, dispersing itself, and cannot be conserved in a coherent form. He is able to practice remote viewing of outdoor locations—but only for short periods of time. This shortcoming frustrates 89-58's handlers, but they believe and hope that his abilities in this regard may improve with time.

If you can bear to watch, the containment vessel is opened twice each week to allow the handlers to clean their asset. He is without fail deeply sedated for this procedure—and remains connected to the doomsday button. He is given a thorough sponge bath, irritations of the skin are treated, the minimal solid waste that he produces is evacuated from the bowel, teeth are cleaned, eyes are examined for infection and then are flushed with antibiotic, and other maintenance is performed. Although 89-58 receives daily low-voltage electrical stimulation of his muscles to ensure a minimal life-sustaining mass, he resembles one of the starving children of any third-world country racked by drought and evil politics. He is as pale as any job on a mortician's table, withered, with elfin bones grown thin from lack of use; and when unconsciously he curls his feeble fingers around the hands of ministering attendants, his grip is no stronger than that of a cradled newborn baby struggling to hold fast to its mother's thumb.

Sometimes, in this profound sedation, he murmurs wordlessly but forlornly, mewls, and even weeps, as if adrift in a soft sad dream.

• • •

At the Shell station, only three vehicles were at the self-service pumps. Tending to their cars, the motorists squinted and ducked their heads to keep wind-blown grit out of their eyes.

The lighting was as bright as that on a movie set, and though Joe and Rose were not being sought by the type of police agency that would distribute their photographs to local television news programs, Joe preferred to stay out of the glare. He parked along the side of the building, near the rest rooms, where huddled shadows survived.

Joe was in emotional turmoil, felt slashed across the heart, because now he knew the exact cause of the catastrophic crash, knew the murderer's identity and the twisted details. The knowledge was like a scalpel that pared off what thin scabs had formed over his pain. His grief felt fresh, the loss more recent than it really was.

He switched off the engine and sat speechless.

"I don't understand how the hell they found out I was on that flight," Rose said. "I'd taken such precautions. . . . But I knew when he remote-viewed the passenger cabin, looking for us, because there was an odd dimming of lights, a problem with my wristwatch, a vague sense of a *presence*—signs I'd learned to read."

"I've met a National Transportation Safety Board investigator who's heard the tape from the cockpit voice recorder, before it was destroyed in a convenient sound-lab fire. This boy was inside the captain's head, Rose. I don't understand . . . Why didn't he take out just *you*?"

"He had to get us both, that was his assignment, me and the girl—and while he could've nailed me without any problem, it wouldn't have been easy with her."

Utterly baffled, Joe said, "Nina? Why would they have been interested in her then? She was just another passenger, wasn't she? I thought they were after her later because . . . well, because she survived with you."

Rose would not meet his eyes. "Get me the key to the women's rest room, Joe. Will you, please? Let me have a minute here. I'll tell you the rest of it on the way to Big Bear."

He went into the sales room and got the key from the cashier. By the time he returned to the Ford, Rose had gotten out. She was leaning against a front fender, back turned and shoulders hunched to the whistling Santa Ana wind. Her left arm was curled against her breast, and her hand was still shaking. With her right hand, she pulled the lapels of her blazer together, as though the warm August wind felt cold to her.

"Would you unlock the door for me?" she asked.

He went to the women's room. By the time he unlocked the door and switched on the light, Rose had arrived at his side.

"I'll be quick," she promised, and slipped past him.

He had a glimpse of her face in that brightness, just before the door fell shut. She didn't look good.

Instead of returning to the car, Joe leaned against the wall of the building, beside the lavatory door, to wait for her.

According to nurses in asylums and psychiatric wards, a greater number of their most disturbed patients responded to the Santa Ana winds than ever reacted to the sight of a full moon beyond a barred window. It wasn't simply the baleful sound, like the cries of an unearthly hunter and the unearthly beasts that it pursued; it was also the subliminal alkaline scent of the desert and a queer electrical charge, different from those that other—less dry—winds imparted to the air.

Joe could understand why Rose might have pulled her blazer shut and huddled into it. This night had both the moon and the Santa Ana wind to spark a voodoo current in the spine—and a parentless boy without a name, who lived in a coffin of steel and moved invisible through a world of potential victims oblivious to him.

Are we recording?

The boy had known about the cockpit voice recorder—and he'd left a cry for help on it.

One of their names is Dr. Louis Blom. One of their names is Dr. Keith Ramlock. They're doing bad things to me. They're mean to me. Make them stop. Make them stop hurting me.

Whatever else he was—sociopathic, psychotic, homicidal—he was also a child. A beast, an abomination, a terror, but also a child. He had not asked to be born, and if he was evil, they had made him so by failing to teach him any human values, by treating him as mere ordnance, by rewarding him for murder. Beast he was, but a pitiable beast, lost and alone, wandering in a maze of misery.

Pitiable but formidable. And still out there. Waiting to be told where he could find Rose Tucker. And Nina.

This is fun.

The boy enjoyed the killing. Joe supposed it was even possible that his handlers had never instructed him to destroy everyone aboard Nationwide Flight 353, that he had done it as an act of rebellion and because he enjoyed it.

Make them stop or when I get the chance . . . when I get the chance, I'll kill everybody. Everybody. I will. I'll do it. I'll kill everybody, and I'll like it.

Recalling those words from the transcript, Joe sensed that the boy had not been referring merely to the passengers on the doomed airliner. By then he had already made the decision to kill them all. He was speaking of some act more apocalyptic than three hundred and thirty murders.

What could he accomplish if provided with photographs and the geographical coordinates of not merely a missile-tracking facility but a complex of nuclear-missile launch silos?

"Jesus," Joe whispered.

Somewhere in the night, Nina waited. In the hands of a friend of Rose's, but inadequately protected. Vulnerable.

Rose seemed to be taking a long time.

Rapping on the rest room door, Joe called her name, but she did not respond. He hesitated, knocked again, and when she weakly called "Joe," he pushed the door open.

She was perched on the edge of the toilet seat. She had taken off her navy blazer and her white blouse; the latter lay blood-soaked on the sink.

He hadn't realized she'd been bleeding. Darkness and the blazer had hidden the blood from him.

As he stepped into the rest room, he saw that she had shaped a compress of sorts from a wad of wet paper towels. She was pressing it to her left pectoral muscle, above her breast.

"That one shot on the beach," he said numbly. "You were hit."

"The bullet passed through," she said. "There's an exit wound in back. Nice and clean. I haven't even bled all that much, and the pain is tolerable. . . . So why am I getting weaker?"

"Internal bleeding," he suggested, wincing as he looked at the exit wound in her back.

"I know anatomy," she said. "I took the hit in just the right spot. Couldn't have picked it better. Shouldn't be any damage to major vessels."

"The round might have hit a bone and fragmented. The fragment maybe didn't come out, took a different track."

"I was so thirsty. Tried to drink some water from the faucet. Almost passed out when I bent over."

"This settles it," he said. His heart was racing. "We've got to get you to a doctor."

"Get me to Nina."

"Rose, damn it—"

"Nina can heal me," she said, and as she spoke, she looked guiltily away from him.

Astonished, he said, "Heal you?"

"Trust me. Nina can do what no doctor can, what no one else on earth can do."

At that moment, on some level, he knew at least one of Rose Tucker's remaining secrets, but he could not allow himself to take out that dark pearl of knowledge and examine it.

"Help me get my blouse and blazer on, and let's go. Get me into Nina's hands. Her healing hands."

Though half sick with worry, he did as she wanted. As he dressed her, he remembered how larger than life she had seemed in the cemetery Saturday morning. Now she was so small.

Through a hot clawing wind that mimicked the songs of wolves, she leaned on him all the way back to the car.

When he got her settled in the passenger's seat, she asked if he would get her something to drink.

From a vending machine in front of the station, he purchased a can of Pepsi and one of Orange Crush. She preferred the Crush, and he opened it for her.

Before she accepted the drink, she gave him two things: the Polaroid photograph of his family's graves and the folded dollar bill on which the serial number, minus the fourth digit, provided the phone number at which Mark of Infiniface could be reached in an emergency. "And before you start driving, I want to tell you how to find the cabin in Big Bear—in case I can't hold on until we get there."

"Don't be silly. You'll make it."

"Listen," she said, and again she projected the charisma that commanded attention.

He listened as she told him the way.

"And as for Infiniface," she said, "I trust them, and they are my natural allies—and Nina's—as Mark said. But I'm afraid they can be too easily infiltrated. That's why I wouldn't let them come with us tonight. But if we're not followed, then this car is clean, and maybe their security is good enough. If worse comes to worst and you don't know where to turn . . . they may be your best hope."

His chest tightened and his throat thickened as she spoke, and finally he said, "I don't want to hear any more of this. I'll get you to Nina in time."

Rose's right hand trembled now, and Joe was not certain that she could hold the Orange Crush. But she managed it, drinking thirstily.

As he drove back onto the San Bernardino Freeway, heading east, she said, "I've never meant to hurt you, Joe."

"You haven't."

"I've done a terrible thing, though."

He glanced at her. He didn't dare ask what she had done. He kept that shiny black pearl of knowledge tucked deep in the purse of his mind.

"Don't hate me too much."

"I don't hate you at all."

"My motives were good. They haven't always been. Certainly weren't spotless when I went to work at Project 99. But my motives were good this time, Joe."

Driving out of the lightstorm of Los Angeles and its suburbs, toward the mountain darkness where Nina dwelled, Joe waited for Rose to tell him why he should hate her.

"So . . . let me tell you," she said, "about the project's only true success. . . ."

Ascend, now, in the elevator from the little glimpse of Hell at the bottom of those six subterranean levels, leaving the boy in his containment vessel, and come all the way up to the security room where the descent began. Farther still, to the southeast corner of the ground floor, where CCY-21-21 resides.

She was conceived without passion one year after 89-58, though she was the project not of Doctors Blom and Ramlock but of Rose Tucker. She is a lovely child, delicate, fair of face, with golden hair and amethyst eyes. Although the majority of the orphans living here are of average intelligence, CCY-21-21 has an unusually high IQ, even higher perhaps than that of 89-58, and she loves to learn. She is a quiet girl, with much grace and natural charm, but for the first three years of her life, she exhibits no paranormal abilities.

Then, on a sunny May afternoon, when she is participating in a session of supervised play with other children on the orphanage lawn, she finds a sparrow with a broken wing and one torn eye. It lies in the grass beneath a tree, flopping weakly, and when she gathers it into her small hands, it becomes fearfully still. Crying, the girl hurries with the bird to the nearest handler, asking what can be done. The sparrow is now so weak and so paralyzed by fear that it can only feebly work its beak—and produces no sound whatsoever. The bird is dying, the handler sees nothing to be done, but the girl will not accept the sparrow's pending death. She sits on the ground, grips the bird gently in her left hand, and carefully strokes it with her right, singing softly to it a song about Robin Red Breast—and in but a minute the sparrow is restored. The fractures in the wing knit firm again, and the torn eye heals into a bright, clear orb. The bird sings—and flies.

CCY-21-21 becomes the center of a happy whirlwind of attention. Rose Tucker, who has been driven to the contemplation of suicide by the nightmare of Project 99, is as reborn as the bird, stepping back from the abyss into which she has been peering. For the next fifteen months, 21-21's healing power is explored. At first it is an unreliable talent, which she cannot exercise at will, but month by wondrous month she learns to summon and control her gift, until she can apply it whenever asked to do so. Those on Project 99 with medical problems are brought to a level of health they never expected to enjoy again. A select few politicians and military figures—and members of their families—suffering from life-threatening illnesses are brought secretly to the child to be healed. There are those in Project 99 who believe that 21-21 is their greatest asset—although others find 89-58, in spite of the considerable control problems that he poses, to be the most interesting and valuable property in the long run.

Now look here, come forward in time to one rainy day in August, fifteen months after the restoration of the injured sparrow. A staff geneticist named Amos has been diagnosed with pancreatic cancer, one of the deadliest forms of the disease. While healing Amos with only a soft and lingering touch, the girl detects an illness in addition to the malignancy, this one not of a physical nature but nonetheless debilitating. Perhaps because of what he has seen at Project 99, perhaps for numerous other reasons that have accumulated throughout his fifty years, Amos has decided that life is without purpose or meaning, that we have no destiny but the void, that we are only dust in the wind. This darkness in him is blacker than the cancer, and the girl heals this as well, by the simple expedient of showing Amos the light of God and the strange dimensional lattices of realms beyond our own.

Once shown these things, Amos is so overcome with joy and awe that he cycles between laughter and weeping, and to the eyes of the others in the room—a researcher named Janice, another named Vincent—he seems to be seized by an alarming hysteria. When Amos urges the girl to bring Janice into the same light that she has shown to him, she gives the gift again.

Janice, however, reacts differently from Amos. Humbled and frightened, she collapses in remorse. She claws at herself in regret for the way she has lived her life and in grief for those she has betrayed and harmed, and her anguish is frightening.

Tumult.

Rose is summoned. Janice and Amos are isolated for observation and evaluation. What has the girl done? What Amos tells them seems like the happy babbling of a harmlessly deranged man, but babbling nonetheless, and from one who was but a few minutes ago a scientist of serious—if not brooding—disposition.

Baffled and concerned by the strikingly different reactions of Amos and Janice, the girl withdraws and becomes uncommunicative. Rose works in private with 21-21 for more than two hours before she finally begins to pry the astounding explanation from her. The child cannot understand why the revelation that she's brought to Amos and Janice would overwhelm them so completely or why Janice's reaction is a mix of euphoria and self-flagellation. Having been born with a full awareness of her place and purpose in the universe, with an understanding of the ladder of destinies that she will climb through infinity, with the certain knowledge of life everlasting carried in her genes, she cannot grasp the shattering power of this revelation when she brings it to those who have spent their lives in the mud of doubt and the dust of despair.

Expecting nothing more than that she is going to experience the psychic equivalent of a magic-lantern show, a tour of a child's sweet fantasy of God, Rose asks to be shown. And is shown. And is forever changed. Because at the touch of the child's hand, she is opened to the fullness of existence. What she experiences is beyond her powers to describe, and even as torrents of joy surge through her and wash away all the countless griefs and miseries of her life heretofore, she is flooded, as well, with terror, for she is aware not only of the promise of a bright eternity but of *expectations* that she must strive to fulfill in all the days of life ahead of her in this world and in the worlds to come, expectations that frighten her because she is unsure that she can ever meet them. Like Janice, she is acutely aware of every mean act and unkindness and lie and betrayal of which she has ever been guilty, and she recognizes that she still has the capacity for selfishness, pettiness, and cruelty; she yearns to transcend her past even as she quakes at the fortitude required to do so.

When the vision passes and she finds herself in the girl's room as before, she harbors no doubt that what she saw was real, truth in its purest form, and not merely the child's delusion transmitted through psychic power. For almost half an hour she cannot speak but sits shaking, her face buried in her hands.

Gradually, she begins to realize the implications of what has happened here. There are basically two. First: If this revelation can be brought to the world—even to as many as the girl can touch—all that is now will pass away. Once one has *seen*—not taken on faith but *seen*—that there is life beyond, even if the nature of it remains profoundly mysterious and as fearsome as it is glorious, then all that was once important seems insignificant. Avenues of wondrous possibilities abound where once there was a single alley through the darkness. The world as we know it ends. Second: There are those who will not welcome the end of the old order, who have taught themselves to thrive on power and on the pain and humiliation of others. Indeed, the world is full of them, and they will not want to receive the girl's gift. They will fear the girl and everything that she promises. And they will either sedate and isolate her in a containment vessel—or they will kill her.

She is as gifted as any messiah—but she is human. She can heal the wing of a broken bird and bring sight to its blinded eye. She can banish cancer from a disease-riddled man. But she is not an angel with a cloak of invulnerability. She is flesh and bone. Her precious power resides in the delicate tissues of her singular brain. If the magazine of a pistol is emptied into the back of her head, she will die like any other child; dead, she cannot heal herself. Although her soul will proceed into other realms, she will be lost to this troubled place that needs her. The world will not be changed, peace will not replace turmoil, and there will be no end to loneliness and despair.

Rose quickly becomes convinced that the project's directors will opt for termination. The moment that they understand what this little girl is, they will kill her.

Before nightfall, they will kill her.

Certainly before midnight, they will kill her.

They will not be willing to risk consigning her to a containment vessel. The boy possesses only the power of destruction, but 21-21 possesses the power of enlightenment, which is immeasurably the more dangerous of the two.

They will shoot her down, soak her corpse with gasoline, set her remains afire, and later scatter her charred bones.

Rose must act—and quickly. The girl must be spirited out of the orphanage and hidden before they can destroy her.

"Joe?"

Against a field of stars, as though at this moment erupting from the crust of the earth, the black mountains shouldered darkly across the horizon.

"Joe, I'm sorry." Her voice was frail. "I'm so sorry."

They were speeding north on State Highway 30, east of the city of San Bernardino, fifty miles from Big Bear.

"Joe, are you okay?"

He could not answer.

Traffic was light. The road ascended into forests. Cottonwoods and pines shook, shook, shook in the wind.

He could not answer. He could only drive.

"When you insisted on believing the little girl with me was your own Nina, I let you go on believing it."

For whatever purpose, she was still deceiving him. He could not understand why she continued to hide the truth.

She said, "After they found us at the restaurant, I needed your help. Especially after I was shot, I needed you. But you hadn't opened your heart and mind to the photograph when I gave it to you. You were so . . . fragile. I was afraid if you knew it really wasn't your Nina, you'd just . . . stop. Fall apart. God forgive me, Joe, but I needed you. And now the girl needs you."

Nina needed him. Not some girl born in a lab, with the power to transmit her curious fantasies to others and cloud the minds of the gullible. Nina needed him. *Nina*.

If he could not trust Rose Tucker, was there anyone he could trust?

He managed to shake two words from himself: "Go on."

Rose again. In 21-21's room. Feverishly considering the problem of how to spirit the girl through a security system equal to that of any prison.

The answer, when it comes, is obvious and elegant.

There are three exits from the ground floor of the orphanage. Rose and the girl walk hand in hand to the door that connects the main building to the adjoining two-story parking structure.

An armed guard views their approach with more puzzlement than suspicion. The orphans are not permitted into the garage even under supervision.

When 21-21 holds out her tiny hand and says *Shake*, the guard smiles and obliges— and receives the gift. Suddenly filled with cyclonic wonder, he sits shaking uncontrollably, weeping with joy but also with hard remorse, just as Rose had trembled and wept in the girl's room.

It is a simple matter to push the button on the guard's console to throw the electronic lock on the door and pass through.

Another guard waits on the garage side of the connecting door. He is startled by the sight of this child. She reaches for him, and his surprise at seeing her is nothing compared to the surprise that follows.

A third guard is stationed at the gated exit from the garage. Alarmed by the sight of 21-21 in Rose's car, he leans in the open window to demand an explanation—and the girl touches his face.

Two more armed men staff the gate at the highway. All barriers fall, and Virginia lies ahead.

Escape will never be as easy again. If they are apprehended, the girl's offer of a handshake will be greeted by gunfire.

The trick now is to get out of the area quickly, before project security realizes what has happened to five of its men. They will mount a pursuit, perhaps with the assistance of local, state, and federal authorities. Rose drives madly, recklessly, with a skill—born of desperation—that she has never known before.

Barely big enough to see out of the side window, 21-21 studies the passing countryside with fascination and, at last, says, *Wow, it sure is big out here.*

Rose laughs and says, *Honey, you ain't seen nothing yet.*

She realizes that she must get the word out as quickly as possible: use the media to display 21-21's healing powers and then to demonstrate the greater gift that the girl can bestow. Only the forces of ignorance and darkness benefit from secrecy. Rose believes that 21-21 will never be safe until the world knows of her, embraces her, and refuses to allow her to be taken into custody.

Her ex-bosses will expect her to go public quickly and in a big way. Their influence within the media is widespread—yet as subtle as a web of cloud shadows on the skin of a pond, which makes it all the more effective. They will try to find her as soon as possible after she surfaces and before she can bring 21-21 to the world.

She knows a reporter whom she would trust not to betray her: Lisa Peccatone, an old college friend who works at the *Post* in Los Angeles.

Rose and the girl will have to fly to Southern California—and the sooner the better. Project 99 is a joint venture of private industry, elements of the defense establishment, and other powerful forces in the government. Easier to halt an avalanche with a feather than to resist their combined might, and they will shortly begin to use every asset in their arsenal to locate Rose and the girl.

Trying to fly out of Dulles or National Airport in Washington is too dangerous. She considers Baltimore, Philadelphia, New York, and Boston. She chooses New York.

She reasons that the more county and state lines she crosses, the safer she becomes, so she drives to Hagerstown, Maryland, and from there to Harrisburg, Pennsylvania, without incident. Yet mile by mile, she is increasingly concerned that her pursuers will have put out an APB on her car and that she will be captured regardless of the distance she puts between herself and Manassas. In Harrisburg, she abandons the car, and she and the girl continue to New York City by bus.

By the time they are in the air aboard Nationwide Flight 353, Rose feels safe. Immediately on landing at LAX, she will be met by Lisa and the crew that Lisa has assembled—and the series of media eruptions will begin.

For the airline passenger manifest, Rose implied that she was married to a white man, and she identified 21-21 as her stepdaughter, choosing the name "Mary Tucker" on the spur of the moment. With the media, she intends initially to use CCY-21-21's project name because its similarity to concentration-camp inmates' names will do more than anything else to characterize Project 99 in the public mind and generate instant sympathy for the child. She realizes that eventually she will have to consult with 21-21 to pick a permanent name—which, considering the singular historical importance of this child's life, should be a name that resonates.

They are seated across the aisle from a mother and her two daughters, who are returning home to Los Angeles. Michelle, Chrissie, and Nina Carpenter.

Nina, who is approximately 21-21's age and size, is playing with a hand-held electronic game called Pigs and Princes, designed for preschoolers. From across the aisle, 21-21 becomes fascinated by the sounds and the images on the small screen. Seeing this, Nina asks "Mary" to move with her to a nearby pair of empty seats, where they can play the game together. Rose is hesitant to allow this—but she knows that 21-21 is intelligent far beyond her years and is aware of the need for discretion, so she relents. This is the first unstructured play time in 21-21's life, the first *genuine* play she has ever known. Nina is a child of enormous charm, sweet and gregarious. Although 21-21 is a genius with the reading skills of a college freshman, a healer with miraculous powers, and literally the hope of the world, she is soon enraptured by Nina, wants to *be* Nina, as totally cool as Nina, and unconsciously she begins imitating Nina's gestures and manner of speaking.

Theirs is a late flight out of New York, and after a couple of hours, Nina is fading. She hugs 21-21, and with the permission of Michelle, she gives Pigs and Princes to her new friend before returning to sit with her mother and sister, where she falls asleep.

Transported by delight, 21-21 returns to her seat beside Rose, hugging the small electronic game to her breast as though it is a treasure beyond value. Now she won't even play with it because she is afraid that she might break it, and she wants it to remain always exactly as Nina gave it to her.

West of the town of Running Lake, still many miles from Big Bear Lake, following ridgelines past the canyons where the wind was born, bombarded by thrashing conifers hurling cones at the pavement, Joe refused to consider the implications of Pigs and Princes. Listening to Rose tell the story, he had barely found the self-control to repress his rage. He knew that he had no reason to be furious with this woman or with the child who had a concentration-camp name, but he was livid nonetheless—perhaps because he knew how to function well in anger, as he had done throughout his youth, and not well at all in grief.

Turning the subject away from little girls at play, he said, "How does Horton Nellor fit into this—aside from owning a big chunk of Teknologik, which is deep in Project 99?"

"Just that well-connected bastards like him . . . are the wave of the future." She was holding the can of Pepsi between her knees, clawing at the pull tab with her right hand. She had barely enough strength and coordination to get it open. "The wave of the future . . . unless Nina . . . unless she changes everything."

"Big business, big government, and big media—all one beast now, united to exploit the rest of us. Is that it? Radical talk."

The aluminum can rattled against her teeth, and a trickle of Pepsi dribbled down her chin. "Nothing but power matters to them. They don't believe . . . in good and evil."

"There are only events."

Though she had just taken a long swallow of Pepsi, her throat sounded dry. Her voice cracked. "And what those events mean . . ."

" . . . depends only on what spin you put on them."

He remained blindly angry with her because of what she insisted that he believe about his Nina, but he could not bear to glance at her again and see her growing weaker. He blinked at the road ahead, where showers of pine needles stitched together billowing sheets of dust, and he eased down on the accelerator, driving as fast as he dared.

The soda can slipped out of her hand, dropped on the floor, and rolled under her seat, spilling the remainder of the Pepsi. "Losin' it, Joe."

"Not long now."

"Got to tell you how it was . . . when the plane went in."

Four miles down, gathering speed all the way, engines shrieking, wings creaking, fuselage thrumming. Screaming passengers are pressed so hard into their seats by the accumulating gravities that many are unable to lift their heads—some praying, some vomiting, weeping, cursing, calling out the many names of God, calling out to loved ones present and far away. An eternity of plunging, four miles but as if from the moon—

—and then Rose is in a blueness, a silent bright blueness, as if she is a bird in flight, except that no dark earth lies below, only blueness all around. No sense of motion. Neither hot nor cool. A flawless hyacinth-blue sphere with her at the center. Suspended. Waiting. A deep breath held in her lungs. She tries to expel her stale breath but cannot, cannot, until—

—with an exhalation as loud as a shout, she finds herself in the meadow, still in her seat, stunned into immobility, 21-21 beside her. The nearby woods are on fire. On all sides, flames lick mounds of twisted debris. The meadow is an unspeakable charnel house. And the 747 is *gone.*

At the penultimate moment, the girl had transported them out of the doomed aircraft by a monumental exertion of her psychic gift, to another place, to a dimension outside space and time, and had held them in that mysterious sheltering limbo through one terrible minute of cataclysmic destruction. The effort has left 21-21 cold, shaking, and unable to speak. Her eyes, bright with reflections of the many surrounding fires, have a faraway look like those of an autistic child. Initially she cannot walk or even stand, so Rose must lift her from the seat and carry her.

Weeping for the dead scattered through the night, shuddering with horror at the carnage, wonderstruck by her survival, slammed by a *hurricane* of emotion, Rose stands with the girl cradled in her arms but is unable to take a single step. Then she recalls the flickering passenger-cabin lights and the spinning of the hands on her wristwatch, and she is certain that the pilot was the victim of a wet mission, remoted by the boy who lives in a steel capsule deep below the Virginia countryside. This realization propels her away from the crash site, around the burning trees, into the moonlit forest, wading through straggly underbrush, then along a deer trail powdered with silver light and dappled with shadow, to another meadow, to a ridge from which she sees the lights of Loose Change Ranch.

By the time they reach the ranch house, the girl is somewhat recovered but still not herself. She is able to walk now, but she is lethargic, brooding, distant. Approaching the house, Rose tells 21-21 to remember that her name is Mary Tucker, but 21-21 says, *My name is Nina. That's who I want to be.*

Those are the last words that she will speak—perhaps forever. In the months immediately following the crash, having taken refuge with Rose's friends in Southern California, the girl sleeps twelve to fourteen hours a day. When she's awake, she shows no interest in anything. She sits for hours staring out a window or at a picture in a storybook, or at nothing in particular. She has no appetite, loses weight. She is pale and frail, and even her amethyst eyes seem to lose some of their color. Evidently the effort required to move herself and Rose into and out of the blue elsewhere, during the crash, has profoundly drained her, perhaps nearly killed her. Nina exhibits no paranormal abilities anymore, and Rose dwells in despondency.

By Christmas, however, Nina begins to show interest in the world around her. She watches television. She reads books again. As the winter passes, she sleeps less and eats more. Her skin regains its former glow, and the color of her eyes deepens. She still does not speak, but she seems increasingly *connected.* Rose encourages her to come all the way back from her self-imposed exile by speaking to her every day about the good that she can do and the hope that she can bring to others.

In a bureau drawer in the bedroom that she shares with the girl, Rose keeps a copy of the *Los Angeles Post,* the issue that devotes the entire front page, above the fold, to the fate of Nationwide Flight 353. It helps to remind her of the insane viciousness of her enemies. One day in July, eleven months after the disaster, she finds Nina sitting on the edge of the bed with this newspaper open to a page featuring photographs of some of the victims of the crash. The girl is touching the photo of Nina Carpenter, who had given her Pigs and Princes, and she is smiling.

Rose sits beside her and asks if she is feeling sad, remembering this lost friend.

The girl shakes her head *no.* Then she guides Rose's hand to the photograph, and when Rose's fingertips touch the newsprint, she falls away into a blue brightness not unlike the sanctuary into which she was transported in the instant before the plane crash, except that this is also a place *full* of motion, warmth, sensation.

Clairvoyants have long claimed to feel a residue of psychic energy on common objects, left by the people who have touched them. Sometimes they assist police in the search for a murderer by handling objects worn by the victim at the time of the assault. This energy in the *Post* photograph is similar but different—not left in passing by Nina but *imbued* in the newsprint by an act of will.

Rose feels as if she has plunged into a sea of blue light, a sea crowded with swimmers whom she cannot see but whom she feels gliding and swooping around her. Then one swimmer seems to pass *through* Rose and to linger in the passing, and she knows that she is with little Nina Carpenter, the girl with the lopsided smile, the giver of Pigs and Princes, who is dead and gone but safe, dead and gone but not lost forever, happy and alive in an elsewhere beyond this swarming blue brightness, which is not really a place itself but an interface between phases of existence.

Moved as deeply as she had been when she was first given the knowledge of the afterlife, in the room at the orphanage, Rose withdraws her hand from the photo of Nina Carpenter and sits silently for a while, humbled. Then she takes her own Nina into her arms and holds the girl tightly and rocks her, neither capable of speaking nor in need of words.

Now that this special girl's power is being reborn, Rose knows what they must do, where they must start their work. She does not want to risk going to Lisa Peccatone again. She doesn't believe that her old friend knowingly betrayed her, but she suspects that through Lisa's link to the *Post*—and through the *Post* to Horton Nellor—the people at Project 99 learned of her presence on Flight 353. While Rose and Nina are believed dead, they need to take advantage of their ghostly status to operate as long as possible without drawing the attention of their enemies. First, Rose asks the girl to give the great gift of eternal truth to each of the friends who has sheltered them during these eleven months in their emotional wilderness. Then they will contact the husbands and wives and parents and children of those who perished on Flight 353, bringing them both the received knowledge of immortality and visions of their loved ones at the blue interface. With luck, they will spread their message so widely by the time they are discovered that it cannot be contained.

Rose intends to start with Joe Carpenter, but she can't locate him. His coworkers at the *Post* have lost track of him. He has sold the house in Studio City. He has no listed phone. They say he is a broken man. He has gone away to die.

She must begin the work elsewhere.

Because the *Post* published photographs of only a fraction of the Southern California victims and because she has no easy way to gather photos of the many others, Rose decides not to use portraits, after all. Instead, she tracks down their burial places through published funeral-service notices, and she takes snapshots of their graves. It seems fitting that the imbued image should be of a headstone, that these grim memorials of bronze and granite should become doorways through which the recipients of the pictures will learn that Death is not mighty and dreadful, that beyond this bitter phase, Death himself dies.

High in the wind-churned mountains, with waves of moon-silvered conifers casting sprays of needles onto the roadway, still more than twenty miles from Big Bear Lake, Rose Tucker spoke so softly that she could barely be heard over the racing engine and the hum of the tires: "Joe, will you hold my hand?"

He could not look at her, would not look at her, dared not even glance at her for a second, because he was overcome by the childish superstition that she would be all right, perfectly fine, as long as he didn't visually confirm the terrible truth that he heard in her voice. But he looked. She was so small, slumped in her seat, leaning against the door, the back of her head against the window, as small to his eyes as 21-21 must have appeared to her when she had fled Virginia with the girl at her side. Even in the faint glow from the instrument panel, her huge and expressive eyes were again as compelling as they had been when he'd first met her in the graveyard, full of compassion and kindness—and a strange glimmering joy that scared him.

His voice was shakier than hers. "It's not far now."

"Too far," she whispered. "Just hold my hand."

"Oh, shit."

"It's all right, Joe."

The shoulder of the highway widened to a scenic rest area. He stopped the car before a vista of darkness: the hard night sky, the icy disk of a moon that seemed to shed cold instead of light, and a vast blackness of trees and rocks and canyons descending.

He released his seat belt, leaned across the console, and took her hand. Her grip was weak.

"She needs you, Joe."

"I'm nobody's hero, Rose. I'm nothing."

"You need to hide her . . . hide her away . . ."

"Rose—"

"Give her time . . . for her power to grow."

"I can't save anyone."

"I shouldn't have started the work so soon. The day will come when . . . when she won't be so vulnerable. Hide her away . . . let her power grow. She'll know . . . when the time has come."

She began to lose her grip on him.

He covered her hand with both of his, held it fast, would not let it slip from his grasp.

Voice raveling away, she seemed to be receding from him though she did not move: "Open . . . open your heart to her, Joe."

Her eyelids fluttered.

"Rose, please don't."

"It's all right."

"Please. Don't."

"See you later, Joe."

"Please."

"See you."

Then he was alone in the night. He held her small hand alone in the night while the wind played a hollow threnody. When at last he was able to do so, he kissed her brow.

The directions Rose had given him were easy to follow. The cabin was neither in the town of Big Bear Lake nor elsewhere along the lakefront, but higher on the northern slopes and nestled deep in pines and birches. The cracked and potholed blacktop led to a dirt driveway, at the end of which was a small white clapboard house with a shake-shingle roof.

A green Jeep Wagoneer stood beside the cabin. Joe parked behind the Jeep.

The cabin boasted a deep, elevated porch, on which three cane-backed rocking chairs were arranged side by side. A handsome black man, tall and athletically built, stood at the railing, his ebony skin highlighted with a brass tint cast by two bare yellow lightbulbs in the porch ceiling.

The girl waited at the head of the flight of four steps that led up from the driveway to the porch. She was blond and about six years old.

From under the driver's seat, Joe retrieved the gun that he had taken from the white-haired storyteller after the scuffle on the beach. Getting out of the car, he tucked the weapon under the waistband of his jeans.

The wind shrieked and hissed through the needled teeth of the pines.

He walked to the foot of the steps.

The child had descended two of the four treads. She stared past Joe, at the Ford. She knew what had happened.

On the porch, the black man began to cry.

The girl spoke for the first time in over a year, since the moment outside the Ealings' ranch house when she had told Rose that she wanted to be called Nina. Gazing at the car, she said only one word, in a voice soft and small: "Mother."

Her hair was the same shade as Nina's hair. She was as fine-boned as Nina. But her eyes were not gray like Nina's eyes, and no matter how hard Joe tried to see Nina's face before him, he could not deceive himself into believing that this was his daughter.

Yet again, he had been engaged in searching behavior, seeking what was lost forever.

The moon above was a thief, its glow not a radiance of its own but a weak reflection of the sun. And like the moon, this girl was a thief—not Nina but only a reflection of Nina, shining not with Nina's brilliant light but with a pale fire.

Regardless of whether she was only a lab-born mutant with strange mental powers or really the hope of the world, Joe hated her at that moment, and hated himself for hating her—but hated her nonetheless.

SEVENTEEN

Hot wind huffed at the windows, and the cabin smelled of pine, dust, and the black char from last winter's cozy blazes, which coated the brick walls of the big fireplace.

The incoming electrical lines had sufficient slack to swing in the wind. From time to time they slapped against the house, causing the lights to throb and flicker. Each tremulous brownout reminded Joe of the pulsing lights at the Delmann house, and his skin prickled with dread.

The owner was the tall black man who had broken into tears on the porch. He was Louis Tucker, Mahalia's brother, who had divorced Rose eighteen years ago, when she proved unable to have children. She had turned to him in her darkest hour. And after all this time, though he had a wife and children whom he loved, Louis clearly still loved Rose too.

"If you really believe she's not dead, that she's only moved on," Joe said coldly, "why cry for her?"

"I'm crying for me," said Louis. "Because she's gone from here and I'll have to wait through a lot of days to see her again."

Two suitcases stood in the front room, just inside the door. They contained the belongings of the child.

She was at a window, staring out at the Ford, with sorrow pulled around her like sackcloth.

"I'm scared," Louis said. "Rose was going to stay up here with Nina, but I don't think it's safe now. I don't want to believe it could be true—but they might've found me before I got out of the last place with Nina. Couple times, way back, I thought the same car was behind us. Then it didn't keep up."

"They don't have to. With their gadgets, they can follow from miles away."

"And then just before you pulled into the driveway, I went out onto the porch 'cause I thought I heard a helicopter. Up in these mountains in this wind—does that make sense?"

"You better get her out of here," Joe agreed.

As the wind slapped the electrical lines against the house, Louis paced to the fireplace and back, a hand pressed to his forehead as he tried to put the loss of Rose out of his mind long enough to think what to do. "I figured you and Rose . . . well, I thought the two of you were taking her. And if they're onto me, then won't she be safer with you?"

"If they're onto you," Joe said, "then none of us is safe here, now, anymore. There's no way out."

The lines slapped the house, slapped the house, and the lights pulsed, and Louis walked to the fireplace and picked up a battery-powered, long-necked butane match from the hearth.

The girl turned from the window, eyes wide, and said, *"No."*

Louis Tucker flicked the switch on the butane match, and blue flame spurted from the nozzle. Laughing, he set his own hair on fire and then his shirt.

"Nina!" Joe cried.

The girl ran to his side.

The stink of burning hair spread through the room.

Ablaze, Louis moved to block the front door.

From the waistband of his jeans, Joe drew the pistol, aimed—but couldn't pull the trigger. This man confronting him was not really Louis Tucker now; it was the boy-thing, reaching out three thousand miles from Virginia. And there was no chance that Louis would regain control of his body and live through this night. Yet Joe hesitated to squeeze off a shot, because the moment that Louis was dead, the boy would remote someone else.

The girl was probably untouchable, able to protect herself with her own paranormal power. So the boy would use Joe—and the gun in Joe's hand—to shoot the girl point-blank in the head.

"This is *fun*," the boy said in Louis's voice, as flames seethed off his hair, as his ears charred and crackled, as his forehead and cheeks blistered. *"Fun,"* he said, enjoying his ride inside Louis Tucker but still blocking the exit to the porch.

Maybe, at the instant of greatest jeopardy, Nina could send herself into that safe bright blueness as she had done just before the 747 plowed into the meadow. Maybe the bullets fired at her would merely pass through the empty air where she had been. But there was a chance that she was still not fully recovered, that she wasn't yet able to perform such a taxing feat, or even that she could perform it but would be mortally drained by it this time.

"Out the back!" Joe shouted. "Go, go!"

Nina raced to the door between the front room and the kitchen at the rear of the cabin.

Joe backed after her, keeping the pistol trained on the burning man, even though he didn't intend to use it.

Their only hope was that the boy's love of "fun" would give them the chance to get out of the cabin, into the open, where his ability to conduct remote viewing and to engage in mind control would be, according to Rose, severely diminished. If he gave up the toy that was Louis Tucker, he would be into Joe's head in an instant.

Tossing aside the butane match, with flames spreading along the sleeves of his shirt and down his pants, the boy-thing said, "Oh, yeah, oh, wow," and came after them.

Joe recalled too clearly the feeling of the ice-cold needle that had seemed to pierce the summit of his spine as he had barely escaped the Delmann house the previous night. That invading energy scared him more than the prospect of being embraced by the fiery arms of this shambling specter.

Frantically he retreated into the kitchen, slamming the door as he went, which was pointless because no door—no wall, no steel vault—could delay the boy if he abandoned Louis's body and went incorporeal.

Nina slipped out the back door of the cabin, and a wolf pack of wind, chuffing and puling, rushed past her and inside.

As Joe followed her into the night, he heard the living room door crash into the kitchen.

Behind the cabin was a small yard of dirt and natural bunch-grass. The air was full of wind-torn leaves, pine needles, grit. Beyond a redwood picnic table and four redwood chairs, the forest rose again.

Nina was already running for the trees, short legs pumping, sneakers slapping on the hard-packed earth. She thrashed through tall weeds at the perimeter of the woods and vanished in the gloom among the pines and birches.

Nearly as terrified of losing the girl in the wilds as he was frightened of the boy in the burning man, Joe sprinted between the trees, shouting the girl's name, one arm raised to ward off any pine boughs that might be drooping low enough to lash his eyes.

From the night behind him came Louis Tucker's voice, slurred by the damage that the spreading flames had already done to his lips but nevertheless recognizable, the chanted words of a childish challenge: "Here I come, here I come, here I come, ready or not, here I come, ready or not!"

A narrow break in the trees admitted a cascade of moonbeams, and Joe spotted the girl's cap of wind-whipped blond hair glowing with pale fire, the reflection of reflected light, to his right and only six or eight yards ahead. He stumbled over a rotting log, slipped on something slimy, kept his balance, flailed through prickly waist-high brush, and discovered that Nina had found the beaten-clear path of a deer trail.

As he caught up with the girl, the darkness around them abruptly brightened. Salamanders of orange light slithered up the trunks of the trees and whipped their tails across the glossy boughs of pines and spruces.

Joe turned and saw the possessed hulk of Louis Tucker thirty feet away, ablaze from head to foot but still standing, hitching and jerking through the woods, caroming from tree to tree, twenty feet away, barely alive, setting fire to the carpet of dry pine needles over which he shambled and to the bristling weeds and to the trees as he passed them. Now fifteen feet away. The stench of burning flesh on the wind. The boy-thing shouted gleefully, but the words were garbled and unintelligible.

Even in a two-hand grip, the pistol shook, but Joe squeezed off one, two, four, six rounds, and at least four of them hit the seething specter. It pitched backward and fell and didn't move, didn't even twitch, dead from fire and gunfire.

Louis Tucker was not a person now but a burning corpse. The body no longer harbored a mind that the boy could saddle and ride and torment.

Where?

Joe turned to Nina—and felt a familiar icy pressure at the back of his neck, an insistent probing, not as sharp as it had been when he was almost caught on the threshold of the Delmann house, perhaps blunted now because the boy's power was indeed diminishing here in the open. But the psychic syringe was not yet blunt enough to be ineffective. It still stung. It pierced.

Joe screamed.

The girl seized his hand.

The iciness tore out its fangs and *flew* from him, as though it were a bat taking wing.

Reeling, Joe clamped a hand to the nape of his neck, certain that he would find his flesh ripped and bleeding, but he was not wounded. And his mind had not been violated, either.

Nina's touch had saved him from possession.

With a banshee shriek, a hawk exploded out of the high branches of a tree and dive-bombed the girl, striking at her head, pecking at her scalp, wings flapping, beak click-click-clicking. She screamed and covered her face with her hands, and Joe batted at the assailant with one arm. The crazed bird swooped up and away, but it wasn't an ordinary bird, of course, and it wasn't merely crazed by the wind and the churning fire that swelled rapidly through the woods behind them.

Here it came again, with a fierce *skreeeek,* the latest host for the visitant from Virginia, arrowing down through the moonlight, its rapier beak as deadly as a stiletto, too fast to be a target for the gun.

Joe let go of the pistol and dropped to his knees on the deer trail and pulled the girl protectively against him. Pressed her face against his chest. The bird would want to get at her eyes. Peck at her eyes. Jab-jab-jab through the vulnerable sockets at the precious brain beyond. Damage the brain, and her power cannot save her. Tear her specialness right out of her gray matter and leave her in spasms on the ground.

The hawk struck, sank one set of talons into the sleeve of Joe's coat, through the corduroy, piercing the skin of his forearm, planting the other set of talons in Nina's blond hair, wings drumming as it pecked her scalp, pecked, angry because her face was concealed. Pecking now at Joe's hand as he tried to knock it away, holding fast to sleeve and hair, determined not to be dislodged. Pecking, pecking at *his* face now, going for his eyes, Jesus, a flash of pain as it tore open his cheek. Seize it. Stop it. Crush it quickly. Peck, the darting head, the bloody beak, peck, and it got his brow this time, above his right eye, sure to blind him with the next thrust. He clenched his hand around it, and its talons tore at the cuff of his coat sleeve now, tore at his wrist, wings beating against his face, and it bobbed its head, the wicked beak darting at him, but he held it off, the hooked yellow point snapping an inch short of a blinding wound, the beady eyes glaring fiercely and blood-red with reflections of fire. Squeeze it, squeeze the life out of it, with its racing heart stuttering against his relentless palm. Its bones were thin and hollow, which made it light enough to fly with grace—but which also made it easier to break. Joe felt its breast crumple, and he threw it away from the girl, watched it tumble along the deer trail, disabled but still alive, wings flapping weakly but unable to lift into the night.

Joe pushed Nina's tangled hair away from her face. She was all right. Her eyes had not been hit. In fact, she was unmarked, and he was overcome by a rush of pride that he had prevented the hawk from getting at her.

Blood oozed from his slashed brow, around the curve of the socket, and into the corner of his eye, blurring his vision. Blood streamed from the wound in his cheek, dripped from his pecked and stinging hand, from his gouged wrist.

He retrieved the pistol, engaged the safety, and jammed the weapon under his waistband again.

From out of the surrounding woods issued a bleat of animal terror, which abruptly cut off, and then across the mountainside, over the howling of the wind, a sharp shriek sliced through the night. Something was coming.

Maybe the boy had gained more control of his talent during the year that Rose had been on the run, and maybe now he was more capable of remoting someone in the outdoors. Or perhaps the coalesced power of his psychogeist was radiating away like the heat from a rock, as Rose had explained, but just wasn't dispersing fast enough to bring a quick end to this assault.

Because of the blustery wind and the express-train roar of the wildfire, Joe couldn't be certain from which direction the cry had arisen, and now the boy, clothed in the flesh of his host, was coming silently.

Joe scooped the girl off the deer trail, cradling her in his arms. They needed to keep moving, and until his energy faded, he could move faster through the woods if he carried her than if he led her by the hand.

She was so small. He was scared by how small she was, nearly as breakable as the avian bones of the hawk.

She clung to him, and he tried to smile at her. In the hellish leaping light, his flaring eyes and strained grin were probably more frightening than reassuring.

The mad boy in his new incarnation was not the only threat they faced. The explosive Santa Ana wind threw bright rags, threw sheets, threw great billowing *sails* of fire across the flank of the mountain. The pines were dry from the hot rainless summer, their bark rich with turpentine, and they burst into flame as though they were made of gasoline-soaked rags.

Ramparts of fire at least three hundred feet across blocked the way back to the cabin.

They could not get around the blaze and behind it, because it was spreading laterally faster than they could hike through the underbrush and across the rugged terrain.

At the same time, the fire was coming toward them. Fast.

Joe stood with Nina in his arms, riveted and dismayed by the sight of the towering wall of fire, and he realized that they had no choice but to abandon the car. They would have to make the trip out of the mountains entirely on foot.

With a hot *whoosh*, roiling gouts of wind-harried flames spewed through the treetops immediately overhead, like a deadly blast from a futuristic plasma weapon. The pine boughs exploded, and burning masses of needles and cones tumbled down through lower branches, igniting everything as they descended, and suddenly Joe and Nina were in a tunnel of fire.

He hurried with the girl in his arms, away from the cabin, along the narrow deer trail, remembering stories of people caught in California brushfires and unable to outrun them, sometimes not even able to *outdrive* them when the wind was particularly fierce. Maybe the flames couldn't accelerate through this density of trees as quickly as through dry brush. Or maybe the pines were even more accommodating fuel than mesquite and manzanita and grass.

Just as they escaped the tunnel of fire, more rippling flags of flames unfurled across the sky overhead, and again the treetops in front of them ignited. Burning needles swarmed down like bright bees, and Joe was afraid his hair would catch fire, Nina's hair, their clothes. The tunnel was growing in length as fast as they could run through it.

Smoke plagued him now. As the blaze rapidly intensified, it generated winds of its own, adding to the force of the Santa Anas, building toward a firestorm, and the blistering gales first blew tatters of smoke along the deer trail and then choking masses.

The cloistered path led upward, and though the degree of slope was not great, Joe became more quickly winded than he had expected. Incredible withering heat wrung oceans of sweat from him. Gasping for breath, sucking in the astringent fumes and greasy soot, choking, gagging, spitting out saliva thickened and soured by the flavor of the fire, desperately holding on to Nina, he reached a ridgeline.

The pistol under his waistband pressed painfully against his stomach as he ran. If he could have let go of Nina with one hand, he would have drawn the weapon and thrown it away. He was afraid that he was too weak to hold on to her with one arm, that he would drop her, so he endured the gouging steel.

As he crossed the narrow crest and followed the descending trail, he discovered that the wind was less furious on this side of the ridge. Even though the flames surged across the brow, the speed at which the fire line advanced now dropped enough to allow him to get out of the incendiary zone and ahead of the smoke, where the clean air was so sweet that he groaned at the cool, clear taste of it.

Joe was running on an adrenaline high, far beyond his normal level of endurance, and if not for the bolstering effect of panic, he might have collapsed before he topped the ridge. His leg muscles ached. His arms were turning to lead under the weight of the girl. They were not safe, however, so he kept going, stumbling and weaving, blinking tears of weariness out of his smoke-stung eyes, nevertheless pressing steadily forward—until the snarling coyote slammed into him from behind, biting savagely at the hollow of his back but capturing only folds of his corduroy jacket in its jaws.

The impact staggered him, eighty or ninety pounds of lupine fury. He almost fell facedown onto the trail, with Nina under him, except that the weight of the coyote, hanging on him, acted as a counterbalance, and he stayed erect.

The jacket ripped, and the coyote let go, fell away.

Joe skidded to a halt, put Nina down, spun toward the predator, drawing the pistol from his waistband, thankful that he had not pitched it away earlier.

Backlighted by the ridgeline fire, the coyote confronted Joe. It was so like a wolf but leaner, rangier, with bigger ears and a narrower muzzle, black lips skinned back from bared fangs, scarier than a wolf might have been, especially because of the spirit of the vicious boy curled like a serpent in its skull. Its glowering eyes were luminous and yellow.

Joe pulled the trigger, but the gun didn't fire. He remembered the safety.

The coyote skittered toward him, staying low, quick but wary, snapping at his ankles, and Joe danced frantically backward to avoid being bitten, thumbing off the safety as he went.

The animal snaked around him, snarling, snapping, foam flying from its jaws. Its teeth sank into his right calf.

He cried out in pain, and twisted around, trying to get a shot at the damn thing, but it turned as he did, ferociously worrying the flesh of his calf until he thought he was going to pass out from the crackling pain that flashed like a series of electrical shocks all the way up his leg into his hip.

Abruptly the coyote let go and shrank away from Joe as if in fear and confusion.

Joe swung toward the animal, cursing it and tracking it with the pistol.

The beast was no longer in an attack mode. It whined and surveyed the surrounding night in evident perplexity.

With his finger on the trigger, Joe hesitated.

Tilting its head back, regarding the lambent moon, the coyote whined again. Then it looked toward the top of the ridge.

The fire was no more than a hundred yards away. The scorching wind suddenly accelerated, and the flames climbed gusts higher into the night.

The coyote stiffened and pricked its ears. When the fire surged once more, the coyote bolted past Joe and Nina, oblivious of them, and disappeared at a lope into the canyon below.

At last defeated by the draining vastness of these open spaces, the boy had lost his grip on the animal, and Joe sensed that nothing spectral hovered any longer in the woods.

The firestorm rolled at them again, blinding waves of flames, a cataclysmic tide breaking through the forest.

With his bitten leg, limping badly, Joe wasn't able to carry Nina any longer, but she took his hand, and they hurried as best they could toward the primeval darkness that seemed to well out of the ground and drown the ranks of conifers in the lower depths of the canyon.

He hoped they could find a road. Paved or graveled or dirt—it didn't matter. Just a way out, any sort of road at all, as long as it led away from the fire and would take them into a future where Nina would be safe.

They had gone no more than two hundred yards when a thunder rose behind them, and when he turned, fearful of another attack, Joe saw only a herd of deer galloping toward them, fleeing the flames. Ten, twenty, thirty deer, graceful and swift, parted around him and Nina with a thudding of hooves, ears pricked and alert, oil-black eyes as shiny as mirrors, spotted flanks quivering, kicking up clouds of pale dust, whickering and snorting, and then they were gone.

Heart pounding, caught up in a riot of emotions that he could not easily sort out, still holding the girl's hand, Joe started down the trail in the hoofprints of the deer. He took half a dozen steps before he realized there was no pain in his bitten calf. No pain, either, in his hawk-pecked hand or in his beak-torn face. He was no longer bleeding.

Along the way and in the tumult of the deers' passing, Nina had healed him.

EIGHTEEN

On the second anniversary of the crash of Nationwide Flight 353, Joe Carpenter sat on a quiet beach in Florida, in the shade of a palm tree, watching the sea. Here, the tides came to shore more gently than in California, licking the sand with a tropical languor, and the ocean seemed not at all like a machine.

He was a different man from the one who had fled the fire in the San Bernardino Mountains. His hair was longer now, bleached both by chemicals and by the sun. He had grown a mustache as a simple disguise. His physical awareness of himself was far greater than it had been one year ago, so he was conscious of how differently he moved these days: with a new ease, with a relaxed grace, without the tension and the coiled anger of the past.

He possessed ID in a new name: birth certificate, social security card, three major credit cards, a driver's license. The forgers at Infiniface didn't actually forge documents as much as use their computer savvy to manipulate the system into spitting out *real* papers for people who didn't actually exist.

He had undergone inner changes too, and he credited those to Nina—though he continued to refuse the ultimate gift that she could give him. She had changed him not by her touch but by her example, by her sweetness and kindness, by her trust in him, by her love of life and her love of him and her calm faith in the rightness of all things. She was only six years old but in some ways ancient, because if she was what everyone believed she was, then she was tied to the infinite by an umbilical of light.

They were staying with a commune of Infiniface members, those who wore no robes and left their heads unshaven. The big house stood back from the beach and was filled at almost any hour of the day with the soft clatter of computer keyboards. In a week or two, Joe and Nina would move on to another group, bringing them the gift that only this child could reveal, for they traveled continuously in the quiet spreading of the word. In a few years, when her maturing power made her less vulnerable, the time would arrive to tell the world.

Now, on this anniversary of loss, she came to him on the beach, under the gently swaying palm, as he had known she would, and she sat at his side. Currently her hair was brown. She was wearing pink shorts and a white top with Donald Duck winking on her chest—as ordinary in appearance as any six-year-old on the planet. She drew her knees up and encircled her legs with her arms, and for a while she said nothing.

They watched a big, long-legged sand crab move across the beach, select a nesting place, and burrow out of sight.

Finally she said, "Why won't you open your heart?"

"I will. When the time's right."

"When will the time be right?"

"When I learn not to hate."

"Who do you hate?"

"For a long time—you."

"Because I'm not your Nina."

"I don't hate you anymore."

"I know."

"I hate myself."

"Why?"

"For being so afraid."

"You're not afraid of anything," she said.

He smiled. "Scared to death of what you can show me."

"Why?"

"The world's so cruel. It's so hard. If there's a God, He tortured my father with disease and then took him young. He took Michelle, my Chrissie, my Nina. He allowed Rose to die."

"This is a passage."

"A damn vicious one."

She was silent for a while.

The sea whispered against the strand. The crab stirred, poked an eye stalk out to examine the world, and decided to move.

Nina got up and crossed to the sand crab. Ordinarily, these creatures were shy and scurried away when approached. This one did not run for cover but watched Nina as she dropped to her knees and studied it. She stroked its shell. She touched one of its claws, and the crab didn't pinch her.

Joe watched—and wondered.

Finally the girl returned and sat beside Joe, and the big crab disappeared into the sand.

She said, "If the world is cruel . . . you can help me fix it. And if that's what God wants us to do, then He's not cruel, after all."

Joe did not respond to her pitch.

The sea was an iridescent blue. The sky curved down to meet it at an invisible seam.

"Please," she said. "Please take my hand, Daddy."

She had never called him *daddy* before, and his chest tightened when he heard the word.

He met her amethyst eyes. And wished they were gray like his own. But they were not. She had come with him out of wind and fire, out of darkness and terror, and he supposed that he was as much her father as Rose Tucker had been her mother.

He took her hand.

And knew.

For a time he was not on a beach in Florida but in a bright blueness with Michelle and Chrissie and Nina. He did not see what worlds waited beyond this one, but he knew beyond all doubt that they existed, and the strangeness of them frightened him but also lifted his heart.

He understood that eternal life was not an article of faith but a law of the universe as true as any law of physics. The universe is an efficient creation: matter becomes energy; energy becomes matter; one form of energy is converted into another form; the balance is forever changing, but the universe is a closed system from which no particle of matter or wave of energy is ever lost. Nature not only loathes waste but forbids it. The human mind and spirit, at their noblest, can transform the material world for the better; we can even transform the human condition, lifting ourselves from a state of primal fear, when we dwelled in caves and shuddered at the sight of the moon, to a position from which we can contemplate eternity and hope to understand the works of God. Light cannot change itself into stone by an act of *will*, and stone cannot build itself into temples. Only the human spirit can act with volition and consciously change itself; it is the only thing in all creation that is not entirely at the mercy of forces outside itself, and it is, therefore, the most powerful and valuable form of energy in the universe. For a time, the spirit may become flesh, but when that phase of its existence is at an end, it will be transformed into a disembodied spirit once more.

When he returned from that brightness, from the blue elsewhere, he sat for a while, trembling, eyes closed, burrowed down into this revealed truth as the crab had buried itself in the sand.

In time he opened his eyes.

His daughter smiled at him. Her eyes were amethyst, not gray. Her features were not those of the other Nina whom he had loved so deeply. She was not, however, a pale fire, as she had seemed before, and he wondered how he could have allowed his anger to prevent him from seeing her as she truly was. She was a shining light, all but blinding in her brightness, as his own Nina had been—as are we all.